SAGAS OF THE
SPACE WOLVES

SAGAS OF THE
SPACE WOLVES

AARON DEMBSKI-BOWDEN
DAVID ANNANDALE · ROBBIE MacNIVEN
BEN COUNTER · C L WERNER
& MANY MORE

BLACK LIBRARY

A BLACK LIBRARY PUBLICATION

'Engage the Enemy' first published in 2004.
'Twelve Wolves' first published in 2010.
'Reparation' first published in 2011.
'In Hrondir's Tomb' first published in 2012.
'On the Heels of Morkai' first published in 2012.
'Defender of Honour' first published in 2013.
Arjac Rockfist first published in 2014.
Blood on the Mountain first published in 2014.
Iceclaw first published as an audio drama in 2014.
Ragnar Blackmane first published in 2015.
Thunder from Fenris first published as an audio drama in 2015.
'Hollow Beginnings' first published in 2015.
Curse of the Wulfen first published in 2016.
Legacy of Russ first published in 2016.
The Hunt for Logan Grimnar first published as *Space Wolves* in 2016.
'Stormseeker' first published in 2016.

This edition published in Great Britain in 2020 by
Black Library,
Games Workshop Ltd.,
Willow Road,
Nottingham, NG7 2WS, UK.

10 9 8 7 6 5 4 3 2 1

Produced by Games Workshop in Nottingham.
Cover illustration by Toni Deu.

See Black Library on the internet at

blacklibrary.com

Find out more about Games Workshop
and the world of Warhammer 40,000 at

games-workshop.com

Printed and bound by CPI Group (UK) Ltd, Croydon, CR0 4YY

It is the 41st millennium. For more than a hundred centuries the Emperor has sat immobile on the Golden Throne of Earth. He is the Master of Mankind by the will of the gods, and master of a million worlds by the might of His inexhaustible armies. He is a rotting carcass writhing invisibly with power from the Dark Age of Technology. He is the Carrion Lord of the Imperium for whom a thousand souls are sacrificed every day, so that He may never truly die.

Yet even in His deathless state, the Emperor continues His eternal vigilance. Mighty battlefleets cross the daemon-infested miasma of the warp, the only route between distant stars, their way lit by the Astronomican, the psychic manifestation of the Emperor's will. Vast armies give battle in His name on uncounted worlds. Greatest amongst His soldiers are the Adeptus Astartes, the Space Marines, bioengineered super-warriors. Their comrades in arms are legion: the Astra Militarum and countless planetary defence forces, the ever-vigilant Inquisition and the tech-priests of the Adeptus Mechanicus to name only a few. But for all their multitudes, they are barely enough to hold off the ever-present threat from aliens, heretics, mutants — and worse.

To be a man in such times is to be one amongst untold billions. It is to live in the cruellest and most bloody regime imaginable. These are the tales of those times. Forget the power of technology and science, for so much has been forgotten, never to be re-learned. Forget the promise of progress and understanding, for in the grim dark future there is only war. There is no peace amongst the stars, only an eternity of carnage and slaughter, and the laughter of thirsting gods.

CONTENTS

RAGNAR BLACKMANE

Aaron Dembski-Bowden

PROLOGUE

The Allfather alone knew what would emerge from the dust. Whatever was coming, it shook the ground beneath its thousandfold tread.

A horde. A tide. An army.

No matter.

He had faced armies before. He'd faced them, gutted them and sent them back to the pits from which they crawled.

Ragnar leaned on the wall, gauntleted knuckles on the rockcrete battlement, waiting to see what would come and try to kill him this time. Beyond the battlements there was nothing but dust and ash, drowning the fallen city in a cloud too thick for even *Einherjar* eyes to penetrate.

'The surface is lost,' said a voice across the vox.

The voice spoke true. 'I have said that I will hold this wall until sunset,' Ragnar replied. 'So I will hold this wall until sunset.'

'I am not arguing with you, Jarl Blackmane. Merely speaking what I see.'

Ragnar saw it, too. Only a fool wouldn't. 'Is there more?'

'Yes, lord. Nightblade reports the Archenemy has a vanguard within the Lavok tunnels. If the foe is reinforced it will be a murderous fight to get through.'

'Sunset,' he said again. 'A promise is a promise.'

A few more hours wasn't so long to give.

He would hold the city's last bastion until the sun set, buying time for the rearguard of the Cadian 57th to withdraw and reinforce the defenders at Kasr Lavok. If the vox could be trusted – and Ragnar knew well that it couldn't – then the Imperial forces at Lavok could hold for perhaps another two weeks.

Two weeks of breath, bought with Space Wolves lives. There was a time, deep in his tribal past, when he would have been disgusted at such a sacrifice. It would have been nothing but a waste of heroic souls.

11

There was no disgust now. Not even remorse. If he was to die here, then so be it.

To his left and right, his brothers waited along the wall, as lost in the dust as the foe they were about to face. He sensed them, still. Their heartbeats were biorhythmic thunder, and not even the constant shelling and shaking ground drowned them out. Their axes and swords purred, waiting to be revved. Packmates grunted and cursed with one another, always aware of nearby brothers, dust-blind or not.

Their lord stood bareheaded and half-blind in the dead city's heart, his features greyed by the dirt choking the air. Even breathing was a battle here, dragging in smoke-thick air that tasted of burned stone and melted steel. What few living humans he'd seen in the last few hours were sucking their breath through rebreather masks. He and his men needed no such toys, but even he felt his three lungs straining to filter out the filth.

Ragnar turned his gaze to where the sky should have been. Shapes swam up there, silhouettes ghosting through the hazy caul of grit-powder and dust. Sometimes he heard the strangled whine of engines, distorted and distant, never quite matching the shadows that flashed through the choked heavens. The silhouettes themselves didn't bank and veer like fighters and gunships; they swooped and shrieked like living things.

Win or lose the war, Cadia was broken. Every city upon its surface was aflame, strangling the skies with the smoke and dust of a million fallen buildings. It would take a decade just to cleanse the filth from the atmosphere. This was the way a world died.

A figure emerged from the dust to his left. Ragnar recognised the cadence of the warrior's tread, and knew him by the snarl of his armour's joints. The spirits of every suit of armour in the Great Company gave their own unique growls, and a Wolf Lord needed to know his men better than they knew themselves. The mechanics of this battleplate sounded dry and throaty, harsh enough to set a man's teeth on edge.

'Priest,' Ragnar greeted the other Wolf without missing a beat.

'Jarl,' was Ulrik's reply, crackling through the canine-skull helm. The Wolf Priest stood with his lord, looking out over what was once a city, and what was now nothing but rubble. A world's worth of rockcrete powder from broken buildings turned the air to ash. *Something the sagas always fail to mention,* Ragnar thought. *The dust that rises from a dying city, as hundreds of buildings fall to the earth.*

'Do you hear that?' Ragnar bared his teeth in an unlovely smile. 'The marching tread of those who wish to grind us down into unmarked graves.'

'I hear it,' said the Wolf Priest, looking out into the dust as if his eye lenses could pierce the murk. 'The sins of mankind come to drag it down, at last.'

Ragnar spat to ward off ill fortune. 'Is that what they'll say of this day, Slayer?'

'No, jarl. Never in life. The sagas will say that on this day the youngest lord – called Blackmane by his kith and kin – led his bloodied hunters into the jaws of winter.'

Ragnar's laugh cut the air like a bolter crack. 'So this is what it's come to – priests lying like bards. Is my courage so tender that you'd keep the cold truth from me, old father?'

Ulrik didn't laugh, though this time Ragnar was certain he heard amusement in the ancient warrior's tone. 'You asked what they will say of this day, Young King. I told you no lies.'

'And are you guessing what fate has in store, or did you read that future by casting the knucklebones of sinners?'

A howl went up along the battlements, carried from throat to throat, the cry raised to the occluded sky. To human ears it would be no more than a feral call; to Ragnar it was a song of significance and nuance, with emotion and warning in the tale it told.

Shadows – and the suggestions of shadows – were lumbering from the unending dust, too large to be human, many too large to be battle tanks. Things of hunchbacked carapaces and thrashing tendrils of bloody-red iron lashing at the dirty air. Things with bestial heads and monstrous wings, engines of war that drooled petrochemical run-off, with breath of violet flame ghosting between their ceramite teeth.

The first rank darkened from shadow to substance, crawling and stalking closer to the fortress walls. The second rank followed. The third. The fourth. More, and more, and more.

'They are without number,' Ragnar said, with neither awe nor fear. He checked Frostfang's hilt mechanisms one last time, to ensure the blade would rev true. 'At least they respected us enough to send a real challenge.'

'An inspiring speech, my jarl?'

'Ha! Don't think I cannot hear the smile in your voice, Slayer. No speeches this time. I am done with speeches, and our brothers need hear no more of them.'

He vaulted up to the battlement wall, throwing his arms wide as he cried his howl to the unseen sky. Unlike the warning call of a moment before, the jarl's howl ended in raucous laughter. It was taken up as a cheer along the wall as the Wolves heard their young lord's evident mirth.

'No speeches now, kinsmen!' Ragnar roared into the dust. 'What more is there to say that we have not already said? Look down upon the rusted heaps marching to claim our walls. Deny them! Kill them! Break them open!'

Another cheer. As it reached its crescendo, Ragnar gunned his chainsword's trigger. The whine of its priceless kraken teeth chewing the gritty air added a savage drone to the Wolves' howls.

'Come for us!' Ragnar roared at the horde. 'Our blades thirst for the taste of tainted blood!'

'That was almost a speech, my jarl,' said Ulrik as Ragnar's laughter faded again.

The Wolf Lord turned a grin down at his mentor. 'I was caught up in the moment, nothing more.'

The battlements began to shake as the war machines drove their claws into the rockcrete walls, beginning their inexorable climb. Ragnar drew his pistol, aiming down at the distorted shadows. Too far away to fire, but that would change soon. 'Are you ready to die, old father?'

Ulrik took his place at the lord's side, drawing his own pistol. It shivered in his grip as the magnetic coils along its spine thrummed to full charge.

'Today is as good a day as any other.'

'My humourless priest,' said Ragnar, shaking his head. He lapsed into near silence, closing his eyes as he waited, shutting out the tremors of this tortured world and softly murmuring name after name beneath his breath.

The Wolf Priest listened as he always listened, solemn during the jarl's funerary invocation. Ragnar spoke the name of every warrior who had died beneath his banner, forcing memories of each of them to the surface, keeping their sacrifice and valour in his thoughts. Would that every jarl value his men's lives so dearly, Ulrik thought, and remember them with such reverence.

'...Sunchaser,' said Ragnar at last. He took a breath, not quite a sigh, and opened his eyes.

Down the wall, a bolter cracked off a single shot. 'Who fired?' Ragnar shouted to his left. Laughter immediately echoed out among dozens of warriors. 'Answer me! Which overeager simpleton just spat a bolt with the enemy still over a minute out of range?'

'Stonebreaker of the Twice-Proven,' came the reply. 'I saw him shoot, my jarl!'

Stonebreaker's name became a sudden chant, mocked with good-natured jeers and cheers by his brothers.

'When we reach the Allfather's side,' Ragnar called back, 'the first words I speak will be to tell the Emperor you can't shoot worth a damn, Stonebreaker!'

More laughter. Ragnar felt his spirits lift at the sound. Ah, to die along-side such loyal warriors, such fine kindred. A doomed man could ask for no more.

'Your ritual,' said Ulrik. 'I have never told you how much I admire you for it.'

Ragnar narrowed his eyes. 'I don't do it to be admired.'

'I know, Young King.'

The Wolf Lord hawked and spat, sending a gobbet of bloody saliva over the wall. 'You know I loathe that name.'

'Yet others speak it with awe. Every one of your men knows of your rite. They love you for it. Your reverence for the slain speaks highly of you, as does the value you place on their lives. Each warrior fighting beneath your banner knows he will never be forgotten – not just with his deeds etched in stone upon the Hearthworld, but spoken in the soulful ritual of his lord before every battle. That matters to them, Blackmane.'

The young commander found himself uncomfortable under such scrutiny. 'Your words are taking a grim turn, old father.'

'Answer me something, Blackmane. Who among the fallen do you mourn most of all?' Ulrik nodded down to where the war machines crawled beneath them. 'Who among the many slain would you have standing by your side in these final hours?'

Ragnar's naked blue stare met Ulrik's scarlet eye lenses.

'Razortongue,' he said at last.

Ulrik looked at his lord through the red-stained gaze of his eye lenses' targeting framework. Biodata streamed in a continuous feed down both sides of his retinal display. The Wolf Priest said nothing, knowing Ragnar would elaborate.

'For the way he looked at the world.' The jarl gave a dark smile. 'And for what he taught me, if not the way he taught it. *Luck runs out, Blackmane.* I hear him saying it, even now.'

Ulrik nodded. 'I would choose him, as well. I mourned his loss then and I mourn it still. Though I do not miss the arguments.'

PART 1

THE MADNESS
OF ANGELS,
DARK AND LIGHT

I

The edge of the Maelstrom, aboard the warship *Veregelt*
Year of the Grey Promise
960.M41

Redness.

The redness of anger, the redness of shallow and shameful pain, the redness of blood in his eyes.

Voices.

The voices of his brothers, the voices of his enemies. The voices of those who fought by his side and the voices of those who wished him dead.

'Blackmane?'

'Brother?'

'Get him up.'

'Hold your fire!'

'Give the word, Slayer. We'll cut them to pieces.'

'This transgression will not be forgotten.'

'Nor forgiven.'

'Get him up, damn you.'

'Blood calls for blood.'

'Hold your cursed fire!'

'Don't fire! Not unless they fire first!'

Into this storm of conflicting voices, Ragnar came back to himself.

'It is done,' he told the gathered warriors of both Chapters. Silence fell over both sides as they faced each other in the *Veregelt*'s hangar bay.

Before him stood the Dark Angels – sixty-one of them in all – their war-scarred plate cast in the same colour as the deep forests of their annihilated home world. They waited in orderly ranks, squad by squad, marked by sigils and standing beneath standards raised by proud bannermen. Robes and surplices of cream were marked by recent battles, burned away in places, blood-spattered in others. Every warrior had a weapon raised, aiming directly at Ragnar.

And behind him, his brother Wolves. Thirty of them beneath his banner – his to command since Jarl Berek had heralded him as battle leader for the campaign at the Maelstrom's edge.

'Take the *Veregelt*,' the Wolf Lord had said months ago, aboard the flagship *Holmgang*. 'I'll give you a third of the company's packs. Return to me with a victory, Blackmane.'

Victory had come, hard-fought but honestly earned, despite the cold indifference of their Dark Angels allies.

But now this. Chainswords sputtered in idle hands, keenly waiting for the call to come to life. Ragnar glanced down at the body by his boots. A Champion fallen, the corpse headless. The Dark Angel's head, still in its helm, lay on the deck a dozen metres away.

Frostfang purred in its ease, blood dripping from the weapon's teeth.

'It is done,' Ragnar said again. 'The duel is over.'

Only silence met this declaration. All was still, even the cyborg hangar-thralls that had been tending to the docked Dark Angels gunships now watched, motionless.

The blow that had crashed against his face had ripped his cheek open to the bone and torn a flap of skin free, but his blood was already clotting in the stinging, re-filtered air. The wound's relative innocence only made the moment worse. It took all of his teeth-clenching effort to hide the momentary weakness of anger and shame.

Ragnar gestured to the body at his feet. 'Take your dead,' he said to the formation of Dark Angels, 'and get off our ship.'

Six Space Marines stepped forwards. Four of them lifted the body in wordless reverence, carrying it back to their ranks. Another carried the severed head with the same sense of respectful, monkish care. The Dark Angels had no captain, for he had fallen in battle weeks before, leaving command of the Fourth Battle Company to rest upon their Champion's shoulders. Now they were leaderless once more.

One of the Dark Angels approached Ragnar, remaining while the others removed the body. His face was bare, his features blunt, his demeanour one of cold serenity. His armour showed only a sergeant's insignia, but the plating was marked with laurel wreaths and ceremonial bolt shell trinkets denoting valour and marksmanship.

'This transgression cannot stand,' he said.

'What do you want of me? An apology?' The pain that had cobwebbed across Ragnar's face was swiftly fading, nullified by his enhanced physiology and a spurt of battle narcotics injected from his armour's internal regulators. 'Your Champion is dead. Had he been more skilled, he would still be alive. That's the beginning and end of it, Dark Angel.'

The Dark Angel inclined his head, seemingly in consideration rather than agreement. 'The duel was to first blood,' he said, coldly, viciously reasonable.

'Does it matter? It's over.'

'Indeed it is,' the sergeant concurred. 'And you lost, Battle Leader Blackmane.'

Jeers and shouted insults rose from the Wolves' disorderly ranks, but the Dark Angel was implacable. He nodded to the wound upon Ragnar's head, where the hanging flap of skin laid a sliver of his cheekbone bare. 'The duel was to first blood,' the sergeant repeated. 'You bled first.'

Ragnar looked back over his shoulder, where his warrior-packs were throwing derision at the Dark Angels amidst all of the laughter. In reflection, the Dark Angels were perfectly silent, doubtless considering themselves above such trite indignities.

'Listen to me,' Ragnar said, his voice little more than a whispered plea. 'I regret your Champion's death. Truly. But withdraw, sergeant, for this ugly scene will only turn evermore foul.'

'No, Wolf Guard.'

'Are you so blind to reason? We fought and won a war together, cousin. Proudly! Go now and we can avoid staining that glory with bloodshed and further regret.'

The sergeant, standing with his helm under one arm as if on the parade ground, showed emotion for the first time since coming aboard the *Veregelt*. His lip curled, not in feral temper but in simple, human disgust.

'You think we fear the bite of your blades? You have no right to plead for mercy now after committing a crime that demands redress. Blood calls for blood. It is tradition.'

'You... wish to fight us?'

'What I wish is of no consequence, Wolf Guard. This is not about me. *You* lost the duel and ignobly cut down the warrior who beat you. *You* broke the lone tradition that binds us together in the echoes of brotherhood. *You* lost your temper like a newly blooded aspirant, disgracing the primarchs' ritual with foul murder.'

Ragnar's reply was a thing of hissed, hot breath. 'Watch your words, Dark Angel. I've cut tongues from men's mouths for lesser insults.'

'I believe you.' The sergeant's disgust had reached his eyes, infecting the warrior's austere stare with condescending light. 'But blood will have blood, Battle Leader Blackmane.'

Ragnar's fury dissipated. It was all he could do not to laugh in disbelief, even in the gravity of the moment. Even with the sin he'd committed heavy and fresh upon his shoulders.

'You threaten us on our own ship? Allfather's bones, Dark Angel, my men will tear your company to pieces. Already they clamour for your last breaths. Take your threats and go while you're still able. I cannot guarantee your survival any longer.'

'I make no threats,' the sergeant said. 'You are the one threatening us, which might be considered dangerous ground when we yet outnumber you two to one. You violated the boundaries of *Duellum Honestas*. Thus, I challenge you to *Duellum Dolor.*'

'A fight to the death?' Ragnar couldn't keep the surprise from his voice. A line sergeant against a Fenrisian battle leader, in a fight to the death? The Wolves behind him were howling with laughter now.

'To the death, Battle Leader Blackmane. In accordance with our rites of war, you have thirty hours – a single turning of the Calibanite day – to accept the challenge and pay the blood price.'

'And if I refuse?'

'Then you forfeit all honour. If you will not pay the blood price, the Dark Angels will take it from the Wolves, one way or another.'

Pain nullifiers were no salve for the heat of irritation. He had let his temper get the better of him, but it wasn't too late to pull the two forces back from the brink.

It couldn't be too late. *Control, control,* he thought. *Calm.*

'I'm not fighting you, sergeant, no matter how you threaten me. For the final time, get off our ship.'

The Dark Angel replaced his helm with a hiss of locking seals at the collar, and saluted with the two-handed sign of the aquila across his chestplate. The voice that left the helmet's mouth-grille was inhuman and metallic, yet somehow serene.

'Thirty hours, Lord of Wolves.'

II

On the Maelstrom's edge, where reality itself was poisoned by the veil of the warp's tempestuous energy infecting real space, the destroyer *Veregelt* came to life. Row upon row of cannons rattled clear of armoured housings along her spinal battlements, black maws yawning into the void. Turrets, dotted like barnacles along the ship's hull, rotated into firing position at the behest of mind-locked servitors. She turned towards her prey, the equally austere and much larger strike cruiser *Sword of Caliban,* shadowed green where the *Veregelt* was mist-grey.

The Wolves pack leaders met on the *Veregelt*'s bridge, standing before Ragnar as their battle leader slouched in the command throne. With only two exceptions, their mood was justified and jubilant as they stood around their appointed commander.

Ulrik was the first exception, which was no surprise to any of the gathered kindred. The Wolf Priest was almost always grim to the point of solemnity. Black clad and icily serene, he stood with his crozius war maul resting on one shoulder. His face was masked by the helm of artificial bone that legend said had once been worn by Leman of the Russ Tribe himself. With a single word, he could have conveyed a wealth of weariness and disappointment in the young leader's actions, but such wasn't his way. Instead, the only emotion in his question was bald curiosity.

'Was that wise, Blackmane?'

Ragnar had no answer to give, though most of his brethren didn't care. The pack leaders rallied around Ragnar, congratulating him upon his victory.

Valkien – called Foebreaker by his kith and kin – clapped the younger warrior on the back. 'Severed his head in one blow. There's one for the sagas. Even the other Great Companies will laugh about this at the next feast day.'

'And you're so certain it's a matter of mirth?' asked Nalfir Razortongue.

'Cutting a Dark Angel's head from his shoulders is always going to be worth a smile, Razortongue.'

Nalfir was the second of the gathered warriors to show no joy. Ragnar had expected mockery and disapproval from the company's bard, perhaps even a lecture. He hadn't gambled on actual anger. Nalfir tore the torc from his neck and let it fall to the deck with a clatter, where it landed by Ragnar's bloodstained boots.

'Hear me, battle leader.'

Ragnar nodded. 'I listen.'

'As well you should, after this day's pathetic deed.' The others found themselves inching away from Nalfir, the way true wolves will edge away when a hunt-scarred rival bears its fangs at the pack leader. 'If a blood price is owed then the Dark Angels can come and try to take it,' he said, showing his long eyeteeth. 'You must fight.'

Hrolf – called Longspear by his kith and kin, and named for the weapon he once hurled into a sea drake's eye – gave a hesitant grunt. 'Killing their Champion is a deed worthy of boasting. Killing a sergeant with bruised pride is less noble. We've already won the ritual duel – let's leave the fools to nurse their wounded hearts.'

'And what happens when this sergeant falls?' asked Valkien. 'Will Blackmane then have to cut down the next Dark Angel in line, and the next, and the next? When does their stubbornness end?'

Nalfir breathed a curse. 'This is a matter far graver than you all seem to realise. There's a time, my brothers, for spitting on the rites and laws of our cousin Chapters. Many times. This is not one of them.'

Ulrik, oldest of all the gathered warriors, gestured for the young bard to continue.

'Blackmane violated the code between our Chapters,' said Nalfir. 'Life for life, blood for blood, honour for honour. The jarl must fight, and it saddens me to see you all considering anything else.'

Ragnar shook his head. 'This isn't about valour, Razortongue. It's about sanity. I can't kill one of them in cold blood. We're Wolves, above such pettiness.'

Nalfir favoured the jarl with a sneer. 'You're already a murderer, Blackmane. Don't blame your hot blood here and now. He cut you, and you killed him for it. You have no right to preach the difference between valour and sanity with a dead warrior's blood on your boots. You could yield, of course. Surrender to them, offering your life into their hands. They'll kill you quickly, I'm sure. Execution by the fall of a knightly blade. But you wouldn't sacrifice yourself like that... would you?'

Ragnar's lip twitched in reply. 'You judge me, singer?'

'As is my right. I am of the First Pack – Wolf Guard to Jarl Thunderfist as true as you yourself. More than that, it's my place, my *duty*, to judge you. First you kill a Dark Angel in a child's fury, now you want to run from the consequences. They'd have every right to plunge a blade into the *Veregelt's* spine as we merrily fled.'

'Fled?' Hrolf's eyes narrowed. 'It's not fleeing when we've already won.

The jarl calls us to deal with the Flesh Tearers warship. Better to answer Thunderfist and rejoin the company than delay here playing yet more honour games with the Dark Angels. We've waited long enough.'

'You're wiser than your words, Longspear. This is not just any ritual, performed by a nameless and meaningless Chapter with no history. These are the Lion's own sons. What do you think the Sacred Duel is? It's born of our own sense of honour as much as theirs – a tradition that has historically kept our two Chapters from war. It's a release. A bleeding of tension. Every few years, it lances the regrown boil and flushes out the poison.'

'And Blackmane *won*,' Hrolf pressed. 'So a Dark Angel died? Warriors die in duels. Allfather's blood, Blackmane even apologised.'

There were discontented murmurs at that. Ragnar's jaw clamped tight; apologies were rarely given in Fenrisian culture, and a graceless or unnecessary one threatened a tribesman's standing among his men, for only weaklings solved with words what should be solved with red axes and bloodstained snow. All warriors of the Adeptus Astartes strove to be above such simplistic attitudes in the theatre of war, but Fenris ran cold in the Space Wolves' blood. A culture leaves its mark upon all men, women and children within its borders, even upon post-humans who leave their home worlds far behind.

'Enough of your craven whispering,' Nalfir snapped. 'Outside the ship's hull burns the Maelstrom. Dark Angels and Wolves alike have shed blood in purging this storm's spinward edge. Five months of fighting! Now you want to blight the saga by running scared before the Dark Angels' rage.'

'Razortongue,' warned Ragnar.

'What, kinsman? Does my temper displease you?'

'Take a breath, brother. Your blood is up and it's poisoning your words.'

Nalfir's smile was a slowly drawn blade. 'My blood is up? I wasn't the one to carve open one of the Lion's knights because I couldn't control myself in an honourable duel.'

Nalfir saw the tension spread across Ragnar's face, tightening the young lord's features. The other warriors slammed gauntlets to the hilts of weapons, but the bard only laughed.

'So that burns, does it? Well, the truth always has a little sting in its tail.'

'Watch. Your. Tongue.'

'Jarl Thunderfist values me for my honesty. He sent me with you for the same purpose, and I don't give the contents of my chamber's pisspot whether or not the truth wounds you. The Great Company's elders have spoken of the dangers of your temper more than once. Now we all see why.'

He gestured to the others in disgust. 'Look at all of you, cheering our lord for striking down that knightly fool. As if Blackmane losing his temper and violating one of the Chapter's oldest codes of honour is something to celebrate! Do we venerate murder now? You *lost*, Blackmane. You were bloodied first. We all saw it. Why did you strike the Dark Angel down?'

Ragnar spoke through clenched teeth. 'You want the truth? I don't know.

I have no answer to ease your sneering face. He struck me, there was pain... and redness. I remember the fury, and nothing more. When the haze faded, the Champion was dead at my feet.' He spat on the deck, in the Fenrisian custom of warding away bad luck. 'Does that sate your hunger for answers, judgemental one?'

'Sadly, aye, it does. And you're revealed to be no more than an uncontrolled Blood Claw promoted far above his station.'

All were speechless in the wake of those words. Valkien's quick gaze flickered between the gathered Wolves, seeing only stunned silence on their features. Words tumbled through his thoughts, finding no traction on his tongue.

Nalfir wasn't yet done. 'Actions have consequences. We saw you kill like a murderer. Now draw your pretty sword and fight like a warrior. If Jarl Thunderfist were here now, this would be his judgement.'

The bard backhanded Ragnar, swifter than a human eye could follow. The young commander's head snapped to the side and the pack leaders moved as one – half of them restraining Nalfir for his transgression, half of them moving to prevent their battle leader from cannoning his fist into the other Wolf Guard's face.

But there was no blow. Ragnar hadn't moved. He ignored his brothers holding his shoulders and arms, just as he ignored the others forcing Nalfir to his knees in obeisance to await judgement. Ragnar's eyes were cold and still. When he blinked, it seemed an indulgence rather than a necessity.

Nalfir, proud despite his brothers holding his arms wide, stared up into Ragnar's eyes.

'Twenty-five hours remain. Time is not on your side.'

Ragnar breathed through closed teeth. The war between prudence and honour was an ugly one, with no right answers. The others shared his tension, though for different reasons. He saw the savage glint in their eyes and heard the heavy percussion of their drumming hearts. Razortongue's words had stirred them, sure enough. They wanted this. Fenrisian warriors to the core, they wanted to watch one of their own cut down another of their hated allies, earning renown for the Great Company in victory.

The right action for the wrong reason.

And Ragnar wanted it, too. Fenris' ice ran in his veins as truly as it ran in theirs.

We are supposed to be better than this, he thought. *Above it. The triumph of higher ideals over base desires.*

Now he was caught between honour and reason. When honour called for senseless bloodletting, and reason had become the coward's way out.

His men looked on, waiting for his judgement. His first true command, chosen by the jarl, and he stood upon the edge of making a grievous error worse. Giving orders in the heat of battle was one thing. He had a gift for it – it came instinctively, with scarce need to second guess himself. But this? The Wolves and the Dark Angels – an immovable object meeting an unstoppable force, both fuelled by unbreakable tradition.

Even if the Imperium never heard of this duel, and even if both Chapters celebrated their part in it, the fact would remain: Ragnar would have cut down a cousin in cold blood.

He knew what his lord, Berek, would do in Ragnar's place. Berek would accept the challenge – 'just a single foolish warrior,' he'd laugh – and return to the Fang with a Dark Angels helm on his belt, and a tale of bitter honour to tell in the feasting hall.

But what of High King Grimnar? Would he fight with a heavy heart or back down, putting prudence over empty glory?

The truth was, Ragnar had no idea. His rise through the ranks had been so swift, so unprecedented, that in these quiet moments he sometimes found himself lacking an elder's example to guide his way. Berek was far from here and trusted Ragnar to see this war through alone. Ulrik was a spiritual guide, not a commander to follow. The Great Wolf, though beloved and revered by the Chapter, was a distant king whose path didn't often cross with that of his lesser kinsmen.

That left instinct. Instinct served Ragnar well, but it was a bestial gift, ebbing and flowing with the heat in his blood. Most often a blessing, sometimes a curse.

If the Wolves left, they sacrificed all claim to honour, damaging the fragile peace between the Chapters. If they stayed, Ragnar would compound his failure of temper with a true murder, surely breeding further resentment.

'Blackmane,' said Grey Hunter Valkien. 'Perhaps Razortongue is right. It's just one warrior. Just one sergeant.'

'You already killed their Champion,' Hrolf added. 'What difference is one more?'

And so mankind dies while its chosen defenders devour each other.

Ulrik looked on in wordless vigil, radiating neither disapproval nor encouragement. Ragnar practically snarled at him.

'Speak, damn you.'

'And say what, young one?'

'You are the soul of this Great Company. Speak, old father. Guide us.'

'There's nothing to say. You know the stakes, you know the cost. Now you seek a right answer where none exists. You were chosen to lead us, Blackmane. Make your choice. Lead.'

The battle leader was the silent heart of a silent bridge, his tired eyes unable to meet the waiting stares of his closest kindred. Finally his hand closed around Frostfang's grip.

And loosened. He sighed.

Ragnar looked down into his kinsman's eyes, and offered his hand to aid Razortongue's rise.

'I will fight.'

III

Sorael kept his head bowed before the Lion's graven image, alone yet not alone. Robed Chapter thralls chanted their monastic song above him upon the chamber's balconies, their hooded faces turned to the domed ceiling. Their place was to fill this sacred space with holy song, aiding in the Dark Angels' communion. For now they sang of Champion Harrad's glories in life, rather than the ignominy of his death.

Sorael came often to the chapel, more so than many of his brothers. His sword was bared as custom demanded in this sacred place, and each breath he drew carried the tang of incense into his lungs. It was a familiar scent, one that harked back to so many similar moments of quiet isolation and solemnity. He lifted his eyes to the Lion's stone-wrought avatar. His gene-sire's features, cast in stern majesty, stared indifferently down at the sergeant.

'I will die today,' he told the statue. If there was judgement in the Lion's lifeless eyes, it was beyond Sorael's interpretation. It was, after all, just a statue. Sorael saw an image, not an icon – a source of inspiration and reflection, not a conduit for the divine.

The sound of approaching boots prickled at his attention, disturbing his devotion. He didn't rise. There was only one reason he would be disturbed here now, and he'd been expecting them to come.

'Sergeant.' It was Morthiac, of course. They would send no other. No one else of significant rank was left alive.

'Honoured Lexicanium.'

The Librarian knelt by Sorael's side, briefly bowing his head to pay his own respects to the fallen primarch. Like the sergeant, he'd unsheathed his sword to leave the blade bare. Sorael watched the younger warrior, noting the crude flesh-replenishment patches still not taking well across the psyker's throat and cheek.

'Do your wounds still trouble you?' he asked once the Librarian had opened his eyes.

The young Lexicanium touched armoured fingertips to the riven and poorly healed flesh. 'Only with the embarrassment of earning them. The pain and discomfort are meaningless.'

A good answer, Sorael thought. For all his youth – Morthiac was only a year out of the Scout Company – he was still a Dark Angel, cast in the primarch's stoic image. To even stand clad in ceramite meant surviving a hundred wars that would see lesser warriors left dead in the dust.

'Once I am dead, you must lead the Fourth home,' said Sorael.

Morthiac inclined his head, acknowledging the duty. 'There is a chance–'

'Spare me all talk of what might be, and let us focus on what will be.'

'You are a swordsman of no small skill, sergeant.'

'Enough. Once I am dead, honour will be satisfied. War between the Chapters will be averted. It will be your place to ensure the Fourth reaches the Rock. We are wounded and leaderless. Our time in the deep void is over.'

'It shames all of the Fourth,' Morthiac said, 'to return so bloodied.'

Emotion darkened Sorael's face. 'No. That is plainly and deeply untrue. The war was bitter but the enemy was scourged in absolute destruction. We lost eighteen warriors in righteous battle, true. Now their names are known to the Emperor of All and His primarch son. There is no shame there. Master Aralech fell with all honour on the front lines, as did Brother-Chaplain Ectar. Only Harrad's death has a pall cast over it, and the shame of his murder lies with the Wolf Lord, not with the Champion himself. Harrad fought Battle Leader Blackmane with all honour, keeping to the laws of the ritual.'

'Yes, sergeant.'

Sorael looked into the younger warrior's eyes. 'Are my words clear, Lexicanium Morthiac? They must be, for if you are to bring the Fourth before Chapter Command, your voice must speak the unburdened truth.'

'Your words are clear, sergeant.'

Sorael stared hard at the Librarian. 'This campaign was a triumph. Remember that, brother. Chapter Master Azrael must hear that above all else.'

'I meant only that the tragedy at the end of this crusade overshadows the glory of winning it.'

'Indeed. That, unfortunately, may be true. Our Chapter's memory is long, and this is not the first time the Wolves have soured the Primarchs' Truce.' Sorael released a breath, looking down at his reflection in his sword's silver blade. 'Though the Dark Angels are hardly innocent in that regard themselves.'

'You speak of a specific battle?'

The sergeant lifted his gaze once more. 'No, just the back and forth tides of this long grudge. Our penchant for ruthless secrecy works against us, and the Wolves have a way of angering those who would be their allies. If we are careful today, we will end this stalemate without aggravating the rest of our respective Chapters and putting the Wolves and Dark Angels at each other's throats.'

'At the cost of your life.'

'I am at peace with it, brother. There are worse ways to die.'

'You knew the message I brought before I gave it. You knew Battle Leader Blackmane would accept.'

Sorael showed no mirth, beyond a deepening of the wrinkles at the edges of his eyes. 'This Ragnar is a barbarian with poor control over his anger, but it would be profoundly unwise of him to refuse the duel. You saw him against the Bearers of the Word in this campaign, alongside Master Aralech. For all the primitive's flaws, he leads from the front and values the lives of his men. He even apologised to me, when we stood face to face over Harrad's body. A rarity for a Wolf. They detest apologising. It is a sign of weakness in their culture, yet he did so nonetheless, for he knew he had acted in error.'

Morthiac narrowed his pale eyes. 'You admire the warrior who murdered Champion Harrad, and will strike you down mere hours from now?'

Sorael raised an eyebrow in disapproval, about as expressive as he ever was. 'Do not mistake acknowledgement for admiration. Did you wish to speak of anything more, or was the message of Ragnar's acceptance the only matter?'

'The Wolves have asked where we wish the duel to be fought.'

'Sacristan,' Sorael answered at once. 'In the Endymion Cluster, coreward of the Golgothan Wastes. The world is not far from here.'

The Dark Angels had won a battle there against the Traitor Legions, long before Sorael's birth. It pleased him to think of his blood running into the earth of a world once cleansed by his forefathers.

'It will be done, sergeant.'

'Thank you. Now please leave me to prepare.'

Morthiac rose, bowing and taking the traditional three steps backwards before turning his back on the Lion's image. Sorael listened to his brother's retreating tread then, alone once more, he listened to the enslaved thralls singing of the fallen Champion and his life's deeds.

In a few hours, he thought, *they will sing of me.*

IV

Sacristan turned in the silence of space, a frontier world in every way mankind judged such things. Here was a world whose peaceful stillness arose from isolation, though it was a peace that vanished the moment one pierced the planet's atmosphere. The weather on Sacristan was forever in flux, and if it wasn't adamantly hostile to human life, it was at the very least not conducive to it.

Scattered colonies dotted its surface, each one primitively shielded against the blizzards that tore their way across the world's face. Once they had been outposts for a planetary culture that had risen, ruled and fallen after an uprising of the Archenemy's Traitor Legions. Although the Imperium had prevailed in that long ago war, the world never regained its primacy. Now the settlements were independent city-states with little contact with the wider Imperium: pirate fortresses, substandard mining installations or other settlements of equal irrelevance.

A week's flight brought the *Veregelt* into orbit above Sacristan. There, patient as only hunters and penitents can be, Ragnar and his warriors waited. With the empyrean's fickle nature, they might be waiting a week, a month or a decade.

Fortune favoured them. Three hours after the Wolves' arrival their cousins broke from the warp at the system's edge, and the command deck's proximity alarms were music to the bored Wolves' ears. On the occulus, the *Sword of Caliban* was a miniscule dot, near-lost among the star field but broadcasting its identity across standard Imperial channels. At full speed the Dark Angels vessel was only eight hours distant.

Rather than linger on the bridge any longer, Ragnar gathered his warriors and ordered the Great Company to the drop pods for planetfall. He would await his opponent on the surface.

Five ships knifed their way back into reality: a cruiser and four smaller escorts running in unity. All five were armoured in immense plating of filthy cobalt, edged with gold so corroded it looked closer to rotted copper.

The precision of their manifestation was something Ragnar would watch and rewatch hundreds of times in the following years, poring over the grainy archival footage from the *Veregelt*'s gun-picters, always studying the imagery for new nuances and always awed at the artfulness of the vessels' arrival.

Never in his life would he lay claim to a ship captain's mastery of the three-dimensional ocean of deep space, but he had a keen appreciation for the skill, flair and calculating mind necessary to turn void warfare into art. He knew enough to know the difference between training, experience and those who piloted warships with a true gift.

The arrival of the five vessels was a display of utter perfection. They didn't burst from the warp in a shuddering run; they speared their way back into real space with vicious, smooth glides, veering around each other in rolling arcs as they lanced forwards. No Imperial vessels could hold such close formation as they left the warp – that degree of unity was beyond the limits of the Imperium's arcane technology. These warships maintained a fluid dance of cohesion at all times. Warp smoke, formed of clinging hands and tortured faces reaching from poisoned mist, trailed at their rolling hulls.

Like sharks, Ragnar would later think, watching the warships twist and glide in the black, starry ocean. *They move like the Hearthworld's sea-tyrants.*

The five vessels surged forth from the same gash in reality, perfectly positioned behind the *Veregelt*. They ran at the Wolves ship, engines hot, gunports unlocking and unfolding. A tidal roar of dissipating warp energy rolled ahead of them, for even a perfect re-entry into reality couldn't banish all of the monumental forces at play. It struck the *Veregelt* like the crest of a wave, hammering the vessel from its place at high anchor.

At the time, Ragnar knew none of this. His world was one of darkness and noise – sirens wailing in every corridor, in every chamber, reaching his heightened hearing through the metal walls of the boarding assault pod. Automated impact warnings melted together with calls of battle stations.

The pod shivered around him, each warrior's harness rattling in its iron sockets. The shiver became a tremor, and the tremor became a shake. Beyond the boarding pod's reinforced hull, there came a great wrenching whine of protesting metal. Even with the *Veregelt*'s gravitic generators, he felt the shift of weight in his bones.

'We're turning,' Nalfir said, feeling it in the same second. 'Why are we–'

The vox exploded with crew members' voices, all of them calling for the jarl. They spoke over each other, the communication channels jamming.

Ragnar disengaged the release clasps of his restraint harness and hammered the boarding pod's launch-abort plate. The pod began its shuddering journey out of its firing cradle and back down to the hangar deck, gripped in the slow arms of a positioning crane.

Ragnar looked up at the servitor's face cybernetically fused to the pod's ceiling, serving as a crude machine-spirit.

'Override iris seals,' he commanded.

'Please confirm,' said the servitor, dead-eyed, parched-throated and entirely devoid of urgency.

'Override!'

Hangar light spilled in through the opening iris door. The deck itself was still thirty metres below them, drifting closer with ludicrous hydraulic slowness as the crane lowered them. Thralls and tech-adepts were running to their battle stations, buckling themselves into crash thrones or adopting brace positions.

'Battle leader,' came the voice from the bridge he'd been waiting to hear, the voice he'd been calling for across the vox.

'Wayfarer, my brother, speak to me.'

'Raiders from the Maelstrom, behind us. Five ships clad in the colours of the vile Eighth.' Ragnar could hear the command crew shouting beneath Sijur Wayfarer's report, but focused on his kinsman's voice. 'A strike cruiser and four escorts of unidentified predation classes. They broke from the warp on top of us. I've never seen a manoeuvre like it.'

They had been waiting, Ragnar knew. Waiting for the Dark Angels' and Wolves' crusade to end; waiting for the Adeptus Astartes warships to stand alone in the dark, away from the vessels of the Imperial Navy that had accompanied them for several months of patrol and reconquest at the Maelstrom's edge. This wasn't an ambush, nor even a battle. This was a reprisal raid. The last gasp of the bloodied and the beaten, desperate to salvage some pride.

They followed us as swiftly as they could, as precisely as they were able, waiting for us to be alone. Now they strike.

'What of the *Sword of Caliban*?'

'The Dark Angels are passing the fifth planet of the system,' said Sijur. 'The *Sword* is at least six hours away. To stay here is to die.'

The warriors with him in the boarding pod added their shouts of indignation to the aural melee. Ragnar silenced them with a chop of his hand.

Five enemy ships. *Five.* Today was a day for impossible choices, determined to shame him one way or another.

'Time to go,' he murmured.

'Battle leader? Did you speak?'

He took a breath before speaking across the vox again. 'I did. Disengage, Wayfarer. We're running. Order all hands to prepare to repel boarders – the Night Lords will try to take the ship. We beat them back if they board us, and break into the warp as soon as we're able. Make full speed for the coordinates where we're to meet Jarl Thunderfist and the *Holmgang*.'

The other warriors were free of their restraint thrones now, standing behind their young leader.

'The Dark Angels may not get their duel after all,' Nalfir told him. 'Facing them was noble, Blackmane, but facing an enemy fleet alone is suicide. We have to run.'

'I know that,' Ragnar snapped. 'Yet your logic doesn't comfort me.'

'It never does. But I'm not here to comfort you, kinsman.' The bard leaned out of the pod and spat onto the hangar deck, to counter ill fortune. 'At least life with you is never dull.'

Ragnar looked over his shoulder, a Blood Claw's mad humour gleaming in his eyes. 'When I die, let those words be written beneath my name in the Hall of Heroes.'

The boarding pod was low enough to leap from. With a wild howl, he jumped.

Ragnar reached the bridge at a dead run, charging up to the central platform and taking command from Sijur Wayfarer with no more than a nod of acknowledgement. On other Imperial vessels an executive officer might announce 'Captain on the bridge' with no small formality. Aboard the *Veregelt,* Ragnar's presence announced itself. Every eye on the command deck instinctively turned to him, even if only for a moment. He brought an aura with him, wordless and vital, bleeding raw confidence.

Ragnar gripped the dais railing as he leaned forwards, watching the battle playing out across the multisected occulus viewscreen just as he felt it in the deck shaking his bones. The *Veregelt* arced and rolled in its flight, but the Night Lords vessels were jackals biting and clawing as they encircled the bigger ship. Hounding the *Veregelt* was easy, for the carrion-feeders of the VIII Legion had the numbers and speed necessary to steer the Wolves ship to their desires. They forced it to bank and veer to avoid collisions, breaking its attack runs; they dived aside from its broadside volleys, leaving the Wolves battlement cannons roaring their payloads into the empty void.

More tellingly, they were cutting off its escape.

'Like fighting rats,' Sijur said from Ragnar's side. He didn't need to admit the *Veregelt*'s guns had scored no worthwhile hits. If the auspex readings showing scan diagrams of the undamaged enemy ships weren't obvious enough, the illuminating flare of their functioning shields told the tale without any doubt.

Data spilled across the occulus alongside the warring vessels. Targeting calculations changed with each second. Attack vectors shifted and redefined their arcs. Predictive runes flashed alongside ship scans and offered hundreds of probabilities at once. Ragnar's preternatural mind processed the wealth of information at a glance.

He came to two conclusions in the same instant. The first was that Sijur had wisely been fighting defensively, seeking to minimise damage to the *Veregelt* through evasive manoeuvres and returning limited fire when the scarce opportunities presented themselves.

The second realisation was that it wasn't going to work. The Night Lords would cripple them before they could run.

'Our shields fell four minutes ago,' said Sijur. 'Now they're preying on our engines, bringing us down with a thousand cuts. I've been trying to lure them into boarding us early, so they'd hold their fire. That's a fight we might actually win.'

The ship shook beneath their boots with sustained impacts. Tremors ran through the grip rail, into Ragnar's fingers and along his arm. The *Veregelt* was taking a merciless beating.

'What's the status of the *Sword of Caliban?*'

Sijur keyed in a long-distance view of the other Adeptus Astartes warship, a dot of darkness against the infinite void.

'They're hours from maximum weapons range. With the damage we're taking, I can't even be sure they're still heading in this direction.'

Then we're alone. We can't outrun them, we can't outfight them, and no help is coming.

'Very well,' said Ragnar. 'Hail the *Sword of Caliban.*'

The connection took several seconds. When it came, it was flawed by ululating static.

'...mander Blackm...' came an unrecognisable voice.

'This is Battle Leader Blackmane of the *Veregelt*. Sorael, my cousin, it grieves me to abandon our duel.' He swallowed, speaking through clenched teeth. Jarl Thunderfist may well have his head for this. And that was even if the Chapters didn't go to war over it.

'...enemy vessels... retreat...'

'*Sword,* your signal is too broken,' Ragnar replied. 'I pray you hear my words better than we hear yours. The fleet at our position significantly outnumbers us, with or without your aid. Don't engage. Repeat, do not engage. The *Veregelt* would be dead in space before you reached us anyway.'

Sijur met Ragnar's eyes and shook his head. The signal, already weak, was fluctuating into uselessness.

'Sorael,' Ragnar finished, 'forgive me for this dishonour. If we meet again...'

'The link is gone,' said Sijur.

Ragnar growled, venting his anger before speaking. 'Cease trying to seek a way to escape. They close the feigned gaps too swiftly. Come about and focus all fire on the closest frigate.'

'The *Black Prayer.*'

'I care nothing for its name, just kill it. We need to provoke the others into altering their paths.'

As the *Veregelt* shivered, obeying the command of its temporary master, Ragnar watched the void dance taking place through the myriad calculations of flashing Fenrisian runes upon the occulus. He saw the Night Lords' intent the moment they began to move into a new attack pattern.

He pointed at one of the escorts' approach arc. 'That destroyer... The *Vision of Entropy*. It will cut us off, moving between the *Veregelt* and the *Prayer,* forcing us to roll away again and reset our attack run.' Ragnar narrowed his eyes, estimating and calculating as best he could to keep pace with the three-dimensional cogitations taking place before him. 'Don't veer away.'

The warriors around him shared a look. 'Blackmane?' asked Sijur, seeking confirmation rather than comprehension.

'It's our best chance to tear a hole we can slip through. When the *Vision of Entropy* dives across our path to break our attack trajectory, take the ship through it. We risk everything, here. Break through and break free... or let them cripple us.'

'No choice at all, eh?' Nalfir said with a quiet laugh. 'This will almost surely kill us, you know.'

Ragnar unknowingly echoed his Angelic rival. 'There are worse ways to die.'

Baring his teeth, Sijur called down to the helmsmen, 'Ramming speed! All hands, brace for impact!'

The Night Lords vessel *Vision of Entropy* danced alongside the *Veregelt,* taking incidental fire from the destroyer's broadsides as she overtook the wounded Wolves ship. She veered ahead, her shields rippling with dissipating energy, moving into a climb that positioned her between Ragnar's vessel and the Night Lords escort *Black Prayer.*

A predator with millennia of experience, she acted and reacted like a living being as she sailed in the deep void. She ran swiftly, engines hot and screaming into the void, her rearward turrets vomiting torrents of plasma and solid shells against the *Veregelt*'s prow armour. With luck she could survive several minutes of retaliation at this range, holding off the Space Wolves barrage against her own shields.

The expected return volley from the burning *Veregelt* never came. By the time the captain of the *Vision of Entropy* realised why, it was already too late. The *Veregelt* leapt forwards with a furious surge of speed, lancing into the destroyer with the strength of an arrow bringing down a hawk on the wing.

The *Veregelt*'s prow eradicated the *Entropy*'s void shields, bursting them a second before it hammered into the other ship's spine. Battlements crumbled as the Night Lords vessel's superstructure came apart, hopelessly devastated under the weight and velocity of the spearing destroyer.

Hundreds of crew aboard the *Veregelt* were thrown from their feet or out of their restraint thrones. Hundreds more died with their bodies smashed against the walls and deck floors. The warship's prow was a blunted ruin, mangled beyond recognition, and with it she'd lost her forward weaponry array, now crushed beyond any ability to fire. The *Veregelt* carried the *Entropy*'s wreckage with it, the Traitor ship still impaled as it fell apart in exploding hull sections.

The final detonation came with the ignition of the *Black Prayer*'s warp engines, its force threading cracks of fire through the forward half of the wounded Space Wolves vessel.

The surviving Night Lords escorts had spiralled away from the maddened display of force, keeping their distance. Now they struggled to come about and recover the pursuit, as the Wolves ship re-lit her weak shields around her flaming superstructure, and lanced for the hole now torn open in the enemy formation. She trailed detritus and vented roaring air from her wounds, as if rising breathless from a graveyard of wreckage.

And then, with an impossibly silent burst of energy that should never exist in the material universe, the *Veregelt*'s arcane, sacred engines carved open a wound in space and time, and dived within.

The rip in reality dissolved behind her, breaking down into the shrieking, melting faces of ten thousand monsters.

The Wolves were gone.

V

Jarl Berek, Lord of the Thunderfists, was a king without a throne. In this he believed himself to be carved in the image of Leman of the Russ Tribe, the Hearthworld's first and greatest High King. A hundred apocryphal tales told how Russ had also refused a throne, claiming they were the icons of scribes and administrators who demanded respect, rather than warlords and warchiefs who earned it.

When he inherited the *Holmgang* from his predecessor, a great ship-master's seat of wrought black iron occupied the central command dais. Berek's first act upon taking over was to have it melted down and beaten into scorched metal rings, offering them as treasures to his favoured warriors and saving the rest to be granted as rewards in the fullness of time. His Wolf Guard elite wore their rings beneath their armour as torcs around their necks and bands around their biceps. By such gestures were traditions born. To serve in his inner circle now was to 'wear the jarl's iron'.

He was on the command deck when Ragnar approached. Berek stood alone despite the sea of thralls, menials and Chapter-serfs working in teams around him. Their lord ostensibly watched from above, though in truth his thoughts wandered to the great occulus viewscreen with its vista of the starry void. A sleek knife of a ship – the destroyer *Baryonyx* cast in the colours of the Flesh Tearers Chapter – waited for the Wolves to decide her fate. Near her floated the newly arrived and savagely wounded *Veregelt*.

Berek scowled again. He'd been doing that a great deal of late.

'You broke my ship, Blackmane,' was what passed for his greeting.

Ragnar's reply was cold. 'I've come to report, my jarl.'

'So I see. You should have come to me before any other, you know. The next time one of your command reports to me before their commander, it will put me in bleak humour.'

Berek saw the younger Wolf fight back a sneer, not entirely successfully. It still twitched at Ragnar's lip.

'I take it that Razortongue fled to you first, whispering of what happened.'

'He did a bard's duty, and a Wolf Guard's duty besides. He told me of your actions among the Dark Angels, the noble and shameful moments alike.'

'I'm sure he did.'

Berek narrowed his eyes. 'You believe he'd lie?'

Ragnar said nothing.

'If you and Razortongue are unable to be civil with one another, at least keep the grudge between yourselves. If I have to intervene, my judgement will favour neither of you, I promise you that.'

Once more, Ragnar said nothing.

'The shame of the final day isn't enough to eclipse the glory of the preceding months, Blackmane. I'm disappointed in you, true, but not disgusted. However, had you lost the war as well as insulted the Dark Angels, this would be a different meeting. I promise you that.'

'Yes, my jarl.'

'And you know you must honour the duel you swore to fight, come what may. You have to face that Dark Angel... Sorael, was it?'

'Yes, my jarl.'

'Well. Our Calibanite cousins will overlook your excremental manners for a while given the ambush, but honour must be satisfied one day.'

'Yes, my jarl.'

'*Yes, my jarl.*' Berek mocked the younger warrior by mirroring Ragnar's lifeless tone. 'Boy, look what you did to the *Veregelt.*' He nodded over at the image of the two ships on the occulus. 'As if there wasn't already enough misery filling my screen.'

'It grieves me to have added to your weariness, jarl.'

That drew a chuckle, the sound so deep and low that it was almost ursine. Berek's mane of blond hair was plaited into dreadlocks that framed a face hewn from pale rock. He was an ugly creature, make no mistake, and smiling did him no favours.

'Keep your sarcasm to yourself, boy. This is serious and my patience with you is in short shrift.'

'As you say, my jarl.' Ragnar turned his gaze to the wounded *Veregelt* once more, and the void-lost *Baryonyx* beside it. 'What of the Flesh Tearers ship?'

'I haven't decided yet. We found it ten standard days ago, after tracking it for over a month. Word from the Fang reached us soon after.' Berek shook his head, the charms woven into his dreadlocks rattling against his shoulder guards. His next words were growled low. 'They're sending the Slayer.'

'From the Hearthworld?' Ragnar didn't conceal his surprise. Fenris was a quarter of the galaxy away. To reach their fleet out here would take months.

'No. The Slayer sails with Red Moon's Great Company, engaged on the edge of the Pale Stars. Jarl Gunnar has orders to bring the Slayer to us, then sail back alone.' There was no missing the disapproval in Berek's voice. 'The Slayer will remain with us to *advise.*'

'A... great honour,' Ragnar pointed out.

'What's this? A rare moment of tact from you, Blood Claw?'

'A day of wonders after all, sire.'

But Berek didn't smile. 'I like nothing about this, Blackmane. Not the misfortune of finding this wreck, not the Slayer's presence, and I like the colours marking that warship's hull least of all. Honour's End was before your time, little brother, but we saw the Flesh Tearers' true selves that day. I'd sooner trust Razortongue in a dice game than those blood-maddened carrion-feeders.'

Ragnar was captivated. Berek Thunderfist speaking in quiet contemplation was an event few of his brethren would ever witness. The younger warrior kept silent as the Wolf Lord continued.

'It's said the Inquisition's Black Ships have visited the Hearthworld only once in the span of one hundred centuries. Did you know that? The Fang's chronicles record only one inquisitor with Fenrisian blood in all of Imperial history. Just one. Inquisitor Jarlsdottyr was her name. She fought alongside the Wolves in the War of Shame, five hundred years ago. At Great Wolf Grimnar's side, if you can believe that. She even met the Fell-Handed. I've heard him speak of it myself.'

Ragnar felt his hackles rise at the mention of the First High Jarl, Bjorn Russbrother, called Fell-Handed by his kith and kin.

'I've never heard of this inquisitor.'

'Not many have, especially in the last century or so. Her name is spoken with a curse when it's spoken at all. The last time she was seen by loyal eyes, she was fighting alongside the Flesh Tearers. You see?' Berek hawked and spat onto the deck, either in distaste or to banish ill luck, Ragnar wasn't sure. 'That cursed Chapter. Everything they touch goes badly for them. Every time we meet, it ends in broken oaths and spilled blood.'

The younger warrior, still a Blood Claw in raw youth despite his elevation to the Wolf Guard, knew his lord rarely sought the insight of others. Especially not from those who had so recently dishonoured themselves. Ragnar regarded his jarl with a cautious gaze, his words walking the border close to disrespect.

'You fear this warship is another black omen,' he ventured, not quite a question.

'I fear nothing,' Berek replied. In that moment Ragnar felt a curious disconnect – he heard his lord's defiance yet felt the falsehood within it. Berek might not fear anything as a human would feel terror, but like many of the Wolves in the last year, the threat of dark omens had him hesitant and uneasy. Ever since the skies of Fenris turned black.

'Forgive my poor choice of words.'

Berek snorted. 'Omens everywhere. Maybe this *is* fear, eh? How would any of us even know its taste if it was?'

Before the eclipse of Fenris' sun, no Wolf Lord would have spoken this way. Now doubt had crept into the Chapter's blood, and doubt was a threat too insidious to fight. The rune-casters and spirit-speakers had infected every one of the Einherjar's Great Companies with a darkness no battle could banish.

Faced with his kinsman's silence, Berek continued with a growled sigh. 'Every seer, shaman and priest within the Fang tells us we must be watchful. So we watch, as they wish. They sing dirges of the Dawn of the End and the coming of the Wolftime. So we listen and pay heed. Now tell me, Blackmane, why we should deal with this wayward warship. Why not sail away and leave it to rot in the void?'

The test was an unsubtle one, but Ragnar took the rare opportunity to advise his liege lord all the same. He answered at once, speaking the truth without mockery.

'Lesser Chapters would do just that, but you're not a coward, Berek. As much as you despise that warship out there in the void, you're wearier still of flinching at shadows. The eclipse promised darkness and we're right to take it as a warning, but omens should make us cautious, not leech our courage.'

Berek raised a scarred eyebrow once more. Eyes the colour of scorched stone regarded the younger warrior with amusement.

'Pretty words. If I didn't know better, I'd say I sensed a lecture within them. Is that so, young Blood Claw?'

Ragnar occasionally knew when to speak and when to stay silent. It was a skill he was slowly learning.

'Back to your duty, little brother. Between incurring the wrath of the Dark Angels and breaking the *Veregelt,* you've got a great deal to make up for.'

Ragnar remained despite being dismissed. Berek raised a scarred eyebrow. 'Is there something more, Blackmane?'

'Yes, sire. You've not said what our boarding parties found upon the Flesh Tearers warship.'

The Wolf Lord hesitated. 'The Slayer's "request" was for the vessel to remain unchanged until his arrival.'

'Are you saying you haven't already sent boarding parties across several times in ten long days, sire?'

Berek grunted a laugh. 'I'm saying my boarding parties secured the ship without breaking anything. Can you give me the same guarantee?'

Ragnar didn't dignify his jarl's mockery with a reply. 'What of the crew manifest?' he asked instead.

'There's no danger – everything aboard is either dead or in stasis. A thousand menials in all. Ninety-one Chapter thralls in a stasis-locked section of the enginarium. Almost four hundred subsistence-grade work slaves on one of the intestinal decks. Three workshop-barracks were screened by stasis fields, holding two hundred servitors that should still function. Forty-one injured humans in apothecarion stasis pods, all of whom look to be battle-trained serfs. None of the astropathic choir survived. None of the Navigational coterie.'

Ragnar sensed where he was leading. 'What of the Flesh Tearers?'

'Seven,' Berek affirmed. 'Seven of them. In stasis, sealed from the outside, not simply deanimated.'

Ragnar scratched at his unshaven cheek, thinking.

'Tell me why you wish to go,' the jarl said, his flinty eyes narrowing again.

'To see for myself. The virtue of knowing one's enemy, my jarl. No more, no less.'

'I see. Well, I've no objection, but take Razortongue with you.'

'What? Why?'

'Because he made the very same request. And because I'm telling you to do it. It's called an order, Blood Claw. You remember those, don't you?'

'Sire...'

'Now, now. I could have taken your head for your recent failures, boy. Don't even think of arguing with me now.'

Ragnar didn't argue. His glare, however, spoke volumes.

'You're lucky that I like you,' Berek told him. 'Now get out of my sight.'

VI

The two warriors walked through arches of corroded bronze and dirty iron, making their way along the warship's cavernous spinal thoroughfare.

To Ragnar's senses, the whole ship breathed with the scent of faded carrion: chalk and cinnamon on the edge of every inhalation, too faint to be a stench. They were walking through the memory of death, its smell not ripe enough to be recent. Cratered metal pockmarks ran along many walls, showing – along with spent shell casings – the most obvious sign of bolter fire. Las-burns marked the walls like lesser graffiti, showing where the human crew had fought back against the invading enemy.

Bodies populated every tunnel and every aisle, many in unwelcome states of half-life. A servitor, rotted to bones and steel components, slouched against a bulkhead long-since sealed by a halo of orange rust. Its bionic hand still quivered, fingertips scratching uselessly against the metal deck with a curiously organic screech.

One of the Flesh Tearers lay further down the hallway, pinned to the wall by the three massive spears jutting through his chest. His helmet's eye lenses gleamed with active power, confirmed by the whine of his back-mounted power pack, infrequently spitting sparks.

Ragnar bristled as Nalfir went to the impaled corpse.

'What?' the bard asked, seeing his companion's tension.

'This is a tomb of the Adeptus Astartes,' Ragnar chided. 'The Flesh Tearers will have their own rites for revering their dead.'

Nalfir said nothing beyond a derisive snort as he reached under the corpse's helmet, disengaging the release seals on the collar.

'Razortongue,' warned Ragnar. 'The Slayer himself wishes this wreck to remain untouched. That includes the slain aboard it.'

There was no hiss of air pressure as the bard lifted the heavy helmet clear. Still Nalfir said nothing. Ragnar strode closer, gripping his brother's wrist.

'Mere days ago you lectured me on respecting the sanctity of the Dark Angels' rituals. What is different here?'

'Don't be naive, Blackmane. The Dark Angels' ritual is our ritual, too. But the Flesh Tearers are dogs and traitors and wretches, down to the last of the bloodline. Now get your hand off me before I remove it myself.'

Ragnar pulled his hand back with a snarl. He looked down at the corpse.

The Flesh Tearer stared eyelessly back at them, his features rotted down to dirty bones in the ruined armour. Leathery threads of ancient tissue held the bones of his neck together.

'A good death,' he said, gesturing to the three spears lanced into the slaughtered Space Marine's chest. 'Hard, but good.'

Nalfir stepped away with a chuckle, resuming his walk down the wide corridor. Reluctantly, Ragnar offered the dead warrior a nod of respect before following his brother.

A short time later, they came across the first of the slain enemy. A dead Iron Warrior, his ceramite plate torn open by blades and bolts, the body within decayed to a husk. Damage to the bones of the corpse's neck and chest told another tale; Ragnar recognised them at once.

'His gene-seed was harvested.'

It was rare to be able to examine any of the Traitorous Ones like this, and he crouched by the legionary's body, looking over the broken armour with its indescribable runic inscriptions upon the plating.

He sniffed, and though the Traitor was centuries dead he caught the traces of impossible scents. Weapon lubricant made from blood. Blood comprised of acid and promethium. Breath that reeked of forge fires. Forge fires that were fuelled by the shrieks and screams of burning martyrs.

A hundred other impossibilities, each as unnatural as the last. It was the smell of madness. Uncomfortable without being disgusting, addictive without sign of sweetness. The stench of the Great Eye and its twisted denizens.

The Iron Warrior's silver helmet was turned to the side, staring down the corridor into the dark towards the Flesh Tearer's impaled body. The killing blow was obvious: a bolter detonation had torn half of the faceplate free, leaving a visage of broken facial bones within the rough hole.

'Good shot,' Ragnar murmured. He reached for the sundered hole, wanting to turn the helmet and examine the other side. It wasn't a mark or pattern of armour he recognised, even had it not sported twin horns of biometallic ivory.

It was Nalfir's turn to warn him. '*Skitnah,*' said the bard, using the tribal term for 'unclean'. 'Leave it, Blackmane.'

Ragnar hesitated with his fingers an inch from the dead warrior's helm. He rose in a snarl of armour joints, deciding to follow his brother rather than endure another argument.

Their first stop wasn't the bridge. Nalfir's wandering led them to the chapel-barracks where, among full-strength Chapters, several dozen Space Marines might have been quartered between mission assignments.

There were no bodies. Most of the individual chambers were bare of any sign of habitation, and Ragnar suspected that even before its disastrous end the *Baryonyx* hadn't sailed with a full complement of Adeptus Astartes warriors.

The two Wolves moved on, room by room, until they reached one that showed evidence of once belonging to a living being. Ragnar felt a creeping sense of familiarity as he entered, seeing what were plainly a warrior's choice in personal trophies. Broken weapons of alien manufacture chained to the dark walls; a tattered pennant almost eroded to nothingness, its allegiance and symbolism now rendered unreadable; citation scrolls and honour badges, left with careful reverence on the spartan room's shelves.

Needing no permission, the Wolves poked through the absent warrior's personal sanctuary. Ragnar moved to a weapon rack, running his gloved touch across a mounted bolter – a blunt, straight, aggressive Tigrus-pattern, not often seen in the arsenals of newer Chapters. Instinctively, he counted the respectable number of kill-markings scratched along the boltgun's body, before moving on to a shelf of mementos and trinkets scoured from various battlefields. Among them:

Teeth from a chainsword, battered and blunt from the blow that tore them free.

A thin sliver of razor wire, of the kind often found marking out Imperial Guard trenches, was wrapped around a deactivated grenade.

A scorched, damaged flake of chitinous armour from some unknowable alien breed was etched with crude Low Gothic letters, spelling out 'Migar's Folly'.

Ragnar couldn't even guess what stories these items, which had meant so much to the warrior who chose to keep them, spoke of.

'Lykartan,' said Nalfir from across the room. He tapped a decaying scroll with his gloved fingertips. 'The warrior who dwelt here. His name was Lykartan.'

Ragnar turned from the wartime trinkets, hearing the heavy purr of his own active armour. He'd been looking through the rotted remains of thick paper sheets, seeing the mildewed shadows of what were once orbital printouts of an embattled cityscape.

'I'm not comfortable trawling through these relics. This feels like rifling through a tomb.'

'Is that what Berek feels, do you think? When he goes through the chambers of slain kinsmen, deciding how to divide their arms and armour? Choosing which of their own relics to bury them with, when they're interred back at the Fang? Comfortable or not, he faces up to the duty without hesitation, Blackmane.'

Ragnar had never considered such a thing, and admitted so.

'I know,' said Nalfir, evidently without judgement. 'Come, brother. Let's go see if this Lykartan was one of the ones to survive.'

* * *

The stasis engines appeared undamaged. Ragnar marvelled at their architecture, each pylon carved from volcanic glass in the shape of a Cretacian lizard-king, and in turn set within huge niches in the rusted iron walls. More than a group of engines with sacred purpose, the stasis machinery resembled a sculpted rendition of life on a savage world. Each obsidian carnosaur stood many times the height of a man, half sunken into its immense socket. The near-infinite cabling of each engine made up the beasts' veins, just barely visible beneath the black glass skin.

Ragnar had been fortunate enough to walk upon a Blood Angels warship and witness some of the artistic marvels aboard, wrought by the hands of the Chapter's Techmarines. Here, aboard the *Baryonyx,* there was a fusion of the familiar and unfamiliar: the artistry of the sons of Sanguinius coupled with the uncompromising savagery of the Flesh Tearers.

Individual pods lined the walls – they formed the talons of the towering lizard-beasts, leaving the inhabitants seemingly asleep within the great glass claws of monstrous reptiles.

He walked among them for a time, taking stock. The majority of the room was given over to stalagmite columns of grey machinery, reaching up to their sister-systems hanging down as stalactites from the arched ceiling. Their arcane function was beyond Ragnar's understanding but it stood to reason they were linked to some secondary power source, given the ship's near-dead plasma core. Everything here was running on subsistent energy, surviving on borrowed time.

The place felt haunted, in a way. Not with the clarity of hearing voices echoing off the walls or seeing flickers at the edges of his eyes, but in the way an old, old room can soak up the lives of those who once lived within it. It was a place of memory, neither a sanctuary nor a tomb.

Ragnar walked to the stasis pods. Most were empty. Many were cracked or otherwise flawed. Bolt shell craters and las-burns pockmarked more than one, or speckled the walls and floor nearby. The fighting had raged even here before the Flesh Tearers had evidently disengaged from the Iron Warriors and fled for the fools' safety of the warp.

Seven, the jarl had said. *Seven of them in stasis.*

It proved to be true. Seven Flesh Tearers slept, time-locked in their stasis pods, each one helmetless. Their pale faces were visages of wrenching fury, showing lengthened incisors in their eternally snarling mouths. Ragnar thought it strange to see faces of such aesthetic perfection riven by scars and twisted by torment. The Blood Angels and their Successors were regarded by many as the peak of human beauty. Yet here were the Flesh Tearers, hideous in their serenity.

'They're not what I expected,' he called out to Razortongue across the vox. Though in truth he'd not known what to expect. Mournful defiance, perhaps. The darker side of angelic wrath evident in their slumbering features. Not this proud, miserable agony.

Nalfir didn't reply. The Blood Claw didn't care – another detail had caught his eye. Each of the last three Flesh Tearers had parchment scrolls upon his armour, torn into thin strips and forming emblematic crosses, like symbolic bandages.

Ragnar moved to the control panel of the nearest pod, looking over the flickering display. The corpse of a tech-adept, worn down to bones and a threadbare memory of robes, stared eyelessly up at him from the floor. He ignored it, seeking any details of the pod's occupant.

No name was visible amidst the few runic letters that were even remotely Gothic. Most of what Ragnar saw meant nothing to him. One symbol flashed brighter than the others, obvious in its urgency. Two red lines – an X of alarm – pulsing, pulsing, pulsing.

'Razortongue,' he voxed again. 'I've found something.'

Nalfir still didn't answer. Ragnar's quick, keen stare took in the chamber – more a dark metal cavern than a room – but there was no sign of the bard. He sought to tune out the clockwork rattling and laborious clanking of the ancient machinery, seeking his brother's heartbeat and the purr of his armour, but the stasis chamber's automated din made the effort useless. He caught no scents over the spicy dryness of old decay and the coppery blood reek of leaking machinery.

As keen as any Wolf's senses were, they were overwhelmed here. Ragnar felt his hackles rise. He drew Frostfang in a quiet pull.

The weight that would have struck him from behind barely clipped his armour as he hurled himself aside from its shadow. Instinct took over – the Blood Claw skidded across the deck and launched back to his feet in a roar of powered joints. Frostfang's kraken teeth whined as they ate the chamber's cold air.

He faced a Flesh Tearer. The warrior was hunched, sweating in the freezing air, with the too-white skin of his face raked by patchwork scarring. The Flesh Tearer bared lengthened fangs at the Wolf, staring with the shining light of madness in his eyes. Cracked vials clinked against black battleplate where they were chained in place. Honour scrolls sealed in place against the ceramite couldn't entirely conceal immaculately crafted red crosses that resembled wounds upon the armour.

'Traitor!' cried the broken angel.

'Hold...' Ragnar warned, levelling his blade. 'I am Ragnar, called Blackm–'

'*Traitor!*' The warrior launched at him, but Ragnar was ready now. He met the Flesh Tearer, shoulder to shoulder, crashing in a slam of ceramite to halt the other warrior's charge.

'Hold...' he hissed again as they grappled, grabbing at one another's wrists, each seeking to cast the other to the deck. 'Hold... damn you...'

'*Filthy traitor,*' the warrior hissed back, no sign of comprehension in his wide eyes. The Flesh Tearer's pupils were pinpricks, devoid of reason.

Ragnar felt his boots scraping across the metal deck as the warrior forced him back. The Flesh Tearer's strength was immense, beyond any battle-brother he had wrestled with in the past. He fought harder, growling into his foe's ruined white face, only to slide back another metre. His sword was useless in these close quarters; he had to drop it to grip the angel's wrist and prevent the Flesh Tearer from pulling out his eyes.

'Beginning to wish I'd just killed you,' he said through teeth clenched hard enough to ache.

'*Traitor*,' the straining warrior breathed back at him.

Ragnar slammed back against the wall, feeling metal give way. The Flesh Tearer bore down on him with renewed strength and leverage, closing one hand across Ragnar's face. The pressure was excruciating as the fingers closed with vice-like strength. Under the pain, Ragnar could *hear* the squealing strain of his own skull threatening to break.

Instinct almost had him spit his corrosive saliva against the palm covering his mouth, but he'd choke on the chemical stink of burning ceramite... and the acid would take too long to have any effect. He'd be dead before it ate its way through to the flesh beneath the glove.

Ragnar leaned back into the mangled wall, stealing enough room to thunder a kick against the Flesh Tearer's knee. The maddened warrior barely reacted. On the second kick Ragnar kept his boot against the knee joint of his opponent's armour, forcing with all the pressure he could give. All he needed was a second to knock the Flesh Tearer off-balance.

Something clicked in his cheekbone. Then a crackle. Then a wet, crunching snap. Vision in the eye started to darken.

Roaring, Ragnar kicked again, hammering out with all his strength. The Flesh Tearer staggered for barely a heartbeat, but it was long enough to release the Wolf's skull. As the crushing strain lifted from Ragnar's face in a burst of cold, blessed relief, the Wolf cannoned his knuckles against the Flesh Tearer's eye, shattering the socket and jerking the other warrior's head to the side. He bore his maddened opponent to the deck with a leap that would have brought down a Thunderwolf, pinning his enemy beneath him, pounding his fists into the Flesh Tearer's stricken features.

All thought of mercy fled. He beat the angel bloody, breaking the bones of the warrior's face with a flurry of blows. Genetically rich blood splashed across him, making his gauntlets reek, yet still he hammered punch after punch into the Flesh Tearer's skull.

Impossibly, the dying angel answered with a roar of his own, hurling Ragnar off his chest with a monumental heave. The Blood Claw turned in the air, landing in a battle crouch on top of another stasis pod, his boots sending cracks splintering through the reinforced glass.

'*Traitor!*' the mangled warrior screamed at him. Blood bathed the Flesh Tearer's face. One of his eyes had burst beneath Ragnar's fist, popping into pinkish jelly. His fangs had eviscerated his own tongue. He was mad...

yet somehow not feral. Reason was absent from his bloody gaze, but sentience was not. '*Traitor!*'

The Flesh Tearer came at Ragnar again, hurling himself with hands outstretched. Ragnar met him with an elbow to the soft armour at his collar, feeling bone and machine nerves crunch in unison, but the Flesh Tearer's strength and momentum was enough to throw the Wolf down onto the deck regardless.

They went at each other with fangs and fists, boots and butting heads. Blood rained from the angel's broken face, spattering like hot oil across Ragnar's snarling features. The droplets that trickled between Ragnar's teeth tasted petrochemically foul and his mind flared with stuttering, hazy images of memories that weren't his own.

Scales on the hide of some great beast, rippling in the night. An endless battlement wall beneath a burning sky. A winged demigod with a sword of fire. The acrid tang of corrupted sweat. Flame sucked into his lungs. Pain running through him along the network of his nerves.

He managed to free himself by getting one boot on the Flesh Tearer's chest and shoving the frothing warrior aside. Scrabbling away, gasping for breath, fortune had his palm thud down on his discarded blade.

Ragnar brought the blade up as the Flesh Tearer launched upon him again, the warrior's weight driving the air from the Wolf's lungs and pinning him to the deck. Frostfang was trapped between them. He'd missed the killing blow.

'*Traitor!*' the angel screamed into his face, spraying acidic saliva and blood from a fanged maw. Ragnar hauled the trapped blade higher, keeping it between them, the kraken teeth scraping deep gouges across black war-plate.

He couldn't reach the trigger. He almost lost his grip completely as the angel's hands closed like an iron noose around his throat, cracking through the machine tendons of his armoured collar. Now even breathing became a battle. What little air he sucked in tasted of the Flesh Tearer's maddened memories.

He still couldn't thumb the trigger. His vision was dimming when he finally wrestled the dead blade up, pushing the toothed saw blade against the side of the Flesh Tearer's face.

'*Trai–*'

Ragnar cut. He carved with the deactivated sword, the monomolecular-sharpened kraken teeth ripping through the Flesh Tearer's skin, muscle and bone. The warrior's pulped eye was torn from its mutilated socket; the gore drizzle spattering Ragnar's face became a torrent, punctuated with fragments of bone. He carved deeper, sawing the blade back and forth as best as his confines allowed, cleaving down to the grey meat of the brain.

The Flesh Tearer's grip loosened. Ragnar stole the chance to throw the warrior aside and stagger to his feet, wiping the blood from his blinded eyes.

He heard a bolter fire, just once, and his clearing vision was rewarded with the sight of the Flesh Tearer motionless at last, the warrior's head detonated into wet red shards.

Nalfir stood above the body, his bolter's muzzle breathing fyceline mist in the cold air. Ragnar aimed Frostfang at him, the Flesh Tearer's blood burnishing the ancient blade.

'Where in the name of the Allfather were you?'

'In the antechamber,' said the bard with a smile. 'Aren't you going to thank me for saving you?'

'Saving me... You treacherous... I should kill you next!'

'Fine, then. I admit that you killed this poor creature on your own, but that's still no way to show gratitude, Blackmane.'

'You did this.' Ragnar pointed the sword at the corpse on the deck. 'Do you expect me to believe one of the stasis pods coincidentally failed when I walked past? You did this, Razortongue.'

'That's quite the accusation, brother.' Nalfir seemed as calm and composed as ever. 'You should tell the jarl of your theatrical suspicion. Perhaps I'll be given a trial. And when I'm found innocent, for you have no evidence at all, of course... then you can kiss my boots before the entire Great Company and beg for my forgiveness.'

Ragnar barked in wordless rage, which only encouraged Nalfir's smile. 'Temper, temper, Blackmane. Look where that got you with the Dark Angels.'

'I won't take this to the jarl,' Ragnar growled the words. 'I deal with my own grudges. But I'm watching you, "brother".'

'Do whatever you wish.' Nalfir lowered the bolter at last. 'We weren't supposed to touch anything, you know. Look at the mess you've made.'

VII

A week later, eight souls gathered in judgement. Seven were warriors in the grey of a summer storm, one wore the absolute black of a deep night. They met in Berek's council chamber where there were no seats, just as there was no command throne upon the *Holmgang*'s bridge. All were expected to stand in their lord's presence. All were equal – all but one. This last figure, clad in sacred black, said nothing to the others, not even to greet them. He watched and, seemingly, waited.

To walk into the chamber was to walk into the jarl's personal museum and armoury. The Great Company's banners and treasures were housed elsewhere across the *Holmgang* and displayed with righteous, boastful pride. Here the dark iron walls were adorned with Berek's personal glories: the banners of fallen enemy overlords and a host of broken relics taken from lifeless alien hands. All were purified by the Chapter's priests before being put on display.

It was not from any sense of modesty, as his men knew all too well, that Berek kept his trophies away from the Great Company's eyes. For all his bluntness, Berek One-Arm – called Thunderfist by his kith and kin – was not without a warlord's sense of cunning. He chose to surround his elite warriors with his own glories, for they were the ones who were permitted by tradition and law to challenge him for leadership. His Wolf Guard were the kinsmen who had to be reminded of his prowess, and the shame that awaited them if they offered a failed challenge.

The warriors stood in silence around the central table. Its surface was a granite replica of the Chapter's annulus, showing the wolfhead symbols of the current jarls in command of the twelve Great Companies. Each of the snarling effigies bared its teeth in typical Fenrisian defiance, carved proud upon the stone.

Berek called the gathering to order by placing his axe with a dull clank onto the rearing symbol of the Wolf that Stalks Between the Stars.

'Brothers, we have come together to decide the fate of the Flesh Tearers warship that tumbles out there, powerless in the void. Who among you would speak?'

All eyes turned to the figure in black, only to look away when he made no gesture at all. Three of the Wolf Guard reached to their throats and pulled their iron torcs free, dropping them onto the stone table, signalling that they wished to speak. Ragnar was among them. His face had healed, but discolouration yet lingered around the fused eye socket and cheekbone that had been fractured.

'Greylock,' Berek gestured to the first of them. 'Your jarl listens.'

Uller, called Greylock by his kith and kin, was a mountain of a warrior. He was named for the frosted hair growing among the blond by his temple – the legacy of an axe blow that split his skull in the headstrong days of his tribal youth. He weighed in on the warship's fate with two simple words.

'Burn it.'

'A simple solution,' Berek admitted.

The wolf tail talismans hanging from Uller's belt swayed as he shifted his immense weight.

'Burn it,' he repeated. 'To the abyss with the Flesh Tearers. Whatever nobility they once possessed is long gone now. Their instincts are poisoned. Blackmane saw it himself – their first reaction upon leaving stasis was to attack him, and he did well to see that cur dead. Burn their ship and let's be done with this debate. There are wars to fight, my jarl. Wars we should be fighting even as we stand here speaking. The Flesh Tearers already think the vessel swallowed by the void. They are losing nothing that they have not already lost.'

Several of the others rapped their knuckles on the table in affirmation. Greylock retrieved his torc, closing it around his neck once more. Berek nodded as he spoke again.

'Greylock counsels that we burn it in the void and be done with it. Razor-tongue, you next. Your jarl listens.'

Barring Ragnar, the bard was the youngest warrior present, and all of them heard the hot blood in his voice. 'We take the *Baryonyx* back to the Fang.'

Silence met these words. Nalfir pressed on. 'We beseech the Iron Priests to restore enough function to reach Fenris, and once she's docked in the Fang's sky platforms, she undergoes cleansing, repair and an overhaul. Within a year she'll be ready to begin her new life in service to the Chapter.'

No knuckles knocked on the stone table.

'We're not thieves, bard,' said Berek.

'No,' Nalfir agreed smoothly, 'we are victors.'

'Then why do you speak of theft?'

'I speak of plunder, my jarl. I speak of the spoils of war. Consider it a trophy if you prefer.'

There was a smile in Berek's snarl. 'You're toying with words.'

'Am I not a *skjald*? Toying with words is my duty.'

Ragnar would be silent no longer. 'You, who advocated my death-duel with the Dark Angels in the name of honour, now advocate stealing another Chapter's warship?'

Nalfir was unfazed. If anything, Ragnar's protestations amused him. 'The Dark Angels are our Chapter's oldest rival, and our bloodlines run all the way back to the Imperium's founding. They're fools, one and all, but I respect them. They're loyal to the Allfather's Throne. The Flesh Tearers are mongrels and mutants by comparison – cannibals known to drink innocent blood. Did the one you fought not accuse you of treachery? *Traitor,* he called you. They hate us, to our very souls.'

'I hear your words,' Berek assured them both. 'Yet in this matter, theft is theft. It's beneath us.'

'My jarl,' Nalfir cut in, 'I know you hear the wisdom beneath my jests. I know all of you do. Perhaps it breaks with tradition, aye, I'll concede that without a fight. But if we return the ship to the Fang, we still claim right of plunder. Can any of you say it's wise to throw away such a prize? Even a single frigate added to our Great Company's armada...'

He let the words trail away, and while they were ill-mannered and brash, they were undeniably true. Practicality now battled with pride in many of the Wolves' eyes. Even a single frigate represented a monumental addition to any Chapter's fleet, let alone one jarl's personal power. Tentatively, knuckles began to knock.

'Especially,' Nalfir added, 'now that Blackmane's ill-fated command of the *Veregelt* left that proud warship so gravely wounded.'

Ragnar bared his teeth. 'Had I not acted as I did, the *Veregelt* would be in the possession of Traitors, and a third of the Great Company dead.'

Nalfir's smile was unconscionably smooth. 'Yes, we're all aware just how you covered yourself with glory in that campaign, brother. The fact remains that the company would be well served by acquiring another warship. This isn't theft, kinsmen. This is providence.'

All present could see the indecision in Berek's eyes. The craving of ambition burned beneath the colour of honour.

'There's a certain cunning wisdom in your words, bard...'

Ragnar thudded his armoured fist on the table, just once. The sound drew all eyes towards him.

'My iron still lies on the stone.'

Berek grunted an acknowledgement that wasn't quite an apology. 'Speak, Blackmane. Your jarl listens.'

Ragnar's blue eyes slipped from Nalfir like a knife sliding from a dead man's spine. He turned his gaze upon the others.

'We're talking of acts of treachery against another Chapter.'

Nalfir smiled. 'Something you have no trivial experience with yourself, eh?'

'One more word...' said Ragnar, his voice as cold as the ice upon which he'd been whelped and raised. 'Even a whisper, *brother,* and you will regret it.'

Against all odds, the bard fell silent, offering only a smile.

'I know I'm not without flaw in this,' Ragnar continued, 'but what you both suggest is beneath us, kinsmen. You, Greylock, suggest cowardice for the sake of convenience. You counsel the destruction of sacred steel out here in the deep void, where no one will see our sin. And you, Razor-tongue, celebrate dishonour by dressing it in the rags of pragmatism. I at least felt shame for my failures at the Maelstrom's edge.'

'What then do you suggest, Blackmane?' asked the jarl.

The Blood Claw looked to each of his older brothers in turn. 'Tell me of Honour's End,' he said. 'I would hear the full story before I judge where I stand.'

Berek gave a low, displeased growl. 'I was blade to blade with the mad angels that day. I killed one of them myself. He had a hive-dweller's blood on his teeth. The blood of the innocent, Blackmane. All you've read in the archives is true. The Flesh Tearers have a sickness in their souls, and on that day it broke free for all to see. I doubt any of them carry the Allfather in their hearts now. Not truly. Their gene-seed is stagnant and corrupt. It sends venom through their blood. You ask of Honour's End? There's no need, Blood Claw. You saw it yourself when you faced one of them aboard the *Baryonyx* and he came within a breath of killing you. It was that – the very same thing – written across an entire city.'

'A malfunctioning stasis pod is hardly the same as a war, my jarl. Tell me of the battle itself.'

'What else is there to know beyond what the archives say? Would you have me summon a Rune Priest here to let you re-live it, like a whelp on a vision quest? The Flesh Tearers stormed a hive spire, slaughtering thousands of unarmed Imperial souls. In their blind rage, they could no longer tell friend from foe. We stood against them, to defend the civilians. That is the beginning and end of it.'

Ragnar had seen as much, not just from reading the archived reports but from the blurry pict captures of various helmet feeds. Most of such footage was from the imagifiers of Long Fangs, far back from the action, bringing their heavy weapons to bear on the battle below.

'What I've seen in the archives is inconclusive, kinsmen. One might even consider it suspiciously so.' Silence threatened once more as Ragnar trailed away. It was the figure in black who broke the quiet with his husky murmur.

'I was there.'

All of them turned to the warrior in dark plate. Ulrik, the ancient Wolf Priest, met none of their eyes, instead looking at the annulus upon the table as though the stone itself held his memories. The lines on his leathery face could have been carved from dark rock for all the give in his expression.

'I was there the day we drew our blades against our cousins, to pun-ish them for butchering the innocent. I was there, and I claim the right of a warrior's own eyes over the fireside whispers recorded in the archives.'

'Speak, old father,' Ragnar bade him. If Ulrik took offence at the Fenrisian term for a tribe's eldest male, he showed none of it. Perhaps he'd simply heard it enough times from Wolves of every Great Company.

'I am Ulrik, called Slayer by my kith and kin, for I have watered the thirsty earth of five hundred worlds with the blood of the Allfather's foes. We fed the crows that day, as did the Tearers of Flesh. Warriors in the heraldry of both Chapters fell in numbers enough that their broken ceramite carpeted the earth. The blood of the dead ran thick enough to drown the ground beneath our boots.'

'But we won,' Nalfir chorused loyally.

Ulrik's reply was ice itself. 'Warriors who weren't yet born when the battle took place now see the banners and trophies we took from lifeless red hands, and they cry of our great victory. I say we failed that day. We failed to do our duty. The stain of Honour's End clings to the soul of every Wolf who fought there. The shame that we did not stop the Angel's sons sooner, and the regret that we did not wipe them from the face of the gal-axy, like filth from the bottom of a boot.'

Ulrik's eyes were dark like old iron, pinpricked by miniscule pupils. His voice held the rough command of an ancient king's decrees, and his gaze was the serene stare of a guiltless killer.

'I take no pride in the day that the Flesh Tearers' honour ended. It is fair, perhaps, to say you know the heart of the Imperium better than any of us here. We fight the Allfather's wars, but you see into the very soul of His empire. You know that no Chapter would be damned purely for turning their butchers' blades upon innocent Imperial souls. We may hate them for it but we would not rain damnation upon them for that alone. The vio-lence they brought against us is not enough to damn them, for Chapters go to war with one another at the merest provocation. Nor is it simply that they massacred an unarmed population. Their blood-madness runs deeper than even such grave acts. If you rely only on the Chapter's archives, then you will know of a pitched battle fought to avenge the innocent dead. A war raging over the lives of Imperial innocents. But what chronicle ever tells the whole truth?'

'Well...' Nalfir began, though he was silenced by Ragnar's quiet snarl.

'Here is the truth of Honour's End,' Ulrik said with cold fire in his ashen eyes. 'When we fell upon them with indignation and fury, when we sought to punish them for what they had done, dozens died on both sides. And there it ended. Both Chapters were bloodied, but High King Grimnar and Seth, Lord of the Sawtoothed Host, brought us back from the edge of ruin. The skirmish ended before it could become a battle.'

Ragnar was captivated by the sight of the old warrior in the throes of confession. 'The archive lists one hundred and seventy-three dead Wolves,' he said, 'cut down in a single battle. You speak of a skirmish. Two hundred lives is a decade's worth of casualties. That's no skirmish, Slayer.'

'And the archives are correct, young Blackmane. That is the tragedy at play, here. It is why the Tearers of Flesh are truly damned. The skirmish ended with reason amidst the madness. When both sides were calmed by the commands of our lords, a ceasefire should have reigned until both Chapters could withdraw. But it failed to hold. The Flesh Tearers offered to return our slain so we might harvest the gene-seed of the honoured dead. In return, they demanded we surrender their slain warriors to their own red priests.'

Ragnar took a slow breath. 'Allfather's blood. You refused them.'

Ulrik nodded, reliving that long ago day. 'We refused them.'

Even Nalfir, too young to have fought there, looked to the Wolf Priest in silence. Ragnar cursed quietly in disbelief.

'And then?' he asked.

'Then they attacked us. The real battle began, over half a dozen dead bodies. They didn't dare let us examine their dead. Do you see? They must have feared what we would find in their blood. Whatever corruption burns in their bodies is a sickness that steals all reason from them in battle. It is a secret they keep at all costs. Were you to access the archives of the Adeptus Mechanicus, I suspect you would find precious little evidence of submitted gene-seed tithes in recent centuries. They are hiding something. Something terrible. A genetic degeneration, a spiritual cancer... It is hard to say. Were we a Chapter more attuned to the whims of the Inquisition and the Adeptus Terra, we might have offered testimony to have the Flesh Tearers declared *Excommunicate Traitoris*.'

'But we face our foes,' Berek put in with a growl. 'We do not run to the mortals ruling in the Allfather's name and whine for their aid.'

'As you say, Jarl Thunderfist,' Ulrik agreed, passionless in his concurrence.

'But...' Ragnar began.

'*But?*' Berek repeated the word in disbelief. 'You weren't at Honour's End but you've crossed blades with one of them yourself mere hours ago. They're rabid creatures, one and all. You'd be dead now if you'd not struck him down. The Chapter is irredeemable, Blackmane.'

'No redemption can cleanse them of their butchery, sire, but we broke a most sacred tradition at Honour's End. In claiming their dead, we gave them no choice but to attack, whether they were guilty or not. Would the Wolves not have done the same, if another Chapter refused to return the honoured dead of Fenris?'

'It's different,' Uller Greylock replied.

'Utterly different,' Berek agreed.

'Is it?' Ragnar's voice was almost bladed in its gentleness. 'And are there no degenerate strains within our own gene-seed? Are we sons of Fenris purer than pure? Or is there a secret swimming in our blood – one we would kill to protect – as well?'

'I'd advise you,' Jarl Berek said slowly, 'to be very careful with your next words, brother.'

Ragnar's muscles bunched in feral readiness at the threat. His breathing slowed almost to nothing, and he saw the same hunting instinct take hold of the others in the same moment.

'I'm not accusing our bloodline of disloyalty,' he said. 'Only that there are aberrant strains within our own cells – a secret known only among our own kind. Do the Adeptus Mechanicus viziers toiling over our genetic tithes consider it unholy? Do they see it at all? Perhaps their investigations reveal anomalies without definitive results, even after all these centuries. Perhaps they lack the vision to understand the anomalies they discover. Does High King Grimnar even send the tithes? Or perhaps our place as a First Founding Chapter grants us treatment that the Flesh Tearers are denied. Who can say?'

Berek's jaws ground together hard enough to creak. A trickle of saliva ran from the edge of his lips, and his guttural voice sent shivers through the table.

'I no longer like your tone, Blackmane.'

'I speak no treachery, sire. There is something in the blood of the Einherjar that turns the hearts of men into the souls of beasts. We know it as the Wulfen Curse. But what Mars thinks of it, if anything, I cannot even guess. The warrior I fought aboard the *Baryonyx* was no longer capable of thought. Something had turned his mind. If we can learn–'

One warrior's knuckles thudded against the stone annulus. It was Ulrik.

'Enough,' said the old Wolf Priest.

That single syllable echoed with the finality of a funeral bell. Muscles began to ease. Knuckles loosened from the hilts of undrawn swords.

Berek wasn't so easily cowed. This was his council chamber, and the warriors present were his closest kindred, oathed to his word and sworn to his command. Ulrik walked between Great Companies, beholden to no jarl, without the rank to demand anything of any Wolf Lord. But he was also the Slayer, the bearer of Leman Russ' own helm, with his name already written more than a hundred times across the Chapter's legends.

Authority did not always lie in rank and title. Berek relented, releasing the haft of his battle axe.

One by one, Ulrik met their gazes. 'Blackmane speaks wisely.' He turned his ashen eyes to Ragnar. Bone charms and wooden carvings rattled against his armour with even the smallest movement. 'But you also speak incautiously. You're newly ascended to your lord's honour guard, Blood Claw. Act with honour at all times, and never cast a shadow across the bloodline of Leman Russ.'

Ragnar tilted his head to bare his throat for a moment – a Space Wolf's gesture, not a Fenrisian's. 'I recognise my failing and will be sure to correct it.'

Ulrik smiled at the ancient phrase, his face creasing with amusement so brief that it was almost illusory.

'Be it so. Remember, I did not say we were blameless at Honour's End, Blackmane, but no Chapter would be justified in gathering our corpses for their inquisitive knives. We do not warrant such scrutiny. We do not paint our faces with the blood of the men, women and children we are charged to defend. We do not turn our blades on other Space Marines when our guilt is exposed. Whatever secrets the Wolves hold as precious, we keep them to ourselves.'

Ragnar nodded, speaking another old phrase. 'We do not do what is lawful. We do what is right.'

Knuckles rapped against the stone table at last.

'And with that in mind,' Ragnar continued, 'I know what we should do with the Flesh Tearers warship. Destroying it is cowardly. Claiming it is theft.'

'So we should just leave it here?' Nalfir's smile was one-sided, and no amusement reached his stare. 'You would let a prize like this rot in the black?'

Ragnar shook his head. 'No. You're all avoiding the most obvious answer.'

Greylock sensed Ragnar's intent and gave a low chuckle. 'You cannot be serious, Blackmane.'

'Why not?' the Blood Claw replied. 'It's a Flesh Tearers warship.'

'So?' asked Nalfir.

'So... we give it back.'

Havoc erupted in a storm of laughter. Uller even slapped Ragnar on the shoulder in recognition of a great jest.

'Ah, the humour of the young,' Berek said through a grin. 'One of them tried to cut your throat not three days ago, yet now you advocate doing them a great favour.'

Uller was still chuckling. 'Perhaps the youngblood wishes to fill the *Baryonyx*'s belly with our own warriors, so we might leap out in ambush when we're taken deep into Flesh Tearers territory. Is that so, Blackmane? Agree that it is, even if you lie by doing so, and salvage a shred of honour from this while you still can.'

Two souls remained silent throughout the laughter: Ragnar himself and old Ulrik. Ragnar's teeth were clenched throughout the humiliation, the second he'd endured in the same month. His fingers curled on their slow way to becoming fists. He could almost feel his brothers' faces breaking under the hammering of his armoured knuckles.

Ulrik wasn't blind to such things. 'Control your temper, Blood Claw. Say what you wish to say, for even if your jarl is not listening, I am. What do we gain from returning the *Baryonyx* to the Angel's mad sons?'

Ragnar forced his bile back down. His voice was almost calm. 'You said yourself, Slayer, that every Chapter has its sins and secrets. We must be mindful of our hypocrisy in this. Should we sail there to bare our throats and apologise for shedding their blood? No, of course not. We were right to fight them at Honour's End. But that was then, and this is now.'

Nalfir snorted. 'And what has changed?'

'Everything.' Despite leashing his temper, Ragnar spat onto the deck by Nalfir's boots. He was careful, at least, not to let his saliva ducts acidify the sign of disrespect. 'You know what has changed, Razortongue. The sky darkened above Fenris and our priests see grim omens everywhere. Our blades must be turned to worthier foes. Now is the time to resolve this conflict once and for all.'

'Resolve?' the bard laughed again. 'We'll *resolve* this conflict by winning it. By destroying them like the heretics they are.'

'That would bleed the Chapter dry, Razortongue.' Olvec, First of the Wolf Guard – called the Tongueless by his kith and kin for the rarity of his words – added his voice at last. As he spoke, his brow furrowed beneath his crest of age-whitened red hair. 'In destroying the Flesh Tearers we would cripple ourselves almost beyond recovery. Think what you're saying before you breathe your foolish words into our ears.'

Ragnar sensed the shift of tension in the air and went for the kill. 'How many times have we crossed blades with the Flesh Tearers since Honour's End?'

'Too many,' Berek grunted at once. Knuckles hammered on stone in the rhythm of agreement. Unlike the distant disrespect between the Wolves and the Dark Angels, the tensions between the Flesh Tearers and the Sons of Russ all too often spilled out into open conflict.

Ragnar nodded as if they'd proved his point. 'And each time it has turned to blood on the earth, the snow and the sand before any ceasefire or truce could even be considered. We should face them now, not as enemies but as wayward cousins. We must decide if our old brotherhood can be salvaged.'

'You believe we should forgive them?' asked Ulrik.

'My own... rash... actions of late have turned my thoughts somewhat. I'm not speaking of forgiveness, Slayer. Not yet. For now I suggest nothing beyond sheathing our swords for long enough to learn the truth. If the Flesh Tearers are damned, then we have lost nothing by seeing it for ourselves. Swords can be drawn and enemies ended. But if they might yet be our cousins when the Wolftime comes, then I would find out now rather than sell more of our blood and sweat in a wasteful war. We need allies, my kinsmen. We need souls that will stand with us when the last sun rises.'

'Pretty words,' Nalfir sighed with feigned gravity, 'but they will be wasted on those traitors, Blackmane.'

'Traitors is a dangerous word, brother. Whole echelons of the Adeptus Sororitas and the Ecclesiarchy say the same of us. How many institutions decry the Wolves as traitors to the Imperium for the times we've shunned the will of the Adeptus Terra? The rolls of history are hardly bare of black marks. Several cite Einherjar vessels opening fire on other Imperial ships for provocation that surely makes no sense to those outside the walls of the Fang. All to protect our independence. The Wolves once opened fire on an Ecclesiarchy fleet without warning, just for the sin of sailing into orbit above Fenris.'

'To dissuade them from making planetfall,' Berek said. 'They believed we were worshipping pagan gods above the Allfather.'

'We don't tolerate Imperial investigation,' added Uller.

'As is our right,' said Nalfir. 'We've done nothing that other Chapters haven't done. Even your recent foolishness with the Dark Angels wasn't wholly without precedent.'

'Every coin has two sides, bard. That's all I'm saying. We should learn the truth amidst the lies.'

Silence rose in the wake of his words. A long silence, during which he met the eyes of every warrior present, awaiting their judgement.

The stillness was broken with a tectonic thud as Ulrik's black gauntlet thumped down against the stone table. He lifted his fist and knocked upon the stone again, beginning a slow beat of knuckle raps.

The others joined in, one by one. Nalfir was the last, only joining in once the jarl had done so.

'Very well,' Berek said, his eyes unreadable, though his mouth was a thin line. 'You have spoken, my kin, and your jarl has listened. Back to your duties for now. I will give my judgement tonight.'

'I will remain,' said Ulrik. 'You and I will talk more on this matter, Jarl Thunderfist.'

Berek's smile was viciously forced. His teeth were gravestones grinding together.

'Of course, Slayer. Whatever you wish.'

VIII

Nalfir came to Ragnar that night with frost in his eyes and a knife in his hand. Space Marines required less respite than mortal men and slumbered far less deeply. Many simply forewent rest as long as they were able, letting segments of their altered brains close down in succession, resting portions of their minds without resting their bodies at all.

Yet there was something cleansing in true somnolence. Away from the front lines, the warriors of the Adeptus Astartes would sometimes sleep as humans would sleep, resting their senses in true slumber.

It was common for the warriors of many Chapters to keep to their own chambers in their sparse hours of rest. This was not the case with the Einherjar. Within the ranks of the Thunderfist Great Company – and like the wolves of their Gothic namesake – the warriors slept in packs. The central chamber of a barracks hall was a squad's sanctuary, armoury and bedchamber. Servitors and favoured thralls often lived in the same shared space, sleeping when the Wolves were away, serving when the warriors were present.

One of them, an arming servitor, tracked Nalfir's movements across the chamber with a critical cybernetic eye. Its voice was a toneless drone as it acknowledged the Wolf.

'Champion Razortongue, do you require–'

'Sssss,' the bard hissed back. 'Silence.'

Nalfir's unarmoured form landed with a thud on Ragnar's slab of a bed. He crouched above the other Wolf's prone figure, eyes narrowed to vicious slits, tapping the silver knife on his pack-brother's chest. It clink-clink-clinked against the dark contours of Ragnar's black carapace set beneath the skin.

'Blackmane,' he snarled quietly. His fingers tightened around the hilt as he bathed in the urge to shed the irritating Blood Claw's lifeblood.

Ragnar still didn't move. Every breath drew in the scent of the bard's salt-sweat, and the knife's separate, sharp metallic smell. He didn't even open his eyes.

'Blackmane,' the bard whispered, teeth clenched now.

'Go away,' Ragnar murmured, 'or I'll take that knife and pry out both of your eyes.'

'I think not.' Nalfir slid from the slab, twirling the knife across his fingers with the grace of a fireside trickster. 'We should speak, Blackmane.'

Ragnar finally sat up, feeling uncomfortable itches at the armour feed connection ports across his spine and shoulders. They were red and angry, each one like a little wound. It was the first time he'd been out of his armour in months, and with typical timing Nalfir had shattered that chance of well-earned rest.

'Then speak.'

'You're new to the First Pack and hungry for glory. I see it in your eyes. No shame in that, eh? But you're putting your ambition above the needs of the company.'

'If you have a point beyond this posturing, please reach it swiftly.'

Nalfir shook his head and sighed as if he'd never seen anything quite so tragic. 'This is all very selfish of you, Blackmane. We should be sword-brothers, you and I. One pack. One heart. One mind. Not pulling in different directions.'

Ragnar reached up to bind his long hair in its customary hunter's crest, dragging the strands from his face. He knew there would be no more slumber now.

'You woke me for this?'

'No, I woke you to challenge you to a fight.' Nalfir spun the knife, letting it dance over his fingers in a silver blur. Like Ragnar he was unarmoured, barefoot and bare-chested, clad only in rough hide trousers. Scars decorated his dark-skinned body, telling the tales of a hundred battlefields.

'Am I to guess the cause of this challenge?' Ragnar asked. 'Or should I just assume you want to ease your bruised pride because the jarl heeded my words and not yours?'

In a flash of muscle and sinew, Nalfir had the knife against the Blood Claw's throat. The keen silver edge scraped Ragnar's unshaven skin. The bard grinned, face to face with his rival.

'You're an arrogant child, Blackmane. You get a pretty sword from a noblemaiden on Terra and suddenly you think yourself lord of the pack, fiercer and bolder and wiser than the rest of us.'

'Is this bitterness that I was chosen as battle leader?'

'And look how you performed in the role, eh? This is about more than your childish temper. This is about *arrogance*. Do you think I'm blind to your glory-lust?'

Ragnar's teeth showed white in the chamber's faint illumination. 'What I think is that you're pushing your luck, singer. If you're worried about your place in the First Pack, perhaps you should be fiercer, bolder and wiser yourself.'

'Such pretty threats,' Nalfir's honeyed voice was low and snide, 'from an unblooded cub.'

Ragnar moved just as swiftly, dragging his bone knife from a sheath on his shin and pressing the tip to the underside of his brother's jaw. A single ruby droplet ran down the fang dagger, turning the air molten with the chemical spice of Nalfir's blood.

'*Unblooded?*' he breathed into the other warrior's face. 'Keep pushing me, teller of tales. I'll wear your blood as warpaint for a year and a day, so all will know my knife cut out both of your worthless hearts.'

If Ragnar was the promise of fire, Nalfir was the chill of ice on the wind. The bard's spite was a calm thing, deceptively gentle.

'You,' the bard smiled, 'are an upstart, glory-starved infant. A child playing at being a man. A cub playing at hunter, surviving only by your maddening fortune. But luck runs out, Blackmane. Luck always runs out.'

Ragnar's knife answered by pressing upwards, piercing the surface of his brother's skin again, shedding another trickle of genhanced blood.

'I know it was you,' he breathed the words. 'You deactivated the stasis lock on the *Baryonyx*. I know it was you, Razortongue.'

'You know nothing, unblooded child.'

'Call me unblooded one more time,' warned Ragnar, 'and I'll use your honour scrolls to wipe myself after night soil.'

Nalfir leaned closer, his mouth conspiratorially close to the other man's ear. His voice softened to a vicious, falsely sweet murmur.

'*Worthless. Unblooded. Cub.*'

Ragnar threw himself forwards, both warriors crashing to the deck in a tangle of bludgeoning limbs. Around the chamber, thralls and servitors hurriedly backed away. The time of threats and insults was done, now wordless grunts and half-formed curses filled the air, punctuated by the dull thuds of fists striking home and heads cannoning off the iron floor.

The sound of Ragnar's dagger pommel cracking Nalfir's skull was the thunderclap of lightning splitting a tree trunk. The sound of Nalfir's knife driving into Ragnar's guts was the wet smack of a carcass dropping from a meat hook in the butchers' hall. Priceless blood decorated the deck in shed speckles, a trail marking the brothers' warring passage across the chamber.

Nalfir heaved Ragnar's head up by his hunter's crest, using it to slam the Blood Claw's face against Uller Greylock's bare sleeping slab. Once. Twice. Thrice. A smeared and bloody imprint of Ragnar's face looked wildly back up at both of them.

An elbow hammered into the bard's throat, hard enough to close his windpipe in a clench of abused sinew, and a second blow cracked into his chin hard enough to break two of his teeth. Rather than slip free as Nalfir's grip loosened, Ragnar pressed the attack. A moment of potential respite dissolved into further brawling. Both of them had lost their knives. Neither of them cared.

It went on like this for some time. Such was life among the frostborn.

The Einherjar's sagas were filled with bare-knuckle battles between tribe-mates and pack-brothers. Most of them ended with the restoration of good sense and brotherly vows of companionship. Lessons were learned. Rivals became sword-brothers. Men who had been willing to brain one other and spill each other's blood found themselves breathless at the end of their brawl, grinning, laughing, bonded closer than ever.

Not here. The fight ended with an iron table crashing into both warriors, thrown with the force of Fenris' winter wind. The table's edge struck Nalfir's already shattered skull, dropping him as though pole-axed. Ragnar took the brunt of the impact on his back and shoulders, sending him smacking face-first into the wall before he staggered down onto his knees.

Down on the deck, they breathed in ragged, bestial panting.

'Nnnh,' Nalfir grunted through blood-coated teeth. Whatever it was supposed to mean was something no one would ever know.

'Grrrhh,' was Ragnar's equally ineloquent reply.

A warrior in full war-plate stood in the centre of the chamber, his teeth bared at his downed kinsmen. Russ himself had never looked so full of fury.

'Accursed Blood Claws.'

'I...' began Nalfir, '...am not a...'

An armoured boot pounded into the bard's chest, snapping the reinforced genetic fusion of his ribs. The bard's protest dissolved into a wounded and puppyish snarl.

'Be silent,' said the warrior standing above them. 'Both of you, shut your mouths. You've got blood everywhere. It's all over my weapon rack.'

'Greylock...' Ragnar managed to say as he regained his feet.

The older warrior's backhand hit hard enough to tear a mortal man's head free from his shoulders. Tanks ran over helpless enemies with less force. Ragnar tumbled to the deck, boneless and groaning.

'I said *be silent*, both of you. That means your clever tongue, Blackmane, as well as the bard's woeful singing.'

Uller Greylock stalked around the pack's shared chamber, looking over the damage, following the blood spatters with an ursine growl.

'I don't need to be a Rune Priest to read the omens in this blood trail.' He gestured at the smeared profile of Ragnar's face imprinted on the metal pallet slab. 'All the portents tell the same simple truth – you're both useless.'

Uller levelled a bolter directly at Nalfir's face. Frost shone in the older warrior's dark eyes.

'If you believe I won't shoot you, boy, you've gravely mistaken my temper.'

'You wouldn't.' Nalfir bared his bloody teeth. 'Greylock, my brother, we're both First Pack.'

'Which means what, to you?' Uller nodded over to Ragnar. 'You just stabbed your pack-brother in the guts, and he broke your head open in return. Now is a foolish time to call upon pack loyalty, Razortongue. When I said to be silent, I meant it.'

'But Greylock–'

The bolter boomed once. The thunder was near-deafening in the confines of the communal chamber, and the slaves – already cowering in the corners of the room – covered their ears at the detonation.

'You wretch!' Nalfir cried out, clutching the bloody stump where his left hand had been. Uller kept his bolter trained on the two wounded warriors.

'You'll live, fool. It's just a hand. Ask nicely and perhaps the Iron Priests will make you a new one.' Uller tapped the vox-link in his armoured collar. 'Rimefang, this is Greylock.'

'Greylock,' Askarval's voice returned at once, crackling over the vox.

'Get word to the Slayer. He's needed in the Hearth of the First Pack.'

Askarval's only reply was a dry grunt of acknowledgement. Once the vox-link clicked closed, Uller finally lowered his bolter and shook his head.

'Accursed Blood Claws.'

'Stop calling me a–' said Nalfir, but the bolter rose again in the time it took to blink.

'I count one hand still attached to your wrist,' Uller snarled. 'Speak one more word and that number will fall in a way you won't enjoy.'

Nalfir lapsed into wise silence at long last. On the deck, lying on his back and swallowing the taste of his own blood, Ragnar laughed alone.

He opened his eyes when the Slayer entered the room. Ragnar hadn't been truly sleeping, merely immersing himself in the meditative state between slumber and consciousness, quieting almost his entire mind rather than mere portions.

The last two days had dragged – he was healed within hours of his arrival, but he was confined to the starboard apothecarion. A punishment, he suspected, but a practical one. Their elders were keeping him away from Nalfir... and keeping Nalfir away from him.

'Welcome back,' Ulrik greeted him.

Ragnar's body was an artist's canvas of fading bruises and healing knife gouges whitening into shallow scars. The wound across his belly was thicker – a deeper and more jagged reminder of his recent behaviour.

Ulrik turned old, old eyes to the young warrior. His gaze was unreadable. Ragnar had to guess whether he was seeing disappointment or dark amusement, and whether there was a difference either way.

'You're First Pack now,' the Wolf Priest said. 'How swiftly you rise.'

'Is that pride I hear, Slayer?'

Ulrik wouldn't be drawn into such a confession. 'A company's First Pack is supposed to be an example of brotherhood and veteran maturity.'

Ragnar said nothing, which said everything.

'There's talk among the other packs that both you and Razortongue will be sent back to the Fang.'

Ragnar cursed. Sent back in disgrace. An outcast, begging for entry into

another Great Company or serving within the fortress-monastery's hall –
denied any honour – until finally drawing a last breath beneath Fenris'
stormy skies.

No. He didn't dare give it any more thought. He was made for more than
such a shameful fate.

'You have a truly vile temper, Blackmane.'

'So I'm often told.' He flexed his limbs and stretched his muscles, feeling the pleasant crackle of sinew.

'Half of those I've spoken to were ashamed of you for trying to kill a
packmate. The other half were annoyed with you for not finishing the job.
Razortongue is an unpopular soul.'

That, Ragnar thought, *is a very diplomatic way of putting it.*

'As are you at the moment,' Ulrik added. 'Wrecking a destroyer and angering the Dark Angels? Your brothers say that misfortune clings to you like
barnacles on a boat's hull.'

Ragnar's reply was a noncommittal grunt.

'This grudge is beneath you, Blackmane. You're not a petty or trivial soul.
So why this? Why Razortongue?'

'I have no answer worth giving. He baits me as a hunter baits prey. He
even counters my orders on the field of battle. He speaks against everything I say. If I stood before the Allfather himself and said the north wind
blows cold in winter, Razortongue would insist the southern gales were
colder in summer. It's just his way.'

'Maybe so,' Ulrik allowed. 'Or perhaps it is his role in the Great Company.
His place rather than his personality. Where a lord must seem impartial,
the lord's mouthpiece can speak with impunity. Razortongue would hardly
be the first bard and herald to be used by a jarl for such a role.'

'I've thought as much, myself. Yet it feels more than that. More personal.
This isn't the first time he's tried to kill me.'

Ulrik's dark, weathered features twisted in hollow mirth. 'Is that so?'

'There have been other incidents, all since I joined the First Pack. These
are only the latest. He even tried on the *Baryonyx*. The freed Flesh Tearer...
that was no coincidence, Slayer. No one with eyes and a reasoning mind
would believe it was a simple malfunction.'

'You seem so certain, yet you haven't spoken out against him for the sin.'

Ragnar felt like spitting at the very idea. 'I won't flee to the jarl like a
child needing an embrace. I face my enemies myself, on my own terms.'

'If, indeed, he is an enemy. Anger and conjecture is not proof, youngblood. Yet you tried to strike him down, did you not? And what if you'd succeeded? Murder of a packmate is a grievous crime, Blackmane.'

'I didn't try to kill him,' said the Blood Claw with a smile. 'I sought only
to teach him a lesson in respect.'

'He says the same of you.'

'What?' Ragnar found his grin becoming a growl. The low rumble in his throat infected his words, making them a feral threat. 'You've spoken to Razortongue?'

'Briefly. He's confined to the portside apothecarion. They're keeping you on opposite sides of the ship while you recover.'

'I've already recovered.'

'Brave words from a man who was practically disembowelled. I wouldn't go kraken-hunting just yet, Blood Claw, no matter how strong you feel.'

'I gave as good as I took.'

'I know that better than you do,' Ulrik pointed out, 'for I've seen the damage to his skull. But I did not come to speak of what has happened. I came to tell you what will happen now.'

Ragnar nodded, waiting, saying nothing. A chill was snaking its unwelcome way down his backbone. The fact it was the Slayer bearing the sentence didn't bode well.

'Your fate has already been decided,' said Ulrik. 'The jarl informed the Great Company an hour ago. It is time to redeem yourself, Ragnar Blackmane.'

Ragnar gave a wordless, suspicious gaze, that finally broke with an unself-conscious smile.

'I'm not going to like this, am I?'

It took seven weeks to repair and refit the *Baryonyx*. She was far from the sleek void blade she'd been in her prime, but with the reverence and concentration of a host of tech-priests and machine-thralls, it was believed she would sail the warp's tides without coming apart at the seams.

The *Holmgang* and the *Veregelt* were long gone. Jarl Thunderfist's ships had sailed away to fight in the Allfather's name, as was their duty. The jarl refused to wait for the repair's completion, trusting it to those he chose to leave behind.

An Adeptus Astartes frigate sails the black skies with a full crew numbering in the tens of thousands. When the *Baryonyx*'s plasma drives quickened and her engines fired, she was crewed by the several hundred survivors of her long stasis drift, as well as four hundred souls consigned to serve aboard her decks by Lord Berek. The jarl's own ship sailed away four hundred souls lighter – no small sacrifice, even for a ship of *Holmgang*'s size. Doubly so, considering the number of thralls and serfs he'd been forced to donate to the wounded *Veregelt* after so many human crew had died in the brief, brutal ambush at the Maelstrom's edge.

Most precious of all, Jarl Thunderfist abandoned one of his own Navigational coteries to guide the Flesh Tearers warship home. The value of even a single Navigator ranked above the profit of entire worlds, yet Berek left one behind when the *Holmgang* set sail.

Seven weeks alone in the void, undergoing painstaking repair. Seven weeks until her engines finally fired, letting her begin a journey that would take months.

On the command deck – now cleared of corpses and the dust that unburied corpses become – Ragnar stood by the empty command throne. He looked over the thin herd of crew members manning the ornate stations, scarcely enough to manage the ship's basic systems. They would be next to worthless if the *Baryonyx* ran into trouble. Three-quarters of the ship's guns would refuse to fire.

The deck shuddered beneath his boots as the ship finally came alive. The stars on the occulus began to drift.

'Set course for Cretacia,' he called out to the sparse, scattered packs of thralls. As if it needed saying. As if there were anywhere else this ship was destined to go.

He'd studied Cretacia in the hololithic archives, watching it turn in its slow dance, feeling an unexpected stab of familiarity. The world was a sister to Fenris in the way siblings can have everything in common yet look nothing alike. Both were *Inhabitare Mortua* – death worlds in Low Gothic parlance – and fiercely hostile to human life, yet where the Hearthworld was a globe of ice and raging oceans, Cretacia was a sphere of teeming jungles. Its face had showed vile green against the backdrop of stars, almost like corposant in the black. Fenris did the same, though with a glowing visage of blue-white frost.

Ragnar leaned on the guardrail around the central dais, wondering if he'd ever see the Hearthworld again. The isolation of deep, utter separation from his pack and company wasn't entirely new to him – not to a warrior with a past as bloody and colourful as his own – but was always unnerving and forever unwelcome. Pack animals needed time to adjust to being on their own, and a Wolf was no different.

'Are you ready, brother?' he asked over his shoulder.

The other warrior present replied with a false and unlovely smirk. His face was an artist's palette of ripe bruises. A curved cranial plate had been crudely implanted at his temple and cheek to rebind his skull together.

'I'm overjoyed to be coming with you, you know,' said Nalfir Razortongue. 'I'm sure we'll receive the warmest of welcomes on Cretacia.'

INTERLUDE

Cadia – The Tunnels Beneath Kasr Belloc
The Last Turning of the Year's Wind
999.M41

Weaponless and wounded, the warrior fled across the tundra. His boots churned up the snow and shattered the grey rocks beneath his staggering lope, and though he often stumbled, he didn't stop. To stop was to die, slain by the blizzard into which he walked, or the Beast that dogged his heels.

The Beast's roars were growing faint – perhaps drowned by the raging wind, perhaps blessedly fading with distance. He prayed it was the latter, yet feared it was the former. Worse was the sound itself. The Beast didn't cry out like an animal; it shrieked like the singing of a steel blade.

The chill was a force unto itself, a cold beyond cold. Its icy caress ate at him, penetrating his armour and leeching the strength from his bones, as impossible as that was. Never had he felt the bite of such a storm. At least, not since the weakling years of his scarcely remembered childhood. Frost glazed across his armour, cracking when he moved, reforming within the span of a single breath.

No earthly storm, this.

Rocks gave way beneath his lurching tread, the treacherous stones sending him crashing to his hands and knees. He breathed a curse that the wind immediately stole, ripping it from his tongue before he could even hear his own voice.

Behind him, the Beast's metallic clarion rang out once again. Closer, now. Maddeningly close. He hadn't been outrunning it after all.

He dragged himself to his feet, forcing his protesting muscles back into the leaning run. Every breath sawing in and out of his throat inhaled the storm and exhaled the remnants of warmth. He'd forced himself into stasis a handful of times in the past, consciously deanimating his biological processes until settling into artificial slumber. This was different. This wasn't the slowing of life, but the draining of it. His biology wasn't deanimating, it was dying. In his chest, his three lungs were growing slow, freezing into hard, useless chunks of flesh. Both of his hearts were lead-heavy, churning icewater instead of pumping blood.

On he ran. Sluggish blood leaked from the lacerated joints of his battle armour, freezing to ruby ice against the grey ceramite. He couldn't recall how he'd taken the wounds; the wind's bitterness was slowing his mind, sweeping his thoughts out of reach.

When the ground gave way beneath him again, it did more than slip from beneath his boots – it lurched downwards and fell away, all sanctuary suddenly banished. The warrior felt himself sliding, tumbling with the falling rocks. Only a panicked hand slamming into solid stone arrested his drop into a chasm that hadn't existed three seconds before.

He hung there, the muscles of his arm straining and tearing, supporting his dangling weight. Beneath him, only blackness and the roaring of the wind. The chasm was depthless, limitless. It was the wide, lightless maw of the kraken that gnawed upon the world's core.

How easy it would be to let go. To abandon his wounded, freezing husk that promised nothing but another few minutes of frostburned pain before succumbing to this storm of storms, or the sharp, hot end of a death between the Beast's jaws.

No. This bloodless fall into darkness was no way for a warrior to die.

His slackening grip on the rock ledge tightened just as a shadow blackened the sky above him. He looked up, expecting the Beast's flashing fangs, or the blur of its claws. What met his gaze was neither.

His lord stood on the precipice, armoured and armed, his great fur cloak dragged by the blowing wind.

'Blackmane,' said Jarl Berek Thunderfist, crouching to offer his hand to the hanging warrior.

Ragnar didn't take it. Nor could he speak through his closed throat, with his tongue numbed and his lips rimed with ice.

Berek grinned through a frost-whitened beard. He reached lower, offering his gauntleted hand once more. 'Come on, lad. Time to go.'

He slumbered for a time, sinking into black unconsciousness instead of the respite of true sleep. Awareness returned in bleary fits and spurts. His senses would come to life long enough to feel a dizzying, sickly warmth against his skin. He saw the prickling orange light of a nearby fire.

'Blackmane?' came his lord's voice.

Ragnar didn't reply. He couldn't. His tongue was a dead slug between aching gums, his thoughts too slow to form into words.

'Do you know,' the voice asked, 'just how close you came to death? How close you still are? Fight it, damn you.'

His eyes fell closed, drowning him first in nausea, then in nothingness.

The next time he surfaced, he saw a cave's grey walls turned amber by the fire's flickering light. Shreds of a dream slipped from his skull – he saw dark armour and priestly robes; he saw silver steel and he heard it sing with an animal's roar... and then nothing more.

This time, he managed to rise. Armour joints snarled in harmony with the aches in his bones.

The cave was small, a haven rather than a home. Ragnar bathed in the fire's light and heat, breathing it in like life itself. The hot air tasted of blood and ash, but even that was a blessing after the choking tang of snow freezing his throat.

'I was beginning to think you'd gone to your reward at the Allfather's side,' said the hulking figure crouched by the fire.

Ragnar looked at his liege lord, the older warrior stirring the fire's heart with a thick deadwood branch. When the words came, they weren't the ones Ragnar had intended to speak.

'You look no different to the last time I saw you.'

Berek grinned, not looking away from the flames. 'What were you expecting, Blackmane?'

'A corpse,' the younger warrior replied. 'You're dead, sire.'

'Is that so?' Berek tossed the deadwood staff into the flames, letting them eat it with the rest of the bracken.

'I avenged you,' Ragnar pointed out. As his thoughts came together in unreliable strands, he was beginning to doubt he was awake at all. 'I butchered the heretic that shed your lifeblood.'

'Oh.' Berek gave an ursine growl that was likely a laugh. 'How heroic of you.'

Ragnar hauled himself to his feet, only to be met with his lord's murmured warning. 'Careful there, hero. You'll be as weak as a three-day cub.'

As true as it was, Ragnar refused to show it. He sank to his haunches by the fire, opposite his long-dead jarl.

'Where's Frostfang?'

'That little pig-sticker? Who knows. You didn't have it when I found you out in the snow. That's your first question? I expected something more practical from you, Blackmane. Do you even know where you are?'

'Where am I?'

Berek's eyes gleamed, dark and delighted. 'A cave.'

'I see that, sire. Where is this cave?'

'Right here.'

Ragnar bared his teeth in a moment of irritated instinct. 'Where is "right here"?'

'Still got that temper, eh? That'll be the death of you, little king.'

'As yours was the death of you?' Ragnar snapped. 'You, who breathed your last breath spitted like venison at a feast and gutted by traitorous blades?'

Berek laughed, opening his fur cloak to reveal his dented and scratched suit of battle armour. The breastplate was a shattered ruin, carved from throat to groin, scabbed over by a thick layer of ice. Destroyed organs and riven flesh showed, just barely, distorted through the frozen lens.

'Yes, just like me. How are the others, eh? How are my First Pack?'

'They are my First Pack now, lord.'

'They took my iron before they took any oath to you, whelp, so tell me how my brothers fare. By Russ, I miss them still.'

Ragnar drew breath to speak, only to be struck by a sudden pressure in his skull. The air he dragged into his lungs had the chemical tang of shipboard filtrators, and the comforting fire flared into the stare of an artificial sun, acid-savage in his eyes.

'Blackmane?' he heard Berek call.

Ragnar held his head in his hands, to stop his skull coming apart at the seams.

'Blackmane?'

'Blackmane?'

'Aye, Slayer. I live. Merely lost in thought.'

'More like dreaming on your feet. A sign of skull damage, or a serious wound to the mind.'

'All is well,' Ragnar lied. 'I saw nothing. All is well.'

Ragnar leaned against the corpse barricade, forcing the shaking, cramping muscles in his arm to unlock. Ahead of him a literal vista of bodies choked the wide tunnel for fifty metres. Behind him, his men were breathless and bleeding, their flesh wracked and torn. Several sank to the ground where they had been standing, overcome with muscle tremors from fighting for seven hours straight. One of them dragged his mangled helmet clear with a curse and spat out a handful of teeth. Due to adrenaline and pain nullifiers in their bloodstreams, wounds taken hours ago were only now discovered: one of the Wolves touched dirty gloved fingertips to his mouth, realising that the axe blow that broke his jaw an hour ago had also torn out part of his tongue.

At Ragnar's side, one of his Grey Hunters slid down to the corpse-laden ground, sitting on the chest of a slain World Eater. The warrior looked at his own left arm with an emotion somewhere between disbelief and irritation. Infrequent sparks flickered from his cleaved wrist, where his bionic hand had been severed away.

Ragnar forced a smile across his features. 'Better your wrist than your throat, brother.'

The warrior growled a laugh. 'True enough, sire.'

Ragnar clapped an encouraging hand on the warrior's back-mounted power pack, and moved away from the barricade.

His men hailed him as he moved through their exhausted packs. He kept his features set in a sly grin, joking with them, teasing them, mocking those who showed superficial and unthreatening injuries. The grin was important. His men must always see him keen and battle-ready, never beset by doubt or troubled by circumstance. Leaders had to be aware of such nuances.

So he grinned, even down in the underworld of blood-stink and barricades made from dead foes. His eyes blazed with forced focus despite the pain of his split-open and hastily sealed skull. The head wound troubled him more than he dared admit. An hour ago, Ulrik had fused the back of the jarl's skull closed with armour cement. Desperate times called for desperate measures. He'd since decided against mentioning how his mind – and his senses – wandered worryingly close to dreams and delusions.

The region they now held was called the Concourse. There, beneath the generatoria district of Kasr Belloc, they stood against the tides of foes seeking to overwhelm them. The route to Kasr Lavok was already hopelessly strangled. For the whole of the day they'd held the subterranean junctions at the Concourse, where Ragnar's warriors had manned a series of barricaded chokepoints and prepared several fallback positions.

The long day preceding the last stand at the Concourse had been somewhat less glorious. Kasr Belloc was in flames, and just as Ulrik had warned, the tunnel routes to Lavok were so crammed with the Warmaster's filthy, miserable troops that all forward motion by Ragnar's company had been halted in a grind of ceramite on ceramite. The assault failed when the tunnels collapsed, brought down by the Archenemy on top of Ragnar's vanguard.

Since then, all had been silent. The last of the Cadian 57th had managed to reach Kasr Lavok only to find it already fallen. That was the last Ragnar had heard of their fate, and of the city they'd sought to save.

'Nightblade is back, lord,' said one of his warriors. It was Soergar, called the True Cut by his kith and kin. Ragnar slapped his shoulder guard in thanks and turned to the grizzled figure who approached from the deeper dark.

'Jarl,' the Scout greeted him. Not *My jarl*. The Scouts walked beyond the borders of the twelve Great Companies, beholden only to the orders of High King Grimnar. Drekka, called Nightblade by his kith and kin, was a far older warrior than the lord he reported to this eve. He was a walking arsenal festooned with weapons, yet without the bulk of sacred ceramite. His trade was murder in the night, not breaking the backs of foes on the front line.

Drekka's report was terse and to the point. Plainly he expected a swift dismissal after his scouting run, but Ragnar kept the old warrior by his side.

'I need you to push further,' the jarl told him.

'Further towards Lavok?' Drekka's dark face creased with smile lines. 'The tunnels are lost, Blackmane, and the city is dead. Our future holds no journey to Lavok, this I promise you.'

'Not to Lavok, kinsman.' Ragnar outlined his plan. Drekka listened and, as was his way, nodded succinctly to give his agreement.

The jarl thanked him, then dismissed him back to the shadows.

As the jarl moved away again, his Wolf Guard flanked him in silent, pack-born unity. He hid his disquiet from his brother-warriors, but the First Pack was bound to their lord closer than any other. They had always seen what others could not be allowed to witness, and knew him too well for his deceptions to take root in their minds. The others of Ragnar's company had seen their lord fight twice as hard as any man alive in these tunnels only to keep grinning between battles, but the First Pack saw beneath the facade. Their lord was weary unto death. They all were.

Away from the other packs, they gathered around a shimmering hol-olithic display of the local tunnel network generated by the Slayer's hand-held projector.

'We stand at the beginning of the end.' Ulrik gestured to several adjacent passages sweeping around the Concourse's rear. 'I was at the sixth barri-cade with Skyhunter and his men – the rearward tunnels cannot be held for much longer without reinforcement.'

'You old crow,' said Alrydd with a gunshot laugh. He had replaced Razor-tongue as the Great Company's bard four decades before, but he was still fresh to the ranks of the First Pack. 'Aren't you drawn to places of death? You should be pleased by the prospect.'

Ulrik smiled beneath his mask, though none of them saw it. 'Perhaps I am. I'm merely pointing out the realities, young singer.'

Ragnar ended their banter with a chop of his hand. 'Focus. Focus on what matters here and now. Fight the battles we can win. That means holding here, and holding here means holding the Septimal passages as well as the rearward tunnels.' He gestured to a cobweb of flickering passages, as thin as filament and spreading out in myriad directions. 'Here. If we take the crawl-tunnels south of the third causeway, it will lessen the pressure on the rearward passages.'

Alrydd cursed beneath his breath. 'It will be knife to throat in those crawl-chutes. No swords. No axes. No bolters.'

Even Uller Greylock sucked in air through his teeth as if in pain. 'It does smell a little like false hope, my jarl, but I'll go if you wish it.'

'I need you elsewhere, Greylock. Longspear, I ask this of you.'

Hrolf Longspear met his lord's gaze.

'Give me Blood Claws, my jarl, and I'll give you those tunnels.'

Ragnar nodded. 'Take the Twice-Proven. Have them leave their ammu-nition reserves here, divided among the remaining packs.' As he spoke, he looked to Hrolf's features, scarcely lit in the reddish gloom. Longspear showed no unease at the thought of being sent into some of the thickest fighting without a single bolt shell to fire.

'Take those tunnels,' Ragnar said, 'and I'll howl your names to the All-father myself when I stand before his throne.'

'It will be done,' Hrolf promised.

'Greylock?'

'My jarl.'

The jarl's quick, dark eyes danced across the projection again. His gesturing hand followed. 'The Septimal tunnels. That's where I need you.'

Like Hrolf, Uller agreed without hesitation. 'Who holds those tunnels now?'

'The Red Mist and Wyrdbane,' replied Ragnar. 'At last report, Wyrdbane is down to five men.'

Uller paced the rockcrete floor. 'Good men with good blades, but it's fairer to ask them to grow wings and fly than to hold there alone much longer. By your leave, I'll take the True Cut and his Swordkin to stand with them.'

'Done.' Ragnar's reply was immediate. 'Go.'

Uller bared his throat in the private Einherjar gesture of obedience. He was gone a moment later, calling Soergar True Cut and his pack to follow.

It was Ulrik who asked the question none of the others wished to voice. He asked it calmly, without either hope or rancour. A practical man, concerned only with the details.

'Then I assume we've heard nothing of reinforcements?' The moment the words left his wolf-skulled helm, the tunnel shivered around them, raining dust and pebble debris against their ceramite plating. With a little imagination, the growl of distant artillery could be the laughter of giants.

Alrydd looked to the shaking walls. 'The war itself is laughing at that question, Slayer.'

Ragnar smiled at the bard's grim jest. It was the kind of thing Razortongue would have said.

The Wolf Lord took his place at the first barricade, bracing himself against the armoured bodies of the dead traitors piled up to make a waist-high wall. The symbol of a blue-and-green world, an image of Old Earth perhaps, showed on the dead warriors' red armour. A world being devoured between iron jaws.

Ancient Ulrik was at Ragnar's side, his leathery features masked by the wolf-skull helm. He stared, red-eyed, into the darkness of the tunnel across the barricade.

'Dare I ask?' Ragnar asked the Wolf Priest.

Ulrik's laugh was dry and ugly. 'I've cut the red threads of nine Eaters of Worlds today. *Nine.* Can you say the same of yourself?'

'He could say it,' Alrydd said from Ragnar's other side. 'But it wouldn't be true.'

Ragnar's answer was preceded by another grin, one fiercer and truer than those that came before.

'Only three, Slayer. But the day is yet young.'

* * *

The flood came in a tide of shrieking, scarred flesh, and the remnants of Ragnar's Great Company rose to fight it back. The foe's tactic was crude but undeniably effective – flooding the tunnels with worthless thralls to let the Wolves weary themselves slaughtering the hordes of zealous slaves. Even immortal arms can ache, and even immortal hands will tire. Ragnar's men battled with their hands cramp-locked around the bloodstained grips of weapons almost starved of ammunition and fuel.

Bolters were starting to click with empty throats. Chainswords and chain-axes were breaking down, their sturdy mechanisms fouled by human meat, their teeth-tracks thrown from overuse, and their simple hilt engines cough-ing in thirst.

Behind the barricade of butchered bodies, Alrydd fought at Ragnar's right side while Ulrik guarded the jarl's left. The torrent of unwashed men and women ground against the Wolves' thin lines in a gale of spitting, frothing, bleeding flesh. Hundreds of knives and cudgels flashed out in malnour-ished hands only to break upon blue-grey ceramite.

The Wolves saw almost nothing human in the men and women besieging them. To the Einherjar they were a single organism, thrashing and heav-ing like some sickly tide of flesh. To stand against the horde was to fight back an ocean made of meat, bone and rags.

Ragnar killed with every movement of his aching muscles. A fist shattered a dreadlocked man's skull, spilling out the grey sludge within. A sweep of his blade tore a filthy woman's head free from her shoulders. Hammer-ing the butt of his pistol down collapsed the stitched face of the mutated thing scrabbling at his breastplate.

On and on it went, wearing the Wolves down hour by hour.

The vox was beyond worthless, forever lost to screeches of distorted speech, too broken to understand, cutting off in mid transmission. The Wolves learned to ignore it; it was just more background vileness to deal with.

When a break in the tides came, it was scarcely a mercy. Taller figures stalked through the ranks, armoured as the Wolves were armoured, bear-ing fresh weapons while Ragnar's men clutched broken blades.

'Skitnah!' Ragnar roared above the chittering sea. *Skitnah. Corruption. Filth.* The World Eaters were back, and he summoned every one of his war-riors to the barricades.

Alrydd threw his head back in a howl. Hearing their bard still alive at their lord's side, the ragged survivors of Ragnar's Great Company took up the war-cry.

More foes followed. More foes died. It took no time at all to add to the corpse barricades with Space Wolves chainblades singing their reaping song, creating building blocks in abundance.

Ragnar felt strangely exposed fighting without his entire Wolf Guard.

Even the First Pack's newest and bravest blood, Tor – called Wolfheart by his kith and kin – had become a presence ever at his side in recent campaigns. Now he fought only with Alrydd Dirgehowler and Ulrik the Slayer, with his other closest brothers sent away to serve among the other squads. Scattering their skills would inspire the exhausted warriors of depleted packs. Every Blood Claw and Grey Hunter would fight harder in the shadow of the jarl's chosen companions.

Ragnar howled in the heat of the melee, venting his weary rage in a wordless, cleansing cry. His muscles were strained almost to ruin beneath the abused layers of ceramite plating – it was only the twin callings of duty and fury that kept him on his feet. Fury, that any warrior alive believed they would be the one to end his life and legend; duty, for he refused to fall while those who depended upon him yet drew breath.

He killed not with his blade, with his bolter, with his fist, or even with his boot. These were merely tools. Ragnar killed with his heart and soul, pouring himself into every desperate movement, sucking in life with every sawing breath.

Different Wolves fought around him at the first barricade. He rotated the serving packs every hour, keeping them as fresh as he could, sending the walking wounded back to the second barricade in order that they might rush forwards to aid the defenders in the grimmest moments. Their purpose was twofold, though the second duty was far less palatable: should the first barricade fall, the wounded packs holding at the second wall would be the last line of defence.

Only two other figures remained constant. Alrydd was a slow blur at his side, the bard's blade spinning and twisting and cutting and gutting. Ulrik's crozius mace gave a flare of kinetic light and a cathedral bell's clang each time it hammered into yielding flesh. The Wolves nearby fought with the same viciousness, far past the point where ferocity becomes savagery. With their backs to the wall, they became the beasts they were named for.

Another howl sounded above the battle – a breathless thing, closer to a gasping bark than a true, full-throated shout. Without the vox the jarl had no way of tallying his warriors' casualties. They howled now under their lord's orders so that he might keep count of the fallen.

The weight of numbers was ever a threat, even if individual humans were not. These were raggedly armoured ranks of soldiers who once served in the Imperial Guard: soldiers who had thrown loyalty and discipline to the wind yet held fast to their cunning. They tangled his ankles, clinging to his boots and shins. They grasped at his arms and elbows, dragging his defences down. With infuriating regularity, sacrificial fools hurled themselves at his blade, willingly impaling themselves in the hopes of bearing the sword down to the ground with their dying grip.

One of them, the boldest of all, managed to crawl through the corpses littering the floor, avoiding half a dozen stamping Wolves' boots. She rose up behind the front line and launched herself upon the jarl's back, hungry fingers reaching for the lord's hunter's crest to find purchase and cut his throat. Her courage came to naught as she was swatted from the jarl's back by a whirring cut from Alrydd's sword. One of the woman's arms remained in place, the severed limb locked to the jarl's shoulder guard by its hand's death grip. It was shaken loose after a few seconds, tumbling into the sea of butchered bodies piling up around the Wolves' knees.

It was dusk on the surface of this world at war, where day and night still meant something. Beneath ground it was the same unending twilight. Decay played a swift game down there, ripening bodies with rot and adding their sickly sweet smell to the already foul corridors.

As the third day came to its slow, bloody end, Ulrik tore the Helm of Russ from his head, dragging the stinking subterranean air into his lungs.

'We cannot hold,' he said during a lull in the massacre.

'I know.' The battered and bloody figure of Ragnar was using a wolf pelt to clean gore from Frostfang's mechanics.

'Pull the Terminators back from the battle. Use them to dig through the collapsed tunnels.'

'That will take an eternity. We need them at the barricades.'

'It's our only chance, Blackmane. Give the order.'

Rare were the times when the Slayer saw fit to give orders to the Young King. Ragnar shook his head, triggering Frostfang now its blockage was cleared.

'No, old father. You said it yourself, we will never reach Lavok. Getting Greylock and the others to dig like rats in the dark won't change that. Do you think they'd even agree? Slayer, *you* try to tell the company's finest warriors that they have to abandon the fight and claw through dirt instead. See how they take that order.'

Ulrik looked over the barricades at the ocean of dead bodies carpeting the tunnel floor, waist-deep in places. With narrowed eyes, he asked, 'What were Nightblade's orders, jarl?'

'What are any Scout's orders? To walk alone where an army cannot go. I sent him back up to Kasr Belloc.'

'The enemy holds Belloc, north to south and east to west. To surface there would be death, deep behind enemy lines. Even if he escapes the fallen city, the rest of us will not. Why would you do this?'

'He won't seek to escape,' said Ragnar. 'I sent him to chase down the source of the fractured transmission.'

'My jarl,' Ulrik sighed. 'You've sent him to his death at a time when we most need every blade by our sides. This is a waste of life.'

Ragnar turned a cold stare upon his mentor. Rather than reply, he returned to the barricade and prepared for the next assault.

The tide came, broke against them and receded after eleven long, bitter hours.

It is no easy feat to tally the lost lives within a harvest of flesh. Did one Wolf die for every fifty humans? One for every hundred? Who could know for certain? Confusion in such circumstances was forgivable, even among humanity's genetic elite. Eidetic recollections can be deceived when the warriors are too weary to dredge through their memories and count, one by one, the harvest of lives that have ended so far. Time had a way of playing tricks on the minds of those fighting within a shield-wall.

Beneath Ragnar's boots ran a river of blood that needed no poetic licence to bring to life. He stood waist-deep in the butchered dead, hurling them aside as best he could, throwing them against the barricade.

In this brief respite the Wolves once more remained in place, too muscle-sore to move away from the barricade and wade through the sea of the slain. Many dropped where they had been standing, murmuring prayers to the old gods that their ancestors had become. Others beseeched the Emperor, not for salvation – such a prayer would be considered craven beyond reckoning – but demanding that the Allfather turn His holy eyes upon them, witnessing their final acts of courage and glory.

Ragnar remained on his feet, though only barely. He lowered his head, letting the blood and sweat drip from his face. As his eyes fell closed, the stinging ache inside them softened with the sweetest relief. For several heartbeats, he wasn't sure he would ever be able to open his eyes again. Already he could hear the marching tread of more foes drawing closer, their echoing advance becoming a tortured mishmash of sound. These weren't the leather boots of treacherous Guard or the rags of beggar-cultists. A heavy, crunching tread of ceramite boots on stone is a sound like no other. It becomes an orchestra of pealing thunder when enough warriors gather; it was a storm Ragnar knew well.

How long until they reached the barricade? Hard to say. Twenty minutes. Ten. It made no difference, either way. This was, at long last, the end. Every one of the Wolves knew it.

'Don't argue with me,' he murmured through gashed lips, picking up the stray thread of a conversation abandoned over an hour ago. Alrydd understood it at once.

'It's my place to argue with you,' the bard replied. His words could be considered the claim of a wise man or the plea of a cowardly one. Whichever was true, the bard spoke with a razor-tongued sharpness. 'When you're wrong, Blackmane, it's my place to tell you so.'

Every warrior remaining could see how it cost him to say those words. Defying his jarl wasn't something lightly done.

'How am I wrong?' Ragnar paused to spit blood onto the sea of corpses around them. 'Tell me that, if you would.'

'We can kill more of them if we hold here,' said Alrydd. 'Returning to the surface is suicide unless the city is retaken. The barricades here serve us well, and the foe dies in hordes. What else matters now?'

Ragnar opened his eyes to the stinging dark once more. 'Killing more of them is meaningless. Empty glory, Dirgehowler.'

The bard splashed water from his canteen over his face, using the precious liquid to clean his eyes of the foes' poisonous, blinding blood. Once done, he handed the bottle to Ragnar.

'This is a good place to die, brother.'

'A good place, yes. Not a good way.'

'Semantics.'

'You say so? I would rather die clawing my way back to sunlight than harvesting the enemy's lives down here in the dark.'

Alrydd felt too weary to even bare his teeth in a snarl. 'Are you listening to yourself, sire? If we fight our way out, we'll lose the barricades and our fallback junctions. We'll be dead before we even reach the surface.'

'We're entombing ourselves behind walls of the dead. They are barely barricades any more. Just mounds of cooling meat making an ocean of the slain.'

'They're the only reason we're alive now.'

'If I die tonight, singer, it will be by the terms I choose. We are leaving. That's the end of it.'

Alrydd knew as well as any other the futility of arguing with their lord when Ragnar's mind was fixed upon something.

'Be it so, then.' He spat onto the closest corpse. 'I was growing weary of the scenery, anyway.'

Ragnar raised his voice to call the others. 'Kindred! Pack-brothers! To me, all who still draw breath! To me, now!'

Alrydd rolled several bodies aside as he waded through gore to reach Ragnar. 'I hope you know what you're doing.'

'Don't I always?' Ragnar gave a weary laugh at his own words as the other Wolves drew near. In a moment of miraculous restraint, Alrydd let that claim go unchallenged.

'Everyone!' Ragnar called, uncaring how his voice echoed down the tunnels, doubtless to the listening ears of the enemy.

Let the enemy hear. Let them come.

'Leave your barricades and rally to me. Death comes marching towards us now, bearing fresh bolters and readied blades while we scavenge weapons from the cold hands of our own dead brothers. But I reject this death. Do you hear me, kinsmen? I deny it. I *refuse* it. Sharpen the teeth of your swords and cast aside all you cannot carry with you. We'll fight our way to the surface or die trying. And if luck and spite carry us back into the sunlight only to be surrounded by more foes, then I will die in the city above, howling my name to the embattled sky. These are the words of your jarl...'

He let his words trail away, drifting down the corridors. A few seconds passed before he added, in a conversational tone, '...and your jarl assumes you're coming with him?'

They didn't cheer or shout. They laughed. Honest grins split their blood-streaked faces, and the survivors of Ragnar's Great Company lauded their jarl with good-natured laughter.

'Make ready,' Ragnar told them. 'We go forwards, no matter what's in our way. Slayer, the schematic if you please.'

Ulrik raised the projector lens, bleaching the air with the image of the tunnel network. It twitched and flickered, as unreliable as ever.

'We could scatter,' Ragnar said, gesturing at the map. 'We've six hundred and more capillary corridors to choose from, and all likely still feeding enemy flesh towards the barricades. They want to choke us to death down here, that much is clear. If we scatter, there's a chance several of the disparate packs will reach the surface.'

'The odds, though...' one of the Grey Hunters spoke up.

'The odds are against us no matter what we do, Crowcaller.' Ragnar aimed his sword towards the barricades and beyond, where the marching tread drew nearer. 'And whatever we choose, we have little time to make our choice.'

'Still, my jarl... Rats scatter. Vermin scatter. We should stay together.'

Knuckles thudded against breastplates in answer to this. Ragnar fought to hide his pride.

'A tide of iron,' called out another warrior. 'We fight our way to the surface as a great pack.'

More thudding knuckles.

'Your jarl hears your words, Redhammer. What do you say, kindred?'

It was Redhammer who answered again. 'What worth is there in five warriors reaching the surface, my jarl, if all others lie slain beneath the earth?'

Knuckles crashed in agreement upon every breastplate. Again Ragnar had to bite back his proud smile. This was loyalty – brotherhood even unto death.

'I am glad you agree with me, kinsmen. Be it so. We fight together.' Ragnar walked around the projected map, using Frostfang's tip to mark a trail through the shimmering light. 'Learn this route. Every junction and every turn.'

On he walked, leading their following eyes along a path that avoided the city's principal and secondary space ports, as well as entire habitation sectors and barracks-fortress districts. The watching warriors could see one thing with stark clarity – it would take almost a week to fight through the route.

'This path will take us under the foundry district, avoiding where the foe is most likely to be flooding the tunnels. We avoid evacuation centres, major thoroughfares, the bastions of entrenched enemy forces last reported by reliable intelligence. But we will be channelled through several of the subterranean strongholds built by the enemy as they claimed the tunnel network. If we survive, as unlikely as that might be, we will surface at the city's western edge.'

'The coast?' asked Alrydd. Every warrior present marked the bard's tone. The coast had been one of the enemy's primary landing sites outside the city. Emerging there was as much a death sentence as staying here.

'It's the coast,' said Ragnar, 'or the eastern plains in the enemy's heart, or the conquered city itself. Our best chance is to rise far behind their front lines and cut back to our own forces. At least from the coast we can re-establish vox communication with the fleet, or make our way south to Kasr Corollus and link with the Cadian regiments led by the Black Templars.'

'If they even remain alive that far south,' the bard pointed out.

'Everything in life is a matter of *if*,' Uller replied. 'Stay silent if you're incapable of focusing on what matters.'

Alrydd lifted a hand to return an obscene gesture, taking a second to realise it was the hand he'd lost hours before. He looked at his stump for a moment before grunting in irritation. True to form, he made the gesture with his remaining hand instead.

Ragnar continued as if neither had spoken. 'With the city fallen, the odds of us ever seeing sunlight are pathetic at best. We knew that when we volunteered as rearguard to hold the walls and the evacuation tunnels. But it's better to die on the hunt, my brothers, and face the Allfather without turning away in shame.'

As the chorus of thudding agreement began again, Alrydd rose to his feet, adding his words to Ragnar's.

'And remember, we are few enough now that I will be watching every move you all make, recalling all that I see for entry into the sagas. Try not to dishonour yourselves, eh? No one wants their legacies ruined.'

Another ripple of amusement answered the bard's words. The approaching bootsteps almost drowned it out.

'Go then,' Ragnar ordered. 'Make ready.'

As the packs moved away, Ragnar used the filthy robe of a slain human to clean the gobbets from Frostfang's teeth. The marching grew ever louder, its disciplined rhythm unbroken.

Alrydd watched him, speaking softly. 'Do you regret volunteering for this?' the bard asked.

Yes. No. I don't know. There are worse ways to die.

'Perhaps,' Ragnar admitted.

'You shouldn't. Tens of thousands have survived, all because we held our ground in this city for as long as we did. All the militia, all the soldiers. They needed us. A city that would have fallen in hours held for over a month, my jarl. Even if our remains never reach the Chapter's vault we can die proud, and if this is the final time Frostfang will sing in your grip, make her last song echo through eternity.'

You have your moments, bard.

Ragnar finished cleaning the weapon, turning the blade over in his hands, examining it for signs of corrosion. 'May it be so, my brother.'

'It's been an honour to fight with you, sire.'

'The fighting's not over yet.' Ragnar revved the priceless blade. Kraken teeth roared along its edges, eating the air but starving for meat and thirsty for blood. He lifted the sword high and shouted into the darkness ahead, *'For Russ and the Allfather!'*

Dozens of howling warriors took up the cry.

PART 2

CRETACIA,
CRADLE OF DRAGONS

I

Cretacia, Home World of the Flesh Tearers Chapter
The Year of the Red Iron and Rising Storms
961.M41

Weaponless, shackled in energy bindings with his wrists linked behind his back, the prisoner paced his cell. He was as one might expect from any Wolf: proud-eyed and draped in the furs of his home world, with his armour plating encrusted with runic markings that meant nothing to those outside of his Chapter and tribe.

From the levels beneath his boots, the resonant song of metal on metal rang eternally against walls of stone. The prisoner endlessly paced the cell, waiting only because he had no choice in the matter. In the way of those born under wide open skies, he rankled at any notion of captivity.

Not that his capture had come as a surprise, of course. The only surprise was that he was still alive.

He faced his captors when they came for him. One of them was a Chaplain, if the holy rosarius medallion around his neck was any indication, and his dark-skinned features were a visage of pockmarked ruination and cybernetic reconstruction. A ravaged hairline of receding stubble was blighted by badly healed tissue craters and the ugly pebbles of burn scarring.

'You're the most fantastically ugly man I've ever laid eyes on,' the prisoner told him, 'but by the Allfather, I bet you're proud of those scars.'

The Chaplain deactivated the layered refractor fields around the prisoner's cell, one by one. The kinetic-resistant barriers snapped out of existence with fizzing crackles of tormented air. As the Chaplain entered the cell, the prisoner stepped back from the iron doorway with no sign of ill intent in his gaze.

'I seek the High Warrior of your Chapter,' the prisoner said. 'Gabriel Sawtooth, Lord of the Tearers of Flesh and this world's master. Long have I waited to share words with him, face to face and eye to eye.'

'Chapter Master Seth is far from here,' the Chaplain allowed. 'He wages war in the Emperor's name. I am Brother-Chaplain Scarath. You already know Sergeant Vorain. He was one of the boarding party that brought you to me.'

'Priest,' the prisoner said in greeting. 'Pack leader. Hail to you both.'

'Our names will serve. My brothers and I rarely stand by titles. You're the one named Blackmane, yes?'

'To my kith and kin I am Blackmane. Outlanders more often use the name Ragnar. It is our way.'

'Ragnar, then.'

The Wolf bared his teeth in a grin. 'Do you bring thanks at last for the return of your warship? Many were the months we spent sailing it back to your skies. My jarl offered one of his own Navigators for the journey – a prize beyond any other. And you repay us by throwing us into bindings. Cold is the welcome on Cretacia.'

Scarath was more than used to the various dialects and variances in the common Imperial tongue encountered across the galaxy. He could understand Ragnar's words, but they were plainly coloured by the Wolf's culture.

'I am not here to thank you,' said Scarath. 'I'm here to sentence you.'

'Sentence? Ha! For what crime?'

Scarath wondered if this warrior was a particularly dull-witted example of his brethren. The answer, as he saw it, was obvious.

'For the crime of being a Wolf.'

For a moment, Ragnar thought neither of them would answer. Not the scarred sergeant, nor the gaunt and grey Chaplain.

'For the crime of being a Wolf,' said the dead-eyed priest. 'For being a treacherous dog from a Chapter of treacherous dogs.'

'Ah, so you wish to execute me. Now I see which way the wind blows. Continuing the war between our Chapters plainly means more to you than any chance of brotherhood. I assume Nalfir will suffer the same fate?'

The Chaplain, thin-lipped and with his eyes half lidded, spoke in a tone as passionless as his gaze. 'You both died the moment you entered our domain. Just as we would be dead the moment we entered yours.'

For the first time since his imprisonment days ago, Ragnar's temper boiled forth. 'Are you so devoid of honour that you would condemn us to death without once hearing our words? Our Chapters were as brothers once – bloodlines from the purest of sources, descended from the most loyal of fathers.'

Scarath was implacable. 'Times change.'

Ragnar clacked his teeth in Fenrisian emphasis. 'There's a cold truth indeed. If this is how you treat those who would be your allies, then whatever blackness you're hiding in your souls is darker than any of us realised. You're right to kill me. Death is better than the pathetic, terrified hospitality you offer.'

Scarath closed his scarred eyes for a moment, taking a breath. Ragnar couldn't reliably read the gesture – it was either soulful reflection or an attempt to control the rise of anger. No evidence either way presented itself, for when the Chaplain's gaze returned, there was nothing but weary fortitude in his stare.

'We will speak then, for the sake of the archives. Why are you here, Wolf?'

Ragnar hesitated. 'What do you mean? I have told your jailor servitors a hundred times and more. Your apothecaries have filled my bloodstream with truth serums – a violation and a dishonour I have allowed in order to prove my honest intent. Never once has my story wavered.'

Scarath stepped closer, bringing with him the telltale stone scent of old ceramite and the bitter purity of weapon oils. He stood face to face with Ragnar, eye to eye, just as the Wolf had asked for upon greeting him. Honour badges and buzzsaw-shaped trinkets on the Chaplain's black armour glinted in the stark light of the illumination strips running the length of the ceiling.

'*I'm* asking you, Wolf, not my slaves or battle-brothers. *I* am asking you. Scarath of the Flesh Tearers, a castellan of the Black Tower. This is your chance to change your story before you walk the Path of the Setting Sun.'

Ragnar's lip curled. He refused to show the unease creeping its way up his spine. This was a poor, poor way to die, denied a warrior's death in this sunless cell. He didn't fear that fate, but he lamented it all the same.

'I am here to see if there can be peace between us.'

Scarath's reply was immediate. 'You lie.'

'It's no lie,' Ragnar growled. 'I have spoken nothing but honesty every time I've opened my mouth. You're not punishing me for lying, you're punishing me because it is easier than dealing with the truth.'

'Yes,' Scarath nodded. 'That's exactly what we are doing. "Better the enemy you know than the stranger you don't." Do you have that saying on your miserable home world?'

'Something similar,' Ragnar admitted. 'But we recognise it for what it is – the false wisdom of cowards seeking to justify their fears.'

Scarath shook his head. What little emotion had showed in his eyes seemed to drain away. 'What peace do you offer, Ragnar? Do you speak for your Chapter, or for a single commander?'

'Nalfir and I speak for Jarl Berek One-Arm of the Thunderfists. He–'

'He is irrelevant. Your lord is one warrior, leading one company, is he not?'

'You say true.'

'And rather than come himself, showing his sincerity, he sends two warriors too young to have fought at Honour's End. How are we to trust you, Wolf? Even if you speak the truth, you speak only for a single Great Company.'

'Our lord would carry word to the Great Wolf.'

'So you say.'

'We offer a first step on the road back to brotherhood. How can you cast that aside?'

'Because Wolves lie, Ragnar. What guarantee do we have that setting you free would make a difference? We could offer forgiveness to your whole Chapter and yet still the enmity might continue. Do you see? You don't bring peace. You've come to see if we are cursed and maddened, because you believe we are the ones to blame for the day that honour ended. The Flesh Tearers spit on your false apology. We have no patience left for the toothy grins of blind Wolves.'

'Wait,' said Ragnar as the Flesh Tearer turned away. 'Speak, priest. You call me blind. At least tell me why.'

'Is it not obvious? Do you think we've never sent ambassadors to the Fang in the last century? And what became of them? Three returned as severed heads preserved in alchemical fluid made from sea serpent venom. Three never returned at all.'

'I was told nothing of this. I didn't know.'

'And had you known, what difference would it have made? The Flesh Tearers have scourged themselves for decades because of what happened at Honour's End. We mourn every drop of blood that was shed that day. How is it that you Wolves do not? How is it that we grieve and atone, yet the Wolves do nothing but cheer and grin?'

The Chaplain sighed, as weary as if he were trying to explain astrocalculation to a beast of burden. 'How are the Wolves so self-righteous, forever acting without shame or remorse? How do you celebrate yourselves as heroes, even when so much Imperial blood is on your hands? How do you always, *always* believe you are the only white in a galaxy shaded grey? Are you all truly that blind?'

'Chaplain Scarath...' Ragnar took a step forwards. 'There are those among the Wolves who are willing to take their portion of the blame for the darkness between our Chapters. Do not let this chance slip through your fingers.'

'Their *portion* of the blame? For trying to desecrate our loyal dead?' Scarath's hands tensed, twitching closer to the sheathed chaindagger at his belt. 'Your brothers pissed like dogs all over the fraternal codes of the Adeptus Astartes! To the abyss with the Wolves and their *portion* of the blame, Ragnar.'

He turned from the Wolf and moved to the iron door. 'Tomorrow you will walk the Path of the Setting Sun. There's no finer death on Cretacia. Consider that my gift to you, rather than slitting your throat here and now.'

'Sergeant Vorain?' called Ragnar. 'Tell me there is more wisdom within your Chapter than the judgement of this foolish holy man.'

The sergeant met Ragnar's eyes from the doorway, then turned and left without a word.

'Scarath!' Ragnar hurled himself against the closing door. Ceramite armour crashed against reinforced iron, neither giving way.

Bolts turned. Mechanical locks thudded home. The wasp-like drone of refractor fields hummed back to life, leaving Ragnar gritting his teeth and staring at the sealed door with his wrists bound behind his back.

There could be no peace between two Chapters as proud and stubborn as the warriors of Fenris and Cretacia. It galled him to die this shameful death in the enemy's hands, but far worse was dying knowing Razortongue had been right all along.

II

For Vorain, the weeks passed as they always did, in tides of duty and respite. The sergeant's responsibilities were many, and he went about them within the fortress-monastery with a single-minded focus that made him invaluable in the role of warden.

It was a role he despised, loath to be away from the Chapter's active campaigns, yet one he was damned to perform due to his excellence in carrying it out. Remaining on Cretacia was a necessary exile, and one not without honour. None of that made it any more palatable. His blade hungered no less than the swords and axes in his distant brothers' hands. They, however, were allowed to fight. Vorain's fate was to watch over an impregnable castle.

And then the Wolves had come. Scarath had tried and sentenced them without consulting the sergeant even once. Vorain was still unsure just how he felt about the Chaplain's interference. Scarath had overstepped his bounds, without question, but Vorain relied on the older warrior's counsel and guidance in matters of the Chapter's soul.

Peace with the Wolves of Fenris? Truly?

He was a sergeant. He could hardly make such decisions for the entire Flesh Tearers Chapter.

The halls of an Adeptus Astartes fortress-monastery always echoed with the sound of military industry, from the forging of weapons to the chanting and training of the warriors that comprise a Space Marine Chapter. The grey stone castle hewn from the living rock of Cretacia's greatest chasm was no exception. Here, Vorain oversaw the Chapter's past, present and future, while its four battle companies sailed the stars in the Emperor's name.

His world was confined by great arches and curved stone walls. His ears forever rang with the sound of the forges churning out bolt shells, and the hammer-crack of those same shells being fired on the target ranges, hour after hour after hour.

The only thing that set Vorain's subterranean castle apart from other Adeptus Astartes fortress-monasteries was the presence of actual brethren.

Where a hundred or more fully initiated Space Marine warriors might tend to their monastic and guardianship duties within the sanctums of other Chapters, the Flesh Tearers' stronghold was bare of such companionship.

Vorain, along with the changeably choleric and coldly serene Scarath, had fewer than thirty battle-brothers under his vigil, aiding in the training of several hundred aspirants. Over time he had found his capacity for conversation dying out, eroding from disuse.

The training bouts with his Chaplain advisor were at least a source of verbal exchange. Much of the rest of the time, among the primitive brutes harvested as potential initiates from Cretacia's population, speech was somewhat scarce. Even his own brothers spoke with him less and less, sensing his withdrawal from their ranks – partly because of his bitterness at this honourable banishment, partly because they were aware enough to see that the sergeant would surely be promoted to the Chapter's command council before long. The Scout Company had been without a formal leader for several years now.

He often watched the brutes wrestling, fighting with bone daggers beneath the proud banners of Flesh Tearers crusades. These were the very youngest initiates, new to their lives as aspirants yet all muscled and scarred beyond the imagining of most Imperial citizens.

Strange to think that only a century ago Vorain had been one of those primitive tribesmen himself. How small the world had seemed. Waking, eating, hunting, sleeping. *Surviving.* What else was there? He had no way of knowing, then, about the great, wide galaxy and its million threats to mankind.

There was an innocence in that simple savagery. The purity of barbarism.

'There's something we must discuss,' Scarath said as the two of them watched the brutes doing battle. The arched chamber rang with the grunts and curses of the fighting clansmen, the crashing clash of bronze weapons, and the pounding of tribal drums echoing off the high walls. The rancid air stank of sweat, blood and desperation.

'This harvest is useless,' was the sergeant's reply.

'You seem distracted, Vorain.'

The sergeant didn't answer. Vorain had seen little of promise in this newest batch of potential initiates. No future Flesh Tearer stood out from amongst the rabble. Their blood would be running through the floor grates before sunset.

'I said, there's something we must–'

'I heard you.' Vorain was already walking forwards, moving between the packs of embattled tribesmen. Unarmoured, wearing only one of the Chapter's monastic robes, Vorain's face and forearms were bare to their stares. He rolled a headless body over with the edge of his leather boot, pausing to pick up the corpse's fallen axe.

A fine weapon. Its blood-marked blade shone in the hazy light drifting in through the stained-glass windows. Once they had shown a scene of the primarch Sanguinius in all his glory before the Eternity Gate. Now the scene was half lost to darkness, choked by jungle creeper vines growing against the fortress' walls, blackening and strangling the primarch's armour.

The axe weighed next to nothing in the Flesh Tearer's hand, but its presence was soothing all the same. An echo of a time when survival was the only question, and triumph the only answer.

Around him, the tribesmen were slowing in their efforts, backing away from the towering warrior. They faced the demigod in their midst with narrowed eyes and clenched teeth, clutching their weapons tighter.

The Flesh Tearer cast off his robe with a shrug of his huge shoulders. The tribesmen shrank back further, raising their own brutish blades.

There were thirty-one of them in total. It took Vorain fifty seconds to kill them all.

When his bloody work was done, he stood in the middle of the chamber, listening to the lifeblood of the unworthy aspirants sluicing through the grates in the floor. The slashing hiss of running blood soothed his irritated headache somewhat. None of them had managed to even block one blow. No matter how hardy Cretacia bred its hunter-sons, only one in a thousand was worthy of wearing the Chapter's red and black.

Vorain cast the stolen axe to the life-soaked stone floor in disgust.

'Another unworthy harvest after all,' the Chaplain agreed.

Vorain stalked back to him. 'You said there was something we must discuss. I assume you've had word of the Wolves?'

Scarath's war-torn features twisted in mirth. 'After three weeks outside the walls? Their bones will have been picked clean by scavengers and bleached by the sun. We have received word from the stars, Vorain, not from Cretacia's wilds.'

Vorain was instantly alert. He couldn't conceal the hope in his voice. 'Word from Lord Seth?'

'Indeed so.'

The sergeant beat his fists against his chest, crying his exultation to the chamber's high ceiling. Scarath watched, waiting for the cry to die away.

'It's over?' Vorain asked at last. 'We will return to serve in a battle company?' Crying out here in this dungeon wasn't enough. He felt like racing to the battlements and shouting his joy to the night sky.

That rush of emotion died when he saw the flicker of hesitation in Scarath's calm eyes. Scarath bared his metal peg teeth in a commiserating smile that Vorain wanted to carve from the Chaplain's face.

'Our lord informed me that the last batch of reinforcements was of the finest quality to date. In recognition of your exemplary service, you are to be promoted to Captain of the Tenth Company, effective at dawn.'

Vorain winced at the title as much as at the knife thrust of disappointment. 'Captain of the Tenth. We can only field four companies with the

Chapter's full strength. How can there be a Tenth Company without the five preceding it?'

'Tradition,' the Chaplain said.

'Then what of attrition? We die faster than our ranks grow. The Chapter is fading, the primarch's curse eats us alive, and all can see it.'

'Tradition is tradition,' said Scarath, 'and the mandates of the Codex Astartes have served our kind well for a thousand generations.'

Vorain exhaled, soft and slow. A hunter's habit, breathing out carefully so as to go undetected by nearby prey. When he raised his gaze to the Chaplain's, he shook his head.

'No.'

'I thought you would be proud,' Scarath said. 'Brother-Captain Vorain.'

'It's a rank that sits poorly upon my shoulders. What did Lord Seth say of the Wolves?'

'Nothing,' the Chaplain replied.

Vorain turned, fully regarding his brother. Communication with the Chapter's distant forces was rare – available a few times each Cretacian year at the very most, relayed by unreliable deep-space probes and tremulous astropathy. The Wolves had arrived with the *Baryonyx* over a month ago; Vorain had been waiting for contact since.

'And why, Chaplain, would our lord have nothing to say of such a vital matter?'

'Because I didn't tell him. Communications were severed before I had the chance.'

Vorain's open stare became a glare. Scarath was no fool, nor was he a liar, and certainly not petty enough to deny such crucial information to the master of the Chapter. If he said communications had failed, then they had failed. It was hardly a rare occurrence. Even so, it should have been the very first matter raised by the Chaplain. Not this maddening talk of promotion. Vorain found himself so suddenly, swiftly furious that he didn't trust his voice not to shake.

'I have once more relayed word via the astropathic choir,' Scarath assured him. 'The third time, if I may remind you. Emperor willing, word will get through at last.'

Vorain exhaled in a feral snarl. 'I'll conduct the next transmission with Lord Seth myself. I'll demand crusading duties once more. I'm finished with this exile.'

Scarath linked his fingers, patient where Vorain was restless. 'You will be denied, brother-captain. You're too valuable here, too valuable to the Chapter's future. I, and the aspirants, would sorely miss your expertise.'

'You would miss me,' Vorain allowed, 'only because you're unlikely to find another warden so willing to sit in silence and let you rule here.'

'You wound me, brother-captain.'

'I mean no offence.' Vorain retrieved his now bloodstained robe from the slick floor, throwing it over his shoulder. 'And I mean that in all sincerity. The flaw has been with me, Chaplain, not you. I have been timid and bitter, concerned with keeping the peace and doing my duty according only to tradition.'

'Tradition is everything,' the Chaplain pointed out. Once more, Vorain wanted to cut the serenity from Scarath's face with a saw-toothed blade.

'Tradition is nothing but the wisdom of the past,' said Vorain. 'A valuable guide. It's not law, Scarath. We shouldn't live by its every twist and turn. The past is rife with error and ignominy, and our Chapter's past is plainly no exception.'

He turned and made his way for the great double doors.

'Does duty call, brother-captain?'

'It is "brother-sergeant" until dawn,' Vorain replied. 'But think on this, my brother. In mere hours, I will outrank you. A warden in rank as well as in duty. And that makes certain decisions mine to make.'

'Is this the birth of arrogance, Vorain?'

'Far from it. Farewell, Scarath. It's unlikely that we'll meet again.'

The Chaplain surged after his brother, following Vorain up the stone stairs in an armoured stride. His heavy boots thudded into the eroded indentations caused by centuries of ceramite tread.

'What madness is this?' Scarath asked, prickled in his confusion.

'There's nothing of madness in my actions,' said Vorain. 'Only pride. I'll transmit my decision to Lord Seth, then I'll consecrate my weapons one last time, and go into the jungle to find the Fenrisians.'

'They're three weeks gone. Dead, along the Path of the Setting Sun.'

'And I will follow them along it. Fenris and Cretacia are as lethal as each other. The Wolves may yet live out there.'

The Chaplain's hand slammed down on Vorain's shoulder, gripping hard enough to hold the sergeant in place, arresting his defiant march.

'They are *dead*, Vorain. You prove nothing by this pathetic, stubborn sacrifice.'

'No?' Vorain gently removed his brother's restraining hand as if it were the touch of an ignorant child. 'If they live then I will hear them out, just as we should have when they arrived and returned the *Baryonyx* to us. And if they have fallen themselves, then I'll find their bones and return them to Fenris.'

'Fool!' Scarath practically spat the word. 'You weren't at Honour's End. I was, and I tell you, you do them more honour and respect than they would ever give us.'

'They already returned our fallen. The dead brothers aboard the *Baryonyx* were untouched after death. You said so yourself when you interred them in the vaults. Whatever wrongs the Wolves have done us in the past, that was a noble gesture that the Flesh Tearers will at least attempt to return.'

'You are the sworn commander of this fortress, oathbound to oversee the Chapter's future. This desire for suicide is beneath you, Vorain.'

For several moments, the former sergeant said nothing. As the silence stretched into awkwardness, he spoke with a weary sigh. 'How many aspirants die after gene-seed implantation? How many brothers fall in Lord Seth's desperate crusades? How many of our brethren are chained in the Tower of the Lost, screaming their delusions to the granite walls?'

'Meaningless,' said the Chaplain. 'Irrelevant.'

'Far from it. The Wolves have come to us, concerned with their own legacy at the end of the Dark Millennium. I share that fear for my own bloodline, Scarath. You and your Chaplains know the truth better than anyone – our Chapter will be dust within a hundred years. I will not damn us in the present for the sake of a future we'll never see. Helping to end this cold war may be the most valuable service I ever do for our Chapter.'

He turned and walked away, leaving Scarath on the stone stairway.

In his days of aimless savagery, before such ferocity had been directed against the Emperor's enemies, Vorain had been a hunter. A hunter's primary expertise wasn't endurance, strength or even his aim with a thrown spear – it was his ability to track. A tracker could find prey no matter where it fled, and find his way back home no matter how far he wandered from the foothill village.

He had a bolter and an axe now rather than a spear of ironwood, and he wore the dark red ceramite of his Chapter rather than decorating his naked flesh with ritual scarring to resemble the scaled hides of the jungle lizard-kings... But it gratified Vorain to know he could still track quarry in the Cretacian wilds.

He knew it would not be a swift process given the Wolves' month-long head start, and what spoor he found at first was weeks old. Even so, he set out with rare joy fuelling his muscles, feeling free for the first time in years as he moved through the tropical rainforest at a loping, heavy-striding run. The weight of his armour was immense even as its machine-muscles added to his strength, but he could keep this pace up for a week or more if necessary.

Too fast, and he would miss the signs of the Wolves' passing. Too slow and he might never catch up to them.

The Flesh Tearer began by seeking around the fortress-monastery, hunting in concentric circles radiating out from the bastion carved into the cliffs. Not knowing which direction the Wolves had taken left him with no choice but to be meticulous, hoping that time hadn't obliterated every sign of their journey.

Vorain found the first spoor on the second day, as Cretacia's brutal sun fell away and night bathed the jungle black. A trail of footprints had turned almost to stone in deep, dried mud. Whichever one of the Wolves had come this way, the ground had sucked and pulled at his boots, threatening to drag him down. Vorain saw other indentations in the hardened earth – signs of hands grasping for stability – and followed the trail, reading the tale it told.

The Wolf had staggered several times, as evidenced by the depth and twist of the bootprints. He'd reached safe ground at a cluster of trees, clawing his armoured fingers into the huge trunks and hauling himself out of the muck. Next to one of the last bootprints was the shallow mark of what was surely the tip of a scabbard, worn at the hip.

Ragnar, Vorain knew. Ragnar had stumbled in the mud, pulled himself free and headed onwards.

Alone? Of that, the Flesh Tearer couldn't yet be sure.

Vorain tracked the Wolves over the following days by a series of more subtle signs. A faint boot print, weeks old, in a patch of dry venomgrass; the glint of metal buried in the earth, revealed as a spent bolt shell casing once the hunter dug it from the ground with his fingers. Rarely did he chance across spoor as telling as the footprints in dried quicksand again, though what signs he did find told a compelling truth. The Wolves weren't moving away from the fortress-monastery in wayward haste. They were hunting, as surely as he was, staying near to the Flesh Tearers' sanctum. And if they didn't quite move with the competence of hunters born to this world, they weren't going to swift deaths the way Scarath had assumed.

The most obvious signs of their passage were offered by the jungle's flora rather than anything as mundane as bootprints. No matter how careful the Fenrisian tribesmen were, Cretacia was a world with a million forms of life they'd never encountered. A hedge of insect-eater plants had been beheaded, no doubt after they'd snapped their bulbous maws at the Space Wolves' exposed faces. The quills of a poisonous fruit tree were missing on one side, probably spat in futility against blue-grey ceramite when one of the Wolves came too close.

Vorain followed their arcing trail in his careful run, eyes always scanning the undergrowth, breathing in the rotting green stink of the deep jungle. He only concerned himself with caution when he recognised the signs that he was entering carnosaur territory, and in those hours he would proceed in a warrior's crouch, his weapons in his hands. He knew the hum of his active armour would betray him to many of the lizard-kings with their feral senses, but he still moved with care, guided by his hunting instinct. No sense in bringing additional trouble upon himself.

Sometimes he'd hear the ground-pounding tread of a lizard-king nearby, or see an immense shadowed flank pass by through the dense trees. In those moments Vorain would remain motionless, his axe in his hand, knowing even the slightest movement would draw the reptilian predator upon him. Minutes after the beast passed on, when he could no longer hear or feel its lumbering tread, he would move once more.

He couldn't avoid them all. The lesser *deinonykin* raptors, which hunted in shrieking packs, were ever a threat, able to drag a man down in moments, disembowelling their prey with kicks and slashes from the talons on their powerful legs. These, he killed with a barrage of bolter fire the moment he sensed them stalking nearby, finishing them with his axe if they managed to weave aside from the shells and close the distance. As an adolescent human hunter armed only with a spear these creatures had been his bane, among the jungle's deadliest predators. As a Space Marine, they were only a threat to him in groups larger than four or five, and such numbers were rarely encountered within a hundred kilometres of the Flesh Tearers' cliff-side fortress.

Despite the misery of his exile, he found himself enjoying the hunt more and more, day by day. Even in the miserable evenings when the monsoon rains scythed down upon him and he spent the nights tracking and stalking – seeing through the green-tinted display of his helmet's eye lenses – he felt unshackled and free rather than lonely.

Several times he came across the evidence of the Wolves' brief camps. With blades and bolters they had brought down the smaller carnosaurs – the raptor beasts close to the size of a Terran horse – and had cooked the sour reptilian flesh over deadwood campfires. Each time Vorain found the husks of the Wolves' meals, he felt a small pulse of sympathy. Even with the scales skinned away, carnosaur flesh was notoriously vile.

On one occasion he found blood, genetically altered human blood, spattered in dry markings upon the side of a rock. It was too dry to taste in order to glean any insight from it, but the tale was clear enough. One of the Wolves had limped here to rest for several moments after being wounded. Vorain also discovered a tooth, as long as his finger and curved like a crescent moon, lying deep in the brush. For a moment he took it to be a carnosaur fang, but as he turned it over in his fingers he could see it belonged to no Cretacian beast. Nothing in his memory of hunting on his home world had ever shown a fang quite this shape. He'd seen teeth like this only once before, and the memory was starkly clear because it was so recent.

A kraken fang. From Ragnar's sword.

When the second week was on the edge of becoming the third, he made a discovery that sent a chill through his blood. A dead snake, twice as long as a man was tall, its scales marked by raised thorns of cartilage with red blotches on its brown flesh. Its head was pulped; the beast had been crushed and hurled aside in anger, no doubt after it had dropped from the branches above to envenom its prey.

Vorain carefully examined the remains of the viper's mouth, which could open wide enough to swallow his fist without difficulty. He thumbed aside the four ivory daggers it possessed for fangs. One fang was still intact; three were broken close to the roots.

With a crack of bone, he tore the beast's jaws open wider to peer within. The fleshy ducts in the roof of its mouth were inflamed even after its death. It had died seconds after delivering its venom.

A *Grida* serpent. Its bite was more than capable of piercing the joints of a suit of Space Marine battle armour.

Vorain dropped the dead snake back upon the colony of myrmidon insects that had been devouring its carcass, and moved on with renewed purpose.

He found the Wolves the next day.

More precisely, they found him.

III

This world despised human life. As a son of the winter world, Ragnar knew a few things about planets that fought to reject colonisation. Cretacia was Fenris' sister in that regard. It was the Hearthworld's blisteringly hot, venomous reflection.

After a month and a half in the jungle wilds, soreness had given way to aches, and the aches had fledged into pain. The low branches of a tall tree had raked his face days ago, and the scratches that had first seemed harmless were now plump and infected, constantly itching, giving off the cheesy smell of dirty pus. His armour was raked open in several places by the claws of leaping, shrieking lizard-beasts – monsters the size of a Thunderwolf battle mount – and the wounds beneath quick-drying coats of armour cement were inflamed and angry, heating his blood and turning his joints to glass.

His enhanced physiology fought to purify his body of all alien infection, but it was a losing battle. Both of his hearts beat with arrhythmic speed, and he could almost feel his internal organs humming as they resisted whatever poisons were saturating his bloodstream.

The only food he'd eaten in over six weeks was the bitter, stringy flesh of the hunting lizards that attacked them, which did little more than take the edge off his hunger while turning his guts in wrenching twists.

Nalfir was faring even worse. One eye was swollen closed by a sting from a striped insect the size of his thumb. A single second's contact with the vermin had been enough to turn the veins of his face throbbing and black, showing through his sweating skin. Elsewhere he bore several wounds from the teeth and claws of beasts that had managed to pierce his armour plating. His body was working so aggressively to purge the toxins inside him that his bionic hand had failed days before, no longer answering his will.

'My body's rejecting it,' the bard had said when his hand first failed. 'Treating the false nerves and muscles as an intruding infection to be healed.'

They both knew they'd already be dead without their Adeptus Astartes physiology sustaining them, and without the suits of sacred ceramite shielding their flesh. Even with their post-human endurance, they had to eat and drink to maintain their strength. The vermin-rich river water they found, even filtered through rocks and boiled above a fire, had their innards clenching in spasms. Blood-sucking flies followed them in a slow, lazy haze, drunk on the genhanced fluid drawn from their veins.

At camp one night, looking up at the sparse stars through the jungle canopy, Nalfir had adopted a philosophical air.

'If Fenris is a world that seeks to turn the snow red with the blood of its people, Cretacia is a world set on poisoning them, so their meat and bones will feed its cursed earth.'

'A poetic thought. It'd be lovelier if the one voicing it didn't have black vomit drying across his chestplate.'

Nalfir had waved his dead machine-hand, dismissing Ragnar with a grunt of amusement.

Days after his bionic arm had deactivated, a fresh pain bloomed in Nalfir's elbow and shoulder.

'Phantom pain,' Ragnar insisted at first.

'Aye. Perhaps.'

A few hours later, the bionic hand began to clench and quiver, and the pain beneath Nalfir's armour bloomed into agony at his bicep.

'Hurts too much to be imaginary,' the bard said. He could ignore it – he could ignore and fight through any pain, as could all of his kind – but the muscle spasms were an irritant that wore away at his temper. His nervous system was wracked from the planet's abuses, and no longer carried signals from his brain with any reliability. Half the time he walked in sweating delirium, cursing in languages from various worlds across Imperial space.

He followed Ragnar, letting the Blood Claw lead – eating when Ragnar told him to eat, resting when Ragnar told him to rest.

'We're being hunted,' the younger warrior announced one evening, ripe with stinking sweat from the still-vicious setting sun. The two of them were knee-deep in sludge, wading through a marsh.

Nalfir turned his head, spitting a stalactite of thick, bloody saliva. One-eyed and wretched, he staggered then, going down to his waist in the muck. Something like an eel slithered past his thigh, leaving a trail of slime in its wake.

Ragnar offered his hand but the bard knocked it away. As Nalfir hauled himself to his feet once more, he had to clear his throat of bloody phlegm before he could make himself heard.

'Hunted by what?'

'See for yourself.'

Nalfir squinted through the bleary distortion of his remaining eye. Ragnar was indicating... something... in the mud along the shore of the marsh.

When he saw the unmistakable imprint of a power-armoured boot trail along the ground, he blinked uselessly to try to unfog his thoughts.

'We've been circling around. These might be our own tracks.'

Ragnar turned an annoyed glare upon the bard. 'I know where we've walked. These aren't our tracks. Trust me.'

'So our hosts are out here, too.' Nalfir laughed for the first time in weeks. 'They just had to make sure we were dead, didn't they? Couldn't even trust their own planet to do the deed for them.'

'If I'm not back before sunrise,' Ragnar said, 'go on without me.'

'What?'

'Just wait here, Razortongue.'

Nalfir's wounded thoughts were slow. He was having trouble following the Blood Claw's words, let alone the reasoning behind them.

'Wait here,' he repeated. 'But why?'

'Because you're all the bait we have. Stay here and look vulnerable.'

Nalfir snorted, wolf-like and grim, at his brother's command. He hauled himself up the embankment and crashed down to sit on the drier earth.

'That will require no acting at all, I promise you.'

He drifted in and out of consciousness, fighting the whole time to remain awake. Sometimes his bionic hand would lock for an hour or more, sometimes it would shake with tremors from his tormented nerves. Sometimes he would stare for what felt like hours across the marshland, only to realise scarcely ten seconds had passed. Sometimes he'd blink slowly, only to open his eyes and see several minutes had gone by while he dozed in corrupted delirium.

He lurched upright when he heard the thrum of Ragnar's power armour across the water.

'Blackmane,' he murmured. His eyes refused to focus on the approaching figure as it waded through the murk.

'No,' said the voice. 'It is I, cousin.'

Nalfir couldn't stop the sudden smile. His vision cleared as if tuned to his amusement.

'Well, now. If it isn't Sergeant Vorain, the warden of this planet.' He levelled his bolter with his good hand, feeling pride burn hot as he drew an unshaking aim.

The Flesh Tearer stood still as the bolter came up. He had an axe in one hand and his own bolter in the other. Like Nalfir, his armour was scarred by fang and talon, discoloured and bleached by the sulphuric rain. Unlike Nalfir, the flesh of his face wasn't ravaged and pockmarked by venom and poison.

'Razortongue,' he greeted the bard.

'That's my tribal name. You call me Nalfir, Cretacian.'

'Nalfir, then. Are you alone? Where is Ragnar?'

'He's dead.'

'That's a lie, cousin. I would have found his bones by now.'

'Maybe you're just a poor hunter, then. Who can say?'

Vorain tensed, exhaling through his clenched teeth as he fought his flaring temper back down.

'To say a Cretacian cannot hunt is a grave insult, cousin. On this world, only cripples and children are incapable of providing for their clan.'

'We have a similar sentiment on Fenris.' He grinned with blood-pinked teeth. 'Let's say the insult stands for now. I find myself in low spirits. A good argument would fire my blood very nicely.'

Vorain shook his head. 'Your survival is miraculous.'

'And your hospitality is dire,' Nalfir replied. 'We've butchered half of the hunting lizards on this continent – I thought Fenrisian wolves were bad. Everything here is toxic. Every beast is venomous, every plant is poisonous. Even the water teems with parasites.'

Vorain nodded. 'All true, though you've barely scratched the surface. Cretacia's most dangerous beasts stay far from the fortress-monastery. They've learned over the generations that we're not timid about using the castle's cannons on those that come too close.'

'The ones we killed were bad enough. Ugh, and the *taste*.'

'Why did you remain nearby?' the Flesh Tearer asked. 'Most of our banished aspirants move far from the fortress-monastery when they walk the Path of the Setting Sun.'

Nalfir's bloody, toothy smile returned. 'We were seeking any weapon caches or armoury bunkers. Then we were going to fight our way back into your fortress.'

Vorain said nothing for several seconds, realising that the Wolf was speaking the truth.

'How... bold of you,' he said at last.

'We're Wolves,' said the bard, considering it to be answer enough. 'Anyway, *cousin*, I've distracted you long enough.'

The Flesh Tearer whirled in place, three times as fast as any human could move, and it still wasn't swift enough. Ragnar surged from beneath the foul water, hammered the axe from Vorain's hands with a blow from Frostfang, and cannoned a backhand across the Flesh Tearer's face.

The Cretacian staggered back, lifting his bolter only to have it smashed aside by the Blood Claw's great blade. Vorain swallowed as he froze in place, eyes meeting Ragnar's deathly stare. The static teeth of the Wolf's chainblade rested against the Flesh Tearer's throat.

Watery muck ran down Ragnar's war-plate in dark rivulets. His hair was a crest of matted filth and his face was decorated in thick, hungry swamp leeches. Vorain hated himself for being impressed: the Wolf had hidden the sound of his armour by crawling under the marsh water, no doubt for several minutes, to ambush the Flesh Tearer from behind.

'A skilful hunt,' Vorain conceded.

'I suggest,' Ragnar hissed, 'that you make your next words good enough to save your life.'

'You have my Chapter's thanks,' Vorain said, keeping the stare unbroken. 'Our gratitude for returning the warship *Baryonyx*.'

They made cold camp within a nearby cave. A discordant song filled their ears as it echoed off the walls, made from the snarl of their damaged armour joints, the drip of water deeper inside the cavern and the distant reptile cries of Cretacia's ruling monsters.

Ragnar had wiped the worst of the grime from his face after his submerged ambush, though his eyes were dark ringed and shot with blood. There was a wetness in Nalfir's breathing that the Blood Claw suspected didn't bode well.

He was the first to speak, waving a fat blood fly away with a cracked gauntlet. 'Why are you out here, sergeant?'

'It is "captain" now,' Vorain corrected with no emotion whatsoever.

'Our heartiest congratulations, then,' Nalfir grunted, amused at his own weak sarcasm. 'Answer the question, though.'

'I wished to find you, to bring you back.' Vorain gestured outside the cave, at the eternal jungle filling the world from horizon to horizon. 'Unless you wish to remain here, that is.'

'Back?' Nalfir's laugh sounded closer to a gargle. 'To execute us properly this time?'

'No. To return you to Fenris with the Chapter's thanks. And to come with you, as an emissary to speak of a ceasefire in this futile war.'

Ragnar was tonguing at a loose tooth. 'You said it was beyond your authority. Sergeant or captain, you're still not Lord Seth.'

'Your jarl,' said Vorain, 'is one lord among many. His word may not be the word of your whole Chapter. That doesn't make it worthless. It makes it a first step to a reborn brotherhood.' He tapped his knuckles to the aquila on his breastplate. 'I'm just one officer among my Chapter, and I can only speak for the few men under my command. But I give my thanks freely, and acknowledge the great honour in your actions. Our Chapters may meet as foes in the future, but the warriors of our two companies are no longer foes.'

Vorain reached for one of his belt pouches, offering the fallen kraken's tooth to Ragnar. 'I found this.'

The Blood Claw took it with a murmur of thanks. The skin around his mouth was raw and scabbed from being unable to control the production of acidic saliva. The new leech bites were indescribably itchy.

'What changed your mind?' he asked the Flesh Tearer.

'You did. The nobility of your gesture, in coming here.'

'I'd have preferred you to realise that several weeks ago,' said Ragnar scratching at his cheek. One of the leech bites began to bleed under his efforts.

'There's much I cannot say, even here and now, in this moment of sincerity. But I can say this. The truth of the Flesh Tearers is that our gravestones are already carved. We cannot recruit swiftly enough, or reliably enough, to replace the losses we suffer in Lord Seth's crusades.'

Both Wolves were immediately, utterly alert. They stared at Vorain, their sore eyes alight with shock.

'Your Chapter is dying?' Nalfir murmured. He had a storyteller's interest in such a dark concept.

'Not now, but soon. Some Chapters rebuild over many decades, weighing duty, honour, shame and necessity. Some fight on even in the face of destruction. We are among the latter. In a hundred years our bloodline will be but a memory. We fight now not for glory, but to leave a legacy worthy of the primarch who sired us. Lord Seth leads us in crusades across the galaxy, committing us where the battles are bleakest, seeking not to save us, but to save our legacy in the Imperium's eyes.'

Vorain paused, mustering the right words before continuing. 'It was cowardly of me to stand by and let Scarath banish you to die in the wilds. Worse, it was futile. Your deaths would have proved nothing and saved no lives. If I am to die – if my bloodline itself is to die – then I wish to leave this life with more than my enemies cursing our name. This is my first act as captain, this is what I will say if you bring me back to Fenris with you, and this is what I will report to Lord Seth should I return.'

'One might argue,' said Nalfir, 'that your actions are selfish. You care only for how the galaxy will speak your name when you and your brothers are gone.'

Vorain's teeth showed pearl-white in his dark, scarred face. It was almost roguish. 'You could argue that. And there's truth there, I admit. But there's also a practical gain for the Wolves. Remember, cousins, that I'm the one who guides our Chapter's initiates. Their minds are mine to shape. And as I train the next – perhaps the last – generation of Flesh Tearers, they will take shape with the knowledge that at least some Wolves behave with honour.'

Nalfir turned to Ragnar, speaking in slurred Fenrisian. 'There's much he's leaving unsaid.'

Ragnar nodded, exhaling slowly. 'And much we have left unspoken, also,' he said in the same tongue. 'But does it matter?'

Vorain made no effort to interrupt the Wolves as they talked on. He rose to his feet, walking to the mouth of the cave and activating his gorget's vox-link. Communication quality beneath the jungle canopy left a great deal to be desired. When he heard the response from the fortress-monastery, Vorain spoke in the guttural, monosyllabic murmurs used by many Cretacian tribes. In the furthest reaches of history, it might once, barely, have been related to Low Gothic.

'What are you saying?' asked Ragnar.

'Requesting a Stormraven and cataloguing your wounds for our Apothecary,' Vorain replied, artfully neutral. 'We must reach higher ground for the gunship to reach us. The sound of their engines always summons carnosaurs, and there is no way a pilot can land a craft beneath the jungle canopy. Are you ready to leave now, cousins?'

Ragnar rose to his feet. 'The sooner, the better.'

IV

Vorain led the way. He was aware of the punishment Cretacia had inflicted upon the Fenrisians, and took care to keep his pace slow as he guided them up the rocky incline. The loose earth and scree had them using their hands for purchase to prevent them sliding down in an avalanche of rubble. More often than not, when the Flesh Tearer would turn around to mark their progress, he'd see them clambering on all fours, bestial and defiant.

Cretacia's moon was high, yet the humid nights were as merciless as the brutal days. Sweat ran freely down their faces as they huffed for breath in the equatorial heat.

Like dogs, the Flesh Tearer thought.

Nalfir was soon lagging behind. Ragnar remained with him, keeping up a steady stream of conversation and curses. Nalfir didn't join in. He grunted with each step, blood-flecked saliva stringing between his teeth.

Both of his hearts beat out of rhythm now. The snakebite in the back of his leg had been spreading corruption through his shin and thigh for two days but his immune system always fought back, reducing the infection to painful tingling. Now it was a battle just to walk – his entire left leg was stiff and numb. The limp he'd been hiding for two dawns was finally taking hold.

'Just shut up,' he breathed to Ragnar, as they fell further behind Vorain. 'Blackmane, shut up for a moment. Listen to me.'

Ragnar's comradely chatter died away. 'What is it?'

The bard didn't cease his hitching stride. As they reached another stretch of loose scree, he clambered up on all fours, dragging his weakening leg up the rocks, pawing at any grip he could find with his remaining hand. Stone scraped and screeched across his ceramite plating with each metre he climbed.

'I think I'm dying.'

Ragnar's laugh was a gunshot bark. 'Don't be so dramatic.'

'Listen to me, you git.' Nalfir's voice was a slick whisper. 'That accursed serpent that dropped on us from above, two days ago. The one with those daggers for teeth.'

Ragnar recalled it. The huge snake had launched at them from the high branches of a tree, wrapping itself in killing coils around Nalfir's torso, arm and leg. Unable to constrict him in his layered armour plating, the reptile had struck at the softer jointed armour behind his knee. Three of its four jagged dagger fangs had penetrated the joint, sinking into the flesh beneath.

Nalfir paused, blinking rancid sweat from his bloodshot eyes before continuing. 'I can't metabolise the venom. It's killing me.'

Ragnar's grin faded at the seriousness in the bard's tone. 'Speak sense, Razortongue. It was just a snake.'

'Aye, and a frostwyrm is just a snake, too, eh? But we've seen them kill Einherjar with their venom.' He pushed himself to his feet as they reached firmer rock. 'I'm a storyteller. A gatherer of tales. I speak more languages than there are stars in the night sky, brother.'

Ragnar nodded ahead to where Vorain was climbing, fifty metres above. 'You speak Cretacian?'

Nalfir grinned, showing bleeding gums. 'Not that those grunts and clicks counts as much of a language, but aye, I speak it. I studied it years ago. Jarl Thunderfist wished me to be ready to translate if we crossed paths with the Flesh Tearers. That's how I know. It's what Vorain said across the vox.'

'He might be wrong.'

'He might be. I tell you though, it doesn't feel like he is. My blood is on fire, and I can barely see an arm's length in front of my eyes.'

Before Ragnar could reply, Nalfir spat a mouthful of dark blood. 'Allfather's bones, what a stupid way to die. If you tell any of our brothers about this, I swear I'll curse you from beyond the grave. Tell them I died fighting... I don't know. Something huge. With teeth the length of your legs.'

'Cousins?' Vorain called down to them, seeing their pace slowing more and more.

'All is well,' Ragnar called back.

Nalfir gave a boyish snigger. 'Oh, yes,' he murmured. 'Everything is just fine.'

'How long do you have left?' Ragnar asked him.

'I don't know. Not long. The Flesh Tearer sounded surprised I was still alive at all, and I'll say this with no shadow of a lie – it feels like I died yesterday and forgot to lie down.'

The heavens chose that moment to open, with runnels of stinging monsoon rain trickling through the thick canopy above.

'I've had better days,' admitted the bard. Ragnar found himself lost for words.

'Just keep going,' the Blood Claw said after a minute had passed. It earned another bloody grin from Nalfir.

'Your inspiring talk needs work, brother. *Just keep going?* That's how you motivate a wounded kinsman?'

'I'm beginning to wish you'd just die, Razortongue.'

'Ha!' The bard wiped the sheen of putrid sweat from his face with a grimy palm. 'I may grant that wish soon. It would have to be me that was bitten, eh? Not you, oh no. Not you with your damnable good fortune. Luck runs out, Blackmane. Have I ever told you that?'

'Only six or seven thousand times.'

'It's the truth, you know. The jarl believes you're destined for great things, but perhaps he'd abandon that hope if he heard how awful your inspiring speeches are.'

Ragnar scowled at the words. 'What are you talking about?'

'Are you really this foolish, Blackmane?' Nalfir hacked up a gobbet of bloody foam and spat it onto the rocks. 'Why do you think I've been insufferable to you since you joined the First Pack? Who do you think ordered me to bait you and test you every damn day?'

Between the revelation and the sickness, Ragnar's head was reeling. 'The jarl ordered that?'

'Thunderfist is a craftier rodent than the company realises. He has a dozen games and tests like this going on at any time. He's had me baiting you over your pride and ambitions – and your temper most of all. Can't have a Wolf Guard who can't control his fury. Throne aflame, brother, he was furious after you killed that accursed Dark Angel. Had me testing you twice as hard after that. He wasn't sure he could trust you at all any more.'

'The fight in the Hearth of the First Pack.'

Nalfir nodded. 'And aboard the *Baryonyx*.'

'I knew it was you.' Ragnar felt the maddened Flesh Tearer's hands around his throat again; felt the pressure of being crushed beneath the warrior's insane strength. 'I knew you'd deactivated the stasis lock.'

'The jarl's orders,' Nalfir grinned, though it obviously pained him to do so. 'And you survived, eh?'

Ragnar couldn't find the words. 'I... thought you were just...'

'Just a bastard?' Nalfir seemed to weigh the idea in his thoughts. 'Well, I am that, as well.'

'Razortongue...'

'Enough of this. You'll take my axe back, won't you? Greylock made it for me. Gave it to me the day I became First Pack. I'd hate for it to rot here on this swine-pit of a world.'

'Of course, brother.'

'Good. Good. My thanks.' Nalfir pulled himself over a rocky outcropping, and a sliver of blood ran from his nose. He sniffed it back up into his sinuses. 'Not dead yet,' he breathed. *'Not. Dead. Yet.'*

The trees were thinning now, the canopy breaking to reveal the churning grey sky, and no longer shielding them from the gritty hammering of the seasonal rainfall. Ahead of them, Vorain was waiting with his axe slung over his shoulder. When they reached him he cast a momentary look towards Nalfir, who slunk down with his back to the rocks, then spoke low to Ragnar through his helmet's mouth-grille.

'Now we wait.'

V

The Stormraven gunship came in low over the trees, its armour plating already streaked with dissolving paintwork under the wet hammering of the lightly acidic rain. It swerved in the sky with an agility rarely seen in Adeptus Astartes aircraft, lacking the heavyset power and momentum of the much larger Thunderhawk.

The craft was a clenched fist of a thing, its turbines wailing as it drifted in closer. Upon its back, a manned turret rotated in a slow arc, its cannons tracking across the sky in search of prey. The servitor bodily locked into the gun pod spared no focus for anything else. Ragnar suspected it was mono-tasked for that single duty – it would live and die in the turret without consideration or complaint. The slave seemed neither male nor female, simply a malnourished grey human cyborged past concepts of gender, identity and personality.

The gunship's ramp lowered to reveal the compartment beneath the cockpit, giving the image of an opening maw. Racked bolters and crates of ammunition waited in the strip-lit crew chamber.

Vorain was the first to break from the cover of the stone overhang that guarded them from the worst of the rain. He strode out into the storm as the gunship's landing claws scraped and kissed the rocky plateau. The Wolves heard the insectile crackle of his vox-channel as he conferred with the pilot – a silhouette they could only dimly see through the reinforced cockpit pane.

The only warning they had was the shadow passing over the moon. There, and then gone. A blur of all-too-brief blackness.

The assault cannons on the gunship's spinal turret whirred, cycling to life with no chance to fire. The shadow struck from above with a grinding crash of metallic thunder – Ragnar saw something vast, something winged – and then it was gone again, leaving them with the distinctive reek of reptilian flesh and the echoing squeal of tortured metal ringing in their ears.

The gunship's turret was gone, torn away down to its hydraulic roots.

Vorain ran back into their dubious cover, shouting to the pilot across the vox. The Stormraven shuddered as it lifted off again, turbines gasping for altitude, breathing its engine fumes across the Wolves in a charcoal-smelling heat haze.

They were drawing their weapons when the turret crashed down onto the slope below them with a thunderclap – now a thing of abused metal and shattered glass. The servitor spasmed in its restraint throne, still futilely trying to carry out its duties even as it bled to death. Ragnar watched it thrash until it accidentally killed itself, gashing open its throat on a shard of the broken cockpit glass.

The Stormraven didn't seek to escape. The Flesh Tearer pilot brought it around in an agile swing, the heavy bolters on its snub nose opening up to hammer shells into the night sky.

Lightning illuminated the predator as it struck again, turning it from a shadow to a beast for a single heartbeat. Great leathery wings cracked like a Fenrisian longship's sail in a storm wind. Claws like swords flashed through the rain to clang against the gunship's hull, sending it spinning aside, drifting, shuddering to come back under control.

The creature landed on the slope with enough force to send tremors through the rocks. Black eyes gleamed, reflecting the moonlight as it turned its beaked, bone-crested head to the warriors.

'Ptyradon,' Vorain said, voicing the name as a breathless curse.

Dragon, Ragnar thought in the same second. *A gods-rutting dragon.*

Three bolters kicked as one, booming shells towards the creature's densely scaled hide. Every bolt sparked and burst without punching through the beast's flesh. In the face of this torrent of fire, the ptyradon lowered its monstrous head, armoured brow ridges closing over its bulging eyes to protect them, and charged.

Ragnar hurled himself away from the advancing beast and crashed into the gravel scree, setting off a rattling pebble avalanche. Vorain cut the other way, barrelling out into the rain in a dead sprint, reloading his bolter with a slam.

Only Nalfir held his ground. He aimed at the beast's clawed hands at the ends of its wings. Such was its speed that the Wolf missed three shots even at that range, scoring only a single hit to its bony digits.

It was enough. The slightest stumble in the ptyradon's stride allowed Nalfir to throw himself after the Flesh Tearer at the last moment, kicking off with his good leg. Behind him, the reptilian beast snapped its jaws where he'd been standing. He crawled away across the scree, letting his weight carry him down the slope on a tide of rolling gravel.

The gunship banked back above them, angling its nose down, and the heavy bolters did what the Space Marines' more modest fire couldn't – the stream of massive shells pounded through the ptyradon's scaled hide, sending gouts of viscera arcing and steaming into the air.

Shrieking, the beast took to the sky on shredded wings, leaping up to cling on to the gunship's fuselage with talon and claw. The Stormraven's engines struggled under the renewed weight, and with a protracted whine of strained turbines, both the gunship and the monster embracing it plunged to the ground.

They hit the scree and tumbled down, bouncing, rolling and burning. Twenty metres. Thirty. Fifty. Coming to rest in a smoking heap, halfway down the slope.

Stillness reigned. Ragnar aimed his bolter down the incline at the now-motionless dragon. *Almost* motionless. He could see it breathing.

'Razortongue!' he called. The bard was much farther down the slope, spitting distance from the wreckage of the gunship and the wounded monster atop it. 'Climb!'

Nalfir felt so weak that he almost laughed. To have lived for so many decades as an immortal reflection of Russ and the Allfather... and now to be laid low by the stings and bites of jungle vermin. *Climb,* Ragnar had said. Climb? He could barely move at all. It was all he could do to keep breathing.

With a strangely piteous whine, the wounded ptyradon lifted its head, opening its guarded eyes, and glared directly at the bard. This close he could see the bulbous eyeballs weren't colourless after all – they were halved by a slitted reptilian pupil, darker than the milky black of the eyeball itself. What Nalfir had taken for a collar of bone spines around its neck now trembled and began to rise, each of them linked by a membrane of veined flesh.

'*Put your helmet on!*' Vorain yelled from higher up the slope. '*Its venom is blinding!*'

Nalfir had one moment to wonder just where his helmet was – back aboard the *Holmgang,* most likely. As with most Wolves he despised confining his heightened senses and shunned war helms as often as not.

The moment passed, quick as a blink. The ptyradon's neck frills quivered as the beast drew back its head, and it disgorged a stream of thick mucus-like venom in vomited spurts. The ooze splattered across Nalfir's armour as he was reaching, crippled and closed-eyed, for his fallen axe.

'*Don't breathe it in!*' he heard the Flesh Tearer shout. As if he needed another warning.

He heard the beast moving now. Nalfir made a last surging grasp for his weapon. His fingers closed around the axe's haft and he gripped it tight, thumbing the ignition rune on the handle. The power axe crackled to life, the power field around the wide blade sizzling as it superheated the falling rain.

He was blind. One of his legs was dead from thigh to toes. One of his hands no longer worked at all. He was covered in toxic poison-spit eating into his armour plating that sent his lungs into seizures if he even breathed in its scent. His flesh itched and ached from rashes and cracking sores from this unbelievably hostile world. His only companions were one of the Flesh

Tearers who had unjustly banished him to Cretacia's insane wilderness, and his brother Blackmane, who was variously seen as a hot-blooded fool or the jarl's heir apparent, depending on which of the Great Company you asked.

Frankly, he believed Ragnar was a little of both.

On top of all of that, Nalfir was dying from the snake venom turning the blood in his veins to slime, delivered by a serpent with fangs the length of daggers capable of biting clean through the fibre-bundle machine muscles of Mark VII power armour.

He laughed, unable to prevent it, and once he'd started he found he couldn't stop. It drew the brimstone-and-bile scent of the toxic spit into his lungs, immediately causing his throat and chest to burn. Even as his amusement faded to chuckles, he kept his eyes closed tight. Better blinded by choice than with the venom scalding his eyeballs. The result was the same, but it came without the distraction of mutilating pain.

Nalfir Razortongue dragged himself to his feet for what he was sure would be the final time, slashed the air with his axe to loosen his cramping muscles, and blindly turned to face the draconic monster crawling towards him.

Dragging his leg, he stalked towards his fate. Meeting it standing on two feet, as a Fenrisian warrior must.

Ragnar watched Nalfir limping towards the lumbering ptyradon, knowing that his packmate was going to his death. In that moment he made his choice. He wouldn't open fire on the beast. He wouldn't charge down the slope to Nalfir's aid.

The bolter in his hand kicked once, bellowing a single shell into the rain. It impacted and detonated a metre from Vorain's boot, sending up a shower of gravel and shrapnel that rattled across the Flesh Tearer's armour.

'Let him fight,' Ragnar called to his red-clad cousin. Vorain was too far away to hear the Wolf's words, but there was no questioning Ragnar's stern expression. After a hesitation, the captain replied with a closed-fist gesture in Adeptus Astartes battle-sign, signalling his compliance.

Ragnar lowered his boltgun. A Fenrisian tribesman was going to his death. It wasn't for his companions to interfere or intervene. In the tongue of his tribe, ragged from the infection riddling his body, Ragnar called out to the wounded bard.

'May the Allfather welcome you at His side, Razortongue.'

He heard the traditional words shouted over the slash of the rain and the guttural thunder of the beast's breathing. Standing in the beast's shadow, Nalfir grinned. Even without eyes, he knew where the ptyradon was wounded. Like all Wolves, he'd been a hunter before the Sky Warriors took him into the stars. He could smell the blood on its breath from its ruptured organs. He could hear the hitches in its stride because of its injured limbs.

He'd fought blind a hundred times before, in training and in the field:

in impenetrable fog and noxious gases, in the lightless dark of a powerless spaceship hold, in wars upon worlds where the sun never rose. He knew how to hunt and kill without opening his eyes. The beast was fast, but it was almost as wounded as the Wolf himself. Nalfir weaved aside from the first strike, careful not to trust his numbed leg with any real weight. He spun away from the second lashing claw, and leapt over the creature's barbed tail as it pounded across the scree, seeking to knock him down.

He had no bolter, and no idea where it had fallen. All he had was the power axe, and he would only get one chance to use it. Another duck beneath a swiping claw, another weave aside from the beast's thrashing club of a tail.

The shadow that he could feel but not see expanded over him, swelling wide, bringing a sudden chill. A great stinking wind buffeted him as the monster beat its bleeding wings, seeking to rear up for a killing strike. Coming at him with its snapping, crashing jaws.

Now.

Nalfir moved with what little strength remained to him, his axe held low, its blade striking a trail of sparks as it gouged through the gravel. He swung upwards with a vagabond's blow, the kind of deceitful, desperate attack that cleaves beneath a shield-wall and has no place in a duel between honest warriors.

The blow landed. The axe bit, and bit deep. Nalfir roared as its curved blade crunched into the beast's body, burying itself in vile flesh. Foul-smelling gore drenched him in a reeking flood, along with the cold, wet chains of reptilian guts. He had a single second to wrench the axe back, prying the wound open wider, before he was smashed aside with enough force to shatter his breastplate like porcelain and blast the last of the breath from his body.

Nalfir's form thudded and rolled across the scree slope in a mangled tumble, ending its brief journey with an abrupt crash against a rise of wet rocks. A spray of red burst in a splash of colour where the bard's skull struck the stone.

The ptyradon died with far less dignity, thrashing its limbs as its insides roped out in slopping wet coils. Its roars became bleating whines even as it sought to claw its way over to the bard's body. Weaker with each step, with the organic pulp of its innards sliding from the brutal axe wound, the carnosaur collapsed only an arm's length from where Nalfir lay unmoving.

The beast's last breath left its jaws as steam between sword-length teeth. It died there, glaring at its killer's corpse, its reptilian eyes seething with bestial, stupid hate.

Ragnar exhaled at last, not realising until then that he'd been holding his own breath. Vorain came to him, skidding to a stop. His voice was hushed.

'He killed a ptyradon with... with *an axe*. He disembowelled it with a single blow.'

Ragnar felt the welcome burn of pride at Nalfir's last deed, and the reverence in Vorain's tone. He didn't reply. He simply hauled himself to his feet.

'A heroic death,' the Flesh Tearer said, awed.

'A stubborn bastard's death,' Ragnar replied. 'Though in my experience the two are often the same thing.'

Together they approached the Stormraven's wreckage, seeking the pilot of the downed craft. Rather than aid the Flesh Tearer, Ragnar waited, watching the dead beast, daring it to move once more.

'I will summon another gunship,' Vorain said.

'Just one? And if there are more of those things out there?'

'Ptyradons are lone hunters.'

Ragnar wasn't convinced, but he had no will to raise an argument. They made their way over to the ptyradon's motionless form.

'Get the axe,' he said to the Flesh Tearer.

It took the lion's share of his remaining strength to push the beast onto its side, exposing the axe driven deep into its belly. He held it there, his muscles burning with fatigue and infection, his fingers gripping its immense reptilian scales as Vorain pulled the embedded axe free with grunted curses. When Ragnar heard the wet crunch of extraction, he released the beast's hide again, letting the body settle.

In keeping with Cretacia's savage fauna, insect vermin were already gathering at the creature's bulging black eyes, beginning their carrion-feeding on the softest and wettest portions of the dead dragon.

When they climbed back up the scree slope, Vorain carried the deactivated power axe still dripping with intestinal slime.

Ragnar carried his brother's body on his shoulders.

VI

It was a long road back to the Hearthworld. The warp's vicissitudes were as benign as could be, letting the Flesh Tearers frigate *Stygimoloch* make the coreward journey to Fenris without incident. With fair navigational winds, making the journey within the span of half a year was considered a blessing. The *Stygimoloch* was one of the fastest vessels remaining in the depleted Cretacian fleet; she made the journey in a mere four months.

The small warship, crewed by fewer than ten thousand souls, refused to sail deeply into Einherjar territory. A brief pulse of telemetry was broadcast into the Fenrisian System, but by the time a patrol vessel from the Fang reached the system's edge, there was no sign of the Flesh Tearers warship.

An unmarked Aquila suborbital shuttle – a lightly armed transit craft ubiquitous across the Imperium – waited at the location of the telemetry pulse. Its systems were active but it was incapable of covering the distance necessary to reach Fenris under its own power, and only had oxygen reserves for a week of survival. All identification had been scraped from its hull plating.

Only two details returned from an auspex scan of the winged shuttle, seemingly lost in the void. The first was its locator beacon: active and beating like a clockwork heart. The second was the presence of trace life signs: two souls, no more, no less.

When it was brought aboard the Wolves patrol destroyer *Atgeir,* a pack of Grey Hunters surrounded the shuttle in the hangar bay, bolters levelled with customary caution at the lowering ramp. The first soul to descend onto the hangar deck was Blackmane of the Thunderfists, leading a coffin-sized stasis pod behind him. He looked worn and weary, with his armour badly scarred and poorly maintained, and he carried an axe that wasn't his own.

'Blackmane?' asked the Grey Hunters pack leader, recognising the Blood Claw from former feasting days at the Fang.

Ragnar nodded, infinitely weary. 'Hail, Stormtamer. I bring the remains of Nalfir Razortongue, slain in honourable battle upon Cretacia, back to

the Hearthworld.' He took a deep breath, savouring the recycled and repro-
cessed air of the *Atgeir*'s landing bay. 'And I have a tale for the Great Wolf's
ears.'

'Then you're fortunate, kinsman. The Great Wolf guards the Fang this
season, resupplying and recruiting for the Wolves that Stalk the Stars. You
said *Cretacia?* Is this a jest?'

Ragnar managed a faint smile, showing his fangs. 'It's a long story.'

Andar hid his suspicions for now. 'We registered two life signals aboard
the shuttle,' said the Grey Hunter. 'Who travels with you?'

'An emissary,' said Ragnar. 'Lower your guns.'

The second figure appeared in the shuttle hatch, clad in red-and-black
battleplate. He descended the ramp slowly, hands open to show that he
carried no weapons. His scarred features were set in a cautious mask as he
became the first of his bloodline to ever breathe the air of a Space Wolves
ship without boarding it carrying a blade and bolter in hand.

Andar Stormtamer turned to Ragnar, disbelief in his dark eyes. 'He let
himself be taken alive?'

'He's not a captive,' Ragnar said. 'As I said, he's an emissary.'

Andar turned his gaze back to the unarmed warrior and spoke in Gothic.
'The Great Wolf will be told of your presence, Flesh Tearer.'

'Yes. Good,' said Captain Vorain in halting Fenrisian. 'It's time, Wolf-
cousins, to end the war.'

'Today is a day for mad tales,' said Andar, looking to the stasis pod. He
dragged his fingertips across his heart, a traditional sign of sorrow at learning of a brother's passing. 'You say Nalfir Razortongue has fallen. How did
he die?'

Ragnar gave a mirror of Nalfir's own smile, as the bard's words left his lips.
He spoke the lie he'd been told to tell, which was now nothing but the truth.

'He died fighting something huge, with teeth the length of your legs.'

EPILOGUE

At the outset, High King Grimnar had said this would be no war of conquest. 'The Archenemy comes now not for resources, territory, nor even for their accursed ideology. This is the first battle in a war of extinction. They mean to burn Cadia, raze its fortresses, and sail onwards without looking back.'

With empty bolters and swords that cried out for fuel, the survivors of Ragnar's Great Company reached the surface only to be confronted with the truth Grimnar had promised. The city no longer existed. In its place was a purgatory of ash and fire.

They hadn't managed to reach the coast. The tunnels were collapsed, barring their passage, forcing them to surface within the city limits. With his helm on, Ragnar breathed in the sweat-scented recycled air of his armour, but the charcoal reek of the incinerated city found a way into his throat regardless. Gritty and pervasive, the smoke and ash and dust blended together into a dense atmosphere of ruination that choked the entire region.

The city was still aflame. Ragged warbands of the enemy were everywhere, desecrating and destroying all they could find in Kasr Belloc's bones. Thanks to the Wolves serving as rearguard for the city militia's evacuation, there was little in the way of living sport for the foe to amuse themselves with.

The ground shivered with the bellows of distant, and not so distant, artillery, as well as the earthshaking grind of battle tank columns and Titan footfalls moving through the dead city. The enemy were no longer shelling the Kasr in force; there was precious little left standing deserving of annihilation. Now they were simply moving their hordes through the wasteland that remained.

'Move,' Ragnar voxed to the First Pack. Together they advanced in low crouches, stalking through the dust-strangled ruins of the fortress-city. The smoke in the air hid the details of their blood-scabbed ceramite and reduced them to armoured silhouettes in the perpetual ashen dark. Other shadows drifted nearby, some human, some far from it.

Ragnar had scattered his packs upon reaching the surface, staggering their advance in the loosest of formations rather than moving as a horde of dozens. Packs were near enough to come to each other's aid in the smoky darkness, yet not grouped up close enough to make significant blurs on any enemy auspex scanners. As ever, the First Pack led the way.

Nearly two hundred Wolves made planetfall with Jarl Blackmane at the campaign's commencement. By the time they regained the surface, scarcely seventy remained. More were lost as they made their way through the city – some impeded by enemy forces during the journey, and Ragnar believed they might yet survive in the ruins. Others sacrificed themselves to distract and hold Traitor patrols so that the other packs might slip deeper behind enemy lines. Each time the company split apart a fraction more, Ragnar's bitter reluctance grew. The fact he had no choice was irrelevant. The necessity of such sacrifice still pained him. His memorised list of those fallen beneath his banner grew by the hour upon this cursed world.

The Wolf Lord led his men onwards, coordinating the advancing packs with whispers across the short-range vox. For a time, it worked well.

'Jarl,' came a murmured voice. 'To me, sire.'

Ragnar looked back over his shoulder, scarcely seeing Ulrik's silhouette near a fallen wall. When even genhanced vision and a finely tuned retinal display struggled to pierce the murk, things were dire indeed. He crossed the shattered road in a low run and reached the Wolf Priest's side.

'Slayer?'

In reply, Ulrik brushed his armoured palm across a section of the tumbled wall still standing. A crude but complicated rune was marked there, cut into the stone. Scraped with a knife.

'That's... Cretacian,' Ragnar said.

'I know little of their tongue,' said Ulrik. 'Do you know this mark's meaning?'

He did. Ragnar nodded, touching the scratched sigil with his armoured fingertips.

'It's my name.'

'Do you jest, Young King?'

'No, Slayer. It's my name as a Cretacian hieroglyph. *"Mane of Shadow".'* He brushed more dirt away, revealing a series of smaller runic letters.

Ulrik said nothing. He simply waited.

'It's a warning,' Ragnar said. 'Nightblade is dead.'

Razortongue's voice echoed down the years, drifting through his mind. *Luck runs out, Blackmane. Luck always runs out.*

'The Flesh Tearers are in the city. At least... they were. We need to reach the southern promethium refineries.'

'And why is that, sire?'

Ragnar bared his teeth in a rueful, weary grin. 'Because that's what these markings are telling us to do. And an actual mission that involves more than running, hiding and fighting in the dark until we die has great appeal. Gather the packs, Slayer. We hunt.'

The scattered survivors came across Nightblade and his Wolf Scouts soon after finding several more trail signs. Their crucified bodies hung from the statuary of a plaza's dry central fountain, roped to the plain, serviceable Cadian stonework by industrial chains. Each of the corpses had been doused with promethium and ignited while chained in place, burned alive like heretics to hang as blackened husks. Their defilement was complete; there could be no recovery of their gene-seed after such a death, even if Ragnar and his warriors had reached the Scouts hours after their execution rather than days.

Ragnar turned from the ruined wreckage that had once been five of the oldest and bravest veterans within the Chapter. He watched the shadow of something vast and inhuman staggering mechanically several kilometres away, barely visible through the dust and ash to the west. Nothing living was that large, but no Titan moved with such sickly sentience. The sight of it made his skin crawl.

'We should cut them down,' Alrydd said of the crucified Scouts, 'and turn their remains to ash.' When Ragnar didn't answer, the young bard turned to Ulrik, who was master of the company's funeral rites. The skull-helmed priest gave no reply either.

'No,' Ragnar said. Reluctance thickened his tone. 'When we retake the city, I'll burn our brothers myself. But not now. Move on.'

They hunted once more. It was Alrydd, a slender silhouette in his Corvus battleplate, who next called a halt.

'Do you feel that?' he said across the vox, as softly as his rich singing voice allowed.

Ragnar felt nothing until he crouched and pressed his palm to the rockcrete road. There it was: a pulse in the broken stone, like the city's own heartbeat.

Or the footsteps of a walking god.

'Titan,' he hissed across the company's general channel.

Ragnar ordered the packs to scatter further and move into whatever cover they could find. Pickings were ripe in the fallen fortress-city, though no structure would protect them if a Battle Titan took umbrage at their existence. They couldn't remain undetected for much longer, of that Ragnar was certain. That they'd even made it this far on the surface was a miracle, but with the city practically razed there was precious little in the way of resources for the enemy to plunder. Ragnar suspected many of the enemy's warbands had already moved on to hunt fresh meat elsewhere.

With his back to a low wall, the Wolf Lord crouched and concentrated. The ground shivered harder, slowly becoming a tremble, then a rhythmic shake. He narrowed his eyes, almost a wince, as something vast nearby sounded a great war horn across the devastated cityscape. Imperial Titans blared their sirens to alert infantry and warn them out of the way. Whatever this war machine was, it didn't sound as if it were warning anyone of anything. Impossibly, it sounded hungry.

Ragnar pressed himself closer to the wall as the god-walker eclipsed what pathetic moonlight was managing to pierce the occluded heavens. He shifted enough to watch the war engine stride past, several streets away, its armoured shins and massive clawed feet sending the remnants of buildings crashing to the ground, breaking apart into yet more dust.

'Banelord.' Alrydd was whispering, as if there were a chance the titanic machine might hear them. 'I've never seen one outside of the hololith archives.'

Ragnar had. He'd boarded one, in fact. He'd gutted the malformed overseer-pilots with Frostfang, before hurling their corpses from the Titan's cockpit-head. That had been a good day, and a fine fight. Only two of his men had been slain.

Closing his eyes, he focused on slowing his twin hearts, straining to listen past the confining helm that dulled his inhumanly keen senses.

Distant gunfire.

Chanting, singing, praying.

The drumming of falling buildings.

The rolling growl of tanks.

The god-steps of marching Titans.

He cycled through Imperial vox-channels yet again, seeking anything amidst the static. The voices he did hear were cracked and degraded, and he wasn't certain they belonged to Imperial souls.

'Allfather's Throne,' he murmured.

'My jarl?' asked Alrydd at his side.

The Wolf Lord opened his eyes. 'Frequency ochre-five-three,' Ragnar replied. 'Listen.'

'I hear it,' Ulrik said at once. His breathing was a measured, mournful inhale/exhale breeze through his wolf-skull helmet. For reasons Ragnar had no wish to know, the Slayer enjoyed the taste and smell of the dead city. The priest evidently wished to experience it rather than seal his armour completely.

'I hear it, also,' said Olvec. They were his first words in days. 'The enemy.'

'The enemy,' Ragnar agreed.

'At the promethium installations,' said Alrydd, distracted by the grotesque voices in his ear.

All eyes turned to the bard. 'You're certain, brother?' Ragnar asked. 'The refineries were among the first districts to be shelled. There can't be much infrastructure left.' He didn't add that the Cretacian markings were guiding him there, promising salvation. A leader should never let his disappointment show to his men.

Luck runs out, after all.

Alrydd nodded, his head still tilted in distraction. 'They're using what remains to refuel their rearguard armour divisions. As sure as the north wind blows cold.'

As usual, Ragnar decided against pointing out that the north wind here didn't blow particularly cold. The bard's axioms tended to be uniquely Fenrisian sentiments.

Even before its near-annihilation, Cadia had been an ugly world. Its sky was bleached by the rancid corruption of the Eye of Terror, which dominated the entirety of its heavens, day and night. Its whole culture, from art and architecture to morality and virtue, was dedicated to the simplicity and glory of Imperial warfare.

As a war-world, its role was to guard the edge of the Eye of Terror, where reality and the warp met to create the haven of Traitors and daemons alike. Cadia could have been beautiful. It could have been a beacon for enlightenment and progress in a darkening galaxy. Instead, because of where it lay in the Emperor's domain, it was forced to devote its entire existence to reinforcing its planetary defences while feeding its entire militarised population into the byzantine processes of the Imperial Guard.

It was said that Cadian children could strip and clean a Kantrael-pattern lasrifle before they could read. On other worlds such a claim would be a crude exaggeration. On Cadia, it was simply childhood.

Understandably, Cadian shock trooper regiments were among the Imperium's most decorated and highly trained Guard forces. Equally understandably, this left the world as a grey and ugly fortress-planet, with its continents given over to vast Kasr bastion-cities, where life consisted of little more than endless training, drilling and military discipline in place of any other kind of culture.

Even away from the main population centres, the wilderness was home to several thousand castles, training camps, bunker complexes and mountain fastnesses. The cities themselves were blocky, armoured, defensible command centres, often shielded from orbit and designed with one thing in mind: to cost any invader oceans of blood for every metre they managed to take and hold. Gun-towers lined the avenues of every place citizens could gather. Communal barracks ran row upon row, road by road, rather than the skyscraping habitation blocks of other cities on other worlds.

Belloc was no exception to the Kasr tradition. In death it had fulfilled the purpose of its life – though it was now dead, aflame and overrun with the Archenemy's rearguard, it was also the grave of hundreds of thousands of invader soldiers, cultists and slaves. The Warmaster, curses upon his black name, had paid dearly to raze the city. He was paying dearly to burn all of the Kasr; the dark truth was that it was a price he seemed willing – even eager – to pay.

Belloc had been named for the mountain range that cast its alpine shadow across the city nestled in its foothills. In the Kasr's southernmost district, closest to the mountains, Belloc's promethium refineries were a tertiary concern to Cadian High Command compared to eastern manufactories and the great central space port.

It took Ragnar's survivors three hours to reach the boundaries of the refinery sector. Each Wolf moved with renewed vitality, energised by the thought of attacking – at last – instead of waiting and repelling assault after assault in the useless dark or hiding among the bones of the fallen city.

The packs spaced out at various points along the district's walled edges, aiming to slip in undetected. They met no sentries or guards.

Ragnar led the First Pack through a row of wrecked and looted warehouses, with Frostfang in his hands. On they moved, slowed by Uller and Olvec in their Terminator plate, yet refusing to leave them behind. The Wolf Lord listened to his packs' voxed communications with razor focus, picturing their positions in his mind on a hololithic map he recalled flawlessly from memory.

The earliest reports spoke of Land Raiders and Rhinos on the ground in the district's furthest side, watched over by patrols of ceramite-clad warriors. The flames made identifying the foe difficult at such distance.

Ragnar ordered his men to begin the attack. He listened to their spoken oaths as they advanced, feeling the familiar and welcome burn of pride. With surly growls and gentle threats they demanded the Allfather pay heed to their deeds and glories.

The First Pack was lagging severely behind when the vox erupted with reports of initial contact. Grunts of effort and the tinny thunder of bolter fire rang out at once. Ragnar's muscles tightened with the need to run forwards and aid his kinsmen.

Uller and Olvec were stomping forwards in their heavy armour plating, frustration writ across their aged features as surely as it was etched across the face of their young lord.

'Go, damn you!' Uller ordered his jarl. The warrior's empty assault cannon whined in helpless, ammo-starved irritation. 'Just save some for us.'

Ragnar broke into a sprint, Ulrik, Hrolf and Alrydd with him. They emerged from the warehouse into a salvage yard with five towering deactivated cranes, and seven others brought down in the war, littering the courtyard with piles of melted slag and scrap metal.

The enemy were here, it was true. Hundreds of them, carpeting the ground, burst open by bolter fire. Traitorous Guardsmen, a horde of them with their flesh marked by ritual knives, massacred upon the earth.

'Sire!' came Soergar True Cut's voice. Laughing. Laughing hard enough to split open his skull. 'It's–' Distortion stole the rest of his declaration. The vox dissolved into static.

A gunship roared overhead, coming in on howling engines and catching him on open ground, far from cover. Ragnar hurled himself down to the scrap-strewn rockcrete, picturing the gunship opening up with its array of chattering, booming heavy bolters. Spent shell cases would rain upon the salvage yard like metallic hailstones.

But the attack didn't come. The engines kept howling, as the gunship hovered.

'Identify yourself,' came a cold voice in Ragnar's ears, barely distorted at all. The new tones were immediately overlaid by several pack leaders voxing their jarl in the same moment, with the same information.

Ragnar rose from his dubious cover, one hand raised to shield his eyes from the Thunderhawk's scissoring searchlights as they drowned him in illumination. He saw the orange glow of distant fire on dark armour plating, and the winged blade emblem on the gunship's nose. He felt the same mad laughter that was afflicting his warriors also threatening to take hold of his own jaws.

'This is the Thunderhawk *Ophanic Vigil* of the Dark Angels Fourth Battle Company. We repeat, identify yourself.'

'Ragnar,' he said over the sound of his relieved men. 'Jarl of the Blackmane Great Company.'

The gunship began to lower. Its landing claws slid free into landing position, and the forward ramp opened on slow, loud hydraulics. The pilot's voice returned over the vox.

'Your request for reinforcements is acknowledged.' The Thunderhawk slammed down onto the rockcrete courtyard of the salvage yard, grinding traitors' bodies beneath its weight. 'Captain Sorael wishes to speak with you, Jarl Blackmane.'

Fifty-one Space Wolves made it to the Belloc Mountain fortress. Ragnar knew more yet lived in the ruins of the city. He would return and find them, when the Imperium pushed back to retake what remained of the devastated Kasr. Even so, fifty-one was a number to thank the Allfather for.

And, somewhat more reluctantly, to thank the Dark Angels for.

Several thousand Imperial warriors were using the mountain fastness as a fallback base. Alongside the huge regiments of Imperial Guard soldiers were thirty Black Templars, a strike force of the supposedly extinct Shadow Wolf Chapter, an armoured battalion of the Subjugators and a recon detachment of Flesh Tearers Scouts.

Over the coming days, the jarl's warriors would be rearmed, resupplied and reinforced from the Einherjar fleet in orbit.

However, the first soul to greet Ragnar was waiting when the gunship's ramp lowered. Time had changed him, scarring his features more than the Young King recalled, and adding several bronze trinkets and honour badges to the warrior's battered ceramite. He was from a Chapter that cared little for armour ornamentation, however. Little separated him from the appearance of a line soldier.

The Flesh Tearer shook Ragnar's hand, wrist to wrist in a warrior's grip. 'You live,' he said.

'I live, Vorain. How did you know we were down there?'

'It was your hunter, Drekka, who first got word to us. We went into the city to seek him, but he'd already fallen. You saw our warnings?'

'I saw them. The Allfather alone knows how many you must have scratched across the city for us to find even a few.'

'Even I cannot be sure. My Scouts have been ghosting through the ruins and taking heads every day for weeks.'

'Thank you,' Ragnar said, humbled by the gesture. 'We'll speak again, after.'

'After? After what?'

'I must meet with the Dark Angels commander. There's a tradition we must honour.'

The duel began at sunrise, though there was precious little sun and even less in the way of warmth.

The two swordsmen circled one another in the snow. Their boots crunched holes in the white ground as they stepped sideways, blades levelled and ready. Two lords, alike in pride and dignity yet opposites in expression and bearing. Captain Sorael's helm was crested with angels' wings, and his dark armour plating covered in a traditional surplice of knightly reverence as he gripped his blade two-handed. Lord Ragnar was bare-headed and snarling into the wind, his armour cracked and ruined, holding his toothed sword in a single loose fist.

It was a scene that had played out hundreds of times before in the roll of years since the Horus Heresy. The war strangling this sacred world was, for the moment, forgotten – all that mattered were the edges of their blades and the expectant stares of their waiting, watching kindred. All were battered and bloodstained, but those armoured in the blue-grey of clean skies were cheering and howling; those armoured in the green of deep forests were silent and solemn. The Wolves raised their weapons high over their heads as they roared, as if the glint of the setting sun on their war-ravaged blades might catch the distant gaze of the God-Emperor upon His Golden Throne. The Dark Angels had their swords turned down, the points driven into the earth by their boots.

First blood went to Ragnar – a gash across Sorael's stern features – eliciting a colossal roar from the Wolves' ranks. Second and third blood went to the Dark Angel, cutting twin slashes across the Wolf Lord's face, returning the cheek-slice in kind and adding a cut across the forehead for good measure.

The wind tore at Sorael's tabard and Ragnar's filthy hair. Still they circled, clashing their blades together, each warrior testing the other's grace and technique, learning how they moved. No true blows were attempted. Even the shallow slashes across both warriors' faces were delivered for the sake of spectacle and minor insult as they gauged each other's skill. The only strike that would matter in the fight was the final one.

They began to test each other's strength and balance. The two swords met with a ringing crash, a heavier blow than any yet struck. They disengaged after a heartbeat, moving back into their patient circling. The respite between blows was much shorter this time, as the Wolf and the Dark Angel unleashed a stream of heavy, blurring strikes that impacted against the opposing blade, spraying sparks into the winter air.

The exchange lasted several minutes, punctuated by several blade-locks where both swordsmen heaved against each other, pauldron to pauldron or face to face around their trapped, squealing swords. Boots scrabbled on the loose rock beneath the layer of mountaintop snow as they bore their weight against each other every time their blades ground together.

Finally they disengaged for the final time, and the duel began in earnest. Sweeping cuts tore through the air only to be met with artful deflections. Swift thrusts were batted aside with the flat of a blade or the crash of a vambrace.

For all their matched skill, the differences in their fighting styles could not have been clearer. Sorael was a consummate swordsman, blocking, parrying, riposting, his movements the muscle memory of a lifelong soldier. Ragnar dodged aside from blows rather than seeking to block them, relying on a barbarian's powerful killing cleaves rather than a duellist's grace.

Their speed was beyond anything the mortal eye could follow – the two warriors became a single entity of blurred blades and limbs, two or three metal crashes coming in the space between each second. Ragnar would press the attack, advancing and swinging immense slashes like some reaper of life from Ancient Terran myth. Sorael would defend, recover and reply with a lightning assault of cuts and slashes that would put Ragnar back on the defensive. Back and forth it went, one warrior forced to give ground in one moment, then stealing the chance to retake it the next.

Above them the shrouded sky promised more snow. And above the clouds, war still raged in the heavens, just as it still swept across Cadia beyond the brief sanctuary provided by the mountain range.

Dirty, exhausted Cadian shock troopers were soon milling around the ring of Adeptus Astartes warriors. Even their legendary discipline was overcome by curiosity to see two lords of the Space Marines engaged in a life and death honour duel. In an Imperium where countless worlds believed the Adeptus Astartes were the Emperor's mythic angels, to see them in the flesh was rare enough. To see them performing one of their most sacred rites was utterly unprecedented.

Of course, witnessing the duel required seeing through a ring of towering, ceramite-clad superhumans. Cadian drivers brought their Chimera and Taurox troop transports closer, and platoons of soldiers watched by sitting and standing on the armoured hulls of their carriers.

Vorain watched from the surrounding circle, following their movements with a keen stare. He doubted the Imperial Guardsmen with their too-human minds were able to process the speed at which the fight was taking place. It was captivating and mystifying in the same breath. Frostfang's whirring teeth sent up an endless chainsaw whine, coupling with the waspish drone of the power field around Sorael's longer blade.

Vorain had never seen a fight like it. Ragnar had the edge in strength and speed, while Sorael had the benefit of far more training and experience. It was too close to predict a victor. The first to make a mistake would be the one to die.

The Wolf and the Dark Angel battled on, heedless of their audience.

When Ragnar overbalanced on a wild swing, Sorael thrust at the Wolf's breastplate, seeking a killing impalement; the tip of the sword crashed aside from the jarl's chest as Ragnar leaned away. When Sorael was slow to bring his guard back up, Ragnar risked the chance at a head-chop, only for the knight to deflect the blade's edge with his vambrace just enough for the slash to swing wide.

Thirty minutes became an hour. One hour became two. Ragnar was sweating freely, his skin steaming in the mountain cold. Even preternatural muscles weren't immune to fatigue, and the first signs of weariness were beginning to show in both fighters. In the practice cages, both warriors might have been able to fight for a day or more, but both Ragnar and Sorael were poorly nourished from long deployments and carrying their share of wounds from the recent months of warfare.

Their guards were slipping. Not enough to allow a killing blow, but enough to betray the burn of tiring muscles. Sorael managed to trip Ragnar with the length of his blade, and rammed the sword down even before the Wolf Lord had crashed to the earth. Ragnar rolled to the side, thundering a kick against the Dark Angel's forearm, sending the power sword spinning from Sorael's grip with a nasty buzz.

He allowed time for Sorael to recover the blade, using the time to pick himself up from the ground and spit to ward away misfortune. As he recovered, Ragnar met the eyes of the closest Wolves. They were no longer shouting for their lord, or insults at his foe. All present – Wolf, Dark Angel, human – merely watched in something closer to silence, waiting for the inevitable slip that would spell the battle's end.

'My thanks,' said Sorael as he approached again, once more holding his blade.

Ragnar had been just as grateful for the momentary respite. He was tiring fast, and weariness in a duel was always the first step in a slow haemorrhage of confidence. Doubt saw men dead as often as an opponent's skill. Baring his teeth, he forced a cocky grin as he faced the Dark Angel. Masked by his helm, Sorael showed no weariness beyond the subtle tells of his slowing muscles.

Show no weakness, Ragnar thought. *Only defiance.*

Sorael returned nothing but an impartial gaze, despite the fact he was nearly panting, dragging air into his three aching lungs.

Ragnar knew that he had to end this quickly, before he lost the chance to win at all. Dragging in a deep breath, the Wolf Lord attacked fast, holding nothing back. Always advancing, stalking forwards, laying on cleaving swing after cleaving swing against the knight's energised blade. Each crash of Frostfang against the Dark Angel's blade bred flares of migraine light from the tormented power field wreathing Sorael's sword.

The Dark Angel fought back, countering with a whirling dance of sword work, weaving his two-handed blade into a spinning silver barrier before him. Ragnar took a step back, then two, then three... He was giving up the ground he'd only just gained, retreating faster than he'd advanced. His boots thudded into the frozen earth, grinding the snow to powder. Twice he almost slipped as the frost turned treacherous underfoot.

He leaned aside as the aggravated chrome blur of Sorael's sword crackled and spat past his face, missing his eyes by a finger's width. Ragnar had less than a second to taste the burned air of the sword's passing, like ozone on his tongue, before the return strike descended from above.

Ragnar heard the desperation in his own roar as he lifted Frostfang to ward against the falling blade. The two swords locked less than a hand's span from the Wolf's face. Again came the vicious heat of the sword's energy field against flesh.

Throwing the Dark Angel back with a furious howl, he retreated another few steps, breathing heavily, seeking – somehow – to buy time.

Sorael sensed his triumph. Pressing the advantage with a volley of cuts and thrusts, the Dark Angel ended with a decapitating strike, planting his feet to perfection and executing the cut with all the grace and power of the hundred-year veteran he was. Sorael's sword sliced at neck-height, matched to Ragnar's stance and posture, lethal at a mathematically perfect level made possible by a century of experience on the field of battle.

The Wolves and Dark Angels who saw the end coming breathed in as it unfolded; the humans with their slower senses had no idea what was happening until it was already done.

The blade rasped through the cold air, the energy field leaving a curved blur of abused kineticism in its wake.

And tumbled, deactivated and suddenly silent, into the snow.

The Dark Angel stood motionless, one arm outstretched to end the perfect decapitation. That arm ended at the elbow. The severed forearm remained with the sword, and the armoured hand that still gripped the hilt.

Ragnar, on his knees before the Dark Angel, rammed Frostfang upwards. As with Sorael, instinct allowed him to execute his blow perfectly. He could have ploughed it through Sorael's torso, hilting in the Angel's guts and disembowelling his opponent. Instead, the Fenrisian relic sword thrust up, its killing teeth slicing the side of Sorael's neck armour, biting just deep enough to taste blood.

Ragnar rose to his feet, keeping the sword at Sorael's throat. He looked into the Dark Angel's red eye lenses, picturing the warrior's features behind the helm's faceplate.

'It's over, Sorael.'

'It is far from over. This is a matter of Duellum Dolor, Jarl Blackmane. Yield or die – those are the laws that bind us here. It can only be over when one yields and offers his life to the other's blade, or one dies in the duel itself.'

'Then yield.'

'No.'

'Yield, and I'll spare your life.'

'Never.'

Ragnar pressed the blade against his rival's throat, leaning closer. His breath steamed in the icy wind.

'Don't make me kill you. Not after four decades have passed since my sin. You lost, Sorael. It's finished.'

Sorael used his remaining hand to disengage his helmet seals and pull the helm free. Sweating as much as Ragnar, he stood bareheaded and stern in the cold mountain air.

'Then kill me, for I do not yield to you, Lord of Wolves.'

Ragnar could scarce believe what he was hearing. Sorael was meeting the Wolf's eyes now, dark to pale, a stare of stark nobility meeting a gaze of all-too-feral fury. He kept his halved arm held against his tabard, the wound already sealed by his enhanced physiology.

It was the old anger that Ragnar felt now, creeping over his skin like a rash, settling into his skull like an infection. He felt the staring eyes of his men upon him as well as the Dark Angels' eyes and the witnessing gazes of hundreds of Cadian soldiers... watching the Imperium's finest warriors on the verge of murdering each other instead of saving this vital world.

All of the fight had bled from him, leeching all of his strength with it. Adrenaline alone kept him on his feet.

There had to be a way out of this.

Razortongue would know. The thought came unbidden. True or not, the bitter and long-dead bard would have also mocked him mercilessly for getting into this position in the first place.

Ragnar smiled, a crooked and sly bard's smile.

'No,' he said, and hurled the priceless Frostfang aside, letting it sleep in the snow near Sorael's powerless blade.

The Dark Angel's eyes flickered to the fallen weapons, then rested on Ragnar once more.

'No?'

'No,' Ragnar repeated. 'We stand at the edge of the Imperium's End, brothers at each other's throats. Russ' blood, if a Flesh Tearer played a part in saving my life, after all the bloodshed between our Chapters, I'll willingly fight at your side without hatred. Can you truly not do the same? Now, of all times, when it matters most? Look at the sky, Sorael. Look at this world aflame. We stand together now, or we fall apart.'

Sorael swallowed and said nothing.

'For forty years I've carried the guilt and shame of leaving this duel unfinished,' said Ragnar. 'We've finished it now, at long last. I've won it, Sorael. *I* choose how it ends. And it ends with both of our blades in the snow, not bathed in each other's blood. *Yield,* you proud bastard. Tend to your wounds, then fight by my side. I have warriors still trapped in the city. Help me find them, cousin.'

Sorael scanned the ranks of his dark-armoured brethren, then watched the growling, snarling Wolves for the span of exactly nine heartbeats.

Thinking. Dwelling. Deciding.

'I yield,' he said at last. There was a pause. 'And we will stand with you to retake Kasr Belloc.'

The reaction was immediate. The Dark Angels' ranks drew their blades from the earth, cleaning the snow from the steel and sheathing them at once. Their solemn presence melted away, robed warriors returning to their duties in ruthless order, preparing for the next battle.

'My brethren,' said Sorael, 'are not celebratory souls.'

'My brothers are,' said Ragnar, a moment before the survivors of his Great Company howled to the night sky, long and loud.

When the shouting ceased, Sorael cleared his throat. 'I must see if my Apothecary can graft an augmetic replacement to my arm before the next battle. We will speak again before we leave.'

'Wait.' Ragnar offered his hand. His left hand. Sorael took it, gripping wrist to wrist as Vorain had done upon greeting the Wolf Lord upon arrival earlier that day. 'My thanks, Dark Angel, for your aid in the city.'

'Duty,' Sorael replied with a brief smile. It was the first sign of amusement Ragnar had witnessed from the Dark Angel. With that, the captain walked away.

Ragnar watched Sorael's retreating back. 'Their composure never ceases to amaze me,' he said to Vorain.

'They're from cooler, calmer blood than you and I,' admitted the Flesh Tearer.

'Forty years,' Ragnar murmured. 'Four decades of guilt, washed clean in an instant.' He shook his head, overwhelmed by the Dark Angels' stoic madness, yet shamelessly grateful for their part in his company's salvation.

'You were lucky, Blackmane.'

Ragnar turned to Vorain, forgiving him the use of the tribal name. 'You believe so?'

'Even an axeman can judge a fight between swordmasters, Wolf. You were lucky to weave beneath the sword that would have severed your head from your shoulders. You won a duel you should have lost. You beat a foe who was only seconds from killing you.'

'I had him,' Ragnar said, perfectly sincere.

Vorain laughed, the sound rich and guttural. 'Your secret is safe with me, Blackmane.' He gestured to the mountain fortress, to the grounded gunships, to the tank crews with their vehicles, to the rattle-walking Sentinels marching here and there, to the dozens of Flesh Tearers, Space Wolves and Dark Angels in hesitant alliance, cautiously mixing ranks. 'Well, safe with me... and every soul who saw the only reason you dodged the killing blow was because you slipped on the ice.'

'Ah, you lie, Flesh Tearer. You lie like a fireside storyteller.'

'At the speed you were fighting, can anyone be sure what they saw? I know what it looked like to me. Let's speak no more of it, cousin.'

Ragnar didn't argue. Nor did he agree. The Young King smiled as he retrieved Frostfang from the snow.

Luck runs out, Blackmane.

Aye. But not today, singer.

CURSE OF
THE WULFEN

David Annandale

PROLOGUE

They met in the dark of the mountain's roots. Here the night of stone was endless. It was not silent, for things of fur and fang and steel prowled, growling warnings to each other. It was not empty, for within it lay the tombs of legends. The tombs were unquiet. The legends they enclosed were granted only a provisional death. These sagas had not ended. One was ten thousand years old, and its thread carried on.

Three warriors met in the dark, in the tombs. When they saw each other, they were startled. When they saw where they had come to, they were disturbed.

The warrior whose mane and beard were as coarse and grey as a wolf's pelt spoke first. 'Brothers,' Harald Deathwolf said, 'you are well met. I did not expect your company.'

'Nor I,' said Krom Dragongaze. Even in the gloom, his eyes glittered with dark light.

'Nor I,' Ulrik the Slayer echoed. The ancient of the Chapter shook his head. His hair was as white as his gaze was dark. His eyes were shadows that watched and judged. He pointed at the vault door by which they stood. 'There is a purpose in this,' he said.

'The purpose is not mine,' said Harald. 'I did not intend to come here.' He looked at the name inscribed over the door, and was uneasy.

'You did not choose to come to the vaults?' the Slayer asked.

'I did,' said Harald. 'But with no clear design. That is...' he hesitated.

'You walked as if in a trance,' Dragongaze said.

'Yes.'

'So we all did,' said the Slayer. 'But not as we believed.'

'No.' Harald tried to see the last few hours clearly, but it was as if he had only just awakened, a sensation itself almost unknown to him in his centuries as a Space Marine. He had been conscious, yet his perception had narrowed to nothing except his next footstep. He had moved through tunnels and shafts, down and down and down, deeper and deeper into the

137

dark, into the night of stone. 'I had a destination,' he said. 'Though I did not know why I went. The need to be there was absolute.' He could not look away from the inscription. 'My destination was not here.'

'You thought to stand before Bjorn the Fell-Handed,' Dragongaze said. 'I did.'

'And yet we are here,' said the Slayer. The Wolf Priest rested a gauntlet against the vault door, gently, as if not to wake the legend inside. 'We marched to one goal, and arrived at another. This is a powerful omen, brothers. We must take heed.'

'An omen of what?' said Dragongaze.

'I will think upon it,' the Slayer said. 'This much is clear. Something is coming. The force of our compulsion speaks to its magnitude. And when the event arrives, we three must be mindful of the roles we will have to play.'

'It is a warning,' Harald said. 'An omen of doom. How can it be otherwise? We sought Bjorn, but we came here.'

The other two said nothing. They all gazed at the inscription. They stared at the runes of warning and the name of the mad legend, and felt a shadow deeper yet than the night of stone fall over their souls.

Beyond me lies a restless sleep, said the door. *Beyond me lies the madness of wrath.*

Murderfang.

The future stalked towards them, jaws agape.

PART 1

THE RETURN

CHAPTER 1

THE DOOMS ON NURADES

'The sky is blue today, governor.'

Andras Elsener, Lord Governor of Nurades, looked up from the sea of parchment and data-slates on the vast iron table before him. Everything was a priority, and everything had to be decided *now*. And this was merely what he had to wade through for the next hour. It was early in the day yet. The interruption was welcome, though he knew he would pay for the break in his concentration later.

Klein, his major-domo, stood at the chamber window. Elsener's quarters were high in the spire of Hive Genos. The view from his office looked out across the spires of the hive from a point that was frequently, although not always, a little below cloud cover. Sometimes Elsener could see many kilometres of the sprawl of the hive. Sometimes he saw nothing but a choking, industrial grey-brown. Twice in his life he had witnessed the weak disc of the sun visible through unusually thin clouds.

He had never seen a blue sky.

Elsener approached the window in wary awe. Klein seemed just as uneasy. He was about to open the door to the balcony but Elsener stopped him.

'No,' said the governor. 'Wait.'

The sky was clear. The blue was startling. It was searing. As Elsener watched, the last of the cloud cover peeled away like burning paper. The blue became brighter and brighter, though Elsener could not see the sun. The colour became painful. Elsener squinted. Klein shielded his eyes.

And then, though the colour still grew more intense, it also became darker. Blue became violet.

'The Emperor save us,' Elsener muttered.

Violet turned to a dark, grimy crimson. The colour of rotting blood stabbed at the back of Elsener's eyes. He could not look away. At the height of the searing, the sky ignited. Flames burst across the firmament. They were huge, arcing, roiling, as if Nurades had been pitched into a molten cauldron. The sky burned all the colours of the spectrum at once, destroying them with fury. As they died, the colours gave birth to other things, things that existed instead of colours, things that bled the eyes and tore at the mind.

The ground heaved. The central spire of Genos swayed back and forth. Narrower towers collapsed. But new spires rose, piercing up through the layers of the hive, thrusting towards the sky like monstrous daggers, and they were towers of bone.

Elsener saw dots appear in the sky. They fell – dark, tumbling, blazing orbs. Closer, and he saw they were skulls. They were a laughing, screaming hail. Jaws agape, they smashed onto the roofs and walkways and roads. They shattered on Elsener's balcony. Where each landed, its fire spread. It grew taller. It took on a shape. Now it had arms, legs. Now a head. Horns.

Muscle and sinew and blood-red flesh. It carried a sword.

Elsener cried out and hurled himself away from the window. He must not look. He must not see. Already he could feel his brain squirming as if it would change into an animal inside his skull.

Klein shrieked. He clawed at his face hard enough to tear open his cheeks. He clutched at his ragged flaps of skin, then ran at the governor, howling and drooling. Elsener drew his personal laspistol and shot the major-domo through the neck.

Then he ran. He did not look back, not even when the window smashed, and a snarling abomination called out to him in a voice of rattling bone. He knew what would happen if he looked. Perhaps he would die in the next few seconds, but if he did not look, he might yet retain his soul.

He prayed to the Emperor as he charged through the door and down the halls of his residence. He prayed the Father of Mankind would grant that he reached the astropathic choir in time. He prayed someone would hear Nurades' cry for help.

The next time Lord Governor Andras Elsener dared to look at the sky, it was weeks later, and he saw the cry answered.

He saw salvation slash through sky with bloody claws.

In the strategium overlooking the bridge of the strike cruiser *Alpha Fang*, the great predator leaned over a hololithic map of Nurades. A mantle of troll hide was draped over his armour, a trophy made of the prey itself. His gestures suggested contained force. At any moment, they could turn into the strike of a hunter. And moment by moment, he chose restraint. His calm was that of a wolf that had already chosen when and how to attack.

Harald Deathwolf pointed to the sigil for Hive Predomitus.

'We begin there,' he said. The hive was located at the base of a high mountain chain dividing the Lacertus Peninsula from the rest of the continent. 'We break the daemons' hold.' He moved his hand south-west, passing over Hive Genos. 'And push them into the sea.'

Canis Wolfborn looked from the map to the oculus. It showed the void riven by the mad flares of the warp storm, and the planet turning in agony. The atmosphere quivered like maggots. The Deathwolf champion grunted. 'Saving that?'

The huge warrior was more restless than Harald. His mane and beard were a lighter shade and longer, more unruly. If Harald was the wolf assured of closing its jaws on its prey, the Feral Knight was the beast barely held back. The bridge was not his natural domain. He belonged in the field, unleashed and roaring.

'Mistress of the vox,' Harald called without looking up from the map. 'Any traffic planetside?'

'Some, lord,' Giske Ager replied. 'Fragments only. There are brief bursts of coherent data. Orders perhaps. There are many cries.'

Harald nodded. He addressed the assembled Wolf Guard, not just Canis. The Deathwolf huscarls varied widely in age. But whether they counted themselves among the Riders of Morkai, the Thunderclaws or the Redhowl Hunters, they were all riders of wolves, and there was a kinship in their countenance – a narrowed, farseeing, predatory gaze.

'We have answered a plea for help,' Harald said. 'We have not come to enact Exterminatus. This planet will not be lost. I will see it returned to the embrace of the Allfather.'

'A hunt then,' said Vygar Helmfang.

'A great one.'

'Good.' Canis growled in satisfaction and anticipation. His question, Harald understood, had not been an expression of doubt in the mission. Canis wanted reassurance that he would not be cheated of prey by cyclonic torpedoes.

The assembled Wolf Guard also sounded pleased with Harald's deployment strategy. The Lacertus Peninsula was the most densely populated and industrially active region of Nurades. When the Space Wolves took it, they would hold the key to the rest of the world.

Harald wondered if it might also unlock something else. The encounter before Murderfang's vault troubled him. He was waiting for whatever event it heralded to make itself manifest. He did not know if the plight of Nurades meant more than it appeared, but there were unusual circumstances. From what had been gathered from the astropathic shriek that had reached Fenris, the coming of the warp storm had been extremely sudden. A matter of seconds. There was something about that arrival that did not seem like the result of the vagaries of the warp and a chance weakness in the materium.

Harald sensed a larger game behind the incursion. He could not guess what it was, nor what, if anything, it portended for the Space Wolves.

No matter, he tried to tell himself. His Great Company would stamp out the daemonic taint, and end the game before it began.

* * *

The Deathwolves fell upon the daemonic hordes much as the warpspawn had attacked the people of Nurades – with sudden, lightning violence.

The drop pods came first, streaking through the tormented sky in a cluster towards the plain between the mountains and the gates of Hive Predomitus. The Stormwolf gunships followed in their contrails. They hammered the landing site with twin-linked lascannon and heavy bolter fire, annihilating daemonkind in the vicinity.

The flanks of the pods slammed down and the Space Wolves stormed out. Grey Hunters howled their eagerness for war. Their helms bore totemic skulls and tails. Some were fashioned into snarling lupine form. They thundered away, in pack after pack. They hurled frag grenades ahead of them, then followed up the blasts with a stream of bolter fire. Monstrosities disintegrated. The Deathwolves pushed the enemy further back, allowing the gunships to land. Caught in the heat of first blood, the Grey Hunters would have followed their instincts to charge on if their pack leaders had not held them back long enough for the rest of their brothers to disembark.

The wait was a short one. Harald's full company launched a blistering assault on the enemy within seconds of having their boots on the ground.

Before the gates of Predomitus, a mass of horned, scarlet-scaled abominations rioted.

'Swordlings of Khorne.' Canis spat his contempt. His breath came in low growls.

'They have not been idle,' Harald said.

In the midst of the daemons rose tall hills of blackened skulls. Millions of Nuradeans had been sacrificed to Khorne, but the hunger of the god and his servants was unending. From the open gates of the city, the daemons dragged thousands upon thousands of howling victims.

'I can see the hills growing,' Canis said. His face was dark with horrified fury.

'So vast a slaughter,' Harald growled. 'Let our answer be more terrible still.'

The Stormwolf squadrons took to the air, pounding the warpspawn with guns. Lasbeams and shells burned daemons and blew them apart. They cut a seared, smoking furrow through the mass of wyrdflesh.

'The hunt is on, brothers!' Harald called. His roar was a clarion call to war, and Grey Hunters and Wolf Guard answered with a roar of their own. The battle cry thundered from the throats of men and beasts, and the thunderwolf cavalry led the charge into the furrow. Harald was at the front atop Icetooth, with Canis at his shoulder, as the immense Fangir shook the earth as he loped forward. Alongside the cavalry sped the Huntbrothers and the Frostrunners, Fenrisian wolves, some pure animal, others cybernetic hybrids, all of them monsters, flesh with strength of steel and steel with the wrath of flesh.

The cavalry slammed into their lines with the force of a nova cannon.

Tens of thousands of daemons massed on the plain. They were hatred embodied. But they fell back, trampled into oblivion by the wolves, blasted apart by bolter fire. Harald felt the exultant ferocity of war flood his veins. The vastness of the enemy army meant nothing except a near-inexhaustible supply of prey. His view turned from the hills of bodies and the burning towers of Predomitus to the horrors that surged, grasping for him. He swung his right arm out. The storm shield on his forearm smashed horns and skulls. He relished the impact. The jar was solid, crunching. He fired his bolt pistol as he swung. Wyrdflesh erupted before him. With his left hand, he wielded the frost axe Glacius. Its huge, wedge-shaped blade was a single crystal shard. It glinted the blue of razored cold. The edge was as long as Harald's arm. Daemonic flesh and muscle and bone ruptured at its strike.

Moments into the charge, Harald's senses were filled with the stench of roiling smoke and spraying ichor. Daemons howled with unnatural voices. The air shook with the clash of rages.

The swordlings tried to surround the charge and bring the cavalry down in a tide of blood. No matter how many of them rushed in, they could not stop the Deathwolves' momentum, although they exacted a toll. Harald heard the agonised snarls of a thunderwolf and the growls of Rangvald, its rider. He heard the crash as Wolf Guard and beast hit the ground under a mass of clawing, slashing daemons. There was an explosion of bolter fire as the brothers nearby sought to blast the swordlings away from the fallen rider.

'Ride on, brothers,' Rangvald shouted, fighting to the last.

And they did. The charge could not slow for anyone. Its success against such a vast horde depended on relentless violence and speed. With each fallen brother, the wrath of the Space Wolves and the thunderwolves grew, and they smashed the daemons with ever-greater ferocity. Harald saw only red – the red of the abominated flesh, the red of flame, and the red of his anger. Icetooth crushed daemons in his jaws. He smashed them to nothing beneath his enormous claws.

At Harald's shoulder, Canis' snarls were expressions of wrath and laughter. He swept his huge wolf claws back and forth, embracing the enemy with destruction. Every blade was as long as a gladius. Harald glanced to the right in time to see Canis slash a daemon's spine into sections with a single swipe.

'A good kill, brother!' Harald called.

The champion grinned, his yellow eyes blazing. He shouted something back, but all Harald heard was an inarticulate snarl. Canis was already deep into primal ferocity. He was in the realm of the beast now.

It would be easy to join him. Already Harald growled with triumph at each of Icetooth's kills. They were as one alpha predator in the field of battle. The bloody charge was exhilarating. The smoky wind blew back Harald's hair and beard. The beat of his hearts matched the pounding of

Icetooth's paws. The thundering anger of bolters, wolves and men carried him forward. Even the stench of ichor, a miasma both clutching and jagged, was a goad.

The call of absolute frenzy was strong. He held back, though. Not much, but just enough to hold on to his awareness of the wider field of battle.

The Deathwolves battered their way forward to victory and slaughter. The thunderwolf charge blew apart the lines of the Khornate abominations. It reduced hundreds of them to a thick sludge of ichor. The power of the wyrd crackled over them, and the foul liquid did not dissipate. Icetooth's paws splashed through a deepening mire. Their anger could not summon the strength to meet the challenge of the Deathwolves. Without pause, without mercy, Harald cut through the daemons and reached the wall of Predomitus.

He did not lead the charge through the gates. Instead, he turned right along the ramparts, then turned again to smash back down through the horde. At his back, he felt the blasting wind of two gunships. They made low passes before the gates, hammering the ground with heavy bolters and lascannons. The gap in the wall became an inferno. Harald looked back to see volcanic destruction, the earth and bodies heaving skyward. Daemons burned as they flew. The horde within the city could not break out. The other Stormwolves flew in from the rear of the lines to meet the advancing cavalry, scything a swath of annihilation as they came.

A daemon leapt high over Icetooth's jaws. It came down directly at Harald, its sword descending to cut his head in two. He brought up the shield and smashed it aside. He finished it off with a bolt shell to the skull. Icetooth seized another abomination by the neck and bit through with a single clamp of his jaws.

Harald seized the moment to look left. In the wake of the cavalry charge, the infantry was advancing, the speed more deliberate but the destruction no less total. The Grey Hunters were still moving towards the gates, cutting an even wider swath. Harald heard their massed war shouts over the cries of the daemons.

Behind the gunships and infantry came the tanks. Predators, Vindicators and Land Raiders in tight formation became a giant grinder, an unstoppable mass of metal and cannon fire. Icetooth ran towards the explosions. Purifying flame pushed back the wyrd-light.

'Riding close!' Canis yelled, coherent again, his voice still guttural. He impaled a swordling through the throat and hurled the creature away to the right, into the blades of its kin. 'Straight to the blasts?' he asked.

Harald could almost believe Canis was ready to pursue the slaughter right into the tank fire.

'Not quite,' he said. But he grinned at his champion. 'Close though.'

He waited until the smoke was choking, shattered stone was raining down on the field, and the concussions were deafening then swerved off to the right, clearing the way for the tanks. The clanking, booming vehicles moved past the cavalry, rolling over the daemons that had been in pursuit.

Canis growled in disappointment. The field before the Thunderwolves was almost empty of daemons.

'We aren't done, brother,' Harald said. 'We're a long way from done.' He turned Icetooth back towards the wall, and they rode a short distance to the flank of the armour. They came around a hill of skulls, and fell upon another horde.

The abominations were in disarray. They could not mount a counter attack. Their numbers worked against them as they tried to respond to the sudden changes in the Deathwolves' vector of destruction. All the thousands in the plain became fodder for the claws of the Space Wolves. The daemons could not attack at once. They hindered each other's movements as Harald triggered conflicting currents of attack. In their rage and frustration, the creatures fell to fighting each other.

The cavalry charge was unrelenting. Hours into the battle, the Deathwolves raced with the same speed and fury as their initial assault. And when at last Harald called a halt, the nature of the plain had changed. The sky overhead remained a storm of dark, mad flame. Smoke rose from the hills of skulls, and blood pooled at their bases. But the cracked earth was barren. The enemy was gone.

Slaughter and victory. So often, they were the same thing. On this day they were. While the gunships continued to pound the gates of Predomitus, Harald regarded the dead land with satisfaction. This much of Nurades was purged.

Beside him, Canis said, 'A good start.' He was hungry for more.

We all are, Harald thought. His blood was up. The annihilation of the enemy in this first encounter, and the imperative to keep up the pressure pushed the concerns of the war's significance to the back of his mind. The plan of a foe was meaningless if the foe was exterminated. And Harald felt the strength of extermination in his hands. He was a predator unleashed, and there was prey on the other side of the walls.

'Yes,' he said to Canis. 'A good start to the hunt. Let us continue.'

The battle for Predomitus took days. Days of unending massacre. In the stages of the purging, the Deathwolves broke though a crush of daemons at the gates, then moved up the primary thoroughfares of the hive. The war was an interior one now. Only rarely did the company emerge into open air, though the pilots of the gunships kept as close to the position of their brothers as possible, strafing the exposed positions of the hive. They blew up towers where the concentration of daemons was so great that the buildings themselves had begun to distort, rockcrete walls turning into scaly flesh.

In the hive, the daemons answered the challenge of the Deathwolves.

They poured in from halls and chambers. They crashed through skylights and ventilation shafts. They erupted from the floors of the route. The Great Company cut them down. Harald kept up the speed of the attack, moving almost as quickly as the initial charge. There was no chance of surprise when the battle was continuous, as unbroken as the flow of a burning river of blood.

The Deathwolves moved fast, with the savagery of the beasts they rode. But Harald chose the path of their assault with care. Aboard the *Alpha Fang*, he had studied hololithic schematics of Nurades' hive cities. The frenzy of his hunt was tempered by strategy. He embraced the wolf. He fought as if he were one. *As if* he were one. There was a difference. Never to be forgotten.

Once the gate was taken, Harald began the second stage of the assault on Predomitus. He split his forces to take the cavalry and infantry down the narrower passages, while the tanks moved implacably down the main arteries. The smaller routes were large enough to permit rapid deployment, but not so wide the daemons could mass sufficient numbers together to slow the advance. The daemons took the bait, and Harald exterminated them.

'This is the long charge, brothers,' Harald voxed the Great Company as the Wolf Guard and Grey Hunters slaughtered daemons, rejoined the tanks on the great avenues, then split off to repeat the pattern. 'This is how we will take back Predomitus. Our victory rests on momentum and speed. Depend upon that.'

Canis tore a swordling in half then gestured at the vista of towering walls and branching avenues lying ahead. 'This is a vast hunt,' he said.

Harald switched to a private channel. 'We do not seek a complete purge,' he said. That would be impossible. 'It will be enough to break the daemons' grip.' He pointed up and to the left, where the upper storeys of a spire flashed with lasbeam fire. 'Nurades still has uncorrupted defence forces. We will give them the means to mount their war of reclamation, then move to the next target.' He thought the prospect of an unending, savage advance would please Canis.

He was right. The champion howled as he and Fangir hurled themselves at the next group of daemons.

The course of the war took the Deathwolves deep into the underhive. There the concentration of daemons was immense. And in the Industrium Sub-terranal, the abominations mounted a challenge to Harald's advance.

The Industrium was a tangle of passages. Machinery was piled upon machinery in a gloom lit by fiery outgassing, and centuries of construction and decay had created jumbled layers of manufactoria. The millions of serfs who worked the Industrium were gone, transformed or dead. Many regions of the steel maze were ruins, and the dead metal was changing into hungry flesh. But much of the machinery was still active, gears turning, jaws grinding ore, forges pouring out molten metal with the mindless persistence of titanic servitors. The passages here were short, broken, unpredictable. Machinic walls rumbled towards each other, then parted. Angles were sharp, and speed was dangerous, difficult, and still necessary. And here, there were other daemons.

Until now, the Deathwolves had fought only Khornate abominations, howling embodiments of rage. In the Industrium, they encountered daemons of Tzeentch. Instead of roars, mad laughter echoed down the passageways. Voices intoned sentences that hovered on the edge of human meaning. The words scratched at the back of Harald's eyes.

'Silence the tongues of the wyrd!' he yelled, his voice ringing off the iron walls. The lead Thunderwolves trampled the daemonic, misshapen horrors of glistening pink muscle. They came apart beneath claws and chainswords. Flesh parted, darkened to the blue of contusions and reformed. The daemons multiplied in their destruction, but were hammered into oblivion by the bolter fire of the Grey Hunters.

Sudden, inhuman shrieks split the air apart. Airborne daemons, things that were little more than wings and horns and whiplash tails, came screaming around the sharp turns, and flew out from between dark crevasses in the machinery. They were mindless but agile. They fell upon the Deathwolves, lunging in with their horns or slashing past with their spiked tails. They came from all directions, attacked and flew off, then came back.

Harald trusted to the predatory instincts of Icetooth to deal with the daemons that scampered forwards on the floor of the Industrium. He kept his focus on the air, drilling bolt shells into the screaming daemons that swooped his way, raising Glacius to cleave their undersides open if they got by his barrage.

The struggle was composed of moments as disjointed as the space of the Industrium. A war of reckless speed. The pistoning, clanking, smoke-spewing masses of machinery rising hundreds of metres on either side. The ceiling just above Harald's head one moment, invisible in the dark heights the next. No way to prepare for each jagged intersection – nothing for it but to race deep into the whirring saw blades of war. The Deathwolves and the screamers streaking past and through each other, ichor and blood a thick spray in the gloom. The shrieks of the abominations entwined with chants and laughter. The howls of the thunderwolves and snarls of their riders cut though the foul braiding of Chaos with the purity of savagery. War turned into a blur of slashing lethality.

In the depths of the Industrium's maze, Harald became aware of a stronger presence. The attacks of the screamers were too precise for mindless daemons. They were directed by a powerful will. Its whisper travelled through the clamour of battle, slithering worm-like through the interstices of cackle and growl and roar. It spoke to the Deathwolves. It would not be ignored.

Another attack, more insidious, more dangerous.

Slithertwyst welcomes you. Slithertwyst has been waiting. You have been long in coming. Will you make the path interesting? Chains and ropes, manacles and webs, such rattling and struggling and twisting and twisting and twisting. Do you see? You do not see. Hurry, playthings. Hurry and see.

Hissing with secrets, dark with knowledge.

'Shut out the lies!' Harald called to his riders.

But in his heart, he dreaded that somewhere in the daemon's blandishments was a truth more corrosive than any lie.

Shut out Slithertwyst? Silence Slithertwyst? Will you silence fate? Will you shut out your days and ways to come?

On the right, dying metal shrieked. A chain of collapses smothered explosions and a stream of incandescent gas flashed overhead. Harald hunched beneath it. On instinct he turned towards the falling wall. Millions of tonnes of metal toppled towards the Deathwolves. Disintegrating machinery threw out spinning shrapnel. The collapse stretched ahead and behind the cavalry. There was no evading the avalanche – Harald raced towards the certainty of crushing oblivion and it parted before him, a conglomeration with the mass of a hundred Stormwolves tearing to either side like a shredded curtain.

Harald and Canis rode head-on at the daemon that whispered in their souls. Slithertwyst stood astride a screamer. The herald of Tzeentch was a being of limbs and horns and teeth, a huge pink abomination draped in robes of shifting, oily blue. Things sprouted from its body that changed from tentacles to horns from moment to moment. It raised a twisted blade, laughing and whispering at the same time, three more arms spreading wide in welcome to the Space Wolves.

Harald urged Icetooth into a leap. The thunderwolf sailed upwards and came down on the head of the winged daemon, slamming it to the ground. The herald leapt from its wounded steed and flailed at Harald's storm shield with claws and tentacles. The power of the wyrd was in its strength. It hit with serpentine speed and the force of a battering ram, forcing Harald and Icetooth back. The other daemon rose to the aid of its master, and Canis and Fangir fell upon it. Canis slashed the winged monster with his wolf claws, his attack as ferocious as Fangir's, while Harald blocked Slithertwyst's blade thrust with Glacius and fired a sustained volley with his bolt pistol into the daemon's face.

The mass-reactive shells exploded inside its skull. The herald was not a thing of true flesh, but here on Nurades it had a physical reality, and the blasts blew its head into two halves. They hung, deflated sacks of flesh, to either side of the body. The claws scrabbled blindly for Harald, and Icetooth snarled in pain and rage as they dug furrows into his hide. The thunderwolf leapt again, away from the screamer as Slithertwyst's shredded body crashed into the wreckage of burning machinery. The cavalry attacked the thrashing daemon with chainswords and bolt pistols, shattering its body even further. Eldritch flame erupted from where Slithertwyst had fallen. There was a sudden blast, and a foul wind, strong as a hurricane howled through the ruins to batter the Deathwolves.

As they rode through the collapse to the next open passage, Canis said, 'Easy prey.'

The champion was right. They had hit Slithertwyst hard, but Harald had not expected the battle to be so brief.

'Too easy, do you think?' he asked.

'No,' Canis grinned. 'Just poor prey. At least they are many.'

Harald glanced back. The glow of the daemonic fire was fading, the wind dropping. He saw no hint of a resurrection. The whispers had stopped. But for a moment, in the curls of the wind, he thought he heard serpentine laughter.

Canis was satisfied to view the daemons as outmatched, but Harald was not. 'Yet the wyrd is strong on this world,' he said.

Canis didn't answer. He was riding towards his next kill, shouting with feral eagerness.

Doubt gnawed at the edges of Harald's war lust. *There is something I am not seeing.*

Ahead, a swarm of the pink daemons squeezed through a narrow passage. There was no time to contemplate the nature of the herald's demise. The slaughter called, and could not be ignored.

Onwards, then, and onwards, the Deathwolves forever charging, forever cutting through daemonic bodies, ending laughter and chants, purifying every corner they passed in the Industrium's maze.

Taking back Predomitus.

At last, the Deathwolves came through the hive. Their assault, a single run lasting many days, left behind a swath of scoured ruins. The war for the hive was not over, but the balance had tipped towards the mortal defenders. The abomination and the heretic were being burned from Predomitus, and the work would go on until none remained, even if every spire of the city was toppled in the process.

The tide had turned. Harald's cavalry, joined by the heavy armour and the gunships, moved on. Before them, the land between Predomitus and Genos seethed with daemons. They came down from the higher ground, a frothing wave of monstrosity.

'All kinds of filth,' said Canis.

Harald nodded. The alliance of daemons had been hidden by the initial encounter with the swordlings. The presence of the Tzeentchian daemons in the Industrium Sub-terranal had been an ill omen. Now it was confirmed. Wrath and change and plague and excess rampaged over the tortured earth of Nurades. All the shades of the Ruinous Powers were united. 'This does not happen without great cause,' Harald said.

'They want this world badly,' Canis said.

'Do they?' Harald wondered. He thought about the relative ease of Slithertwyst's defeat again. He shook off the speculation. Whatever the purpose of Chaos, the Space Wolves were here to end it.

Though he and his brothers had just come through an exhausting campaign, he rose on Icetooth's back as if fresh to the battlefield, Glacius held high.

'Brothers!' he called. 'Let us hunt again!'

The Emperor's predators tore over the land to slake their thirst for war.

Weeks, then. After Predomitus, weeks of battle across the length of the Lacertus Peninsula. Always forwards, never retreating, cutting through daemons, and pushing them towards the sea, taking back the world they had stolen. The grind of battle in the hive now expanded to an entire region, with kilometres gained each day, but so many more to go, and an entire world infested.

Harald did not look towards an end of the campaign. He concerned himself with the victory of the moment, and of the steps necessary to reach the end. In seeking to counter his strategy, the daemons aided him. They brought more and more of their forces to bear against the Deathwolves, and so they hurried their extermination.

Forty days after the siege of Predomitus, the Deathwolves crested a ridge and caught their first glimpse of the sea, still hundreds of kilometres away. Below, the land dropped away gradually into an arid, rolling plain. It was a cauldron of daemons. Harald paused. He looked upon a heaving mass of beings, a nightmare drawn for the darkest sagas.

'A fine hunt,' Canis said. His face and beard were matted with ichor, and his armour was scored with burns and the marks of otherworldly blades. 'Glorious.' He looked towards the daemonic legions, his hunger for battle as strong as ever.

'Can a hunt be too glorious?' Harald said.

Canis turned to him in disbelief. After a long moment, he laughed, as if deciding Harald was joking. 'Never,' Canis said.

At the moment the champion's laughter ended, Harald thought he heard the echo of another, sibilant voice. Harald glanced around. Slithertwyst's final mockery haunted him.

Every day of the campaign, he watched for the daemon's return. In the corner of his left eye, he saw a dark pink movement. He looked. There was nothing there.

'What did you hear?' Canis asked.

'I thought I heard the daemon who taunted us in Predomitus.'

Canis looked puzzled once more. 'That cannot be. We banished it. Tore it apart.'

Yet it laughed. 'And why Nurades?' he said, finally asking the question out loud. 'What is the meaning of this incursion?'

'Its meaning?' Canis said. 'What does it matter? The daemons' purpose dies with them.'

Does it? It must.

Yet it laughed.

He shook his head. 'You're right, Wolfborn,' he said, trying to convince himself. 'Deathwolves!' he voxed to the company. 'We push to the sea! Leave only death in our wake!'

They poured down the slope. A storm of claws and guns descended on the daemons.

Harald was unable to savour the taste of the victories as they came. The questions gave him no peace. Even in the thick of battle, as he roared and slew, they lingered, as insistent as they were half-formed.

Onward. Forwards. Weeks of war. Weeks of slaughter. The beasts forever unleashed, claws and fangs ripping the unholy foe apart. The infinity of the enemy merely an infinity of prey.

Canis exulted.

Harald doubted.

On and on. Endless.

Until there was an end.

The Lacertus Peninsula came to an abrupt halt. The restless sea hurled itself against sheer basalt cliffs hundreds of metres high. Caught in the tormented energy of the warpstorm, the waves rose to half that height, battering the cliffs with such force the spray drenched the land above. The wind howled with voices. It raged against the Space Wolves as they cornered the daemonic hordes. The abominations of the Ruinous Powers shrieked and gibbered, their voices entwining with the wind and waves.

They fought in vain. The true tempest came from Fenris.

Harald turned his doubts into rage as he and his brothers crashed into the final hordes. On all sides, the Deathwolves howled with triumph. After weeks of incessant battle, they attacked as if fresh to the battlefield. Their prey had nowhere to turn. They tore into the daemons with furious joy. Ichor and spray drenched Harald as he and Icetooth savaged them, and Glacius seemed to sing in his hand. He barely felt the impact of his blows. He cut through skulls and chopped torsos in half. He crushed spines with his storm shield. He fired into explosions of disintegrating wyrdflesh.

Canis laughed with merciless ferocity. Harald joined him. So did the entire cavalry, and then the infantry. The cliffs resounded with the terrible laughter of alpha predators.

Harald and Icetooth plunged forwards, and forwards again, until there was no forwards any longer.

The shattered daemon army plunged over the edge of the cliffs. Monstrous forms struggled through the air. Waves like mountains rose to swallow them, Nurades in its anger taking its tormentors into the violent depths of the sea.

The Deathwolves' laughter rode the thunder of the surf.

Lord Governor Elsener met with Harald Deathwolf and Canis Wolfborn in one of the defence spires of Hive Genos. Elsener's quarters had been destroyed early in the incursion. He had barely escaped the tower's fall. None of the astropaths lower down had been as fortunate. Their cry for help had been their last act, and it had opened them fatally to the power of the warp. Elsener had witnessed their daemonic transformation. He had witnessed much since the start of the war. He had seen thousands of hive militia and all but a handful of his Tempestus honour guard give their lives in the defence of a chapel redoubt in the centre of the hive. He caught sight of his reflection in a glassteel window as he approached the chamber. What he had seen was branded on his face. His eyes were sunken and his skin was grey and lined with the deep scars of a soul's trauma. He saw the face of a man who would not live long past the end of the war.

The Emperor grant I see the liberation of Nurades, he thought.

He entered the room, leaning on a rough cane he had fashioned from the shaft of an ornamental pike. The chamber was a turret emplacement midway up the tower. It was large enough to serve as a command centre, and it was intact. Heavy bolters stood in the vaulted apertures facing north, south, east and west. They guarded the approaches over the rooftops of the lower hab complexes. Or the ruins of those complexes. Much of Genos was a smouldering ruin. But it had been cleansed.

The sky was dark with the smoke from the fires. It was free of the lunatic brilliance of the warp storm. As the war swept upwards from the Lacertus Peninsula on the inhabited northern land mass of Nurades, the strength of the storm faded. It had been many days now since Genos and Predomitus had been free of the terrors of that light and its rains.

Waiting for the lord governor was the liberation of Nurades. Elsener's breath caught. Two colossal warriors faced him. Their armour carried the stench of war. There was the acrid sting of fyceline, and the disturbing trace of slaughtered abominations in the streaks of ichor. And the aura of dangerous animals. They were human, yet their features were so rough-hewn, their hair so wild, that Elsener felt he had stepped into the presence of massive beasts.

He feared them almost as much as the things he had been fighting for weeks.

Elsener bowed, eyes averted. 'My lords,' he said. 'Nurades thanks you for the salvation you bring.'

Deathwolf grunted. 'Your survival does you credit, Lord Elsener.' He turned to the hololith table that had been brought to the chamber. 'We have some questions for you.' The table displayed a map of Nurades' polar regions. 'The war grows fiercer the further north we go,' Deathwolf said.

With an effort, Elsener forced himself not to imagine a plague of horrors even worse than that which had attacked Genos.

'The abominations are more numerous, and more resolved to prevent our advance,' Deathwolf continued. He tapped the map where runes indicated some form of complex. 'What is this? I have found no records about it.'

'Borassus,' Elsener said. He swallowed and leaned more heavily on his cane. 'We expunged the records, but we have yet to erase its memory from our culture. It is a fortification. It is cursed.'

Wolfborn snorted. 'What on Nurades is not?'

'Borassus has been a place of shadows for centuries. It has been shunned since long before the warp storm came.'

'So it will be all the worse now, you believe,' Deathwolf said.

'How can it not be?'

Deathwolf nodded. 'We take note of your warning. No son of Fenris takes the word *curse* lightly. So Borassus is where we must go. If the Ruinous Powers seek to prevent us from reaching it, its importance is clear.' He spread his hand over the polar regions. 'There are no settlements for over a thousand kilometres in any direction. No prey for the daemons. Borassus is their anchor point on this continent. From what you say, it may also be a gateway for them. We shall take it, and cleanse this world.'

The skies were clear over Borassus as the Stormwolves arrived. There was no smog of heavy industry in this empty region, a land of barren rock and deep cold. Nor were there the unholy flames of the warp storm. Even as the Deathwolves had prepared their assault on the fortifications, the convulsion around Nurades had subsided. The storm had passed. The materium was reasserting itself. The night of the Nurades' pole was a clean black and the stars were jagged silver. Twice the size of Luna, Nurades' moon cast a light heavy with silence over Borassus.

A hundred kilometres to the south, the heavy armour of the Deathwolves battled a massive surge of daemons in the mountain pass that was the primary access point to the Borassus region across land. With the attention of the forces of Chaos drawn to that struggle, Harald ordered an air insertion into the target zone. Now the Space Wolves came in waves of gunships, disembarking on a wide plain before the main gate of the fortifications.

As his cavalry and infantry assembled, Harald eyed the battlements, outlined in black by the vast sphere of the moon. The complex of bunkers, towers and ramparts made him think of broken tusks and fangs. Borassus hulked, quiet and black, waiting. The main gate was a ruin. The way in was clear. He saw no movement.

Standing beside him, Canis said, 'This place is not dead.' His fangs were bared. Icetooth and Fangir growled. Their hackles were raised.

'It waits for us,' Harald agreed.

The cavalry of the Deathwolves advanced with caution. Harald could not lead a charge with no enemy in sight.

The Space Wolves passed through the ruined gate. Beyond was a large staging ground. Some of the barracks surrounding it had fallen in on themselves. Rockcrete walls had tumbled as if smashed by a huge fist. Bunkers were squat shapes, at regular intervals in the space between the walls and the great hulk of the central keep. Cold light and deep shadow washed over them. Their doorways and turret apertures gaped, idiot mouths and blind glares. Harald sent squads ahead to check the nearest buildings. They found only darkness inside.

The Deathwolves moved deeper into Borassus. Wind whispered over the ground, cold with loss. The tread of thunderwolf paws and ceramite boots echoed against the walls, and desolation embraced the company.

The door to the keep had fallen too. Harald slowed when he saw the entrance was blocked with rubble. The interior of the keep appeared to have collapsed. He scanned the upper levels of squat towers. Rows of apertures stared back at him; more dark, empty eyes.

The eyes blinked and snarling light burst from them. It lit the ramparts of the keep. On the roofs of the bunkers, as if a concealing curtain had been ripped away, flame daemons of Tzeentch now whirled their mad dance and hurled daemonic fire at the company. *They've been there all along*, Harald realised. Some great sorcery had kept them hidden.

The blasts hit everywhere across the Deathwolves' formation. A fireball of coruscating blue streaked past Harald's shoulder. It hit Aluar, enveloping the Grey Hunter. Power armour, flesh, bone and muscle mutated and fused with such explosive energy that he passed from a thing of bleeding angles and howling mouths to ash in a fraction of a second.

On all sides, reality cracked. An army appeared in mid-charge, tearing through the brittle veil of the real. The staging ground was empty and then it was full. A stampede of juggernauts barrelled into the Deathwolves' flanks. They were massive beasts of crimson hide and crimson armour with horns that were as long as their jaws. Some horns were spikes, while some were in the shape of serrated axe blades, and behind each was the force of a speeding tank. They pierced ceramite. They chopped through ribs. They impaled thunderwolves through the throat.

Riding high on their monstrous steeds, Khornate swordlings swung their blades down onto damaged armour. They exulted with each skull they severed, holding high their crimson offerings to Khorne.

Slower and more numerous than the behemoth cavalry, thousands of daemons of Nurgle closed in. They were a sea of droning, chanting pestilence. Weeping sores covered their bodies and maggots dropped, squirming, from their blades. They came to smother the Deathwolves in the embrace of the grandfather of disease.

'Form up!' Harald voxed. 'Push them back!' Icetooth and Fangir lunged towards the stampeding Khornate daemons.

'Cowards, depending on surprise,' Canis snarled.

It worked, Harald thought. 'Then we'll render their tactic futile,' he vowed. The trap had been sprung. He would take the Deathwolves out of it now. The beast in his heart swore this, though the cold tactician reckoned the odds and knew how this night would end.

The scarlet behemoths attacked the Space Wolves flanks. There was no way forward. The ruined keep was a cliff wall. The only chance was to break the brunt of the assault and reclaim mobility.

'We must push to the rear,' Harald said to Canis. He poured bolt shells into the skull of a leviathan until its head burst. It fell heavily, carving a furrow in the stony ground, rolling over and crushing its rider.

'A retreat?' Canis asked. Fangir dodged a charge and dug his claws into the monster's scales. Canis decapitated the swordling with a swipe of his right hand and impaled the behemoth's neck with the wolf claws on his left.

'A manoeuvre,' Harald said. 'With a change of prey.'

'Brothers!' he shouted into the vox. 'Rend the daemons of plague apart!' He began to turn Icetooth around. A juggernaut launched itself at the thunderwolf. Icetooth twisted around, brought his head down and latched his jaws onto the beast's throat. He bit with steel-crunching force. Daemonic ichor poured to the ground as the juggernaut bellowed and tried to shake free. Harald batted aside the sword daemon's weapon with his bolt pistol and slammed Glacius into the abomination's midsection, cutting it in half. It dissolved into steaming, scarlet foulness. Icetooth tightened his grip on the juggernaut. His claws smashed through its armour. Harald turned his axe at the exposed flesh, hacking deep into the body of the monster. It reared backwards with a strength born of its impending doom. Icetooth rose on his hindquarters with it. The juggernaut tried to roll over and crush its tormentors, but it was evenly matched with the thunderwolf. As if he was as furious with the ambush as his master, Icetooth refused to release his prey. The juggernaut fell back on all fours and Icetooth tore its throat out. It slumped down, and Harald cut off its head.

The huge daemon's body collapsed in on itself. Its scales rusted, then flaked to dust, and its flesh melted into a foul muck. As its mass disappeared, Harald had the room to manoeuvre. Beside him, Canis and Fangir finished the other behemoth. Fangir clawed all the way through the flank, loosing a flood of snapping, shrieking, burning viscera. Canis cut deeper with his own blades until he severed the skull. The daemon's roar of pain and rage choked off and the monster vanished in an explosion of ichor. Moving to the left and right flanks, Wolf Lord and champion barrelled down the line of the Deathwolves, adding their might to that of each brother locked in a struggle, blunting the assault of the daemon cavalry.

'Back to the walls! Back to the plain!' Harald ordered. 'There we will run the abominations down!'

The Great Company changed its direction. The Deathwolves fought through the jaws and crush of the Khornate monsters. They fought through the barrage of warp flame that fell in their midst, destroying their brothers through lethal metamorphosis. And they moved against the plaguebearers.

Overhead, the Stormwolves strafed the ramparts with helfrost and las. Stormfang gunships punished the daemons on the ground. Great beams created swaths of absolute zero temperatures. Some of the daemons caught in the fire managed to move, their unnatural being performing the impossible, yet they crumbled apart as they advanced, reduced to dust before they could be free.

The Tzeetchian flame daemons retaliated in force. Across the fortifications, half of them redirected their fire at the gunships and assault craft. Warpfire engulfed engines. It turned wings into fangs. Before Harald could reach the rear lines, multiple volleys of the unholy flame gripped the fuselage of a Stormfang, transforming it into something scaled and flexible. Engines screamed and the gunship whirled. Its sudden flesh changed again. It became glass. The forces of its violent movement shattered it. Ship and crew vanished in an explosion that lit the dark with light natural and unnatural.

Harald and Canis rejoined each other as the Deathwolves struck hard against the plague daemons. The abominations at the front disappeared in mid chant, annihilated by the massed rage of the Space Wolves. The cold polar air became dank and humid with rot. Even as they disintegrated, the daemons fought back, releasing a wall of noxious vapour ahead of them.

The Deathwolves advanced into the sea of disease. Though the behemoths continued their attack, they had lost the advantage of speed. They were bogged down as they waded through the plague daemons. The Great Company drew closer to the gate, and the freedom of movement beyond.

Warpflame surrounded the Stormwolf *Guard of Frostheim*. A score of flame daemons hit it at the same time. Its frame subjected itself to conflicting forces of such power it froze in mid-flight. Madness held it suspended over the gateway. It bulged and contracted. It writhed. Eyes tore open and bled along the fuselage. The underbelly split wide. Its teeth gnashed, and then it screamed.

'*Back!*' Harald roared.

The company's movement stalled. A mass so great could not reverse course that suddenly. The Space Wolves reacted with perfect discipline, yet for fateful seconds they neither advanced nor retreated.

Guard of Frostheim fell. A combusting assemblage of metal and flesh crashed into the ground before the gate. The incinerating blast washed over the Deathwolves. There could be no turning for Harald, and he leaned into the explosion, fastening his grip on his mantle as Icetooth crouched low, howling at the destruction. The cowling of an engine cart-wheeled over Harald's head. It came down in the Grey Hunters behind him, both blade and meteor. A wind of ignited plasma and burning immaterium raged around him. It sought to devour him. It failed, repelled by his cloak. Made from the hide of the ice troll king he had slain, it defied all flame.

The sound of the explosion was so huge that it drowned out the cries of the dying, yet Harald knew his brothers were being consumed. He could feel the loss in his soul. In grief and rage, he rose before the gale of *Guard of Frostheim*'s death had fully abated. Icetooth's hide smouldered. Patches of fur and flesh had been burned down to muscle. Matching his rider's fury, he answered Harald's command and lunged upward.

'With me, brothers!' Harald voxed. 'Gather and face the foe together. Let the abominations break against the rock of our strength! Cavalry, pre-pare to rush the enemy towards the keep! Infantry, break with us and scale the walls.'

The gate was rubble. There was no egress from Borassus. Scores of dae-mons had vanished in the crash, for all the difference that made. The tide of plaguebearers still ran high.

The beast in Harald could not silence the tactician. The breakout attempt had failed. The last chance to escape the trap had fallen with *Guard of Frost-heim*. One last charge, then. One last bellow of rage against the enemy. If the cavalry drew the greater part of the daemons away from his brothers on foot, perhaps the Deathwolf infantry would survive to rejoin the heavy armour to the south. If the saga of the company's thunderwolves ended here, let it be a fitting conclusion, a song echoing with the death of count-less unholy foes.

Sensing vulnerability, the daemon horde redoubled its attack. The roar-ing beasts shook the ground in their raging hunger. A clamour of tolling bells urged the plague daemons on. Blades of disease and blades of wrath hacked at the Space Wolves. Harald's warriors gathered around him form-ing a wall of snarling beasts and ceramite-clad giants. The constant barrage of warpflame struck more down with every second. The daemons of Khorne and Nurgle pressed in, the closing of a vice.

Canis Wolfborn had come through the explosion with his face a single massive burn. His armour was scorched black. His eyes shone with proud anger. 'Predators to the last,' he said to Harald.

Harald nodded. Canis was ready for the inevitable, eager for the kills he would yet be granted this night. This was good, it was right. Harald raised Glacius in his last defiance.

'For Russ!' he called.

'For the Wolftime!' the company answered.

For us, it has come, Harald thought.

He felt the hair on his arms rise. He was surrounded by foulness that would drive mortals insane, but something else in the night made him react as if to an unknown threat.

A flicker rippled over the daemons. It looked like uncertainty.

Shadows streaked across the rooftops before huge silhouettes struck the flame daemons and tore them apart. The warpfire barrage came to a sudden end. In its wake came a deluge from the air. It was ichor. So many daemons were destroyed in a matter of seconds that their end was a rain upon the battlefield. Harald blinked. The shapes were monstrous, but not as strange as they should be. He heard growls, deep and ferocious, and his blood stirred with recognition.

His olfactory senses responded to the scent of kinship.

'Brothers...' Canis said with stunned awe.

'How?' said Harald. This isn't possible, he thought. The shapes were too big. Too misshapen.

And yet...

He would wonder later. On every roof of Borassus, the daemons were being exterminated.

Harald signalled the charge, and already it was no longer desperate. The Deathwolves howled their challenge as they attacked.

The figures on the roofs howled back.

No, Harald thought again. He cracked the skull of a behemoth wide open, stitched a swordling from head to belly with bolt shells, and again he thought *no*, torn by hope and unease before the impossible.

Now the ramparts of Borassus were free of daemons. The figures that could not be familiar leapt to the ground. They attacked the rear ranks of the daemons, butchering their way towards the Deathwolves. They used no firearms. Some had punch-daggers. They attacked with the pure savagery of the animal, shredding the enemy with their hands. Their clawed hands.

A greater monstrosity overwhelmed the daemons. The Deathwolves fought with the boiling rage of near defeat. Their every howl was answered by the giants approaching them. Now the momentum was with the thunderwolves. Now it was the daemons who were surrounded.

Now it was the daemons who were doomed.

The end was inevitable. It came quickly. And when the last daemonic remains were dissolving in their foulness, Harald faced the creatures who could not be there.

The heavy moonlight reigned over Borassus again. Its quiet was broken by the predatory breathing of giants.

The monsters were hunched as if ready to spring. They did not. They held back – for the moment.

Canis was growling in unison with the thunderwolves.

Harald looked at him. 'You called them brothers,' he said.

Canis nodded, shook his head. He grimaced in confusion. 'They are, but... their scent is strange. It is *old*.' His fists opened and closed. He was caught between the signals of kin and threat. He was on the threshold of attacking.

'Hold fast, brother,' Harald said. His weapons held low but at the ready, he advanced towards the creatures who had saved his warriors. With every detail he took in, the vertigo of unreality grew stronger. They were huge. Very tall and massively broad, they dwarfed Harald. They were beasts.

They were wolves.

They hunched forwards as if running on all fours came naturally to them, and indeed their arms were long. Their faces too were elongated and hirsute. Their fangs were huge, and their maws so lupine Harald wondered if they could speak. There were still aspects of the human in the monsters though; he saw in those faces the thing he had tried to deny but could no longer. He saw the familiar. He saw *kinship*. He smelled it too, beneath the tang of combat stimulants and thick bestial musk.

The wolves wore armour. How did the firmament not crack wide open to see such armour in this place and in this time? It was battered, patchwork, barely held together by rough welds, damaged almost beyond recognition. Almost. It was a faded slate grey, the colour of ancient history. The insignia were visible, though close to vanishing beneath battle scars. They were Fenrisian. They were known to Harald. They were known to every Space Wolf. Their memory had been faithfully preserved.

They had not been seen for ten thousand years.

'This cannot be!' a Wolf Guard shouted. For a moment, Harald thought the words were in his head.

No, he thought. This cannot be.

The 13th Great Company. Lost to the warp in pursuit of Magnus after the fall of Prospero.

The immense warriors grouped around the largest of them all. The night rumbled with low, wary growls. Harald maglocked his weapons. He held his hands open and away from his sides. He approached the alpha. The great beast watched him with amber eyes. He was so huge that his moon-cast shadow swallowed the Deathwolf.

Harald held the gaze of those eyes, even as he had to crane his head back. I do not come to attack, he thought, but I do come to command. He knew this was necessary. Yet he was closing in on a myth. It was an effort to keep the awe he felt from his face.

He was only a few steps away now. He saw the beast's features in more detail. The traces of the human were clearer. The shape of the eyes, of the brows – more and more he saw the lineaments he knew in his brothers, and in his own reflection.

He accepted the truth of what he saw. The murmurs and warning growls of the Deathwolves behind him were an assurance he was not hallucinating.

Harald stopped before the alpha. He stood straight, his gaze unwavering. The great beast's chest expanded as it took a breath. The alpha rumbled.

Harald braced.

The beast lowered his head and dropped to one knee. So did all the others. The threat of the moment passed as they acknowledged a new alpha.

Though he dreaded what these revenants portended, Harald was mindful of the debt he owed them too. He placed his hand on the giant's shoulder and bid him rise.

'Who are you?' he asked.

The monster's jaw struggled to shape a name. 'Yngvir,' he said.

'Are you loyal to the primarch?' Harald asked.

'We... are... brother.' The rasp was entirely animal. Only the words were human. 'We... are... Wulfen.'

Why Nurades? Harald thought again. Now you know. He looked at the ranks of the Wulfen, and felt he was gazing into a future seized and made bloody by the jaws of the past.

CHAPTER 2

THE COUNCIL OF WOLVES

Dark Angels Company Master Araphil came to Borassus to hunt for truth. A war had come and gone, and it had left behind shadows. Summoned by Scouts, his company had pierced the warp storm and entered orbit over the polar circle of Nurades. At that moment, the world had still been overrun with daemons. By the time the landing was complete, the daemons were gone. How?

The marks of battle were everywhere amid the ruined fortifications. The struggle here had been ferocious. The buildings and the ground were scorched and blasted. The walls were pocked with the distinctive impact craters of bolter shells. Other Space Marines had been here. Who?

Until a few moments ago, the most urgent question had been where Sergeant Arhad and his Scouts had gone. They had vanished from all vox and auspex readings before Araphil's company had arrived at Nurades. Now Araphil had partial answers, although dark ones. The shadows were deep, but he would hunt out what they concealed.

He stood in a bunker, surrounded by the remains of the Scouts. The bunker had become an abattoir. The bodies were dismembered, heads torn in half. Viscera had been thrown against the walls and hung over the ledges of gun apertures. Even in the cold of this region of Nurades, the atmosphere of the chamber was clammy with the stench of blood. The Scouts' armour had long, parallel rents. The sign of claws.

Who has done this? That was the urgent question. The obvious answer was *daemons*. Araphil mistrusted it. For all the savagery, for all the butchery, the kills were too clean. Where were the signature desecrations of the Ruinous Powers? It was conceivable that the sheer brutality was a form of Khornate rage. Araphil was unsatisfied with that answer too. He sniffed. His neuroglottis detected the faint trace of animal musk beneath the overwhelming odours of vitae and of bodies turned inside out. Araphil could believe animals had been at work here but he could think of none native to Nurades capable of overcoming even a single Scout.

Outside the bunker, squads moved through the wreckage of Borassus, seeking truth and secrets. After he had been called here, he had commanded the scene be left to him alone. He wished to commune with the space and the dead on his own. He moved deeper into the bunker, taking in each corpse, recording each name with a prayer and a promise of vengeance, eyeing the wounds and the manner of death. He kept his emotions in check.

Observe. Judge later. Observe now. Let the shadows speak. Let the dead give their answers.

To his right, there was a mound of body parts. Were there three victims there, or five? Perhaps portions of more. Something inside the mound moved. The motion was slight, a weak spasm. It was enough to dislodge a hand. Araphil knelt. He cleared away the fragments of corpse until he found the whole body beneath. It was Brother Dolutas. He was difficult to recognise: his face had been clawed to the bone. His armour was peeled back over his ravaged chest and broken ribs. Araphil looked closely, and Dolutas took a breath. It was weak, shallow. It could have been a sigh before dying. Then it came again.

'You have been strong, brother,' Araphil said softly. 'Apothecary!' he voxed. To the Scout he said, 'Be content. We are here to give you strength now.'

A blinking light midway down Dolutas' right flank drew Araphil's gaze. A servo-skull lay there. Its lower half was smashed and its gravitic impellers were wrecked, but one eye blinked red, red, red. The memory light. The servo-skull had preserved a recording.

Red, red, red, the eye blinked.

Answers, answers, answers.

'There are other wyrdstorms,' Logan Grimnar announced. 'Storms with the same empiric signatures as the one over Nurades. The astropaths are emphatic. Some died as they confirmed the nature of the storms, and their flesh was marked by the same wyrdflame burns in each case. The storms are scattered, yet they are unmistakable.'

Silence fell over the Wolf Lords of Fenris as the implications of those words sank in. Around the periphery of the Hall of the Great Wolf, heroes of the Chapter stirred. Serfs froze, sensing a rise in tension. It was, Harald thought, as if a great wind were gusting through the Hall. The totems and pelts on the walls did not stir, but the thunderwolves crouched at their masters' feet raised their hackles. A raven took to the air above Ulrik the Slayer. Its caw echoed across the hall.

In the centre of the vast space was the Grand Annulus. Set into the floor were thirteen wedge-shaped stone slabs, each marked with the runes and insignia of a Great Company. The Wolf Lords stood upon the territorial markers of their authority. One of the slabs was obsidian. It bore no markings. It was the painful absence on the Annulus, the break in the circle. It was the place belonging to the lost 13th Company, and so it represented all the lost. Only now the lost had been found. Harald's gaze kept returning to it. So did the eyes of the other Wolf Lords.

Krom Dragongaze broke the silence, speaking the question on every mind. 'What do the storms portend?' he asked.

Grimnar turned to Ulrik the Slayer, standing at his side. He nodded. The Wolf Priest advanced to the centre of the Annulus.

'I have spoken with Yngvir,' he said with a voice ancient yet strong like grating stone. 'Though his speech is difficult, he was clear that there are more of his brothers coming. *On the wings of storm.* Those are his words.'

'And this return,' Dragongaze said before anyone else could respond, 'if these Wulfen are indeed the Thirteenth, why now? How has it happened? What does it mean?'

The Slayer waited several beats before answering. Now the silence in the Hall was total. 'The omen of the Wulfen is clear,' he said. 'If they have come back, can Russ be far behind?'

The Hall of the Great Wolf erupted.

'How can we be sure?' Gunnar Red Moon demanded. 'Where is the proof? How do we even know the Wulfen are what they claim to be?'

'Their existence speaks for them,' Sven Bloodhowl answered. 'As do their deeds. They saved Lord Deathwolf.' He looked at Harald. 'You who are brother to more wolves in your company than any of us must feel the truth of our kinship with the Thirteenth.'

Harold gave Bloodhowl a long look. The other Wolf Lord was much younger than he was. His hair and beard were a rich brown, and cut short. His symmetrical, rock-jawed features were indeed much further from the lupine than Harald's. He would feel the complexities and risks of the warrior's relationship with the beasts less acutely.

'We are kin to wolves,' Harald said. 'We are *as* wolves. We are not wolves. You can see what they have become.'

He kept his tone moderate, but his words enflamed tempers even more. The Wolf Lords moved towards the centre of the Annulus as they shouted at each other. Harald held back. He had expressed his doubts, said what he had to say. The monstrosity of the Wulfen gave him pause, and there were too many unanswered questions about what had happened on Nurades. He could not easily accept the Slayer's pronouncement, though he could not dismiss it either.

The other Wolf Lords were far more vehement.

'Lord Deathwolf is right!' Kjarl Grimblood said. 'Look what they have become! An omen indeed! A dark one!'

'How do we know they are really Wulfenkind?' said Egil Iron Wolf. 'Why not mutations? After so long in the warp, their Canis Helix could have suffered terrible damage.'

Erik Morkai snorted. 'Monsters or not, what does it matter? They fight well. They're good weapons.'

'Nothing more?' Bran Redmaw rounded on Morkai. 'Is that the depth of your thought and honour? And my war packs, are we the same to you? Savages to be used up as needed?'

'You hot-blooded fool, did I say that?'

'You as good as did,' Redmaw told Morkai. 'If that is all you can see in the Wulfen, you are more blind than I ever imagined!'

The voices rose in anger. Harald looked to the Slayer. The Wolf Priest was regarding him silently. Harald thought of the meeting in the vaults. That was the first omen. How did the Slayer interpret that night? How did he believe it linked to the return of the Wulfen? Harald was convinced the link was there. He could not divine its meaning, nor could he shake his unease.

'The Fell-Handed!' Krom was saying. He said it again, cutting through the shouts. 'We must consult Bjorn the Fell-Handed. He *knew* the Thirteenth. He was there before the company vanished.'

All eyes turned to Ulrik the Slayer. He shook his head. 'Bjorn will not awaken,' he said.

'Good omen or ill,' said Ragnar Blackmane, 'we must find the others.'

No one disagreed.

Grimnar strode forward. The Wolf Lords stood still. They waited for the Great Wolf to speak.

'Our task is clear,' he said. 'We will seek out and return our brothers to Fenris. Whether they are cursed, or whether their arrival means Russ will soon be at our side again,' he nodded once to Ulrik, 'we will know in the end. And know we must.'

Harald nodded at this.

'Brothers, make ready. We sail the Sea of Stars with the Wulfen to gather the Thirteenth Great Company!'

As the Wolf Lords left the Hall, Dragongaze drew Harald aside. 'You're worried,' he said.

'I believe the Slayer and I see very different omens in the Wulfen. He sees what we lost, and what we hope to have again.'

'And what do you see?'

'What we might become if we are not vigilant. I see what we might lose.'

'You think the Wulfen are harbingers of disaster?'

'I'm sure they are harbingers. I don't know of what. That is my concern.'

'Our meeting before the Murderfang...' Dragongaze began.

'Yes,' said Harald. 'I was thinking of that too. It is linked to Nurades. But how? What drew us there. Krom, a daemon laughed at us as we vanquished it.'

Dragongaze was silent for a moment. 'Yet you purged the daemons,' he said. 'You defeated the Ruinous Powers.'

'Even so, the daemon laughed.'

'Daemonic malice?' Dragongaze suggested. 'It sought to sow doubt.'

'Yes,' said Harald. He met Dragongaze's eyes squarely, and did not hide the depths of his concern. 'It succeeded.'

At war in the world beneath sleep, above death. The struggle eternal. Ten thousand years now, fighting from plane to plane, an unending march.

I tarry until you come again, father.

The loss of the body is no loss of self. The agility of youth forgotten in the great hulk that fights in the kingdom above sleep. But here, in the land between, there is speed again. The fury of spirit matched to the echo of form. The echo of a sarcophagus, a coffin of false death and infinite war.

All echoes here. Shadows of form and thought, cast by the weight of things in the other realm, the one above sleep. The roots run deep. The war runs deeper. So long without surcease, but what need for rest here, in the kingdom beneath?

None.

Only battle.

On the echo ramparts of the echo fortress, fighting an enemy who are not echoes, whose flesh is the stuff of echoes.

I must wake. I must speak to my brothers.

A flood of daemons, a sea lapping at the hexagrammic shadow.

There can be no waking yet. The sea is rising.

The daemons must be fought.

The prey tried to fight back. Lasgun fire struck the Wulfen. The beasts ran directly into the fire, roaring. They were twice the size of the puny human figures, and much faster. They ripped arms from torsos and heads from necks. Blood fountained across the scene of the massacre and paving stones shook under one monster's feet as he rushed an opponent. He wielded an immense frost axe. He sliced the body in half with a stroke so powerful the blade buried itself in the wall behind then freed it and held it aloft with both hands. The slaughter was complete. The Wulfen pack howled as one.

They looked up to the gallery where Logan Grimnar stood with the Iron Priest Hrothgar Swordfang. The Wulfen panted, their breath steaming, blood coating their muzzles and armour. They were surrounded by the torn flesh and scattered viscera of the training servitors. They were the image of mindless savagery.

The beasts lowered their heads and took a knee, bowing to the supreme alpha.

'Good,' Grimnar said.

That was enough. The Wulfen rose and loped from the training arena.

'Their new armour looks well,' Grimnar said to Swordfang.

'Thank you, Great Wolf,' the Iron Priest said. 'Their Mark II relics were beyond repair. We completed the Mark VIII size modifications four days ago. They were reluctant to part with their remnants, but they have adapted.'

'Has communication improved?'

Swordfang's servo-arms moved back and forth equivocally. 'A little,' he said. 'Serkir, the one with the frost axe, is interesting. He is volatile. He can be almost articulate in short bursts. At other times, language escapes him completely. He understands more than most of the others, I think.'

'A leader?'

'He is subordinate to Yngvir. He might do well with his own pack, though.'

Treaded servitors entered the arena from low access doors. Their arms had been replaced with floor-scraping blades. Blank-eyed, unemotional, they began the disposal of the bloody remains.

'The weapons the Wulfen were using,' Grimnar said. 'I saw no firearms.'

'No,' said Swordfang. 'They appear to have no aptitude or taste for them.'

'Those swords and axes, they look familiar. But I don't recognise them from our arsenals.' They were too huge. They were impractical for any warrior who wasn't as outsized as the Wulfen.

'They are from our walls, Great Wolf.'

Grimnar blinked, surprised, as he realised what Swordfang meant. Immense relic weapons had hung on the walls of the Fang for millennia. Grimnar had regarded them as he did the heroic tapestries. They were heraldry, ornamentation, ancient objects to be honoured.

'What inspired you to take them down?' he asked.

'Serkir seized the axe himself as we crossed a hall to the training grounds,' Swordfang said. 'He cut a statue in half with it. He seemed familiar with its balance. So did the other Wulfen when I ordered the gathering of other such weapons. They wield the weapons as if the blades were forged for this express purpose.'

'What are you suggesting? That they were already in their current form ten thousand years ago?'

'I do not think so. The remnants of the power armour they wore show signs of stress, suggesting they burst through it when they changed.'

Grimnar frowned. 'I do not understand.'

'Nor do I. Then there are the grenades. I instigated a full search for all relics scaled to the proportions of the Wulfen. We found many swords and axes. Enough for the entire company, should all the brothers be found. The grenades, however, are not just suited to the hands of the Wulfen. They are suited to their brains.'

'What do you mean?'

'I was not sure the Wulfen would be capable of using explosives. Firearms are too complex. Nevertheless, we included the grenades in the trials. We discovered they are not on timers.'

'Impact fuses?'

'No. An impulse trigger.'

'Those are very rare,' Grimnar said.

'These are rarer still. I attempted to operate one. I cannot. But the Wulfen can do so without difficulty. The triggers associated with these grenades are attuned to the specific neural patterns of the Wulfen.'

Grimnar digested this in silence for a long moment. 'What do you conclude?' he asked Swordfang.

'I cannot conclude anything,' Hrothgar answered. 'We are faced with two possibilities. Either the phenomenon of the Wulfen existed in our deep past, though there are no records or tales of their existence, in or out of the Thirteenth Company...'

'Or?'

'Or these weapons were forged in *anticipation* of the coming of the Wulfen.'

The thought stole Grimnar's breath. Had this moment been building for ten thousand years? 'They were foretold?' he asked.

'I know of no such prophecy.'

'Nor do I.' That did not mean none existed. So much had been forgotten over a hundred centuries. If in some way the Wulfen were not just returned but long awaited, then Ulrik the Slayer's interpretation of the omens must be correct.

Grimnar did not want to contemplate the implications if the Wolf Priest were wrong.

The launch bays of the Fang vibrated with the roar of gunship engines. Squad after squad embarked in the assault craft. The bays were open and the wind of Fenris shrieked inside, freezing the skin, biting deep, stirring the blood to the hunt and to war. The sky beyond was streaked by the contrails of the gunships that had already left, ascending to the strike cruisers waiting at low anchor. One Great Company after another departed Fenris to set sail on this most portentous of hunts.

All but the Tenth. The Drakeslayers would remain.

Krom Dragongaze stood on an observation platform above the bay, unblinking in the backwash of motors and the merciless fangs of the wind. He stared into the bay. He did not turn his head until, in the corner of his eye, he saw Grimnar approach. Then he faced the Great Wolf.

'The Fang is yours,' Grimnar said.

'While all the other Wolf Lords depart on this most vital of missions.'

'Fenris cannot be left undefended.'

Krom lowered his head in acknowledgement. There is no need for a Wolf Lord to remain as castellan, he thought. Or for an entire company to be sidelined.

As if reading his mind, Grimnar said, 'I gave this task to you and the Tenth for a reason.'

Krom waited, saying nothing.

'You were reckless on Alaric Prime,' Grimnar said.

So this is punishment for the Sanctus Reach, Krom thought.

'I need to know you will keep faith in your oaths,' said Grimnar.

Krom bristled. He struggled to remain silent. He succeeded. Just. Grimnar continued, 'There is no question of loyalty or ability. The issue is discipline.'

The urge to protest was strong. Krom's frustration was motivated by more than slighted honour. The meeting at the Murderfang's vault haunted him; the portents were multiplying. Though the Slayer's talk of Russ' return was compelling, it did not satisfy Krom. Harald's part in the unfolding saga was already fateful. Krom had no doubt that more was to come. He and the Slayer had yet to learn their roles. The Wolf Priest would find the thread of his destiny in the Sea of Stars while Krom would remain here and wait. There was something he must do. There was a reason he had been among the three to be led to that encounter. It must have something to do with the Wulfen. How could he do what fate required of him, whatever that was, if he was cantoned on Fenris?

No matter. There was no choice. The Great Wolf had spoken and Krom's path was clear. He quashed his protestations and nodded once, his face immobile as stone.

'I make my oath that Fenris will be secure,' he said. 'The Drakeslayers stand fast.' He was called to this task, and he would fulfil it. Glory was as nothing compared to an oath and redemption.

'I am pleased to hear it,' said Grimnar. 'A pack of the Wulfen will remain with you. Iron Priest Swordfang will continue his examination of them. There are many questions that need to be answered. We will not learn all of them on the Sea of Stars.'

Krom nodded once more. He wondered how he should interpret the news that not all the Wulfen would depart. He watched Grimnar walk away. A minute later the Great Wolf appeared in the bay below, surrounded by Ulrik the Slayer, the High Rune Priest Njal Stormcaller, and the champion Arjac Rockfist. The legends marched up the assault ramp into the Thunderhawk that would transport them to the battle-barge *Allfather's Honour*. The roar of the transport's engines built to deafening levels, then it shot out of the launch bay.

The fiery wind of its departure was the last one. Krom remained as he was, watching the final Stormwolves climb while the bay doors rumbled together, shutting out the gale of Fenris. Premonition crawled over his flesh. His hackles rose. When the doors clanged, the ring of iron against iron was the doleful slam of a sarcophagus lid.

He knew then that fate would still find him.

PART 2

THE HUNT

CHAPTER 3

WHITESTALKER

The mechanism had not moved in centuries. It was inert, an assemblage of cold shadow and utter immobility. Nonetheless, its daily care was observed as a duty sacred and vital. Armatures and spheres of brass and silver and gold gleamed in sepulchral perfection. Its gears were anointed with holy oil. In all the millennia of its existence, there had never been a single moment when it had been left unobserved.

On this day, the Speculum Infernus moved.

A data-servant called out in alarm at the first sight of action. A single cogwheel, a few centimetres across, stirred. Within seconds, its revolutions were a blur. Larger and larger nested wheels began to turn. From the eight corners of the great device, tall sceptres crackled with eldritch lightning. Inside the periphery, spheres rotated and travelled along complex, elliptical, intersecting revolutions. Fluted bronze pipes released scalding steam, giving voice to a hissing choir.

An alchemy of movement, an omen of metal.

On the north side of the Speculum, gargoyles of gold perched on a cluster of silver pedestals. Mechanical wings unfurled and jaws opened wide in expressions of blind hunger. Data-parchment streamed from between the fangs. The servants gathered the parchment, averting their gaze from its runes and sigils. The dooms inscribed thereon were not for them to understand.

This was a mercy.

In the Citadel of Titan, the Prognosticars of the Grey Knights gathered to read the dooms. The sanctified mechanism of the Speculum Infernus shook and scribed, steamed and prophesied. It told of warp storms. It revealed connections.

The Grey Knights beheld the terrible confluence of events. They were forming a single immense shape, its meaning as unspeakable as it was inescapable.

And then, even as the Great Companies of the Space Wolves spread out across the galaxy to gather their lost kin, the Brotherhoods of the Grey Knights departed Titan on quests just as grave and urgent. The Space Wolves travelled the lines of a pattern. The Grey Knights sought to arrest its manifestation.

Elsewhere, darkness laughed.

Fimnir. Spartha IV. Dragos.

The sites of the hunt. World after world engulfed by the sudden warp storms, their empyrean signatures so distinct and so identical that they seemed to be the flowerings of a single tempest.

Hades Reach. Atrapan.

The Great Companies fell upon worlds tortured by the revels of daemons. On every planet, billions of subjects of the Imperium had no hope until feral salvation dropped out of the skies, and rioting madness gave way to war.

Suldabrax. Emberghul.

Grimnar assigned strike force names to the companies. Sagablade. Whitestalker. Iron Hunt. Kingsguard. These were not individual crusades. They were the stepping stones of a single mission on a scale rarely mounted in the history of the Chapter. The struggle on each world was enough to inspire legends in the local cultures that would last until the Wolftime. The victories were the stuff of sagas on Fenris, but they were important only in the measure of the totality of the hunt's success. The Space Wolves came to find the Wulfen. The crushing of the Ruinous Powers was a means to an end.

The surviving populations who found themselves returned to the Emperor's Light were fortunate bystanders. Had the storms that blighted their planets been of a different nature, their help would have had to come from other sources, if it came at all.

On one world after another, the Space Wolves pushed back the armies of Chaos. The splintered 13th Great Company was gathered up. The Wulfen were transported to the rallying point in the Anvarheim system. Aboard the strike cruiser *Coldfang*, under the command of Battle Leader Hjalvard, the beasts were prepared to re-enter battle, integrated into the other Companies. The 13th, for now, could not function as a unified company.

News of each success reached the other companies quickly. The Wolf Lords learned of the growing numbers of Wulfen in the ranks of their brother commanders. The victories urged Wolf Lords to greater feats.

On the *Alpha Fang*, as Strike Force Whitestalker prepared for its campaign, Harald received the reports of the hunt. He watched the tally of Wulfen warriors climb, more of them all the time, their presence growing in the martial body of the Space Wolves.

His unease grew.

'We will find every Wulfen brother before any other Imperial force,' Grimnar had declared.

'This we swear,' all the Wolf Lords had answered.

If we succeed, Harald wondered, what then?

He did not speak the question aloud. He had taken his oath.

He came close to voicing the question once. During the *Alpha Fang*'s transit through the immaterium, he asked Canis, 'What do you make of the Wulfen?'

'Strong warriors,' said the Champion.

Canis was the most feral of the Deathwolves. He was perhaps the closest of Harald's brothers to the Wulfen. Harald wanted to know if Canis felt more distance or kinship to the monsters.

'Anything more?' he asked.

'The beast is strong in them.'

'Too strong?'

Canis did not answer right away, his heavy features deep in thought. That he had to think before answering, that he seemed uncertain, was disconcerting.

'They control their frenzy,' he said at last.

'Aye, they do,' Harald said.

The conversation went no further, then. But as Harald was heading to the bridge to make ready for the drop back into the materium, Vygar Helmfang caught up to him and raised the question himself.

'Lord Deathwolf,' said the Wolf Guard, 'I understand there is no question of the Wulfen's loyalty.' *For now*, hovered unspoken in the air between them. 'But their nature...' He groped for words. 'Their form and their actions do not always coincide.' Vygar grimaced, displeased with his own formulation.

Harald understood what he meant. Any brother he had known who had even come close to resembling the Wulfen's physical form had been completely consumed by battle frenzy. He could think of no case where a Space Wolf had been capable of anything approaching calm while in that state.

They control their frenzy. Canis' comment took on greater weight.

Vygar was one of the oldest of the Wolf Guard. In the field, he fought with tenacious ferocity. He was also one of the best strategists in the company. Centuries of battle had tempered him into a warrior who understood the value of forethought. His experience and his caution were the qualities Harald prized in his strike force. And Vygar's concerns were dovetailing with Harald's own.

'You believe their nature is much more complex than some might think,' Harald said.

'I believe we know very little about it, yet are acting as if we do.'

'We are being watchful, brother. All of us.' He had faith that this was so. Even Ulrik, in his enthusiasm, was vigilant. He clapped Vygar on the shoulder plate. 'We will be vigilant together.'

Vygar nodded that he had understood. Harald was agreeing with the need for great care.

* * *

And so the *Alpha Fang* came to Svardeghul, a world of ore, an industrial cinder transformed into a malignant tumour.

The strike cruiser and its escorts translated from the immaterium into the midst of the warp storm surrounding the world. The crews of the vessels were braced. Even so, the shock struck hard. The tempest shrieked through the wounds of reality. It strained the Geller fields to breaking point. Madness found its way through fissures in the defences. It shook the hulls and laughed down corridors. Two frigates were lost. One, the Gladius-class *Roar of Asaheim*, passed before the *Alpha Fang*'s oculus. It had turned to glass. The entire vessel was a crystalline sculpture thousands of metres long. It reflected and refracted the convulsing light of the storm. Hull and weapons, decks and crew, all were translucent. The engines were silent. The vessel moved forwards with the momentum of its death.

Harald's lip curled in anger as he took in the malign beauty of the lost frigate. The doom was insidious in its art. He could not but see an ill omen in the spectacle. Then the energy of the storm took the ship. The *Roar of Asaheim* shattered, vanishing in a glistening shard cloud.

On the bridge of the *Alpha Fang*, consoles melted. A weapons-system servitor's head exploded into a mass of writhing tendrils. Feingar, pack leader of the Coldeye Scouts, stood over a hololith map with his counterpart Lokyar Longblade. The tendrils reached for Feingar, tangling around his arm. Cursing, he ripped them from his armour and crushed them to white pulp beneath his boots.

Damage reports from the fleet flooded in. Static and the sounds of claws against bone disrupted the vox transmissions.

It was several minutes before there was enough order restored on the vessel for auspex scans of Svardeghul to be possible.

'Anything?' Harald asked the mistress of the vox.

'Nothing coherent at all,' said Ager. She stood straight and to attention, but her face was grey. She alone had heard what came from the planet. She had not relayed any traffic through the vox-speakers, shielding the bridge from further madness.

She confirmed what Harald already knew from the view in the oculus. Svardeghul's only remaining ocean, remade into sludge by millennia of manufactoria effluence, was now flesh. Maws thousands of kilometres long opened and closed. This world was lost to the Imperium forever. But somewhere below, there were brothers to rescue.

Harald watched Svardeghul's agony, doubting the wisdom of his mission, but he gave the orders for it to begin.

Before the storm, Svardeghul's cities had walked. They were rigs the size of mountains. Supported by eight immense pistons, they walked the planet with seismic steps, transporting their tens of millions of workers. They moved from one ore deposit to another, sucking the planet dry of its resources and sending them off-world to feed the unending hunger of the

Imperium's machinery of war. Some of the cities still walked. Augur scans revealed they had come to life. Their inhabitants had been crushed into the vitae circulating through the arteries of blind, howling monsters. Others were tottering ruins, making their slow march across the blasted land while the last of their shrieking populations were consumed by the daemons.

Wherever the augurs picked up even a semblance of conflict, Harald sent elements of Whitestalker to search for the Wulfen. He had assembled the strike force from his most experienced warriors. Even the Blood Claw band, the Deathhowls, were veterans compared to their brothers of the same rank. It would not be long before they ascended to become Grey Hunters.

'Our target is Rig Delta,' Harald told the Riders of Morkai, the Wolf Guard who would accompany him. 'It is the capital, and it has fallen silent.'

'No others have done so?' Vygar asked.

'No.' His hunting instincts were pricked by the anomaly. 'I would know why.'

'So great a fall,' said Lokyar, awed.

Harald would have marked the rare occurrence if he had not felt a chill silence in his soul. He had seen vistas of destruction beyond counting. He had seen few where vastness and suddenness were so conjoined.

The Deathwolves had made their landing before the ruins of Rig Delta, and found that it too had made a landing. Against the north end of the wreckage, a vertical precipice three thousand metres high rose above the rocky plain. Lokyar gazed back and forth from the top of the cliff to the titanic wreck. The city was so huge, even its broken corpse was almost as high as the fall it had taken.

'All the controllers of the city's march must have been killed,' Lokyar said. 'There was no one to stop it from walking over the edge.'

'Or it was made to do so,' Harald said. What daemon would not have rejoiced at causing such a catastrophe?

Portions of the great pistons still jutted skyward, driven through the base of the rig by the impact. Broken into jagged shafts, they fell away from each other, funerary columns of ruined, industrial majesty. Mining drills, refineries, manufactoria and habs were smashed into an indistinguishable mass, a hill of twisted, compacted metal. The city slumped away from the cliff, a leviathan spilling its machinic body across the plain. Promethium burned, filthy pyres lighting the contours of the rig, pooling at the bottom of the ruins into a lake. Black smoke roiled upwards towards a sky in the grip of the warp storm. Crimson and violet clouds formed into daemonic visages, their laughter tainting the air with a sick, clammy thunder.

Blood mixed with the promethium. It fell in cascades from the sharp angles of the city and flowed across the plain. Its stench was greater than the fire. The Space Wolves' nostrils were filled with the death of millions. Bodies were everywhere, burned and crushed. They spread out for many thousands of metres on all sides of Rig Delta, a great scattering of leaves hurled to the winds when the fall came to its terrible end. There was the stink of the daemon too. Ichor dripped from collapsed frameworks. It coated the sides of machines turned into abstractions of iron and plasteel.

There was no war here, though. The event had come, and the fate of Svardeghul had moved on.

The Deathwolf drop pods had come down on the west side of Delta Rig, three quarters of the way down the length of the ruin. While the Death-wolves mustered, the Wulfen moved a short distance away and gazed off to the south. The wind blew in ever-shifting gusts, pushing the flames first one way, then the other. When it began to come from the south, the Wulfen set up a howl. They hunched further forward, as if preparing to run prey to ground. Yngvir loped back to Harald.

He stopped a respectful distance from the Wolf Lord. He lowered his head, a gesture of deference to his superior, but still Harald had to look up to meet his eyes.

'Brothers...' Ygnvir said, pointing south.

'You have their scent?' Harald said.

Ygnvir grunted. 'And daemons... War.'

'Lead us, then. We will follow.'

Harald, Canis and the Riders of Morkai mounted the saddles of their thunderwolves. Lokyar's Stalkers headed off close behind the Wulfen, a lethal and silent advance guard to scout the terrain ahead and report back by vox. To Norvald Iceflame, sergeant of the Deathhowls, he said, 'Take *Runeclaw*. I want the Blood Claws held in reserve.'

Norvald's eyebrows rose. 'As you will, Lord Deathwolf.' He glanced towards his band, waiting a short distance away.

'They can rest assured that they'll get their fill of enemy blood,' Harald said in answer to the unspoken question. 'But I want cooler heads at the tip of the spear. Some... difficult decisions may lie ahead.'

'They'll understand,' Norvald said. 'The promise of battle is enough.'

'Good. And vox the other hunting parties. Have them converge on our position.'

'Aye, Lord Deathwolf.' Norvald marched towards the Stormwolf, gestur-ing for the Deathhowls to follow.

The core of Strike Force Whitestalker began its advance. Behind the Riders of Morkai marched the Nightwolves and Morkai's Hunters – Harald's most battle-hardened Grey Hunters. Behind them and on the flanks, giv-ing themselves a clear line of fire, were the Icefangs. They were Long Fangs of the Deathwolves. Veterans and marksmen, though the spirit of the wolf was strong in their souls, so too was the ice of Fenris in their blood. Their judgement was as sharp as their lack of mercy.

The Wolfkin ran along the entire flank of the company. Some packs of Fenrisian wolves ranged further ahead with Lokyar's Stalkers. Whether augmented with cybernetic limbs and jaws, or still in their natural state, they were all monstrous predators. They were the true beasts of Whitestalker, brothers to the Space Wolves but still a species apart. When Harald looked ahead to the baying Wulfen, he saw the line blurred, and it troubled him.

The Deathwolves left the ruins of Rig Delta behind. They travelled fast over the barren landscape. Nothing grew. There was only the rocky plane, broken by jutting outcroppings. Above, the air twisted with warplight, and sigils formed, conjuring madness. They dissolved into howling faces. All were monstrous, distorted, yet they also bore traits that were familiar, as if the souls of fallen comrades were trapped in the sickened skies of Svardeghul.

The Deathwolves ignored the faces. They ignored the attack. They were on the hunt. Nothing would divert their course.

'The scent so soon,' Canis said as they rode. 'A good start again.'

The champion did not often initiate conversations. 'Too easy, you think?' Harald asked.

Canis shrugged, but his eyes were shrouded, uncertain.

Too easy, Harald thought again. An entire world to search, and the Deathwolves were on the trail of their quarry on the first attempt, almost as soon as they had landed. He had followed his intuition, guided, he wanted to believe, by some sound reasoning. Even so, he did not rejoice in the sign of quick success. He distrusted it.

Why have we found the scent so easily? He was suspicious of his own intuition.

The hunt had travelled fewer than ten kilometres when Lokyar voxed Harald that the quarry was in sight, locked in combat with a daemonic host. '*The Wulfen are eager to aid their brothers.*'

'They must hold until I give the order,' Harald said. He urged Icetooth to greater speed. The rest of Whitestalker kept pace. Soon they reached the top of a ridge, where the Scouts had managed to hold the Wulfen back from engaging.

Harald looked down the slope to the region designated on the Svardeghul maps as the Shatterfields. The land the Deathwolves had just crossed was desolate, but it was a region that had yet to be scoured of its ore. Now they had reached the border of a vast area that had been worked to death. The Shatterfields had once been plains but now the surface was broken by a cracked-glass network of ravines. Between these, slag heaps reared their blackened heads. Isolated from one another, an army of sullen hills stretched to the horizon.

The ridge sloped down to a large plain flanked by heaps to the east and south, and a zig-zagging line of ravines to the west. The ground resembled the cracked, disintegrating skin of an enormous reptile. It was here the Deathwolves found the war. A large band of Wulfen fought an army of daemons. Outnumbered many times over, the Wulfen had retreated to the base of a slag heap in the south. They were partway up the slope, surrounded by jagged monoliths of discarded rock. Their position was strong; the daemons could not rush them in a mass. The Wulfen held them at bay. Hordes of pink Tzeentchian nightmares clambered over each other and the rocks only to be torn apart, each broken daemon reforming into two blue abominations. The Wulfen hurled the new, wailing creatures into their kin, knocking them back further.

'Like Nurades,' Canis said.

'Indeed,' said Harald. The daemonic horde was as varied as it was vast. 'I do not like this unity.'

Moving up through the pink horrors were daemonettes and creatures of Slaanesh. The daemonettes' strides were long and graceful, while the fiends leapt and galloped. As agile as the Tzeentchian abominations were clumsy, the Slaaneshi daemons crossed the battlefield in a feral joy of dance, their song turning slaughter into dark pleasure. They were fast, and the obstacles of the ruined earth could not slow them. They pounced on the Wulfen, trilling their chorus of exquisite murder. Their pincer limbs struck at the throats of the 13th Company. The fiends jumped over the stones, their long stinger tails stabbing through ancient, disintegrating armour. The Wulfen hit back with claw and blade, with frenzy and rage, dismembering and cutting daemonettes in half. Ichor coated the stones as broken monsters dropped back down the slope, dissolving. Yet they kept coming, more and more joining the attack, and they were taking their toll. Severed Wulfen heads arced through the air, raining blood.

Attacks from the air were just beginning. Burning chariots of Tzeentch swooped over the hills. Pulled by shrieking winged abominations, mounted by huge flame daemons, their edges scorched and sliced, while the flame daemons poured wyrdfire over the Wulfen, seeking to incinerate their reality.

'Our brothers stand strong,' Canis said. He looked at Harald expectantly.

'They do,' said Harald. He saw in the 13th Company the indomitable spirit of true Space Wolves. And he saw the unrestrained savagery of monsters.

'If we do not act...' Canis began.

'I know,' Harald said. 'They will fall.' The Wulfen could not withstand the sustained assault from land and air much longer.

Yngvir and his brothers were straining to tear down the slope. Harald did not give the order.

He hesitated. He was torn between two duties – to his oaths, and to his Chapter. He had sworn to rescue the Wulfen. But the more he saw of them, the more he dreaded what their ultimate impact on the Space Wolves would be. And again, there was the ease with which they had been found. The victories on Nurades sat less and less well with him. At the back of his mind, the laughter of Slithertwyst echoed still.

Harald felt Canis' eyes on him. He glanced at the Champion. There was no judgement there. Canis was waiting to see the path the Deathwolves would take.

All Harald had to do was nothing, and this splinter of the 13th Company would cease to be. If the Wulfen were a threat, it would diminish now by this much.

His instinct was to turn away. Against all his practice, against all his history of war, against everything he had been commanded to do, this was what his spirit urged him to do.

Then Harald looked at Yngvir, and thought of the debt his company owned the Wulfen.

His oaths were sacred. The Great Wolf had spoken. This was the path upon which the Space Wolves had embarked. It could not be changed at this juncture. Harald would travel it with all his brothers, and do what he must.

He raised Glacius. He said nothing, and his silence itself was a command. Even the Wulfen understood, and their growls quieted. Then he slashed down with the frost axe.

Strike Force Whitestalker charged down the slope with the Riders of Morkai in the lead. The only sounds came from the pounding of ceramite boots and wolf paws, and they were drowned out by the singing and chanting of the daemons. The horde was unaware of the destruction that streaked across the broken landscape towards it. Fifty metres from the daemonic ranks, the enemy was a wall of unnatural bodies – heaving, writhing, ululating. The singing filled his mind with images of excess and disease. The stench of open wounds, rotten meat and sickening blooms filled his senses. Harald snarled, hurling the foulness from his lungs. He raised his bolt pistol.

Another signal. All along the lines of the wedge-shaped phalanx, gun barrels pointed in the same direction.

Harald fired. So did all of Whitestalker. The air around Harald went dark, the dread light of the warp storm suddenly cut off by the immense hail of bolter shells. The hammering concussion of thousands of barrel reports overwhelmed the daemonic choir. The shells slammed into the mass of pink daemons and they exploded into smaller blue twins. The barrage tore these apart just as quickly. The mass-reactive shells punched through the slender forms of the daemonettes and fiends, exploding their silhouettes.

The Space Wolves stormed into the fray. Moments after the gun fire, the jaws of wolves and the chainblades of Space Wolves shredded the abominations. The Wulfen bayed their challenge, and it was answered by their brothers under siege. Yngvir's pack struck with the ancient weapons gathered from the Fang. Swords as long as spears and axes with blades as wide as a mortal human cut an ichor-spraying swath through the daemons. Harald saw the enemy destroyed as thoroughly as if the weapons had been sanctified power blades. Yngvir eviscerated a brace of pink daemons with slashes of his twin frostclaws. He wielded the relic blades with a perfect savagery. Ichor fountained over him. His jaws were agape in bestial delight.

The Wulfen slaughtered the forces of the Ruinous Powers with a force that stirred Harald to awe. The light of explosions and energy bursts flashed off their new armour. They embodied a terrible glory. However monstrous they were now, they had fought alongside Russ. Warriors from ten millennia past had returned to the battlefield. Their mere presence was an echo of the Imperium at its height.

And of the height of its agony.

Whitestalker took the daemons by surprise. Harald roared with brutal satisfaction as he saw the enemy react with disarray to the attack. Creatures of nightmare confronted a nightmare of their own. The Deathwolves barrelled through the rear lines, spreading their destruction outwards, striking out from the flanks while the front of the wedge pushed deeper and deeper into the daemonic ranks. Advancing more slowly, the Icefangs kept up the punishing barrage of heavy weapons fire. Lascannons incinerated abominations in blasts of searing white, leaving nothing behind but foul ash and dissipating sparks of wyrd energy. Heavy bolters punched through the pink daemons with such explosive force that the shattered bodies could not reform into their blue counterparts.

As if the World Wolf itself had seized the enemy host within its jaws, Whitestalker cut the daemon numbers in half in a matter of seconds. All the Deathwolves joined the Wulfen in howls of war and triumph.

The daemons responded. While their ground forces fell and dwindled, the aerial assault intensified. The skies filled with burning chariots and a swarm of screamers. The chariots flew along the flanks of the Space Wolf phalanx, huge flame daemons unleashing streams of wyrdfire. The Deathwolf advance slowed as the warriors jinked from side to side, seeking to avoid the blasts. Some did not. As Harald and Icetooth raced between two parallel explosions of flesh-corrupting fire, he heard a shout of soul-torn rage, and was engulfed by a sudden cloud of grey ash. The particles that had once been brother warriors settled on his armour and in his beard. Icetooth howled in distress, shaking it off. Harald beat his fist once against the totems on his chest, willing the souls of his lost brothers a swift journey to the land of the dead, and promising them vengeance.

The winged, screaming abominations cut back and forth across the Space Wolf lines. They flew low, hunting together. As if lured by the great spiritual strength of each warrior, they clustered their attacks around a single victim. Their shrieks pierced ears and souls, horns stabbed into the seams of armour and spiked tails whipped in with severing force. Arterial blood shot skyward, mixing with ash and corrupting flame. Heroic sagas snapped to an end as heads bounced off shoulders to be ignominiously trampled to mulch on the ground.

'Now, Norvald!' Harald voxed. 'Tear this foulness from the air!'

Runeclaw roared into the Shatterfields. It flew low, its engines shaking the battlefield. Lascannons and heavybolters streaked fire and destruction over the heads of the Space Wolves and a storm of energy and explosions shredded the flying daemons. The gunship's embarkation ramp dropped open and the Deathhowls hurled themselves down into the battlefield. They bayed their eagerness to be at the enemy's throat and hit the ground running, tearing along the flanks. Half the pack savaged the daemons on the ground while the other half turned their fire on the chariots and screamers. They were joined in the effort by the Icefangs. The Deathhowls' skill with their bolt pistols was lethal, but the impact of the shells was dwarfed by the cataclysm of plasma and lascannons. The air over the Shatterfields burned. It hurled daemons to the ground, their bodies blown apart, their materiality evaporating.

Harald was deep in a maelstrom of annihilation. He and his Deathwolves were the anger of the storm. Abominations swarmed over each other in the effort to halt the advance. They rushed to their extermination. The blue crystal of Glacius' blade flashed through scale and flesh. Every swing was more savage than the last, and Harald poured his fury into the weapon. Every impact and slicing crunch was vengeance and justice. He destroyed with every blow. Whatever his doubts about the wisdom of the mission, his hunger to destroy the daemon was as furious as ever. His charge was destruction made absolute. As he witnessed the supernova rage of the Wulfen, he drew upon it, and his own ferocity climbed to new heights.

The daemons fell, and fell, and fell. They were nothing but meat in the jaws of the wolves of war. Their numbers dwindled. The Deathwolves approached the base of the slagheap. The besieged Wulfen were still taking casualties, but they fought with the spirit of imminent victory. Many of the daemons attacking them turned back down the slope in an attempt to stop the crushing, devouring storm.

They were trying to stop fate itself. They failed.

A pair of flame daemons, caught up in a paired whirlwind dance, rose in a spinning leap from the rocky slabs below the Wulfen's position. Their jump took them over Harald, and just below the lethal barrage of *Runeclaw* and the Icefangs. They came down on either side of Vygar Helmfang. He tried to retaliate, but as he lashed out with his wolf claws, bellowing defiance, his armour and his flesh deliquesced. They dripped from his bones together, a mass of pink and blue-grey and frothing blood.

'Lord Deathwolf!' he cried. 'Preserve our Chapter!' His voice disappeared into the gargling coughs of a drowning man. His beard and face flowed together and poured off his skull. His skeleton burst into terrible growth. Serpentine clusters of bone spurs struck out of his frame with the speed of a scorpion's tail. They plunged their barbed ends into the neck and spine of his thunderwolf. The beast howled with its master. They collapsed to the ground, rolling and fusing into a mass of brittle, self-constricting tentacles and organic sludge. The cries of agony went on much longer than should have been possible.

Vygar was avenged before he truly died. The other Riders of Morkai fell on the flamers, their blades hacking the daemons apart in seconds. Fury unslaked, the Deathwolves attacked the rest of the daemonic horde with grief transmuted to devastation.

The daemonic army dwindled even further.

A solitary screamer flew high above the fray, dodging the fire of *Runeclaw*, dropping lower only for brief moments. On it stood a herald of Tzeentch. Harald only had momentary glimpses of it. The daemon controlled the actions of the army below with gestures and calls whose syllables thundered and hissed at once. The words coiled at the edge of Harald's consciousness, and he could not decide if they were familiar or not. He did not want to believe this was Slithertwyst again. The Deathwolves had destroyed the material form of that daemon fully. And yet... And yet...

It did not matter, Harald thought. Not here and now. All that mattered was the destruction of the enemy.

The air around the herald cleared again, and the daemon reached out to the east, its claws splayed. It pulled at the air as if hauling in chains. From the other side of the slagheaps came a huge clanking of gears, and the pounding of great masses. Over the peaks came four towering daemonic engines. Arachnid limbs of iron punched craters into the earth with each step. Their upper bodies were behemoths of twisted, bulging muscle, devastation made flesh; they were machines of war and they were beings of hatred. Their colossal limbs wielded claws that could crush a tank, and swords the height of a Space Marine. They stuck to the high ground, looping around to the south, then descended, spreading out to surround the Wulfen. The engines stepped over the broken monoliths without noticing their presence. Swords crackled eldritch energy as they came down, cutting through rock and flesh with equal ease. The daemons moved with the majesty of death. There was no rush to their attacks. They were ponderous but inevitable.

The siege was over. The enemy was larger than the fortress. But the Wulfen were fast. They ran at the monsters, dodging the blows, although some were crushed to pulp between claws. One of the possessed walkers was armed with a monstrous cannon. It fired, and the concussion almost knocked Harald from Icetooth's back. Huge shells thudded into the ground, erupting with fire that burned the materium and the wyrd. Wulfen and daemon alike vanished in the explosions.

The devastation could not stop the Wulfen. Their brothers died, but as the daemon walkers focused on their victims, the rest of the pack shot between the legs and leapt up to slash the torsos and arms of the daemons.

The cannon-wielding behemoth reared back. It clawed at the beings who dared attack it. It bellowed like a wounded bull pulling one of the Wulfen from its chest. Ichor poured to the ground in a flood. The possessed walker sank talons half a metre long into the torso of the warrior. It aimed its gun at the lupine blur on the ground, disdaining the two Wulfen stabbing punch daggers into the metal of the barrel.

They jumped away the moment before it fired. Multiple shells surged through a barrel punctured and no longer true. The daemon stalker's material reality turned against it. The shells exploded at once and the daemon's arm and head vanished in the blast. The body weaved back and forth until it collapsed against the monoliths at the base of the heap.

The Deathwolves broke through the last of the daemons between them and the Wulfen. Pink horrors and daemonettes and flamers were still on the attack, but there was little they could do now. The Space Wolves dominated the field, and now they roared over the wall of debris and joined the fight against the daemon engines.

Harald and the Riders of Morkai attacked the legs of the nearest colossus. Thunderhammers chopped and battered the limbs while Harald and Icetooth smashed at a right foreleg. The limb rose high over Harald's head then stabbed down. Icetooth leapt aside as the leg pulverized rock. Harald swung Glacius, and the force of the blow reverberated through his arm and down his spine. The frost axe bit deep. Metal buckled. The monster stamped and circled, sweeping its claws after the Wolf Guard. Iron shrieked, and one of the legs tore away. The daemon stumbled to the side and its aim went wide. Its head leaned forward, a huge, skinned beast shrieking its outrage. Harald met its eyes. He answered its roar and emptied his bolt pistol's clip into the monstrous face.

The shells punched through the daemon's skull. Geysers of flesh shot out the back of its throat and neck. Its roars turned into gurgles of agony. The impacts jerked it backward.

Battle on all sides of Harald exploded at once. The world was fractured by the pounding pillar-sized limbs and the booming of sorcerous cannons. Yngvir's Wulfen swarmed over another daemonic engine with their relic weapons, overwhelming it with their fury and opening molten wounds in its body with their great blades. The largest of the new Wulfen pack, standing on the shoulders of a possessed walker, tore the daemon's head from its body. Two of the great daemons fell. Anger, grief and baying triumph surged as one through Harald's spirit. The events at the periphery of his awareness were sudden and vast enough to pull a small portion of his attention away from the leviathan he fought.

Only a fraction. He never turned from the abomination's wrathful eyes.

It was enough. The claw came in from his left, a blur he turned too late to face. It closed around him and jerked him aloft, off the back of Icetooth. His arms were trapped in the daemon's grip. He could not move. The daemon walker lifted him high. Now its eyes shone with malevolent triumph. Its shattered jaw streamed ichor and its mutilated visage contorted in a snarl as it rejoiced over the downfall of its tormentor. It began to squeeze.

It spoke, somehow forming words despite the canyons of its injuries.

'You will not behold the game's end, Harald Deathwolf.'

Mountains pressed in on Harald's chest. His armour cracked. It split. Blades of broken ceramite cut though his carapace and into his flesh. His fused rib plates splintered. He could not breathe. Pain was a blackness spreading from his core, seizing his consciousness, splintering his thoughts.

'You will never learn your purpose.'

The full length of his frame cracked. He felt a more terrible crushing take place as his internal organs began to rupture. The blackness crept over his vision and the world receded behind a thickening veil. Only the terrible fire of the daemon walker's gaze penetrated it.

The slow, inexorable constriction paused. It relaxed by a fraction. With a supreme effort of will, Harald pushed the blindness away. One of the Wulfen had leapt up and seized the end of the daemon's claw. Through sheer bodily strength and mass, he was holding the arm down and pulling the tips of the claw apart. The daemon walker growled in disbelief. The Wulfen's ancient, ruined armour was little more than scraps now. The muscles of his arms bulged with strain and his fangs gnashed. He was beast far more than human, yet he acted with selfless heroism. Bit by bit, the halves of the claw began to part.

Denial, anger and disbelief twisted through the hollow thunder of the daemon's words.

With a sudden jerk, the Wulfen opened the claws wide. Harald fell to the ground. On his knees, his vision streaking with red and grey, his breath whistling as he dragged oxygen in over floating ribs, he saw the Wulfen twist the claw clockwise. Metal groaned, then screamed, and so did the possessed walker. The Wulfen kept turning the claw. The daemon tried to pull away but sparks and ichor cascaded over the Wulfen and, with the grating of flesh and the ripping of metal, the entire forearm came away. The daemon stalker howled, its black essence jetting out of its stump. The Wulfen turned, spinning, gathered huge momentum, and flung the claw with the force of a meteor into the daemon's head. The edge of the claws smashed the skull between the eyes. A mindless cry rose from the colossus. A sulphurous stench, the death rattle of a volcano, wafted across the battlefield. The daemon smashed the stones beneath it with the force of its fall.

Harald struggled to his feet. He spat blood. His arms were numb, but he had not lost his grip on his bolt pistol and Glacius. He straightened, ignoring the flashing agony throughout his body. The Wulfen warrior howled over the body of his titanic foe. He turned to face Harald. He nodded, acknowledging his debt and his gratitude, and the Wulfen loped away in search of more prey.

Harald followed. He could still raise his frost axe, and as Icetooth came to his side, he waded into the last of the battle. There was little prey now to find. With the great daemons destroyed, the remaining daemons were badly outnumbered, their struggle hopeless. They fought on, as if their purpose had been to die at the hands of the Space Wolves all along.

Harald looked up. The air battle had ended. There were no more flying daemons and no sign of the herald. Harald listened intently, trying to hear past the clamour of final slaughter for the echo of dark laughter. He could not find it. Perhaps there was none to hear.

He was not convinced.

The silence of bloody peace at last came to the Shatterfields. Harald watched the Wulfen of Whitestalker reunited with their brothers. Twice now, he thought, the Wulfen have saved your life twice. The debt is a heavy one, and you thought about leaving them to the daemons.

Yet he felt no shame. He mistrusted the impulse to gratitude.

Twice. Such a great debt. Can this be fate? Coincidence?

More and more traces of a pattern. He could see fragments, but he could not link them. The pattern refused to shape itself into meaning.

Harald looked upon the scene of victory, feeling the cancer of unease gnaw at his soul.

At war, beneath sleep, above death.

I must wake.

But no. The daemons climbing the wall. Leading them, a giant, a vastness of rage and wings. Landing blows in the psychic wall of the Fang.

I must wake.

But not now. Turn the fury against the daemons. The shadow of an assault cannon firing, firing, firing.

The dream-echoes of daemons exploding to nothing under its power.

The giant climbing against the hexagrammic shells.

There is no waking yet.

Only the battle beneath sleep, above death.

The pict screen was black. Vox traffic had fallen into a silence deep as the void. It was as if Krom was trying to communicate with a tomb. He put the earpiece down and looked down at the huscarl.

'How long?' he asked. Around him, the activity of the Fang's augur and vox complex had acquired a troubled intensity. Kaerls struggled in groups at their stations. While one fought with controls, others waved totems and made signs of warding, seeking to banish the disruptive spirits.

'We lost contact with Frostheim ten minutes ago,' said Albjorn Fogel. The overall supervision of the facility was his responsibility. He was an old man, and the skin of his face was like thick leather. It barely moved. But his forehead was creased now with concern. 'Before that, it was Svellgard. It fluctuated in and out of contact for an hour.'

'The problems have been system-wide?'

'Yes, lord. They were so momentary and scattered at first we did not think this was anything more than aetheric flaws in the vox.'

Krom pointed to the pict screen. 'Not just the vox now,' he said.

'That is so. In the last hour, we have begun to experience outages of all auspex readings as well.'

'Is there a pattern?'

'None beyond increasing frequency and duration. When the blackouts end, the vox operators at the other end report no malfunctions with their equipment. They believe we are the ones shut down.'

'No reports of possible enemy activity?'

'None at all, lord.'

Krom worked to keep the frustration from his voice. 'Very well,' he said. 'You will update me every hour of the situation.' He thought for a moment. 'You say Frostheim's silence has been the longest yet?'

'That is so.'

'I wish to be informed the instant vox is restored.'

'Yes, lord.'

Krom left the chamber. He was near the peak of the Fang, and he followed a gallery that led to a turret platform. He pulled back the iron door, then stepped into the howling wind. He looked up through rarefied air into the night sky. The stars were dagger points of cold light.

The cold numbed his exposed skin but could not numb his frustration. Duty held him on Fenris, and the links to the other worlds of the system were fraying. The rise in the incidents had the earmarks of an attack, but it was one he could not counter. There was no provenance and no enemy. As long as the worlds and moons of the Fenris system came back into contact, signalling nothing amiss, his hands were tied.

Even if the news from the system was bad, his oath held him to the Fang. Should Frostheim or Midgardia or any other Fenrisian world go dark, should they fall to enemy hands, the attack would almost certainly be a diversion. Fenris would always be the real target. To break his oath and take the bait, leaving the Space Wolf home world defenceless, was a crime too monstrous to contemplate.

And yet. He stared into the unforgiving black of the void above, and knew that something worse than his most dire speculations was approaching. His fists tightened in frustration. A low growl rumbled in his chest.

He stood on the turret platform for a full hour. Then two.

Frostheim remained silent.

CHAPTER 4

A SYMMETRY
OF BLOOD AND STORM

The battle-barge *Allfather's Honour* was at low anchor over Vikurus. It had translated from the immaterium three hours before, holding a stationary orbit over the city of Absolom. Aboard, preparations for invasion reached completion. The Kingsguard were about to descend.

Ulrik entered the bridge's strategium, where Grimnar sat in a throne carved from a single block of Fenrisian granite. 'An astropathic message from Sven Bloodhowl,' Ulrik said.

'Strike Force Sagablade was successful on Tranquilatus?' Grimnar asked.

'They were. They also encountered Dark Angels.'

Grimnar muttered a curse. 'Many?'

'A company's worth. They were already at war with the daemons when Sagablade arrived.'

'So they saw the Wulfen.'

Ulrik nodded.

'The fates have been kind to our hunt thus far,' said Grimnar. 'But the Dark Angels... That is unfortunate. There was contact?'

'Yes. With the Ravenwing. Bloodhowl reports the Dark Angels demanded our Wulfen brothers be turned over to them. Daemons attacked before shots were exchanged. Sagablade extracted the Wulfen during the battle.'

Grimnar's slow intake of breath was as close as he came to wincing. 'To depart in the midst of a struggle is hard. Bloodhowl acted wisely.'

'The Dark Angels would not agree,' said Ulrik.

'No, they would not,' said Grimnar. 'We will deal with those consequences in due course.' He paused, thoughtful. He looked at Ulrik, his eyes troubled. 'A well-timed daemonic attack,' he said. 'I know what Lord Deathwolf would say about that.'

'And that is?' Ulrik asked.

'That it could be interpreted as daemonic intervention on our behalf.'

Ulrik shook his head. 'That interpretation would be mistaken.'

'So I would prefer to believe, Slayer. Convince me. Was the fortunate event chance?'

'It was the chance created by inevitable fate.'

Grimnar's eyes burned in the shadows of the chamber. He leaned forward. 'Say on, old one.' For a moment, he was once again the young warrior eager for the veteran's insights.

'The Thirteenth Company has returned to the materium. That event itself is so great, it has convulsed the warp. It is so great, it cannot transpire without leading to events just as great. The Wulfen come to us in advance of Russ. They will reclaim their rightful place on the Grand Annulus. Nothing can stand in the way of this resolution, and certainly not the Dark Angels. If agents attempt to stop fate, chance itself will be forced to intervene. Do you see?' Ulrik asked Grimnar. 'If it had not been the daemons, it would have been something else. Fate cannot be denied. The abominations were pawns of destiny on Tranquilatus.'

'It is true our course is clear here too,' Grimnar said.

'Aye. The Stormcaller was unequivocal.' The High Rune Priest's scryings had allowed no uncertainty. The Wulfen would be found in the shrine city of Absolom. None of the other strike forces had had targets so precise revealed to them. One after the other, they had triumphed, and Wulfen packs were being transported to the Anvarheim system and the waiting *Coldfang*.

The Kingsguard strike force had had far to travel, and was among the last to arrive on station. The string of successes before immense odds were still more evidence, as far as Ulrik was concerned, that he was correct in his interpretation of the portents.

Grimnar stood. 'To battle, then, Wolf Priest.' He bared his fangs in an eager, predatory grin. 'To battle.'

'Are you sure about this?' Sammael asked. Standing in the antechamber to the astropathic choir of the strike cruiser *Silent Oath*, the Grand Master of Ravenwing stared at the parchment in his hand.

'We are certain of its recipient, yes.' Master Astropath Asconditus raised a cautious hand. The old man was bowed, his gaunt, sallow face deeply shadowed by his cowl. 'Not as to its meaning. The message is open to multiple interpretations.'

'This message is ambiguous,' Sammael said. 'It can be interpreted many ways.'

'None, with your pardon, are good,' Asconditus said.

Sammael did not reply. He looked at the message again. Transcription, already subject to the vagaries of the warp and astropathic interpretation, was rendered even more doubtful by the message's fragmentary nature. '*Leave no sign*,' he read.

Asconditus spoke up again. 'A question? A statement? An order? All are damning, Grand Master. There are only shadows here.'

'And there is no doubt about the provenance?'

'None. It was sent by the battle-barge *Allfather's Honour*.'

The Space Wolves' flagship was communicating with the Wolf Lord Sven Bloodhowl on the *Bloodfire*. Sammael was not inclined to think well of the Space Wolves. For that reason, he was wary of his instincts. He had to be sure of the truth before acting. But after Tranquilatus, he was finding it difficult to disagree with Asconditus.

The antechamber was dark, its vault invisible in the shadows. Even so, Sammael saw light dawning on the situation that had been developing since Nurades. The light was cold. What it revealed was unclean.

The bestial slaughter of the Scouts who had been stationed to protect the Dark Angels' interests on Nurades. The pict from the recovered servo-skull revealing a massive shape with the Fenrisian insignia on its armour. The presence of the mutated beasts on Tranquilatus. The craven behaviour of the Space Wolves, escaping with their monsters during a daemonic attack.

'We bear witness to an accumulation of damnation,' Asconditus said, as if reading Sammael's thoughts.

'We must be cautious,' said Sammael.

'But if the Space Wolves have mutated...'

Sammael shook his head. 'We must be sure.'

Asconditus' voice dropped to a whisper. 'With respect, Grand Master, aren't we?'

Sammael did not wish to be. Whatever he thought of the Space Wolves, they had been fierce warriors for the Imperium. If they had become unclean, the loss would be terrible. The cost of dealing with the fallen Chapter would be even worse.

'What news from the Rock?' he asked. Perhaps new truths had been unearthed, ones that would point away from this dark path. 'Has Scout Dolutas been located?' The survivor of Nurades had disappeared before regaining consciousness.

'Not according to the last report.'

'He must be found!' Sammael said. It was impossible that a Dark Angel could vanish on the Rock. Not by accident. And if it were not an accident, then there was an enemy who had penetrated the citadel, and *that* fact led to its own set of terrible implications.

'There is something else I must ask,' Asconditus said.

'What is it?'

'I have heard that on Tranquilatus, daemons attacked at just the right moment to benefit the Space Wolves.'

Sammael hesitated, but Asconditus' train of thought was growing harder and harder to resist. 'In effect, that is so,' he said. 'I consider that a coincidence.'

Asconditus bowed his head. His silence was sceptical.

Sammael left the antechamber and made for the bridge. The *Silent Oath* was already making all haste for the Rock. The thought ate at him that darker shadows had already reached it.

And that his worst surmises about the Space Wolves still fell short of the truth.

The Kingsguard came to Absolom. Logan Grimnar's strike force descended in squadrons of Stormwolves and Thunderhawks. As the gunships approached the shrine city, they split up, the flights heading for their designated target zones. Each warrior-band had its contingent of Wulfen to help track their kin.

Ulrik watched Absolom grow larger through a viewing block of the Thunderhawk *Helwinter Judgement*. Despite the smoke billowing upward from hundreds of blazes, at first the city seemed almost intact. The glory of its architecture had not been destroyed. Absolom was a shrine city; the placement of every stone had a religious purpose. The veneration of the Allfather was made manifest in cathedrums built for hundreds of thousands, in mile-wide processional avenues of gleaming marble, and in colossal statuary. Many times larger than an Imperator Titan, the statues were both monuments and habs. They were human in form, some robed, others armoured. They were the qualities of the Emperor given solid form. The Guardian of the Imperium, the Master of Mankind, the Destroyer of the Heretic and the Xenos, the All-Seeing, the Exterminating Sword. Before the warp storm, their limbs and torsos had housed tens of thousands. Their skulls were the chapels where worshippers would look out with the eyes of a god, and contemplate a yet greater one. The upturned palms were landing pads, which now received one squadron of Stormwolves.

Helwinter Judgement led its flight of gunships between the shoulders of the colossi. Closer up, Ulrik could see the damage. The face of one statue had been utterly destroyed, and its skull was now an eerie, hollow darkness. Flames licked from the eyes of another. As *Helwinter* flew past, he had a brief glimpse of ongoing slaughter inside the great habs. Mortals were hurled from shattered windows. Things of horn and claw rioted through the fires.

'The daemons have not overthrown the towers,' Njal Stormcaller said. He sat next to Ulrik in the Stormwolf's troop hold. The High Rune Priest glared at the vista of the tormented city. In the rumbling, shaking hold, the air crackled with ozone. Pressure built around the Stormcaller. His rage was building.

'It pleases the daemons to keep them intact,' Ulrik said. He gestured at magnificence turned malignant. 'The place of highest worship turned to unholy purposes.'

'Aye. The desecration is all the more complete.'

'Foulness from within the sacred,' Ulrik said.

Stormcaller nodded, as if coming to a new understanding. 'And the Wulfen are our great hope fighting within the foul,' he said. 'A striking symmetry.'

Ulrik waited.

'The omens multiply,' said Stormcaller. Though his anger at the daemons did not diminish, his eyes shone with anticipation. 'Surely Russ *is* coming,' he said.

Good, Ulrik thought. It was clear the High Rune Priest saw the truth of the Wulfen.

'They shall rise from the daemonic maelstrom as they tore away from the grip of the immaterium,' Ulrik said. 'There is repetition here. The Wulfen bursting through one threshold after another.'

Lower now, roaring through more densely interlaced structures. Arched bridges traced delicate paths through the air between cathedrum towers and free-standing prayer galleries. Ulrik caught more impressions of Absolom's pain. The city's defenders had lost, but some still lived, and fought on. At the peak of one narrow arch, a trio of Sisters of Battle was surrounded by plaguebearers. The daemons of Nurgle slowly trudged up from both ends of the bridge. There were hundreds. The Sisters cut them down with bolter and flamer as they came near. There was space for no more than two or three of the daemons at once. The heroines of the Imperium could hold out as long as they had ammunition, but the stream of plaguebearers was unending.

Helwinter Judgement strafed the east side of the arch with its lascannons. It burned away a huge swath of the abominations. Then it left the bridge and the struggle behind.

'That bought them a little time,' said Stormcaller.

'Aye,' said Ulrik. 'No more than that, though.'

Lower still. Now the Stormwolves slowed as they made their final descent into the Grand Assemblis. The square was a few thousand metres on each side, the parvis of four grand cathedrums. Statues of the saints were scattered about it, their placement and orientation given the appearance of chance, as if they were living pilgrims making their way towards the houses of worship. They were an illusion of calm in the midst of nightmare. Blood daemons of Khorne rampaged through the square, cutting down desperate squads of militia. The mortals fought, but there was no hope for them. They were now only prey for the swordlings, slain for sport.

There were many mortals present in the Assemblis, however, many tens of thousands. They lay in mounds a score of metres high. Some of the heaps were on fire, bodies slowly turning to ash and smoke. Others squirmed and heaved. The dead flailed their limbs as if struggling against a new pain, one worse than any they had known alive. Wyrdfire skittered over the mound, running like water, destroying the lines between rot and metamorphosis.

Around the periphery of the square were pict screens. Once they would have broadcast images turning officiating ecclesiarchs into heroes twenty metres high. Now they screamed madness.

The gunships came down into the square. Their lascannons and twin-linked heavy bolters scorched the Assemblis, blasting the landing area clear of the swordlings. Assault ramps dropped, unleashing the Kingsguard before taking off once more to continue their purging assault.

Ulrik charged into the square, part of the collective howl of rage. Grimnar led the charge aboard *Stormrider*. The thunderwolves Tyrnak and Fenrir pulled the war chariot, as eager to lay waste to the foul enemy as their master. With a roar, beasts and warrior fell upon the blood daemons. In Grimnar's left hand was his storm bolter. He attacked with such ferocity that it seemed the enemy exploded into body parts and a deluge of ichor on all sides of *Stormrider*.

The paving stones shattered beneath the tread of the Venerable Dreadnoughts Haargen Deathbane and Svendar Ironarm. Daemonic forms vanished in the heat of Haargen's multi-melta. Svendar lumbered forward, a mountain of walking death, his great axe and blizzard shield striking down the daemons with the force of a rockslide. Where he walked, he left a wake of crushed, disintegrating bodies. The crushed forms of the abominations sank slowly into the pools of their liquefying essence.

And there was Murderfang.

The Stormfang *Drakesbane* shadowed the advance of the Kingsguard. Its heavy bolters chewed through the mobs of swordlings, but they were incidental targets. Its helfrost destructor was trained on Murderfang, ready to fire if needed. The Dreadnought's rage was absolute, a thing of shredding madness. The warrior was as unpredictable as a rabid wolf. There was always the danger that the path of its rampage would take it through the bodies of its brothers.

On this day, Ulrik did not believe that danger existed. He followed close behind Murderfang. He saw a purpose now in his meeting in the vaults with Dragongaze and Deathwolf. The feral Dreadnought was himself an omen of the Return, and here he led the charge to recover more of the 13th. Even the Great Wolf followed Murderfang in this charge.

Ulrik brought his crozius arcanum down with exterminating force, banishing the unclean with the symbol of Fenris' spiritual strength. Ichor splashed against his totems. Swordlings snarled, but the snarl of the Wolf Helm of Russ was greater than theirs, and their anger turned to agony before they fell. Ulrik fought with wrath, in the name of what was to come. He had lived so long, and perhaps it had always been decreed that he would live to see these great moments arrive for the Space Wolves.

The return of the 13th Company. The return of Russ.

Events were aligning. The portents were clear. The future was unfolding as it should, as it must, and Ulrik rejoiced to bear witness to it.

The vox speakers of the sarcophagus distorted Murderfang's howl. The rage rattled and shrieked across the Grand Assemblis. The Dreadnought pounded forward, his terrible gauntlets reaching for the sword-wielding Khornate daemons. The abominations attacked, swords clanging against the sarcophagus. They were rushing to their doom, but they were the essence of rage given bodily form, and they could do nothing else. The beast met them with his murderclaws. Blades the crystalline blue of xenos ice crackled as they slashed through daemonic flesh. The daemons came at Murderfang by the score but he tore them apart without pausing in his battering run. He turned to wherever he saw the greatest concentration of abominations. His momentum was relentless. He was a machine of perpetual slaughter.

There were thousands of the swordlings in the Assemblis when the Kingsguard descended. Shortly, only stragglers remained. Then there were none. Daemons shrieked from the galleries and spires of the cathedrums, but the square was purged. The few surviving mortals clustered together, staring at the Space Wolves with awe and caution. Even the ruinous shrieks coming from the pict screens could not tear their attention from Murderfang. They regarded him with terror. They could barely walk, yet it was clear they would attempt to flee if they came within the Dreadnought's gaze.

Deprived of foes, Murderfang paused. The Wulfen of the Kingsguard gathered near him, as if sensing kinship. Ulrik moved to the front of the Dreadnought. The face visible within the sarcophagus was contorted by a rictus of eternal rage. The eyes were wide, glassy, bloodshot, agonised. There was no personality there, yet for the first time in his memory, Ulrik saw Murderfang blink. He sniffed the air. So did the Wulfen.

Stormcaller joined Ulrik. The High Rune Priest's psyber-familiar, Nightwing, landed on his shoulder. It shook its feathers free of gore and cocked its head, training its bionic eye on Murderfang.

'He senses more Wulfen,' Stormcaller said.

'As you predicted,' said Ulrik.

'I have never known him to stop of his own accord before.'

'Nor have I.'

A change came upon Murderfang's eyes. Something more than bloodthirst entered them. There was recognition. Ulrik's soul was elated at that sign of consciousness.

Everything aligns, he thought. The chapters of the great saga unfold before us.

Murderfang and the Wulfen turned to face south, then thundered towards the cathedrum named the Dome of Penitents.

Ulrik raised his crozius and howled in triumph. A short distance away, *Stormrider* followed the feral pack. Tyrnak and Fenrir were eager to follow the baying of the Wulfen. Over the triumph of the wolves, Grimmar's voice called to the Kingsguard. 'Our kin await us, brothers!' He pointed forward with the Axe Morkai. 'Forward! We shall be reunited amid the destruction of the daemonic foe!'

The strike force followed in the wake of Murderfang. The Space Wolves passed between the screaming pict screens, then beneath the towering arch that marked the processional ramp to the cathedrum. The gunships broke away as they approached the entrance. *Drakesbane* and the Stormwolves flew higher. They strafed the open platforms and stained glass windows of the dome wherever daemons dared to show themselves.

The ramp was wide. The golden doors were colossal, monuments in their own right, so that hundreds of penitents at once could pass through them. There would be room enough for *Morkai's Howl* and *Fire of Fenris*. The Land Raider and Redeemer rumbled up behind the Kingsguard, tanks of legend adding their ferocity to the hunt.

Murderfang slammed into the doors. The impact threw them back. The Space Wolves stormed into the Dome of Penitents.

Just before he crossed the threshold, a flint of silver high in the air caught Ulrik's attention. He paused and looked up. The gunship assaults sent dust and smoke bursting from the dome. The sky was obscured. He faced ahead once more. He could not shake the impression of having caught a glimpse of something dangerous yet sacred.

Inside the dome, the legions of the Ruinous Powers awaited the Space Wolves.

A space of glittering sanctity had become a cauldron of violence, massacre, sacrilege and madness. The floor of the cavernous auditorium was heaped with the bodies of worshippers, ecclesiarchs and Sororitas. Shrines lay overturned and shattered. The frescoes of the dome had been defaced with blood, entrails and fire. Cherubim had become disembowelled corpses. Stars were now the blazing eyes of warp-born behemoths. Beneath the centre of the dome, a golden figure of the Emperor, over twenty metres tall, still stood, sword raised as if in defiance of the storm of abominations that rioted through the cathedrum.

The sounds of two greetings washed over the Space Wolves. Daemons roared, hissed and gabbled. Plague, wrath, excess and change fused into a choir of evil, a noise damp yet burning, powerful yet diseased. The second greeting was no less triumphant. Howls of war came from high above, in the Celestium Galleries. At the level of the Emperor's sword, walkways cut across the width of the dome, gossamer-thin in the immensity of the space. Suspended on those iron threads and leaping between the archways of the galleries, Wulfen battled daemons. They moved constantly, speed and slashing fury keeping them from being overwhelmed by the flood of abominations.

In the auditorium, the daemons surged forward. Murderfang was already deep into the rising tide. He trampled scampering daemons of Nurgle and the pink creatures of Tzeentch. His claws dismembered sword daemons of Khorne and the fiends of Slaanesh. The wave foamed around and past Murderfang, surrounding the Kingsguard as the strike force charged deeper into the cathedrum.

A vast shape landed before the statue of the Emperor with cratering force and filled the air with marble shrapnel and dust. The walls of the cathedrum shook with the impact. The horned daemon stretched to its full, towering height. It spread its wings. It raised an axe large enough to cut through a tank and a monstrous serpent of a whip. The axe blade dripped blood. Bits of flesh clung to the barbs the length of the whip. The colossus of rage bellowed, and its roar was the sound of worlds drowning in the blood of mindless hate.

It had already reduced much of the Celestium Galleries to ruin. Columns and walkways were shattered. The bodies of Wulfen lay in the wreckage and blood rained down upon the Emperor, streaking his visage with red tears.

The huge daemon strode towards the Space Wolves. Its footsteps boomed. The lesser abominations intensified their attacks. Creatures of the four Ruinous Powers revelled in the approach of the greater daemon, the Khornate abominations most of all. Their infernal cannons fired from the far side of the dome. Burning, laughing, flaming skulls bombarded the Space Wolves. The bones exploded, spreading streaming fire over the hulls of the advancing Land Raiders. *Fire of Fenris'* twin-linked heavy bolters churned the air with exploding stone and fountains of ichor. *Morkai's Howl* attacked with its own flames, sending a stream of purifying fire over scores of daemons.

Ulrik gathered a sense of the full battle in quick, frozen glimpses. The daemon wave was massive. There was no possibility of grand strategy, only the struggle against the nearest foe, survival measured from one second to the next. He buried the crozius in the skull of a blood daemon at the same moment as he incinerated the torso of a fiend of Slaanesh with his plasma pistol. A wall of evil pressed in, reaching for him with claws and talons. Tongues of wyrdfire fell on him, but he was strong in faith and anger. His wolf amulet blazed and an aura of pulsing red and blue surrounded him. The blows of the daemons could not land on him. He waded deeper into the horrors, laying waste to the creatures of the warp. The baying and snarls of the Wulfen fired his blood. He killed with the furious abandon of a Blood Claw, yet he remained conscious of the weight of history on every moment of the struggle. Thousands upon thousands of years had worked towards this battle, itself one more step towards the fulfilment of a greater destiny.

'Strike the daemons down, champions of Fenris!' Ulrik shouted. 'For Russ! For his return!' He howled, and his cry was taken up by the rest of the Kingsguard. The Space Wolves surged forward, feral, annihilating.

Did the daemons before him hesitate before Ulrik's savage joy? Did they wonder at the bone snarl of his helm and the power of his shout?

He thought they did, and well they should. He butchered his way forward, determined to reach Grimnar's side and face the huge daemon together.

The giant came closer, its eyes fixed on Logan Grimnar. It snarled in anticipation. Caught up in the battle frenzy, the Wolf Guard Drengir charged the daemon. Without taking its gaze from the Great Wolf, the Khornate horror smashed Drengir aside with its axe. The Wolf Guard flew backwards, colliding with the statue of the Emperor. Marble, armour and bone broke together. Drengir landed on the flagstones, motionless, and disappeared beneath the claws and hooves of the lesser daemons.

Bellowing vengeance, Grimnar leapt from *Stormrider*, the Axe Morkai raised high, a challenge and answer to the daemon's weapon. The instant Grimnar's boots hit the flagstones, other daemons rushed him. Arjac Rockfist and the Wolf Guards punished them for the temerity of their interference. They cut a swath through the abominations, clearing the path for Grimnar. A new page in the saga of the Great Wolf was about to be written.

Lightning exploded between Ulrik and the scene of the approaching duel. Njal Stormcaller was moving forwards too, summoning an electrical storm, burning the daemons to ash.

A shriek came at Ulrik from above and behind, the high pitch carving the sound from the deeper, deafening clamour of the war. His reflexes responded before his conscious mind understood the nature of the threat. He turned in time to see a burning, airborne chariot pulled by two of the shrieking winged daemons.

A Tzeentchian herald rode the chariot. The pink-hued abomination was robed. In its left hand, it clutched a black tome that burned with blue wyrd-fire. Its right hand held a staff whose head was an edged, twisted crescent, the symbol of its dark god. From the herald's chest came a third hand, which pointed mockingly at Ulrik. The daemon laughed at him. It lowered its staff as the screamers angled in for their attack. It shouted in its unholy tongue. Ulrik rejected the words, refused to let them take on meaning. He understood well enough why the herald laughed, though. It was pointing the staff at his crozius. In its form, the Tzeentchian daemon was a hideous parody of his own sacred role.

Ulrik made ready to silence that laughter. Behind him, Grimnar and the great daemon traded blows, Axe Morkai and axe infernal clashing with such force they unleashed blinding flashes of eldritch power.

The winged horrors dived. A coruscating nimbus formed around the pink daemon's third hand.

Ulrik waited until the chariot's infernal steeds were committed to their angle of attack before he moved. At the last second, he ducked low and ran forward, firing a plasma salvo upward. He passed under the winged creatures as his bursts melted through their underbellies. Their shrieks became stuttering wails. They crashed to the floor, dragging the chariot down with them.

The rapid thunder of Grimnar's storm bolter boomed from the centre of the cathedrum. Shells exploded against the Khornate daemon's breast-plate. The colossus staggered back a step.

The daemon was raising its axe to counterattack when the upper portion of the dome exploded. Tonnes of rubble fell, smashing walkways. Galleries collapsed. Wulfen and daemons fell with them. Two gunships in silver-grey roared into the cathedrum, heavy bolters and assault cannons pounding the abominations, and descended to where Grimnar and his foe reeled under the rockcrete avalanche.

They were Stormravens. The Grey Knights had come to Absolom.

Ulrik felt his eyes widen. The eruption of the sons of Titan into the battle had the quality of a fevered vision. In the fraction of a second, his reaction passed from stunned surprise to wariness.

Do they know about the Wulfen?

The herald and the titanic daemon looked up as the Stormravens descended. The giant snarled, but the Tzeentchian abomination laughed. The Chapter of the Adeptus Astartes most fanatically devoted to the exter-mination of daemons had joined the battle, and the herald laughed.

The chill finger of premonition reached into Ulrik's hearts. Dark portents were taking shape before him. He could not see the pattern they formed. He could only tell it was present. In this moment, all he could do was seek to disrupt it by ending the herald's celebration.

Grimnar acted on the great daemon's moment of distraction. Ulrik saw him run forward and bring the Axe Morkai down against the abomina-tion's whip arm. The blade flashed the blue of purest cold. It cut all the way through the limb. Ichor jetted from the daemon's stump. The giant roared more in wrath than in pain.

Ulrik reached the herald as it clambered from the fallen, screaming char-iot. The daemon hissed in outrage. Its middle hand, glowing with warp energy, struck him in the chest. Daemonic power encountered the ward of his wolf amulet. There was a flash of searingly black lightning, and the blast staggered Ulrik and the pink horror. The daemon retaliated with a second, more powerful blast from its staff. Concentrated wyrd energy hit Ulrik at the same moment as the giant daemon struck Grimnar in the chest with a massive cloven hoof, smashing the Great Wolf down.

A fist of madness wrapped itself around Ulrik and took him to the ground too, assaulting his consciousness with visions of the impossible and mon-strous. He fought the sights. Other pink abominations jumped on him. The daemonic mass held him in place while claws battered at him. Witch energy sought to transform his armour into something weak.

Ulrik heard the shouts of his brothers on all sides. They called his name. They trained bolter fire on his attackers. The daemons were too numerous. They came at him faster than the other Space Wolves could destroy them.

Ulrik felt as if the fell beings would shove him through the ground to the molten core of this world. '*Fenris!*' he shouted, calling upon its icy ferocity. He raised his right arm, hurling back a scrabbling daemon and smashing the skull of another with the crozius. The pressure on his chest lessened. He fired a single shot of the plasma pistol. At point blank range, the burst washed over him. Its terrible incandescence burned into his armour. Damage runes screamed red and blinked out. The purity of the fire disrupted the wyrdflame. Agony cut through the visions. The spell of transformation dissipated. Ulrik smashed the crozius back and forth, crushing daemon flesh and form. He rose from the midst of the nightmares, howling a hunter's fury.

Ahead, beyond the herald of Tzeentch, the Grey Knights had dropped from the Stormravens. They surrounded the huge daemon and Grimnar.

'Lord Grimnar!' their captain shouted. One of his paladins blocked the daemon's killing axe blow with his sword. 'I am Stern of the Grey Knights! I demand your immediate surrender!'

Before Ulrik, the herald laughed.

'You are wrong to exult, abomination,' Ulrik snarled. 'You are already defeated.'

Grimnar answered Stern by leaping to his feet even as the daemon killed three paladins with a single strike of its wyrd-imbued axe. Stern attacked the daemon himself, forcing it back another step with blows from a sword whose power lit the space of the cathedrum with silver lightning. The Great Wolf charged into the fray and buried the Axe Morkai in the great daemon's chest, where ichor from the earlier wound still dripped. The daemon's breastplate collapsed. The monster staggered.

The Tzeentchian herald blocked Ulrik's charge with its staff. It wielded the weapon with two hands while the third held the book aloft. The daemon began to chant. The air snapped. Eldritch energy built up. The colours of the cathedrum smeared. It seemed as though the entire Dome of Penitents was turning around Ulrik, faster and faster, losing all consistency, becoming a maelstrom of stone and glass. The colours interwove, growing brighter, more brittle. Cracks appeared in the air, spreading and connecting. Thin ice was about to shatter. A foul wind blew from the cracks, howling directly into Ulrik's soul.

The pink daemon was opening a portal to the warp.

From a great distance, he heard the baying of the Wulfen. He snarled, becoming one with their savagery. His beast leapt at the throats of his enemy. He brought the crozius down on the centre of the staff at the same moment as he fired the plasma pistol at the book. The staff snapped. The herald's chanting ceased. It screamed. The air screamed. The materium screamed. The maelstrom spin ceased and the colours of madness became an explosion of blood. The cracks in the real became mere scales of illusion, and they flaked away in a storm of ash.

The Dome of Penitents was solid around Ulrik once more. Roaring, he smashed the crozius against the herald's skull. The daemon's body parted with a hideous, tearing crunch. Ulrik sent a plasma blast into the gap between the halves. The herald's ululating babble turned into a duet of pain as the body split all the way, becoming two blue horrors. One jumped at Ulrik and wrapped its limbs around his neck. Wyrd energy lashed down his frame. The other abomination wailed as its twin grappled with Ulrik. It stretched out its arms, seeking reunion.

Ulrik pulled his right arm back, and smashed the crozius into the spongy flesh of the blue horror's head. It reared back, but kept its grip around his neck. It did not see the pleading of the other daemon. Ulrik trained his plasma pistol on the creature's maw and fired a rapid burst. The heat of a sun exploded inside it and its being evaporated.

The remaining blue horror dropped its arms. It regarded Ulrik, its old eyes knowing what would come next. He had destroyed the heralds. This remnant could do nothing against him. The daemon opened its jaw wide as he brought the crozius in for the final stroke of annihilation. He raised his other hand to block the blue creature's attack, but it did not try to seize his fist and the crozius in its maw. It laughed instead.

He smote the abomination with a single, devastating hit, the crozius crackling with lightning, the very anger of Fenris purging the materium of the unclean thing. And the daemon laughed. It burst apart, spraying liquefying flesh in all directions.

The laughter echoed for several seconds after the daemon was gone.

Harald said the fiend called Slithertwyst had laughed too. The thought was troubling. It was a dark echo.

'This is our saga!' Grimnar was shouting. He severed the other arm of the daemon. The monster collapsed. 'Our fight,' Grimnar said, and sent the gigantic head rolling. 'Our business.'

Ulrik marched through the ruin of the chariot to stand with Grimnar as he confronted the Grey Knights. The struggle against the daemons was ending. With the destruction of the colossus and the herald, the rest of the abominations were vanishing under the firepower of the tanks and Kingsguard elements further out from the the the statue of the Emperor. The daemons were disappearing more quickly than they were being destroyed, Ulrik thought. They were abandoning the field. They knew they were defeated.

Or else their work is done.

The Ruinous Powers united. The forces of the Imperium divided. Ulrik saw the catastrophe forming. He saw why the herald of Tzeentch might have laughed in the end.

Stern was speaking of heresy and mutation as Ulrik drew near. Such an old refain. Such a tedious refrain. Ulrik had encountered versions of the same accusations hurled at the Space Wolves throughout his centuries of service. There was nothing new in them.

What was new was the impasse.

'These things came from the warp, and only my brothers and I are fit to judge if these kin of yours are corrupt. They must be handed over to us immediately, as must any others you have recovered. We will see to it that they reach Titan safely,' Stern said.

'Never,' Ulrik muttered under his breath. His pulse beat in his ears. A growl rose in his chest. He eyed the Grey Knights, and faced the inevitable. They were fanatics. They could not be turned from their path. They had come to take the Wulfen. There was only one way to stop them.

'Stern, I'm sure you think you're being very reassuring, but there's as much chance of you taking the Wulfen as of me giving my crown to a blubber-seal. I'd see our brothers dead before I handed them over to be cut apart and studied,' Grimnar said.

'Forcing your cooperation at this juncture would prove costly,' Stern warned.

Even as Ulrik kept his arms lowered, he adjusted his grip on his pistol and the crozius.

Grimnar and Stern were still speaking. The words were nothing more now than the ritualistic prologue to battle. Around the circle, the stances of the Space Wolves were shifting. In moments, the blood would flow.

'I would have thought,' said Stern, 'considering the current situation around Fenris, you would want all the friends you could get, Great Wolf.'

Ulrik stared at the Grey Knight. His limbs went numb with premonition.

'What situation?' asked Grimnar.

Stern answered, and transformed Ulrik's premonition into horror.

CHAPTER 5

UNVEILING

The decks of the *Coldfang* vibrated from the snarls. The walls thrummed with feral rage. The roars were growing louder. Hjalvard pounded down the halls of the strike cruiser, convinced he would find disaster at the guard post. The thought made his lips pull back in anger. His pulses were a double-beat of incipient battle frenzy. His skin crawled. His jaws ached as his fangs pushed further out from his gums. As he rounded the final corner, he was charging to attack.

But the barrier held. Vintir was at his post. The door behind him was sealed. The Grey Hunter raised his power sword, but he did not run to meet Hjalvard's rush. 'Battle leader!' Vintir shouted.

Stop! Hjalvard thought. His rational mind wrestled with the beast. *Stop!*

He turned at the last moment and slammed his fist into the wall, cracking the stonework. He breathed through his nose, forcing himself to move slowly, to be still. If his body calmed, perhaps his spirit would too.

He had headed here merely on an inspection. He had almost precipitated the very disaster he had dreaded.

The contagion is growing, he thought.

When he felt he could speak without snarling, he faced Vintir.

'All is well,' he said, hands up as if it were Vintir and not he who had needed placating. 'Have they tried to come through?' he asked. Above all else, he had to keep the Wulfen off the main decks.

'They are remaining below,' said Vintir. 'I think there have been some fights for dominance, but I believe the pack leaders are keeping them in their quarters.'

'For now. And you, brother? How are you faring?'

Vintir grunted. 'As long as I'm not challenged...'

Hjalvard nodded. 'I've issued standing orders. No access to the Wulfen quarters, and no access to this corridor. We will keep the situation contained.' *For as long as possible*, he almost added. He could only trust his

203

coolest-headed warriors to be outside their own quarters now, let alone stand guard on this choke point. He could barely trust himself now.

His vox bead crackled for his attention. 'What?' he snapped.

'*There are ships translating into the system, lord,*' an anxious huscarl said. '*The* Allfather's Honour, *the* Alpha Fang, *the* Bloodfire *and the* Wolfborn. *The Great Wolf is hailing us.*'

'I'm on my way,' Hjalvard said. He looked at Vintir. 'The fleets are returning.'

'Is the hunt finished?'

'Pray that it is, brother.'

The hold below was more filled than the rest of the Space Wolves knew. It held more than just the Wulfen now.

In the *Alpha Fang's* hololith chamber, an encrypted channel opened to the five strike cruisers. Harald Deathwolf and Canis Wolfborn watched the flickering image of Hjalvard describe the situation aboard the *Coldfang*. The battle leader's every word was dreaded confirmation. Harald grimaced. He had never before felt such pain at being proven correct.

'*We are overtaken by madness,*' Hjalvard said. '*Already seven Grey Hunters have fallen to the curse. The transformation has taken them. They are Wulfen now.*'

'*The mark is upon us all,*' Ulrik put in, the ancient voice hard and rasping as a glacier's crawl. '*The change can come to us at any time.*'

'*In combat!*' Hjalvard protested. '*In the heat of battle! The only struggle on the* Coldfang *has been between brothers! The more Wulfen come aboard, the worse it has become. Tempers are explosive. The training cages are wet with blood. I have restricted almost my entire force to quarters. My ship is a tinder box. It will take very little for it to explode.*'

Hjalvard's tones were harsh with strain. His breath kept turning into a growl. There was a softness to some of his consonants, as if he was finding it difficult to close his lips over his fangs.

'This is what I feared,' Harald said. 'The Wulfen are a curse.'

There. He had made his declaration. It was no longer a supposition, no longer a warning. The danger the Wulfen presented was clear. What had yet to be revealed was the full extent of the threat.

At his words, the hololithic figures burst into static, reformed, and burst again as the Wolf Lords shouted over each other. Ulrik the Slayer's image remained still, dark with intensity. Egil Iron Wolf and Sven Bloodhowl, bloodied from their struggles on Mygdal Alpha and Tranquilatus, sided with Harald.

'*Aggression is spiking on my ship,*' Iron Wolf said.

'*And mine,*' said Bloodhowl.

Grimnar spoke, silencing the others. '*The Stormcaller subjected our kin to every test he knows, Deathwolf. I insisted on it. There is no Chaos taint here. None!*' he said.

The image of Ulrik the Slayer nodded once, as if that was an end to the matter, but Harald had noticed a sliver of doubt in Grimnar's voice.

'*Perhaps not,*' said Iron Wolf, '*but there is something amiss. Some sickness, perhaps? My optic augurs read biochemical hyperactivity in my warriors. Their blood stirs…*'

'*We make warp for Fenris at once,*' Grimnar thundered, cutting him off. '*And upon our arrival, the Wulfen will fight at our side. The Space Wolves will defend our home world, and we will do so together! Do you mark that ship that has joined our formation?*'

'I do,' Harald said. The grey hull of the battle-barge reflected the light of Anvarheim with a bleak purity.

'*Our fleet is accompanied by the Grey Knights,*' Grimnar continued as if Harald had not spoken. '*Will you trust the encryption of this channel when the likes of them are present? Will you call our brothers cursed when they might hear? They demand we turn the Wulfen over to their tender mercies.*'

'Then we should do so, and excise the curse from our ranks,' said Harald.

Hjalvard had kept out of the debate of the Wolf Lords, but he grunted now in agreement.

'*No,*' said Grimnar, more quietly now. '*We need them. Fenris needs them. Even the Grey Knights have agreed to suspend their demands for the time being.*'

'*Then why are they here?*' Lord Iron Wolf asked.

'*They have offered their aid. I have accepted.*'

'The threat is grave then,' Harald said. He knew it was, since Grimnar had sent the order to all vessels to return to Fenris. Harald, Iron Wolf and Bloodhowl had already been making for Anvarheim when they received the message. The rest of the Wolf Lords had to cease their hunts and return. For Grimnar to accept the Grey Knights' offer of aid, the crisis must be extreme.

'*Captain Stern's astropaths intercepted a message from the Fang,*' said Grimnar.

'They did?' said Harald.

'*Only they could have,*' Grimnar replied. '*So little was left. Listen.*'

The recording played over the vox feed. The message was garbled and broken. The fragments were insufficient to permit a transcription into written language. Instead, the voices of the astropaths summoned portents through sound. They conjured symbols through the phrasing and tone. That was enough. In his mind's eye, Harald witnessed visions of storm and collapse, of fire and of an infinity of rioting, inhuman forms.

'And we would bring the Wulfen back with us?' he protested. 'Don't you see, Great Wolf, the role they have played in this disaster? Fenris is attacked while we have been scattered over the Sea of Stars, in pursuit of beings who bring out the most uncontrollable side of ourselves. Will we compound our folly now?'

'*They saved your life, Lord Deathwolf,*' Ulrik said.

Yes, Harald thought. Twice. He was mindful of his debt. Each word he spoke against the Wulfen felt like a frostblade plunging into his sense of honour. *There is no debt to the unclean,* he reminded himself. *There is no debt to the cursed.* There was no comfort in those words. Even so, his greater duty was to the survival of the Space Wolves, and he would not flinch from the path he must walk. 'What better way to be introduced to the heart of our Chapter?' he said.

'*You are wrong,*' said Ulrik. '*They are the necessary counter to the threat. If we abandon them, we abandon Russ. If we fight without them, we invite disaster.*'

'*Enough,*' Grimnar said. '*The decision has been made.*'

Harald shook his head. He muted his vox bead and looked at Canis. The champion shrugged.

'They fight well,' Canis said.

'They do,' Harald agreed. *But for whom?* he added silently.

'*There is more,*' said Grimnar.

More? Harald thought. *This isn't enough?*

'*I am unencrypting the hololith transmissions. Brother-Captain Stern warned me of something else on Vikurus. Prepare to receive pict data from the battle-barge.*'

A few moments later, Stern said, '*You have been speaking a long time under encryption.*'

'*We have,*' said Grimnar. His tone dared Stern to object.

'*The attack on Fenris is not the end game,*' Stern said, as if Grimnar had not spoken.

The electro-missive from Stern arrived. The pict screen above the tacticarium table displayed a schematic of the galaxy.

'*The warp storms associated with your... kin... are not random occurrences.*'

'We never thought they were,' Harald said.

'*You misunderstand me. Their locations are not random. The afflicted worlds were chosen for a reason.*'

The warp storms appeared on the schematic, a disease of whirling sigils.

'*Look,*' Stern said.

More data was added to the maps. With the exception of the warp-struck worlds, the galaxy faded into the background. Lines appeared, connecting the storms. Harald squinted. Even in this form, the pattern was an assault. A coil of tendrils looped from Atrapan to Hades Reach, split to grasp Irkalla and Dragos in jagged talons, fused once more to pierce Spartha IV. On and on the lines went, from world to world, a foul unveiling. A symbol came into being on the pict screen. The image shook. Static ate into the galaxy, though the lines remained strong. They vibrated. They began to pull free of the screen itself.

Then the data feed terminated. The pict vanished.

'*The complete symbol is dangerous even as the most basic schematic,*' Stern said. '*And it is being drawn over the breadth of the galaxy.*'

'What is it?' Harald asked.

'*It is vengeance.*'

'You've encountered it before?'

'*Records of it. No one in the Imperium has seen it for ten thousand years.*'

Ten thousand years. The past again, forever reaching out, forever clawing the present.

'And when was it seen then?' said Harald. The question was ceremonial. In the depths of his soul, he knew the answer.

'It was only ever used by the sorcerers of Prospero.'

Harald reached out to the blank screen. He slashed a finger across it as if he could disrupt the vanished pattern. As if he could destroy the pattern coming into being across the Imperium, and even now devouring the worlds of Fenris.

The symbol was the signature of the Crimson King.

PART 3

THE RITUAL

CHAPTER 6

PLANETFALL

Frostheim and its moon, Svellgard.

Midgardia.

And then Valdrmani, the Wolf Moon. The enemy was on the doorstep of Fenris itself.

The system cried out for its saviours. Krom heard. Held by his oath, he could do nothing.

Frostheim fell into its infernal silence, but Svellgard howled before it followed. The vassals garrisoning the World Wolf's Lair saw the seas vomit up millions of daemons. They had a brief moment to call out to Fenris, to give voice to their horror, before they were swallowed up.

Krom heard. He could do nothing.

Midgardia was the inverse twin of Fenris. Where Fenris was glacial, Midgardia was a hothouse. Fenris' winds blew with bone-scraping purity, whereas Midgardia's air was foetid and thick with spores. Fenris permitted only the hardiest, most brutal of life forms to survive on its surface but Midgardia was a lush, fungal jungle, an explosion of life in such super-abundance that it was a riot of all-consuming competition. The population of Fenris was sparse. The people of Midgardia were many. When the warp rifts opened in the air and below the ground, unleashing the daemonic hordes on the surface of the cities and in their subterranean warrens, the massacre was not over in an instant. There was time for the Ruinous Powers to savour their work. There was time for Midgardia's militia to attempt a defence, and so there was time to experience the death of all hope. The population of Midgardia screamed as it was overcome. The scream was the death cry of millions. It resounded across the Fenris System. It was compounded of such horror and agony and fear that it seemed as if it should send the very Wolf's Eye into eclipse.

Krom heard. He could do nothing.

And Valdrmani. Like Frostheim, it fell quiet. There was a different quality to its silence, however. Frostheim went down first, and when the rifts opened across the system, it was clear the ice world had been the start of the attack. Valdrmani went down at the same time as Svellgard and Midgardia. There was only the briefest of cries, suddenly cut off. Or, it seemed, contained. Communications were dead between Fenris and Frostheim. But the astropathic choir of the Fang detected something in the aether of Valdrmani. The silence was tense, stretched to the breaking point. Something was building up, and when the silence could no longer contain what grew, the scream would dwarf all others.

Verthandi, mistress of the astropathic choir of Fenris, came to Krom and told him what was sensed, and what was to come.

Krom heard. He could do nothing.

He patrolled the defences of the Fang. The Drakeslayers stood on high alert, ready to destroy the enemy when it came to Fenris. They longed to take the battle to the daemons, but to where? To which world first?

No rifts had opened on Fenris. Krom saw, in the sparing of the Space Wolves' home world, the lineaments of a trap. The agony of the other worlds tested him. The need to storm to their aid threatened to tear him in half. But his failure on Alaric Prime held him to his oath; he would not abandon his post and see Fenris devoured by the daemonic as the rifts opened, mocking his pride and his arrogance.

He pushed the astropaths beyond their limits. It was the only action open to him. Grimnar and the other Wolf Lords must know what had been heard on Fenris. They had to be recalled. The choir sent out the call. It was torn to shreds by the rifts. No aetheric communication could leave the system. Even vox transmissions no longer worked, except over limited distances.

Impossibility was a poor excuse. The message must be sent. Astropaths died, the blood of their minds pouring from their eyes and ears.

'We cannot,' Verthandi told Krom. She could barely walk now. She was supported by serfs on either side.

'You must,' Krom told her. 'You will.'

When he was not on the ramparts, he stood in the shadows of the stone gallery above the choir, bearing witness to their efforts. He saw the cost of what he demanded. He saw a form of heroism different from the battlefield glory he and his brothers knew. It was no less real. The astropaths were the only active combatants on Fenris. He watched them with respect and envy.

There was no way to know if any of their efforts were successful. There were no messages that arrived from outside the system. There was only the wait for the return of the hunters. The hope they would hear. And the endless, grinding frustration.

Krom waited. He stood fast. And while he kept faith with his oath, the worlds of the Fenris System screamed.

* * *

The wolves returned to the fold in fury. The individual fleets had purged world after world in the hunt for the Wulfen. Now they arrived as one, descending with all their might on a single system. Their own home.

But the Fenris System was no longer theirs.

The ships translated from the warp, yet the warp did not leave them. It was here, in the rifts unleashing infinite foulness on their worlds. The fleet emerged from the Mandeville point at the edge of the system. Even with the ships in close proximity, vox communication was growing difficult. Attempts to make contact with the home world failed. Assembling a coherent picture of the situation was difficult. It was not impossible, however. The aetheric disturbances caused by the rifts over the occupied worlds were so severe that there was no doubt where the fury of the wolves would be directed.

'We shall make simultaneous strikes,' Grimnar announced in the hololith chamber of the *Allfather's Honour*. 'The Firehowlers will retake Svellgard. The Deathwolves, Frostheim. Lord Iron Wolf, together your company and the Kingsguard are bound for Midgardia.' Every sentence the Great Wolf spoke resounded in the chamber like the beat of a huge war drum. The Great Wolf's frame seemed to vibrate from the horror and rage within.

Ulrik shared the wrath. No words could encompass the crime that had occurred. No words could describe the punishment that was coming.

The Great Wolf paused. He exchanged a look with Ulrik. The High Wolf Priest knew what Grimnar would say next. All the Wolf Lords did. Their hololithic images were still. They waited for the blow to their pride.

When Grimnar spoke again, his voice was no less resonant than it had been before. If he must make this request, it would be done with power. 'Brother-Captain Stern,' Grimnar said. 'We would be grateful for your aid in purging Valdrmani.'

'*It shall be done,*' Stern voxed.

'*And the Wulfen?*' Lord Deathwolf asked.

'To each strike force, a murderpack.'

'*We risk having our companies consumed by frenzy from within.*'

'It is *done!*' Grimnar roared. 'We will use every weapon and every warrior to reclaim our worlds. Chaos seeks to weaken us. We will counter it with unity. We will not deny any brother the honour of fighting to reclaim our system.'

'Lord Deathwolf,' Ulrik said. 'The Wulfen have not been brought to us by Chaos. They have returned to us to fight this greatest threat.'

'*I hope you are right, Slayer,*' Deathwolf replied. '*We will know very soon.*'

Beneath sleep, above death, the giant daemon on the ramparts.
  Its sword high in hunger and triumph.
  No. You come no further.
  A duel of thought and dreams and lightning. The sword striking through

the echo-sarcophagus. The assault cannon shadow pounding nightmare
flesh. The noble savagery of Fenris stronger than the abomination's wrath.
The fell hand seizing the daemon's limbs.

The crushing of wrath's form.

The daemon broken, the wave hurled back.

Only for a moment. The wave rising again, and with it a terrible shadow.
An echo of a scream not yet heard. It has the shape of doom.

The daemon laughing in defeat. Taunting. Revealing a horror all the worse
for its truth.

The silver templars will die. Their death is your end.

The doom gathering definition.

I see it. I see it!

They must be told.

Wake! Wake! Wake!

Two summons came for Krom within seconds of each other. Albjorn Fogel
voxed from the augur complex. The fleet had returned. Multiple ships had
translated into the system. Contact was impossible, but their radiation signatures and warp displacements were unmistakable. Krom raced from the
astropathic choristrium.

'One vessel is unknown,' Fogel was saying. Before he could continue, the second summons overrode the first. It came from deep in the roots of the Fang.

'Lord Dragongaze,' Hrothgar Swordfang voxed, *'Bjorn the Fell-Handed*
is awake!'

Krom felt the winds of fate howl around him. A culmination was at hand.

'On my way,' he told Swordfang. To Fogel he said, 'Keep trying the vox.'
He changed direction, heading for a grav-lift. It dropped him thousands
of metres, accelerating to near free-fall in seconds, then gradually slowing
in the final minute, depositing him in the centre of the mountain's ancient
labyrinth. In the only vault that still held a Dreadnought, he found Hrothgar Swordfang and other Iron Priests, along with a group of Wolf Priests.
'You finally succeeded,' he said. They had been trying to wake Bjorn since
Harald had returned from Nurades.

'No,' said Hrothgar. 'This is not our doing. He woke of his own accord,
and called for you.'

Krom approached the enormous war machine. The oldest hero of the
Space Wolves did not move. There was no sign of consciousness until
Krom was a few metres away. The monolith lowered slightly. Optic augurs
regarded him, relaying his image to the mind inside.

'Krom Dragongaze,' said Bjorn. The voice seemed as old and deep as
the Fang.

'You wake to aid us in our hour of great need, venerable brother.'

'No. I sleep still.' Bjorn spoke slowly. His words seemed to come from
a measureless distance. 'I must sleep. There is war there that only I can

fight. The threat is dire. We stand on the brink of destruction. You must go to Valdrmani.'

'I am bound by my oath to remain,' said Krom. 'The Great Wolf and our brothers have returned from the hunt. They will drive the abominations from our system.'

'They have not come alone.'

'That is so,' Krom said, startled. 'A battle-barge we have not identified.'

'Silver,' said Bjorn. 'Grey Knights.'

The priests stirred in surprise and anger. Those warriors were not welcome on Fenris.

'They make for Valdrmani,' Bjorn continued. 'They will die on Valdrmani. Their fate will determine ours. You must go, Dragongaze. Warn them. Save them. Save us.'

'I have sworn an oath,' said Krom.

'Break it, or doom us,' Bjorn told him.

'What awaits them?' Krom asked.

The Dreadnought was still. Krom sensed his consciousness recede to a place beyond reach. The vault was again filled with the silence that lived between sleep and death.

Krom realised he didn't need an answer. It was enough to know the Grey Knights would fall into a trap. *Their fate will determine ours.*

The fleets led by the *Allfather's Honour* and the *Wolfborn* entered low orbit over Midgardia. Its atmosphere was thick, forever clouded. The surface was invisible. To the eye, there was nothing to announce its taint. The vox was more revealing – faint traces of human screams mixed with the monstrous howling of inhuman tongues.

Ulrik stared at the cloud cover through the oculus. Anger at the desecration suffused his blood. He was eager to be on the ground. Eager to eradicate the abomination. Eager, too, for the Wulfen to prove their worth, to at last assume their proper role amongst the Great Companies. They would be fighting for something much more than the recovery of their kin. They would be fighting for the salvation of Fenris and the Space Wolves.

The Wolf Lords were increasingly wary of the Wulfen. The spreading aggression was a challenge. What they did not understand, Ulrik thought, was the nature of the test. Fury was in the blood of the Space Wolves. They were stronger with the return of the Wulfen. So was the fury. We must learn to channel it, he thought. We must remake ourselves. Then we will be ready for Russ when he comes again.

'Augurs,' Grimnar said.

'Readings confirm two rifts,' the vassal officer answered. 'They are located near the Magma Gates. One above ground, one below.'

'Good.' Grimnar touched the vox console beside the command throne. 'Is Strike Force Fenris ready?'

'*We are,*' said Egil Iron Wolf.

The last of the ship-to-ship transfers had taken place just before the battle-barge and strike cruiser reached their positions. Grimnar had sent his heavy armour to join the Ironwolves, while Egil's Terminators and recovered Wulfen had come aboard the *Allfather's Honour*.

'Good.' Grimnar stood. He joined Ulrik at the rail overlooking the bridge. 'Let it begin!' he roared. His wrath was a storm. It held and expressed the rage of every Space Wolf. 'Strike Force Fenris, you are the hammer that shatters the enemy's skull. Strike Force Morkai, we are the frostblade between the ribs. Now, let thunder fall!'

'Well done, lad,' Ulrik said quietly. 'Well done.'

The orbital bombardment began. The lance batteries of both ships fired into the atmosphere. The target zone was before the walls of the Magma Gates. The enormous fortress complex would withstand the attack. Anything outside on the walls or on the ground within several thousand metres would not.

Spears of lasers plunged through the cloud cover. The air heated to red. A fierce wound appeared on the shifting, opaque face of Midgardia and fury seared the planet. The attack was continuous. The view in the oculus shifted to display the *Wolfborn*. Along the length of the hull, shafts of concentrated destruction lashed the world below.

We are bombarding our own worlds, Ulrik thought. It has come this far. The pattern has ensnared us this far. But no longer.

With the purifying destruction of these strikes, the Space Wolves were breaking the snare. Dark machinations had created the vulnerability of the home system. The wills behind the warp storms had used the Wulfen to lure the Great Companies away. Ulrik would grant Harald that much. That lure, though, would be the seed of the foe's destruction. No one could use the brothers of Fenris against each other.

This is our trial, he thought. There is yet another pattern at work, a glorious one, and we approach its culmination. We are being tested. We must prove ourselves worthy of Russ and of the saga into which he will lead us.

He stared at the lance fire so fiercely, his vision contracted to the blaze of those vertical suns. He blinked, jolted from his reverie of faith when half the batteries ceased fire. The *Wolfborn*'s bay doors opened. Stormwolves launched. They flew down in formation, their dives so steep they were almost in parallel to the lasers. A new series of short bursts lit the hull. The drop pods plunged into the atmosphere. They too were a bombardment, a living one, and their reach would be far greater and more destructive than that of the batteries.

Grimnar clapped Ulrik's shoulder. 'Fenris has begun its work,' he said.

'It's time Morkai was about its own,' Ulrik growled.

The Great Wolf and the High Wolf Priest left the bridge. They took a grav lift down through the towering superstructure of the battle-barge. On the same level as the launch bays, they entered a huge chamber amidships.

The Terminators of the Kingsguard and the Ironwolves stood along the periphery of the teleportarium's platform. The rest of the Great Company formed concentric rings of Grey Hunters, Long Fangs, Blood Claws and Scouts. Inside those rings were the Lone Wolves. At the very centre were the Wulfen of two companies, and in their midst were the massive sarcophagi of Haargen Deathbane and Svendar Ironarm. The Venerable Dreadnoughts stood guard over Murderfang. He had been subdued with helfrost after the departure from Vikurus. Wrapped in adamantium chains, he was conscious once more. The presence of the Wulfen appeared to have the same effect as in Absolom. Ulrik thought Murderfang was calm, but perhaps it was the patience of a predator about to spring. Whatever the truth, it was possible to bring him here.

The teleportation was risky. Only Terminator armour had homing devices. The Iron Priests had communed with the machine spirit of the ancient teleportarium. With the Terminators' homers marking the full spread of the strike force, the Iron Priests believed it would be possible to send the full complement of warriors into the subterranean warren of Morkai's Gate with an acceptable degree of safety. Most of the complex's population lived below ground. The tunnels and caverns were large. The maps were detailed and accurate. There was no uncertainty to the coordinates. The risk came from the turbulence created by the warp storms.

Grimnar and Ulrik strode across the teleportarium platform to the centre. The Wulfen watched their approach. They dropped their heads before the Great Wolf, acknowledging the supreme alpha. Their battered armour and punch daggers had been replaced using the stores of new, Wulfen-adapted equipment aboard the *Coldfang*. They were restive, clawed hands opening and closing. Their jaws were wide, lips curled back over their gums. The tension of such a large murderpack bled into the rest of the strike force. Ulrik felt the contagion. He could not dismiss it. His heartbeats accelerated. His teeth were on edge and saliva flooded his mouth. His righteous anger over the daemonic incursion lost some of its focus, becoming a beast of its own. He needed to fight. He needed the warm spray of his prey's blood.

He clutched the totems hanging at his waist and fixed his gaze on the crozius arcanum. *This is the trial. This is our truth. The rage is ours. It is mine.* There was no curse here, only the reality of the Space Wolves, the truth of the spirit that had grown larger and more ferocious with the return of the 13th.

'Let the enemy feel our claws at their throats!' Grimnar called.

In the control gallery in the upper reaches of the chamber, the Iron Priests saluted and began their task.

There were pylons at each of the four corners of the platform. They were tall, engraved with sigils holy to the Omnissiah. They curved inwards, their tips pointing towards the centre of an invisible dome over the strike force. The pylons came to life, energy spiralling up their height, building to a blinding intensity at their points. The air grew taut. There was the sharp smell of ozone. The Wulfen howled, their manes bristling.

The shift happened.

A split in the materium.

The eyeblink of reality.

Ulrik experienced the jolt of being and non-being. He was in the *All-father's Honour*, and then he was in the high cavern before the great underground gates of the fortress.

And the Wulfen were maddened. Maniacal howls filled the cave. The monsters of the 13th Great Company leapt forward, claws out, fangs gaping.

In their midst, Murderfang exploded into violent movement, a thunder of frenzy and war.

In the *Alpha Fang*'s strategium, Harald gathered the Wolf Guard, Feingar of the Coldeyes and Norvald Iceflame around the hololithic display of Morkai's Keep.

'The ship we detected in orbit translated into the warp before we could identify it,' Harald told his officers. 'However...' he tapped the vox. An auspex recording played back. The vox traffic on Frostheim was active. It was scrambled by the proximity of the rifts. Enough was intelligible, though. Dark, twisted voices emerged from the speaker.

'Traitors,' Canis spat.

Harald nodded. 'There are more than daemons below. Our true enemy begins to show his face.'

'Who are they?' Feingar asked.

'Still unidentified.'

'Just one ship,' said Canis.

'Yes,' said Harald. 'They have Morkai's Keep, but we are many.'

'What about the defences?' said Norvald.

'Inactive.' Harald distrusted the new turn of luck, but the readings were clear. Fate was at last favouring the Space Wolves. 'Sensor auguries have detected no energy readings from the gun emplacements. The wyrd stirs in the heart of the keep, but its outer walls are dead.'

'If that is true,' Feingar said, 'the attack must have occurred very recently. A poor strategy to leave yourself vulnerable to retaliation.'

Harald agreed. His loathing for the Traitors did not mean contempt for their skill in the battlefield. They were not fools. It would not do to treat them as such. The assumption that the Traitors had only just taken Frostheim troubled him, even though it was the only plausible deduction. He did not second-guess the augur readings. He had to act based on the information he had.

And he needed to act. The idea of Morkai's Keep in traitorous hands was insupportable. The enemy was forcing the Space Wolves to attack their own fortifications. Harald's limbs thrummed with anger. He would fall on the

Traitors and make them curse their own existence. Every second of waiting was indefensible.

He saw the same furious anticipation in the faces surrounding the tacticarium table. The bloodiest, most violent retaliation imaginable was
required.

Harald made a claw of his hand and held it above the centre of the hololith. 'We drop into the heart of Morkai's Keep,' he said, 'with the full fury
of Whitestalker. They would use our walls against us. So we will ignore the
walls. Drop pods first, Stormwolves following in a steep descent, providing
covering fire for the drop pod troops. Our primary target is the command
chamber. Retake it and exterminate the Traitors.'

There was nothing subtle about the strategy. It was designed as a brutal
hammer blow, fuelled by rage. Harald's anger was too great for anything
else. So was that of his brothers. The Wolf Guard roared as one, and clapped
their fists to their pauldrons.

Revelation hovered before Harald's eyes. He saw the salute as a thin
veneer. The truth was the roar. The truth was the beast. He saw the mark
of the wolf on all his brothers, and in himself. He saw the division between
human and animal vanish altogether. He saw what he had been warning
against, and fighting against.

He saw that the contagion had reached him too. The insult of the
Traitors was too great. The war anger was too strong. The beast was
claiming him.

He saw all this, and then he didn't. The revelation sank beneath the red
sea of wrath.

He answered his brothers with his roar, and then he marched from the
strategium.

A few minutes later, Harald and one pack of Thunderclaw Wolf Guard
with their thunderwolves were aboard *Runeclaw*, streaking through the
frigid atmosphere of Frostheim. He looked through one of the forward
viewing blocks. The air was clear. Visibility was excellent. He could already
see, on the plane of white below, a small shape, barely more than a dot,
but jagged, clearly artificial: Morkai's Keep. Ahead of *Runeclaw* and the
other Stormwolves, the drop pods left contrails of fire in their wake. Searing claws stabbed towards the fortress.

Harald felt calmer than he had aboard the *Alpha Fang*. The hunt was
on, and soothing the rage of frustration. His earlier revelation rose in his
mind. He pushed it aside, consciously this time. Those thoughts were useless to him now.

The surface of the planet drew closer and the uniform white acquired
texture. The cracks of crevasses and the shadows of mountains appeared,
outlined by the reflected light of Svellgard. Morkai's Keep grew. Its blocky
form gathered strength.

Harald's calm bled away again. His senses sharpened. The hunger built.

Closer. The distant mountain ranges cleared. The mesa of the keep filling the view. The concentric walls of the keep marking the target.

Strike Force Whitestalker fell towards the silent fortress.

Silent no longer.

The walls of Morkai's Keep erupted with light, the barrel flashes of dozens of guns. Lascannons and vortex missiles struck at the drop pods. The lethal flowers of flak blossomed in such density that the keep vanished beneath their blackened crimson. The huge shells of macro cannons roared through the squadrons. Drop pods exploded, vanishing in expanding fireballs. Other pods had their sides sheared off and were sent into uncontrolled, tumbling falls, shedding wreckage and warriors as they spun.

Proximity alert klaxons shrieked.

'*Turn that off!*' Harald shouted over the clamour. The alarms were pointless now.

In the cockpit, Iron Priest Veigir obeyed. The klaxons fell silent. Now Harald could hear the uproar on the vox. Curses mixed with snarls and electronic shrieks.

'There were no energy readings!' Veigir shouted. 'How can the guns be active?'

'What matters is they are,' Harald said. 'Stormwolves, provide covering fire for the drop pods,' he ordered. 'There is no evasive action to be had. We are committed.'

Straight down, into the cauldron. The anti-air fire was so intense that the sky was a single explosion. The Space Wolves had designed the armaments of Morkai's Keep to annihilate any attack by air or by land, and now it fulfilled its duty. Other, darker weapons added their destructive force to the las and missiles and flak. Wyrdflame billowed and writhed between the explosions. Harald saw a drop pod fall into a concentrated burst of the mutagenic horror. The pod collapsed in on itself, crushing its occupants, then turned itself inside out, becoming a thing of giant, bulbous organs. It continued to change as it fell. It had no form any longer. It was a constant flow of transformation.

The Stormwolves sent out a stream of lascannons and heavy bolter fire. They sought to take out the turrets, but they were firing blind through the storm of flame. The drop pods were in the direct line of fire, hampering the gunships' retaliation, and even they were disappearing from sight. There was only the cauldron, the roil of the air tearing itself apart.

The vox traffic was a cacophonous litany of disaster, of drop pods blasted from the sky, of shells and las punching through the hulls and wings of the Stormwolves.

'Hold fast, brothers,' Harald exhorted. 'We are still hunting! Our claws will tear the enemy from the sky!'

There was nothing else he could do. He was helpless until the gunship reached the ground. He bit back his curses. His fury was indeed strong, but it had nowhere to strike as he gazed at the unfolding of a rout.

Runeclaw dropped below the flak barrier. Morkai's Keep came back into sight. It was unbreached. Only a few drop pods had landed within the ring walls. They were isolated. Their surviving Deathwolves were being chewed up by ground-defence turrets. Beyond the walls, the rest of the pods were spread out across the glacier.

The configuration of the battle changed again. Winged shapes burst from the flanks of the glacier and screamed upward to meet the Storm-wolves. They were armour-plated predators, both engines of war and yowling daemon.

'Machine drake!' Veigir shouted.

Angular jaws parted to reveal autocannons. They added their fire to the anti-air guns, flying in towards the Stormwolves on the flanks. Their shells cut across the deadly stream from Morkai's Keep. At the very moment the Space Wolves attempted to change their angle of approach, veering away from the fortress to defend the scattered troops, they were caught in a shredding, interlocking barrage.

Once again, there was no chance of evasion.

The turrets below ceased shooting as the machine drakes screamed into the midst of the Stormwolves. The blistering rate of fire from the six-barrel autocannons pummelled ships already battered by the descent. Vessels that had been the subject of song for millennia turned into meteoric balls of flame. The death of heroes roared over the landscape, shedding wreck-age and bodies. The squadron turned its guns on the daemonic engines. They took their toll. *Runeclaw* unleashed a coordinated burst of las and bolter, both twin-linked pairs pulverizing the gunship's target at the same moment. The blasts decapitated a flyer. Its head plummeted towards the ground. The body careened off in a wild, whirling spin. It collided with another corrupted flyer, tangling their wings. Both fell, flames erupting from the body and ruptured engines.

Harald punched the bulkhead and snarled as he saw the enemy bleed at last. Then huge talons plunged through the roof. Wyrd energy crack-led around them as they contracted and crumpled ablative ceramite and adamantium. The machine drake peeled the roof back and screamed in triumph. Entwined with that shriek were others, the souls of a crew long succumbed to damnation howled pain and terror and rage. The scream slammed through the troop compartment of *Runeclaw*, overwhelming even the roar of the invading wind.

Icetooth and the thunderwolves howled. They struggled against the har-nesses bolted to the deck. Deathwolves fired upward, bolter shells by the score punching into the blue, glowing armour of the machine drake. Explo-sions rippled along its underbelly. It shrieked again, with anger now, and opened one of its talons, releasing the sheared roof and reaching into the hold to crush the tiny warriors who dared cause it harm. Harald brought up his storm shield and smashed it into the leading claw. The shield's energy field exploded with a rage of its own. The impact jolted down the length of his frame, hard enough for the deck to crack beneath his boots. The talon jerked, momentarily halted, and Harald spun, bringing Glacius against it with a blow to shatter mountains. He severed it and ichor and promethium flooded the hold. Now the flyer screamed with its own pain. The sound ignited the air and a firestorm engulfed the Deathwolves. Contemptuous of the flames, Harald struck again, hitting the centre of the talon, opening a split that travelled up the side of the monster's limb. Energy lashed out in every direction. Fire raced into the engine's wound.

Pain engulfed the sentient machine. It yanked its wounded limb from the gutted Stormwolf, and, still clutching the hull with one talon, folded its wings and dropped into a vertical dive. The sudden shift in mass turned *Runeclaw* over in the air. Harald jammed the storm shield into the torn bulkhead and held on to keep from plummeting through the gap in the roof. Most of his brothers were still in grav harnesses. They dangled upside down, shooting at the machine drake. *Runeclaw*'s engines thundered with strain as Veigir fought against the pull. He slowed the drop, but could not right the ship. Another flyer streaked past on the port side, autocannon shells puncturing the wing and engine nacelles.

The flight surfaces were all but destroyed. Two of the engines had exploded. The gunship's fall was accelerating as the machine drake pushed it down to an annihilating smash.

Bolter shells dug into the daemon ship's plating but it kept its grip on the Stormwolf. The talons were out of reach of Glacius. He could not attack without slipping his arm from his shield and falling from the gunship.

In the midst of wind and flame, the Thunderclaw Kollungir dropped his bolter and yanked off his helmet. His eyes were wide and red and mad. He howled, insensate with rage. The howl went on and on. Harald could not hear it over the whine of the remaining engines. He could feel it though. His blood pounded in answer. Kollungir's jaw lengthened and his hair and beard coarsened. He shook his head back and forth, snapping with lethal fangs, and his face projected forward until it was no longer human – it was a muzzle. He struggled with his gauntlets until they too fell away, revealing fingers that ended in huge claws. He tore his harness apart. Still howling, his body transformed by a frenzy that went beyond war into the most primal being of the Space Wolves, he leapt through the roof. He fell on the daemon's clutching talon and attacked it with stabbing, slashing, biting fury.

The contagion spread to a second Thunderclaw. Leifir ripped himself free as well and followed his brother. As he jumped, Harald saw there was nothing left of the rational in his eyes. He was lost forever to the beast within.

Leifir and Kollungir were flesh. They attacked a thing of metal and wyrd-born sorcery. Yet they drew blood. They pierced the hide of their prey. The foul mix of ichor and fuel sprayed into the hold. Fire bellowed.

The daemon engine roared in outrage and released *Runeclaw* before peeling off to starboard.

Two figures fell, clawing at air.

Freed, *Runeclaw* went into a spin. It tumbled and rolled, a ruin in free-fall. The wind at last put the fire out. Harald held tight to the wedged shield as he was thrown back and forth. He caught glimpses of the ground through the open roof. Once again helpless to act, he damned the decisions that had brought Whitestalker to this point, ambushed and blasted from the sky.

We rushed.

We did not stop to think we might be deceived.

We only listened to the fury of our beasts within.

We are falling to the curse.

Twisting, falling end over end. The glacier rushing up.

The engines stuttering, firing in bursts as Veigir struggled to slow the descent.

The world a maelstrom.

Wind and speed and fury.

A sudden, terrible crash.

CHAPTER 7

NOVA

Krom stood with Hrothgar Swordfang at the entrance to the Wulfen quarters. Serkir faced them. He held his frost axe with both hands. There was an eager glint in his eyes, but his hackles were not raised. His stance was not aggressive.

'Take them,' Hrothgar urged. 'Use their strength. Seeing them in combat will be invaluable.'

'There are more urgent considerations,' Krom reminded the Iron Priest, who nodded in acknowledgement. Krom would have hesitated to stop here, however briefly, if not for two reasons. The *Winterbite* would not yet be ready for launch. And there was fate. Even now he worked to divine the meaning of that gathering before Murderfang. The Wulfen had a role to play in the events unfolding in the Fenris System. He could no more deny that than he could the coming of winter.

Serkir focused his gaze on Krom. He struggled to form words. 'We... must... go...' he said, the final word trailing off into a growl, one that was not a threat, but instead a shudder from his deep being, a response to the call of destiny. He shook himself, then repeated, 'We... must... go... to Valdrmani.'

Krom gave Hrothgar a sharp look. 'What have you told them?'

'Nothing.' Hrothgar was startled too.

Krom turned back to Serkir. Fate had spoken to the Wulfen too, then. Serkir knew what he must do. His words were so close to Bjorn's. Krom's decision was clear; there was no choice at all. For the first time since the departure of the hunt, he breathed more easily. The fate that had been closing in was here, and he was free to take up arms against it.

Krom made for the grav lift with Hrothgar at his side and Serkir leading the pack behind. They rose to the peak of the Fang. In the final stages of the ascent, the walls of the lift shaft vibrated with the deep thrum of the *Winterbite*'s engines powering up. The vibration became thunder when the doors opened and Krom entered the space dock.

The crew of the *Winterbite* had begun a crash preparation for lift-off the instant Krom had given the order. Anchored to the dock, the Nova-class frigate was small and light as warships went. It was still a mountain tethered to another. It rumbled now like a volcano on the verge of eruption. It too was eager for the battle to be joined.

Waiting for Krom were the warriors of Fierce-eye's finest. They had assembled as soon as Krom had given the order for mobilisation: Beoric Winterfang and the Wolf Guard in terminator armour, Hengist Ironaxe at the head of the Grey Hunters, Egil Redfist and his Blood Claws. They were the elite of Krom's Great Company. They were a pack of hunters hungry for war. The icon of the sun wolf on their pauldrons seemed to snarl in frustration at having been held back so long.

'The Great Wolf has unleashed us?' Beoric asked.

'No,' said Krom. 'He has returned, but we still have no contact. Bjorn the Fell-Handed sends us to the rescue of the Grey Knights.'

'*What?*' said Egil, astounded.

'They are heading into a trap on Valdrmani,' Krom told him. 'If they fall, our Chapter will suffer a mortal blow.' With that he crossed the dock at a fast march, past vassals and servitors completing the final tasks before the launch. He strode up an embarkation ramp into the mustering bay of the *Winterbite*. The ramp rose behind the last of the warriors, slamming shut with a reverberating clang.

'Beoric and Hengist, you are with me on the bridge. The rest of you, remain here with our brothers of the Thirteenth Company. The journey will be brief. Action will be immediate.

'Shipmaster,' he voxed as he strode from the bay. 'We are aboard. Is the ship ready?'

'*Just now, lord.*'

'Then launch.'

He broke into a run. He felt the power of the engines run through the halls of the frigate like fire through his blood. The decks trembled, then his weight multiplied, g-force pressing down as the ship hurled its great mass towards the sky. Krom did not slow. He and his brothers charged towards the bridge as if reaching it would bring them to their target sooner.

The *Winterbite* did not have far to travel. Merely the distance from Fenris to its moon. But Krom had been conscious of time flowing away from the moment Bjorn had returned to the silence of his war beneath sleep. No seconds had been wasted. The frigate had departed the moment it could. But for every one of those seconds, the Grey Knights had drawn closer to Valdrmani, and none of the hails from Fenris had been answered.

The Grey Knights could not be warned. The only hope was that they could be stopped.

Not enough time, Krom thought. Not enough. It was as if he could picture the Grey Knight ship knifing through the system, approaching the moon while he still had not left the upper atmosphere of Fenris.

He burst onto the bridge. The oculus showed the void and the face of Valdrmani. Already the moon was visibly growing closer. Its fall into silence had been a special torture for Krom. There were hundreds of thousands of citizens in the Longhowl domeplex. They were on the threshold of Fenris. Krom should have been able to reach out from the peak of the Fang and strike at the daemonic foe.

'How close are the Grey Knights?' he demanded.

The augur officer looked up. 'They have already arrived.'

No time.

The distress call was clear now. The signal the astropaths of Titan had so painfully pieced together from the shreds that escaped the warp was whole. Precise, focused, it came from Valdrmani, not Fenris, broadcast from Long-howl. The cry went out on sub-warp frequencies too. When Stern switched to its channel on the vox, he could listen to the full message. He did so again as he boarded the Stormraven *Deimos Glaive*.

'They're still calling?' Brother-Librarian Carac asked. The shadow of his psychic hood accentuated the angles of his long, sharp features.

'They are.'

'It isn't automated?'

'No.' Stern drew the grav harness over his shoulder. 'The words repeat, but there are variations in the voice.' It was hoarse, exhausted, sometimes almost inaudible.

'Don't they see us?' said Xalvador.

'The speaker is not a Space Wolf,' said Stern. 'These are mortals. I doubt they will believe in their salvation until it is upon them. So let us be about it.'

The Stormravens launched. They shot away from the bays of the battle-barge. Below, Valdrmani awaited. Stern knew that Chaos rioted on the moon, though it presented a face of emptiness and silence. The surface was a desert of red dust, never to be moved by a wind. There was no atmosphere. The domes of Longhowl became clear.

'No breaches,' Carac said.

'So it would seem,' said Stern.

There was no vapour of escaping air from the domes. Their forms were intact.

'Strange the daemons should take such care,' Carac mused.

'Deaths by sudden cold and asphyxiation are too merciful to be enjoyed,' Stern said. 'If the incursion began inside Longhowl, the enemy would not need to force an entry.'

Even as he spoke, his answer dissatisfied him. Another reason came to him in the next heartbeat. If there were corrupted mortals in the enemy ranks, they would need air. And if that were true...

The signal, he thought.

In that moment, the signal changed. It became a single word.

'*Welcome*,' the voice said.

Then it laughed. Well it might. The subterfuge had been perfect. In an instant, Stern beheld the enormous implications of what had been done. The enemy had simulated a broken distress call that had passed every test of authenticity the Grey Knights had used on it. Worse, he now saw dire purpose in the fact that *only* the Sons of Titan had succeeded in intercepting it. The signal had been imperceptible to the Space Wolves because it had been aimed specifically at the Grey Knights.

The Space Wolves were not countering the enemy's plan by returning to the Fenris system. They were fulfilling it, lured by means of the Grey Knights to arrive at the appointed time.

We were lured too, Stern thought. The enemy wants us here.

Now.

At this very spot.

The laughter became a maniacal howl. The signal cut out.

In the centre of Longhowl was a huge cylindrical tower. It stood higher than any of the domes. It split open, revealing the barrel of an immense gun.

The nova cannon fired.

Destruction had a royal majesty. The eternal night of Valdrmani exploded into ruby-coloured day. A multitude of energy columns shot out of the barrel at once. They lanced into the void, and into the core of the Grey Knights vessel sitting in low orbit.

The battle-barge was still fully visible through the Stormravens' viewing blocks. Now it was lit by the terminal beam. Stern watched the display in horror. He watched annihilation unfold in silent grace.

The light seared so brightly, it seemed to burn the void itself. It sliced through the battle-barge from underbelly to superstructure. The ship held its form for a long, slow moment that was less than the single beat of a heart, then the bow began to dip. The stern moved forward.

The battle-barge became two. The light between its identities expanded, becoming brighter yet, becoming the cry of plasma, the wail of a sun's birth and of a sun's death. The shockwave rippled over the length of the vessel. The wave travelled outwards. It reached Valdrmani. The Stormravens were beyond its greatest force. Even so, it hammered them with its passage. The engines of *Deimos Glaive* howled in protest. A great fist shook the gunship, blurring the view of the battle-barge, then passed. The fire from the heart of the ship blossomed. It swallowed the halves before they could begin to tumble. They disintegrated in its jaws. The light hurled the pieces away.

A monstrous dawn flared over the face of Valdrmani, then faded. The nova cannon ceased fire and night returned, illuminated by a sombre fireball in the heavens. And then the rain came. The broken, burning pieces of the vessel began their fall to the surface. Flung with the force of the battle-barge's death, many streaked moonwards at immense velocity.

They were comets of broken vaults, vast marble columns becoming broken spears, meteors of adamantine slag. A head ten metres across, from the bow's statuary, smashed through *Bane of the Magi*. The gunship exploded, becoming more of the rain of wreckage.

The domeplex would survive. It was designed to withstand such impacts. The Stormravens were not.

'Get us down!' Stern ordered. He stared at the domes, willing the gunships to descend faster. The Grey Knights were exposed to the hurtling debris of their ship. Longhowl would give them the necessary shelter.

And the even more vital chance at revenge.

The Wulfen leapt towards Ulrik and Grimnar. They were a mass of fangs and blades. They were larger than any other Space Wolf. Ulrik saw what only their enemies had witnessed until now. The utter madness of violence coupled to an unparalleled physical force of war. The Wulfen were a fury that could not be stopped.

Ulrik did not blink. He kept faith with the 13th Company.

The Wulfen leapt over his head. Murderfang stormed after them, his vox speakers shrieking, overloaded by the howling insanity within. On instinct, Ulrik and Grimnar moved aside to let him pass.

Two seconds had passed since the teleportation.

The last of the disorientation leaving him, Ulrik turned in the direction of the Wulfen charge. They had passed through the ranks of Strike Force Morkai like a clawed wind.

'They are frenzied,' said Grimnar.

'The teleportation process,' Ulrik surmised. There was nothing but the animal in them now. Yet they knew the enemy, and fell upon the abominations.

The Space Wolves had arrived on target. The cavern was the grand entrance to the underground settlements of Midgardia. Behind, the ground sloped gradually back up to the surface. Ahead, huge iron doors engraved with the two heads of Morkai opened onto the warren of tunnels. From the dark within came daemons. The unholy unity that had prevailed upon the other worlds beset by the warp storms held true here – daemonettes, plaguebearers, pink horrors and the swordlings rushed out together. The Wulfen tore into them before the first Terminator opened up with storm bolters.

Two seconds, that was all. Then the rest of Strike Force Morkai joined the assault.

The fire of the Wulfen was among them all. Ulrik felt it in his blood and in his bones. As he drove a plaguebearer's head between its shoulders, he could feel the pull to the feral, stronger than it had ever been. His jaws ached as his fangs sought to push out from his gums. Every breath was a snarl.

'The gift is upon us, brothers!' he shouted. 'Rejoice! We are among the blessed of Russ!'

The flood of daemons was immense. They attacked with a lethal unity. The speed of the daemonettes and blood daemons was a distraction, demanding a response to their attack while the plaguebearers closed in with inexorable patience to deliver their heavy blows. The pink horrors kept their distance. They hurled sorcerous bolts into the fray. Mutating light struck the Space Wolves.

Brothers died. Some went down to scores of wounds inflicted by blade or claw. Others collapsed with their lungs foaming out of their mouths and nostrils. And there were those who succumbed to the mutagenic fire. Their armour became a gnawing cartilage. Their flesh became a vortex of change that ended only with death, when it slid off their skeletons to pool on the cavern floor.

Ulrik heard the cries of sagas cut short. And he raged.

Far more sagas grew longer in deed and glory. For every brother who fell, dozens of daemons were rent asunder, blown apart and crushed. The battle was ferocious. It was also brief. His armour covered in ichor, his breath turning into a snarl, Ulrik suddenly found there were no more abominations to destroy. The cavern was awash with foulness. Bodies lay in heaps. Their forms were slowly melting into nothing.

Inhuman whispers and babbling came from deeper in the tunnels. The Wulfen and Murderfang were about to run through the doors after their prey.

'*Halt!*' Grimnar roared.

The Wulfen stopped in their tracks. The slaughter of the daemons had eased the confusion caused by the teleportation. Killing was something they understood, and this had been a good hunt. Ulrik saw traces of rationality return to them. They bowed to Grimnar. Murderfang, still under the influence of their presence, waited also. Unintelligible mutters growled from his vox speakers.

'The enemy is on the run, Great Wolf,' Njal Stormcaller said.

'And we will keep him running. Our wait will be short.'

Volkbad Wulftongue stepped forward. 'Indeed,' he said. 'I am in vox contact with elements of the defence forces. The Midgardians are coming to join us.' The leader of the Shieldbrothers spoke approvingly. The Terminator pack dwarfed any mortal, but they could appreciate valour even in that humble form.

'They are still fighting?' Ulrik asked.

'Barely. What remains of their units are converging on this point.'

The mortals arrived a few minutes later. Some found their way down from the surface. Most came from the tunnels. They were ragged from battle. Their uniforms were torn and caked in mud, dust and blood, and their eyes were haunted. They had beheld sights no mortal should even imagine.

Their exhaustion fell away as they entered the Space Wolves' presence. Their determination was renewed, though they gazed fearfully at the Wulfen.

While the mortals gathered, forming themselves into something like squads, Grimnar spoke over the vox with Egil Iron Wolf. Several times, Ulrik heard him ask the Iron Wolf to repeat himself. Communications were going to be difficult even over these relatively short distances.

When Grimnar was done, he asked Wulftongue, 'Are you able to track the teleportation homers on the surface?'

'There are some fluctuations of the signal,' Wulftongue said. 'It is strong enough for now.'

Grimnar nodded. 'Well enough,' he said. He raised his voice to speak to the full company. 'Strike Force Fenris has taken the Magma Gates,' he announced. 'The Iron Wolf is ready to advance. Now we will reclaim Midgardia. As above, so below. We advance together, scouring each zone of the abomination. The daemon will find no refuge, nowhere to regroup. Brothers, *to war!*'

With those words, he loosed the Wulfen. They ran into the tunnels, Murderfang close behind. The tunnels were barely wide enough for the passage of a Dreadnought, and his roars were bounced around the narrow stone confines, echoing ahead, a horn blast of doom.

The Space Wolves followed. Past the doors, there were three tunnel entrances. Rather than reduce the effectiveness of the company by restricting his warriors in tight confines, Grimnar divided the strike force between the three passages.

'All must be cleansed,' he declared.

Ulrik moved with Grimnar and his Wolf Guard down the central tunnel. He was one step behind the Great Wolf, ahead even of his champion, Arjac Rockfist. The Wulfen were howling much further ahead. Ulrik needs to have them in his sight. He needed to bear witness.

They encountered no daemons for the first hundred metres, only their bodies, shredded by the Wulfen. Then the tunnels branched again. And then again. And again. At each intersection, Grimnar divided the strike force further. The smaller squads could advance more quickly. The Space Wolves spread through the caverns of Midgardia. The great scouring had begun.

Daemons lurked in the darkness. They attacked from the shadows, lunging out from side passages, ventilation shafts and crevasses in the walls and cave roofs. They were scattered. They stood no chance. Flamers, bolters, thunderhammers and the Stormcaller's conjured lighting burned them to ash or smashed them to pulsing flesh in pools of ichor. They barely slowed the advance.

'Where are they all?' Arjac asked as he smashed a plaguebearer against a wall with Foehammer. The daemon slid to the ground, its upper torso

and skull turned to mush. 'Not all at the surface, I hope. No sport in that.'
The Man-Mountain marched by himself just behind Grimnar. His huge
frame filled most of the tunnel.

'They will be closer to the habitation zones,' Ulrik said. 'Where there is
prey.'

The tunnels thus far were access routes, exhausted mining seams, and
maintenance shafts. The few larger caverns the Space Wolves had passed
were warehouses and turbine rooms where huge fans created wind for the
underworld, circulating the air. They had seen a few mutilated remains,
but very few signs of the citizens of Midgardia. Ulrik presumed they had
sought shelter in their homes. Concentrated together, they would have
presented desirable targets for the daemons – so many victims, so many
to suffer and to see others suffer in turn.

Massacres that would now be avenged.

More tunnels, more divisions, more speed. The Wolf Guard caught up to
a pack of Wulfen. Daemons appeared and died in seconds.

Hours into the advance, Ulrik heard Grimnar call Egil Iron Wolf's name
several times, then curse.

'What news?' Ulrik asked.

'None now,' Grimnar said. 'Not for some time.' He cursed.

'They were advancing well.' The Iron Wolf's forces were moving entirely
in armoured vehicles. The mist at the surface was so corrosive it could
dissolve armour.

'Until they reached a swamp. The daemons have been hitting them hard.'

'They can't free the tanks?'

'This is what I hoped to learn. I've heard nothing for almost an hour. In
his last vox transmission, the Iron Wolf was cursing about spores eating
through armour and flesh. Now he doesn't answer. We have no vox contact with the surface.'

'How far have we come without their cover?' Ulrik asked. If the tan-
dem advance had broken down, Strike Force Morkai would be much more
exposed to a counter attack.

'Wulftongue has lost the signal,' said Grimnar. 'We cannot tell where
Strike Force Fenris is.'

'If we purge...' Ulrik began. He was interrupted by the angry growls of
the Wulfen. 'The enemy is close,' he said.

They heard the daemons before they saw them. There was a rasping
sound, as though the tunnels had begun to breathe. The noise grew louder,
becoming the skittering of claws, the dragging of blades, the snarls and
chanting of thousands of abominations. A great tide was coming in from
all directions.

The tunnel ahead of Grimnar's squads curved to the left. The air filled
with a cloying odour. It worked its way through the rebreather of Ulrik's
helm, reaching behind his eyes. It sought to lull him. It invited him to lay

down arms and surrender to a dream of excess. He snarled, shaking free of the unclean illusion. The Wulfen howled and raced forward, enraged by the malevolent scent.

Grimnar raised the Axe Morkai. 'Rend the abomination limb from limb!' he shouted. The Space Wolves charged as one. They rounded the corner and barrelled into a huge cluster of Slaaneshi fiends. The daemons lashed out with pincers and stingers and ceiling vents disgorged flamers. They fell in the midst of the Space Wolves, the fire of change washing over the warriors.

Bells began to toll. From behind came the monotone chants of the plague daemons. They hacked at the Grey Hunters bringing up the rear. Fell blades cut through ceramite. Disease ate at the souls of heroes.

The Space Wolves hit the daemons with fire and blade. The Wulfen cut abominations in half with single blows of their relic weapons. Mounted on their backs, the stormfrag auto-launchers responded to the neural impulses of the Wulfen. The grenade explosions were huge in the tunnel. They blasted craters of flesh, splashing the cavern walls with wet, broken chunks of daemon.

A daemon dropped in front of Ulrik. His momentum carried him through the full burst of its wyrdflame. Change seized him. It sank claws into his being and sought to remake him. It fought with another force of transformation. The gift of the Wulfen was there. He felt the beast rage against the daemonic influence. Its hold on his soul was deeper. The flames could not touch him. He retaliated with a different flame, incinerating the form of the daemon with plasma.

The wrath of wolves overwhelmed the plague of daemons. Grimnar's squads stormed over and through the enemy. The more daemons there were, the more prey there was. The advance did not slow. It accelerated. A cleansing flame of bestial rage swept through the tunnel.

Ulrik emerged from the wave of daemons covered in ichor. He paused for a moment to take in the state of his brothers. There had been losses, and there were serious injuries. These were only fuel for anger. Terminators and Wulfen thundered on. On the squad channels, Ulrik heard how easily breathing turned to growls. The gift was growing stronger. So were the warriors.

He ran on forward again, catching up to Grimnar. 'The spirit of the wolf burns high in our brothers,' he said. 'We cannot be stopped.'

The Great Wolf's face was grim. 'I fear the Iron Wolf has been, or worse,' he said. 'The daemons have had the opportunity to mass a counter attack.'

'What of the rest of Strike Force Morkai?'

'Stymied, I think. I cannot reach all of them. Those who answer cannot yet break through the ambushes.'

'So only we are advancing.'

Grimnar nodded. 'So it would seem. We strike on,' he said. 'We will plunge our claws into the enemy's heart and rip it out.'

'The others will triumph too.'

'They will,' Grimnar affirmed. He growled with such conviction, it seemed to Ulrik the words themselves had the power to shape reality.

Though the tunnels continued to branch, Grimnar no longer divided the force. The squads plunged down the larger passages. Here they had liberty of movement along with the power to smash the foe. The daemons attempted repeated ambushes. They were torn to pieces for their pains.

The temperature climbed as the Space Wolves moved deeper and deeper underground. They reached settlements built into large caverns. Streams of lava flowed across the floors and interconnected walkways and living platforms hung from the ceilings. The people of Midgardia had lived inside their forges, suspended above a killing heat and had braved molten death the way the people of Fenris confronted the cold. The mining and manufacturing communities were small. Each had been home at most to a few thousand. They were all empty now, broken tombs. Pieces of bodies littered the platforms. Flesh without bones was draped across thresholds and hung from windows. Flayed skeletons were suspended from metal frameworks, still dripping blood. They were coated with oozing, viscous slime and buzzed with otherworldly insects. The metalwork on the walls of the suspended habs had been defaced and the engravings of wolf heads and hammers had been gouged by claws. The new markings formed runes that writhed in the corner of the eye.

The deeper the Space Wolves went, the worse and more elaborate the desecrations became. Bodies were fused together into altars of bone. On the central platform of one settlement, a dozen mortals had been assembled into a single rune. Ulrik smashed the sculpture as he marched past. The violence he did to the dead was a necessary evil to free their souls of these new, cursed bonds.

He could not read the runes. No human could without suffering moral damage. Even so, the traces of meaning scraped at the edge of consciousness. The same four runes kept repeating. These were names. Their frequency was increasing, as was their size, as if the names were being shouted louder and louder.

A summoning.

'We are seeing pieces of a ritual,' he told Grimnar.

'Ongoing?'

'It has been completed,' Stormcaller answered. 'The energy of the wyrd is present, but fading. Something grave has already transpired.'

They went through more settlements, deeper beneath the ground, the air wavering in the heat, the tunnels flickering orange, lit by lava now always close at hand. There were more ambushes. The daemons attacked now at wherever the passages were at their narrowest and movement most restricted.

There was blood. Brothers fell. But so did each wave of abominations, utterly extinguished.

Settlement 529 was larger than the others the Space Wolves had traversed, though it too occupied a single cavern. A fallen sign by the access walkway read *Deepspark*. The citizens had given 529 a name. There were none now to speak it. The community was another grave. There were fewer bodies here and none were intact. All were burned, as if the cavern had become a giant crematorium.

The Wulfen moved cautiously along the wide metal walkway. They growled warnings, their hackles up. There was no threat visible, but Ulrik could feel the imminence of presence. Something pressed hard on the air, stretching the membrane of reality.

'The foe is close,' Stormcaller said.

'From what direction?' Grimnar asked.

'I cannot tell. From the wyrd.'

Ulrik glanced over the railing of the walkway at the floor of the cavern. He hissed at what he saw.

'That is why,' he said, and pointed. The lava channels had been altered. They had become the four runes. Molten rock flowed through unholy names.

'The four runes are joined,' Stormcaller said. 'Four names have become one. We approach the heart of Midgardia's torment. The great powers of Chaos have united. The hordes we are fighting are commanded by a unity of daemon lords.'

'Then their destruction will be Midgardia's liberation,' said Grimnar. 'Do you hear, craven scum?' he bellowed. 'The sons of Fenris have come to rip you from this realm! You do well to hide, but do not think you will escape us!'

The squads reached the centre of Deepspark. The platform was large and had acted as a town square. A chapel to the Allfather and hall of sagas were built on opposite sides. Walkways and metal suspension bridges converged onto it, creating a nexus point in the web of iron paths.

The membrane tore.

Warp rifts opened up over four major walkways. Behind the Space Wolves and ahead, to the left and the right, reality wailed and disgorged a legion of abominations. This was more than an ambush. Daemons bounded and lurched over the bridges, clamouring for the blood of heroes.

Four hordes. Four armies of the Ruinous Powers. Towering over each were four princes. The rifts tore wider at their arrival and the cavern trembled with the sounds of their names, becoming a volcanic fanfare. Lava erupted from the runes. Tongues of rock licked up towards the walkways. The edges of the channels contorted into lips. Grinding voices paid tribute to the forces that gave them life.

Mordokh.

Arkh'gar.

Tzen'char.

Malyg'nyl.

The names were attacks. Each syllable stabbed behind Ulrik's eyes. And though he had escaped the meaning of the runes, their constant repetition had left its residue on him. When the names sounded like the tolling of granite bells, he knew what they were. He knew the daemons. They insisted upon it. They marched to collect their choice prey, and they would have their victims die in the knowledge of what great being had brought them low.

Grimnar laughed. He raised the Axe Morkai with both hands. It flashed with its own wyrd energy, hungry to punish the daemons with the same force that embodied them.

'Good sport at last, brothers!' he roared. 'For Russ! For Fenris!'

'*For the wolftime!*' came the answer. It turned into a howl that shook the cavern to its roots. From vox speaker and bestial throat, the howl went on and on.

Rage and animal hunger were one.

Ulrik rode the fury of the gift. Its fire consumed his thoughts. At the Great Wolf's side, amidst brothers who had fought for ten thousand years, he charged towards the princes of damnation.

Anger. Instinct. Reason.

Harald acted on all three in the moments after *Runeclaw*'s crash. The gunship hit with brutal impact, but there was no time to recover. Anger gave him the impetus to leap to war. Most of his Wolf Guard had survived. So had their mounts. They battered their way out of the ruin.

Instinct had him lead his brothers to the side of the gunship facing away from the fortress walls and gun emplacements.

Runeclaw had landed on a ridge a short elevation above the battlefield. Harald followed reason and climbed onto the roof to see the extent of the disaster. Instinct again granted him speed. He was exposed for a few seconds only, and they were enough. What he saw made the anger burn ever higher.

Reason held him back from pointless recklessness.

Instead, he saw the need for the meaningful kind.

The Deathwolves had lost the coherence of any formation. They were in scattered squads at best. Some fought on their own, the only survivors of the drop pods destroyed in mid-flight. He saw two other things, which his reason seized upon.

He saw the enemy. There were Khornate daemons, but it was not those fiends who held the redoubts and turned their huge batteries on the Deathwolves. It was not daemons who had concealed the energy signatures of the defences. The enemy who used human weapons was on the field now, picking off the individual Space Wolves, eroding the strength of Whitestalker. Mobs of mortal cultists were loose upon the glacier, harassing Wulfen and

Deathwolves. They were the thralls of vicious masters in horned, distorted power armour. The Traitors were clad in blue and green.

Alpha Legion.

Traitors and worse than traitors. Beings so consumed by deception there was nothing left. They defiled the honesty of war.

He felt the revulsion, the hatred. Instinct and anger sought to hurl him roaring from the roof. Reason prevailed. And it was thanks to reason he understood the other crucial sight: another stricken Stormwolf streaking overhead, its engines burning. It left a contrail of black smoke as it came in at an angle over the battlefield, overshooting Morkai's Keep. Harald made out its markings. It was *Sigurd's Might*, carrying Feingar's Coldeyes, one of the packs of Wolf Scouts.

The gunship disappeared beyond the fortress. Harald dropped down from *Runeclaw*'s roof. As he leapt onto Icetooth's back, he pictured the geography of the glacial mesa. The fortress did not rise from the centre of the plateau. It was built at the edge of the glacier's flank. Where *Sigurd's Might* had gone down, there was only the greater drop to the wastes below.

Unless…

There was an ice ledge that jutted out partway down the ice cliff. If fate had smiled and the gunship had come to rest there…

Harald switched the vox to a private channel. 'Feingar,' he said.

In the background, he heard groaning metal. Then Feingar said, 'Yes, Lord Deathwolf.' His voice was calm, assured. The voice of a warrior who knew exactly what his task was. 'We have already begun.'

'Good,' Harald said and ended the communication.

The Thunderwolves awaited his orders. He said nothing about Feingar. The Alpha Legion were masters of misdirection and deception. To deceive them, there could be no communication with the Coldeyes. He had to keep the knowledge of what might happen from all. Even from himself, if he could.

Meaningful recklessness.

'We storm the gates,' he told the Thunderwolves. 'Take the field, and call our brothers to us. We will gather our strength once more, and our hammer will batter the foe to extinction.'

Do not think about Feingar, he told himself. Do not speculate. Ride to destroy the Traitors. Let it suffice, and it will do more than that.

He turned Icetooth and charged down the slope from *Runeclaw*. Canis and the others followed. They joined in his war cry. The wolves bayed, as enraged as their riders.

Harald rode hard for the centre of the plain. Turrets turned his way. Shells chewed up the glacier, stitching a line of craters as they sought the Thunderwolves. Ice exploded in dagger shards. But Harald's pack was fast. It defied the gunners and barrelled towards the Traitors. The shelling veered away towards other targets, avoiding the new masters of Frostheim.

The Thunderwolves fell upon a squad of Alpha Legion warriors who had surrounded a wrecked drop pod. They were pouring bolter fire into three Grey Hunters struggling from the ruin. The Space Wolves still fought, but their wounds were crippling. Two more of their brothers lay motionless beside them, their blood staining the ice crimson. The clamour of the shells covered the approach of the Thunderwolves. One of the Traitors turned at the last moment and received Glacius full in his helm's grille. Harald's strength and Icetooth's speed drove the blade through the armour and out the back of the Traitor's skull.

The Thunderwolves cut through the squad's line, killing three upon the instant. They turned and circled the others, strafing them with bolt pistols. The Alpha Legionnaires were caught between the fire of the riders and their former victims. They fought back with bolters millennia old. At the sight of the archaic models, Harald thought again of the Wulfen's ancient weaponry. His mind saw dark connections to be made, but he rejected them for now. All that mattered was to kill and to fight on.

As the Thunderwolves cut down the squad, the battlefield responded. Using his peripheral vision, Harald saw many brothers struggling to converge on his position. The Wulfen fought with blind rage. There was no order there.

Not all Deathwolves were making for him. Lone figures loped across the ice, howling and changing, consumed by the curse.

So many dead. So many transformed.

He rounded on the Alpha Legion with renewed fury. He let his anger strike for him. He did not let it become him. His anger was human, and so it must remain.

As the last of the Traitors went down, Harald turned to find the next kill. It found him instead. With autocannons blasting, a daemon engine emerged from behind the ruins of the drop pod. The round-bodied monster walked on two legs, had arms and a thing that might have been a head – Harald could not imagine what machine it might once have been before corruption and possession had transformed it. Now it was walking destruction, a thing with the drake's maw and autocannon limbs. The head dug its teeth into the buckled hatch of the pod and tore off a chunk of metal as if it were flesh, before devouring it. At the same time, its arms opened fire. Shells of phosphor blazed across the ice and into the Thunderwolves. Brother Onarr and his wolf blew apart. The flaming remains pattered down to the glacier. Harald and Icetooth tore through the falling flames, heading down and left, towards the other side of the drop pod.

The dire engine devoured more wreckage, then took a heavy step forward. Its feet punched deep holes into the ice and the surface melted from the monster's infernal heat. It did not let up in its fire, turning the area around the drop pod into a storm of phosphor and exploding ice. The Grey Hunters saw their rescue turn to their destruction. They turned their guns on the monster. It turned its attention to them. They disappeared in the hail of autocannon shells, their armour vaporised.

Harald rounded the drop pod and came up behind the beast, leaping from Icetooth and landing on the engine's back. The monster's carapace was a heavily shielded sphere. The beast responded to his presence by turning sharply to the left and the right, trying to shake him off. Harald hung on, grasping the grille of one of the vents. A searing wind blew from the internal furnace, scorching his face. The monster's arms and neck flailed, but Harald was out of their reach. He lunged forwards and grabbed hold of the edge of the carapace from where the plated, articulated neck emerged.

The other Thunderwolves circled the engine. Two more packs had joined the fight and their bolt pistol fire hammered against the carapace. The explosive shells did no more than crack the surface. The fiend stamped and roared, firing in a circle. Incandescent death pursued the Thunder-wolves. It found two more.

Cursing, Harald held on to the carapace with his left hand and, with his right, he pulled krak grenades from his belt. He thrust them into the join between the neck and body, fixing four grenades to the beast, clustering them on the same point. Then he jumped away from it.

He landed on his feet. He was inside the circle of the monster's fire. Its blind maw craned down at him, inorganic teeth snapping.

The grenades went off, one after the other, melting through the plates of the neck, tearing open the beast, reaching its burning core. A geyser of flames shot out from the base of the neck. The daemonic engine staggered. A machinic scream of pain tore itself from its throat. Its autocannons fell silent. Then it fired again, without a target now, blasting at the entire world in its agony. The shells were of its body, and it consumed itself in its pain. The fire jetted higher, pushing the wound wider, until the monster cracked in half. Harald shielded his gaze from the searing light. The beast disap-peared into its own pyre.

Icetooth bounded over the crevasses opened by the shells. Harald climbed onto his back once more. He led the charge anew. There could not be pause, no chance for the turrets to acquire the Thunderwolves as targets.

Harald became the gravitational pull of the battlefield. Riding down the centre of the glacier towards the gates, he was visible to all, and he pulled his scattered brothers towards him. The enemy sought to block their gathering, the keep's batteries and daemonic cannons smashing Deathwolves to pulp and ashes. Cultists swarmed over them. Traitors picked off lone figures with cold precision, but they too were caught by the gravity. They responded to the threat of the Thunderwolves, and closed in.

The Wulfen and the Deathwolves who had fallen to the curse were nearer too. They followed the path of frenzy. It led them to the groupings of prey.

Batteries on the left and right converged fire, two gatling cannons and a battle cannon creating an impassable curtain of shredding, pounding shells before the gates of Morkai's Keep. There was the line, Harald knew. If the Thunderwolves reached that point, they would go no further. Even so, he urged Icetooth to run faster. Keep up the pressure, he thought. Keep the enemy's focus.

He had stolen the battle's momentum from the Alpha Legion, despite their massive advantage in armament and position. The advantage was temporary. The Alpha Legion had time. Stalemate would result in the Traitors' victory.

Meaningful recklessness, he thought. And so he led the charge as if the artillery barrage meant nothing.

There were enemies still to kill before the terminal point. Ahead of him was a band of elite Traitors butchering Long Fangs. Off to the right, a lone Alpha Legion warrior moved through the struggling Deathwolves like a serpent of lightning. He was a blur. In the rush of his own speed, Harald could not catch more than a brief glimpse of the warrior. He left a wake of blood, Grey Hunters and Blood Claws falling to his assault. A handful of Wulfen and Blood Claws, enraged by this viper of war, abandoned the effort to reach their Wolf Lord and turned on the nearer foe. Turret fire dogged their movements. They were wounded and slowing as they tried to surround the Traitor. He welcomed them to their end. Harald saw the circle tighten. He looked away at the nearer band of Traitors, coming into reach within seconds. When he checked again, severed heads lay on the glacier. Only two Wulfen still fought, and one had lost an arm.

The sight of that single killer spiked Harald's rage. There, he was certain, was the lord of the Traitors, and the cause of Frostheim's suffering. Harald's rage urged him to turn Icetooth from his path and hunt the warlord down.

Reason held him back.

His place was before the gates. There were more of his brothers fighting their last here. And these Traitors were closer.

'Fenris!' Harald roared as the Thunderwolves raced through explosions of ice shards. He pulled Glacius back, preparing to pay the Alpha Legionnaires in kind and decapitate the first warrior in his path.

He swung. The axe blade whistled through empty air. His target had moved with sinuous grace. The entire band shifted their focus as if the Thunderwolves had been their goal all along, and the Long Fangs merely bait. Harald's foe was suddenly at Icetooth's left flank. His bolt pistol cracked. Shells slammed into Harald's shoulder plate and ceramite splintered. The impact knocked him from Icetooth and onto his back. A Traitor aimed a power sword at his neck, the weapon flashing with wyrd energy, but Harald rolled to his right, firing his bolt pistol to the left. The glacier hissed where the sword struck. There was no sound of his shots finding their mark. He leapt to his feet and the sword was in front of him, plunging towards his chest. He knocked it aside and sidestepped, and a bolt shell exploded against his left shoulder.

A sudden fog surrounded him. It was a smear of jagged black and white. He could not be sure how many Traitors he fought. They moved like a single being, one opponent always in his weak spot. From some unknowable distance, he heard Canis call his name, then snarl. Weapons clashed on all sides, invisible beyond the wall. The sword, one or many, stabbed and slashed. He blocked most of the strikes, but the Traitor, one or many, had the advantage of speed. Blows hit home, cutting through the seams of his armour. When he struck back with Glacius and bolt pistol, he attacked nothing but air.

One or many, they were wearing him down.

In the distance, a bellow of pain that descended to a gurgle.

Feingar, make your move, he willed.

A blinding flash of energy. Silver pain sinking between his ribs.

Feingar, we are out of time.

CHAPTER 8

RITUAL'S END

Flies.

Flies and blood.

Blood and change.

Change and pain.

The daemons' gifts to the mortal realm filled Deepspark. Four princes of Chaos marched to war, and there was no aspect of the cavern that was not one with their corruption. The floors of the walkways squirmed and bit. The rails rotted and burst with sprays of venomous spores. The walls of hab-huts ran with smoking blood. Death sang its music of seduction, inviting the mind to the contemplation of the sensuousness of blood, the decadence of severed limbs, the headiness of butchered meat.

And in the midst of the manifold tortures of corruption, there was the gift. The purity of the hunting animal. The total abandon of bloodletting, yet bloodletting not without purpose. Threats must be extinguished. Prey must be run to ground. There was no corrupt pleasure in the kill. There was no shrieking, mindless vengeance. There was necessity. There was instinct.

The arm of the warrior and the fury of the beast.

Ulrik saw and understood all this. The war in Deepspark was an avalanche of sensation and revelation. He fought through walls of daemonic flesh. His body acted on instinct so rapid and urgent that his mind barely registered his actions. In his left hand, his plasma pistol fired and fired and fired, the rhythm of the bursts stopping just short of the critical overheating – blast after blast of destructive light, incinerating the skulls of abominations, melting their torsos. His crozius smashed form and devastated flesh. Plague daemons, Khornate swordlings, the clawed dancers of Slaanesh and the pink nightmares of Tzeentch pressed in on him, struggling against each other to strike the killing blow. He waded deeper and deeper, cursing them in the name of Fenris and its spirits. His voice was raw with the power of his anger.

He bellowed, though he did not hear his own words. No speech could be heard over the fire of storm bolters and white-noise roar of flamers,

echoing and building against the cavern walls. Ulrik reacted to the daemonic strikes, countering them and retaliating with killing force, yet the
eyes of his spirit looked past the immediate foe. His struggle was to reach
the daemon prince ahead of him. It was the one embraced by the runic,
soundless cry of Tzen'char. It had a form. It was winged. It had limbs. It towered over the lesser daemons of its horde. But its form seemed contingent
on the whims of its will and the moment. Its movements had a swift, stuttering quality, as if fragments of time kept falling away. Its arm was raised,
and then its talons were impaling one of the Wulfen without it ever bringing the arm down. As Ulrik drew nearer to its position on the platform, he
saw an impossible depth to the daemon's shape. To stare into its being was
to see an existence stretching far beyond this place and time. The depths
twisted and coiled and branched. Each flicker of its being brought a different version of the daemon from elsewhere. The closer Ulrik came, the
more he had a sense he was approaching an incarnated labyrinth.

He had to reach the daemon. He had to fight alongside the Wulfen, who
had surrounded the abomination. This struggle was a fulfilment of destiny.
This was what the Wulfen had returned to fight. The gift of their bestial fury
was the answer to the curse of the daemons. They had clawed their way
through and over the lesser foes, straight to the creators of the madness.

And they were being cut down.

No, Ulrik thought. No.

He would not let them fall. He howled, and the beast raced through his
veins. He would tear through the abomination before him with his bare
hands.

At his shoulder was an even greater roar. Logan Grimnar barrelled into
the horde. His face was contorted. His eyes were red and blazing. His fangs
were bared.

The way forward became clear to Ulrik. The frenzy of the Wulfen must
not be contained, but embraced and channelled. It was spreading now,
and it would destroy the abominations before them. It would be Midgardia's salvation.

Ulrik's howl became a cry of savage joy.

The blow hit the side of his head. It was so powerful it seemed to strike
his entire frame. It knocked him to the floor of the platform. He fell on his
back and darkness crept in at the edges of his vision. It withdrew, but the
cavern spun. His limbs did not obey his commands.

The daemon prince of Nurgle loomed over him. Beneath a faceplate,
its mouth gaped in a leprous, contemptuous grin. Flies poured out from
beneath its teeth. It lurched away from him, its jaw unhinging to spew a
vast swarm of insects over the Space Wolves.

Ulrik struggled to clear his vision. Feeling was returning too slowly to
his arms and legs. The blow from Mordokh had been more than physical.

Rise. Rise and hunt.

The beast gave him strength. He started to move. He still could not see clearly. The war was a dizzying vortex. The platform rocked and suspension cables parted with a vicious twang and a walkway covered in struggling Space Wolves and daemons fell to the lava below.

A lithe, reptilian presence stood over him. The Slaaneshi prince held the eyes of Ulrik's brothers in one hand. It reached towards his helm with the other.

And then its face split in half. The Axe Morkai was deep in its skull.

Grimnar, baying his wrath, struck faster than Ulrik had ever seen. He moved with the speed of the unleashed predator.

The change was taking hold.

Rise.

Hunt.

Ulrik snarled. Crimson fury flooded his mind. He lurched to his feet. His vision at last began to clear, and Grimnar had already moved to a new target. Malyg'nyl was on its knees, elegant claws struggling to hold its head together. The Khornate Prince Arkh'gar clashed with Grimnar. Already the daemon was bleeding.

Yes, Ulrik thought. He staggered forward to the Great Wolf's aid. The gift takes us to victory. 'We will open the way for Russ!' he shouted. 'We shall–'

Laughter cut through his words. Tzen'char spread its wings. It spoke a sentence that flickered and looped through the labyrinths of existence and madness as the daemon's form did. A scream of the immaterium howled from the centre of the cavern. A flash of unlight cut through Ulrik's armour and slashed his flesh. Bleeding from a hundred cuts, he kept his feet. He blinked his eyes clear.

The daemons were gone.

On the platform and walkways, Terminators and Wulfen stopped in mid-strike.

The shriek of the wyrd passed. It was replaced by the rumbling crack of stone. The walls and ceiling of the cavern split. A web of crevasses spread and joined. All of Deepspark shook as the end approached.

Ulrik howled his denial. But the wounded, weakened body of Midgardia did not care for prophecy. The cracks built to thunder, the thunder to a mountain's roar, and then everything fell.

Fell into the crushing dark.

A shape ripped through the fog.

Massive. A thing of sinew and claws and fangs.

A monster of the bloody past and of the uncertain future.

Yngvir slammed an Alpha Legionnaire to the ground. He stood on the Traitor's back and seized his helm then twisted and yanked back, tearing off the Traitor's head. He held his trophy high, blood raining down upon him, and howled.

The fog began to break up. Yngvir lashed out into the fading limbo, and suddenly he was holding another enemy by the arm. The Traitor turned his blade against Yngvir. The Wulfen was the equal in speed to the Traitor. With the fluidity of the perfect kill, he released the Traitor, evaded the blow, and countered with his relic frost claws. He struck with both arms, shattering the Alpha Legionnaire's armour and plunging the huge blades through the Traitor's carapace and into his hearts.

Now the fog was gone. So was the intricate, interlocking choreography of battle that had turned the band of warriors into a single being. Yngvir had broken their unity. Harald struck, and this time he found his target. Glacius severed the sword arm of the warrior before him. The Traitor stumbled back, spraying blood. He raised his bolt pistol. Harald plunged his axe blade through the Traitor's chest.

Around him, the Thunderwolf cavalry brought down the enemy with the full savagery of vengeance. Every blow Harald landed had a richly satisfying impact.

And all the time he thought, three times. Yngvir had saved his life three times. He owed a transcendent debt of honour to the warrior he believed to be cursed.

An explosion shook the upper levels of Morkai's Keep. Armourglass blew outward. The turrets fell silent. At last, Harald heard Feingar's voice on the vox once more. '*The Keep is ours, Lord Deathwolf.*'

Harald stood back from an Alpha Legion corpse. He yanked Glacius from the skull. He looked over the battlefield.

'Your Scouts have given us victory,' he told Feingar.

The elite Traitors were slaughtered. With the artillery down, the superior numbers of the Deathwolves were now turning the tide. A new inevitability had come to the glacier. Harald pushed aside the thought of how many brothers had been lost. There would be time to mourn and celebrate their sagas when the war was won.

He looked for the Alpha Legion warlord. There, a few hundred metres away. He had lost the purpose in his movements. He hesitated, motionless in the midst of the battlefield's eddying smoke.

Are you wondering what has happened to your guns? Harald thought. He pounded across the glacier towards the warlord. Are you wondering what happened to your victory?

The warlord's hesitation was fatal. He was a motionless target. He did not see the enormous silhouette close in on him through the smoke. Icetooth slammed into the Traitor with the force of a tank. The warlord fell, rose again to defend himself, managing to strike the thunderwolf once before Icetooth brought him down with finality. The crack of a snapping spine sounded over the glacier.

Icetooth stood guard over his prey until Harald arrived. The Traitor reached for his lost sword, but he was broken. He could not move. He looked up at Harald. 'The ritual is complete, lapdog,' he said. 'Killing me won't change anything.' Empty insults, empty defiance. The Traitor sought some shred of pride, some measure of dignity at his end.

Harald granted him neither. 'Maybe not, but it'll make me feel better.' With a single blow from Glacius, he decapitated the Alpha Legionnaire.

Harald kicked the head away from the twitching body. He had not lied – the execution was satisfying. It did make him feel better.

Then he looked out across the glacier, at the blood and the cost, at the rampaging Wulfen, and at his transformed brothers. He thought about his debt to Yngvir, and of the contagion that had shut down strategic thinking.

Damnation and salvation. He did not know how to separate them.

Or if there was still time to do so.

The three Stormwolves flew through the tumbling wreckage of the Grey Knights vessel. As they angled towards the surface of Valdrmani and made for Longhowl, chunks of the battle-barge became a hard rain upon the moon. There were few remains of any size. Compared to the vessel that had been, Krom was passing through the ashes of cremation.

On the bridge of the *Winterbite*, he had seen the ruby streak of the nova cannon shot, the flash. By the time the frigate had reached the far side of Valdrmani, the fires had faded. There had been nothing but the night of the void, the ashes, and the terrible absence.

Too late, he had thought. Too late. You held true to your oath too long.

Then the augur array had detected the fading signature of engines on the surface of the moon.

The Stormwolves flew close to the domes and passed over the landing site of the Stormravens. The gunships were intact.

'Smoke rises from the main gates,' said Hrothgar, looking through the viewing block.

'A good sign,' Krom said. 'They went in fighting.'

The Iron Priest gestured at the domeplex. 'A big area to search.'

Krom nodded. 'We'll make for the nova cannon emplacement. We can start there. I would want vengeance for my ship.'

'Aye,' said Hrothgar.

'*Lord Dragongaze*,' Egil Redfist voxed from his Stormwolf. '*Bolter flashes three hundred metres to port.*'

Krom had been focusing on the column of the cannon. He looked down in the direction Redfist had indicated. The Blood Claw leader was right – a spot midway down the height of the dome strobed with the distinctive lightning burst of gunfire.

'Take us there,' he ordered.

The squadron dropped, closing in until it was flying almost flush with the anti-rad crystalglass skin of the dome. The interior of Longhowl was lit with a sick glow that pulsed slowly from red to green to bone-grey. Monstrous shadows cavorted. They grew in number the closer the gunships came to the flashes.

'Good,' Krom said when they reached the position. The word felt strange to utter. When had he last been able to look at anything and declare it *good?* He had just passed through the dust of a Grey Knights battle-barge. He beheld the settlement of Fenris' moon overrun by daemons. And now he saw a small band of Grey Knights surrounded by daemons led by a blood-thirster. The Grey Knights were moments from being overwhelmed. Even so, Krom said, 'Good.' The battle was not over.

There was still time.

'On my signal,' Krom voxed to all three Stormwolves, 'breach the dome.' Over an open channel, he broadcast, 'Grey Knights! Incoming! Brace!' Then he said, '*Now.*'

Skyhammer missiles and lascannons struck the dome. The battle flashes vanished behind the greater blaze of explosions and the dome wall burst outwards, turned to powder in the violent decompression. The atmosphere of the dome rushed out, carrying with it the daemonic horde. Las and twin-linked heavy bolters pulverised the enemy cloud. More missiles streaked towards the bloodthirster as it sailed out, carried by a wind more powerful than its wings. It disappeared in the multiple blast.

'Take us in,' Krom said when the last of the daemons were scattered over the surface of Valdrmani.

The three Stormwolves flew in through the huge breach. Their assault ramps dropped before they had finished settling. Krom strode down first. His Fierce-eye's Finest followed.

The Wulfen came last.

The Grey Knights said nothing but headed for the nearest exit from the void-struck quadrant of the dome. Even when both armed parties were on the other side of a sealed bulkhead and in a full atmosphere again, they remained silent. Krom eyed them and their captain. He could list a dozen reasons effortlessly why he had contempt for their order, but their actual presence was impressive. It was more than the superlative Aegis armour and the perfection of the Nemesis power weapons. The cold nobility commanded respect.

Krom felt the strength of the captain's gaze even beneath the Grey Knight's helmet. When the captain's attention passed from Krom to the Wulfen, Krom chose that moment to laugh.

'You can embarrass us with thanks a bit later,' he said. 'Once our work is done. I am Krom Dragongaze, Wolf Lord of the Drakeslayers. My men and I are honoured to fight at your side.'

The Grey Knight captain looked a few moments longer at the Wulfen. Serkir held them in order. Low growls issued from their throats, but their attention was focused beyond the Grey Knights. The captain faced Krom.

'Brother-Captain Stern of the Third Brotherhood,' he said, and held out his hand. Krom did the same. They clasped forearms.

'We have to move quickly,' Stern said. 'Whatever the daemons are doing, it is almost done.'

As the tension of the immediate moment passed, Krom noticed the growing pressure behind his eyes. It throbbed with the pulsing of the unnatural light. 'There is something...' he began.

'Yes,' said Stern. 'You feel it, then. There is a ritual at work on this moon.'

There were two exits from the storage bay in which the Fierce-eyes and the Grey Knights found themselves. Stern headed for the one on the left.

'What sort of ritual?' Krom asked. He signalled for his warriors to follow. The Grey Knights had fought their way this far. They would have done so for a good reason.

'I do not know, as yet. I believe the destruction of our vessel is part of its work, however. Every event since the formation of the warp storms has been part of a foul pattern. The ritual is reaching the critical point. We cannot permit its completion.'

'How do you know this? Or that we must go in this direction?'

'Are you a psyker, Lord Dragongaze?'

'I am not!' He made a sign of maleficarum.

'Yet you can feel the energy. Imagine, then, my experience of it.'

Time, Krom thought. In the end, there was even less than he had dreaded.

Lord Skayle had fallen silent.

In the astropathic choristrium of Longhowl's command sanctum, Hekastis Nul walked the circumference of the glyph, musing about the silence. The Dark Apostle felt little concern. It did not matter to him whether Skayle lived or died. Nul would be dead himself in a few minutes. But his anticipation of the great moment was acute, and his preparations were complete. He filled the remaining seconds by contemplating the implications of his lord's defeat. Perhaps the Dogs had reclaimed Frostheim. Maybe Svellgard too, or at least established a foothold there. Unless they had performed Exterminatus on their own moon, it was impossible that they should have banished millions of daemons in so short a time.

'Did you lose Frostheim, Lord Skayle?' Nul mused aloud.

Standing around the glyph, his cultists bore witness as it approached its great flowering. The astropaths of Longhowl were alive, after a fashion, but they no longer had flesh or minds. Imprisoned in their cradles, their power, their pain, their sanity and their selves had been siphoned into the glyph. They were melted, deformed figures, still convulsing in agony, still screaming, kept alive by the hunger of the thing they were feeding.

'If the Dogs have Frostheim,' Nul reasoned, 'they now have hope. If they have hope, what follows will be richer still. Therefore, Lord Skayle, your death is part of our pattern.'

The power in the choristrium spiked. So did Nul's anticipation. He stopped pacing and looked at the glyph, standing between two of his cultists.

The glyph was daubed in daemons' blood. It occupied the centre of the choristrium, embracing the astropathic cradles. Its light was as painful to behold as a sun's. The light in the chamber had ceased to shift colours. Now it was a jade of mind-stabbing intensity. Soon the glyph would bring about an apotheosis of pain, and with it, the end of the Space Wolves. The blast that would destroy Longhowl and all within was no more than a by-product of its true goal.

The goal was the vision – the vision that would travel across the galaxy. The vision of Grey Knights murdered by the Space Wolves. The vision for the entire Imperium.

The final moments slipped away. As they did, the Dark Apostle felt another tension begin to fold and cut the air. A being that was many and one was coming from many directions and none. The Living Labyrinth approached.

Nul said, 'I am glad, master, you have chosen to witness the moment.'

On the other side of the choristrium, his wards at the entrance collapsed, banished. Their sudden release of energy blew the doors apart. Shredded metal flew across the dome. The dogs who did not understand they were already dead rushed in.

You are too late. I will show you.

Hekastis Nul stepped into the glyph.

Energies erupted around him.

Beyond the doorway, Krom saw the fate of his Chapter reduced to seconds. He charged into the chamber. By his oath, he would prove those seconds to be enough.

'*Cultists!*' Stern voxed. '*In cover behind the cradles.*'

'Petty little men,' said Krom as lasgun fire streaked his way. 'Drakeslayers!' he called. 'Put them down!'

The Space Wolves spread out through the room. Their fire wreaked monstrous havoc on the mortals. The cultists were armed, and shot back, but the effort was futile. They did nothing to slow their execution.

'Kill them all and kill them now!' Krom ordered. Faster, he thought. Faster. He streaked around the circumference of the chamber, his axe cutting down another cultist with every step. He was a scythe. He fired into the cradles as he ran, killing the astropaths too. His one thought was to stop the energy flow into the glyph.

'*Commendable vehemence,*' said Stern. '*Lord Krom, keep them busy. My warriors and I will finish this. Brothers! The Rite of Nullification!*'

The Wulfen and the Fierce-eye's Finest hit the humans of the choristrium like a cyclone of bolter shells and blades. The air filled with a deluge of blood, but the energy was still building. Green light lashed out from the centre of the glyph. The pressure was so intense, Krom's ears began to bleed. The dome of the choristrium cracked. The walls and floor vibrated, on the verge of shattering outward. The seconds were falling away to nothing.

The Grey Knights began their counter-ritual, moving into the glyph. Hurry, Krom thought, glancing away from the killing to see their progress. They were moving with deliberation, marching directly into the blazing energy, pushing against it. The wyrd lashed out. It could not keep them away.

Hurry, Krom willed. There is no time.

There was a concussion at the centre of the glyph. For a moment, Krom thought the end had come, but it had not. The pressure still mounted. The light strobed with madness and shrieked with rage. From its blinding core came a Dark Apostle of the Alpha Legion.

Stern plunged into battle with the Traitor.

Krom was less than a quarter of the way through his run of butchery. There were hundreds of cultists, scores of astropaths. His warrior blood cried out to attack the Traitor, but he did not. His oath had kept him inactive on Fenris so he might be here, now, at this most critical juncture. His duty to Fenris now was massacre.

Even the Wulfen did not turn to the greater prey. They understood. Without the energy from the cultists and the astropaths, the Dark Apostle was a single figure, all but powerless.

Drain the glyph.

So much blood. So many mortals dead now, and yes, the terrible light wavered. The rhythm of the searing pulses of jade light slowed. It became syncopated. The light began to fade.

Now the last of the cultists was cut down, and the cradles of the astropaths were all destroyed. The Dark Apostle was on his knees, impaled by Stern's sword. He was shouting. He shrieked the name Tzen'char. The sound of the name hurt Krom's eyes.

But the light was fading. The light was...

No...

No!

The energy built once more, faster and more terrible than before. More than blinding. The dome of the choristrium seemed to melt and shake at once. Reality tore, and the chamber filled with daemons. The air around the contours of the glyph vomited into existence pink horrors and flame daemons by the hundreds. A firestorm of wyrdflame hit the Space Wolves. Blood Claws turned to glass and shattered. Wulfen were devoured by new maws on their own bodies. The daemons fell on the Grey Knights, disrupting the counter-ritual. The Grey Knights cut down the abominations as fast as they attacked, but they attacked without cease. The flood would come until the purpose of the glyph was fulfilled.

The blast was imminent. Krom's mind filled with jagged fragments of betrayal and mutation.

The wyrd roared with awful birth, and the dread owner of the name howled by the Dark Apostle appeared. It stood before Krom at the edge of the glyph. Majestic in triumph, Tzen'char spread its wings.

'*Stern!*' it roared. The Grey Knight looked up.

Krom charged at the daemon. He rammed his shoulder into the abomination's back. It was like running headlong into a mountainside. The impact stunned him, but the daemon fell. He emptied his bolt pistol into its skull. Suddenly he was staring at the front of the daemon. The maze of its being reassembled its configuration in the blink of an eye. It was prone, and then it was standing, and its sword had pierced Krom's left shoulder. His pistol arm went numb. He stepped forward into the blade, moving to within striking distance again, raising his axe.

The daemon laughed. It raised its right hand. Energy danced from the claws, as blinding as the unholy light of the glyph.

Serkir leapt at Tzen'char. His frost axe came down on that right arm. It bit deep. The labyrinthine being shifted again. Serkir's blade went all the way through and struck the floor. The daemon's arm was untouched. Serkir's attack had gained Krom one second more of life.

And the daemon laughed. The sorcery on its talons became a roaring nimbus as it reached for Krom.

He could see nothing except the light. The burning, destroying light.

Except now the light was filled with prayer. And the daemon was screaming.

The malignant jade shattered, replaced by the purity of silver.

The energy of the wyrd came apart, broken from the inside. Stern was there. Stern had entered the eye of the wyrdstorm. Krom had turned the daemon's attention away, and the Grey Knight had stabbed his holy sword into the centre of the glyph.

Tzen'char screamed. All the daemons screamed.

The build-up of energy was reversed. Even the glyph shrieked.

The light of judgement consumed all that was unholy.

EPILOGUE

It had been Scout Dolutas, wounded almost to death by the savagery of mutated Space Wolves. It had not even had to speak to deliver its message to Araphil, to give him the answers he dreaded. The Dark Angels had seen the images held by the skull. They had been reluctant to draw the terrible conclusions, but their thoughts had been inexorably pulled towards that chasm. They had taken the bait, and the great event had begun.

It had been Master Astropath Asconditus. Into Sammael's ears it had delivered questions and suspicions, all constructed around the tiny fragments of another lie. It rejoiced in the perfection of its art as Sammael, reluctantly, slowly, but inevitably, had walked still further down the path.

Then that form of Asconditus had served its purpose too. Another kill, another disappearance on the Rock. The little touches gave it so much pleasure. It watched the Dark Angels begin to suspect an alliance between the Space Wolves and a daemonic party. It tried to remember when it had last tasted such delight.

Now it was the seneschal Vox Mendaxis, and it waited upon Grand Master Azrael. Events were proceeding so perfectly, it had no need to act for the moment. There were no messages to twist. No orders to misinterpret. Azrael had the facts: Chaos taint in the entire Fenris system, Space Wolves transforming into Wulfen. Nothing but the truth.

Azrael was still regrettably hesitant. For the moment, though. Only for the moment.

Under the hood of Vox Mendaxis, the Changeling suppressed a smile.

The vox system was working again in the damaged command centre of Morkai's Keep. The unit was a powerful one, and some of the interference had diminished. Harald established contact with Sven Bloodhowl, holding the World Wolf's Lair on Svellgard. The Iron Priests of both companies used the signals from the two fortresses to amplify each other.

And now he heard Krom Dragongaze's voice, too.

Harald stood at the gaping hole in the command centre's wall. He looked up into the night sky of Frostheim while he spoke to Dragongaze.

'Brother,' he said, 'it is good to speak to you.'

'*And you. What news of the Great Wolf?*'

'None. Communication with Lord Iron Wolf has been fragmentary. The situation on Midgardia is dire. All contact with Grimnar's strike force has ceased.' He paused. 'The Iron Wolf says there was an earthquake...'

'*I will not believe it,*' said Dragongaze. '*We have hope now. Let us use it well. We purged Valdrmani. We will free our other worlds too.*'

At the augur bank behind Harald, Feingar shouted, 'Vessels translating in-system!'

Harald rushed back inside. 'Who?' he asked.

'Dark Angels,' Feingar said. He tapped the augur network's pict screen. One reading after another appeared. 'Ultramarines. Iron Hands...' More than a dozen different Chapter runes appeared over the vessel signals. Then came those of Knightly houses. Then mass transporters of the Astra Militarum. The fleet was immense.

'Dragongaze,' Harald said, 'Are you picking up the same signatures?' He had so many doubts. There had been so much deception. He had to be sure.

'*We are,*' the Fierce-eye said. '*It looks like a substantial portion of the Dark Angels fleet before we even count the rest.*'

'It *is* their fleet,' Feingar said. Then his eyes widened. He pointed to a rune many times larger than the rest. 'Russ,' he swore. 'That's the Rock!'

Doubts. Patterns. Dooms within dooms. Harald felt the events click together like the gears of a terrible machine. As Feingar updated the positions of the fleet minute by minute, Harald returned to the breach once more. He watched the sky.

He witnessed the passage of a moon, one that did not belong in the Fenris System.

He saw the movement of stars he knew to be warships.

He was still watching when the sky flared, and the bombardment of the Fenris System began.

LEGACY OF RUSS

Robbie MacNiven

THE LOST KING

The World Wolf's Lair, Svellgard

Logan Grimnar – the Fangfather, the Old Wolf, the High King of Fenris – was dead.

So the daemons said. They howled and shrieked and gibbered the news from warp-spawned throats that shouldn't have been capable of intelligible words. But the servants of the Dark Gods had never concerned themselves with nature's constraints.

Logan Grimnar is dead!

'They lie,' Sven growled. The young Wolf Lord was clutching his doubled-headed battleaxe, Frostclaw, with such intensity that his whole armoured body was shaking. 'They *lie*.'

'They are warp-scum,' Olaf Blackstone said. 'Lying is the sole reason for their existence.' The white-pelted Bloodguard stood behind and slightly to the right of his lord, yellow eyes surveying the bleak hills that lay barely a mile across the icy sea. Those hills now undulated with a living carpet of daemons, like an infestation of lice swarming over a rotting skull. They had appeared not half an hour before, crawling like primordial nightmares from the depths of Svellgard's oceans. They were massing for an attack, cohorts of lesser daemons marshalling beneath the nightmarish banners of their gods, and as they did so their deranged shrieks carried across the cold waters to Sven and the rest of his Firehowler Space Wolves.

'They're trying to provoke us,' Olaf said. 'Hoping we divide our forces.'

Sven Bloodhowl opened his mouth to reply, then paused as the hammering of bolter fire broke out behind him. His Great Company were still purging the last of the defences at the heart of the World Wolf's Lair, burning the shrieking daemons from their holes with gouts of blazing promethium before mowing them down with bolter fire.

Progress reports trickled back constantly over the vox as the noose tightened around the last wyrdspawn left in the depths of the fortified missile control nexus. Nine packs, the entirety of Sven's Great Company, were stalking the bunkers, redoubts and weapon emplacements arrayed in concentric circles around the rockcrete keep dominating the island's centre. They would not stop until they had hunted down every last creature from the first daemonic wave to have overrun the island.

'I'm provoked,' Sven said as the bolter echoes were snatched away by Svellgard's cruel wind. 'What's the status of the Drakebanes?'

'Ten of the pups still able to wield a chainsword.'

'And the Firestones?'

'Only five. Wergid is among the dead. The survivors are still hungry though. As are our Wulfen.'

'Then you shall lead them, Olaf. Vox Torvind, Kregga, Uuntir and Istun. Have them return from the central bunkers and assemble here. And two Thunderhawks.'

'The *Godspear* and the *Wolfdawn* have both refuelled and rearmed. They are inbound from the fleet, expected arrival in ten minutes.'

'Then they shall be the vehicles of our wrath. A wolf should never suffer a liar.'

In truth, Sven had not killed enough today. His heart still raced and his fingers itched. The thought of wyrdling filth defiling not just Svellgard, but all the worlds of his home system, brought up an instinctive urge to lash out. He had not had word from any of the other battle-zones for hours – as far as he was aware Harald Deathwolf was still consolidating on nearby Frostheim, while Egil Iron Wolf and the Great Wolf were engaged on Midgardia. The daemonic taunts reached him again from across the narrow sea, and he shuddered.

They were wrong. Logan Grimnar was not dead. He couldn't be.

'To attack is unwise, my jarl,' Olaf said, still watching the nearby island. 'There are doubtless more such filth spawning from the rifts below the waves all about us. If we split our forces we invite annihilation.'

Sven turned to face his old packmate, and although rage still burned in the Wolf Lord's grey eyes, his tattooed features and strong, stubble-lined jaw were clenched with a tight smile.

'Are your fangs getting too long for all this, Olaf?' he asked. The Bloodguard champion returned his gaze levelly, without expression, too old to be so easily drawn.

'Don't tell me a hundred-odd kills are enough to sate you for one day?' Sven pressed. 'If the Bloodguard aren't with me I'm sure the Oathbound would take your place? Or the Firewyrms?'

Olaf still said nothing, but there was a chill whisper of naked steel as his wolf claws slid free from his gauntlets.

'If you wish to teach monsters not to lie,' the Bloodguard said, 'then I will be as happy as ever to assist with the lesson.'

* * *

Seven miles south of the Magma Gates, Midgardia

'Logan Grimnar is dead.'

The daemon choked on the words, a flood of writhing maggots spilling from its locked jaw. Egil Iron Wolf slammed his boot down on the fallen plaguebearer's skull, smashing it to a grey, squirming pulp.

'Strike Force Morkai, come in,' the Iron Wolf snapped into the vox. His only answer was static discord. It had been the same for over an hour now. He fought back the urge to stamp down again on the plaguebearer as it sank back into the ooze that had once been the jungle floor.

'*My jarl, we must return to the* Ironfist.' The voice of Conran Wulfhide, the pack leader of his Ironguard, cut in over the link. '*We can't stay out here. This entire place is toxic. It will eat us alive.*'

Egil knew Conran was right, but still he hesitated. The purple spore jungles of Midgardia had been transformed beyond all recognition by Nurgle's rotting touch, once-mighty trunks now swollen with blight and infested by gigantic maggots, their leaves turned black with decay. The ground underfoot had been reduced to a foetid, cloying pus-bog that writhed with worms and sightless, snapping maws. Egil's Great Company had been battling through the corruption for hours, part of the two-pronged counter-attack designed to sweep the wyrdlings off Midgardia and retake its subterranean cities. The offensive, however, was becoming bogged down in every sense of the word.

Even worse, the runic *Juvjk* script that flashed across Egil's visor warned him that the poisonous fug clouding the air was rapidly stripping away layer after layer of his power armour. Even reinforced ceramite, sealed by the Iron Priests and blessed by the Wolf Priests, was no match for Midgardia's acidic air. The rest of Egil's Great Company was faring no better – howls of agony occasionally interrupted the vox chatter as the nightmarish atmosphere penetrated an unfortunate warrior's armoured joints or ate through his visor's lenses, causing flesh to blister and slough away in just a few heartbeats. Egil had ordered all packs to withdraw to the sealed interiors of their transports while he continued to try to make contact with Strike Force Morkai. With the Great Wolf, Logan Grimnar.

'Back to the *Ironfist*,' Egil finally said. Around him heavy bolters and lascannons hammered and cracked as the armoured might of the Ironwolves sought to keep the shuffling, slime-soaked Nurgle Tallybands at bay. For the past hour the droning wyrdspawn had showed little desire to close with the spearheads of Egil's stalled advance, apparently content to soak up their firepower among the blighted trees and let the spores of the infested jungle do their work for them. Egil had been forced to halt his grinding offensive when the vox had lost all contact with Grimnar's own thrust, which was supposed to have been keeping pace below, following Midgardia's labyrinth of underground tunnels and passageways. Communication had been intermittent right from the beginning, but now it was gone entirely. And the counter-offensive wasn't even a day old.

Egil was the last member of the Great Company to return to his transport, slamming the sealing rune on the hatch behind him. Within *Ironfist's* red-lit hold Conran and the five other members of his pack waited, their grey battleplate befouled with a thick layer of pestilential filth. They were all that remained of Egil's Ironguard. His Terminators had been lent to Grimnar when he had descended into Midgardia's depths with the Champions of Fenris. He felt their loss almost as acutely as he did that of the Great Wolf himself. He activated the cogitator monitor bolted above the hold's crew hatch, uploading the latest combat schematics to its gently pulsing screen display.

His Great Company had been divided into four Spears of Russ, one for each point on the map. Fists of Predator and Vindicator battle tanks supported Rhinos, Razorbacks and Land Raiders filled with the foot-packs. They'd punched out from their base at the Magma Gates and swept all before them. Now, they were stalled and separated, the blinking runes representing each Spear static and beset by assaulting icons.

The Midgardian defence forces acting as their reserves were suffering even worse, their fragile human physiologies no match for the deadliest of the Plague God's diseases. Egil watched their casualty percentages for a moment, seeing them tick up steadily with each passing second. Even the most basic military mind would have acknowledged that their position had become an impossible one. The Iron Wolf activated his vox, blink-clicking to add the Ironwolf pack leaders from all four Spears to the channel.

'This is Egil,' he said. 'Without word from Strike Force Morkai the gains we have made over the past two hours are no longer tenable. We must assume it is possible for wyrdspawn to infiltrate our interior lines through the unguarded tunnels below us. If they successfully break our Midgardian defence force reserves then each Spear of Russ will be cut off from the Magma Gates' landing zones, as well as each other. I am therefore ordering Strike Force Fenris to withdraw by packs towards the Magma Gates. Once there we will commence a staggered withdrawal into orbit, starting with the defence forces and ending with my own Spear. Pack leaders, acknowledge.'

As confirmations trickled back down the link, Egil had to fight to stay silent. His cold, calculated orders, so characteristic of the Iron Wolf, concealed the war which raged in his armour-plated breast. Logically a staged withdrawal was the only option. Strike Force Fenris had stalled deep inside an utterly inimical environment, was on the brink of overstretching even as it was outflanked, and the enemy's numbers showed no sign of decreasing. To continue to advance ran the risk of seeing his entire Great Company overrun and annihilated, their remains eaten up by Midgardia's hideous plague jungles.

But the Old Wolf was missing, somewhere below. If Egil took a backwards step now he knew he would be forever remembered as the one who had abandoned Logan Grimnar. If he saved his Ironwolves by ordering a retreat, he damned himself forever in the eyes of his brothers. He snarled with frustration and keyed the vox again.

'An addendum to the previous orders. Conran Wulfhide of my own pack will be assuming command of the Strike Force with immediate effect, until my return.'

Conran's head snapped up, and he began to protest. Egil carried on, speaking over him.

'I will be taking the remainder of my Ironguard underground, to re-establish contact with the Great Wolf. The evacuation from the Magma Gates is to proceed as previously outlined. Within that framework, all pack leaders are to defer to Conran as though he speaks with my own voice. Is that clear?'

More affirmations, and now complaints too.

'*Let the Cogclaws come with you, lord,*' Kjartan Stone-eye said over the vox. '*My pack have been firing blind into spore clouds and wading through daemon spoor all day. Let us continue the Iron Hunt, lord, I beg you.*'

'*Is what the wyrdlings are chanting true?*' Nokdr Iceclaw of the Snow-fangs asked before Egil could respond. '*Is the Great Wolf dead?*'

'That is what I'm going to disprove,' Egil said. 'And the rest of you will follow my orders, or Russ help me I will tear the fangs from the jaws of each and every pack leader in this Great Company. Show some discipline, Ironwolves.'

'Lord–' Conran began. He'd stood and was facing the Iron Wolf, bowed slightly in the hold's confined space. Egil raised a gauntlet before he could go any further.

'I know what you're going to say, Conran. There are no other options. I cannot let us all die here, and Midgardia's depths are no place for an armoured column. But nor can I abandon the Great Wolf. You will take the Ironwolves to the Magma Gates, and I will see you all again on the bridge of the *Wolftide*.'

For a moment it seemed as though Conran would argue, but instead he just shook his head, his jaw locked and gauntlets clenched.

'The nearest recorded entrance to the Midgardian underworld is three hundred yards south-west of this position,' Egil said, activating a map uplink on his visor's display. 'Directly towards the nearest Tallyband. It's an old mine chute, designate Beta Eleven-Seven. The *Ironfist* will take us that far, and then you will assume command and get my Wolves clear of this hellhole. Understood?'

Conran nodded, saying nothing, no longer looking at the Iron Wolf. Egil knew better than to push his obedience any further. He linked to the Land Raider Crusader's internal vox.

'Torvald, all guns live. For Russ and the Allfather, take us forward!'

* * *

Morkai's Keep, Frostheim

Canis Wolfborn crouched, ignoring the ache in his joints. The day's blood-letting had been long and fierce. His armour bore the scars of daemon blades and bolter rounds alike, and the foul ichor splattering its surface had only just begun to crust. The champion of Harald Deathwolf reached out and grasped the corpse before him by the pauldron, rolling it onto its back.

The body was that of Snorri Redtooth, one of the Grey Hunters belonging to Erenn Frostwolf's pack. Canis only knew as much because he recognised Snorri's musk. The Grey Hunter's head was missing.

Nor had his pack-kin been any more fortunate. Canis had been track-ing their corpses deep into the vaults of Morkai's Keep for almost an hour. The only one he'd yet to find was Erenn himself.

The bodies of the Grey Hunters were certainly not alone down in the keep's depths. Through betrayal and vile maleficarum the forces of Chaos had seized the Space Wolves fortress, presaging the beginning of the dae-monic incursions across the system. In the furious battle to recapture the stronghold from the treacherous Alpha Legion, fighting had spilled down into its lowest levels. Canis had counted half a dozen Space Wolves bod-ies, mostly Blood Claws whose names he'd forgotten, though he recalled their scents. They were outnumbered by the rag-clad cultists that carpeted the vaulted halls and corridors. All around the mark of furious retribu-tion was clear, in the bloody hacking and tearing of chainblades and the vicious, gory detonation of close-range boltfire. There were even three Alpha Legionnaires, the stale stench of ancient corruption coming off their bodies turning Canis' stomachs.

But all of them had fallen at least two hours previously. Snorri and the rest of the dead Grey Hunters were fresh.

Canis carried on down the corridor, noting the location of Snorri's body on his vambrace marker. Behind him Fangir, his loyal thunderwolf, padded silently. Canis could sense the huge animal's tiredness mirroring his own, by its slow, heavy panting. The beast's wiry fur was matted with blood, and not all of it belonged to the enemy. But there was no time to stop. Not yet. Like the thunderwolf, Canis had caught a scent. There was something still down here, something that shouldn't be.

At the end of the corridor open blast doors marked the entrance to the keep's main armoury. On its threshold Canis found Erenn. The pack lead-er's cuirass had been split by a blow of incredible force, and his breastbone carved open, exposing the bloody mess of the Wolf's inner organs. Inside the armoury more cultists lay butchered, but none of them could possi-bly have dealt such a wound.

Two other doors branched off from the entrance, one to the left and one to the right. Canis closed his eyes and inhaled, opening his senses. There was still something lurking beneath the acrid stench of weapon discharges,

the reek of stale sweat, the tang of blood and the pack musks of his fellow Wolves. Something at once sickly sweet and bitter, wholly unnatural.
He had caught it at the entrance to the vaults, as the rest of Harald's Great
Company had begun the process of collecting their dead and incinerating heretic corpses. He had slipped away from the grim work, his instincts
bristling. The fight was not yet over.

The smell was coming from the right-hand door.

It was the entrance to a munitions shaft, the floor sloping downwards into
darkness. The lumen strips overhead had failed. Canis began to descend,
trusting to his sense of smell. Even for a Space Wolf it was keen. Canis
was a natural-born predator, the only member of the Deathwolves able to
match their lord, Harald, in the Great Hunt. Shadows were nothing to him.

There were no more bodies. It seemed as though the fighting had passed
this section of the vaults by, though that didn't explain why the blast door
had been lying open. The unnatural smell grew stronger, a wyrdling stench
that caused the Space Wolf's hackles to rise.

Ahead he sensed rather than saw the shaft coming to an end, widening
out into what he assumed was a munitions bunker. Behind, Fangir began
to growl, the throaty noise reverberating through the narrow space. Canis
slid his wolf claws free.

There was a noise from ahead, his taut senses making it sound hell-
ishly loud. The skitter of claws on rockcrete. The stench grew even worse.

'Wyrdlings,' he snarled softly to Fangir. His suspicions had to be right.
Harald needed to be warned. He keyed his vox.

That was when the first daemon launched itself, screeching, from the
darkness.

Longhowl, Valdrmani

For the first time in a long time, Krom Dragongaze found himself on his
knees.

It was not an injury that had driven him down, though blood still trickled from the rapidly clotting wound in his shoulder. The daemon prince's
blade had bitten deep, but the Wolf Lord had suffered worse. No, it was the
realisation of just how close they had all come to annihilation.

Even before he had joined the ranks of the Sky Warriors, death had held
no fear for Krom. But there were worse things in the galaxy than death. As
the daemonic invasions had spilled out across the system, Longhowl, the
primary astropathic beacon on the Wolf Moon of Valdrmani, had come
under attack.

The fact that the Chaos-tainted glyph planted in Longhowl's choristorium
would probably have obliterated Krom had never figured in his thinking as
he'd led the assault to destroy it. What had driven him to his knees was the
knowledge that, if he had failed, the sigil's infernal wyrdling power would

have lanced a false image of his Space Wolves slaughtering Imperial subjects into the mind of every psyker in the Segmentum. The illusion would
have cemented the belief that the sons of Russ had turned traitor, and set
the Imperium's might against the whole of Krom's Chapter. The thought
made his flesh crawl with disgust.

A silver gauntlet, blackened by fire, appeared before the Wolf Lord. He
clasped it and allowed himself to be hauled up by its strong grip.

'Well met, Dragongaze,' said Captain Stern. The Grey Knight had removed
his helmet, his noble features streaked with sweat. His armour was still
smoking from the hellish wyrdfire which had engulfed it, the marks of
warding and protection inscribed into the silver aegis plate glowing bright.

'It is over?' Krom asked as he looked around. Moments before, the
choristorium had been packed with howling daemons and the wailing, melted remains of the station's possessed astropaths. Now it was
a scorched, ichor-splattered wreck, the astropaths reduced to skeletal
husks in their burned-out cradles. The Chaos glyph that had been the epi-
centre of the warp ritual was split and broken, the multihued light that
had blazed from it now doused. Krom remembered Stern forcing his way
through the icon's wyrdflame and plunging his crackling force sword into
its heart, shattering it. The moments that followed were a blur – blinding
light, shrieks of frustration and terror, a splitting pain that still throbbed
dully behind Krom's eyes.

But the daemons were gone. They had won.

'It is over,' said Stern. Around the edges of the purged choristorium Grey
Knights and Space Wolves alike were picking themselves up. Not all who
had fallen rose again.

'We must establish contact with Fenris,' Krom said. 'Send word that the
daemons have been thwarted, and that we are both still alive. That should
give those who doubt us reason enough to reconsider.'

Stern nodded. The ritual was supposed to have set the Wolves and the
Knights against one another, but even with the daemonic plot defeated
there was no telling how the Imperium was responding to the events in
the Fenris System. Massive warp incursions, mutation among the Adeptus
Astartes, rumours of treachery – something had set out to destroy the Space
Wolves, and it had come diabolically close to succeeding.

'I must return to the Fang,' Krom continued. 'I cannot leave it unguarded
a moment longer.'

'Then go with my thanks. Your assistance here was invaluable,' Stern said.
'If you had not left Fenris to come to our aid I could never have stopped
the ritual in time.'

'Bjorn the Fell-Handed saw you trapped and killed,' Krom said. 'I would
not have left the Fang on any word save his.'

A vox blurt interrupted Stern before he could respond. The signal's ident
code belonged to Krom's flagship, the *Winterbite*.

'*My lord, we are receiving a priority message from the Fang,*' said the voice of one of the ship's huscarls.

'Patch me through,' Krom ordered, turning away from Stern. After a moment's static the voice of Albjorn Fogel, chief vox huscarl of the Fang's communications array, spoke to him over the link.

'*My lord, our long-range augur sweeps have detected a large fleet translating in-system. The signifier codes are all Imperial. Thus far we've identified strike cruisers and battle-barges belonging to the Ultramarines, Iron Hands, Marines Malevolent, Doom Griffons and Shadow Haunters, along with capital ships of the Imperial Navy's 32nd Obscurus sub-fleet, Knight carriers from House Mortan and six Astra Militarum mass transporters. We also believe...*' Fogel trailed off.

'Go on,' Krom said.

'*My lord, one of the signifiers belongs to the fortress-monastery of the Dark Angels. We believe the Rock arrived in Fenrisian realspace approximately twenty minutes ago.*'

'Hail them,' Krom said.

'*We've tried, lord. They refused to even acknowledge the signal connection. Our ships around Midgardia, Svellgard and Frostheim are also reporting no contact.*' Krom broke the connection for a moment to look at Stern.

'A crusade fleet has just entered the system,' he growled. 'Led by the Dark Angels.'

'It's as I feared,' Stern said. 'Supreme Grand Master Azrael has been shadowing your Chapter since he learned of your... genetic anomaly on Nurades. I suspect he believes the Space Wolves to be tainted.'

'Fogel,' Krom snapped into the vox.

'*Yes, lord?*'

'Raise all shields and prime defensive batteries. Advise all our fleet assets throughout the system to do likewise. I am returning to the Fang immediately.'

'*Yes, lord. Are we on a war footing?*'

'Not unless they fire first.'

'You need to take me to the Rock,' Stern said. 'If they won't open their vox-nets to any communications from us I must speak with Azrael directly.'

'Your battle-barge is ashes, Stern,' Krom said. 'If you wish to leave this moon you are welcome aboard *Winterbite*, but I am going direct to the Fang. I have already sullied my oath by abandoning it to come here. I will not compound my dishonour further by leaving the Hearthworld to the mercy of fools and zealots.'

'As you wish,' Stern said. 'But once there I must request the use of one of your ships.'

'And you shall have it,' Krom said. 'It would be well if you reached Azrael before he reaches me, because Allfather protect him if he launches a single strike against any part of this system.'

* * *

The Rock, in high orbit above Midgardia

The primary command bridge of the Rock was a cavernous place, full of faded glory and shadows that had lain undisturbed for ten millennia. At its heart a great tiered dais rose, each stone step carved with intricate figures telling the long history of the First Legion. The top of the ziggurat bore a throne of brass and steel, bristling with data ports and holo-screens, vox uplinks and runebanks. There sat Azrael, Keeper of the Truth, Supreme Grand Master of the Dark Angels and all of the Unforgiven. Face set beneath his white cowl, he surveyed the bridge below without expression.

Serfs, servitors and data-slaves scurried to and fro amidst tiered ranks of cogitator banks and oculus viewscreens, while menials toiled in the communication pits sunk around the dais, backs bent double, blind to the cold stone columns that rose around them to the distant, vaulted ceiling. The air was thick with darting servo-skulls and fluttering auto-cherubim, their censers filling the air with the cloying smell of warpbane and other sacred unguents. The rattle and chime of cogitators, the crackle of vox horns and the throaty machine cant of the bridge's choir of course-chartists echoed back endlessly from the stained crystalflex of the viewing ports opposite Azrael.

The bridge, in all its cold stone majesty, dwarfed even the greatest ships of most other Space Marine Chapters. Azrael noted a few of his fellow Adeptus Astartes casting glances up at the highest reaches of the ceiling, swathed in darkness far above. They were assembled around a large, circular holochart near the central nave, laid out before Azrael's dais. The chart itself was beaming a grainy green representation of the Fenris System into the smoky air, the orbs representing Midgardia, Fenris, Frostheim and their attendant moons revolving slowly around the pallid sphere that was the system's sun, the Wolf's Eye. As the briefing began the display flickered, overlaid by red and blue sigils and arrows that plotted the arrival of the crusade fleet.

It was an impressive undertaking, Azrael thought. A stark reminder of the danger that developing events posed to the Imperium. Normally a crusade fleet took far longer to bring together, never mind fully deploy. Azrael recalled the Antarika Crusade, which he had participated in when he had still been a battle-brother in Sergeant Nefalim's tactical squad. It had first been approved by the High Lords of Terra two centuries before Azrael had even been born. It took two hundred years to assemble the full fleet assets, petition the Adeptus Mechanicus and the knightly households for support, and divert Space Marine Chapters from operations elsewhere. The crusade's nominal leaders had died and been replaced three times over, and entire Army Groups of the Astra Militarum had been disbanded and recruited afresh before the vanguard of the battlefleet had even left its docks.

The force Azrael had brought together was smaller than that of Antarika, but it was still fearsome. Contingents from fourteen Chapters, two Imperial Navy sub-battlefleets and three Astra Militarum Army Groups. Further forces had sworn to assist and were en-route, including Titans of the Legio Dominatus. Only a figure of Azrael's considerable standing and experience could have summoned such strength with so little notice.

Below him, that strength was exemplified by the fourteen Space Marines attending the final operational overview. Among their heraldry Azrael could see Howling Griffons and Red Consuls, the vicious yellow of the Marines Malevolent, the grey battleplate of Shadow Haunters and the silver of one of his Chapter's own successors, the Guardians of the Covenant. Besides those physically present, two of the Adeptus Astartes were represented by throbbing blue hololithic displays – Captain Epathus of the Ultramarines Sixth Company and Iron Captain Terrek of the Iron Hands Clan Company Haarmek. They were both already bound for the world of Frostheim, on the far edge of the system, leading a detachment of the crusade fleet's might.

Interrogator-Chaplain Elezar led the briefing. Azrael had given him the task on the advice of Asmodai. The Master Interrogator-Chaplain had been impressed by his apprentice of late, and Azrael knew how difficult it was to earn the favour of the grim Master of Repentance. Even now he towered like a silent revenant beside Azrael's throne, observing Elezar without comment.

'Midgardia,' Elezar was saying, a gesture highlighting the sphere spinward of the Wolf's Eye. 'The second largest of the Fenris System's three planets, and the world we are currently entering high orbit above. Its surface was formerly a toxic jungle, classed as a death world. The Midgardian natives lived below the outer crust, in cavernous subterranean hive cities.'

'*The past tense is noted, Brother-Chaplain,*' Terrek the Iron Hand said, his voice crackling from the vox horn built into the holo-display projecting him. '*What fate has befallen them?*'

'Long-range augur scans indicate the surface of Midgardia has suffered a near-total daemonic infestation. Of the situation underground we have no idea.'

'*Haven't the Wolves tried to purge it?*' Captain Epathus of the Ultramarines asked, his own holo-form flickering.

'With two Great Companies, including that of Logan Grimnar himself.'

'*And what has become of them? Of Grimnar?*'

'We are still collating information from intercepted vox transmissions and high-yield surface scans, but it seems their counter-attack was a complete failure. The Great Company known as the Ironwolves are currently evacuating the planet, while the fate of Grimnar and the Champions of Fenris remains unknown. They were last recorded battling the infestation in the caverns below the planet's surface.'

A murmur passed through the Space Marines. Elezar pressed on.

'Valdrmani, the Wolf Moon, Fenris' only satellite,' he said, indicating the orb slowly circling the white-and-blue sphere of the Space Wolves home world. 'Intelligence reports that a battle-barge of the Grey Knights Third Brotherhood was destroyed in orbit by a nova cannon sited near the astropathic beacon known as Longhowl. Whether that was due to the daemonic incursion, or represents treachery by the Space Wolves, is currently unknown, as is Captain Stern's status. Pict footage remotely extracted from Longhowl's databanks shows vessels leaving the battle-barge for the moon's domeplex before it was destroyed. If daemonic forces have indeed overrun Valdrmani, it may well be that they are attempting to implicate the Wolves for whatever has befallen Stern.'

'They need hardly try,' Captain Vorr of the Marines Malevolent spat. 'If the stories of the Wolves'... mutants are to be believed.'

'That is an accusation that will be further investigated as soon as time allows,' Azrael said. The muttering among the assembled Space Marines died as he spoke, his deep voice carrying easily across the hectic bridge.

'Right now securing the Fenris System against daemonic incursion is our foremost priority. Once it has been purged, we shall hold the Wolves to account for what they have tried to hide from us. From the Imperium.'

The Dark Angel's cold words left a gulf of silence in their wake. After a moment Elezar continued.

'Frostheim, the third and final planet of the Fenris System. It is the site of Morkai's Keep, which was recently seized by heretic forces before being retaken, it seems, by Harald Deathwolf's Great Company.'

'*What heretic forces?*' Terrek demanded.

'We are still gathering intelligence on the matter. Frostheim is orbited by a natural satellite called Svellgard. The moon's surface is dotted with a number of small islands, sites for a powerful orbital defence battery known as the Claws of the World Wolf. These were recently recaptured from a daemonic infestation which appears to be originating from beneath Svellgard's seas.'

'Are the weapon systems still operational?' asked Bohemund, captain of the Doom Griffons Fourth Company.

'As far as we're aware, yes. Brother-Captains Epathus and Terrek are both en-route there with their brethren as we speak, supported by the Imperial Navy's Four Hundred and Eighty-third Obscurus battlefleet sub-detachment and an Astra Militarum Army Group. They will stabilise the situation.' Both Epathus and Terrek's holo-forms nodded their confirmation, the motion causing them to flicker.

'And if the Wolves do not wish to be "stabilised"?' Vorr asked.

'Then they shall be taught a long-overdue lesson in how to cooperate with their brethren,' Elezar replied. Unnoticed, a smile ghosted across Azrael's lips. He could see why Asmodai favoured the young Interrogator-Chaplain.

'Besides their presence on the system's three planets and two moons, sector defence data-files show that the Wolves maintain two Ramilies-class star forts,' Elezar continued, 'designated *Gormenjarl* and *Mjalnar*. Contact was lost with both soon after the incursion began.'

The rest of his words were drowned out by the voice of Azrael's vox seneschal, Mendaxis, speaking in the Supreme Grand Master's ear.

'*Sire, we have just detected a ship signature not registered with the fleet breaking into realspace coreward of our position. Initial scans show it was last registered as a private vessel associated with the retinue of Lord Inquisitor Banist de Mornay.*'

Azrael's expression remained stoic, but his grip tightened fractionally on the skulls carved into his throne's flanks. Beside him Asmodai, listening to the vox exchange, turned sharply to look at Azrael. De Mornay, the Supreme Grand Master thought. So the old fool yet lived. Of course he'd followed them here.

'*He's hailing us,*' Mendaxis said.

'Accept it,' Azrael replied. 'Throne vid only.'

A small screen, framed by the wings of the aquila, rose from the throne's arm. For a second the monitor fizzed green with static, before resolving itself into a face Azrael had hoped never to see again.

When he had first met Lord Inquisitor de Mornay the man had been a paragon of Imperial strength – young, iron-jawed, steel-eyed, his red hair cropped close, more accustomed to flakplate than the robes of his ordo. But a century had taken its toll, rejuvenat processes or not. Now the face that occupied the screen was sagging into fat, the jaw-line more jowl-line, one eye rheumy with cataracts.

'*Supreme Grand Master Azrael,*' said de Mornay, his deep voice crackling through the vox horn set below the screen. He was smiling. '*I am glad to see you again.*'

'I cannot say the same,' Azrael replied. He didn't have time for the Inquisition's games, especially not the ones that de Mornay loved to play.

'*Am I interrupting something?*'

'The crusade fleet is currently preparing to fire-bomb the surface of Midgardia.'

'*May I ask why, aside from the fact that Midgardia falls under the control of the* Vlka Fenryka? *I'm sure your primarch would be proud, if I recall my Progenium history lessons correctly.*'

'The planet has fallen to a daemonic incursion.'

'*How do you know?*'

'Augur sweeps, vox intercepts, strategic analysis data, the visions of my Librarians and the fact that a Space Wolves Great Company is currently fleeing the surface.'

'*The Champions of Fenris?*'

'No. We believe it to be the Ironwolves.'

'*But the Champions are also on Midgardia, aren't they? Led by Logan Grimnar himself?*'

'Our vox transcripts report all contact with him has been lost.' De Mornay was silent for a moment before speaking again.

'*I would like to request an immediate audience.*'

'Your rosette will do you little good, de Mornay,' Azrael warned. 'I am not some cowering Militarum general or docile planetary governor. If you wish to speak, it will be on my terms, not yours.'

'*I see the sons of the Lion are as cooperative with His Holy Ordos as ever,*' de Mornay replied, acid creeping into his voice.

'I will humour you this one time, de Mornay, as a token of goodwill towards the Inquisition. But don't expect anything more from me. Few Chapter Masters would grant you the privileges I do.'

'*Expect me within the hour.*'

Azrael cut the link without another word. He knew de Mornay well enough to understand that rebuffing him would only heighten his determination. Better to lure the fool into the Lion's den and show him the consequences of his beliefs first-hand.

Below him Elezar was describing the intention of the Chapter to fire-bomb Midgardia's surface. The muttering of the assembled commanders showed it was as unpopular among them as it had been with de Mornay. Azrael keyed his personal vox.

'Dismiss them,' he ordered Elezar.

Without showing any sign of having heard Azrael over the link, Elezar began to bring the briefing to a close.

'De Mornay is here because of us, not the Wolves,' Asmodai said, his voice hissing quietly from the maw of his grim, black skull helm.

'Without a doubt.'

'We must keep him at arm's length.'

'Have no fear, brother. I intend to.'

Below the dais the thirteen Space Marine commanders were departing, each one bowing briefly towards Azrael before they left. Himmaeus of the Knights of the Covenant was the last to exit the bridge, exchanging a curt nod with his Supreme Grand Master before passing through the blast doors. Azrael rose and descended from the dais, Asmodai following him like a shadow woven from nightmares.

'Brother Elezar,' Azrael said. 'How do you find our brethren's appraisal of the coming operation?'

'Approving, for the most part,' the Interrogator-Chaplain said, stepping away from the holochart and bowing as Azrael joined him. 'Though our decision to bomb Midgardia met with ill feeling. It does not sit well with them to burn the planet with the Great Wolf still unaccounted for.'

'Of course. It is not what I would wish to do, but we have no alternatives. Midgardia's surface is now so infested that only warpspawn could possibly exist down there for any length of time. The entire strength of this crusade would be liquidated if we sought to make planetfall, and we cannot let the warp rifts on the surface grow any further. It must burn, all of it.'

'Yes, my lord,' Elezar said. 'They will all accept our decision, I have no doubt.'

'*Sire,*' Mendaxis interrupted him. '*Lord Inquisitor de Mornay's shuttle is requesting docking clearance.*'

'Grant it,' Azrael said tersely. 'And send Brother-Sergeant Elija to escort him personally. Tell him there are to be no deviations, they are to come straight here.'

'*Yes, sire.*' Azrael glanced at Asmodai.

'A necessary evil, brother,' he said. The Master Interrogator-Chaplain didn't reply.

Sergeant Elija brought Lord Inquisitor Banist de Mornay to the bridge borne aloft on a cushioned vital-support palanquin which was welded to the backs of two tracked servitor units. Behind him came a train of disparate creatures. There was a lithe-looking, black-armoured Sister of Battle, her eyes staring with fiery intensity from a flame-scarred face. Alongside her was a limping, blue-robed lexmechanic, borne down by a great stack of data-slates and scrolls. Tugging on his robe-tails was a long-limbed Jokaero, taking in the grim splendour of the Rock's bridge with simian fascination. A dead-eyed cherubim wove and darted overhead on buzzing rotor wings, trailing more parchments.

Behind them all shuffled an emaciated figure, naked bar a soiled loincloth, its wiry body stitched with scars and stimm-injection ports. Rather than hands, its arms ended in crudely grafted electro flails, currently trailing inert along the floor. Its head was covered by a red hood and bound by a riveted visor stylised into the shape of the Inquisitorial I. The faint sound of soothing plainsong drifted from its lobe implants.

Azrael grimaced in disgust as he watched the arco-flagellant limping after its owner.

'Greetings, Supreme Grand Master,' de Mornay called as his palanquin crossed the bridge, rumbling awkwardly around ranked cogitator pews. As he spoke, the lexmechanic started to scramble for a free slate and autoquill.

'You would bring an abomination like that aboard the Rock?' Azrael demanded, eyes still on the arco-flagellant.

'We all do the Emperor's will,' de Mornay responded. 'And I've made poor VX Nine-Eighteen here enact that will in many terrible ways down the years. It's good for him to get out.'

'Emperor's... will...' muttered the lexmechanic, autoquill now scratching furiously across a data-slate.

'Your appearance is as sudden as ever,' Azrael said dispassionately. 'And unwelcome. Why are you here, de Mornay?'

'The arrival of anyone bearing a rosette ought to be sudden, Supreme Grand Master,' the inquisitor replied, palanquin rocking to a halt before the Dark Angels. He shifted his ageing body fractionally, the wires binding him to his moving recliner's life-support systems rattling. 'And only unwelcome if you have something to hide.' Except for the Sister of Battle, his retinue clustered behind him like a herd of frightened grox calves.

'Something... to... hide...' the lexmechanic repeated, still writing.

Though he remained silent, Azrael could feel Asmodai's anger emanating like the chill of the void beside him.

'That doesn't answer my question.'

'Ah, but I believe it is my prerogative to ask the questions here.'

'The... questions...' the lexmechanic said.

'Hush now, Peterkyn,' de Mornay muttered before continuing. 'I can sense you are going to make this audience both brief and impolite, so I will speak plainly. Firstly, there are loyal subjects of the Emperor still on the planet below us. The planet you intend to incinerate.'

'Massed evacuation is unfeasible,' Azrael replied. 'The populace would need to be quarantined and screened en-masse for warp taint. There is manifestly neither the time nor the facilities for such actions.'

'While civilian losses are regrettable,' de Mornay made a point of glancing at Asmodai, 'I was referring more to the burning of an entire Great Company of your fellow Adeptus Astartes.'

'Fire-bombing Midgardia will not damage its underground habitats,' Azrael said. 'And that was Grimnar's last recorded location. If by the Emperor's will he yet lives, he will be unharmed.'

'And when he emerges he'll be stranded in a toxic ash waste.'

'If you have an alternative suggestion, Lord Inquisitor, by all means share it. I would have thought that as a member of His Holy Ordos you would have rejoiced at the mass annihilation of mankind's darkest foes.'

'Rest assured, nothing pleases me more,' de Mornay said. 'But less so if the victory comes at the price of one of the Imperium's greatest leaders.'

'I never thought I would live to hear the Inquisition praising Logan Grimnar.'

'Times can change, Azrael. As can the topic of conversation. What were you doing on Nurades?'

Azrael's jaw clenched.

'We were purging one of the Emperor's worlds of daemonic infestation.'

'And just how many daemons did you banish there? Did the Wolves leave any for you? An entire Lion's Blade Strike Force deployed to cleanse an infestation that had been wiped out days earlier?'

'Is this a line of questioning, or just an opportunity for gross insults? Your grudge-bearing does you no credit, de Mornay. I don't need to humour you, not even for a moment.'

'What were you looking for in the polar ruins, Azrael? What were your Scouts guarding?'

'That squad was inserted ahead of our main strike force. If you have any real questions, de Mornay, I suggest you start by asking the Wolves how they died. That is what we first came here to redress.'

'There is no evidence the Wolves have attacked Imperial citizens. Can the same be said of your Chapter, Azrael?'

'Their monsters butchered a squad of my Tenth Company,' Azrael snapped, his reserve finally eroded. 'We have pict footage of it.'

'Shame you don't also have footage of how the sole survivor of said butchering disappeared,' de Mornay shot back. 'And from within the depths of this very fortress-monastery no less. Something here is not what it seems.' The inquisitor's gaze swung across the bridge, lingering on the communications pit where Mendaxis was bending low to review a spool of data parchment.

'Choose your next words carefully, de Mornay.'

'I smell the reek of the warp here, Azrael.'

Beside him he felt Asmodai shudder at the inquisitor's damning words. Azrael turned and stilled him with a gesture.

'This audience is over,' he said. 'Get off my bridge.'

'You don't end audiences with the Inquisition, Azrael,' de Mornay said. 'And your bridge is as much a part of the Emperor's realm as anywhere else in the Imperium. There are no jurisdictions here, not for one bearing my seal.'

Azrael turned. It was not a sharp movement, neither sudden nor violent, but it was undoubtedly laden with threat. He took a single step forward, so that even on his palanquin the aged inquisitor was dwarfed by the Angel's armoured form. The vast bridge went suddenly quiet.

'I grow tired of your games,' Azrael said softly. 'Your prejudice against my Chapter is well known. The mission that brings us here is not only entirely legitimate, it is desperately vital to the fate of the Imperium. We can do without your pathetic past grievances.'

'I will make my own judgement on that matter,' de Mornay said, putting his palanquin into grinding reverse. 'We shall speak again soon, no doubt.'

'If we must,' Azrael said grimly. 'Brother-Sergeant Elija will return you to your shuttle, immediately.'

As the inquisitor and his retinue retreated the voice of Mendaxis clicked again in Azrael's ear.

'*Sire, we are receiving fresh intelligence from Midgardia.*' There was a pause.

'Go on.'

'*It would appear that Logan Grimnar...*' Mendaxis hesitated again.

'What? Speak.'

'*Sire, Logan Grimnar is dead.*'

Seven miles south of the Magma Gates, Midgardia

Midgardia's spores had eaten away the external pict recorders, so Egil Iron Wolf was blind to the firepower of his command tank as it rolled towards its objective. He could well imagine it though. A stream of assault cannon rounds kicking up spumes of filth from the milky pus-bog, bursting shambling, slime-slick plaguebearers like overripe fruit. Swathes of bolt-rounds sped from the glowing barrels of the *Ironfist*'s hurricane bolters, smashing through spore-trees, lancing plague beasts like boils and cutting giant flies out of the air. The pitch and roll of the heavy transport added a tale of pulped and crushed wyrd-scum, ground beneath aquila-stamped tracks.

Egil had witnessed similar sights many times down the centuries, and still it thrilled him. His brethren in the other Great Companies revelled in the sensation of axe and chainblade chopping meat and bone, and the clash of steel on ceramite. Egil had always considered his passions similar, but for him the glory of battle was not only in the muscle behind a blow, it was in the unbending metal that dealt it. Cog, track, bulkhead and burning engine, in the armour of his Great Company he saw the unstoppable strength and lightning speed of Russ himself. Wrath was so much more potent when it was clad in iron.

Perhaps that was why he was pursuing his current course. Iron did not bend and it did not break, except beneath the most terrible of forces. He would not acknowledge that these wyrdspawn, these beasts bred from a madman's nightmares, were stronger than he was. He wouldn't give them the privilege of forcing him to abandon his Great Wolf. He would not bend, and he would not break.

'Destination reached, lord,' Torvald's voice crackled over *Ironfist*'s intercom. 'Ramps ready to drop on your mark.'

'As soon as we're clear, rejoin the task force,' Egil said. He glanced back at Conran. Unlike the rest of the Ironguard, he sat in one of the hold's restraining harnesses, his expression stony.

'I will see you aboard the *Wolftide*, brother,' Egil said.

'With the Great Wolf,' Conran added, nodding. 'May Russ and the Allfather be with you.'

The time for words passed. Egil's servo-skull, Skol, hovered at his shoulder, its tiny antigravitic motor buzzing. He checked his armour was properly sealed and banged the disembarkation rune above the Land Raider's forward hatch. It flashed from red to green. Wolf claws slid free, a thought sending energy crackling down the wicked blades.

There was a thump of mag-locks and a hiss of decompressed air. The ramp fell forward and light, sickly and pale, flooded the troop compartment. Egil charged out into the rot jungle, a howl on his lips.

Two seconds to assess his surroundings. Skol looked left, the skull's implanted vid feed uploaded directly to the Wolf Lord's bionic eye. Egil went right. Ten paces ahead, the corroded remains of the entrance to a Midgardian mineshaft yawned. *Ironfist*'s hurricane bolter sponsons were still hammering.

Only a handful of plaguebearers were between the Land Raider and the mine entrance. One died with Egil's claws in its throat, gargling on its own ichor. Moln Stormbrow, the first of Egil's Ironguard to follow the Wolf Lord from the hatch, pulverised another with a swing of his thunder hammer as it made a clumsy swipe for Skol.

'Into the mine,' Egil barked, bursting a squealing nurgling underfoot. 'Now!'

Olaf Ironhide, the final member of the Ironguard, splashed out into the jungle's quagmire. *Ironfist*'s ramp immediately began to rise, and the tank was reversing before the opening was even sealed, great tracks throwing up fountains of pestilent, sticky spume. The noble war machine was almost unrecognisable from the outside, drenched in oozing filth, its thick armour plating pockmarked by ichor and spore clouds. The pain its machine-spirit must have been suffering caused Egil to bare his fangs beneath his visor as he gutted another droning plaguebearer.

With their lord at the centre, the Ironguard sprinted the last few yards to the mine's corroded metal overhang. Egil's auto-senses stripped away the darkness within, picking out dead lumen globes and a rudimentary lift mechanism leading down into the mine proper. Its winch and cables, however, had long been eaten away. A servitor controller hardwired into the shaft's activation panel was little more than bones and rusted metal, its vat-grown flesh desiccated by Midgardia's spores.

'Borgen, hold them off,' Egil ordered. 'There must be a secondary point of access.'

Borgen Fire-eye planted himself at the mine's entrance and unleashed his combi-flamer on the daemons gathering outside, spitting oaths and curses at the wyrdspawn even as he set their rotting flesh ablaze. The rest of the Ironguard spread out around the lift chute, hunting for another path downwards. Egil's visor display was already being lit by red, flashing runes telling him the toxic air was eating away at his armour's sealant, while Skol's gleaming cranium was becoming visibly more pitted and scarred with each passing second. They had to get belowground, and fast.

'Here, my jarl,' Bjorn Bloodfist said. 'A machine-ladder running parallel to the lift.' Egil hurried to the Ironguard's side, and saw that he was right. A smaller shaft entrance, including a heavy ferroplas ladder designed for lowering mining machinery, led down into a darkness so deep even the scans of Egil's augmented eye couldn't penetrate it.

'Will it hold?' Orven Highfell asked as they looked at the ladder, the doubt in his voice obvious.

'It will have to,' Egil said, turning to Moln. 'Collapse the entrance,' he ordered.

'Jarl?'

'Do it! We need to descend, but it will take time. We cannot afford a pursuit.'

Moln hefted his hammer, and replaced Borgen at the mine's entranceway. As Fire-eye checked his weapon's promethium level Stormbrow swung his crackling weapon at one of the overhang's support beams. The decaying timber gave with a splitting crash, and Moln ducked back just in time to avoid the thunderous fall of the mine's entrance.

Egil already had his feet on the machine-ladder's rung clamps. The ferroplas groaned beneath his power-armoured bulk, but held. He began to climb downwards. There was no time to think, no time to assess the situation or calculate risk percentages. They had to get below before Midgardia's corrupt atmosphere poisoned them all.

And besides, every second wasted was another second not knowing the fate of the Great Wolf.

Mouthing a silent prayer to the Allfather, Egil led his pack into the darkness of the underworld.

The Rock, in high orbit above Midgardia

For the most fleeting of moments, when the inquisitor had first arrived on the bridge, the thing wearing the flesh of Vox Mendaxis had known the closest sensation to fear a creature such as it ever could.

The unsettling sensation was soon replaced by the thrill of a close escape. For a second, as the human's eyes had fallen on it, the creature had fancied its flesh would unravel and its daemon-form would burst into holy flame. The Imperium's storytellers would have enjoyed that. The purifying aura of His Chosen Servant burning away the disguises of the corrupt and scorching their evil plots from existence. The ridiculousness of it almost made the Mendaxis-thing giggle out loud. The inquisitor was just a man, and like all men he had ultimately failed to see what was right in front of him.

It was growing bored in the communication pit. It had been masquerading as the vox seneschal since the crusade fleet had entered the warp, bound for Fenris. But now, with the inquisitor's departure, Azrael had returned to his bauble-throne above while the bridge busied itself with preparing firing solutions for Midgardia. Briefly it had toyed with the idea of following the inquisitor back to his shuttle and killing him and his simpering little herd of sycophants. A void pilot who accidentally opened both airlocks in transit perhaps? Or a tragic carbon monoxide leak in the transport bay?

But no. Of the many, many skeins of Fate that wove themselves around such undeniably titillating acts, none of them furthered the task the Mendaxis-thing was here to complete. It chided itself. There would be time aplenty for such games afterwards. Once the Wolf and the Lion had torn each other's throats out.

Finally, the balance of Fate on the bridge Changed. The one known as Interrogator-Chaplain Elezar turned from the holochart he had been scanning and made for one of the bridge's vaulted exit gangways.

Azrael was deep in conversation with his skull-helmed Master Interrogator-

Chaplain, and no one else had the authority to stop the vox seneschal. The Mendaxis-thing rose from the pit and followed lightly in Elezar's wake. As it went it wondered whether any of the labouring menials around it would note that, although it appeared to walk, the body of Mendaxis was in fact floating a fraction of an inch above the bridge's worn flagstones. Such little touches amused it still further. There really was no cure for mankind's blindness.

Elezar passed through hissing blast doors and left the bridge. The Mendaxis-thing slipped after him just before the doors slid shut. Ahead, so real that it seemed to impose itself upon the Mendaxis-thing's vision, Fate's weave spread, a beautiful multi-hued tapestry spun by its master. And all the threads that were tied to Elezar's mag-boots led him to his private reclusiam-cell. That much was now inevitable, and the Mendaxis-thing felt the gratification of knowing it had locked them both into the correct path.

All that remained to do was pick which body it would greet the young Interrogator-Chaplain with.

The Warp

They would have made him their master. Beastlord. Wolfheart. The Wild King. They would have crowned him with savagery and robed him with hunger. He refused. He was not like them. Not yet.

That truth pained him, he could not deny it. There was something inside, something in all of them, that refused to ever be tamed. While the hearth-fires burned low it would rather be hunting in the snow, while weapons lay at rest it would rather sink fang and claw deep into preyflesh. Even some of those he had known the longest had succumbed to it. Scarpelt and Harok, Haghmund and Olfar. Long-fangs and grey-pelts all, given over to the Beast Within. They said the same thing, each one of them. The Wolftime was coming. Leadership was needed. Would he join them?

That was not his way, he reminded himself over and over. There was savagery, yes, but it was cold, calculated, unleashed only when the moment was right. The savagery the others now possessed burned bright, was blind to reason. It was the hungry rage that flung the wolf into the huntsman's trap.

They were late. The warp was playing its usual tricks, seeking to confound and infuriate them. Fury made the Beast stronger. It made more of his warriors turn. They had been bound for the Fenris System for what felt like a lifetime. The other Great Companies were already there, already fighting, already dying, already writing their sagas on Midgardia, Svellgard and Frostheim. The thought pushed him even closer to the edge. He took a long, shuddering breath, trying to clear his head.

Soon they would be home. Whether it would be as beasts or as men, he did not know. There was only one certainty. He would make all those who defiled Fenris pay.

THE YOUNG
WOLF'S RETURN

The Rock, in high orbit above Midgardia

Interrogator-Chaplain Elezar knelt, his black power armour's artificial fibre bundles whirring and clicking softly with the movement. The ceramite of his knee plate grated against the stone floor of the reclusiam-cell. Wordlessly, he genuflected to the only object occupying the tiny space except his meditation cot – the winged sword sigil of the Dark Angels, set in brass relief upon the bare wall.

For a moment he was silent and still, the only sensation the distant vibration of the Rock's mighty plasma drives, many levels below. He let conscious thoughts drip from his mind, like the tallow wax from the ten thousand candles flickering in the Basilica of Repentance. He could feel the beating of his primary heart and the hum of his active battle-plate, throbbing in rhythmic sympathy with his vital signs. Outside, his genhanced hearing detected the approach of armoured footfalls, but he ignored them. Like a prisoner in the Rock's deepest dungeons, he chained his mind in impenetrable darkness, link by link, seeking the oblivion that would let him give proper and meaningful veneration to the primarch and the Emperor.

Just as words formed on his lips, he heard the hiss of his cell door behind him. In an instant he was back on his feet, but the oaths died in his throat as he turned towards the figure who had interrupted his private worship.

'My apologies, Brother-Chaplain,' Azrael said, stepping into the small space. The door whispered shut behind him.

'Supreme Grand Master,' Elezar said, bowing his head. 'No apologies are needed. You simply surprised me.'

'And that in itself no mean feat, I am sure,' the hooded master of the Unforgiven said, returning Elezar's bow with a nod. 'I wished to speak with you privately, and I could think of no better place than this. It concerns the nature of our hunt, and the exposed position we find ourselves in.'

'Yes, lord. What do you wish of me?'

'We must remain ever-vigilant, Brother Elezar. Our enemies circle us like wolves, looking for any sign of weakness, waiting for the opportune moment to strike.'

'I understand, lord. My vigilance is unfaltering.'

'That is true,' the Supreme Grand Master continued, pacing behind him. 'You have been chosen for great things, Elezar. You are indeed blessed.' The Chaplain turned.

'I am glad you believe so. I live to serve the Chapter and the Emperor.'

'Of course, of course.' Azrael continued to circle him. 'It is decided then. You shall help me to announce it.'

'Announce what?' Beneath the shadows of his cowl, Azrael smiled more broadly than Elezar had ever seen him smile before, spreading his arms as wide as the cell's confines would allow.

'His return, of course.'

'Whose return? I don't understand.'

But Azrael didn't reply. Like a bolt of lightning, he struck Elezar, and the Dark Angel knew no more.

Aalsund Island, Svellgard

The impact of Sven Bloodhowl's boot pulped a daemonette's skull with a hideous crunch. The Wolf Lord landed atop the body as it came apart, the impact grinding the remains into Svellgard's hard-packed tundra.

The counter-attack was going in hard. The wyrdlings were still amassing on the islands around the World Wolf's Lair missile control base, their shrieks and screams vibrating the cold, wind-lashed air. Sven, as ever, led from the fore.

There was no space to swing Frostclaw. They were all around him. The Wolf Lord used his short chainsword, Firefang, to gut the clutch of she-daemons pressing as close as lovers, spinning in a tight, ichor-splattered circle. That gave him more room. He gripped Frostclaw near the top of its haft, using the frost axe in tight, hard chops. Claws and talons rained down on the Wolf's armour seeking weak points, scarring the mist-grey plate silver. None found their mark. Sven was a master of this form of warfare; surrounded, he kept moving, kept killing, until he'd carved out half a dozen yards of space. – enough room to slip his hand further down Frostclaw's slick handle and start swinging it properly.

That was when the real slaughter began.

Sven laughed as he killed. The battle-joy was on him, the axe-song that sung more sweetly than the fairest *skjaldmaid*. Either side of him his Blood-guard matched their lord, each one a blur of controlled fury. They had dropped from *Godspear*'s open hold on pillars of fire, their jump packs keening. Together they'd fallen like the warrior-kings of the old sagas, bolts of lightning hammering into the nest of wyrdlings crowning the island's peak. For a few long, bloody seconds, each Space Marine was alone amidst a sea of tentacles, claws and snapping maws.

They relished it.

Olaf Blackstone's wolf claws savaged wyrdflesh left and right, swiftly matting his long, white pelt with stinking ichor. Torvind Morkai, the youngest of all Sven's Wolf Guard, wielded his rune-carved Fenrisian blade in a blinding arc, his swordsmanship so swift that crimson daemons burst apart in fountains of gore before they could even bring their brass-hilted blades to bear. A dozen yards away Kregga Longtooth smashed his crackling power fist into the chassis of a nightmarish Khornate artillery piece, its yawning skull-maw cannon useless at such close range. A single blow sent twisted metal and shattered skulls slamming into the nearest daemons, flinging the entire infernal device onto its side with a shriek of grinding, broken warp-tech.

Nearest to Sven himself were Istun and Uuntir, the former cleaving open the skull of a bloated plague beast with a blow from his twin-headed power axe, the latter using his scarred storm shield to batter a clutch of twisting, writhing horrors back onto the blades of the frenzied swordlings behind them. Any that tried to squirm round his guard were met with efficient blows from the Wolf Guard's thunder hammer, each short strike accompanied by the fearsome weapon's booming discharge.

As he killed, Sven was only half aware of the carnage unleashed by his personal champions. They were his retinue, his chosen, skilled even among the ranks of his Great Company's three Wolf Guard packs. Each was a warrior-king, their flesh and armour inked and carved with runes telling of their numberless sagas, their blades notched but ever-keen. Sven had slaughtered tyrants and broken armies with them at his side for almost a century.

This was merely sport.

'On my mark, disengage,' he ordered, grunting as Frostclaw bit through the rotting hide of a plaguebearer, cleaving the shambling monstrosity from collarbone to groin. *Godspear* passed above the melee, bolters hammering death into the undulating sea of terrors surrounding the Space Wolves. The Thunderhawk's disembarkation ramp was still down.

'Mark,' Sven said, activating his jump pack, Longbound. With a burst of supercharged power it slammed him through the downdraft of the Thunderhawk's turbofans, the sudden acceleration drawing a growl of exhilaration from his throat. The young Wolf Lord angled his leap over the edge of *Godspear*'s ramp, auto-stabilisers thumping as he hit the deck. With a skill that spoke of decades of experience, his Wolf Guard followed him up, directly into the gunship's hold. He made way for them, keying his vox as he looked down into the swarm of shrieking monstrosities.

'Drakebanes, do you think you can do better?'

The Skyclaws answered with chainswords and howls rather than words. In twos they pitched over the ramp of *Wolfdawn*, the other Thunderhawk holding station a little further down the slope. Jump packs flared as they neared the ground, only fractionally arresting their freefall. There was a string of brutal crunches as they slammed into the daemons below, the impacts audible even over the scream of *Godspear*'s engines.

Sven watched them closely as the Thunderhawk banked round, its bolters still raking those daemons swarming over the hilltop. As far as the Wolf Lord was concerned, age and experience came a poor second to battle-hunger and skill. The promotion of the likes of the young redhead Torvind to his Bloodguard, straight from the ranks of the Blood Claws, was a perfect example of his philosophy. The Drakebanes had already fought hard today to purge the missile-launch nexus that was the World Wolf's Lair, but beneath the eye of their vigorous young jarl none would tire. The surface-to-orbit weapon silos buried deep beneath the tundra of Svellgard's islands were vital to the system's defences. They could not be overrun, especially not the control centre that constituted the Lair.

'Young Veslar shows promise,' Olaf said, joining Sven at the open ramp. If it weren't for the daemonic gore that clogged his wolf claws and covered him from boot to topknot, there would have been no indication that the old Bloodguard had been locked in furious combat mere moments before.

'I prefer Mourkyn,' Sven said, watching as the Skyclaws carved their way through the wyrdlings covering the lower slopes. Mourkyn was using his jump pack for repeated short combat leaps. Even from a distance his bared face was visibly twisted with battle-glee as he pounded down again and again into the creatures scrambling to get at him, splitting skulls and snapping spines with his armoured weight.

'He'll rupture his pack if he keeps that up,' Olaf said stoically. 'The boy needs to learn to respect the spirits of his weaponry. And besides, Veslar shows more leadership. The pack follows him instinctively.'

That much Sven couldn't deny. Veslar was at the heart of a small wedge of three other Skyclaws, the improvised formation forging ahead of the rest of the Drakebanes as they made for the island's peak. They moved with a natural fluidity, covering one another's weaknesses, striking together wherever the daemonic tide eddied or parted.

'We don't need leadership as long as you or I live, Long-tooth,' Sven joked, straight-faced. The flashing of an incoming transmission rune interrupted his observations. It belonged to Yngfor Stormsson, leader of the Firemaw Long Fangs, currently overseeing the last purging of the Lair from its central control keep.

'Speak,' Sven ordered.

'*My jarl, the Lair is under attack,*' Yngfor said. '*More wyrdspawn are emerging from the seas all around. As many as before.*' The thudding of

heavy bolters and the whine of recharging plasma cannons was audible
in the transmission's background. Sven cursed.

'Assume defensive positions,' he said. 'Occupy as many of the bunkers
as you can. We are returning immediately.'

'*Yes, my jarl.*' Sven cut the link.

'Trouble?' Olaf asked.

'Just say it,' Sven replied. '"I told you so."'

'They're attacking the Lair again?'

'Yes, again.' Sven brought up the Drakebanes on the vox-net.

'Your fun is over, pups. We're returning to the Lair. It would seem this
wyrdling filth doesn't know when to give up.'

Morkai's Keep, Frostheim

The wyrdling that came at Canis Wolfborn took the form of a woman. The
similarities were only fleeting, for its hands ended in a pair of snapping,
crab-like claws, and its flesh was mottled a dark purple. Worst was its face –
a fanged, shrieking visage that twisted with hate as it flung itself at the
Space Wolf.

His instincts had been correct. While the rest of Harald Deathwolf's Great
Company had been busy collecting and burning heretic dead from the
battle for Morkai's Keep, he'd tracked more wyrdspawn into the depths of
the ancient fortress. The place had not been fully purged after all.

The thing was fast, but so was Canis. In the tight space of the munitions
shaft the daemonette had little chance to use its unnatural agility. The
Space Wolf plunged one set of wolf claws into the creature's slender torso,
while its own talons dragged jagged scars down his battleplate. The thing's
scream turned to a shuddering gasp as it came apart in a burst of sickly
sweet smoke, its physical form unmade by the killing blow.

It was not alone.

More daemonettes darted from the shadows of the munitions bunker,
the air now thick with the cloying reek of their vile perfume. Canis could
only take a couple of steps back up the shaft before they were on him. He
sliced off one slender arm where smooth warp-flesh met claw-bone, filling the tight space with a spray of purple ichor.

'Fangir,' he snarled. His thunderwolf was behind him, and in the sloping
corridor there was no hope it could get its bulk past Canis, but there was
room enough for its snapping maw. It plunged past the Wolfborn, fangs
clamping around the daemonette's head. The kill gave him the split-second
he needed. He keyed his vox.

'The vaults of the Keep are overrun. All packs, lock on my position.' Further words were lost in the screaming of another lunging daemonette.

Inch by inch, Canis fought his way backwards. The servants of the Dark
Prince threw themselves on him in ones and twos, too fast and frenzied

for him to properly disengage. Nor were they just Slaanesh's breed now. Red-scaled swordlings, rancid plaguebearers, gibbering pink and blue horrors – by the time Canis and Fangir had backed their way to the top of the shaft, he knew he had not just stumbled across an isolated nest of daemonic infestation. There was still a warp rift open, deep in the vaults of Morkai's Keep.

He disembowelled a swordling as it lunged at him, its wicked black blade glancing off his breastplate. The daemon burst apart in a shower of stinking offal. Beside Canis, Fangir snapped off the head of another daemonette as they started to burst out of the shaft's confines.

As he reached the Keep's armoury corridor, fresh howls filled his ears. These, however, were instantly familiar to him. Chainswords roaring, the Blood Claws of the Deathhowls rushed to his side, the scent of their pack musk instinctively reassuring. At their sides came the lesser wolves – Yorri, Vela, Scarr, three of the many Fenrisian beasts Canis counted as his pack-kin.

'Stem this tide of filth,' he barked at them. Neither the Deathhowls nor the wolves needed any further encouragement. They laid in with blade and fang, the confined space resounding with the crunch of torn flesh and bone, and roars from throats both daemonic and mortal.

'*Canis, what's happening?*' Harald Deathwolf's voice snapped in his ear. The Wolf Lord was still supervising the clean-up operation out on the Keep's upper walls and surface bastions, ordering the burning of heretic dead and the honouring of the Great Company's fallen. Canis used the space created by the arrival of the Blood Claws to step back out of the melee and answer him.

'There are still wyrdlings in the vaults. Too many. If we do not purge them now they will resurface in even greater numbers than before.'

'*I am on my way. Hold firm.*'

The scrape and scrabble of more claws behind him made Canis spin, fangs bared, a single savage swipe of his claws shattering the hellsword stabbing at the small of his back. The Khornate daemon hissed, resorting to its talons as it went for his exposed face. Canis leaned back with an agility that belied his armour's bulk, servos whirring. The daemon's lunge carried it onto one set of wolf claws, and the strike of the second bisected its horned skull. As it burst apart more of its snarling kin pressed at him, flooding upwards from another munitions shaft opposite the first.

'Deathhowls, to me!' Canis roared.

The Blood Claws answered, and Morkai's Keep shook with the fury of battle. The vaults were crawling with terrors, savaging one another in their desperation to shed mortal blood. Inch by hacking, growling, grunting inch the Space Wolves managed to fight their way to a level higher, into a service corridor, before the press of wyrdflesh around them became too great. That was when Harald reached them.

The Deathwolf's arrival was announced by Ynvir's howl. The great Wulfen led his Murderpack into the heart of the monstrosities attempting to over-whelm Canis and the Blood Claws, bursting with frenzied strength from the confines of a grav lift at the far end of the service corridor. Frost claws glittered in the blinking illumination of the plasteel tunnel as they carved a bloody arc through the nearest spawn.

'*Well met, Canis,*' said Harald's voice over the vox. A moment later the Deathwolf jarl himself emerged from the lift in the wake of his Wulfen's assault, flanked by his dismounted thunderwolf cavalry, the Riders of Morkai.

'To the Deathwolf,' Canis shouted. With Fangir, the Fenrisian wolves and the surviving Blood Claws by his side, he cut his way towards Harald. The Wolf Lord cleaved his own path with his frost axe, Glacius, chopping down one writhing horror after another or battering them aside with his storm shield. After a few moments of brutal killing, nothing stood between the two brothers.

'The lower levels are infested,' Canis panted, grasping Harald's forearm. 'They are becoming more numerous and powerful with every moment. We must seal them off. Otherwise the whole Keep will fall.'

The Wolf Lord's reply was lost amidst the crash of falling rockcrete and the shriek of rent plasteel. A dozen yards down the corridor, a section of the wall came slamming inwards beneath the impact of a Khornate murder-engine. The machine, part hell-forged metal, part wyrd-spawned flesh, forced itself through the gap and onto the nearest pack of Wolves, its cog-jaw grinding through power armour as though it were wet vellum.

Canis muttered an oath and spat to ward off the thing's evil, feeling his transhuman body flush with a fresh surge of adrenaline. At last, a beast worthy enough to be hunted.

More daemons followed in the wake of the growling engine of destruction, capering pink and blue horrors that gibbered and brayed with insane glee.

Canis hurled himself at the juggernaut before it could rampage any fur-ther, catching it in the flank as its teeth sawed through the midriff of a screaming Deathhowl. His wolf claws jarred off the machine's red-plated side, leaving nothing but blackened scorch-marks. Reeking of burning blood and molten metal, the thing emitted a howl like the scraping of steel on bone. Canis struck again, with all his might. With a crack of discharging energy, the claws extending over his left fist shattered against the jugger-naut's armour, their power shorting and sparking.

The machine had difficulty turning itself in the packed corridor, but its sheer bulk forced the Space Wolf back. A snap of its jaws passed inches from his exposed face, the heat that radiated from the thing's infernal maw singeing the blonde hairs of his beard.

A familiar snarl sounded beside the Wolfborn, and he felt a weight push him aside. At full stretch, Yorri the wolf lunged down the corridor, leaping on top of the juggernaut's spiked shoulders as it ground round to face Canis. Vela and Scarr were behind it, the packmates darting through the melee to savage the monstrosity threatening their brother. The machine beast roared again, trying to buck Yorri off its back, but with scrabbling claws the wolf held on. And bit down.

The Fenrisian wolf's iron-hard fangs locked around the juggernaut's neck, just above its brass collar. Scarr darted beneath the creature, snapping its own jaws up around the underside of the juggernaut's throat. Cables and tendons snapped, spraying oily ichor and the defiled blood of the thousands sacrificed to summon the daemon engine. The construct's roar was cut off with a gristly snap. The wolves hung on.

Behind Canis there was a howl as Fangir powered into a brace of swordlings, red flesh disintegrating beneath the savagery of the great thunderwolf's assault. He half turned to assist his wolf-brother, but the juggernaut before him was not yet finished. It heaved its bulk forward with a choked snarl, slamming Scarr back against the wall. The wolf yelped as it was impaled by the great blade crowning the machine's snout, leaving both it and the daemon pinned against the wall as they died. Yorri and Vela whined with sympathy, tearing open the remains of the juggernaut's throat.

That was when the horrors following it through the breach leapt for the two remaining wolves, boneless arms flailing wildly as the air ignited around them. A dazzling gout of multihued wyrdflame engulfed Yorri, and it howled as its ichor-matted pelt ignited.

'*Yorri!*' Canis roared, and threw himself towards his packmate. Laughing manically, the horrors leapt into his path, each one shattering into a million multi-coloured shards as Canis struck at them. Their flames curled and licked around his body like living tentacles, singeing his battleplate black. Mere feet ahead, Yorri writhed in agony, rolling off the top of the defeated juggernaut. Vela added its howl to that of its kinbeast as one of the swordlings battling Fangir slammed its hellsword through its throat, butchering the snarling animal.

The sight of his wolves dying woke something primal inside the Feral Knight. He shuddered as he struck down more of the Tzeentch daemonspawn, a keening, inhuman noise rising in his throat. Agony spiked through his body, aching in his skull, clawing behind his eyes, biting at his fingertips. There was a crunch as he felt the fangs in his jaw distend, ripping his gums and choking his throat with the taste of his own blood. Sweat broke out across his body as his secondary heart kicked in, and his pupils dilated. The sounds of fighting faded into nothingness.

Within him the curse of the Wulfen snarled and snapped, howling to be free.

His fist shattered the last pink horror. He stumbled to Yorri's side, the wolf now scrabbling blindly across the corridor's floor. It was immediately clear that the creature Canis had once counted as a packmate was no more. The wyrdling flames had not burned its fur and flesh – they had wrought something far worse. Even as Canis watched, the wolf's body split and broke, changing and mutating beneath the kaleidoscopic flames. A new snapping maw tore itself open in the beast's underbelly, and fresh blue eyes stared wide with agony along its flank. Spines burst free along its back and one hind leg bristled with silvery scales. The sickening stench of the warp filled Canis' hyper-sensitive nostrils.

He howled and brought his boot down on what had once been Yorri's skull, even as horns split and distended it. Still the beast twisted and yelped as the power of Chaos tore through its body. No longer thinking, Canis stamped down again and again, then started to tear into his former packmate with his lightning claws, rending open rippling flesh and cutting apart burst organs. He howled again, face and beard splattered with blood and spittle, fangs bared as he ripped asunder the creature he had once called his brother.

Finally the flames died. Finally Yorri's flesh stopped writhing and twisting. Finally the amorphous, bloody thing that had once been the proud Fenrisian wolf lay still, joining Vela and Scarr in silence. Their hunt was at an end. Canis slumped to his knees beside the deformed carcass, and howled his loss.

The howl was answered. In unison the wyrdlings assaulting the Space Wolves from either end of the corridor shrieked, pausing to vent their praise even as they were slaughtered with blade, bolt and fang.

And afterwards, for a few seconds, there was silence. Canis heard the long, slow scrape of claws in the breach behind him. Shivering with blood-lust and pain, he stood.

A swordling, larger than any he had ever seen, picked its way through the rubble of the hole smashed in the corridor wall. Its scaly, gore-red hide was armoured with plates of beaten brass and steel, while around its throat a chain thick with shattered ribs dangled. Skulls hung from more chains hooked into the flesh of the monster's unarmoured back, clattering against one another like some parody of a cloak. In one fist it gripped a jet-black, wickedly barbed hellsword, almost as long as Canis was tall. The rune of the Blood God burned white-hot in the centre of its horned, elongated skull.

'Wolfborn,' the thing hissed, a black, forked tongue darting from between razor-sharp teeth. 'I am Korvak Bladelord, the Red Paladin, Herald of Khorne. I have been sent to claim your skull for the throne of my master.' As it stepped into the corridor the Tzeentchian warpfire left by the banished horrors hissed and sputtered, cringing away from the bloody aura of another god's champion.

Canis had no words for the creature. All was blood and pain and snarling, unkempt rage. He howled and lunged.

Korvak moved with the speed of a creature born from a killer's nightmare. In a flash its great hellsword was locked with Canis' right-hand wolf claw, energy snapping and crackling up the black blade's length. Canis punched the shattered remains of his left-hand claw into the thing's belly, a blow that had banished more of Korvak's daemonkin today than he cared to count. But the Herald was suddenly no longer there. Its sword was flashing downwards in a great arc, wielded as easily by the red-skinned wyrdmaster as another man would swing a short sword.

Canis dodged, but the blow still cracked off his left pauldron, splitting the ceramite. The Wolf attempted to push forward inside the daemon's guard, shoulder-first, but again Korvak was not where he had been a heartbeat before.

The air itself seemed to be vibrating, and the splitting ache in Canis' skull was getting worse. For a moment reality seemed to shimmer and shift, like a heat haze trapped in the corridor's confines.

'*The warp rift is widening,*' Harald's voice crackled over the vox. He was back near the grav lift, the press so tight he'd been reduced to using his shield over Glacius to snap bones and break skulls. '*They're growing more powerful. We must withdraw.*'

The words didn't register with Canis. He was hunched over, panting, face contorted by a snarl, glaring at the daemonic Herald which now stood a half-dozen paces back through the breach.

'Surrender to the rage that beats through your veins, Wolf,' Korvak hissed. 'You are no less a beast than your fallen pets.'

Canis lunged again, and again cut only air. The stomach-turning stink of the wyrdrealm was overwhelming now, like burning copper twined around rancid meat. The air undulated, and the realisation that the walls themselves had begun to bleed pierced the fug of savagery clouding his mind. It ran in thick, red rivulets, streaking the pale plasteel and pooling underfoot. Reality itself was unravelling around him.

And suddenly Korvak was behind him. Canis tried to turn, tried to snarl his defiance and spit in the monster's face, but it felt as though he was battling through tar. The hellblade found its mark with an ease that spoke of countless millennia of warfare – parting the armour plating below his backpack as though it wasn't there at all. Searing through him like a bolt of fire, biting deep into his spine.

The Feral Knight fell to his knees with a grunt, blood pouring from his mouth to stain his beard red. He choked. Korvak was suddenly before him again, skull trophies clattering. Duellist turned executioner, the Herald raised his sword with a small flourish, Canis' blood steaming as it ran off its scorching black surface. He tried to bring his claws up one more time, fangs bared, spitting bloody defiance.

The hellsword fell. And the wolves of Fenris howled.

The Underworld, Midgardia

The first thing Egil's boot touched was bone. There was a snap as he dropped the last few feet down the mining shaft, servos humming. He realised as he landed that he'd splintered the ribcage of a desiccated cadaver, lying directly below the machine-ladder that had led them underground.

How had it all come to this? From spearheading an armoured counter-attack out of Midgardia's Magma Gates, to crawling into the planet's under-world in search of Logan Grimnar and his Kingsguard. Egil spun, claws unsheathed, their actinic energy illuminating a small patch of blue light around him.

Nothing. His bionic eye whirred as it sought to pierce the musty darkness, auto-senses straining. Skol's inbuilt stab-lumen beamed ahead, picking out a low tunnel of heavy metal struts and hard-packed grey dirt. More fresh corpses, clad in the decaying remains of mining overalls, littered the plas-board flooring.

'Clear,' Egil breathed, stepping forward in time for Moln to drop down behind him. The big Wolf Guard landed heavily, grunting as his power armour's servos absorbed the impact.

'This looks like one of the Seven Hells,' he growled as he took in their new surroundings, making way for the next packmate to drop down from the machine-ladder.

'Things are going to get tight,' Egil allowed, stepping over to where Skol had illuminated a patch of wall near the shaft entrance. A plastek-sheathed map had been hammered into the packed earth, along with a slew of yel-lowing output dockets, tariff chits and work progress schedules. Egil spent a few seconds scanning it all with his bionics, blink-saving the image and analysing its markings.

'This tunnel will slope downward for just under a mile,' he said. 'At its end is a larger service intersection, Twenty-Nine B. From there we can pick up one of the highway transit routes that connect the underground hives.'

'Where are we taking it?' Orven, the last of the pack to drop down, asked.

'The Great Wolf's last recorded position,' Egil said. 'The uplink log had him entering Settlement Five Hundred and Twenty-Nine. The Midgardians call it Deepspark. It lies two miles to the south, and almost a mile deeper.'

'Deeper,' Moln growled. None of the Wolves enjoyed the claustrophobia of underworlds like Midgardia.

'We must find Logan Grimnar,' Egil said. 'And as many of his Kingsguard as possible. It is inconceivable that they have all been lost.'

'Then let's tarry no longer,' said Borgen Fire-eye. 'I shall take point.'

'With Skol,' Egil said, a thought-impulse sending the servo-skull hum-ming a few feet down the tunnel.

'Keep your helmets on,' the Iron Wolf cautioned as they set off. 'These bodies can't have fallen more than forty-eight hours ago, despite the stage of their decay. Even at this level the air is toxic.'

'At least there's a good reason to keep going down then,' Bjorn Blood-fist growled. Low, grim laughter greeted his words, and Egil smiled briefly. Despite the ongoing fear over the Great Wolf's whereabouts, he no longer

felt the doubts that had plagued him above ground, amidst the spore
jungles. His Great Company were clear of this hell, and he was doing all
he could to find his lord.

Even if they all died down here, alone and forgotten, that had to count
for something.

Its True Name was unpronounceable to tongues of flesh and blood, but
mortals knew it as Sourgut. Phugulus was a great believer in addressing
his Tallyband on a mortal-name basis, so it was Sourgut that the Herald
of Nurgle called on as he gestured at the collapsed entrance of the mining outpost.

The great beast of Nurgle dragged itself through the sumptuous pox-bog
to the broken timbers, and emitted a pungent belch.

'Give him room,' Phugulus ordered, waving his plaguebearers back from
the diseased beast. The words had barely left his split lips before Sourgut heaved like some monstrous slug, the daemon's whole body tensing
and contracting. With an ugly bellow, the beast spewed a violent torrent
of green-grey sludge, writhing maggots and rotting offal at the shattered
entranceway of the mine.

'Fine work, Sourgut,' Phugulus crowed, a trio of the puffballs pockmarking his back bursting with delight. The motion set off those members of
the Infested Tallyband closest to their leader, swiftly filling the Midgardian
jungle air with yet more daemonic spores. Sourgut warbled contentedly
and belched again.

The acidic contents of the bloated beast's stomach worked quickly.
In barely a minute it had eaten through the felled timbers blocking the
entrance, burning a path into the mine. Phugulus waddled inside without
hesitation. They'd need haste if they were going to catch up with their visitors. It really was inexplicable, just how fast the wolf-men in their metal
boxes had left. Praise be to the Grandfather that at least a few had decided
to stay. Why they'd chosen to go down the mine was beyond Phugulus, but
he had no doubt that following them was the right thing to do. He'd heard
much from his kin of Midgardia's fabled underworld. It would surely struggle to match the fecund glory he and his spore clouds had brought to the
surface jungles, but if he didn't see it himself he'd never know.

The interior of the outpost was empty, but the boot prints of the
wolf-men in the mulch underfoot weren't difficult to follow. They all led
to a heavy-looking ladder shaft, its depths lost in darkness. As the Tallyband clustered into the mine behind him, Phugulus paused at the shaft's
edge, his peeling features contorted by a grimace. Almost absentmind-
edly, he fumbled beneath a greasy fold and plucked a squirming nurgling
from his diseased flesh. The slimy daemonic mite tried to gnaw the Herald's worm-like fingers, but his skin had long ago lost the ability to feel
anything, for good or for ill.

'How deep is it?' he asked the creature. It stared at him for a second with wide, imploring eyes. Then Phugulus tossed it over the side. It squealed shrilly as it fell, its own spore-bags popping with fear. The Herald leaned forward, cocking one ear as the noise rapidly faded into the shaft's depths. There was a distant *splat*. He leaned back, grinning.

'Shallow enough! Down we go!'

Wolftide, *in high orbit above Midgardia*

Conran snapped his fingers at the nearest bridge huscarl and pointed at the open vision port. A swarm of spacegoing vessels filled the crystalflex glass, framed by the blotched, ugly purple orb of Midgardia.

'Hail them again,' the Wolf Guard ordered. The huscarl was no doubt thinking that they'd already tried a dozen times, but he clearly knew better than to question the filth-splattered, grim-faced Space Wolf. He bent to the vox bank, snapping commands at his scurrying kaerls.

'How long have they been here?' asked Kreg of the Ironjaws. The Long Fang pack leader had accompanied Conran to the *Wolftide*'s bridge as soon as their Stormwolf transport had docked. In truth Conran was thankful for the white-pelt's presence. He had railed against Egil's decision to give him command of the Ironwolves not simply because he'd wished to accompany his jarl on what would surely be a saga-worthy strike into the underworld, but also because of the pressures of command. The knowledge that the fate of the entire Great Company now rested on his actions gnawed at him. That, and the Great Company's fleet, arrayed in a defensive spread around their flagship, the *Wolftide*.

The last aerial transports bearing the evacuated Ironwolves had docked with the flagship minutes before, but what was he to do next? Simply sit and wait for word from Egil, even while Sven and Harald's Great Companies fought the wyrdspawn filth on Svellgard and Frostheim? And what of Midgardia itself? He surely could not compound the shame of the Ironwolves' retreat by having them break from orbit and abandon the world? He'd already ordered the Great Company's ships to open all available holds, hangar bays and storage spaces to as many of the planet's human refugees as could still be evacuated from the Magma Gates. Now that their protectors had left them, the last human settlements would surely fall to the tide of decay sweeping the jungles. The Sky Warriors had failed their vassals.

'The system's augur sweeps report that they broke from the warp a little over six hours ago,' Conran said to Kreg, still glaring at the vessels beyond the vision port. There were dozens of them, great and small – bristling Imperial Navy capital ships, like the spires of great Ecclesiarchy cathedrals cast adrift in space, flanked by the sleek, armoured bulkheads of Adeptus Astartes strike cruisers and lumbering, grox-like Astra Militarum mass transporters. And in the midst of them all, the great spire-tipped planet-shard

that was the Rock, the mobile, warp-capable fortress-monastery of the
Dark Angels.

The sight should have thrilled any loyal servant of the Imperium. Conran
felt only uncertainty warring with his rising anger. They hadn't asked for
this, and his instincts told him nothing good would come of it. The presence of the Dark Angels alone was enough to make him distrustful. He
spat onto the deck, warding off their evil with the old Fenrisian custom.

'We're reading activity among the crusade fleet,' called one of the kaerls
manning the *Wolftide*'s cogitator tiers. 'Several of the Imperial Navy's capital ships appear to be diverting power towards their weapon systems.'

'What?'

'They're preparing to fire,' Kreg said. Even the old Long Fang sounded
incredulous.

'At what?' Conran snapped. 'Triangulate their likely targeting coordinates!'

'There's nothing...' the kaerl trailed off. 'Unless they're locking onto Midgardia itself.'

'Vox!' Conran barked. The huscarl at the communications bank turned
to him, face grim. He shook his head.

'The crusade fleet is still refusing to acknowledge our signal.'

'Gunnery, all weapons live,' Conran snarled, turning to the weapons station. 'I don't care if you have to drop our shields to do it in time, I want our
full arsenal online right now. Vox,' he turned back to the huscarl, 'contact
the rest of the fleet and tell them to do the same.'

'Do you have a target designation, sire?'

'No, just get our weapons red and make sure those bastards see them.'
He snarled at the crusade fleet, fist clenched subconsciously around the
hilt of his mag-locked chainsword. 'This is one message they won't be
able to ignore.'

The Rock, in high orbit above Midgardia

For a rare moment on the primary command bridge of the Rock, nobody
knew what to do. After giving orders to the fleet to prepare firing solutions
for Midgardia, Azrael had retired to the fortress-monastery's inner chambers with Asmodai, undoubtedly to deliver final commands to his captains.
Normally Vox Seneschal Mendaxis would have spoken on behalf of the
Supreme Grand Master, and communicated with him directly in the event
of an emergency. But when the augurs reported that the Space Wolves fleet
sharing Midgardia's orbit was suddenly powering up its weapons batteries, there was no sign of the seneschal.

Brother-Sergeant Naamiel, commander of the bridge's security detail and
the only Space Marine present, sent a flurry of vox messages to the Captain of the Watch, but had no authority to decide whether or not to start
a civil war on his own initiative. Messages from the rest of the fleet began

to light up the vox banks, reports of Imperial vessels being target-locked by Space Wolves ships sending the communication pits into a flurry of panic-laced activity.

Just as it seemed someone somewhere was going to give the order to fire, Interrogator-Chaplain Elezar strode onto the bridge, skull helm glinting in the green light thrown by the cogitator screens, pict feeds and oculus vid-screens surrounding him.

'Report,' he said.

'Brother-Chaplain,' Naamiel said, bowing briefly to the grim figure. 'Our scans show the Space Wolves have started to target elements of the crusade fleet. They are hailing us, however we are still complying with the Supreme Grand Master's order not to make contact with them.'

'Where is the vox seneschal?' Elezar demanded.

'We don't know, Brother-Chaplain.'

Elezar seemed to survey the nearest cogitator pews for a moment, inscrutable behind his leering helm. Then he gestured curtly to Naamiel.

'Accept their signal. Vox only.' Naamiel hesitated for a moment before nodding.

'Yes, Brother-Chaplain.'

Elezar strode to the nearest communications pit and accepted a brass-wired vox horn handed to him by a stooped Chapter serf. A feral voice snarled at him over the link.

'*What are you doing, Dark Angel? Why are your blades drawn?*'

'Who am I addressing?' Elezar replied.

'*Ironguard Conran Wulfhide, acting pack leader of the Ironwolves. I demand you power down your fleet's weapon systems immediately, in the name of Russ and the Allfather.*'

'The Wolf has no authority over the Lion,' Elezar said. 'You have abandoned Midgardia. We are going to purge its surface before the situation there degenerates any further. The warp rifts deforming the planet cannot be allowed to become any more unstable.'

'*My jarl Egil Iron Wolf is still planetside,*' snapped Conran's furious, animalistic voice. '*As is the Great Wolf himself. I swear by every oath ever uttered, if a single one of your ships fires upon Midgardia this fleet will tear you apart.*'

'We will not fire on you, Wolf, unless you fire on us first. But we have no evidence any of your lords yet live on Midgardia. We cannot wait any longer for them to re-establish contact.'

'*I am going to the surface.*'

'What?'

'*I am taking a Stormwolf to the surface, right now. If you fire-bomb Midgardia, you knowingly kill me, not to mention the tens of thousands of Imperial citizens still trapped there. Your vox banks will have recorded this discussion, as have ours. If you still fire on Midgardia your treachery will be known to all.*'

'Do as you wish,' Elezar said. 'Our duty is clear. The bombardment begins in approximately thirty minutes, and where you are then is of no concern to us. Should your fleet fire on ours we shall respond in kind. It should be clear from our relative strengths that if you pursue such a course of action you will end up losing your fleet as well as your planet.'

The vox horn clicked. The serf who had handed it to him bowed at his feet.

'Lord, they have broken the connection.'

Elezar tossed the horn to the hunched slave and turned to Naamiel.

'Do not accept any more signals from them, or any other Wolf forces in-system. The Supreme Grand Master will return shortly.'

As it paced once more from the bridge, the Elezar-thing shuddered imperceptibly. Hidden behind its false helmet, as though mimicking the skull's leering smile, the creature known as the Changeling grinned from ear to ear.

Longhowl, Valdrmani

Longhowl possessed few survivors. When the daemons had burst into reality on Valdrmani – within the sealed interior of the moon's population domeplex – the human defence forces had been caught totally off guard. It had been murder in its purest and most unadulterated form. Men, women and children had been massacred by blade and fang, claw and warpflame, the habitation blocks running red, the screams echoing back for days off the domed roof high above. When Stern's Grey Knights and Krom Dragongaze's Fierce-eyes had finally banished the daemons back to the warp only a handful of Longhowl's former inhabitants still lived, shuddering in basements and cellar tunnels, half mad with terror and despair.

'They need to be quarantined,' Stern said. He was watching the vid feeds in Longhowl's command sanctum. Across the dozens of screens looped images of the domeplex's interior played out in grainy black and white. The daemons had left the habitation a wasteland of corpse-littered streets and buildings with walls twisted and morphed by warpfire, warm human flesh melded with cold rockcrete. Into the nightmare left in the daemons' wake, the survivors were only now slowly beginning to emerge.

'I know full well what you mean by that,' Krom said, his eyes on Stern rather than the screens. 'You will kill all of them, rather than run the risk that even one may live and bear the taint of the wyrd elsewhere.' Stern turned to Krom, meeting his gaze unflinchingly.

'You are correct.'

'I will not assist you with murder,' Krom said. 'Are you going to do it all by yourself, Grey Knight?'

Stern said nothing. The situation was clear enough to both of them. There were not enough of Stern's knights to search out and corral Longhowl's traumatised survivors, and nor was there any time. Those who yet lived weren't going anywhere.

'The Stormwolves are here,' Krom said. 'If you want to leave this moon I suggest you and your brethren board them with me.'

'Lord Dragongaze.' The voice of one of Krom's Wolf Guard interrupted him. The warrior was standing by the command sanctum's primary vox banks. 'The Fang is hailing us.'

'Give it to me,' Krom said, taking the vox horn proffered by the Wolf Guard.

'*Lord, it's Albjorn Fogel,*' crackled a voice over the link. '*Your vox huscarl on* Winterbite *told me you were at Longhowl's command sanctum. I thought communicating there directly would ensure a better connection.*'

'What is it?' Krom demanded of the Fang's chief communications officer.

'*I am receiving an urgent transmission from the* Wolftide, *Egil Iron Wolf's flagship. Priority Black.*'

Krom felt his hair bristle at the words. Few situations were dire enough to require the Chapter's highest encryption level.

'Is it the Great Wolf?' he asked.

'*I don't know, jarl. I thought it best to patch you through direct.*'

'Do it.'

Static flooded the vox horns mounted on the communications array. A voice drifted and wove through it, as though from a great depth, tiny but insistent. There was a louder squawk of distortion, and then the voice cut into audible focus.

'*Lord, it is Conran Wulfhide, of Egil Iron Wolf's pack. I am currently transmitting from his flagship,* Wolftide.'

'Well met, Conran,' Krom said, making an effort to keep the urgency from his voice. 'What news?'

'*Lord, Midgardia is lost, and with it my jarl Egil and the Great Wolf. They are both beneath the Magma Gates, cut off from all communication. Do you know of the crusade fleet that has invaded our system?*'

'I have had the huscarls in the Fang and aboard my own ships try to communicate with them for hours,' Krom growled. 'They refuse all contact.'

'*I spoke with one of the Lion's sons on the Rock not twenty minutes ago. They intend to fire-bomb Midgardia.*'

'Those treacherous fools,' Krom spat. 'I knew they intended some sort of madness. Have you tried reasoning with them?'

'*Yes, lord. They will not turn from their course. I have told them I am going to Midgardia myself, and if they intend to burn the surface they will burn me with it. I would rather die than abandon those still there to the flames of their own so-called protectors.*'

'Do whatever you can to buy time,' Krom said. 'I cannot abandon the Hearthworld, but Captain Stern of the Grey Knights will soon be on his way. He knows of the wyrdlings behind this trickery. He will talk the Lions out of their own stupidity.'

'For the sake of us all, I hope so, lord.'

A claxon suddenly began to wail throughout the command sanctum, and augur lecterns around Krom lit up with insistent lights.

'What in the Allfather's name is that?' Krom snapped. The vox clicked. It was the *Winterbite*, overriding Conran's transmission.

'My jarl, we are detecting more ships breaking in-system. We are still triangulating the coordinates. As of yet, no identifiers.'

'World Wolf's balls,' Krom swore. 'What now?'

The Void, Fenris System Edge

Like a spear tip shattering a shield, the *Holmgang* smashed back into realspace, reality buckling and splitting around it. Geysers of screaming, fang-filled light streamed from the ship's Geller field, sucked like scum down a drain as they were dragged back into the immaterium.

The battle-barge was not alone. A heartbeat after its return to reality it was joined by the strike cruiser, *Veregelt*. Six smaller escorts of the Chapter Fleet followed, tearing themselves free from the wyrdrealm in formation around the two capital ships.

Shields up and gunports open – the Young King had come home.

'Status,' Ragnar barked from the *Holmgang*'s command dais, gauntlets clenched as his blue eyes swept the bridge below.

'All other vessels are reporting successful re-entry,' shouted an anonymous voice from one of the vox pits. 'They are disengaging Geller fields and standing by for your orders.'

'We are being hailed by the automated system monitors,' said another of the kaerls, manning the barge's communications array. 'They request immediate ident codes.'

'Transmit them,' Ragnar ordered.

'Augur sweeps are still triangulating,' said a senior huscarl. 'Forty-seven per cent complete.' The Wolf Lord ground his fangs together, trying not to make his need for haste any more obvious.

'Lord, we are being hailed by the astropathic beacon on Valdrmani. The transmission signature belongs to that of Lord Dragongaze.'

'Put it up on screen,' Ragnar ordered. The visual feed hanging above the centre of the bridge flickered into life, the vox horns suspended from the ceiling either side of it hissing with static.

After a moment the stern visage of Krom Dragongaze swam into view. As ever he looked every inch the Fenrisian warlord – his blue-grey battle-plate edged with gilt and draped with pelts, his fiery red hair bound up in braid-knots, his bionic optic implant – the so-called 'fierce eye' itself – burning with crimson intensity. Ragnar immediately noted the blood crusting around the rent in the Wolf Lord's right shoulder plate.

'Ragnar,' Krom said, voice cut through by distortion.

'Dragongaze,' Ragnar acknowledged, inclining his head.

'*You're late.*'

'The false currents of the wyrdrealm have been confounding my Navigators for days.'

'*We need you, Young King,*' Krom said. His voice sounded heavy. '*We've had no word from Bran Redmaw or his Great Company. They must still be adrift. There is a hell-spawned plot afoot, and I fear it is far from foiled. It has already come too close to succeeding here at Longhowl.*'

'Is the Hearthworld secure?' Ragnar demanded. 'The Fang?'

'*Yes. I am returning there as soon as this transmission is finished. We do not fare so well elsewhere though. The Iron Wolves have been forced to abandon Midgardia.*'

'It is lost?'

'*Along with the Great Wolf himself. Egil has stayed behind to search for him below the Magma Gates, but we have had all communications with both broken.*'

'We will purge Midgardia,' Ragnar snarled, clutching at the wolf-tail talisman hanging from his holstered bolt pistol, 'fight our way into the underworld, and find the Old Wolf. I won't stop until every last wyrd-damned monstrosity has been banished back to their miserable hell pits.'

'*There's more,*' Krom said, shaking his head at the young jarl. '*Seven hours before your arrival an entire crusade fleet translated in-system. It is led by the sons of the Lion. Even the Rock is here.*'

'Damn them,' Ragnar said. 'Can the fools not see beyond their own petty grudges?'

'*We have identified over a dozen Chapters accompanying them,*' Krom continued. '*And they are refusing to communicate with us. The majority of the fleet is currently taking up position in Midgardia's orbit, though we've identified vessels belonging to the Ultramarines, Iron Hands and Shadow Haunters en-route for Frostheim and Svellgard. Harald and Sven's Great Companies are still battling the wyrdling scum there.*'

'We don't know if this fleet comes as friend or foe?'

'*I have just received a transmission from Egil's flagship. One of his Wolf Guard claims the Dark Angels are preparing to burn Midgardia from orbit.*'

'With the Great Wolf still unaccounted for? They wouldn't dare!'

'*There are none to stop them,*' Krom pointed out. '*Egil is lost with the Great Wolf, Sven and Harald are fully engaged on Frostheim and Svellgard, Bran is still sailing the sea of stars. Grey Knights of the Third Brotherhood under Captain Stern are about to depart for the Rock, but I do not know if they will arrive in time, let alone whether I trust them to fully dissuade the Lions. And I cannot leave the Fang. It was one thing to travel here to the Wolf Moon, but Midgardia's orbit has put it on the far side of the system. I cannot risk leaving the Hearthworld defenceless, not with so much wyrd trickery afoot.*'

'I will go,' Ragnar said. 'And I will tear the throats from anyone fool enough to attack one of our worlds. Once I have stopped them I will descend onto Midgardia and find the Old Wolf and Egil.'

'*Beware, Ragnar,*' Krom said. '*There is foul play at work. I came to Valdrm-ani to assist Stern's Knights despite my oaths. If I hadn't, a wyrd ritual in this very domeplex's choristorium would have convinced our allies, and maybe even the Imperium at large, that we had turned renegade. These wyrdling monsters aren't merely attacking us. They are trying to turn us against ourselves.*'

'They won't have to try hard if the crusade fleet fire-bombs Midgardia,' Ragnar growled. 'I am going there with all speed. I will see you when this is all over, Krom.'

'*Find him, Ragnar.*'

'I will, Fierce-eye,' the Young King promised. As the screen went dead he smashed one gauntlet into the other, the crack of ceramite bringing the whole bridge to a standstill.

'Helmsmen,' he snarled. 'Plot a course for Midgardia.'

LYING IN FLAMES

Morkai's Keep, Frostheim

'*Canis!*'

Harald Deathwolf's roar came too late. Glacius was embedded in the chest of a disintegrating plaguebearer and his storm shield was raised as rusting blades stabbed and slashed. Canis Wolfborn knelt, bleeding his last at the far end of the corridor. Harald saw the black wyrd-wrought steel of his executioner, a Khornate Herald, rise above the press.

Then Fangir struck. The thunderwolf moved like a charge of lightning through the melee, painted red with the gore of the swordlings it had torn apart. As the hellsword fell the faithful beast slammed into its wolf-brother's side, knocking Canis over. The daemon's sword struck, and there was a yelp of pain.

'Canis!' Harald repeated, shouldering his way through the manic fight, the shock of his storm shield blasting combatants from his path. Ahead Canis lay unmoving, blood pooling beneath him. Fangir writhed beside him, the Herald's sword lodged deep in its shoulder. With a snarl of fury the Khornate daemon wrenched the weapon free and struck the huge thunderwolf again, cutting into the meat of its flank. Fangir twisted and howled.

Harald wasn't going to reach them in time. He cleaved apart a brace of capering pink wyrdspawn, grunting as the frost axe carved through their shimmering, ever-changing flesh. They were getting tougher, stronger, faster. Reality in the vaults of Morkai's Keep was starting to disintegrate, unravelling beneath the sheer, stinking, gibbering weight of the daemonic onslaught.

The Khorne Herald stabbed Fangir again, seeking to lance the monstrous thunderwolf's heart. Protecting Canis with its body, the huge beast was unable to attack properly. Its fur was dark with its own blood. Harald couldn't get close enough.

An explosion rocked the corridor, throwing the Deathwolf into the shoulder plate of one of his Wolf Guards. A section of wall to his right came crashing down, the rubble burying the nearest daemons and splitting the skull of an unfortunate Blood Claw. Harald braced himself, ready for yet another flood of wyrdlings to come bursting through the gap.

But instead of gnashing, shrieking horrors, the swirling smoke of the breach was ripped apart by the thunder of bolter fire. Muzzle flashes and the lightning-crackle of activated power fists lit hulking shapes as they pushed through the rubble, their sheer size knocking the breach wider. Terminators, armoured in black, a white gauntlet sigil adorning their right pauldrons. Iron Hands.

The tide turned. Trapped in the corridor's confined space, the daemons could do nothing but throw themselves at the new arrivals. Standing firm, with legs braced and backs straight, the Iron Hands gunned the unarmoured monstrosities down, the hammering of storm bolters and the whir of assault cannons almost too loud even for Harald's auto-senses to filter.

'*Wolf Lord, this is Sergeant Baalor of Clan Company Haarmek. I advise you to fall back to our position immediately.*'

'Not without Canis,' Harald snarled at the Iron Hand over the vox. 'Death-wolves, to me! Ravening Jaw pattern!'

His Wolf Guard, the Riders of Morkai, snapped shut around their lord, using the space torn by the Terminators' fusillade to finally establish some sort of cohesion. Like a fang piercing rotting meat, the small wedge of Wolves punched through the last remaining daemons between them and Canis.

The Khorne Herald was waiting. It stood over Fangir's prone body, dripping with the thunderwolf's blood, its guard down and arms outstretched in challenge.

'Face me, Wolf,' it hissed, looking directly at Harald. 'And die.'

'Maybe next time, daemon,' Harald spat. His Wolf Guard stayed locked around him, power weapons crackling with lethal energies, as their jarl knelt beside Canis.

His visor was still reading vital signs. The Wolfborn's hearts were labouring, and his eyelids flickered as his sus-an membrane forced him into a regenerative hibernation. It looked as though the daemon's thrust had severed his spine.

'You need a Wolf Priest,' Harald told Canis, hoping he was still capable of understanding him. 'Don't try to move.'

'Fangir,' Canis murmured, the words barely leaving bloody lips.

'He's coming too,' Harald assured him, and then turned to his Wolf Guard.

'Send that thing back to hell,' he snapped, nodding at the breach. But the Khornate daemon had already gone. The rest of its kin were dissolving. Harald slung Glacius across his back and bent to heft Canis across his shoulders, his armour's strength-enhancing servo bundles whining in protest. 'Bring the thunderwolf,' he added. Two of his Riders, Gunnar Felsmite and Denr Longblade, hefted the limp animal between them.

'*We are departing, Wolf,*' the monotone voice of Sergeant Baalor crackled over the vox. '*With or without you. None of us can remain down here
any longer.*'

'We're with you,' Harald growled, grunting with the strain of carrying
the Wolfborn. 'Deathwolves, withdraw to the Iron Hands.' The Terminators
parted to allow the retreating Space Wolves through, never once interrupting their mechanically precise bombardment of the daemonic creatures
scrambling after them.

Outside Morkai's Keep a storm was building. It had come from the east,
heralded by a wind that howled and bit with the feral savagery of the
World Wolf itself. Thick, ugly clouds had turned day to night, and snow
had started to swirl and eddy across the glacial plateau where the bleak
fortress hunched.

Iron Captain Terrek of Clan Company Haarmek stood like a statue
forged from black ceramite and silver steel, impervious to the elements
that clawed at him. He gazed up at the fortress' bastions, the lenses of his
bionic eyes peeling away the thickening snow to reveal weapons damage and battle scars. Outside the walls the corpses of traitors and heretics
had been heaped in dark, rapidly freezing piles, awaiting a flamer's kiss.
The remains of others still lay scattered across the great glacier's surface,
uncollected. The Space Wolves had been interrupted before they could
finish their purging.

'*Clan Commander, we have him,*' clicked a voice in Terrek's ear. It was
Brother-Sergeant Baalor, normally commander of Tactical Squad Baalor,
now leader of the composite squad of Terminators assembled to retrieve the
Wolf Lord Deathhowl. Terrek acknowledged the message with a blink-click
of his lenses.

'You've found him?' asked a sibilant voice. Terrek glanced briefly down at
the Shadow Haunter Scout Sergeant, Arro, crouched at his side. He and his
four Initiates had drawn their camo capes up over their heads like cowls,
leaving only the pallid flesh of their lower faces and the nubs of their nas-
cent fangs visible beneath the snowy folds.

'We have,' Terrek confirmed.

The Shadow Haunter infiltrators had returned five minutes earlier, with
news that Terrek had already guessed at. The defences of Morkai's Keep
were no longer tenable. The Iron Captain had deployed his Terminators
on the recommendation of the other Chapter's Scouts, teleporting them
into the Keep's vaults to retrieve the Wolf Lord. He'd served alongside the
Shadow Haunters before, and though their combat doctrines and personal
outlooks were inefficient by the standards of the Iron Hands, their disparate approach to warfare had yielded some analytically exceptional results.
If his grey-clad allies said Morkai's Keep was lost then it undoubtedly was,
regardless of all the fire and fury of the Space Wolves.

The sounds of combat within the fortress reached Terrek's audio receptors, carried by the howling wind. Bolter fire, chainblades, throaty war cries and the unnatural sounds made by the neverborn as they fought, bled and died. The noises were eclipsed momentarily by the shriek of three afterburning turbofans as a black-plated Thunderhawk gunship banked overhead, coming in to land beside the three already occupying the glacier's edge. The warriors of Terrek's strike force – six squads – stood at parade rest in the shadows of their heavy transports, the snow piling up on their towering, immobile frames.

'*We are at the gates,*' Baalor voxed. Terrek and the Shadow Haunters waited. The main entrance to the Keep lay open before them, the rail lines that would have sealed the huge adamantium blast doors sitting inert. The enemy had come from within.

'I have a visual,' Arro said. The Haunter's advanced eyesight had detected movement – shapes emerging from beyond the gate, striding implacably though the deepening snow. Soon Terrek could discern three of his Clan Company's sergeants – Baalor, Zernn and Haamel – bedecked in the archo-mechanical glory that was Tactical Dreadnought armour. Behind them came a bloody mass of figures in the blue-grey ceramite of the Space Wolves. The three remaining Iron Hand Terminators, Krevvin, Horst and Thall, brought up the rear.

Terrek's steel-plated jaw clenched as he saw the ichor-stained creatures loping in the midst of the Space Wolves. Too savage-looking even for their barbaric Chapter, the animals' distended, muscle-bound frames were clad in archaic scraps of armour and their limbs bristled with dark fur. Even at rest their features were contorted into beastly, leering snarls, their fang-filled maws drooling with spittle. They moved hunched over, stooped like predators, almost as though they mocked the firm and unbending posture of the Iron Hands leading them. These then were the mutants the Dark Angels had warned them about. He fought to swallow his disgust, and opened a vox-channel with the motley pack.

'Wolf Lord Harald of the Deathwolves,' he said. His bionics scanned unfamiliar runic markings and pelt totems, picking out the figure most likely to be the leader. The one he settled on carried one of his pack-kin over his shoulders, the fallen warrior's blood streaming down the Wolf's grey armour to leave a red trail in the snow. Behind him two more Wolves hefted the carcass of a huge, furred Fenrisian beast between them.

'I am Harald,' the Wolf said, stopping before Terrek as his Terminator sergeants took post either side. 'And who in the Allfather's name are you?'

'Iron Captain Aleron Terrek, Clan Company Haarmek, of the Iron Hands.' The words issued flat and lifeless from the bionically augmented warrior's vocaliser. 'And this is Scout Sergeant Arro of the Shadow Haunters Tenth Company.'

With a grunt of effort Harald laid the body he'd been carrying in the snow before the Iron Captain. A quick optical scan by the Iron Hand revealed, to his surprise, that the Wolf still lived. Just.

'He needs an Apothecary,' Harald said. 'As does his wolf-brother.' He nodded back at the huge beast being reverently lowered by his packmates.

'That creature is his brother?'

'We are all brothers, machine-man.'

'Where are your own Apothecaries?'

'My Wolf Priest is with the rest of my Great Company,' Harald said, his impatience with Terrek obvious. 'Still fighting inside the keep. I am going to rejoin them.'

'You will do no such thing,' Terrek said, his voice remaining monotone. 'You will vox your squad leaders and order them to withdraw immediately.'

Harald took a step towards him, his visor's red lenses level with Terrek's optical hardware.

'We've fought all day to purge this fortress of wyrd-taint,' the Wolf said, the words a snarl rasping from his helmet's vocaliser. 'Morkai's Keep belongs to the *Vlka Fenryka*, given by oaths and secured by blood. We will not abandon it, not after so many sagas have been written in its defence.'

'Then you will all die,' Terrek said simply. 'Morkai's Keep has been target-locked from orbit by my battle-barge, *Iron Requiem*. I have instructed its gunnery crew to open fire in exactly... twenty-one minutes and eighteen seconds. The ship's bombardment cannon will level this glacier, and seal any of the warp filth that survive far below the surface.'

'You cannot,' Harald said, turning from the expressionless visor of the Iron Hand to the silent, cowled menace of the Shadow Haunters. 'You would not dare strike at the sovereign territory of the sons of Russ!'

'My Clan's most senior Iron Father will attend to your dying brother,' Terrek said. 'We will make... repairs. But only if you cooperate.'

'This is outrageous!'

'This is logical. Your keep has fallen. You require my assistance. I, however, do not require yours. Extracting you was merely a courtesy, and one that I extended with considerable risk. Had my Terminators not successfully teleported into your vaults and brought you clear, my squads would have lost their sergeants at a stroke.'

It was apparent the Space Wolf wasn't listening. He was pacing in the snow like some caged animal, every distant howl and clash of steel still echoing from the keep attracting his gaze. Terrek had taken more than enough of the hot-tempered warrior's foolishness.

'Our fleet intercepted a transmission from this world's moon, Svellgard,' he said. 'It seems the Wolves of your kinsman, Sven Bloodhowl, are also beset.'

Harald stopped his pacing and faced the Iron Hand once more.

'The World Wolf's Lair is under attack again?'

'Yes. Seemingly with even greater force than before. As soon as we have dealt with the incursion here, my Clan Company and I will be bound for Svellgard. There are already other elements of the crusade fleet en-route.'

'What crusade fleet?'

Terrek's response formulae faltered, and he glanced at Arro. The Shadow Haunter Scout simply shrugged.

'Wolf, we have much to discuss.'

The World Wolf's Lair, Svellgard

Sven Bloodhowl no longer laughed as he killed. Now he did it with furious intent – not the primal rage of his Wulfen Murderpacks, but with the lock-jawed, stone-eyed determination of a warrior seeking vengeance.

Torvind was dead. When the Thunderhawk *Godspear* had taken them back to the World Wolf's Lair, Sven had been able to see just how massive the new horde assailing it was. The sea around the missile control complex churned and foamed as ten thousand fanged and clawed nightmares dragged themselves up from the deeps, the wailing cacophony of their voices like a gale battering at the bunkers and redoubts from every side.

As *Godspear* banked round to land, the Wolf Lord had seen the first wave of the daemons' new assault succeed. A cohort of red-scaled swordlings poured up the rocky knoll that dominated the southern tip of the island, flooding towards its fortified vox-mast like a rising, blood-soaked tide. From the open hold Sven had watched the stab of bolter fire and plasma beams as the Grey Hunters assigned to the mast's defence – the Blackfangs – died to a Wolf.

Worse was to come. Emerging from the thrashing waters below came clanking monstrosities – twin Soul Grinders, climbing the craggy cliffs on segmented, arachnid-like mechanical limbs. From the knoll's top their maw-cannons would have an unrestricted line of sight across the whole island.

Sven had led the counter-attack. He and his Bloodguard had dropped from *Godspear*'s hold as they had done innumerable times before, jump packs blazing, power weapons wreathed with disruptive energies. The Soul Grinders had broken and died, one shattered by Kregga Longtooth's power fist, the other by Uuntir's thunder hammer, the enraged daemons possessing the war engines dissipating into the ether.

But it was a trap.

More wyrdlings darted from the waters lashing the crag, these ones impossibly fast. On sleek, lithe-limbed mounts, the Slaaneshi seekers had scaled the rocks in a matter of heartbeats and were upon the Bloodguard before they could rally to their jarl.

Alone, the Space Wolves fought with their customary skill, strength and savagery. This time it would not be enough. Accompanying the mounted daemonettes came a soporific fogbank that rolled in off the sea.

Purple-tinted and cloying, the unnatural miasma worked its way through their armour's vents and numbed the Wolves' razor-sharp senses, slowing each thrust and riposte, deadening each blow. Sven had found himself alone in the impenetrable fog, swinging Frostclaw at nothing, the ululating shrieks of the creatures darting around him making him shudder with strange, unnatural gratification.

He didn't see Torvind fall, and perhaps that was for the best. Under such conditions, it could not have been a death befitting such a warrior. When the young Drakebanes powered into the mist with their own jump packs howling, banishing the vile wyrdcraft with fresh blades and bolters, Olaf had discovered Torvind lying prone at the foot of the vox-mast. His helmet was discarded and his white features frozen in an expression of wide-eyed joy, framed by his long red mane. The cut running across his throat, ear to ear, had been made with a blade so fine his flesh had closed shut after its passing, sealing in the blood. As Olaf, still dizzy from the daemonette's wyrdling musk, probed the wound it had finally come jetting out. He realised the blow had cut the young Bloodguard's throat right back to the bone.

The knoll could not be defended, that much was obvious. Sven, his Bloodguard and the few remaining Drakebanes had withdrawn to the island's interior defences, and the Wolf Lord had ordered his Vindicators to turn their cannons on the vox-mast. A salvo of heavy siege shells had sent the rocks crashing into the sea, denying them as a vantage point for more daemonic artillery.

All that had only been the beginning. The daemons were relentless. From defence turrets and hardened bunkers, rockcrete redoubts and plasteel-plated bastions, Sven's Bloodhowls gunned them down. Salvoes of bolts burst plaguebearers like oversized boils, or reduced swordlings to a red mist. Lascannon beams seared through clanking, whirring daemonic war machines while bolts of plasma vaporised flocks of undulating, manta-like sky-screamers as they swooped down with snapping maws. When the tide rose too high, the stink of promethium vied with the pervasive reek of the wyrdrealm as flamers burned the filth away. The odour of melting wyrdflesh was the worst thing Sven had ever smelled.

And it was all for nothing. On and on the daemons came, cohort after cohort pulling themselves, drenched, from the surrounding sea like some madman's parody of accelerated evolutionary progress. It didn't matter how many were banished back to the wyrdrealm. It didn't matter how long it took them to gain the stony shingle, and then the cold, bare earth between the beach and the outer bunkers. All the spawn from a galaxy-spanning hell were flooding up through the three ever-widening rifts beneath Svellgard's oceans. The Bloodhowls could have fought for millennia and not vanquished a fraction of their attackers.

'Input the missile launch codes,' Sven ordered Yngfor Stormsson, whose Firemaw Long Fangs occupied the keep at the heart of the Lair. 'And rig the central silos for demolition. I am contacting the fleet. We are evacuating.'

'*Lord, communications have been intermittent since the vox-mast was felled,*' Yngfor reported. '*And it will likely be another half hour before we can even begin to extract.*'

'Then we'd better start now,' Sven growled. 'I'll hold them off.'

And so the jarl led his eighth sally of the day into the daemonic host. Frostclaw keened, reaping wyrdflesh with every stroke, neither warp-forged steel, leathery hide nor hardened scales any protection against its razor-ice edge. In his other fist the whirring teeth of Firefang glowed white-hot, a biting blur of fury that shrieked as it sawed through chitin and bone.

Sven killed mechanically now, the fires of his battle-song extinguished. Torvind's death, and the deaths of all the others who had been dragged down beneath the maddening tide, counted for nothing. Svellgard was lost. The Firehowlers had failed.

'*Lord, communication from the fleet,*' said Yngfor over the vox. The rest of his words were lost on Sven as he was forced to duck the swipe of a beast of Nurgle's meaty worm-maw, the flailing blow catching the top of his jump pack and causing him to stumble. He righted himself with a snarl and plunged Firefang into the pestilential monstrosity's swollen belly, revving the chainsword violently. Reeking offal, chewed maggots and flayed meat battered at him, drenching him in toxic green sludge. He kept sawing until the beast had stopped squirming, up to his knee plates in eviscerated daemonic guts.

'Repeat,' he snapped into the vox. Then, suddenly, Yngfor's message became irrelevant. He realised what the Long Fang had been trying to tell him.

Their salvation was at hand.

Overhead, the blank, slate-grey skies were being inscribed with fiery contrails, like a hundred meteorites burning through Svellgard's upper atmosphere. It was a sight he'd seen many times in over a century of warfare, and yet still it thrilled him. He prayed to the Allfather that there would never come a day when it did not.

Above him, an orbital assault was beginning.

'Yngfor,' he voxed. 'Forget my last orders. All packs are to hold their ground. Help is on its way.'

The Void, Fenris System

The strike cruiser's name was *Star Drake*, and its shipmaster was the youngest in the Space Wolves Chapter Fleet. He was called Ranulf, and he was a big-boned, blond-haired warrior who seemed ill at ease in the void, pacing around his bridge like a beast that had not been fed for days.

Captain Stern watched him without comment. The Grey Knight stood immobile beside the Wolf's command throne, hands behind his back, waiting. They had left the upper orbit of Fenris less than an hour ago, Stern's dozen remaining silver paladins occupying the cells reserved for the packs of Wolves that were the *Star Drake*'s usual cargo. Krom Dragongaze's parting words echoed through Stern's thoughts.

'Ranulf will take you to the Rock,' he had said. 'He's wasted above the Hearthworld, without any foe to face. He hungers for glory.'

'I seek negotiation,' Stern had cautioned. 'Not battle or glory. The last thing we need is to give the Dark Angels any more reason to doubt the loyalty of you or your kin.'

'He's simply to transport you to the Rock,' Krom had said. 'Then he will join Egil Iron Wolf's fleet above Midgardia. You are not responsible for him.'

For that, Stern was thankful. The Space Wolf hadn't stopped moving since they had broken from orbit. He spoke only in grunts, not so much hostile towards his passenger as indifferent. The two other Wolves who commanded the ship's serf crew seemed similarly distressed. One was overseeing the watch at the enginarium, whittling runes into a wooden token with single-minded intensity. The other stalked the ship's lower decks, apparently without purpose, snarling at any who got too close.

Stern placed one gauntlet on the hilt of his sheathed nemesis force sword.

'How is our progress, shipmaster?' he asked.

Ranulf was down among the cogitator tiers of the bridge's lower level, momentarily out of Stern's line of sight. There was a long pause before the Wolf called back up to him, his voice sounding hoarse.

'Tolerable, daemonhunter. Another three hours will see us within short-range hailing distance of the fleet around Midgardia.'

'My Brotherhood appreciates your assistance in this matter,' Stern said, wondering what the Wolf was doing.

'Anything that lets us strike back at these treacherous fools,' came the halting reply.

Stern wondered briefly whether Ranulf was referring to the daemons that infested the system, or his supposed brother Adeptus Astartes in the crusade fleet above Midgardia.

'I will take my leave, for now,' the Grey Knight said. 'I must brief the Knights of my Brotherhood on the situation we might expect once we reach Midgardia.'

There was no reply. Stern turned to depart.

Below him Ranulf crouched, hidden between the cogitator banks, fists clenched, eyes screwed shut, his whole body shaking in mute strain. The kaerls around him stared at their lord in silent, wide-eyed terror, edging along their benches away from him.

Slowly, a growl began to build, deep within the Space Wolf's chest.

Stern was halfway towards his commandeered cell when the inter-ship vox-net exploded.

At first it was just screaming. Stern's sword was in his hand instantly, energy crackling up the blade.

'Brothers, report,' he demanded. All his Knights were still in their cell blocks. None were any more aware of what was happening than he was.

The screaming worsened. It was no longer just a single voice, and no longer just on one frequency. On three separate channels, the sounds of indiscernible Fenrisian pleas drowned out all other communication.

Stern checked the channel sources. The bridge, the enginarium, and sub-deck seventeen, deep in *Star Drake*'s bowls. Realisation struck him just as he heard the first feral snarls over the vox. His blood ran cold.

'Artemis, Gideon, Ethold, deploy to the engine deck immediately,' he ordered. 'Simeon, Osbeth and Caldor, track vox-channel nine-eight-two-oh. Everyone else rendezvous on the bridge.'

'*What is it, brother-captain?*' Gideon asked. '*I sense no warp taint here.*'

'You're right,' Stern said. 'It's worse.'

He sprinted for the bridge, bursting through the open blast doors just as a flood of screaming kaerls poured in the opposite direction. The leadmost scrambled to make way for the silver-armoured warrior as he thrust between them, eyes on the monster prowling the deck below.

The monster that had once been Shipmaster Ranulf.

The Space Wolf had succumbed to his kind's inherent curse. The warrior's armour was now split and twisted around fresh growths of muscle, his gauntlets broken by wicked claws. The shipmaster's face was barely recognisable, a contorted mess of blond fur and fangs. Yellow, lupine eyes stared wildly up at Stern as he sensed the Grey Knight's arrival.

'*It's the Space Wolves,*' Caldor voxed as the other Knights made the same discovery. '*They've gone berserk.*'

'Don't kill them if you can help it,' Stern said. He slowed as he reached the metal staircase leading from the upper half of the bridge to the lower, deactivating his force sword as he went.

'Ranulf,' he said to the Wulfen. 'Do you remember me, Ranulf?'

The Wulfen snarled. It had killed. There was blood on its claws and matted in its beard.

'I know you do not recognise my scent, Ranulf,' Stern said, spreading his arms, opening his guard. 'I am not one of your pack. But remember my voice. I am your cousin, Space Wolf.' He halted a dozen yards from the Wulfen, the beast seemingly frozen to the spot.

A half-dozen kaerls, cowering beneath their clattering cogitators, chose that moment to run.

'No!' Stern barked at them, but too late. The thing that had been – or maybe still was – Shipmaster Ranulf leapt as they passed, a feral howl tearing from the monster's throat. Two of the serfs went down beneath its claws, screaming. Blood splattered across their workstations.

Stern activated his sword once more and sprang forward, features set.

Lowly Chapter thralls or not, he would not allow any more innocent Imperial blood to be shed.

Ranulf turned with a speed even the Grey Knight captain couldn't match, claws slashing across his silver breastplate. Stern grunted at the impact, swinging his sword around as he sought to keep the Wulfen at bay. The beast, however, had no time for finesse. Ducking the swing, it wrapped two arms around Stern's midriff and heaved. The Grey Knight found himself going down beneath the creature's sweat-stinking weight, servos protesting.

The two Space Marines struck the decking grille with a crack. Stern immediately regretted trying to talk to the beast face to face and leaving his helm mag-locked to his belt. The Wulfen pinned his arms and tried to savage the Grey Knight's skull with its fangs. Stern could only turn his head away, bloody drool splattering him.

Somewhere, a claxon began to wail. Red emergency lighting bathed the bridge. He felt the deck shift fractionally beneath them.

'Brother-captain!' The voice of Alacar, one of Stern's brothers, caused the Wulfen's head to snap up. Six Grey Knights occupied the upper bridge, force weapons activated, storm bolters levelled.

Stern used the opportunity the distraction afforded him. He head-butted the Wulfen. The creature grunted as its head snapped back, fangs crunching, its grip on Stern's arms loosening a fraction. The Grey Knight ripped one gauntlet free and, as the Wulfen's head came back down, eyes filled with raging madness, he pressed two fingers to the creature's scalp.

'Enough,' he enunciated, driving a spike of his will, blindingly bright, into the beast's mind. His psychic soul flare illuminated more than he'd expected, more than just the animalism displayed by the creature's behaviour. Fear, sorrow, pain. Above all, awareness, no matter how base. Whether he'd wanted to or not, Stern could not deny that the creature was still a Space Wolf. Ranulf was still there.

And Ranulf now slumped, suddenly limp, across Stern. He was unconscious.

The other Grey Knights reached his side. With some difficulty they dragged the sprawling Wulfen off their captain. Stern found his feet.

'Brothers, report.'

'*The enginarium is secure,*' crackled Gideon's voice in his ear. '*But we had to put the Wolf down. Brother Ethold is wounded, and the engine systems themselves were damaged before we could purge the mutant.*'

'Ethold?' Stern asked.

'*I'll live,*' came the big Grey Knight's response.

'How bad is the damage to the engines?' Stern glanced at the red lights still blinking across a slew of the bridge's cogitator banks.

'*I don't know, brother-captain. The mutant killed a number of tech-priests. The remainder are assessing the damage as we speak.*'

'Have them shut off those claxons,' Stern ordered. 'Caldor, status?'

'*Our Wolf is also dead, brother-captain. He threw himself from a stanchion when we cornered him. Some sort of madness gripped him.*'

'They are cursed,' Alacar said beside him. 'We should kill this one, before it awakes.'

'That is not our decision to make,' Stern said. He cast around the bridge, his genhanced senses picking out the hiding places of its surviving crew.

'You,' he snapped, pointing at an old man in the pelt-trimmed robes of a huscarl, trying to cower behind a holochart. 'Where are this ship's holding cells?'

'Deck theta-nine, lord,' the serf stammered. 'That's the main brig.'

'You will lead my battle-brothers there with this prisoner, as soon as you have told me what this means.' He gestured at the flashing rune banks of the nearest cogitators, and then at the wolf-headed claxon horns that still howled from the bridge's arching roof.

'Lord, the enginarium has gone into lockdown,' the huscarl said. 'Any weapons fire on the drive deck could trigger it. It will need to be overridden.'

'You can do so?'

'With time, lord. But there may also have been damage done to the control mechanisms.'

'What are you saying?'

'That without basic repairs our projected course will take twice as long to achieve.'

'Where can such repairs be effected?'

'Our enginseers would likely be sufficient, lord. But it may be quicker to seek assistance from the nearest docking station.'

'And where would that be?'

'We will need a moment to triangulate our exact location.'

Stern waited in silence as the huscarl bent over a rune bank, wizened fingers tapping away. After a few moments the claxons shut off, though the lights continued to wink urgently. Slowly, more wide-eyed kaerls began to emerge from their hiding places.

'Return to your stations,' Stern ordered. 'Now.'

'I have our coordinates, lord,' the huscarl said, sliding a freshly inked data chit from a cogitator's imprint port. 'It would appear...' he paused to scan the slip of paper, then looked at Stern's boots, uncertainty radiating off him.

'Speak,' Stern commanded.

'The closest station is a Ramilies-class star fort, *Gormenjarl*. It is part of the system's defence network.'

'Contact it immediately. Inform them of our requirements.'

'That's the problem, lord,' the huscarl said, still not meeting the Grey Knight's steely gaze. 'All contact with both *Gormenjarl* and the system's other Ramilies, *Mjalnar*, was lost at the start of the daemonic incursions. Our signals go unanswered.'

Stern gazed out into the star-studded expanse stretching away beyond

the *Star Drake*'s open vision port. The problem was clear. They were partially stranded hours from their destination, and time was running out.
But everything about *Gormenjarl* boded ill.

'How big is the Ramilies' defence contingent?' Stern asked. The huscarl
paused, scanning his cogitator screens.

'Six platoons of Imperial Navy armsmen and a single pack of Grey Hunters. The ones on rotation when contact was lost were the Redpelts of Lord
Kjarl Grimblood's Great Company.'

It was surely a trap. The onset of the Wulfen curse at such an inoppor-
tune moment could not be coincidence. What if the Space Wolves' genetic
instability really was warp-tainted?

But that did not change things, Stern told himself. Not yet. The Dark
Angels had to be stopped before they started a full-scale war with the
Wolves. The carnage such a conflict would unleash could only serve the
Ruinous Powers. Once the situation had been stabilised, then the Wolves
and their bestial defect could be subjected to judgement.

Stern had to get to the Rock as soon as possible. And that meant braving a daemon's schemes.

'Chart a new heading,' he said to the huscarl. 'Get the engines back online
and divert as much power to them as you think they can handle. Take us
to *Gormenjarl.*'

The Void, Fenris System

At times like these, standing aboard the bridge of the battle-barge *Holmgang*, Ragnar Blackmane felt truly helpless.

For a Fenrisian warrior, born and bred beneath clear, cold skies on the
banks of icy seas, the confinement of void travel was akin to the worst sort
of imprisonment. In his younger years the Wolf Lord had spoken with officers of the Imperial Navy who had relished the endlessness of the galaxy
beyond their ships' bulkheads and vision ports. They talked of limitless
space, of the ultimate expanse, a wanderer's quest that could last forever.

Ragnar saw none of that in the starry darkness he now gazed upon. Only
nothingness. The way his pack brethren referred to it – the Sea of Stars –
was a misnomer, a lie told to comfort their instinctive dislike of the void. It
was nothing like the beautiful, windswept seas of the Hearthworld. It was
worse than desolation, worse than abandonment.

Truly, it was a void, nothing more and nothing less. It trapped him in
a box of adamantium, his sword-skill and battle-lust rendered impotent.
The killing was done by others, by gunnery thralls and range finders, target locks and servitor breach-loaders, none of it glorious, all of it torpid
and impersonal. The Young King's only hope during void engagements was
for the savagery of a boarding action. Those, he allowed, were rare, sweet
fights. Then a warrior's speed, his strength and his fury meant everything.

But even those few seconds of blood and steel couldn't eclipse the shuddering monotony of voidborne travel.

Ragnar hadn't moved from the centre of the *Holmgang*'s bridge since his fleet had translated in-system. After hailing Krom he'd tried to raise Sven on Svellgard and Harald on Frostheim. His efforts to make long-range vox contact had failed, though he'd reached Harald's flagship, in orbit above Frostheim. The ship's chief vox huscarl had reported vessels belonging to the Iron Hands, Ultramarines and Shadow Haunters moving into orbit, making no threatening moves towards the Space Wolves fleet but refusing all offers to communicate.

Right before the end of the last transmission the huscarl had reported an Ultramarines strike cruiser and a trio of Astra Militarum mass transporters breaking away from the fleet in the direction of Svellgard, orbiting on the far side of Frostheim. At the same time Iron Hands Thunderhawks had been picked up heading for low orbit on a trajectory that would take them to Morkai's Keep. Whether they went to assist Harald Deathwolf's warriors or purge them, Ragnar didn't know. The thought that loyal cousins may at that very moment be tearing at one another's throats because of some wyrd-spawned trickery made his entire body shake with anger.

As far as Midgardia was concerned, information was even patchier. The crusade fleet there, led by the Rock, dwarfed the one taking post around Frostheim and Svellgard. The Space Wolves ships in orbit appeared leaderless – on the rare moments when the *Holmgang* was able to establish reliable contact, the reports from the huscarls were conflicting and confused. Logan Grimnar was lost. Seemingly now Egil Iron Wolf was too. There were rumours the crusade fleet was about to unleash Exterminatus on Midgardia.

Loudly and without shame, Ragnar damned the waiting to the Seven Hells.

At last, a change in the soul-searing monotony. Augur beacons chimed, and kaerls scurried to and fro beneath the bridge's dais as data was collated.

'What is it?' Ragnar demanded, staring out into the void, the nothingness, as though his keen eyes would have been able to pick something out of the endless emptiness.

'A ship just entered our furthest engagement proximity zone, lord,' said a huscarl, bowing to the Young King.

'What ship?'

'Our cogitators are working to identify it right now, but it appears to be Imperial.'

At the moment that counted for very little. Ragnar bared his fangs in annoyance as he waited for the chattering cogitators to finish their arcane computations.

'I have it,' said a second huscarl, peering at the fuzzy green display of a data-slate. 'The ship is a fast cutter, New Star pattern, but appears to have been extensively modified. It's transmitting an ident-signal...' He paused for a moment. 'But it's blank, my lord.'

Ragnar's expression darkened. He watched the red blip representing the anonymous vessel drawing fractionally closer to the Space Wolves fleet on one of the bridge's holocharts, like a seaborne minnow darting cautiously towards a great Fenrisian kraken. There were few ships in the galaxy that bore blank ident-signals, and fewer still that would dare approach an entire Space Wolves fleet on a war footing.

'There are no other ships within striking distance?' the Young King demanded, eyes darting across the charts and the oculus feeds.

'No, lord.'

'Extend the augur range and scan again. I want to be certain.' Even at the best of times, the appearance of such a vessel didn't bode well. And these were far from the best of times.

'Lord, it's hailing us. Vox only.' For a moment, Ragnar hesitated. Then he gestured at the communications array.

'On speakers. Let's hear him.'

The voice that addressed the crew of the *Holmgang* was one Ragnar felt he'd known all his life – firm, uncompromising, self-assured. It was the voice of the Imperium, cracked with age but still smouldering with resolution. It was exactly what the jarl had feared, as soon as he'd seen the blank markers of the mysterious ship's designation.

'*Greetings, Lord Blackmane,*' it said. '*My name is Lord Inquisitor Banist de Mornay of the Ordo Hereticus, Segmentum Pacificus Divisio. Aboard the* Allsaint's Herald.'

'Lord Inquisitor,' Ragnar acknowledged. 'You've come from the crusade fleet, I take it?'

'*Not exactly. More like in spite of the crusade fleet.*'

For all the voice's apparent strength, it could not disguise its frailties from Ragnar's keen senses. The Wolf could detect the slight wheeze that came with aged, failing lungs and the soft, wet slap of fleshy lips. While de Mornay's tone retained much of what must have once been a considerable will, Ragnar doubted the man's body had stood the test of time so well.

'Your ship comes here seeking me,' the Young King said. 'Why? What business have you with the *Vlka Fenryka*?'

'*Noble Wolf, I do not know how much you are already aware of,*' de Mornay answered. '*But time presses, so I will speak plainly. The Dark Angels have not come here to banish daemons. They are here because they are convinced – all of them – that your Chapter is harbouring the curse of a mutation far beyond the limits sanctioned for Adeptus Astartes gene-seed. And, as you can gather from their following, the Imperium at large appears to have been persuaded by them.*'

'The Imperium, but not you, Lord Inquisitor?' Ragnar demanded. De Mornay didn't reply, and the Young Wolf let the silence stretch. The accusations of mutation had left him pale-faced with anger, but he swallowed it, bit back at the beast snarling inside him. They were already lacking friends as it was. Cementing his Chapter's isolation would not help any of them.

'Why are you here, de Mornay?' he repeated.

'Suffice to say for now that I believe the Dark Angels' interest in your... unfortunate secret conceals one of their own, one which surely must be far darker than what your wolf-brethren are currently struggling with.'

'You speak in riddles, inquisitor,' Ragnar said. 'I already count Lukas the Trickster among the ranks of my Great Company, I wouldn't want you to give him competition.'

'These channels are undoubtedly being monitored, Wolf Lord,' de Mornay said. *'Yes, even with your ciphers and encryptions. The Inner Circle sees much, and hears even more.'*

'You are beginning to sound senile, inquisitor. What is this madness you speak of?'

'I request an audience with you directly, Lord Blackmane. Aboard your ship.'

The sudden demand caught Ragnar by surprise.

'Into the wolf's lair?' he said slowly. 'Don't you believe any of the stories you've heard? Do you think you would be safe?'

'Not safe,' de Mornay allowed. *'But at least certain. Discussing matters face to face would be preferable to this. Your Chapter wards others away with the appearance of savagery, but your souls are not dark. I know Chapters that are.'*

'You would rather a wolf's lair than a lion's den,' Ragnar said, smiling grimly. 'Very well, Lord Inquisitor. We will receive you. And perhaps venture into the den together.'

Sub-orbit, Midgardia

Midgardia wasn't hailing him.

Conran was not surprised. Normally a descent upon the Magma Gates would have required dual-level clearance codes and at least one vocal scan. But the only thing that spoke to him now over the vox was static.

The non-encrypted channels were a mess. Control of the airspace above the planet had collapsed completely. There were dozens of fliers aloft, from sleek unicutters to swollen cargo sows. They gave Conran's Stormwolf a wide berth, not merely because of an instinctive fear of the Adeptus Astartes, but because his was the only transport headed planetside while the rest fled.

'This is foolishness,' said Kreg's voice for the eighth time.

Conran didn't reply. The Long Fang had almost physically blocked him from leaving *Wolftide*'s bridge.

'What does the lion care for one wolf?' he'd demanded.

'It's not one wolf,' Conran had snapped back. 'Logan Grimnar is down there. Egil Iron Wolf is down there. Our jarls, our champions, the greatest living heroes of our Chapter. I will not be the one to abandon them.'

'You cannot help them down there,' Kreg had said. 'Hail the Rock again. Try one last time.'

But Conran could take no more. He would not scream hopelessly into the void while his packmates died.

The same loyalty clearly did not occupy the minds of the citizens of Midgardia. The landing plates and docking spires of the Magma Gates, rising above the blotched purple canopy of the surrounding spore jungles, were awash with people seeking salvation. Looking to the skies for landers that would never come. The Wolves in orbit had already taken on board what they could. As the Stormwolf banked overhead Conran saw the muzzle-flash of small-arms fire as a mob of refugees attempted to rush an area of the plates cordoned off for upper-spire dignitaries. The guards – privately hired muscle, no doubt – cut down the initial rush, but could not reload fast enough to stop the next. Conran lost sight of them as they were swamped by a sea of scrambling, screaming men, women and children.

The Space Wolf had seen such sights many times before. Civilian panic and disorder had been a feature of almost every war zone he had ever fought in. But this was not some crater-scarred war world in some distant frontier system. This was Midgardia, sister planet to noble Fenris itself, part of the Space Wolves' fiefdom. The thought sickened him.

'*Conran,*' said Kreg again over the vox. Conran cut the channel.

He banked left, angling the transport for the highest point of the Magma Gates, the planetary governor's control spire. Finally, he received a challenge, if only an automated one. A servitor demanded a string of ident-codes over the vox. Conran gave them, and was cleared to land. He noted with surprise that Governor Sandrin's private shuttle, a gleaming chrome autowing, was still sitting idle on its docking strut.

Conran let the hardwired auto-servitor pilot the Stormwolf down, releasing his restraint harness and standing by the cockpit hatch. There was no one to greet him at the landing strut. Blast doors led from the plate into the control spire proper. Even this high above the canopy, the corrosive effect of Midgardia's daemon-enhanced spores was obvious. Metal rusted and flaked and the blast doors opened with juddering reluctance, as though they hadn't been used for decades. Below, the purple jungles stretched in an endless sea, discoloured now with foetid shades of green, a smog of ugly yellow-tinted spores hanging over the deformed canopy. The Wolf Guard didn't linger outside.

He stalked the council chambers and corridors of the spire, his senses on edge. How far had the wyrd-taint been able to spread since they'd evacuated? Judging by the panic being exhibited on the public docking plates he assumed the enemy had at least penetrated the Magma Gates' outer bastions.

The control spire, however, seemed utterly deserted. That was until his auto-senses detected the sound of raised voices emanating from Governor Sandrin's personal chambers.

The rooms themselves were not the sumptuous things other planetary rulers might have enjoyed. The Magma Gates were more military garrison and administrative hub than a governor's palace. Sandrin himself was not an Imperial Commander in the true sense of the title. It was the Space Wolves, and not the High Lords of Terra, who had appointed him as Governor of Midgardia, just as it was the Wolves that had appointed every one of the planet's rulers since the Imperium had first granted the Chapter full rights over the Fenris System.

Sandrin himself was a competent enough man, a hard-working, long-suffering administrator who preferred a clerk's ink-stained apron to his fur-trimmed robes of office. Yet it was the latter he was wearing now, standing beside the unmade bed in his private sleeping chamber. His angry words masked Conran's approach.

'I won't tell you again, Melain, I'm not leaving! Take the children and the shuttle. Go straight to the Wolf fleet in orbit, they'll give you sanctuary. But I must stay.'

'Why?' Melain wailed. The governor's wife was knelt before her husband, still in a dishevelled nightdress, face swollen with grief and streaked with tears. Two children, eyes wide with frightened bewilderment, stared on from a chair in the corner of the room. The older of the two, a little girl, was the first to notice Conran. She screamed.

Both parents turned, faces etched with fear. The realisation that it was one of the Adeptus Astartes, and not some foul daemon standing in their doorway, didn't do much to lighten their expressions.

'Governor Sandrin,' Conran said. 'I did not think to find you and your family still planetside.'

'I-I won't leave,' Sandrin stammered. 'It would be a dereliction of my duties as an Imperial citizen and a betrayal of my oaths to your Chapter and to Fenris. In ten thousand years no governor has abandoned Midgardia.'

'Your courage does you great honour,' Conran said. 'But surely we cannot ask the same sacrifice from your family. I know what is coming through the spore jungles in this direction. I certainly would not wish my kinsfolk to experience it first-hand.'

'I won't leave my husband,' Melain said, defiance hardening her grieving expression.

'Yes, you will,' Conran said. 'For the sake of your children. I will take you onboard my own Stormwolf. You will be delivered safely to the flagship of my lord Egil, in orbit above.'

'He sent you to retrieve us?' Sandrin asked.

'No. He is still deep in the underworld. I came on my own initiative. A misguided faction of our fellow Adeptus Astartes has been threatening to fire-bomb Midgardia's surface. It seems we cannot stop them without drawing blood. I had hoped my presence planetside would make them reconsider. I cannot simply sit in orbit any longer while this world is burned to ash.'

'We have been betrayed?' Sandrin asked incredulously.

'I fear so, governor, though just by whom or what I do not yet know. Let me escort your family outside.'

'At least come to the shuttle,' Melain begged. Conran saw the resistance in the governor's pinched eyes, but after a moment he glanced at his two offspring and nodded.

'Hurry,' Conran said.

Melain gathered the children by her side, and the four followed Conran back to the landing strut, their wiry, pale Midgardian bodies dwarfed by the towering Space Wolf.

'The atmosphere is becoming ever more toxic,' Conran warned before the strut's blast door. 'The air itself has been infected by the Archenemy's presence. We must be quick.'

The family nodded. Conran raised a gauntlet. 'On my mark.'

He hit the door's release rune. Beyond it, they didn't get far.

The Space Wolf was only a half-dozen yards across the strut's plate when the little boy's shriek brought him up short.

'What's that?'

The Wolf had seen it too. A spear of light, flickering with the burning of contrails, stabbing down from orbit. It struck a few miles east of the Magma Gates. Fire blossomed, a conflagration that mushroomed like the jaws of the great Fire Wolf, consuming all around it.

'Allfather protect us,' Conran said.

Above, the crusade fleet opened fire.

The Warp

They challenged him. He would not be their king, so they came for him one by one. Old friends and Long Fangs all. He put them down, each in turn, stripped of his battleplate, hair matted, his body streaked with blood and sweat, panting from between bared fangs.

Was he still so different from them? Was there still any point in resisting? Even when they submitted? Even when knees bent, and throats were bared in subservience?

He accepted their fealty, though his whole body itched to join them. Surrender to the gnawing, black, clawed thing inside him.

But no, no. Resist. You are more than a beast, though you may no longer look or think it.

The daemons came for him next. The wyrdrealm knew of their approach, and of the threat they posed. It had already tried to slow them, to delay their arrival in the Fenris System. Now it attacked the fleet's Geller fields. Things with snapping tentacles and a thousand weeping eyes materialised onboard their vessels. With rending claws and howling beast-oaths, each one was sent straight back to the hell that had spawned it.

The warp could try its trickery for eternity, but fate was inexorable. Nothing would stop the Redmaw now.

THE BROKEN CROWN

Exfill Shaft twenty-nine point seven two,
the Underworld, Midgardia

Egil and his Ironguard had barely gone a hundred yards before their vox-links picked up a squeal of transmission code. It was gone in a heartbeat, vanishing once more into Midgardia's cavernous depths. Fifty yards later there was another blurt.

'Press on,' Egil ordered, fighting to keep the frustration from his voice. Logan Grimnar was down here somewhere. Some of his Kingsguard had to have survived as well. The Iron Wolf would find them, or his bones would remain beneath Midgardia for eternity.

The tunnel they were taking was painfully low and narrow, requiring the Space Wolves to stoop almost double as their pauldrons ground against its crumbling dirt flanks. The air was close and hot, and the scuffle of ceramite through muck, the hum of power armour and the panting of his packmates filled Egil with a claustrophobic, fang-baring impatience. Until the vox squealed a third time.

'Come in,' Egil snapped, click-cycling through half a dozen channels as he hunted for a solid connection. They could not be alone down here. There had to be survivors.

Ahead, Borgen Fire-eye added fuel to his hopes.

'Bolter fire,' the Wolf Guard said. 'Not far away.'

Moments later the familiar thunder reached Egil's auto-senses, echoing down the tunnel to him.

'Keep going,' the Iron Wolf ordered.

They did so, snarling with the effort of forcing their way along the mining exfill shaft. Egil's dirt-caked armour tracked his rising adrenaline, a growl building in his throat. His decision to come down into these infernal depths had been justified. There were still fellow Wolves down here. Surely Logan Grimnar was among them.

Finally, the vox made proper contact.

'*Not an inch, brothers,*' came a growl, followed immediately by the crash of more bolter fire. Egil heard the echoes of the shots bouncing down the tunnel ahead. He recognised the voice.

'Brother Lenold,' he said. 'It is Egil, of the Iron Wolves. We are inbound on your location. What's your current status?'

'*By the primarch, it's good to hear you, lord,*' Lenold responded. '*We're holding shaft intersection Twenty-Nine B. There's wyrd-scum everywhere.*' The rest of his sentence was cut off by a howl, and the furious revving of a chainsword.

'Hold fast, Champions of Fenris,' Egil said, then switched to the inter-pack channel. 'Borgen, how far?'

'I can see the end of the tunnel,' the Wolf Guard replied. 'More plague filth.'

'Into them, brothers.'

Egil saw the light of lumen strips stabbing around the silhouette of Borgen ahead of him, and moments later the rasp of the Wolf Guard's combi-flamer and the sickly stench of burning promethium reached him. He followed his Ironguard out into intersection Twenty-Nine B.

It was a cavernous meeting point for monorail lines and mining shafts, plasteel beams and bare-wired lumen strips providing a hub for half a dozen separate excavation sites, along with grav lifts to the surface, rappel-lines to lower levels, and rail routes to the nearest of Midgardia's subterranean hive cities. Egil and his pack burst from one of the smaller exfill shafts running north to south, catching a brace of shuffling plague daemons in the flank as they dragged their swollen, rotting bodies towards the knot of Space Wolves at the intersection's centre. Skol, Egil's iron-plated servo-skull, counted two-dozen Adeptus Astartes as it hummed overhead, the image from its miniaturised caster transmitted directly to Egil's bionics.

'We have you, brothers,' the Wolf Lord voxed as Borgen's combi-flamer ignited the nearest plaguebearers, their sonorous chants turning to deep-throated wails as their diseased flesh melted from their canker-ridden bones.

'*It's coming again,*' Lenold voxed back. '*Brace yourselves!*'

'What is–' Egil began, but didn't need to finish. He felt the earth around him shudder, dirt cascading from the intersection's high, steel-ribbed ceiling. Then the ground a dozen yards ahead heaved upwards, splitting apart a monorail track with an ear-shuddering clang. Something surged through the blast of earth and shattered stone, fang-filled maw agape, dragging its long, prehensile body up through the hole it had burrowed into the intersection.

'*Plague wyrm,*' Lenold voxed. '*Bring it down!*'

'Borgen,' Egil snapped. The Ironguard was already bringing his weapon to bear, spearing a lance of liquid flame at the huge, nightmarish wyrm as it dragged the last of its fleshy folds from its maw-tunnel. It was at least two-dozen paces long, and as thick around its centre as any of Egil's warriors. The parts of it that weren't caked with Midgardian soil were the corpse-white of a creature that had never known sunlight, and hideous, disease-blotched organs were visible pulsing through its membranous flesh. It made a gargling, squealing noise as it cringed away from Borgen's flames, twisting with ghastly speed towards the Wolves fighting back to back at the intersection's heart.

'It's headed your way,' Egil voxed.

'*Destroy its burrow,*' Lenold replied. '*Quickly!*'

Egil saw why moments later. There were things crawling up out of the wyrm's maw-hole – plague beasts and nurglings, clawing arm over arm, scrambling on top of each other as they dragged themselves up from Midgardia's depths.

'Changing canisters,' Borgen said, anticipating his jarl's orders as he screwed a fresh fuel cell into his combi-flamer.

'Grenades,' Egil shouted. He hammered his boot into the spilled guts of the first plaguebearer to stagger up out of the pit, slamming it back down into the yawning, writhing hole. In the same breath he snapped a frag grenade from his belt clamp and pitched it after the wailing daemon. There was a crump and a blast of shredded, rotten meat and black ichor jetted up from the burrow.

'Close it,' Egil ordered. 'Send these monsters back to the wyrdrealm.' His Ironguard rallied to him, power weapons carving apart the plague daemons even as they scrabbled for a foothold in the intersection. Then Borgen stepped up to the edge, his combi-flamer reloaded. With a *thump-whoosh* he flooded the hole with liquid flame, roasting the things choking it. The sickening stench of burning wyrdflesh filled Egil's nose, penetrating even his armour's filters.

'The hole is losing integrity,' Moln warned.

A second later Egil felt the earth shift beneath him. He threw himself back just in time as the hellish burrow collapsed in on itself, dragging the edges down into a sucking, crushing vortex of grey muck. Borgen, standing close to the centre, was too slow to avoid being caught in the earth's unyielding grip.

'Brother!' shouted Orven, lunging after the falling warrior. He managed to snatch onto the edge of his backpack, but the pull of the collapsed hole was too strong. It dragged Borgen further down before Orven could get a better hold on him. The Wolf Guard choked on muck as he drew breath to bellow defiance. In just a few seconds he was gone, the settling dirt showing no sign of his passing.

Bjorn and Moln hauled Orven back before he too was dragged down. Egil cursed and spat. It was not the sort of death he'd have wished on the rashest, most obstinate Blood Claw, let alone a warrior whose sagas had filled the halls on many a feast night.

'*It's escaping!*' Lenold's voice over the vox tore his attention away from the dirt scar that had become Borgen's grave. The wyrm had buried its hardened, fang-filled head into one of the intersection's walls and was rapidly squirming its way back into the underground. Egil saw the flesh in its side bulge and twist horribly, and realised that it had swallowed one of the Champions of Fenris whole. The warrior was struggling to escape the creature's gut, even as its bile melted the flesh from his bones.

Lenold and his Wolves pursued it, chainswords ripping at pale flesh and bolt-rounds blowing chunks from its body in bursts of stinking yellow slime. It regenerated every blow, its vile flesh reknitting seconds after each strike. With horrific speed, it had twisted itself into its fresh tunnel, leaving the Champions of Fenris behind.

'That is the third time that infernal beast has struck,' Lenold snapped. 'I cannot say if it was the same one, or whether there are many. Its wounds heal as soon as we make them.'

'It's how the wyrdlings have been traversing the underworld,' Egil surmised, eyes on the churned earth of the collapsed tunnel.

'Your arrival was timely, lord,' Lenold said, pacing across the intersection to clasp Egil's arm. Around him the Champions of Fenris clustered. They were universally dirt-grimed and bloody, the armour not befouled by Midgardia's depths scarred silver by the strike of blade and talon. Even the half-dozen Wulfen slinking among their number were panting and breathless, their tough bodies criss-crossed with fresh wounds.

'Where is the Great Wolf?' Egil asked. 'Where is Logan Grimnar?'

'We do not know,' Lenold said. 'He pressed too far ahead with his Kingsguard and the Slayer. Going by his last vox transmissions he had penetrated Deepspark and engaged a large infestation of wyrdspawn there. Then the lower tunnels collapsed and we lost all contact.'

'The surface is even worse,' Egil said. 'We could not hold what ground we gained. I ordered my Great Company to withdraw to the Magma Gates and then into orbit.'

'Yet you are down here with us?'

'Just my Ironguard and I. Would you have abandoned the Great Wolf in a place such as this?'

The question required no answer.

'At least the air isn't befouled down here,' Bjorn observed. 'Not yet, anyway.'

'Where are the rest of the Champions,' Egil asked Lenold, 'if Grimnar was only with his Kingsguard?'

'Lost, scattered. The vox-links are almost useless this far down. What you see here are the remnants of three packs – my Wulfborn, Korvald's Fangbrothers and Fjyr's Stormbringers. We've been getting scraps of transmission from Tormund's pack to the south. We were on our way to link up with them when that damn wyrm struck. The daemons follow in its wake.'

'You've tried all available routes into Deepspark?' Egil asked. 'Are all the tunnels collapsed?'

'All on these levels, and the lower ones. We hoped to try higher once we had consolidated our strength.'

'I fear we will grow weaker rather than stronger the longer we delay,' Egil said. 'I have never seen wyrdlings attack with such relentlessness.'

'They sense their victory is close,' Lenold growled.

'Then let us prove them wrong. Where is the nearest tunnel to the upper levels?' Lenold pointed at a grav lift at the far end of the intersection.

'This far down most of the mechanisms still seem to be intact,' he said. 'It will be faster than trying to take the tunnels, and risk the plague wyrm striking again.'

'We will use the lift then. Will you and your pack come with me?'

'Without a moment's hesitation, Jarl Iron Wolf. I will not see the light of the Wolf's Eye again until the Great Wolf has been found.'

Low orbit, above Frostheim

Fire parted Frostheim's storm-clouded heavens, its light reflecting from millions of snowflakes as they swirled and eddied around the bleak crags of Morkai's Keep. It fell not as an inferno, not indiscriminately like a shower of blazing meteors. It was a single beam, a lone rapier-thrust of crackling power delivered from low orbit by ancient targeting savant-engines and warriors who were now more machine than man. It struck the uppermost towers of Morkai's Keep and split the ancient, frozen citadel right down to its casements.

Harald Deathwolf watched the destruction in silence. He had raged and snarled enough, firstly to the impassive black visor-plates of the Iron Hands, then via vox to the Ultramarines Captain Epathus, the Shadow Haunters Captain Slythe, and an Astra Militarum general whose name he didn't remember. All in vain, the Wolf Lord reflected as he watched the Iron Hands battle-barge, *Iron Requiem*, destroy his Chapter's fortress from orbit. The ancient vessel's lance strike pierced Frostheim's cloud cover, and in his mind's eye Harald saw bastions melting and explosions blossoming through the ancient bulwarks with fiery finality. He saw daemons incinerated and charred to ash, burned in the keep's collapsing vaults in their thousands. It was not enough. Grimacing, he turned away from his flagship's viewing port.

'Put me through to Stolvind's lair,' he ordered the vox huscarl.

'*Lord?*' asked Stolvind the Wolf Priest over the link.

'How fares Canis?'

'*He is stable, my jarl. His wounds are grievous though. Considerable augmetic surgery will be required if he is to walk again, let alone fight.*'

'Is he awake?'

'*Intermittently. His sus-an is flickering between wakefulness and a cata-tonic state. All he has done is ask about his thunderwolf.*'

'How fares Fangir?'

'*He lives too, though it will be a long time before he is healed enough to bear his wolf-brother into battle again.*'

'Your skills do you credit, Wolf Priest,' Harald said. 'We were right to refuse the Iron Hands' help. Keep me informed.'

'*Yes, lord.*'

'Sire,' called another huscarl from the communications pit beneath Harald's bridge throne. 'The crusade fleet is beginning to break from orbit. Their projected destination is Svellgard. It would seem the Ultramarines and elements of the Astra Militarum mass transporter fleet are already in orbit above the moon.'

Harald bared his fangs in anger. Svellgard. Frostheim's moon and the loca-tion of the World Wolf's Lair, the control hub for the orbital defence batteries buried among the satellite's many bleak islands. The last transmissions from the moon's surface had suggested Sven Bloodhowl and his Great Company were still locked in a brutal battle with the invading wyrdspawn there.

'Vox *Iron Requiem*,' Harald ordered.

'We've tried, lord. No response.'

'Any other ship in the crusade fleet then. Adeptus Astartes, Imperial Navy, Astra Militarum, Imperial Knights, I don't care. Get me someone.'

'Lord, they have all locked us out of their communications channels again. They won't even receive our incoming signal code.' Harald cursed.

'Set a course for Svellgard immediately,' he ordered. 'And try to raise Lord Bloodhowl. We must not let what has happened on Frostheim repeat itself there.'

The World Wolf's Lair, Svellgard

'*Harakonari an tellika regala!*'

The Konndar-dialect battle cry of the 51st Harakoni Warhawks rang out across the vox-nets of the Space Wolves and the bleak skies of Svellgard as they began their airborne assault. It had been preceded by twenty minutes of fury – carpet-bombing by Marauders of the Imperial Navy's 111th Seg-mentum Obscurus Atmospheric Fleet, and ground attack runs by Vulture gunships of the 88th Tactical Wing. By the time the Harakoni Warhawks had started to jump from their Valkyrie transports, there were few dae-mons left on the islands surrounding the World Wolf's Lair.

Still, the soldiers of the Astra Militarum met bloody resistance. Warhawks died, ripped apart by claws and talons, run through by warp-forged steel, ground beneath iron-spiked wheels or disintegrated by gouts of bile, boiling blood and molten metal. Others fell by the hands of their own comrades and commissars, minds shattered by the horrors they found themselves facing. But the hammer of the Emperor, once swung, could not be prevented from falling. Some of the platoons among the first drops – the one-way ticket boys – survived long enough to create little las-studded bastions of resistance among the tide of insanity. The air cover focused on these defensive points, strafing the monsters around them before they could amass the numbers needed to overrun the Warhawks' positions among the crags and tundra of the islands.

Then the second wave made their drop, grav-chutes flaring, las-carbines snapping bolts of crimson death at the warpspawn. Less than an hour after Sven Bloodhowl had first spotted the beginning of the assault in Svellgard's skies, the Lair's three surrounding sister islands were declared secure.

Reinforcements continued to arrive. The gunners and equipment of the 155th Royal Cantabrian Light Artillery were dropped via Valkyrie as the Warhawks started to dig in. In a matter of minutes six batteries of fixed-position Earthshakers had been assembled on the peaks of the islands, creating concentric points of fire support for each neighbouring landmass. The air shuddered with percussive thunderclaps as they began to shell the beaches of the Lair, still awash with daemonic invaders.

'Keep up your fire,' Sven snarled at his Great Company over the vox. 'Drive them back into the sea.' The Firehowlers obeyed. Caught between the pounding bolters, plasma guns and streaking missiles of the Space Wolves and the shuddering explosions of the Astra Militarum's heavy artillery, the daemonic assault disintegrated. Earthshaker strikes sent up great gouts of sand and grit, laced with burning globules of warp-flesh and ichor. The air shimmered as whole cohorts of wyrdlings were unmade, vanishing from reality with howls of fury, pain and hungry denial.

Finally, the big guns fell silent. Sven ordered his packs to cease fire moments later. There were no more daemons left on the beaches of the World Wolf's Lair, the stony stands shimmering as their corpses vanished back into the immaterium.

'Raise them on the vox,' Sven ordered, gazing out at the neighbouring islands. More aircraft were arriving, bigger transports carrying light armour, sentinel walkers and prefabricated flakboard bulwarks. A wing of matt-grey Thunderbolt heavy fighters streaked low overhead, banking south as they scanned the choppy seas for the next assault.

'They're not responding,' Olaf Blackstone growled. 'All vox-channels have been closed and locked since they landed that artillery.'

The euphoria of a battle won cooled rapidly. Looking out at the distant barrels of the Earthshakers studding the islands' ridges, Sven felt a sudden foreboding creep over him. There had been no Astra Militarum elements in-system last he'd heard. Where had they come from?

'Raise the fleet,' Sven said. 'They must know more than we do.' The vox squawked in his ear.

'*Lord Bloodhowl*,' said a familiar voice.

'Lord Deathwolf,' Sven replied, scanning the transmission's source. 'You're no longer on Frostheim?'

'*No. Morkai's Keep has fallen. I am bound for the World Wolf's Lair.*'

'Fallen?' Sven echoed, disbelief warring with sudden anger. 'How can that be? I thought you'd purged the Alpha Legion traitors and their wyrd-spawn allies?'

'*It was not the heretics who took it,*' Harald Deathwolf replied. '*Do not communicate with anyone until I arrive. And maintain your defensive positions.*'

'What is happening, Deathwolf?' Sven demanded.

'*I will explain in person, Bloodhowl. There is maleficarum trickery at work.*'

Star Drake, *the Void*

Gormenjarl. A mountain cast from plasteel and adamantium and set adrift in the void. It filled the viewing ports of the *Star Drake*, the light of the Wolf's Eye glinting from its gargoyle-edged bulkheads and the gaping maws of its defence batteries. Those weapons could blaze with enough firepower to decimate a fleet, yet now they lay inert, as silent as the star fort's vox-channels.

'Still nothing?' Captain Stern demanded. The huscarl shook his head, eyes not leaving his blinking instrument displays. Stern watched *Gormenjarl* through the *Star Drake*'s open ports, imagining its defences flaring with sudden life. Their shields would hold for less than a minute, and the weight of ordnance would leave the proud Space Wolves strike cruiser a listing, gutted wreck in the time it took for them to fire a single salvo.

But the guns stayed silent.

'Maintain the docking vector,' Stern ordered. 'And inform me of any contact. I will be with my brethren in bay alpha-one.'

As Stern strode from the bridge he keyed his personal vox, opening a private channel with Brother Theo. Alone among the Brotherhood, Stern had ordered him to remain aboard the *Star Drake* and guard the unconscious Wulfen confined to the ship's brig.

'Any change?' Stern asked.

'*None, brother-captain,*' Theo replied. '*The beast still slumbers.*'

'You are to ensure that remains the case,' Stern said. 'And if you do not hear from me within the next hour, you are to take this ship to Midgardia and demand an audience with the Dark Angels. Do not let this madness continue, brother.'

'*I understand, brother-captain.*'

Stern closed the channel, confident Theo would carry out what may be his final orders. The other eleven Grey Knights were waiting for him in the cavernous corridor that acted as the *Star Drake*'s primary docking bay, standing in a tight circle with heads bowed and force weapons held at rest. Brother Latimer was leading them in the Canticle of Absolution, the Six Hundred and Sixty-Six Secret Words, the High Gothic cant ringing back eerily from the bay's ceiling. The Space Wolves Chapter-serfs manning the bay hung well back, staring at the huge silver-plated warriors with undisguised fear.

Stern took his customary space within the circle, taking the lead from Latimer with practised ease.

'No despicable trickery will thwart us, no Damnation will bring us low.'

'There is no peace for us,' the rest intoned as one. 'For an eternity we strive.'

'Though mere mortals in His service, everlasting shall be our True Duty.'

'*Et Imperator Invocato Diabolus Daemonica Exorcism!*'

Stern finished the oath-prayer of the Grey Knights with the Benediction of the Third Brotherhood.

'*Itur in fauces iumentorum. In os gehennae. Imperator dei estis lux. Vestri sumus foedus inite gladio. Gloria tibi in saecula.*'

Into the jaws of the beast. Into the mouth of hell. God-Emperor, you are our light. We are your sword. Glory to you forever.

The chant finished, its echoes rebounding one last time from the ship's walls before they too fell silent. As one, the Grey Knights raised their heads and came to attention.

'Brothers,' Stern said, addressing them without his helmet. 'We are about to walk into a trap. Beyond those blast doors is a Ramilies-class star fort dubbed *Gormenjarl*. No communication has been received from its crew since the outbreak of the first daemonic incursions in this system. We must assume the worst. Our objective is to secure this docking spine and protect *Star Drake* while its crew effect repairs. If possible, we will then attempt to purge any taint that may have manifested within the star fort.'

'Brother-captain, isn't our objective to reach Midgardia?' asked Brother Gideon. 'If the star fort is infested then purging it will slow us down considerably.'

'Which is why we will only go on the offensive if it is practical,' Stern replied. '*Gormenjarl*'s current trajectory is taking it past an extensive asteroid field known as Alpha Eleven-Nineteen, lying spinward of Fenris itself. If the opportunity arises I will attempt to storm the fort's command deck and reroute it into Eleven-Nineteen. If a realspace collapse has occurred onboard *Gormenjarl* then we cannot afford to leave it open, regardless of the situation on Midgardia.'

'*My lord.*' The huscarl's voice blared over the bay's vox rig. '*We are moving into our final docking position. You will be able to break the atmospheric seal and board* Gormenjarl *within the next five minutes.*'

'Brothers, make ready,' Stern ordered. 'Wrathhammer formation. I will take point.'

His Grey Knights assembled in a wedge around him, standing before the heavy, wolf-stamped blast doors of the docking bay, snapping home storm bolter clips and murmuring prayers to the spirits of their armour and weaponry. Stern pulled on his helmet, clamping and locking it with his gorget seal. A blink and the retinal visor display of his auto-senses came online, filling his vision with targeting reticules, vox-channels and vital signs. Around him he felt *Star Drake* shudder, its adamantium hull groaning and straining as its helmsman eased it into contact with *Gormenjarl*'s main docking spine. It was almost as though the venerable strike cruiser had no wish to touch the foreboding, silent star fort.

One last long, agonising moan rose from the ship's metal, and there was a distant, shuddering thump that reverberated up through Stern's boots. Then all was still.

'*Stand by,*' the huscarl's voice crackled over the vox.

'*Post tenebras lux,*' Stern said. After darkness, light. His Brotherhood echoed him, and as one they activated their nemesis force weapons, holy energy surging and sparking up glaive, sword and halberd.

A warning claxon shrieked. The light above the blast doors blinked red. Stern's grip on his force sword tightened. There was a thump of disengaging magnetic seals, a pressurised hiss, the grating of autobolts and servo-locks. The light above the doors blinked green.

The blast doors rolled back, and Brother-Captain Stern led his paladins' charge. Straight into the mouth of hell.

The Void, Fenris System

'Are you sure this is wise, lord?' asked Sister Marie. Her hawkish features – scarred by the flamer burns so common among members of her Chamber Militant – were set in a familiar expression of disapproval.

Lord Inquisitor Banist de Mornay shifted fractionally on his auto palanquin, the vitae cables plugged into his flesh flexing with the movement, and tugged the trapped hem of his dark red robes out from underneath him. The deck beneath his recliner's tracks shuddered as the shuttle clamped onto the hull of the larger vessel beyond the docking bay's blast doors.

'We should have activated the mark seventeen exo-plate,' Marie continued. 'At least then you would have rudimentary protection from these animals.'

'The Wolves are not our enemy here, Marie,' de Mornay said, his voice chiding. 'Many wish us to believe they are, but we must not be swayed by their lies. Do not allow them to influence your judgements of these warriors.'

'They are harbouring mutants,' Marie pressed, unable to even utter the last word without her features twisting with disgust. 'The Dark Angels do not lie about that, and you know it.'

'The genetic heritage of the *Vlka Fenryka* is a complex one, that I grant,' de Mornay said. 'But we must examine the outcomes of actions, regardless of what we perceive their intent to be. Thus far the Wulfen seem only to have acted alongside their battle-brothers, and exhibit very little animosity towards the God-Emperor's servants. They are fighting as hard as any of us to rid this system of daemonic taint. That in itself must count for something.'

'I merely worry about my ability to protect you in a ship full of beasts,' Marie said. 'We should have brought VX Nine-Eighteen as well.'

'Sometimes a subtler touch is required,' de Mornay said. He had ordered the rest of his in-field retinue to remain aboard *Allsaint's Herald*. 'The last thing we need right now is to antagonise our hosts. We require them if we are to make progress, after all these years.'

Marie said nothing, but de Mornay could feel the distaste radiating off the Adepta Sororitas. He could not wholly deny that he didn't share that disgust. Genetic impurity, especially amongst the hallowed ranks of the Adeptus Astartes, was something he'd struggled to uproot for decades. To wilfully overlook evidence of mutation went against his instincts as a member of the Ordo Hereticus. But for now there were greater matters at stake – and darker secrets to unravel – than the curse of the Wulfen. In their eagerness to persecute their old rivals the Dark Angels had left themselves exposed. De Mornay had waited a long time for such an opportunity to present itself. All he needed now was muscle.

Hydraulics whined and thumped, and the blast doors leading from his private shuttle's docking strut into the Space Wolves battle-barge ground open. A single figure waited for them on the other side, wreathed in decompression steam. He towered in the blue-grey power armour and furred pelts of the Space Wolves, and though his unhelmeted head was a latticework of old scars and blue knotwork tattoos, his eyes were disarmingly calm and grey. Seeing de Mornay's cable-covered servitor-palanquin rolling through the venting steam, he bowed.

'Lord Inquisitor, well met. I am Thierulf Bloodhanded. I have been sent by my jarl, Ragnar Blackmane, to escort you to the *Holmgang*'s bridge.'

'The pleasure is all mine, Thierulf,' de Mornay said, making the sign of the aquila. 'By all means, lead on.'

He had heard it said that every Wolf Lord shaped his Great Company to his own dominant personality. Travelling through Ragnar Blackmane's flagship, de Mornay could well believe it. The Space Wolves he passed were more often than not young, armour and blades inscribed with new kill markings, and had that hungry look about them that had Sister Marie's hand fixed to the hilt of her holstered combi-flamer almost every step of the way. One snarled at de Mornay as they passed, holding the inquisitor's gaze long after most would have flinched away. As they neared the upper decks he became aware of an ever-increasing pack of Wolves following them. Despite his outward confidence, he felt cold sweat pricking across his body, anticipation setting his pulse racing. His fingers brushed his plasma pistol in its ornate leather holster, strapped to the palanquin's flank.

'Pay the pups no mind,' Thierulf said, as though reading de Mornay's thoughts. 'They've just been caged for too long. The currents of the Sea of Stars have been fickle of late. I was starting to think we'd never make it home.'

'You're aware of what's happening throughout the system?' de Mornay asked.

'Aware enough. Wyrdling scum are attacking everything bar the Hearthworld itself, and the sons of the Lion are trying to intervene with a crusade fleet. Meddling where they're neither wanted nor needed, as ever.'

'I'm here to try to do something about that,' de Mornay said.

Thierulf made a growling noise. After a second the inquisitor realised he was laughing, albeit mirthlessly.

'All depends what you want out of it in return, pyre-builder.'

'Who ever said anything about wanting something in return?'

'It's always so with your kind. Here, we've arrived.' Thierulf came to a halt before a wire-mesh grav lift, and entered a string of codes on the rune lock.

De Mornay spent a moment looking at the jagged lines of the Fenrisian *Juvjk* script on the lock. He had to remember to have Peterkyn create an auto-upload file for that language. An understanding of it was looking increasingly useful.

'I should return to my pack,' Thierulf said. 'They are grown restless in this torpid transport. Take the lift to the bridge level. My jarl Ragnar will meet you there.'

'My thanks, Wolf,' de Mornay said, rolling onto the lift platform as its grille door juddered open. 'We will doubtless both do the God-Emperor's work again soon enough.'

'Allfather be praised,' Thierulf grunted, and hit the activation rune. The doors snapped shut, and the lift began to rise with a low whir.

'If they mean to slaughter us, now is when they'll do it,' Marie muttered.

De Mornay allowed himself a smile, glancing briefly up at the pict feed monitoring the lift's occupants.

'Your suspicions make me think you've served in my retinue for too long, honourable Sister,' he said. 'Regardless, we shall soon discover whether your beliefs are well-founded. Into the wolf's lair...'

The grav lift chimed as it reached the *Holmgang*'s highest level, the bridge that lay at the top of the ship's command spire. The doors opened once again, and the hubbub of an Imperial warship's control nexus washed over the two Inquisitorial operatives. It was stilled by a deep growl, a growl that became words.

'Welcome, Lord Inquisitor de Mornay. It's rare to have a visitor from the ordos aboard my ship.'

De Mornay rolled his palanquin onto the bridge, assuming the mask of haughty indifference he had relied upon for so long. In his profession it did no good to show weakness or fear, either to friend or foe. But beneath the dozen predatory eyes that observed his arrival, indifference was a difficult appearance to maintain.

The bridge of the *Holmgang* was a cavern-like space, its walls and high ceiling cast from Fenrisian stone, carved with intricate scenes of the battles and the mythic adventures that the Space Wolves knew as sagas. Lumen globes flickered in alcoves or hung suspended from chains overhead, their light battling the green glow of cogitator screens and augur arrays. Chapter-serfs in plain blue-and-grey shifts bent over their workstations, fingers tapping at rune banks or adjusting heavy brass levers and gauges. Huscarls, their robes trimmed with fur, paced the walkways between the stations, monitoring the ship's vital signs and its progress through real-space and relaying pertinent information to the command dais. That raised platform of seemingly primordial rock dominated the bridge's centre, the rune-carved stone throne at its top draped with heavy pelts. Upon it, like a techno-barbarian warlord from the darkest days of the Age of Strife, sat the figure that could only be the Young King. Ragnar Blackmane.

His grey battleplate was trimmed with gold, and hung with fang tokens. A dark wolf pelt was draped over his right pauldron, while a green gem glittered at the centre of his Belt of Russ, the relic that marked out all Wolf Lords. He wore no helmet, his long, black hair and sideburns lending his features a wild look. The appearance was only accentuated when he grinned, revealing vicious canines.

'You are a bold one, witch hunter,' he said as de Mornay ground to a halt before the throne, Marie at his side. 'I like that. But will I like the reason you are here?'

Ragnar was not the only Space Wolf on the bridge. Half a dozen of his pack leaders stood around his dais, their pelts grey, their eyes surveying de Mornay with something akin to hunger. Native Fenrisian wolves also prowled the bridge, seemingly at liberty to come and go as they pleased. They sat and watched the two interlopers with as much restrained savagery as their transhuman wolf-brothers.

'Any true son of Fenris would approve of the reason that I am here, my lord,' de Mornay said to Ragnar. 'Defending your Chapter's honour, recovering your Great Wolf and purging your native system of daemonic infestation. That is what I am here to request your assistance with.'

'That may be,' Ragnar said. 'But I doubt that's the only reason you have sought out my fleet.'

'Why else would I seek an audience in person?'

'To discover if the rumours are true.' Ragnar grinned again, a savage expression that carried with it little warmth. 'I can tell you now, they are. Sverri!'

A low growl answered the Wolf Lord's summons. De Mornay followed the sound to the far side of the bridge. Emerging from the shadows of a strategium cell came a creature seemingly born from the wildest and most savage of imaginations.

It bore only a passing resemblance to the other Space Wolves on the bridge. It was larger, and its iron-hard muscles bristled with bestial black hair. It wore less armour, what battleplate it did possess appearing archaic and timeworn. Its lower limbs were more like those of the Fenrisian wolves that padded around the bridge, distended and claw-toed. Its features were even more terrible – they were no longer recognisably human. Its nose was flattened and nostrils flared, while its predatory yellow eyes were sunk into a heavy brow. Its hair was long and matted, and its thick jaw was studded with rows of fangs that jutted out over its lower lip. As it moved towards Ragnar's throne it adopted a loping, hunched gait, claws scraping on the bridge's stone floor.

De Mornay felt Marie freeze beside him. He held up his hand, afraid the Adepta Sororitas would be overcome by disgust and draw her weapons. He was in no doubt that such a move would spell immediate, bloody death for both of them.

'My lord,' the thing Ragnar had addressed as Sverri snarled, struggling to form the syllables between jutting fangs and heavy, panting breaths. With some difficulty, it knelt before the throne.

'Sverri, this is Lord Inquisitor de Mornay of the Ordo Hereticus,' Ragnar said, looking at de Mornay. The inquisitor could sense the Wolf Lord studying his reaction, searching for the revulsion he expected. Sverri also turned to look at de Mornay, in a half crouch, watching him with the wary caution of a beast sizing up an enemy. Judging whether it was predator or prey.

'Lord Inquisitor, this is Sverri, pack leader of my Great Company's newly adopted Wulfen Murderpack,' Ragnar finished the chill introduction.

De Mornay held Sverri's calculating, lupine gaze. It was the oldest law of nature. To look away would be to show weakness, and weakness was more often than not fatal.

'The Wulfen are not my concern,' de Mornay said slowly. 'Not yet, anyway.'

'So why are you here?' Ragnar demanded. 'I do not have time for the Inquisition's games. As you yourself have said, my home system is beset and my lord Grimnar is missing. Speak plainly or get off my ship.'

'The Dark Angels above Midgardia intend to fire-bomb its surface,' de Mornay said. 'They must be stopped before they go any further. Azrael and his Inner Circle have remained unaccountable to the Imperium for too long.'

'So your hand is revealed,' Ragnar said. 'The lion is the one you're hunting, not the wolf.'

'After a manner of speaking, yes.'

'But why?'

'It is a grim tale,' de Mornay said, 'and we have little time for it.'

'You will get nothing from me unless you explain yourself,' Ragnar said. De Mornay sighed and nodded.

'Then I will be brief. Fifty years ago I was bringing word of a greenskin invasion to the Calva Senioris System, in the Narthex Nebula. The foul xenos struck before a defence could be organised, and I was left leading an underground resistance. The Dark Angels and Silver Eagles were dispatched to spearhead a liberation, but one of the Angels, an Interrogator-Chaplain named Asmodai, received word of my resistance movement. He attacked our camp, slaughtered loyal Imperial citizens, and would have killed or captured me had I not proven my membership of the ordos before his battle-brothers.'

'Why?' Ragnar asked. 'Why would he attack you?'

'I have spent the past five decades asking the same question,' de Mornay said. 'You may scoff now, Wolf, but once I was a fine young warrior, active on the God-Emperor's front lines, striving to enact His will and banish the darkness that forever threatens our Imperium. After Asmodai's atrocity I went directly to the home world of the Silver Eagles and told their Chapter Master everything. That the Dark Angels had butchered fellow servants of Terra, and that many Silver Eagles had also fallen after Asmodai abandoned their fight against the orks to pursue me.'

'And what did the Silver Eagles do then?' Ragnar asked. He was leaning forward in his throne now, eyes fixed on the inquisitor. The Wolves, de Mornay remembered, loved their sagas.

'The Silver Eagles did nothing,' he said, letting the bitterness in his voice show. 'Or next to nothing. They would not confront the Dark Angels. They merely petitioned Supreme Grand Master Azrael. He claimed he would censure Asmodai. I doubt any censure was ever carried out.'

'The sons of the Lion have always been a secretive brotherhood,' Ragnar said. 'They have little honour, and I would not trust one of their battle-brothers as far as I could throw him. That being said, you are the inquisitor, not I. If you cannot bring the Angels to justice yourself I do not see how I can help. I have a war to fight.'

'Our paths are linked now, Lord Blackmane,' de Mornay pressed. 'And they have been ever since the Dark Angels decided to invade your system. I believe they are not only here for your...' he hesitated, glancing at Sverri, who seemed to be following the discussion with a silent, animalistic understanding.

'I believe they are trying to misdirect the Imperium,' de Mornay continued. 'They were hiding something on Nurades, a relic perhaps. If your Chapter hadn't purged the daemons infesting that world we may never have realised it, but I have never seen the Dark Angels move with such decisiveness unless the Inner Circle felt threatened. I want to end the insanity that infects this system. I want to confront Azrael, and I'm not strong enough to do that alone.'

'You will start a civil war,' Ragnar said doubtfully. 'I would not listen to a wyrd-damned word uttered by one of the Lions, but nor would I expect them to listen to me. I would add nothing to your negotiations bar the threat of my Great Company's presence.'

'Then let me do the talking,' de Mornay said. 'I simply wish your fleet to accompany me to Midgardia. Unless I'm badly mistaken, that is where you're headed anyway.'

Ragnar exchanged glances with his Long Fangs. Sensing his opening, de Mornay kept speaking.

'In ancient times the sons of Russ were the Emperor's executioners. All Legions feared you. The same cannot be said today. The Dark Angels treat you like animals, to be baited, trapped and shamed. They may well have already opened fire on Midgardia. They will not stop until the Fenris System is naught but ruins and ash.'

'We are indeed bound for Midgardia,' Ragnar allowed, again fixing de Mornay with his unsettlingly bestial gaze. 'And you may accompany us. I do not know what we will find there, but it seems as though the rest of the Imperium has turned its back on us. I would be a fool to scorn an inquisitor offering an alliance during such times.' De Mornay bowed his head.

'If it is any consolation, I do not believe your Wulfen are warp-tainted, Lord Blackmane,' he said. 'And regardless, their judgement can wait. For now, we have to stop this madness of Angels, before we slaughter each other at a daemon's behest.'

The World Wolf's Lair, Svellgard

Harald Deathwolf's Thunderhawk put down on the landing pad jutting from the Lair's central control keep. Sven's Bloodguard joined Harald's own Riders of Morkai, forming an honour guard as they led the Wolf Lord into the command chamber. Sven Bloodhowl was waiting for him.

'Lord Deathwolf,' he said as Harald stepped into the room. Low and plated with plasteel, its illumination pulsed dully from emergency lumen strips lining the walkways, from the monitors of vox arrays and from the Lair's missile targeting systems. A holochart dominated the centre of the chamber, currently deactivated.

'What in the name of Russ is happening?' Sven went on as Harald joined him at the edge of the chart.

'Wyrd-damned treachery, that's what,' Harald growled. 'We were locked in battle with wyrdling scum in the vaults of Morkai's Keep when a strike force of Iron Hands made contact with us. Their captain told me he would destroy the keep from orbit, whether my warriors still garrisoned it or not.'

'What sort of madness is that?' Sven growled. 'Did they succeed?'

'Morkai's Keep is a ruin,' Harald said. 'Resisting would have resulted in the annihilation of my Great Company. Believe me brother, I considered it.

I have tried to raise the Fang, and the Great Wolf on Midgardia, but I have heard nothing. I can only assume this fleet is but part of a larger incursion.'

'Are they here for the Wulfen?' Sven asked darkly.

'I can see no other motive. They are too numerous to be a response to the daemonic incursion. Such a force must have been gathering for weeks prior to the invasion. Have they tried to contact you?'

'I've heard nothing,' Sven said. 'The Astra Militarum have occupied the nearest islands. Their artillery is zeroed in on us, but they won't communicate. The daemons have been driven back, but they will soon return. Their numbers are unending. I fear the warp rifts below the oceans are widening. The scans say there are at least three down there.'

'I am going to order my Great Company to deploy here, in full strength,' Harald said. 'I have given up enough of our Chapter's territory today. I will not evacuate again.'

'Won't they repeat what they did on Frostheim?' Sven asked. 'An orbital bombardment would achieve two objectives for them. It would wipe out both us and the wyrdlings.'

'If that's to be our fate I will die with my boots in the dirt of one of my Chapter's worlds,' Harald said. Sven looked him in the eye for a moment, before a fanged grin split his tattooed features.

'And if need be the Bloodhowls will burn alongside you, brother. Whatever is to happen, we will make the Saga of Svellgard one that will be sung in the feast halls of the Fang for millennia to come.'

Ramilies-class star fort, designate Gormenjarl

Stern's worst fears had been realised. *Gormenjarl* had become a gateway to hell.

Mankind's collective nightmares had been made manifest onboard the star fort. The walls of the docking bay had twisted and melted like candle wax, plasteel and adamantium now studded with fleshy maws that snapped and spat, or clusters of eyes that wept black ichor. The decking underfoot flowed and shifted like quicksand, the metal molten and writhing, or plated with fresh growths of chitin. The air was heavy with sweat vapour, and vibrated with some gigantic, hellish heartbeat.

'Brothers, purge this filth,' Stern roared as he swept through the *Star Drake*'s blast doors, his nemesis force sword inscribing a crackling white arc through the shuddering air. The first daemon to meet his blade, a red-skinned bloodletter, disintegrated beneath the blow, its hellsword shattered into a hundred black shards.

The Grey Knights stormed what had once been the star fort's docking spine, storm bolters hammering death into the warpspawn packing the arching corridor, the roaring flames of Brother Tomaz's sanctified incinerator torching the tainted walls and filling the air with the stench of roasted daemonflesh. Stern led his brethren in the Chants of Admonishment, the strength of their hatred and the purity of their faith like a physical force that sent daemons shrieking and scrambling back down the corridor.

'To the far end,' Stern voxed. 'Secure the junction.'

At the end of the corridor the spine split into two sub-routes, both leading deeper into *Gormenjarl*'s guts. There the corruption was even worse. The floor, walls and ceiling now resembled the tract of some foul creature's intestinal organs, carpeted with flesh that throbbed and pulsed with unnatural life. Stern stamped down on a bloodshot eye that glared up at him from what had once been the deck, bursting it in a spray of milky ichor. Around him his brothers stood firm, the protective wards edging their silver aegis armour blazing white with heat. The very air of the star fort pulsated and bent around them, as though the tainted atmosphere was seeking to avoid contact with the holy paladins.

'We hold here,' Stern ordered. 'Bulwark formation.' He blink-changed channels. 'Huscarl, how long before *Star Drake* is void-worthy again?'

'*We are reactivating the engine blocks right now, sire,*' the Space Wolves thrall replied, voice choppy with static. '*After that we will need to couple with the star fort's external coolant array. The systems estimate fifteen minutes.*'

'Make it ten,' Stern ordered, and cut the link.

The level of *Gormenjarl*'s infestation was worse than even he had expected. There had to be a warp rift open at the star fort's heart. That meant another front in the war for the Fenris System.

'We must seal away this filth, before it can spread any further,' he voxed to his brethren.

'If we are to seize whatever remains of the bridge, it will take all of us to get that far,' Gideon replied. 'We would leave the entrance to *Star Drake*'s docking bay undefended.'

'Besides, if we adhere to our previous plan, I doubt we would find any way to redirect the star fort into the asteroid field,' Tomaz added as he jetted a fresh gout of blessed promethium into a clutch of squealing horrors. 'If the level of corruption on these external levels is this bad, I assume the inner command centre is completely lost.'

Stern impaled a lunging daemonette, banishing the creature in a blaze of light. He knew his brethren were right. They were too few to fight their way to the root of *Gormenjarl*'s infection. Even holding the docking spine looked like a desperate task.

'But if the star fort's directional controls no longer work,' Brother Artemis voxed, 'then will its targeting systems? Or its shields?'

The thought was interrupted before it could gain traction. A terrible sound bounced down the flesh-corridors towards the Grey Knights. It was a howl, at once chillingly familiar to Stern, and yet horribly different. It was distorted, as if by vox interference, rising to an unnatural pitch before diving to throaty depths. The eerie sound sent the daemons ahead of the Grey Knights into a frenzy, throwing themselves onto the Space Marines' blades and bolters. Not in rage, Stern realised, but in desperation. In fear of whatever was coming down the twin corridors behind them. The words of the huscarl earlier, aboard the *Star Drake*, came back to him. A pack of Grey Hunters, the Redpelts.

'Brethren, brace!' he shouted.

Gormenjarl's complement of Space Wolf defenders still lived, but in the most nightmarish way imaginable. And now they were coming for the silver-armoured interlopers.

Transit line four hundred and three,
the Underworld, Midgardia

Transit line four hundred and three was the primary level-one subsurface route into Deepspark. The grav lift took Egil and his ragged retinue to a maintenance station half a mile from what had once been the subterranean hive's entrance. As he stepped into the wide, tracked tunnel, the vox display on the edge of Egil's visor uplink finally showed signal connectivity.

'All Imperial forces, come in,' he said, setting the vox tuner to roam.

'We should be able to make contact with the surface this high up,' Lenold said.

'That's what I'm attempting to do,' Egil replied. 'It may take time to lock onto a signal though. We should proceed.'

The Wolves set out, following the dual rail lines that wound their way through the dirt-walled tunnel. Skol buzzed ahead, its pict feed relayed directly back to the Iron Wolf's bionics.

'Signs of fighting,' he said as he walked, scanning the walls with his remaining unaugmented eye. 'Recent. Also, the air is showing higher spore toxin content.'

'The nearer to the surface we are, the higher it'll be,' Bjorn said.

'Even more so if plague wyrdlings passed this way recently,' Lenold said darkly.

'And they may well have,' Egil said. 'Skol has found something.'

It was a body. A Grey Hunter, slumped across one of the tracks, fingers frozen in claw-like rigor mortis. The blood from the wound piercing his breastplate still glistened red.

'Dredwulf,' Lenold said grimly, kneeling beside the fallen Hunter. 'From Storrie's pack. They were the nearest to catching up with the Great Wolf before he was cut off.'

'The body is not old,' Egil said, eyes scanning the dark shadows that flickered beneath the tunnel's wan lumen globes. The keen senses of the Wolf Lord, even enhanced by his augmetics, detected nothing. 'They must be close.'

'We should press on,' Lenold said.

'Agreed.'

Further down the tunnel, Egil's vox finally picked up something. A blurt of signal code cut across the long-range frequency.

'I've detected an Imperial transmission,' he said, coming to a halt. 'From the surface. I'm locking on now.'

'I'm getting it too,' Lenold said. 'Seems to be coming from the Magma Gates.'

'Conran,' Egil said as his Ironguard's identifier rune lit up on his visor. 'It's a looping non-verbal distress code.'

'You still have part of your Great Company on the surface?' Lenold asked.

'I shouldn't,' Egil said. 'Conran was ordered to lead the withdrawal of the Ironwolves in my absence. He shouldn't still be on Midgardia.'

'Or transmitting,' Lenold noted. 'Do you think something has befallen the Magma Gates? Can it be possible that they are already overrun?'

Egil snarled with annoyance. Surely Conran would not have disobeyed his orders to lead the retreat? If more of his Great Company were still on Midgardia, wouldn't he pick up their vox transmissions as well? But if only Conran had come back, then why? And what fate had befallen him if all that remained was a distress transmission?

A growl from ahead broke his train of thought. While the rest of the make-shift pack had halted, the remaining Wulfen had slunk further down the line. Now their bestial warnings echoed back up the tunnel.

'They've found something,' Lenold said. Egil felt his pulse quicken, hairs bristling with a sudden sense of foreboding. He led the pack at a run along the tunnel.

The Wulfen had discovered more bodies. Four of them, more of Storrie's Grey Hunters. Dismembered, still bloody. If they had taken any wyrd-spawn with them, the creature's bodies had already melted back into the immaterium. The Wulfen were clustered in a tight circle at the centre of the group of bodies, crouched over something, snuffling and growling in obvious distress.

'Stand aside, wolf-brothers,' Lenold commanded, parting the circle. They scrabbled back in the dirt, letting out a low, mournful moan.

'What have they found?' Egil demanded, reaching Lenold's side. Skol darted overhead, stab-lumen picking up the object the Grey Hunters had died defending. The Iron Wolf caught his breath as the light shone back off gilded metal.

It was Fellclaw. The huge thunderwolf's plated skull, the one that had been borne aloft on Logan Grimnar's back ever since he had slain the mighty beast during his Trail of Morkai almost a millennium ago. Its gilding was battered and befouled with muck and blood, and a number of fangs had snapped off.

'The Great Wolf's crown,' Lenold muttered. 'Then he's been this way.'

'Or Storrie's pack found it elsewhere and were carrying it with them,' Egil said.

'Either way, he is not lost. Surely he lives.'

Egil said nothing. Lenold bent to retrieve the gilded skull, lifting it with reverence. 'He is close. I can feel it.'

'Something else is closer,' Egil said as his visor lit with warning runes. 'The toxicity levels in this tunnel just rose threefold.'

'*Lord,*' Moln voxed. '*We are detecting movement back down the tunnel.*'

'I can smell them,' Lenold snarled. 'More plaguespawn.' Around them, the Wulfen began to howl. Egil's wolf claws slid free.

'Brothers, to me!'

INFURNACE

They had been Wolves once. Grey Hunters, experienced warriors, their pelts flecked with silver and their armour etched with runes that told of great and bloody sagas. But they were Wolves no more. The things that came at Brother-Captain Stern and his Grey Knights down the flesh-corridors of *Gormenjarl*'s primary docking spine wore only a semblance of their old selves, a mocking half-facsimile. Blue-grey battleplate was now bent and twisted around fleshy growths and scarred with the runes of an altogether darker tongue.

The transhuman physique of the Space Marines had been similarly bent, changed to better suit the purposes of the insane things that now wore the Wolves' flesh. Arms ended in bony claw-growths, snapping maws or spine-rimmed tentacles. Vox grilles had become slavering jaws, and visor lenses blinked with raw eyelids. Lower limbs were double-jointed or cloven-hoofed. One beast's bare arms were covered in a million tiny chitin spines that gave the appearance of a bony fur pelt, while another had atrophied, leathery pinions sprouting grotesquely from the seal of its backpack.

They had once been the Redpelts, *Gormenjarl*'s Space Wolves garrison. Now they were monsters, possessed by the daemons that infested the star fort, their bodies broken and abused, refashioned with no heed to nature's constraints.

And they came straight for the Grey Knights, slavering, snapping and howling.

'Stand firm, brethren,' Stern shouted, raising his nemesis force sword. 'Suffer not the unclean to live!'

The two sides, silver paladins and possessed warp-wolves, met with a crash of ceramite and snapping bone. The foremost daemon, a thing with a red-pelted wolf's head and crab-claw arms, went straight for Stern. The Grey Knight captain met it with a downward slash of his force sword, silvered steel cleaving through warped plate to hack off one of the monstrosity's snapping limbs. The thing didn't even flinch, latching the other claw around Stern's right fist. The vice-like grip sheared cleanly through his wrist-mounted storm bolter and bit through his vambrace, drawing blood. Stern grunted and lunged forward, driving his blade into the creature's abdomen. The combatants locked. Even after running it through, the possessed Wolf still fought, lupine jaws distending with unnatural ease as they snapped and slavered at Stern's helm.

Stern spat strings of words from the Rites of Exorcism, channelling the holy willpower of his collected Brotherhood into his blade's psyker-sensitive steel. The stab of energy was infinitely more potent than the physical edge, tearing deep into the daemon wearing the Space Wolf's flesh. Like shadows ripped apart by a sudden flood of light, the warp creature was banished back to the immaterium. The defiled body of the Wolf slumped against Stern, dead, infected blood pattering down the daemonhunter's silver armour. Stern pushed the body off, commending its lost soul to the Emperor.

Around him, his brothers fought for their lives. They had been trained almost from birth to destroy warpspawn. From their blades – adamantium-tipped, forged from blessed silver and blessed by holy water – to their aegis armour – inscribed with catechisms of hatred and wards of faith, and anointed with sacred oils – every inch of their being was repellent to the creatures that scuttled and crawled in the darkest corners of mankind's imagination.

But the things they fought now were not purely daemonic. They were an unholy melding, a dark union between the physical and that which should only have existed in nightmares. The flesh of the possessed Wolves did not cringe from purifying silver, and it did not vanish back to the warp when pierced by righteous steel. The speed, strength and savagery of the Space Wolves, itself a match for the battle skill of Stern's brethren, had been augmented a hundredfold by the dark cunning and unholy vigour of the things that had come from the warp.

The Grey Knights struggled to match them. Force weapons clashed with chitin and twisted steel, and claws raked at silver power armour. One of the possessed had locked multiple jaws around Brother Lucan's gorget, tearing open the ceramite with ease and gorging itself on the flesh of the Space Marine's throat. Brother Wilfred slammed his force glaive into the creature's scaled flank, bellowing in High Gothic. Still it hung on. Lucan was on his knees, blood jetting from the savage wound. Wilfred rammed his storm bolter into the side of the thing's skull and fired, disintegrating it with a blast of hexagram-inscribed bolts. Beside him Brother Tomaz had wreathed another of the former Space Wolves in the white flames of his incinerator.

The thing howled, the sound more like four voices than one, all shrieking together. Even as the flesh melted from its deformed bones it came on, clutching Tomaz in a fiery embrace. The Grey Knight kicked the charred remains away in time to take a blow from another possessed Wolf's hammer-like bony appendage. The impact dented his helmet and slammed him back into the fleshy walls of the docking spine.

Stern parried the chainsword of another possessed. The weapon had melded with the Space Wolf's arm, black ichor now oiling the spinning saw-teeth. Stern's sword locked with it, the tendon-rotor screaming, the teeth jammed as they tried to chew through the blessed steel. The possessed thrust forward, using its unnatural strength to drive Stern back, vox grille snapping with freshly sprouted fangs.

'Brother-captain!' Alacar bellowed from behind Stern. 'Down!'

The Grey Knight reacted without thinking, dropping to one knee with his sword still locked. He felt the weight of Alacar's charged force hammer swing overhead. The crackling weapon struck the possessed squarely in the face, pulverising its horned skull and slamming the body back down the corridor with a concussive blast of released energy.

There was no time for thanks. Stern turned his rise into a lunge that impaled the two-headed horror leaping at him. More daemons were attacking in the wake of the possessed. A back-cut cleaved apart another of the Tzeentch horrors in a blaze of multi-coloured light. A hellsword caught him in the thigh plate, scoring a shallow wound above his cuisse's seal. A second hacked deep into his right pauldron, scarring the book-and-sword sigil of his Chapter. Stern parried another blow, his sword a silver blur as he kept two hissing bloodletters at bay.

'*We're losing ground,*' Gideon shouted over the vox, moments before a hellsword punched into his gut.

'Tomaz, Ignition pattern,' Stern snapped, throwing Gideon back with a thrust of his pauldron. 'Scourge formation. Slowly.'

Tomaz adopted a braced stance and unleashed his flamer in a wide arc, covering the corridor from one side to the other. The walls themselves shuddered and writhed beneath the purifying heat. The warp-wolves howled and shrieked as their flesh ignited, while the flames licked harmlessly across the armour of Stern's paladins. As one the Grey Knights stepped back, heeding their brother-captain's orders to disengage. Artemis, Alacar and Wilfred snatched the fallen bodies of Lucan and Gideon as they went, the remaining six knights closing protectively around them.

Tomaz's flames didn't check the possessed for long. If anything, it only drove the daemons into a greater frenzy. They tore through the docking spine, bodies still wreathed in fire. The Grey Knights opened up at point-blank range, hammering them with mass-reactive bolts.

'Report?' Stern snapped into the vox.

'*A few moments more, lord,*' came the strained voice of *Star Drake's* huscarl.

'You don't have them,' Stern said, parrying the raking claws of a burning, bolt-riddled possessed with a sucking maw for a head. 'Open the blast doors.'

Pace by pace the Grey Knights continued to retreat. When the warp-spawn pressed too close, the supportive fire of Wilfred, Alacar and Artemis from the rear ranks cut them down, while Stern, Osbeth, Simeon, Caldor, Tomaz, Ethold and Latimer hacked, slashed and stabbed unceasingly at the frothing, snarling tide. Behind him, Stern heard the grate of the docking blast doors rolling open.

'Tomaz, burn them again,' he ordered. The fact that the possessed were still clawing at them showed how powerful the warp rift at *Gormenjarl*'s heart was. They had to close it, and there was only one way to achieve that now.

'*My last canister,*' Tomaz voxed, before stepping up once more. The roar of holy flames and the shriek of warpspawn filled the corridor once again. The Grey Knights used the precious few seconds to turn, dragging their wounded back into the *Star Drake*.

'Hold them here,' Stern ordered as he reached the doors. 'We can give the crew a few moments more.'

As Tomaz backed through the opening, jetting the remains of his incinerator's promethium canister after him, the other nine Knights halted at the blast doors and unleashed a hail of silver-tipped storm bolter rounds. The corridor immediately in front of the door disintegrated in a hail of torn, burning flesh and detonating shells.

'*We've done all we can, lord,*' the huscarl's voice crackled in Stern's ear.

'Disengage from the docking spine,' Stern ordered. 'Now.' He slammed the sealing rune next to the blast doors. The heavy adamantium juddered shut just as Tomaz stepped inside, his incinerator sputtering a few last drops of liquid fire. Moments later there came the hammering and shrieking of things on the other side, furiously attempting to claw their way inside the *Star Drake*.

'Caldor, Osbeth, take Lucas and Gideon to the medicae bay,' Stern ordered. 'Everyone else remain here, Overwatch pattern. Ensure there is no breach. I am going to the bridge.' There was a thump and a moan of metal as the Grey Knight spoke, and the sounds of pounding from the far side of the blast doors trailed off.

'We're retreating?' Ethold called after Stern as he strode towards the docking bay's grav lift. The big paladin was slicked with dripping, stinking ichor, fists locked around the haft of his force glaive. Stern didn't look back.

'No.'

The *Star Drake*'s bridge was a hive of activity. The huscarl Stern had given temporary command to was standing atop the command dais, snapping orders to his kaerls. In the open vision ports Stern saw *Gormenjarl* hoving into view as the ship detached itself from the docking spine and swung about to face it.

'Were repairs completed?' Stern asked as he strode onto the bridge. The huscarl bowed hastily.

'We still cannot route full power to the plasma drives for fear of overloading them, lord, but to all intents and purposes, yes. The coolant coupling was eighty-five per cent complete when we detached. We should make far better time now. Do you have a heading?'

'Not yet,' Stern said. 'Reroute power to the forward bombardment cannon. Lock onto the star fort, I don't care where. Just hit it.'

'Affirmative, lord,' said the huscarl, before barking orders to the gunnery station. Deep in the *Star Drake*'s bowels whips cracked and chain gangs heaved in the hellish half-light as they dragged a vast bombardment shell into the breach of the strike cruiser's primary cannon. The ship's machine-spirit, manifest in the probing of its sensory arrays and augur masts, easily acquired the huge target presented by *Gormenjarl*.

'Bombardment cannon loaded and locked, lord,' a gunnery kaerl called.

'Fire,' Stern said.

Swallowed by the void, there was no sound of any discharge, but the flash of the mighty weapon reflected back from the fort's gleaming bulkheads, and the tremor of its recoil reached the bridge's decking plates. Seconds passed. Then part of the star fort's gaping docking space blossomed outwards, eerily silent, the armour plating blown apart by the point-blank shot and spinning away with a curiously majestic slowness.

'You were right, Brother Artemis,' Stern said, smiling grimly. '*Gormenjarl*'s shields no longer function.'

He turned to the gunnery station. 'Huscarl, direct all firepower at the structural weak points. I want to have dealt it crippling damage within the hour. And have your communications pit patch me through to the Fang immediately.'

The Fang, Fenris

Lord Krom Dragongaze's footsteps led him into darkness.

A part of him knew he should not venture into the Vaults. It was a cursed place, an icy shaft buried deep into the roots of the mountain. A place of cracked, worn statues and sealed doors, their mechanisms frozen solid with ice. The power had long ago failed, and even the great geothermal reactor coils that helped keep the Fenrisian death-chill from the Fang's corridors had never reached this deep. This was beyond the Underfang and the Halls of the Revered Fallen, a place marked on few maps, and remembered in even fewer living memories.

Krom trod the rock-carved corridors with care, the active hum of his power armour painfully loud in the stony depths. He held a lumen orb in one hand, its pale light picking out the graven alcoves and craggy stairways before him. In a place like this, even the Fierce-eye didn't want to trust to his senses alone.

He passed three ward-doors before he reached the chamber he sought. He had to search the depths of his long memory to conjure up the correct pass-codes, and he felt the static buzz of hexagrammic wards and power shields as he passed through each one. Beyond the last lay a great, vaulted room. Krom's orb failed to even pick out its ceiling. The stony glare of a hundred forgotten Wolf Guard stared down at Dragongaze from their plinths lining the chamber's walls, while row after row of metal caskets filled its open floor.

Krom glanced at his visor display, but it told him little. The vox, the chrono counter and his tracking signal had all failed him. He could have passed into another dimension as far as his auto-senses were concerned. All he had was a temperature reading well below freezing, his spiking vital signs, and targeting reticules continually flashing a warning red as they picked up the false outlines of the ancient statues. He deactivated them with a blink, trying to ease his jagged heartrate.

'Why are you here,' he growled to himself. Even though he hadn't vocalised it beyond his helmet, the words seemed to echo about in the frozen, lost chamber. There was no reply, but he knew the answer anyway. He could not sit and wait in the great halls of the Fang while the rest of his Chapter fought and bled across the other home worlds of the Fenris System. He had to try to learn the truth. Perhaps, down here, there would be an insight into the curse that plagued them.

The casket he was seeking was the nearest to the ward-door. It was the last one to have been brought to the haunted depths, laid to rest less than four centuries earlier. Krom approached it, his lumen orb flickering, as though reluctant to go any further. The casket was large – steel bound in brass and big enough to hold Snegga the Giant, the broadest warrior in Krom's Great Company. Its flanks were inscribed with ancient, intricate runic script while a carving of the World Wolf was inlaid on its lid. Krom brushed his fingers against it, and felt the throbbing power of an active stasis field within.

The Wolf Lord set his orb down beside the casket and unlocked the gauntlet from his left hand, laying it beside the orb. Then he drew his combat knife, and nicked the razor steel against the back of his hand. A single line of blood ran down his forefinger. He held it against the gene-lock panel set into the casket's flank. There was a whir as the mechanism matched and confirmed the genetic heritage of the sons of Russ. Then there came a thud of bolts, and a hiss of pressure sealant as the casket's heavy lid slid slowly back on auto-hinges. Krom kept his combat knife out.

At first, with the lumen orb still on the ground next to it, the casket's interior was just a well of power-charged darkness. Krom's auto-senses were stripping the shadows away when a single small lumen in the casket's top blinked on. What it revealed inside was a horror.

The Great Wolf had saved it four centuries earlier, on the frigid world of

Lumerius. The vile traitors of the Black Legion, led by the insane butcher Fabius Bile, had been hunting for it, desperate to seize its genetic material and fashion an army of nightmares to augment their dark strength. Grimnar and the Champions of Fenris had gotten there first, putting the traitors to the sword and rescuing the casket. It had been taken here, to the deepest vaults of the Fang, and here it had lain undisturbed ever since, sleeping the ages away in the frozen darkness. Fang-brother, the Lost, Herald of Russ. *Wulfen.*

The creature had been locked in the casket's inbuilt stasis field, its claws out, features twisted in an eternal, bestial snarl. Krom bent forward to look into its eyes, seeking something more than animal hunger in them. As his shadow fell across the Wulfen he got the distinct sense that the thing was looking back at him, aware, every muscle silently straining against its enforced paralysis. The Wolf Lord straightened hastily.

It was not a Space Wolf. Perhaps it had been once, but the heraldry of its ancient power armour belonged to the Wolf Brothers. Theirs was a tragic tale. The only Successor Chapter ever founded by the VI Legion, the genetic legacy of Russ had proven to be too volatile to be replicated beyond Fenris. According to half-remembered, half-believed legend, the Wolf Brothers had been riven by the curse of the Wulfen. Those not killed had been scattered by the tides amidst the Sea of Stars. The few that still survived were hunted, whether by a misguided Imperium, or darker powers.

Grimnar had gotten to this one just before the forces of Chaos had latched their claws around it. The thought of the warped geneticist Bile capturing a Wulfen for his experiments was a terrible one. Looking down at the stasis-frozen body of the feral creature, Krom sought reason in its form. Legend held that the Wulfen's return presaged that of the primarch himself. Certainly the old Wolf Priest Ulrik had thought as much. Others had been less certain.

It had long been feared that evidence of the instability of the Canis Helix within the genetic code of the Space Wolves could be used by other Imperial factions to damn the Chapter. Now just such a scenario was playing out, with the Lions occupying the system. What had brought the Wulfen back? Had they returned to combat the daemons infesting the system, or were they in fact a part of the Dark Gods' schemes, unwitting pawns in a plot to annihilate the Rout once and for all?

'*Lord,*' said Vox Huscarl Fogel, transmitting from the Fang's communications hub. Krom started, taking a step back from the casket. His vox had re-established a connection. Sudden anger flushed through him. What had he hoped to achieve by coming down here? There could be no insight into the curse. The Wulfen were animals, pure and simple.

'Speak,' he ordered Fogel.

'*Lord, Captain Stern is on the long-range vox. He has urgent news.*'

'I'm on my way.'

He looked down one more time into the Wolf Brother's eyes. They glared back at him. He wondered for a moment whether, in truth, his own gaze was any less unsettling. Then he hit the sealant rune, and watched the casket's heavy lid lock back into place. The thud of the internal clamps echoed through the chamber. Krom refastened his gauntlet, picked up the lumen orb, and left.

The Fang's primary communications array was hushed when the Wolf Lord arrived. He was handed a vox horn and receiver by Fogel.

'Stern,' Krom said into the horn. 'Report. What's happened?'

'*Grim tidings,*' the Grey Knight replied. '*I am aboard the star fort* Gormenjarl. *We have recently discovered a full-scale daemonic infestation. My brethren and I are too few to purge it, so we are currently bombarding the fort from afar. The infestation has disabled the structure's weaponry and shield capabilities.*'

'Has Shipmaster Ranulf consented to this?' Krom demanded.

'*No,*' said Stern. '*That was the second matter that needed to be discussed. Your shipmaster has succumbed to your genetic... curse. I've had to confine him to his own ship's brig. His two crewmates also turned, at the same time. We had no choice but to slay them.*'

Days earlier news that the Grey Knights had killed his brethren – Wulfen or not – would have sent spikes of rage stabbing through Krom's thoughts. Now though, he felt nothing. He had fought tooth and nail alongside Stern's silver paladins, saved the soul of his Chapter with their help. The blank, feral glare of the Wolf Brother had held nothing of the *Vlka Fenryka's* martial upbringing and nobility, only its darker, more bestial side.

'We need more men,' Krom said. 'If what you say is true, Stern, then we must ensure control of *Gormenjarl's* twin, *Mjalnar*. We cannot afford to leave it infested with wyrdlings.'

'*Aren't all forces engaged, besides your own?*'

'Not all,' Krom said. 'Not quite.'

The Void, Fenris System

'Do you trust him?'

Ragnar sneered. 'I'd as soon trust one of the wyrdlings. He's a member of the ordos. He exists to persecute and lie. Have you ever heard of one of his breed who didn't despise our Chapter, and all because we strive to protect mankind? Because we dare to honour the reason for our very existence?'

Olvec the Wise, Ragnar's Wolf Guard Battle Leader, nodded. 'He seemed open enough with his motives though. If his tale was true, he despises the Lions. He would use us as a weapon against them.'

'And well he may, if they burn Midgardia. If they want a war, they'll have one.'

The two Wolves were conferring privately in the *Holmgang's* shrine to Morkai. The place of worship, like much of the ship, recalled the Chapter's primal roots – though the decks and ceiling were plasteel plate and iron mesh, the walls were clad in rugged, dark grey stone, mined from the flanks of Asaheim. The lumen strips, running down the length of the room's edges, were dimmer in this less-visited part of the ship, with much of the power rerouted to the plasma drives. They threw long shadows over the pelt-heaped stone altar, and cast the features of the two Wolves into jagged contrast. Ragnar's eyes gleamed coldly.

'Do you believe the inquisitor's tale,' Olvec asked, 'about Interrogator-Chaplain Asmodai?'

'There are many such stories about the sons of the Lion,' Ragnar said. 'They are a dark brotherhood. It is little surprise that they should clash with the ordos. And now the ordos have come to us. Clearly this de Mornay knows the value of his enemy's enemy.'

'He was a warrior once,' Olvec said. 'He has the bearing still, despite his age. I smell blood and steel about him.'

'That is at least to be commended,' Ragnar allowed. 'Regardless of whether he intends to use us or not, any who wield a blade in the All-father's name are useful at a time like this.'

'We are beset,' Olvec agreed. 'And the packs are hungrier than ever. Wyrdspawn or the Lions, whoever we next bare our claws against will suffer.'

The *Holmgang*'s intercom command channel clicked in Ragnar's ear. Olvec watched as his jarl received the vox huscarl's message.

'To the bridge,' he said after breaking the link.

'Trouble?'

'Dragongaze is hailing us again. Perhaps he's grown bored, sitting alone in the Fang.'

The half-jest fell flat. They hurried to the command deck. Krom greeted them from the static-washed display of its main vid feed.

'*It's the Grey Knights,*' he said.

'What of them?'

'*Captain Stern has just sent me a transmission. Our Ramilies star fort,* Gormenjarl, *has been infested by wyrdlings. His Brotherhood is too few to purge it, so he's destroying it from afar with one of my ships. We believe* Mjalnar *may also have been overrun.*'

'Have you hailed *Mjalnar*?' Ragnar asked.

'*There's been no contact made with it since the incursions began,*' Krom said. '*I fear the daemonhunter is correct, and if he is we cannot afford to leave a mobile warp rift open in the heart of the system.*'

'My fleet is the nearest to *Mjalnar*'s current location,' Ragnar said, glancing at one of the bridge's glowing holocharts. 'But it would delay our arrival at Midgardia.'

'*We have no choice, Blackmane,*' Krom said. '*There is still no word from Bran Redmaw, and all our other forces are fully engaged. You alone can meet this threat.*'

Ragnar grimaced, but nodded. 'Very well, Fierce-eyes. My packs will purge *Mjalnar*. Pray to the Allfather its communications have simply failed, and our brethren yet garrison it.'

'*I shall,*' Krom said. '*But there is other news from Stern. He discovered* Gormenjarl'*s plight after he went there seeking repairs. Apparently Shipmaster Ranulf, of the* Star Drake, *succumbed to the curse along with two others. They damaged the ship before they could be stopped.*'

'Are you telling me not to trust my own Wulfen?'

'*I'm telling you to be mindful of those who have not yet turned, Young King,*' Krom said. '*Whether we accept them into our ranks afterwards or not, having experienced warriors devolving into half-beasts only weakens us.*'

'I have more than just the curse to be mindful of, Dragongaze,' Ragnar said. 'Have you heard of a Hereticus inquisitor by the name of Banist de Mornay?'

'*I have not, why?*'

'His ship has joined my fleet en-route to Midgardia. He seeks to enlist my help in bringing the Lions to heel.'

'*The last thing we need now is the Inquisition's meddling,*' Krom growled.

'He claims to believe our Wulfen are free of warp taint. That could make him a valuable ally.'

'*Or he could turn on us as soon as he's used us to settle whatever grudge he has with the Dark Angels,*' Krom said. '*Tread carefully, Blackmane.*'

'Don't I always, Dragongaze?' Ragnar smiled grimly. Krom didn't respond. The transmission ended.

'Get me the inquisitor's ship,' Ragnar ordered his vox huscarl. 'Tell him I am changing course.'

Svellgard

Wrath had arrived. It burst into existence in the depths of Svellgard's oceans, tearing itself free of one of the warp rifts that had pierced the moon's seabed. For the first time since creation, it brought light to the icy deeps. It burned white-hot, the fury of its god made manifest. Blood and screams and war-steel had drawn it here, a memory of the fury of Wolves, and now it would do its god's bidding.

The waters around it began to churn and boil. Already billions of gallons from Svellgard's seas had plummeted through the warp rifts and into the madness of the immaterium. The islands that housed the Claws of the World Wolf were growing steadily larger, the waters receding from the shores and exposing fresh, jutting rocks, gleaming like bone spiking out from desiccated corpses. Through the flushing tides the monstrosity known as Infurnace blazed. Ahead of it lay the World Wolf's Lair, and a fight worthy of the Blood God.

* * *

The Void, Fenris System

Mjalnar was transmitting. It was not, however, an intelligible signal. The Wolf fleet circled the unresponsive Imperial star fort like a pack sniffing at a frozen corpse, hackles up and fangs bared, wary.

'Boost the audio,' Ragnar ordered from the *Holmgang*'s bridge throne, leaning towards the vox array. The noises emitting from *Mjalnar* came through more clearly. Except they were not really noises at all. The Wolf Lord was reminded of being plunged underwater, and having crushing pressure reduce everything to a sort of constant, muted rumble. It set his hairs on end and sent a strange, icy chill creeping along his shoulders.

'Cut the link,' he said. 'And pull alongside. I want to board immediately.'

Mjalnar filled the *Holmgang*'s viewing ports, a mountain of silent adamantium threat. Transmission lights and guidance beacons still winked from its crenelated masts and spires, and the star fort's great guns had been run out. Of actual life, however, there was no sign.

'Lord, Inquisitor de Mornay is hailing us,' a vox kaerl said.

'Speakers,' Ragnar ordered.

'*What happened to our need for haste?*' de Mornay demanded.

'There are some duties even the Inquisition cannot countermand,' Ragnar replied. '*Mjalnar* is a mighty battlestation. If it has fallen, it must be retaken. If it is overrun, it must be destroyed.'

'*Every second we delay, Midgardia burns,*' de Mornay said.

'Do you think I don't realise that?' Ragnar snarled. 'Do you think I don't ache to close my fist around the throats of those threatening my Chapter's worlds? My Wolves have waited too long to pass this kill by. If you wish to face the Lions alone then by all means, carry on to Midgardia. But my packs are my own, and we are boarding *Mjalnar*. Are you still with us, *inquisitor*?'

There was a long pause. Ragnar sneered. Then the reply crackled over the vox, heavy with finality.

'I will see you onboard the star fort, Lord Blackmane.'

The World Wolf's Lair, Svellgard

The seas were retreating. Sven watched them rather than the Thunderhawks and Stormwolves of Harald's Great Company as they landed amongst the bunkers, bastions and turrets of the World Wolf's Lair. He had already transmitted data links pinpointing where his lines were weakest. Harald's warriors would fill the gaps accordingly, Firehowlers and Deathwolves manning the parapets and fire slits side by side. But the joy such a gathering of Wolves would normally have brought Sven was eclipsed by the mystery of Svellgard's receding seas.

'The wyrdling rifts must be widening,' Olaf Blackstone said, pointing at the expanse of sodden wet sand that now stretched away from the Lair's shingle. 'The water is disappearing into the immaterium.'

'At least we'll see the bastards coming,' Sven growled. He pointed to a patch of ocean further out, a choppy channel that ran between two of the Lair's neighbouring islands. It looked as though a bank of fog or steam was rising from the waves, creating a swirling cloud on the near horizon. 'And what about that?'

'Russ only knows,' Olaf replied. 'Send the *Godspear*?'

'Agreed. Have the area scanned. We've enjoyed enough wyrd-damned surprises.'

'Affirmative.'

'*Lord, I'm getting movement,*' said Yngfor the Long Fang over the vox. 'Contacts coming ashore from the south.' Sven opened a channel to Harald.

'Are your packs in position, Deathwolf?'

'*They are, Bloodhowl. Let the wyrdlings come.*'

'We'll make them regret the day they sought to claim Svellgard,' Sven said, switching to the company-wide channel.

'All packs, fire at will.'

Boarding Torpedo Fifteen-B, approaching Mjalnar

Ragnar flexed his arms and shoulders. He felt the servo bundles that gave life to his power armour whir in response to the motion, while the true flesh and muscle of his transhuman physique stretched. He had been trapped in the voidborne prison of his flagship for too long. The hunt called to him. He could already feel the wyrdling scum snapping in his grasp, shrieking as he sent them back to the empyrean. He realised his gauntlets were clenched, and let out a long, slow breath. The chrono display counting down in his visor's top-right corner still read over a minute before the boarding torpedo impacted into the star fort's flank.

He finished recounting the names of his dead pack-brothers. It was a ritual he had observed for a long time, and he knew it gave comfort to his Great Company as well as to himself. To know their jarl valued their lives, counted them as true kin whether amidst the fires of battle or the feasting halls of the Fang, hardened the bonds of pack loyalty. The Blackmanes were all as one.

He drew *Frostfang*. The ancient chainsword felt like an extension of his physical form, his fist closing with familiar certainty around the worn handle. His fingers itched to flick the activation stud. Hidden beneath his helmet's faceplate, he grinned.

'You're grinning, aren't you?' said Tor Wolfheart.

'And you're not?' Ragnar replied. 'I have ached for this, brother. At last we will join the other Great Companies in the defence of our home worlds.'

Twenty seconds. He knew he didn't need to say anything to the

Blackpelts, his Wolf Guard. They understood what was coming. Like the Allfather's burning warspear, they would plough into the diseased heart of the wyrdspawn infestation, banishing it from the material universe, utterly wiping away the taint of their existence.

Five seconds. The boarding torpedo shuddered as it impacted into *Mjalnar*'s flank, latching on with razor limpet clamps. There was a muffled *whoosh* of heavy meltaguns, followed by the thud and whir of disengaging locks. The pod's assault bay was bathed in bloody red light. Ragnar released his restraint, feeling his adrenaline spiking, breath coming in pants through his armour's filtration systems.

The blast doors opened, revealing a circular hole that dripped with molten steel, the edges still glowing from the melta blasts. Ragnar triggered *Frostfang*, his vox-amplified howl blending with the chainsword's savage roar. He leapt through the boarding hatch, fangs bared. Straight into a deserted service corridor.

And not a daemon in sight.

The World Wolf's Lair, Svellgard

This time, the creatures of Chaos assaulting Svellgard's beaches struggled. With the addition of Harald's packs to Sven's defences, the weight of firepower had doubled. The receding tides had left the dark cohorts with more open ground to cross before they could reach the outermost defences of the Lair. Squealing and roaring wyrdlings were cut to pieces even as they dragged themselves, dripping, from the icy waves. The Earthshaker artillery added their firepower from the nearby islands, their strikes sending up great plumes of water and brine as they shelled the gradually expanding southern edge of the Lair. Fifteen minutes into the assault, Sven's biggest concern, watching from the ramparts of the Lair's central keep, was monitoring ammunition expenditure.

That all changed with a message from *Godspear*.

'*The island channel is experiencing a huge temperature spike,*' the pilot voxed. '*Something in the water is giving off an energy signature. And it's moving towards the Lair.*'

'What fresh maleficarum is this?' Sven growled. 'Keep tracking it.'

'*Lord, it seems to be rising to the surface. I–*' the pilot got no further. The water beneath the vapour fog heaved. Something vast powered from the sea and into the steam-wreathed air. Great, bat-like pinions unfurled, and black coal-flesh that smouldered with hate-fuelled heat burst into white flames.

With a roar that shook the rockcrete beneath Sven's mag-boots, a burning Bloodthirster lunged upwards at *Godspear*.

Sven could only listen to the pilot's startled, frantic oaths as he tried to evade the greater daemon. He watched the Thunderhawk bank desperately, but the fire-wreathed monstrosity was infinitely lither in the air.

The huge axe it wielded inscribed a fiery arc through Svellgard's grey sky, and smashed into one of the *Godspear*'s wings. The single blow cut clean through its armour plating, throwing out a spray of fat sparks. The gunship immediately lurched to one side, its servitor-controlled bolters blasting wildly into the air in all directions. It started to spin out of control amidst a plume of fire and black smoke.

'Infurnace,' Sven breathed. He recognised the greater daemon. All the Wolves did. Its crude, fiery likeness could be found carved across the saga knotwork in four of the great halls of the Fang, recounting the epic battle between it and the Wolf Lord Kjarl Stormpelt, many millennia past. Infurnace was a tale every Blood Claw knew, one of the near-mythical monsters that reared its head from the depths of the Chapter's glorious past. And now it had returned, to help write new sagas with fresh blood.

The greater daemon had only just begun. It lashed out with a chain-whip grasped in its other fist, the heavy, white-hot links snagging the damaged Thunderhawk's remaining wing. With a roar like a forgesmith's hammer-strike, it twisted its mighty body in mid-air, directing the *Godspear*'s erratic plunge towards the shoreline of the closest island.

Sven made out the tiny figures of Astra Militarum troopers vainly attempting to scatter as the Thunderhawk's burning shadow screamed over them. The Bloodthirster's chain snapped free, and the *Godspear*'s wrecked remains hammered into the island shingle. It ploughed a deep furrow in the shore, obliterating a section of makeshift flakboard barricades and wiping the platoon manning them from existence. Then the gunship exploded, a blossoming fireball that blazed across the island's beach, as though in sympathy with the fiery monster that had caused it. The blast took more troopers with it, demolishing the western side of the island's defences.

Infurnace didn't even pause to survey its handiwork. Wings beating, it launched itself through the air, straight towards the World Wolf's Lair.

Ramilies-class star fort, designate Mjalnar

Ragnar and his Blackpelts stood just beyond the hatch of their boarding torpedo, weapons drawn. Nothing moved to oppose them. The service corridor was old, and quite clearly deserted. The ceiling was a mass of bared coolant piping, and the walls were naked plasteel, inset with cobwebbed lumen orbs. Rust discoloured every surface, and there was a distant hissing where steam escaped from a ruptured pipe. Although the corridor was clearly timeworn and abandoned, there was no wyrdling stench about it.

'Morkai's heads,' Ragnar spat, feeling his system flush with rage. 'Where are they?'

No one answered. The old lumen orbs flickered once, but remained mute.

'Maybe the star fort is free from taint,' Uller Greylock growled. 'Maybe the Grey Knights were wrong.'

'Then where are the crew?' Ragnar asked. 'Why haven't they been responding to our transmissions?' He blink-clicked his visor's vox display. 'All boarding packs, come in.'

'*Hostor's Spears, here.*'

'*Maegar's Pack, affirmative.*'

'*Asgeir's Allslayers here, my jarl.*'

'Contacts?' Ragnar demanded. Negatives crackled back at him, the Blood Claw pack leaders sounding as confused as he was. A rune in his visor lit up, and Ragnar switched channels to accept de Mornay's incoming transmission.

'*A trap,*' the inquisitor said. '*It has to be.*'

'What makes you so sure?'

'*The crew surely wouldn't have simply abandoned the station.*'

'We will soon find out,' Ragnar replied, switching back to his pack-wide channel. 'Hostor, take your Claws to the escape shuttle bay, it should be a hundred yards down the corridor on your left hand.'

'*Yes, lord, on our way.*' Ragnar switched back.

'De Mornay, what's your current location?'

'*It appears to be an outer munitions shaft for the spinward-facing weapons batteries,*' de Mornay replied. '*It's deserted though.*'

'Hold there,' Ragnar said. 'My Blackpelts and I will join you.'

'*Affirmative.*'

Ragnar met de Mornay at a junction leading to the weapons batteries. The inquisitor was still mounted on his palanquin, but his ageing body was now armoured in flakplate, and an archaic-looking brass-cased plasma pistol rested in one hand. Alongside him stood his grim-faced Adepta Sororitas bodyguard, clad in the midnight-black Purgation pattern power armour of the Order of Our Martyred Lady.

'You know the star fort's layout?' de Mornay greeted the Wolf Lord.

'It falls under the auspices of the Chapter Fleet,' Ragnar replied. 'It's part of the system defence network. All pack leaders have access to its schematics.'

'So what do you propose we do?' de Mornay asked. 'There's something wrong about all this.' He gestured with his pistol down the deserted corridor behind the Blackpelts.

An update from Hostor clicked in Ragnar's ear before he could reply.

'*Lord, only half of the escape shuttles are accounted for. Six have jettisoned.*'

'There are shuttles missing,' Ragnar told de Mornay.

The inquisitor frowned.

'The riddle grows more complex. If they were all present I would assume the crew to have been slaughtered. But if they evacuated, this place may genuinely be deserted.'

'But why would they leave?' Ragnar asked aloud.

'The central command deck may tell us,' de Mornay said. 'It must have audio and visual logs?'

'And more. It should have recorded the escape shuttles' projected routes. And from there we can set the fort on a more useful course than its current trajectory. Towards Midgardia, for example.' He opened a channel to the three Blood Claw assault packs that had boarded with him.

'Converge on the command deck. I want this riddle solved.'

Transit Line four hundred and three,
the Underworld, Midgardia

They'd found them. Phugulus emitted a blast of noxious spore clouds and pointed excitedly down the rail tunnel. The little pack of Wolves had led them to a larger one, and now they'd combined into a single force. Truly, the Grandfather was good.

Behind the daemonic Herald his plaguebearers were dragging themselves from the tunnel burrowed by Garr'nokk, the Great Plague Wyrm. Garr'nokk himself was writhing down the rail line towards the Wolves already, his many maws snapping and drooling hungrily. Chewing dirt was clearly not enough – the noble beast was desperate for flesh and blood. Phugulus waved after it.

'Let us bless these great warriors with diseases befitting their might,' he bellowed at his chanting plaguebearers. 'Onwards, dear friends, onwards!'

The plague-recitals of the Infested redoubled in volume and urgency as they set off in Garr'nokk's wake, Phugulus struggling to keep his diseased bulk near the head of his Tallyband. He could see more than just a fortunate gathering of soon-to-be-blessed wolf-men ahead. He could see the whole glory of a new realm ripe for the Grandfather's benedictions. The Midgardian underworld was overly humid, yes, but it was certainly earthy, dark and dank. All manner of mould, fungi and rot could be cultivated in its depths. By the time he returned to his Grandfather's garden he would have a host of wondrous specimens to present.

The possibilities jostled for attention in the Herald's thoughts, so much so that he barely even noticed when the Tallyband crashed into the howling Space Wolves.

The knot of Wolves gathered around Logan Grimnar's fallen crown turned, weapons revving to life. The air was thick with spores, misting their view further back up the transit tunnel. Shapes were limping through the rancid smog, shuffling and moaning with throaty, bile-choked voices.

'The wyrm,' Lenold snarled. Egil followed his gaze, and saw that the huge daemonic wyrm had returned. It writhed down the tunnel with a hideous peristaltic motion, its blind maws agape. And, once again, a clutch of rotting lesser daemons were following in its wake, using the tunnel gnawed by his multi-fanged jaws to traverse Midgardia's underworld.

'Take the beast,' Egil said. 'We'll close the tunnel again. Then we can

purge that foul thing together. It must not be allowed to escape this time.'
Lenold only nodded, already moving to meet the wyrm head-on.

Egil launched himself into the plaguebearers crawling through the tunnel
in the rail highway's wall, his Ironguard beside him. They had to be quick.
The counter on his visor showed the toxicity levels in the air rising rapidly.
This Tallyband had clearly brought the surface's corruption with it into
Midgardia's depths.

The Iron Wolf's power claws shredded the first plaguebearer he reached
for, its rancid form disintegrating into a puddle of decomposing sludge.
Egil went through a second and a third, snarling with rage. The memory
of the Great Wolf's broken crown lent every blow a furious, unstoppable
strength. How dare these weak, putrid monsters threaten his Chapter with
destruction? How dare they seek to turn and warp everything the Wolves
had defended for so many millennia?

The plaguebearers parted before him, their endless, maddening chants
for once falling silent. One of their number pressed to the fore. This one
was larger, standing a head taller than the things around it. Its frame was
bloated and riven with suppurating sores, its lone, cyclopean eye blinking
with an unnatural intelligence from beneath one curling horn. It gripped a
pockmarked broadsword in its fist, worm-fingers writhing around the hilt.
It was a Herald, a leader of the Tallybands. Egil raised his wolf claws, their
power snapping, acknowledging the challenge.

The Herald struck.

Ramilies-class star fort, designate Mjalnar

'The fastest route to the command deck from here is via the barracks blocks,'
Ragnar said. 'Kraken formation, don't hesitate to engage if you make contact. Inquisitor...' He turned to face de Mornay. 'Stay close, but don't get in
the way.' De Mornay simply shrugged.

'Lead on, Lord Blackmane.'

The Blackpelts set off, Ragnar at the fore. They followed the service chute
to a side door that led to a mesh walkway, passing over a vast set of throbbing coolant spheres, used to douse the star fort's heavy artillery when it
glowed hot from repeated use. Beyond it lay a communications sub terminal. The vox banks had been shut down, their screens blank, horns silent.

'That explains why we've not been picking up a signal,' de Mornay said.
'But why deactivate them?'

'We'll find out soon enough,' Ragnar growled. He was following the
heads-up schematic display of *Mjalnar*, overlaid with the three runes representing the other boarding packs. The system was suffering some sort
of interference – the runes showing the locations of the Blood Claws kept
blinking from existence, then reappearing nearby, yet only fractionally
closer to the command deck at the star fort's heart. Ragnar voxed them,

but all reported good progress. And still there was no sign of life, wyrdling or otherwise.

Beyond the vox terminal was the barracks block. Ragnar glanced into one of the cells as they passed. Its bunk beds were pristine, and kit bags still sat in files along the floor. It was as though *Mjalnar*'s crew were all still present, but had simply become invisible. The Wolf Lord snarled with frustration.

The vox transmissions from the other packs were similarly unhappy. Maegar reported he'd come up against a dead end that didn't exist on the schematics, and had been forced to turn back. Asgeir made a similar report moments later – he'd found himself in a medicae bay that supposedly didn't exist. The pack leader's voice was strained, and Ragnar caught the sound of snarling in the background. The noise shook a growl from his own throat, and his Blackpelts responded in sympathy. They were all hungry, all frustrated.

They passed through the barracks, the command deck just ahead. Ragnar punched in the runes on the security doors, haste forcing him to re-enter them twice. His grip on *Frostfang* tightened. The doors slide back to reveal…

The outer service corridor. The same one they'd first entered *Mjalnar* through. The hole bored by their boarding pod's meltas still gaped in the far wall, its molten edges now jagged and hardened. Ragnar just stared.

'The schematics must be wrong,' Tor said, voice choked. 'Outdated.'

Ragnar realised he was panting. His vision flickered, colours flashing in and out of focus, like a pict caster switching between high and low resolution. He could smell blood, coppery and insistent. His jaw ached, and his fingers itched. Anger flooded his mind. This wasn't what they were here for. This wasn't what he'd endured the Sea of Stars for. Fenris was beset and his warriors were wandering the corridors of some damn, deserted star fort. He needed to kill, now. They all did.

'It's a trick,' de Mornay was saying, attempting to penetrate the fug of bloodlust that was gripping the Wolves. 'They're trying to confound you. Trying to trigger your curse. This star fort is as infested as the one the Grey Knights purged.'

'A… trick…' Ragnar grunted, shaking his head slowly. No. Blood. He needed to spill blood. He could taste it in his mouth. His fangs were starting to distend. *Frostfang* was screaming at him to kill.

'They're here!' de Mornay shouted, plasma pistol whining with charge. 'All around!' The sudden crackle and the scent of ozone cut through Ragnar's consciousness. The Young King gasped and blinked, as though only just waking from a long, dark nightmare. He realised ozone was not the only thing he could smell. The unmistakable stench of wyrd-taint was suddenly everywhere.

Shrieking with rage, the daemons broke their illusion and flung themselves upon the Space Wolves.

* * *

The Rock, in high orbit above Midgardia

Far below, fire billowed and spread. The Elezar-thing, the Changeling, watched it from the Rock's vast, stain-tinted bridge viewing ports. From so far away, it looked like an insignificant thing at first. The deathstorm missiles unleashed by the Imperial Navy's capital ships were like little shards of starlight, quickly lost on their way to the surface. They bloomed again amidst Midgardia's purple shades, little pricks of light set against the diseased darkness. Only when those pinpricks eventually began to meet and cluster did they truly start to spread. The Changeling didn't bother to control its grin, masked as it was by Elezar's skull helm.

The flames grew and flourished, until they had embraced a third of Midgardia's visible surface, black ash clouds starting to obscure the upper atmosphere. A part of the Changeling wished it could be down there, experiencing the raw, chaotic annihilation in person. Perhaps, in a different existence among one of Fate's many other paths, it would walk the surface of Midgardia during its fiery execution. It would see the inferno devouring the planet's diseased, infected foliage, bursting blighted bark and setting light to the surfaces of the pus-bogs. It would see Tallybands sent blazing back to the warp, just as the fires roasted the human people of Midgardia and gutted the spires of the Magma Gates. Only into the underworld would the flames fail to reach. That did not concern the Changeling. There would be more than enough time to deal with those lost Wolves.

Grandfather Nurgle would be infuriated by the torching of his new possession. The thought only fuelled the Changeling's delight. In all of Creation and Uncreation, only its master knew the final form of the tapestry it wove from Fate's threads, but even the small patch the Changeling saw before it was glorious to behold.

The Elezar-thing snapped its gaze away from the sight of the burning world. It had let its thoughts drift. There was still work to be done. Swiftly, it turned from the viewing ports and paced from the bridge, back towards the Interrogator-Chaplain's cell.

Midgardia was only the beginning.

Iron Requiem, *in high orbit above Svellgard*

Iron Captain Terrek reached out and touched the soul of the machine. The Clan Commander felt the spirit of his battle-barge rise up from the depths as he finished plugging himself into *Iron Requiem*'s command throne, neural links, spine cords and gene-coils, draped with purity seals, binding him to the centre of the bridge. Terrek always found it a thrilling sensation, to commune so directly, so intimately, with something that had never known the weak constraints of the flesh.

Iron Requiem was ancient. It had forged through the stars and brought the Emperor's light to the darkest reaches of the galaxy for almost eight thousand years. Yet the soul of the machine was anything but old and sluggish. It spoke to Terrek freely, as an old friend, of its pride at the successful lance strike against Morkai's Keep, twinned with its shame at unleashing its weapons upon brother Adeptus Astartes. Terrek quietened its fears. The Space Wolves were at best mutants, and at worst traitors. They were barbarous savages who had run rampant through the stars, unchecked by any authority, for far too long. Now the Iron Hands would help bring them to heel.

Terrek had deactivated his bionic eyes. Now he saw directly through the *Iron Requiem*'s augur arrays, the data fed back to him in a steady stream through the throne's many ports. Svellgard hung below them, a little blue-grey orb framed by the vast, icy sphere of Frostheim behind it. Around the orb clustered what looked from a distance like swarms of airborne insects. With a thought Terrek increased the augur magnification, picking out individual ships from among the fleet that hung around the moon. Most were Astra Militarum mass transporters and Imperial Navy battleships, but Terrek also noted the proud blue heraldry of a sleek Ultramarines strike cruiser.

As per the agreed plan, the sons of Guilliman had not yet committed any of their squads to Svellgard's surface, allowing the Astra Militarum and the atmospheric aircraft of the Imperial Navy to secure the island beachheads. They would be sufficient to assess the threat, and from there decide whether to reinforce the Wolves or destroy them with their moon. Only once the enemy's main strength had been pinpointed would the Angels of Death commit themselves. As a strategy it was both simple and logically optimal. The Clan Company's Iron Father had gone so far as to compute an eighty-seven per cent likelihood of success.

Such figures brought Terrek as close to pleasure as was possible nowadays, but unknown factors still remained. One of those was playing out even as *Iron Requiem* joined the rest of the crusade fleet around Svellgard. Terrek noted multiple sensors tracking a powerful energy signal on the surface below. Visual scanning was struggling to map a reliable image of the thing causing the disturbance. Whatever it was, it appeared to be neverborn in nature. Terrek filtered the garbled Astra Militarum vox messages being translated back to their commanders in orbit. Fire. Death. Rage. Terrek assessed and dismissed each keyword in turn. Wings. Axe. Blood. Daemon.

Greater daemon.

Bloodthirster.

He felt even the mighty spirit of *Iron Requiem* shudder as they made the joint realisation of what was attacking the Claws of the World Wolf below. One of Khorne's mighty champions had burst into being beneath the moon's cold waves. That could only mean the warp rifts were even more unstable than they had initially calculated. The sooner he acted the better.

His implants calculating range, azimuth, diffraction and speed projections, the Iron Hands captain began to plot another firing solution for his battle-barge's lance battery.

WOLF TRAP

The very walls of *Mjalnar* shuddered and shifted, plasteel plating suddenly as insubstantial as a heat mirage. Through the haze came wyrdlings, their blades and claws reaching for Ragnar and his Space Wolves.

'Blackpelts, to me!' Ragnar roared. Normal forces would have been annihilated by so sudden and horrific an ambush. The Blackpelts, however, were far from normal. Back-to-back they fought, Tor Wolfheart and Alrydd the Bard, Uller Greylock, Hrolf Longspear and Svengril the Younger. With bared fang and wild eye they smote the creatures of Chaos, the warped corridor ringing with Fenrisian steel and crackling disruptor fields, snapping bone and snarled oaths. They were the Young King's most favoured warriors, chosen as much for their brutal sword-skill as for their combat experience. Against them the lesser daemons of the wyrdrealm, for all their rage, could do little.

And they were as nothing compared to their lord. Ragnar was a blur of unrestrained, natural-born violence. He'd abandoned the protective knot of the pack, striking out further down the corridor. Normally a Wolf Lord's personal retinue would have striven to defend their leader, adopting a formation that covered his back and protected his blind spots. But the Blackpelts knew better than to try that when the battle-joy had taken hold of their Young King.

Ragnar killed. It was simple. It was brutal. It was a terrible thing to watch, something that even his Wolf Guard treated with reverence. He was a blur of perpetual motion, never hesitating, never stopping, not even thinking. It was instinctive, deadly, the result of transhuman genetic engineering and the warrior conditioning of an already martial race, combined with over a century's bloody battlefield experience. *Frostfang*, Ragnar's ancient chainsword, was a blur, a halo of tearing teeth that left a haze of viscera hanging in the air around the lunging, spinning shape of the Wolf Lord.

He danced the warrior's dance, darting death that sawed through limbs and skulls and torsos and sent clutches of nightmares tumbling back to hell together.

Inquisitor de Mornay was only half aware of him. His plasma pistol was in one fist, venting steam from its coolant valve as he fired down from his palanquin. Sister Marie stood behind the rocking platform, hammering her combi-flamer into the mass of bug-eyed, snapping monsters clawing at them. Her black power armour was pitted and scarred, its holy surface befouled with a sheen of dripping ichor. She was reciting the Thirty-Third Prayer of Revelatory Salvation in low, hard tones as she killed, eyes gleaming with the fires of a warrior given sacred purpose. When the tide rose too high she triggered the flamer, and the corridor was filled with the stench of roasting warpspawn and the dancing light of blazing promethium as it ate hungrily at the shrieking creatures.

Subconsciously, the inquisitor was regretting not bringing the arco-flagellant, or donning his exo-plate. A part of him had hoped the rumours of *Mjalnar*'s corruption would prove to be unfounded, and the last thing he'd wanted was VX Nine-Eighteen rampaging through the star fort's narrow corridors. That was a mistake he wouldn't make again.

The daemons screamed with fury, enraged at the fact that their trick had been discovered. Without the intervention of de Mornay they would have driven Ragnar and his packs to the brink of turning, the Wolves' frustration with the star fort's seemingly endless, deserted corridors leading to the triumph of the Canis Helix. The Young King would have become the Young Beast.

And then, as sudden as it had begun, the ambush was over. The last daemons flickered and vanished with fading howls. The walls were whole once more, painted with dripping slime and riddled with bolt-rounds. Ragnar twisted to a stop in a low crouch, *Frostfang* held upwards, its kraken teeth still revving. The Wolf Lord remained frozen for a second, fangs bared, a single twitch all that was needed to trigger another killing spree. But none came. He stood and deactivated the chainsword, wiping a globule of shorn wyrdmeat from the casing.

'I needed that,' he growled.

'We can't stay here,' de Mornay said. His plasma pistol whined as it recharged, hot in his gloved grip.

'We aren't going to,' Ragnar said. 'Pack, on me.' He keyed his vox. 'Report.'

'*It's an ambush, lord!*' shouted Hostor over the link. The sounds of fighting were clearly audible in the background.

'The whole station is a trap,' Ragnar replied. 'Objective remains the same. Secure the command deck.'

'*Understood,*' said Hostor, the word underpinned by the sound of a revving chainsword.

'The other packs?' Uller asked as Ragnar broke the link.

'Unresponsive,' the Wolf Lord said grimly. 'World Wolf pattern. We have an objective to secure.'

'Where are you going?' de Mornay demanded as the Wolves moved off down the corridor.

'The command deck, of course,' Ragnar called back. 'Via the nearest vox terminal. Someone has to warn the rest of the Chapter that those Grey Knights were right.'

'The place is infested,' de Mornay said. 'We'd be better off evacuating and bombarding the station with your fleet.'

'I've seen worse cases of corruption,' Ragnar said. 'Haven't you, inquisitor? Besides, do you think that little scrap was enough to satisfy me?' The Wolf laughed.

Glowering, de Mornay rolled his platform in the pack's wake.

The World Wolf's Lair, Svellgard

'All packs, focus fire!'

Sven didn't need to clarify the target. The burning Bloodthirster was hurtling through the air like a comet, aimed unerringly at the heart of the World Wolf's Lair. It roared a challenge as it came, the sound seeming to shake the whole moon to its core. The receding waters around the island churned as yet more daemons joined the assault, answering the great slaughter-lord's defiance. For a moment, just a split-second, Sven thought he understood what it meant to be a mortal, armoured only in plates of metal, facing down the molten, white-hot fury of a god's avatar. He wondered if Jarl Stormpelt had known the same feeling when he had duelled the same monster, all those centuries ago.

Bloodhowlers and Deathwolves opened fire as one, filling the air with death. Bolter rounds, streaking missiles, spears of plasma and heavy las hammered at the greater daemon, ordnance enough to decimate an army in seconds.

It didn't even slow. Missiles burst in the air before they could strike, detonated by the thing's infernal heat. Hard rounds became molten spray that pattered from its craggy black hide. A demolisher cannon shell detonated in front of it, the shrapnel barely touching it. The daemon burst through the smoke with its roar still ringing through the fire-streaked air, its blazing eyes fixed on the control keep. On Sven.

'Leave me,' the Wolf Lord said. Olaf looked at him, saying nothing.

'Do not question my orders, long-tooth,' Sven growled, turning to face him.

'Do not question our loyalty, pup,' Olaf replied, unsheathing his wolf claws. Around him the other Wolf Guard activated their own weapons, the air filled with snapping blue energy.

'I will not have the greatest of the Firehowlers die here,' Sven said. 'I am going to order Yngfor to target this keep and launch one of the World Wolf's Claws.'

'It would be minutes before it struck,' Olaf countered. 'You're a tolerable fighter on a good day, pup, but do you really think you can keep that piece of wyrd-dung busy for that long?' The rest of the Bloodguard growled their agreement.

'Bloodhowl!' The voice interrupted Sven before he could respond. He turned to see Harald Deathwolf pull himself from the access hatch up onto the keep's battlement. The big Wolf Lord was grinning.

'Not you too,' Sven said.

Harald just laughed and slammed a hand into his pauldron. His Wolf Guard, the Riders of Morkai, were following him out onto the parapets.

'That's one big beast,' Harald said as he watched Infurnace's fiery approach. 'I want its skull for my hall. Maybe I'll take the name Stormpelt, eh?' The Riders of Morkai snarled and beat fists against their breastplates. The Bloodguard responded in kind, the two grey-pelted packs facing one another down like feuding Blood Claws.

'Yngfor,' Sven snapped into the vox, linking to the depths of the keep, where the Long Fangs were helping to coordinate the fire support.

'*We can't stop it, lord,*' the Long Fang said over the background thunder of heavy bolters. '*Nothing can touch it.*'

'Cease fire,' Sven ordered. 'And launch one of the Claws. Lock onto this keep's coordinates.'

'*But lord–*'

'Don't argue,' Sven said. 'Just do it. Then get to the secondary command bunker.' He cut the link.

Harald had activated his frost axe, the disruptor field snapping along Glacius' twin heads.

'It will kill us all,' Sven said.

'It'll kill you, Bloodhowl, you fangless pup,' Harald said. 'Not me. I told you, I want its head.' He pointed Glacius at the oncoming daemon, and howled a challenge.

Despite himself, Sven grinned. He activated Frostclaw.

Infurnace struck. Its great, cloven hooves slammed into the keep's parapet. Rockcrete crumbled, slamming back into the Wolf Guard. Sven bowed into the wave of debris, auto-stabilisers struggling to keep him upright, feeling the wreckage hammer and score his armour. The daemon found purchase on the edge of the battlements and cracked its whip, the chains rattling. It roared its defiance in the Wolves' faces, the heat like a melta's passing shot. The air shimmered and wolf pelt tokens singed and caught light.

Harald struck first. Glacius was an arc of ice carving through a furnace's heat, straight towards the daemon's head. The blow never landed. The Bloodthirster moved with a speed that should have been impossible for a creature of its size, smashing aside Harald's blow with the spiked haft of its own burning axe. The Wolf Lord stumbled, and a strike from the creature's whip slammed him down onto his back.

Gunnar Felsmite was the first to die. The Wolf Guard threw himself at the monster, his claws sparking. One set buried in the thing's thigh, cracking the black skin. Flames burst from the wounds. Gunnar twisted the claws free a split-second before the daemon beheaded him. The jetting blood steamed in the super-heated air.

Denr Longblade was next. He swung his longsword up in a parry, but the axe simply carved through the steel and then down through ceramite, flesh and bone, cutting the Space Wolf in half.

Nils Ironclaw and Fior Frostmane died together, both gutted by a single vicious swing. The blow struck Sven too, meeting the head of Frostclaw. The force of it rung down through the axe, throwing it from the Wolf Lord's numb grasp.

A single second's opportunity. A moment amidst the fire and blood. Fangs bared, Sven threw himself inside the greater daemon's guard and thrust Firefang up. The chainsword's teeth bit deep into its lower torso, chewing through brass plate and wyrdflesh. Sven thrust harder with both hands, roaring as he forced the blazing sword up to its hilt.

'I am a Firehowler,' he snarled. 'I am a son of the Fire Breather. You cannot burn me.'

Infurnace backhanded him, the blow sending the Wolf Lord grinding across the parapet's bloody rockcrete in a shower of sparks. He came to a stop next to Frostclaw. He managed to get a hand on its haft again before the Bloodthirster's whip lashed out, chains snapping around his outstretched vambrace. With a grunt Sven found himself dragged up onto his knees. The rockcrete beneath him cracked and split as the beast dug its hooves in.

'*Sven!*' Olaf's wolf claws slammed down on the whip's taut length. The chains shattered and Sven slumped back, hand still on the haft of his weapon. Infurnace roared as Istun swung his power axe at the beast's back, hacking into flesh that had the consistency of coal. It spun with its terrible speed, and the Bloodguard narrowly ducked a swing of its axe.

'You've done enough,' Olaf snarled, dragging Sven to his feet.

'Yngfor,' Sven voxed.

'*Still inputting the coordinates, lord,*' the Long Fang replied.

'Then do it faster!'

'*Lord, you'll destroy half the island!*'

'You have to go,' Olaf snarled in Sven's face. 'Some of the Great Company must survive.' Behind him Istun bellowed with pain as the Bloodthirster's huge axe cleaved through his right arm. Uuntir slammed his thunder hammer into the beast's knee, but even that mighty weapon did little more than crack its dark skin. Flames licked from the wound as Infurnace shattered the Bloodguard's storm shield with a single stroke.

'Firehowler!' It was Harald. The Wolf Lord's nose was bloody and broken, and his eyes blazed with battle fury. But instead of pointing at the greater daemon, he gestured upwards. Sven followed his finger.

Directly overhead, a patch of Svellgard's slate-grey clouds was flaring with a blood-red light. A second later the voice of his flagship's vox hus-carl, in orbit above, crackled in his ear.

'*Lord, a ship of the crusade fleet has just launched a lance strike against Svellgard's surface.*' Suddenly it made sense. Sven looked at Harald.

'Run.'

Transit line four hundred and three, the Underworld, Midgardia

The transport tunnel resounded with screams and the tearing of flesh. Around Egil Iron Wolf his brothers fought, back and forth across the rail lines of the sub-crust highway, hacking and chopping into the resilient, dead flesh of the plaguebearers. The necrotised daemons felt nothing, and hacked back at the Wolves with their own rusting blades, trying to drive them against the packed earth of the tunnel wall.

The Nurgle Herald that challenged Egil was no warrior. The Iron Wolf real-ised that, to his surprise, as he darted back from the daemon's first clumsy swing of its pitted broadsword. It was obese and rotten to its core, reduced to shuffling after the Wolf Lord as it tried to swipe at him. Its blade would not kill Egil. But the miasma of filth that surrounded it might.

The Iron Wolf lunged, razor-fast, the wolf claws of his right fist blazing with power. They punched through the daemon's breast with ease, four points searing through pox-scarred flesh, yellow fat and cancer-gnawed bones. Egil ripped downwards, spilling a slew of vile innards, seething with fat maggots.

The Herald laughed.

Egil's visor was awash with red runes. The air around the Herald and his infernal Tallyband was hyper-toxic. Pulsating puff-ball growths infesting the plaguebearers' skin were bursting and popping all around the embattled Space Wolves, clouding the air with a noxious fug of green daemonspores. His auto-senses told him his armour was literally disintegrating, layers of ceramite being eaten away every second. When it was gone, he'd be a puddle of rotting matter in the time it took to draw breath.

Egil thrust desperately at the Herald with both fists, its broadsword clanging uselessly off his pockmarked breastplate. The wolf claws tore deep again, carving up its engorged folds, spilling pus-blood and writhing worms. The thing just tried to stab him again. It was impervious. A move-ment flickered through the spore cloud behind it.

'Go back to the wyrdrealm, you rancid scum,' Egil snarled as he embraced the Herald, both sets of claws locked deep inside its noxious body. A warning sound wailed in his ear as his armour lost integrity, the ceramite gone, the shaped plates of adamantium and plasteel beneath stripped almost to their servos. His breath caught, intake filters clogged with green slime. The Herald was laughing again. It leaned into Egil's helm, worm-tongue caressing his audio receptors.

'I am Phugulus, wolf-man,' it croaked. 'And I come bearing a message.'

Egil buried his claws deeper, trying to find something vital, pushing against a seemingly impervious mountain of decay. The daemon's phlegm-choked words echoed around his skull.

'*Logan Grimnar is dead.*'

'Moln!' Egil roared, and flung himself backwards, claws sliding free of the weeping flesh. The daemon stumbled, and a bolt of blue lightning split the green smog behind it. It struck the Herald's horned skull with a thunder-clap that echoed back from the highway tunnel's sloping walls.

Phugulus exploded. Moln's charged thunder hammer, swung two-handed, burst the bloated monstrosity like a huge ulcer, sending out a shockwave of gory pus and burning meat so thick that it physically drove Egil back a pace. The Herald's demise was met by a wail from its plaguebearers.

'Krak grenades, collapse the hole,' Egil snapped, slashing down the near-est lesser daemons as they tried to recover. He was rewarded seconds later by a trio of splitting detonations as anti-tank grenades collapsed the maw-tunnel the plaguebearers had crawled in through. He shouldered another daemon to the ground and stamped hard, snapping first its ribs and then its neck. More fungal balls burst as the daemons died, but with-out the Herald the air's toxicity readout on Egil's visor had already begun to drop. He swung at another plaguebearer that had buried its blade in Olaf Ironhide's knee joint, cutting its head from its shoulders as Olaf ripped the blade free.

'It's nothing,' the Ironwolf grunted as a scream split the tunnel's chok-ing air.

The plague wyrm still lived. It was being hammered by the Champi-ons of Fenris, its loathsome white flesh riddled with bolt-rounds and torn by chainswords and wolf claws. Yet still it healed, its unnatural physiol-ogy impervious to even the most violent blows of the enraged Wolves. Its fang-ringed maw snapped hungrily at them, driving part of the pack back. Judging by the shape bulging grotesquely halfway down its gelati-nous gullet it had already snapped up one of the Space Wolves, his scream now silenced.

'That thing must die,' Egil said. 'We cannot let them infest any more of the underground. On me.'

The Ironguard fell upon the wyrm's twisting, writhing length. Their power weapons carved out great chunks of flesh and stinking, misshapen organs, cursing the thing back to the wyrdrealm as it splattered them with sizzling yellow slime. Egil aimed a strike for the folds beneath the Wolf who was being slowly swallowed, slicing the membranous skin open. Like some foul parody of a birth, the remains tumbled from the wound in a cascade of steaming digestive juices.

The Wolf started screaming again.

Egil stabbed down without hesitation, piercing what remained of his skull and ending his blind, acid-melted agony.

'In the Allfather's name, die!' came a shout. Throwing caution aside, Lenold had flung himself directly towards the wyrm. As it reared before him he emptied his bolter on full auto into its maw, howling as he blasted apart fangs and flesh in a storm of mass-reactive shells.

The wyrm struck, snaking down beneath Lenold's barrage to snap at his legs. The sudden, sinuous strike pitched the Wolf from his feet. In an instant the Champion of Fenris was half locked in the thing's shattered jaw, bolter falling from his grasp as he sought purchase on its slippery skin. He grunted in pain as its sucking maw grated through his power armour.

'Lenold!' Egil threw out both hands, claws retracting as he grasped onto the Wolf's vambrace. His armour hummed and whirred as he dug his heels in, battling the daemon's strength. It twisted and shook its head like a hound, dragging Lenold a foot deeper into its acidic gut.

'Give... me... a grenade,' Lenold managed between clenched fangs.

'I'll have to let go,' Egil snarled.

'Do it.'

Egil released Lenold's vambrace. In an instant the Champion of Fenris was dragged down by the thing's horrific peristalsis, but not before the Iron Wolf was able to smack a primed krak grenade into his gauntlet.

'Back!' Egil barked. He threw himself away from the wyrm, dragging the nearest Champion with him. The tunnel highway echoed with the thunder-clap of a detonation, and once again a jet of stinking offal splattered the Wolf Lord. He scrambled back to his feet, wiping yellow viscera from his visor's lenses.

The wyrm was headless, but still far from dead. It writhed madly in a pool of its own effluvium, as though still seeking bodies to devour. Even as Egil watched he could see its flesh growing and reknitting, the nubs of half-formed fangs sprouting around the decapitated skin.

'Focus your attacks,' he ordered. 'Start fighting like one pack and we may finish this damned thing.' He triggered his claws again and swung for the daemon's gaping wound.

Together Egil, his Ironguard and the Champions of Fenris ripped into the plague wyrm's remains, hacking and stabbing and slicing at the wound torn by Lenold's sacrifice. Beneath the savage fury of the Wolves, even the daemon's powers of regeneration were not strong enough. The sons of Russ fought on, drenched helm to boot in wyrdling filth, ripping the thing apart with their gauntlets, ploughing waist-deep through pulsing, sucking flesh. Egil's claws finally tore through the last hunk of its meat, splattering it in dripping chunks against the tunnel's wall. He spread his arms and loosed a rare howl, turned mechanical-sounding by his vox amplifiers. The Ironguard and the Champions joined him, united in their slaughterous exaltation. The noise echoed eerily down the tunnel as the stinking remains of the wyrm shimmered and, finally, flickered from existence.

The hunt for the Great Wolf would go on.

Ramilies-class star fort, designate Mjalnar

Ragnar beat the horror's head against the side of the vox station. The thing simply giggled, gibbering some arcane nonsense. With a snarl the Wolf Lord swung *Frostfang*, splitting apart the amorphous pink flesh and revving the weapon until the thing imploded into nothingness. From the nothingness, popping into being like a conjurer's trick, two lesser blue horrors lunged at him. He beat them both down with his chainsword, spitting on their shifting remains. Finally, they too vanished from reality.

'Room secured,' Ragnar growled, panting.

With the maleficarum trickery broken the vox terminal hadn't been far from their boarding point, but nor had the way been easy. More daemons had dropped from a service hatch, mottled black furies with fluttering wings. Confined to the corridor, they'd been butchered in seconds. The beast of Nurgle in front of the terminal's doors had been a more difficult challenge. De Mornay had eventually vaporised its bloated skull with a plasma bolt after Sister Marie's combi-flamer had set it alight.

The vox terminal beyond had been filled with capering horrors, who let out an almighty cacophony when the Wolves blasted their way in. Ragnar had kicked the first in the face as wyrdfire had begun to coalesce around its flailing arms, smashing it into a hundred glass shards that reflected back crazed images before they vanished.

The rest of the horrors soon followed. Svengril and Tor secured the far door while Ragnar activated the star fort's vox uplink. After a moment the monitors blinked into life, and a low hum permeated the room. The glow underlit Ragnar's smile.

'This is Ragnar Blackmane to all *Vlka Fenryka*. The Ramilies-class star fort designate *Mjalnar* is currently subject to a daemonic infestation. It is being cleansed. Repeat, it is being cleansed. All forces take note, but no reinforcements are required.' He ended the recording and waited while it uploaded to the beacon, the transmission cogitator rattling.

'"No reinforcements are required",' de Mornay echoed. He sounded incredulous.

Ragnar shrugged.

'The corruption isn't as bad as Krom made out it would be.'

'You nearly tore each other apart,' de Mornay said, looking from Ragnar to the Blackpelts who crouched tense, silent, waiting for his next order.

'That was before we found an enemy to fight,' Ragnar said, without a hint of irony.

'Give me the vox horn.'

'What?'

'I said give me the vox, I need to send a transmission.'

'To whom?'

'You forget yourself, Wolf,' de Mornay snapped, his voice suddenly loud. 'I am a member of the God-Emperor's Holy Inquisition. The sum total of those I answer to in this galaxy is nil, bar Him on Terra. Now *give me the warp-damned vox horn!*'

One of Ragnar's Wulfen growled at him. De Mornay turned to the bestial warrior, eyes blazing.

'Be silent!' he barked. The Wulfen took a crouched pace backwards, eyes wide. Its packmates whimpered.

Ragnar stared at the inquisitor. For the briefest moment, he could see the fiery young warrior that had resisted the Dark Angels on Calva Senioris, still bloodied, still unbowed. Wordlessly, he passed the vox horn to him. The disparity in sizes between the towering, armour-plated, ichor-streaked Wolf Lord and the old, palanquin-bound mortal only emphasised the latter's strength of will.

'This is Lord Inquisitor Banist de Mornay, Ordo Hereticus, Divisio Segmentum Obscurus, ident code four five seven, seven three eight alpha. Voice scan initiate.' Ragnar looked at his pack-kin, all staring at the glaring inquisitor. The voice scan must have come back positive, for de Mornay continued.

'Requesting clearance to all data files on ordo forces currently operating within the Fenris System, priority A-one.' He entered a string of galactic coordinates and location tag-codes. 'Combat group Omicron, Ordo Malleus Chamber Militant Third Brotherhood. Establish link.'

Ragnar's surprised expression was replaced by a frown as de Mornay spoke again.

'Captain Stern, this is Lord Inquisitor Banist de Mornay of the Ordo Hereticus, currently transmitting from the star fort *Mjalnar*.'

'What're you doing?' Ragnar demanded, but de Mornay ignored him.

'Yes, we've met resistance. Corruption level three beta or kappa, no higher. But I suspect it will grow worse the deeper we get.'

Ragnar turned his back on the inquisitor and gestured to Tor. 'Take point, we're moving on.'

The Blackpelt nodded eagerly, punching the door's activation rune. Beyond it lay another empty corridor. Ragnar scowled.

De Mornay caught up with them quickly, palanquin grinding and juddering on its servitor tracks.

'What was that?' Ragnar said without bothering to look at the inquisitor.

'I called in reinforcements.'

'I told you we don't need any. I have six more packs waiting with the fleet, they only need a word from me to board and storm this accursed place.'

'Then forgive me if the thought of being surrounded by your Wolves isn't the comfort it was before I saw you nearly turn into ravening monsters,' de Mornay said. Ragnar snarled, but the retort died in his throat as the walls shuddered, and a fresh wave of wyrdlings launched their ambush.

The Void, Fenris System

Stern cut the vox-link and turned to the *Star Drake*'s gunnery huscarl.

'That's enough. I have new orders. Helmsman, set a course for *Mjalnar*'s last recorded location. I shall provide more detailed coordinates momentarily.'

As the Space Wolves serfs scurried to do their new masters' bidding, Stern returned his gaze to the strike cruiser's viewing port. Beyond it *Gormenjarl* drifted through the sea of stars. The mighty Ramilies was no more. It listed, oxygen venting from its shattered spires and bulkheads, surrounded by a halo of burned, broken debris. Its gun decks lay blown apart and its docking spines twisted, while a single ruthlessly accurate, point-blank strike from *Star Drake*'s main cannon had demolished its command deck and whatever slinking, squirming horrors had lurked in the darkness within it.

The star fort was still far from completely annihilated, but it was badly wrecked. Stern had tagged it with a priority beacon, forbidding entry to it by Inquisitorial mandate. When time allowed, the Emperor's servants would return to finish the job he had started. For now, though, he was needed elsewhere.

'Brethren, perform the Rites of Cleansing and rearm. We are not done yet. Give thanks and praise to the Emperor that He has blessed us with further purpose this day.'

The World Wolf's Lair, Svellgard

Like a spear cast by the Allfather from distant Terra, a lance of fire fell from Svellgard's heavens and destroyed all it touched. The pillar of flame ignited the grey clouds, burning them away and leaving a halo of radiance around its crackling shaft. It struck the very heart of the island housing the World Wolf's Lair, slamming down onto the parapets of the central fire control keep.

Infurnace burned. The monstrous greater daemon had proven impervious to every hard round and munition fired at it. Against the force of a concentrated lance strike, however, even it was not untouchable. The ultra-heavy energy beam caught the Bloodthirster at its heart. As the battlements around it shattered, Infurnace stood transfixed, hooves braced and arms spread wide, its roar of fury melding with the thunderous crack of the beam's impact. The daemon began to disintegrate, flesh turning brittle, bursting apart, wings snapping and becoming ash. The light of the lance strike engulfed it, as the walls of the keep melted and collapsed.

As swiftly as it had come, the pillar of energy blinked from existence, its thunderclap rolling across the ever-receding sea and echoing back from the nearby islands.

The noise woke Sven. For a moment the impact with the dirt had combined with the sensory overload of the lance's strike to short out even his enhanced senses. His chrono display told him he'd been unconscious for a little over thirty seconds. In that time the keep had gone, replaced by a crater of fused rockcrete blocks and melted plasteel girders.

The Wolf Lord dragged himself to his feet. Beside him Harald stirred, blinking in the aftermath of the strike. Clotting blood on his brow had joined that of his broken nose, matting his hair. Sven had grabbed him when he'd realised what was happening and triggered his jump pack, Longbound, driving the modified dual-vector thrust Valkyris pattern to full turbo. According to his visor display the strain had momentarily shorted out the pack's lift capacity. Kregga and Olaf had both leapt clear as well, dragging a pair of Harald's Riders of Morkai with them. Of the rest of the twin packs, however, there was no sign.

Frostclaw was embedded in the stony earth a few yards from the deep furrow that marked Sven's brutal landing. The Wolf Lord limped to the axe and tugged it free, absently noting the injuries scrolling across his visor. A twisted right calf and two fractured ribs, along with a sprained left hand. He tried to flex it but could not. Pain flared momentarily before it was overwhelmed by the stimms pumping through his body. He gritted his fangs. Focus.

The edge of the crater where the keep had once stood was smoking. Sven hefted his frost axe and limped towards it. He heard Olaf call out behind him as the Bloodguard gathered his wits, but he ignored him. His wounds throbbed, but he ignored them too. He had to know.

His jump pack recharged with a ping, its rune blinking green again. He reached the crater's lip, mounting the rubble of its outer edge with some difficulty. Beyond, he found himself looking down into a tangled bowl of wreckage, the keep's remains melted and fused together by raw heat.

At its centre stood Infurnace.

At first Sven thought the daemon had been petrified. It stood with its arms wide, its flesh now ashen and stiff, its wings gone. Like some nightmarish statue, it reigned in silence over the devastation surrounding it, a testimony to total annihilation in a galaxy of eternal war.

Then it moved, its horned head turning fractionally to face Sven, ash drifting from it. The Wolf Lord saw the fires that still smouldered, deep in the cracked pits of its eyes.

Sven howled, and triggered Longbound. The pack flared in harmony with the Firehowler's rage, launching him at full turbo into the pit on a pillar of fire. Infurnace moved, but only slightly, as though battling its own paralysis, parts of its burned form breaking and crumbling. It could not stop the Wolf, not now. Sven struck it from above, boots-first, the impact shattering whatever remained of the daemon's spine. In a great cascade of ash and sparking embers he crashed through the greater daemon, and Svellgard's cruel wind finally whipped its remains away. For a moment, the Wolf Lord's advanced hearing detected the distant echo of an angry roar. Then the last of the dust settled, and all was still.

Sven rose from his crouch amidst the wreckage, and turned slowly back towards the crater lip. The crack in his fused ribs ached. Harald, Olaf, and the surviving Bloodguard were standing looking down at him, splattered in grime, blood and ichor. Sven bared his fangs.

'Find out whose ship did this,' he snarled, pointing at the rubble beneath him.

Iron Requiem, *in high orbit above Svellgard*

The machine-spirit of *Iron Requiem* thrilled with the knowledge of another successful strike. Hardwired into the ancient warship via his command throne, Iron Captain Terrek felt the ship's exaltation as his own. It brought joy to a soul that had not experienced such an emotion in over a century, momentarily warming cold synth-skin and making the Iron Hand's auto-heart thud a little faster. For a moment – just a fraction of a second – the Iron Captain remembered what it had been like to be human.

And then the moment passed, a statistical anomaly, subsumed and made irrelevant by the cold, hard reality of the present. The Space Marine shifted in his throne, data cables rattling. It would not do to become so engrossed in the triumphs and failings of his own flagship, no matter how tempting. As much as it vexed him, his duties demanded more than a purely machine instinct.

Still, the exhilaration was not entirely misplaced. The lance strike had been accurate to a thousandth of a degree, a noteworthy achievement even for the *Requiem*'s venerable targeting systems. It had also resulted in the annihilation of the target. The heat signature being emitted by the never-born entity no longer registered on the *Requiem*'s powerful augurs. The flow of information Terrek was constantly receiving via his auto-senses estimated that fatal collateral damage consisted of no more than two to three dozen individuals and some rockcrete and plasteel command structures. Again, for a lance strike into the heart of a contested battlefield, it was an excellent final result. One to be replicated, and swiftly.

Terrek requested further data. It flowed to him without hesitation, ramping up his sensory input, his mind a blur of scrolling, ever-changing digits and statistical readouts. Beneath the frenetic activity of his neural nodes, his deeper consciousness swam, torpid, heavy and cold. He would like – it considered – to petition the Iron Council for a transferral to the position of Master of the Fleet. The current Master was reaching the end of his independent productivity, weighed down as he was by almost half a millennium of augmentations. Given his experience and machine-bred aptitude in the field, Terrek considered the likelihood of the success of his application to be as high as seventy-eight per cent.

Such thoughts did not register with the main thrust of the Iron Captain's attention. He was busy communing with the other ships of the fleet, touching upon their machine-spirits directly without having to waste time going through the tedium of vox-channels and the sluggishness of fleshy minds, so prone to misunderstanding and obstinacy. There could be no delay. They had to strike, as the old Medusan phrase went, while the iron still burned. He estimated a window of opportunity no wider than a few minutes, after which the optimality of a full-scale orbital bombardment would begin to decrease.

As though in answer to his thoughts, a worrisome miscalculation reared its ugly head amidst the stream of data codes. Something nagged in the Iron Captain's ear. It took him a moment to realise it was the click of his personal vox. A transmission.

As though from a dream, the drifting, distant voice of his vox seneschal reached him. He dismissed the tiny man with a single, raised silver digit, already aware of the contents of his message.

'Epathus,' Terrek said, his voice, for a moment, indistinguishable from that of a mind-wiped translation servitor.

'*Iron Captain,*' the Ultramarine replied. He was currently onboard his own flagship, now holding station on the other side of Svellgard, between the moon and Frostheim. Even over the vox, he managed to somehow sound altogether more human than Terrek.

'I am preparing firing solutions, brother-captain,' Terrek said, struggling to draw his mind far enough out of the machine cant to formulate a diplomatic response. 'I must not be disturbed.'

'*Firing solutions for targets on the surface of Svellgard?*'

'Your logic is flawless on this occasion, brother-captain.' The last word bore a suffix of binary code, a sudden blurt that Terrek had to clamp down on, like a tick. A shadow of discomfort passed through his thoughts, soon gone.

'*With respect, such a course of action has been advised against by the rest of the crusade fleet, including Supreme Grand Master Azrael,*' Epathus said. '*Except in the direst of circumstances.*'

'I compute the three identifiable warp rifts below Svellgard's oceans to constitute dire circumstances,' Terrek replied.

'*But shelling the Wolves from orbit on one of their own moons would represent another,'* Epathus countered. *'They will already be furious at the damage your first strike has caused.'*

'The damage may have included as few as two-dozen casualties.'

'Two-dozen too many in their eyes, I assure you.'

'Four times as many are likely to have perished at the hand of the greater daemon assailing them had I not struck.'

'A fact that will only antagonise them even further. I have served alongside the Wolves before, Iron Captain, on Granthia Nine. Depriving them of a great kill is considered a grievous insult.'

'That is wholly illogical,' Terrek said, feeling the faintest stirrings of anger flicker in the depths of his neuro-circuitry.

'But it stands,' Epathus said. *'If you want an unchecked bombardment now, you risk initiating a full-scale civil war. Their twin fleets in orbit alongside us will retaliate, and that will only be the start.'*

The numbers had stopped. They hung in their thousands in the air around Terrek, blinking insistently. An algorithm left incomplete did not portend to good things, and the Ultramarine's interruption had pushed his calculations beyond their time threshold. By now it was likely that the Space Wolves had sought shelter in their lair's subterranean bunkers. Casualty ratios from an orbital bombardment would be slashed by over two thirds.

Terrek could no longer destroy both the neverborn and Svellgard's Space Wolf defenders at a single stroke.

Why he would want to do so was not entirely certain, beyond the fact that his logic engines had traced the reason for the crusade fleet's existence back to the persecution of the sons of Russ. Terrek was simply attempting to cut out the wasteful intermediary experience. The Ultramarines, however, clearly possessed less foresight. He scratched at one of his few remaining patches of human flesh, white and scarred beneath the housing of his right cranial bionic optic.

'Very well, Epathus,' he said. 'I commend myself to your alternatives, whatever they may be.'

'Not an orbital bombardment,' the Ultramarine said. *'But an orbital assault. Let us demonstrate to the Wolves the power of the Imperium, and what happens to the enemies of that power. That will show us where they truly stand.'*

> *Transit Line four hundred and three,*
> *the Underworld, Midgardia*

Egil wiped green daemonspoor sludge from his helmet's vox grille and the thermal waste dissipaters on his backpack, switching to his armour's internal oxygen reserve with a thought-impulse.

'If more of them carry their infections down here we won't be able to continue our hunt for the Great Wolf,' Moln said grimly. Like all the Space

Wolves still with Egil, the few scraps of his armour not coated in a crusting layer of slime shone scarred silver, stripped to the lowest layers by the nightmarish atmosphere.

'I agree,' said Orven. 'If the surface has been completely overrun we do not have long before they begin to infest these tunnels as well.'

'But is it overrun?' Bjorn wondered out loud. 'What of Conran's signal? It comes from the Magma Gates, does it not?'

Egil nodded, but stayed silent. Conran's distress transmission had been weighing on him since he had detected it. Suddenly things had grown complicated again. Had his Great Company evacuated Midgardia as he'd ordered? Or did Conran's presence point to a larger contingent of Ironwolves? If not then why was he here? And what had caused him to loop a remote distress pattern from the peak of the Magma Gates?

Suddenly, his quest for the Great Wolf did not look so noble, or quite as selfless. He had abandoned his own Great Company, his own pack-kin, during a difficult and dangerous operation. He had left them leaderless. Such an act harmed the integrity of the whole strike force. Even now he could feel the distress of the surviving Champions of Fenris as they sought guidance following Lenold's demise. When pack leaders died and the links in the chain of command were shattered, the warriors of Fenris returned to their instinctive state, giving deference to the alpha. Until one established itself, a leaderless pack could be prone to prevarication and ill-considered decisions. Egil could feel just such uncertainty creeping through the Wolves now, in the Champions and even among his own Ironguard.

He glanced at Grimnar's battered, gilded thunderwolf skull. It was cradled in the claws of a crouching Wulfen, the beast looking up earnestly at Egil. For a moment the Iron Wolf considered the paradox, of the symbol of one of the greatest Wolves ever to have lived being held in the malformed hands of something that they couldn't even be sure wasn't wyrd-tainted. Egil realised, however, that it had taken a moment's introspection to come to that conclusion. When he had first seen the Wulfen with the Great Wolf's broken crown, he had seen only a wolf-brother guarding one of their Chapter's sacred relics. The other Wolf Lords could yet disagree, but Egil knew he had come to accept the place of his cursed brethren within the ranks. They were all one.

The thought made up his mind. He addressed the combined pack.

'We are returning to the surface,' he said. 'If only momentarily. We must discover what is occurring there, how we might be of assistance, as well as resupply and receive reinforcements. If the situation is stable, we shall return here immediately to resume our hunt.'

As he'd expected, there were some growls of challenge. He faced them down, as unbending as the iron that marked his crest.

'I am a Wolf Lord, leader of eleven packs. Honour demanded I come here seeking our lost king. I do not deny, I desired it in my own hearts as well. But I cannot spurn my duties any more. I must see to my Great Company and coordinate the defence of this world, or whatever remains of it. I have promised to return here as soon as I am able, and I cement that now with an oath, before you all. I swear I will find the Great Wolf.'

The growls became more approving, and there were nods, even among the Champions of Fenris.

'Those who wish to stay here can remain, and continue the hunt,' Egil went on. 'But I shall be taking the thunderwolf's skull. I will keep it safe, until I can give it back to Logan Grimnar in person, and tell him the saga of the brave Wolves who fought and died to preserve it.' More approval. Egil knew from long experience that now, more than ever, it was time to show strength and certainty. He turned away from the pack, drawing up a chart of sub-level one on his visor. The nearest route to the Magma Gates began at a tunnel branching eastwards from the highway, a hundred and fifty paces back up the rail line. Egil began to walk.

Behind him, the entire pack followed.

Ramilies-class star fort, designate Mjalnar

Something terrible had taken up residence in what Ragnar's visor schematics called Strategorium Six-A. Before hell had overturned reality onboard *Mjalnar* the room had served as a small strategic amphitheatre, plasteel tiers lined with cogitator lecterns encircling a large, central holochart.

What had once been a space reserved for grave military discourse was now a playground for creatures with no fixed form. Horrors of Tzeentch leapt, skittered and cartwheeled around the buckling chitin plates that had been the strategorium's seat tiers. Above the holochart, like a nightmarish projection, a more powerful daemon had manifested in the shape of a huge, disembodied eye – a throbbing, lidless, veined orb with an iris that shimmered and changed with kaleidoscopic intensity, passing through every colour in the spectrum in a matter of heartbeats. The jet-black well of the slit pupil at the heart of the storm of colours seemed bottomless, fathomless, as equally impossible as both finite and infinite realities. Even just glancing at it, Ragnar felt a splitting migraine burst and flare behind his own eyes.

De Mornay was right. The nearer they drew to *Mjalnar*'s tainted heart, the worse the corruption was becoming.

'Blackpelts, into them!' Ragnar roared.

His Wolf Guard needed no encouragement. Howling oaths and spitting for luck, they flung themselves into the strategorium, slaughtering the nearest horrors without hesitation. Ragnar made straight for the wyrdling eye at the centre of the chamber, not meeting its gaze, focussing on each individual creature in his path as he split and carved and cut them into shards of riotous colour.

'Ragnar, wait!' shouted de Mornay from the chamber's entrance. His warning came too late. Over the now-familiar stench of the wyrd, Ragnar caught the distinctive, chlorine-like smell of ozone. A second later a thunderbolt of purple lightning snapped up out of the daemon eye's pupil.

The bolt struck Tor Wolfheart square in the breastplate, slamming him back into the side of the tier behind him. The Wolf slumped, his armour smoking, and for a moment Ragnar thought the Blackpelt was dead. Then he stirred, and Ragnar felt a rush of relief. It was short-lived.

Tor began to scream.

The Wolf Guard lurched forward onto his knees, his bolt pistol and power axe clattering to the deck. Gauntlets scrabbled at the breastplate where the lightning had earthed itself. Then the metal armour cracked, splitting the plate's embossed wolf's head. Tor's screaming grew worse.

Ragnar could only watch as something that looked like a fleshy maw ripped itself open in the Space Wolf's chest. The power armour cracked further, and the Wolf's organs began to thrust up out of his broken chest bones in a wash of blood. The terrible wound seemed to spread, ripping its way from Tor's thorax to his groin, the armour peeling back grotesquely. The Wolf Lord realised the Blackpelt was literally being turned inside out.

It was Sister Marie who ended the Wolf's misery. She engulfed Tor in a jet from her combi-flamer. The Wolf's screaming as the fire roasted his deformed body sounded almost relieved compared to what had come before. Finally he stopped, the once proud warrior reduced to indiscernible, burned flesh.

The daemonic eye unleashed its lightning again. The purple bolt cracked into the chitin flooring a yard to the left of Svengril the Younger. Fleshless, raw hands burst up out of the smoking impact, grasping at the Wolf's boots. Snarling, Svengril stamped them to a bloody mulch.

'Take cover,' Ragnar shouted, dropping down behind one of the cogitator lecterns ringing the strategorium's centre. The Wolves and Marie did likewise, de Mornay rolling his palanquin back out of the chamber.

'*We need reinforcements,*' the inquisitor voxed.

Ragnar didn't respond.

The horrors capering around the eye shrieked and bawled with insane laughter as their master fired again. A third bolt hammered the lectern Uller Greylock was crouched behind. In an eyeblink the cogitator was transformed into a cloud of multi-coloured butterflies that dispersed into the wyrd-charged air. Uller, wide-eyed, found himself sheltering behind nothing. The power of the daemonic orb's mutating energies crackled and snapped around it, and the horrors laughed all the harder, like children delighted with their parent's trick.

Howls interrupted them. The sound came from two of the four corridors branching off from the chamber, bouncing and echoing back from its high dome. Ragnar felt a thrill of relief, and rose in time to see his Blood Claws bust into the strategorium from two opposite sides.

Except they were no longer his Blood Claws.

What had once been Maegar's Pack and Asgeir's Allslayers were now something else. The mark of the Wulfen was unmistakably on them. They'd discarded their helmets and much of the armour plating on their legs and forearms, revealing wicked claws and bristling fur. They ripped into the strategorium like a primal tide, fangs bared, muscles straining as they savaged the horrors around the eye.

The thing attempted to defend itself. More lightning snapped from its centre. Wulfen convulsed, one collapsing with a howl as its bones were transformed into jelly, another choking as both arms ran and melted together into a fleshy tentacle that then proceeded to strangle the writhing Wolf to death. Another bolt struck like a chain, bouncing between three of the former Blood Claws. One was turned instantly into a frozen statue of glittering, multi-coloured gems, another collapsed as its blood was transformed into amasec, and the third simply vanished, leaving behind a small silver eye token.

Such warping, unnatural powers would have broken the sanity of most attackers instantly. To the Wulfen it only served to heighten their instinctive blood-fury. The two Murderpacks hit the centre of the chamber at the same time, leaping up onto the holochart from all sides. The eye managed one last bolt – turning a Wulfen into an open book that caught light and blazed away to nothingness – before their claws reached it. The thing deformed and burst with stinking, clear liquid as the Wolves' talons raked its cornea, ripping into the retina, gouging down to the vitreous centre. The daemonic pupil dilated, the slit of black nothingness widening, and with a wet thud it detonated, showering the chamber in gelatinous chunks.

The Wulfen howled their victory. Ragnar dropped down into the holo-pit, approaching them tentatively. The murderlust was still in their lupine eyes, and he knew himself how difficult such passions made it to differentiate between friend and foe, or understand when the battle was over.

One of the Wulfen on top of the chart, still splattered in the daemon eye's viscera, leapt down to face Ragnar. For a second, the beast held his gaze. Then it bowed. Only then did Ragnar recognise pack leader Maegar.

'Lord,' the transformed warrior managed to grunt from between its fangs. Ragnar felt an unexpected upsurge of remorse. This was his fault.

'Well met, Brother Maegar,' he said quietly, putting a hand on the Wulfen's slime-slick shoulder. It seemed to shudder, but maintained its deferential pose.

'Could not... control pack...' Maegar growled. 'Asgeir dead. One pack now.'

Ragnar understood. Beneath the strain of being led in circles through the infested star fort, Maegar and Asgeir's Blood Claws had succumbed en-masse to the curse. In the fighting to reach the strategorium Asgeir had fallen, and now the Wulfen had instinctively banded together into a single Murderpack.

Ragnar realised they were all staring at him, suddenly silent. It was no different to meeting the glare of a pack of wild Fenrisian wolves. Ragnar let his own gaze slowly travel over them, grip tightening fractionally on Maegar's shoulder.

'It is good to see you again, brothers,' he said, slowly and clearly. 'Now on, to the heart of this place. The wyrdling stink is still strong in the air. I would see it purged.'

As one, the Wulfen snarled their approval.

The Magma Gates, Midgardia

Egil reached sub-level seven before Olaf Ironhide collapsed. The pack assumed defensive positions as the Iron Wolf moved back down the transit line to the fallen warrior's side.

'The rot,' the Ironguard growled between gritted fangs. He nodded down at his leg. Despite the enhanced clotting agents in Space Marine blood, the injury dealt behind his knee plate by the plaguebearer's sword was still leaking a discoloured, yellowish fluid.

'Skol,' Egil said, supporting Olaf up into a sitting position. The servo-skull buzzed over the Space Wolf's leg, the bio-scanner implanted into its left eye socket bathing the scarred silver plates in a wash of green light. After a moment it blinked out, and the results uploaded to Egil's bionics.

'The organics of your left leg are severely infected,' he said after a moment.

'I know, lord. The damn spores got in.'

Egil nodded. 'I'm no Wolf Priest, but the limb is ruined and the infection will spread if we don't remove it. If it hasn't already.'

'You do it, lord,' Olaf said. He thrust his Fenrisian rune sword towards the Iron Wolf. Egil took it.

'Bjorn, help me with the plate,' he said. The two Wolves stripped the remains of the power armour from Olaf's leg. The stink of rotting meat filled the air as the final part was lifted away. Skol's stab-lumen lit up the ruin that had been the Ironguard's limb. The flesh around the initial wound had completely sloughed off, revealing yellow bone pitted with infection. The rest of the leg was rotten with fast-working decay. Some skin came off along with the power plates, revealing the dark-veined muscle beneath. Pus welled up from the injury, and the skin further up the limb was as white as a Fenrisian helwinter.

'Do it,' Olaf urged. 'Quickly.'

Egil didn't hesitate. While Bjorn lifted the leg, the Wolf Lord slid Olaf's combat knife in a circular motion around the Space Marine's upper thigh. Dark, infected blood pattered on the tunnel transit's dirt floor. The flesh parted, and Egil began to cut into the meat of Olaf's limb with his sword. The Ironguard grunted, hands clutching handfuls of dirt. His body would be flooded with stimms and counterseptic while his secondary heart kicked

in, countering the bloodloss. It would all be in vain if Egil didn't finish the
amputation before the infected leg corrupted the rest of the Space Wolf.

He felt the Fenrisian blade grate as it struck Olaf's femur. He triggered
the weapon's disruptor field, blue energy wreathing it and cutting through
the bone in a heartbeat. Olaf gasped, but still didn't cry out. Egil cut the
power to the blade, not wanting to further widen the wound, and cleaved
through the remaining muscle with a grunt. Olaf slumped back.

'Let it clot,' Egil said. 'Moln and Orven will help you.'

'One will do,' Olaf growled.

'Orven.' Egil gestured at Highfell, who bent to help Olaf onto his remaining leg. The blood from his stump had already slowed to a trickle, the flow
stemmed by the Space Marine's Larraman cells.

'We go on,' Egil said.

The grav lifts into the Magma Gates' depths were no longer functioning.
The pack was forced to go from one supply transit to another, entering the
surface settlement through a network of low service corridors and forgotten storage bunkers. By the time they reached sub-level one the signs of
burning were obvious.

The pack slowed as it reached the surface level, becoming more cautious.
The vox offered no inkling as to what awaited them beyond the underworld.
All the channels were dead, a wall of static. All that existed was Conran's
remote emergency beacon, blinking from somewhere in the Magma Gates'
command spire. A grim, sinking feeling settled over the Wolves as they
began to climb through the Gates' main levels.

Everything had suffered fire damage. Walls, floors and ceilings were
blackened, and smoke still rose from twisted, melted machinery that occupied the service levels. Fire smouldered in places, and the air was dark and
heavy with a pall of ash. They started coming across bodies too – at first
just a few blackened bones, but more the higher they went. Soon the corridors of the Magma Gates were wall-to-wall with blackened skeletons,
their contorted, grasping death-postures speaking of the agony and desperation of their final moments. They had been burned alive, en-masse.

'Something terrible has happened here,' Moln growled as they climbed a
blackened stairwell towards the higher levels. Egil didn't reply. The air was
thick with burned flesh, but the stink of wyrdlings, that sickly smell that had
invaded his senses for hours, was suddenly absent. The only occupants of
the Magma Gates were the sightless, scorched skeletons of thousands of its
citizens and defenders.

'Conran's signal is near,' Egil said. 'Two more levels up.'

'If he was caught in this damnable fire we'll find only ash,' Moln grunted.

'I pray to Russ you're wrong, brother.'

They passed through a council reception chamber, elegant rustbark
furniture reduced to charred stumps, the formerly plush carpet now a

few fused strips around the flaking walls. Overhead, a ceiling fresco representing the Fenris System had been darkened by smoke, but had remained otherwise miraculously untouched. Egil blink-saved an image of it on his bionics as they passed underneath and reviewed it as they climbed to the next level.

He lingered on the blue-and-white orb of Fenris, and then on the sky-blue of Frostheim, and its darker attendant, Svellgard. Finally, the purple orb of Midgardia, occupying the centre of the painting. Classification *Terrum Mortis*, death world. Six and a half billion souls, eight hundred and ninety-two settlements, a production output of timber, toxins, minerals and, of course, warriors. Wolves had died defending it many times before, and each time the invader had been defeated. The Magma Gates, the greatest above-ground settlement, the conduit between the underworld and the surface and one of the planet's bastions of Imperial authority, had never fallen.

Until now. Even if no attackers stalked the hallways, corridors and sleeping blocks, it was apparent that the Magma Gates were only a husk, gutted by whatever infernal fire had been unleashed upon them. It would have been easy to ascribe the grim destruction to foul maleficarum, but the accusation didn't sit well with Egil. The creatures of the wyrd loved to corrupt, to twist and defile. They loved perverting the order of mankind, loved mocking it with their insane parodies. They were bred from humanity's greatest fears and insecurities, and from such things they drew strength. Destruction – at least the unthinkingly total, undiscerning, anonymous ruination Egil saw around him – did not befit the servants of the Dark Gods. There was no defilement here. Death alone reigned, a charred ash-spectre.

They found Conran. His remains were in one of the Planetary Governor's apartments, adjacent to a shuttle landing strut. His armour was singed black. Egil broke the neck seal, and found badly cooked meat within. The emergency beacon was still transmitting from his gorget. Egil cancelled it.

The body was not alone. Cradled between Conran and the wall were a jumble of bones. Skol's scan showed four distinct sets of remains, male and female, of varying ages. It looked as though Conran had been attempting to shield them when the firestorm had rushed down the corridor.

'Take him,' Egil said to two of the Champions of Fenris, pointing at Conran. He looked at the bones the Wolf was cradling. A glance at the planetary overview files saved into his auto-sense data backup showed that the current Governor of Midgardia, Wellim Sandrin, had a wife and two children.

Moln's shout from the far end of the corridor broke the Wolf Lord's pondering. The Ironguard had stalked to the blast doors leading out onto the spire's landing strut. Finding them half open and the mechanism burned out, he'd stepped onto the platform.

'Morkai's heads,' he swore loudly as he saw what lay beyond. Egil joined him, checking his armour was still properly sealed as he stepped outside of the Magma Gates' shell.

He didn't need to ask the reason for Moln's curse. What had happened to the settlement became suddenly clear. What had happened to all of Midgardia became clear.

The planet burned. From horizon to horizon a towering black thunderhead – like an endless mountain range – blossomed up into the sky. Between it and the spire, a vast plane of grey stretched – ash, bristling with the stubs of a million burned and charred trees. The wind that whipped at the two Space Wolves shifted vast dunes of ash and filled the air with thick, swirling dust and sparking embers. The sky overhead was as choked as the ground below, creating a ruddy twilight underlit, in the distance, by the inferno that continued to consume the rest of the planet.

Midgardia's spore jungles – tainted or not – were no more. An irradiated, windblown desert now surrounded the Magma Gates. The daemons were gone.

Without a word, Egil sent a hailing message to the *Wolftide*'s vox array, now blinking green in the top left of his visor.

Iron Requiem, *in high orbit above Svellgard*

The Wolf wanted to talk. In fact, judging by a scan of the stress levels in his voice, he wanted to kill.

Terrek wasn't listening to him. Keys words pinged in the Iron Hand's backup mem-bank, logged for later review: *outrage, revenge, traitor, betrayal*. Beyond that, the Iron Captain had only briefly recorded that he was talking to Sven Bloodhowl, Wolf Lord of the Firehowlers Great Company. One day it may be relevant. Just not now.

Terrek's primary concern was for his deployment schematics. The entire might of Clan Company Haarmek was to be combat-dropped on Svellgard within the next hour. Current strength stood at ten squads, besides his own – six tactical, two devastator, two assault, along with another of bikers and the supporting armour. The venerable Dreadnought elders, slumbering in the battle-barge's hold-sanctums, would not be awakened for so simple an operation.

It had already been planned out in detail. Terrek had spent the time in-transit to the Fenris System with a choir of stratego-servitors, assessing all the potential war zones, the likely opposition, and deciding upon the best means of engagement. Now he aligned the preparation matrix for the moon of Svellgard with a high-priority neverborn incursion. Only one element required the reanalysis he was currently undertaking – that the Space Wolves were now to be considered non-hostiles. Despite what the Wolf was saying to him over the vox.

The orbital assault algorithm was almost complete when a wailing intrusion snapped at his attention. He was dimly aware of bridge serfs scurrying and shouting around him, beyond the ghostly vision of his machine self.

His probes located the problem without their garbled messages, shouted over the screaming of proximity alarms.

There was another fleet translating in-system.

They were home.

THE WILD KING

The Void, Fenris System

In a surge of shrieking wyrd-light, Bran Redmaw and his Great Company returned to Fenris. The warp spat them out off-course, dangerously deep inside the system, trailward of Frostheim. As his flagship's kaerls sought to triangulate their exact location, transmit ident codes and establish vox contact, Bran paced his bridge from one end to the other, bare, blood-encrusted fists clenching and unclenching.

He had thought they weren't going to make it. The wyrdrealm's maddening waves had mocked them, tossing and turning his fleet's vessels with bows of gibbering insanity, scattering them and ripping them away from their destination. As his Navigators had battled to hold on to the beacon of the Astronomican, Bran had been engaged in his own fight, with those he'd once counted as brothers.

They were still his brothers, he reminded himself. Regardless of the wounds they'd dealt him. Regardless of how they now looked, thought and acted.

'Lord, we have established a vox connection with Lord Deathwolf,' called a vox huscarl. 'His signal is currently being rerouted from Svellgard via his flagship.'

'Accept it,' Bran said, pacing to the communications station. Harald's lagging voice came through on a tide of static.

'*It's good to see you on our sensors, Redmaw.*'

'And good to be home, Deathwolf,' Bran replied. 'How goes the fight?'

'*It stinks. Young Bloodhowl and myself are on Svellgard. The place is crawling with wyrd-dung. Fenris is quiet, and we've heard nothing from Midgardia.*'

'My scanners are reading a large non-Chapter fleet in orbit above you,' Bran said, glancing over the readouts flooding back on the monitors and oculus vidscreens from his fleet's augur probes.

'*Aye, and that's only the half of it. It's a crusade fleet, elements from four-teen different Chapters along with Russ-knows how much Militarum and Navy support, all come to call us to heel. A lance strike by one of their ships nearly ended both Bloodhowl and myself. They refuse to communicate with us.*'

'They're here for the Wulfen,' Bran surmised, fists clenching harder.

'*And more than reluctant to help with our little wyrdling problem. We're hard-pressed down here, Redmaw.*'

'My warriors are hungry for a kill,' Bran said. 'If Fenris is indeed secure we will deploy in full to support you.'

'*That may turn the tide,*' Harald said. '*Hurry.*'

As the connection ended Bran gazed out of the viewing port. Its blast shutters were rattling back, exposing the glittering expanse of the Sea of Stars beyond. The ship's bridge was reflected back in the thick layers of crystalflex, and Bran caught sight of himself towering beside the brass-edged vox banks. It was not a vision he was familiar with. His helmet was off and his dark hair lay unclasped, thick around his shoulders. He'd stripped off his pauldrons, rerebrace, vambrace and gauntlets, revealing thick arms that were criss-crossed with a latticework of fresh cuts and sheened by a slick of sweat.

They only respected strength. Bran had shown it. Even that would not be enough though, if they were not released to the hunt soon. Bran had promised to reinforce Svellgard as though he had a choice – the packs would demand he struck out at the nearest enemy, whether he'd wanted to deploy them to the moon or not.

A crusade fleet. That made matters even worse. How his brothers would react to his return had been worrying enough. He hadn't dared consider what the wider Imperium would do when they discovered what had become of Bran's Great Company during their warp transit. Confronting the wyrdspawn would surely mean confronting those who had come to accuse the Wolves too.

But that was a risk he was going to have to take eventually. Battle called, and with it a release of the primal hunger that had been building among the Redmaws. He called up his helmsman, eyes still locked on his own savage reflection.

'Set a course for Svellgard.'

Ramilies-class star fort, designate Mjalnar

The Wulfen had caught the scent of the wyrd just beyond the command deck's blast doors. They howled and gnashed their fangs as Ragnar entered the rune lock code, their eyes wide and wild with murderlust. The Young King turned to face them as the door rumbled open.

'Kill them,' he said. The Space Wolves charged.

The daemons answered the Wulfen's howls with ones of their own. *Mjalnar*'s command deck was crawling with them, the star fort's cogitator control tiers – divided into gunnery, docking, directional, enginarium, vox and shield bays – playing host to cohorts of capering blue and pink horrors. The air was filled with the snap and crackle of changing, wyrdling energies, and shoals of undulating Tzeentch sky-screamers circled in the vaulted dome above. At the heart of the bedlam rose the primary control platform, the air above it rent and shimmering around a writhing portal that resembled the scaled form of a great, coiling fish. Lightning whipped and lashed from the warp rift, and even as Ragnar watched, more cavorting pink wyrdlings materialised beneath it with a crack of incandescent light.

At the centre of the control platform a large figure sat, occupying the station commander's throne. Ragnar tried to focus on him, but the air around the figure, seated directly below the warp portal, seemed to bend in on itself, like a mirror repeating its own reflection endlessly. It confounded Ragnar's eyes and made his headache redouble.

'Kill them,' he repeated through clenched teeth.

The Space Wolves stormed the deck, setting upon the Tzeentch wyrdspawn standing between them and the portal. Ragnar led his Blackpelts, cutting left and right with *Frostfang*, heedless of the claws that scraped and scratched at his scarred battleplate.

Behind the rush of Wolves, de Mornay hauled his palanquin to a halt and slotted a vox antennae back into his platform's chassis. It was time.

'And this is why we didn't bring the exo-plate, Sister,' he said to Marie. 'Deploy the beacon.'

The Adepta Sororitas reached into an alcove beneath the palanquin's recliner, set back from the engine unit that powered the servitor's treads. The device she pulled out resembled a small metal casket, easily held in two hands, with a key panel and a blinking input system inset on one side. She activated it with a mem-code and a small rod extended from the top with a click.

'Place it there,' de Moray said, pointing his plasma pistol at the area of decking just beyond the blast doors. Marie put the device down on the ichor-slashed grille carefully, and stepped well back. A light beamed from the las-scanner on top of the casket, momentarily covering the space around it in a green grid. De Mornay's grip on his pistol tightened, and he found himself mouthing a prayer he hadn't uttered in a long time.

The las-scanner blinked red two, three, four times, and then became a constant green. The grid vanished. De Mornay waited, breath held, trying to ignore the howls and shrieks of the combat raging all around him.

And then, with a crack, Brother-Captain Stern and his Grey Knights arrived.

Stern had cleared de Mornay en-route to *Mjalnar*. As was so often the case with representatives of the Inquisition, even the encrypted information available to the Chamber Militant was fragmentary and incomplete. Banist de Mornay had been an operative under the late Lord Inquisitor Sebastian Cornwel for seven years, his interrogator for nine, and a full inquisitor for almost fifty. He'd held the rank of Lord Inquisitor for the past dozen. His data entries spoke of strenuous, unstinting service. Malar Nine, the Crusius Campaign, the Delphoid Purges – de Mornay had served on the front line in almost as many cleanse operations as Stern in the past six decades.

The data logs also hinted at more unsavoury activities. The incident files had been wiped, but following a period stationed in the Narthex Nebula fifty years previously de Mornay had spent a great deal of time seemingly operating alongside the Dark Angels. Formal complaints from the Chapter to the Segmentum's Inquisitorial Divisio headquarters seemed to show that the sons of the Lion were less than happy with his presence. For whatever reason, de Mornay appeared to have an obsession with them.

That, however, was not Stern's concern. For a moment the after-memory of the teleportation overcame him – the sucking, gelatinous grasping of tentacles against his silver armour, the searing bone-chill of the void, the stomach-knotting sense of dislocation. He'd always hated teleporting. De Mornay's homer had guided them true though, from the pentagram-inscribed, energy-charged chamber aboard *Star Drake* to the bloody, battle-rent command centre of *Mjalnar*.

The Grey Knights were moving the moment they snapped into existence onboard the star fort, spreading out in an Exodus offence pattern from around the teleport beacon. Stern analysed the situation in a heartbeat. The command deck was awash with Tzeentch warpspawn, their corruption emanating from a crackling silver split above the chamber's control platform. A powerful daemonic entity dominated the same platform, its warding trickery so strong even Stern's aura was unable to pierce it and discern its true nature.

The Wolves battled their way towards the creature and its portal, most of them transformed mutant beasts. Stern saw immediately that they were fighting their way into a trap. In their haste to storm the platform they'd exposed their flanks. Shimmering, shapeless things riven with unholy light were drifting to envelop them, while a shoal of blue sky-screamers detached from the flock circling above to swoop down on the Wulfen's heads.

'Brethren, split and cleanse.' Stern ordered. He went right with Caldor, Alacar and Latimer, while Tomaz, Wilfred, Artemis, Ethold and Osbeth went left.

The flamers of Tzeentch met them. From their many sightless heads, from gaping maws and from the flaring ends of quad-jointed limbs, multi-hued warpfire spewed to engulf the charging Knights. The flames themselves screamed as they flowed around the silver paladins, grasping and snapping at them like the sinuous appendages of a living creature. Such an inferno would have reduced unwarded mortals to gibbering hunks of twisting, mutating flesh and blasted bare the sanity of the most devout Imperial servant. Stern felt the warding aegis engraved into his armour vibrate as it turned the daemonic energies aside. He spat one of the Prayers of Contrition as he thrust through the warpfire, nemesis sword a scything white arc.

The first flamer came apart beneath the holy steel, its own fires turning in on it and eating it up. Stern's brethren were beside him, their anointed weapons crackling with power as they cut apart the ever-changing monsters. They closed around him, united in a recital of the Canticle of Absolution. Stern threw a glance at the centre of the chamber.

The Wolves' advance had stalled.

Ragnar cursed when he saw the Grey Knights materialise amidst a flare of teleportation lightning. He'd known the inquisitor would go behind their backs at some point. There would be a reckoning with him when this was all over.

If any of them made it off the command deck alive. The sky-screamer came at him from above, filling the energy-charged air with the shriek of its passing chitin spines. Ragnar met it with an upswing of *Frostfang*, the chainsword's scream matching that of the airborne daemon as it sawed the thing in two, spraying the Blackpelts with stinking purple viscera. More of the creatures dived down at them, their manta-like bodies rippling on the invisible currents of the warp.

The Space Wolves' attack was blunted. Horrors pressed in from all sides, splitting and multiplying, bathed in hellish wyrdlight that threw crazed shadows across the embattled chamber. The sleek sky daemons above them struck in shoals, swooping at an angle so that their frills of spines and drooling maws skimmed the top of the melee. The Wulfen paid for their feral desire to remove their helms, their unprotected faces gouged and torn by the passing screamers.

'Stay tight!' Ragnar bellowed at the nearest Wolves, slashing through another blue horror that leapt at him, all flailing arms and yawning mouths. 'Aim for the platform!'

Behind him he heard a grunt, and half turned to see Hrolf Longspear stumble, blood spilling from where a horror's claws had succeeded in breaking the thigh seal of his armour. Uller Greylock was also injured, his helmet buckled where a screamer's passing blades had hammered into him. The Grey Knights were on their flanks, wreathed in wyrdflame as they hacked at the sea of madness. It would not be enough.

It was Hostor who saved them. His Blood Claws, the only one of the three boarding packs to have resisted the curse of the Wulfen, burst onto the command deck from the far side of the melee. Their howls joined with the pounding of bolt pistols and the roaring of chainswords as they speared into the fight around the control platform. Almost immediately Ragnar felt the shuddering press of morphing wyrdflesh around him lessen as the Tzeentch daemons turned to face the new threat.

'Blackpelts, forward!' he barked, shouldering his way through the fight. The platform's stairs lay directly ahead, devoid of enemies, the eldritch energies of the silver warp portal coruscating above. Behind him he could hear his Wolf Guard struggling to keep the way clear, a fresh tide of wyrdlings breaking against their blades and armour as the creatures realised the Wolf Lord's intentions.

Ragnar parted a final horror with a swing of *Frostfang*, stamping on the thing's dissipating remains as he lunged for the stairs. He took the metal rungs three at a time, alone now, his fangs bared. The air ahead shimmered and warped, images repeating themselves, patterns shattering and reforming around the faceless, dark thing that sat beneath the warp portal's swirling quicksilver centre. Ragnar flung himself at the twisting barrier with a howl.

And stopped. Silence gripped him, sudden and complete. The frenetic bloodletting of the command deck was gone. Here, in a perfect sphere of unreality centred beneath the portal, all was calm and still.

The star fort's command throne lay before him. A figure sat upon it, huge, brooding, clad in baroque power armour and a horn-crested helm. The blue battleplate was trimmed with gold and inscribed with hundreds of leering daemonic heads, the eyes regarding the Wolf Lord with a mocking glint as he stumbled to a halt.

As Ragnar stopped the figure spoke, voice silky and slick with ten millennia of vile deeds.

'Hello again, Young King,' said Madox.

Iron Requiem, *in high orbit above Svellgard*

More Wolves.

The augur arrays of the Iron Hands battle-barge had detected another fleet moving in-system. Their projected course took them to Svellgard, and the section of the crusade fleet surrounding the moon. Data logs showed the ships as belonging to the Wolf Lord Bran Redmaw's Great Company.

Terrek scanned the information, noting the class and size of each approaching vessel. With the fleets of three Wolf Lords combined above the moon their voidborne assets would outnumber those of this portion of the crusade fleet. And that was without factoring in the destructive power sitting dormant in the silos buried beneath the craggy tundra of Svellgard's islands. The Iron Captain cut the link with Sven Bloodhowl – who was still raging impotently at him from the moon's surface – and opened a channel to Epathus, back aboard the Ultramarines flagship.

'We should petition Grand Master Azrael for reinforcements,' he said.

'*Perhaps,*' Epathus allowed. '*But I have just explained the situation to Harald Deathwolf. He is in agreement with our projected assault plan.*'

'I do not trust the Wolves,' Terrek said, his flat machine tone giving the statement no inflection.

'*We have little choice other than to seek their assistance, for now. The forces at our disposal are insufficient for purging Svellgard alone.*'

'No force need be exerted if we destroy the moon from orbit.'

'*Such an act will not be sanctioned by the rest of the crusade, Terrek. It would mean the destruction of the Wolves' orbital defence systems, and would likely cause catastrophic damage to Frostheim as well.*'

The Iron Hand felt a surge of annoyance throb through his circuitry. He suppressed the unworthy emotion. The Ultramarine's words had some merit. Regardless of where their loyalties lay, the Space Wolves currently occupied a powerful system-defence nexus. Destroying it would mean destroying valuable Imperial facilities whose ancient, sacred mechanisms ought to be recaptured intact.

'I will transmit a request for reinforcements to the Rock,' he said. 'Then we shall begin planetfall, as per the prearranged assault plan.'

'*I shall see you on the surface, Iron Captain,*' said Epathus.

The World Wolf's Lair, Svellgard

'Machine-loving, cogbrained, traitorous wyrd-scum,' Sven spat. 'I hope your servo-loving mother burns in the Seven Hells for the rest of eternity.'

The vox-link to the Iron Hands battle-barge had been cut over a minute earlier, but that didn't stop the Wolf Lord's invectives from echoing around the bunker. Eventually, Harald placed a hand on his fellow jarl's shoulder.

'What?' Sven snarled, rounding on him in the confined, red-lit space of the Lair's secondary command bunker.

'I've just spoken to the Ultramarines captain, Epathus,' the older Wolf Lord said. 'He's uploading a planetary assault overview to our systems right now. They're going to spearhead a counter-attack.'

'Yngfor is dead,' Sven said. 'And his pack with him. I'll kill that Iron Hand traitor myself!'

'Afterwards, Young Wolf,' Harald said. 'Right now we have more pressing concerns than vengeance.'

The thudding of bolter fire from outside the bunker's reinforced walls underscored his words. Since the destruction of Infurnace the daemonic assaults had only increased. The outer bastions were hard-pressed and the combat channels were overwhelmed with reports of rising casualty rates and unsustainable ammunition expenditure. The ocean-eating warp rifts were still widening. If left unchecked, Sven knew they would swallow the whole moon, and create a cataclysmic rent in reality that would surely rip apart the entire Fenris System.

'What do the sons of Guilliman want?' he asked eventually.

'They've identified three primary warp portals from orbit. They'll attack one, the Iron Hands the second and we'll strike at the third. An orbital bombardment will help seal them and clear us a path.'

'They're as likely to try to wipe us out as seal the rifts,' Sven snarled.

'That may be, but at the moment we have no choice but to trust them. As long as we try to hold the daemons, their numbers will only multiply. We have to go on the offensive. Also, Redmaw is on his way.'

'He's finally arrived in-system?'

'With all his fleet. Now is the time to strike.'

'And afterwards, hold these misguided fools to account for what they've done,' Sven added.

'Aye, that we shall, brother.'

Wolftide, *in high orbit above Midgardia*

The Wolf Lord had returned to the iron-clad bridge of his flagship, boots ringing from the metal underfoot. Kreg bowed, eyes averted. 'I could not stop him, lord. I tried.'

Egil didn't respond. He was looking past the Long Fang, out of the *Wolftide*'s viewing ports. At the crusade fleet, clustered around the brooding, tower-studded bulk of the Rock. The Iron Wolf's expression was dark.

He had returned minutes earlier, retrieved along with his pack by one of his flagship's Stormwolves. They'd brought Conran's remains with them, and the Great Wolf's battered crown.

'Conran tried to reason with the Lions,' Kreg explained. 'He believed if he proved there were still Wolves on Midgardia they wouldn't burn it. He went himself.'

'They know he went?' Egil asked quietly. 'They know he was on the surface when they began the bombardment?'

'Yes, lord, he told them. We have the vox transcripts.'

'And they knew I was still planetside as well? That I was hunting for the Great Wolf?'

'Yes, lord.'

'Gunner,' Egil said to one of his huscarls. 'You have a lock?'

'We do, lord,' the huscarl said.

'Conran ordered us to load and lock all batteries before he departed,' Kreg explained. 'It was how we convinced the Lions to talk to us in the first place.'

'Hail them again,' Egil ordered.

'We cannot, lord,' the vox huscarl said, shaking his head. 'The entire fleet has sealed us out of its channels.'

'Gunner, what are you locked onto?' Egil asked.

'An Imperial Navy Lunar-class cruiser, lord. *Wrath of Man*, part of the 483rd Obscurus battlefleet sub-detachment.'

'Message from bridge command to the forward bombardment cannon,' Egil said. 'Maintain current target. Open fire.'

* * *

Ramilies-class star fort, designate Mjalnar

Ragnar said nothing. Madox laughed, an oily, chilling sound that filled the bubble of unreality occupying the centre of *Mjalnar*'s command deck.

'You seem surprised, Wolf,' the Thousand Sons sorcerer said. 'Is it really so strange that you should find me here, at the heart of all your frustrations?'

'You're dead,' Ragnar said, pointing *Frostfang*'s idling blades at him. 'I drove the Spear of Russ through your faceplate.'

'A fine strike,' Madox said, laughing again. 'I remember it well!'

'This is a trick. An illusion.'

'Existence itself is an illusion. Life is a trick.'

'I'm not here to bandy words with bad memories,' Ragnar snarled, striding towards the Chaos Space Marine.

'Of course. You'd be in danger of actually learning something if you did.'

'You have nothing to teach me, wyrdling.'

'What about the fate of Midgardia? I could tell you that it burns with fires set by Angels.'

'Be silent.'

'I could tell you the Lion's son dances on the end of a daemon's strings. I could tell you the Iron Wolf has turned his guns on the Corpse-Emperor's warships.'

Ragnar raised his chainsword, snarling.

'I could tell you he's coming back,' Madox said, but Ragnar wasn't listening. *Frostfang* fell, a planet burned and died, and darkness took the Young King.

The Rock, in high orbit above Midgardia

Azrael sentenced Vox Seneschal Mendaxis to be auto-scourged, when time allowed. The punishment made the Changeling grin privately, for the fate that had already befallen the Supreme Grand Master's real vox seneschal was far worse.

The Mendaxis-thing had returned to its communications pit, suitably penitent. Its inexplicable disappearance earlier had infuriated the normally detached Dark Angel. None thought to wonder where Interrogator-Chaplain Elezar had now gone. He was surely in his reclusiam-cell, praying.

The Changeling was glad of the change of flesh. It provided the perfect opportunity for more distractions.

'The captain of *Wrath of Man*, lord,' it called up to Azrael, seated on the Rock's bridge throne. 'He's been fired upon by the Space Wolves battle-barge *Wolftide*!'

'A warning shot?' Azrael demanded.

'It struck him amidships, lord. His port shields have taken damage.'

'What of–'

The Supreme Grand Master's question went unfinished. Auspex arrays across the Rock's oculus viewscreens and the ranks of cogitator pews lit up with a storm of warning symbols. Somewhere a claxon began to wail.

'Sire, the entire Space Wolves fleet has just opened fire!' shouted an Augur Chief. 'Imperial Navy assets are reporting direct hits!'

'Message to the entire crusade fleet, all ships are to hold fire,' Azrael snapped. 'And open a channel with the *Wolftide*.'

'Yes, lord,' the Mendaxis-thing said. 'I shall see to it personally.'

He turned in the bottom of the communications pit and snatched a vox horn.

'Patch this through to crusade fleet elements,' he ordered the communications serfs hardwired into the stations around him. 'All ships be advised – they may fire at will.'

Wrath of Man, *in high orbit above Midgardia*

The *Wrath of Man* rocked like an Old Terran ship in a sea swell, its shields flaring around it with vigorous blue light.

'Another hit, captain!' shouted Lieutenant Renmann. 'Port shields reporting thirty-one per cent integrity!'

'I can see that Lieutenant, thank you,' Captain Krief said through clenched teeth. 'Kindly reduce your voice to a level befitting that of an officer of His Divine Majesty's Imperial Navy, and then get me a secure channel with the Rock.'

The reprimand barely had an effect on his wide-eyed subordinate. The young Third Lieutenant scampered across the bridge to the vox bank, where communications deck officers in pristine white uniforms were scrambling to acknowledge the flood of engagement data coming in from the rest of the fleet.

'Sir, signal from the Rock!' he shouted, waving a comms chit at the captain. 'Fleet assets are to engage at will.'

'God-Emperor preserve us all,' Krief said, leaning against the brass railings of his control platform and staring out of the viewing ports at the Space Wolves fleet. Had it really come to this? Even as he asked himself the question another bombardment cannon strike impacted against the *Wrath of Man*'s shields. He felt the deck shudder beneath him, and the bridge's lumen globes blinked dangerously.

'Sir, port shields at nine per cent integrity!' Renmann squealed.

'Hard to port,' Krief said heavily. 'Gunnery, man the forward lances, and prepare torpedo bays one through six.'

Wolftide, *in high orbit above Midgardia*

'Lord, all ships are reporting successful hits,' said the vox huscarl. The bridge of Egil's flagship was thick with the backdraught of weapons discharge and the stench of macrocannon propellant.

'Have them cease fire,' Egil said, eyes scanning the readouts of the bridge's oculus viewscreens. 'And check that link with the Rock. Tell me they've opened communications.'

'Lord, scanners report incoming fire,' shouted a frantic kaerl from the augur bay. 'Lances and torpedoes!'

'No change with the Rock,' said the vox seneschal. 'The channel remains closed.'

'May the Deathwolf devour them all,' Egil snapped. 'Message to all ships, resume fire. And have all hands brace for impact.'

The Rock, in high orbit above Midgardia

'Lord, our Imperial Navy assets are returning fire,' said the Augur Chief.

'What?' demanded Azrael. His voice carved through the hubbub of the Rock's bridge. 'Order them to cease at once. Mendaxis, link to me directly.'

'Of course, sire,' the Mendaxis-thing said, no longer even bothering to hide its grin from the dead-eyed serfs around it. It coupled the Supreme Grand Master's throne vox cord to the broadcasting terminal, taking its time about it.

'There appears to be a transmission fault, sire,' it lied.

'Secondary vox then,' Azrael snapped to one of the communication sub-pits. 'Link me!'

It was all the Changeling could do to stifle a laugh.

Wrath of Man, *in high orbit above Midgardia*

'Sir, communication from the Rock!' shrilled Lieutenant Renmann. 'All ships are to cease fire immediately!'

Captain Krief looked up from the damage readout on his control lectern, peering through the organised chaos that dominated the Imperial Navy bridge.

'Clarify,' he ordered.

'Order clarified,' Renmann replied after a moment. 'All ships cease fire!'

'Have the Adeptus Astartes taken leave of their senses?' First Lieutenant Oppen asked. His words were punctuated by another shuddering impact. Krief's eyes darted back to the damage readout scrolling across his lectern's monitor. The shields were on the brink of shorting out. Like the other half-dozen Navy vessels nearest to the Space Wolves fleet, his ship was now fully engaged. To break the firing cycle and power down or even stall the targeting sequences would guarantee defeat, should the Wolves maintain their fire. By the time they were fully operational again, the fearsome armaments at the Space Marines' disposal would have already transformed them into a listing, burning wreck.

'We are not subordinate to them, captain,' Oppen pressed. 'The Imperial Navy answers to none but–'

'I'm aware of the hierarchy of the fleet, thank you, First Lieutenant,' Krief snapped. 'Now kindly return to your post. You too, Mister Renmann.'

Another strike rocked his ship. His soul groaned in counterpoint to the agony of the overburdened shields. He'd captained the *Wrath* for the past twenty-five years, Terra-standard. When the venerable Lunar-class cruiser suffered, he suffered, and its triumph was his own. To take her out of what was on the brink of becoming a life-and-death fistfight with what could surely now only be a band of renegades and traitors went against every Navy-given value ingrained in him.

But ignoring orders also went against his nature, and regardless of Oppen's bombast, Krief was under no illusions as to the position he occupied within the crusade fleet. Oppen could answer to the Angels of Death if he wanted.

'Message to gunnery,' Krief said. 'Ceasefire, effect immediate. And pray to Him on Terra that those warp-damned Wolves do the same.'

Wolftide, *in high orbit above Midgardia*

'Lord, they've ceased fire.' The huscarl's voice was breathless. Egil's flagship seemed to have gone quiet, still and silent like a weary predator, waiting to see if the killing was done.

Egil watched the bridge's blinking auspex displays and the oculus visuals, expecting them to flare red and furious once more with interstellar ordnance. He felt the deck beneath him shudder with release as *Wolftide*'s bombardment cannon fired again. The monitors, however, remained a sterile green.

'Lord,' said the vox huscarl. 'The Rock... is hailing us.'

'Order to all ships,' Egil said slowly. 'Ceasefire. And accept the link. Bridge speakers.'

The *Wolftide*'s command deck was overlaid with static as the vox horns came online. After a moment a voice, hard and cold as a basilica's keystone, broke through the interference.

'*Do you want to die, Wolf?*'

'Supreme Grand Master Azrael,' Egil said. 'I see you've finally found the transmit button on your vox set.'

'*Choose your next words carefully. Why did you just open fire on an Imperial fleet?*'

'Why did you just fire-bomb one of the Allfather's worlds?'

'*I am not here to chase your tail, mongrel. You have two hours to withdraw your fleet from orbit and proceed to Fenris, where you shall await the Imperium's judgement for what you have done here.*'

'The Imperium's judgement, or the Lion's?' Egil demanded. 'Withdraw your forces from this system within the next two hours, and we will discuss your actions from a less fatal distance.'

Egil was aware that they were mirroring each other. Near annihilation would be mutual. The Iron Wolf had opened fire not just because Conran and the murdered citizens of Midgardia had been crying out for vengeance, not just because the Lions had violated their sovereign territory, and not just because they had put the Great Wolf in danger. He had done it to buy time. He had no idea how large the crusade fleet was, or whether it had engaged other Great Companies elsewhere in the system. Until Azrael had said it, he didn't even know that Fenris hadn't suffered the same fate as Midgardia.

The Iron Wolf, logical as ever, had seen the Wolves under attack, and he had responded. Now that he had checked them, the time had come to discover who the real traitors were.

The Lions, or the Wolves.

Svellgard

From the grey heavens, the weight of the Imperium's wrath fell upon Svellgard.

First it was firepower. The precise strike of *Iron Requiem* had been nothing next to the weight of ordnance unleashed by the combined fleets in Frostheim's uppermost orbit. Lance strikes, melta torpedoes, augur-guided macrocannon shells – they ripped and shredded Svellgard's clouds and shook its islands to their bedrock.

The bombardment was centred on three different sectors, around the edges of the warp rift anomalies pinpointed by the fleet's scans. There the corruption was at its worst, the sucking, swirling oceans seething with nightmares of blubbering flesh and grasping tentacle-limbs. Cohorts of lesser daemons pushed their way through the morass of submerged warp-flesh, all massing in the direction of the World Wolf's Lair. Until the orbital barrage began to annihilate them, splitting apart the ocean waves and flinging great pillars of evaporated water skywards.

As the great guns of the Imperium's fleets continued to hammer Svellgard's deformed deeps, more contrails filled the air. The objects fell with almost as much force as the macroshells, but their payloads were considerably more deadly. They struck in clusters near two of the three portals, hammering the exposed seabed close to where the receding waters still lashed and foamed.

Drop pods. Their flanks fell, armoured figures deploying from their cramped interiors with experienced ease. To the north of the World Wolf's Lair, the blue battleplate of the Ultramarines, to the east, the black and silver of the Iron Hands.

Thunderhawks followed the drop pod assault down, leaden with armour support. Bolters flashed and barked as the Space Marines secured their landing zones, the concentrated firepower more than enough to banish the daemons dragging themselves from the surf towards them.

The world the Adeptus Astartes found themselves fighting in was a strange one. Even as the oceans retreated they left behind hundreds of choppy micro-oceans in the lower depths of what had once been the sea-bed. An advance route was planned out across uplands of craggy exposed bedrock, thick with dripping growths and writhing aquatic life.

Few of the growths of life were without the hideous stigmata of Chaos.

The Space Marines cleansed as they went, the Ultramarines with a Codex-approved combination of pre-planned advances and individual unit flexibility, the Iron Hands with remorseless implacability. All the while, the capital ships maintained their bombardment from above, hammering the things crawling up out of the rips in reality, searing away Svellgard's seas with fiery wrath.

The Space Wolves were the last to join the assault. Harald and Sven waited. When Epathus asked why, Harald claimed they were giving Bran Redmaw more time. In truth, they wanted to ensure the crusade fleet deployed its strength to attack the warp portals, and not the World Wolf's Lair. Only when heavy Astra Militarum troop shuttles had started to plough through the lower atmosphere did the Wolf Lords give the signal.

'I'll see you afterwards, Deathwolf,' Sven said, clasping his brother's vambrace.

'Enjoy yourself, pup,' Harald replied, returning the warrior's grip. 'For Russ and the Allfather.'

The Wolves went on the offensive. The weight of daemonic attackers around the Lair's shores had slackened considerably as the wyrdspawn turned to protect the rifts. Harald and Sven led their packs from the defence networks and bunker tunnels with vengeful howls, thundering out into the cloying wet sand. Only then did the Wolves' ships in orbit join the bombardment, hammering the wyrdlings around their objectives – the largest portal, south of the Lair.

The Astra Militarum were joining the attack against the other two. Valkyrie airborne assault carriers picked up the Harakoni Warhawk detachments defending the islands around the Lair and deposited them via short grav-chute drops onto the new front lines. The Ultramarines and Iron Hands found their gradually ever-more exposed flanks bolstered by platoons of airborne infantry in black combat fatigues and tan-coloured carapace flak-plate, salvoes of semi-automatic lascarbine fire snapping out from the rugged shoals and dunes that had once been the seabed.

Heavier ground troops were landed behind the front, around the drop zones initially secured by the Angels of Death. To the north, the 443rd Adraxian Legion and the 15th Naimen Armoured, to the east, the 16th Kattak Grenadiers and the Sixth Virillion Steelborn. The Guardsmen followed in the wake of the Space Marines, burning and slaughtering remaining pockets of infestation with the application of massed, point-blank firepower.

Above them, the Imperial Navy added yet more weight to the fight.

Thunderbolts and Lightnings screamed from the fire-scarred skies, peeling off from their squadrons one by one to strafe the never-ending hordes shuffling from the receding deeps. Higher up, wings of Marauder bombers rumbled, their payloads pockmarking the already-ragged landscape.

The Navy did not enjoy air superiority for long. The clouds soon played host to rippling shoals of blue and purple sky-screamers and flocks of black-fleshed furies, as well as bigger, indefinable things with beating or buzzing pinions and darting talons. They latched themselves onto wings and fuselages, claws splitting open cockpits and hauling pilots, screaming, out into the air, to be devoured or thrown to their deaths. The fighters closed around their bombers in response, painting the sky with beams of las and thudding trails of autocannon rounds that bisected the daemonic flocks. The Adeptus Astartes joined the battle for Svellgard's skies as well, Thunderhawks and Stormtalons churning out bolter fire in support of the Navy formations.

Beneath, like reflections in a bloody river, the battle raged. Only in the south did the Wolves remain unsupported, fighting on with only the orbital strikes of their fleet to help clear the way. Sven led from the head of his Skyclaws, his face a rictus of ichor-splattered determination. Gone was the laughing warrior who thrilled at the roar of his chainsword and the crackling power of his frost axe. Gone was the young Wolf who staked a battle's success on the number of heads taken, and struggled to outdo the antics of his youngest, most savage pups. Now he killed in near silence, grunting with each powerful swing of Frostclaw, ignoring the ache of his split rib-plate or his useless left hand.

Olaf Blackstone fought at his side, lightning claws a blur of charged razor-steel, finishing anything his Wolf Lord didn't send screaming straight back to the immaterium. The Skyclaws pressed into the heart of the wyrdling legions, chainswords howling and flamers roaring, infected by the grim, killing fury of their jarl. The daemons parted before them.

'Not too far, pup,' Harald said over the vox. He was astride Icetooth once more, the huge thunderwolf slick with wyrdling gore, snapping and snarling through a clutch of wailing daemonettes. Around him the remainder of his Riders of Morkai had also mounted their Fenrisian war beasts, the savage fang at the tip of the attacking Deathwolves. The Firehowlers, however, were pulling ahead.

Sven didn't respond. He hit the turbo on Longbound, letting the jump pack slam him almost horizontally across the slime-slicked seabed. He struck a brace of horrors as they tried to summon their mutating flames to stop him, the things disintegrating beneath the impact of the power-armoured warrior. Frostclaw lashed out – a glittering, icy arc in the ichor-misted air – to reap more wyrdling un-lives. A moment later and Olaf was at his side once again, slamming down on his pack amidst the melee. Still the Firehowlers pressed on.

And around them, stronger than the rising tide, the daemons surged.

Terrek slammed his power fist into the snapping, living jaws of the skull cannon's chassis, feeling the warp-forged steel buckle and split beneath his energy-wreathed gauntlet. The discharge of the disruptor field tore through the neverborn engine, blasting it apart in a blizzard of burning metal and shattered bone.

'Status,' the Iron Captain demanded as his squad pulled apart the screaming construct's remains.

'*The machine-spirit is in pain, brother-captain,*' came Morex's reply over the vox. '*I estimate the supplications will take five minutes more.*'

'You have them,' Terrek said, inputting the delay into his visor's combat matrix and switching to the Clan-wide channel.

'This is Terrek to all squads. Hold.'

The Iron Hands stopped as abruptly as deactivated servitors, before automatically taking up defensive positions along the exposed reef they found themselves straddling. Behind Terrek the Clan's Iron Father, Morex, was applying his cog glaive to the disabled tracks of Land Raider serial two-one-one-six-A, designate *Black Vengeance*. The blazing daemonic skulls fired by the living cannon just destroyed by Terrek had dented the tank's adamantium hull and shattered the links of one of its heavy tracks. Bolters and lascannons still blasting, it had slewed to a ponderous halt atop the reef's crest.

'*Captain, what of the humans?*' Sergeant Baalor voxed. '*They are still attempting to advance.*'

'Let them,' Terrek said after a split second's analysis. 'If they make headway now they may be able to keep pace with us when we resume the advance.'

'*Acknowledged, Clan Commander.*'

Terrek could well imagine the frantic vox calls inundating the Guard officers, and their uncertainty over whether to halt alongside the silent, black-armoured automata, or whether to press on unsupported. Terrek would not permit them to halt. Pausing to maintain the integrity of his Clan's advance was imperative, but stalling the entire offence against the eastmost warp portal would be wasteful.

While he waited, the Iron Hand reviewed the progress of the other counter-attacks. The Ultramarines were lagging, too focussed on maintaining contact with their supporting units. Epathus' squads had interspersed themselves among the Militarum, bolstering the width of their thrust towards the northern portal whilst weakening the tip of the spear, centred around Epathus and his Sternguard. That was the difference between Guilliman's offspring and those of the Gorgon – the former always engaged with at least two objectives: to win, and to minimise the losses of their allies. The machine-minds of Iron Captains like Terrek were unhindered by such dangerously indulgent concerns. Without victory, the lightest losses were damning. With it, any losses were acceptable.

The Wolves were doing no better. Though their progress towards the southern portal was impressive, the sigils blinking across Terrek's visor were without any form of coherence. The savages were launching a blind, all-out charge towards the largest of the three warp rifts, plunging through a veritable sea of neverborn. Even the most favourable analysis had them being cut off, surrounded and annihilated long before they reached their objective.

'*Praise the Machine.*' Morex's monotone exaltation interrupted Terrek's assessment. '*The iron is willing, brother-captain.*'

Terrek glanced back to see *Black Vengeance* rolling forwards once more, greasy smoke churning from its rear exhaust ports.

'All squads, resume,' Terrek voxed. Like a pict feed that had been unpaused, the Iron Hands rose and went forward once more.

Ramilies-class star fort, designate Mjalnar

A world burning. Darkness.

Ragnar's eyes snapped open. There was a face above him, square-jawed, scarred, the eyes a stony grey-blue. The Wolf Lord's hand came up instinctively. It was intercepted by a fist of silver steel.

'Daemonhunter,' Ragnar said, snarling up at the Grey Knight kneeling over him. 'Where are my Wulfen?'

The Knight said nothing, but released his hand, and offered an open palm. Ragnar took it, and allowed himself to be pulled to his feet.

'Safe,' the Knight said. Ragnar gazed around, blinking. His packs were clustered around him – Blood Claws, Wulfen and the Blackpelts, watching their lord attentively. For the first time since boarding *Mjalnar* he realised his head was clear. The throbbing ache that had split his skull was gone.

As were the daemons.

'Where is Madox?' Ragnar demanded.

'Who?' the Grey Knight responded. Ragnar looked up at the control platform. The command deck was slashed with ichor and littered with Space Wolves dead, but of the Tzeentch wyrdlings there was no sign. The platform itself was deserted, the command throne empty, and only a livid scorch mark on the domed ceiling told of the former existence of the warp rift.

'What happened?' Ragnar asked.

'When you stormed the platform you broke the daemon's glamour,' said the Grey Knight. 'You fought and slew the Tzeentch Herald at the heart of the corruption. When you banished it the warp portal collapsed in on itself.'

'I saw a vision,' Ragnar said, staring up at the empty throne. 'Someone I have not seen in a very long time.'

'Lies and deceit,' the Knight said. 'Even more than his brothers, the Changer loves trickery and illusion.'

'Madox said Midgardia is burning,' Ragnar said. 'I saw it. Fires set from orbit, eating up everything. He said a daemon is behind the Lion's actions.'

The Grey Knight exchanged a glance with de Mornay. The inquisitor's face was grim.

'Regardless of the daemon's trickery, we must press on to Midgardia,' he said. 'For all our sakes. Brother-Captain Stern, will you take passage on my vessel?'

'Gladly, Lord Inquisitor,' the Grey Knight said. 'Once we have retrieved our two fallen brothers from *Star Drake*. Lord Blackmane may also wish to take custody of the Wulfen we've left locked in the brig.'

'You truly mean my Murderpacks no harm?' Ragnar asked, not bothering to mask his suspicion. The surrounding Wulfen watched with silent, rapt intensity, like children observing an Emperor's Day ascension play.

'There are more pressing matters at hand, Lord Blackmane,' Stern said.

'And when there aren't?'

'I cannot promise you won't hear from me again.'

'We can discuss such delicate matters en-route.' De Mornay said. '*Mjalnar* is cleansed. I will set an Inquisitorial quarantine marker, and then we must be on our way. Before the situation in this system deteriorates even further.'

'I fear it already has, witch hunter,' Ragnar said, seeing again the fire-wreathed world the thing disguised as Madox had forced into his mind. 'I fear it already has.'

Svellgard

The Wolves died.

They did so in ones and twos. They did it well, fighting their way towards the southernmost warp rift with gore-streaked weapons in their fists and oaths on their lips. But they died all the same. Swordlings matched Blood Claws blade for blade, power armour little defence against the wicked edges of their scalding black weapons. Purple-skinned daemonettes danced between the packs, ducking and weaving with preternatural grace around the clumsy swings of chainswords before darting in to slide claws and slender knives through the weak joints between ceramite plates. Limping Tallybands of rancid Nurgle wyrdspawn soaked up the thunderous firepower of Grey Hunters and Long Fangs, shuffling onwards even as bolt-rounds burst their necrotised flesh apart.

A trio of juggernaut-mounted swordlings hammered over a reef outcrop, shattering the exposed, growth-covered bedrock before slamming into the ranks of the Nightwolves. The Grey Hunters went down, innards pulped by the colossal impact of warp-forged steel or gored on the spikes and wicked blades covering the monstrous daemon machines. To their left, a pack of red-skinned Khornate hounds clashed with Harald's Fenrisian wolves. Iron-hard jaws locked around the frilled throats of the flesh hounds, while the daemons' savage claws raked through tough grey pelts. Yelps, snarls and howls ripped apart the ragged air of Svellgard.

Above the swirling pack battle, a burning, spinning bladed disc shackled to two undulating sky-screamers tore through the Stormbringers as the Skyclaws were mid-leap, bisecting a trio of the young Wolves. Their jump packs detonated, the burning remains plummeting back down to the exposed seabed. Floating a foot above the disc's spinning, sigil-etched surface, a Herald of Tzeentch cackled and wove its long, charm-hung arms in an indecipherably complex pattern, spitting pink and blue wyrdfire indiscriminately into the fight below.

The Space Wolves offensive buckled, but it did not break. It fought back. The melta and plasma guns of the Nightwolves hummed and spat, searing molten holes in the plate armour of the juggernauts and vaporising their red-scaled riders. Harald lead his shock cavalry back to support their packmates, Space Marines and wolf-brothers fighting side by side, the thunderwolves snatching up Khornate death hounds in their great maws and savaging them. Bloodhowl's Ravens, Sven's twin Land Speeders, swooped in behind the flying Tzeentch chariot, rune-etched hulls glowing in the after-burn of the unnatural flames that trailed behind its spinning form. Their multi-meltas found a target lock, and the strange sky chariot and its daemonic rider detonated like an exploding firework, punching a glittering cascade of colours across the battle-wrought sky.

'Deathwolves, rally!' Harald shouted, turning Icetooth in a tight circle and swinging his ichor-splattered frost axe above his head. Beside him Vygar Helmfang hefted high the Great Company's Wolf Standard, the Ravening Jaw rampant on its rippling field of red silk. The Deathwolves fought their way to their lord, bolters hammering, chainblades a frenzy of ripping, cutting teeth as they sawed their way through the wyrdflesh tide.

'Pup, bring your packs together,' Harald growled over the vox. 'We need to consolidate before we–' the Wolf Lord was interrupted by a hammering discharge. Something slammed into Rudr the Black's thunderwolf, Stonejaw, blasting it apart in a shower of bloody meat and burning fur. As the Rider of Morkai scrambled to find his feet amidst the steaming viscera of his mount, another projectile slammed low overhead, nearly cutting the Wolf Standard in half. Harald's keen eyes caught a split-second impression of it – a brass-plated skull, jaw agape, trailing wyrdfire.

'Skull cannons,' the Wolf Lord barked, following the missile's trajectory. Atop a spine-studded shoal a hundred yards ahead, a battery of daemonic artillery had ground up from the surf, the maws of their bone barrels flaring with bloody light. Another of the living guns fired, smashing apart a shaft of barnacle-encrusted rock just to Harald's right.

'Grolf,' Harald voxed. 'Bring those things down.'

'*No, lord,*' came the response from the Long Fang Ancient. '*We're too hard-pressed.*' Harald spotted his two heavy weapons packs, the Stormbrows and the Icefangs, off to the right fighting hand to hand with a clutch of gibbering, mutated spawn. Grolf's snow bear cloak picked him out at the centre of the melee, the white pelt matted black with ichor.

'Ynvir!' Harald bellowed. The huge Wulfen was at the head of his Murderpack, dripping with wyrdling viscera as he ripped into a fresh cohort of horrors. At the sound of his lord's voice he turned, his pack thrusting past him with savage hunger. Harald pointed Glacius' dripping head at the battery of cannons as they fired again, shattering the air around him with burning, cackling skulls.

'Silence those engines!' Harald shouted.

Ynvir moved off immediately, his pack moving to protect him with the feral instincts of bonded hunters.

'Vygar, Rudr, keep the company together,' Harald ordered his two remaining Wolf Guard before urging Icetooth forward. The thunderwolf plunged through the combat, forcing its way to the Wulfen's side as they ripped a path towards the skull cannon battery.

The hellish weapons fired again, their living, daemonic projectiles splitting apart a trio of Wulfen, splattering the rest of the Murderpack with their gore. Harald roared and swung Glacius again and again, cleaving apart the swordlings at the base of the shoal. Around him Wulfen fought and died, impaled on black hellswords even as they ripped open red, scaly flesh with claws and fangs. Ynvir pushed the furthest, his frost claws a blur of primal fury. Again, with a shrieking discharge the cannons fired, and more Wolves died. Harald howled.

Then the shadows struck. They flickered from the darkness of what had once been an underwater cavern, bored into the shoal's flank. Silver steel flashed in the grey light, and the hissing swordlings manning the skull cannons died. The machines, sentient and savage, ground round on spiked wheels, maws snapping, but the shadows darted back out of reach. Melta bombs flared, and the daemon engines came apart, blasted to molten slag, the skulls embedded in them split and shattered.

The Wolves pressed forward. The swordlings around them shimmered and blinked like a faulty viewfeed, the dark will binding them to the material plane fading. As the Khornate cohort finally vanished Harald found the shadows at his side. He recognised them.

'Bloody work, Space Wolf,' said Scout Sergeant Arro. His camo cape, pulled close around him, was slick with steaming strings of gore, and his alabaster features were streaked red. Harald recalled the Shadow Haunter Scouts from outside Morkai's Keep.

'What are you doing here?' Harald demanded. Beneath him Icetooth growled, wary of the cloaked figures crouched around them.

'We were sent to track you,' Arro said. 'But Corax forgive me, I cannot stand by and watch brothers dying like that.'

'The Iron Hands sent you?'

'Crusade command sent us. But they don't understand the extent of the incursion here. Consider us at your disposal, for now.'

Harald grunted. Before he could respond, Sven's panting voice broke in over the link.

'*Deathwolf. They're behind us. Soul Grinders. We need you.*'

'Brothers,' Harald snarled. 'On me.'

FATE UNBOUND

The Rock, in high orbit above Midgardia

The bridge of the Rock was a scene of chaos, and the Changeling rejoiced. It had done its work well. Azrael was locked into a dead-end argument with Egil Iron Wolf, and his underlings were at his mercy. Or, more accurately, the mercy of the bridge's comms chief, Vox Seneschal Mendaxis.

The communications pits heaved with activity as vox serfs attempted to contact the crusade fleet, the channels overlaid with orders to cease fire and demands for clarification. The augur banks were still picking up the occasional lance strike as Navy captains continued to respond to the Space Wolves barrage, in defiance of the confused messages emanating from the Rock. Amidst the disorder the Changeling sent out codes that further distorted what was happening – little blurts of static that cut up vital messages, contradictory targeting data-speech, new heading requests.

Through it all he listened to the conversation crackling back and forth between Azrael and Egil Iron Wolf. Each was demanding that the other stand down, the Dark Angel ordering the Wolves to withdraw to Fenris, while the Wolf was ordering the crusade fleet to disengage and leave the system. Neither appeared to be listening to the other. The Changeling cut and chopped the link at opportune moments, fighting furiously not to burst into laughter.

Such games amused it. They were a distraction, it was true, but for now the thing wearing Vox Seneschal Mendaxis' flesh had nothing better to be doing. The plans were in motion, turning and changing within themselves. The actors necessary for the play to begin were on their way, but until they arrived the Changeling would have its idle fun. It sent fresh firing coordinates to a squadron of Navy Sword-class escorts, locking them onto their Wolf counterparts. A flurry of clarification requests came back. Grinning, it ignored them and broke the data-link.

The air around the figure of Mendaxis shimmered for a moment, the blemish on reality visible only to those with attuned warp-sight. The

Changeling shuddered in its false skin, feeling the swirling skeins of Fate around it constricting. Of the thousandfold paths laid out by its master, more and more were slipping away, the few that remained yawning like the maws of hungry parasites as they sought to latch onto the present and take their place as the future.

The air shuddered again. It was drawing nearer. On a distant world, a ritual the Changeling had first set in motion a century before was reaching its climax. The Rock was bound with powerful wards, but the Changeling had done its work well, breaking the necessary ones with the help of its master. The fortress-monastery was still a difficult place to be, the sacred seals long ago woven by the Lion's Librarians, making the daemon's borrowed flesh crawl, while the incense that filled the bridge's air caught in the back of its throat. The games were a pleasing distraction from such discomforts. Soon, however, its patience would be rewarded. Soon they would be here – the Silver Fool, the Young King, the Angel Hunter – and then the real games could begin.

Svellgard

Svellgard's oceans died, and its islands churned with battle. As the three Imperial strike forces forged towards the trio of warp rifts sucking away the moon's seas, only one faltered. The Wolves were alone.

Sven's jump pack carried him up onto one of the Soul Grinder's segmented, arachnid-like limbs. His auto-stabilisers whirred as he cut the pack's turbo, using its momentum to throw himself along the twisted warp-steel and up towards the daemon engine's cockpit. The metal there was bent and deformed with growths of pulsing purple skin, sprouting at the top into a mouth-like cannon. The war machine's fleshy upper arms snatched for him, one vast meat-fused mechanical claw carving overhead. Sven ducked the swing and then triggered Longbound again, bounding up onto the top of the machine's pulsing turret.

His boots dug into skin as he landed, the thing's pistons shrieking like tortured voices as it attempted to twist its bulk and throw him off. Face contorted with hatred, Sven began to hack at it with Frostclaw. He started with the maw cannon, the axe's ever-keen edge hewing through metal and the meat entwined around it. The engine emitted a machine roar, trying to reach him with its vast claws, but the Wolf made the angles impossible. He began to beat at the top of the turret itself, hacking through thick folds of muscle and chitin growths to reach the corrupt metal beneath.

The rest of his Skyclaws were assaulting the Soul Grinder simultaneously, chainswords striking sparks from its mechanical limbs. One of the young Wolves was snatched up in its claws, his scream cut brutally short as the huge blades scissored shut, bisecting him. Sven hacked harder, a howl building in the back of his throat.

Below he was dimly aware of the arrival of the Deathwolves, Harald's ichor-soaked warriors pitching into the melee alongside his own. A second Soul Grinder took a Vindicator's demolisher shell to its turret, blowing out in a blizzard of twisted wreckage. Below Sven Frostclaw finally bit into metal, scarring the black steel. He swung again, with all his strength, fangs gritted. The frame shattered beneath him, and an ear-splitting shriek, like steel scraping along steel, rushed from the machine's wound. Sven smelled rotting meat and burning copper. He triggered Longbound.

The Soul Grinder stumbled and finally collapsed, its infernal bulk crushing a Skyclaw too slow to leap backwards. The air above the rent in the machine shimmered as the daemon possessing it escaped, vanishing back into the immaterium with one last piercing shriek.

Sven touched down beside the twitching wreckage, shaking and panting. The daemons had recoiled at the engine's death, massing their strength near the foot of the dune the Firehowlers were battling across. Harald pulled Icetooth to a stop beside the staring young Wolf Lord.

'We need to consolidate,' the Deathwolf said. 'Our losses have been too heavy.'

Sven said nothing, still staring into the distance, jump pack idling, streams of black gore slipping down his armour.

'Take up position on the brow of this dune,' Harald said. 'Let the Wulfen and the Claws hold them back long enough to reform the packs.'

'You yourself said we can't hold them,' Sven said. 'If we stop going forward, we die. All of us.'

'But we can buy time,' Harald said. 'And right now, no matter how hard you fight, pup, time is our only true hope.'

The Holmgang, *in high orbit above Midgardia*

The bridge of the *Holmgang* was hushed and tense. It was immediately apparent the moment vox contact was established with the ships above Midgardia that Ragnar's fleet was too late. Amidst the total breakdown in communications discipline, one thing was made clear by the fleets anchored in high orbit – Midgardia was burning.

Ragnar said nothing. Madox's vision had been true – before him, beyond the crystalflex ports, the death world was smeared with great whorls of black ash, its once-purple surface now a barren grey shot through with the flickers of fires so vast they could be viewed from orbit. More flames flared nearer, in the void between the ships already clustered above the planet. The crusade fleet and the Wolves defending Midgardia had turned on each other. The realisation made the Young King sick to the pits of his stomachs. He had failed.

'Lord Egil Iron Wolf is hailing us from his flagship, *Wolftide*,' Ragnar's vox huscarl said quietly. He motioned for the Chapter-serf to accept the link, not taking his eyes off Midgardia.

'*Lord Blackmane, well met.*' Egil's voice came through choppy and distorted, the range still extreme for ship-to-ship uplink communication.

'Lord Iron Wolf,' Ragnar said. 'Tell me my eyes deceive me.'

'*They do not, Blackmane. The Lion has burned Midgardia.*'

'And now you burn the Lion?'

'*They must be stopped.*'

'And they will be,' Ragnar growled. 'I swear it to you. But this may not all be their doing. There is dark maleficarum at work here, Iron Wolf. I have seen it.'

'*I have no doubt, Blackmane. There are wyrdspawn everywhere.*'

'And closer than we may think. I have enlisted the help of the Grey Knights. They will put a stop to all this.'

'*You would trust the daemonhunters?*' Egil asked. '*What of our Wulfen? Recall that they sought us out on Absolom not so long ago in order to persecute us.*'

'Krom saved their lives above the Wolf Moon, and I fought alongside them on *Mjalnar* to purge the wyrd-taint that had taken root there. They have had the chance to condemn us, but they have not.'

'*Not yet. Perhaps they are not strong enough to right now.*'

'They could have joined the crusade fleet against us. They know more than just the Wulfen are at stake here.'

'*And how can they be of any help to us?*'

'They will lend weight to our cause when I enter the Lion's den,' said Ragnar. 'Even the Angels cannot ignore the sons of Titan.'

The Rock, in high orbit above Midgardia

Azrael glared down at the holochart auspex from his command throne. For hours the runes representing the crusade-fleet assets and those of the Wolves had remained largely static, overlaid with intermittent trajectory paths. Now, however, the Rock's augur ports, already busy trying to track the spluttering half-engagement playing out with the Iron Wolf's fleet, were blinking red with warning lights. New sigils were appearing within the chart's sphere, multiplying with each static-wash update. Another Space Wolves fleet was approaching combat-effective range. The initial scans said it belonged to the Great Company of Ragnar Blackmane.

Azrael knew the name. The impetuous young Wolf Lord had encountered the Unforgiven on a number of occasions in the past century. Few of those occasions had been positive in nature. Azrael had read the reports.

Nor was Ragnar's fleet alone. Azrael saw the sigil representing *Allsaint's Herald* blink into existence, and had to suppress a surge of rage. Of course de Mornay would return, with a pack of tamed hounds to do his bidding.

'The meddling fool has brought pups for his dirty work,' Asmodai hissed from beside Azrael's throne, reading his Chapter Master's thoughts.

'I should have known he would. It makes no difference. We shall break from orbit and make for Fenris. That should sharpen the minds of these animals.'

'Lord, we are being hailed by *Allsaint's Herald,*' said Vox Seneschal Mendaxis, cutting in. 'Shall I accept?'

'Negative,' Azrael said. 'We have no time for–'

'*Greetings, Supreme Grand Master,*' crackled de Mornay's voice before he could finish.

'Mendaxis, I said–'

'*Before you break the link, you should be aware I have members of the Ordo Malleus' Chamber Militant onboard this vessel. Just in case you were considering firing on us as well as the Wolves.*'

'We are not the traitors here, de Mornay. You are the one parlaying with mutants.'

'*Enough of your thunder, Azrael. Even you can't deny this situation has gotten far out of hand. You have lost control of your own fleet. Let us speak, face to face, and resolve all this before it degenerates any further.*'

'I do not see how you can help. You will simply seek to further your own misguided agenda, as ever.'

'*You will receive us aboard the Rock, Azrael. I have the power to declare you* excommunicate traitoris, *you and your whole Chapter. Don't believe I won't use my Inquisitorial edict.*'

'Your threats are as ridiculous as they are ill-conceived, de Mornay. But we have come to expect that.'

'*Lord Azrael.*' The voice on the other end of the vox was suddenly different – heavy and leaden with grim, restrained power.

'Who is this?'

'*I am Captain Arvann Stern of the Grey Knights Third Brotherhood. I am here on the business of my Chamber Militant. I would speak with you in person, Supreme Grand Master.*'

For the first time since entering the Fenris System, Azrael felt a flash of uncertainty.

'You are accompanying de Mornay?'

'*We are with the Lord Inquisitor, yes. He has our protection, naturally.*'

'You may come aboard, but he may not.'

'*If we are to resolve this situation without shedding the blood of any more of the Emperor's servants, I strongly suggest he comes as well. As does a representative of the Wolves. This madness has gone on for long enough.*'

'They will try to intimidate us,' Asmodai muttered. 'It is ever their way.'

'*We will come alone,*' Stern said. '*No retinues. We seek only to discuss what has happened here.*'

'If there is any attempt to censure my Chapter–'

'*There won't be. The destruction wrought here has been the work of the Archenemy. Together we shall root out their taint and banish it back to where it belongs.*'

Azrael was silent, watching the markers blinking on the holochart below him, and the oculus viewscreens scattered across the bridge's expanse. Even with Ragnar Blackmane's arrival, the Wolves above Midgardia were still heavily outgunned by the crusade fleet. The Rock alone would have been a match for them. But the presence of the Grey Knights had pierced the fug of confusion and recrimination that seemed to be shrouding Midgardia's orbit as thoroughly as the ash clouds now choking its atmosphere. Azrael could not deny that since unleashing the firestorm, matters had been spiralling out of control. The freefall had to be arrested, even if that meant having to court the Wolves and rebuff de Mornay's latest misguided accusations in person. He keyed the transmission rune in his throne's armrest.

'I shall expect you within the hour,' he said, and cut the link.

Below, the Mendaxis-thing smiled.

Svellgard

It was *Iron Requiem* that struck the killing blow. That, and the combined firepower of two Imperial Navy cruisers, *Reducto Ignis* and *Pride of Galthamor*. Guided by the venerable battle-barge's ancient locking beacons, the three capital ships speared Svellgard's eastern warp portal with a direct orbital bombardment.

Terrek's Clan Company contained the neverborn as the ships rained annihilation on the maw they were clawing up out of. The Iron Hands had formed a cordon of ceramite and steel, bolters thundering death at anything that crawled from the great, discoloured whirlpool that marked the portal's heart. Nor did they stand alone. The Astra Militarum, bloodied but unbowed after their struggle across the bared seabed in support of the Space Marines, added their fire to that of the Angels of Death, a blizzard of fizzing las-bolts finishing anything that managed to breach the curtain of hard rounds laid down by Terrek's automaton-like brethren. Imperial Knights were with them now too, half a dozen striding through the deeper surf, bright heraldry gleaming in the dying light. Their heavy weapons barked and roared, lacerating the daemonic cohorts with irresistible firepower before they could form to attack.

Despite the destruction, the barrage laid down by the ground attack forces was insignificant next to the power of their fleets. The spines and chitin fangs that thrust above the waves, marking the edge of the portal's maw, snapped and shattered. Svellgard's swirling ocean was thrown into further turmoil by each burning lance strike and each super-heavy munitions shell, the waters foaming and erupting in towering columns. The concussive boom and crash of the roiling sea utterly smothered the howling of daemons and the hammering of mortal weaponry. It did not quite, however, drown out the exultations which blared from vox casters, laud hailers and every human throat. The daemons shied away from the holy litanies as assuredly as they did the bolts and las.

Terrek monitored the portal's closing from atop the hull of *Dark Vengeance*, the mighty Land Raider rocking beneath the Iron Captain as it was hammered by surf thrown up by the continuing bombardment. It was perched on a battle-scarred reef jutting above the maelstrom churning through the rift maw. The Iron Hand's bionics scanned the waves, reading the energy output torturing Svellgard's deepest points. The neverborn did not have long, his calculations estimated. Even as he watched, those still flinging themselves on the sons of the Gorgon flickered, their material forms unravelling beneath the twin assaults of fire and faith. They attacked with a frenzied abandon only immortal nightmares could enjoy, but they were banished all the same.

The tactical readout put the Ultramarines on course to close the northern portal within the next hour. The data from Epathus' assault was ultimately much the same as that transmitted by Terrek, only slight deviations in time and casualty ratios separating the twin strike forces. The same could not be said for the Wolves.

The Shadow Haunter Scouts had stopped reporting back half an hour earlier, but the auspex uplinked to the readout showed their attack had stalled completely. The two Great Companies had merged on top of what looked like an exposed coral dune, the green wolf's head runes on the display surrounded by a thick sea of blinking red contact markers. Estimated losses for the combined force stood at just under half, and the figure rose even as Terrek monitored it.

At the current rate of daemonic incursion, the Iron Captain gave them two more hours before they were completely overrun, give or take a twenty-minute margin of error. And that thought did not worry him in the slightest.

A hellsword punched through Sven's battleplate. The blow was like a spike of fire being driven into the Wolf's side. He grunted with the impact and the sudden rush of pain, his body flushing with painkiller stimms. The swordling tried to claw through his helmet's lenses with its other hand, shoving the blade deeper as it did.

Sven cut its head off. Black ichor fountained across the Wolf, and after a moment the thing flickered and vanished, sword and all. Sven bit back a moan as blood flowed from the wound in his side, battling to blank out the pain.

He was tired. His thoughts, still coloured with the arrogant exuberance of a young Firehowler, railed against the idea of admitting it, but it stood as a fact, incontrovertible despite his own *skjald*-worthy battle-lust. He had been fighting for days without rest or sustenance. His armour was scarred and in need of maintenance, the servos whirring and heaving, the auto-senses lagging fractionally. His body was no better; it was bruised, cut and bleeding, his hand still sprained and his rib-plate now split in two places. A swooping pack of furies had also managed to rake a wound through the seal of his right pauldron. His vital readouts told him the hellsword had just pierced his oolitic kidney. The wound was far from fatal – his genhanced biology was already rushing to clot and reknit the damage – but the sudden pain had brought home the reality Sven had been denying.

They were all going to die.

If Harald knew it he wasn't admitting it. The Deathwolf was marshalling the defence of the northern and eastern side of the coral shoal, directing the ordnance of the Predators and a trio of Land Raiders at its base as they poured fire into the onrushing wyrdspawn. Sven's heavy armour did much the same on the opposing slopes, while the bloodied packs gathered themselves further up, checking bolt magazines and dragging thick chunks of daemonic viscera from their chainblades.

Sven counted the heads of the Skyclaw pack around him. Four of the youths still stood. Olaf, his brow a crusting mess where a daemonette's claw had caught him earlier, was his last standing Bloodguard. Kregga still lived, but had been almost gutted by a Khornate murder engine. He'd been dragged to the hill's crest where the Wolf Priests were seeing to the Wolves' wounded. The rune on Sven's visor representing his vital signs display pulsed weakly.

The Skyclaws were staring, and he realised abruptly that he'd been clutching the wound in his side, gauntlet slick with his own blood. He snarled at them, like a pack leader, and they averted their gazes.

'*Not long now, pup,*' Harald's voice crackled over the vox.

'Before the last of us vanish beneath this tide of filth?' Harald didn't respond. The air around Sven throbbed as a macrocannon shell from low orbit turned the seabed two hundred yards south into a roiling ball of flame. The Space Wolves ships had shifted their firepower from the southern portal to the wyrdlings flinging themselves at the stalled ground advance. Even their great weapons would not be enough. Time, the basis of Harald's desperate strategy, was running out.

Then Sven's short-range auspex display lit up, and finally everything changed.

Shuttle Forty-Eight Nine-B, in high orbit above Midgardia

The Rock made *Gormenjarl* and *Mjalnar* look like reclusiam outhouses set alongside a fully fledged Ministorum basilica. It completely filled the pict feeds of the *Herald*'s shuttle, a craggy planetoid of black, crater-scarred stone studded with bristling spires. Defence turrets, communication uplinks, augur shafts and the yawning maws of spacedock ports were set alongside the crenelated structures that presumably housed the Dark Angels chapel-barracks, armoury cells and training towers.

A whole fleet could have rearmed and refitted safely within the Rock's bowels. The light of the Wolf's Eye reflected back from a thousand arched, stained crystalflex viewing ports and the barrels of a hundred super-heavy defence-system weapons. Light throbbed from the fortified planet shard too, idling in its vast plasma drives and warp engines, and flickering with actinic energy where its ancient force shield shorted and sparked. Crowning it all was the Angelicasta, the Tower of Angels, a great bastion-pillar of dark, shattered stone and flying buttresses surrounded by a cluster of cathedral-sized ruins.

Looking upon the ancient spaceborne monolith, even Ragnar felt a pang of doubt. The fortress-monastery of the Dark Angels matched the Fang in its towering, seemingly indestructible bulk. It represented the original might of the First Legion, a throwback to mankind's sundering, the days of wrath and ruin when brother had fought brother and the fate of the galaxy had stood poised on a razor edge.

'Into the Lion's den,' the Wolf Lord muttered.

Neither Stern nor de Mornay answered. Both were watching the visual feeds alongside Ragnar, their faces grim. For the first time since Ragnar had met him, the inquisitor had welcomed them aboard his shuttle standing up, rather than slumped in his palanquin. He was clad in a suit of humming mark seventeen exo-plate, thick with vitae-support coils and strapped-on life pumps. His torso was shielded with reinforced layers of flak, while an energy-conversion pack plugged into his back plates powered the armoured leg callipers and limb braces that held him firm. Though the inquisitor was pale with the obvious strain placed upon his ageing body, he seemed to draw a grim pleasure from Ragnar's surprise when he saw him.

'Try to keep up, Wolf,' he'd said, patting the plasma pistol locked to his hip. Now, as they drew near the Rock, Ragnar noted the inquisitor's knuckles were white beneath the plasteel tendons of his exo-armour, his scarred body clearly charged with anticipation. Once again the Space Wolf wondered at the man's obsession with the Dark Angels. The relationship between the ordos and the Adeptus Astartes was often fraught, but de Mornay seemed to have dedicated his entire life to hounding the Lions. Ragnar wondered how much longer they'd permit him to chase them.

'We go to negotiate, not fight,' Stern said.

'They're often very similar, good captain,' the inquisitor replied. 'Both should be conducted from a position of strength. That's something you learn quickly once you join the ordos.'

The shuttle docked, sliding through a deactivated section of the force shield and into the waiting maw of one of the Rock's ports. Ragnar released his restraining harness as the landing probes brought the transport to a shuddering halt. The main hatch disengaged with a thud of clamps and a whine of hydraulics, venting gouts of steam. Beyond it the docking bay was scattered with dead-eyed haulage servitors and scampering Chapter-serfs in discoloured white shifts. Gargoyle-headed vox speakers inset into the bare stone walls blared servicing orders and screeds of data updates.

A single Dark Angel waited for the three arrivals, the white cowl of his habit drawn up. He gave a short, stiff bow as they stepped out onto the bay.

'Lords, my name is Sergeant Elija. If you will follow me.' He turned without waiting for them, pacing off towards a grav lift. Ragnar glanced at Stern, but the Knight's face was unreadable. They followed.

If the Fang was a tribal lair carved into Asaheim's cold stone, then the Rock was an ancient cathedral long abandoned. Elija led them down echoing corridors thick with dust and through antechambers overlooked by the towering statues of hooded angels. The floor beneath was flagged with stones and the heavy brick walls bound with shafts of age-dulled plasteel, while the ceiling overhead was vaulted and choked with deep shadows. Burning, spiked braziers flickered at intervals down the corridor, their light seeming to deepen the foreboding gloom. The only signs of life – though it was a cruel jest to call it such – were the servo-skulls that occasionally hummed past, or observed them with blinking optics and empty sockets from brass charging ports set high on the corridor walls. Until they came to the bridge, they met no one.

Ragnar wondered whether the apparent desolation was just for show. He could feel the humming power of the charged asteroid vibrating through the surfaces around him, and distant booms and clunks occasionally shook pattering motes of dust down from the vaults overhead. He knew there were hundreds of Adeptus Astartes and tens of thousands of serfs above, below and around him. Either the Dark Angels wished to hide their strength, or unsettle their visitors.

And despite Ragnar's burning dislike for the sons of the Lion, their efforts were not wholly in vain. An air of unutterable melancholy hung over the entire fortress-monastery, an ache of the heart that had gone on for far too long. For the first time, the Space Wolf felt something more akin to remorse rather than spite when he considered the Unforgiven. While the halls of the Fang echoed with exuberant boasts, *skjald*-songs and the sounds of feasting, the Rock lay in cold, sepulchral silence, alone in the void.

The silence at least was banished when they reached the primary bridge. The plainsong chants of course-chartists warring with the crackle of vox horns, the rattling of cogitators, the blaring of alarm systems and the whir of augur pickups and oculus viewscreens, the scuffle of hurrying feet and the frantic murmur of situation reports finally gave evidence of activity. Elija led the trio through the feverish workings of the vast, echoing command hub, Stern at the fore, de Mornay limping at the rear in his walking armour.

Their path led them to a great, hooded figure, overseeing the ceaseless work from a throne centred atop a dais that rose from the surrounding communications pits like some ancient ziggurat. Beside the throne stood a second figure, similarly clad in a white habit, the black battleplate and screaming-skull helm marking him out as one of the Dark Angels'

Interrogator-Chaplains. Both figures surveyed Elija as he stopped beneath the dais and struck his gauntlet against his breastplate in salute.

'Welcome, Brother-Captain Stern,' said the figure on the throne. He rose and descended the stairs, servos humming. All the while he looked only at the Grey Knight, eyes dark and piercing beneath his cowl.

'Supreme Grand Master Azrael,' Stern said, nodding his head in a brief show of respect. 'My thanks for receiving us here.'

'You left me little choice, Grey Knight.'

'Choice is a luxury few of us possess.'

'That much is true.' The Dark Angel and his Chaplain reached the foot of the dais, facing the interlopers. Throughout the exchange they had pointedly ignored both Ragnar and de Mornay. The Wolf Lord felt his anger spike. He could sense the inquisitor beside him struggling to hold his tongue.

'My Master Interrogator-Chaplain, Brother Asmodai,' Azrael said, introducing the reaper-like figure beside him.

'Explain your presence here, daemonhunter,' Asmodai said, words slipping like serpent's venom from his black, cowl-shrouded helm.

'There is something wrong with this place,' Stern said. 'I felt it as soon as I stepped onboard.'

'Do not abuse my hospitality,' Azrael said. 'I have brought you here in good faith.'

'Then indulge me, lord.' Stern cast his hard gaze across the bridge. 'I have hunted the filth of the warp for as long as you have been Master of your Chapter. My kind are trained to root out taint, and my warp-sight knows when they are near.'

Ragnar noted that the holy etchings on the Grey Knight's silver aegis had started to glow dully.

'Recently there have been a... number of inexplicable incidents,' Azrael said slowly, as though unwilling to admit as much. 'One of our Scouts disappeared from the apothecarion, and a number of the Chapter-serfs have been acting strangely. Even our Master Astropath is unsettled. My own vox seneschal has been–'

'Where is he?' Stern interrupted, hand dropping to the hilt of his force sword.

Azrael glanced at the primary communications pit and frowned. His gaze travelled up, and caught the back of Vox Seneschal Mendaxis, trailing data cables and readout scrolls as he walked brusquely towards the bridge's open blast doors.

'Mendaxis!' Azrael barked. 'Where do you think you're going?'

Stern's blade rasped from its scabbard, and the air was suddenly full of static charge. Mendaxis didn't look back, but darted through the doors, far faster than any human being should have been able to move.

'*Daemon,*' Stern snarled.

* * *

Svellgard

Like the Wolf That Stalks Between Stars, the Redmaws fell from the void upon Svellgard. The vox thrilled with howls and snarls, and the words of Bran himself.

'Hold firm, brothers. The Lost have returned.'

Drop pods struck the seabed to the south of what should have been the site of Sven and Harald's last stand. Wulfen burst from them as soon as their flanks dropped, driven into a maddened frenzy by the confined spaces. Four Murderpacks ripped into the daemons north of the warp rift, their howls echoing up to their embattled brethren.

The rest of Bran Redmaw's Great Company – those who had resisted the curse – followed. They fought their way from their pods with savage efficiency, bolters hammering the knots of daemons not already broken apart by their sudden, brutal arrival. Thunderhawks sped low overhead, raking the lesser daemons with more bolter fire, their forward cannons blasting apart the larger engines and writhing spawn. Within minutes the drop zone was secure.

Sven and Harald had no need to confer, either with Bran or each other. Together they ordered their bloodied packs forward, fuelled by the wild strength of warriors who had learned their immediate deaths were not yet inevitable. They led from the front, trying to outpace each other, frost axes an icy blur in the cold, ichor-saturated air. Darkness was falling, and the last gleam of the Wolf's Eye touched upon the tarnished armour of the three Great Companies as they came together near the rift's swirling, churning edge.

The killing did not end there. The daemons flung themselves at the Wolves with even greater fury than before, heedless of their fate, desperate to rip flesh and shed blood before they were thrown from the material universe. But they found their fury outmatched. Bran's Wulfen – almost half his Great Company – were savage even for their cursed kind. They fought on despite the gravest of wounds, seemingly sustained by the purity of their hatred. The legions of the Dark Gods could not stand before them.

As the circle finally tightened around the last rift, the ships of the Wolves' three fleets combined their armaments, raining fire down into the hellmaw. Together Sven, Harald and Bran hurled the wyrdspawn back into their watery abyss, while the colossal tear of weeping flesh and bone that had burrowed from the darkest dimension into Svellgard's reality was unmade by orbital annihilation. On the Wolves fought, killing now on instinct, exhaustion driving out conscious thought and leaving room only for the swing of blade and the slash of claws.

And then, suddenly, Sven found no more wyrdflesh for Frostclaw's slick edge. He spun, snarling, expecting to be struck from behind, fearing some fresh maleficarum.

Instead he realised he was staring back at the remains of his pack – ragged, panting, bloody in twilight's last light. The anger and the hatred that had sustained him was suddenly gone, and he fell to his knees amid the surf, head bowed.

It was over.

And yet, in truth, it had barely begun.

The Rock, in high orbit above Midgardia

The Changeling laughed freely as it fled. It darted down the bridge's main access corridor and then right, through a sub-shaft, the doors sliding open with a flick of the Mendaxis-thing's hand. Around it Chapter-serfs scrambled to get out of the way, wide-eyed with shock.

Throughout the Rock, warning claxons began to wail. The vox piece still fitted to the Mendaxis-thing's ear was alive with frantic chatter. Through it all, the furious voice of Azrael boomed.

'*Stop that thing!*'

The Changeling managed to control its mirth long enough to spit a string of arcane syllables, grotesquely distorting the Mendaxis-thing's mouth in order to utter the unnatural words. The vox-link clicked and went silent, the channel killed as assuredly as if the transmission stud had been flicked. The daemonic entity bound to the scrapcode virus the Changeling had uploaded from the primary communications pit had awoken. It would take weeks of machine-psalms and recoding before it was banished and the Rock's internal communications systems were functioning again.

The giggling daemon vaulted down a plasteel stairwell and knocked a serf out of the way. At the daemon's touch the man screamed and convulsed, flesh breaking out into hideous, bloody growths. The Changeling didn't even notice, barging through one door and then down another flight. Around it reality was a blur, a haze of multiple possibilities overlaying and interlocking with each other. Its goal lay down, deep down, amidst the stygian darkness of the Rock's forbidden crypts and vaults.

Soon the distant ritual would be complete, and its master's plan one step closer to glorious, irresistible, ever-changing fruition.

They found Mendaxis in a long-disused venting shaft for a reserve thermal coil. His neck had been snapped and he'd been stripped naked, his wizened body hung upside down from a coolant pipe and carved bloody with dark sigils. The corpse was weeks old.

Interrogator-Chaplain Elezar was there too. He'd been struck so hard that his skull helm had fractured. He still lived, but his sus-an membrane had forced his body into a regenerative coma, and he was immobile. Azrael snapped orders at a train of anxious Chapter-serfs to have him taken to the apothecarion. The hunt resumed.

'This way,' Stern said. He pounded down a flight of stairs, ceramite ringing off steel, the air heavy with the static charge of his force blade's disruptor field. Azrael and Ragnar were right behind him. The Wolf Lord had *Frostfang* out, its rotor idling throatily, while Azrael had drawn the Sword of Secrets, the power weapon's ancient obsidian blade crackling with its own energy field.

Asmodai and de Mornay followed, the inquisitor in front, struggling in his whirring battle-suit. Having the Master Interrogator-Chaplain stalking directly behind him set the inquisitor's whole body on edge, and with every step a part of him expected to feel the Dark Angel's ignited crozius arcanum slam into his back.

Below, Stern pushed deeper, through another set of blast doors that, until recently, had been firmly warded and sealed. There were few warp entities capable of penetrating the psychic defences of a fortress-monastery as ancient as the Rock, and even fewer capable of surviving there for any length of time. Whatever the thing was, it had left behind a trail. Its passing would have been invisible to untuned mortals; Stern, however, had the witch sight.

A cloud of spores, glowing with a luminous, sickening light, hung in the air before the Grey Knight, marking the corrupting influence of Chaos. Azrael had commanded his Librarians to attend him, but the whole of the Rock's hardwired vox-network had unexpectedly shut down, undoubtedly evidence of further daemonic tampering. The corridors of the Rock would need to be thoroughly cleansed once the threat had been removed, but until then the passing taint was the only way of tracking the daemon.

That, and the scattering of hideously mutated, mewling bodies it left in its wake. Ragnar killed each deformed horror with a swift thrust of *Frostfang*, while Stern and Azrael pressed on. They could hear the thing's laughter echoing up from the levels below, mocking and childlike.

'It's headed for the vaults,' Azrael said. 'We can't let it reach them.'

'What is it trying to achieve?' de Mornay called after him.

'Let's stop it before we find out.'

'Lower your blocking shield, Supreme Grand Master,' Stern said. 'Allow my brethren to teleport aboard. We could cut it off.'

'No. We will find this trickster eventually, with or without your help.'

The trail led them through the Rock's gloomy structures, out into a processional way lined with graven statues of hooded, skeletal angels. The great force shield crackled and spat lightning overhead. At the far end of the way vault doors loomed, just one of a number of entrances leading deeper into the fortress-monastery's hidden depths. The doors themselves were carved in the likeness of more angels, features hidden by their cowls, broken swords in their fleshless fists. Two Deathwing Terminators, looking for all the world like two more towering, bone-carved statues in their off-white Tactical Dreadnought armour, stood either side of the heavy doors. They raised their storm bolters as the party approached.

'Lower your weapons,' Azrael snapped. The Terminators hesitated before doing so.

'Lord, you... only just passed this way,' said one of the hulking Deathwing.

'We have been compromised,' Azrael replied. 'There is a shapeshifting warp entity on the loose. He could be any one of us. No one is to enter or leave here alone, is that clear? Only when there is more than one of us. Even if the Lion himself demands passage, you are to halt him.'

'Yes, lord.' The Terminator's red lenses swung across Ragnar, Stern and de Mornay, lingering on the inquisitor. 'And what of these three?'

'They are with me,' Azrael said. 'For now.' The Dark Angel pulled his cowl back, stepping up to the door's retinal scanner. It blinked, and there was a gentle hiss as the great Angel-crafted slabs of adamantium rolled smoothly back.

Beyond, darkness. It took a second for even Ragnar's advanced senses to adjust. Below, a stone stairway led to a second set of great doors, similarly inscribed with the Chapter's *angelica mortis* heraldry.

Azrael hesitated at the top of the stairs, a hand snatching Stern's pauldron before he could descend. He looked back at Stern, Ragnar and de Mornay, his dark eyes holding each gaze in turn.

'Down here, you must stay by my side at all times. There are places you cannot go.'

'Wherever the warpspawn are found, there shall I smite them,' Stern said, reciting one of his Ordo Malleus canticles. Azrael said nothing, but removed his hand. Asmodai leaned in close to de Mornay, words hissing from the shadows of his cowl.

'I'll be right behind you, inquisitor.'

Into the darkness they went.

Soon.

The realisation thrilled the Changeling. To an immortal such as it, time was everything and nothing – the warp made it eddy and shift in inconceivable patterns. And to the Changeling, the past century of painstaking preparation had felt like an aeon.

It slid through another ward gate, its muttered incantations burning away the hexagrammic seals. It no longer laughed. Matters had become serious. The games were over. Fate, the very essence of the future, was writhing about it like a great, slippery sea creature. It had to snatch onto it, grasp it, latch its yawning maw to the present, so that its silver tail became the future, stretching out into infinity.

It was deep down now, so close to the core of the Rock that even the throb of the mobile fortress-monastery's engines was a distant, tiny tremor, fainter than the last beat of a dying man's heart. The air around it shivered, as though the musty, ancient place found its presence repellent.

It was directly below the Tower of Angels. It passed through mouldering, lightless crypts and ancient armouries, the blades and battleplate thick with cobwebs. Even the Angels dared not tread here, bound up in their own superstitions. The Changeling could sense the revulsion Azrael felt as he accompanied a trio of outsiders into the most sacred depths of his home, twinned with his fear. He knew exactly what the daemon's intentions were.

A cavernous, bare rock tunnel took the daemon back up a level, out of the Angelicasta's depths. The sweet, slow-burning taste of lingering pain and despair lured it on, filling its warp-flesh with vigour. It would be their salvation. And through them, it would take despair from these few, and give it to the many.

A cluster of dungeon vaults lay ahead, just some of those that pierced the Rock's cold heart. The green ceramite and white cloth that encased the Changeling were serving it well. None dared doubt the veracity of the Supreme Grand Master himself.

More guards fooled. With the entire vox-network disabled it was impossible for Azrael to get news of the imposter to travel ahead of the daemon itself. By the time they realised their mistake, it was already outside the first reinforced hatch. Outside the very first of the cells holding the Fallen. The dungeon's anteroom was circular, two-dozen heavy, barred doors each leading off to an individual holding block. Each one was flanked by graven statues, their broken swords inscribed with active warding runes. To the Changeling's warp-sight, the very stonework bled despair, agony and regret, the tendrils of emotion a delicious aroma to the hungry daemon. Its borrowed hand reached for the gene-lock of the first hatch.

Where it stopped. A shudder – a rare sensation – ran down the Changeling's borrowed spine, the shadow of an instinctive reaction born from its time wearing mortal flesh. Skin prickled and the servos in the illusion of its power armour whirred as its fists clenched. Around it, for the first time since it had set events in motion, Fate buckled.

There was something at the far end of the cell corridor. The Changeling could not so much see it as sense the absence of the aether around it. To the daemon's warp-sight, the thing was really an un-thing, a black void without tangible thoughts or emotions to define it.

The daemon tried to look upon the un-thing with Azrael's flesh-eyes. It was diminutive in size, its form hidden beneath the thick folds of a bone-coloured cloak, as though in imitation of the Lion's sons. The shadows beneath its deep cowl were utterly impenetrable, as dark to mortal eyes as its soul-presence was to the Changeling's warp vision.

It did not move. It did not have to. The Changeling found itself taking a step back, the daemon's flesh quivering. Fear was something the Changeling could not feel, only feed upon, but the sight of the un-thing watching him from the shadows caused the daemon an indefinable, icy discomfort.

The Changeling could not stay here. It could go no further. This part of the wider plan was unnecessary anyway, a mere addendum to the ritual that would carry the daemonic trickster away, and drag the Lions with it. The Changeling doubled back the way it had come, the cells untouched. Fate's weave morphed, the future a newborn, fresh entity.

Behind it, the Watcher in the Dark remained silent and unmoving. It was still there, unseen, when back within the Angelicasta's depths the Lion, the Wolf, Knight and Angel Hunter finally caught the Changeling at bay.

Svellgard

The madness was gone. The skies above Svellgard no longer blazed with firepower, and the ocean's remains lapped at their new shores, tides calm once again. The great tracts of barren, exposed former seabed steamed in the evening light while the tundra of the islands – now hilltops – gleamed coldly.

'Well met, Redmaw,' Harald said. His fellow Wolf Lord nodded, face and forearms streaked with wyrdling ichor.

'Likewise, Deathwolf. It is good to finally bloody the Murderpacks.'

'The curse has struck you hard, brother.' No comment had been made of Bran's savage appearance. The Wolf Lord merely nodded, looking out over his packs. They still prowled with hungry intent around the crags and shoals of Svellgard's former seabed, their wyrd-hate unsated.

'It was a long voyage here, Deathwolf,' Bran said eventually. 'I am just thankful we made it at all.'

'Our companies owe you life debts,' Harald said, glancing over to where Sven was pulling himself back onto his feet with the assistance of his Blood-guard, Olaf. The vox in Harald's ear clicked.

'*It's Arro,*' said the Shadow Haunter. Last the Wolf Lord had seen of the sinister descendant of Corax, he and his sole remaining Initiate had been battling alongside Feingar and his Coldeyes Wolf Scouts. '*The crusade forces have been ordered to evacuate the surface immediately. You may wish to do the same. I suspect another bombardment is imminent.*'

'They wouldn't dare,' Harald said, fighting to keep the weariness from his voice. 'After all this, they couldn't now strike us from orbit.'

'*I cannot claim to know their minds, Wolf Lord. But your Chapter are the executioners of old. Tell me, if you were loosed upon mutants, would you stop anywhere short of total annihilation?*'

The Rock, in high orbit above Midgardia

'Brothers,' said the Stern-thing.

'Daemon,' Stern replied, raising his force sword. Ragnar, Azrael, Asmo-dai and de Mornay came up short behind the Grey Knight, staring at his twin, a perfect reflection dominating the far end of the corridor.

The Stern-thing's face twisted with a wild grin, an expression that looked utterly unnatural on the Knight's graven features. Ragnar activated *Frost-fang* at the same time that Azrael and Asmodai brought up their own blades.

'Stay back,' Stern said, pacing towards the waiting daemon. 'There isn't room enough for all of us.'

As much as it pained him, Ragnar saw the daemonhunter was right. The corridor was a narrow one, the paladin's silver pauldrons almost scraping its stone walls. The grin on the opposing Stern-thing's face remained fixed.

'I was beginning to wonder if you would ever catch me, brothers. It was getting lonely down here, amidst the–'

Stern struck. If any of them had expected the daemon's trickery to unravel, they were to be disappointed. The Stern-thing met the real Grey Knight blade for blade, and both weapons flared with equal force, bolts of lightning arcing and snapping at the surrounding walls. The two warriors drew back as one, the movements perfectly mirrored. The daemon's mimicry was sickeningly accurate.

'Begone, foul warpspawn!' the Stern-thing bellowed, abandoning its grin in favour of a theatrically grim expression. 'Back to the black pit from whence you crawled!'

'I have not come here to be mocked,' Stern snarled, and slashed. Again the blades clashed.

'Speak not unto the daemon,' the Stern-thing said, all fake earnestness as the two parted once again. Ragnar was thankful the narrowness of the corridor prevented them from circling one another. He doubted he'd have been able to keep track of the true Stern.

And then, the thing changed. There was a blaze of light, diffracted and kaleidoscopic. Ragnar snarled and averted his eyes. When he looked again, Madox glared back at him over Stern's shoulder, baroque armour gleaming in the glow of the lumen orbs.

'Everything I told you was true, Wolf,' the Thousand Sons sorcerer said, voice dripping with disdain. 'Why didn't you listen? You could have saved Midgardia. You could have saved your Great Wolf. And now he's gone. *Logan Grimnar is dead.*'

Ragnar took a pace towards the daemon, fangs bared. Azrael snatched him by the shoulder.

'Rein in your savagery, Wolf. It's trying to trick us.'

'Is it, Lion?'

This time the voice was as cold and cutting as serrated steel. The corridor was abruptly plunged into darkness, the actinic lightning of Stern's, Azrael's and Asmodai's weapons the only illumination. When the dull lumen orbs flickered on a second later, the thing had changed once again.

Now it was clothed in a manner not dissimilar to the Dark Angels, white robes hanging over ancient, black power armour. The thing's hood threw its features into deep shadow. An ornate, heavy-looking blade hung from a scabbard, draped from chains behind twin pistol holsters.

'I am here to make you answer for your crimes, Keeper of the False Truth,' the figure said. 'I am here to make you repent. In the name of the Lion–'

Azrael's roar drowned out the daemon's words. The Master of the Unforgiven thrust violently past Stern, obsidian blade lunging for the hooded figure. It darted back, the crackling light of Azrael's sword illuminating a vicious grin beneath the cowl.

'Stop!' Stern bellowed. 'You don't know what you're dealing with!'

Ragnar felt his hairs prick as the Grey Knight thrust a fragment of his will into the command, charging it with psychic energy. Azrael shuddered to a halt, face contorted with fury. Stern pushed him aside.

'I know what you are,' the Grey Knight said, addressing the daemon. 'Even in the realms of the warp it would be impossible for anything else to do what you have done here, Changeling.'

'Don't be so sure, corpse-worshipper,' the hooded Space Marine said. Then, still grinning, he exploded. Bloody meat and shards of ceramite scythed towards Stern, Azrael and Ragnar, evaporating as the illusion came undone. Something unfurled itself from the space where the Adeptus Astartes had been, spreading feathered pinions, its beaked head stooped against the corridor's low arches. It screeched, the sound piercing Ragnar's ears and shaking the rock around him. For a moment even Stern stood transfixed, staring up at the crouching, blue-feathered Lord of Change.

'M'Kachen,' the Grey Knight breathed.

+Who else?+ The greater daemon's words thrust directly into their minds, accompanied by a peal of mocking, avian laughter.

'No,' Stern said through gritted teeth. 'Your lies are at an end, Changeling.'

'We are buried in lies here,' the daemon taunted. 'They're all around us.'

It made a series of arcane gestures with its claws. There was an ear-splitting crack, and a sudden fissure appeared in the stonework to the right of the greater daemon. Sickly, diffracted light blazed from it, followed by a phantom gale that tugged at the habits and cowls of the Dark Angels. The M'Kachen-thing croaked a series of unutterable syllables and the cracks split wider, bursting apart in a hail of shattered stone. The portal blazed with eldritch energy, the howling of a realm of pure madness grating from the jagged, broken stone like a million razor blades.

Horrors bounded from the infernal light. The dank air filled with their mad gibbering, and warpfire sparked and ignited in the corridor around them.

'Stop them,' Stern shouted. 'I will banish the trickster.'

Asmodai struck first, roused to righteous wrath by the presence of warp filth in the Rock's most sacred depths. The ghost-wind snapped at his white-and-green habit, making it billow around his black armoured form. He swung his crozius arcanum in a crackling arc, the wings of the holy weapon wreathed in white energy. Daemons disintegrated before him, their unnatural flames breaking and spluttering harmlessly around the

Interrogator-Chaplain. The rosarius hanging from an adamantium chain around his neck, crafted in the likeness of the hooded Angel of Protection, blazed with golden energy as it shielded him from the dark warp magics.

Ragnar and then de Mornay fought to join him, pressed against the corridor wall. The Wolf Lord carved through one pink horror after another, *Frostfang* reducing them to writhing ectoplasmic blobs. Even as he killed them their swirling remains reformed into smaller blue horrors, sneering and snapping at him as they tried to claw through his power armour.

De Mornay fired his plasma pistol into the twisted mass coming from the portal at point-blank range, a prayer on his lips. The incandescent bolts of blue energy vaporised the leading clutch of daemons, but still they came. Soon the pistol was burning in the grip of the inquisitor's exo-gauntlet, steam venting from the carbon-adamant ventilation casing and the magnetic accelerator coils ribbing its spine glowing blue with overuse.

Down the corridor, Azrael and Stern fought the Changeling. It was a blur, toying with reality as it battled the two Space Marines, the borrowed flesh of the greater daemon seeming to shift and twitch like a faulty viewfeed as it phased away from its attackers. The Angel and the Knight rained blows on it, their weapons wreathed with power, but the daemon matched each and every one with a long silver staff. A riposte dented Stern's pauldron and scarred Azrael's breastplate, ripping his habit.

The thing was fast. Azrael recklessly lunged into its guard, the black obsidian of the Heavenfall Blade punching like a lance towards the thing's shifting core. It moved again, but this time too slow to properly avoid the sudden strike. The Sword of Secrets caught the Changeling in the flank, the ancient weapon searing through feathers and flesh alike. The M'Kachen-thing let out a screech and snatched at the Supreme Grand Master. Left exposed by the lunge, he found his arm gripped in the greater daemon's avian claws. It twisted viciously, and there was an audible snap before it flung the Dark Angel bodily back against the chamber's far wall.

Stern thrust forward, force sword blazing with white light. The winged greater daemon parried the blow with its staff, deceptively spindly arms bolstered by the strength of the warp. Stern locked in place, servos groaning as the two strained.

Azrael found his feet. He took the Sword of Secrets in his left arm, his right broken by the daemon's claws. As Stern pinned the creature's guard the Dark Angel seized the opportunity to lunge in beneath the Grey Knight's raised weapon, but his thrust never connected with the daemon's lower limbs. It spat a string of twisting syllables, and the Dark Angel was forced to his knees by a sudden flood of pain. His secondary heart kicking in with a jolt, he snarled with agony as he tried to force his burning limbs to obey his commands. The Sword of Secrets slipped from his grasp, the obsidian blade clattering and shorting as it struck the dusty stone floor.

Ragnar saw the Supreme Grand Master battling to rise and Stern held in place. He dragged himself free from the press of horrors, gouging a path through their flailing bodies. Asmodai fought on, feet planted before the portal, the Angel of Vengeance that tipped his crozius arcanum dealing death from its deadly wingtips with each stroke. The press of daemons had forced de Mornay up against the wall, his overheated pistol abandoned, servos straining as he sought to grapple with two horrors forcing themselves upon him with their snapping, drooling maws.

'I abjure thee,' Stern was snarling, wreathed in white fire as he pitted his psychic strength against that of the Changeling. 'I banish thee. I cast thee out of His Holy Realm.'

The daemon echoed his words with its own dark litany, the titanic energies building between them threatening to shake apart the whole tunnel. Azrael managed to force his way back onto his feet once more, teeth gritted against the pain suffusing his body. He clutched the Sword of Secrets in one shaking gauntlet.

Ragnar smashed apart the last horror between him and the Changeling. Stern was still pinning its staff with his own blade. He saw his opening. A prayer to Russ on his lips, the Young King swung *Frostfang* for one of the daemon's straining limbs.

The ancient chainsword bit true. The daemon's shriek matched the weapon's roar as it juddered through warp-woven feathers and flesh. Light blazed once again. The phantom wind redoubled in strength, accompanied by the crash of more splitting rock. His auto-stabilisers activated as he fought to stay upright, a gauntlet going up to shield his eyes.

Through the blaze he saw silhouettes. Stern was standing tall, his sword held high. The greater daemon was gone, replaced by a hunched, multi-limbed figure. Behind it reality had further come apart, the stone of the tunnel wall now disintegrating into nothingness. Beyond it Ragnar caught an impression of tall, broken turrets and snapping pennants. The view seemed to plummet, morphing and changing into a bare stone chamber occupied by armoured figures – unmistakably Adeptus Astartes. They stood waiting on the other side of the rift, their features indiscernible in the blazing light that ringed it.

The lesser daemons howled and shrieked. The invisible wind ripped at them, tearing their coruscating flesh away in great globules, sucking them back into the portal that had birthed them. De Mornay managed to tear himself from them as they were whipped away into oblivion. Asmodai crushed the morphing skull of one more with his fist before it was dragged back into the immaterium.

The figure stepped through after its disintegrating minions, as though struggling in a gale. The portal shimmered. Ragnar managed to take a pace towards it, his howl torn away by the wyrdwind. Stern was at his side, the daemonhunter still bellowing his sacred oaths. Azrael managed to reach out too. The Sword of Secrets lunged, almost piercing the veil of reality as the hunched creature slipped away.

And then it was over. Like wakefulness asserting itself after a vivid dream, both the light and the gale vanished. The momentum of the Space Marines carried them forward, but rather than plunge through the rift and into the mysterious chamber, their gauntlets struck scorched stone. The warp portals were gone, the only evidence of their existence the burn markings on the tunnel wall. And the faintest sound of giggling laughter, echoing away into nothingness.

Stern slumped against the wall, even his prodigious mental strength spent. Azrael grimaced, extending his broken arm until bones cracked and snapped back into alignment.

'I was blind,' the Dark Angel said bitterly as the stimms kicked in, as though speaking to the Rock itself. 'I was fixed so firmly on Fenris I could not see the snares set about my feet.'

'About our feet,' Ragnar said, gazing at the burn marks on the wall. 'We have all suffered from this wyrdspawn's trickery.'

'It will pay,' Azrael said. 'For such mockery, I will hunt it to the edges of realspace and beyond.'

'Before you do that, I think we would all benefit if you withdrew your ships from here,' de Mornay said. The inquisitor was shaking and pale with pain and exhaustion, only held upright by the scarred frame of his armour. 'There has been enough misplaced bloodshed already.'

Azrael looked at the inquisitor and then at Ragnar, his dark eyes holding the Wolf's bestial gaze.

'The Imperium will not allow you to harbour mutants. If we do not call you to task, another will. Then our actions here may seem lenient.'

'There are proper channels,' said Stern, sheathing his force sword. 'A conclave of the ordos should be called and the matter debated openly. I have witnessed the wolf-beasts with my own eyes. Without them, this system would have fallen to daemonic infestation. I can find no trace of warp taint upon them, only grievous genetic anomalies.'

'I agree,' said de Mornay. 'As terrible as they seem, I would be dead without them. They must be judged openly, and with due process.'

Azrael was silent for a moment more. When he spoke again it was with brusque finality.

'The crusade fleet will withdraw to the system's edge while the situation is assessed. I will have my Librarians scour this place. If they can pick up the daemon's spoor, they may be able to track it to wherever it went. I believe it is still within the material plane. We cannot permit its continued existence, and I won't allow its acts here to go unpunished.'

'It will lead you on a pointless dance of destruction,' Stern warned. 'It is known in our grimoires as one of the most devious of all the Trickster God's servants.'

'All the more reason to destroy it,' Azrael said. 'Until we can, though, and until the time is right to sit in judgement, I shall order my fleet assets to disengage from Fenris.'

Iron Requiem, *in low orbit above Svellgard*

The dark bridge of the Iron Hands battle-barge hummed with power, the atmosphere crackling with pent-up energy. The lance batteries were almost fully charged.

Terrek watched the Space Wolves on the moon below, picking out their positional markers with the machine-mind of his hardwired auto-senses. He sat once again in *Iron Requiem*'s command throne, linked directly to the ancient warship, his cold steel body inert as his thoughts communed with *Requiem*'s spirit. It was tired but exhilarated, the air of the bridge heavy with the smell of discharge and las after-burn, the battle-barge's great guns still glowing hot in their open ports. It had been a righteous hammer today, a purger of the unclean, a destroyer of the impure.

Its holy work was not yet done.

The Wolves below were beginning to evacuate, perhaps sensing what was to come. They were too slow. Terrek had returned to his flagship almost an hour earlier, as soon as his objective on the surface had been completed. There was no time to be lost. While the Wolves were still clustered in battle array, they presented an optimal target.

Epathus had refused to join him in the strike, and there was no word from the Shadow Haunter Scouts still on the surface. It did not matter. Where others flinched, the Iron Hands remained unbending. *Requiem*'s firepower would be more than enough, and with their surface assets destroyed the Space Wolves fleets would be left open to his squads' boarding pods and teleport strikes. By the time dawn touched the dark side of Frostheim, Terrek would have reclaimed both the world and its moon for the Imperium.

The iron was hot. It was time to strike.

Terrek realised the bridge serfs were pleading for his attention. He understood why a moment later, as a priority vox signal beamed into his consciousness, flowing directly from the *Requiem*'s communications banks into his mind via his cortical plug. He blink-scanned the message.

+ + inter-fleet transmission ref. 97/19/RDM + +
+ + sender: Gloriana-class battleship *Invincible Reason* + +
+ + ident-code 7697: callsign Lionsword + +
+ + *This is Supreme Grand Master Azrael to all crusade fleet elements. All ships are to disengage with immediate effect. New heading coordinates are being transmitted. There are to be no hostilities conducted against the*

Space Wolves from this moment onwards. Repeat, all ships are to disengage immediately. Stand by for further orders. + +

  + + message ends + +

Terrek felt a rush of anger even his detached thoughts struggled to suppress. *Iron Requiem* responded in sympathy around him, the engines flaring fractionally as the ancient vessel shared its brother's dismay. The moment was now. The iron burned. The renegades were exposed, their mutants at the crusade fleet's mercy.

More data streamed through his thoughts. The Ultramarines ships were breaking from orbit. Even as he assessed their likely heading, the rest of the crusade fleet began to depart. Terrek buried another surge of anger.

Without the rest of the fleet to support them once hostilities resumed, the statistical likelihood of a decisive victory over the Wolves began to drop. The urge to strike, to purge the foul taint of the unclean, still burned bright, warming his cold augmetics and throbbing through his synth-organs. His own internal logic systems, however, would not permit him to override a direct order from Crusade Command. The judgement of the Wolves would have to wait.

With a thought, Terrek began to power down the lances.

The Fang, Fenris

There had not been so many Wolves on Fenris since the great hunt for the Wulfen had begun. Six Great Companies – even ones as bloodied as the Firehowlers or the Deathwolves – made the halls blaze with life. The warriors feasted and boasted and drank, and tried to forget that Midgardia was ash, and Longhowl an abattoir, and Svellgard a wilderness of rock and mud pools, and Morkai's Keep a ruin.

Their lords could not so easily ignore what had happened in the war zone that the Fenris System had become. They gathered in the Hall of the Great Wolf, in the heart of the Fang. The vast chamber was cold, its craggy, pelt-draped walls only half lit by a few lumen braziers. At its centre lay the great stone slabs of the Grand Annulus, the flickering light picking out the wolf crests of the Great Companies inscribed upon the twelve blocks, and the scorched, unmarked darkness of the thirteenth.

Sven, Harald, Krom, Egil, Bran and Ragnar stood upon their respective slabs. They all still wore their battleplate, the ceramite scarred and pitted. Each tried not to glance at the empty stone bearing the carving of the Night Runner – Logan Grimnar's crest.

'I request I be allowed to return to Midgardia immediately,' said Egil Iron Wolf, shattering the chill silence. He held the battered, gilded skull of Fellclaw, the Great Wolf's crown, in his hands. Skol hummed around his shoulders, the servo-skull's pict recorder blinking.

The other Wolf Lords were silent. 'I made an oath,' Egil went on. 'To return. The fires set by the Angels did not reach into the subterranean levels. The Great Wolf is still down there.'

'And we will find him,' Krom said quietly.

'So let me go.'

'We all wish to go,' Krom said. 'But we cannot abandon the rest of the system. The crusade fleet remains active on its edges. They are simply waiting for official sanction before returning.'

'Kjarl Grimblood's Great Company is projected to arrive in-system soon,' Ragnar said. 'Let him go to Midgardia. We cannot forsake it.'

'I will join Grimblood alone if need be,' Egil said. 'My Great Company can remain here in defence of the Fang, if that is what you all wish.'

'We must secure Svellgard as well,' Sven said. 'The Claws of the World Wolf may be needed if the crusade fleet returns. And the vaults of Morkai's Keep should be scoured.'

'And what of the doppegangrel-spawned wyrdling trickster that caused all this?' Krom asked. 'And the inquisitor you claimed would assist us, Ragnar?'

'De Mornay departed after the Lions,' Ragnar said. 'I do not believe he will ever stop chasing them. As for the wyrdspawn, I saw it with my own eyes. I suspect it was the Changeling, the same filth that infiltrated the Fang after the Great Wolf first disappeared, and impersonated him on Dargur. Russ only knows how long it had secreted itself aboard the Rock. Even the daemonhunter, Captain Stern, could not fully banish it.'

'The Lions will hunt it,' Krom said. 'We have more pressing concerns.' None needed to say what those concerns were. The Wolf Lords' eyes were drawn to the single, scarred black slab of the Annulus, the one unmarked by any sigil. That of the Thirteenth Company. The Lost. The Wulfen.

'Let us not think ourselves so superior to our kin,' Bran said, looking at each of his fellow lords in turn. He had donned his armour once more, though a wildness still glinted in his eyes, burning yellow in the half dark. 'Let us not imagine this curse – if we must call it that – is an affliction visited upon our Thirteenth Company alone. Can any of us here deny that we have felt its pull long before the reappearance of our brothers? Would any here face me and claim that this deficiency has not been with them every day since they first bore our primarch's gene-seed? We do not understand the Thirteenth, so we fear them. But at the same time, we know them, for who among us has not seen our closest brothers join them? Who among us cannot see ourselves mirrored in them?'

'The right and the wrong of it all can be debated with more time than any of us currently possess,' said Harald. They were the first words he had spoken, and all eyes turned to him.

'It is clear we must work to discover a means of artificially restraining the influence of the Canis Helix,' he continued. 'But one thing is certain. We stand at one of the darkest points in our Chapter's history. The greatest powers of the warp have conspired to destroy us. Not only the Imperium at large, but us specifically. A tide of filth fouler than any I have ever seen has engulfed our worlds. We have resisted, as is our way, yet I believe this saga has only just begun. I cannot say whether the Wulfen are our salvation or our doom. Before Svellgard I believed the latter. But since then my mind has been clear. Cursed or not, I would rather die beside my pack brothers – all thirteen companies – than ever raise Glacius against even a single one of them.'

There were growls of approval from the other Wolf Lords. Harald went on.

'Our Chapter has suffered many losses, and those not yet fallen stand on the brink of madness. Morkai's Keep is a shattered ruin, and the surface of Midgardia an ashen wasteland, its population – our own subjects – wiped out. The Great Wolf is gone. Many of our allies believe we are both lost and damned. Treachery stares us in the face, while defeat snaps at our heels. Other warriors would despair. But not us. We are greater than any wyrd-spawned plot or jealous mortal's lies. We are the Allfather's chosen, his rough-pelted warhounds, the scourge of the heretic and the bane of all traitors. Our sagas sing of ten millennia of triumph, and we will be sure to add to them yet. For Russ, and for the Wolftime.'

He looked at the heart of the Annulus, at the spherical stone inscribed with the crest of the Space Wolves Chapter itself.

'Fenris endures.'

THE HUNT FOR
LOGAN GRIMNAR

Ben Counter

PART ONE

FEAST OF LIES

For the first time in many years, Logan Grimnar was exhausted from battle. He had held off the tau for nearly three days as the xenos had sent unending packs of attack-beasts and swift hover-tanks to harass the Space Wolves.

The aliens had paid dearly for the chance to tire out the Great Wolf of Fenris. Hundreds of tau and their alien auxiliaries lay among the rocky canyons covering the surface of Dactyla. Now, as the Great Company faced the xenos outside, Grimnar stood on the threshold of the temple he had come to this world to find.

'Can the Great Company stand?' asked one of Grimnar's champions. Each of the half-dozen warriors was taken from the Chapter's Wolf Guard, armed with Terminator armour and their pick of weaponry from the Fang's armoury. It was rare that anyone would speak to Grimnar so bluntly, and Grimnar still had ample fury in him to round on the warrior.

'You know better than to question the resolve of our brethren,' he snarled. 'They will stand as long as they have to. And we will ensure that is not for long. Follow me and speak no more.'

The temple was more ancient than the Great Crusade itself. Echoes of a long-dead xenos empire's architecture broke through the living rock of the tunnel complex beneath the ground. Even as Grimnar led his champions down further, he could hear the reports of tau pulse rifles and the replying volleys of bolter fire.

They were Space Wolves, and the tau were as drained by the running battle as Grimnar and his brethren were. The Great Company would hold. The tau assault would be blunted. He knew this because this was the place the runes had described, and Grimnar would not return from this hunt empty-handed.

'There,' said Grimnar, indicating a symbol cut into the wall. It resembled a serpent coiling around a skull. 'Njal Stormcaller cast that rune as I watched. We are close. Just a little further.'

Grimnar felt the weight of the Axe Morkai as he walked. The warrior he had once been would have dearly loved to lay it down and rest, but those were the thoughts of a lazy pup and not the Great Wolf, so he forged on until he came upon a massive circular slab of rock blocking the way ahead.

Without a word, Grimnar put a shoulder against the rock and pushed. The Wolf Guard joined him, adding their strength to his. The slab rolled aside, revealing the way into the chamber that lay at the heart of the complex.

Purple light bled from the vault. Grimnar's autosenses were not enough to shut down the glare completely, and he held a hand in front of his face, squinting. The Wolf Guard had their storm bolters ready to open fire on any enemy that might emerge from the temple's core, but they held their fire.

They saw what Grimnar did. And in that moment, all the weariness of battle was gone.

Ulrik's watch included the dawn hours, when the blood-red light of Fenris' sun broke across the glacier-bound mountains. It was the season of fire, when Fenris came closest to its star and the equatorial oceans boiled. In the environs of the Fang there was no warmth, but the ground heaved and cracked like distant thunder as the glaciers experienced a rare thaw.

'It will be today,' said a voice behind Ulrik. It was that of the Wolf Lord Krom Dragongaze, whose Great Company had the duty of manning the Fang during the Thirtieth Great Hunt. Krom wore his trophy rack on the back of his power armour, surrounding his ruddy face with a halo of jangling bone. The orange ridge of hair along his scalp was dark in the reddish dawn light. 'Do you not think so, Lord Slayer?'

'Perhaps,' said Ulrik. He anticipated the return of the Great Companies as much as any at the Fang, and yet he could not let the emotions of a Fenrisian close to the surface.

'I can smell it,' said Krom. 'My Great Company is restless. It is not a glorious task, to serve as housekeepers here while the rest of the Chapter is on the hunt. I must fight to keep them focused, and yet I itch to be let off the leash myself.'

'Sometimes,' said Ulrik, 'we must keep the wolf caged.'

'That is not as easy for us as it is for you,' said Krom shortly.

Ulrik kept looking into the distance. He wore, as always, his armour's skull-faced helmet, and so Krom had no chance of reading anything from his face. Ulrik let the silence fall, broken only by the distant moan of the thaw and the cries of frosthawks wheeling overhead.

'Forgive me,' said Krom. 'I spoke out of turn.'

Ulrik did not move to face the Wolf Lord, and instead pointed a finger up towards the colouring sky. A silver streak was just visible there, like a falling star, a thread of precious metal suspended.

'The *Canis Pax*,' said Ulrik. 'You were correct, Lord Dragongaze. It is today.'

The *Canis Pax* carried with it the Great Company of Alaric Nightrunner, known to the rest of the Chapter as the Silent Howlers. They descended in a fleet of shuttles from their strike cruiser and landed among the eyries of the Fang, and were met by a host of thralls to assist with their docking procedures and get the first glimpse of the trophies they had brought back. The brothers of Krom Dragongaze's Great Company, the Drakeslayers, lined the processional down towards the cell blocks and sparring halls of the Fangs, saluting Nightrunner's battle-brothers on their return. Behind them walked Alaric Nightrunner himself, cutting as dashing a figure as there was among the Space Wolves, with skin the colour of beaten bronze and thunder hammer swinging at his hip. Alongside Nightrunner's Company marched the Rune Priest Njal Stormcaller, by some accounts the most powerful psyker the Space Wolves had fielded for thousands of years.

Everyone there cried out the same question: what trophy had the Silent Howlers brought back to Fenris? No Wolf Lord ever returned from the Great Hunt without a new prize to be displayed at the Fang as a symbol of the Space Wolves' relentlessness at the hunt. Alaric did not carry a new skull or captured banner, and met all questioners with the same knowing smile.

Ulrik was not among the honour guard. This was a time for the Space Wolves to be uncaged and to let their spirits run wild. They needed times like this. They did not need a presence like Ulrik standing over them to remind them of their duties. Instead, the Wolf Priest spent several hours in the Reclusiam, drafting missives to be sent out by courier-thrall to the most loyal tribes of Fenris. Each one called for them to send an emissary, one of the wise and powerful men permitted to know of the Chapter's workings, to the outskirts of the mountain fortress' hinterland, where a shuttle from the eyries of the Fang would transport them to the inaccessible peak. There they were to hear of the exploits of the Great Hunt, and take the tales they heard back to their tribes.

It was part of the cycle that brought new blood into the Chapter. The youthful warriors of Fenris learned of the Space Wolves' heroic deeds and sought to emulate them in the endless battles between the tribes and with the furious indigenous life forms of Fenris. The Wolf Priests, led by Ulrik, chose the most valiant, and brought them into the Chapter to be put through the Blooding and made into Space Wolves. The myth of the Space Wolves was as crucial a part of the process as the warlike Fenrisian stock, and the Great Hunt served to create new legends that grew and spread with every telling.

Elsewhere in the Fang, for nineteen days Alaric Nightrunner kept his silence. In that time three more Great Companies, those of Bran Redmaw,

Gunnar Red Moon and Sven Bloodhowl, arrived home laden down with the trophies they had taken. Finally the emissaries from the tribes arrived, and Ulrik led them wordlessly into the fortress – wise men and warlords, the soothsayers and patriarchs of their clans. The call went out for the Space Wolves to gather in the Great Hall and hear the sagas of the Great Hunt. The first to take the place reserved for the saga-teller was Alaric Nightrunner.

Ulrik presided over the feasting. There was only so much of the leash that could be given to a Space Wolf. Five Great Companies were present in the Great Hall and Fenrisian ale was flowing, a concoction of fermented plant life lethal to an unaugmented man. It was strong enough to affect a Space Marine in spite of his enhanced capacity to filter out toxins, so Ulrik was ready to intervene in case boasting and challenging turned to bloodshed among the battle-brothers. Ulrik stood in his black, skull-faced armour, silent while the cheering and drinking songs of the Space Wolves battered against him like a sea wind.

Alaric Nightrunner approached the enormous fireplace to a tremendous cheer. The tribal emissaries applauded too, and among them Ulrik recognised the First Spear of the Bear tribe, a muscle-bound warrior carrying a kraken-tooth lance, and the hooded emissary of the Stargazer tribe. The Frost Wyrm tribe, the Flint Striders and the People of the Burning Sea had also sent representatives. Not all the tribes had answered Ulrik's call, but many had. Whatever tale Alaric was about to tell, it would soon be heard by all of Fenris.

Alaric heard the cheering for a minute, then motioned for quiet. The noise lowered enough for him to be heard.

'I carry no trophy for you,' he said. The battle-brothers cried out in dismay. 'But that does not mean I have disgraced the Great Hunt. Far from it! No, I have a tale for you, and fear not, there will be plenty of reason to pour yet more of Fenris' bounty down your gullets.

'Our hunt took us to the edge of the Ghoul Stars, where the void is as clouded as a corpse's eyes. The *Canis Pax* was my steed and my brethren were sharpening their blades for the chase. The region is haunted by warp predators and the ghosts of fallen xenos empires, and there is always worthy quarry to be had! Njal Stormcaller, whose casting of the runes guided all the Great Companies on the Great Hunt, stood by my side, and he looked upon the diseased void with great relish. He foresaw the foes all but begging to be put to the bolter and the chainsword. And I had my thunder hammer and spear ready to take the foremost head!'

The brothers of Alaric's Great Company cheered and pounded the feasting table. The Space Wolves of the other companies shoved the Silent Howlers and jeered, but they could not drown out the celebration.

'And we were not disappointed! But it was not some void ghost or spectre that we found. No, the quarry found us. Which of you has not faced the accursed tyranids upon the battlefield? The shadow across the stars, the Great Devourer? You all have cause to hate the tyranid, and indeed I have left a thousand of their foul warrior-beasts headless and gutted in my wake. And yet, I had never faced them like this.

'The *Canis Pax* was pursued by a great hive ship of the tyranids. This monstrous, living thing was like one of the whales that live in Fenris' deep oceans, but vast enough to swallow the *Canis Pax* whole! And indeed, that is what it intended, for it hounded us for many leagues across the void.

'The hive ship loosed its spores, and they fell upon the hull of our strike cruiser. I despatched the brothers of my company to face the boarders, and furious battle raged on the *Canis Pax*! Elbow-deep in dark ichor were my brethren, their snarls of rage punctuated by the sound of chainblades through chitinous armour. And what tales of heroism I could tell you of the hours they fought! Time and again they fended off the tyranids as the xenos tried to breach the bridge and engine rooms. They led counter-charges to the alien beachheads, where the raw void had bled into the decks.

'Hundreds of tyranids were slain. The smaller creatures attacked in waves. The warrior-creatures that serve as elites and officers among their kind directed them, and were singled out for combat and destruction by the pack leaders of the Silent Howlers. I took my place outside the bridge, and beside me stood the Stormcaller. He called on the World Wolf to open his jaws, and a score of tyranids tumbled into the void he conjured! He bade the lightning fall upon the enemy, and a brood of warriors was charred to smouldering chitin by the sky's fire that answered! And as the enemy charged, I killed one with every spear-thrust, and crushed a skull or a ribcage with every swing of my thunder hammer. Thus did the first prey of our Great Hunt fall, and it was good!'

'But brothers, it was not enough, for the hive ship itself was closing in. If we did not destroy it, it would consume us. Even if we outpaced it, there might have been a million warrior-beasts in its belly to send against us. And though the brethren fought with fury, some were brought down and slain. Howl the names of Agmundyr Iron Talon, Kari the Swift and Hrolfyr Bearhide! For they reaped a toll of the xenos filth before they fell.'

Alaric Nightrunner's Great Company howled a long, high note of mourning for the fallen. The other Space Wolves did not harangue them now. Alaric grabbed a flagon from the table beside him and poured the foaming ale down his throat in one, and at his signal the Silent Howlers did the same.

'And when the fight paused,' continued Alaric, 'I turned to the Stormcaller. To him, I said, "We cannot destroy this hive ship alone. Our torpedoes cannot penetrate its hide, and its presence so close prevents us from jumping into the warp." And the Stormcaller replied, "Is this Alaric Nightrunner who speaks? The Wolf Lord most renowned for his cunning, for whom no battlefield conundrum is too obscure? Use that cunning, my lord, and with wisdom seal its fate!" Thus did Njal Stormcaller speak to me, and I was much chastised by his words, for they were true. But in that moment, I knew the solution.

'Imagine, my brothers, the void, befouled by the presence of the Ghoul Stars. The hive ship pursues the *Canis Pax*, and disgorges more boarding spores with every moment. And now, when the hour is darkest, a hero emerges! A Stormwolf gunship flies from the strike cruiser's fighter decks, and it is painted with the heraldry of the Wolf Lord, Alaric Nightrunner! Can you see it, my brothers?

'Then a hatch opens, and the Wolf Lord himself steps out onto the hull. White vapour streams from the faceplate of his helm. He carries the spear with which he slew the Frost Worm of Jormun Glacier. He holds it above him, and though none can hear him in the void, he is yelling obscenities at the hive ship, and demands it fight him one to one, spear against void-borne might!'

The Silent Howlers were laughing now, whooping between swallows of Fenrisian ale. They began banging the tables rhythmically, a drum roll that shuddered the floor of the Great Hall. Alaric was posing with his spear, holding it above his head as he brandished it at an imaginary hive ship.

'The hive ship closes in. Its jaws open in a grin wide enough to swallow the *Canis Pax*. Deep within its gullet are colonies of tyranid filth, tens of thousands of them roosting in the cavern of its mouth, thousands more crawling between its teeth to pick at the morsels of its last meal. The Storm-wolf flies closer, the Wolf Lord draws back his arm to strike... and he is gone!'

The laughter stopped. The Great Hall was suddenly silent as every Space Wolf there imagined the hive ship's jaws closing on the Stormwolf, swallowing the gunship and the Wolf Lord alike.

Alaric held them there, extending the moment of silence for as long as he dared.

'And then... boom!'

The Silent Howlers erupted. Ale spattered on the walls and floor as they held their flagons aloft.

'I give you Njal Stormcaller,' exclaimed Alaric over the din. 'The greatest worker of wonders ever born to Fenris! For it was he who created the illusion of the Stormwolf, and of myself atop it, waving my spear as if I meant to harpoon that great whale of the void. And that illusion was wrapped around a most tasty morsel – a cyclonic torpedo, a deep detonation warhead, such as the *Canis Pax* uses to rake the flanks of its prey. The hive ship's hide was too stout to let the torpedo through, but once the beast had swallowed its prey, I gave the order to detonate!

'The warhead must have gone off close to the beast's brain pan. Instantly, it became ill-coordinated and slow, and faltered in its pursuit. And those of you who know the tyranid well are aware of how the lords among them coordinate the lesser beasts from afar. The hive ship controlled the creatures assailing the *Canis Pax*, or else its brain was used to transmit the commands from whatever distant horror leads their fleets. The control was broken, and now the tyranids on board the *Canis Pax* became unfocused and panicked, striking about at random or seeking to flee. And what Space Wolf could resist such a hateful foe, suddenly so ripe for the killing?

'So I led my brethren in falling upon the tyranid. It took three hours to finish the task. Three hours of butchery and revenge! I must have taken two hundred hormagaunt heads, and a dozen warrior-beasts fell beneath my thunder hammer and spear. There is joy in the hunt hard-run and well-fought, it is true, but I cannot deny the pleasure of the hunt that falls upon the prey when it has been made weak and desperate. And when the *Canis Pax* was free of the xenos taint and its decks were awash with dark blood, we turned to the hive ship.

'Its jaws lolled open. It drifted without purpose. I ordered the *Canis Pax* to turn about and unload its missiles and torpedoes down the beast's ruined throat. Its innards were blasted through, and it vomited forth a mighty torrent of torn xenos flesh and dead tyranids. How could such a sight be so foul, and yet so glorious? Thus was the death of the hive ship, and thus did the Great Company of Alaric Nightrunner take its quarry in the Great Hunt!'

Alaric gave a grand bow and the battle-brothers of his company chanted his name. Alaric accepted their acclaim with exaggerated humility, laying his spear on the floor before them as they cheered.

'Wait!' cried a voice. Krom Dragongaze's face was flushed with drink, and no doubt with anger that he had not had the chance to bring such a tale back from the Great Hunt. 'You tell a fine story, Lord Nightrunner. But every lord on the Great Hunt must return to the Fang with a trophy of his kill. I see you carry no new baubles. Where is your trophy?'

'Lord Dragongaze,' replied Alaric with a smile. 'You have but to look.' He pointed to the large windows at one end of the Great Hall, which led onto a balcony looking out over the snowy hinterland of the Fang.

Ulrik followed the gaze of every Space Wolf. Through the windows, a pair of Stormwolf gunships came in low over the peak of one of the Fang's sister mountains. Between them was strung an enormous object that took shape as the mists were blown away by the engines – it was a titanic length of curved bone, lined with thousands of teeth. It was several hundred metres long, and looked to be part of a much, much larger skull.

The ships lowered the jawbone onto the peak, where it became lodged between spurs of snow-capped rock.

'The jawbone of the hive ship,' said Alaric Nightrunner. 'Presented to my brothers of the Fang.'

In the hours of feasting that followed Alaric Nightrunner's story, the Great Companies of Erik Morkai and Egil Iron Wolf arrived back at the Fang, accompanied by fanfare and feasting as before. Ulrik again stood back from the celebrations, and watched from the Great Hall's balcony as Engir Krakendoom's shuttle fleet descended to the eyries.

Ulrik saw that Njal Stormcaller had joined him on the balcony. The Rune Priest's fierce, wind-burned face was not flushed with drink. Ulrik had noticed him abstaining from the Fenrisian ale.

'How straight was Lord Nightrunner's tale?' said Ulrik. 'I will not contemplate he lied, but his are the tales that gain and lose much in the telling.'

'True enough,' said Njal. The various rune-stones and bone trinkets hanging from his robes jangled in the chill wind as he watched Lord Krakendoom's shuttles coming in to roost. 'All that he said happened, happened. He did not say that my casting of the runes led him to the Ghoul Stars, where there was no sign of our true quarry. He did not disclose the great disappointment I saw in him that he had brought down his enemy with a ploy from afar, rather than slaying a champion of the warp that in single combat, or some xenos corruptor whose death marked the freedom of a human world. But yes, his tale was straight enough, as it goes.'

'Krakendoom is almost as garrulous as Lord Alaric,' said Ulrik. 'I expect he will demand the saga-teller's place next.'

'And he is not shy to call out those who do not match his exploits. Perhaps you will be needed in the hall before long.'

'No doubt,' said Ulrik. 'I have broken up scraps between him and Dragongaze since they were Blood Claws.'

Already there was a commotion in the Great Hall as the first of Engir Krakendoom's Great Company, the Seawolves, took their place among the revellers.

'Let us hear what he has to say,' said Ulrik.

'Think of the foulest place,' said Engir Krakendoom. 'Think of the most noisome pit, the rankest orifice of a world you have ever been to. Now think of it twice as filthy, three times as foetid, four times as brimming with vermin! The world you think of now is Sorixyn IX. And there the Great Hunt led us, and though it was a world benighted and embattled, the Seawolves leapt right into this sea of filth! For there the soldiers of the Imperium fought, and there were enemies that needed killing.'

Krakendoom's Great Company had a reputation for fierce ship-to-ship combat prowess, and they wore that reputation on their armour as kill-markings and memorials of engagements. Many of them wore now the skulls of the lizard-like pests that infested the jungle world of Sorixyn IX, and more than a few wore ork skulls or finger bones as trophies of their last battles. They were as boisterous as ever, cuffing and wrestling with one another as their Wolf Lord spoke.

'The Imperial Guard on Sorixyn were veterans of death world campaigns, and yet this world was preying on them as if they were newborn pinklings! And their foe was the ork, that most resilient of vermin, which was moving at will through the dense jungle hunting man and beast. Truly, if there was ever a world that cried out for the tender touch of the Space Wolves, it was this one.

'The Seawolves fell upon the orks where the fight was fiercest, and many were the life-debts pledged to the sons of Fenris by regiments of the Imperial Guard in return for their deliverance! At Foulfester Ridge and the Blackleaf River we left heaps of the orkish dead in our wake. Our Stormwolves strafed the crude orkish airfields and our packs rampaged through their mech-yards and supply trails! But there was one foe that could not be fought with the tactics of drop pod and bolter volley. No, this was a creature whose legend was as dangerous as an entire war-host of greenskins, whose existence eroded the will of the Guardsmen more than the cruelty of the jungle or the savagery of the ork. And they called it the Thousand-Handed One.

'While my brethren joined the Imperial Guard in fending off the orks, I made it my duty to hunt down the Thousand-Handed One. For was this not an omen, to have such a quarry placed in my path while upon the Great Hunt? It was for such a hunt that I was born. Why, you ask? Because of this nose!

'This nose, my brothers, is as keen as any blade in the armouries of the Fang. This nose has slain more foes of mankind than the guns of a battleship! There was no corner of Sorixyn this Thousand-Handed One could flee to where I would not sniff him out. It was among a heap of slain Guardsmen that I picked up his scent. And what a scent it was! Who among you has not experienced the stench of the ork?'

At this, a disgusted groan and angry grumbling rose from the Space Wolves. A quirk of the Chapter's gene-seed, one inherited from the Primarch Leman Russ himself, was an exceptionally well-developed sense of smell. There was indeed nowhere to hide from a Space Wolf once he had the scent, and he could close his eyes and sense a world picked out in smells instead of colours. Engir Krakendoom prided himself on a sense of smell that had tracked a Fenrisian werekraken across a stretch of fjord and glacier, and many a Space Wolf could proudly claim feats of olfactory prowess.

And it was true that orks stank. Ulrik himself could remember his first whiff of the greenskin. It was something that truly never left a Space Wolf's memory.

'Yes, you know it well,' continued Krakendoom. 'That hint of spoiled offal. That mixture of sweat and stale ordure. The fire of the filth that clings between its fangs! The pus and rot of its battle-wounds! When the Wolf-time comes, when I stand beside the Emperor and Lord Russ to fight the final battle, I shall rejoice to know that soon I will never have to smell an ork again!

'And the Thousand-Handed One had a very particular scent of its own. Its name came from the men's hands it took as trophies and wore about it everywhere it went. It had the smell of death on it as well as the orkish stink. And so I followed it through the jungle, through gullies choked with foulness and across pools of bubbling sulphurous bile. Sorixyn IX tried to stop me as best it could with its own exotic smells, be it the rot-lily or the carrion of a fallen scarasaur, but I did not relent.

'And I was being hunted in turn. The Thousand-Handed One knew I was after it, and it had my trail, too. We circled one another through the jungle, closing and drawing away, each seeking the perfect terrain to strike. Were we equally matched? Was this a quarry whose prowess in the hunt matched that of Engir Krakendoom?

'It was many days after I picked up the trail that I found a dark and foetid hollow. I knew the Thousand-Handed One was at least half a day away. I judged the place perfect to lure in my prey and subject him to a lethal array of death traps. I set up deadfalls and snares, spear-throwers loaded with the springs of young saplings, spike pits and tripwires, using every scrap of field knowledge I had learned in decades upon the battlefield. And at the end of this gauntlet I waited, the bait for this trap, feigning injury and exhaustion such as would make me an irresistible feast for the savage ork.

'But the Thousand-Handed One was not a son of Fenris. It knew not the honour of the hunt, the respect granted to the prey, the bond between hunter and quarry we learn while barely out of the cradle. It cared nothing for a clean kill, face to face. No, it was a coward. And once it divined my location, it called on the greenskin artillery on a nearby hill to bombard my position with a firestorm of furious shrapnel!'

The Space Wolves hissed and spat to hear of the dishonour of the greenskins. It was said that a long time ago, in the age of the Scattering, human encountered ork for the first time and instinctively came to a place of mutual hatred. Orks had just enough concept of civilisation to delight in tearing it down, and enough sense of honour to wantonly breach it whenever they could.

'And yet,' said Krakendoom, calming the grumbling with an outstretched hand, 'I was no fool. Of course I knew the greenskin would call on its big guns to flush me out. Of course I knew the Thousand-Handed One would cast away all the honour of the hunt and take its cheap kill while it could. And so I had prepared a way out of my death trap, a tunnel through the rocks that broke from the clinging mulch of the jungle floor. It was just big enough to admit my mighty frame, and as the shells whistled down I crawled through it and out into a nearby valley where the artillery could not find me.

'For hours the shells fell. The sky was black with smoke, and lit with the red lightning of explosions. A terrible thunder rolled across the jungle! Yet I was unharmed, and in that valley brimming with foulness, I waited. Predators fled from the thunder, but they saw in me a fellow hunter and gave me a wide berth.

'Finally, the fires no longer fell from the sky. As the echoes died, I heard the war cries of the greenskins as they moved through the remains of my death trap. And I caught the scent of the Thousand-Handed One, at the head of a band of orks, and I knew they were searching for my corpse.

'Yes, the Thousand-Handed One was looking for me. And it found me! I leapt from my hiding-place, no longer content to skulk like a lizard in the undergrowth. For the first time I saw the Thousand-Handed One up close, and what a beast it was! Twice the height of a Space Marine and three times as broad, a hulking monstrosity such as had terrorised the whole battle zone of Sorixyn IX. Chains of severed hands hung around it. Its enormous fangs were crusted with filth and gore. It carried an axe well-stained with the blood of Imperial Guardsmen, and its dark green skin was as gnarled as the bullet-scarred trees of the jungle.

'Across the smouldering ruin of the jungle our eyes met, and the Thousand-Handed One knew it had been outfoxed. For a moment it showed the honour of the prey, just enough for it to bark angrily at the other greenskins who followed it so they shied away and did not intervene. I drew my mighty frostblade, its teeth carved from those of the kraken I slew with my own hand. The ork hefted its axe, a weapon huge enough to fell the mighty jungle trees with one stroke. And we charged.

'Can I speak truly of the fury of our battle? Though I take quick to the tale, I do not have the words. If the greenskin had found its mark, it would have hewn me in two. But I did not give it the chance. I called on every feint and swordsman's trick I learned in the sparring halls of the Fang, even those tricks my people taught me when I was but a stripling boy in the halls of the Devil Lynx tribe. Never have I faced such a foe, and never have I dredged so deep within myself to solve the riddle of the blade before me.

'But the Thousand-Handed One was an ork, and I was a son of Fenris. Angered at being outwitted by me, it sought to split me from crown to fundament with a mighty downward swing of its axe. But I rolled out of its way and the axe was buried in the charred ground. I rose to my feet, drew back my blade, and with a howl of revenge I plunged it into the back of its skull!'

The Space Wolves cheered. There was little they enjoyed more than to hear of the death of such a xenos.

'The blade came out of its mouth, and the matter of its brain sprayed from between its teeth!'

More cheers.

'And when I tore my frostblade free, its skull was emptied, its eyes dull, its axe hanging limply from dead fingers!'

The Seawolves whooped and howled and banged their tankards on the table. With a smile, Engir Krakendoom reached into a leather bag hanging from his waist and took out a pair of withered, gnarled green hands, each three times the size of a man's, severed at the wrist.

'This is the trophy I bring back to the Fang!' he exclaimed. 'The hands of the Thousand-Handed One!'

Ulrik watched over the placing of the ork's severed hands in a niche in one of the Fang's many trophy halls. Over the millennia, trophies almost beyond counting had been brought back by Space Wolves who had taken a notable kill or achieved a crucial objective. A band of thralls curated them, keeping the rolls of which trophy was taken from which foe and by whom.

The emissaries of the tribes watched the interring of the hands in a crystal display case, for they would take the story back to their tribes of the astonishing, exotic things the Space Wolves took or cut from their foes. The youths of their tribes would seek to win the eye of the Space Wolves, some of them would win trophies of their own, and the cycle would continue.

With great pride, Engir Krakendoom watched the thralls close the lid on the display case. The ork's hands took their place alongside the battered helmet of a Thousand Sons traitor and the severed arm of an accursed eldar farseer. The Seawolves howled in triumph as Krakendoom's offering to the Fang was added to the spoils of the Thirtieth Great Hunt.

Wolf Lord Berek Thunderfist emerged from his shuttle carrying the war-glaive of an eldar pirate, one he had personally slain while his Great Company stormed the space hulk *Vivisector*. Shortly after him arrived the Great Company of Harald Deathwolf. Harald had the head of the rebellious governor of Triskel Secundus, carried with mock gravity on a pillow of bloodstained velvet. Finally Kjarl Grimblood arrived, his Great Company badly mauled in a brutal clash with a warband of Night Lords traitors, and he brought two dozen blasphemers' hearts to adorn the trophy halls of the Fang.

Only the Great Wolf Grimnar had yet to return. Almost the entire Chapter was at the Fang, a rare enough occurrence, and so Ulrik watched carefully over the Great Hall as the feasting and drinking continued.

None could say who would take to the place of the saga-teller next. It was not unknown for Wolf Lords to fight a duel over the right to tell the next tale, wrestling with hands and bared teeth alone, or instigating an ale-fuelled brawl between their companies. Beneath Ulrik's gaze, none would dare fight now, but still the tension was there. Berek Thunderfist, normally reserved among the Wolf Lords, might relate one of his fabled episodes of bluster and bravado when the ale flowed and seek to seize the attention of the Great Hall. His Great Company certainly encouraged him to do so, but for the time being Thunderfist was content to sit and tear with his teeth at the hunks of meat the thralls brought up from the Fang's lower reaches.

One of the tribal emissaries stood and walked towards Ulrik. It was the emissary of the Stargazer Tribe, in his dark blue hooded robes. The Stargazers were rarely seen outside the mountain pathways they knew so well, and though Space Wolves had been recruited from among them they were few in number and suited more to serving as lone Wolf Scouts than as packmates among the Blood Claws and Grey Hunters. Ulrik had walked among them seeking candidates for the Blooding before, but not for some years. It had been a surprise that the Stargazers had sent an emissary at all.

'Lord Slayer,' said the emissary. 'I have heard much of the exploits of the Great Hunt to tell to my people upon my return. They will seek to make war to catch the eye of the Fang, and so we will become strong. For this reason you brought me here. But I see now that you give the teller of tales a sacred place, as is our custom too. May I petition you for a turn to speak?'

'This is an unusual request,' said Ulrik. 'Thralls of the Fang are permitted to tell a saga, for indeed Leman Russ bade the Chapter grant the greatest respect to he who tells it. But for someone outside the Fang to be given the honour is rare indeed.'

'I understand,' said the Stargazer emissary. 'But for now, no Wolf Lord is minded to take his place by the fire, and I feel it would benefit the battle-brothers greatly to hear a voice from the world of the tribes they have left behind. It will remind them who they are.'

'Then take your place, emissary,' said Ulrik. 'You have shown no fear in speaking with me. I shall show you the respect that is due to an elder of your tribe. Tell your tale.'

The emissary bowed in thanks, and shuffled to the place by the fire. By the looks of him he was old, well past the age of a warrior, which on Fenris meant he had been a fierce and tenacious man in his youth to have survived so long. Bone fetishes and runestones jangled as he walked, the implements of the soothsaying and divinations for which the Stargazers were known.

The babble of conversation died down as the Space Wolves realised the old man was about to address them. They were curious to hear what such a man would say, for only the oldest Long Fangs had heard someone from outside the Fang regale them with a saga.

'My people read the stars,' began the emissary. 'Though we divine the future in many ways, it is among the stars that we find the most profound truths. The Crone Fenris looks down at us with her thousands of eyes, and in that glittering void we seek to understand things that are distant in space or time. My people have read from the stars a tale that I believe concerns you here, for having heard the sagas of your exploits, I realise the night sky has granted us a glimpse into the Great Hunt.

'On the extreme edge of all things there lies a rocky and harsh world, one devoid of life in its natural state, named Dactyla. And yet there is life there now, an alien that men call the tau, and in great numbers he has colonised this world. For what purpose I cannot say, for none can understand the mind of the xenos, and curses on him who tries. The runes your own seers read led one of your number, the Great Wolf Logan Grimnar, to Dactyla, and it took many months for him to arrive there. He rejoiced, for there were xenos to slay, and the Great Wolf loves nothing more than fresh xenos blood on his axe. There he bade his Great Company set about the xenos with much fury, as if exacting revenge for some unknown wrong, and the tau fled in terror as the Space Wolves descended from the sky.'

Ulrik had not expected this from the emissary. He did not think word of the particulars of the Great Hunt was known among the peoples of Fenris – and yet Grimnar had indeed set off for the Eastern Fringe, following the runes cast by Njal Stormcaller on the eve of the hunt. The Stargazers were known for their prowess at reading the past or the future, and sometimes events in the present that were far away, but nevertheless Ulrik had not heard of one divining distant events in such detail.

Whatever Ulrik thought, the place of the saga-teller was indeed sacred, as Leman Russ himself had decreed. So the Wolf Priest respected the emissary's right and listened on.

'Yet the tau waxed great in number,' the human continued, 'and called many more to the battlefront. Lord Grimnar wished not to become mired in war, for he had not come to take the heads of the tau but to seek the quarry of which the runes had spoken. So he gave the order for his battle-brothers to fight on the move, through the valleys and tunnels of Dactyla, fending off the tau as he strove on for his destination.

'The Grey Hunters met the tau advances with walls of bolter fire. The tau sent forth giant suits of walking armour and tau warriors armed with weapons that could fire from a league away. They sought to race ahead of the Great Company and lay ambushes, but the Blood Claws fell upon them as they laid their explosives and dug their foxholes. Tau blood flowed on upon the black stone of Dactyla, and yet the tau did not relent.

'Svalgar Brokentooth was the first to fall to the tau. His wargear failed him, and a shot like an arrow of bright energy found his primary heart. He was the first, but not the last. Though the Great Company covered many leagues at a bound and evaded every tau attempt to bring them to battle, yet one by one Space Wolves fell. And as the running battle continued, they had no time to mourn their dead. They committed the names of the fallen to memory, took their gene-seed and wargear, and forged on, for the Great Wolf would not let his quarry go.

'Finally, Grimnar espied his goal. He had not known what form it would take, but now he saw it was a mighty gate hewn into the rock, the threshold of a temple older than mankind. It was graven with symbols from a language that had not been spoken in millions of years. Surely this was the place the runes had spoken of, and Grimnar's prey lay within.

'The Space Wolves stood with their backs to the gate, and made ready to defend the temple against the tau. The xenos had brought in squadrons of mighty armoured suits and metal beasts from their base on Dactyla, and now these stood arrayed against the Great Company of Logan Grimnar. The Long Fangs shot down a xenos machine that flew like a steel eagle, and it spiralled down into a squad of Fire Warriors in a ball of flame. Great was the celebration to see the aliens burn! And yet more were cresting the ridge above the Space Wolves with every moment.

'Grimnar chose six heroes to accompany him. Six mighty champions of his Wolf Guard, to stand with their lord while the Great Company fought. He threw open the gates to the temple that had stood closed for aeons, and entered.

'From outside, the sound of battle reached the Great Wolf's ears. The tau had surrounded his brethren and it seemed attrition alone would seal their fate. Just as the noble predator is cornered by a pack of scavengers on the winter ice, so did the Space Wolves face a foe many times their number. And just as that great beast is slain not by one mighty blow but by a multitude of tiny bites, thus the Space Wolves' doom appeared to them. The tau did not fight face to face and fist to fist like the men of Fenris, but from a great distance with arrows of light, and soon more Space Wolf dead were added to the tally to be mourned when the battle was done – if any Space Wolves remained to remember them.'

The Space Wolves grumbled and glowered. Any talk of falling to the xenos was cause for anger, and now they were hearing of it from a tribesman from outside the Fang. Even though it was just a tale the emissary was telling and they had no way of knowing its truth, the words carried a certainty to them. Ulrik knew he would have to watch them carefully, for already the emissary had strayed into dangerous territory. When it came to protecting the good name of the Great Wolf, the Space Wolves might need to be discouraged from turning to violence.

'In the temple, the Great Wolf felt the leaden ache of long battle in his limbs. He had fought for so long, and yet the greatest test he felt sure was now to come. His champions were resolute, yet he knew they, too, were at the point of exhaustion. They had all fought for many times the hours any of us among the tribes could, and even Space Wolves can only fight for so long.

'In the depths of the temple was a great portal. Grimnar and his champions hauled aside the stone barring the entrance, and looked upon a great chamber with walls of amethyst. In the centre of this chamber was a sarcophagus, huge in size, inscribed with rough-hewn runes. To Grimnar's shock they were in the tongue of Fenris, an old dialect and yet one he could read. They spoke of the heroic deeds of he who was within, and a dread curse on those who had put him inside. Grimnar bade his champions remain by the doorway, and approached the sarcophagus himself. He shattered the sarcophagus lid with a blow from the Axe Morkai, and looked on the corpse within.

'It was a sight the Great Wolf knew well. He had seen that mighty countenance many times in the histories of his Chapter, but now it was withered and dry, with skin aged like desiccated leather. He also knew well the wargear in which the corpse had been buried, the dark and dull grey livery of the ancient Space Wolves Legion, the mighty frostblade that lay beside the body now tarnished and blunted with neglect.

'Logan Grimnar sank to his knees. He let out a terrible howl of abandonment, and in his heart truly he knew despair for the first time. For the Great Hunt was over. Logan Grimnar, the Great Wolf and High King of Fenris, was looking upon the corpse of the primarch Leman Russ.'

The uproar was furious. Space Wolves yelled insults and curses at the emissary. Krom Dragongaze threw one of the great feasting tables on its side, spilling heaps of meat and gallons of ale onto the flagstones. A young Blood Claw drew his combat blade and stepped towards the fireplace, face creased with anger.

'No!' yelled Njal Stormcaller. 'The place of the saga-teller is sacrosanct! Sheathe your blade, Brother Freigar!'

'This cur has blasphemed in all our hearing!' retorted Erik Morkai. The Dark Wolf, as he was known, glared from beneath his mane of black hair, fury in his equally black eyes. 'He speaks of the death of Leman Russ. But Russ swore he would return to us, at the Wolftime! To say he is dead is to defy the very word of the primarch!'

'It was Russ who commanded that no man lay a hand on the teller of the tale,' argued Berek Thunderfist. 'Though my fury is stoked, I shall choke it down. I bid all my brethren do the same.'

'This man is not even of the Fang!' yelled Brother Kulfrarg, a Long Fang of Engir Krakendoom's Great Company who was one of the longest-serving pack leaders in the Chapter. 'Who will curse us for spilling his blood? Who will call us to heel?'

'The Stormcaller and the Thunderfist speak true.' Ulrik the Slayer did not have to raise his voice for it to cut through the din. The brothers quieted their anger when they heard the Wolf Priest speak up. 'No man may harm the teller of tales.' Ulrik stepped towards the emissary, who through the uproar had not moved or spoken a word. 'But I stand apart from the rules of the Chapter. The bindings of Russ' rules do not hold me as they do you.'

Ulrik tore the hood from the emissary's face.

Where the face of the Stargazer tribe's emissary should have been, there was instead an endless and starry void, as if the entire universe could be glimpsed therein. Galaxies spun in the darkness, and stars were born and boiled away to nothing. Empires could have lived and died in the time it took Ulrik to tear his eyes away, mindful of becoming transfixed by the vastness of the sight.

Ulrik's crozius arcanum, the power weapon that served as the badge of the Wolf Priest's office, was in his hand. Its power field crackled into life as he brought it around in a vicious, bisecting strike up into the emissary's torso.

The emissary was gone, flitting in a heartbeat to a place several metres away. The crozius thrummed as it swiped through nothing. Already the Space Wolves were bringing out their knives and bolt pistols, but as shots cracked across the Great Hall the emissary vanished from one point to the other, impossible to pin down or hit. Brother Freigar, the Blood Fang, dived at the emissary but he was caught in a tendril of psychic power and flung against the wall.

The shape of the daemon was no longer that of a man. It was a spectre, its shape formed by the folds of the cloak whipping around it. It had four arms, three of them on one side of its body, multicoloured flame flickering around its hands. The other hand pointed a long, black talon down at Brother Bjarki of Thunderfist's Long Fangs. Bjarki was thrown into the air and slammed into the ceiling, tumbling back to land with a smack on the stone floor.

'Hold, daemon!' Njal Stormcaller jumped up onto one of the feasting tables, blue-white light flashing around him as he called a lightning bolt to each hand. He hurled one bolt like a javelin and the daemon, its robes whipping around it, teleported out of the bolt's path. The second bolt slammed into the ceiling of the Great Hall and cast out a crackling cage of electricity, trapping the emissary in bars of raw energy.

'The words of the daemon are lies!' shouted Ulrik. 'You seek to bring us despair but we see through your untruth!'

The daemon turned its empty face towards Ulrik. 'There is no deceit,' it said in a dark, liquid voice, 'as cruel as a truth disbelieved.'

Blue-black power was gathering between the daemon's hands. Njal's cage held it now, but in moments it might be free.

'By the jaws of the World Wolf, be devoured!' yelled Njal. He drove his staff into the floor and a black fissure opened up in the air, the maw of a crack in reality. Like a crevasse running across a glacier, it roared towards the daemon.

The jaws of the World Wolf was a particularly Fenrisian application of psychic might, an exhortation for the spirit of Fenris itself to swallow the enemy and condemn him to an oblivion more profound than destruction. Njal Stormcaller had a mastery of the power that no other Rune Priest had ever approached. The battle-brothers knew it was coming and dived out of the way as the fissure streaked across the Great Hall.

The daemon cackled and the lightning cage shattered. Ulrik felt the shockwave hitting him, lifting him off his feet to slam him into the wall behind him. He stayed conscious through the impact, willing himself to observe what happened.

The daemon held up a hand and the fissure stopped just before it was swallowed up. The daemon started to reel in the blackness, winding it like thread into a sliver of black lightning that echoed those Njal had called forth. Then, as if mocking Njal, the daemon hurled the bolt at the Stormcaller.

Njal yelled as the bolt hit him between the eyes. His cry choked in his throat and he toppled to the ground.

Ulrik was on his feet now. The crozius was hot and angry in his hand. The daemon turned to him again.

'Despair,' the daemon said. 'The truth, the lie, it is all the same. It is all despair.'

The thing that had claimed to be the Stargazer emissary shifted form into a swirling blue-black bolt of energy, and hurtled off through the window of the Great Hall, over the balcony and out across the snowy landscape of the Fang's hinterland. Ulrik ran to the balcony rail and saw it vanish behind the mountains, off past the peak where the hive ship's jawbone lay.

The Space Wolves rushed to the balcony. Bolt pistols chattered as they fired after the daemon, but it was long gone, swallowed by the Fenrisian sky.

Ulrik turned from the window. Njal Stormcaller lay by an upturned table, face down on the flagstones. Ulrik turned him over and checked his life signs from his armour – the Rune Priest was alive, but his hearts were hammering arrhythmically. Ulrik took a vial of stabilising serum from the many compartments and pouches around his waist and injected one into the Stormcaller's neck. His heartbeats became slower and more regular. Njal's face, burned to leather by the winds of Fenris, took on a little more colour as Ulrik checked his pupils.

'What manner of thing was the intruder?' asked Wolf Lord Krom Dragongaze, walking over from the furious mob of Space Wolves by the window.

'Take the Stormcaller to the apothecarion,' said Ulrik. 'See to it yourself. Then I will seek your answers.'

Ulrik knew the vaults of the Fang better than anyone in the Chapter. He had to own that knowledge alone, for among its treasures were books of lore that could not be entrusted to anyone save a Wolf Priest. One of them was an account of the mad mind-wanderings of a nameless warp-prophet, where he described a being that came to him in his dreams. It was a being with a face of stars, one that could take on many forms, and dictated to the prophet a million-line poem that drove men mad.

Another was a tome proscribed by the Inquisition but recovered by the Space Wolves from a raid on an apostate cardinal's palace. It was a catalogue of the beings which the cardinal had summoned from the warp and had bargained with for obscene pleasures and ancient secrets. One of those beings was a thing that took on the shape of anyone the cardinal thought of, and mocked him with what turned out to be the truth of his violent death at the Space Wolves' hands.

There were others. Glimpses here, mentions there. It had many names but the title most often given to it was the Changeling. A creature born of the will of the Lord of Change, the warp power of knowledge and lies. An agent of the purest Chaos.

There was no mystery as to how the Changeling had entered the Fang. Ulrik had invited it. Perhaps it had been masquerading as the emissary of the Stargazer tribe for years before it got its chance to stand before the Space Wolves and weave its fiction. Perhaps it had taken over the emissary's form after Ulrik had sent the word out, and had left the real emissary frozen in a snowbank or thrown in dismembered chunks into the sea. Whatever the case, it had used Ulrik to enter the Fang and take up the place of the saga-teller in the Great Hall.

Ulrik knew anger well. It was impossible to grow up on Fenris and not know it. The chief Wolf Priest had to keep his anger caged, bolted down and restrained, so it did not overwhelm him and drive him to the same destructive and reckless acts he dissuaded in the rest of the Chapter. But he felt that caged wolf growling now, inflamed by the rage and disgust he felt at having been the Changeling's means of penetrating the heart of the Fang.

Ulrik banished these thoughts as he stood over Njal Stormcaller. The Rune Priest was still comatose. All the fury of the World Wolf had been driven back through Njal's mind and had forced his brain to shut down. The Wolf Priests and the apothecarion thralls would ensure his body was looked after, but only Njal himself could put his mind back together. Ulrik had never seen the Stormcaller as vulnerable as he looked now, stripped of his armour beneath the Wolf Priest's shroud, wires and tubes hooked up to the autosurgeon and medical cogitator beside him.

'We will find it, brother,' said Ulrik. 'We will bring it to justice. Many have tried, but it has chosen us as the means of its destruction. And the sons of Fenris will deliver.'

The only reply was the ticking of the cogitator's autoquill, scratching out the beat of Njal Stormcaller's hearts onto its reel of parchment.

'It lies,' said Ulrik. 'That is how it sows destruction. Its tale of Russ' death was a lie. If we do not believe that, we are lost.'

There is no deceit as cruel as a truth disbelieved.

The daemon's words were intended to create the fissure of doubt in the Space Wolves' mind, to make them wonder if Russ really could be dead and the prophecy of the primarch's return meaningless. It wanted to force them onto the path that would lead them to despair. While Ulrik lived, the Changeling would not succeed.

'But the brothers are beginning to ask the question,' continued Ulrik. 'And there has been no sign of the rest of the fleet in the sky. They ask why the Changeling came to us, and what it intended with its lies of Russ' death. And above all, they ask the question to which I must turn my own mind.'

Ulrik had not spoken it out loud, but here, with only Njal Stormcaller to hear him, he gave it voice.

'What has become of the Great Wolf?'

Ben Counter

PART TWO

THE CAGED WOLF

Ulrik's breath misted in the chill heart of the Fang. The Vaults of Rest had to be kept cold to preserve the delicate technology down here – and to keep the slumbering bodies from putrefying in their sleep.

Ahead of Ulrik was one of the huge war machine berths. The stone was lined with cogitator screens and archeotech devices that clicked and whirred in the half-darkness. Set into the berth, linked to the Fang with hundreds of cables and hoses, was a Dreadnought. Even asleep and without its arm-mounted weaponry, its brutal shape, like a bipedal tank, spoke of danger and fury.

Ulrik placed a hand against the Dreadnought's sarcophagus. The ceramite plating was caked in frost.

'Brother Bjorn,' said Ulrik. 'Your Chapter has need of you.'

Ulrik's words echoed around the vault. There was no other reply.

'You walked with Leman Russ,' continued Ulrik. 'You were there when he left us, and you heard his promise to return. Now a daemon has woven lies that claim Russ is dead, and it seeks to shake our spirit with such deceit. You could end our disquiet, brother. If you stand amongst us and tell the sagas of Russ, the Changeling will find no purchase in our hearts.'

Ulrik was aware he was being watched. The Chapter thralls who worked in these vaults were a strange and uncommunicative breed, used to working in the near-dark and quiet of the Fang's deeper layer. They waited in the shadows now, their deference to Ulrik the Slayer shown by their silence. The Dreadnoughts in these vaults needed constant care to ensure their systems continued to support the mortally wounded Space Marines interred inside, and waking a Dreadnought required hours of tech-rituals. These thralls, though they were rarely seen by any of the Space Wolves, had as sacred a duty as anyone in the Fang.

'But it uses the flesh of truth to clothe its lies,' said Ulrik. 'It speaks of how Logan Grimnar, the Great Wolf, found the corpse of the primarch on the Eastern Fringe. And it is true that Grimnar has not returned from the Great Hunt. He is long overdue back at the Fang, and none can say where he is. So we must find him, even though the trap laid by the Changeling is as clear as day. We must walk into the jaws of the Great Enemy, Brother Bjorn, for I see no other way. Unless you can counsel us to greater wisdom. Unless you can awaken, brother, and speak.'

Bjorn did not reply. The Dreadnought did not move. Ice had encrusted the hydraulics of the legs and the mountings of its shoulder units. Bjorn had not awakened for years, and the time between his periods of activity had slowly grown longer over the centuries. How long before he woke again? A decade? A century?

'Inform me of any change,' Ulrik said to the thralls lurking in the shadows, and headed back towards the upper levels where the Wolf Lords were gathering. If there had been a chance to seek the ancient Bjorn's counsel, it was gone now. Bjorn was unable or unwilling to stir, and now Ulrik only had one decision he could make.

The eleven Wolf Lords of the Space Wolves were gathered in the Repository of Battles. The circular chamber was lined with shelves holding books of battle-sagas and campaign histories. Thousands of conflicts were described there, from the Horus Heresy to the Great Hunt the Chapter had just completed. The lords stood around the huge circular table, waiting for Ulrik. A conclave of all the Wolf Lords would normally take place in the Great Hall, before the whole Chapter, but not this time.

Ulrik entered. Eleven pairs of eyes glanced down in respect. Even the Wolf Lords acknowledged the authority of Ulrik the Slayer, for the Wolf Priests were set aside in the structure of the Chapter, a parallel chain of command that could overrule any of them on the rare occasion it became necessary.

'Does he wake?' asked Berek Thunderfist.

Ulrik did not need to answer that question. 'With the Great Wolf still lost to us and the Changeling having made its play against the Chapter,' said Ulrik, 'there is no excuse for inaction. And yet the Changeling has made its way among us once, and Njal Stormcaller still lies comatose because of it. I cannot leave the Fang unguarded when the daemon has shown itself cunning enough to breach our walls at will.'

'Then leave an honour guard,' said Engir Krakendoom. 'As we did for the Great Hunt. Name which one of us shall remain and the rest shall tear the galaxy apart until we find the Great Wolf!'

'No,' said Ulrik. 'You shall all remain. The Changeling's objective is to break the will of the Space Wolves. If we fragment across the galaxy, it will prey on us one by one. The Chapter will stand united. If the Changeling wants to break us, it will have to break us all at once.'

'I will not abandon the Great Wolf to his fate,' snarled Lord Morkai.

Ulrik did not flinch before Morkai's glare.

'The Great Wolf will return to us,' he said, 'as surely as Leman Russ will at the Wolftime. I will see to it in person. I shall take a small and swift force and travel to the Eastern Fringe, following the route laid down by the Stormcaller's rune-readings, and I shall find Grimnar. You, my brothers, will defend the Fang and the spirits of your Chapter. That is where your keenest duty lies. The Changeling will make his move against us again, and soon, and you will all be here to meet him.'

'You would have me skulk here, when the Great Wolf is lost?' Krom Dragongaze slammed a fist into the table. 'The Changeling knew of the Great Wolf's destination. Fell powers have closed in on him. He battles daemons and traitors and Throne knows what else, and yet we are to sit and watch over the Fang like so many nursemaids?'

'You are,' said Ulrik. 'That is my command. In the absence of the Great Wolf Grimnar, it is my voice that carries the authority of Leman Russ.'

'You can try to stop us,' said Morkai. 'But our lord needs our assistance, and woe betide anyone who stands in our way.'

'Ready the fleet!' demanded Engir Krakendoom. 'Arm the ships! We leave with the dawn's breaking!'

'Wait!' shouted Berek Thunderfist. 'It was Ulrik the Slayer who took me from my tribe and made me a Space Wolf. He did the same for most of you, too. It was under his tutelage that you became what you are today. I trust him more than I trust myself. If it is his word that he alone seek the Great Wolf then I shall bow to it, much as it may pain me.'

'If we are all of a mind,' retorted Morkai, 'then what force in the galaxy can stop us?'

'Leman Russ bade all of us kneel to the word of the Wolf Priests,' said Berek, 'and yet how often has Ulrik used that authority? It is rare indeed that he stands against any one of us. I have faith that if he now overrules us, there is a good reason for it.'

'And which of us,' said Lord Bran Redmaw, 'knows the mind of the Changeling? All we can be sure of is that it wishes to kindle despair within us. It is a cunning creature and we will surely make its work easier if we stampede across the galaxy in our rage. When the Changeling comes for me, I would have you, my brothers, by my side.'

'Whatever you choose,' said Ulrik, 'whether you obey the word of Russ or usurp it for your own will, make the decision soon, for neither Lord Grimnar nor the Changeling will wait for us.'

None of the Wolf Lords spoke up. For a moment it looked like Krom Dragongaze would voice defiance of Ulrik, but the moment passed and he swallowed his words.

'Then I will select a strike force from your Great Companies,' said Ulrik, 'and take the *Canis Pax* as my ship, for it is among our swiftest. I will leave before the breaking of the dawn. The rest of you, make fast the defences of the Fang and ensure the spirits of your brethren are made ready. The Changeling will make its move against us again, and you will be ready for it when it comes.'

The warp was angry.

Ulrik could feel it. He had made many voyages through the immaterium, slipping into the parallel dimension to travel vast interstellar distances, and each time he had felt the uncleanness of the warp cling to him. This time, as the *Canis Pax* plied its inconstant tides, he could almost hear the scratching of a million predators at the hull of the strike cruiser. In the time between moments, he was sure he caught the distant whisper of something dark following the ship hungrily, lusting after the morsels inside.

For his strike force, Ulrik had selected one pack of Blood Claws, led by Lief Stonetongue, two packs of Grey Hunters under Hef Sunderbrow and Tanghar Three-Finger, and a number of Wolf Guard. Baldyr White Bear, Wsyr Flamepelt, Olav Brunn, Thord Icenhelm and Brok Oakenheart were all veterans equipped with Terminator armour who had seen just about every form of war that existed in the galaxy, and had served in the retinues of their Wolf Lords for untold years. Ulrik had selected them for their experience, and because he had seen them ascend through the ranks of the Chapter since their initiation rites. He could trust them to obey him without question. They had brought a small armoury with them on the *Canis Pax* – Rhinos and a Land Raider assault tank, along with a clutch of drop pods for an orbital assault and a Stormwolf gunship to support them from the air. It was a necessarily small force, but one ready to cope with anything that waited for them on the Eastern Fringe.

Baldyr White Bear was on duty watching over the bridge as Ulrik walked through the blast doors. Shipmistress Asgir was at the helm, a woman so gnarled with age it seemed the starch of her Naval uniform was the only thing holding her up.

'Lord Slayer,' said Asgir as Ulrik approached. 'It's as rough as a kraken's hide out there. Something doesn't want us to get through.'

'Are we making better time?'

'We've reached the jump point,' replied the shipmistress. 'It's been damnably slow, though. Navigator Morone is on the verge of speaking in tongues, I am sure of it.'

Ulrik imagined the ship's Navigator, his third eye pressed to the sensorium that looked out onto the warp, mind churning as he was assailed by the insanity that only he could comprehend. 'Breach real space as soon as possible,' said Ulrik. 'We are expecting to be in hostile territory when we emerge.'

'The *Pax* has another few crash breaches in her,' said Asgir. 'Not sure about her crew, but they'll live with it.' The shipmistress smiled, showing some missing teeth. A lifetime ago she had been trained at an officers' school of the Imperial Navy, but after serving with the Space Wolves for so long a little of Fenris had rubbed off on her.

'I do not like the smell of this,' said Baldyr White Bear. His Terminator armour was well-scored with old battle wounds – its previous owners had refused to remove the scars, and Baldyr continued the tradition. Baldyr had the tall crest of violently red hair and forked beard typical of the White Bear tribe, for though he was a Sky Warrior now, he had never strayed too far from the traditions of his tribe. 'There are dark forces threatening us.'

'Warp ghosts,' said Asgir. 'The voidborn are talking of it. The crew think it doesn't reach my ears but I hear everything that happens on my ship. If a shoal of ghosts has caught our trail, it could be what's slowing us down.'

'Not that,' said Baldyr, shaking his huge battered head. The servos of his Terminator armour sighed as he folded his arms. 'Not something that's following. Something that's waiting for us.'

'Lord Slayer,' said Shipmistress Asgir. 'We're at the immaterium zenith. There's no time like the present.'

'Make ready for crash breach,' said Ulrik.

Alarms blared throughout the strike cruiser. The crew's training would have them securing loose gear before finding the safest footing they could. The bridge crew were firing up the real space navigation cogitators while strapping themselves into the bridge's restraints. Ulrik activated the mag-locks on his armour's sabatons, clamping himself to the deck, and watched the viewscreen for the first sight of the Eastern Fringe.

The *Canis Pax* shuddered violently as the Geller fields around the ship flared and the warp drive ripped a hole in the veil between dimensions. There was a sense of a sideways lurching, a nauseating shift in balance, and the image of a stretch of real space crackled onto the viewscreen.

The stars stopped halfway across the screen, for this was the very extreme of the Eastern Fringe, where the galaxy ended. Everything beyond was empty void, with only the smears of distant galaxies to suggest there was anything out there at all. Tales described how men went mad when they reached the edge of the galaxy and suddenly realised how insignificant it was to be a human being.

Ulrik did not feel insignificant. Any part of him that might have once been in awe of oblivion had long since been tempered into something stronger.

The purplish half-disc of a planet hung to one side of the viewscreen: Dactyla, a cold and rocky world in distant orbit around a dying star.

'Shipmistress, we have contacts in the void,' said the crewman at the comms helm.

'Is it the *Eternity Fang*?' asked Asgir.

The crewman scanned for a sign of the Great Wolf's ship.

'Xenos,' he replied.

'Bring them onto the viewscreen,' said Ulrik.

The image shifted again, cycling through several magnified views of blurry shapes against the blackness. The final one resolved into a spaceship as large as the *Canis Pax*, surrounded by a shoal of smaller escorts. Its lines were smooth and streamlined, as if designed to swim through an ocean, and its red hull panels were mottled like the skin of a fish.

'Xenos indeed,' said Ulrik. 'Tau.'

'I fought them at Kolhelo Reach,' said Baldyr White Bear, darkly. 'Slippery and cunning things. And the daemon said Grimnar faced the tau here.'

'The daemon mingles its lies with the truth,' said Ulrik, 'so that weaker men believe them.' But in spite of his words, Ulrik's teeth gritted when he recalled the daemon's words. Everything the Changeling had said had so far been proven true.

'The tau are contacting us,' said a crewman. 'They're requesting... a summit.'

'A summit?' asked Ulrik.

'One of theirs, one of ours.'

'Tell them I have no need to match wits with an alien. We shall take what we came here for and leave.'

'More contacts,' said the crewman at the navigation helm. On the spherical holo-display above his cogitator, several red warning runes were flaring up as the *Canis Pax*'s sensors picked out more tau ships around Dactyla.

'Reading one tau capital ship,' said Shipmistress Asgir, looking up at the viewscreen. 'The *Canis Pax* is a fine ship, Lord Slayer, but that xenos craft is her equal. And she's not alone.'

'You wish to speak plainly, shipmistress?' said Ulrik.

'We cannot break through, my lord,' said Asgir. 'Not here. They have many times our tonnage in the void and they can hit us from a damnably long way away. We'll be drifting metal before we get to high orbit.'

Ulrik made a show of thinking on this for a long moment. In truth, he was quelling the wolf that snarled inside him. The greatest challenge for any Wolf Priest was to cage that inner beast, so he could offer counsel and even overrule the lords of the Chapter without his reason being warped by his anger. It was an unnatural thing to do, for rage was as intrinsic to Fenris as the storms that tore across its glaciers. But it was a necessary blasphemy, for no Wolf Priest can do his duty with the wolf running rampant.

'Contact them,' said Ulrik. 'They have the advantage, for now. I will speak.'

The arranged location was a shuttle anchored halfway between the *Canis Pax* and the tau fleet. Ulrik waited in the passenger compartment as a ship of the same size, also unarmed, approached. The hull rang as the xenos craft docked with the *Canis Pax*'s shuttle. Ulrik could hear the hiss as the airlock pressurised.

Ulrik had come here alone. Even the shuttle's pilot was a monotask servitor instead of a crewmember from the *Canis Pax*. Ulrik was taking a risk in making himself vulnerable before the xenos like this. It might be a war machine or even an explosive device that greeted him when the airlock opened. But the tau usually observed the protocols of negotiation, if only so their treacheries could be sewn all the more cunningly. It was not a question of Ulrik trusting the tau to honour the rules of the parley – it was knowing that it was in their interest to do so.

The airlock opened. The creature that walked in had a basically humanoid shape, except for the hoofed shape of its feet and the four digits on each hand. Its heavily embroidered golden robes hung over a set of body armour with plates painted deep red. A sheathed knife was mounted on the side of its chest-plate, and the faceplate of its helmet was a featureless bone-coloured oval. Aside from the knife, which looked ceremonial or like a badge of office, the being was unarmed.

A pair of hovering drones accompanied the alien, the disc-shaped devices ringed with eye-like sensors. No doubt they were transmitting everything to the tau fleet.

'What are you?' said Ulrik.

The tau removed its helmet to reveal a face with blue-grey skin, a lipless mouth, a vertical slit in place of a nose and large eyes like polished black stones.

'I am Shas'el Dal'yth Sona Malcaon,' the alien said, in slightly accented Low Gothic. 'Commander of this fleet. This world is under the protection of the Tau Empire.'

'Your kind work in castes,' said Ulrik. 'You're not the ambassador caste.'

'Our water caste ambassador was lost in action,' replied the shas'el. 'Thus, I speak for the Tau Empire here.'

'What do you want with this world?'

The shas'el's expression changed, but Ulrik couldn't read the alien's face. 'I have answered your questions. I would have my openness reciprocated. Who are you, and why are you here?'

'I am Ulrik the Slayer of the Space Wolves, a son of Fenris. I am seeking one of my own, the Great Wolf Logan Grimnar.'

'This will be the *gue'ron'sha* who made war on my people,' said the shas'el, 'without warning or cause.'

Ulrik did not flinch, but the tau's words hit hard. The Space Wolves had been here at Dactyla, and they had fought the tau. It was just as the Changeling had said.

Eventually, the story would reach a lie. It had to. The Changeling could not have told a complete truth if it had wanted to. It was a deceiver by nature, and it could not change that nature any more than Ulrik could stop being a Space Wolf. Every step closer to the end of the story brought Ulrik closer to the truth, and when he had it, whatever plan the Changeling had laid would unravel.

'I have no wish to fight you,' said Ulrik. 'When we have the Great Wolf, we will leave.'

'And then you will return,' said the shas'el, 'and exterminate us. This is the way of your Imperium.'

'We will–'

'You will leave,' interrupted the shas'el. 'You will not make demands of us. You will not be granted shelter on our world, nor a petition to our rulers or mercy from our guns. Turn your ship around, Space Wolf, and leave, or you will be blasted from the void. There is no need of the water caste's words here. There is no need for negotiation. You will obey us or you will die. This is the Imperial way of diplomacy, is it not? You should know it well.'

'Let us recover our dead,' said Ulrik. 'This is no more than you would ask of us.'

'We would ask nothing of you,' said the shas'el. 'I called for this meeting so I could see you face to face, one warrior to another, and avoid more unnecessary bloodshed. If you possess any of the honour of which your Imperium likes to speak, you will preserve the lives of your people and swallow your pride, and leave this world to the Tau Empire that is sovereign over it. Were I water caste I would speak on, no doubt, but I am fire caste, and I see only war. So the talking is done.'

Shas'el Malcaon turned and walked back to the shuttle's airlock, twin drones in tow.

'Wait,' said Ulrik. 'You cross one Space Wolf, you cross us all. We are not like the humans of the Imperium you may have encountered in the past. We will swear an oath and pursue you to the end of the galaxy.'

'You *are* at the end of the galaxy, Space Wolf,' replied the shas'el. 'And we can bear a grudge as well as you.'

The airlock door hissed closed.

'They are telling the truth,' said Shipmistress Asgir. 'They can destroy us if they wish.'

'This is one of the fastest ships in fleet,' replied Ulrik. 'Can we outrun them?'

Asgir looked between the faces of the Space Wolves assembled in her ready room. Their huge armoured bodies crowded the normally spacious room, which was hung with antique star charts and the accumulated trophies of a lifetime commanding ships in the void. Ulrik was accompanied by his force's pack masters, Hef Sunderbrow and Tanghar Three-Finger, and the Blood Claw Lief Stonetongue.

'We can outrun their capital ship,' said Asgir. 'But the rest of their fleet will get around us to block our path. Wherever we go, they can bring us to bear and hammer us with their weapons.'

'Can we not shelter on the far side of Dactyla?' asked Lief Stonetongue.

The members of a Blood Claw pack were typically few in years, for the recklessness of a young Fenrisian was suited to the Blood Claws' close combat method of war. Stonetongue was much older than his charges, for he had proven so proficient in up-close butchery that he had not moved on to the Grey Hunters as most Blood Claws did. The lower half of his face was tattooed blood-red, as was typical of the Stonetongue tribe, and he wore a jangling collection of enemies' fingerbones from rings though his ear. 'Redmaw's flagship pulled that off in the Battle of Ghul Mar Reach.'

'Redmaw wasn't fighting the tau,' replied Asgir. 'We could get to the sensor shadow behind Dactyla, but we're being constantly scanned from planetside. The tau have an installation down there that would be watching us every mile of the way. No one on the *Canis Pax* can make ordure without the aliens knowing.'

'An installation,' said Hef Sunderbrow, one of the Grey Hunter pack leaders. 'Just one?'

'The planetary scans say it's a single command centre with several sensors covering all angles of the planet,' replied Asgir.

'A command centre we can destroy,' said Lief Stonetongue.

'Not from orbit,' said Asgir. 'Their fleet would shoot us down before we got close. And they'll have the place covered with enough point defence to seal it up.'

'Good,' said Stonetongue. 'It's never satisfying to win a battle from orbit.'

'Speak for yourself,' said Asgir. 'Vaporising xenos from a thousand miles away is what keeps me warm at night.'

'Loath though I am to deny the shipmistress' proclivities,' said Tanghar Three-Finger, 'I would be much aggrieved to leave Dactyla without wetting the rocks with some xenos blood.' Three-Finger was solid and predictable, a Grey Hunter who bowed to the chain of command. He had no imagination, but he was trustworthy, which to Ulrik was as valuable a quality. His shaggy mane of red-brown hair hung down over the many honours pinned to his armour.

'How long can the *Canis Pax* survive if the tau move against us?' said Ulrik.

'If they throw everything they have?' said Asgir. 'Twelve hours. After that we'll be spent, and those flat-faced grox-rutters will be free to do whatever they want to us.'

'Then we will make twelve hours enough,' said Ulrik. 'Three-Finger and Sunderbrow, remain on the *Canis Pax* to repel any boarders.'

'And where will I be?' asked Stonetongue, with a dangerous smile.

'With myself and the Wolf Guard,' said Ulrik. 'On Dactyla.'

Dactyla was as bleak a rock as existed in the galaxy. Its dying star was a smouldering red eye that bled a painful light. The planet itself was a knot of broken rock jammed together into a jagged sphere. The world had once held a sizeable Imperial population, as evidenced by the husks of cities still clinging to its intact land masses. Some time after settlement the planet had been pushed and pulled by a sudden burst of conflicting gravities, shattering the surface and forcing its abandonment. Now it was dead and empty, the dried-out skeleton of a world scattered with ruins.

Njal Stormcaller's rune-readings had brought Logan Grimnar to this place. Throne knew what was on this planet worthy of the Great Wolf's attention. Ulrik knew that whatever it was, it was not the corpse of Leman Russ. Nevertheless there had to be something on Dactyla, something that pulled at the threads of fate strongly enough to have Njal's runes point the way.

Perhaps Dactyla's secret was the same thing that had stoked the tau's interest here. Their structures dotted the rocky world, gripping the mountain peaks or floating anchored in Dactyla's thin upper atmosphere. It seemed that even the industrious xenos were only just clinging to the planet, the spindly transmitters and scanners like scraps of spider web about to blow away on a solar wind.

One of the few stable points on the planet was the southern pole, where a broad plateau of rock was covered in shattered and fallen Imperial ruins. Once a mighty city had stood here, but now only ruins remained. It was here that the tau had set up the heart of their operations, a series of connected domes protected by drone turrets and a hangar of fighter craft. The *Canis Pax*'s scans had suggested a conventional gunship or shuttle landing would be suicidal, as the tau were a technologically adept race and their anti-air weaponry would swat such a craft out of the sky.

Thankfully, the Space Wolves did not do things conventionally. The *Canis Pax*'s complement of drop pods was prepped and loaded into the launching bays, and as the strike cruiser fled from the tau fleet past the disc of Dactyla, they were deployed.

Twelve minutes later, just beyond the predicted range of the tau air defences, they landed in a deep, black-shadowed valley, and the Space Wolves invaded Dactyla for the second time.

Lief Stonetongue crept back from the top of the ridge. His Blood Claws waited with uncharacteristic patience just below the ridge. The thin air of Dactyla necessitated the wearing of helmets, even though Blood Claws often showed their bravado by going into battle bare-headed. They had painted their faceplates with the black and red stripes they typically wore as warpaint.

'Drone patrol's passing,' voxed Stonetongue. 'But we can't get in unseen. The xenos will be alert to us in a few minutes.'

'Then we shall teach the tau how to fight,' replied Ulrik. He was further down the ridge with the Wolf Guard, huge in their Terminator armour, beside him. 'Lead the charge, Brother Stonetongue.'

Lief Stonetongue let out a long, rising howl, amplified through the force's vox-net. The Blood Claws joined in, and as the sound reached a crescendo Stonetongue lifted his power sword high and let its energy field leap to life. At the flash of the power field the Blood Claws pack sprinted up the slope and onto the plateau.

It would have been better to do this with the strike cruiser's armoured vehicles. It would have been better to land the drop pods right on top of their target. But the tau had not given the Space Wolves either option, and so the Blood Claws led the way across the open ground towards the complex deemed most likely to harbour the tau command centre. The strike force could not even use the Stormwolf gunship for air cover – the xenos would bring it down in a heartbeat. This had to be done on foot.

'Where are you, xenos?' snarled Stonetongue as he ran. 'My sword-arm will grow lazy without alien flesh to carve! Would you see my brethren grow fat and indolent, like overfed dogs? Present yourselves and let us teach our bodies discipline by sundering yours!'

The Wolf Guard followed, creating a formation around Ulrik. Their purpose was to protect him as much as it was to play their part in destroying the tau. A tau drone streaked towards the Space Wolves and Brok Oakenheart shot it down with a burst of fire from his assault cannon, the report of the gunfire a strange high thud in the thin air.

The closest dome, one of the smaller outlying structures, lay a short sprint from the Space Wolves. A section of the dome slid aside to reveal a cadre of tau fire warriors armed with long-ranged pulse rifles, flanked by a squadron of a dozen drones each equipped with a pair of automated guns. The tau squad leader activated a handheld device and a series of armoured panels sprang up along the ground around the dome, creating instant rows of cover behind which the tau took shelter.

'Down!' ordered Ulrik.

Lief Stonetongue had been on the brink of ordering his Blood Claws to charge in, heedless of the gunfire, to get to grips with the xenos. The tau had superior ranged firepower but up close they could crumble – Stonetongue knew it, and must have been slavering to reap his tally of death in hand-to-hand combat. But by the time his Blood Claws got there they would have been riddled with pulse rifle fire. They might win out, but at the cost of battle-brothers Ulrik could not afford to lose. Not here. Not like this. Every Space Wolf was worth a hundred of these aliens. Ulrik ordered them to seek the shallow cover of the plateau's dips and scattered rocks, and they obeyed in spite of their instincts.

'Wolf Guard! Open fire!' Ulrik pointed towards the tau with his crozius, but the Terminator-armoured Space Wolves beside him did not need much instruction. Oakenheart spun up the barrels of his assault cannon as the other Wolf Guard took aim with their storm bolters.

The assault cannon hammered into the armoured barricades. Storm bolter fire spattered around the tau, who dived into cover as bolter shells burst in miniature explosions. Two drones fell, caught in the metal storm.

'Now, Blood Claws! Break them!'

The fire had streaked over the heads of the Blood Claws. Now Stonetongue's brethren leapt to their feet, following up with bursts of bolt pistol fire as they ran. Several of the Blood Claws hurled frag grenades which burst in glittering blasts of shrapnel. By the time the young warriors hit, the tau were barely back on their feet.

Most of the tau had not fired a shot. Gun drone fire fell among the Blood Claws, but there was nothing Ulrik could do about that. He had to trust in their wargear to keep them safe for these few dangerous seconds, and ensure that any who fell would live on as their gene-seed was harvested.

Stonetongue vaulted the barricade. He pounced upon the tau squad leader, who was distinguished by turquoise-coloured flashes on the panels of his red armour plating. Stonetongue crushed him to the ground and followed up with a downwards thrust of his power sword. In the flash of the sword's power field, Ulrik saw the silhouettes of the other Blood Claws leaping into the fight.

It took seconds. The Blood Claws ripped through the tau. While each fire warrior was a deadly soldier when looking down the sights of his pulse rifle, he had no way to fight back when up close with the raging Blood Claws. Arms were torn from shoulders. Chests were carved open with chainswords. The squad leader's torso was almost obliterated, leaving a lower trunk and the scorched stumps of his arms and head as the power sword's field seared through flesh and bone.

The Wolf Guard did not join in the charge. They stayed beside Ulrik, shredding the hovering drones with bursts of fire. Armed with storm bolters and Oakenheart's cannon, the Wolf Guard sported the firepower of many times their number of unaugmented soldiers.

With the drones scattered and broken, Ulrik joined the Blood Claws at the barricade. They had performed well. Tau blood was pooled liberally on the ground and sprayed across the walls of the dome entrance. Inside the dome, along with banks of alien technology with a purpose Ulrik could only guess at, was the sealed doorway into the covered passageways that connected the domes. The way in.

'Un-bar the gate, Brother White Bear,' said Ulrik.

Baldyr White Bear was armed with a chainfist, a massive power gauntlet with a chain-toothed blade extending from the back of the hand. He rammed the blade into the doorway, and the teeth and power field acted in unison to chew rapidly through the reinforced tau construction. In seconds a rectangle was cut away large enough for a Terminator-armoured Space Marine to move through.

Already Ulrik could hear alarms and orders in the tau tongue blaring across the base. The assault had begun scarcely two minutes ago, but the xenos were already reacting. The tau were swift and intelligent in the methods of war. They were adaptable and they possessed exceptionally advanced technology. Fenrisian fury would have to win this fight, fury and speed.

Ulrik felt the wolf inside him snarling at the back of his mind. It wanted to be loosed, to lead him rushing through the tau base killing every alien he found, dragging Stonetongue's Blood Claws in his wake. But he could not open up the cage. He was the counterpoint to Stonetongue's recklessness. Without him, the Space Wolves were nothing but headstrong dogs haring after every prey they found, running straight into the gunsights of the tau Fire Warriors.

Ulrik was first through the breach. The passageway was lined with pipes and cabling, and branched off into a web of connected tunnels. At the centre of the web, the scans had suggested, was the eye without which the tau would be ignorant to what was going on over Dactyla. Ulrik's task was to blind it. If he could not, the *Canis Pax* would be destroyed and Logan Grimnar would stay lost.

'They're trying to get around us,' voxed Baldyr White Bear. 'I can smell them. They think they can corner us like vermin in a nest.'

'Keep moving and do not let them funnel us into a crossfire,' replied Ulrik. 'They cannot match us in prowess. They seek to best us with cunning.'

'There was never a xenos so cunning as my blade!' snarled Stonetongue through the vox. Ulrik knew the tone in his voice well – his wolf was loose, guiding him headlong. A Space Wolf full of such fury could not be stopped.

Ahead of the strike force was a set of massive blast doors, sealed in response to the Space Wolves' assault. They were near the centre of the complex now, and there was only one way forward.

Baldyr White Bear did not need ordering to set about the blast doors with his chainfist. These held up better than the previous doors and sparks showered as Baldyr ground his way through the armoured slab. The Space Wolves found what cover there was among the coolant pipes and crates of war materiel.

Ulrik glimpsed a tau warrior at the far end of the corridor behind them, ducking behind cover. This one was accompanied by a handful of drones armed with long-barrelled variants of the fire warriors' pulse rifles. Its helmet had a set of glowing orange lenses on the front that looked like targeting or magnification equipment.

Mobile projectors were pushed into the corridor, and above the projectors sprang fields of a shimmering milky haze that obscured the tau moving into position. A pulse rifle shot punched through the haze, boring through the wall beside one of Stonetongue's Blood Claws. Another caught one of the Blood Claws in the shoulder and sent him sprawling, roaring in pain and anger, to the floor. Two shots hit the Wolf Guard Wsyr Flamepelt, one shearing through his greave. His dropped to one knee, grunting angrily through gritted teeth.

'We are not trapped like prey,' roared Stonetongue. 'They have cornered a predator, and we will turn and devour them!' He had his power sword drawn and the Blood Claws were making ready to mount a charge. 'Blood Claws, Fenris' fury, this floor is far too bare of alien heads!'

Ulrik grabbed Stonetongue by his collar and slammed the pack leader against the wall.

'You will not charge into their guns,' said Ulrik, his voice low but powerful. 'We stay together. We fight as one. Let them string us out and we will be slain one by one. Bury your anger. We are not here to give your men's lives for a few more alien dead.'

More shots hit home. Another of the Blood Claws was hit in the throat and clutched at where the shot had caught the join between helmet and collar. Flamepelt took a shot full on his shoulder pad – he was barring the way to Baldyr White Bear, shielding his fellow Wolf Guard with the wall of his armoured body.

Bolt pistol fire was stuttering down the corridor in return, but the tau were impossible to target properly through the light-bending field. Oakenheart's assault cannon hammered bursts of fire, but they were random, too, and the sniper drones kept firing. Every third shot seemed to wound a Space Wolf – one sliced a good chunk from Ulrik's shoulder pad, and sheared one of the vents from the backpack of his armour.

Finally, after what seemed like hours, Baldyr White Bear shouldered aside a section of the blast doors. Ulrik led the way through, more sniper fire pinging and shrieking through the air behind him.

Beyond was unmistakeably the nerve centre of the tau operations on Dactyla. The huge circular room was full of concentric cogitator banks of advanced alien design. Screens were everywhere, with those on the curved surface of the dome overhead showing enormous orbital displays. Information streamed across each screen, making for a glittering constellation of colour.

The tau had prepared for the Space Wolves. Waiting behind the banks of cogitators was a band of creatures who did not resemble the tau at all. They were insectoids almost seven feet tall, clad in vibrant blue carapaces. They had clawed talons and buzzing wings, and each had six compound eyes set into its mandibled face. More than a dozen sheltered in cover, each with a bulky blaster weapon and segmented body armour of unmistakeably tau design.

'Auxiliaries,' voxed Baldyr White Bear as he entered the nerve centre. 'Xenos from the Tau Empire. Vespid.'

Ulrik vaulted one bank of consoles as the first fire came down. The vespids rose into the air, firing from every angle, and whining shots burst around the Wolf Priest as he sprinted and rolled.

Flamepelt was next into the room, supported by Oakenheart. He fired up into the vespids with his storm bolter, shooting down two that were too slow to dart out of the way of the stream of explosive shells. The vespids fell, wounded, and Lief Stonetongue led the Blood Claws in falling on them. Then Thord Icenhelm and Olav Brunn of the Wolf Guard followed, sending chains of storm bolter fire chattering across the dome, forcing the vespids down into the range of the Blood Claws' chainswords.

Xenos blood sprayed across the consoles. Stonetongue leapt off a cogitator and grabbed a vespid's trailing limb, dragging it down and slicing the creature clean in two through the abdomen with a slash of his power sword.

Tau reinforcements were making it into the command centre. A squad of fire warriors were accompanied by more auxiliaries, these ones the lanky, avian creatures the Imperium knew as kroot. Beside the orderly tau, they had a feral look, and were festooned with feathers and trinkets. They carried knives of bone and bronze for the kind of up-close fighting the tau themselves eschewed. One of the kroot was holding back a trio of animals with the same savage, scaly appearance. They snarled like attack dogs, and their master let them off the leash.

The kroot hounds bounded towards the Space Wolves. Ulrik felt the weight of his crozius arcanum in his hand, the power weapon an emblem of a Wolf Priest's authority. The gilded wolf's skull head was surrounded by a power field, crackling blue-white.

One kroot hound leapt at Ulrik. Its beak-like maw opened wide to snap down on him. Ulrik met it with a swing of his crozius, shattering the bony jaw and driving it back into the creature's brain. It was dead when it hit the ground, and by the time the second hound closed in, Ulrik's plasma pistol was in his hand.

The weapon kicked as superheated plasma burst in a plume against the kroot's shoulder. It burned through skin, muscle and bone, and the kroot hound thudded to the floor a yard from Ulrik. As the pistol's power coils recharged, Ulrik ducked forwards and drove the crozius down into the beast's spine. The power field disrupted the gristle holding its vertebrae together and its upper back disintegrated.

The Blood Claws hit the kroot in a thudding, brutal melee. Chainswords sawed into kroot flesh. Xenos knives sought out joints and seals in power armour. Lief Stonetongue stayed up on the console, slicing down with his power sword at the kroot who tried to surround him.

'Wolf Guard!' ordered Ulrik. 'Bring down the fire warriors! Cleanse this place!'

The Wolf Guard hammered bolter shells at the tau. Pulse rifle fire spattered back in return but the Wolf Guard did not duck and scrape for cover as other troops might have – they were relentless, trusting in their armour to hold as they advanced towards the tau.

The tau were disciplined and skilled soldiers. They were veterans of countless battles, exemplars of their species' way of war, but they had not faced anything like the Wolf Guard before.

Flamepelt roared through the pain of his injuries and smashed into the broken cogitator housings, firing as he went. Baldyr was beside him and Oakenheart took up the rear, ripping out volleys of autocannon fire. The dome was full of bursting shrapnel and through it the Wolf Guard advanced until they were within power fist range.

Flamepelt was bleeding from several pulse rifle wounds, but the pain just seemed to give him more strength. A swing of his power fist caught one tau square in the chest and smacked the resulting gory mess against one of the huge orbital display screens, shattering the image of the stars over Dactyla and spreading xenos blood across the wall. Flamepelt cracked another tau's skull with a downward swing of his storm bolter.

Baldyr swatted aside the last kroot hound with his chainfist. The creature was thrown across the dome in pieces. Ulrik ran in behind Baldyr to get among the tau, blasting one point-blank with his plasma pistol as the glittering arc of his crozius scattered three more.

It took a lot to keep the wolf caged in the thick of the fight. The Space Wolves were not here just to take alien heads – their mission was to blind the tau sensors watching Dactyla's skies, and Ulrik could not let the force get split up here pursuing the enemy for its own sake. The son of Fenris wanted to embrace the berserker rage of his people and paint this place with alien blood, but the Wolf Priest reined it in and focused.

The leader of the fire warriors was trying to direct his disintegrating squad from the rear, snapping shots from his rapid-firing carbine as the Wolf Guard closed in and the kroot line threatened to collapse under the Blood Claws' assault. Ulrik picked him out from the fray and waded through the fight towards him, shouldering aside the fire warriors who tried to bar his way.

The tau leader backed away towards the doorway through which he had tried to storm the dome, firing as he went. Pulse fire cracked and thudded against Ulrik's breastplate as he pursued. The tau glanced behind him, then back at Ulrik, and in that moment the Wolf Priest saw that he had changed.

Where there had been only the blank surface of the tau's visor, now there was a pool of formless dark. It plunged down through the tau's skull and into another reality, where ancient stars boiled away and new nebulae bloomed into existence. It was a glimpse of infinity, a vision of the void beyond the void, and it could ensnare a man's mind with the endless possibilities it promised.

It could not ensnare Ulrik. He had one of the strongest minds of any son of Fenris, moulded by the icy embrace of his home world and tempered by battles with the fiercest of daemons. He would not fall into the vision's trap, or feel despair. He was a Wolf Priest. He was the Slayer.

Ulrik tore his eyes away and shook the fog from his mind. He had glimpsed the same thing not long ago, when he had torn the disguise from the imposter speaking in the Great Hall of the Fang.

A daemon. The Changeling. It was here, on Dactyla.

Ulrik barely noticed as he smashed aside a kroot that leapt at him with its blades outstretched. He did not acknowledge the fire warrior who was crushed beneath his armoured feet as he ran. He saw nothing but the daemonic presence, and heard nothing but the echo of the Changeling's laughter as he had heard it in the Great Hall.

The wolf was loose. Ulrik felt its shackles breaking in his mind. Its howl filled his consciousness. He was running through the chambers of the base now like a hunter pursuing his quarry across a Fenrisian glacier, past banks of alien technology and the scattering bands of tau labourers. The fire warrior leader was just ahead – on open ground Ulrik could outrun the alien, but the base was cluttered and the creature knew his way.

The daemon had followed the Space Wolves to Dactyla, to spring whatever trap it had prepared for them there. Ulrik had outwitted it by ordering the bulk of the Chapter to remain on Fenris. Now it was time to finish his victory over the daemon by trapping and destroying its physical form. If the Changeling could feel regret, it would regret ever having picked out the Space Wolves as the target for its games.

His quarry bolted through a doorway and the door descended behind him. Ulrik slid beneath it and caught it on his shoulder, roaring as he forced it back open. The motors of the doors screamed and smoked as he pushed his way through.

He was outside the dome now, on a stretch of rocky plateau between the base's structures. Ruins of ancient Imperial buildings filled the area. Overhead, silvery fire streaked across the sky as the *Canis Pax* led the tau fleet in an intricate dance. Shipmistress Asgir was keeping the strike cruiser alive against the firepower of the whole tau fleet. When the Changeling was defeated, then Ulrik could worry about assisting with her battle in orbit. For now, his objectives had changed.

A pack of kroot emerged from one dome, interposing themselves between the Changeling and Ulrik. Ulrik crashed into them, bowling half of them over with the force of the impact. They carried long rifles with blades attached to the barrels which they wielded like halberds. Ulrik parried one and shattered the knee of the kroot who held it with a downwards strike of his crozius. The power field leapt up and his follow-up strike into the kroot's chin took the alien's head clean off its shoulders. Ulrik whirled, catching two more in crozius' arc, casting them broken and bloody across the rock.

Ahead, another section of dome slid aside. The fire warrior being puppeted by the Changeling disappeared inside. From the dome strode a bipedal battlesuit twice the height of a Space Marine. One arm ended in an energy cannon and the other held a circular shield that cast a force field around it. On the side of its armoured chest was an oversized combat knife in a sheath, worn not as a weapon but an emblem of rank. Ulrik recognised it through his fury.

Shas'el Dal'yth Sona Malcaon. The tau leader who had demanded the Space Wolves leave Dactyla or die. One more tool of the Changeling.

The wolf inside Ulrik howled. If Ulrik had to go through this alien too, then he would. He was a Space Wolf. The blood of Leman Russ burned in him. Nothing could stand before him when he was gripped by the fury.

Ulrik batted another kroot aside. They scattered as the battlesuit approached, propelled on incandescent jets from the exhausts mounted on its back. The suit crunched to the ground just ahead of Ulrik and took aim with its cannon. Ulrik rolled to the side as a tremendous burst of energy ripped into the ground beside him, blasting a deep trench through the rock.

Ulrik was back on his feet. He leapt at the battlesuit. This was a machine designed to keep foes at a distance, and to capitalise on their vulnerability as they fled. Ulrik would not flee. He found a handhold between two armour plates and swung up towards the battlesuit's head, an armoured rectangle fronted by a nest of glowing lenses. He drew back his crozius and rammed it into the battlesuit's eyes, letting the power field discharge to blast the head apart.

The battlesuit's shield arm had an oversized hand that now reached up and closed around Ulrik's thigh. It threw him off and he landed hard, skidding on his back along the rock. The battlesuit was reeling, blinded.

Ulrik was barely able to focus enough to check his body for injuries. He was battered, but he'd suffered nothing that would keep him from fighting. The rest of his mind was taken up with the rage.

He would tear this machine apart, piece by piece, and when the morsel of alien coward inside was revealed, he would rip it open and hold the bloody chunks up to the sky.

The power field of his crozius had recharged. This time it would tear off the battlesuit's arm or split its torso open. Ulrik ran at the machine, taking advantage of its blindness to cross the arc of its cannon.

A panel on the battlesuit's chest opened up like a hatch on a spaceship. Inside, lit by the winking readouts of the battlesuit's controls, was the shas'el. A faint pane of clouded air suggested an energy field that kept the cockpit's atmosphere pressurised in Dactyla's thin air. The tau's lipless mouth was open and the warning lights inside his cockpit were reflected in the liquid black of his eyes.

He saw Ulrik just in time to bring the shield arm around. The energy shield flared as Ulrik slammed into him at full speed. He bounced off and sprawled on the rock. The shas'el brought the shield down like a guillotine blade into Ulrik's abdomen. Trapped against the rock by a weight of shimmering energy, Ulrik struggled like an insect on a pin.

The battlesuit's cannon swung around to aim at him. If the tau ever smiled, Shas'el Dal'yth Sona Malcaon smiled then.

Ulrik forced his arm out from under him and drew his plasma pistol. The weapon was powerful enough to sear a hole right through solid power armour, but its power coil needed a few seconds to recharge after each shot. That meant Ulrik only had one pull of the trigger.

He fired straight up. The bolt of plasma hit the shield generator and the energy field crackled out of existence. Ulrik rolled out of the way as the cannon fired into the ground at the battlesuit's feet.

The explosion lifted Ulrik off his feet and threw him against the battlesuit's leg. Ulrik stayed conscious and aware as the side of his breastplate buckled with the force. His inner armour of fused ribs cracked, and shards of bone were driven into his chest cavity. He felt every one, needles of fire shrieking through him as his organs were burst and lacerated.

Ulrik hit the ground and gasped in a breath. His torn lungs flared in pain. Beside him was a glowing crater in the ground where the cannon had vaporised rock. Ulrik still had his crozius in one hand and pistol in the other. He holstered the pistol, ignoring the pain from the torn muscles down his side.

The wolf inside Ulrik was not quietened by the pain. He only heard it louder now. He reached up and grabbed the lower edge of the battlesuit's open cockpit, pulling himself back up to the level of the shas'el.

Ulrik was face to face with the alien. The shas'el looked surprised to see Ulrik still living. As Ulrik brought his crozius back for the kill, he caught the reflection of his skull-faced helm in the tau's large black eyes.

The reflection changed. The shape of the wolf's skull distorted and broke apart in a spray of stars. Galaxies spun away and thunderheads of glowing stellar gas boiled out from an endless void. Millions of years spiralled away in chains of dying stars.

Ulrik was almost lost. Again, he forced his mind away. A terrible realisation was breaking at the back of his mind.

He heard distant laughter, and he understood.

Something slammed into Ulrik's side. He fell away from the cockpit and hit the ground by the crater again. The tau fire warrior, the one Ulrik had pursued from the command centre – the Changeling – had run up and knocked him away from the shas'el.

Ulrik's injuries cried out again. The shas'el turned to face Ulrik. The image of the void rippled across the fire warrior's helm and the shas'el's face, and Ulrik heard that laughter again, ringing from some dark place.

Of course the Changeling was not on Dactyla. The daemon was on Fenris, lurking at the threshold of the Fang, waiting for its chance to invade the minds of the Space Wolves. It had cast an illusion to distract Ulrik and force him to make himself vulnerable in a way that no Wolf Priest ever should. Because the Changeling knew Ulrik's one weakness.

The caged wolf. The rage of Fenris. The Changeling knew it was inside Ulrik, and that when it ran loose all the mental discipline the Wolf Priest had created would shatter and be forgotten.

Ulrik rolled onto his front. His strength was bleeding away as he crawled.

The anger was gone now, and he could feel only pain. He had suffered physically before – he had no fear of pain alone. But the pain was a reminder of how completely he had been outfoxed by the daemon. It had known every move Ulrik would make, the exact way to make him forget himself and become the furious son of Fenris that lay inside. He had split off from his battle-brothers and made himself vulnerable, and got himself cornered alone by the enemy in a way that would have had him scolding the most ignorant of novices.

The fire warrior backed off. The battlesuit manoeuvred to stand over Ulrik now, the face of the shas'el visible in the open cockpit. The battlesuit lifted a massive armoured foot, and raised it over Ulrik.

In that moment, when death became certain, a strange emotion surfaced somewhere amid the pain and regret. It was a peculiar form of admiration – nothing positive, nothing that suggested forgiveness or kinship. But nevertheless, Ulrik could not help but acknowledge the sheer cunning of the Changeling, the way it had found the one weakness in a man who should have no weakness at all. For all Ulrik took pride in being a Fenrisian and a son of Leman Russ, his homeworld and his primarch had engendered in him the flaw in his mental armour that the Changeling had exploited.

The battlesuit's foot rushed down to crush and destroy.

Beyond the battlesuit, the void was streaked with starship fire. And somewhere among those stars, Ulrik realised with what would surely be his last thought, lay a Fenris now open to the predations of the Dark Gods.

Steve Lyons

PART THREE

EYE OF THE DRAGON

The pressure on Ulrik's chest suddenly eased.

The shadow of the gargantuan battlesuit above him – the shadow of death – unexpectedly disappeared.

He could barely see or hear past the alarms in his helmet. His auto-senses were in overdrive, diagnosing the damage to his armour, to his body, mostly telling him what he already knew. They told him only one thing that mattered: he was alive. His wolf amulet had protected him from being crushed, though it couldn't have done so much longer.

The venerable Wolf High Priest had been spared to fight yet another day. He muttered a grateful prayer to the Allfather, as he looked for the agency through which his will had been done here.

The sky of this dreary alien world was screaming; its ground was trembling. Drop pods in blue-grey livery, the Space Wolves' colours, were plummeting through the clouds, striking the ground like meteors. One of them had landed just behind the battlesuit, the force of the sudden impact throwing it off-balance.

Ulrik forced his battered armour, and his equally battered body, to move. Before the battlesuit's shas'el pilot could regain control – before that heavy foot was raised to crush the life out of him again – he dragged himself out of the dirt and staggered away from it. His damaged lungs burned with every breath of air he gasped in.

The battlesuit loosed a volley of plasma rounds after him. They were comfortably off-target, though Ulrik felt their heat washing over him.

The first of the pods opened to disgorge fresh Space Wolves upon the battlefield. Ulrik recognised a few of them, saw the badge of the Sun Wolf on their shoulders and knew who must have brought them here; as if he hadn't suspected it already.

Of all the twelve Wolf Lords, only one would have disregarded the High Priest's orders and followed him here. Only one would have been so eager to prove himself – for the thousandth time – in action.

That one had just saved Ulrik the Slayer's life.

Krom Dragongaze's red cloak billowed around him as he stepped out of the drop pod. Its violent landing had sent cracks through the hard earth, but his gilt-edged artificer armour had easily absorbed the brunt of it.

He heralded his own arrival by firing a volley of explosive bolt-rounds into the air. In his other hand Krom clutched his signature weapon, Wyrmclaw, a huge double-bladed frost axe. It only took him a moment to choose his target.

'Take out the battlesuit,' he roared into his comm-bead.

Towering above all else, the tau machine was an irresistible lure to him, particularly as it was already damaged. The battlesuit's head had been staved in and its pilot had thrown open its chest hatch in order to see. As a bonus, it seemed to have beaten the Wolf High Priest. The prospect of succeeding where Ulrik the Slayer had failed made Krom's mouth water.

His orders were received and understood by his Wolf Guard, his company's fiercest warriors. With the exception of the Old Wolf's Kingsguard, Krom's Wolf Guard was the largest among the Great Companies – thanks to the example he set for his warriors, he was quick to claim.

They leapt from the drop pod a breath behind their lord and fanned out around the enemy, bolt pistols and storm bolters rattling.

'Keep your distance,' their pack leader cautioned them over the vox-net. 'One of those things can shatter power armour with a blow, but we have the advantages of speed and agility over it. Best to weaken its defences with ranged fire, then move in for the kill.'

That was Beoric Winterfang, always the calm voice of reason. His age and wisdom had been cited by some as a useful counterbalance to Krom Dragongaze's hotheadedness, but he was one of Krom's disciples all the same, and as loyal as the rest of them.

'Sometimes, I wonder if you have wolf's blood in you at all,' Krom grumbled to himself, not for the first time. Beoric's centuries of distinguished service, however, demanded his respect.

The battlesuit shuddered and reeled beneath the Wolf Guard's sustained assault. It was anything but helpless, though. It snapped up a giant arm – more precisely, a multi-barrelled cannon attached to its shoulder joint – and unleashed a blinding storm of plasma rounds upon its assailants.

There was scant cover to be had, so there was little the Space Wolves could do to evade the white-hot fire that swept over them. They could only weather the onslaught as the markings and adornments on their armour blistered and burned.

Jormund Thunderclaw, a head taller than the others in more durable Terminator armour, pushed his way to the front of his battle-brothers. He planted his feet in the ground and brought his cyclone launcher to bear. A cluster of krak missiles screamed out from over his shoulders to blaze a laser-guided path towards their substantial target, bursting against the battlesuit's energy shield and engulfing it in noise, fire and smoke. Its cannon continued to lash out, but half-blindly now.

Many of Ulrik's strike force were recovering their wind, and the rest of the tau had begun a hasty pullback, finding themselves outmatched. The remainder of Krom's Drakeslayers – his Blood Claws, Grey Hunters and Long Fangs – were harrying their foes' heels, speeding their retreat. The High Priest had rejoined the battle too, in spite of his injuries.

Krom pierced the miasma around the construct with a narrow-eyed glare. His nostrils twitched at the scent of burning electrics. The battlesuit's cannon had been silenced. Any moment now, he judged, its pilot would make a break for it, try to trample his way over the blue-grey perimeter that was tightening around him. Krom saw his chance and took it.

Ignoring Beoric's sage advice – as was his right – he charged, lips peeled back from his fangs and axe awhirl above his head.

Wyrmclaw was edged with the ground talons of a Fenrisian ice wyrm; its blade cut harder than diamond and was lent additional power by the arcane runes carved into it. Krom smashed the blade into the battlesuit's right knee joint, where a missile had already struck. For a moment, the axe remained lodged there, drawing out more smoke and furious sparks. It wasn't enough.

The pilot glared down at him from the battlesuit's chest cavity, its black eyes inhumanly cold. Krom threw himself with all his strength, all his fully-armoured weight, shoulder-first against the pylon of the battlesuit's right leg. Already off-balance, at last it fell. Krom recovered his axe with a wrench as the suit toppled away from him.

His Wolf Guard joined him now, at Beoric's command. They swarmed the felled machine, hacking through its sputtering shields with frost blades and power weapons. They dragged the hapless pilot from its cockpit and were snapping, howling, vying for the honour of tearing out its throat.

Within minutes of Krom Dragongaze's arrival, the battle was won. He puffed out his chest with pride and turned to face Ulrik.

'You're welcome,' Krom grinned.

'I told you to stay behind at the Fang,' Ulrik snarled.

'I had a feeling I might be needed here,' Krom answered him, brazenly.

Ulrik subjected him to his grim helm's full glower. Most men – even those of Fenris – would have flinched from its judgement in fear. Not Krom, though. It was not for nothing that he was known as Dragongaze, or the Fierce-eye.

Krom's head was bare, with bright russet hair sprouting from his scalp and chin, spilling over his gorget in plaits. He met Ulrik's searing gaze with equally fiery red orbs of his own, and showed by the twitching of his lips that he relished the contest. The wolf-skull totem that he wore on his back loomed over his own skull. It appeared to be leering at Ulrik too, eye sockets full of insolence.

'We have idled too long at the Fang,' said Krom. 'My Drakeslayers are impatient to bloody themselves again, after missing out on the Great Hunt.'

A growl formed at the back of Ulrik's throat, but he let the matter drop. He had made his point – for what good it might do, what good it ever did – and Krom's disobedience had saved him, after all. His death would have wounded the Sons of Russ grievously – especially with the Great Wolf still missing.

Olav Brunn padded up to him. 'High Priest, the tau may be licking their wounds for now,' he counselled, 'but they will doubtless regroup and attack again. If the Great Wolf is to be found here–'

'Grimnar came here,' interrupted Krom, 'to this planet?'

'To explore the ruins of the city here, we believe,' Ulrik confirmed, 'and Olav is right, we may not have much time to search for him.'

Krom nodded and turned away from him abruptly. He fixed his eyes on the mildewed walls of the city across the plateau, as if he expected them to wither as most men did in the heat of his glare. At the same time, he barked into his comm-bead, jolting his Great Company into action.

Ulrik gave the same orders to the members of his smaller force. The Drakeslayers, however, were hungrier and better rested than the High Priest's battle-brothers and, spurred on by their Wolf Lord, they took the lead.

Krom had his Wolf Guard form up around him and loped towards the crumbling city gates himself. He made sure to beat the Wolf High Priest through them.

The city reeked of dust and decay, making Krom's nose itch. Its streets were narrow and winding, lined by the skeletons of half-demolished buildings. He felt hemmed in. A heavy silence had rushed in to fill the void left by the end of the battle, and the grey sky seemed a long way away.

The city had not been lived in for long before the Dactylan catastrophe had forced its evacuation. It felt lifeless, soulless, sterile. *An ill place for hunting.* Few feet, Krom knew, had trodden these streets in many decades, even centuries.

Few feet, he thought, *and yet some...*

The dust had been disturbed, and recently. There were too many trails to separate one from another, so he dispensed with the business of trying to follow them. He had his company fan out across the rubble. If there was something to find here – a clue to the Great Wolf's whereabouts or Grimnar himself, perhaps crippled and in need of assistance – a Drakeslayer would find it or he would know the reason why.

Krom rounded the curve of a great mouldering dome, long since laid low by spiny roots that had risen up beneath it, thrusting outward triumphantly through its shattered doors and windows, only to then succumb themselves to age and blight.

A junction loomed, at which five narrow roads corkscrewed away from each other. Krom split his Wolf Guard into packs and chose the central route for himself: the one least likely, in his judgement, to loop back towards the walls.

Scant minutes later, however, he caught familiar scents on the breeze and came face-to-face with six battle-brothers, treading the same road as him but in the opposite direction. *This place is a maze,* he thought sourly. A man without his wolfish instincts – and less importantly, his armour's auto-senses – would have lost himself by now.

The first discovery was made by a novice Blood Claw. His voice burst over the vox-net, proud and hungry to impress. A moment later, Beoric Winterfang delivered a more measured report from somewhere further eastward. The content of his message was much the same as that of the Blood Claw's. Each had come upon the site of a recently fought battle – and each had found its casualties.

'I recognise Uri Stormhammer,' Beoric voxed. 'A staunch member of the Old Wolf's Kingsguard. He has been dead for some days.'

'Then Grimnar *was* here,' Krom replied. *And may be yet.*

'My lord, I see another corpse,' chimed in the eager Blood Claw. 'It's a Space Marine, my lord, but not of Fenris. He bears the symbol of Caliban.'

Krom's top lip curled at the mention of the Space Wolves' ancient rivals.

'We have Dark Angels here too,' Beoric confirmed. 'One has clearly been felled by a chainsword – and, my lord, I see no tau. We have no tau bodies here.'

That could only mean one of two things. It was inconceivable that any Space Wolf had fallen without taking at least one of his enemies with him. So, had the tau simply removed their dead for burial? It was not impossible, but they had engaged Ulrik's force outside the city – and so far, Krom had detected no fresh tau scents within it.

He clenched his fists inside his gauntlets. It had been a long time since Krom had gone toe to toe with a Dark Angel – and then he had certainly proven which of them was superior. He would relish the chance – an excuse – to prove it again.

He took a moment to consider that happy scenario. Another vox, however, demanded his attention. He recognised the voice of Egil Redfist, the Blood Claws' commander.

'Lost contact with three of my Wolves,' he reported ominously. 'I'm sending you details of their last known location and leading my pack there now.'

So, there were still enemies – living enemies – hiding in the city. Dark Angels? *No,* thought Krom, *they wouldn't lurk in shadows.* Tau? *Perhaps...*

But the hairs on his neck and down his spine were tingling, as they had been, he realised, since he had passed through the crumbling gate. The air had a scent, a taste of something he couldn't quite define, but it clawed at the lining of his nose and prickled his throat.

Krom Dragongaze's instincts were never wrong. There was something evil here.

'This one can still be saved,' said Wsyr Flamepelt.

He was speaking of a grey-haired Long Fang, whose hand he had seen protruding from beneath a pile of stones, whose body he had uncovered.

The Long Fang's wounds were deep, but his enhanced physiology had staunched the bleeding and slowed his metabolic rate to less than a crawl. It might be weeks or longer before he woke – Space Marines could remain in healing comas for centuries – but wake he would.

'Too late to tell us what happened here,' Ulrik grumbled.

He ordered that the brother be returned to the *Canis Pax* where he could be properly tended to, then strode away, his heavy brow furrowed beneath his helm.

He had voxed Krom Dragongaze, and knew that the Drakeslayers had found more bodies. *Not enough to suggest a massacre,* he considered, *but cause for concern nonetheless.* What had happened to Logan Grimnar that had kept him from tending to his wounded or burying his dead? *For that matter, what brought him – the Dark Angels too, not to mention the tau – to these festering ruins in the first place?*

'Another Dark Angel over here,' Olav Brunn grunted. This one was far beyond helping. His armour was seared and dented; he lay crumpled against the foot of a spiral staircase that led nowhere.

Ulrik cast a shrewd eye over the corpse, seeking clues to the mystery. The Dark Angels and the Space Wolves had long been rivals, but fighting one another to the death was quite another thing. Unless, he concluded, the Angels had been touched by the taint of Chaos. He studied the body closely, but the Space Marine, Ulrik satisfied himself, was only what he appeared to be.

He updated Krom on his situation, eliciting a cruel bark in response. 'I make that seven of theirs to five of ours,' the Wolf Lord boasted. *Thus far,* thought Ulrik. Unlike Krom Dragongaze, he didn't see everything as a competition.

He was listening, with one ear, to a vox-report from the *Canis Pax* in orbit. He had instructed its shipmistress to make continuous scans of the planet's surface. He voxed the news to Krom.

'The tau are regrouping on the plateau, with a dozen more battlesuits. There may be advance parties searching inside the city already.'

Could the tau have ambushed Krom's missing Blood Claws? he wondered.

Krom snarled, 'Good. Let them come.'

'No,' snapped Ulrik, feeling his gorge rising again. 'We cannot let the tau delay us here. Save that battle for another day. We need to find what we came to this benighted world for and get out of here. Do you understand me, Krom?'

'As you will,' the Wolf Lord allowed thickly, then broke off contact.

Ulrik took a breath and reminded himself of the Fierce-eye's more admirable qualities. He had certainly had to recite them often enough. The Great Wolf had repeatedly threatened to expel Krom from his Chapter; either that or rip out his throat. It had been the High Priest's thankless task, each time, to ask him to reconsider.

It was Ulrik – an old wolf even then – who had recruited Krom and overseen his training. He had seen Krom's belligerence and bouts of fiery rage as weapons worth tempering. The many great victories that Krom had since won, the foes left bloodied in his wake, the unshakable loyalty he inspired among his Drakeslayers, all of these things showed Ulrik's choice to have been the correct one.

And now I owe him my life...

A sudden flurry of vox reports assailed his ears. At the same time, he heard the unmistakable sound of gunfire coming from the north-east, deadened by the intervening stone buildings, and then more gunfire, this time from the south.

The Space Wolves were under attack.

At the very first gunshot, Krom bolted into action.

He sprinted across the dead city's narrow roads, through the shells of its sundered buildings, scrambling over heaps of debris. He came up short, letting loose a howl of frustration, as a solid wall rose to block his path. He turned and pushed his way back through the Wolf Guard who were following at his heels, seeking a way around it.

He reached the site of the battle too late. It was almost over.

A half-pack of Grey Hunters had surprised a tau scouting party. There had been six tau to three Space Wolves, but the xenos were unskilled in hand-to-hand combat and their attackers had been upon them before they could use their pulse rifles.

Four tau had been efficiently dismembered; the remaining two had fled in opposite directions for their miserable lives. The Space Wolves would have chased them down without a thought – and Krom would probably have joined them – had Beoric Winterfang not arrived at that moment and instructed them to stand fast.

'The High Priest said we weren't to let the tau delay us,' he reminded Krom calmly, in response to the Wolf Lord's murderous glare. 'Nor would it be wise to split our forces any further than we have, until we know more about the threat we face.'

The knowledge that Beoric was right did nothing to assuage Krom's anger.

He unleashed it upon the nearest viable targets, the Grey Hunters. He raged at them for letting the tau escape, not being faster, stronger, more alert. 'When we return to the Fang,' he swore, 'you'll each spend a week training with the Blood Claws, learning to use those blades – and should I ever witness such a clumsy display again, I'll beat you black and bloody myself. No excuses. I will not have–'

He broke off, realising that was his voice was competing with a new sound.

He whirled around as a craft plunged, whining, out of the sky behind him. It was small and black, the shape of an arrowhead. It bore no Imperial design. Nor was it tau, judging by its harsh lines and angles. It was coming right at him – a suicide run, Krom thought, and he bellowed at his men to scatter and leap for cover.

The craft pulled up short of the ground, tilting to evade the surrounding buildings by a hair; it was more manoeuvrable than Krom had imagined it to be. He glimpsed a pilot behind its glacis, saw two more heads poking out of a weapons emplacement at its stern.

'What in the warp is it?' he cried.

Then the gunners got to work, strafing the street ahead of them with thousands of tiny, sharp projectiles spat from a long-nosed cannon. Krom had ducked into an archway, letting its intricate stonework bear the brunt of the assault. Some splinters ricocheted off his armour, however, and a few stuck in it: slender, quivering shards of crystal, glistening with neuro-toxins. He knew what he was facing now.

Beoric, with his centuries of experience, had seen it at once.

'Eldar!'

The shadow of the craft flitted over them, its belly almost scraping the Space Wolves' heads. Its gunners rotated their cannon to spray out more shards in their wake, forcing the Drakeslayers to scramble for new defensive positions.

Crouched in his archway, Krom emptied his bolt pistol in the enemy's direction. His targets were the gunners' exposed heads, but at this range, through a blizzard of poisoned needles, they were nigh on impossible to hit.

'Use your weapons, you sons of dogs,' he bellowed at his Wolf Guard and Grey Hunters alike. 'Bring that damned thing down, and you might just show me you have iron in your blood, after all.'

The black xenos craft, following the road's curve, had disappeared behind a dome; that gave them some respite from its splinter cannon at least, a precious moment to regroup. Krom could hear its antigravity engines, however – quiet by any normal standards but loud in the city's silence. It hadn't gone far.

He pulled two crystal needles out of his forearm, one out of his chest. He dashed them to the ground, where they shattered. He reloaded his bolt pistol.

He heard Wolf High Priest Ulrik's voice, insistent, through his comm-bead.

'I have reports of gunfire from your position. What's happening over there? Krom!'

Krom drew his breath to answer him, but held it. *He can wait another moment,* he thought, *for better news.* Other voxes were coming in, in any case, competing with each other to be heard. Egil Redfist, in search of his missing Blood Claws, had come upon a xenos ship too, and three more Space Wolves packs, spread across the city, had likewise suddenly found themselves under fire.

Russ, they're everywhere at once, thought Krom. *How is that possible?*

The black craft had climbed out of the maze of streets and banked steeply around; now it came swooping in again, snapping the spire off a square tower as it skimmed over it. For a second time, the Space Wolves found themselves fixed in its cannon sights; this time, however, there was one important difference.

This time, Krom Dragongaze knew what was coming, and he was ready for it.

They leapt from inside the broken buildings, behind the archways. They appeared on balconies and parapets and at the shattered windows of crumbling towers.

Ulrik cursed himself for a novice. He had caught their scent on the wind but misjudged their proximity, concerned about the brothers he had been rushing to assist. He had shouted a warning in the moment the ambush was sprung, and this alone had kept his pack – six-strong at present – from being entirely surrounded. Still, they were badly outnumbered.

He counted over twenty of them: dark eldar warriors in flexible, black armour. Spikes bristled from their shoulders, knees and elbows, horns from their conical helmets. Like all their kind, they had a sun-starved pallor to their skin – those few that showed their faces – and yet they were muscular and lithe, with their tapered ears and chins, filed teeth and silken black or white hair.

'Their weapons are strong, but their armour is weak,' Ulrik bellowed. 'Hit them fast and hit them hard. For Russ!'

But even as he led the charge to battle, he voxed an appeal – to anyone, any Space Wolves who weren't already themselves besieged – for reinforcements.

The black craft came around for another strafing run: its third.

Krom had feared it might not. His men were well entrenched in doorways and windows along each side of the street – good sniping positions. They had shattered the pilot's glacis and, he felt certain, winged one of the gunners. He had thought the dark eldar might change their tactics, perhaps even turn tail.

They had drawn blood, however, and they had a thirst for more.

Ulvar Razorfang had ventured too far out of hiding to line up a perfect shot. The splinter cannon had snapped around towards him in a heart-beat, and its crystal shards had shredded him. He had reeled back into his doorway, hitting a wall hard – he was still propped up against it. He hadn't moved in over a minute.

At least three other Space Wolves were wounded – Krom Dragongaze among them. Like Ulvar, he had chosen to take a risk and had been pun-ished for it. This time, he told himself, he would be faster. *No excuses.*

Crouching beneath his stone arch, he judged the skimmer's approach by the whining of its engines. When it was almost on top of him, so close that it had to level out of its dive and its cannon couldn't target him for a second, he made his move.

This time the climb was easier, because Krom could use the handholds he had punched into the stone already. The numbness in his left shoulder, however, was spreading along his arm into his fingers. Aloud, he cursed the splinter that had found the gap between his gorget and his pauldron, momentum driving it through his power armour. He had yanked out the stem, but the tip had embedded itself in his flesh.

What if the poison spreads to my primary heart?

He didn't like to think about that. He clambered onto the top of the archway, and this time his timing was near perfect. The skimmer was right there, almost within his reach. Had he lifted his head a second earlier, it would likely have taken it off. Indeed, another ship – with normal engines – could have fried him in its backwash.

The dark eldar gunners hadn't seen him. They had their backs to him, focusing on the targets strewn across the street ahead of them.

A lesser man – even some Space Wolves, such as Beoric Winterfang – might have taken a moment to think, to assess the situation, and thus been too late to act. Krom trusted his instincts, which had always served him well. He let them guide him now and made the jump. For a heady second, he flew.

Not fast enough! Like a shadow, the black skimmer slipped out from underneath him. Krom howled, reaching for it with straining arms and fin-gers. His numb left arm threw off his balance, and suddenly he was flying no more but falling. He felt a stab of emotion – not fear, never fear, but shame.

And because Krom Dragongaze refused to bear that shame, because he couldn't fail in front of his pack, somehow his flailing hands found pur-chase after all. They caught on a snare chain, trailing from the skimmer's port wing. He bit back another howl – this one of pain – as his injured shoulder was almost wrenched out of its socket.

The sudden addition of Krom's plummeting weight threw the craft into a spin; caught unawares, one of the gunners pitched over the side and fell past him. The craft wasn't high enough for the fall to be fatal, but the nine Space Wolves waiting below would see to that.

It was taking all of Krom's strength to cling to the chain, but he had to climb it; dangling in mid-air, he was horribly exposed. As the skimmer levelled out, its wingtip struck tortured sparks off the marble skin of a tower – whether accidentally or in a frantic attempt to scrape him off, he couldn't tell.

He willed his arm to work, to haul him up the chain and onto the skimmer's stubby wing. It lurched as he planted a foot on it, and its engine pod trailed black smoke. The surviving gunner saw him and wheeled the cannon around towards him. Krom fixed the alien with a menacing glare and half-charged, half-stumbled into its turret.

He wrestled the xenos for control of the splinter cannon. Dark eldar were quick and they were agile – but in a contest of strength, he had a servo-assisted edge over them. The gunner surrendered its cannon and snatched instead for a flail at its hip.

Krom left his axe slung across his back. He grappled with the xenos, pinning its spindly arms to its sides. He felt its lightweight armour cracking in his pincer grip, and only wished he could see the frightened face of his enemy beneath its black, impassive helmet.

Somehow, it squirmed free of him for a second, but it was struggling to draw breath. It reached for its flail again, but Krom delivered a brutal, backhanded blow with his gauntlet, which almost took its head off. As the xenos reeled, Krom barged it, leading with his good shoulder. It tried to brace itself, but a fortuitous lurch of the skimmer betrayed it and sent it tumbling after its late partner.

The dark eldar flipped head over heels in mid-air; it would land on its feet, but the craft was flying higher now than it had been and the impact would likely shatter the xenos' bones.

The pilot had managed to lift the skimmer's nose and drag it up above the rooftops, but was struggling to keep it there. Krom drew his axe, intending to cut his way into the sealed cockpit, but was forced to make a grab for the cannon instead. The black skimmer plunged into a barely-controlled dive and careened around the narrow streets, scraping a wing against a building here, ploughing through a mast there.

The engine pod was coughing up gouts of flame; Krom could see through the glacis that the pilot was losing a fraught battle with its controls. It was only by the Allfather's will that they hadn't been spread across the city already.

Krom had no choice. He had to jump for it.

Russ, but these xenos are fast – or are my injuries slowing me down?

Ulrik was flanked by a trio of dark eldar. They lashed at him with blades that telescoped into razor-studded flails at the flick of a wrist, making them impossible to parry. In contrast, they evaded each blow of his energy-wreathed crozius, seeming almost to be enjoying the dance. Their eyes shone fervently in the slits of their tapering helmets; above these, each wore the jagged symbol of their warrior kabal. It was not one that Ulrik recognised.

He described ever wider arcs with his weapon, trying to keep them at bay, but they darted between his swings and raked at him again. So far, the force field generated by his amulet had absorbed most of their punishment, but they were wearing him down, and his lungs were feeling the strain again. Ulrik had to change his tactics or he would lose this fight.

The next time a flail lashed out at him, he entangled his crozius in it and yanked on it sharply. His intention had been to disarm, but the wielder clung to its weapon stubbornly, which led to a brief and decidedly one-sided tug of war. As the xenos stumbled into him, off-balance at last, the Wolf High Priest swiped at it with his free hand, sending it reeling into one of its fellows.

In the process, he left his back exposed to the third, and its lash sliced through his fur-trimmed cloak and flayed a layer of ceramite off his forearm.

He had opened a gap in the dark eldar's circle, however, and he lowered his head and powered through it before they could regroup. He drew his plasma pistol, wheeled around and fired at them as they leapt after him, flattening his back against a stone wall so they couldn't surround him again.

The odds were still against him, but he suspected that was about to change.

Ulrik counted three brothers felled by flails and venom blades, and two others by splinters fired from the shadows – but many more had responded to his summons, most of them Drakeslayers. *I may owe Krom my life again!* The battle was spreading to engulf a city block, and the Sons of Russ were no longer on the defensive. They had begun to claim a few kills of their own.

Some packs across the city were not faring half as well. Reinforcements hadn't been able to find them in time. The vox-channels had been clogged with their voices a moment ago, but one by one they were falling ominously silent. Ulrik hadn't heard from Krom, but he had contacted Beoric Winterfang and had learned that his Wolf Guard had also been attacked.

They appeared so suddenly, with no warning at all, thought Ulrik, *and my ship's scans didn't detect them. Could it be...?*

The dark eldar were bringing in additional forces too. A pair of hulking, slavering beasts had joined the melee, dwarfing the humanoid combatants of both sides. Ulrik had encountered their like before. They resembled colossal, violet-hued apes, many-eyed and many-toothed with barbed tails and massive, razor-sharp claws.

A lean figure hovered above these clawed fiends on an anti-gravity skyboard: a dark eldar beastmaster. It was driving its charges onward with judicious lashes from a crackling whip. Its chest was bare, its belt hung with animal skulls, and it wore a shamanistic mask that resembled the monsters' own features – perhaps one of the arcane methods by which it asserted its dominance over them.

Two packs of Krom's Grey Hunters engaged the beasts. Ulrik voxed them across the battlefield.

'Bloody them and you'll send them into a berserker rage,' he warned them. 'Take out their master first, and they're as likely to turn on the dark eldar as not.' *Far easier said than done,* he knew.

His own three opponents were upon him again with their flails. Ulrik turned the red-eyed, snarling visage of the Wolf Helm of Russ upon them; one of them faltered for an instant, and he stove in its skull with his crozius.

He filtered a single voice out of the babble that filled his ears: '– saw they were outnumbered and fled from us. We ran some of them down, but the rest seemed to melt into the shadows. We have four Blood Claws down. As we arrived, they... the xenos were loading our battle-brothers onto a black skimmer.'

They're using hit-and-run tactics, Ulrik realised, *keeping the bulk of our forces disoriented – and divided – while they pick off our stragglers, one pack at a time. And take them where?* He feared he knew the answer to that question.

It was time he took the offensive.

Three dark eldar warriors had been enough to keep him on the back foot; two was a different matter. Ulrik lunged at them, taking the blows of their flails, whirling the sacred crozius – his weapon, but also his badge of office – end over end. One of them managed to dance out of his path, but the other did not. These xenos were fast – but so too were the Sons of Russ.

Ulrik roared as he battered his enemy repeatedly, giving it no time to draw breath, splitting open its helmet and driving it into the ground. When he was done, he rounded on his remaining opponent – to find it gone.

It had not left alone, he realised. No more than a handful of dark eldar lingered on the battlefield – some had fallen, but not enough to justify the drop in numbers – and their snipers' heads had vanished from the surrounding windows.

His battle-brothers hadn't noticed yet, or were just too preoccupied to care. The clawed fiends had scented their own blood and been driven into a frenzy, as Ulrik had predicted they would, and it was taking every man at hand to contain them.

He couldn't see the beastmaster. *Had he been shot down or had he withdrawn with the others, leaving his charges behind?* He tried to vox Krom Dragongaze, but received no answer again, so spoke to Beoric Winterfang.

'I assume the *Ironpelt* is in orbit?' he asked, referring to the Drakeslayers' strike cruiser.

'It is, High Priest,' Beoric confirmed.

'Contact your shipmaster. Have him launch his Thunderhawks.'

'High Priest, the tau–'

'I know. Our scans told us the same. I don't need those ships to land, just to look as if they might. I'll have my own gunships join them.'

'A distraction,' said Beoric.

'Keep the tau's air defences busy for ten minutes, then withdraw.'

Ulrik didn't wait for any further questions. Switching to another frequency, he issued a series of orders to his own shipmistress, Asgir. At the same time, he reloaded his plasma pistol. With that done, he bellowed his war cry again – raising an answering howl from as many Space Wolves as could hear him – and returned to the fray.

The smoking wreckage of the black craft was strewn all about him.

Krom could no longer feel or move his left arm at all; on top of that, he had twisted his back and scraped his armour, ricocheting off walls and outcroppings on his way to the ground. Repair cement had patched up the damage to the armour; the damage to his body would require more time and care.

He voxed Beoric, on a frequency that allowed the other Drakeslayers to overhear him.

'I've dealt with the xenos craft. Its crew are dead.' He made the boast sound almost casual. 'Making my way back now; I need a fix on your location.'

Krom didn't reveal how close to death he had come, how soon after his leap from the skimmer it had smacked into the near-intact stone wall of a tower.

Its pilot may have crashed deliberately, he thought, knowing it was dead either way and desiring to take its killer with it. He considered digging the dark eldar's corpse out of its mangled cockpit, so he could spit on it.

His impromptu flight had carried him deeper into the ruined city. All was quiet here now the wreckage had settled – but he feared that wouldn't last. Beoric and the others were over five miles away from him. *Too far.* He had their bearing now, but would still have to find a route through the streets to reach them.

'We should come to you,' suggested Beoric. 'There are more of us. It would be safer. You should take shelter until we–'

The Wolf Lord cut him off with a contemptuous snort. 'If you expect Krom Dragongaze to hide like a mewling–'

He froze as he felt his hackles rising and heard an all-too-familiar whining noise from above and behind him.

'What is it?' hissed Beoric through his earpiece. 'My lord?'

'Another skimmer,' he answered through his teeth. 'It's seen me.'

For a moment, Krom was ready to stand and fight. His right forefinger was curled around the trigger of his bolt pistol before he knew he had drawn it; through narrowed eyes, he glared along its barrel at the black shape bearing down on him. He had brought down one dark eldar ship today, why not another?

He hadn't been hurt last time. Nor had he been alone.

Krom had no choice, but that didn't mean he had to like it. He put off the decision as long as he could, perhaps a second too long. He emptied his magazine in the enemy's direction and hurled violent curses at them – futile gestures both, except for giving vent to his impotent fury. The black craft levelled out, careering between the city's stone husks. Its cannon began to spit, its poisoned darts tearing up the road in front of him.

Krom turned tail and ran for his life.

One of the two clawed fiends had finally fallen.

Even thrashing about in its death throes, it had continued to bloody its claws and fangs and knocked at least two Space Wolves off their feet. It couldn't beat back all of them, however, and a dozen chainswords hacked at the beast until it shuddered and fell still, dark blood matting its violet fur.

Ulrik had remained on the edge of the melee, firing into it when he had seen a clear shot, reserving the rest of his attention for matters else-where. In the sky he could see distant blossoms of light, the only signs of the pitched battle being fought up there. Occasionally, a ship – one of the combatants – would dip into the atmosphere and his enhanced hearing would detect the faint roar of its engines.

At last, he heard the sound he had been waiting for.

'Rolling Thunder to Wolf High Priest Ulrik,' a voice rumbled in his ear. 'I've made it through the tau blockade. Descending towards the abandoned city now.' Simultaneously, he heard engines above his head, deep and throaty, and saw their contrails burning across the heavens.

The remaining clawed fiend was mortally wounded, too angry and stupid to accept that it was dead. *The Drakeslayers are capable and numerous enough to take care of it,* Ulrik judged, *as their commander would no doubt insist if he were here.*

He broadcast a general-frequency vox to his own forces, those fighting the monster alongside him and those further afield. He told them to disengage from their battles, those that could, and prepare to rendezvous with him at coordinates to follow.

He was contacted by *Rolling Thunder*'s pilot again, on cue: 'I've identi-fied a possible landing site, a plaza, on a bearing of oh-seven-four degrees, two point one miles from your vox-signal. It'll be a tight squeeze, but I think I can–'

'I'll meet you there,' barked Ulrik.

Russ, don't let me die like this!

Krom hurtled around another sharp bend in the road. He saw a narrow gap between two buildings and plunged into it. It opened onto a circular plaza, where the dismembered legs of mildewed bronze statues still clung to broken plinths. He was too exposed here.

He glanced over his shoulder. He couldn't see the black skimmer but could hear its whining engines zeroing in on him. He turned back the way he had come, squeezing back between the buildings in the hope of confusing his pursuers.

As soon as he reached the road again, however, they pounced on him. Krom howled as his back was peppered with poisoned splinters. *Don't let me be cut down from behind, running like a frightened man-cub. Don't let that be how I am remembered. Let me meet my killer face to face and die with his blood on my claws.*

He was lucky this time. His armour saved him, preventing the needles from reaching his flesh.

A window loomed in front of him. Without stopping to think, he dived through it. His twisted back betrayed him. He landed on his numb left shoulder, sending a jolt of pain through him. His armour automatically upped his medication, but he countermanded it, needing his senses to be sharp. Splinters thudded into the far side of the wall behind which he was sprawled. At least he had found temporary shelter.

He couldn't stay here.

Krom scrambled away from the window, avoiding the shafts of grey light that streamed in through the roof. He crouched in the shadows and sniffed the musty air. His keen eyes pierced the gloom, exploring the innards of the dome in which he found himself. Its shell was relatively intact, but its internal walls had crumbled. There were plenty of egress points, designed and otherwise.

He could hear the dark eldar craft circling above him. No doubt they would direct ground troops to this spot to root him out. He couldn't afford to rest. He had to move, to get away from here, before they arrived.

He picked a window and loped across the rubble towards it, being sure to stay out of the light. He flattened himself against the wall and waited. When he judged that the skimmer was at the farthest point of its circuit, Krom bolted. He tumbled, head over heels, through the window, landed on his feet and ran. He was counting on taking his pursuers by surprise, on his reflexes being sharper than theirs were.

He wasn't fast enough – or they were too fast. Barely had he taken six steps when the skimmer was riding on his tail again, swooping down on him like a giant bird of prey, its cannon firing. More than one of its needles penetrated his armour this time, and buried themselves in his back.

Krom staggered and almost fell. He realised that the nearest cover was too far ahead of him, so turned back while he could. He scrambled through the same window he had emerged from, back into the broken dome. This time, he knew there would be no escaping from it. He was trapped here.

He couldn't reach the splinters in his back with only one hand. The injectors in his armour were flooding his system with anti-venoms, trying to counteract the dark eldar toxin – but the only thing holding it in check, he felt sure, was the rage bubbling white-hot in his veins. He embraced that rage like a brother.

He refused to let his legs fold underneath him. He kicked out at what was left of the walls instead, demolishing them and punching a fresh hole in the side of the dome. He voxed Beoric Winterfang, because he needed to scream at someone. 'Where are you?' he demanded. 'Do I have to slaughter every xenos on this planet by myself? What in Russ' name do I keep a Wolf Guard for?'

From Beoric there was no reply. Krom's hearts, both of them, were pounding in his ears as if competing with each other. The skimmer still circled overhead. The dark eldar troops, their warriors, would be here soon, he knew. All he cared about now was being on his feet to greet them.

He found a place in the shadows to crouch, from where he could watch every entrance to the dome. He clutched his bolt pistol in his right hand, though he had to concentrate to keep it from shaking. He would cut down two, maybe three dark eldar before they knew where he was. Then, when his gun was empty, the rest would come to him and Wyrmclaw would deal with them.

They would find him surrounded by the gutted corpses of his enemies, and would know that a battle worthy of legend had been fought here. The Sons of Russ would toast the memory of this day at many feasts to come.

They would long tell the tale of Wolf Lord Krom Dragongaze's last stand.

The narrow streets were empty again, which was no more than Ulrik had expected. It was typical of the dark eldar to spring a surprise attack then retreat with their spoils while their victims were still disoriented. *Not this time,* he vowed.

Rolling Thunder's engines now drowned out all other sounds for him; her wolf's-head shadow blotted out the light momentarily as she passed over him. She was a Stormwolf, an assault ship capable of carrying sixteen Space Wolves into battle.

Ulrik loped around the corner of another fractured hab-block, the five members of his Wolf Guard at his heels. The Stormwolf was sitting there, waiting for him. She almost filled the cramped plaza in which she had put down, wreathed in her own exhaust smoke, looking battered but defiant – as indeed she always had.

Its pilot, Rogan Bearsbane – a ruddy-faced, heavy-set Iron Priest sporting a voluminous beard – flashed him a grin from the cockpit as he lowered the boarding ramp. Ulrik waved his battle-brothers ahead of him, and was pleased to see others – more than he had expected – streaming into the plaza to join them.

One group of three wore the badge of the Sun Wolf. They were members of Krom Dragongaze's Wolf Guard, though neither the Fierce-eye nor Beoric Winterfang were among them.

A Wolf Guard by the name of Beregelt squared up to the High Priest. 'You're taking a gunship in pursuit of the dark eldar's captives.' It wasn't a question.

'The Great Wolf was here,' said Ulrik. 'If they took him–'

Beregelt interrupted him, boldly. 'We're coming with you.'

Ulrik growled at him, 'I have as many Wolves as I require.'

'They have our Wolf Lord cornered,' said Beregelt, stubbornly. 'Beoric is leading a pack to his side, but I fear they may not reach him in time, especially not if there is a gate to the eldar labyrinth in these ruins.'

Ulrik nodded. 'It may be what brought the Great Wolf here.'

It didn't surprise him that Beregelt knew of such matters. The Wolf Guard had served long enough to have seen many things.

'You plan to follow the dark eldar through that gateway,' said Beregelt. Again, it wasn't a question. 'Lord Krom would want his Wolf Guard aboard that ship.'

And just how was Krom separated from his Wolf Guard, Ulrik thought to snarl, *especially after I cautioned him against being reckless?* He bit back the words. *Now is not the right time.* 'Very well,' he conceded gruffly, then turned his back.

He climbed aboard the waiting gunship, and left Beregelt and the Drake-slayers to follow him as they wished.

They had come at him from nowhere.

Krom Dragongaze cursed them, cursed the splinters in his back, the neurotoxin in his system, cursed himself most of all for his weakness. He had closed his eyes, unwittingly, for a second: long enough for them to strike.

The poison had tightened his chest, making it difficult to breathe. His pulses were irregular, his secondary heart pumping frantically to compensate for his failing primary. He had prayed for his enemies to find him soon, lest he die first and be denied his blaze of glory.

He had rested his brow against a half-demolished wall, though he didn't remember doing so. His auto-senses warned him that the temperature in the dome had dropped sharply – but, insulated by his armour, he had paid them little heed. He had thrown back his head with a shuddering breath as the cold had touched his lungs. His eyes had snapped open and he had found himself beset.

They were unlike any dark eldar he had encountered before.

They were similar in build and facial features, but their skin was ebony-black rather than milky-white. They had marked themselves with tattoos, which flowed like oil, forming one hideous, blasphemous shape after another. The creatures were wrapped in pale robes, blood-spattered and stinking of death – fashioned, Krom realised, from layers of flayed skin stitched together.

They slashed and thrust at him with sickle-shaped blades, wielded with the precision of surgical knives, but they also tore at him with fangs and claws.

Krom dropped his pistol. He hadn't had a chance to use it and knew he probably wouldn't again. He drew his axe. He wasn't sure how many opponents he was facing: one second he thought there were only three of them, the next he was sure there were five or more. They seemed to phase in and out of the shadows around him.

Shadows...

He *had* heard tell of creatures like these, long ago. Was it Ulrik who had spoken of them at some point, early on in his training? *Tales told by lesser men,* he had thought at the time, *to frighten their young.* How had the High Priest named these semi-mythical creatures? He remembered now: *nightfiends!*

It was whispered that they could spring from any man's shadow. *Is that how they crept up on me?* Krom wondered. The way the darkness appeared to deepen around them, as if they were sucking light out of the world, he could believe it.

He felt cold emanating from their very souls, and when he swung Wyrmclaw at them, even when he was positive that its blade had cleaved their flesh, often they remained unbloodied. They were swift – as swift as their dark eldar brethren – and he feared that the poison in his body was slowing him down, but it wasn't only that. It was almost as if these creatures were shadows themselves.

He screamed at them until his throat was raw, hurling every curse he knew at them. He called them cowards and challenged them to face him like warriors, one at a time. The only sounds they made in response were vile hisses. Their blades and claws continued to slice through him, chilling his flesh where they touched it.

Krom fought back as fiercely as ever he had. His tiredness, his shortness of breath, were almost forgotten. His armour had dosed him with stimulants, but nothing could replace the natural rush of battle. Still, his efforts so far were proving futile. Worse, he had the impression that the shadow-skinned creatures were holding back. They could have slain him by now, but instead they were sporting with him.

The thought enraged him, and he whirled his frost axe with renewed vigour and laughed as he felt it biting into flesh and splintering bone at last. The tones of the creatures' hisses changed, then – they sounded affronted, as if they had the right – and some of them melted away, to leave but three arrayed in an arc before him. These three raised their arms, their talons pointed at him like spears.

Krom managed to take a single step towards them before he was struck by another wave of freezing cold.

He tried to raise his good arm to protect his face, but found he couldn't. He was paralysed and the nightfiends were swarming him again, more of them than ever. They wrenched Wyrmclaw from his helpless fingers; for a

moment he thought they would use it to take his head, but they had something worse in mind.

They encircled him, grabbed at him, tipped him backwards off his feet.
They shouldered his power-armoured weight between them, and Krom
would have howled in rage at this humiliation had his lungs not been
frozen.

The cold – or was it the poison? – had spread behind his eyes, stealing
his senses from him one by one. Inwardly, he railed at the indignity of his
fate: to be shamed in this manner, to be made a wretched hostage. Out-
wardly, there was nothing Krom Dragongaze could do as the icy shadows
claimed him.

Ulrik sat in *Rolling Thunder*'s passenger compartment, knee to knee with
Olav Brunn, Beregelt and Leoric Half-ear, a Rune Priest he had requested
join them in case they had need of his particular talents. Ulrik blocked out
the deafening roar of the Stormwolf's engines as he spoke to Asgir, on the
orbiting *Canis Pax*, by vox. He had instructed his shipmistress to make continuous scans of the abandoned city and keep him informed of the results.

'I see them, High Priest,' she reported. 'Dark eldar Venom skimmers in
all sectors. They're fading in and out... I can't get a lock on them...'

Allfather be praised, thought Ulrik, *we still have time.*

Rogan Bearsbane voxed him from the cockpit. 'I have eyes on a skimmer and am in pursuit. We can't match it for manoeuvrability, though.
It's weaving in and out of the buildings, even through them. If it wants to
shake us off, it only has to–'

'High Priest,' Asgir cut in on him. 'Something else. Three signatures closing in... no, taking up positions around you, matching your course and
speed.'

'The tau?' Ulrik guessed.

The shipmistress confirmed it. 'I'm reading them as Manta gunships.'

The dark eldar are their enemies as much as ours, he thought. *They are
watching us to see what we will do. More likely, they have guessed we won't
be their problem much longer.*

'Russ' teeth!' Rogan spluttered, suddenly, and he slammed the Stormwolf into a steep, banking turn.

At the same time, Asgir reported that a new icon had erupted onto her
tactical hololith. The accompanying data, however, was gibberish.

Ulrik pushed himself up from his seat and pressed his eyes to the slats
of a narrow viewport in the forward hatch. From this limited perspective,
however, he was too late to see anything of import. 'What is it?' he barked
at his pilot. 'What did you see?'

'Down in the ruins,' Rogan answered. 'Some... some xenos artefact. It
had three curving pylons, like claws. Then suddenly, between them... It
was like... like staring into the heart of the warp itself.'

'What about the skimmer?'

'It flew into that... High Priest, what is it?'

'It's a gateway,' said Ulrik. 'And your orders remain the same. Our captured battle-brothers are aboard those ships. The next one to approach that portal...' He had switched to a general frequency, allowing his brothers to hear him. 'You will follow them through.'

For the first time, Rogan demurred. 'High Priest, are you certain-?'

Beregelt sat forward. 'They may have taken Lord Krom in there,' he said, quietly.

That seemed to settle the matter. Some of the other Space Wolves exchanged uncertain glances, but none raised a voice in protest. Nor did Rogan speak again, but Ulrik felt the Stormwolf coming back around.

'We don't know what's in there,' Leoric warned.

Ulrik turned to Beregelt. 'Vox the rest of your company. Tell them where we're going and that we may not return. They are to wait six hours; then, in the absence of further contact from either of us, return to the Fang.'

He was likely wasting his breath. With the dark eldar gone – and even without Krom to lead them – the Drakeslayers would probably find an excuse to re-engage the tau. *So, let them. It is none of my concern,* he thought.

He peered out through the narrow viewport again. He saw the portal ahead of them, just as Rogan Bearsbane had described it. It was as if the xenos construct had torn a hole in the surface of reality itself – and beyond it...

He could barely look at its blinding, hateful light, even with his eyes protected by the Wolf Helm of Russ. He made the sign of the aquila across his chest and silently asked the Allfather for his guidance. This was either a monumental act of courage or one of insanity; he couldn't tell which.

But the Great Wolf may be in there...

Ulrik offered another prayer – aloud, this time, for all to hear – that the Allfather might still be able to watch over them where they were about to go, so far from the things they knew. Then a dark eldar skimmer dropped into his line of sight, span into the light and was completely swallowed by it. He voxed his pilot, 'There it is. Go! Go!'

Rolling Thunder plunged into the seething portal.

And left the tangible universe behind it.

PART FOUR

DARK CITY

His opponents had never stood a chance.

Most likely, thought Krom Dragongaze, *they were never meant to.*

There had been six of them to his one – slobbering ghouls with flat eyeless faces and rows of trembling nostrils. They had come at him in flurries of claws and teeth, blunting both against his armour. The last one had wrapped its mouth around his forearm, clinging to him tenaciously for all its wounds. He tore it free and dashed it to the floor.

Throwing back his fiery mane, he loosed a howl of triumph to the heavens.

Then his victory soured in his throat. The crowd's roars washed over him, reminding him where he was. He knew what they wanted from him. The last of his enemies was twitching at his feet. They were baying for him to hurt it again. They wanted him to torture it, to eke out its dying agonies.

He spited them by staving in the ghoul's skull with his maul, though this was an undeserved mercy. The dark eldar's cheers turned to jeers, their fine features twisted in displeasure. *Russ, if only I had my pistol,* thought Krom.

He was barrelling towards them before he knew it.

He jumped off the finely balanced, polished bone disc of the stage. He ploughed through knotted coils of razorwire. He vaulted onto the high wall that separated him from the crowd. He came as close as he ever had to getting over it. Then whips enwrapped his arms, his legs, his throat, as they always did. Krom knew it was useless to struggle against his captors, and yet, wreathed in the red mist of rage, he always did.

The whips crackled with profane energy, and his nervous system burned. The slave masters yanked Krom back into the arena and he writhed in the black sand, convulsing helplessly, coughing up foam and flecks of blood.

The sky of Commorragh had a sullen crimson cast. It rested heavily on the tips of the arena's jagged spires and the brooding ziggurats overlooking it. Shrivelled black suns glared balefully down at him. When Krom had first arrived here, another prisoner – a dishevelled Imperial Guardsman – had told him he would see no other sky for as long as he lived, which would be until he met his match in combat. 'Then it will be a long life,' Krom had boasted. He hadn't seen the Guardsman again.

The crowd had forgotten him already. Other battles were in progress across the various stages, offering them many more opportunities to sate their lust for suffering. A member of the wych cult that ran the arena was carving up a tau fire warrior. Krom wondered if it too had been captured on Dactyla. Beyond them, he saw clawed fiends, a battered-looking Chaos Terminator – and a figure in a filthy pale robe and black power armour.

Krom's weapon was torn from his nerveless fingers. Six slave masters hauled him away through one of the many dark portals that led to the arena's bowels. By now, the descent through the foetid passageways, with their pulsing, green-tinted light, was a horribly familiar one. His footsteps rang off the floor, which felt like marble but was black with sickly-looking veins coursing through it.

An iron gate hissed open for him, and Krom was thrown to the floor of one of the gladiatorial cells. Unable to lift his hands to catch himself, he landed like a sack of grain. He found his voice in time to curse his gaolers as they locked the gate behind him.

It was several seconds before he could lift himself into a sitting position, propped against the wall. He hated letting his cellmates see his weakness, even though they were as battered as he was. He snapped at them, telling them to lift their chins and square their shoulders, show that they would never be bowed, and they shuffled to obey him.

'What did they have you fight?' asked Jormund Thunderclaw.

'Some manner of ghoul,' Krom spat, and he described in detail how he had slain each of them in turn. 'I almost butchered my audience too. I was close enough to smell their fear, see myself reflected in their eyes. Next time...'

'Allfather be praised, we still have that,' Jormund rumbled. 'Though we may die here, still we can despatch many more of His enemies ahead of us.' It disturbed Krom to hear him talking like that.

Each of the Space Wolves bore the marks of the slave masters' lashes, but Jormund's Terminator armour was in the worst state of them all. He had fought so hard to begin with. The slave masters, however, had wrapped him in chains that, like their whips, crackled with dark energy. They had stripped out his heavy weapons and shattered his servo-motors, until it was all he could do to stand.

The thought that Jormund was learning to accept his fate made Krom rage. He wanted to leap to his feet. He wanted to yell out to his Wolf-brothers. Three of them shared his cell. There were more in the others. He wanted to remind them that they were the Wolves of Fenris. Most of them were members of his own company, the Drakeslayers. He wanted to tell them to rise up, break through their bars and tear out their gaolers' throats.

'Brother Dreadhowl,' he recalled. The young Blood Claw had been taken to the arena some time before him. Krom hadn't seen him there, but that meant nothing. 'Did he... Has he returned?' No one answered his question. No one had to.

Krom had given up trying to count the days he had been here. His auto-senses suggested that a month and a half had passed, but each of his brothers had a different tally. For the first few days, or weeks, he had been sure that the rest of the Drakeslayers would follow him here. No matter that their journey was impossible – for him, for their Wolf Lord, they would find a way to make it.

He knew now that no one was coming. If he was to escape this hellish place, it would be up to him alone. So what if his captors had the upper hand for now? What if the red sky was teeming with dark eldar ships? And beyond that sky, outside of this dark city...

Krom had been brought here unconscious. Some of his brothers had been awake for the journey, however, and they had spoken of the horrors...

They were lost.

The gunship *Rolling Thunder* had followed a dark eldar skimmer through an energy-charged portal. Now, she was barrelling her way through a realm of...

It was impossible to describe.

Ulrik the Slayer crouched in the troop compartment, peering through a narrow forward viewport. The Stormwolf's sensors couldn't process the data they were receiving, so couldn't be trusted. Other than an occasional fleeting glimpse of their prey, Rogan Bearsbane, their pilot, had only his instincts to guide him.

'It's like flying through an ice storm,' he said. His voice sounded strained over the vox-net.

'We can't afford to lose that skimmer,' said Ulrik, tightly.

He had thought this would be something like flying through the warp. It was worse than he could have imagined. Through the viewport, he too saw snow and ice, but he knew – perhaps thanks to the relic helm he wore – that nothing they were seeing was real – not as humans understood reality. He couldn't look into the face of the raging storm for long; it made his eyes ache. Even when he screwed them shut, he could feel the unreality's substance, like static, in his head.

There are brother wolves aboard that craft, the High Priest reminded himself. *I did the right thing, going after them – whatever the outcome.*

'They've seen us,' Rogan growled over the vox. 'They're weaving, trying to throw us off their tail. They're smaller than we are, more manoeuvrable. It's only a matter of time before they make a move we can't match.'

Ulrik grimaced and pressed his eyes to the viewport again. *Rolling Thunder* had dropped back onto the skimmer's tail, but her engines were howling in protest at the abuse they were receiving.

Then a hole gaped open in the heart of the static storm – a deep, black hole – and the skimmer banked and plunged assuredly into it. Rogan tried to follow it, but the storm closed in again and suddenly he was flying towards what looked like a sheer ice face. He unleashed a stream of colourful curses as he pulled up sharply. 'I don't see any sign of them. We've lost them!'

In the troop compartment, more curses filled the air. The Drakeslayer Beregelt was more stoic; still, he gripped the sides of his seat almost hard enough to crush them. His own fate didn't concern him, Ulrik knew, rather that of his captured Wolf Lord.

Ulrik slammed his crozius arcanum into the deck plates, so its winged wolf-skull head crackled with sacred energy. 'Are we so easily beaten?' Ulrik roared. 'Should we cower here, whimpering over the slightest setback? We *will* find our brother Wolves, if we have to wade hip-deep through dark eldar corpses to do it.'

'Tear this foul realm down around their twisted ears!' cried Thord Icenhelm.

'For Russ!' bellowed Ulrik, and the others joined their voices to his. He wished he felt half as confident as he sounded.

It was the High Priest's duty to maintain his brothers' morale, even when, privately, he feared their cause was hopeless – that they might be trapped in this godless realm forever.

Two more days passed, maybe three – Krom couldn't tell – before the slave masters came for him again.

They didn't have to call his name. Everyone knew whom they wanted. He had counted their footsteps as they approached his cell. Six dark eldar always arrived to fetch him, more than for anyone else. He was already standing, waiting for them, when the gate hissed open.

They beckoned to him, speaking harshly in their obscene language. A handful of the senior gaolers had translating machines, which they used to communicate orders to their prisoners. The rest had other ways of making themselves understood.

These six had their whips readied in case of trouble. Had Krom tried to fight them, he knew they would have flayed him gleefully – before dumping him, half-insensate, in front of his assigned opponent anyway. He had barely survived the experience last time.

They took him through the green-veined passageways again. They passed rows of sealed gates, from behind which he heard the occasional muffled howl of pain, anguish or rage. He could hear the roars of the arena crowd growing louder.

Two more Wolves were waiting, each with his own escort, in the cramped muster area. On the closest stage in the arena, a pair of fleshless monsters with clawed tendrils were tearing into each other, urged on by the lashes of their beastmasters.

'Did you hear about Brother Silverpelt?' Beoric Whitefang asked him, bleakly. 'They put him up against a monstrous spider with blades on its legs.'

When Krom had first been delivered to his cell, he had been dismayed to learn that Beoric too had been caught, although he was secretly comforted by his Wolf Guard commander's stoic presence. He suspected that Beoric had allowed himself to be captured, so as to remain at his lord's side.

Krom nodded. 'I hear he removed all eight before the spider's poison killed him.' It was important that such stories, and the names attached to them, were remembered. Beoric knew nothing of Brother Dreadhowl, however, when Krom asked him. It seemed that no one had witnessed his fate, so his story would remain untold.

An appreciative roar swelled from the arena crowd. Another contest had ended, on one of the further stages. A minute later, its victor was brought inside, walking upright and proud, and Lars Thorgil was marched out to replace him.

Krom had seen the black-armoured figure before, but never close up. Now he could see quite clearly the winged sword emblem on his robe and the skull-shaped faceplate beneath his hood – the stranger was a Dark Angels chaplain. Krom's lip curled involuntarily. Krom hated the Dark Angels and their mysterious ways. His experience of them had left him with an impression of secrecy and superiority. He couldn't trust them because they only trusted themselves – and as rumour would have it, they couldn't even trust some of the brothers in their own ranks. It was true that an age before there had been tension between Leman Russ and the Lion. It was also true that while the primarchs forgave each other, there were many in their legions – and the Chapters that followed – who could not forgive.

In the arena, the beast fight had reached its bloody conclusion. The victorious creature was being driven away by its master, while shackled human slaves hosed the loser's remains from the stage.

Then it was Krom's turn to fight.

He was taken by the arms again and marched out beneath the sullen sky. His appearance was greeted by an audible thrill of anticipation. His stomach turned at the thought of his audience being so pleased to see him. They knew he would give them a good show.

Something was different this time.

He was taken to a stage at the farthest edge of the arena. In the midst of the tiered seating, an expansive podium overlooked him. Squatting upon its lip was an ostentatious ebony throne that, tonight, was occupied. The arena's ruler was in attendance, surrounded by obsequious servants and sycophantic cronies.

Krom was struck by the creature's beauty, but was instantly disgusted with himself. *It is an evil beauty,* he thought, *a glamour to disguise a monstrous soul.*

The queen was as much a warrior as her followers, clad in barbed leather armour that left her thighs and stomach exposed. She wore a sword belt hung with fetishes, and an elaborate leather headdress.

She saw him looking and returned his gaze coolly, with a twinkle of amusement in her eyes. She had had him brought before her, he realised suddenly. He was fighting at the queen's pleasure, for her entertainment, tonight.

Krom looked for a weapon. There were plenty strewn across the stage and around it, though few of any quality. He chose an axe with a serrated metal head, because nothing better was available. It was a poor replacement for his own. Wyrmclaw had been prised from his fingers while he lay unconscious. It lay somewhere in the arena, too large and heavy for most to wield it – Ragnek Halfhand had seen it.

His opponent made her entrance to the arena. She was a gladiatrix, a female arena fighter. She wore similar leathers to her queen, although her outfit was less elaborate. As she strode into the arena, Krom's lips curled back from his fangs. Until now, he had only been pitted against other prisoners. To finally face one of his captors... He had longed for such an opportunity.

He fixed the gladiatrix with a smouldering glare as she strutted towards him. Her dark eyes met his, unafraid. Her jet-black lips smirked at him. He prickled at the creature's arrogance. Tightening his grip on his axe, he began thundering towards her before she had even fully mounted the circular stage. He let her see his teeth and feel the full force of his lungs.

The gladiatrix had drawn a pair of swords that had been concealed in her bodice. No scrabbling for weapons in the dirt for her. She sidestepped his charge and slashed at him, cutting into his right vambrace. Krom snarled as he swung his axe again, but the gladiatrix pirouetted away and was suddenly behind him. He whirled to face her as her twin blades stabbed towards his eyes. He barely batted them away before they blinded him.

He lunged beneath the gladiatrix's swords, trying to tackle her. She back-flipped away from him, landing in a taut crouch across the stage, her black lips taunting him. The crowd that had cheered for the Wolf Lord a minute ago screamed now for his enemy to cut him, to let them taste his dying agonies.

He embraced the white-hot rage that they stoked in his chest, let it energise him but not control him. He had to keep his wits about him.

He hacked, sliced and thrust at his opponent doggedly. She evaded each blow with a grace that made him feel slow and clumsy. *Russ, this is like battling the nightfiends!* he cursed, remembering the shadowy creatures that had beaten him and brought him here. But there had been many of them, Krom reminded himself, and he had been slowed by wounds and poison when he fought them.

He eased back deliberately, making the gladiatrix come to him. He would show her – and her baying supporters – that he could be quick too. She obliged him, and her blades whirled around his ears like turbines. Krom twirled his axe, gripped the haft with both hands and parried each attack with its chipped head, metal striking sparks off metal.

The gladiatrix overreached herself and his haft caught her wrist, breaking the bone. She dropped a sword, and Krom followed through by shattering her nose with his elbow. Startled, the eldar wheeled away from him and dropped into a defensive crouch again. She wasn't smirking any longer, but Krom, with the taste of his opponent's blood on his lips, was leering like a beast of prey.

They circled each other, narrow-eyed and alert for an opening or sign of weakness from the other, each tuning out the crowd's impatient demands and biding their time.

Krom's eyes kept flickering over the gladiatrix's shoulder to the queen on her ornate throne. She was craning forward eagerly, moistening her lips with her tongue. Then her gloved hand glided across a rune panel in her armrest, and the throne itself rose into the air and edged over the podium's lip, straining closer to the spectacle before it.

Krom's opponent on the stage took advantage of his momentary distraction. The gladiatrix flew at him again in a flurry of razor-edged metal, scoring his armour and forcing him onto his back foot. He defended himself against her, but kept an eye trained on the queen.

In that moment, for the first time in too long a time, he saw a story worth the telling. Krom Dragongaze recognised a deed worth giving his life for.

He went on the offensive, hammering at his opponent with more brute force than precision. As before, his blows came nowhere close to landing – nor were they meant to. He drove the gladiatrix back towards the edge of the stage. Then, as she whirled out of his grasp, he leapt off the stage and, with all his might, he hurled his axe towards the queen's slender white throat.

To his dismay, she caught the hurtling projectile.

He barely saw her hand move – she just plucked the axe from the air. Krom had lost his weapon and turned his back on an enemy for nothing.

He heard her footsteps running up behind him – too late. The gladiatrix leapt onto his back and slipped her blade behind his gorget, into the side of his neck. If she expected the pain to cripple him, however, clearly she didn't know the Sons of Russ.

Krom reached over his shoulders, snatched his foe's head in both hands and wrenched her off him. He slammed her into the stage, breaking her bones, divesting the creature of her second sword and expelling the breath from her lungs. He held her down with one massive gauntlet over her face, almost smothering her.

The crowd roared once again for Krom Dragongaze. *They don't care who wins,* he realised, *as long as someone suffers – even if it's one of their own.*

This time, he gave them what they wanted.

He kept the wriggling, spitting gladiatrix pinned down, her agility no use to her now. He drove his free fist into her, shattering the rest of her bones and pulping her flesh. When the creature could take no more and passed out, Krom tore her still-beating heart from her chest and displayed it to his audience defiantly.

His gaze remained fixed on the queen and her hovering throne. He bared his fangs and snarled at her, conveying the unmistakable message: *You're next!*

She raised the axe to her mouth, unperturbed. She ran her tongue along its blood-encrusted edge, seeming not to care that she cut herself in the process. Then, casually, she snapped the wooden haft in two and tossed the parts back into the arena.

Blood was spurting from Krom's neck. Even his Larraman's organ couldn't staunch the flow entirely. He was forced to clamp his gauntlet over the wound. He needed the ministrations of a Wolf Priest. There were no priests here, however.

The dark eldar slave masters were moving in around him with their whips. Fatigued and weakened by blood loss, he was unable to resist them.

Ulrik blinked and remembered where he was.

He felt as if he had been trapped in a waking dream for weeks, but his chrono informed him that it had been less than a minute.

He wrenched his gaze away from the viewport. Still, tendrils of harsh, white light streamed through it, tearing at his eyes. *When men look upon the unfiltered warp,* he thought, *it drives them mad. Perhaps the same is true of this realm?*

His brothers were shifting uncomfortably in their seats, some of them cradling their heads in their hands, shrinking away from the light. He almost ordered the viewport blocked, but he had to be able to see what was out there.

Leoric Half-ear, the Rune Priest, was sitting in a meditative pose, his eyelids flickering.

'I see... I see the pathways, but they're tangled together,' he said, 'and I see...' Whatever Leoric saw, it was so terrible that he could not speak of it. His face was pale and clammy with sweat.

Olav Brunn was staring out of the viewport, in a trance. Ulrik leaned forward, seized him by the shoulders and shook him. He waited for the Wolf's eyes to focus. 'Have faith,' he commanded, augmenting his voice to reach all of them, whatever their states of mind. 'Remember, the dark eldar endure in this realm. They build their cities here. Are we, with the Allfather's light to guide us and protect us, not stronger than they are?'

He opened a vox-channel to Rogan Bearsbane in the cockpit. Ulrik couldn't imagine how he was coping up there, with no respite from the realm's madness. Indeed, he sounded confused, distracted, on edge. The High Priest talked to him, trying to reassure him and keep him focused. It was only because of Rogan's piloting skills that they were still alive.

'If you can find a place to land...' he suggested, hopelessly.

Rolling Thunder was buffeted fiercely, and a series of violent cracks – like the shifting of massive quantities of ice – reverberated through its structure. The Space Wolves looked to the hull above their heads, anxiously.

'No place... there's no place for us here,' murmured Leoric. 'We're not welcome... We should leave before... before we are...'

Then, suddenly, they were flying straight and level again, and the hateful light had faded. It was like a weight had been lifted from Ulrik's soul. He heard Rogan Bearsbane's breathless voice: 'The storm... Thank the Allfather, the storm is lifting.' Ulrik looked through the viewport again. *Have we found our destination, after all?* he wondered. *Or have we somehow blundered our way back into realspace?*

All he could see was blackness.

Then, he felt gravity tugging at his stomach, and realised that *Rolling Thunder* was in a vertical dive. Rising up to meet her were the ruins of an ancient city that looked like it was constructed from a lattice of bones, suffused with a soft internal light.

'I can see them sheltering behind their walls.' Leoric whispered. 'I see them dancing, laughing, feasting... but they are dust.'

Ulrik blinked and suddenly the city was bright and young again, its streets teeming with shadowy phantoms. Then it dropped away rapidly as Rogan raised the gunship's nose. The tendrils of the icy storm ensnared them once more and the city was gone.

Some of the others had seen the phantoms too. Beregelt turned to Ulrik, his incomprehension written on his face.

'Time means nothing here,' the High Priest growled, and the thought could have driven him – even him – to despair. Not only did this realm span known space, its passageways crazed between the layers of reality like capillaries – they extended into past and future too. He lacked the knowledge to navigate it.

He recalled the legends he had heard of those – such as Jaghatai Khan – who had tried before him and been lost. *We could fly for centuries, millennia,* Ulrik realised, *and never find our captured battle-brothers, never meet another living soul, never find a way out.*

He suppressed a shudder. *Perhaps we already have.*

A disturbance rippled through the gladiatorial cells.

Krom felt his hackles rising. He clambered to his feet and strained at the bars, trying to see outside. He hadn't slept for as long as he had been a prisoner, but he had shut down his brain one section at a time to rest it. This allowed him to remain alert, but he knew it also left him prey to waking hallucinations.

Am I seeing things now? Krom wondered, as a familiar figure stalked towards him through a sickly green haze. If he was, then his brothers were seeing the same. They were on their feet in each of the surrounding cells, unleashing howls of protest. The eldar queen paid them no heed. She had locked gazes with Krom, and they held each other's eyes until she came to a halt – a step away from the point at which he could have reached through the bars and gutted her. She addressed her entourage of grovelling serfs and slave masters in their own language, in a voice like splintering ice that made Krom's teeth itch. He spat curses at her, to drown her out as much as anything. The slave masters snarled at him and brandished their whips in threat.

The queen hadn't taken her eyes off him. Krom felt, as he had in the arena, that she found him amusing – which enraged him all the more. She spoke curtly to her escorts again, then turned on her heel and stalked away from him, the howls of the captive wolves echoing after her.

The slave masters came back for Krom a short time later. They normally gave him longer to recover between contests – his neck still throbbed as his body struggled to heal the gash in it, and any strenuous activity was likely to tear it open again. They beckoned to Jormund Thunderclaw too, who rose with difficulty in his crippled suit of armour.

The journey took longer than it had before. Jormund moved slowly and unsurely, and no amount of threats or punishment could make him go any faster.

'You should feel honoured,' a slave master told Krom as they walked. His words emerged from a vox-grille slung around his neck. 'Janaera herself is impressed with your prowess in the arena.'

'I couldn't care less what your bitch queen thinks of me,' Krom snarled.

'She has named you favourite of her warriors.'

Krom bridled. 'A Wolf of Fenris belongs to no one, even less so a–'

The slave master talked over him. 'Impress the Grand Archite and she may choose to extend your life.'

'Tell your "Archite" to face me fairly in combat herself. Let her see my prowess close up instead of watching like a cringing cur from the shadows.'

'You will end your days here all the same, but you could see more of them. The ruling succubi arrange the arena bouts, and for a favourite of theirs they will–'

Krom spat in the dark eldar's face. It snarled and its whip lashed out at him. Brother Jormund started forward, affronted by this slight to his lord, but Krom motioned him to stand down. He wiped a trail of blood from his cheek with the back of his gauntlet, and bared his fangs in a grin.

Getting under his captors' skins may have been a tiny victory, but still he savoured it.

In the muster area, he was handed a double-bladed frost axe, its keen edge gleaming. Wyrmclaw! He looked at it in surprise, expecting some trick. He took the proffered weapon all the same. It felt good, it felt familiar – it felt right – as his fingers closed around it. It felt like an extension of his hand. He had missed it sorely.

'There is some advantage in being the Grand Archite's favourite, after all,' said Jormund, wryly. 'She wishes to see you at your best, evidently. Perhaps she will return my missile launcher to me too. *Then* she will witness a spectacle.'

The slave masters said nothing to that suggestion. Instead, one of them produced a skeletal key, unlocked the massive shackle that encircled Jormund's left arm and began to unravel the heavy chains that bound him. Krom saw the relief in his battle-brother's posture as he was able to straighten his back and square his shoulders.

The next thing he knew, the trailing chains were being wrapped around *him*.

Krom tried to protest, but the slave masters tightened their cordon around him. They clamped the shackle around his left forearm, tightened and locked it. He was bound to Jormund now, a triple length of chain stretching barely more than an arm's length between them. Whatever was waiting for them out in the arena, they would face it together.

They were taken to the farthest stage, as Krom had expected.

It took them an age to reach it. He and Jormund struggled to coordinate their movements. More than once, Krom was almost pulled over by the larger, heavier Terminator. Some members of the crowd laughed and jeered at them. A fat, rotten, purple-skinned alien fruit burst against Krom's pauldron.

They rounded a stage that was bordered by bone-carved pylons, like fangs around a daemon's mouth. The podium came into view and Krom's eyes darted to it. Sure enough, the Grand Archite was draped across her throne.

He and Jormund had found a rhythm now and made better progress, though Jormund's right foot dragged behind him. They clambered awkwardly onto the circular stage and their escorts withdrew to the shadows. Jormund reached for a giant, spiked mace, almost yanking Krom off his feet again in the process, to the crowd's amusement.

Krom took out his anger on the eldar queen. 'Come down here and fight me,' he bellowed up at her. 'You enjoy the taste of pain? I will treat you to agonies like you've never before imagined. I will tear out your black heart with my teeth.'

His words were likely unintelligible to her, but his tone and gestures certainly conveyed his meaning. Still, the arrogant expression on the Archite's pale face didn't flicker. Krom considered hurling his axe at her again.

He was distracted, however, by a sudden flurry of activity behind him. Half a dozen dark eldar, led by a beastmaster, were hauling a new combatant across the arena. It was fighting them all the way. Even their whips couldn't subdue the raging creature. They had been forced to bind it, as they had Jormund, with chains.

Krom saw a spiny carapace and six powerful limbs, and knew right away that he was looking at a tyranid organism. 'A genestealer,' he muttered, darkly.

'A broodlord,' muttered Jormund, 'to judge by its sheer size and the shape of his head.' His voice sounded strained, which boded ill.

With much pushing, lashing and cursing from the slave masters, the creature was dragged up onto the stage, whereupon it immediately grew calmer. Krom saw a glint of intelligence in its beady eyes. It seemed to understand that the two armoured figures across from it were being offered up to it as prey.

The beastmaster had the broodlord's chains removed, and its captors hastened away from it. It dropped into a crouch. A slobbering, spiny tongue, as blue as its hide, flicked out between its fangs. Krom felt a palpable wave of dread washing over him, almost strong enough to freeze his feet to the stage. Jormund stepped in front of him, thinking to shield his Wolf Lord, but Krom pushed him aside.

The monster sprang at them – and rebounded with a high-pitched screech as Wyrmclaw sliced into its hide. Its clawed feet skittered on the stage's smooth surface, and it leapt at Krom again. This time, he splintered its exoskeleton. He would have done more, had the chains that bound him to Jormund not snapped taut.

Still, the monster flew at Krom a third time, a fourth and again, until Wyrmclaw inevitably missed its mark – glancing off the monster's shoulder. Then it was upon him. Razor-sharp claws shredded his armour and gouged at his face. The monster's jaw dropped open, wider than Krom would have thought possible, and he recoiled from its unholy breath. He couldn't fight it on so many fronts at once.

He thanked the Allfather, then, that he wasn't fighting alone.

Krom was wielding his axe two-handed, tugging on his battle-brother's arm with every swipe. That had made it difficult for Jormund to join in the fight thus far. Now, however, the Terminator delivered a crushing mace blow to the broodlord's spine. When that didn't deter it, he tried to drag it off his Wolf Lord by its throat, which at least afforded Krom some respite from its breath. The monster's claws continued to tear at him, however, as it thrashed in the Terminator's grip, tearing up his greaves with its hind feet.

Krom wrenched himself free of it at last, though he lost his right pauldron and a clawful of flesh in the process. The broodlord squirmed out from between Jormund's massive arms to slash and snap at him. Krom had no time – and could gain no space – to lick his wounds. Jormund staggered beneath the monster's vicious onslaught, and so the Wolf Lord staggered too. Then the broodlord turned and flew at him again. *It thinks me the weaker of the two of us because I am smaller,* he realised, and bridled at the insult.

Krom smashed his axe blade into the monster's head with all the strength he could muster. He thought he might have snapped its neck – but if he did, it barely noticed. Its claws ripped into him again, and Krom knew his only hope now was to fight in the manner of the monster – with desperate abandon, surrendering himself to the feral part of his own nature, clawing, biting, kicking, gouging.

The red mist descended upon him, and he welcomed it.

Krom wrestled with the broodlord on the ground, though he had no memory of falling. There was blood in his eyes, his nose, his mouth; his armour had been rent, his regal red cloak was in tatters and the gash in his neck was gaping open again.

Jormund came to his rescue once more. Krom heard the repeated impact of metal against flesh, the broodlord snarling and spitting, and suddenly its smothering weight was lifted from him. The wolf part of him didn't want to let it go, and it howled in thwarted anguish as the creature was wrenched out of his hands. He reached after it, but blood rushed to his head and made it spin.

The stage was sticky with blood that was definitely, at least in part, his own. His fingers found Wyrmclaw's haft and closed around it. He hadn't even been aware that he had dropped it. His auto-senses screamed warnings in his ears, but he muted them. His auto-medicae was running dry of painkillers. Slashes from the broodlord's claws criss-crossed his armour and had cut searing trails into his flesh.

He could hear Jormund and the monster fighting, but the sounds – like the roar of the crowd – seemed somehow distant from him. He tried to use the chains that connected him to Jormund to haul himself up. They were slack; he didn't understand why. Somehow, he managed to get his knees underneath him and clambered laboriously to his feet. He stood, unsteadily, blinking, and realised that the fight was behind him.

Jormund was on top of the broodlord. He was holding it down with one knee and the ragged stump of his right arm. Incredibly, Krom realised, it had hacked off the Terminator's forearm, divesting him of his mace and the chain's shackle alike. Jormund's left hand, however, had a grip on the monster's head, his index finger sunk up to the knuckle in its eye socket. He slammed its head into the stage repeatedly, sending splinters of bone and gobbets of brain tissue flying.

Krom lurched towards them, a defiant roar rattling in his chest, his axe raised. The broodlord's claws were tearing open Jormund's sides. Krom aimed for its elbow joint – *an arm for an arm*, he thought – but his blade hewed into the stage instead. He couldn't tell if his target had moved or if he had simply misjudged its position. He was struggling to focus past the dark red blotches in his vision.

Jormund Thunderclaw sagged, and his limbs splayed out underneath him. He was at least comatose, if not dead – either way, the dark eldar would burn his body.

The broodlord was faring little better. Its remaining eye rolled back into its head, and Krom heard it struggling to breathe. Its claws twitched weakly and it couldn't drag its mangled body out from beneath the Terminator's crushing weight.

He sagged to his knees beside it. He took over where Jormund had left off, hammering at the monster's head. He blotted out everything else, blotted out the arena crowd and thoughts of his brother's demise. It took all his focus, all his strength, to cling to consciousness, to raise his axe and bring it down, beating out a steady rhythm.

Krom felt heavy hands on his shoulders. He shrugged them off, but they returned in greater numbers, rougher and more insistent. It was over. His enemy was dead. It had died some minutes ago. He had pulverised its skull. He had lost his left gauntlet and pulverised his knuckles too. The crowd had grown tired of him, seeking out other spectacles. The slave masters had come for him, to return him to a cell. Until the next time.

It took four of them to carry him, and he struggled against them all the way. The portal to the cells swam ahead of him and, belatedly, he remembered the Grand Archite. *Is she still watching me?* He was sure he could feel the creature's cool gaze on his back. He could imagine her smirk as she enjoyed his humiliation, drank it in.

At least she saw, at least they all saw, that I won, he consoled himself. With that thought, he allowed the beckoning darkness to claim him; and, for the first time in more days than he could count, Krom Dragon-gaze passed out.

Time had become elastic. Seconds had stretched into days and weeks, while months and years had passed by in the space of minutes.

At some point, another portal loomed in front of them, filled with fire. Flames hotter than the core of a star reached through it and licked at *Rolling Thunder*'s hull, threatening to draw her in. Cold beads of sweat were forming on Ulrik's brow, although he had the protection of both the Storm-wolf's ceramite plating and his own armour.

Rogan's skilled and violent handling of the controls saved them. Shearing away from the inferno, they were snatched by the static storm's capricious currents again. Their port wing scraped against something all too solid. As *Rolling Thunder* screamed in agony, Ulrik could only pray that she wouldn't be torn asunder.

'The Allfather is with us,' he assured his brothers as the buffeting finally abated. He said nothing of the vision he had glimpsed inside the fire. It had lasted a fraction of a second, no longer, but it was scarred upon his retinas: a twisted, leering, monstrous face.

Perhaps he had only imagined it...

They ploughed on through a nest of giant insectile creatures, which pursued them angrily for some distance. Repeated bursts from their helfrost cannon eventually discouraged them, but one latched onto the hull. Rogan scraped it off against a wall of ice, but lost the starboard cannons in the process.

Another hour, a month, a decade sped by. The storm clouds funnelled around them, plunging them into a tunnel barely wide enough to fly through. Shadowy creatures invaded the troop compartment, cackling with gleeful malevolence.

Leoric sat bolt upright. 'The warp,' he intoned, 'it's straining at the barriers... seeping in through the fissures...'

Ulrik had drawn his pistol, but the words jolted him to his senses, made him realise that the Rune Priest was seeing only phantoms. 'Don't look at them!' he yelled. He screwed his eyes shut, but still he could feel the ghosts battering at the barriers around his mind, every one of them bearing the face he had seen in the flames.

'The Allfather is our shield,' the Wolf High Priest declaimed, lighting up his crozius. He recited a litany of protection, entreating all those present to join in. Two of his brothers had succumbed, however, one foaming at the mouth, the other trying to claw out his own eyes, while Rogan was screaming gibberish over the vox-net.

Time passed.

Ulrik found himself praying with Rogan, guiding him back to the light. Emund Firetooth, a novice Blood Claw, was beyond such help – Beregelt had granted him the mercy of a bolt round to the temple. The phantoms had receded when they had left the tunnel behind them. Still, Ulrik felt the itch of their intangible claws behind his eyes, at the base of his brain.

Leoric furrowed his brow in concentration. 'I see something,' he said, 'but we have to hurry. We have to–'

'Did you see Lord Krom and the others?' Ulrik asked quickly. 'Can you take us to them?'

Leoric shook his head. 'No, I did not see them. I thought I saw the way *back*.'

Ulrik's hearts sank. He met Beregelt's eyes and saw the same dismay reflected in them. Inwardly, he railed against the idea of turning tail, of abandoning his brothers to their fates – not to mention the missing Great Wolf whose trail had led them here. *But what about the brothers aboard this ship? I am responsible for them too.*

He gave Beregelt an almost imperceptible nod. The veteran Drakeslayer lowered his gaze to his feet, but understood.

'Don't try to resist it,' Leoric said. 'Let it take us where it will. It wants us gone.' Olav Brunn relayed his words to Rogan Bearsbane.

'We shall return for them,' Ulrik swore in a quiet but resolute growl. 'Somehow, one day, we shall return for-'

'*Russ's teeth!*'

Rogan threw the Stormwolf into a lateral spin, forcing the Space Wolves to cling to whatever they could reach. Ulrik scrambled to the viewport again, as something huge and blue and grey careened out of the static towards them.

'High Priest!' Beregelt strained forward beside him, his pale yellow eyes widening in astonishment. 'Isn't that... Wasn't that...?'

'Another gunship,' Ulrik breathed.

It was already gone, peeling away from them into a pocket of icy mist. They had come a hair's breadth from a collision, close enough that Ulrik was left with an afterimage of the pilot's ruddy, red-bearded face gaping at him open-mouthed through his glacis. He had recognised that face. He had recognised the gunship too. It seemed impossible – but what had Leoric told them? *I thought I saw the way back.* He remembered his own words too: *Time means nothing here...*

'We're almost there,' Leoric said, unable to conceal the relief in his voice despite himself.

Ulrik opened a channel to Rogan Bearsbane. 'Maintain our course,' he said.

'But High Priest, I saw-'

'I know what you saw, Brother Rogan. Maintain our course. The Allfather is with us, he has found us even here – and he will guide us out of the storm.'

Already, Ulrik could feel the turbulence around them easing. A solemn hush descended in the troop compartment, and for a long time – or a short time, it was still impossible to know – the only sound to be heard was that of *Rolling Thunder*'s engines.

At last, Rogan's voice buzzed in Ulrik's ear again, more composed than it had been. He reported a gap in the storm ahead of them. Through the gap all was black, but Rogan said he thought he could see the pinprick sparkle of stars, real stars. Ulrik turned to Leoric, who nodded sagely.

'Take us through the gap,' Ulrik ordered, though the words weighed heavily on his heart. After all they had endured, to be spat back out into real space... It was almost more than he could bear. He had failed in his mission – he was no closer to finding Logan Grimnar than he had been. As for Krom Dragongaze and the other captured Space Wolves...

They would have to save themselves.

Krom was woken by the hissing of the cell gate. The slave masters had come for him again. Ragnek Halfhand protested that it was too soon, that Krom needed more time to heal – but the Wolf Lord silenced him with a glare. Wolves did not beg.

Jormund's sacrifice had left Krom, for one of the few times in his life, despondent. Many may have been surprised to hear it, but there was a limit to the Fierce-eye's arrogance, after all. He had tried to do his fallen brother justice. He told how fiercely he had fought, and how well – in graphic detail, with embellishments to cover what he had not seen – and ensured that the story was spread. He had set his pride aside, giving Jormund due credit for saving his life. He wasn't sure what good it would do.

Jormund Thunderclaw's story would die between these walls. As would the stories of too many others. Krom remembered the Guardsman he had met on his first day here, and knew he had spoken truly. Not even the mightiest champion left the arena a victor. The only way out was in defeat and death – at least, according to the dark eldar's rules.

His right knee had seized up. His damaged servo-motors were no help to him as he struggled to stand. He began to understand how Jormund must have felt, a prisoner of his own armour. Two slave masters took Krom under the arms and hauled him roughly to his feet. He shrugged them off. He intended to keep his dignity, at least.

He had only three escorts today. He walked unaided between them. He considered snatching one of their whips. He was sure he could take one, even two of them down before they subdued him. Defiance meant certain death, however. He preferred to take his chances – such as they were – in the arena.

The muster area was unusually crowded. A dozen Chaos cultists were waiting there, chained together. They sneered and cursed at Krom, straining to reach him. He bared his fangs at them in return. They had the look of new arrivals, unbloodied and still strong. Krom took some solace in the likelihood that they were about to die.

As they were herded away, another combatant was led through, back towards the cages. It was the Dark Angels chaplain. He turned his head to look at Krom. He offered no greetings, nor even acknowledged the other's presence. His armour was dented and scored, but he appeared to have weathered his ordeals well, on the whole.

Krom glared at him, but had no chance to speak as the slave masters were jabbering at him excitably, prodding him with their whip handles, and – sooner than he had expected – it was time for him to fight again. He took a deep breath, gathering his depleted energy, focusing his willpower.

Impress the Grand Archite and she may choose to extend your life...

They hadn't given him Wyrmclaw this time. Had the queen grown tired of him already? *So what if she has?* he thought stubbornly. *The span of my life is for no xenos scum to determine. Not while I have breath in my body and strength to fight.*

Krom lifted his head, squared his shoulders. He made the sign of the aquila. Then he stepped out beneath the crimson sky of Commorragh and let the roar of the xenos crowd wash over him.

The arena had been restructured during his absence. The polished stages had been removed to create a single fighting space that stretched from one arena wall to the other. The large surface was covered in sharp black sand that crunched beneath his boots. The eldar were clearly planning for this fight to be a grand finale, Krom realised grimly.

As he crossed the huge space, he glimpsed the queen's throne. It was empty. Her absence stoked his anger. *I'll give these xenos a show like they have never seen before,* he swore, *one to leave them cowering in fear of the Allfather's might!*

In the centre of the arena, he found the chained Chaos cultists waiting for him. His lips twitched at the prospect of being the one to slay them.

The cultists weren't alone, however. Dozens of other combatants were being herded from their cages. There was a group of tau fire warriors to Krom's left and beyond them, two groups of Imperial Guardsmen. There were orks to his right, including one hulking warboss with a scarred pit in place of its right eye, and a Traitor Space Marine in tarnished black and gold. *A Black Legionnaire!*

A slave master prodded Krom in the back, mistaking his surprise for trepidation. He shrugged it away from him with a snarl.

Krom was weighing up the traitor, intending to engage him first, when a roar went up from the crowd and he realised that he had misjudged the situation. He was not expected to fight his fellow prisoners. Rather, his true opponents came wheeling out of the sky towards him. The slave masters withdrew and Krom dived for the nearest axe – but the traitor reached it before him, snatching his prize out from under his nose. He dropped into a crouch, empty-handed.

Suddenly, they were all around him – a gang of young dark eldar males, heavily-inked and leather-armoured. There were thirty or more of them, whooping and screeching, poised atop skyboards, which they steered with their feet. They hacked at their prey with double-bladed polearms, and had already eviscerated a pair of cultists.

Two of the hellions flanked a tau and lifted it off the ground between them. Then they were gone, escaping into the sky again, out of reach.

The attack left the grounded combatants in disarray. The surviving cultists pulled this way and that, hampered by the chains that bound them to a pair of bloody corpses. The orks were snatching up every weapon in reach, hurling them at the circling predators. Krom made a grab for an ancient-looking chainsword, while he had the chance.

The hellions were putting on an aerial display. They repeatedly tossed their luckless victim to one another, much to the crowd's delight. Only when the tau was battered, broken and partially dismembered did they fling its body away from them with casual contempt. As they swooped on the arena again, however, Krom was ready for them.

Three skyboards hurtled towards him. He sprang to meet the centremost of them, hoping to surprise its rider. He brought his chainsword down in a double-handed smash, which the hellion parried, by a hair. The dark eldar swerved away from Krom, the jagged edge of its board clipping his foot. He landed heavily on his injured leg and crashed onto one knee.

The hellion hooked a bone pylon with its polearm, whipped its board around and flew at him again. One of the orks saved him, though that surely hadn't been its intention. It appeared as if from nowhere, barrelling through the Chaos cultists, pouncing on the low-flying dark eldar with a murderous howl. It had run out of weapons to throw, without thinking to keep one for itself, but its meaty fists alone could crush bones.

The skyboard veered between two pylons and flipped over, depositing one hellion corpse and one thrashing-mad greenskin in the dirt below. Slave masters rushed to drive the latter back into the centre of the arena.

The other hellions were gone again, but for one other that had become separated from its board. The cultists swarmed over it, denying it the chance to stand. About a third of the prisoners had fallen. Krom realised that the hellions had picked off the weakest of them. Most of the tau warriors and several Imperial Guardsmen lay among the dead.

The hellions swooped again, but this time their tactics had changed. They focused their attacks upon a single target. They swarmed around the Chaos Space Marine like angry insects, stinging with their polearms. Swatting at them furiously, he cleaved one through the stomach and caught a second in the throat with his elbow and flipped it backwards off its board.

Once again, the cultists swarmed the fallen hellion.

At last, a hellion swooped carelessly into Krom's reach. Bones ground together inside his patched-up left gauntlet as he swung his whirring blade, and he sucked in air between his fangs. It was worth the pain, however, to open his enemy's throat.

The Black Legionnaire had claimed a few kills of his own, as had the orks. When the hellions withdrew, this time, only twelve of them remained. It was less than half their original number. They had whittled the traitor down, however, leaving him to bleed out from a hundred cuts and gouges. They performed a victory circuit of the arena, garnering wild applause, giving Krom and the other remaining prisoners – a handful of Guardsmen and cultists and three orks, including their warboss – a minute to collect themselves.

Krom took charge, barking at the Guardsmen to form a defensive circle, back-to-back. The hellions attacked for the final time, and for Krom, the next few minutes were a blur of ducking, diving, swiping and screaming. He was at the centre of a maelstrom, barely able to react to one threat before the next came at him from another direction. He didn't dare stand still for a second, so he pushed his battered body as hard as he could to keep moving, keep fighting, stay alive. The sand of the arena was slick with blood, and more than once he slipped and almost lost his footing.

Through a red haze, he saw the ork warboss' neck being severed. He saw the last of the Imperial Guardsmen speared by three polearms at once.

There were dark eldar bodies on the ground too, however, several of them thanks to Krom's efforts.

Then his sputtering chainsword was parried so fiercely that it span out of his broken hand.

He found himself in a crouch in the middle of the stage, surrounded by mutilated corpses. The final hellion was plummeting towards him, cackling madly. He propelled himself forward, diving beneath the oncoming sky-board, landing facedown – as he had planned – beside the Chaos Space Marine. He prised the axe out of the traitor's dead fingers, rolling onto his back as the skyboard whipped around again. He hurled the weapon at the skyboard's underside. Its blade lodged deep inside the board's workings, sending it careening out of control, skipping and spluttering across the sand, taking its rider with it.

It was over, and Krom was alive. He was the sole survivor.

He tried to stand, but a fresh gash in his side that he didn't recall sustaining – combined with his old, unhealed injuries – rendered him temporarily incapable. He fell back to his knees. With his hearts hammering in his ears, at first he didn't hear the ominous thrill that rippled around the arena.

A shadow blotted out the sky's sullen light. Krom raised his head to find a blurry shape looming over him. He couldn't tell if it was beast or machine, or a perverted amalgam of both. A pale, muscular torso was hunched inside an armoured carapace, which bristled with implements of war and torture.

It had no legs but hovered, like the skyboards, on anti-gravity motors. A thick, segmented tail coiled over its head, a twitching xenos weapon grafted onto its end like a sting.

Whatever this unholy contraption was, Krom was in no state to fight it. Even if he could, there would only be more behind it. His fate had never truly rested in his own hands, after all. The Grand Archite had decided the time and manner of Krom Dragongaze's demise, as soon as she had ceased to be entertained by him.

And that time, it seemed, had come.

Rob Sanders

PART FIVE

THE DARKNESS
OF ANGELS

The Dark City rang with the sounds of battle and butchery. From the serrated spires of High Commorragh to the insanity of the Middle Darkness, the miserable industry of the Old City to the degradation of the Sprawls, things were suffering and dying. It was home to the murderous and those they would murder. It was a hellish cityscape of barbed wonder and torment, in which the alien and the depraved lived, died and enjoyed the perversity of everything inflicted in between. Above the corpse-thick slurp of the city's rivers, the slave revolts of the gateway ports and the dimensional flux of the shadow districts, the cacophony of death rose.

The arenas spread like a dark cancer out from the razored towers and crooked pinnacles of High Commorragh. Dominating the Sprawls, they drew the bloodthirsty and depraved for kilometres around – alien deviants who filled their worthless lives with their daily fix of death and howled their rabid encouragement from their terraces of black stone. They spat curses in a language of shattered syllables that contorted their thin lips and haunted their features with a wretched fury. They wagered in flesh – that of their slaves, their rivals and their own. They pushed, shoved and screamed at each other as the violence of the arena spread through the auditoria. Knives flashed in the darkness, gutting and slitting. Victims bled their last, stamped into the ground by feverish throngs of xenos intent on commanding the best views – views of alien beasts, the gore festival of traps, and prisoners reduced to the brute desperation of murderous survival.

Krom Dragongaze was one such prisoner. A figure stumbling through the black sand of the arena, the grey of his plate stained crimson with wounds suffered in the course of never-ending battle. He fought through fatigue and loss of blood.

The dark eldar arena was a crowded circus of death. Blinking blood from his eye, and with plaits of copper-coloured hair slick with gore, the Wolf Lord could see bodies of Space Wolves in the arena. Krom tried to summon some anger or indignation. This was no way for Wolves to die. But the Sons of Russ did die this way. All over the galaxy. When a brother of the Space Wolves died, it was not asleep in his cell. He died badly, as some savaged mess on an alien world or bolt-mulched corpse at the foot of a traitor. Still, as deaths went, this was not a good one.

Krom screwed his eye shut. He tried to blank out the pain of loss, his personal agonies and the baying, pale-faced hordes of the auditorium. If he was going to die, he would die like a Wolf. In the moment. Savage and deadly before the end. Opening a bloodshot eye and the shattered remnants of a sizzling optic, the Space Wolf beheld the doom that had been chosen for him.

Whipping up the arena sand into coiled wisps with its anti-gravitic motors, a huge, gladiatorial abomination drifted towards him. Looking like a fat, floating black scorpion, the sickly construct was hunched with a thick, armoured shell – with weaponised claws and rearing tail. It clanked and crunched with the rancid change of internal gearing. It belched a light black smoke, while flasks of unspeakable fluids bubbled in the shell-ports. It was ramshackle in nature and dripping with the filth of past atrocities, but nonetheless the monstrosity gave the impression of indomitable efficiency.

The thing seemed unhurried, as though relishing the howls of encouragement and bloodthirsty expectation from the audience. A macabre fusion of pallid flesh and murderous machine, Krom's opponent was a semi-sentient torture device – a twisted thing that knew only the delights of a slow death and success measured in screams. It existed to inflict myriad agonies. Festooned with tools of pain, it appeared to Krom less as a gladiatorial killer than a cybernetic butcher, intent on chopping him up a piece at a time until there was nothing left.

Krom spat blood at the arena sand and clenched his fists so hard the joints cracked. Spent. Battered. Doomed. The Space Wolf's hands itched for weapons that were not there. His plate, once a thing of beauty, was a rattling wreck. All he had was the nature of the beast that clawed at his soul and growled to be released.

'It's all I need...' Krom hissed through bloodied lips.

The Wolf Lord didn't wait for his opponent. He weaved across the arena, his boots crunching in the black sands as he stepped lightly through the dead, giving the pain engine's flesh-fused weaponry some difficulty in tracking him. The alien deviants in the audience whooped their savage expectations.

As Krom ran towards the half-machine, he felt the thing betray a moment of primal uncertainty. Things the size of a Space Wolf didn't usually go on the attack. They usually ran screaming from its scything hook and liquifiers. The Wolf Lord would not. As he took his last few steps, he felt his hearts beat in time with whatever stitched fusion of piston-plugs and muscle pumped wretched filth around the pain engine's veins. He felt for its movements and intentions.

Allfather's wounds, Krom thought to himself, *this thing is fast*. The scything hook cranked around in its bone-socket and flashed for the Space Marine. The crowd seethed with delight. Krom rolled across his pauldron, the hook sparking off his ruined backplate. The momentum carried him to his feet just in front of the pain engine's armoured head. The Space Wolf smashed his fist down at the metal beast. He hit it again and again, his gauntleted knuckles scuffing and cracking against the thick helm. The engine clunked, whirred and gushed hydraulic fluids as it drifted back. Krom's bare knuckles had barely dented the plate, however, and the thing came at him with the nozzles of its claw.

The Wolf Lord did not want to find out what came out of such weapons. Flipping head over boots, Krom landed messily on the sand, just clear of the nozzles. Such a demanding manoeuvre required strength and concentration and the punishing arena fights had stripped him of both.

Again, Krom had a moment to appreciate the monstrous engineering of the pain engine and its recoiling reflexes. Striking out with the nozzled limb while turning on its whirring gravitic motors, the pain engine swung around a set of chain-flails attached to the bottom-plate of the weaponised claw. Running on retractable chains, weighted hooks tore around in an expanding arc. Where they got purchase, the flails ripped sections of plate from Krom's back and embedded themselves in the slabs of muscle about the back of the Space Wolf's shoulders. His pack sparked with the damage inflicted by the cruel hooks.

The hooks sank deep and burned inside his body with some kind of smeared poison. Krom roared, although he was not surprised. Every razor-sharpened edge or cruel point in this foetid, alien place seemed laced with some kind of burning residue or mind-clouding toxin. It was all part of the lethal nature of this dread city. His limbs felt stricken. His breathing was laboured and his hearts thumped to an irregular rhythm. His mind was an addled ache, struggling to stay conscious. Whatever the venom was, it was overcoming his engineered body's ability to resist its perilous effects. Krom knew that the venom was unlikely to kill him. The pain engine would do that eventually. Like everything else in the crowded coliseum, the venom was a form of theatre. It reduced the transhuman perfection of humanity's finest to a dazed hulk – a tranquilised beast to be played with for the audience's satisfaction. Once the gladiatorial machine had shown off its skills and clunking supremacy, however, the mob would demand death. Something spectacular.

Turning, Krom did the only thing he could – he grabbed the chains. With a wild fury, Krom leaned into the agony of the embedded hooks and hauled the chains around. The pain engine began to move, its anti-gravitic motors causing it to drift around. Without legs or tracks, the monstrous fusion of flesh and machine had no traction on the arena sands and floated around with the centrifugal force of the Wolf Lord's swing. The thing gushed rank liquids through its lines and streamed smoke. It swung out further until suddenly the chains locked, running their course.

Krom felt a tortuous tug through the running lines. Breathing deep and clenching his teeth, he prepared himself for the worst. Letting go of the chain-flails, Krom allowed the drifting bulk of the pain engine to fly off towards the arena wall. The embedded hooks tore free through the Space Wolf's flesh and suit, pulling him off his feet and into an ugly fling across the sand. As the hooks and chains retracted, the pain engine struck the wall. Bouncing off black stone, the thing's shell casing split.

Dark eldar spectators ran to the arena edge to look down on the damage. Krom tried to get up. Muscle raged red hot across his back. Strips of skin hung down through shattered plate. All the while the Space Wolf's mind swam with the plethora of poisons his genetically engineered body was trying to process. He saw the pain engine belch smoke and eject some kind of liquid effusion from its cybernetic body in a squirting stream. The thick fluid hissed on the sand.

While clutching his back, Krom gestured with the fingers of his other hand for the pain engine to try again. The arena crowd went wild. Krom couldn't tell whether his actions were being celebrated or reviled. It didn't matter. He was dead for certain now. All about him he felt the weight of his plate. His damaged pack was faltering and the powered suit dying. He would be soon to follow.

The pain engine rattled towards him. Its hook glinted through old blood and filth, still impossibly sharp. Chain-flails snapped back into place and the pair of nozzles forming the claw of the other appendage dribbled a foul concoction in deviant anticipation. The drips and slurps created smoking pits in the sand, giving Krom the impression of some kind of acid.

As it drifted at speed towards him, the pain engine's tail contracted and the screw-shaped barrel spat a stream of static at the Space Wolf. Krom dived to one side. It was an ugly manoeuvre, the Space Wolf driving his suit on with the pure brute force of his body. He turned to see the static thrash at the sand where he had been standing. Rolling again in the sluggish suit, the Wolf Lord couldn't avoid a second, silent blast. The horrific weapon made no sound, but Krom was noisy enough for the both of them as the static hit him in the chest. He fell back spasming and screaming. His body was wracked with the excruciating agony the weapon had visited upon him.

Krom clenched a ceramite fist out in front of him. His whole body trembled with pain, and his suit was like an anchor dragging him down.

His teeth chattered uncontrollably. He punched the sand and roared the agony away. As the effect of the weapon began to fade, Krom's blurring vision returned to clarity. The flat of the merciless hook flashed before his face, smashing him to one side. Krom forced his faltering plate on. He crawled underneath the metal beast, feeling the pulse of the gravitic motors wash over him. The thing turned on the spot, as Krom somehow got to his feet and staggered away.

He heard a discharge of liquid as something spat from the appendage nozzles. Krom tried an evasion but failed. Without his powered reflexes he was merely a Space Marine buried in ceramite. Poison, exhaustion and blood loss were taking their toll. Sliding on the sand, the Space Wolf only half managed to avoid the liquifiers. The foul concoction spattered ahead of him, turning the arena floor to a cloud of steam.

Some of the liquid struck his pauldron and arm, however, and began to eat through the ceramite. While his plate hissed furiously near his face, Krom tore at the seals and locks of the pauldron and plate sections. There was no time for ritual or respect. Hooking his gauntlet under the shoulder plate he ripped it off before clawing the ceramite from his upper arm. He felt the flesh-burrowing burn of several droplets that had eaten their way through. Skin, muscle and bone seethed and a feral roar issued from the Wolf Lord.

He stumbled away from the engine, trying to clear his pain-addled brain just long enough to enact some kind of retaliation. He didn't get a chance to. The metal monstrosity drifted up behind Krom and, firing the stinger pod on its tail, once more blasted a static stream of agony into the Space Marine.

Krom roared, stricken and held there by the agonies coursing through the entirety of his body. The pain engine wasted no time in angling its hook. Coming up behind the paralysed Wolf Lord, it brought the hook up through his ruined plate and back flesh with a sickening thud. Lifting Krom Dragongaze up on the brutal weapon, the pain engine turned, idling on its gravitic motors. It presented Krom and his suffering to the crowds for inspection. For entertainment.

The sounds of disappointment from the crowd rose to the darklight suns hanging in the Commorrite sky. The cut-glass syllables of abuse rained down on the arena. Improvised missiles pranged off Krom's plate and the engine's metal shell while members of the audience demonstrated their detestation by tearing off cloaks and presenting weapons – as if they were going to climb down into the arena. They were stopped, however, by a cordon of coliseum guards: warrior females dressed in leathers.

The Space Wolf could not tell whom the crowd were disappointed with – him for failing or the pain engine for providing them with entertainment not twisted enough for their appetites. Allowing his agonised gaze to travel up from the commotion, up through the spiteful ranks of the arena audience, Krom could make out the sheltered box manned by slave-servants

and coliseum guards. Ragged banners streamed from the structure depict-
ing a serrated shadow, the symbol of the queen's coliseum cult. The queen,
who had been absent until now, was summoned back to her throne by the
hollering of her audience. If she wanted to remain in power, she had to
make sure they were getting a good show. Krom bridled at the sight of her.
She was clad in extravagant barbed leathers, the uniform of a gladiatrix.
Her theatrical headdress revealed eyes steely with focus, while her body-
suit left little to the imagination. She stared down at the Wolf Lord as the
pain engine presented its offering. The decision was hers.

Krom faded in and out of consciousness. The pain was unbearable. He
had barely the strength to open his eyes and poison raged through his
body, afflicting his mind. His limbs felt like lead, his suit was dead and his
movements on the hook an agony.

The queen hesitated over the decision.

The terraces of the coliseum were growing riotous. Dark eldar flashed
the sharpness of their teeth and blades, savagely pushing one another.
There seemed to be a difference of opinion regarding the quality of the
day's entertainment. Female guards in leathers, sporting pistols with long,
tapering barrels, were moving through the mobs of disgruntled xenos, ready
to mercilessly put down any rioting. With the coliseum in uproar, discon-
tent infectious and the audience seconds away from becoming part of the
entertainment, the dark queen had little choice but to act.

Giving a signal of savage disdain, the queen ordered a section of prisoner cages opened. With bars parting and a hydraulic wall of spikes
moving through the cells, more prisoners were forced out onto the arena
sands. Crucified upon the hook and held high above the arena floor, Krom
Dragongaze beheld his replacements.

Part of him hoped for Space Wolves – although he would take no solace
in his brothers being thrust into this arena of torture and humiliation – but
he could hear his Drakeslayers roaring their fury and throwing themselves
at the bars of cages that would not break. They had not been let loose.

The prisoners were a miserable gathering, mostly humans, emaciated,
dressed in rags and showing signs of terrible mistreatment. There was a lone
eldar, horribly scarred but stoic. Krom spotted a servant of the Machine
God in rust red robes, limping on a shattered bionic. All torturer's fodder
for the pain engine. Then Krom saw them. The dark queen's gambit. Three
transhumans, like himself. One he recognised as the Dark Angels chaplain he'd seen a few times being brought to and from the arena. His filthy
white vestments were draped over his battle-scarred black plate, the hood
pulled up to partially conceal his distinctive skull helm. With him was one
of his brothers, a librarian in blue armour.

The monster advancing from the furthest cage might have once been
a Space Marine but he was no angel of the Emperor. The armoured figure was decked in spikes and the perversity of blood red plate. A Chaos

Space Marine uncaged. A World Eater let off the leash. His face-flesh was daemon red and a single horn erupted out of the side of his head, winding about his skull like a crown. He had the fixed smile of a maniac, drunk on the violence to come. Violence he fully intended to inflict in the name of his fell patron.

Marching up to the priest of Mars, the World Eater smashed the hobbling construct to the sand with obvious relish. Sinking probing fingers into the base of the priest's back, the Chaos Space Marine ripped the priest's spine up out of cybernetic flesh. The metal spine dripped with blood and oil and carried with it an armoured cranium housing the victim's half-brain and cogitator. Shaking wires and interfaces loose, the World Eater took a few experimental swings with his improvised flail. As he marched for the pain engine, Krom had no doubt that the maniac had every intention of destroying the monstrous machine – and then everyone else.

The pain engine lowered its hook and allowed Krom to slide off. Hitting the sands like a pile of scrap, the Wolf Lord let out a bellow of agony. The mobile torture machine drifted overhead, advancing towards its new victims. It would no doubt return later to inflict further horrors on him, the Space Marine thought, for the crowd's edification and entertainment.

Krom summoned reserves of strength he didn't know he had. He felt as though the hook had split him in half. Like an infant animal, he tried to stand. He staggered and fell. He could do it, but it was agony. He crashed back down on the sands in the pain engine's gravitic wake. Everything hurt. Poison coursed through his veins. His shoulder still seared with the acid working its way through his flesh, and his back felt as if a red hot iron had been thrust into it.

He heard screams. Prisoners were dying. The dark eldar pain engine was nothing if not an artist. Like a true gladiatorial showman and torturer, it had zeroed in on the weak for the entertainment of easy kills. It instinctively knew the transhuman prisoners would be more of a challenge and that therefore their suffering should be left until last.

Dragging his forehead off the sand, Krom witnessed what happened when you faced the xenos pain engine without the benefit of a Space Marine's engineered body and training. Men died horribly. The monstrous fusion of flesh and machine wanted to show off the full range of its torturer's tools. Prisoners were hooked through the belly, the scything blade ripping slowly up through the sternum and out through the jaw. They were shredded by the poisoned hooks of the arm-mounted chainflails. Some bled to death on the sand, while others were dragged across the ground by chains. Several were left to tremble, convulse and die where they lay as the poison ravaged their mere human constitutions.

Spitting sand from his lips, Krom saw that the cruel xenos audience were satisfied. The queen's gamble seemed to have paid off. The conflict on the terraces had given way to masochistic delight. Those spectators eager

for blood were getting it. Those demanding more challenge and torment
for their time and coin were back on the edge of their seats with expectation. Even the leather-bound guards had stopped to soak up the death
and suffering.

The screams grew louder, echoing about the coliseum and rising above
the city as the pain engine deployed its other instruments of torture. Prisoners either distracted by former abuses or fixed to the spot with present
terrors were sprayed down with acid from the engine's liquifier guns. Like
wax sculptures, the thrashing victims dribbled to the sand to form puddles
of red and white. Within seconds there was little left of them but the echo
of their dreadful suffering.

For a moment it looked like the eldar might put up a fight, but then the
xenos decided to run. He shouldn't have, Krom decided, as for the relish
of the audience's racial hatred, the pain engine hit him again and again
with the agonising static from the screw-shaped barrels mounted upon
its overhanging tail. The ghoulish dark eldar were treated to the prisoner
scratching at himself on the ground, experiencing more pain than he could
bear. After an appropriate show of agony, the prisoner died of his torments.

As the last of the human prisoners turned and ran from the pain engine,
the wretch found himself face to face with the World Eater. Swinging his
metal skull around on its titanium spinal column like a morning star, the
Chaos Space Marine stove in the prisoner's skull. The victim fell before the
spiked might of the World Eater, and the traitor splattered the prisoner into
the sand with stamps of his gore-speckled boots.

As the two Dark Angels looked on, the gladiatorial pain engine glided up
between them and the Blood God's champion. The Interrogator-Chaplain
offered an open gauntlet towards the World Eater to indicate that the
pain engine was all his. The maniac's smile broadened – a simultaneous
acknowledgement of the offer and the fact that he was looking at a dead
man.

The World Eater broke into a powered run. As the pain engine accelerated to meet him it reached out with its hook. Smashing the limb to one
side with his flail, the Chaos Space Marine began to beat the machine back
furiously. Ducking beneath a storm of lacerating hooks, the World Eater
allowed the chain-flails to pass overhead before hammering the engine with
the reinforced cranium of the tech-priest. The xenos audience screeched
with excitement and pain lust.

As sparks flew from the liquifier appendage, the traitor's improvised
weapon failed him, the metal skull detaching from the priest's blood-slick
spine. Stamping at the pain engine with his boot, the World Eater seemed
unstoppable. The brute became a feverish storm of powered kicks and
punches. With a kick knocking the gladiatorial machine back on its gravitic field, the maniac picked the metal cranium up from the sand, carrying
the weapon like a primitive might a rock. The stinger pod on the engine's

tail recoiled, sending a stream of static torment at the Chaos Space Marine. The World Eater didn't move.

'Again!' the traitor roared, an infernal echo to his voice. The weapon seemed to do nothing to the monster. The cybernetic menace blasted the World Eater a second and a third time, each time to bawling encouragement from its opponent.

The World Eater yelled and ran at the clanking contraption. Knocking aside the engine's flaying hook with the metal skull, he proceeded to smash at the armoured shell until the cranium too came apart in a shower of circuits and brains. His maniac's smile now horribly contorted with rage, the World Eater grabbed the side of the pain engine. Pushing upwards with a furious heave, the Chaos Space Marine flipped the construct over.

Without the stability of its gravitic motors, the horrific fusion of flesh and instrument of torture landed on the thick plate of its hunched back. Sparks flew and the mechanism belched black smoke. It rolled across the sands, each time attempting to right itself. With gravitic motors getting a fix on the ground, the pain engine came to a stop. Shell-mounted flasks were smashed and the monstrosity's hull sizzled and steamed with its own foul fluids. The liquefier appendage showered the sand with sparks and the stinger pod hung at a crooked angle on its segmented metal tail.

Krom watched as the impossible happened. The World Eater wasn't finished. He stormed towards the pain engine, intent on ripping the gladiatorial machine apart. He would probably have done so, if it hadn't been for the stuttering stream of acid the pain engine spattered into his face. With its mechanism damaged and feed lines broken, all the monstrous machine could send the Chaos Space Marine's way was the acid left in its liquefier guns. The World Eater had never screamed before but as the acid spray ate through his face, he heard the sound of his own suffering echoing in his ears.

'Get him up,' Krom heard from behind him. 'Get him up.'

It was the two Dark Angels. As the brother in blue put Krom's arm across his back, his compatriot grabbed his other arm and hauled the Space Wolf off the floor. Krom tried to shrug the Dark Angels off him but his heavy plate, its sluggish servos and fibre bundles resisted.

'Can you fight?' the Interrogator-Chaplain said, his syllables clipped with a nobility of purpose.

'My plate has no power,' Krom growled, almost like an accusation.

'Can you fight?' the Interrogator-Chaplain demanded again, his courteous tone laced with authority.

'Have you ever met a Wolf who wouldn't?' Krom bit back.

'Not yet,' the Dark Angel admitted.

The three Space Marines stopped as they saw the pain engine, billowing black smoke and bleeding fluids, surging across the sands towards them.

'Which is as well, for I fear this will require all three of us. Our tainted friend got things rolling but we shall have to finish this monstrosity.'

Krom wasn't sure he could trust the Dark Angels any more than he could his captors – the rivalry between the Wolf and the Lion was far from dead. Krom was a creature of immediacy, however. He lived and fought in the moment. Necessity made for strange allies and alliances.

'We shall put an end to this show,' Krom promised, through his pain. That was all he was willing to say.

'Brother Othniel will flank right, myself left,' the Interrogator-Chaplain told Krom.

'And me?' the Space Wolf growled with disgust.

'You will wait for an opportunity,' the Dark Angel assured him. 'We shall create one if we can.'

As the pain engine rattled noisily on, the Interrogator-Chaplain and Othniel dragged Krom across the arena, the toes of the Wolf Lord's boots creating a pair of trenches in the sand. As the machine got close, the Dark Angels dropped Krom without ceremony and peeled off to the sides. Clattering to the ground, Krom pushed himself up on his arms. His plate was like an armoured coffin about him. As the Dark Angels stalked around the pain engine it turned slowly on its gravitic motors, hovering near Krom like a hound defending a buried bone.

Suddenly the Dark Angels ran at the monstrous engine, their robes flowing after them. Othniel reached the gladiator first, skidding to a stop just before the throat-tearing swipe of the machine's hook. Surging for the weaponised appendage, Othniel balanced the might of his powered blue plate against the hydraulics of the bone-fused limb. The pain engine struggled, but Othniel held fast, forcing the armoured thing back across the sand. Unlike the World Eater or even Krom himself, the Dark Angel's attack lacked ferocity, but he more than made up for that with stalwart determination.

The Interrogator-Chaplain came from the other side, jumping up onto the side of the pain engine's armoured shell. Leaping across its hunched back, the Dark Angel cleared the monstrosity with knightly elegance. The pain engine, however, fired the screw-shaped barrels of its stinger pod. Unable to raise the barrel on its broken tail, the pain engine missed the Interrogator-Chaplain and blasted itself in the back.

As the thing drifted backwards towards Krom, Brother Othniel released it. With its gravitic motor stuttering about him, Krom looked up at the pallid flesh of the pain engine. It was muscular, clammy and horrifically interfaced with the dark machinery. With tendons taut and the pain engine's organic muscles flexing horribly, the Wolf Lord couldn't tell whether the thing was in some kind of private agony or ecstasy. Then Krom saw his opportunity. The pain engine's brawny neck ran into its armoured helm, but under its jaw the Space Wolf spotted a weakness. He had to be fast, however, before the monstrosity recovered and slaughtered them all.

Forcing the fingers of his powerless gauntlet straight, Krom thrust his palm up through the abomination's throat. Helped by the backwards drift of the thing, Krom punched his hand like a claw up inside the pain engine's armoured helm and skull. The construct spasmed, the muscles of its chest and arms contracting. Smoke belched from the machine and fluids were expelled from all its ports. In that second, Krom Dragongaze knew he had it. With disgust-fuelled violence the Space Wolf reached up inside the engine's xenos skull and crushed the twisted thing he found inside. Alien gore poured through the holes in its helm onto the sand.

The monstrosity's gravitic drive stuttered and failed. Withdrawing his bloody gauntlet, Krom heaved himself and his dead plate to one side, moments before the motor failed and the pain engine came crashing down on the arena sands, a smoking wreck.

As Krom lay there, staring up at the dark Commorrite suns with the dark eldar audience screaming for more blood, the Wolf Lord felt the Dark Angels over him once more. Grabbing him by his plate, they hauled him to his feet. The Wolf Lord shrugged them off. As he went to fall again, the Interrogator-Chaplain supported him. Scowling, this time Krom allowed the Dark Angel to help him.

Amongst the audience there was movement. Columns of coliseum guards were filing down through the terraces. Dressed in leathers and carrying a combination of electrified nets and bidents, the dark eldar appeared ready to secure the arena. Jets of flame spouted from nozzles set in the arena wall, growing in length and power. The raging inferno turned blood and sand to glass, forcing the remaining prisoners to gather in the centre of the arena.

The Dark Angels helped Krom across the sand in his dead plate, away from the unbearable heat of the flames. The survivors became a throng of silhouettes. The flames corralled them together before dying suddenly in a great whoosh of heat. As his eyes adjusted to the vanishing glare, Krom saw that the coliseum guards had run up in place of the flames. They encircled the survivors with their number. For the first time, Krom realised that the maniac World Eater was still alive – although a horrifically disfigured mess, roaring into gauntlets he used to cover what was left of his face. The Wolf Lord and the Dark Angels would have killed the traitor, if it hadn't have been for the dark eldar surrounding them.

The xenos held crackling nets, while presenting the twin tips of their forked spears in a circle of death. As the leather-clad guards closed on the Space Marines, Krom bridled. He was exhausted from the prolonged demands of survival in the arena but his victory already had him bristling with a desire to savage his alien captors. From behind, the Dark Angel Interrogator-Chaplain spoke.

'If you choose to fight,' he said, 'then the Dark Angels shall fight with you. Know, savage prince of the Wolf King, that our lives will be forfeit. I appeal to you. Return quietly to your cage. From there we can make plans for our liberty.'

Krom spat blood at the sand in disgust, the spittle hanging from his chin whiskers.

'Wolves weren't meant for cages, Angel,' Krom growled back at him.

'There is no honour dying like this,' the Interrogator-Chaplain told him.

'I will kill every xenos that tries to lay their filthy hands on me,' Krom rumbled.

'Of that I have no doubt,' the Dark Angel said. 'But what do you think they are going to do when the corpses of the alien dead are at our feet?'

'They will flood the arena with flame,' Krom admitted, managing to shake the effects of the poison from his head.

'The cages offer us a chance, at least,' the Interrogator-Chaplain said.

The dark eldar guards tightened the circle about them, the double blades of their spears tapping the plate and dimpling the barbarian flesh of the Wolf Lord. Krom glared his hatred up the length of the weapon at the guard ready to thrust it through his chest.

'Alright, Angel,' Krom said, raising his arms in the lifeless plate with difficulty. 'We do this your way.' The Wolf Lord turned the hatred in his eyes on the Interrogator-Chaplain, who nodded the blankness of his skull helm in silence. 'But I hope you are caged with me,' the Space Wolf snarled.

Surrounded by a forest of spears, the Space Marines were escorted back to their cells. The barred compartments were built into the arena wall so that prisoners could see what was expected of them during the dread games. The cells were little better than the escort, with spikes and razored shafts projecting inwards, limiting the movement of the prisoners and frustrating attempts to batter down the barred doors or rush their gaolers.

Krom wasn't surprised that the dark eldar took such measures. Compared to even the brawniest of the dark eldar beastmasters, clutching their whips and the chains of their chimeric creatures, the Space Wolves were hulking demigods. They drowned the wretched aliens in their shadows.

Returned to the cells with the remaining members of the Drakeslayers, Krom arrived to grim acknowledgments of 'My lord'. The Space Wolves had seen what Krom had been forced to suffer out on the sands and had gone wild in their cells. Now they met their captain with grave, whisker-lined faces in the gloom and eyes that burned like candles in the night.

One face that was not there was that of Jormund Thunderclaw. Krom had lost so many of his brothers that his friend's face was now but a ghostly memory, fading further with each new loss. Krom bit back his bitterness. He had to look out for the brothers that still lived.

Hengist Ironaxe's features looked greyer and more drawn than usual, while Rorven couldn't help a mumbled exclamation of 'By the Allfather' at the extent of Krom's injuries. Haegr Fangthane came to the bars, despite his own wounds, and Brorn Grindalson even reached out to touch the Wolf Lord's ruined plate in reassurance. The Space Wolf was forced back by the thrust of a dark eldar spear. Ulf Horghast, Lars Thorgil and Ingrimm Thunderfell growled, spat and kicked at the bars of their cell, drawing the attentions of the xenos to them instead.

'You would do well not to antagonise them, brothers,' the Interrogator-Chaplain told them as he helped Krom along. Grundar Greymane gave him the winter bleakness of his eyes.

'By the Allfather,' Greymane spat. 'My Wolves would savage them all.'

Krom tottered, the poison still potent in his blood and his plate dragging him down, but the Interrogator-Chaplain caught him.

'I believe you,' the Interrogator-Chaplain said. 'But not today, they won't.'

Krom did not get his wish. The dark eldar guards forced the Interrogator-Chaplain to help the Wolf Lord into a cell with his own – Grundar Greymane, who continued to spit blood, and an unusually reserved Beoric Winterfang. The Interrogator-Chaplain and Brother Othniel were placed in the next cage.

Sitting in the cell, with the points of spikes scraping against his plate and cage-spanning blades beneath his chin, Krom had some time to consider whether he had been right to submit to incarceration. Beoric was no Iron Priest, but with time to kill, the leader of Krom's Wolf Guard went to work doing what he could with his lord's plate and damaged power pack. After he had managed to restore partial power, the suit was still a drag on Krom's bestial reflexes but allowed him some protection and manoeuvrability. Meanwhile, Grundar did his best to tend the Fierce-eye's terrible injuries.

Feeling well enough to move around the tiny cage, the Wolf Lord kicked away a bowl of slop the gaolers had provided to ensure the prisoners kept up their strength for the spectacle of the show. Krom suspected all the food and water they were given was drugged to keep the dangerous Space Marines sedated until they were once more required for the arena. He had ordered that all such offerings be ignored. The Drakeslayers did not need such comforts. The spilling of blood was their mead and the righteous butchery of the Emperor's enemies their sustenance.

As the hours passed under the gloom of the imprisoned stars, Krom regained his strength, his coordination and his mind. It had been a battle – every bit as torturous as the one fought on the arena sands – but eventually he felt his engineered body starting to break down the alien poison, though who knew what side effects it still might have.

Krom watched as prisoners from other cell sections were marched out into the arena to fight for their lives against a menagerie of alien beasts and the small army of warrior women that called the coliseum their home. Crowds came at all hours to shriek, hiss and soak up the merciless violence of the arena. The dark eldar came for their fix of death, perverse pleasures to fill the rancid emptiness of their hearts.

When he wasn't watching the gladiatrix and their monsters, studying their murderous craft, Krom turned his attentions to the cages in which he and his men had been housed. He found Beoric Winterfang, the leader of his Wolf Guard, staring at him. His eyes were glazed with regret, and he quivered with an animal fury bubbling below the surface. Krom knew what was coming.

'I failed you,' the sergeant said finally.

'You fail yourself, sergeant,' Krom told him, 'if you entertain such fantasies – for I know it would be a fantasy indeed, if Beoric Winterfang failed anyone.'

'My lord,' Beoric said. 'It is a failing to not be at your side when you need me.'

'Then I was wrong,' Krom told him with a grim smile. 'You're always failing me. Why, only three days' past, my mug of mead was just beyond my reach. The day before that I noticed a mark that needed polishing on my plate.' Krom looked Beoric in the eye and tried to draw a similar smile from his sergeant.

'Only yesterday,' Krom went on, 'I needed to answer nature's call. I looked around. Where were you, sergeant? Where were you?'

Beoric managed a weak curl of the lips, but his eyes still spoke for the guilt he felt at not fighting by his Wolf Lord's side in the arena.

'You jest, my lord,' the sergeant said, 'but your life was left in the hands of untrustworthy Angels.' Beoric gave the Interrogator-Chaplain in the next cage the daggers of his eyes. The Dark Angel nodded slowly at the Wolf Guard sergeant, as though he were acknowledging some thanks or compliment. As Beoric went to get to his feet, Krom grabbed his arm and pulled him back down.

'My life was in the most capable hands of all,' Krom assured him. 'My own.'

'It's my opinion, my lord,' Beoric said.

'And I respect that, but opinions are like chin-whiskers. We all have them,' Krom said. He looked over at the Dark Angels. 'Present company excepted. If you want to worry about something, sergeant, worry about getting out of here.'

Krom stared at the Dark Angel in his dark plate, hood and filthy robes, who hadn't said a word since they had been returned to their cells.

'So, Angel,' Krom called across the spiked death trap of the cell. 'You have been making plans, I assume.'

'It's what they do,' Beoric said. 'Scheme, plot and conspire.'

The Interrogator-Chaplain said nothing. He was lost in something like prayer.

'Plans for our liberty,' Krom reminded him.

'Have faith, Fenrisian,' the Interrogator-Chaplain told him.

'I'm not interested in faith,' Krom spat back, the hackles on the back of his neck rising. 'Faith can't cut through bars, Interrogator-Chaplain. Faith cannot be wielded like a weapon in the hand or vanquish enemies like a bolt round to the head.'

'I cannot argue with that logic,' the Dark Angel said. Krom waited for more from the Interrogator-Chaplain but he returned to his solemn silence.

'I don't know why I'm even talking to you,' the Wolf Lord growled. 'I should never have listened to you in the first place. We face hundreds of warriors in the arena, thousands in this damned amphitheatre and millions in the monstrous city beyond. Your counsel has simply added a locked cage to those obstacles.'

'You forget the flames...'

'A man can walk through flames, Interrogator-Chaplain,' Krom said. 'Bars, less so.'

'You complain like a dog,' the Dark Angel said.

'That might be less of an insult than you imagine, Angel,' Krom said. He growled to himself. 'It's only a matter of time.'

'You're not wrong,' the Interrogator-Chaplain agreed. 'An opportunity will present itself. It is in the nature of opportunities to do so.'

'A plague take your opportunities,' the Wolf Lord said. 'The Sons of Russ come for us. They are on their way.'

Krom thought he heard something familiar on the foetid coliseum air. He turned his head and put an ear between the cold metal of the bars. The Wolf Lord tried to filter one sound from another. The suffering of prisoners in the surrounding cages. The death and spectacle of the arena. The raucous appreciation of the audience as the blood sports played out before them. The sound of the Dark City beyond the coliseum terraces – murderous perversion and the sating of alien appetites. Then he heard it. The rumble of rocket engines, turbofans and afterburners. The distant and distinctive roar of Adeptus Astartes gunships on an attack run.

Staring up through the bars, over the wicked terraces of the coliseum and through the serrated towers of the Dark City beyond, the Wolf Lord thought he spotted the silhouette of Thunderhawks against the gloom of the Commorrite suns. As they blasted towards the city outskirts at attack speed, the grey of their hull plating became clear.

The Space Wolf stood transfixed as his brethren dropped from the sky. The Wolves were coming. The Emperor's executioners, falling like the blade of an axe on the Dark City. Coming for Krom and his Drakeslayers.

The Space Wolf Thunderhawks announced their arrival with the flash of dorsal-mounted battle cannons. Krom visualised the dark eldar of the labyrinthine shardscape watching from their leaning towers, stripping bodies in the alleyways of the Sprawls and picking through the ruins of the Commorrite outskirts. They would look up at their stolen suns, and see the streaming silhouettes of the gunships, arriving to deliver the Emperor's justice to this benighted place. There would be panic. Havoc would reign supreme. The sadistic would come to know no mercy. Slavers would know the wrath of the enslaved. The raiders would become the raided...

Krom found himself gripping the bars of his cage. His teeth were bared and he was licking his lips. He shook his head to clear it and looked again up at the sky. The Space Wolves were not coming to rescue them. Such fantasies were probably the result of some remnant of the poison in his veins or just the potent desire for vengeance. Instead of Thunderhawks, Krom realised that he had been staring at a constellation of shadowy blots drifting across the webway sky.

'Nobody is coming for us,' the Interrogator-Chaplain said. He seemed to read Krom's mind. 'Not the brothers of the First. Not the Wolves of Fenris. The webway is an alien environment: another dimensional reality, even. We cannot cross such a realm in our mighty warships. We've tried. Innumerable vessels, hopelessly lost or spat back out upon the galactic plane. Some say that forgotten gods and primarchs still roam the labyrinthine expanse of its passageways. It is a place of elegance and alien intuition that we couldn't hope to understand, let alone navigate.'

'It sounds like you have given up, Angel,' Krom snarled. 'And that is something a Wolf can never do.'

'I'm glad to hear it, brother,' the Interrogator-Chaplain said. 'Do you think you are the only Adeptus Astartes with unfinished business in the galaxy? I firmly believe that we can escape our present incarceration, this city and perhaps even this alien realm. It is simply a matter of waiting for the inevitable. Before the suns set on this benighted place I am sure we can find a way to help each other out of these less than ideal circumstances.'

Krom had a pithy response prepared, but he stopped himself. He was too proud to truly acknowledge what he owed the stranger, but also too proud to fail.

'Shall we work together, then?' Krom said.

'We are all of the Emperor's blood,' the Interrogator-Chaplain said.

'So are many who have betrayed such a covenant,' Krom said. The Wolf Lord had killed enough renegades and traitors in legionary plate to know.

Once again the Interrogator-Chaplain seemed lost in thought.

'Of course, you're right,' he said, his words heavy and knowing. 'A Wolf's wisdom indeed.'

'What about him?' Krom said. 'Is he of the Emperor's blood?'

The Interrogator-Chaplain looked across at the cage containing the World Eater. The monster sat silent in his spiked, blood-red armour. His face was a ghoulish mess, a gore-stained skull with a single remaining eyeball staring right through the Interrogator-Chaplain, through Krom, and his own agonies.

'He is not for this world,' the Interrogator-Chaplain said. 'By all that is right and true, we should finish off what's left of him, but I fear we won't get that far. He won't give us a choice.'

Krom nodded his agreement. The pair went silent for a moment, only the clash of blades and the deviant roar of the crowd filling the space.

'And just so you know,' Krom corrected the Interrogator-Chaplain, 'I don't think that those suns ever go down.'

A roar of appreciation from a new crowd of dark eldar sadists drew Krom's attention. The coliseum was spilling over with pale-faced spectators, their features sharp and cruel. Extra leather-bound guards had been rushed out onto the arena wall with razorflails, impalers and bidents. As the screeching applause continued, Krom came to understand that some new gladiatrix, torture machine or monster had taken to the arena.

As the Space Wolves and Dark Angels came to the bars, it became clear, at least, who some of the combatants would be. With an agonising clunk, the barred entrance to their cages rose.

'Eyes open, Drakeslayers,' Krom said. 'Round two.' As spiked panels began to ratchet through the cells, forcing the Space Marines back out onto the sand, Krom felt Beoric Winterfang at his back. The Wolf Lord's plate felt like sluggish scrap about him.

'Do you hear that, Fenrisian?' the Interrogator-Chaplain asked. 'That's the sound of opportunity knocking.'

'Now all we have to do is find the door,' Krom said.

As the Space Marines ventured out onto the blood-wet sand, Krom remembered the World Eater. Turning, he saw the skull-faced maniac advancing upon Brother Othniel and the Interrogator-Chaplain.

'Chaplain,' Krom warned.

The Dark Angel turned and Othniel put himself between the Chaos Space Marine and his chaplain.

'Traitor,' the Wolf Lord called, his voice burred like an unfinished metal edge. 'After, yes? Supposing any of us survive this – whatever it is.'

'Whatever it is, this barbarian will survive it,' the Interrogator-Chaplain warned. 'Best we kill him now, while we have the numbers.'

'Won't we need him if we start losing those numbers?' Krom asked.

The Interrogator-Chaplain and the World Eater stared at each other with burning eyes.

'The agony of choice,' the Interrogator-Chaplain said.

An alien roar of nerve-shredding intensity and bombast took the Space Marines' attentions off the World Eater. Krom felt the sand quake beneath his boots. Something big was crossing the arena. As the prisoners emerged they saw the monster they were expected to fight.

It was a xenos horror, the height and bulk of a three-storey bunker. Despite its size, it moved with predacious assurance on its colossal hooves. A chitinous abomination, the beast was all armoured shell, fang-filled maw and bio-weaponry: a powerful tail, terminating in a hammer-head thagomizer; shoulder-sprouting battering rams; a monstrous crusher-claw and a huge, wrecking-ball symbiont that draped from its other appendage on a fibrous tendril-cord of twisted tendon and sinew.

'Sergeant?' Krom said.

Beoric Winterfang hesitated, then understood what the Wolf Lord was asking. 'It's a tyranid,' Beoric said, identifying the beast for the rest of the Drakeslayers rather than Krom. 'Carnifex sub-type. Some kind of stone-crusher or siege creature.'

'Weaknesses?'

'None,' Beoric answered honestly, 'as I recall.'

'Remember Delta-Phrakaasi?' Krom asked.

'We had Land Raiders, missile launchers and grenades,' Grundar Grey-mane said.

'What I wouldn't give for some grenades,' Haegr Fangthane said.

'We can't kill this,' the Dark Angel Interrogator-Chaplain said.

'Oh, I don't know,' Krom said. 'You could talk it to death.'

'We're not meant to kill it,' the Dark Angel said. 'It's meant to kill us, one by one, for entertainment.'

'No torture, no suffering?' Krom asked.

'Suffering was earlier,' the Interrogator-Chaplain said. 'Something to stimulate the appetite. This is the main course – and these deviants can't get enough of a sudden and bloody death.'

As the Space Marines spread out on the black sand, brawny beast-masters wrangled the monstrosity on huge chains connected to hooks embedded in the creature's armour plating. The thing was clearly an arena veteran. One of its shoulder battering rams was smashed at the top and had a metal spike hammered into the stump as an extra weapon. The creature had lost an eye and wore a leather hood over the punc-tured orb like a bird of prey.

Sections of chitinous shell that had been ripped away had been staked back into the creature's flesh and bound with coils of razorwire.

'What if we tried to topple it?' Ingrimm Thunderfell said. 'I've seen these things go down before.'

'Right,' Grundar Greymane said, 'but then what? We can hardly punch it to death.'

'We could go for the other eye,' Ulf Horghast offered.

'It's a tyranid,' Winterfang reminded him. 'It could be trailing innards from its headless body and it would still be lethal.'

'Interrogator-Chaplain?' Krom asked.

'This beast could be a solution, rather than a problem,' the Dark Angel said.

'Agreed,' Krom said. 'We've got to stop playing this game for the xenos and start playing it for ourselves. That thing is a biological siege engine, but it's cut off from its species. It will be confused and easy to draw. Let's spread out and direct its talents – perhaps get it to take out one or two of these walls and provide us with an escape route.'

As the beastmasters released their chains, the tyranid monstrosity began stomping towards its prey. The dark eldar audience hissed their excitement – the unstoppable tyranid construct was clearly an arena favourite.

'Understood?' Krom asked.

'Yes, my lord,' the Drakeslayers returned.

'For the Allfather,' Krom said.

'For Russ,' his Space Wolves roared, before spreading out across the arena.

Moving towards the arena walls, with the dark eldar guards in all their svelte repugnance watching over him, Krom waited for the carnifex that was thundering across the arena towards him.

'Interrogator-Chaplain,' Krom called. 'I know your Chapter likes its secrets, but you can at least tell me your name before we die.'

'Balthus,' the Interrogator-Chaplain told him. As they prepared for the alien horror to reach them, the pair saw the World Eater stride out into the middle of the arena. 'Would you look at that?'

'Maniac,' was all Krom had to offer on the spectacle.

As the carnifex charged across the sands, shaking the walls of the arena, Krom watched the World Eater walk out before it. He was curious what the Blood God's champion was going to do. Within horrible seconds, the Wolf Lord found out. As the monstrous tyranid screeched its way across the killing ground it stamped down on the World Eater with the splayed hoof of a chitinous leg. With the full weight of the monster hammering down on the Chaos Space Marine, plate was crushed, bones ground to meal and what was left of the World Eater's hate-curdled flesh splattered into a sand-soaking mess on the arena floor. If ever the coliseum had told a cautionary tale it was now. Krom was glad he hadn't authorised a more direct attack.

'Remember,' he called across to his Drakeslayers as they spread out along the wall. 'Do not engage. Be a moving target. Direct the beast's attentions at the wall.'

As the tyranid approached it skidded in the sand. Krom could see that the beast was reluctant to get any closer to the perimeter wall, no doubt having been doused in flame by the projectors one too many times.

'Run!' Krom ordered, and run the Wolves did. They needed to disorientate the monster enough for its instincts to overcome its conditioned wariness of the wall. Stomping through the sand with powered steps, the Drakeslayers spread their number and tried to stay ahead of the alien abomination. Its grotesque head, filled to the brim with daggered teeth, reached out from a clinkered nest of chitinous plating. Bringing up its hammerhead tail and angling its shoulder rams parallel with the ground, the thing stretched its neck and opened its mouth. Two colossal tusks erupted from its bottom jaw, waiting to guide prey in.

As the young Kjarli Tyrvald set the pace, drawing the creature on, Hengist Ironaxe ran the gauntlet of an about face. Turning and accelerating back along the wall the way he came, he caught its attention. Scrambling heavily through the sand, the beast reached out with its crusher-claw. Pushing himself off the wall, to the spiteful abuse of spectators and arena guards alike, the Space Wolf ran between the monster's legs. As the heavy crusher-claw struck the wall where Hengist had been, spidery cracks spread through the wall section. A guard lifted the telescopic shaft of her bident but the incensed organism wasn't interested in her.

Pivoting on its hooves, the beast roared its strange, tyranid ire before setting off after Grundar Greymane. As Grundar criss-crossed paths with Ingrimm Thunderfell, the horrific beast stomped its way along the wall. As Thunderfell held its attention, the tyranid's shoulder-column spike scouring a trench through the stone, Brother Hrothgar attempted to take up the chase. Uninterested in new prey, the carnifex charged down on Thunderfell, tearing away wall-mounted spools of razorwire and arena torture racks.

'Ingrimm,' Krom roared. 'Don't look behind. Just run!'

It didn't help, however. The tyranid's neck stretched out and the beast swept the Space Wolf up in its plate-mangling jaws. Krom watched another of his Drakeslayers die, disappearing into the creature's maw.

Krom heard the cruel laughter of the audience and felt something wet hit the back of his head. Turning, he saw that the dark eldar guard behind him, a thing of extravagant hair, shredded leather and alien nakedness, had spat at him. Wiping the spit from his scalp with his gauntlet he pointed a thunderous finger at the guard. She flashed a needle-toothed smile of derision.

The Wolf Lord felt it before he saw it. The quake of the beast approaching. Hrothgar had tried to lead it away from his doomed brother and the wall, only to have the abominate alien construct run him down. As it reached out with its crusher-claw, other Space Wolves ran in, daring the beast to chase them.

'Here, you mound of galactic spoilage,' Krom roared, waving his arms. 'Here!'

The tyranid snatched Brother Hrothgar up in its crusher-claw and snapped the huge appendage shut. What came out between the mashing force of the claws was beyond description.

A predator spoiled for choice amongst a bounty of kills, the thing simply wouldn't stop, thrashing and turning like a creature half its size. Space Wolves, drawn in to save their brother, now found themselves within reach of the beast's monstrous claw, snapping maw and swishing tail. Knocking an escaping Lars Thorgil into the sand with a pounding ram of its shoulder column, the tyranid pinned the Space Wolf to the ground with a hoof. As Thorgil roared, the carnifex leaned in with its horrific jaws and bit the Space Marine in two.

The tyranid's tail swept around as the creature re-orientated itself. Beoric Winterfang was there. As promised, he hadn't left his captain's side. As the hammerhead end of the tail came around, the sergeant ran at Krom. Knocking the Wolf Lord out of the thagomizer's path, Beoric was struck with the full force of the creature's tail. Hammered across the sands like a rag doll, he landed some distance away, a tumble terminating in a pile of shattered plate. As Krom got back to his feet, Grundar Greymane and Hengist Ironaxe made it over to the sergeant. After a brief inspection, Grundar nodded an indication that the Space Wolf was alive. Signalling with two armoured thumbs to the sky and then two pointing fingers, Krom gave them the order to get the sergeant away from the tyranid and the death that surrounded it.

'Fenrisian,' Interrogator-Chaplain Balthus called. 'The wall.'

Krom nodded. The coliseum boomed with the malicious jubilation of alien spectators. The carnifex screeched its disorientated desire to end them all. Like all tyranid spawn, it had been constructed to kill until nothing about it was left living. Krom had no doubt that the monstrosity would act upon such instincts, given the chance.

Picking up Hrothgar's helm, a gore-filled receptacle that had rolled across the sand, Krom emptied the contents onto the arena floor before throwing the helmet at the beast. Bouncing off its chitinous skull and leather hood, the helmet got the tyranid's attention. Everything so far had run away from the stomping, snapping nightmare. It looked at Krom with the predatory blankness of its remaining eye. Kicking at the black sand, Krom sent a cloud of dust spiralling up about him. It was enough. The huge creature leant into an acceleration. As its maw crunched on what was left of Lars Thorgil, it pounded the arena floor with death-hungry steps.

As Krom ran towards the wall, his plate grinding and pack sparking with the effort, he saw the guard who had spat at him looking down the length of her spear at him. The Wolf Lord felt the arena shake with the steps of the monster behind him. He counted the closing quakes beneath his own footfalls. Then there it was: the delay he had been waiting for.

Skidding down through the blood and dust, Krom put his rattling plate down on the ground. Sand turned to glass where the flame projectors had roasted the arena perimeter, taking Krom onwards. As he crunched to a stop, the soles of his boots hit the wall. There was a whoosh. The monstrosity had stopped to swing the wrecking-ball symbiont attached to its appendage. The weapon swung on a thick tendril of tendons, constricting to destructive tautness. Instead of obliterating the Wolf Lord, the wrecking-ball struck the wall, dashing into the stone.

Rock dust billowed out across the sand. Chunks of stone fell about Krom, further denting his plate. Hooking his thumbs under a large piece of rock, the Wolf Lord heaved, his powered arms faltering.

Through the maelstrom, Krom heard coughing. A slender silhouette bled into focus. It was the dark eldar guard. Having fallen from the wall, she was now back on her feet and aiming the twin blades of her impaler at Krom.

'Fenrisian,' Krom heard Balthus call a warning through the murk.

Krom released his grip on the boulder.

The dark eldar coughed again before baring her sharpened teeth. She was going to enjoy slipping her spear into the Space Marine's throat. The tyranid's tail cut through the rock dust like an aftershock, the work of the wrecking-ball unfinished. It broke the guard, the hammer-head thagomizer smashing her aside and into the wall. Pushing at the boulder, Krom managed to lift it enough to scrape his armoured legs free.

Scrambling up the mound of rubble, the Wolf Lord climbed through the improvised exit he had created. Beyond, he could hear the seething threats of nearby spectators and the clack of boots as guards converged on the breach.

Blinking the dust from his eyes, Krom sniffed the air. He smelled fuel. Some foul chemical accelerant. The Wolf Lord allowed himself to skid back down the scree. He once more heard the crunch of something approaching across the sand. Turning, he picked up a sizeable chunk of stone and held it over his head. The carnifex punched through the rubble, its chitinous battering rams surging up at Krom. It scrambled up at the Space Wolf, crusher-claw and death trap maw snapping. Hurling the boulder down on the tyranid beast, Krom shattered the stone on the thing's armoured head.

Krom leapt from the rubble as the monster blinked some semblance of sense and murderous instinct back into its skull. Landing, the Space Wolf felt the servos and hydraulics in his suit protesting. As he pushed himself to his feet and ran from the wall back into the arena, the carnifex did the opposite. Scrambling on up the scree slope and over the demolished wall, the tyranid sensed prey beyond the settling dust. Victim hordes. A captive audience. As Krom ran from the monster, he found Interrogator-Chaplain Balthus and his Drakeslayers closing on the breach.

'Back!' he roared. 'Get back!'

The explosion blasted Krom from his feet and sent him skidding on his chestplate across the arena floor. The Space Marines were knocked back, losing their footing on the sand. Rolling onto his side, Krom watched a fireball reach up towards the sky. As the carnifex had tried to breach the perimeter wall, something implanted in its flesh by the beastmasters had set off the flame projectors. A fail-safe device to prevent the monster escaping. The wrecking-ball had ruptured the tanks of exotic fuel in the decimated section of wall so when the tyranid tried to cross the projectors set off the leaking accelerant.

Getting to his feet, Krom stumbled away from the raging wall section with his Drakeslayers. After a few moments the carnifex re-emerged, a furious inferno of chitinous flesh. It stomped out of the flames, shrieking from within the blaze. In a blind rage of raw suffering, the abomination ran across the arena.

The Wolf Lord expected that such a spectacle – a wall breach, an explosion and a gladiatorial monster aflame – might have grabbed the attention of the audience. He was wrong. Looking across the ghoulish faces of the spectators, he saw that they were looking up. Peering up at the sky also, Krom could see why.

The shadow he had seen earlier – the blot on the miserable heavens upon which he had projected fantasies of Thunderhawks, rescue and city-wide slaughter – was a shadow no more. The Wolf Lord's instincts had been right. The flying craft had been on a trajectory for the coliseum. They weren't bringing salvation from beyond the webway, however, but enemies from within.

Krom watched as an attack flotilla of dark eldar grav-craft, skiffs and barges emerged from their optical shielding and circled above the coliseum like a stirred-up swarm of insects. All aethyrsails, razorvanes and black bulwark plating, the raiding vessels crawled with Commorrite warriors. Like the coliseum guards and gladiatrix, they were all female savages, dripping with blades and black-hearted cruelty. The differences were subtle but they were there. Something in the way the killers wore their leathers, their hair and malicious intent. Unlike the coliseum cult, whose banner bore a serrated shadow, the pendants trailing from the raiders displayed a black talon, the symbol of a rival cult.

While the longer and more extravagant craft carried out their impossible manoeuvres with a sickly hiss, smaller gunships and transports screamed by, overladen with lithe murderers. Trophy racks braced terrified prisoners across the prows of the vessels and scaling nets allowed mobs of dark eldar to climb down into the coliseum crowds, while others dropped like poison from the skies – leaping from swooping craft with dire grace to land in the arena.

Krom watched the deviant warriors of the Serrated Shadow and Black Talon clash. They shredded one another with tapered pistols, impaled foes on bidents, slashed with wicked knives and cut through crowds with razored flails. The audience was not spared the horror and within moments the entire coliseum was a free-for-all, with spectators drawing blades and pistols of their own.

'I think the show is over,' Krom said of the madness.

'Or just beginning,' Balthus added.

The Interrogator-Chaplain narrowed his eyes. The prisoner cages were firing. With cage doors rising and advancing spikes forcing prisoners from their captivity, the arena was suddenly awash with gladiatorial prospects, all released at the same time, looking warily at each other and the riotous slaughter taking place on the terraces above. The sand suddenly rippled up about the Space Marines.

'Look out!' Krom called.

A length of razor wire running across the arena, carefully hidden, had been cranked to flesh-slicing tautness. One moment Brother Ragnek was there, the white of his battle-gritted teeth showing through his beard. The next, the Space Wolf crashed to the arena floor in two pieces.

Krom tasted blood in the back of his throat mixed with the bitterness of adrenaline. He waited for another wire to sever him but it didn't happen. All across the sands, a razor sharp web of death sang to a metallic strain, making the arena more dangerous than ever. The newly liberated prisoners backed towards the arena wall but the perimeter only offered the illusion of safety. Movement sensors situated below the surface of the sand set off shooting spikes, streams of mutagenic gas and gouts of projected flame. As more razor wires criss-crossing the sand twanged to tautness, heads were whipped off, limbs lost and bodies cut in half by a network of sprung cables. Krom saw blundering victims torched, speared and transformed into formless abominations of bubbling flesh by the wall defences.

Krom had seen such traps deployed before. He had heard the audience roar its bloodthirsty delight at their murderous activation. He had not seen all of the traps deployed at once, however. It did not play to suspense or the theatrical nature of the coliseum.

'A malfunction?' Balthus asked. The place had turned into a full-scale murderous riot, with dark eldar guards and raiders cutting each other down with barrel and blade.

'Or prisoner stock being purged,' Krom said grimly. 'Perhaps these wretched xenos want to deny us to their back-stabbing cousins. Are we going to wait to find out?'

Balthus and the Wolf Lord looked back at the raging inferno that was the wall breach.

'The flames?' the Interrogator-Chaplain said, shrugging. 'You said that we could walk through them.'

'I didn't actually think that we would be doing it,' Krom growled. He led the prisoners through the carnage of the arena and the corpses, both human and alien, that littered the blood-soaked ground. Away from the clean-sliced corpse of Ragnek Halfhand and visions of gladiatorial gore. Towards the raging swirl of heat and flame through which their escape route lay.

An armoured skiff swept in between the Space Wolves and the breached wall. Several of the grav-craft above, circling like vultures, had seen the liberated prisoners flood the arena death trap. Driven by a desire to secure such stock or simply to enjoy the arena's gladiatorial bounty, female raiders dropped from their skyborne chariots in their leathers, whipping blades and flails about them.

The warrior women who had athletically landed before the Space Marines smiled with malicious beauty. Their leader, a vision of intoxicating repugnance, waggled a finger back and forth in mock remonstration, even her long nails filed to serrated shivs.

The warrior women worked their murderous way across the sands. A whirlwind of envenomed blades and black leather armour that barely covered the lithe obscenity of their xenos forms, they athletically negotiated the death trap of the coliseum. They leaped and rolled beneath triggered razor wire. They danced through the fired spikes with a cruel grace while executing freed prisoners with unparalleled skill and merciless bladework. Each artistic death resulted in a fountain of orchestrated gore as the dread beauties closed on the Space Marines.

'Brothers,' Krom seethed. 'Break them.' He and his Space Marines would be playthings for the xenos no more.

The new dark eldar stepped elegantly through the cadavers and body parts left behind. Krom knew that they were playing with the unarmed Space Marines. He swore by the Allfather, through sharpened teeth, that he would be ready – ready to disappoint her, her kindred and the howling hordes who had come to watch him and his men die. The Space Wolves would survive the alien madness of this nightmare realm and make it their solemn pledge to end all pirates, raiders and deviant dark eldar that crossed their path.

With a creak of their gauntlets, the closest of his kindred rushed the leading warrior woman. They intended to bury the murderess and her blade maidens in plate and Fenrisian muscle. The dark eldar of the Black Talon were too fast, however, and anticipated their clumsy attack. Invited it. Revelled in it. Moments later, heads had left shoulders, hearts had been skewered and blades bleeding venom had turned proud Space Wolves into convulsing corpses still foaming at the mouth.

As blades sang through plate and gauntlets smashed, more warrior women dropped to the ground. Young Kjarli Tyrvald was turned into a streaming blur of blood and brains by the half-naked dark eldar heralds who flanked their mistress with swirling razorflails. While the lead murderess leapt cables and elegantly butchered fleeing prisoners with a double-bladed glaive, her heralds blessed her path with spilled blood. Advancing with razorflails swinging about them in slaughterous arcs, the warrior women were like a pair of bloody hurricanes. Appalling in their beauty and calm like the eye of the storm, they controlled the speed and reach of their weaponry, swinging the blades of the flail expertly about their bodies.

Krom stumbled back before the deadly arc of one weapon, watching for the change of its air-shredding passage. The dark eldar whipped the razorflail about her, tearing it through the sand at Krom's feet before leaning into an arc that sent the weapon searing above the Space Wolf's ducked head. He pulled back – just in time for the end of the other flail to hiss off the surface of his chestplate. It was a dance of death and Krom had been invited to be part of the entertainment. He knew there was little he could do to combat such a deadly weapon. It couldn't be deflected; it could only be dodged for so long. He needed to turn the razorflail against its wielder.

The Wolf Lord readied himself. Once again he would have to draw the enemy in.

He allowed the weapon its terrible arc and embraced its flesh-tearing impact. The weapon sliced into his side, cutting through his plate and ripping into muscle and carapace. Krom roared as the flail bit into him. Snatching it like a rope with both gauntlets, the Space Wolf hauled on the length of the weapon with all his feral might. The herald lurched forward, off-balance. Refusing to let go of her gore-dribbling weapon, the dark eldar was torn towards Krom and he was ready for her. Opening his right gauntlet like an outstretched claw, he brought it down on the warrior's head. Tearing his armoured fingers through the bone of her slender skull, Krom brained the xenos, smashing her down into the sand.

The Wolf Lord stood over the corpse of the dark eldar and pulled the length of the razored flail from his side. Blood ran down his grey plate from the clean slice. A shriek brought Krom back to the moment. The second herald, who had been dicing fleeing prisoners with her own razorflail, had seen her sister felled. Running at Krom with her flail tossed about her like a lasso, she issued a mind-splitting war cry.

Stomping through the black sand, Krom accelerated to meet her. As the herald's razorflail came around in a devastating arc, he made a clumsy swing of the same weapon in his hands. Entwining and tangling, both flails were quickly abandoned. Krom had not intended anything else but was surprised at how ready the dark eldar was to release her main weapon. By the time the knotted flails thudded to the ground, the warrior had already drawn a pair of thin, willowy blades. She ran down on the Space Wolf, her weapons like extensions of her lithe body.

Krom intended to smash straight through the warrior with his engineered strength and the bulk of his armour. The dark eldar leapt, however, jabbing at the Space Wolf like a scorpion. He felt the blade squeal between his plates and stab through slabs of muscle. Hitting the ground, the herald rolled before slashing the monomolecular edge of her blades across Krom's pack and pauldron.

The Space Wolf reached out for her with grasping fingers but the dark eldar moved with alien reflexes and a dreadful grace. She was incredibly fast, her painted face a vision of hateful concentration. She weaved and ducked. She leapt and cartwheeled. With each feint and manoeuvre the tip of her blades came in, slipping through Krom's defences to skewer his flesh.

The Wolf Lord's grey plate became a bloody, punctured mess. Krom waited, gritting his sharp teeth through the pain. As one of the dark eldar's blades squealed between two pieces of plate, he tensed, closing the seal about the sword like a clamp. Clinging to the blade for just a moment too long, the herald's hand was still clutching the hilt when Krom grabbed it.

Crushing the delicate bones against the hilt of the weapon with his gauntlet, Krom saw the savage concentration on the face of the xenos shatter.

As she brought her second blade up to slash his face, Krom tore her arm around. He felt the crunch of the herald's shoulder. This time the dark eldar let out an involuntary screech. With her back to him, the dark eldar tried an awkward stab at the Wolf Lord's throat. Leaning back away from the gore-stained point, he tugged the warrior back towards him with her broken arm. Lifting his leg he kicked out at the herald. Servos fired and fibre bundles contracted, sending a powered kick and the sole of an armoured boot into the warrior woman's back.

Krom heard the back break. Her screams were joined by those of the xenos audience. Her blade fell from her hand and her slender body fell after. Paralysed, the dark eldar looked up at the Space Wolf from the floor. She was an untidy heap of broken bones and burning hatred but Krom would not leave her unfinished. Towering over her he pulled her blade from where it was still trapped in his plate. The Wolf Lord flung it down at his opponent, sending it thudding into her chest. Krom watched the blade and the dark eldar's armoured bosom rise and fall one last time before all was still.

The lead dark eldar gladiatrix moved with barefoot grace through the carnage of the arena. Corpses, both human and alien, littered the blood-soaked ground. She turned the double-bladed glaive about in her hands like a dancing girl with a baton as she stepped over the butchered corpse of Haegr Fangthane.

Like a predator scenting prey, she started gaining speed. Holding the shaft of her glaive streamlined along the length of her body, she moved lightly through the carnage. As she ran on she casually twirled the weapon, cleaving a deranged prisoner that came at her in two from the jaw to the hip. She skull-stabbed a fleeing Tarellian and smashed to pieces some captured cybernetic abomination.

Krom tore the short, cruel blades from the bodies of her svelte handmaidens. They were light and alien to his grip. His furious steps took him towards the murderess. With a roar he struck out for her, the short blades clutched like daggers in his gauntlets. The stabbing lunge had every right to rip the dark eldar gladiatrix apart and spill her alien innards on the sand, to turn the perfection of her abominate form into a ruined carcass. It was not to be, however.

The gladiatrix was all silky, unnatural speed and Krom's opponent simply wasn't there as his vicious attack was launched. Somersaulting the Space Wolf, the dark eldar landed behind him. As the Wolf Lord turned, she brought one of the blade-heads of the glaive around and smashed a blade from his hand. Spinning, the other blade came around to slice down through the ceramite of Krom's ruined pauldron. He felt the weapon bite into the flesh of his shoulder and the burn of some caustic coating bleed from the metal.

Krom would not be put off. Instead of withdrawing, the Space Wolf moved in closer. With his remaining blade clutched against his chest, ready to thrust forth and gut the gladiatrix, he reached out with his free hand. A leather strap, a chain or a lank limb, anything to get an anchor on the alien warrioress. Flipping back, she escaped the clawing grapnel of his gauntlet, the shaft of the glaive turning and twirling. Sparks flew from the back of the armoured hand as his gauntlet was smacked away. The flat of the second blade batted Krom's remaining weapon free from his grip.

Before he could react – his movements a slow-motion nightmare – the gladiatrix had jabbed with her glaive, the blade flashing forth in place of her retreat. Gouging a hole in the Space Wolf's grey plate at his thigh, the shaft came at him again and again. Each thrust was a different angle, the glaive darting forth through Krom's grasping defences and retracting before he could lay his fingertips on the weapon. A flashing stab through the cabling of the Wolf Lord's midriff. One to the muscle of the right arm. A deeper gouge to the chest. The spinning blades of the glaive glinting in the dull, darklight of the captured suns, ready to take Krom's head. The Wolf Lord imagined the fountain of gore that would follow. The murderous ecstasy of the dark eldar about them.

Krom looked up into his killer's eyes. They sparkled with hatred and glee. Her taut musculature rippled beneath the pallor of her skin.

As the glaive came around, Krom ducked his head. As he did so, one of his red plaits bounced upwards, only to be sliced free by the blistering passage of the glaive blade above him. He bellowed as he pushed himself up from the sand. It was an ugly lunge. His hands came up, his fingers grasping for the dark eldar's slender neck.

Momentary disappointment crossed the gladiatrix's face. She pulled the glaive back and spun it overhead, intending to cleave the blade straight down through the Space Wolf. The shaft of the weapon hit Krom's outstretched gauntlets. Locking his fingers about its length like a vice, the Wolf Lord held her there. The gladiatrix's body contorted about the glaive, every muscle of her sickly slender form contracted to bring the weapon down. Krom's arms burned from the wicked stab wounds the dark eldar had visited upon him. His lips retracted about his sharp teeth and a low growl issued forth from his chest. He would deny the gladiatrix her death fetish.

Krom heard footsteps approaching across the sand. His gaze was locked with his enemy. He dared not look away. A moment's distraction could end him. He entertained the possibility of more warrior women, padding forth in bare feet to stab and gut him as their murderess held him in position. The sand-crunching steps were heavier than the coliseum killers, however. An angel of death approached.

Krom watched as the gladiatrix's headdress was knocked from her head. Her face was suddenly covered by filthy, dun white material, pulled so tight that the Space Wolf could see the sharpness of her alien features through it. It was the Interrogator-Chaplain – come to end the xenos. A punishment suitable for the crime of the alien's mere existence.

With the hem pulled across her throat, Krom saw the dark eldar's mouth open in a silent scream, her sharp teeth piercing the material. As the chaplain hauled back on the material cutting across the gladiatrix's throat and covering the abominate beauty of her face, Krom realised that he was strangling the alien with his own robes. The dark eldar released her glaive, which remained in the Wolf Lord's vice-like grip, and tore feverishly at the material with her stiletto fingernails. There was little she could do, however. The garrotting robes were held by one of the Emperor's Angels. The power of his engineered muscle and determination to do his xenos-eradicating duty were more than a match for the fell skill of an alien murderess.

The gladiatrix began to thrash. For her it was no longer about air. The chaplain was breaking her neck. She smashed the sharpness of her elbow uselessly into her enemy's plate. She clawed at him and his hood-buried helmet. As he lifted her up off her bare feet, ready to end the arena's deadly champion, Krom saw her spasmodic hands reach for a thin blade in her belt. Snatching it up, the warrioress made ready to stab the chaplain. Krom saw the discoloured metal and the concentrated venom that smoked from the blade. It was not like the glaive. The glaive was a show weapon. Something to please the audience with its twirling glint. Something to slow down opponents in preparation for a theatrical kill. The knife, however, looked like it could kill at the slightest nick or slice.

With his hearts thudding in his chest and mind swimming with blood loss and doom, the Wolf Lord willed himself to his feet. He thrust the double-bladed glaive back at the gladiatrix, slamming the blade into her chest. The chaplain released his quarry and stumbled back as the tip of the blade erupted from the dark eldar's back. As he backed his filthy robes went with him, revealing the cold shock on the face of the warrioress. As her knife tumbled from her fingertips, landing blade first in the sand, a trickle of blood made its way down her face from the corner of her thin lips.

The Wolf lord roared and lifted the gladiatrix above his head, holding her there as she died, the impaled warrior woman working her horrible way down the blade and shaft of the weapon. But there was no audience to applaud his efforts or shriek its displeasure. The arena was a nest of pistol-blasting, blade-stabbing havoc. Black Talon raiders. Dark eldar guards of the Serrated Shadow. The deviant wretches that made up the coliseum audience and Commorrite citizenry. All were at each other's throats, while two dark queens fought through the vicious slaughter.

Krom saw the coliseum queen in the spikes and extravagant leathers wielding an impossible length of barbed blades about her nightmare form. Her opposite was a lean killer, whose flesh was powdered theatrically to whiteness. She wore black boots and gloves that reached up her legs and arms. The gloves whipped with finger blades like razored wings, threatening to dice anything that got too close. Krom dropped his trophy, sickened by the alien butchery.

Above the warrior queens, shrieking skiffs visited blistering destruction upon the coliseum with exotic grav-craft mounted cannons. As bombs dropped from the gunships and blade-vaned barges, Krom hauled Interrogator-Chaplain Balthus forward.

'Incoming!' the Wolf Lord barked to what was left of his Drakeslayers, but as the bomb hit the arena floor it did not explode as he expected. Instead, a sizzling storm of dark energy tore up the sand, growing to form a dome of immaterial transference. As reinforcements in leathers, clutching tapering pistols, blistered forth from the globed gateway, Krom could see that it was a portable portal used to rush further troops into the coliseum.

Krom looked to Balthus and Grundar Greymane, who had Sergeant Beoric over one pauldron.

'Do you hear that?' Krom said. 'I hear knocking.'

Grundar looked unsure.

The Interrogator-Chaplain wasn't about to abandon such an opportunity.

'It's death to stay here,' Balthus said to the Space Wolves.

'It could lead anywhere,' Grundar said.

'Anywhere but here,' the Interrogator-Chaplain shot back.

'I don't think we have a choice,' the Wolf Lord said, moving towards the nearest portal. 'Space Wolves: to me!'

As a walk became a run and both Space Wolves and Dark Angels converged on the sizzling dome of unnatural energy, dark eldar came at them. Splinter shot blasted from pistols ripped at their plate and warrior reinforcements put themselves and their blades between the prisoners and their escape route. The Space Marines would not be put off their path, however. They barged their way through the surprised xenos, and before the dark eldar could stop him, Krom had plunged into the interdimensional static of the portal. It washed over him like rising waters, filling the Wolf Lord with a feeling of pain and dreamy disconnection. For a moment his heartbeats died away and his stomach plunged in all directions at once. What felt like an eternity passed in several agonising seconds, as Krom emerged from the other side of the searing dome.

His plate immediately registered the cold. It bit at his flesh through the mangled suit. Balthus, Brother Othniel and Grundar followed. Everything was quiet but for the evil hiss of the portal. They found themselves in a dark chamber, the architecture of which was twisted and rachidian. As the other Drakeslayers made it through the portal, Grundar laid the unconscious Sergeant Beoric down on the floor and made a brief inspection of his injuries. He was out cold, but apart from cracked plate and similar damage to his ribs and black carapace, Beoric looked like he was going to make it.

The Space Marines spread out to search the chamber.

'Rorven,' Krom said to the Space Wolf. 'Watch the portal – wait, where's Hengist?'

Looking about the drawn faces in the chamber it was clear that Hengist Ironaxe was not with them.

'He was last to enter,' Rorven said. 'He was behind me and then–'

Krom made to enter the alien portal once more. He would not leave the Grey Hunter behind, not while he still lived.

'My lord, wait,' Grundar Greymane said, reaching out for him. At that moment a silhouette blazed through the interdimensional static. The Space Wolves tensed. Hengist Ironaxe appeared, his forehead betraying several deep gashes he had not had moments before. He clutched in his gauntlets something that Krom had never thought to see again. Wyrmclaw. The Wolf Lord's rune-carved frost axe.

Krom cracked the caked blood about his face with a smile.

'We thought we had lost you, brother,' he said.

'I thought you had lost this,' Hengist told the Wolf Lord, 'until I saw some xenos looter leaving the cell block with it.'

Taking the frost axe and admiring the blade, he took the Grey Hunter by the fist and held him there in appreciation. He looked behind Hengist at the unnatural energies of the portal.

'Rorven, Hengist,' Krom said. 'Find a way to destroy that damned thing.'

As the Space Wolves searched, they found nothing but bodies. Dark eldar, with their throats slit and hearts cut out. A swift and brutal massacre had taken place – presumably by the Black Talon reinforcements that had entered the arena from the portal. Other than the dead, the building into which the Space Wolves had walked was deserted.

'Fenrisian,' Interrogator-Chaplain Balthus called. Following the voice, Krom and Grundar found the two Dark Angels out on a spiked watch-balcony. Looking around, Krom saw that they were standing on a crooked tower that stabbed up into the dust-choked void. The darkness of the sky was all nebulous reds and blue, reflected in the sulphuric snow that clung to the tower and caked the rocky twilight below.

'We're out of the webway?' Krom said. It sounded like a question but was more of a statement. Balthus didn't bother to answer.

'This must be a dark eldar outpost,' he told Krom. He pointed out the Serrated Shadow banners that fluttered in the gelid breeze. 'A supply tower or base of piratical operations.'

The Wolf Lord nodded: 'We found bodies.'

'Some private war of xenos cults or clans,' Balthus said.

'Vicious dogs, eh,' Krom said. It was one thing to attack a rival cult and their coliseum, but to launch reinforcements from the very bases from which the coliseum expected their own was especially black-hearted. For all the Space Marines knew, however, it could have been a daily occurrence in the Dark City.

'See that?' Balthus asked, pointing up towards a bright collection of five stars, like a rash blotting through the nebulous dust of the system.

'They look close,' Krom said.

'They are,' Brother Othniel said, the light of the stars reflecting off his blue plate. 'It's a quintuplet system – two binaries and a lone companion. Rare – and therefore easy to identify.'

'So,' Krom said. 'Where are we?'

'At a guess, one of the rocky, outlying moons or dwarf planets of the Skarapaz System,' Brother Othniel told him.

'I've never heard of it,' Krom admitted.

'Which is probably why the xenos pirates are using it for a system outpost,' Balthus said.

'It's not far from Harrow Worlds,' Othniel said.

'Damn, that's close,' Krom said. 'My Wolves hold station over Dactyla.'

'The Angels of the First are not too distant, either,' Balthus said. 'Now we are free of the webway, Brother Othniel will use his talents to contact the Librarians and astropaths of our respective fleets.'

Krom grunted and extended a grey gauntlet.

'My thanks,' he told the Interrogator-Chaplain. 'For this. For the arena.'

'Without cooperation, I am certain that we would all be dead,' Balthus said plainly. 'Emperor knows we have both lost brothers. But I take your hand anyway.' The Interrogator-Chaplain took Krom's gauntlet and the Space Marines shook on their shared deliverance.

'Hopefully,' Krom said, looking up at the dust-streaked heavens, 'we would have made our primarchs proud.'

Balthus nodded slowly.

'When our brothers arrive,' the Dark Angel said, 'I fear our truce will come to an end.'

'Yes,' Krom agreed.

'For what our legions could never see,' the Interrogator-Chaplain said, 'was that the Lion and the Wolf were so similar in their differences. It is a blindness and burden that their sons bear to this day.'

'Aye,' Krom said, peering up into the blackness of the void. 'A darkness indeed.'

'Yes,' Balthus said. 'The darkness of Angels.'

Rob Sanders

PART SIX

THE WOLF WITHIN

An ornament hanging silently in the void, the Space Marines strike cruiser took station above the tiny world of Skarapaz XVIII.

'It's the High Priest,' Sergeant Beoric Winterfang announced, identifying the vessel from its rugged outline. Still recovering from his injuries, the sergeant held his shattered ribs as he spoke. It was painful, but he did not let on. 'Ulrik is here. Grandfather Lupus has come for us.'

Krom Dragongaze joined the sergeant out on the frozen rock of the unassuming world, sulphuric snow crunching beneath his boots. The plummeting temperatures would have killed any normal man. To the dark eldar who had made an outpost on the outlying world, it was no doubt a painful fetish. To Fenrisians, it was nothing. The mild chill of a world orbiting far from its five suns.

The pair watched as a Stormwolf gunship dropped from Ulrik's cruiser, the *Canis Pax*, and made its way across the surface of the rocky planet.

As the Stormwolf came in to land, Krom read the name *Rolling Thunder* emblazoned on the gunship's scarred side. It was a venerable craft and the veteran of many furious engagements. Putting down on the outpost's primitive launch pad, the gunship whipped up snow and grit about it. Walking up behind the Wolf Lord and his sergeant were Grundar Greymane and the surviving Space Wolves. Behind them were Interrogator-Chaplain Balthus of the Dark Angels and Brother Othniel, the Librarian who had sent word of their location to both their Dark Angels brethren and the Wolves stationed over Dactyla. It was the Sons of Russ, however, who had received the message and come for their kindred.

Grundar Greymane started the chant, which was picked up by Sergeant Beoric and the Space Wolves about him. Before long it became a roared mantra.

'Lupus, Lupus, Lupus...'

The transport compartment ramp lowered as the *Rolling Thunder* landed and cut its engines. A Space Marine emerged. It was not the High Priest, but the Wolf Guard Beregelt. He smiled at seeing his master.

'My lord,' the Space Wolf said. 'Ulrik the Slayer offers you greeting.'

'We are obliged to you and the venerable Slayer,' Krom said, as Ulrik's men filed out to assume a cordon about the gunship. Ulrik himself, a vision of doom in his wolf skull helm and furs, stepped off the ramp last, out onto the rock and snow.

'Lord Dragongaze,' Ulrik greeted Krom. 'Scion of the Sun Wolf – it is a pity we should meet in such a benighted place.'

'You are well met, wherever duty finds us,' Krom told him honestly.

Ulrik's optics settled on the Dark Angels behind.

Krom glanced back and forth between the two. 'This is...' he hesitated.

'Balthus,' the Dark Angel said. He gave the Slayer a slow nod, which the Wolf High Priest returned with suspicion.

'And Brother Othniel,' Krom said, 'who was responsible for determining our location and summoning aid.'

'Yes,' Ulrik said, his breath misting about him. He let the word hang there in the freezing air. 'You can't imagine how surprised we were to receive your message from an Angel of the First.'

'The Interrogator-Chaplain and Brother Othniel were instrumental in our escape from the xenos.'

'Yes,' Ulrik said again. 'You look like hell.'

Finally the Slayer stood aside, extending an arm towards his gunship. Sergeant Beoric and the surviving Drakeslayers filed between them and into the troop compartment. The Space Wolves were eager to get weaponry back into their hands and join their brothers under the High Priest's command.

'Interrogator-Chaplain,' Ulrik acknowledged, using the appropriate term of address, as the four of them mounted the ramp. The door closed on the dark eldar outpost and the tiny, frozen world of Skarapaz XVIII. The engines fired and the *Rolling Thunder* took off.

'Incoming transmission,' Beregelt told Ulrik. 'It's the shipmistress, my lord.'

'Shipmistress Asgir,' the Slayer said, changing vox channels. 'This is Ulrik. Our mission has been a success. We have extracted Lord Krom and his Drakeslayers. Prepare the ship. I want you to make way as soon as the gunship is aboard.'

'The *Canis Pax* stands ready to receive you, Master Ulrik,' the shipmistress voxed back.

As Balthus and Brother Othniel came up behind, Beregelt and another Wolf Guard took them by the plate of their forearms and slapped a pair of manacles on the two Dark Angels. The Interrogator-Chaplain did not resist, instead simply giving Ulrik the blank gaze of his skull-helm optics.

'Is that really necessary, High Priest?' Krom felt compelled to say. He had expected some friction, perhaps harsh words from the High Priest, who had lived long enough for the rift between their two Chapters to become a prejudice, but Krom had not anticipated such measures.

'The Angels fought side by side with us. They have already known with us the cold touch of bar and chain.'

'And they will know it again,' Ulrik the Slayer said, 'if they are to board the *Canis Pax* with us.'

The Space Marines in the troop compartment reached out for bars and supports as the Stormwolf banked. Before Krom could protest, the compartment voxhailer came to life above his head.

'High Priest,' a voice crackled across the voxhailer. It was the Space Wolf pilot, Rogan Bearsbane. 'I have targets.'

'Targets?' Ulrik said.

'Out here?' Krom echoed.

'The strike cruiser augurs told us nothing of this,' the Slayer said.

'They do now, my lord,' the pilot said. '*Canis Pax* reports the approach vector between us and the cruiser crowded with enemy vessels. They were cloaked by the dust and some kind of alien field technology.'

'Do you have numbers?' Krom asked.

'Hundreds of fighters and assault craft,' Rogan Bearsbane confirmed, as the Stormwolf swerved this way and that on the approach.

'And our foe?' Ulrik asked.

'Xenos pirates, High Priest.'

'Dark eldar,' Interrogator-Chaplain Balthus said.

'Too many for a raiding party,' Krom said. He looked at Ulrik. 'There must be larger vessels in the area – veiled, like the attack craft.'

The Slayer reached up and clunked a thick switch on the voxhailer.

'*Canis Pax*, are you monitoring this?' the High Priest asked.

'Aye, my lord,' Shipmistress Asgir returned. 'We are awaiting your instructions.'

Krom gave the Slayer a grim look. His Drakeslayers had been dogged by misfortune. Now they had brought the same misfortune down on the High Priest and his venerable strike cruiser.

'Have the navigation officer plot his solutions and ready the warp engines for immersion,' Ulrik ordered.

'But, High Priest,' Asgir protested. 'We can't leave you behind.'

'You won't have to,' the Slayer insisted. 'Have the flight deck prepare for our arrival.'

'The enemy crowds the approach, my lord,' the pilot insisted, as Ulrik threw the vox switch back. 'They block our progress with their darkness.'

'We are the claw that tears its way through such darkness,' Ulrik the Slayer told him. 'We make way for the Emperor's light. Proceed.'

'Yes, my lord.'

Krom held on as the *Rolling Thunder* accelerated away. He heard the boom of harpoons and grapnels smashing against the gunship's armoured hull as the dark eldar craft attempted to gain purchase. He looked up as thick spiked chains rattled cacophonously across the top of the Stormwolf.

Krom felt the gunship swerve suddenly to avoid a collision, pull up and then plunge into a further acceleration. Balthus stumbled back a little, his manacled gauntlets struggling to find anchorage on the compartment wall. Ulrik watched the Dark Angel, his optics burning bright, while the Space Wolves assigned to watch over him stuck close like a shadow. Krom felt the gunship's skyhammer missile launcher fire again and again, before hearing the whoosh of detonations and a prang of debris wash across the hull. The explosions were followed by the searing blast of lascannons, underscored by the rhythmic chatter of heavy bolters. Krom marvelled at the number of targets the gunship crew were contending with. Rogan Bearsbane had not been exaggerating. The *Rolling Thunder* was punching its way through a veritable swarm of twisted dark eldar ships. Krom heard the rattle of heavy grade splinter fire shattering its way across the gunship.

'Prepare for impact,' the Space Wolf pilot called across the vox.

Krom readied himself. Everyone inside the compartment lurched forward as the *Rolling Thunder* smashed through the blizzard of dark eldar fighters and boarding craft. A shockwave passed down the superstructure of the gunship from the armoured prow to the engine columns. Space Wolves were knocked forward, their mag-locked boots clunking to new anchorage. Even Ulrik staggered, and the Dark Angels were forced to steady themselves as best they could with their manacled hands. Alarms and klaxons fired in the compartment, indicating the collision.

'Report!' the Slayer barked into the wall vox.

'The *Rolling Thunder* is clear,' Rogan Bearsbane confirmed. 'But the enemy intends to pursue.'

'Prepare for evasive manoeuvres, on the shipmistress' mark,' Ulrik said as the Stormwolf accelerated again. The Slayer changed channels. Shipmistress?'

'Standing by, my lord,' Asgir replied.

'Load and prime your weaponry,' Ulrik said. 'We have company. I want you to welcome them with the primarch's own thunder. Do you understand?'

'Yes, my lord. Understood,' Asgir said.

Krom moved up amongst his surviving Drakeslayers, checking in with his brothers. The blood and filth on their faces and the sorry state of their plate told him how much they had suffered. They were not beaten, however. The arrival of their brother Wolves had re-energised Krom's men. As he moved through them they returned his enquires with an obedient eagerness. In the dark eldar arena they had been cornered animals: tormented and caged. Now, back among the ranks of Russ' own, their eyes glinted with a predacious pack mentality. Their score with the dark eldar would not be settled with bolt and blade, however. The xenos challenge would be answered in fire and thunder.

Krom felt forces tear at him as the *Rolling Thunder* banked sharply to avoid streams of dark energy from pursuing fighters. The Wolf Lord could only imagine the swarm of dark eldar ships pursuing them. Vehicles of spike, blade and serration, trailing chains and razored anchors. Slave ships laden with miserable specimens forced to fight. Torture craft brimming with dark eldar warriors.

'*Rolling Thunder*,' Shipmistress Asgir said, her voice intruding on the compartment from the open voxhailer. 'Cannons in range. You are cleared to leave your plane of approach and enact evasive manoeuvres.'

Krom felt the Stormwolf ascend. Already blasting through the void at maximum speed, the pilot put the gunship into a steep and sudden climb.

'You are cleared to fire, *Canis Pax*,' Ulrik told Asgir.

'Very good, my lord,' the shipmistress answered before the vox communicated the ear-splitting boom of the strike cruiser's cannonry firing in monstrous unison. The Space Wolves in the compartment added their roaring cheers to the firepower, willing the pursuing swarm of dark eldar craft to be decimated.

'Status?' Ulrik demanded.

'The enemy have sustained catastrophic losses, my lord,' the shipmistress said, 'but so great are their number that their pursuit continues.'

'Shall we never be rid of this alien scum?' Krom rumbled.

'I'm priming the gundecks for another broadside,' the shipmistress told him, but the Slayer seemed to have lost interest.

'Belay that,' the High Priest ordered. 'One day the Wolves will return and raze the dark place that spawned these foul xenos to the ground, but today our escape must be clean and complete. Have the flight decks cleared for a high-speed landing. Make way, Shipmistress. I want my ship on a translation approach by the time we arrive.'

'I await you on the bridge, my lord,' Shipmistress Asgir said.

'Rogan, take us in,' Ulrik commanded.

The compartment rolled to one side as the *Rolling Thunder* changed coursed. Krom held onto the section wall. Firing its mighty sub-light engines, the *Canis Pax* pulled away, forcing the gunship, and presumably the pursuing pirates, to change the angle of their approach to meet the moving strike cruiser. The voxhailer crackled with the pilot's countdown of the reducing distance.

'Brace for impact!' Rogan Bearsbane said finally. Krom put himself behind the Dark Angels to prevent them falling back. He saw that Ulrik noticed this gesture, although the High Priest said nothing. Krom felt the gunship bounce beneath his mag-locked boots. The pilot had brought the *Rolling Thunder* in at speed and on her armoured belly to save the landing gears. A horrific shearing sound passed through the compartment as the gunship skidded across the flight deck, leaving behind a shower of sparks. Krom prepared himself for the impact, but it never came. The gunship drew to a soft halt, lamps inside the compartment flashing. The ramp slowly lowered to the deck.

As Ulrik and his Space Marines filed out, Krom hit the stud on the voxhailer.

'My compliments, brother,' he told Rogan Bearsbane, before exiting with his Drakeslayers.

It felt good to be back on the void-chilled iron of a Space Wolf deck. It was only now, however, that Krom could truly appreciate what the Space Wolves had passed through. Krom beheld the swarm of dark eldar craft. Like an ink stain spreading across vellum, the dark eldar approached through the nebulous dust of the system – the obscurity in which they had lain hidden. Krom turned to see Ulrik behind him, taking in the dread spectacle. Interrogator-Chaplain Balthus and Brother Othniel were with them, under guard. The Slayer turned to leave, heading for the bridge. There was no time to lose.

'Bridge, this is Ulrik,' he said into his helmet vox. 'Get us out of here. All I want these xenos wretches to see is the blaze of our engines until they can see it no more.'

'Understood, High Priest,' Asgir returned.

'With me, Lord Dragongaze,' Ulrik said. 'Bring your prisoners.'

Krom bit back a snarl. He looked at Balthus and Brother Othniel and the Space Wolf guard that the High Priest had put on them.

'This way, Interrogator-Chaplain,' Krom said, leading them off the flight deck. Looking to Beoric Winterfang, he added, 'Sergeant, get yourself and our Drakeslayers to the Apothecarion.'

'And you, my lord,' Grundar Greymane said, for indeed, Krom was a mess.

'I will be along shortly,' the Wolf Lord said. 'In the event of a boarding action, you should be where you are most needed: defending this ship.'

As the mighty *Canis Pax* made its manoeuvres, Krom accompanied Ulrik and the Dark Angels to the strike cruiser's command deck. The danger Krom had brought upon the High Priest and his ship became ever more apparent on the bridge, where reverse lancet screens revealed black tendrils of smaller craft reaching out for the *Canis Pax* like a monster of the deep. As the strike cruiser completed its turn, the shipmistress ordered the warp engines primed.

Ulrik growled to himself as the blaze of a full burn torched countless vanguard fighters and alien boarders intent on being the first to reach the *Canis Pax*'s hull. With the rumble of engines passing through the deck, both Space Wolves and Dark Angels watched as the dark cloud of raiders receded, the xenos pursuit craft no match for the colossal engine columns of the Spaces Wolves strike cruiser.

'Forward screens,' Shipmistress Asgir called as deck serfs took the *Canis Pax* at full speed towards the system's Mandeville point. The bridge lancet screens admitted the bottomless glory of the void. The bridge lamps flickered. Runebanks and command deck cogitators faded for a moment and tripped in their workings, before returning to functionality. Deck serfs and servitors began calling out warnings as their instrumentation fed them new data. The shipmistress moved down the line of machines, checking the readings for herself.

Krom didn't need the *Canis Pax*'s augurs and scanners. Standing with Ulrik, he could see the three vessels growing on the forward screen. The ships surfaced from the warp, piercing the static super storm of a dimensional transference. The opening bled colour as an agitation of alternate realities rubbed against one another. Even prow on, coming straight at the *Canis Pax*, Krom could make out the belligerence of Adeptus Astartes cruisers, the vessels smashing back into reality. The noble green of the hull was unmistakable. They were the proud vessels of the First Legion.

Ulrik the Slayer snarled.

'Strike cruisers, my lord,' Shipmistress Asgir reported. 'They are arming their prow weaponry.'

Krom turned, but Ulrik was fast, even for a Space Wolf of half his age. The High Priest had grabbed Interrogator-Chaplain Balthus by his robes and slammed him back into the command deck wall. Even the Space Wolves guarding the Dark Angel were surprised at the sudden violence of Ulrik's movements.

'A little surprise for us, Interrogator-Chaplain?' the Slayer said, their skull helms almost touching.

'You seem surprised,' Balthus replied evenly.

'Ulrik,' Krom called, grabbing both by the arms, trying to prise them apart.

'Do you know why they call them *Interrogator*-Chaplains?' Ulrik asked Krom.

'Ulrik...' Krom said.

'They judge and are judged,' the High Priest spat. 'They are happy to keep their secrets while they expose the secrets of others.'

'And I'm sure you have plenty,' the Interrogator-Chaplain intoned.

'My lord, we must act,' Shipmistress Asgir warned. Krom Dragongaze feared what the Slayer's next order would be.

'Intensify forward shields,' Ulrik barked, his blood-bright optics burning into Brother Balthus, 'and ready the prow cannon. We shall end this before it begins.'

'Ulrik, don't,' Krom said.

'First blood shall be ours, brother,' Ulrik told Krom before looking back at the Dark Angel. 'For 'tis a dangerous thing to corner a wolf...'

It was too late, however. In that moment, looking through the lancet screens, Krom knew that he had been wrong. He saw the flash of the vessels' prow cannons, engaging in unison.

'The Dark Angels are firing,' Shipmistress Asgir confirmed from her augurbanks and cogitator.

Krom stared at Interrogator-Chaplain Balthus in disbelief.

'Fire!' Ulrik the Slayer roared. Letting go of Balthus, he clasped his gauntlets around the pulpit rail, projecting his fury at the attacking Dark Angel vessels on the lancet screens.

Krom Dragongaze prepared for impact. Fired upon by three Dark Angel strike cruisers, the *Canis Pax* was about to take an incredible hit. The Space Wolves ship could even be destroyed. With the Wolf High Priest bellowing orders across the command deck, Krom grabbed Brother Balthus from where Ulrik had abandoned him. Snatching the Interrogator-Chaplain by the robes, Krom held him against the bridge wall. Something didn't seem quite right to Krom, however. Like a scent out of place or a too-easy kill, the attack simply didn't make sense. The Dark Angels seemed to know Balthus was on board and yet they would fire on the ship carrying him.

Krom grabbed for anchorage on the bridge wall and engaged the magnetic soles of his boots. The blasts rocketing away from the three strike cruisers converged upon the *Canis Pax*. They would hit any second.

'Prepare for impact,' Shipmistress Asgir called to her command deck, clutching the pulpit rail near her command throne.

But the impact never came. The *Canis Pax* didn't buck or shake. Wiring didn't cascade from the ceiling or flame roll through the section. Deck serfs and servitors were not knocked from their consoles and Space Wolves did not rage at the mendacious Angels.

A light rumble went through the strike cruiser's superstructure as the blasts rocketed down the length of the *Canis Pax*. Ulrik stared at Asgir and then about the command deck.

'They missed,' the shipmistress said.

'Not likely,' Krom said.

'Aft feeds,' Ulrik barked.

With a sizzle of static, Asgir had a deck serf change the lancet screens to a pict-feed of the strike cruiser's rear. Magma bomb warheads streaked behind the *Canis Pax*, and they did indeed appear to have missed.

But then their true target revealed itself. From amid the swarm of dark eldar fighters and assault craft the *Canis Pax* had left in its wake, three larger vessels were pursuing them. They had managed to avoid the *Canis Pax*'s augur arrays and pict feeds by using some kind of exotic field technology to obscure their presence, but now they were shedding their ambush shielding.

Firing upon the pursuing shadows, the Dark Angel strike cruisers had turned the disguised torture ships into crackling tempests of erupting destruction. Krom got the brief impression of graceful, spindly craft – all blade-vanes and willowy darkness. One moment the piratical cruisers were stealthily moving up behind the *Canis Pax*, like great black scorpions of the void ready to strike – the next they were a chain reaction of ghostly explosions. As the ships detonated with alien energies, the shattered architecture flew in all directions, like a primed grenade of wicked, gargantuan shrapnel.

The bridge was silent. Krom looked to Brother Balthus, who gave him an emotionless stare. The Wolf Lord released his hold on the Interrogator-Chaplain.

'Ulrik,' Krom said, when no one else spoke. The Slayer put up his gauntleted hand.

'Screens,' Ulrik growled. The lancet screens returned the bridge to a view of the closing Dark Angel cruisers. The *Canis Pax* had struck the centre vessel with a blast of its own, turning the starboard sections of the dark green cruiser into a battle-scarred mess of mangled architecture and rupturing detonations. Ulrik ordered, 'Open a channel with the Dark Angel cruisers.'

'Which one?' Shipmistress Asgir asked.

'Any bloody one,' Ulrik said. 'And be lively about it.'

'Balthus,' Krom said. There was necessity in the Wolf Lord's voice. The situation had to be salvaged. The Emperor's Angels had fired upon one another. Damage had been done. Lives had been lost. The appearance of treachery once more dogged the Adeptus Astartes. Krom would not allow such misfortune to escalate. 'Interrogator-Chaplain, please.'

When Balthus spoke, his words were heavy and cold, like the pitted steel of an ancient weapon. He pointed with a ceramite finger.

'The *Calibos*,' he said, identifying one of the vessels. 'The ship you opened fire on is the *Semper Fortis*. Mine is the *Repentance*.'

'Channel open,' Asgir reported.

'*Repentance*, this is the *Canis Pax*,' Ulrik said. 'Please respond.'

Static proceeded from the bridge voxhailers.

'*Repentance*,' the Slayer pressed, 'I am Ulrik, High Priest of the Space Wolves. Your flotilla has sustained damage at my hand, but your destruction was not our intent. The galaxy is broad and wide and the mistakes made within its borders are many. This is one such mistake. We thought we were under attack and responded, as any of the Emperor's blood is engineered to do. We seek parley to repair the damage we have done and atone for the offence committed. Please respond.'

Once more the Space Wolves' patience was rewarded with static. All the while the Dark Angels vessels grew larger in the lancet screens. Krom turned on Brother Balthus.

'Tell them,' the Wolf Lord insisted.

The Interrogator-Chaplain, however, said nothing.

'We have two of your brothers among our number,' Ulrik said, the annoyance obvious in his aged voice. 'A Chaplain and a Librarian that we should like to return to you.'

Krom detected it first. Something in the air. A heat without temperature. The sizzle of scorched reality.

'Teleporter signatures!' Shipmistress Asgir called out. While the Space Wolves had been concerning themselves with making contact, the Dark Angels had simply transported themselves aboard. A lead mist bled into manifestation on the command deck. Shapes in bone white terminator armour appeared on the bridge. Boltguns were primed as the Dark Angels peered down barrels and muzzles at their Space Wolf targets. The Space Wolves on the bridge, in turn, thrust their own weapons with ferocity and shock at the armoured interlopers.

Krom marvelled at the perfect execution of the boarding. He grabbed Brother Balthus once more by the filthy material of his robes and pulled them apart to reveal a teleporter homer on the Interrogator-Chaplain's belt. Balthus must have had it on him the whole time.

Krom snarled, to himself rather than Balthus, but that didn't stop a Dark Angel officer thudding the muzzle of his bolt pistol into Krom's temple.

Balthus shrugged off the Space Wolf's grasp, straightening his robes.

'It doesn't have to be this way,' Krom said, as Balthus moved through the stand-off, uncaring of the boltguns and furious glares being cast across the command deck.

'Angels are dead, Wolf,' the officer hissed through his helmet's vox-grille.

'We have all lost brothers to the desperation of these shared circumstances,' Krom said.

'We share nothing,' Brother Balthus said.

'But we could,' Ulrik suggested quietly. He stared at the Interrogator-Chaplain. 'We have worked side by side in brotherly accord against a common foe.'

'You opened fire upon our vessels,' the Dark Angels officer said, his words sharp like the blade that sat in the scabbard on his belt.

'We thought we were under attack,' Krom said.

'You were,' Balthus told him, 'but not by warriors of the First.'

'Forgive me,' Ulrik the Slayer said. The word seemed unnatural proceeding from the cracked lips of such a venerable Space Wolf. 'Is that not what you are empowered to do, Interrogator-Chaplain? Forgive me. For it was my vessel that opened fire upon your own. My order that authorised that attack. Forgive the blunt words of diplomacy, that catch on the sharpness of my teeth and are an ill-fit for the mouth from which they come. Forgive one, like you, of the Emperor's blood – who wishes a brotherly alliance out here, where the void is empty and humanity's foes myriad. Accept a mistake for what it is and together we shall lay your kindred to rest.'

Krom looked from the High Priest to the Interrogator-Chaplain. Balthus had stopped wandering across the bridge and was now staring out through the screens at the Dark Angel ships holding the *Canis Pax* in their sights.

'Interrogator-Chaplain–' the Dark Angels officer began.

'We are Adeptus Astartes all,' Krom interrupted. 'We have all come to this miserable corner of the galaxy on the Emperor's business.'

Balthus turned to face them. He seemed to have reached a decision.

'Very well. I seek a traitor of the Alpha Legion,' the Interrogator-Chaplain began. 'He has escaped from our custody and is to be punished for his many crimes – but first we have to find him, and that task has proven... challenging.'

'We seek someone too,' Ulrik said. 'The Great Wolf. We hunt for him as he hunts for our Lord Russ. I know that in the past our fathers have not always seen eye to eye. I know that in the stormy present our Chapters have had precious little upon which to build brotherly love. I would ask you, Interrogator-Chaplain, to allow for a future in which our two Chapters work together for the accomplishment of separate deeds. Allow the Space Wolves, in recognition of the losses you have suffered at our hand, to hunt down your quarry with you. In turn, permit us to learn what we can of our lost leader from this transgressor – for the arrival of the Great Wolf with his warrior host in this wretched region of space will not have gone unnoticed.'

For the longest time, the Interrogator-Chaplain did not speak.

'Stand down,' he told his Dark Angels finally. The officer hesitated before re-holstering his pistol. The barrels of aimed boltguns drifted slowly towards the floor before the chaplain's orders were conveyed to the *Calibos*, the *Semper Fortis* and the *Repentance*. Balthus nodded to Krom and then to Ulrik, the Wolf Lord and High Priest returning the solemn acceptance. 'Once more,' Balthus told them, 'the galaxy shall witness the sons of the Lion and the Wolf hunting together.'

Krom could feel the lightness of his steps. It was welcome. His injuries were still healing and his artificer plate had only benefitted from the most basic of repairs. As he ran the suit still rattled about him and his armoured boots pounded the marble underfoot to shattered stone. On the low-gravity world of Stratovass Ultra, however, his plate weighed significantly less than it did on Fenris, or aboard the *Canis Pax*.

The Blood Claws of Squad Greymane ran beside him with Grundar following, a ravenous pack of Fenrisian wolves snapping and seething on adamantium chains. The beasts had the scent and were leading the Space Wolves through the mighty spirehalls and palatial pinnacles of Eyriax – the capital hive city of Stratovass Ultra.

Interrogator-Chaplain Balthus had brought them there on the trail of the Alpha Legionnaire, Sathar the Undone. The *Ironpelt* had followed the *Canis Pax* to this world from Dactyla. Ulrik the Slayer and Sergeant Beoric Winterfang had remained with the Space Wolves vessels, while Brother Othniel and the other Dark Angels had returned to the *Repentance*. The strike cruisers, both Space Wolf and Dark Angel, held station high above the hive world. Meanwhile, Krom had unleashed his Fenrisian beasts and the neophytes of his Drakeslayers on the world's surface. With the Interrogator-Chaplain's gathered intelligence and the hunter's instincts of the Space Wolves, Krom was confident that they would catch Sathar the Undone.

Planetfall had taken them to the rusted dunes of Stratovass. The traitor's scent had led them through the stilt shanties in the capital hive's towering shadow. The Space Wolves had followed Sathar up through the Chartist dry docks, where the skeletal frameworks of merchant freighters, haulage brigs and tenders were under construction.

Krom had got his first look at their quarry in the nest of cloud-swathed spires that reached up from the surface of Stratovass like a spiked crown. Sathar was a broad, imposing figure in dark armour and robes, his face lost in a hood. Great bat-like wings erupted from the space between his backplate and pack, but it was impossible to tell whether they were real appendages or a theatrical affectation. Carrying the broad blade of a sword that was almost as tall as him, Sathar was fleeing through the vaulted halls and palaces of the spires. Krom caught sight of him on one of the myriad walkways extending between the nest of towers, moments before he disappeared in the clouds.

Without the pack of wolves and the keen senses of the indefatigable Blood Claws, they would have lost the traitor, since the clouds of Stratovass didn't only bury the palace towers in a beautiful haze but manifested within the spirehalls, high corridors and great chambers.

As the wolf pack snaggled and snarled their way through the luxurious accommodations, their claws tore up rugs and flagstones. Grundar Greymane let the beasts have their head and run on their adamantium chains. His Blood Claws, young and short of hair, whiskers and fangs, moved through the palaces with a feral grace. In the low gravity, the slick glide of their movements took them over ornate furniture, through stained-glass windows and up grand staircases with ease. They were the headstrong Sons of Russ and the Emperor's genekin, with nothing to fear from even the most powerful of the hiveworld's inhabitants. Heavy-set, with a lifetime's worth of muscle and experience, Grundar and his Wolf Lord were slower and more measured in their movements, with Brother Balthus in his fresh, streaming robes coming up behind.

'Grundar,' Krom said. 'Bring him down.'

The Drakeslayers were so close. They had hunted the renegade up through the hive. Cornering him in the pinnacle palaces, the Space Wolves had given their quarry nowhere to go. Krom could not risk the possibility of the Legionnaire reaching a launch pad or pick-up from a terrace balcony.

At his Wolf Lord's order, Grundar Greymane released one of his Fenrisian beasts. The wolf surged away from the pack, finally at liberty to run its prey down. The Space Wolves followed the creature as it weaved through pillars, bounded balustrades and made short work of hall expanses. It disappeared into the mists hanging in the palace chambers but its fellow beasts, still on Grundar's chains, showed the way.

Suddenly Krom heard the most awful sound. The shriek of a beast in agony and shock, followed by a dismal moan of death that echoed perversely through the misted chambers. It wasn't long before the Blood Claws found the wolf. It had been skewered through the jaws and the length of its body, by what Krom could only imagine was the Chaos Space Marine's monstrous blade. Striding through the mist-cloaked antechamber, Krom found himself outside on a platform. Three bridgeways, made of chain and lightweight metal planking, spanned the gap between the palace tower they were in and the other spires reaching up out of the clouds. The jangling walkways themselves were lost in the haze.

Behind him, Grundar's wolves snapped and spat, while the Blood Claws caught their breath and awaited orders. Laying his gauntlet on the chains of one bridge and then the others, Krom felt for the tremble and bounce of a recent crossing.

'This one,' the Wolf Lord said. A Blood Claw with a mane of red hair and side whiskers went to follow but Krom put his hand up. Sending a jangle through the chain walkway with his gauntlet, the Wolf Lord waited. He looked at Brother Balthus, who gave a nod of approval. A sharp clang cut through the cloudy obscurity in which the hive spires were lost. The sound of metal upon metal. Krom stepped back, the chain feeling suddenly loose in his grip. He listened for the sound of the falling walkway, the tangle of metal and chain cut away by Sathar the Undone on the other side. The traitor had waited for them, feeling for their crossing as Krom had done before intending to send the Wolves plummeting to their deaths. Stratovass Ultra was a low gravity world but a fall from the towering hive spires of the Eyriax would still mean certain death.

Krom studied the other two walkways. They vanished into the mist, so he could not be sure where they led. He turned to Balthus.

'You've pursued this traitor before,' Krom said to him. 'What is the best course of action?'

'We'll separate and entrap him,' Balthus said. 'I'll go this way.' He indicated the walkway on the right. 'You take your Wolves by the other route. We shall cut him off and attack from all sides.'

Krom nodded, and without another word Balthus set off across the jangling walkway. He was quickly swallowed by the looming mist.

Krom moved over to a Blood Claw called Skvaldigar Frostfang, an eager Drakeslayer whose scalp was a nest of short braids. He knew Skvaldigar to be savage and hungry for promotion.

'Brother,' Krom said, 'do you think you and your Claws can make that jump?'

Skvaldigar grinned, showing his needle teeth.

'Or we'll die trying,' the Blood Claw said.

'Bring me that traitor,' Krom ordered. 'Alive.'

It was the Wolves' best chance to corner him. The Blood Claws would attempt to jump across to the mist-wreathed spire while Krom, Grundar and the Fenrisian beast pack traversed the chain walkways between their tower and another. From there they could cross back to cut their quarry off.

'Grundar, with me.'

Krom led the way towards another chain walkway. The jangling bridge drooped between the tower and the central spire. Grundar reached the light metal of the planks first, dragged on by the ferocious insistence of the wolf pack.

Looking back, Krom could see the hazy silhouettes of the Blood Claws leaping from the spire. In the low gravity of the hive world, their bounding steps took them far across the open space between the towers of the Eyriax. Krom lost the Blood Claws as they dropped through the clouds. The Wolf Lord knew that as the Space Wolves hit the tower lower down they would sink their gauntlets into the elaborate architecture and latch on. Then they would scramble up the side of the spire and surprise Sathar the Unbound from below.

Krom and Grundar ran, the wolves snapping ahead of them on adamantium chains. The walkway led them up onto another spire platform and in through the glorious, gothic antechambers of the planetary governor's palace. The outlying spires through which the Space Wolves had worked their way had been largely deserted. The ruling elite of the tower top villas and palaces had abandoned the musty grandeur of their homes to pillaging servants and exotic pets left to pick over the food of their banquet tables.

Before they had reached these ostentatious dwellings, Krom and his Drakeslayers had moved up through the industrial sectors and rancid habs of the capital hive. There the Space Wolves had encountered mayhem. Sectors in full riot. Manufactorums ablaze. Hivers screaming for lost friends and family members. The city was alive with reports of stalking monsters, things of claw and fury that tore hivers apart. As Krom and his Drakeslayers moved up through the levels in pursuit of Sathar, the Space Wolves received no warm welcome. Workers in rubber suits and underworld wretches in rags and tattoos ran from the sight of the Space Wolves in their imposing grey plate. Grundar had questioned such behaviour but Krom had put the reaction down to the presence of the Chaos Space Marine and his compatriots.

The havoc that afflicted the capital hive had not been restricted to the riots and butchery of the underhive and mid-levels. The villas and palaces of the high and the mighty had been affected also. Unlike the hivers far below them, the planetary governor of Stratovass Ultra and his inbred kindred could leave and seek sanctuary in nearby hives. As Krom moved through the decimated door of a banquet hall, he got a taste of what the hive nobility had left behind.

As the two Space Wolves moved through the governor's palace with its dust-thick halls and ghastly décor, Krom's nose detected the coppery tang of death on the air, the unmistakable smell of slaughter. Grundar's wolves picked up on it also, dragging him along on their unbreakable chains.

The air in the hall was thick with a red mist. Walls, paintings and tapestries were splattered with gore. The floor was slick with blood, while mounds of bodies and body parts sat like small islands in a sea of gore. Rusted chains criss-crossed the floor, with manacles still attached to hands and arms that were no longer connected to torsos. Krom was no stranger to slaughter, much at his own hand. He was a Space Wolf, one of the Emperor's executioners. But this was something else. The huge hall had been full of people. They had not been killed out of necessity with bolt and blade. They had not even been sacrificed with cultish ceremony. They had been savaged. Torn limb from limb. The chamber had the feeling of an agriworld abattoir: the rawness of blood and fresh meat was overpowering. Krom licked his dry lips. He tasted the death that waited for him there.

'Grundar,' Krom said as the wolf pack nuzzled their way around the piles of mutilated corpses and across the bloody expanse of the banquet hall floor. Grundar Greymane looked about him.

'The doors were locked and reinforced from the outside,' the Space Wolf said, confirming what Krom was thinking. He cast his gaze across the bodies in their ragged, gore-soaked clothing. 'The chains. Hivers imprisoned in the palace halls. Some kind of ritual perhaps?'

Krom had encountered many false prophets and Chaos cults on myriad doomed worlds. He had interrupted dread ceremonies where bloody sacrifices had been used to bring forth monstrosities from the beyond. This did not seem to match those experiences.

'Where's the paraphernalia? The faithless heretics who would benefit from such dark arts?' Krom asked.

Grundar hauled back on the chains of the drooling wolves and moved a dismembered arm over with the tip of his boot. Mind-aching symbols and scripture were carved into the skin of the ragged limb.

'Perhaps they brought forth an abomination that wreaked havoc upon those that summoned it,' Grundar hypothesised.

Krom took in the slaughter.

'No,' the Wolf Lord said finally. 'The doors were barred from the outside. Whether these wretches were meant for sacrifice or not, I don't think they got that far. No summoning took place. Something else got to them first.'

'You can bet the Interrogator-Chaplain's quarry or his accursed allies are behind this,' Grundar said, before his wolves began pulling on their chains and barking furiously. Their sudden savagery was turned on the end of the chamber where the hall opened up into a balconied area where banqueters would have once talked and relaxed after their meals.

'My lord,' Grundar said, responding to the animals' ire.

Krom already had his bolt pistol clutched in one grey gauntlet. At the wolves' warning, he quickly drew Wyrmclaw. The glazed blades of the frost axe reflected the red of its bloody surroundings.

Suddenly the light from the balcony died. An armoured figure had landed, a silhouette against the bleak mist, the figure's rippling cloak and bat's wings filling the opening. It was the Interrogator-Chaplain's quarry: Sathar the Undone, the heretic Krom and his Drakeslayers had hunted up through the Eyriax hive. The traitor had embraced his darkness indeed. As a silhouette he cut a figure of ragged ruin. Sathar bled danger and a rank-hearted confidence into the air. His plate was a thing of twisted beauty, buried in a hood and robes that cloaked the monster's dread presence.

Grundar and Krom's pistols came up as snarls crossed their faces.

'Stay where you are,' Grundar Greymane barked as he struggled to hold back the ravenous pack on their adamantium chains, 'or I'll blow you in half.'

Like Sathar, Krom knew this to be an empty threat. They were to hunt down and take the traitor alive for Brother Balthus. Even to the Space Wolves, the Chaos Space Marine was much more valuable alive. He might be able to tell them much of the Great Wolf's location and activities in this dismal corner of the galaxy.

The traitor retracted his wings and rose from his landing crouch. In his hands he held the unwieldy length of a crusader's blade. With dark confidence, Sathar walked towards them. Grundar leaned into his aim.

'I mean it,' the Space Wolf told him through gritted teeth.

Krom stared at Sathar the Undone as he entered the hall. Turning from silhouette to an advancing menace, the Wolf Lord could see that their quarry was much twisted by Chaos. His cloak was a withered patchwork of flayed skin, while his wings were in fact scaled like those of a mythological serpent.

Krom slipped his pistol back into its holster and laid a gauntlet on Grundar's arm, prompting the Space Wolf to lower his own weapon. Sathar took his imposing blade in two hands and began to move the length of the sword about him in practised movements. The Wolf Lord felt bile rise up the back of his throat. He wanted nothing more than to allow Grundar to blast the heretic back off the balcony or to cleave him in two himself with Wyrmclaw. The arrogant traitor had led them on a pointless chase. He had evaded the Blood Claws, who were perhaps still climbing up to intercept him. He must have eluded Brother Balthus, and now he had intercepted Grundar and Krom when they were attempting to do the very same thing to him.

Krom would make him pay for such hubris. He readied his frost axe, taking several experimental swings. Sathar the Undone needn't have arms or legs to repent his transgressions to Brother Balthus or provide the Space Wolves with information.

'So you are the wolf that's been snapping at my heels,' Sathar said, his voice like a snake's belly across the sands.

'And you are the traitorous wretch whose stench we have been tracking,' Krom returned.

'If Balthus has engaged the assistance of the VI Legion, then his standards must have fallen,' the traitor said.

'Speak not to me of who has fallen, heretic,' Krom growled. He tipped the head of his axe at the slaughter that surrounded them.

The accusation produced a nasty chuckle from Sathar the Undone.

'You think this was me?' he asked. 'I'm here to halt the progress of this mindless barbarity. That's why I left my brothers in waiting.'

The mounds of dead flesh either side of the Space Wolves began to tremble and collapse. Butchered torsos, heads and dismembered limbs tumbled down as the armoured figures hidden beneath rose. Krom turned and Grundar with him. The wolves went mad, snapping and drooling at the hidden warriors. Boltguns came up as the figures shrugged off the gore. The blue-green of their monstrous plate ran black with blood. Krom waved the blade of his axe from one foe to another, holding them in his sights.

'Drop it,' an Alpha Legionnaire hissed, stepping forward through the dead. Krom looked around at the Chaos Space Marines.

Sathar nodded at Krom.

'Do it, Wolf,' Sathar told him.

'You heard him,' Krom said to Grundar Greymane, as he placed Wyrmclaw carefully on the floor. 'Drop it.'

As Grundar released the chains of the beasts in his charge, the wolf pack surged away. Leaping in all directions, the wolves tore at the Alpha Legionnaires. Bolters thundered and the beasts of Fenris snarled. Wolves died, blasted back and torn apart by bolter fire. Others rattled their teeth and claws against cursed ceramite before being battered aside. Krom Dragongaze's reflexes were no less swift than the ferocious beasts. Grabbing Wyrmclaw, he brought the frost axe around with sudden violence, stepping over the body of a blasted wolf. Chopping down, he turned the boltgun of the Alpha Legionnaire who had issued him orders into a cascade of shattered parts. Grabbing the shaft of the axe, Krom pivoted the weapon around and smashed it into the warped detailing of the Legionnaire's faceplate. Following the turn around, Krom smashed the axe blade through the helm, leaving an arc of gore in its path.

Assailed by wolves on all sides, the Alpha Legionnaires sent bursts of fire wide. With streams of bolt rounds blazing through the bloody haze of the banquet hall, Grundar picked up his bolt pistol. Hammering bolts into the chest and faceplate of the nearest Legionnaires, the Space Wolf crouched below streams of gunfire meant to blow his head from his shoulders. A Chaos Space Marine grabbed him suddenly from behind, seizing him in an expert hold. The final bolt rounds of his pistol blasted into the marble of banquet hall pillars. Grundar saw a knife flash before him, the Legionnaire aiming to slice the Space Wolf's throat. Growling as much to himself as his attacker, Grundar fought like an animal, tearing at his foe's plate and arms. While the Alpha Legion warrior adapted his powered hold, moving with elegant determination between death-dealing techniques, Grundar simply relied upon the rage of the animal inside him.

Ripping and clawing at the Legionnaire with his gauntlets, Grundar turned within his enemy's grasp. Prising his arms free, the Space Wolf tore the serpent-styled helm from the Legionnaire's face. His dead reptilian eyes burned with some inner corruption. The Alpha Legionnaire benefitted from expert training and was a master of martial invention. He had an elongated lifetime of battle experience and the boon of some darkness at work within him. He could have killed Grundar a thousand different ways. Trapped in the Legionnaire's hold and with a blade slicing for his throat, the Space Wolf knew only one.

Instead of pulling away, Grundar lunged for the Legionnaire. Holding him by the warped stylisations of his breastplate, Grundar heaved him in close. Opening his mouth, his sharpened teeth glistening, the Space Wolf tore the Legionnaire's throat out with a single, disgusted bite. Allowing the Alpha Legion warrior to crash to his knees, Grundar stumbled back, spitting gore from his blood-spattered lips.

With the thunder of boltfire echoing about the hall, Krom smashed a blazing weapon aside with Wyrmclaw. Heaving the frost axe with the firing fibre bundles of his powered plate, the Wolf Lord chopped down through a Legionnaire's chest. Turning with lupine grace, Krom dodged the furious blast of a boltgun as another Legionnaire advanced with his weapon tucked into his pauldron. The frost axe came around, smashing the Chaos Space Marine's weapon from his hands. Whirling about, Krom buried the blade in the Alpha Legionnaire's head.

Krom ducked as a final Legionnaire came up behind to smash the butt of his boltgun down on the Space Wolf. Krom crashed down onto his armoured knees, dragging the axe and the corpse in which it was embedded with him. Savagely jabbing the axe hilt back, Krom cracked the plate of his attacker in the midriff. Pivoting on one knee, the Wolf Lord hacked at the Legionnaire's leg. The Chaos Space Marine dropped his weapon and reached down for the grievous wound but Krom completed the cut with another chop through the knee.

As the Alpha Legionnaire fell, Krom rose from the bloody floor. Staggering, he reached out for a pillar to steady himself. He saw Sathar the Undone swing the tapering length of his crusader sword, cutting one bounding wolf out of the air before splitting another in half. The keen blade slipped through the fur and lean Fenrisian meat, silencing the beast's roar. Krom continued where the animal had left off, a roar building in his chest. He pointed the blade of his frost axe at the traitor before pushing himself away from the pillar. Stomping his way into a run, with blood splashing about his footfalls, Krom launched himself at Sathar the Undone. Stamping up a mound of bodies, the Wolf Lord jumped – taking full advantage of the hive world's low gravity. Bringing the axe down on the renegade, Krom felt a bone-rattling jar pass through his body as Sathar brought up the length of his crusader blade to meet his blow.

The traitor heaved back at Krom, prompting the pair to circle each other with powered steps. The optics of Sathar's helm burned into the Space Wolf, while Krom returned the stare with the piercing gold of his eye. The Wolf Lord snarled his intention to annihilate his opponent while Sathar was calm, his exertions resulting in a helm-grille hiss. Simultaneously, they launched their attacks.

The differing fighting styles of the two combatants made for awkward and uneasy combat. Krom hacked and wheeled about with Wyrmclaw, attempting to rake through armour and slash his enemy to ribbons. It was savage and instinctive: the unleashing of the beast within. Sathar, conversely, moved with practised sweeps of his long blade. With a knightly martial elegance, he propelled the blade about him, or held it aloft to absorb the frost axe's savage blows. He thrust and stabbed with the length of the blade, using it like a spear to weave through Krom's defences. As the Space Wolf heaved, chopped and smashed at Sathar in a fury, the tapering tip of the renegade's blade punctured plate and flesh, striping the grey of the Wolf Lord's armour with the red leakage of fresh wounds.

Krom brought Wyrmclaw down on the Chaos Space Marine's blade and fancied the weapon creaked. Heaving down on the haft of the frost axe, the Wolf Lord leant in, baring his teeth at Sathar's faceplate. The traitor held him there, however, the crusader blade trapped between them. Pushing Krom back, Sathar whipped the weapon around with serpentine speed and determination. As Krom came straight back at him, the sword was ready – surging forward to skewer the Space Wolf. Krom was ready too. With blistering savagery, he backslashed the oncoming blade aside, smashing his axe blade through the weakened section of metal.

The crusader sword shattered, prompting Sathar the Undone to stagger back in surprise. Krom would not relent, however, and stamped out, burying the sole of his armoured boot in the traitor's gut. Krom heaved his axe over his head and down at Sathar, who just managed to get the remains of his blade and its crossguard between him and the descending Wyrmclaw. The two held each other there for a moment – still, like statues.

'No!' Grundar Greymane roared as a staccato of bolt rounds hammered into his Wolf Lord. The shock and surprise registered on Krom's snarling face almost immediately. He had taken the shot in his side, the pipes and lines of his armoured midriff a sparking mess. As his arms and plate faltered for a moment, he looked down to see the Alpha Legionnaire whose leg he had hacked off still on the floor. The Chaos Space Marine had reached for his boltgun and in agony aimed it up at Krom from the floor. The Legionnaire was dead seconds later as Grundar ran at him, bringing his boot down barbarically on the back of the Chaos Space Marine's head and snapping his neck.

The murderous strength behind Wyrmclaw was lost for a second and Sathar pushed the weapon back. It gave the renegade just enough room and opportunity to withdraw the wicked remnant of his blade and thrust it at the surprised Wolf Lord like a dagger.

The shattered, stabbing stump of the blade scraped the Wolf Lord's breastplate and would have pierced his hearts had it not been for Grundar Greymane's thundering advance. Stamping through the carnage of slain Legionnaires, butchered wolves and hiver corpses, Grundar hammered into Sathar. Getting a gauntlet to the traitor's armoured wrist, the Space Wolf interrupted the deadly advance of the shattered blade and tore it away from its path of murderous destruction. The Chaos Space Marine was knocked back by the Space Wolf cannoning into him and it was all Krom Dragongaze could do to clutch his bolt-blasted side and watch Grundar knock Sathar the Undone through the stone of the balcony balustrade. Seconds later the pair were gone, wrangling with each other in a death grip and falling from the edge.

Clutching the rawness of his injured side, Krom staggered over to the ruined balustrade and peered down through the clouds. He searched for Grundar Greymane and their sworn enemy but the clouds had swallowed them as they plummeted through the spire heights.

Out of the haze about the tower, Krom saw figures appear. Blood Claws, leaping from the opposing spire where they had failed to find Sathar the Undone. They clawed for purchase on the busy architecture of the palace walls, holding there for further orders as the remainder of their number sailed across the open space.

Bent double over the demolished balustrade and peering down over the edge of the balcony, Krom heard footsteps coming up behind. In agony, the Wolf Lord hauled himself up and around to meet the threat but found Interrogator-Chaplain Balthus working his way through the slaughter. The Dark Angel looked down at the bodies of the Chaos Space Marines.

'Where have you been?' Krom demanded.

'I was searching for him in the mist,' Balthus replied.

There was something in the Interrogator-Chaplain's tone that gave Krom pause. Balthus had proved himself honourable time and again, and yet... Krom could read nothing in the blank skull helm that stared back at him.

'Well, you were wasting your time looking out there,' Krom snarled.

'You had him?'

'Had him,' Krom confirmed, 'and lost him.'

As he approached, Balthus nodded down at Krom's stomach wound.

'You're injured,' the Dark Angel said.

'I'll live,' Krom assured him, looking over the balcony. He grunted. 'I'm not sure I can say the same for the traitor you hunt.'

Grundar Greymane tumbled down through the cloud. He clawed at his foe, tearing at his cloak of flayed flesh. They fell past the rushing blur of over-elaborate architecture. Stratovass Ultra might have been a low gravity world but it still *had* gravity – enough to drag the Space Wolf at increasing speed towards the splattering embrace of the rockcrete surface.

Suddenly, the whooshing obscurity of the cloud became a storm of whipping lines and cables. Cords snapped and lines slashed about Grundar's armoured form. As he hit the metal of a support line he abruptly stopped. Plate crumpled and the air was knocked out of his lungs. Falling to one side, the Space Wolf plummeted through a further net of cords and cables stretching between the palace tower and sub-spires.

Sathar the Undone was torn from his grasp, the traitor tangled in the lines. With the fingers of his gauntlet grasping for his enemy, Grundar plunged away. The irregular outline of the tower seemed to reach out for him: vanes, statues and balconies. He smashed down through the stone of an ornamental bridge and punched a hole through decorative banners advertising the ancient Houses of the Eyriax Hive.

The lines and wind-lashed banners did enough to break Grundar's fall that when he hit the roof of a sub-spire, the Space Wolf merely crashed through the crumbling tiles, bouncing off the metal bracings of the superstructure. With smashed plate and bones, Grundar rolled off the steep tower roof and once more found himself plummeting.

The fall was short-lived, however. With a grunt of agony, the Space Wolf hammered into the marble of a balcony floor. With the stone shattered beneath him like a tessellation, Grundar rolled onto his chest. He found it difficult to breathe, his black carapace and ribs broken.

The Space Wolf had fallen back into the central spire. He was confident of that. The balcony of another great hall – one of many in the labyrinthine grandeur of the hive palace. Blurred vision began to focus to a grim crispness. There was movement. A multitude in motion. Sound that hurt Grundar's sensitive ears. Groaning. Screaming. The horror of death, shrieked seconds before the fact. The Space Wolf's nose also picked out the pungency of sweat and fear. The sharp tang of blood spilled. The rawness of flesh ripped open.

The hall was a cacophony of panic and slaughter. Like the chambers above it was crowded with victims. They jangled with chains that prevented them from running. They fled in confusion and dread, each in their own direction before being torn back by the restrictions of their shackles. The whites of their eyes and the frantic futility of their movements told of their terror. The cultish symbols freshly carved into their hive-grimy flesh was evidence of the sacrificial horror to come.

Then Grundar heard it. Something harsh and half-remembered. A sound that called out to the animal part of him. The monstrous part of him. The part that was Russ. Like a tsunami of gore, blood fountained for the hall's high ceiling as unseen abominations moved through the sacrificial throng. Chains were slashed and victims snatched up before being thrown through the air. Heads spun off in whirls of blood.

Grundar imagined some of the horrors he had faced in his long service to the Allfather. Xenos abominations. Chaos Space Marines twisted into monstrosities. Daemonic entities crafted of infernal whim. As the slaughter moved towards Grundar, the Space Wolf tried his vox-link.

'Greymane to command,' he hissed with effort. 'Come in.'

The channel was silent. It was not a good sign. 'Greymane to command. Lord Dragongaze, receive.'

Like everything else about the suit of powered armour, the vox-link was smashed. Then he saw it. As a throng of terrified hivers were turned to chum before his eyes, an armoured figure ventured forth from the blood-bath. Grundar Greymane's hearts leapt at the sight of grey plate and the sigil of the wolf's head, proudly displayed on a gore-spattered pauldron. Hunched like some wild beast burdened by its own savage nature, the creature wore neither helm nor gauntlets. It was as if its plate was a remnant of a forgotten age, unable to contain the animal fury within it. Its hands were dripping grapnels of blood-matted fur and wicked claws. The thing's maw was crowded with blood-stained fangs and its facial hair slick with gore.

Grundar searched for some scintilla of humanity in its rage-bright eyes. Some flicker of nobility or recognition. He failed to find it. Grundar, however, recognised his brother-beast. By his grey plate, caked black with old gore. By the legionary sigils that still adorned its armour. By the curse that drove mind and flesh to acts of animal barbarism. By the features of Russ, worn like a mask over the rage of a monster unbound. Unbridled. Unstoppable.

It saw him. Grundar Greymane, Son of Russ and proud wolf of Fenris. Reflected in the burning urgency of the monstrosity's eyes, he was a victim, taunting the beast with breath and pulse. He was flesh to be torn with tooth and claw. Gore to be adorned. A thing to be savaged.

'Brother...' Grundar Greymane managed. He knew his killer. The Space Wolves knew them as the Wulfen. Lost brothers bearing the genetic curse that made them more beast than man. The sacrificial slaves that had been assembled in the palace of the planetary governor might have been intended for some bloody ceremony orchestrated by Sathar the Undone and the Alpha Legion. They had found their terrible end not at the edge of a heretic's blade or some monstrous abomination brought forth by the warp. No – the wretched hivers had come to know death sudden and savage, by fangs that slashed open their throats and claws that ripped through their torsos.

'Brother–'

It was too late. The Wulfen was upon him. Not one but several creatures. Tearing. Raging. Roaring. Grundar's smashed plate was nothing before their ferocity. His fraternal flesh was a site of frenzied butchery.

And then it was over. The horrific sound of his torso being ripped apart was gone, as was the thrash of jaws. The Wulfen were gone, launching themselves back into the terror and bedlam of the main massacre.

Grundar lay there. His face was awash with his own blood. His innards – mulched and shredded – decorated his savaged form. His mind faded. He drifted down into the darkness of encroaching death. The surrounding butchery became nothing as the Space Wolf was acquainted with the intimacy of his end.

'Greymane, this is command,' the Space Wolf's vox fizzled. It was Krom Dragongaze. 'Grundar, where are you?'

Grundar tried to speak. To form at least one word. A word with which to warn his Fenrisian brothers of the horror to come. To tell his Wolf Lord that Wulfen were there on Stratovass Ultra. 'Greymane, please respond.'

The mangled lips of the Space Wolf's slashed face could not form the sounds. The warning burned within Grundar's mind but his torn throat and his mouth full of blood would not answer. With such failure afflicting his shredded hearts and Krom's words in his ears, Grundar Greymane let the darkness take him.

C L Werner

PART SEVEN

SCENT OF A TRAITOR

The grizzled Wolf Scout leaned close to the wall, his nose half an inch from the grimy surface. His face scrunched back in a bestial grimace as his nostrils flared, taking in the manifold odours of the hive. Lopt Redtooth closed one eye as his mind identified the superfluous smells, separating them from the scent he was hunting for. His other eye, long ago replaced by a bionic mechanism, clicked and whirred as it kept the dimly lit corridor in focus.

Ulrik watched the scout work. Of all Krom's Drakeslayers, it was Lopt who was best suited to this task. He had the instincts of a thunderwolf when it came to following a trail, something more primal than skill and experience could bestow. He had honed his abilities tracking ice trolls through the black caverns beneath Asaheim, bringing back the scaly ears of the monsters as trophies. Unlike the wolves of Fenris, however, Lopt had the mind of a man, able to interpret what he smelled in ways beyond the capacity of any beast. This was why Ulrik had given the duty of following the trail to the scout instead of one of the mighty canines. In this task, intelligence would prove as vital as speed.

Lopt lifted a tiny tube of paper from the ground. It was only the most minute of fragments, crushed and burnt, further stained by the industrial grime that caked the walls of the alley. Ulrik could smell nothing but the smoky residue of charred plant fibres rising from the discarded lho-stick. The Wolf Scout, however, was able to pick through a maze of odours to find the scent hidden underneath.

'The same man,' Lopt said, his bionic eye still prowling the shadowy corridor. 'There's more fear to his scent now. I think he knows he's being hunted.'

Krom Dragongaze grinned at Lopt's words. 'If he knows he's being followed, he'll go to ground. He'll go where he feels safe.'

Beregelt stroked the fur of the great Fenrisian wolf at his side. He had taken charge of the beasts since their former master, Grundar, had been lost. 'Say the word, and Vangandyr will run the heretic down.' A low growl rattled at the back of the animal's throat, as though it caught the meaning of Beregelt's words and was eager for the hunt.

'Lopt's nose has brought us this far,' Krom said. 'I'd not offer him insult by letting Vangandyr steal his catch.'

Ulrik took the lho-stick from Lopt, turning it over in his armoured hand. There were a dozen Space Wolves ranged along the corridor, with many more spread out through the district. This region of the hive city was a labyrinth of maintenance shafts, service ducts, transport channels and load-paths used by the processing plants and factories to conduct raw materials from the ring of collection centres outside the hive. There was a confusion of walkways, alleys and sneak-tracks that squirmed their way between the hab-blocks and industrial complexes – tier upon tier of trails for the Space Wolves to prowl, rising in successive layers up into the spires some miles above. It was a lot of ground to cover. Formidable as the Drake-slayers were, Ulrik would have welcomed more help.

The Wolf Priest could sense the unease in Krom's words and knew the question the Wolf Lord wanted to ask. The Space Wolves had discovered the trail of their prey when they found the Traitor Space Marine's scent on some hive-serfs. Through Lopt, they had been able to track one of the menials away from the scene of one of the gruesome sacrifices that had been plaguing the hive.

If this hiver were indeed to lead them to the traitor, Sathar, then the Dark Angels would want to be there. After his trail had been lost three days ago, Interrogator-Chaplain Balthus had gone his own way, arguing that they stood a better chance of finding their quarry if they split up. Now that the Space Wolves had picked up this scent, it was Ulrik's duty to let the Chaplain know, but he hesitated.

It seemed that before his escape from their custody, Sathar had learned much about the Dark Angels and their tactics. Familiarity with his hunters was how the traitor had been able to elude the Dark Angels for so long. If Ulrik informed Balthus of the trail they were following then the Dark Angels would demand to lead the pursuit. The traitor would be ready for them and the hunt would be a failure. Ulrik had a duty to his allies, but he felt a greater duty to the Allfather to bring down this traitor. Of equal importance was the information Sathar might have – there was a good chance that he knew what fate had befallen Logan Grimnar.

Ulrik turned towards Krom. 'This trail has been given to the Sons of Russ to follow. The burden is upon us. We will share the victory with the Dark Angels, but not the hunt.'

This seemed to satisfy Krom. 'My other packs will gather on the flanks and run alongside the trail Lopt has found. The prey will not slip past,' he growled.

'The hive-serf we track may have been deceived,' Ulrik cautioned the Wolf Lord. 'It may be that our quarry is innocent of treachery. Keep that in mind.' The last was spoken with emphasis, his voice carrying to the Space Wolves further down the corridor. They had an obligation to defend the Allfather's servants. It would taint the glory of their purpose should they allow innocent blood to stain their tracks. Ulrik suspected that the Dark Angels wouldn't be so reserved in their own methods.

At a gesture from Krom, Lopt hurried along the alleyway. The Wolf Scout seldom paused to examine his surroundings now, more certain of the trail since finding the lho-stick. When the path ascended up gantries or dropped into service tunnels, Lopt gave voice to a quick bark to alert the rest of the pack, then swiftly pursued the scent.

In a short time, a low snarl sounded across the vox. Ulrik recognised the distinct pattern of Lopt's voice. The meaning was clear. The Wolf Scout had cornered the hive-serf.

'My warriors will cordon off the area,' Krom told Ulrik. 'We'll hold on to anybody who even thinks about leaving.'

A menacing growl rose from Vangandyr.

'I don't think any runners will get far,' Beregelt said, tightening his hold on the wolf's chain.

Ulrik nodded. Though a Space Wolf could stalk doppegangrels and ice wyrms across the tundra with the stealth of a snow panther, the bowels of a hive city weren't ideal for stealthy manoeuvres. The hab-blocks around them were teeming with inhabitants and the presence of dozens of giant warriors of the Adeptus Astartes wasn't something that could be hidden from them. The hive-serfs knew the Space Wolves were there, and that knowledge had sent them cowering inside their hab-units. Any that emerged from hiding now would only be those with some vital purpose. Those perhaps seeking to warn their dark master.

The snarl of small arms fire rang out from around the bend. Lopt barked a hasty warning over the vox, then fell silent. Ulrik could pick out the distinct report of the scout's bolt pistol mixed into the chatter of stubbers and shotguns. The Wolf Priest drew his plasma pistol and glanced over at Krom. The Wolf Lord was already motioning his retinue to spread out in support of Lopt.

'Looks like the serf stopped running,' Krom growled, fangs gleaming in a fierce smile.

'Try to take him alive,' Ulrik advised.

Like grey shadows, the Space Wolves fanned out. Beregelt led Vangandyr down an alleyway, two other Wolf Guard climbed up into a maintenance gantry and another pair rushed along a side street. Krom led the last of his retinue in a charge directly towards the sounds of combat. Ulrik followed the Wolf Lord's course.

The ambush had caught Lopt at the junction of three streets, a broad ramp at one end of the crossroad rising up into the next layer of the hive city. The fugitive he'd been tracking must have slipped word to comrades somewhere along the trail, and it was here that the hivers had decided to spring their trap. Converging upon the scout from three sides, the mob had forced the Space Wolf to take cover behind one of the plasteel columns supporting the rampway. From this improvised fortification, Lopt was delivering staggered fire. He was careful to shoot just enough to keep the mob back, but restrained himself from inflicting enough casualties to send the ambushers into flight. His purpose was to keep them right where they were until the rest of the Drakeslayers could secure the area and cut off any avenue of retreat.

A fierce, booming howl thundered from the Space Wolves as they rushed into the junction. The ambushers, a motley mixture of drab hive-serfs and garish gangers, were thrown into confusion as the huge power-armoured warriors charged towards them.

'Strength is honour!' a tattooed ganger shrieked as he spun around and aimed a snub-nosed stubber at Krom. Before the man could shoot, Krom's pistol barked, the shot ripping through the ganger's knee and hurling his maimed body out into the street.

The mutilation of their spokesman set the rest of the mob into furious retaliation. Men dashed out from behind pillars and pipes to blaze away at the Space Wolves with shotguns and pistols. One, wearing nothing but a breechcloth and a crazed grin, charged at them with a massive chainsword clenched in his fists. From a nest of conduits and pipes overhead, a man swathed in a dark cassock sniped at the Drakeslayers with a lasrifle. Darting about the edge of the ramp, a pair of burly ruffians in the coveralls of factory workers lobbed firebombs at the Wolf Guard.

Bullets and solid slugs clattered harmlessly from the thick ceramite armour. A sweep of Ulrik's crozius disarmed the ganger with the chainsword, leaving the mangled hiver screaming in a pool of his own blood. A burst from Krom's pistol brought the sniper crashing down from his nest above the junction. Wading through the pools of flame left by the firebombs, the Space Wolves pushed their assault against the mob.

'Strength is honour! I shall be worthy!' The cry was accompanied by a searing surge of flame that went sizzling past Ulrik's shoulder. One of the Drakeslayers cried out, dropping back as he was engulfed by a torrent of flames.

Ulrik sprang towards the hiver with the flamer. He was a brawny man, his muscles swollen with chem stimulants. There was a latticework of tattoos covering his face, a writhing mixture of swords and snakes entwined around an aquila. There was a vicious gleam in the thug's eyes, the look of a cornered ice-vermin that fights despite its fear because it knows it has no other choice. Ulrik could see his opponent trying to discharge another blast of flame, but the weapon was sputtering.

'Submit to the Allfather's justice,' Ulrik warned, swatting the flamer from the hiver's hands with his crozius. 'Repent and you may find mercy.'

Terror transfixed the hiver's visage as he stared up into the Helm of Russ. 'I shall be worthy,' he almost sobbed, reaching a hand to his neck. Ulrik just had time to spring away before the hiver detonated the grenade hanging from his necklace. The brunt of the explosion caught him in the shoulder, sending him sprawling in the middle of the street.

Ulrik started to rise, but was struck from behind. Looming above him was an enormous ganger, nearly as large as a Space Marine. The filth of mutation disfigured the man's body, lending him an idiot expression as well as a prodigious musculature. The mutant held a plasteel girder in his hands and as the Wolf Priest tried to stand, the ganger brought the bludgeon down again. As his head bounced against the street, Ulrik could see several hivers rushing towards him to take advantage of his distress.

'Only strong is worthy,' the mutant dullard slurred as he brought the girder crashing down again.

'You aren't strong,' Ulrik snarled back. The old Wolf swept his leg underneath the mutant's, pitching his foe to the ground. A kick of his boot smashed the ganger's face and a blow from his maul pulverized the man's left arm. Ulrik left the groaning wreckage and turned to face the pack of hivers coming for him, only to see that they had already been intercepted. Emerging from an alleyway, the huge bulk of Vangandyr smashed into the men. The gigantic wolf locked its jaws around one hiver's leg, tossing him aside with a twist of its head, then spun around to crush another man beneath its lupine bulk. Beregelt wasn't far behind, his fire discouraging those the animal had failed to send fleeing.

The ambush had been turned upon itself. With more Drakeslayers converging on the position, none of the mob would escape. When it came time to interrogate those they captured, however, Ulrik found there was little they could tell him that he didn't already suspect. Sathar had preyed upon the hivers, pressing them into a cult of his own creation. Hive-serfs from the factories and gangers from the underbelly of Eyriax had been drawn into the traitor's service, acting as his eyes and ears within the city in exchange for the protection and power he promised them.

The one detail that did interest Ulrik was how the hivers relayed information back to their master. They communicated by passing intelligence through Ecclesiarch collectioners, laymen who prowled the hab-blocks seeking contributions for the endowment of shrines and temples.

The Space Wolves looked more closely at the sniper Krom had brought down from the ceiling. Lopt bent over the body, sniffing at the monk-like cassock. His face wrinkled in distaste at the pungent reek clinging to the robes. There was a greasy mix of incense and promethium so prominent as to almost blot out the man's own scent.

Ulrik nodded as the Wolf Scout gave his report. There was one place in particular where such a curious combination of smells could be expected. A snarl rattled at the back of his throat as he considered the audacity of the traitor to conceal himself in the very shadow of the Allfather.

Ponderous in its dimensions, the crematorium was an incongruous medley of temple and factory, a place where the dead of Eyriax were brought for final disposal, and where mourners came to pay their last respects. Bronze iconography a hundred feet wide adorned the outer walls, displaying the symbols of the Ecclesiarchy and scriptures from the Imperial Creed. Statues of saints and martyrs stood within niches cut above each doorway, their granite faces slowly crumbling beneath a patina of soot and industrial grime. Great vents in the roof spewed a greasy grey smog into the air, a mixture of fuel and incense with a strong undercurrent of burning flesh. A steady flow of load-carriers drove around the immense structure, bearing stacks of metal caskets to the receiving bays at the back of the building.

Ulrik didn't need to see the Drakeslayers to know that they were moving into position. He could *feel* them all around, could smell their eagerness, hear the impatience in their breath. Krom had dispatched them to cover every approach to the target, not leaving so much as a maintenance hatch without a team of Space Wolves ready and waiting to smash it open.

'Inside will reek,' Krom reminded Ulrik. The Wolf Lord held his grey helmet in one hand, contemplating it with a calculating eye. 'The wolves will be utterly overcome by the stink. We'll have to leave them out here. I've ordered the Drakeslayers with the sharpest noses to stay with them and to act as reserve. They'll be more use out here keeping guard than they will inside. If our prey slips through, they'll be ready to pick up his trail.'

'You give this traitor a great deal of credit,' Ulrik said.

Krom laughed. 'He's managed to evade the Dark Angels for a long time. That makes him better than them. Although it doesn't mean he's as good as a Space Wolf.'

At Krom's command, the Drakeslayers mounted their assault. The doors and hatches fronting the building crumpled under the armoured boots and whirring chainswords of the Space Marines. Howling their battle cries, the giant warriors surged into the crematorium.

Krom's Wolf Guard smashed the ornate double doors of the main entryway. Ulrik rushed into the wide reception hall beyond, stunning the robed attendants inside by the abrupt violence of his entrance. Crying out in shock, their faces transfixed by a mix of awe and terror, the men prostrated themselves before the black-armoured Wolf Priest. In their quivering babble, he could hear appeals to the God-Emperor for protection and forgiveness. Briefly Ulrik wondered if their imprecations were sincere or if these men were also minions of Sathar. The Space Marines following behind Ulrik swept past the shivering attendants, sparing them small notice as they pursued the sounds of activity beyond the hall.

A thrill rushed through Ulrik's veins, the primal eagerness and anticipation of battle that had been with him ever since he was a Blood Claw. The sensation was dulled beneath the layers of restraint and experience he'd acquired over his many centuries of service to the Chapter. Impulsiveness and instinct didn't control him. They were tools, assets to be tapped into and focused towards the objective at hand.

Sathar the Undone. Ulrik's lips curled back in a snarl as he contemplated their prey. He could still remember Svane Vulfbad, the turn-pelt renegade who'd betrayed the Space Wolves and taken much of his Great Company down the path of Chaos. It was easy to appreciate how fiercely the Dark Angels despised traitors. Yet their hate hadn't been enough to catch their enemy, any more than the Space Wolves had been able to visit justice upon Vulfbad. That was why Ulrik had advised Krom to stage an immediate assault on the crematorium. The Dark Angels might have displayed more caution, waited until they were certain of catching Sathar before committing themselves. That would give the traitor time to prepare. With a sudden assault, Sathar might be caught off-guard.

The Drakeslayers stormed the sanctuaries and chapels that ringed the reception hall. Each chamber was filled with crowds of mourners, come to offer prayers for departed family and friends. Ancient pews groaned under the weight of the sombre throngs while still more hive-serfs stood in the aisles and along the walls to make their representations. Waxen seals affixed to each mourner's forehead proclaimed the serial number of the casket that had received the departed they had come to honour. Scrolls pinned to their sleeves displayed the amount of their contribution to the Ecclesiarchy's coffers to petition a personalised eulogy for the deceased. Behind the stone altar at the fore of each chapel, a lay-priest chanted a litany for the dead, sometimes pausing in his droning chant to utter a special commendation for the spirit of someone whose grieving family had been especially generous in their tithe.

When the Space Wolves intruded upon these chambers, disrupting the mortuary rituals, mourners and lay-priests alike were thrown into alarm and confusion. It took but a single snarled command to send them rushing out into the reception hall and from thence into the streets beyond. Seeing the hurried exodus, Ulrik noted cloaked figures emerging from shadowy alcoves. Obscure and sinister in their aspect, the lurkers made no move to obstruct the Drakeslayers. He could guess their purpose – guards to monitor the funerary ceremonies and report anything suspicious to their dark master. It was likely they'd already informed Sathar that the Wolves had come. The best way they could serve their master now was to delay the Drakeslayers by arousing their suspicions. It would be no small effort to extricate the sentries from the mass of frightened mourners.

'Forget Sathar's rats,' Ulrik voxed the other Space Wolves. 'If we need to find them later, we'll set the wolves on their track. For now we hunt bigger game.'

Behind the crematorium's outer chambers lay the Halls of Eternal Dreaming. The contrast was that of day and night. From the sombre sanctuaries and chapels, the Halls expanded into a vast cavern of machinery, a cathedral of industry rather than spirit. Rotating belts slithered between great vats and presses. Hooks and mechanical claws swung above, their gruesome talons poised to seize the bodies that were laid out upon the belts. Immense oven-like furnaces squatted at the far end of the hall, flames crackling behind the steel grilles. Huge pipes pumped fuel into the furnaces, drawing promethium and other incendiary chemicals from mammoth tanks clustered about the opposite side of the building. A brigade of pallid servitors shuffled around the machinery and the furnaces. With the aquila branded into their foreheads and their bodies covered in strange cloaks that at once suggested the coverall of a labourer and the cassock of a pilgrim, the servitors were twisted parodies of the human form. Arms replaced with grasping claws of iron, legs substituted for whirring treads of steel, each of the attendants was part machine, programmed to perform his duties with neither complaint nor fatigue. They didn't react even as the first of Krom's Blood Claws came loping into the factory, simply continuing to operate the machinery they had been assigned.

'Damn this incense,' Krom cursed behind his helm. 'It's enough to set the oldest Long Fang on edge!'

With the incense saturating the air, the Space Wolves found their vision murky and their sense of smell overwhelmed. Ulrik had expected the incense to be an obstruction, but he hadn't anticipated it to have such a pernicious effect. For the first time a troubling thought came to him. He had tried not to underestimate Sathar or to let contempt for the traitor cloud his judgement. Even so, he wondered if he had given their prey enough credit.

The groan of heavy chains grinding their way through pulleys thundered overhead. Ulrik swung around, watching as a massive cauldron was hauled across the hall on a suspended rail. The immense metal vessel abruptly lurched to a stop, hanging for an instant above a pack of Grey Hunters making their way along the factory floor. The Space Wolves scattered as the hook supporting the cauldron released it. Gallons of bubbling chemicals slammed into the floor, spilling over the ferrocrete foundation. Noxious liquid splashed across the Grey Hunters, sizzling against their ceramite armour.

Across the crematorium, other mechanisms suddenly developed violent faults. The doors of a furnace swung open and sent a blast of flame searing across the advance of some Blood Claws, forcing them to leap back and swat at the burning wolf-pelts and talismans hanging from their armour. The nozzle of a sprayer meant to bathe corpses in purifying unguents burst and sent a stream of liquid streaking across the hall with enough force that a pack of Long Fangs were knocked off their feet.

'Damn that traitor! Does he think he can stop us with these petty tricks!' Krom aimed his bolt pistol at a nearby servitor, exploding the half-machine's head. The servitor slumped beside the flywheel it had just started to turn, arresting the opening of a furnace door.

'Stay alert,' Ulrik warned. 'Don't let your warriors lose focus.'

He knew his order would be difficult to follow. The whole of the factory was descending into a bedlam of amok machinery. Hydraulic claws dropped down from the ceiling, scrabbling for the Space Wolves below. Pneumatic pincers slashed at the Drakeslayers from behind banks of pressure gauges and lubricant feeds. The rattle of bolters and the screech of chainswords rose in answer to the rampaging machinery.

Some of the servitors now shambled away from their machines. One, holding a great hydraulic hammer clenched in its metal claws, lunged at a Wolf Guard, the head of its tool-turned-weapon cracking the pillar behind the Space Wolf as he dodged from its path. A kick of the Drakeslayer's boot crumpled the servitor's leg, pitching it to the floor. A burst from the Wolf Guard's bolt pistol exploded its head in a spray of blood and lubricant.

Across the factory floor, the Grey Hunters were confronted by a murderous file of maintenance servitors. Each of the automata had a tank of caustic purifiers bolted to its back, hoses snaking out from the canister to connect with the wide-nozzled sprayer that replaced one of its arms. The servitors sent blasts of acidic granules billowing out towards the Grey Hunters, forcing them to take cover behind a bank of machinery before retaliating with a withering fusillade of bolter fire. Engulfed in a cloud of shimmering granules as the canister burst, one of the servitors was quickly consumed down to the bone as its flesh dissolved.

More servitors moved to the attack, turning a medley of instruments and tools against the Drakeslayers. The whirring abrasives of buffers and grinders scraped across ceramite as automata emerged from storage lockers, surprising one of the Blood Claw packs. The young Space Wolves replied with bolters and swords, tearing through their ambushers in a riot of violence. Servitors with promethium projectors turned against a squad of Long Fangs, sheets of rolling flame sizzling against their armour and blackening their tribal talismans before a missile barrage obliterated their attackers.

Something more instinctive than thought made Ulrik turn away from the fray and towards one of the great presses where the ashes of hive-serfs were compacted. Above the gigantic press, standing upon an elevated walkway, was a lone figure.

Gripping his crozius and plasma pistol a little tighter, Ulrik rushed forwards. When the lurker started to climb higher into the maze of gantries and walkways that stretched across the crematorium, the Wolf Priest gnashed his fangs in frustration. If there was some passage connecting the roof of the building to the next level of the hive, their prey could avoid the warriors Krom had left outside. He'd gain a valuable lead. Ulrik didn't intend to grant the traitor such an opportunity.

The hulking presses loomed before him as Ulrik hurried after his quarry. Leaping over one of the conveyor belts that brought boxes of ashes from the furnaces, the Wolf Priest found himself at the edge of the descending ram. Beyond, he could see the stairs leading up to the walkway. Without a flicker of hesitation, Ulrik sent a ball of plasma searing into the pipes fitted to the side of the press. Oil and fluid erupted from the broken tubes, spraying across the hall. Ulrik dived under the dropping ram, crawling across the bottom of the press. The loss of fluid retarded the descent, causing the plate to lose impetus with each passing second. Just the same, Ulrik felt his backpack squeezing him before he wormed his way free. His boots were barely clear before the heavy ram completed its descent and struck the base with a dull metallic boom.

The thunderous impact wasn't enough to blot out the other sounds that now drew Ulrik's attention. The rattle of bolters had increased, but there was a difference in the reports now, a shift in quality that warned Ulrik not all of the weapons being fired were from the armouries of the Fang. The Dark Angels – had they come to help the Space Wolves or to contend their right to the hunt? Ulrik cast the question aside. Interrogator-Chaplain Balthus could argue his case after the traitor was caught.

The Wolf Priest charged the stairs, lunging up them in great leaps as he took advantage of the planet's low gravity, hurtling across the first walkway and rushing up to a second. A lupine snarl of satisfaction rumbled at the back of his throat when he spotted his prey ahead. The lurker had lingered instead of fleeing. He'd stayed to gloat over the Drakeslayers and the confusion his menagerie of traps had wrought. That was a mistake he was going to regret most dearly.

'Sathar!' Ulrik cried out in challenge. 'Your days of mocking the Allfather are over! Justice has come for you on the fangs of wolves!'

The traitor turned. He wore a heavy cloak that appeared stitched from human skin, but the garment wasn't enough to hide the bulky power armour he wore beneath it or the great leathery wings that sprang from his back. The helm that peered out from beneath the cloak's hood was pulled out into a beak, the optics fashioned from a yellow transparency that somehow lent them a jaundiced quality.

'I hear you bark, but can you bite?' the traitor snarled. Sathar lunged at Ulrik with the jagged edge of his broken blade. Krom had shattered the sword with Wyrmclaw when the two had fought in the governor's rooms, but the original had been so huge that the remnant was still the size of any normal blade, and just as deadly. The weapon seemed to soak up the shadows around it, blurring its outline as it came slashing towards the Wolf Priest. Narrowly was he able to dodge aside as the blade came smashing down, shearing through the framework and sending a tangle of twisted steel crashing to the floor far below.

Ulrik retaliated, bringing his maul around. He tried to shatter the sword again, but Sathar was too fast, feinting and veering away. A hiss of amusement rasped from Sathar's helm as the traitor struck at Ulrik once more. This time the blade slashed through the guardrail a few inches from the Fenrisian, the severed length of the rail whipping back at him like a snake.

Bringing his crozius crackling across the walkway, Ulrik sent a mass of torn metal flying into the traitor's face. Sathar staggered back, his broken sword incapable of fending off the spray of debris.

'I don't duel traitor scum,' Ulrik growled. He leaped across the pit his maul had gouged in the walkway floor, springing at the traitor like a thunderwolf.

Sathar's sword lashed out, striking at the supports connecting the walkway to the ceiling. The blow sheared through the metal girders. The walkway crumpled, part of its length sliding away to hang forlornly from the rearward span. In an instant, Ulrik found only empty space beneath him. Without hesitating, he hooked the flange of his crozius in the angle between support and walkway, using his momentum to turn his fall into a flip. Pivoting, he flung himself over the guardrail and onto the walkway behind his foe. By his own action, Sathar had trapped himself between the Wolf Priest and a plummet to the factory floor below.

Still there was fight in the traitor. Raising his sword, Sathar rushed towards Ulrik. The Wolf Priest fired his plasma pistol. The impact ripped the weapon from Sathar's hands and pitched it down into the crematorium.

The traitor took a step back and reached for the bolt pistol holstered at his side. A snarl of warning rose from Ulrik.

'Balthus wants you alive, but that's the only thing he said about your condition.'

Sathar moved his hands away from the gun.

'So you have caught me,' he said, slowly pointing his hand to the factory below. 'Or have you? It is a tricky prospect when the hunter finds himself trapped.'

Ulrik could hear the sounds of conflict raging below, the battle cries and combat orders swirling through the inter-squad vox channel. Krom was trying to redeploy his Drakeslayers, to answer the ambush that had suddenly engulfed them. From his vantage point high above the factory floor, Ulrik had a better appreciation of the situation than Krom. He could see how disunited and scattered the traps had left the Space Wolves. More than that, he could see the enemies his battle-brothers now faced. Not a rabble of cultists or rebels, but a force of Space Marines. Even in the fumes of the crematorium, he could tell they weren't Dark Angels.

'You aren't the only one with friends,' Sathar said. 'For now, my associates are only trying to keep them busy. It will be much different if they decide to apply themselves in earnest,' he cautioned.

'Your traitor friends are outnumbered,' Ulrik scoffed.

Sathar shook his head. 'They would surprise you. Besides, they need only hold your comrades long enough for us to talk.' His voice dropped to an unctuous whisper. 'I know who you are seeking, who it is you are really hunting.'

Ulrik took a step towards the traitor, his maul ready to strike the turncoat down.

'You know nothing,' he snapped, rage boiling within his heart at Sathar's effort to manipulate him.

'Logan Grimnar,' Sathar said, thrusting the name at Ulrik as though it had the bite of his lost sword behind it. 'That is who you were looking for before you were distracted by Balthus.'

'You know nothing,' Ulrik repeated, but even he could hear the lack of conviction in his voice. Sathar had planted a seed of doubt in his mind. Did the traitor really know something? Could he let this chance slip away?

The traitor glanced back down at the factory floor. 'If the fighting gets much worse, I worry that my associates may want to press the issue. Make your choice while it is still yours to make.'

A sick feeling boiled inside Ulrik's stomach. To even contemplate a compromise with something like Sathar was an outrage. He would carry it with him as a blight upon his honour for the rest of his days. Yet if there was truly a hope of picking up Grimnar's trail again, he had to take it. His own honour was small concern beside the welfare of the Chapter.

'I'll hear you out,' Ulrik said. 'Call off your dogs.'

'I'll keep my pistol, just to reassure myself of your sincerity. If you are so inclined, you can try to disarm me once you've listened to me,' Sathar told him. 'Comrades!' he spoke into his vox bead. 'I am captive of the Space Wolves! There is no purpose to further fighting. Withdraw. Withdraw and proceed as planned.' The traitor swung around to Ulrik. 'I have called off my dogs, now call off yours.'

'Lord Krom, I have taken the traitor,' Ulrik spoke into his helm's vox-bead. 'Do not pursue the others. We must remain committed to our cause and not spend our resources on distractions.'

The Wolf Priest glared at Sathar. He knew whatever the traitor wanted to say would be designed to tempt him. He also knew none of it could be trusted. He'd need more, something he *could* trust.

'Send Leoric Half-ear to me,' Ulrik said. Whatever deceit was in the traitor's words, the Rune Priest Leoric would be able to sniff out the truth in his mind.

Sathar the Undone led the Space Wolves into a concealed chamber above one of the crematorium's sanctuaries. Ulrik grudgingly admired the craft with which the traitor had hidden his refuge. Even knowing it was there, he was hard-pressed to spot the break where a carved finial in the sanctuary pivoted to expose the elevator leading up to the room. The niches in the walls and the stone plinths arrayed about the room made it clear that the place had been intended as a mausoleum at one time, a place to inter those too wealthy and privileged to have their remains reduced to fertilizer. Now the mausoleum was given over to Sathar's use. Light shone down upon the chamber from panels fitted into the ceiling, illuminators designed to mimic the clean light of unpolluted skies long-since extinct above the surface of Stratovass. Flickering through the warm glow of dawn, passing onto the bright blaze of noon, the panels sent a panoply of shadows wheeling about the room.

The walls were adorned with star charts, the niches converted into caches of data-sheets and pict-slates. Upon the stone plinths were assembled curious devices and artefacts – trophies and mementos that must have been claimed by Sathar during his wanderings across the galaxy. Some Ulrik recognised: the narrow helm of an eldar witch-prophet, the severed talon of a giant genestealer, the broken blade of an Inquisitor's power sword with the grim iconography of that organisation engraved upon the guard. Others were things beyond even Ulrik's vast understanding. Among these was a three-foot-tall prism of black glass. There was an oily, creeping atmosphere about the object that made the Wolf Priest's hackles rise. Leoric Half-ear removed his helm and glared at the thing.

'You can smell the stink of the warp even over the reek of the furnaces,' the Rune Priest growled in disgust.

'A curiosity I came upon rather recently,' Sathar said. 'I haven't had a chance to study it properly, but you must agree it is unique.'

Leoric was peering closer at the glass now. 'There are... things moving inside,' he muttered. 'I can almost...'

The traitor laughed. 'It is dangerous to peer into the abyss unless you know what to look for. You can never be certain what might be looking back.'

Ulrik drew the Rune Priest away from the dark prism. At his touch, Leoric shook his head, as though stirring from a stupor. 'I came to hear about the Great Wolf, not abominations from the warp.' His face contorting into a lupine snarl, he drew his pistol and aimed it at the tainted relic.

'That might be unwise,' Sathar warned. 'I have taken great pains to prevent a doorway to the warp from opening in this city. Shoot the prism and you may accomplish in a heartbeat what the slaves of Chaos have been trying to achieve for months now.'

Ulrik gripped Leoric's arm, pushing the bolt pistol downwards. 'Leave the prism for now,' he told the Rune Priest. 'I need your talents focused upon the traitor. I need to know how much he says is lie and how much is truth,' he elaborated over their private vox channel.

Ulrik's eyes glared from the depths of his skull-helm as he turned towards Sathar. 'Speak quickly, traitor. Balthus is waiting.'

Sathar leaned against one of the plinths. 'Again you call me "traitor", but I tell you I serve the Emperor more completely now than you could possibly understand. A profound revelation came to me, an epiphany. It is this – to destroy monsters, you must become a monster. To defeat the enemy, you must turn its weapons against itself. There can be no measure afforded for honour and morality. All that matters is victory, however it is achieved. Turn Chaos against itself. Use the instruments of heresy to destroy the heretic.'

A low, threatening growl rumbled from behind Ulrik's mask. 'For such madness you abandoned your heritage?'

The runic talismans chained to Leoric's armour shivered with eerie energies as his psychic powers reached out to probe Sathar's thoughts. 'The vermin's mind is consumed by his delusions. Even now he imagines himself a servant of the Allfather.' The Rune Priest's voice seethed with revulsion over the vox.

'You wouldn't understand,' Sathar repeated. 'It is beyond your ability to understand. You have deluded yourselves with conceits of honour and morality. You couldn't possibly appreciate what it means to–'

Ulrik sprang forwards, seizing Sathar by his robe. 'I've heard enough of this madness. Tell me about Logan Grimnar. Where is the Great Wolf?'

'The key to that information isn't so easy. You will have to work for it,' Sathar pointed at Leoric. 'Your Librarian will tell you I don't lie when I say that I am not responsible for the ritual murders afflicting this city. I have fought against those responsible, but now they are driven to an outrage of such scale that it may be beyond the abilities of my resources to overcome. We need your strength, the ferocity of the Space Wolves, to guarantee victory.'

'You're not only mad, but a fool to think we would aid you,' Ulrik snapped. He tightened his hold upon Sathar, dragging the traitor towards him. 'There can be no compromise with a heretic.'

'Wait!' Leoric's voice crackled with hate, his eyes shone with bloodlust. 'I have seen into his mind. The enemy he would loose us against. The leaders controlling this cult. They are of the brood of Magnus!'

Ulrik felt the blood pumping through his hearts blaze with a vengeful fury as he heard the traitor primarch's name. There were no foes in the galaxy the Space Wolves despised and hated more than the murdering sorcerers of the Thousand Sons. The old Wolf Priest could feel the savagery of the Canis Helix rippling through his flesh, responding to the magnitude of his rage. By an effort of will, he subdued the primal energies, forcing them to recede back into the darkest corners of his being.

'This is why you were certain we would help you,' Ulrik seethed. He felt like a beast lured into a trap, baited by his own instincts. How deep did Sathar's machinations go? Had he intentionally lured the Space Wolves here so that he could exploit their hatred of the Thousand Sons?

'No. You will help me because it is the only way to find your Chapter Master,' Sathar said. 'The Thousand Sons command House Morvane, an entire merchant guild corrupted and sworn to the Ruinous Powers. Their leader, a sorcerer called Medeb, has crossed paths with the Great Wolf. My spies have kept me informed of the cult's activities for some time now. So far the cult has attempted only minor rituals, lesser obscenities to test the waters. Tonight, however, they intend a far greater abomination.'

'Convenient timing,' Ulrik told the traitor.

Sathar nodded. 'It is because Medeb knows you are here. I was able to hide my presence from the sorcerer, but the same cannot be said of you and the Dark Angels. Medeb intends to open a doorway to the warp, a channel between Stratovass Ultra and the Eye of Terror. Medeb was cautious before, uncertain that the doorway could be stabilised. Now he has cast aside such reserve. Whether the door remains or not, he will open it all the same.'

Ulrik looked over at Leoric. The Rune Priest shook his head. 'It is what the traitor believes to be true,' he said. 'But that is only perception, not reality.'

'Would you lose the chance to find the Great Wolf because you will not believe me?' Sathar asked. 'If you need further convincing, let this speed your thoughts. I trusted to the honour of the Space Wolves to allow me to speak with you, but I knew there could be no such compact with the Dark Angels. So to gain their aid, my associates have laid a false trail for Balthus. The Dark Angels will follow that trail thinking it will lead to me, but instead they will find the cult. They will be destroyed if they fight alone. Only by combining our forces can victory be assured. If the Space Wolves don't fight, then the Dark Angels will meet their fate. It is in your power to spare them an ignoble doom.'

'You scheme without honour,' Ulrik snarled at Sathar. 'You offer a despicable choice and then explain that it isn't a choice at all. Save Eyriax, save the people, save the Dark Angels, but only if you cooperate.' The Wolf Priest slapped his hand against the plasma pistol holstered at his side. 'Whatever happens, you will be beside me. The first sniff of deceit, the first hint of betrayal, and you can be certain of one thing. I will burn a hole though that scheming brain of yours big enough to fly a Thunderhawk through.'

'I would expect nothing less from Ulrik the Slayer,' Sathar said. 'But do not be too keen to make an enemy of me. There will be foes enough for all of us where we are going.'

Thrusting out from the side of Eyriax, many miles above the surface of Stratovass, the spire of House Morvane was a soaring tower of plasteel and crystal rivalled only by the residences of the planetary governor and the High Ecclesiarch in magnificence and extravagance. Masts of meteoric iron bound in electro-runes of the Adeptus Mechanicus defended the spire from lightning and discharges of the polar aurora. Chemical misters sprayed solutions across wall and roof to combat the ravages of smog and pollutants. Leering gargoyles fashioned from lunar granite shielded the tower from psychic and spiritual malignancies.

It was this last defence that had failed in its purpose. Blessed and sanctified by all the saints, the gargoyles couldn't protect a place that freely welcomed corruption, that invited the powers of darkness into its halls. What had driven House Morvane to swear themselves to Chaos was unknown. Fear, ambition, revenge – it didn't matter what had lured the merchant guild into heresy. All that was of consequence was that they had been tempted and they had failed the test.

As the Space Wolves prowled along the darkened service corridor, stealing down the maze of passages that wound their way between the opulent galleries and chambers used by the merchants themselves, the hair on Ulrik's arms bristled. Whatever cause had led them to this defilement, it couldn't justify such obscenity.

Ulrik glanced over at Sathar, feeling even greater disgust for the traitor. Sathar had been chosen to transcend humanity, to receive the greatest gifts the Emperor could bestow upon his servants. He had become a Space Marine, superhuman in body, mind and spirit. To him had been bestowed a legacy of honour and courage that was beyond the grasp of common man. He had been entrusted with relics steeped in the blood and bravery of heroes, sacred wargear that had led his battle-brothers to victory in a thousand wars. All of it had been thrown away, cast aside because of a delusion, a madness that through heresy Sathar could find still greater purpose. If not for the oaths he had sworn, if not for the information he might have, Ulrik would like nothing better than to end Sathar's perversion here and now.

The smell of blood drew Ulrik's attention away from the cloaked traitor. A quick click across the inter-squad vox told him that Lopt's scouts had encountered guards in the corridor. Patrolling well ahead of the Drakeslayers, the scouts were thorough in their elimination of any resistance they found. The main body of Krom's warriors would find the remains slumped against the walls, tunics and surcoats stained with gore. Sometimes there was the slash of a knife, other times the bodies bore the marks of tooth and claw. Lopt was too cautious to allow his pack to risk the report of a bolt pistol and too swift to give their victims a chance to fire a shot of their own.

'Your scouts are to be commended,' Sathar remarked. 'I don't think a rat could slip past them.'

Krom ignored him. 'How long have you been watching this place?' The Wolf Lord gnashed his fangs in a fierce display. 'You seem to know all its secrets, all the hidden trails. Just remember this, heretic – if this is a trap, you die first.'

'It won't be a trap,' Ulrik said. He glared at the traitor. 'A trap would be almost honourable. No, he waited for us. He waited for someone to run this risk so he wouldn't have to. He'd try to contain the cult, keep them from going too far, but actually destroying them was a task he intended to leave to others.'

Sathar shook his head, the optics of his helm focusing on the Space Wolves all around him, each warrior seething with loathing for the traitor in their midst. 'You forget, I share the same risks as you,' he reminded Ulrik.

'Yes, and that worries me even more than whatever evil the Thousand Sons have been conjuring,' Ulrik said. 'At least they make no pretence about who and what they are.'

The traitor laughed. 'There is a saying from ancient Terra – the enemy of your enemy is your friend.'

'There is a Fenrisian custom that a broken sword is never reforged,' Ulrik said. 'It is thrown into the sea, a dead thing. There is no trust for something that has already betrayed one master.' He looked across the Drakeslayers, appreciating far better than Sathar how greatly they were struggling to restrain the instinct to destroy the traitor. 'Do not tempt your doom,' he warned. 'It will find you soon enough.'

'Perhaps all of us,' Sathar said, gesturing to a mark hidden in the gilded scroll work that adorned the sides of the corridor. 'A sign left by my spies. We are near to the Grand Arcade overlooking the Chancellery of House Morvane. Your brothers need hold back but a little longer. Soon they will have foes enough.'

Almost as Sathar spoke, muffled sounds reached the keen senses of the Drakeslayers: a dolorous, reptilian susurration of many voices raised in a grisly chant. Beneath the chanting, more vibration than sound, was the clamour of primitive drums and woodwinds. Ringing out above the ghoulish cadence was an invocation, an inhuman appeal that raved and shrieked with piteous horror. Every Space Wolf felt his hair crawl in agitation, felt his hearts quicken in response to the abject threat laced within the noise. The cult had started their terrible ceremony, their profane appeal to the powers of Chaos.

Lopt slipped back down the hallway. He stopped before Krom and Ulrik, giving the leaders a hasty report.

'We've found a door in the wall ahead,' the scout sergeant said. 'It opens upon an arcade overlooking a hall the size of the *Ironpelt*'s docking bay.'

'Enemy numbers?' Krom asked, fingering the hilt of his sword.

'Hundreds,' Lopt answered. 'A dozen or more Thousand Sons among them.'

'Just as I promised,' Sathar stated. 'It would seem you have your work cut out for you.'

Ulrik rounded on the traitor. 'If the Allfather wills us to be victorious, I will yet deliver you to Balthus. Until then, you remain in my keeping.' The last was uttered in a low growl, a reminder not just to Sathar but to the other Space Wolves. The Chaos Space Marine was Ulrik's responsibility and he intended to carry that burden through.

The Drakeslayers hurried up the corridor. Lopt's scouts were deployed around a door hidden in the wall, fashioned so that it merged seamlessly with its surroundings. Part of the scrolling slid down at Lopt's touch, revealing a hidden recess and an angular nub of ivory projecting slightly from the exposed panel. At a gesture from Krom, Lopt pulled the ivory nub, drawing out a rod-like shaft of metal. In response, the concealed door receded into the wall.

The instant the door slid open, the sounds of the ritual swelled to an almost deafening fury. Smells of boiling fat, smouldering offal and singed hair struck the sharp noses of the Space Wolves. A slimy, insidious chill pawed at them, sinking through their ceramite armour with an intensity that had nothing to do with physical temperature. It was the icy clutch of sorcery, the frigid emanations of the warp itself, a malignant pulse that offended the soul. Leoric Half-ear winced in momentary pain, fingers tightening around his rune staff with such force that the ancient relic groaned beneath his touch.

'They must... be stopped,' the Rune Priest whispered as he tried to shake off the psychic emanations. He waved away the Grey Hunters who moved to offer him aid, pointing a commanding finger towards the Grand Arcade.

The Drakeslayers began to filter out onto the arcade. It was a broad, colonnaded hallway overlooking the vast expanse of a courtyard below. Tier upon tier of arcades rose upon three sides of the court while the far end was given over to a colossal sheet of crystal. Tinted with a crimson lustre, the crystal looked out upon the storm-swept skies. Strange lightning crackled and flashed beyond the panes, ribbons of electricity snaking out to crash against the iron rods projecting from the walls.

The Chancellery itself had been designed for the obscene rites of House Morvane. Broad enough to accommodate the immense throng of cultists, the centre of the court was dominated by a raised platform cut into a nine-sided wedge. From each angle of the nonagon a smouldering brazier of brass and bone rose, the impaled husk of a butchered sacrifice slowly roasting above the chemical flames. A macabre pattern of indentations cut into the floor allowed blood from the victims to flow through the hall, pouring down the gutter-like slits to form weird patterns and arcane symbols. In the middle of the platform, a ring of rough stones was arrayed, their pitted surfaces aglow with eldritch harmonies. It was here, among the stones, that the despicable priesthood of the cult performed their abominable rites and a grinning hierophant shrieked the inhuman invocation that dominated even the clamour of the chanting thousands who filled the courtyard.

Ulrik glared at the vile scene, feeling the abhorrent energies the cultists had evoked. His eyes locked upon a clutch of towering figures who held themselves away from the main throng – observing rather than partaking of the ritual unfolding around them. There was no mistaking the fluted vanes that fanned out from the sides of their helms or the golden accents that adorned their ancient armour. At their head stood a sorcerer carrying a staff.

They were the children of Prospero, the archenemy of Fenris. The Thousand Sons.

'They're here,' Krom snarled, hate dripping from his fangs. 'And here they die,' he vowed. The Wolf Lord started to swing around to snap orders to the Drakeslayers.

Whatever deployment Krom intended for his warriors, whatever strategy he planned to seal off the courtyard and prevent the heretics from escaping, it all came crashing down in an instant. Far below, beneath the tier that flanked the arcade on which the Space Wolves stood, the steel doors sealing the entrance were ripped from their fastenings, blown inwards by powerful explosions. The huge portals careened across the hall, mutilating scores of cultists as they tore through the throng, crushing dozens more as they came smashing down. The grisly chant exploded into a cacophony of alarm and outrage; the eerie drums and flutes fell silent. Only the diabolical invocation persisted, somehow rising louder and more malignant than before.

Through the shattered doors huge warriors in bone-coloured armour rushed. The Dark Angels had arrived, pursuing the trail Sathar had left for them. The Space Marines, confronted by the obscene spectacle of the massed cultists, exhibited no mercy.

'Purge the traitor's flock!' Interrogator-Chaplain Balthus' voice boomed, joining his battle-brothers in righteous fury.

'A bit ahead of my projections,' Sathar grumbled, as he watched the Dark Angels cutting down robed cultists with flaring power swords and the explosive shells from boltguns. Still, the traitor had a dour tone when he turned to Ulrik. 'They will need your Wolves if they are to survive.'

Before Ulrik could comment, he saw the cultists begin to react to the attacking Dark Angels. From beneath their robes, the heretics produced a motley array of weaponry. Stubbers growled while slender laspistols sent beams of energy searing across the hall. Crazed worshippers threw themselves at the hulking Space Marines, knives and hatchets clenched in their fists. A few cultists, amok with their obscene devotion, reached into the braziers and scooped the blazing chemicals onto themselves. These living torches, tortured screams ripping from their lungs, hurled themselves upon their attackers.

These weapons were no match for power armour, though. The Dark Angels pressed their attack, penetrating deeper into the hall. It was then that the first of them fell, stricken not by bullet or blade, but by the malignant energies leaping from the mind of a black-robed psyker. The malevolent conjurations sent the Dark Angel crashing to his knees, blood spilling from the vents in his helmet. An instant later, the hulking warrior fell unmoving to the ground.

'Long Fangs along the gallery! Target the Thousand Sons!' Krom bellowed. 'Grey Hunters, strike down the psykers! Blood Claws and Wolf Guard, with me!'

As he roared out the last order, Krom swung up and over the balustrade. It was a simple matter for someone who had climbed the craggy slopes of Asaheim's mountains to lower himself from one tier to the next. With their Wolf Lord leading the way, the Drakeslayers followed, eager to join the fray.

Ulrik caught hold of Sathar, pulling the traitor behind the cover afforded by the balustrade. Steel and stone were shredded as a concentration of bolter-fire peppered it. The Thousand Sons had noted the arrival of Krom's warriors and were taking action to stem their descent. Several Blood Claws were sent hurtling to the floor below as shells slammed into them or ripped apart the columns they were climbing. In the next instant, the arcade trembled as the Long Fangs loosed a barrage of lascannon and missile fire at the Chaos Space Marines. Ulrik could feel the impact of their concentrated fire as a still greater tremor, yet when he looked out from behind the shattered balustrade, the Thousand Sons were unharmed.

'The enemy is not without protection,' Leoric snarled. 'They use sorcery to shield themselves from our guns.'

'Nor is that their only trick,' Ulrik swore. Below he saw the Thousand Sons sorcerer – surely the one called Medeb – stalk away from his comrades. Sparks crackled all around him as the fire from the attacking Dark Angels smashed against his arcane shield. Medeb pointed his staff towards the Dark Angels standing between him and the platform. Instantly, the Space Marines were flung back, sent flying across the hall by some unseen force.

'Our fight is down there,' Sathar declared, his words surprising Ulrik. The traitor was already swinging out over the side of the balustrade, shells tearing into the column beside him.

'Try to counter their sorcery,' Ulrik told Leoric as he pursued Sathar.

The moment the Wolf Lord showed himself, a shell slammed into his shoulder, splitting the pauldron. He lost his grip, hanging by one hand from the balustrade. Instinctively, he swung his body, using the momentum of his near-fall to propel himself towards a column on the tier below. More fire from the Thousand Sons struck at him, pitting and splitting the column. Again, Ulrik was forced to rely on his finely honed reflexes, casting himself out and away from the exploding stonework. His leap brought him slamming against another column thirty feet below, his armoured fingers digging gouges in the stone as he tried to arrest his momentum. Still the Chaos Space Marines pursued him with a vindictive fusillade, pushing the old Wolf to another hurried leap and another violent drop. The low gravity of Stratovass Ultra lessened the impact, but couldn't entirely compensate for his fall.

Finally Ulrik reached the floor. He'd been spared the attentions of the enemy when he dropped the last couple of tiers. He quickly saw the reason.

The Thousand Sons were falling back towards the ring of stones, pursued by a pack of Blood Claws. It was an eerie contrast – the young, ferocious Space Wolves and the ancient, lifeless pawns of Prospero. The Thousand Sons moved with an uncanny gait, neither organic nor mechanical in nature. There was little of the Space Marine left within the warriors of the Thousand Sons, just a malignant essence and dust.

Ulrik swung around, looking for Medeb. He found the fiend stalking among the stones, using his psychic powers to send charging Drakeslayers and Dark Angels flying. The sorcerer was striving to protect the cult leaders and especially the hierophant who continued to give voice to the profane invocation.

That invocation was now exhibiting its effects. Strange energies coruscated from the middle of the platform, whipping around the standing stones. The malignant forces rippled harmlessly about the armoured forms of the Space Marines, but against the bare flesh of the cultists the results were far more pronounced. Some of the heretics exploded in bursts of blood and bone, while others wilted into puddles of quivering flesh. Yet more were transformed, their bodies twisting and contorting into grisly new shapes. Arms erupted into masses of tentacles, heads expanded into fanged maws dripping with venom. One cultist shrivelled into a reptilian dwarf while another bloated into a feathered giant. The mutated throng renewed its assault against the Space Marines, striking out at Dark Angel and Space Wolf alike.

Ulrik met the assault of a hideously mutated creature. The thing rushed at him, crackling and laughing, its body already crumbling away as rampant mutations boiled through its flesh. A brutish paw slashed out, narrowly missing the side of his helm. Ulrik swept his crozius across the beast's breastbone, collapsing the loathsome spawn like a balloon. For an instant, the thing tried to resist the annihilating force of the crozius, then with a snarl it sank into a puddle of oozing corruption.

'Nicely done,' Sathar's voice rang in Ulrik's ears.

The Wolf Priest spun about to find the traitor beside him. His cloak was slashed and torn and his armour stained with blood – little of it his own. 'I tried to keep up with you, but it is daunting to keep pace with a wolf on the prowl.'

Ulrik gestured at the carnage unfolding all around them. 'I understood that your fellow traitors would be lending a hand. Perhaps they aren't as loyal as you think them to be.'

'They are in reserve,' Sathar said. 'And I fear we will soon need them.' As he spoke, the traitor aimed his pistol at Medeb, but the shot was diverted from its target, shearing away from the sorcerer to blast apart one of the cult leaders.

'We'll have the sorcerer soon,' Ulrik declared.

Krom and his Wolf Guard had joined the assault against the Thousand

Sons. Already two of the ancient traitors had been destroyed, their armour distorting in a blast of warp energy. Balthus and several of his Dark Angels were forcing their way through a cordon of giant mutants to reach the periphery of the platform.

'They'll be too late,' Sathar swore. 'He knows he's finished. Now he wants to take everyone with him.'

Ulrik saw what Sathar meant. Medeb turned upon the cult hierophant, cutting the cultist down with a sweep of his staff. The invocation, however, didn't falter. It was immediately taken up by Medeb himself. Now the cadences became more strident, less nebulous. There was imperative behind the spell now – not an appeal but a command. The sorcerer was pouring his own spirit into the conjuration, ripping asunder the barriers between reality and the immaterium.

Pulses of hideous power now spilled from the platform, rushing down among the remaining cultists. None were left unchanged, their bodies distorting in the most atrocious discord. The mortally injured, the hideously maimed: wherever a spark of life yet lingered, the greedy daemons swept in to control and reshape it.

Orbs of gibbous light dissipated from the midst of the circle, expanding and swelling until they assumed monstrous shapes. Beaked fiends bounded across the hall, immolating victims in blasts of daemonic fire while fish-like horrors fluttered up into the arcades upon winged lobes.

The battle had turned, the rampant horde of mutants and daemons forcing the Space Marines back. The Dark Angels became surrounded, and packs of Drakeslayers were cut off from their battle-brothers. All through the hall, the conflict degenerated into isolated combats pitting superhuman endurance against inhuman malevolence. A towering nightmare, its feline body bristling with psychic fires and spectral flames, charged through a swathe of Wolf Guard to snap and claw at Krom. Only the Wolf Lord's reflexes kept the beast from landing a killing blow. Across from the embattled Krom, Balthus was similarly beset by a serpent-like fiend with six heads, the flattened husk of a Dark Angel caught in its coils.

'I fear it is time to deploy my assets,' Sathar told Ulrik. 'Try to remember who is the enemy.' The traitor issued orders into his vox bead.

Sathar's signal brought an almost immediate response. His associates, the resources he'd kept in reserve, had been lingering on the periphery of the Chancellery. Now they filed into the great hall, deploying along the lower arcades. Like the ones Krom and Grundar had fought in the governor's rooms, they were from the Alpha Legion. Ulrik could scarcely believe he was in this hideous situation – fighting alongside the traitors he longed to tear apart.

Yet as disaster loomed, it was the Alpha Legion who brought relief to the reeling loyalists. From the lower arcades, their fire raked the mutant throng. The great crystal face of the window was shattered as missiles came shrieking into the courtyard to batter the largest of the monsters. Ulrik had a fleeting impression of a gunship circling through the storm.

With the sudden onslaught of the Alpha Legion throwing the cult into disarray, Ulrik saw his opportunity. Medeb had overplayed his hand and exposed the nature of his ritual. He was the key; without him the spell would lose focus. Perhaps the gate would even shut itself entirely.

'I'm going for the sorcerer,' Ulrik told Sathar, nodding at the traitor's pistol. 'Cover me... or at least don't shoot me in the back.'

Ulrik knew if he hesitated, his chance might be lost. For the moment, the forces raging across the hall had left a breach. Any instant might see it close again. He had to act. Lunging forwards, the Wolf Priest hurtled up the platform. He felt the rampaging energies of the gateway rippling around him. Some of the Fenrisian talismans he bore were reduced to ash by the eldritch assault. Only by holding his crozius before him was he able to force a path through the maelstrom. Even then, he found his progress barred. The Thousand Sons, those still animated by the spirits bound within their armour, moved to intercept him.

Raising his plasma pistol, Ulrik sent a ball of energy searing through one of the Chaos Space Marines. The ancient armour exploded, burst apart by the fury of the escaping spirit. He scowled at his spent weapon. The plasma would need time to cool before it could be unleashed again. That left two opponents in his way. As one, the ghostly warriors lifted their boltguns and took aim at their foe. Ulrik glared back at them. He might reach one, but doing so would leave him open to the other.

Snarling a prayer to Morkai the death wolf, Ulrik sprang towards the enemy on his right. His crozius swept out, smashing across the Chaos Space Marine's helm, splitting it open. The traitor staggered back, an uncanny light bleeding out from the crack in its helmet. The boltgun fell from its fingers and it pitched backwards, collapsing in a burst of warp energy.

Ulrik was surprised to find that the other had failed to fire upon him. The closeness of Sathar's scent told him that the traitor must have intervened, striking down the Chaos Space Marine before it could attack.

'Leave Medeb to me,' Ulrik warned Sathar. The sorcerer had to be taken alive, had to disclose what he knew about the Great Wolf.

Medeb saw Ulrik coming. Until the last moment, the sorcerer maintained his invocation, keeping the daemonic gateway open as long as possible. It wasn't until Ulrik brought the crozius swinging towards his head that Medeb ended his incantation. Bringing up his staff, he blocked the energised mace. Sparks erupted from the antagonistic energy fields, the unholy emanations of the warp-infused staff straining against the sacred properties of the crozius.

'You find no victory here, cur of Russ,' Medeb taunted. 'All you can do is meddle.'

Ulrik glared into the beaked mask of his foe. 'Magnus said the same thing before we burned your world.'

Twisting the crozius around, he brought his boot crashing into the sorcer-er's gut, pushing his foe back. When Medeb swept his staff around to parry, Ulrik ducked beneath his adversary's strike, pushing the staff away, and struck the sorcerer's left wrist. Ceramite, flesh and bone were obliterated in an instant, pulverised by the destructive field surrounding the crozius.

The stricken sorcerer stumbled back, staring in disbelief at his severed hand. As he started to raise his staff to retaliate, the Wolf Priest's crozius crashed down upon it. Instead of merely breaking the staff, the impact caused it to explode, unleashing the malefic energies Medeb had drawn into it. The resultant blast obliterated the sorcerer's head, leaving only a smoking stump behind.

Ulrik scowled down at the dead sorcerer. Drained by the ritual he'd per-formed, Medeb had been unable to protect himself from his own power. It was a fate the traitor deserved, but with his destruction the Space Wolves had lost the hope of picking up Logan Grimnar's trail.

The discord of battle still raged through the courtyard, the Dark Angels and Space Wolves finishing the daemons and mutants conjured by House Morvane's ritual. The Alpha Legion, Ulrik noted, had already withdrawn, stealing back into the shadows before they could be confronted by those in service to the Allfather.

Sathar had remained behind.

'You have kept your word to me,' he told Ulrik. He gestured to where Balthus was despatching a knot of cultists. 'But you must break your word to him.'

'Never,' Ulrik snarled at the traitor. He reached for his plasma pistol. The weapon was ready to fire again, ready to cripple Sathar if he tried to flee.

'I know you will,' Sathar said. 'It is why I took such a risk. You aren't hunting me.'

Ulrik's voice became a bestial growl. 'You said Medeb had crossed the Great Wolf's trail,' he declared.

'So he did, but I think you'll agree killing him was necessary,' Sathar said. 'Besides, there is a better way to track down your Chapter Master. Trust that I can help you find him. Even a Space Marine must sometimes show a little faith.'

Ulrik was sickened by the debate that tore at him. What should he choose – his duty to his Chapter or his obligation to his allies? Sathar might be twisted, but the traitor hadn't yet told a lie. If he said he had knowledge of Logan, then he probably did. It was his hold-card, the piece he had kept off the table until he could use it to buy his freedom.

'What do you offer?' Ulrik demanded.

Sathar smiled.

'The prism,' he said. 'Have your Librarian stare into it, only this time have him think only of your Great Wolf. The vision he finds in the lens will guide you. Of course, the prism is a thing of the warp. If Balthus learns of it, he will demand its immediate destruction. He will consider anyone who uses it tainted and corrupt – heretics to be destroyed.'

The revulsion boiling inside him was unlike anything Ulrik had ever experienced. Duty and obligation fought within him, but he knew where his loyalty must fall. 'Go,' he snapped at Sathar. 'If our paths ever cross again, I will show you no mercy.'

Sathar nodded and hurried across the platform towards the shattered window. 'If our paths cross again, old wolf, it will be by my design.'

Ulrik saw the traitor leap through the broken window, his grisly cloak whipping about him as the polluted winds of Eyriax lashed at his body. Sathar's lunge brought him to the wing of the Alpha Legion gunship. The Wolf Lord's last sight of the Traitor Space Marine was of him being pulled into the aircraft as it peeled away and rose into the smoggy sky.

C L Werner

PART EIGHT

WRATH OF THE WOLF

As he accompanied Interrogator-Chaplain Balthus up into the old mausoleum above the crematorium, Ulrik considered the strange events that had
brought him to this place. Every creak and groan that rattled through the
elevator gnawed at him, worrying at his conscience, reminding him that it
was the traitor Sathar who hid from the light of the Emperor, not Balthus.
Yet circumstances had conspired to make the Wolf Priest honour his compact with the Traitor Space Marine over his alliance with the Dark Angels.

The smell of blood and battle was still in his nose. It hadn't been so long
ago that he'd stood in the halls of the corrupt House Morvane, fighting
alongside Sathar against the cultists and their masters from the Thousand
Sons. The sorcerer Medeb had been prevented from opening a doorway
between Stratovass Ultra and the Eye of Terror only through the agency of
Sathar and the Alpha Legion. It wasn't recognition of that service which had
moved Ulrik to forsake his agreement with Balthus and allow the traitor
to escape. It had been the clue Sathar had provided the Space Wolves... a
clue that might lead them to Logan Grimnar and his vanished companions.

The moment the elevator reached the traitor's abandoned refuge, Balthus was prowling around the plinths, studying the niches in the walls. The
Dark Angels had removed everything once the Space Wolves had told them
about Sathar's lair. Even so, Balthus was paranoid that they had missed
something. At least, that was his excuse for bringing Ulrik back with him
to the mausoleum. Now that they were alone, the Dark Angel felt at liberty
to voice the suspicions that had been growing in his mind.

'The agreement was that we should help one another in our hunts. The
sons of Caliban have kept their side of the arrangement. Can the same be
said of the sons of Fenris?' Balthus asked.

The Interrogator-Chaplain stalked through Sathar's stronghold like a predator on the prowl, studying every inch as he went. At the moment, the Dark Angel seemed more like a Space Wolf than a product of the Lion's gene-seed. The resemblance impressed upon Ulrik that for all their differences, there were many points of kinship between the two Chapters. They fought to protect the same Imperium and their loyalty was to the same Emperor. They should be united in purpose. Instead, as had happened so often in the many millennia since the Heresy, they were at odds.

'Be careful, Interrogator,' Ulrik advised. 'Calling the honour of the Space Wolves into question is a reckless thing. Such accusations are typically answered by blade and claw. You are fortunate that I've been around long enough to make allowances for those who speak before they think.'

Balthus stood beside one of the plinths. It was the same one upon which the prism had stood. The Dark Angels had seized the dataslates, star charts and other paraphernalia that Sathar had left behind. After permitting the traitor to escape, Ulrik had felt duty-bound to give the Dark Angels every possible clue that might put them back on the traitor's trail.

Every clue, except one. The prism had been removed before the Dark Angels were shown Sathar's lair. Even now, it was hidden inside the Stormwolf, the *Rolling Thunder*.

'The Angels have ever been a temperamental lot,' Balthus declared. 'Some do indeed speak without thinking. It is left to Wolves to act without thinking.' He spun around, facing Ulrik, the optics of his helm glowing like embers. 'Sathar was here! So close I could reach out and touch him! You caught his scent, found his lair! We were so close...'

'Thwarting the ritual the Thousand Sons were orchestrating was more important,' Ulrik said. 'Every soul on this world was imperilled. Had we delayed even a moment, there is no saying how dire the consequences would have been. You lost six of your battle-brothers in the fight against House Morvane. How many more would have been slain if we'd ignored the cult and pursued Sathar instead?'

'Only because he saw no profit for himself in their triumph!' Balthus scoffed. 'I tell you, there is no villainy Sathar would not commit. Six battle-brothers, a hundred battle-brothers, they would be a small sacrifice to bring this monster to justice!' The Dark Angel walked across the chamber towards the entrance where Ulrik stood. 'Forgive any insult my anxiety draws from my tongue. You cannot understand the frustration, the disappointment this has brought upon me. There is nothing more important to me than putting an end to Sathar's infamies. Here, the hunt has come closer than ever. I am not too proud to accept that we came so close because of our comrades from Fenris.'

Ulrik clapped his hand on Balthus' shoulder. 'I know what you would ask of me, but it is impossible. We are sworn to our own hunt. We have vowed to seek out the Great Wolf and learn what has befallen him. There is nothing that can make us turn away from our purpose.'

The Dark Angel brushed Ulrik's hand away. 'Then you have found some new clue to your Chapter Master's fate. I suspected as much. I will not ask how you came by such information or where.' He turned around and pointed at the plinth. 'I will not ask you why Sathar only took with him the object that made that imprint in the dust and left everything else behind for us to recover. No, I won't ask such things of you.'

Balthus marched past Ulrik. 'Just as you will not be turned from your hunt, neither will I stray from my own. I *will* find Sathar. When I do, I will ask him these questions. Then we of Caliban will better understand the ways of Fenris.'

Ulrik watched the Interrogator-Chaplain as he stalked away into the battle-scarred halls of the crematorium. He knew Balthus would be as good as his word.

The corridors of the crematorium were silent now. Save for some enforcers conducting an investigation into the subversion of the facility's staff, the place was empty of activity. It would be some time before the damage inflicted on the factory could be repaired and the disturbed machine-spirits appeased by the tech-priests. The Ecclesiarchy had already dispatched some of its less influential clergy to begin recruiting a new cadre of laymen to fill the positions vacated by Sathar's minions.

Emerging from the crematorium, Ulrik made his way back to the *Rolling Thunder*. The gunship had landed in the centre of the plaza, its formidable grey bulk filling the space. Crowds of nervous hivers were gawking at the ship and the fabled Adeptus Astartes who were making their last inspections before their departure. As Ulrik crossed the square, Krom Dragongaze approached and fell into step beside the Wolf Priest.

'I've stashed that damned curse-stone the traitor gave us on the gunship,' Krom reported. 'It'll take a sharper eye than Balthus' to find it.'

'Let's not put that to the test,' Ulrik said. 'He's just suspicious enough to try.'

'Once it's on the *Canis Pax* and Leoric Half-ear sniffs out what we need from it, I'm of a mind to toss it out an airlock,' Krom said. 'The sooner we're done with the thing the better.'

Ulrik could appreciate the Wolf Lord's sentiment. The prism was a thing of the warp, thus pernicious and deadly. Before the Rune Priest exposed his mind to the visions locked inside the crystal, Ulrik wanted to sanctify Leoric with prayer and ceremony, to invoke the Allfather's blessing and safeguard him against the horrors that awaited him.

'Let us move swiftly,' Ulrik advised. 'Leave this planet and set Leoric to his ordeal. The sooner we can find Logan Grimnar's trail, the sooner we can reclaim our honour.'

It had taken Leoric Half-ear considerable effort to unlock the secret of the prism. The process had been far more difficult than Sathar had implied, and Leoric had discovered the prism to be a treacherous and conniving thing. It put visions and distractions in his mind, continually trying to tempt him away from his purpose. Every fleeting glimpse he was afforded would be smothered beneath a flood of noise and distortion. Whispers scratched at his brain, voices clawed at his soul, intelligences malignant and inhuman tried to reach into him from the warp-tainted glass. A less disciplined will than that of a Space Marine would have collapsed under the strain – driven to madness or worse. But Leoric was able to prevail against the deceits of the prism and at length unlock the knowledge the Space Wolves needed.

In the prism, Leoric saw the planet to which Logan Grimnar's strike cruiser, the *Eternity Fang*, had gone after it left Dactyla. He saw the ship apparently destroyed, annihilated by some cosmic force, but he also saw that the Great Wolf and his companions hadn't shared their ship's fate. They'd made planetfall. What became of their brothers after that, Leoric couldn't say. Even his stamina had reached a point near collapse. It was enough for their purposes that the Space Wolves had managed to identify the planet.

Dargur was a world recorded in the sagas of the Fang. The blighted, forsaken planet had played a role in the first Great Hunt. A wasted sphere orbiting a crimson dwarf just within the Eye of Terror, it had been the place of battle and horror for millennia. The Great Wolf Bjorn had led his warriors there in search of their primarch, finding instead only daemons and the remnants of a debased xenos civilisation.

Now it was to this desolate world that Logan Grimnar had led his own Great Company. Ulrik wondered if his old friend had discovered new evidence that Russ had visited Dargur or if he had been led here by the same broken trail Bjorn had followed so long ago. That the Great Wolf had failed to return to Fenris, or at least send word back to his Chapter, was proof enough that some distress had befallen the Champions of Fenris.

Penetrating the Eye of Terror was formidable enough a task. Even the most powerful navigators didn't risk straying too close to this cosmic blight. It was a place where the energies of the warp bled out into physical space, distorting the laws of reality and providing sustenance for all manner of daemonic horrors. Complicating the ordeal still further were the jumbles of asteroids littering the system, the shattered remnants of Dargur's sister worlds. Around Dargur itself there was a ring of semi-daemonic satellites, perverse constructs of a vanquished xenos' science.

Ulrik was impressed by the skill Rogan Bearsbane exhibited as he steered a path through the satellites. Rogan displayed an uncanny facility for detecting which of the defence drones were inactive and which yet possessed a flicker of malignance within their corroded frames. Only twice was the ship hit during its descent to Dargur's surface. The damage wasn't sufficient to cripple the ship, though Rogan was leery of tempting the fates again until full repairs were made. Some of the other Stormwolf gunships were battered far worse before they reached the surface.

Making planetfall on Dargur was an accomplishment devoid of victory. Ulrik could smell the uneasiness that gripped his warriors as he watched them ready themselves to disembark. They couldn't forget that this was the world Bjorn had visited in search of Leman Russ. They couldn't forget that his hunt for the primarch had failed. Would they too find only defeat here?

'All is in the hands of the Allfather,' Ulrik told his warriors as he moved among them. 'If you prove yourself worthy of triumph, then he will grant it to you.' He reached out and took a wolf-tail talisman a Blood Claw held towards him, bestowing his blessing upon the totem before returning it.

Near the hatchway, Ulrik found Leoric waiting for him. The Rune Priest had driven wolf-bone talismans into his forehead, the runes etched into each marked with his own blood.

'The dreams are quiet,' Leoric told Ulrik when he felt the Wolf Priest's eyes on him. 'The spirits of Fenris have subdued the cries of Chaos.'

'For how long?' Ulrik wondered, unconsciously brushing his fingers across the heft of his crozius.

Leoric closed his eyes and bowed his head. 'Long enough to lead us where we need to go,' he vowed. Blood trickled down his face and over his lips. Dragging one finger across his mouth, he daubed the image of claws across his cheeks. It was an almost forgotten custom, sealing his promise in blood.

Ulrik slammed his hand against the stud that controlled the *Rolling Thunder*'s hatch. The rumble of groaning plasteel and servo-motors filled the hold as the doors opened. The lower ramp shuddered outwards, folding upon itself as it slammed down on the surface of Dargur.

Ulrik recalled vividly the data recorded about Dargur in the sagas. He remembered, too, listening to Bjorn describe the place when the Dreadnought was roused from his rest. The descriptions hardly compared to what he saw now. The caprices of the Eye of Terror had wrought awful changes upon the cursed world. The sky was a purple bruise blotched by ugly stains of black and ochre, smudges too nebulous to rate being called clouds. The earth was a waste of black dirt, parched and barren. It lay around the gunship in an undulating course of hills and gullies. Beyond, in the distance, scabrous formations reared up into the sky, monstrous growths of rock that might have been the skeletal echo of mighty mountains. The sun, sullen and spiteful as it loosed its crimson glow upon the planet, reminded Ulrik of a kraken's eye – watchful and fearsome.

The other gunships were landing nearby. Scarcely had the *Wolfhowl* settled upon the desolate ground than the ramp came slamming down and Krom Dragongaze launched himself forwards in a great leap that carried him several feet from the hatchway. He crashed down in the grimy black dirt, a cloud of dust rising all around him.

Krom rose from his crouch, Wyrmfang clenched tight in his right hand while a fistful of dirt trickled through the fingers of his left.

'Daemons of Dargur!' he bellowed. 'Cower in your lairs! Hide in your holes! The Space Wolves have returned and I, Krom Dragongaze, have brought them!'

The defiant howls of their lord brought Krom's Wolf Guard charging down the ramp. Ulrik and Leoric adopted a more measured pace. The horrors of Dargur, they were sure, would still be waiting for them.

As he reached the ground, Leoric fell to his knees. Carefully, the Rune Priest reached into a wolfskin bag hanging at his side. Muttering an invocation to the spirits of Fenris, he cast a handful of tiny bones onto the ground, then leaned over them, studying them with a cautious eye before probing them with one armoured finger, turning them from side to side, examining each angle as it was exposed.

Other Space Wolves came over to observe Leoric consulting the bones. Wherever they fought, however far they travelled, the traditions of Fenris bound them, gave them the strength to defy any adversity. When Ulrik looked into the exposed faces of Blood Claws and Wolf Scouts, he saw the uneasiness of tribal superstition there, but he also saw a gleam of hope.

'Well, do the spirits tell you anything?' Krom asked as he stood above the Rune Priest.

Leoric looked up, snatching the bones from the ground in one fist. He pointed towards the horizon. 'The howl of Fenris is strongest in that direction,' he said. Each word seemed to fight for purchase on his tongue and his face was marred by the strain his divinations had inflicted.

Krom nodded. He brought Wyrmfang up and pointed the blade to the west. 'Lopt and the scouts to the fore!' he commanded. 'Keep your noses keen for the scent of our brothers! Keep your eyes sharp for the claws of our enemies!'

Forming up around their Wolf Lord, the Drakeslayers set out across the desolate wastes of Dargur. Ulrik gathered his strike force and followed Krom towards whatever doom lay before them.

'Troll-sucking vermin!' Krom bellowed as his axe swept through the ropey neck of a shrieking slytherfang. The twelve-foot reptile slopped away from Wyrmfang, splashing across the rocks in writhing sections. All around him, the Space Wolves were beset by a swarm of the mutated creatures, a slithering horde that had erupted from the ground in a seething mass of fangs and coils.

Ulrik slammed his foot down on the neck of one reptile, breaking its spine and pushing organs out of its mouth. A second creature perished as the field of his crozius blackened its scales and vaporised its blood. The thing flopped about for a moment in a mindless display of agony.

Beasts though they were, the attack was staged like a carefully planned ambush. Not until the Space Wolves were in the very midst of the swarm did they crawl out from between the broken rocks. They'd waited until they could bring their full strength against the Fenrisians, displaying a patience beyond simple vermin. That fact troubled Ulrik immensely. Throughout their trek across the wastes of Dargur, from the hills of dirt to the scummy swamps of amber slime and now these flatlands of stone slabs, creatures of every description had harassed and tormented them. Not with the stubborn tenacity of beasts, but with the deliberate persistence of a higher intelligence.

It was an impression that Ulrik couldn't shake as he watched the swarm of reptiles crawl from their burrows and hurl themselves at the armoured Space Wolves. The beasts attacked without fear or hesitation, dying by the droves on the blades and claws of the Fenrisians.

Ulrik smashed another of the reptiles with his maul. The vermin didn't represent a real threat to the Space Wolves, at least not one that could drag them down in battle. It was the constant harassment that was taking its toll, wearing away at the discipline of the Space Wolves, provoking more and more the savage instincts that were the legacy of the Canis Helix. With each attack they became that little bit more reckless and feral in their reactions. Bit by bit, the cohesion that made them a company of warriors was being eroded.

The last of the slytherfangs perished upon Krom's axe. The Wolf Lord glared at the dying creature, then flung its carcass from him and threw his head back in a victorious howl. The cry caught in his throat as he spotted something in the sky overhead.

'Beware, brothers!' Krom shouted. 'The enemy falls upon us from above!' Ripping his bolt pistol from its holster, he sent a burst of fire streaming upwards.

From the sky, a great flock of ebon-winged horrors swooped downwards. Heedless of the bolter fire that rose to greet them, the monsters descended, sickening shrieks rising from their misshapen beaks and fanged jaws. Fiery ichor dripped from their torn flesh, sizzling as it struck the rocks below. Like the mutant lizards, the winged fiends threw themselves at the Space Wolves with an amok ferocity, but unlike the reptiles there was a malicious determination burning in their eyes. More than mere beasts, the foes the Drakeslayers now faced were entities of the warp – daemons.

One of the furies fell upon a Blood Claw, raking the warrior's exposed face with its claws, tearing away great ribbons of flesh. Another sank its talons in the shoulder of a Grey Hunter, seeking to drag the armoured Space Wolf with it as it rose back into the sky. Both daemons soon discovered the folly of their efforts. The Blood Claw, ignoring his ghastly wounds, caught the flying foe with his chainaxe, ripping it apart in a welter of gore. The Grey Hunter, lifted a few feet into the air, fired a burst from his bolt-gun that exploded the fury's head and sent fragments of its skull clattering across the rocks.

Everywhere, the Space Wolves were wreaking havoc upon the daemons, yet still more of the horrors came. Ulrik swept his crozius into the faces of shrieking furies, the sanctified field of energy shattering their obscene essence and exploding them in bursts of sizzling ichor. Leoric, raising his rune staff, drew upon the ancient powers of Fenris, calling lightning from the diseased sky to immolate clutches of winged daemons. Krom, roaring his defiance, brought axe and bolt pistol against the flock of enemies that dived down upon him, littering the rocky shelf with dismembered fragments that slowly steamed away into crumbling bits of cinder.

Amidst the carnage, a sudden impulse gripped Ulrik, drawing his attention to one of the furies. The daemon soared about the periphery of the fray, but unlike its fellows, the fiend refused to commit itself to the battle. A primal instinct of warning flared through Ulrik's mind, crying out to him that the circling fury represented a threat greater than the entire flock. Ignoring the daemons swarming around him, the Wolf Priest aimed his plasma pistol at the soaring creature and sent a ball of fire blazing towards it.

Either by chance or infernal design, one of the other daemons dropped down between Ulrik's shot and his intended target. The stricken fury exploded in a dazzling coruscation of fire and light, the charred remnants of its wings flittering to the ground like falling leaves. Ulrik's target dropped down, streaking for the earth some distance from the battle. Ulrik saw it shift and change as it fell, transforming into one of the slytherfangs before hitting the ground and slinking away into a rocky crevice.

Ulrik knew that this creature was the guiding intelligence behind all the harassing attacks the Drakeslayers had endured. He had seen for himself the formless doppelgangrels of Asaheim, shape-shifting haunters of the forests. This, however, was something even more dangerous, a malignant entity that could both change its form and command lesser creatures to obey its commands. His thoughts turned back to the daemonic Changeling, the monster that had mocked them within the Great Hall itself.

Had the fiend followed them? Had the Changeling been dogging their trail from the very beginning? Ulrik wasn't certain if that possibility was less troubling than the other: that the Changeling had been waiting for them on Dargur all this time.

The Drakeslayers were exterminating the last of the furies, Long Fangs burning them out of the sky with heavy flamers and frag missiles. The rocky shelf was stained with their odious residue, a mephitic vapour rising from the greasy stains left by their dissolution. Ulrik took a step towards the hole into which he'd seen the shape-shifter disappear. He shook his head in dismay. It was doubtful the thing had lingered, even more doubtful that it had maintained the same form. He might search for days without finding the creature's trail. And if it truly was the Changeling, then any delay at this point would put the entire hunt in jeopardy.

'Lord Ulrik!'

The Wolf Priest turned as he heard himself being called. He could see a pack of Blood Claws gathered around the prostrate form of a comrade, the mangled carcasses of several furies scattered around him. There was a hideous rent in the fallen Space Wolf's chest plate, strips of meat caught in the torn ceramite. Even at a distance, Ulrik could smell the stink of death rising from the stricken Blood Claw. Already the warrior was standing before the Gates of Morkai. There was nothing that could be done for him, but by harvesting his progenoid glands, Ulrik could ensure the warrior's legacy lived on.

Sombrely, Ulrik removed the Fang of Morkai from his belt and began to recite the prayers that would commend the fallen warrior's spirit to the Allfather. He wondered, before the hunt was over, how many more times he would be called upon to harvest the legacy of the dead.

Hours after the attack by the furies, the Drakeslayers saw an end to the rocky flatland. The cracked shelves of stone gave way to an eerie vista – a vast forest of crystalline trees. The crimson light of Dargur's sun sent weird reflections shimmering from the angular facets of the translucent trunks and branches, creating the mirage of a rolling sea. As soon as the forest came into view, Lopt and his scouts set out ahead of the main body, intent upon ferreting out any unseen hazards that might be lurking ahead.

They didn't have long to discover the threat the forest posed. As Lopt drew near, the crystalline trees hurled slivers of themselves at him. The shards sheared through the rocky shelf and several stabbed their way into the scout's armour before he could retreat back out of their range. Lopt's comrades took hold of the old veteran, helping him reach the rest of the Drakeslayers. The ferocity with which Lopt was cursing his misfortune told Ulrik the scout was in no danger. Morkai wouldn't allow anyone with that much anger into his halls.

Briefly, the Space Wolves considered going around the forest. Leoric consulted his runes again, but his divinations directed them through the obstacle, not around it.

Krom pulled at his beard a moment, peering into the shimmering forest. Even his vaunted stare could discern no hidden secret amidst the strange trees. 'We've enough weaponry to level a few miles, but this stuff might stretch on for hundreds before we see the other side. I find myself wishing we had a psyber-raven. A view from above would be worth a gallon of mead right now.'

Ulrik studied the forest ahead of them. Everything was still, exhibiting an eerie silence. A thought occurred to him. Taking a rock from the ground, he tossed it into the trees. As it clattered against one of the crystalline stalks, it gave off a loud crack. Instantly the trees loosed a salvo of slivers. A second stone, tossed with more care, landed on the sandy soil without sound. This time there was no barrage from the trees.

Behind the lupine Helm of Russ, Ulrik smiled.

'The trees lack eyes to see, but in some fashion they are able to hear.' He nodded towards Lopt, who was being attended by the other scouts. 'Lopt must have made a sound that drew their notice and so they fired upon him.'

Krom ground his fangs together.

'Lopt is the best hunter I have,' he said, his voice lowered so his words of praise wouldn't reach the other Drakeslayers. 'He can sneak into a thunderwolf's den and steal her cubs with the mother sleeping right beside them. If he made too much noise to slip past these trees, then none of us will be equal to the task.' The Wolf Lord paused, a toothy grin appearing on his face. 'Maybe the answer isn't less noise, but more.'

Without further explanation, Krom stalked towards the forest, angrily waving back his Wolf Guard when the warriors would follow him. Step by step, he approached the trees, eyes locked upon the tracks left by Lopt, judging when he'd be close to where the trees had reacted to the scout. When he reached the spot, the Wolf Lord stopped. Facing the crystal growths, Krom threw back his head and howled.

The howl Krom gave voice to didn't sound from his own throat, or at least so it seemed to the Drakeslayers watching him anxiously from the rocks. The noise appeared to reverberate out in the midst of the forest, a trick of ventriloquism the Wolf Lord had employed to amuse his entourage many times before in the halls of the Fang. Now the trick deceived more than the ears of Space Wolves. The trees, reacting to the howl, cast splinters not towards Krom, but at the distant spot from which the howl seemed to issue.

Still throwing his howl, Krom began to walk towards the trees. He crossed the line where Lopt had aroused the forest. Steadily Krom pressed onward, still howling, still meeting no resistance to his own advance. When he'd pressed several feet past the point where Lopt was attacked, he stopped howling. Turning around, he sprinted back towards the rocks. Crystal splinters flew at him, dogging him until he was out of range.

'There's the riddle solved!' Krom laughed, walking proudly before his warriors. 'The trees can be tricked! Give them a choice of targets and they will strike at the loudest!'

'I should think the Drakeslayers aren't eager to lose their Wolf Lord,' Ulrik told Krom. 'Unless you think there's someone louder than you.'

Krom chuckled at the Wolf Priest's humour. 'No, old one, we'll not howl our way across. We'll blast our way across.' He pressed his hand against the grenade dispenser on his belt. 'We toss a grenade out among the trees to either side of our path and while they're busy shooting at the noise, we slip through.' He shrugged as he conceded one point against his plan. 'Might be slow going, but at least we can be sure of seeing the other side.'

As the Wolf Lord had feared, progress through the forest was a slow, tedious affair. But it was progress. Each set of grenades the vanguard threw kept the trees occupied long enough for the column to gain twenty or thirty yards at a run. Speed rather than caution dictated the pace during the brief spurts between grenades. Ulrik was impressed by the cohesion with which the warriors executed the arduous operation. The Space Wolves froze in place with an almost mechanistic precision whenever things were quiet. Beregelt had already taken the precaution of muzzling Vangandyr and the other wolves.

After several hours of the gruelling advance, one of the vanguard nudged Ulrik and nodded at the trees ahead. The crystals here had grown thinner, exhibiting a less concentrated pattern of growth. Beyond them could be seen rolling dunes of emerald sand. Krom's ploy had worked – they were through the forest.

Ulrik started to turn, intending to signal to the rest of the company that they were almost out of the forest. As he did so, however, a dark shadow fell across him. The Wolf Priest bit down on the instinct to cry out as he felt powerful talons snatch at him and drag him up into the sky with a sickening lurch.

Craning his head back, Ulrik could see that his attacker was a giant rodent-mosquito creature. There was a monstrous impression of intelligence in its gem-like eyes, a hint of malignant mockery as it stared back at him. He was caught in the grip of a daemon.

The Wolf Priest drew his plasma pistol as the daemon-fly carried him out over the forest. A crackle of sadistic mirth oozed from the creature's proboscis. The pincers gripping Ulrik abruptly loosened their hold, sending him crashing downwards. As he fell into the midst of the hostile forest, he fired a shot at his foe. The ball of plasma seared upwards, but already the unnatural substance of the daemon was morphing into a new shape, shrinking and twisting into a moth-like being that darted from the path of his shot. The Changeling circled once, as though to assure itself of its victim's distress, then sped away towards the horizon.

Crashing down through the mineral branches of the trees, the crystalline growths themselves broke the impetus of Ulrik's fall. On their own, the spiny shards were incapable of piercing ceramite plate. It was the murderous velocity with which they were impelled towards prey by the trees that made them a threat. The violence of his descent sent a loud clamour ringing out through the forest. From every direction, trees hurled slivers at the sound.

Ulrik was shielded from the worst of their attentions. The trees he'd struck in his fall had been denuded of spines on those facets that faced him. Instead of posing a direct menace, the disarmed trees became his bastion, absorbing the impacts of the slivers flung at him from deeper in the forest. Even so, many slivers crashed against his armour and three pierced through to dig into his flesh, stabbing him in calf, thigh and forearm. Worse, the ground all around him was strewn with brittle fragments that crumbled at the slightest weight, the crackling sound drawing further salvoes from the forest.

The Changeling had flown him far from his comrades, well into the expanse of crystalline spires. Even if they picked up his trail, Ulrik doubted that there were enough grenades in the whole company to reach him and make it back out. He prayed Krom would have sense enough not to risk it. Finding Logan Grimnar was more important than rescuing a foolish old wolf who'd let himself be caught by a daemon's wiles.

Ulrik noticed a sound in the distance. It was the slicing, rending discharge of spines from some of the trees. At intervals, the noise was repeated. He strained his ears, trying to catch the explosive clamour of grenades, but it eluded him. Instead, after a time, he began to hear a faint howl. It was a voice he recognised – that of Krom Dragongaze. Ulrik had known the Space Wolves would never leave him. At the same time, Krom wasn't willing to put the entire hunt at risk and send the whole company back into the forest. It was typical of his pride and bravado that he'd taken it upon himself to seek his missing mentor.

The howls drew closer. Finally Ulrik could see Krom picking his way through the trees. A few spines were caught in his armour and blood dripped from a wound in his side, but the Wolf Lord still presented a miraculous sight. He scowled when he saw the litter of crystal lying all around Ulrik. With one hand he motioned for the Wolf Priest to keep still. Throwing another howl out amongst the trees, Krom brought one boot stamping down on the fallen shards. The crackle of crushed crystal wasn't enough to distract the trees from his feral cry. Krom waved Ulrik forwards.

Tense minutes followed as the two Space Wolves started back along the trail Krom had blazed. Again and again, the crystalline trees sent their slivers knifing towards them. During a pause, Ulrik shared a worried look with Krom. They still had far to go, yet the violence of the trees was becoming more pronounced. It seemed like the things were adapting to Krom's trick and turning their attentions to the real prey. A shake of the Wolf Lord's head told Ulrik that his friend had reached the same conclusion. As things stood, they'd be ripped to pieces before they made it out.

Abruptly, the trees around them shivered with agitation. They began to loose their shards at some distant point. It was inexplicable, for Krom hadn't thrown one of his howls in that direction. The two Space Wolves knew better than to question their good fortune, however. Whatever had distracted the trees, they would exploit it. Swiftly they dashed ahead, rushing through the grisly trees. Despite their reckless haste, the mineral growths continued to ignore them, firing instead on some target in the distance.

It seemed a boon from Morkai himself that the trees remained indifferent to the Space Wolves until they were clear of the forest. Among the emerald dunes beyond, Ulrik could see their comrades waiting for them. The warriors raised their arms in a silent cheer when they saw the two heroes emerge from the forest. Even with such cause for celebration, they had sense enough not to risk provoking the trees.

Turning his head, Ulrik considered the crystal trees and the peculiar agitation that had come upon them. As he looked out over the strange forest, a faint sound reached his ears. Bitterly, he dismissed it as a trick of the wind – for it seemed to Ulrik that he'd heard the howling of a wolf somewhere in the distance.

The emerald dunes fell away behind the Drakeslayers, giving way to a somehow even more desolate landscape of crumbling mesas and jagged ravines. So bleak were the surroundings that Leoric felt a sense of foreboding and paused the march so that he might consult the bones again. Once more they followed his divinations, their trail leading them through a haunted land of rock hoodoos and burbling geysers.

The march came to an abrupt halt when the land fell away into a wide canyon, stretching away as far as even the sharp eyes of Krom could follow. Lopt walked to the edge of the fissure and tossed a stone down. The rattle and clatter of the falling rock ended in a steaming sizzle. The Space Wolves peered down to watch as the rock dissolved in a mire of corrosive sludge that carpeted the bottom of the canyon.

'Morkai take this cursed planet,' Krom growled. 'It seems there's no choice but to go around this damned pit.'

Ulrik shared the disappointment and disgust of his battle-brothers. They'd come through many ordeals to reach this place, travelled far from the halls of the Fang in search of the Great Wolf. Now, when every warrior began to sense the end of their hunt, Dargur had thrown yet another obstacle in their path.

'There's a bridge across,' Lopt offered. The scout indicated a narrow span some thirty yards below the rim that stretched across the middle of the canyon. It was almost ethereal in its slenderness, barely three feet across and scarcely half as thick. The winds in the canyon appeared to have eroded it down to this state and it looked like one more good gale would send the entire span crumbling into the acidic sludge below.

Yet as he studied the bridge, Ulrik was struck not by its fragile appearance but by the material from which it was made. Doubting his eyes, he turned to Leoric.

'Isn't that the same crystal Sathar's prism was made from?'

Leoric was discomfited by the mention of the prism, but the Rune Priest closed his eyes and stretched out his hand. Bone fetishes and tiny runestones dangled from his fingers on leather straps, each talisman shivering in a spectral breeze as Leoric muttered an incantation. After a moment the charms grew still once more and he opened his eyes.

'You are right,' he told Ulrik. 'There is a resonance between that bridge and the prism. The harmony is too distinct to be accidental. The crystal was cut from this span.'

Ulrik turned away, staring out across the expanse of the canyon. The

Space Wolves would lose too much time trying to get around the obstacle. The bridge represented the only alternative, but it looked so feeble that even he was hesitant to put it to the test.

The Wolf Priest thought again of Sathar and how the traitor had insisted that he and his Alpha Legion allies remained loyal, albeit in their own deviant fashion. Something Sathar had said came back to him, an admonition that even a Space Marine needed to have faith. Advice? A challenge? Or was it the traitor's way of testing Ulrik's trust? Had Sathar sent them this far only to bait them into this trap? Just how far was the traitor prepared to go?

'I'm going down,' Ulrik told Krom.

'It'll never hold,' Krom swore. 'If you insist on testing the thing, let one of us do it. The Drakeslayers will mourn a lost comrade, but all the Fang will mourn Ulrik the Slayer.'

'I have made my choice,' Ulrik said. 'Sathar knew about this place. I am certain of it. He brought us here as a test of our faith.'

Krom was unconvinced. 'At least let us fashion a rope to haul you back if you're wrong.'

Ulrik lowered himself over the edge of the gorge, sinking his claws into the rock.

'To doubt is to question your own resolve,' he said. 'Faith is to be without question. The bridge will hold, because I believe it will hold.'

Lining the edge of the canyon, the Space Wolves watched as Ulrik picked his way down the side. He could smell the agitation in their scent, the concern that wracked them. There wasn't one who wouldn't have offered himself in the Wolf Priest's place, and there wasn't one who lacked the respect to accept his decision to act on his own. They could only watch as he slowly descended to the crystal bridge.

When Ulrik's boots came to rest upon the narrow span, he felt a thrill course through his body. There was an almost electric shock, a numbing surge that pulsed through his armour. He could feel a dull hum rushing up his feet. The old wolf smiled to himself. This was how the span maintained its cohesion, not through the solidity of its construction but from the magnetic flow of energy that ran through it.

'It is stronger than it looks, brothers,' Ulrik called up to his comrades. He actuated the mag-clamps built into his boots, finding they gripped the bridge as readily as they would the hull of a starship. 'The clamps in your boots will hold you fast to the surface. Let me cross first, then follow one at a time.'

The excited barks and boasts of his comrades rang down from above. Ulrik couldn't quite embrace the acclaim. The Space Wolves were celebrating his courage when it was his belief they should be praising. His faith in a traitor's words, his trust in his own instincts to tell deceit from truth. To venture out onto the span was an act of courage, but not the kind many of his brothers would understand.

* * *

The canyon was hours behind them when the Space Wolves noticed the eerie change that had come upon the sky. Upon the purple horizon there now shone a jaundiced glow, a leprous blemish that cast its eerie rays into the atmosphere. Leoric closed his eyes and gripped his rune staff tight. The icy winds of Asaheim flowed about him as the Rune Priest drew upon the magic of his familiar spirits.

'There,' Leoric hissed through clenched fangs. 'Within that glow our hunt will end.'

'In victory or disgrace?' Krom asked.

Ulrik interposed himself between Wolf Lord and Rune Priest.

'Some questions are best left unasked. If we feed Morkai this day, will knowing it make us retreat from our purpose?'

Krom shook his head at the admonition. 'You suggest I am either a fool or a coward,' he grumbled. 'Only Ulrik would be so bold.'

'Of all your many faults, my friend,' Ulrik said, 'foolishness and cowardice are not numbered among them. I only advise that warriors fight the better if they do not feel the hand of destiny or the claw of doom hovering over them.'

The Wolf Lord pulled at his long beard, digesting his mentor's counsel. 'I recant my question, Leoric. Let the future see to itself. Whatever shape it takes, it will bear the marks of our claws!'

The Space Wolves moved out across a blighted plain, shrivelled clutches of cacti the only evidence of life. Gradually, as they drew nearer to the glow, the plain became peppered with jagged heaps of stone, toppled megaliths of almost unfathomable antiquity, their angles contorted to suit the aesthetics of an alien geometry. The scars of an ancient battle marked the fallen constructions, ragged craters blown by missiles and melted pits left by plasma guns. The Space Wolves thought of their Chapter's history with this world and of Bjorn's long-ago foray against the xenos inhabitants who claimed Dargur as their own.

Ahead, the Space Wolves could see the desiccated shell of an alien structure, a colossal building with great soaring columns and the decaying fragments of tremendous spires. The moons of Dargur hung in the heavens above, casting their rays down upon the ruin and evoking the eldritch glow from its broken walls. The sight put the Fenrisians on edge, provoking their primal repugnance of all things marked by Chaos.

'It is a temple,' Leoric whispered. Blood trickled from the bones he had set into his forehead and there was a ghoulish shine in his eyes, reminding Ulrik of Sathar's prism. 'Here the Thnalys held their murderous bacchanals and paid tribute to the Ruinous Powers. Here they sacrificed nations to placate the Dark Gods and preserve themselves from the corruption of the warp.'

'Bjorn put paid to their xenos wickedness ages ago,' Krom declared.

Leoric fixed his shining gaze upon the Wolf Lord. 'Where the Chaos Gods have been honoured once, they may be honoured again.'

Before the Rune Priest could explain more, Lopt came running over to report to Krom. The Wolf Scouts had ranged ahead of the main pack, patrolling the terrain ahead lest Dargur spring still more surprises on them. What he had was a surprise, but for once it was a pleasant one.

'I've caught the Great Wolf's scent,' Lopt said, tapping the side of his nose. 'It hangs heavy about the ruins. The place is thick with the smell of Fenris.'

Krom clapped the scout on the shoulder and smiled at Ulrik. 'The hunt draws to its end,' he declared. 'We've found the Great Wolf and his companions.'

'Yes,' Ulrik agreed, 'but we don't know what holds them here. That is a riddle we've yet to solve.'

'It will be solved,' Krom growled, drawing Wyrmfang. 'It will be solved with blades and guns! No, old wolf, do not try to hold me back. For too long our kin have been kept from us. Now let whatever force holds the Great Wolf discover what it means to trifle with the Sons of Russ!'

Ulrik could feel the rest of the Drakeslayers rising to the agitation of their Wolf Lord. The hunt had been long and arduous, dragging them across the stars. Now that the end was in sight, their discipline was being overcome by their more feral instincts. The Wolf Priest made an appeal to Krom, playing upon the respect and admiration in which the young Wolf Lord held his old mentor.

'Now, at the end of things, is when caution is most needed,' Ulrik warned. 'We must spy out the terrain, discover what it is that has kept Logan Grimnar from returning to the Fang. We must learn the challenge that awaits us.'

Slowly, grudgingly, Krom bowed his head and returned his axe to his belt. 'As ever, old wolf, your wisdom makes me feel like an impetuous Blood Claw fresh from the Trials of Morkai.'

There was still a smell of impatience in Krom's scent, in the scent of all the Drakeslayers, but for the moment, at least, it was curbed, held in check by their discipline.

'Then let us find what has befallen the Great Wolf and see for ourselves how this hunt will end,' Ulrik said. He motioned for Lopt to lead them towards the ruins, to follow Logan Grimnar's scent into the alien temple.

It was only a matter of minutes before the Space Wolves stood beneath the temple's shattered roof. They crept around the cyclopean columns, slipping into the shadows of broken walls. To their right rose a great shelf-like tier of platforms, to the left the crumbling rubble of a gargantuan altar. Before them, arrayed in a great concentric spiral, were jagged pillars, their capitals still supporting fragments of the collapsed roof.

Details of the architecture held the interest of the Space Wolves for but the briefest moment, however. It was the figures chained to the pillars that claimed their attention – massive, hulking shapes far larger than the hooded men that pranced around them with gleaming knives. The hearts of each Space Wolf froze when their eyes settled upon one of the captives.

None of them could mistake the snowy mane of hair or the long pleated moustaches, the sharp hawk-like nose and thick craggy brow. They had found Logan Grimnar and some of his warriors. The missing Space Wolves had been taken prisoner, stripped of their armour and readied as sacrifices. The Fenrisians had been savagely beaten, many of them slumping unconscious in their chains.

'The ritual on Stratovass Ultra,' Leoric hissed. 'They are seeking to perform the same rite, using the lives of our brothers to fuel their spell!' Blood stained his face, bubbling up from the runes etched into the wolf bones piercing his flesh. 'There is something more. A presence...'

The Rune Priest's distress was unnoticed by the Drakeslayers. Krom and his warriors had heard Leoric's words, and that had been enough for them to abandon all restraint. Seizing their weapons and howling their battle cries, the pack rushed towards the pillars, intent upon freeing their captured brothers and annihilating the enemies who dared to hold them prisoner.

Ulrik cried out to Krom, urging the Space Wolves back. His words were too late, however. They were already committed, and hurled themselves upon the foe with the ferocity of thunderwolves. Axes and swords sheared through the hooded men, and claws slashed the cultists to bloody ribbons. Bolt pistols barked, exploding heads and chests with each shot. The cough of a flamer was punctuated by the shrieks of burning heretics.

The Wolf Priest rose from the stricken Leoric, shaking his head in dismay. Lost in their fury, the Drakeslayers were oblivious to the ease of their combat. They didn't question how such feeble foes could have overcome Logan Grimnar and his warriors. The realisation would come to them soon, but by then Ulrik feared it would be too late.

Below, Krom had reached the pillar to which Logan Grimnar was chained. Casting aside the gory remains of a cultist, the Wolf Lord brought his axe whipping around to sever the Great Wolf's bonds. As he did so, there was a thunderous crash and a blinding flash of purple light. Wyrmfang was torn from Krom's hand and sent clattering across the ground. He glared at the pillar, then barked a warning to his warriors. So near to their comrades, so close to victory, and their triumph was being snatched away from them. Some infernal barrier surrounded the captives, a sorcerous shell they couldn't pierce.

Anger and frustration gripped the Drakeslayers. They lashed out at the corpses around them, venting their fury. As their rage swelled, monstrous laughter rippled through the temple.

Upon the tiers, armoured shapes appeared, manifesting with such suddenness that it was as though a veil had been thrown aside. There was no mistaking their gilded armour and the vane-like crest that framed their helms. They were Traitor Space Marines of the Thousand Sons. Dozens of them spread out across the tiers, their guns trained upon the Space Wolves below.

Towering over the Thousand Sons, a malicious cackle still bubbling from its blackened beaks, was an even more monstrous foe, an enemy steeped in the worst infamies recorded in the sagas. It had the withered body of a colossus, great wings stretching out from its back, mighty talons tipping each of its shrivelled claws, and two heads perched upon scrawny, vulturine necks, their eyes swirling pits of magic and madness. Clasped within one monstrous fist was a massive staff of ivory and gold, a monstrous tome of obscene lore chained at its apex.

Ulrik felt a surge of loathing and horror rush through him. The thing was nothing less than the Oracle of Tzeentch, the daemon known as Kairos Fateweaver.

The daemon lord's mockery reverberated through the shattered temple, each echo adopting fresh nuances of cadence and tone. Kairos stretched forth its staff, the pages of the ghastly book rustling in an arcane wind. It pointed the staff downwards at Krom.

'Thirteen to feed the spell,' the daemon's left head cried while its counterpart shrieked the same words in reverse.

From the heights of the tiers, the Thousand Sons opened fire upon the Space Wolves. Ambushed by the Chaos Space Marines, the Drakeslayers scrambled for cover, seeking shelter behind the pillars and the shattered rubble from the altar.

Still on the periphery of the temple, Ulrik and his strike force seemed to have gone unnoticed by the Thousand Sons and their daemonic master. Hastily, Ulrik split his command into two forces, sending half the warriors to circle around the temple and strike the opposite flank. He would lead the rest against their foe from the nearer side. He had no delusions about the kind of damage they could inflict upon so many Chaos Space Marines and a greater daemon, but he hoped they might sow enough confusion to grant Krom and his warriors enough respite to recover.

As Ulrik led his handful of warriors towards the side of the temple, he found that their presence wasn't as unnoticed as he'd hoped. Spheres of purple light crackled through the air overhead, swiftly coalescing into vicious ray-like shapes. Swimming through the air on lobed flukes, the grisly daemons shrieked wrathfully.

Knowing the daemons had taken from them the element of surprise, the Space Wolves unleashed a fusillade of bolter fire into the monstrosities. Ulrik blasted his plasma pistol into the flying daemons, burning one of them from the jaundiced sky. For every daemon they brought down, it seemed there were two left to swoop down upon them. The Wolf Priest saw one Grey Hunter crushed to the ground beneath a screaming fiend. A Blood Claw had one of his arms bitten in two by the snapping jaws of another.

Ulrik met his own attackers with his crozius. The maul crackled as it tore through one diving daemon, exploding it in a burst of ichor and light. A second monstrosity had its fanged maw ripped open by the weapon, its mangled form lifting back into the air with broken fangs dripping from its mouth. The third daemon-ray, however, prevailed where the others had met failure. Its hurtling mass slammed into Ulrik, smashing him to the ground. The Wolf Priest could feel its jaws snapping against the back of his helm, trying to find some weakness it could exploit.

A fierce howl rang out and the daemon's crushing weight no longer pinned him. Rolling onto his side, Ulrik saw a feral shape of fangs and claws ripping into his daemonic adversary. He blinked in disbelief at the battered war-worn armour that clung to the savage figure, recognising it to be an old pattern of power armour.

Similar fearsome creatures were helping the others, springing up from behind the rubble to pull daemons out of the sky. Hairy, half-human brutes crushed the daemons to the ground and savaged them with flashing claws, ripping gibbets of corrupt flesh from their monstrous bodies. One of the daemons, seeking to flee, was burned from the sky by a bolt of crimson lightning.

Ulrik turned from the grim spectacle of the feral creatures to see the warrior who'd saved him. He found himself gazing upon an old Rune Priest, his patched armour displaying a riotous disarray of styles and patterns, each piece daubed with protective marks and runes.

As for the bestial fighters, Ulrik wondered, could they be Wulfen? The afflicted beasts were rarely seen. Driven wild by the fault in their gene-seed, they were a secret source of shame that the Chapter usually tried to keep hidden. Ulrik had never heard of the creatures amassing in such a number – apart from in the case of the fabled Thirteenth Company...

'My thanks for your intervention, but my brothers are beset by enemies within the temple,' Ulrik told the Rune Priest.

The old warrior nodded his head. Turning towards the ravening Wulfen, he uttered a sharp bark. The half-human creatures swung around, locking eyes with the Rune Priest before loping off once more. They hurled themselves at the walls, digging their claws into the old masonry and pulling themselves upwards. Ulrik watched them climb for a moment, then rallied his own men and hurried to the gap that had been their objective.

When the Wolf Priest reached the base of the tiered platforms, he found the Thousand Sons slowly advancing upon Krom's besieged forces. The twin-headed Kairos hung back from the fighting, content to direct its minions and loose the occasional spell against a hapless Drakeslayer. The ambush was slowly closing around Krom, forcing his warriors to abandon the cover of the altar as the Chaos Space Marines brought their heavy weapons to bear.

Then, from their rear, the Thousand Sons found themselves beset by a foe even more ferocious than the Drakeslayers. The Wulfen came charging down the platforms, flinging themselves upon the stunned traitors with animalistic viciousness. Bestial claws ripped into gilded armour, tearing it from the ancient traitors. Finding only emptiness within the armour increased the frenzied wrath of the Wulfen.

The Thousand Sons retaliated with emotionless precision. While a few of their warriors moved to form a perimeter, those behind unleashed a withering stream of fire into the feral warriors. Two of the Wulfen were ripped apart under the salvo. A third was reduced to a mangled pile of meat even as he was pulling down one of the Chaos Space Marines.

It was Ulrik and his warriors who now aided the Wulfen. Their fire served as a distraction to the Thousand Sons, diverting some of their attention away from the feral creatures. When Leoric and the rest of the Space Wolves appeared at the far side of the temple, the fire from the Thousand Sons was split still further. Unlike their monstrous allies, the Space Wolves were able to duck back down behind the outer walls and gain some protection from the vengeful attentions of their foes. Even so, the Chaos Space Marines were leeching away at their strength, picking off the odd Grey Hunter or Blood Claw who was too slow to seek the protection of the walls.

With their foes reeling from the surprise assault of the Wulfen, Krom rallied his own warriors. Rushing out from behind the pillars, the Drakeslayers added their fire to the savage assault unfolding in the tiers. It was the Thousand Sons who now found themselves trapped. They fought with the determination of the damned, but their casualties were mounting. One after another their shattered armour was clattering down from the tiers and the dust of their mortal essence was drifting away on the wind.

Kairos glared with its gibbous eyes at the packs ravening all around it. A spell from one of its talons reduced a Grey Hunter to a charred smear. A bolt of flame from one of its beaks transformed a Long Fang into a pile of steaming meat. From its staff, a crackling whip of power flayed flesh and fur from one of the Wulfen, leaving its bloodied carcass strewn across the temple. More and more, however, as its minions fell, the daemon was compelled to employ its magic to defend itself, to ward away the salvoes of missiles and bolter fire that were directed against it.

In the midst of the carnage, Ulrik spotted one of the Thousand Sons turning to fire at a chained Space Wolf. The Chaos Space Marine blew apart the captive's head. The sight filled Ulrik with rage. Snapping a shot from his plasma pistol, he blew apart the murderous traitor.

Ulrik turned to the nearest of the Wulfen, locking eyes with the ferocious creature. More by gesture than word, he indicated to the feral warrior his plan.

'Try to break their chains,' he told the half-beast. The Wulfen growled, but to his relief went loping down towards the pillars. Ulrik prayed to Morkai that these strange warriors would be able to succeed where Krom had not before any more of the Thousand Sons decided to kill their prisoners.

'Krom,' Ulrik called out across the vox. 'Have your warriors cover the Wulfen. I'm hoping he can break the chains.'

Ulrik's command was quickly executed. Krom's Drakeslayers concentrated their shots on the Thousand Sons who were trying to bring down the Wulfen loping towards the pillars. The Chaos Space Marines were forced back, denied the opportunity to pick off their target. The Wulfen reached the temple floor and sprang to the nearest pillar. As Ulrik had predicted, his claws had no problem seizing hold of the chains and breaking them. The first of Logan Grimnar's companions was free.

Other Wulfen now seized upon Ulrik's idea. Great as their savagery towards the Thousand Sons had been, loyalty to their pack was an even greater force within them. In ones and twos they broke away from the fighting, rushing down to free the Champions of Fenris.

A grisly shriek of rage rose from the beaks of Kairos. The huge daemon lunged for the Wulfen, seizing the warrior moving to break the chains binding Logan Grimnar. Fateweaver's clutch transformed the snarling fighter into a bloody paste. While the Wulfen perished, Krom rushed to finish the job, Wyrmfang once more in his hands to strike a blow against the Great Wolf's chains. Kairos saw him and lashed out, seeking to seize hold of the Wolf Lord.

Before it could act, Kairos was assaulted by an elemental storm. Thunderous bolts rained down upon the daemon, driving it back. The fiend fixed its baleful gaze upon Leoric. The instant Leoric faltered, Fateweaver sent magic of its own blasting into the Space Wolf. He cried out as the destructive energies seared through him. His eyes exploded in a blaze of fire, the flames swiftly reducing his face to a leering skull.

Fixated upon Leoric, Kairos now found itself beset on all sides by its other foes. Those Wulfen not freeing the captives were helping to dispatch the last Thousand Sons. The full force of the Drakeslayers was now turned upon the Lord of Change. Shrieking in rage, the giant monster reached out with its claw, tearing a hole in the air behind it. The next instant, the creature had slipped through the rent in reality.

'Don't let it escape!'

The command rang out across the chamber. All eyes turned upon the bloodied figure of Logan Grimnar. This time Krom's axe had succeeded in breaking his chains. The Great Wolf waved his fist at the vanished daemon. 'It holds more of our brothers beyond the barrier!'

Ulrik was the first to reach the boiling rent through which the daemon had vanished. The Rune Priest who led the Wulfen was the second. Closing his eyes and raising his staff, the Wulfen compelled the rent to stay open. He cast an imploring look at the Wolf Priest, urging him on. Ulrik didn't hesitate, but rushed through the portal.

Beyond the doorway was another world, a ghastly ruin of floating plateaus suspended within a skyskape of shimmering incandescent vapour. Close to the rent, surrounded by broken battlements, was a circle of petrified trees, their stony bark etched with sinister, cabalistic designs. To each of the trees, just like the pillars in the alien temple, one of Logan Grimnar's Great Company was chained. Ulrik stared in shock when he saw that one of the captives had an all-too familiar mane of snowy hair and long pleated moustaches. Somehow, in this world, Logan Grimnar was still a prisoner!

Kairos was stalking towards the trees when its left head swung about, eyes widening in surprise as it saw Ulrik running out of the rent.

'I did not foresee this.' The daemon's voices somehow conveyed a tone of unease. It started towards Ulrik, raising its staff. Then it reeled back, crying out as it saw other warriors rushing out of the rent. The Wulfen howled with fury as they caught the daemon's scent, charging at the monster in a frenzied mob.

With the daemon focused upon the Wulfen, Ulrik charged for the pillars. Raising his crozius, he brought the maul cracking against the chains binding Logan Grimnar to the stone. An electric shock coursed through his body, almost tearing the crozius from his hand. Staggering back, Ulrik tried to fight down the numbness that dragged at his mind. It was the sight of the Great Wolf, the confidence that shone in his eyes as he saw Ulrik beside him, that gave the Wolf Priest the determination to fight through the effects of the sorcerous shield.

Tightening both hands about the grip of his crozius, Ulrik brought the weapon crashing against the chains once more. Again there was a tremendous shock, a searing pain that flared through every nerve in his body. This time, however, the chains snapped. Logan Grimnar's body sagged forwards, but the Great Wolf had enough strength left in him to keep from crashing face first into the dirt.

A baleful roar thundered across the floating plateau. Ulrik spun around, putting himself between the source of that enraged cry and the weakened Great Wolf. Kairos fixed him with each of its baleful eyes. The daemon's malignance slammed into Ulrik like a physical blow.

'You'll not cheat me of my prize,' Kairos snapped. A sphere of swirling flame erupted from its outstretched claw, leaping towards the Wolf Priest.

Ulrik held his ground, ready to die to protect Logan Grimnar. As the fiery sphere hurtled towards him, he could feel his skin blister inside his armour. Before it could engulf him entirely, the malefic conjuration dissolved into a fizzle of sparks. Ulrik saw one of the Wulfen climbing his way up the daemon's arm, tearing feathers and flesh away with each rake of his claws. The sudden attack had broken the monster's concentration, sparing Ulrik at the last moment.

'Make for the portal,' Ulrik told Logan Grimnar, gesturing towards the rent. 'I'll keep the daemon busy.' Before the Great Wolf could object, Ulrik was already rushing towards Kairos.

The Fateweaver plucked the Wulfen from its savaged arm. The feral warrior's body writhed in a hideous fashion as Kairos focused its malignance upon him. Bones rippled in obscene displays, flesh bubbled and flowed like water. What had been a fearsome warrior was reduced to a confusion of ruptured tissue under the daemon's magic.

Kairos' right head spotted Ulrik as the Wolf Priest came charging towards it. The fiend shrieked in primordial rage, dipping its staff to direct the relic's hideous power against him. Before the daemon could work its magic, Ulrik threw himself forwards in a desperate lunge. His arm wrapped about the ivory and gold length of the staff. He could feel the mutating energies of Kairos' conjuration rippling through the shaft and seeking to penetrate his own armour.

'Foolish mortal!' Kairos cackled, peering at the Wolf Priest. 'You cannot hurt me.'

Ulrik glared back at the daemon, the fiend that had caused his Chapter so much sacrifice.

'Maybe not,' he barked back, 'but what about this!' He slammed his crozius down against the immense tome lashed to the ivory rod. Ancient pages were ripped free by the blow, sent skittering away across the plateau.

Kairos cried out in shock, lunging after the torn pages. Laughing, Ulrik repeated his attack, ripping another fistful of sheets from the tome. The daemon's left head fixed upon him, the eyes blazing with unspeakable hatred. It started to raise its claw, to pluck him forcibly from the staff, but even as it did, the daemon's right head shouted in alarm. The Wulfen that had been darting about its legs, biting and clawing at the fiend, now gave up that pursuit, instead rushing after the scattered pages.

'My book,' Kairos squawked. Whirlwinds sprang from its eyes, whipping around the Wulfen, trying to catch the pages before the savage creatures could.

Ulrik seized upon the daemon's distress, sending still more pages fluttering away from its book. Kairos, unwilling to risk any magic that might harm his precious pages, could only try and shake its foe loose by whipping its staff back and forth.

Ulrik endured the vicious motion, biding his time until he saw his chance. As Kairos shook the staff towards its body, the Wolf Priest released his hold. Momentum sent him crashing against the daemon, the flanges of his crozius slashing the feathered flesh of its shoulder. Ulrik grabbed a fistful of Kairos' robe, trying to use it to arrest his fall while he brought his maul cracking against the fiend's neck. Ichor oozed up from the gash he inflicted, but before he could strike again, the daemon used its mighty wings to rise into the air. The huge pinions beat at him, breaking his tenuous hold and sending him plummeting to the plateau.

The Wolf Priest felt bones break as he slammed into the ground. Clenching his fangs against the pain, he forced himself up, drawing his plasma pistol and making ready to meet the daemon's next assault.

The attack didn't come. Conjuring more of its whirlwinds, Kairos was focused upon snatching the pages Ulrik had knocked loose from its tome.

'Keep today, whelps of Russ. For I have seen tomorrow!' Kairos roared.

Again, the daemon stretched forth its claw, ripping a hole through reality into which it could retreat.

Ulrik glared after the escaping daemon.

'Take heart that you thwarted its purpose,' the weary voice of Logan Grimnar came to Ulrik. He turned around to find the venerable warrior limping towards him. Behind the Great Wolf came the rest of his warriors, freed from their chains by the Wulfen. 'Its intention was to open a permanent doorway between the Eye of Terror and Fenris. By using the spirits of Space Wolves to power its ritual, the daemon could have created such a gate.'

'Will it try again?' Ulrik wondered.

Logan Grimnar frowned. 'We'll have to make sure it doesn't get the chance.' He scowled at the rent through which Kairos had retreated. 'If I had my armour and the Axe of Morkai, I'd chase the wretched creature down right now.' He turned a worried look to Ulrik. 'Did you find the rest of my warriors? Are they safe?'

Ulrik started to answer when he saw a figure emerge from the rent leading to Dargur. It was the old Rune Priest in the ancient armour. As he joined them, he bowed low to Logan Grimnar. A low growl rattled at the back of the wizened warrior's throat as he pointed firmly at the Great Wolf and then at the portal to Dargur. Tapping himself on the chest, he pointed to the rent through which Kairos had fled. Both portals were slowly starting to close.

'I think he means us to hurry back to our comrades and leave the pursuit of Kairos to his pack,' Ulrik said.

Logan Grimnar didn't seem to hear the Wolf Priest at first, staring instead at the symbol adorning the Rune Priest's armour.

'We must hurry, my lord,' Ulrik said, recalling the scene he'd left behind. It was impossible that Logan Grimnar could be both here and on the other side of the rent. One had to be an imposter. Which one was the problem that now faced him.

Logan Grimnar said something to the Rune Priest. Ulrik couldn't make out his words, but the only response was a shake of the warrior's head and another gesture towards the portal Kairos had escaped into. Frowning, the Great Wolf nodded.

'Brothers, let us be gone from this place,' he called to the other Space Wolves.

Ulrik waited until the last of Logan Grimnar's warriors was through before slipping into the rent himself. It seemed to be collapsing around him as he clawed his way between worlds. Reality itself was bleeding away, and for a hideous moment he felt the enormity of nothingness reach out for him. Then something far more physical caught hold of him. A fierce grip closed about his arm and pulled him from the rent.

'I'm not staging another Great Hunt to look for you,' Krom cursed as he dragged Ulrik from the rent. The wound in reality closed up behind him. The Wolf Priest had narrowly escaped being lost within the void.

'You'd have the Great Wolf to help you,' Ulrik said. The comment brought a severe look to Krom's visage.

'Which one?' he grumbled. Krom pointed at the Space Wolves Ulrik had sent through the rent. Logan Grimnar stood among them. But there was another Logan Grimnar who stood with the captives rescued on Dargur. Of the two, it was the Logan Grimnar of Dargur who presented the more convincing aspect, arrayed as he was in power armour and with the Axe of Morkai clenched in his hands. He glared at the Logan Grimnar Ulrik had rescued.

'You've been gone six days,' Krom reported. The Wolf Priest shook his head. It was almost unbelievable that so much time could have passed here when it had only been a few moments on the other side. If the Logan Grimnar of Dargur was an imposter, he'd had a good amount of time to convince the other Space Wolves otherwise.

All around them, weapons at the ready, stood the warriors who'd risked so much to rescue these men. They were a grim sight, their faces hard – for these were warriors who'd just had the taste of victory turn to ash in their mouths.

'One of our Great Wolves is an imposter,' Ulrik said. 'If I hadn't gone through the rent, its deception might have succeeded.'

Logan Grimnar of Dargur pointed at his opposite. 'Or the daemon decided upon this deceit only when its plan here was thwarted. If it can't open a doorway between here and Fenris, the next best thing would be to leave one of its minions in control of the Fang.'

Logan Grimnar from beyond the rent bared his fangs. 'You wear my armour and hold my axe. Tell me, if you were a cunning daemon, would you leave such things within reach of the Great Wolf or would you have them available for your spy?'

'There is one certain way to tell them apart,' Ulrik abruptly declared, stepping between the two Logan Grimnars. 'We can have Krom's wolf Vangandyr sniff them. A daemon might be able to trick a Fenrisian's senses, but it can't deceive a cyberwolf.'

Both of the Great Wolves frowned when Ulrik made his statement. It was the Logan Grimnar of Dargur who answered first. 'We are both so drenched in the stench of Chaos, I would be surprised if he knew the scent of either of us.'

The Logan Grimnar from beyond the portal laughed. 'A nice effort, but you are fooled,' he told his double, 'for Vangandyr is a thunderwolf, not a cyberwolf.'

'I knew I could count on you to know your wolves,' Ulrik said. He spun around, his crozius slamming against the imposter's hand even as he began to lift the Axe of Morkai. An inhuman wail of fury sounded from the false Logan Grimnar as its stolen visage began to slide and flow into a soup of twisted flesh. The Changeling lashed out from within the Great Wolf's armour, a writing coil of voidstuff whipping about Ulrik's neck. Before it could tighten, the real Logan Grimnar pulled the Axe of Morkai from the ground and brought its magic blade chopping down. The daemon's distorted head went flying from its shoulders to land among the standing stones, where it faded to nothing. The coil wrapped about Ulrik's throat lost coherence, writhing and ebbing away. The empty shell of power armour crashed forwards with a clatter onto the ancient stones.

'Do you think it's dead?' Krom asked Ulrik.

The Wolf Priest shook his head. 'With daemons it is never easy to tell.' Inwardly, he doubted the Changeling was gone, merely abandoning a disguise it no longer had use for.

Logan Grimnar stood glaring down at his armour. 'Taking my face is one thing, but taking my armour is too much. I'll have to polish it for a decade to get the stink out.' Looking up, the Great Wolf smiled at the warriors who had come so far and risked so much to find him.

'Brothers, let's be on our way,' Logan Grimnar declared. 'It's been too long since I've had the smell of Asaheim in my nose and the taste of Fenrisian mead on my tongue.'

As the Space Wolves withdrew from the alien temple, bearing their wounded and carrying their dead, Ulrik felt his eyes drawn to the mound of stone beneath which they'd entombed the fallen Wulfen. Somehow it felt wrong to leave them behind.

'You seem troubled, old friend,' Logan Grimnar told Ulrik when he caught him looking back towards the cromlech.

'They were brothers in arms,' Ulrik said. 'It sits ill with me to leave them here.'

'This was their hunting ground,' the Great Wolf said. 'Their work here is not complete.' Logan Grimnar shifted uneasily in the borrowed armour he wore.

'They were of our gene-seed? They were Sons of Russ?' Ulrik asked. 'Were you able to communicate with their leader?'

Logan Grimnar nodded slowly.

'What did you ask their Rune Priest?'

'I asked him if they were the Thirteenth Great Company,' Logan Grimnar answered. 'He said that Great Company is a legend.' The Great Wolf stared into Ulrik's eyes. 'And a legend is how they must remain.'

Ulrik nodded, casting one last look at the cromlech. 'Yes, they are legend,' he said.

BLOOD ON THE MOUNTAIN

Ben Counter

PROLOGUE

The first Ulli had seen of Alaric Prime was a topographic map projected from the holomat servitor mounted on the floor of the gunship. Now, as the rear ramp of the *Skjaldi's Lament* slid open and the icy wind roared in, Ulli could see the holo-briefing had not done this world justice.

A gleaming panorama of frost and white sunlight flooded the gunship's interior with light, as bright as a magnesium flare. Here, above the layers of cloud, this world's sun reflected up into an ocean of pale fire. The star Alaric, this world's sun, burned icily in a mantle of the most extraordinarily vivid blue.

The peak of Sacred Mountain burst up through the light ocean, a mighty spear of snow-capped stone that pinned Alaric Prime to the sky. No wonder the people of this world, settled in the distant reaches of the Dark Age of Technology, had bowed to this peak as the physical manifestation of the Emperor's will. When the Great Crusade brought Alaric Prime into the Imperial fold, it had been to the vastness and perfection of Sacred Mountain that the Imperium had been compared. The mountain shone as if plated with silver, a counterpoint to the sun above.

Ulli Iceclaw felt his eyes sting as his pupils contracted, his augmented senses correcting to prevent the snowblindness that any normal man would have suffered. The freezing air lashed against his face, whipping the wolf's tooth necklace around behind him. The many trappings of a Rune Priest – talismans from Fenrisian graves, teeth and bones for scrying, books of battle-prayers and meditations – jangled on his belt.

'They say Terra's sky was that colour,' said Brother Tanngjost, who held onto the handrail overhead beside Ulli. 'A long time ago. It is like that in paintings and poems.'

'Tanngjost Seven Fingers was probably there to see it, the old dog,' said Saehrimnar Brokenaxe. Saehrimnar was grinning beneath his expanse of red-brown beard. He was still strapped into the gunship's grav-harness and had his weapon, the pack's massive heavy bolter, across his knees.

'Not so old I cannot learn some new tricks,' retorted Tanngjost, pointing at his packmate with one of the remaining fingers on his mutilated hand. 'Like boxing a fat upstart's ears!'

Ulli ignored the bickering. It was tension being let off, and in spite of the barbs the pack needed it. They had been together a long time, some of them since they had first come to the Fang as hopeful young Fenrisian warriors, and without some levity they would become jaded and stagnant. Instead the Rune Priest looked back into the passenger compartment, towards Aesor Dragon's Head.

'Pack leader!' called Ulli over the roaring wind. 'What do you see?'

Aesor unfastened his grav-harness and joined Ulli at the ramp. His long, sharp face was as complete a contrast to Tanngjost's as the blinding sky of Alaric Prime had been to the gloomy interior of the gunship. Aesor's was young and unscarred, while age had lined Tanngjost's face as deeply as the battlefield scars that covered his cheek and one side of his jaw. When the people of the Imperium imagined the Space Wolves, the mighty warriors of Fenris, it was Aesor they imagined.

'A battlefield,' said Aesor. 'A butcher's block unbloodied. A blank parchment for us to write our glories upon. I see what every son of Fenris desires, a place for us to descend and bring the Emperor's justice.'

'There goes the Company,' said Tanngjost, leaning forward for a view of the cloudscape beyond the gunship's engine. Streaks of burning light were punching down through the clouds, trailing ripples of flame. They were drop pods, each one in the pale grey livery of Fenris with the black wolf's head stencilled on the side – the symbol of Ragnar Blackmane's Great Company. The same symbol Pack Aesor wore on the shoulder guards of their armour.

'Wish them Russ's speed,' said Aesor, 'and they will wish us his fury. Their battle is on the slopes below and the ballads of this war will speak of what they do. But we shall have our own saga, and though fewer will hear it, it will be ours alone. Pack Aesor! Give thanks, for again the galaxy gives us what we crave! It gives us war!'

'War!' cried Aesor's packmates in response, like a toast drunkenly roared in the Great Hall of the Fang.

Ulli could feel the fury in them, tempered in the bonds of brotherhood. A Rune Priest could not help pick up the vibrations from the men around him – no psyker could, for psychic power was rooted in human emotions as much as human will. The relish Pack Aesor felt at the coming battle thrummed at the base of Ulli's skull, infectious, eager to be released.

'You know what I see, Rune Priest?' said Fejor Redblade, seated at the back of the compartment. He lifted the sight of his customised bolter to his eye, as if picking out a distant target on the upper slopes of Sacred Mountain.

'What, Fejor?' asked Ulli.

Fejor smiled, revealing the overgrown canines of a Space Wolf. 'Piles and piles of dead orks,' he said.

ONE

Strikeforce Stormfall hit Alaric Prime hard. Beneath the clouds, the massive battle in the shadow of Sacred Mountain had entered its first stages. According to the briefings just before the gunship had launched, the orkish invasion force had made landfall in their hundreds of thousands, crashing to the surface in hollowed-out asteroids and barely space-worthy hulks that had landed more by luck than judgement. Orks cared nothing how many they lost to get to a planet's surface – each death just meant more mayhem for the rest of them. The numbers had been sufficient to force a beachhead there, and now the Imperial forces were desperately trying to contain a growing mass of orks rampaging out from their landing sites. Imperial Knights, war machines crewed by Alaric Prime's warrior aristocracy, had blunted the ork breakouts, but they could not fight on forever.

It was the orks' own war machines that made the difference. Orks could hammer together an engine of war from wreckage faster than the Imperial Guard could get their own tanks loaded and fuelled. Anything the Imperial defenders destroyed just became more spare parts for the greenskins. The Imperial Guard had plenty of veterans who had faced greenskins before and they reported this orkish invasion had with them more armour and greenskin engineers than they had ever seen. That was the extent of the intelligence on the ork invaders on Alaric Prime.

The greenskins had come to this world with numbers and purpose. It was no accident that they had landed at Sacred Mountain, the most storied place on this planet. They had to be defeated here, or Alaric Prime would be lost.

That task of relieving the defenders had fallen to Ragnar Blackmane and the Great Wolf Logan Grimnar. Blackmane was the young king, a future Great Wolf omened as grandly as any who had ever walked under the moons of Fenris. Grimnar was the Chapter Master and the Lord of the Fang, and while he had more battles behind him than in front he was still a terror of the Emperor's enemies. Together they were the greatest warriors from a Chapter whose lowliest members were ferocious masters of war. They brought with them most of their respective Great Companies, supported by aircraft, armoured formations, and specialists like the Rune Priest Ulli Iceclaw.

The great battle would be for the lower slopes amongst the greenskin landing sites, where there was a great tally of orkish heads to be reaped by chainsword and frost blade. There Blackmane and Grimnar would cover themselves in greenskin blood and hundreds of Space Wolves would glory in the ferocious joy of it. But on the upper slopes, where that battle would be a distant din, Ulli Iceclaw and Pack Aesor would wage a war of their own.

It was Starkad and Fejor who took the lead; Fejor, with his hunter's eyes, and Starkad with the experience of surviving in places just like this. The snow flurries kicked up by the *Skjaldi's Lament* swallowed the guide and the sniper as they jumped down from the gunship. Ulli and the rest of Pack Aesor followed, Ulli reading the winking green runes projected onto his retina by the auto-senses on his armour. In the whiteout he wore his helmet and the icons told him his packmates were nearby, advancing alongside him, close enough to come to one another's aid but far enough to avoid a single missile or landmine taking out more than one.

A Rune Priest stood apart from the rest of the Chapter – he was a psyker, training alone with the secrets of warpcraft. But here he could hunt with a pack of brothers alongside him, and the joy of that cut through the distance he had to maintain. Ulli's mind was shared between the Rune Priest and the son of the Fenris, and the Fenrisian's heart grew to be a pack hunter again.

'I'll keep the peak between us,' came a vox from Sigrund, the Space Wolf who piloted the *Skjaldi's Lament*. 'No greenskin filth will take potshots at my gunship! I shall make for return when the charges are blown and I shall not tarry, so be quick!'

'Don't doze off,' replied Saehrimnar. 'We won't be long.'

'I can see the structure ahead,' voxed Fejor. 'I'm taking cover. The greenskins hold it.'

'Advance, and be swift,' said Aesor. 'The snow will settle.'

Ulli emerged from the whiteout to see Fejor crouching by a rock, Starkad beside him peering through a pair of magnoculars. The pair had reached the edge of a long, sheer drop, a shoulder of the mountain, marking a stage of the ascent towards the uppermost peak behind them.

The departing engines of the gunship were replaced by the roar of rushing water. Below the ledge, a great lake reflected the pure blue of the sky. A dam blocked off what had once been a plunge down a sheer cliff face that vanished into the tops of the clouds hundreds of metres below. Several sprays of water gouted from the dam, the force turning hydroelectric turbines inside the dam that shuddered the rock beneath Ulli's feet.

The dam itself was a massive slab of rockcrete, its curved parapet mounted with battlements wrought into scowling masks like the face-plates of archaic armour. Chunks had been torn and blasted away, bundles of cables crudely slung from the breaches onto the shore at the far side of the lake. There squatted an orkish encampment, ringed with barricades of scrap steel cannibalised from the landing craft that had brought the orks here. The dam powered smoky workshops and motor pools of ramshackle vehicles – tanks, transporters, even aircraft that looked barely sky-worthy parked alongside a rocky airstrip marked out with burning fuel drums. A central building, apparently the bulk of a crashed spacecraft, glowed with bursts of blue-white power and the odd crackling and thrumming from it reached even across the lake to Ulli's ears.

'By the Moon-Wolf's frozen rump,' growled Saehrimnar. 'Our greenskin friends have been busy.'

'They are vermin,' said Tanngjost. 'Once they get a foothold they spread quickly, and they are Hel itself to winkle out. Even so, these orks are not such fools as we imagine. They took the dam early and are powering their workshops. See? War machines for the fight below – a second wave to strike from these upper slopes, where our brethren will not expect it. Blackmane was wise indeed to send us here.'

'I see a dozen greenskins on the dam,' voxed Starkad.

'Barely even sport,' said Fejor.

'Be thankful the enemy gives us such a quick victory,' said Aesor, 'no matter how much you love to shed his blood, Fejor Redblade.' Aesor turned to Ulli. 'Rune Priest. What do you make of our options?'

Ulli unlatched the helmet of his armour. The cold air in his throat felt good, much like the Fenrisian chill on the battlements of the Fang. He breathed in, reading the air. The Codex Astartes, that manual of Space Marine tactics, stated that the helmet of power armour should be worn at all times, but a Space Wolf knew that his nose was as powerful as his eyes and a battlefield could reveal as much by smell as by sight. He caught machine oil, sweat, the chemical traces of metal melted in a crucible. The mountain itself smelled pure, snow and ice and cold rock.

'Move in swiftly,' he said. 'No need to soften them up. Take them on at close range. That is how the ork loves to fight, too, but it will give the greenskins in the camp no time to respond. We must be in and out before they can scramble those warbikes and flyers. My apologies, Brother Fejor, but there will be no long-range kills made unseen, not for the moment.'

'I agree,' said Aesor. 'Starkad, scout us a way in. The rest, be ready to move. Kill close and swift. Ulli, bless our blades for this one.'

No one even mentioned that Aesor would take the pack's first kill on Alaric Prime. It was not the sort of thing that needed saying.

The honourable first blood was taken from the greenskin lurking in the dam's cavernous interior, serving as what passed for a sentry among the orks. Aesor's footsteps were lost amid the roar of the turbines and rushing water, and the ork did not hear them until the Space Wolf was three paces away. The ork didn't have time to bring its gun barrel up as Aesor brought his frost blade down past its face, the serrated edge slicing down into its shoulder. The frost blade was cut from a kraken's fang, and held an edge that could slice through the armoured predators of Fenris's oceans. It passed right through the upper chest and spine of the ork, and out beneath its arm. The two chunks of the ork's body thudded to the floor, the red-black mass of its organs slithering out across the rockcrete.

The rest of the pack bounded after Aesor as he ran past the fallen ork into the dam's interior. Crude orkish technology was everywhere, bolted to turbines or drawing off the power generated by the dam into masses of cables and pipes. Starkad carried one of the squad's demolition charges and Tanngjost the other, strapped to the backpacks of their armour. A stray shot could detonate one – it was not a task taken on with relish.

'Here,' said Ulli as the pack rounded a turbine housing. 'We're halfway across the dam. A breach here will do the most damage.'

'Set the charges,' ordered Aesor. 'Fejor, watch our backs.'

Starkad and Tanngjost began fixing the charges, one to the outer wall and one to the inner. A breach in both would flood the dam and send the torrent draining down through the cliff, hopefully taking the rest of the structure with it. Ulli was no engineer himself, but the Iron Priests of Strikeforce Stormfall had devised this mission and assured him that a strong enough explosion in the right place would bring the whole thing down, starving the ork encampment of the power needed to get their war machines running.

Ulli's thoughts were broken by the howling above him. He glanced up to see an ork looking down from a length of pipework a couple of storeys above, bellowing in alarm. Ulli instinctively drew his bolt pistol from its holster but before he could fire Fejor had taken the shot, punching a stalker bolt round through the ork's forehead and blowing out the back of its skull. The body tumbled to the floor.

Another howl took up the alarm, then another, a chain of them echoing down the length of the dam. Enough war-cries were raised to be heard over the turbine din.

'The enemy wants us,' said Aesor. 'He can have us!'

'Rune Priest,' said Saehrimnar, hefting his heavy bolter level with Ulli's chest. 'Bless the Widow, Brother Ulli!'

Ulli laid both hands on the housing of the heavy bolter Saehrimnar called the Widow. The weapon was too big for anyone unaugmented to carry, and it took a particularly well-built Space Marine to lift it with the ease that Saehrimnar did. Ulli felt his palms tingle with the familiar heat, as if he were laying them against the door of a blazing forge.

Ulli drew the psychic energy needed for the rune striking, calling it down from his mind's rare connection to the warp. He felt the darkness of that realm slithering at the back of his head, its tendrils probing at the mental defences a Rune Priest built up during decades of testing. That darkness was as familiar as the fire spiralling around his arms and out through his palms, the coils of heat and cold running around the inside of his armour as its warding circuits drew off the excess psychic power.

In his mind he formed two runes, taken from the language with which the tombs of Fenris's ancient kings were inscribed. One rune was strength and fury, both honour and the honour-breaking rage, the strength and curse of Fenris's people. The other was focus of mind, decisiveness, the will and the knowledge to strike with certainty. It was the necessary quality of a king, and when applied to steel it meant accuracy and sharpness.

The metal beneath Ulli's hands buckled and he drew them away. Where his palms had been, the two runes were now raised up from the metal. They glowed blue-white with the energy of their making, energy Ulli had drawn from the warp and forged with his mind.

'My thanks,' said Saehrimnar with a grin. 'Fitting garb for the queen of battle!'

The war-cry of the orks rose to a single wailing bellow, dozens of their voices raised as one. Ulli could hear the rumble of their feet on the rockcrete.

'Brothers, are we set?' demanded Aesor.

'I am,' said Starkad.

'A few moments,' said Tanngjost. He was still fiddling with the detonator on the demolition charge.

'Starkad, help him,' ordered Aesor. 'I would be gone from this place.'

Through the darkness the greenskins approached. Dozens of them loped through the broken machinery and rubble that choked the dam's interior. Orks were humanoid, but there the resemblance to man ended – their skin was dark green leather covered in scars and scabs, heads hung low on massively muscled torsos. Mouths crammed with too many teeth to fit snarled under red piggish eyes. Every movement was power and anger, for every ork was born with a lust to despoil and destroy that never waned until they died.

'What sons of a hundred oathbreakers stand before Brokenaxe?' yelled Saehrimnar. 'What waits for you beyond death that you are so eager to see it?' He cocked the movement of his heavy bolter, levelling it at the approaching horde. 'Do you hunt for oblivion? Fenris obliges!'

The heavy bolter bucked in Saehrimnar's hands as it rattled off a chain of fire, the barrel flare strobing in the darkness. The din of the gunfire echoed off the rockcrete into a wall of noise. Ulli's runes glowed hot on the weapon's housing as shots burst among the orks, ripping open bodies, throwing chunks of torn flesh and limbs into the air.

The other Space Wolves returned fire. Aesor blazed with his bolt pistol. Tanngjost, relieved of his task preparing the charge, stood and unholstered his custom bolter. He added a volley of his fire as Ulli did with his own pistol. Fejor switched to full-auto and sent half a magazine of stalker shells into the orks.

'Done!' yelled Starkad into the vox.

Behind the bulk of the horde, smouldering in the shadows, was a great dark shape looming and huge. Ulli felt the crackling psychic mass of the orks, a pulsing insanity like a fire or a stormy ocean, and among it a massive upwelling of rage.

Aesor grabbed Saehrimnar's shoulder guard and turned him around. The unspoken order was given and the pack withdrew, firing as they went towards the exit behind them. Saehrimnar sent out short volleys now, aiming as he moved, the bolter shells drawn to their targets by the power of the runes Ulli had inscribed on the gun.

'What a treat to be shot right through!' yelled Saehrimnar Brokenaxe between volleys. 'Feel the breeze on your lungs, my friend! Feel the mountain air on your guts!'

The return fire was ill-aimed and without discipline. The ork preferred to fight up close, and most used guns to soften up enemies and make noise as they charged. A shot rang off Ulli's shoulder guard as he took aim at a charging greenskin and put a pistol round through its skull.

The rage was growing. Ulli had faced orks before, but he had never felt this. In the swirl of combat he could not focus on it to divine what it was, but even the glimpses he had of it spoke of a scale and intensity beyond the psychic field that always surrounded a mob of orks in battle.

Pack Aesor emerged into the snowy glare outside the dam.

'Do it, Starkad!' ordered Aesor. Starkad hit the detonator switch in his hand and twin plumes of rubble and dust erupted from the centre of the dam. The sound hit a moment later, the ground shuddering, hot air roaring from the dam entrance.

Orks charged out of the dam onto the snowy mountainside. In ones and twos, the Space Wolves fell on them and cut them to pieces. Starkad drew his twin drake's-fang daggers, spinning and lunging as he punctured abdomens and severed spines. Saehrimnar clubbed one greenskin to the ground with his heavy bolter, and the creature was finished off by Aesor's frost blade thrust through the small of its back.

One ork barrelled towards the Rune Priest. Ulli's axe was in his hand. The weapon had runes of his own making inscribed on its blade and they glowed with anticipation of bloodshed. The power field around the weapon sparked into life, energy rippling across the blade. The ork was a larger one than most, a leader in whatever tribal system passed for their society. Its face was painted with a crude representation of a white skull, its gnarled fangs were tipped with iron and it wore a filthy mass of skins and matted furs. It was armed with a cleaver-like weapon, its rectangular blade well pitted with old blood.

Ulli ducked its first blow, letting the weight of his body and armour drop him out of the cleaver's arc. He struck upwards with his axe, burying it in the ork's chest. He balled up a flare of psychic power, born of anger that this alien would dare single him out, and let it burst up through the psychic circuit in the axe. The power burst out through the blade, adding itself to the force of the discharging power field.

The ork was blown clean in two. Scorched meat and organs rained across the snow. The upper half landed some distance away, the legs and abdomen flopping wetly to the ground in front of Ulli.

He could not deny how good it felt. Ulli set himself apart from the ferocious Blood Claws, or men like Saehrimnar who revelled in the kill – but Ulli was still a son of Fenris, and the lust and glory of battle was in his blood.

The ground rumbled as the dam gave way. A new waterfall burst through the break, taking half the crumbling structure with it as it poured down the cliff face to plunge through the clouds. Ulli glanced around to see the orks who had made it out of the dam were dead or dying, the last of them shot down by a short burst of fire from Tanngjost.

Ulli could hear the bellowing of orks trapped inside the dam, and the rushing of water inundating the whole structure.

He could hear something else, too. The roar of unfamiliar engines from the direction of the lake. From the camp across the lake a black speck was rising on a column of grey-black smoke, the drone of its engines growing louder as it approached.

'They have aircraft,' voxed Ulli.

'Russ's teeth,' snarled Fejor. 'I'll never understand how they learned to fly.'

'Break and take cover!' called out Aesor. The pack was already moving, scattering for the scant shelter of boulders and rises of rock. Behind them the peak of Sacred Mountain rose craggy and covered in snowy outcrops, but the slope by the lake was open. There was nowhere a man the size of an armoured Space Marine could hide, not from a strafing run from above.

Ulli ran for a rock that barely reached his waist. He was suddenly so open to attack he might as well have been wearing nothing but the ox-hide loincloth a supplicant wore on his Blooding. He glanced back and saw the ork aircraft knifing across the lake, swooping low. Massive cannon were mounted below its wings and a cluster of fat bombs hung under its belly. The craft had a blunt, lopsided look, the panels of its hull apparently salvaged wreckage, its pilot showing a grin of yellow fangs behind the cracked glass of the cockpit. How such a thing could even fly was beyond Ulli's understanding. It was as if the orks willed their war machines into motion, and fuelled them with their need to destroy.

The cannon opened fire. Bursts of flame and smoke jetted from the aircraft's wings. Explosive shells burst deafeningly along the near shore of the lake, and in a second or two they would fall amongst the exposed Space Wolves.

Ulli felt the hot blast of exhaust washing down over him as he was bathed in the roar of an engine. The cockpit of the ork aircraft shattered, throwing shards of glass and broken machinery behind it in a glittering tail. The ork craft angled upwards, wrenched out of its trajectory, and the shots from its cannon sprayed uselessly towards the mountain's peak. The aircraft spiralled away, its pilot dead, vanishing among the upper slopes and leaving nothing but a contrail of filthy smoke.

'I leave you for five minutes!' came Brother Sigrund's voice over the vox. 'Five minutes and already you need me to save your mangy pelts!'

Skjaldi's Lament banked around over the lake, the lascannon mounted under its nose still glowing from the volley that had shot down the ork. Sigrund brought the gunship down towards the slope, the rear ramp already opening.

'No whelp ever welcomed its mother's milk as we welcome you, Brother Sigrund!' laughed Tanngjost.

Beyond the landing gunship, the centre section of the dam was completely gone. The lake was rushing through the breach, the edge already receding from the shore as the meltwater drained away.

'You made a bloody great mess,' voxed Sigrund. 'As always.'

'Board, brothers,' ordered Aesor. 'I would not tarry here.'

'A shame,' said Tanngjost as he lugged his heavy bolter towards the gunship. 'I'll miss the mountain air.'

And again, welling up below his feet like the molten heart of the mountain itself, Ulli could feel that hate. A rage unbounded, waxing upon itself. It had the stink of the ork, but blacker and stronger, the monstrous will of the greenskin race distilled and made pure.

Smoke billowed at the entrance to the dam, from which howled the rush of water through the breach. The rockcrete entrance was suddenly shunted out of alignment, the lintel forced upwards as a great dark shape emerged through the smoke.

Ulli saw then what that hatred looked like, given a physical form. It was an ork, but that word did not seem to do the thing justice. It was enormous in size, twice the height of a Space Marine even hunched over, as broad through the shoulders as a tank. Its shape was composed of muscle and fang, its skin tattered with scars and almost black with age and smoke stains. Its jaw was so heavy as to look deformed, even among the orks, crammed with too many fangs to fit. Its eyes were burning coals set into pits of scar tissue.

Ulli had faced giant orks before. The larger the ork, the more powerful it was among its tribes and warbands, and so the hugest specimens formed the greenskins' leadership caste. This one, however, brought with it the psychic wailing of hatred and madness that spoke of the roiling, diseased ocean of rage it had in place of a mind. And there was a terrible intelligence to it, the last attribute one might give to the greenskin. On its back – no, *in* its back, fused to the spine and ribs, protruding from the skin and muscle – were metal protrusions like antennae, around which crackled blue-white arcs of power. It crackled across the ork's steel gauntlets and the metal plates riveted to its skin as makeshift armour. Cogs and flywheels spun amongst the machinery, generating the bursts of power. Sparks ground into the rocks, and snow vanished to steam as it stepped onto the lake shore.

In its arms it carried a weapon that would not shame a main battle tank, a cannon with five rotating barrels connected to an ammunition hopper full of loose shells. Like the aircraft, like everything the greenskins built, it looked like something that should never work, or at the very best that should have blown up in its user's hands as soon as the trigger was pulled. But the will of this thing was enough to make the weapon work as it levelled the barrels at the *Skjaldi's Lament*.

'Hear the thunder straight from Fenris!' bellowed Saehrimnar as he brought his heavy bolter up. He blasted a chain of fire at the ork, and the shots hammered against its massive frame.

The fire sparked off the armour and thudded into its flesh, but the ork was not even pushed onto the back foot. Explosive bolts were swallowed up by the mass of scar tissue and muscle, and the barrel of its cannon came down to aim at Saehrimnar.

The return fire was scattered wild. One shot caught Saehrimnar in the thigh and blew the ceramite open, revealing the wet redness of muscle underneath. Saehrimnar sprawled, his blood spraying onto the white snow.

Ulli was closest to Saehrimnar. He broke cover and sprinted to his fallen packmate, before the ork could bring its cannon to bear again. It could throw out a massive wall of fire but its recoil was such that the ork had to brace itself before it could finish off Saehrimnar. It would be enough time, Ulli was sure of that. He had the instinct of a seasoned warrior; he knew the cruel science of bullets and bodies. It would be enough.

Ulli grabbed Saehrimnar around the waist and hauled him off his feet. He backed towards the rock he had tagged as cover – it wasn't much against the air attack but it would provide shelter from fire at ground level.

Ulli saw the ork out of the corner of his eye, leaning into its gun to keep it level. It was even stronger than Ulli had imagined.

There would not be enough time.

The gun roared. Ulli felt the massive calibre shells ripping past him. The ork's face was illuminated in the muzzle flare.

Saehrimnar's head and upper chest burst. Ulli was thrown back, a torrent of blood and gore hitting his face. The weight he carried was suddenly less, for a good portion of Saehrimnar's body was gone.

The ork turned back to the gunship, which was rotating in place to aim its nose cannon. The ork brought its weapon to bear first. The barrels blazed and a dozen shots punched through the cockpit, stray rounds bursting among the fan blades of one engine. The engine tone rose to a scream and the craft wheeled out over the lake, belching smoke.

'Sigrund!' voxed Aesor. 'Brother Sigrund!'

The *Skjaldi's Lament* pitched into the lake and vanished, drawn under and out of sight by the currents rushing towards the breached dam.

Across the lake, a flotilla of craft had set sail. They were ramshackle motor launches and hovercraft, wreathed in oily smoke, teeming with greenskins from the camp. They held tribal banners high and waved their cleavers and guns, eager to clean up whatever the air assault had left alive.

'Fall back!' ordered Aesor. 'Take to the peak! The upper slopes!'

The ork turned back to the Space Wolves. It shouldered its gun and drew from among the machinery on its back a blade as long as an oak trunk and as wide as a Space Marine. The jagged length of the weapon was corroded and spattered with old black bloodstains. The time for killing from a distance was gone – it wanted its next kill up close.

Ulli hefted Saehrimnar's body onto his shoulders and vaulted over the boulder behind him. The lakeside slope became jagged and broken a good long sprint away, the gradient increasing sharply as the knife-like ridges and outcrops rose towards the mountain's peak. The giant ork could take any of them it wanted if it could outpace them, but that would limit it to one or two. If the pack of Wolves stayed where they were and fought it, they would still be on the shore when the rest of the greenskins arrived.

The scream of tortured engines reached Ulli's ears. The *Skjaldi's Lament* rose from the waters, lurching like a wounded sea creature. Behind the shattered windshield, Brother Sigrund wrestled with the controls as he forced the gunship's nose to point at the ork. A handful of shots blasted at the beast, most missing, one burning through an armour plate and into the greenskin's flank.

The ork bellowed and took up its cannon again, and with a final volley shattered the front end of the gunship. It vanished into the waters, Brother Sigrund having got in a final insult to the creature that killed him.

Ulli used the seconds Brother Sigrund had bought him. He ran for the cover of the rocky slopes, willing his body to ignore the weight of Saehrimnar's corpse on his shoulders and the heat of the blood that ran down his face.

The ork's frustrated roar echoed around the mountainside, mingling with the tumult of the new waterfall and the grinding of the ork flotilla's engines.

It hurt Ulli to flee. But the pack would not survive a battle here, exposed, one of their number down and the orks assaulting in full force. Their shame would burn hot, but it would not go unanswered. In that moment, Ulli knew the giant ork had to die, or the stain on Pack Aesor's honour would never be washed away.

TWO

Pack Aesor gathered an hour later. The way had been hard going, the steep slope forcing them to climb as much as run. But Space Wolves trained in the treacherous foothills of the Fang – they lived in a mountain and it was natural for them to negotiate such terrain. Even before they had been chosen by the Wolf Priests to undergo the tests that made them Space Wolves, some of the pack had lived among tribes who hunted and made war among Fenris's mountain ranges. It was difficult, but it was more difficult for the greenskins, who pursued them slowly up the slopes in an ill-disciplined throng with their enormous leader at their head.

Starkad was waiting for the rest of them on a shoulder of rock where they could gather, snatch a few moments of rest, and plan their next move. He was a natural pathfinder and had made the best progress. Ulli, weighed down by Saehrimnar, was last.

Saehrimnar's head and neck were gone, and most of his chest. The gene-seed organs, which could be preserved and implanted into new aspirants, were gone as well. They had been seated in his throat and chest, from where they regulated the many augmentations of the Space Wolf's body. Saehrimnar would not give those sacred organs, crafted from the flesh of the primarch Leman Russ himself, to the next generation. His legacy had come to an end. It was the worst coda to a bad death.

There was little time for words, and none of the packmates had much inclination to say them. Saehrimnar had been the quickest among them to speak. Without him, the silence he left said more than any of them could. The pack buried Saehrimnar under a cairn of loose stones, and Aesor took up his heavy bolter.

Starkad pointed up the slope, to where a squat rockcrete bunker occupied a ledge. It was the best shelter they would find up here, probably built by the Knight Houses of Alaric Prime to aid their exploration of the vast mountain.

As the pack made their way in silence towards the bunker, Ulli hoped the orks would not think to search the pile of stones and defile what they found there.

In the light of the guttering fire, the man's eye seemed to be sunk so far into his head that his face was little more than a skull with the skin stretched over it. He wore a rebreather mask, adding oxygen to every breath to compensate for the thin air at this altitude. Looking at him, Ulli thought how easy it was to forget that an environment like this, so natural to a Space Wolf, could be lethal to an unaugmented man.

Pack Aesor had found the man in the bunker, huddling by his fire. It looked like he had been there for days, living off a few packs of emergency rations, waiting to die up there on Sacred Mountain. His name, he had told them, was Frith.

'Time was,' he was saying, his voice almost lost in the shrill wind outside the bunker, 'they were kings of this world. My masters were this world's master. You see this?' he held out an emblem pinned to the lapel of his tattered uniform, a pair of compasses on a field of red enamel. 'House Varlen. Their sons had the most resplendent Knights on Alaric Prime. I, we, we would have followed them through the warp and into the heart of Chaos itself. But now?' The man coughed out a laugh, and Ulli wondered how old he was. He could have been anything from twenty to sixty. 'Now these... these animals have come down from the sky and made us all into normal men.'

Tanngjost looked down from the bunker's firing slit, where he had mounted Saehrimnar's heavy bolter. 'The greenskins don't have your world to themselves any more,' he said. 'The Space Wolves have come to Alaric Prime. Two companies of us. There's not an ork in this galaxy that can stand up to Blackmane and the Great Wolf.'

'And how many of you are there?' said Frith. 'A hundred? A thousand? The orks are vermin. They breed! There will always be another one around the next rock. You could kill a million of them and there would always be more.'

Behind Frith, Starkad drew the long, thin spike he used to clean the barrel of his bolter.

'You were a mechanic?' said Ulli hurriedly. 'For the Knights?'

'A retainer,' said Frith. 'Like all the line of my father. I served Baron Vigilus Varlen, Second Son of his House. I kept his steed, the *Dominus Vult*. Never did a finer Knight walk this world! I hung her with banners of Varlen's victories and polished her crimson flanks! But she has fallen, Angels of Death. She fell and is gone! How can this world prevail if even the *Dominus Vult* can be prey to the vermin?'

'How did you lose her?' asked Aesor.

'The ork,' said Frith. 'The one ork.'

'You saw it?' asked Ulli. 'Their chief, from the camp by the dam?'

'They must have their gods,' said Frith, ignoring Ulli. 'They must look like that ork did. The baron faced him on the mountainside. I watched from our command truck. Already I was thinking how I would bleach the vermin's skull and hang it among the battle honours. But it was not just a brute! A brute, the baron could have killed. It was cunning. It did not fight an honourable duel.'

'It's one of their engineering caste,' said Aesor. 'But I've never heard of one the size of their warlords. Not an auspicious combination.'

'There were more of them,' continued Frith. 'We saw them sneaking up but we were too slow. They infected my master's steed.'

'Infected?' asked Ulli.

'With a disease,' said Frith, leaning over the fire, the flame glinting off his sunken eyes. 'A disease of the metal. The *Dominus Vult* went mad! I heard the master screaming. She stalked off into the mountain, and blackness bled from her. Then she was gone, and the vermin was laughing. We fled and scattered. I ended up here. I know not where the other retainers are – most likely they are dead. Perhaps I will walk out and take the mountain's embrace. This is holy ground, Angels of Death. That was why my master took to these slopes, in case the greenskins defiled it. And they have. The mountain weeps.'

'A machine-virus,' said Aesor. 'I have never known an ork to employ such a thing.'

'Orks are animals,' said Fejor. Ulli noted with some gratitude that Starkad had put his blade away. 'That is beyond them.'

'They are animals who can cross interstellar distances,' said Ulli, 'who can capture a hydroelectric dam and use it to churn out war machines within hours. There is a cunning to the creature we faced. It is not like the other greenskins. Its hatred masks it, but there is a... a depth there. An intelligence.'

'I have known you a long time, Ulli Iceclaw,' said Tanngjost, 'ever since Phalakan. But even now, knowing that you see what you see, it raises my hackles.'

'Well, you aren't the one who has to see it,' replied Ulli.

Tanngjost grunted in agreement, and turned back to the firing slit to keep the watch.

Frith's chin sank down to his chest and he closed his eyes. Only the misting of his breath on the inside of the transparent rebreather mask suggested he was alive.

'I take it we cannot raise the Great Company,' said Ulli.

'Not with the gunship gone,' said Aesor. 'Its communicator could reach Blackmane's command. Our vox-net is not strong enough. On level ground with no interference, yes, but up here we are on our own. They will realise when we do not return, but I doubt our brothers will have the warriors to spare to come and rescue us.'

'Then we are on our own,' said Ulli.

'When are we not?' replied Fejor.

For a long moment the only sound was the crackling of the fire and the whistling of the wind.

'Tell me of Phalakan,' said Aesor, looking at Ulli across the fire.

'Your packmates must have spoken of it,' said Ulli.

'I would hear of it from you,' said Aesor. His voice was level and Ulli could read nothing from it.

'A battle against the eldar,' said Ulli. 'Tough going. We lost many brothers. I was apprenticed to the Rune Priest Torgrim Splitbeard. We were cut off and I found myself fighting back to back with this ingrate here.' Ulli jabbed a thumb at Tanngjost. 'And Saehrimnar. The eldar made Tanngjost rather more handsome.'

'I shall ever be grateful to whatever alien it was,' said Tanngjost, idly scratching the spiral scars on his face as if they itched with the memory. 'I paid him back in kind but I was a bit too generous. There wasn't much left of his head at all.'

'Saehrimnar broke his axe in the fight. The xenos were damned fast, back-flipping and dancing all around. So he picked up a heavy bolter from the ground and shot them all down. We called him the Broken Axe after that.'

'And you?' asked Aesor.

Ulli knew Tanngjost from Phalakan, but that had been a long time ago and Aesor had become their pack leader after that. Aesor didn't know Ulli, and it seemed that the word of his older packmates wasn't enough for him. Ulli bristled at that, a little of Russ's blood reminding him that he was still a Space Wolf, even if he studied in the Rune Halls instead of feasting in the Great Hall. But he could not blame Aesor for his caution. They would have to rely on one another up here, each one placing his life in the hands of all his packmates. Trust had to be earned hard in such circumstances.

'I put the runes on their guns,' said Ulli. 'When their bolters ran dry, I put them on their knives and chainswords. When their blades were dull, I put them on the rocks, and we dashed out the aliens' brains. Few of us lived, but live we did, and Ulli Iceclaw became worthy of the Blood of Russ. I might not boast like the Wolves of your pack, Aesor Dragon's Head, but I have earned the armour that is my pelt and I am proud of it.'

Aesor nodded, the ghost of a smile on his face. It struck Ulli then how, unlike the older Space Wolves who were covered in scars, Aesor was unblemished by war. Almost unblemished, that is.

'Tell me of your ear,' Ulli said.

Behind him, Tanngjost chuckled quietly. Starkad, who was resting in a dark corner, broke a smile, which did not happen very often.

Aesor looked for a moment as if he would curse out Ulli for his presumption, and perhaps if Ulli had been a member of Pack Aesor he would have. But the moment passed and Aesor shrugged.

'You have good eyes,' he said.

'You would not hide your scars by choice,' said Ulli. 'You are not some perfumed Blood Angel ashamed of the marks of battle. It is something that weighs on you. And if you would know about me, then I would know about you.'

Aesor swept the hair back to reveal the dark red snarl of scar tissue where his left ear had been. 'Before my Blooding,' he said, 'many of us were taken to the foothills of the Fang to look on the place where we would be tested. One of the other aspirants joked he would bet his kraken-tooth knife that I would be the first corpse brought back. I lost my temper, Ulli Iceclaw, and in the scuffle I bit off his ear. My people took tributes from the barbarian tribes of the Shark's Reach fjords, and we did not take kindly to insults. And I was young.'

'I see,' said Ulli. 'And he took your ear in recompense?'

'Ulli, Ulli,' said Tanngjost. 'I thought you were supposed to be the smart one?'

Aesor shook his head. 'No. I tore it off myself. I was taught to pay my debts, and not to visit on any man an insult we would not accept ourselves. My Blooding was delayed a week and I stood guard on the walls of the Fang in only a loincloth as punishment. I hide this scar because I would not have it bandied about that Aesor Dragon's Head is not to be insulted, for if that happened I would not know what my brothers truly thought of me. But I could not have it repaired either because then I would not bear the wound I had earned as one I dealt to my brother. So I hide it as best I can, until some sharp-eyed and inquisitive soul decides to point it out.'

'Then I would say we have both satisfied our curiosity,' said Ulli.

Starkad snapped to alertness, his bolt pistol suddenly in his hand.

'What is it?' asked Aesor.

'I can hear them,' said Starkad.

Starkad was from the nomad tribes who walked a belt of glaciers on Fenris, carving survival from the endless ice. They were trackers and pathfinders without compare, many of them serving as Wolf Scouts unless they were too pack-minded, like Starkad. Their senses were considered exceptionally sharp, even amongst a Chapter who could hunt by scent alone. When something caught Starkad's senses, the pack paid attention.

'Footsteps?' asked Fejor, unshouldering his rifle ready to set up at the firing slit. 'War-cries?'

'Engines,' said Starkad.

Ulli pushed open the bunker door as Starkad stamped out the fire. The wind was a thin, shrill whistle but underneath was the grinding of many engines, low and throaty. On a lower slope he could make out a lumbering shape, and as it came closer it resolved into a squat, ugly machine crawling up the rocky slope towards the shoulder of rock on which the bunker sat. The machine was something like a huge, flattened tank, but in place of tracks it had sets of rotating bladed wheels that dug into the rock and hauled it upwards. A crew of orks scrabbled across the machine's hull, throwing out chains with grappling hooks to draw tight and keep the tank stable as it climbed.

Hitched to the back of the rock-crawler machine, dragged by ropes and chains, followed dozens of orkish warbikes being towed in the machine's wake. The warbikes were painted in red with the sigils of a crude skull painted in blue. Their riders' leathers and goggles were well stained with oil and smoke. Some of the bikes were fitted with sets of cannon, the kind of crude, loud weapons that orks loved. Ulli guessed about thirty of them were being towed up the mountain.

He could feel the low *thrumm* of orkish minds, bestial but united in purpose. And beneath that, the dark foundation of their rage, the echo of their leader's mind.

'By Magnus's broken teeth,' swore Tanngjost, watching from the doorway beside Ulli. 'They didn't waste any time. Where do they get all this junk from?'

'Some build, some lead, most fight,' said Ulli. 'It is as if someone created the greenskins for war. Their mechanics can make a gun or a war machine from a handful of nuts and bolts. Their leader is more adept than most, it seems. Blackmane was wise to send us here. If it continues, it could turn the battle below.'

'Pack leader,' said Fejor. 'I would cover their assault from above us. I can take out a driver or gunner.'

'Agreed, brother,' said Aesor. 'But do not give yourself away for the sake of one more shot.'

Fejor left through the door, staying low as he ran for the snarl of broken rock and fissures that led to the uppermost slopes.

The grinding of the rock-crawler's engine changed pitch and the machine slowed to a halt, the orks on board hurling grappling hooks to keep it chained to the slope. The host of warbikes behind it gunned their own engines, whooping with the anticipation of speed and destruction.

'They're insane,' said Tanngjost.

'Their rank and file are,' said Ulli. 'Their leader knows exactly what it is doing.'

The first warbikes screamed up the few metres of slope that remained, reaching the sliver of level ground on which the bunker stood. Snow sprayed out behind them as the orks crouched over their handlebars, lips peeled back over yellow fangs.

Tanngjost ducked back into the bunker and manned the heavy bolter. Aesor and Starkad aimed their guns through the firing slit beside him. Ulli stayed by the door, using the rockcrete construction for cover and drawing his bolt pistol.

The heavy bolter opened fire. The lead bike was struck in the front wheel and fairing, pitching nose-first into the snow and catapulting the rider from his saddle. His body impacted against the rocks near Fejor with a crunch of bones.

The survivors drew cleavers and clubs, whooping as they banked to sweep around the bunker. Another fell, caught through the forehead by a shot from Starkad's pistol. Heavy bolter fire took down another before the bikers roared around to the other side of the bunker.

Ulli held his rune axe tight, feeling the psychic circuitry of its blade echoed in the shape of the sigils he drew in his mind. He judged the tone of the shrieking engines and leaned out from the doorway, bringing his axe up just as the first ork rounded the bunker.

The rune axe hacked into the ork's chest and shoulder. Ulli didn't need to force his willpower into the axe to shatter bone and shred neurons – the ork's own speed buried the axe deep enough to cut through heart, lung and spine, and the body that thumped into the wall of the bunker beside Ulli was dead before it hit. Ulli wrenched the axe out and brought it up in time to parry the swing of a cleaver from the next biker.

This one wore a mass of teeth hanging from leather strips around its neck, its muscular body cut deep with ritual scars. Its face was painted with blue skull markings. It slewed around to charge at Ulli again, as Ulli knew it could not resist doing.

The ork expected Ulli to duck, so it brought its cleaver down low as it swung. Ulli jumped instead, with an agility granted by the muscle-fibre bundles that let his power armour echo his every movement. He crashed into the ork knee-first, throwing it off the back of its bike and landing on top of it in the snow. He drew back his axe and brought it down into the ork's skull, splitting its surprised face in two.

More bikes were cresting the slope, mounted with cannon slung on either side of the rider. They were slower and their aim was wild as they sprayed shots almost at random. Splinters of rockcrete rained down as they peppered the bunker's side with fire. Tanngjost ignored the incoming fire, loosing off bursts from the heavy bolter to claim two, three more as they roared towards him.

One bike careered out of control and pitched over the side of the mountain. Two more crashed into one another and as the surviving rider got to his feet, Fejor sniped it through the throat from his hiding place above.

The orks were seeking to encircle the bunker, but they had to slow down to negotiate the wreckage of the bikes whose riders Ulli had killed, and soon Starkad was beside him, wielding chainsword and bolt pistol to bring down the bikers. When cornered like this, the level-headed nomad of the Gautreksland glacier vanished and pure Space Wolf came to the surface. Starkad fought with his teeth bared and hands bloody. He rammed his chainsword through one ork's chest, ripped the blade out and threw the wounded greenskin to one side. Another ork leapt down from its bike to leap on Starkad from behind, but Ulli willed a wave of psychic power into

the rune on his axe that represented the Fenrisian word for flight and swiftness. A crescent of glowing energy swept out from the blade as he swung
it, its leading edge as keen as the axe itself, slicing off the ork's arm at a
distance of several paces.

Orks were scrambling from the wreckage of their bikes, taking cover
from the heavy bolter fire in the rocky slope. Some refused to leave their
machines, slewing around to hammer fire at the bunker even as they were
shot down and wrecked.

Ulli was finishing off an ork on the ground with the spike on the butt-end
of his axe when he caught a scent on the cold wind. It was one he had
smelled before, a mix of old blood and chemicals, decaying flesh and dense,
choking musk. He yanked his axe out of the ork's chest and raised his nose
to the sky, trying to catch the scent again.

'What is it, Rune Priest?' asked Starkad.

'I smell warpcraft,' growled Ulli.

'We have them scattered,' voxed Aesor. 'Hold your ground and break
them against us.'

'They are not finished,' replied Ulli.

The clanking of great metal feet rang off the rocks, and Ulli saw a huge
armoured hand finding purchase at the top of the slope. The orks clinging to the back of the rock-crawler machine whooped and cheered as the
face-mask of a massive steel head rose up behind it. The face was wrought
into the shape of an eagle with deep green lenses for eyes. Its shoulder
guards were in the shape of golden-feathered wings and the torso was
inlaid with the intricate heraldry of an ancient and powerful house of Alaric
Prime.

It was an Imperial Knight.

THREE

Ulli had never seen a Knight in the steel before. Once whole legions of them strode at the head of Imperial armies in the ages of the Great Crusade, the Heresy and the early centuries of the Imperium. Now the secrets of their construction were known only to the Adeptus Mechanicus and only a few aristocratic houses maintained and piloted them. They were bipedal war engines that echoed the enormous machines of the Legio Titanicus, but smaller and more agile, the linchpin of a way of war that was almost extinct.

This one was sick. Ulli could tell that at the first glance. Glistening black oil ran from its joints, like corrupted blood, running from its eyepieces and the joints of its armoured body. The green and gold paint was blistered as if by disease, with pits and craters like old wounds turned bad.

Behind it clambered the giant ork mechanic, and in one hand it held a chain hooked to a collar around the Knight's neck. It was a master leading a slave, and it brought with it the stink of witchcraft and that upwelling of rage that seemed to shake the mountain under Ulli's feet.

'Is that the *Dominus Vult*?' demanded Aesor inside the bunker.

A shuddering Frith appeared at the firing slit. 'No,' he said, his eyes wide with horror. 'It's the *Aquila Ferox*. Emperor on high, they got the *Aquila*...'

'Whatever it is,' said Tanngjost, 'this heavy bolter won't dent it and that thing on its arm is a battle cannon. It will crack this bunker open.'

Ulli ducked back into the doorway to shelter from the fire still coming down from the scattered orks. The bikers had been sent to keep the Space Wolves pinned down in the bunker while the Knight reached them. The greenskin was not stupid, and it could call upon the corruption of the warp.

'Rune Priest,' said Starkad, sheltering beside Ulli, 'we have need of you.' He was holding out the final demolition charge, a spare in case the detonator failed on one of the charges they planted at the dam.

'Brother,' said Ulli, 'I cannot...'

'We will all die,' said Starkad, 'if you do not.'

Ulli looked into Starkad's face. He was one of the newer members of the pack, and had not been a Space Wolf when Ulli had fought alongside Tanngjost and Saehrimnar at Phalakan. Ulli did not know the young Grey Hunter well, but he had seen in him a calm and analytical war mind that could turn to a Fenrisian fury when cornered, a pathfinder who could pick out a trail through the roughest terrain and scout the most cunning enemy. The Chapter would do ill to lose him. But there was no regret in his face, and no pride at being the one to stand alone. There was just the certainty at what had to be done, and that he was the one who had to do it.

Ulli placed a hand on the casing of the demolition charge. He formed the sigils of strength and reckless fury on it, indiscriminate destruction and anger without form. It was not a complicated symbol but it was one that needed raw power, dredged up from the well at the back of Ulli's mind that was usually kept sealed by the mental discipline of a Rune Priest.

The glowing rune in the shape of a fist was etched onto the explosive's casing, and Ulli's hand smouldered with the effort.

'Cover him,' ordered Aesor.

The Knight reached the top of the slope, its gait lopsided and uncertain. One arm ended in a battle cannon, a weapon normally carried by the main battle tanks of the Astra Militarum. The mountainside shuddered under its feet.

'Metal beast!' bellowed Tanngjost from the bunker. 'Steel will melt and bend in the forge of war, but flesh and bone will not! And greenskin filth! Your kind are a disease, and in my hands I hold the cure!'

The ork mechanic turned at the sound of Tanngjost's voice, its face creasing with hatred. It pointed and bellowed towards the bunker and the enslaved Knight followed it, the battle cannon turning to aim. Tanngjost opened fire and heavy bolter fire *spanged* off the Knight's armoured chest, throwing out sparks but doing no damage.

Starkad sprinted from the doorway, pistol in one hand and the demolition charge in the other. Ulli's rune left a glowing trail in the air as Starkad ran.

If Ulli could bury his axe in the ork's skull, would he kill it? Even if he channelled every drop of psychic power through the blade, was that well of warp-born darkness too great for a Rune Priest to overcome? Ulli had never encountered an ork corrupted in this way before. He had never even heard of such a thing. How could he fight it?

Starkad reached to within a few metres of the Knight before the ork saw him. It roared and stomped up proud of the rocks, drawing the rotator cannon it had strapped to its back to make the climb. Ulli broke cover and ran at an angle to Starkad's path, letting a white-hot flow of power course from his mind into the axe. The weapon was hot in his hand and it was suddenly heavy, the strength of his arm temporarily drained as it was forced out of his body and into his mind.

Ulli leapt and brought his axe down, as if delivering a killing blow to the back of a prey-animal's neck. The blade of psychic energy was projected from the axe, a crescent of white light. It hammered into the ork's gun and shattered its casing, sending components spinning everywhere.

Ulli gulped down air. He abhorred the moment of weakness that followed such use of his power. He saw the ork throwing the broken weapon aside and growling in frustration – but it was not stalking towards Ulli for revenge. Instead it stayed fixated on Starkad, who was now in the shadow of the Knight.

'Here!' yelled Ulli, knowing it was useless. The distraction had bought a few seconds, but not enough for Starkad to do his work. Instead Ulli ran for the ork, his axe for the moment just a mundane weapon until he could catch his breath and feel the psychic power flowing through him again.

The Knight's cannon hammered a volley of shots into the bunker. Unaugmented hearing would have been deafened by the din – as it was Ulli's senses were overloaded for a moment by the noise. Chunks of the bunker vanished in bursts of flame and debris, laying open the interior.

Silhouetted by the muzzle flare of the battle cannon, Starkad clamped the charge to the leg of the *Aquila Ferox*. The ork loomed down on him, bringing his cleaver up to hack Starkad in two.

Ulli dived into the ork's side, tackling the alien shoulder-first. It was an unyielding wall of muscle and scar and Ulli barely knocked the ork back half a pace. He hacked at it with his axe and buried the weapon deep in the ork's shoulder, but the ork flexed the muscle of its arm and forced the blade out. For a moment Ulli was looking into the ork's eyes, and behind them he saw the infinite darkness of the warp, tinted red and boiling over with hate.

The ork aimed a backhand swipe at Ulli and caught him square in the chest. Ulli was thrown off his feet, head reeling with the impact, and it was instinct that made him throw his hands out to find some purchase in the snow and rock. He arrested his momentum just as his feet swung out over the precipice, a moment before he would have slid over the edge and into a fall hundreds of metres down through the clouds.

The charge detonated. The concussion wave hit Ulli before the sound and nearly threw him the rest of the way off the edge. The impact slammed against his ringing head and everything went red for a moment as the mountain shuddered.

Fragments of rock rained down over Ulli. Through the dust and snow thrown up by the blast he saw the *Aquila Ferox* listing to one side, one leg completely gone below the knee where Starkad had planted the charge. It put out a hand to steady itself but the ork's corrupting machine-sickness had made it slow and ill-coordinated. It toppled to the ground beside Ulli, the greater part of its weight hanging over the edge. It slid across the icy rocks and fell. Ulli heard the sound of stone on steel as it was battered against the side of the mountain and plunged through the cloud layer.

Ulli shook the sense back into his head. Somehow he still held onto his axe – another warrior's instinct. He used it to push himself to his feet.

The shape of the ork emerged from the smoke. In one massive paw it held Starkad up in the air, brandishing him towards the ruined bunker. Starkad's face was streaked with blood and his armour was torn and cracked, but he was conscious. He saw the ork's maw opening wide.

The ork bit down on Starkad's upper body. Its fangs sheared through ceramite and bone. Starkad's head and shoulders disappeared down its gullet. Blood and organs spilled down its chest as the ork threw the body aside.

Ulli could feel its glee. It relished this, not just killing, but killing a foe in front of that foe's allies. The very hatred Ulli felt for the ork brought it joy.

'To the slopes,' said a voice behind Ulli. In the chaos it took him a moment to recognise it as Aesor. 'Upwards. More are following.'

Ulli could hear the engines now, more bikers and war machines crawling up the slope towards the ruined bunker. Through the smoke of the Knight's assault he could see Tanngjost, the insensible Frith thrown over his shoulder, breaking from cover to join Fejor in the rocks above.

'We're running out of mountain,' said Ulli as Aesor helped him to his feet.

'Then we will make our stand at the top,' said Aesor, 'and bleed the greenskins white as they follow us. Move, Rune Priest. Move!'

For the first time, what remained of Pack Aesor could appreciate just how many greenskins followed the mechanic who led them. They had swarmed out of the camp by the mountain lake, thousands of them, released from the workshops to take up whatever weapon they could find and hunt down the Space Wolves.

Two more crawlers ground their way up to the ruined bunker, one bringing more bikers, the other scores of orks clinging to its upper hull. Other orks made the journey on foot, clambering through the ice and snow. From the glimpses of the greenskins massing below, Ulli estimated three to four thousand of them, many hauling their bikes after them, others loaded down with heavy weapons. Ulli saw no more corrupted Knights, for which he dared to be grateful.

Above the Space Wolves now was nothing save for a long snowy climb up to the very peak of Sacred Mountain, a gnarled spear of rock pierced with black caves. When the pack reached that peak, there would be nowhere left to climb.

Frith trudged alongside the pack as they moved. He was slow, but his weight was a fraction of a Space Marine's and he did not have to watch his footing so carefully in the snow.

'I should not look upon it,' said Frith, pointing up at the peak. 'It is a sacred place. Only those who pilot their own Knight may make this journey. We are unworthy.'

'Speak for yourself,' growled Tanngjost.

'What is in there?' asked Aesor.

'In there?' said Frith.

'This is more than just a mountain. It might be the tallest on this world but the Knight Houses are not cowering savages to bow before a mere mountain. I have heard tell the lower reaches were opened up, and there was found the means to summon us to Alaric Prime, but the peak is a mystery.'

'We keep it to ourselves.'

Aesor paused in his climb and turned to Frith, fixing the retainer with a look that Frith couldn't return. 'We could leave you,' said Aesor, 'if you would rather keep it to yourself.'

Frith squirmed for a moment, but Aesor did not have the air of someone who let such things slide. 'It is said that the Omnissiah put his greatest secrets in the peak,' said Frith. 'He walked here before men did. And when the Knightly Houses came, He left them ninety tablets of pure carbon carved with the admonishment never to tread upon the peak. When we are worthy, when we can hear the Omnissiah's truths and not corrupt or abuse them, then the peak of the mountain will open up to us. That is why our noblest sons make this journey and halt at the threshold, to show the Omnissiah they still hold true to his commandment.'

'And now there will be greenskin filth running all over this place,' said Fejor, who was listening in from his place in the lead a few paces ahead.

'I cannot think of it,' said Frith, 'I must not.' Ulli noticed the labour of his breath and remembered that while a Space Wolf did not care about altitude, an unaugmented human would suffer as the air got thinner. Without rest Frith would probably die before the sun rose the next morning, and he would not get any rest.

'I smell smoke,' said Fejor. Aesor held out a hand and the pack halted. They were in the lower reaches of the long snowy ascent, a trudge of perhaps two hours up to the rocky spike of the summit. Ulli followed Fejor's gaze and saw a smudge of grey against the ice-blue sky.

'It's the ork aircraft,' said Tanngjost. 'The one Sigrund shot down. Our greenskin pilot made friends with the side of this mountain.'

'Take a moment to think,' said Aesor. He kneeled in the snow and ran his hand through it, picking up a handful. 'This is fresh snowfall, on top of old. See up ahead. Near the peak? The snow is cracked where the slope has shifted. It won't come down with our movement but it wouldn't take a lot more.'

'An avalanche,' said Tanngjost. 'Wouldn't mind dropping half the mountain on a few orks.'

'There,' said Aesor, pointing to the side of the pack's path, where a dip in the slope formed a snow-choked valley. 'The orks are many but they are slow and move at different speeds. They will gather there before striking out for the peak. And above them is an avalanche begging to be set off.'

'Set off by us,' said Fejor. 'That ork death trap never dropped its bombs. If they didn't go off on impact then they'll still be there.'

'A fitting tribute to Brother Starkad it would be,' said Tanngjost, 'if we could set off a few more explosions in his name.'

Starkad's death flashed in Ulli's mind. He did not dwell on the deaths of brothers, setting those thoughts aside to be unravelled at the mourning rituals back at the Fang where the fallen were remembered. But the sight of Starkad's body disappearing down the greenskin's gullet, the alien's growl of satisfaction at the taste of a Space Wolf's flesh, those came to Ulli's mind unbidden.

'We have to take out their leader,' said Ulli. 'If that thing lives, it'll bring its warpcraft to the battle and the Imperial Knights will become weapons in its hands.'

'Leave that to me,' said Aesor. 'Fejor speaks true. Between Sacred Mountain and the greenskins we have everything we need. We will not make our last stand on this peak, brother. The greenskins will be making theirs.'

FOUR

The pilot's body was a tangle of skin and flesh, torn open first by gunfire and then by the impact that pancaked the fighter craft's nose back into the fuselage. Smoke was coming from one of the engines that had been torn clear of the main body and burst into flames. The snow was stained a dirty grey by the spill of fuel and oil.

'How can they get anything like this to fly?' asked Tanngjost, peering into the wreck's innards. 'It's just flotsam and junk.'

'The greenskins believe it will fly,' replied Ulli. 'Maybe that's enough.'

Fejor wrenched a sheet of steel away from the hull, revealing the bomb load crushed into the fuselage. 'A couple look intact,' he said. 'Tanngjost, your help, brother.'

Aesor and Ulli kept watch as the packmates unloaded the intact bombs. The bombs were as crudely made as the rest of the craft, just metal barrels with fins welded on and filled with explosives. It was a miracle they had not all detonated on impact.

'Do you see them?' asked Aesor.

All Ulli could see was the long white expanse of the slope, then the snarl of frozen rock that led down to the ruined bunker and eventually the distant blue glimmer of the lake. 'No,' he said, 'but they are there.'

'Greenskin scouts,' said Aesor, pointing towards a dark cleft in the rock where Ulli could just make out movement. 'Received wisdom states the ork is too stupid to scout ahead. That it simply charges headlong into anything put in its way. But you noted the cunning in the creature that leads them, Rune Priest. What you sensed, I now see with my own eyes. When the assault on the bunker failed, it changed plans. Now it seeks to trap us and hunt us down, and leave us no hiding place. It has its scouts pick out the best routes up the mountain, so its forces will not become bottled up and congested.'

'But you do not have any admiration for it,' said Ulli.

'No, brother,' said Aesor, 'for it tries to match wits with a hunter of Fenris.

Better for it that its greenskins charged blind and raging up at us, for then at least they would have the advantage of shock and fury. No, it has never hounded a quarry like us. It has no trick or tactic that I did not learn as a child of my tribe, let alone a warrior of the Space Wolves.'

'It left no gene-seed for us to take from our dead,' said Ulli. 'Not from Starkad or Saehrimnar.'

'You think that was deliberate?'

'I can conceive of few better ways to dispirit Space Marines than to kill our brothers in such a way that the flesh of Russ cannot be passed on.'

'A coincidence,' said Aesor. 'And crimes for which it will be punished. It should be grateful that we are visiting no more than death on it.'

'There is more going on in that creature's skull than you realise,' replied Ulli. 'The machine-virus was born of warpcraft, and wielded with deliberation and focus. Our enemy is no greenskin brute that rules by size and strength alone. That is why it must die, Aesor Dragon's Head.'

'And so all discussion of our foe will be rendered irrelevant,' said Aesor, 'for die it shall, and then there shall be nothing going on in its skull at all.'

Tanngjost trudged towards them from the wreck. 'There are two bombs that are still intact,' he said. 'Fejor's rigging a detonator. They were using a chemical mix as explosives, and bloody volatile too. If it wasn't so cold here it would go up if you breathed on it.'

'Thank Sacred Mountain, then,' said Aesor, 'for another weapon.'

Ulli thought of the cold, and looked around for Frith. He saw the man crouching out of the wind by the side of the wreck, holding the lapels of his uniform around his face. He was going to die, and Ulli thought about mentioning that fact to Aesor – but there was nothing the Space Wolves could do to prevent it, no shelter to provide for him or fuel to build a fire.

Ulli wondered if Sacred Mountain was an auspicious place to die, if it would be a failure in the eyes of the Omnissiah or a blessed end under His gaze. The Space Wolves did not cleave to the Imperial church or the many variations of the Imperial creed, or to the worship of the Omnissiah, that facet of the Emperor as a god of knowledge and revelation. Ulli did not understand religion of that kind – he had read the runes from tombs of Fenrisian kings venerated as ancestors by the people of his home world, but he did not himself believe their ghosts came to lead the souls of fallen warriors to the afterlife as many tribes did. And the Emperor, while the greatest man who had ever lived and the father of the Space Marines in a literal and figurative sense, was not a god in his mind as the Imperial church would have it. Did it bring comfort or dread to imagine the Omnissiah glowering down to judge at the moment of death? Was there even room in Frith's frozen mind for matters so weighty?

It was not long before Fejor and Tanngjost had buried the bombs at the top of the fractured snow field, where the upper layer sat precariously on an older fall of icy snow. The detonation would bring it all down, sweeping into the narrow defiles that would serve as paths upwards for the greenskins. More of the orks were gathering now, the hardiest and fastest climbers, lurking behind ridges of stone ready to make the final push upwards. Behind them smoke rose from the engines of bikes the other orks were manhandling over the rough climb, ready to scream up the flat slope.

'The bombs need no help this time,' said Tanngjost, 'and our pack leader's frost blade is as keen as it ever will be. But alas, the heavy bolter was destroyed at the bunker and all I have is my darling Frejya. Rune Priest, would you?'

Tanngjost held out his bolter to Ulli. It was a heavily customised model, an older marque from some ancient armoury of the Fang. Its casing was inlaid with red and gold, marked with silver eagle's heads to mark notable kills the weapon had taken. Tanngjost had even had the weapon's name inscribed on it.

'It has been too long, Lady Frejya,' said Ulli. 'Last time I saw you, you were out of shells and Tanngjost was beating an eldar about the head with you.'

'She might not be refined,' said Tanngjost, 'but she's still my girl.'

'What does she wish of me?'

'She is jealous of Brother Fejor's range,' said Tanngjost. 'Not his bite, for sure, for she can blow a hole in any greenskin big enough to spit through. But she'd rather not have to wait until I can see the reds of their eyes.'

Ulli laid his hand on Frejya's casing. He could feel the years on the weapon, the countless alien and heretic lives taken by her, the joy that a Space Wolf took in the decimation of his enemies. Such a weapon took the runes well because half the work was already done – it was already infused with meaning and history, with a patina of age and bloodshed. Ulli created the rune in his mind, taken from the tomb of a long-dead Fenrisian prince who could shoot a snow hart through the throat from leagues away. Distance, accuracy and cold-heartedness were enwrapped in the symbol now being raised up in light and steel.

'Fine raiment,' said Ulli, 'for a fine lady.'

Gunfire was stuttering up from below. The orks weren't trying to hit anything, or even fire ranging shots. The noise and the fury was its own reward, raising the blood of the greenskins until they were in a raucous battle-frenzy, with war-cries echoing up from the throng. They were starting the climb up the slope, falling over one another in their eagerness to get to grips with the Space Wolves.

'Can you see their leader?' voxed Aesor.

'Not yet,' replied Fejor, who was crouched in the wreckage of the crashed aircraft, surveying the enemy through the scope of his sniper rifle.

'Not right,' said Aesor. 'Greenskins lead from the front.'

'This whole army could be swept away,' said Ulli, 'but if that creature survives, all our work here will be undone.'

'Is it among them?' asked Aesor.

Ulli knelt in the snow and put a hand to the ground. Though his psychic discipline was not the reading of minds or the perception of the warp, his psychic sense could still react when the touch of the warp was strong enough.

It was there. The dark and monstrous stink of warpcraft, filtered through the mass of hatred that each ork possessed in place of a mind. It pulsed through the rocks and the air. It stained the clear sky. Ulli felt filthy just to perceive it.

'It's here,' said Ulli.

'Much as I would love to try,' said Fejor, 'I doubt we can wade through this many greenskins to get to it.'

'Then as Russ hauled the Iron-Scale Kraken from the ocean to best it on land,' said Aesor, 'just as Hef Shattertusk lured forth the Beast of the Black Fjord, so shall we bring the enemy to us.'

Above the Space Wolves' position was a promontory of rock, sprouting from the base of the rocky spindle that formed the mountain's peak. Aesor ran to it and stood on the edge, drawing his frost blade. Ulli could imagine that image in stained glass adorning a chapel, built by Emperor-fearing citizens to honour some act of deliverance from the Space Wolves. Very few of the Chapter were handsome, but Aesor was definitely among that few.

'Beast of Sacred Mountain!' Aesor bellowed. 'I know you can hear me! You have slain my brothers and I have slain yours, and who is either of us to leave such work undone?'

Aesor's words echoed up and down the mountain, as if Sacred Mountain itself were calling out the greenskin. A few whooping war-cries reached Ulli's ears from below.

'My frost blade has not drunk its fill!' continued Aesor. 'And there is space for another skull above the fire of the Great Hall! I think yours will fit perfectly, greenskin. And so I call you out! You will find no fiercer quarry on this planet, you will find no sword keener than mine to test your own! I call you out, and I know you hear me true!'

The orks howled and bellowed, and fired randomly up in the air. And then the din subsided.

Ulli had never seen greenskins cowed into obedience, not when they were chanting their war-cries and ready to spill blood. But these threw themselves face-down into the snow or scurried to the side as the horde parted.

The greenskin leader walked out from the throng. The mountain seemed to shake under its feet. It pointed up at Aesor and bellowed, the sound carrying on the wind like a roar from the warp itself.

'Do it!' yelled Aesor.

Fejor shouldered his rifle and jumped down from the wreckage, where the detonator had been rigged to the bomb load.

The ork grinned and the contraptions on its back glowed blue-white, spraying sparks and arcing into the ground. With a sound like a clap of sudden thunder, it vanished.

The orks around it were thrown aside by the shockwave. A blast of air tinged with the steely taste of ozone and blood hit Ulli, heavy with the greasy feel of warpcraft.

'It exploded,' said Tanngjost.

'It teleported,' replied Ulli.

The air was torn apart. The ork appeared on the promontory a few paces from Aesor, bellowing as it brandished the massive cleaver in its fist.

Aesor saluted with his blade – a foolish gesture, but a feint. The ork lunged at him, bringing the cleaver down to cut the pack leader in two. Aesor dodged to the side and turned the cleaver with his frost blade – a mundane weapon would have been shattered but the kraken-tooth blade turned the cleaver aside and the weapon was driven into the rock beside Aesor's foot.

Aesor leapt into the ork, planting a foot on its knee to propel himself upwards. He grabbed one of the beast's fangs with his free hand and head-butted it in the bridge of the nose. Cartilage cracked and the ork reeled.

'Say the word,' voxed Fejor from the wreck.

'Stand by,' replied Ulli.

Aesor vaulted off the ork before it could tear him off and dash him against the rocks. The separation was enough for Tanngjost to draw a bead with Frejya and blast a volley of shots into the greenskin. Shots punched into the mass of gnarled green scar tissue, but only angered the creature more. It hauled the cannon off its back, the barrels cycling as it levelled the weapon at Tanngjost. The ork had patched the weapon back together using ill-matched spare parts and chunks of welded steel plating. There was no way it should have worked, but there had been no reason for the ork aircraft to fly either.

The cannon blazed. Tanngjost sprinted for the rocky base of the mountain spire as shots erupted around him, throwing columns of snow into the air.

Aesor lunged at the ork. His frost blade was aimed at the place where its heart should have been. But the ork was fast, far too fast for a creature of its size. It brought its cleaver down into the path of the blade and caught Aesor's arm in the crook of its elbow, levering Aesor to the ground. It let its cannon fall to the rock as it drew its fist back.

Ulli's axe was in his hand. He had not willed it – it was a reflex action, wired into his hindbrain. Psychic power was pooling into the weapon, illuminating the runes on its blade. They were runes from the ancient peoples of Fenris, sigils of keenness, valour and ferocity, glowing bright against the dark steel.

The ork drove its fist into Aesor's chest. Ulli heard the ceramite buckling and the stink of warpcraft was suddenly sharp and real, the savage joy of the ork making its corruption flare up.

Ulli charged at the ork. This time he dropped at the last instant, knowing the ork had the cunning to anticipate the attack. The ork's cleaver swept over Ulli and he hacked the axe deep into the ork's thigh.

A force weapon, such as the rune axe, was not just a badge of a Rune Priest's rank. The psychic circuitry built into it was attuned to the wielder's mind, a conduit for the raw psychic power created by accident of birth and merciless training under the Rune Priests of the Fang. When that power flowed through the blade, it killed. It did not wound or sever – it sheared the enemy's soul away, annihilated his mind in the torrent of willpower.

Ulli let his mind flow through the axe now, the killing wave, the flood of mental fire, to shred the greenskin's mind from the inside.

A great black wall of hatred met his mind. The psychic force crashed against it like an ocean against a cliff. Ulli was thrown back, mentally and physically, hurled onto his back with his vision greying out and fireworks of shock bursting in his mind.

The mass of warp-born corruption had welled up and thrown him aside. The darkness inside the ork was more powerful than Ulli had realised. It was not an ork at all – it was a vessel for that darkness, brimming over with raw hatred that found form in the greenskin's savagery and lust for war. Ulli had faced daemons and witches, and sorcerers of the dark gods on the battlefield, but he had never felt such a magnitude of raw corruption.

'Fejor!' gasped Ulli into the vox, and his own voice sounded far away. 'Do it!'

'Thirty seconds!' came the reply.

Aesor was on his feet. The breastplate of his armour was crushed and split, and blood ran from his mouth. The ork lashed at him with its cleaver and Aesor parried, duelling with the creature blow for blow. They were both fast, both strong. The ork had the greater reach and power, but Aesor's frost blade was the finer weapon and he had the skill of a Space Marine and master swordsman. Ulli rolled onto his front and pulled himself to his feet, picking up his axe from the ground – the weapon's blade was smouldering and the snow around it had melted away.

Aesor was forced back a step. The ork slashed at Aesor at waist height with enough power to cut the Space Wolf clean in two. Aesor jumped back and sliced in response, the frost blade cutting off a good chunk of armour on the ork's shoulder and revealing oozing red muscle beneath the gnarled skin.

Fejor was running to join Tanngjost by the spire. Ulli glanced behind him and gauged the distance to the wreck. He was a little too close, and scrambled across the slope out of the blast radius.

Frith crouched beside the wreck, head in his hands and shivering.

'Frith!' yelled Ulli. 'Move! Move!'

Frith didn't respond. Perhaps fear made him insensible to what was going on around him. Perhaps he knew full well what was happening, and chose not to flee.

The bomb exploded. The wreck, Frith, and a good portion of the mountainside vanished into a column of grey snow and flame. The ground seemed to liquefy under Ulli's feet and he pitched onto his face.

The greenskin stumbled back. Aesor leapt onto its chest, frost blade drawn back to spear it through the heart. The ork grabbed Aesor with one hand, its massive fist enclosing his waist, and slammed him into the rock head-first.

The side of the mountain shifted and slid downwards. Ulli couldn't even imagine how many tonnes of snow had been dislodged, now gathering speed as it rumbled towards the ork horde below. The greenskin mech turned at the sound to see the avalanche seething downwards.

Ulli took the chance. He sprinted for Aesor, who lay on the rock at the greenskin's feet. Ulli grabbed the collar of Aesor's armour and hauled him away towards cover.

The ork looked back around to see Aesor out of reach. Its face split into a grin, of all things, and it laughed – it laughed to see its quarry escape and its army seconds from destruction. Liquid corruption, oily and black, was slathered around its fangs and glinting in its eyes. It reached behind it and worked the controls of the contraption in its back.

The ork vanished again, leaving the taste of burning metal in its wake. Ulli thought it must appear ahead of him, at the base of the pinnacle, cutting him and Aesor off from the cover of the mountain's caves. But instead, the flash and sound of the teleport came from below. The greenskin appeared in the midst of its army again, in the path of the avalanche that by now had taken the entire slope's worth of snow with it in one boiling mass.

Ulli was sure he could still hear the greenskin laughing as it activated another of the devices it had built into itself. A dome of crackling golden energy leapt up around it, flaring and spitting with arcs of electricity, encompassing a good third of the ork army.

It was a forcefield. The damn thing had a forcefield. Ulli cursed inwardly as he dragged the reeling Aesor towards Tanngjost and Fejor at the nearest cave entrance.

The ork horde vanished in the whiteout. Ulli waited at the entrance to watch, and sure enough, after a few moments of stillness the snow hissed and boiled away, revealing the perfect circle where the forcefield had protected the ork army from its fury. In the middle of hundreds of greenskins their leader stood bellowing orders and pointing up at the pinnacle.

Hundreds had died. Maybe thousands. But more than enough remained. Ulli spat in the snow and headed into Sacred Mountain, knowing the orks were following.

FIVE

Not even the Knightly Houses of Alaric Prime knew what lay inside the peak of Sacred Mountain, nor who had built it or why. The intelligence the Space Wolves had on the world suggested only that it was an archeo-tech site, full of technology from the Dark Age before the coming of the Emperor, when human innovation ran untempered and great wonders and terrors were made. A few legends suggested those who entered the peak never returned, which made it a less than ideal shelter for Pack Aesor, but one slightly more appealing than facing the orks in the open.

Inside the cave the pack found walls of smooth metallic stone cut into enormous blocks, dark and shot through with silver lines that suggested circuitry. Along the ceiling ran broad metal pipes that looped in and out of the stone. Panels of black crystal made up the floor and sections of the walls, still polished and reflective even after Throne knew how many centuries exposed to the elements. Flurries of snow blew in from outside and melted against the stone, for it was slightly warm to the touch, and Ulli could just feel a faint vibration as if from a power source running deep down in the mountain.

There was no sign of anyone having set foot in here. The cave led down into the body of the mountain, in a wide winding spiral lined with silver glyphs of some ancient tech-language. It was better shelter than nothing, but for real cover the pack would have to move further in and find a defensible location. They had time until then, but not much.

Fejor was kneeling over the stunned Aesor, trying to get his buckled breastplate off so the pack leader could be checked for injuries. Ulli leaned against the wall, watching the snow swirling outside and listening to the orkish war-cries and bike engines.

'How many did we get?' asked Tanngjost.

'Half,' said Ulli. 'Maybe more. A good tally for us this day.'

'But you do not rejoice in it, Rune Priest.'

'No. The true enemy lives. With luck it will follow us up here and spare our brothers below a few more hours of whatever evil it can wreak among the Knights. That is scant recompense.'

'We gave it a bloody good fight,' said Tanngjost.

'That would be enough for an Imperial Guardsman with a lasgun and bayonet,' replied Ulli, 'to tell himself while he waits to die. It is not enough for a Space Marine. We cannot claim valour as victory, or endeavour, or a fight well fought. Only victory is victory to us, and we are not victorious.'

'Does a man have to be miserable to join the Rune Priests,' said Tanngjost, 'or is it just you?'

Ulli tried to raise a smile, but could not. He could only think of the *Aquila Ferox*, corrupted and lumbering at the greenskin's command, and how a whole legion of them might look advancing on the great companies of Ragnar Blackmane and Logan Grimnar.

'How dare you?' came a voice from behind Ulli.

Ulli turned to see Aesor standing behind him, his damaged breastplate hanging loose, one shoulder guard buckled and split. Aesor's face was pallid and his eyes sunken, as if he had not slept for days, and Ulli could feel the anger in his eyes – a hot, red tint, flickering behind the pack leader's mind.

'I do not understand, brother,' said Ulli.

'How dare you deny my combat against the enemy!' snapped Aesor. 'The greenskin was mine to fight! The kill was mine, and you denied it to me!'

'You were wounded,' said Ulli, keeping his voice level. He had not seen Aesor like this before, but somehow it was not a surprise – that proud predator had always been there, lurking behind Aesor's eyes, waiting to uncoil.

'I could have taken it!' retorted Aesor. 'I was hurt, but it was distracted. A few more seconds and I would have been on my feet, as I am now, and I would have taken its head!'

'You would have died!' replied Ulli, louder than he had intended.

'Then I should have died!' shouted Aesor. 'I should have fallen in single combat with the beast, a glorious death that would crown the legacy of Aesor Dragon's Head! Do you think I want to become old and lame like this crippled ancient here?' Aesor jabbed a finger at Tanngjost. 'That may be enough for you, but not for me. I was chosen for greatness. I was destined for glory. Now I have been denied it. How many times do we court a death like that, in single combat with a lord of xenoskind? A death deciding the fate of a whole world? Of such things are the sagas of my people written. I might never see it again. My saga might never be written. And that sin I leave at the feet of Ulli Iceclaw!'

'That is why you fight?' asked Ulli. 'For glory, for a song to be sung of you when you die? What of your duty to the Emperor, to the citizens of His Imperium?'

'A billion die every moment,' snarled Aesor. 'What good does it do me to die for billions of ignorant scum who will never know my name, and who will be dead the next day? Only glory remains. Only glory is worth dying for. That is what you robbed from me. I do not expect a Vulture Clan deviant to understand.'

Ulli did not reply. He could not. Aesor spat at Ulli's feet and walked deeper into the cave, around the curve which led into Sacred Mountain.

'Pack leader!' shouted Tanngjost after him. 'Brother Aesor!'

There was no reply except for Aesor's footsteps, echoing as they faded away.

Tanngjost leaned against the cave entrance. 'He had no right,' he said.

'He is the pack leader,' said Ulli. 'He has every right.'

'But that does not mean you have to agree with him.'

'It does not.'

'Is what he said true?' asked Fejor, still sitting where he had been working on Aesor's armour.

'That I am a lame old cur?' said Tanngjost. 'Alas, it is. If no enemy can finish the job, this old body will fall apart of its own accord soon enough.'

'I meant about the Vultures.'

Tanngjost gave Fejor the kind of look a Wolf Priest might give a boisterous young Blood Claw, when that Blood Claw was bandying insults that others present might take too seriously. But Fejor showed no contrition on his face. If he realised the seriousness of the question, he did not care.

'It is,' said Ulli.

'I did not know any Vulture Clan yet lived.'

'Hold your tongue, Fejor Redblade,' said Tanngjost. 'I might be old but I can knock the fleas out of your hide.'

'Peace, Tanngjost,' said Ulli. 'The truth holds no fear for me. The Wolf Priests descended on the Valley of the Burning Stones and exterminated my people. And rightly so, for they were deviant witches to the last person. Five were young and strong enough to be salvageable. Three were found corrupted and were abandoned in the snow to die. One did not survive his proving. The last one was me. I have come to terms with it, yet none will speak of it to me. Such an origin is ill-starred indeed and those brothers who know it doubtless assume I would be moved to violence to hear it mentioned. Aesor probably hoped I would strike out at him, so he would have reason to fight me.'

'You are my brother, Ulli Iceclaw,' said Tanngjost. 'No matter what clan whelped you. You are Vulture no longer, not since you returned from your Blooding a Space Wolf. Aesor might not say the same, but I do.'

'Fejor, set up here,' said Ulli. 'Find something to build a barricade we can defend. We can fight at this cave entrance, where the orks can only assault with a few at a time. There may be somewhere more defensible further in that we can fall back to.'

'I should find Aesor,' said Tanngjost. 'I fear for him. He was always proud, but not like this.'

'Then we are both headed inside,' said Ulli. 'Time to see what the Knights of Alaric Prime were forbidden to look upon.'

'If I smell greenskin,' said Fejor, 'I'll vox.'

Within the peak of Sacred Mountain was a single great machine, a vast and terrible construction around which ran a spiralling pathway. Shafts of massive pistons soared away in every direction, massive cogs meshed in the shadows and the ever-present thrum of power got louder the further in the Space Wolves went.

Everything about it was ancient. The very air smelled of centuries. Drips of condensation had made stubby stalagmites on the floor and here and there the smooth grey stone was cracked where the mountain had shifted.

'Throne knows who built this,' said Tanngjost as he and Ulli emerged onto a long walkway crossing a depthless black gulf, crossed with cables and pipes. On the other side, hexagonal columns framed the entrance to a cave of crystalline datamedium, glittering with flickers of power and information.

'We built it,' said Ulli. 'Another mankind, who existed before the Emperor brought reason to our species. A mankind who had never looked into the gulf that delving too far could open up.'

Ulli paused halfway across the bridge. Something smelled off. It was something like the stink of warpcraft the ork mech had upon it, but far more subtle, cold where that had been hot, metallic where that had been bloody.

Ulli drew his bolt pistol and moved warily. Tanngjost followed, training Frejya across the crystalline cavern ahead.

At the threshold of the cavern, Ulli saw the huge metallic foot outstretched. He backed against one of the crystal pillars and glanced around, to see the whole massive steel form sprawled on the floor of the cavern. The winking datamedium lights picked out the gilding on its armour plates, and the glistening black oil that oozed from its joints. It was humanoid, three times the height of a Space Marine when it had stood, with massive-calibre guns mounted on the backs of its arms. On its back was an open hatch that led into a cramped one-man cockpit, from which spilled bundles of cables. Its armour plates were lacquered a deep red, emblazoned with the coat of arms of a Knightly House of Alaric Prime.

'It must be the *Dominus Vult*,' said Ulli.

'It looks like it crawled in here to die,' said Tanngjost, approaching the fallen Imperial Knight. He aimed Frejya into the cockpit as he checked inside. 'And I think we have made the acquaintance of Baron Vigilus Varlen.'

Inside the cockpit was a corpse, the face blackened by electrical burn. The eyes had burst and the sockets were charred pits, and the lips were drawn back over shattered teeth. The scorched remains of a red uniform clung to the chest, covered in tatters of gold brocade and a rack of medals that had melted into blobs of gold and silver. The body looked fused to the fittings of the cockpit, the hands indistinguishable from the twin control yokes and the legs and lower body lost in the tangle of pedals and pipework.

The black fluid had pooled in the cockpit and fingers of it had reached up into the body, running like dark veins up the arms and neck. Up close Ulli could see the same fluid trickling from every seam and join in the Knight's body, oozing in questing fingers across the floor. Threads of it ran through the datamedium where it met the wall, and there the glittering lights had dimmed like stars blotted out by a dark moon moving across the sky.

'Corruption,' said Ulli grimly. 'Do not touch it, brother. It is not just a machine-curse the greenskin inflicted on this machine. It is a physical corruption too, born of the warp. I have not seen such a thing before, but I know the source by its smell. It would take an Iron Priest as well as me to exorcise it.'

Tanngjost knelt down and held a hand over the floor, tracing the shape of a swirl of spilled corruption. 'Here,' he said. 'A footprint. Power armour. I might not track as Starkad could but these eyes are not grown dim just yet. The trail goes this way.' Tanngjost followed the marks to a black smear on the wall. He stumbled here, and put a hand out to steady himself.

The temperature dropped several degrees at once. Ulli's grip tightened on his bolt pistol, and he spun at the sound of metal grinding on stone behind him. The faceplate of the *Dominus Vult* was shaped like the helm of archaic plate armour, with triangular eyeslits over a featureless shield-shaped plate. The eyes were glowing a dim blue, guttering as if a hot flame burned inside the Knight's head. That flame seemed to focus on Ulli, and he was certain the head moved imperceptibly, corrosion and warped metal grinding as the servos forced themselves back to life.

'Brother, beware!' said Ulli and turned back to Tanngjost. But Tanngjost was not there.

Where the datamedium cavern had been, now there was a rocky valley open to a sky that was overcast with grey-white cloud. Packs of carrion birds wheeled over the jet-black mountain peaks that bounded the far end of the valley. It was a dark and chill place where the sun only reached for an hour a day, choked with huts made from whale bones and the flayed skins of enemies unwise enough to raid the narrow mountain passes.

Beyond those peaks were cairns and watchtowers built to warn the unwary of these mountains' tribes, scattered with the skulls of men who had traded with them, shown their captives mercy or tarried with one of their women. Of all the evils, conspiring with the mountain tribes to produce more offspring was the worst, for they carried with them a taint worse than madness, disease or dishonour.

Memory caught hooks into the back of Ulli's mind as he spotted the heap of corpses at the end of the valley. A battle had been fought here, swift and total, with some huts fired, others trampled down, and blood slick on the heaps of bones and trash on the valley floor, but the bodies had all been gathered up into that one heap. Hundreds of bodies were piled up there. The figures that stood around the heap were at once strange and familiar to Ulli, for the youth who had first seen them had not known what they were. They were taller than any man, wearing armour the same colour as the clouded sky, hung with pelts and bone charms. Some wore helmets, as if to ward off the stench of the valley's evil, others went bareheaded to reveal faces burned by decades of wind and lined with battle-scars.

Ulli the Space Wolf, however, knew who they were. They were Wolf Priests of the Fang, among them men he would encounter and recognise years later among his battle-brothers. Neither would acknowledge the connection, but those Wolf Priests knew full well that Ulli was the skinny, filth-streaked creature they had spared. It was a lifetime ago. It was not to be spoken of.

One priest threw a burning brand onto the pile. The bodies must have been doused with accelerant for they caught fire immediately. The bodies vanished in the flames, casting more light than the Valley of the Burning Stones had ever seen.

Everyone the young Ulli had ever known was in that ball of flame. The other youths spared by the Wolf Priests were ones he did not know, for the strongest of the valley's young were kept separate lest they join their powers and try to break from the clan's authority. Even here Ulli had been feared, because he had the strength to one day overthrow the Vulture elders and take the Valley of the Burning Stones for himself.

Ulli realised his arms were bound behind his back. He had been thrown into the remains of a burned hut, among the blackened bones of the valley's defenders, who had fallen to the Wolf Priests in a few exchanges of gunfire and force blades. Strung along the valley walls above him were more scorched bones – not the recent battle-dead but the sacrifices the Vulture Clan had made to their gods, chained to the rocks and burned in a ritual that gave this valley its name.

The memories hurt. Ulli the Space Wolf's memory was crammed into the young Ulli Vulturekin's skull, sharing a space too small for it with the youth's terrified, angry, confused mind.

Two of the Wolf Priests approached Ulli, their armoured feet crunching through the bones. Though the youth did not understand their Fenrisian dialect, the Space Wolf did.

'We should take this one back to the Rune Priests,' said one. He had a long and battered face, like a length of driftwood.

'No,' said the other. He had a black beard streaked with grey. Ulli recognised the face of Vortigan Breakbone, a senior Wolf Priest who had often presided over the feasting in the Great Hall. 'This one will never be clean.'

Breakbone levelled a bolt pistol at Ulli's chest.

Cold hands grabbed the back of his neck.

'Rune Priest!' shouted Tanngjost. 'Brother Ulli!'

Ulli was shoved against a chill stone wall. His head bounced against the hard surface. The crystal chamber swam back into view and Vortigan Breakbone's gun barrel was replaced with Tanngjost's face, eyes intense, jaw set.

'I slipped,' gasped Ulli. 'I was weak, just for a moment. Forgive me, brother.'

'Your eyes rolled back and you staggered about. You were speaking a language I did not know.'

'The corruption here is strong. It can entangle more than machines.' Ulli put a hand to his chest unconsciously.

'What did you see?' asked Tanngjost.

'The past. Do you still have Aesor's trail?'

'Yes. He headed further in. There are many paths ahead but I think I can follow him. I would not do it alone.'

'Then we must move on. The greenskins outside will not wait for me to pull myself together. On, brother, on.'

SIX

The datamedium was the information core for an enormous factory, cramped and folded as if ready to unfurl into a vast foundry. Machinery of brass and stone rose in bewildering configurations, with the only light from trickles of glowing data that wound around their crystal pillars. Ulli could make out a huge brass oculus that might grind open for an army of war machines to march out of, huge turbine blades arranged in a spiral that speared down into the darkness, generators and forges that smelled as if they had lain cold for thousands of years.

Aesor's trail was barely perceptible, but drops of corruption led further into the tangle.

'What will this be when it awakens?' said Tanngjost as he trained Frejya's barrel across the shadows.

'The only ones who know that are those who built it,' replied Ulli. 'If it is a weapon and the greenskin corruption takes this place, we could lose this whole world.'

Ulli's vox chirped. 'They are at the threshold,' came Fejor's voice through a crackling vox-channel. 'I can stand my ground a moment but I must fall back.'

'Damnation,' said Tanngjost. 'They don't waste time.'

'We will be with you soon,' voxed Ulli. 'Faith, brother.'

'Take your time, Rune Priest,' came the reply. 'I can kill awhile at my leisure.'

Tanngjost turned to head back the way they had come, through the data cave and across the bridge.

A shifting darkness darted from nearby and hit Ulli hard in the side, knocking him off his feet. He threw out a hand to brace his fall but he found nothing and slithered off the edge of an engine block, clattering down through layers of machinery.

Ulli knew Aesor Dragon's Head by the smell of him, tainted now with a metallic impurity something like old blood.

Aesor landed on top of Ulli, hands around Ulli's throat. Ulli caught a glimpse of Aesor's teeth bared, discoloured black, the whites of the pack leader's eyes stained with dark threads like spilt ink. Ulli lifted a knee and levered Aesor off him, throwing him aside.

Ulli took stock of his environment. There was enough room to fight, but obstacles and impediments jutted out from every angle. The two Space Wolves had landed on an assembly line, with jointed brass arms and blocks of stone poised to stamp and press. Underfoot was a conveyor belt of steel segments.

'Brother Aesor, you have taken leave of your reason!' called Ulli. He tried to spot Aesor among the machinery but everything was tangled and confused, his mind ringing, the opaque blanket of corruption lying over his senses. 'I am a Space Wolf, a brother of the Fang, as you are! We have found corruption here and it is your enemy. We can fight it together.'

'Ulli Vulturekin dares speak of corruption?' came the reply. Ulli was only vaguely aware of its direction. 'You were steeped in it! You were born to it!'

Aesor stalked out of the shadows. He had his frost blade drawn, a trickle of blackness running down the kraken-tooth blade. Ulli got his first good look at what had happened to Aesor. The warp-born virus had found purchase in him, latching on to some impurity just as it had tried to latch on to Ulli's memories. Aesor's cheeks and eyes were sunken as if in death. The oily darkness oozed from the corner of his mouth and the joints of his armour. The stink on him was overpowering.

'This is not you,' said Ulli. 'Aesor is in there, fighting to be free. I can exorcise this from you, my brother. I can...'

'They killed you!' roared Aesor.

And though he tried to will it down, the old pain flared in Ulli's chest. The pain of those scars that had never completely healed, where the Wolf Priest's bolt pistol had blasted a burning hole in rib and lung.

They had executed him. They had shot Ulli Vulturekin dead and thrown his body on the back of a pack animal, to be dissected at the Fang so they could understand the debasement of the Vulture Clan.

But he had not been dead. Not quite. And the strength that kept him alive had marked him as strong enough to become a Space Wolf.

'Speak not of me,' said Ulli. 'The warp-virus clouds your mind. Think on yourself. Think on becoming pure. You are imprisoned, but you can be free. Aesor Dragon's Head is no enemy of the Fang! He is a hero who will tear apart the filth that infects him!'

'And I suppose,' replied Aesor, 'that if I do not, you will put down this diseased runt for the good of all?'

Ulli took out his rune axe. While a bolt pistol could kill with a good shot to the head, the rune axe gave him a better chance of an incapacitating or killing blow – but against a master swordsman like Aesor, it still wasn't a very good chance. 'I have my duty,' he said.

'You still do not understand, Vulture's cur,' said Aesor with a smile. 'I cannot die.'

Ulli had studied the ways of combat enough to know the lunge was coming. It was a thrust to the upper chest, a killer if it hit true. Aesor's frost blade lanced up at Ulli through the darkness. Ulli knocked it to the side and Aesor stepped inside his guard, driving a knee up into Ulli's side to knock him off guard, then hooking Ulli's left arm and throwing him over his shoulder. Ulli rolled as he hit the steel of the conveyor and Aesor followed with a downward thrust intended to skewer Ulli through the back. Ulli spun on his stomach, kicked Aesor's front leg out from under him and felt the frost blade shearing off a chunk of his shoulder guard as it missed by a hand's breadth.

The two were a pace apart again as they sprang to their feet, each shuddering with the tension as they guessed and second-guessed the move the other would make.

'I will not grow old and crippled like Tanngjost,' said Aesor, more corruption slithering from his mouth. A tear of it ran down the side of his neck and Ulli realised it must be running from the scar where Aesor's ear had been. 'I will not become bitter and unheard. This flesh cannot rot. There is nothing in my future save glory and a glorious death. This is what a Space Wolf is supposed to be.'

'You have fallen,' said Ulli. 'The true Aesor can rise again.'

'I am perfect,' came the reply. 'None can rise any higher.'

Ulli let his psychic sense probe the edges of Aesor's mind. It was like touching a live electrical wire. Dangerous spurts of pain sought to drive him away as the jealous corruption built its mantle around Aesor's soul. It was pride that had let it in – a Space Marine's sin, pride and the anger at that pride being wounded. Aesor had been at his most vulnerable when he had come across the greenskin's machine-virus, and it had used that moment of weakness to infect him as it had infected the *Aquila Ferox* and the *Dominus Vult*. As it had so nearly infected Ulli himself.

Aesor made the first strike again, a slashing arc at waist height. Ulli drove the frost blade off with the head of his axe but that was not the real kill-stroke. Aesor spun and brought the blade around in a figure of eight, the edge slicing down at Ulli's shoulder. Ulli ducked to one side and Aesor closed, headbutting him in the bridge of the nose.

Ulli fell back a step. His psychic sense shattered and a thousand flecks of perception flickered in his mind's eye. For a split second, he was insensible.

Ulli brought his free hand up to grab the frost blade he knew, by some hindbrain instinct, was aimed at his chest. He caught the blade as it slid in and felt the cold line of pain across his palm as the edge sliced through the ceramite of his gauntlet.

The blade was turned aside just enough to miss his primary heart and the real target, his spine, which if severed would leave him paralysed. The point nicked his heart and punctured one lung, passing out through the backpack of his armour.

Ulli gasped. The breath opened the wound up more and heat flooded into the void the cold had left, as blood filled the ruptured lung.

'That is for the insult, Ulli Vulturekin,' said Aesor. 'For the glorious death you stole from me. But the Wolf Priests did not take the time to make sure you were dead. And they failed again when you awoke and they let you live. They should have cut your throat and burned your corpse. The task they failed on that day, I will finish on this.'

'Only if you die afterwards,' gasped Ulli. He was still on his feet but the cold numbness was spreading through him where his armour dispensed painkillers into his bloodstream. 'Aesor Dragon's Head will only do to a brother what he will inflict on himself.'

Aesor paused. His hand went to the place where his ear had been.

'No,' he said. 'You are no brother. You are...'

The moment of indecision had been just long enough for Ulli to draw his bolt pistol. Before Aesor could react the barrel was up and Ulli blasted three rounds into Aesor's chest.

Aesor fell back. The breastplate of ceramite, buckled as it was, was more than enough to keep the shot from penetrating flesh and bone. But the impact threw Aesor off balance and the shock would addle even a Space Wolf's senses for several seconds.

Ulli threw himself shoulder-first into the tangle of machinery beside him. His weight snapped robotic arms and sent components pinging in all directions. He forged through, seeking a way off the conveyor and out of Aesor's reach. His upper body was numb and his arm would be slowed – he would be second best against Aesor in hand-to-hand combat at the best of times, but wounded he might as well lie down and die if he stayed to face him. He had to get away, to regroup, and seek out his brothers.

He forced his way through the knife-sharp edges of broken machinery, and felt his footing fall away. He pitched forward into darkness, his armoured body clattering off cogs and pistons as he fell. His head spun and he could not tell up from down until he landed, hard, on the pitted steel surface of a giant cold furnace.

Ulli Vulturekin wanted to lie there and wait for the pain to wash away. But Ulli Iceclaw was more than that witch-boy had been. He was a Space Wolf. Pain meant nothing save for the chance to overcome it. And both Aesor and the greenskins still threatened his brothers. He got to his feet, feeling the wound in his chest flare up with the movement.

Ulli had come to rest a long way down, with the thin light of the data-medium barely reaching his surroundings. His superior vision could just pick out the outlines of the huge cylindrical forge beneath him, its door yawning wide enough to admit a tank, with gigantic steel pipes and cables leading up into blackness.

BEN COUNTER

Ulli willed a fragment of his psychic power into the rune axe he still clutched. The runes on its blade glowed blue-white and cast deep, long shadows around him. He could make out more of his surroundings, including one fuel pipe that led upwards in the direction of the datamedium cave and the chasm. From that direction he could hear muted gunfire and yelling greenskins, as Fejor and Tanngjost fought their battle against the attacking orks. There was no sight or sound of Aesor.

Ulli ran through the patterns of pain across his body. He was battered and bruised from the day's fighting even without the wound Aesor had dealt him. His nose felt broken and he had to breathe through his mouth. The sword wound was deep enough not to hurt in the right way – not sharply, like torn skin and muscle should, but with the dull, cold throb of shock and severed nerves. His stomachs turned with it. Every augmentation and sleep-taught survival instinct fought to keep him functioning as a warrior.

He walked along the pipe, then climbed as it got steeper. He could feel the humming of Sacred Mountain running through the steel, rising and falling in a long, slow pattern like an immense heartbeat. And in the dark cold smell of stone and steel, he could detect the note of corruption that had come to this place with the *Dominus Vult*, seeping and growing.

Perhaps Sacred Mountain was strong enough, and would expel it like a body expelled sickness. Ulli hoped so. There was majesty to this place, even dormant. He understood, cradled in the mechanical darkness, why the Knightly Houses of Alaric Prime had looked on it with such awe. The first of them to explore Sacred Mountain, hundreds of generations ago, had looked on it and realised they were not yet ready to understand what it held, and ever since had stopped just short of the summit in recognition of something greater than themselves.

Huge stalactites of datamedium hung down, columns of jagged crystal fluttering with millions of lights. Even dormant, Sacred Mountain's machine-spirit was alive, running through billions of calculations every second. Perhaps it knew it was invaded, by greenskins without and the machine-virus within. Ulli clambered onto an adjacent bundle of wires to get a closer look, for the scent of the corruption was stronger here, but with a hint of ash and burned skin.

Fingers of blackness ran down the column, but instead of reaching further down, with every moment they split up and turned into dark blotches, indistinct and fading. Lights gathered there, flaring like distant fireworks, and the tendrils of the virus were turned back or dissolved into nothing.

'You fight back,' said Ulli as he watched. 'The Knights are not strong enough, but you are.'

He could feel the anguish of the virus as it was held back from the deepest cores of Sacred Mountain's data systems. It was a fury and a frustration, skittering at the back of his mind, the sound of a prisoner screaming dulled by the walls of his cell. It was not just a collection of machine-code and warp incantations – it was a living thing, drawn from the warp and mutilated by the greenskin mech until it served as a slave weapon. Ulli could taste the concoction of anger and pain, frustration and hatred, all boiling through every dark tendril.

It had almost got him. It had found a way in, and had it not been for Tanngjost, perhaps it would have taken Ulli's reason as it had Aesor's. The wound in his chest throbbed in response to the thought. He clambered upwards, towards where a glimmer of light punctured the shadows and the sounds of battle grew louder.

Ulli had reached the entrance to the datamedium cavern, leaving a trail of coagulated blood behind him as if he had dropped handfuls of rubies to mark his path. He hauled himself up onto level ground and leaned against the cave wall. The face of the *Dominus Vult* stared up at him. The fire behind its eyepieces was extinguished. Black rivulets bubbled over the edge of the open cockpit, and liquid corruption had almost immersed the scorched body welded inside.

'Fejor, Tanngjost,' said Ulli into the vox, aware that his voice was croaking and weak. 'Report, my brothers.'

'They attack!' came Tanngjost's voice in reply. 'Wave after wave! We have fallen back to the chasm. I thought you lost, Rune Priest, but we could use your axe with us!'

Ulli hurried through the cavern and across the bridge. At the far side, gunfire hammered and echoed across the mountain's interior. He could make out the distinct cough of Fejor's suppressed bolter rounds, and the chatter of Frejya fired at full-auto. And he knew well the sound of bolter shells hitting greenskin bodies.

Across the bridge, Fejor and Tanngjost had drawn wreckage of ruined ork bikes and fallen debris into a barricade. Both Space Wolves crouched there now, reloading their weapons between waves of orks. The corridor ahead of them, leading back up to the mountainside entrance, was so choked with ork bodies the floor was completely hidden and they lay three deep against the walls.

'Brother Ulli!' cried Tanngjost as Ulli approached. 'Alas, you have missed the first of the killing. But there will be more than enough to make up for it. The greenskin must honour us greatly to give us so many targets for our firing range!' His face fell. 'You are wounded.'

'You are not parade-ground-ready yourself,' replied Ulli. Both Tanngjost and Fejor were covered in ork blood, and their armour was dented and scored from a dozen close calls. Their faces were bloody, some of it their own. 'I have two working hands, both with trigger fingers. I can fight.'

'It is your mind we need as much as your hands,' replied Tanngjost.

'What of the Pack Leader?' asked Ulli. 'He has lost his mind. He dealt me this blow and I could not pursue him.'

'He vaulted our barricade and ran on,' said Tanngjost. 'There was darkness on him, and not just the corruption. What has happened to him?'

'The same that happened to the *Dominus Vult* and the *Aquila Ferox*. It almost happened to me, brother.'

'I always thought,' said Fejor, 'that if one of us was to fall, it would be me. No right mind takes such pleasure in killing as mine. Of all of our pack, it was Aesor I would have trusted to stay righteous, and to be the one to put me down when I fell.' He broke a smile, the first time Ulli had seen him do it, and a very different man showed through for a moment. 'But I do not think I have long to wait before the greenskin does that job for him.'

'If Aesor brings this disease back to the Chapter,' said Ulli, 'we could lose much more than Alaric Prime.'

Greenskin war-cries echoed down from the mountainside, rising and falling rhythmically. Steel clashed on steel. Engines revved.

'They're coming again,' said Tanngjost. He checked the load in his weapon. 'Frejya is thirsty,' he said. 'We are running low on ammunition. This one will be settled with teeth and knives.' He drew his pair of combat knives and held them out to Ulli. 'My two little girls,' he said. 'When their mother tires of the fight, they will finish it.'

Ulli let the old runes form in his mind. A Fenrisian prince, a famed hunter and horseman, had been buried in a tomb inscribed with sigils of swiftness, prescience of combat, and the knowledge to strike once and for the kill. These runes appeared on the blade of one knife and glowed deep red. The other received the symbols of spite and revenge, for they came from the monument to a queen of Fenris who, in ages past, had been quick to anger and to seek vengeance, and whose rule lasted a hundred years as a result.

Tanngjost's old face, with old spiral scars and fresh battle-wounds, was lit up by the light of the runes. They glittered in his eyes. 'Just what they needed,' he said.

Fejor rarely fought with his chainsword, always killing at long range when he had the option. But he had only a few stalker shells left, and so he handed his chainsword to Ulli for rune-striking. It was a compact marque, used on boarding missions and other occasions where close confines made a longer weapon a liability. It resembled a workman's tool more than a Space Marine's weapon of choice. Ulli gave it runes of raw power and strength, steadfastness and the ignorance of weakness, taken from the great necropolis of Fenrisian fortress-builders.

The roaring of engines signalled the approach of the greenskins. The din grew louder and mingled with the screaming of the orks, whipped up into a killing frenzy.

A single ork was a stupid and ill-disciplined creature. But orks, a tribe or army of them, when directed by one with willpower and cunning became a green tide that no defence could stand against. That was how they fought, wave after relentless wave of them, brutality incarnate. That was how their leader intended to grind down the last Space Wolves who stood against him on Sacred Mountain.

They did not care how many of their own they lost. There were always more orks.

The orks must have fought among themselves for the right to be the first in this wave. The winner was a scarred veteran, its lower jaw replaced with a slab of jagged metal, clinging to the handlebars of the smoke-belching bike beneath it. It had a massive industrial claw clamped over its left arm and waved it like a banner as it hurtled towards the barricade.

Two of Fejor's last few stalker shells knocked the greenskin off its bike, sending it somersaulting backwards off the saddle. The bike careened off the wall and skidded on its side into the barricade, throwing wreckage everywhere. The bike screeched past Ulli in a spray of sparks. A dozen orks charged in the biker's wake, wielding cleavers and hammers. Ulli blasted at them, unable to miss the wall of green flesh with a volley of bolter shots. They fell and tumbled, but more followed, yelping with joy that they were the new front line.

Tanngjost jumped up onto the remains of the barricade. 'My blades are far too sharp!' he yelled. 'Which of you will help dull their edge?'

And then the orks were on them. A howling press of bodies, of cleavers rising and falling, of teeth and claws raking at power armour. Ulli lashed out with his axe, feeling the shudder up his arm as a head came free of its shoulders. His backstroke cut through an arm.

Ulli had always been apart from his fellow Space Wolves. He was a Rune Priest, and they all held their own counsel, but even among them Ulli was the one who had been marked for extermination and had survived. It was the word of Ulrik the Slayer, the most respected Wolf Priest in the Chapter, that had saved him from being clubbed to death and thrown into the Fang's incinerator. Though none of them spoke it out loud, many in the Chapter thought Ulrik had taken too great a risk and should have completed Ulli's execution himself. And so Ulli had never been close to the heart of his Chapter, never the foremost reveller at the feasting, never held up as the image of a Space Wolf.

But he was still a Space Wolf, and deep within there was the spark of Leman Russ's own fury that Ulli could not deny. It rarely came to the surface but it was there, scratching at the back of Ulli's mind. It was the savage-born warrior, the berserker, the sheer joy of battle that had driven the Primarch to so many victories. It was at odds with the studious mind of the Rune Priest, and so Ulli had caged it, but it had never left him. And in the scrum of greenskin fury, he set it free.

He let the joy of battle kindle inside him as he brought his axe down on the head of the ork that lunged at him, splitting its skull down to the jawbone. It caught fire as he rammed his bolter into the mouth of another ork and blew out its throat. By the time two greenskins leapt onto him and tried to pin him to the ground, he was aflame with it.

Ulli howled with joy. It overcame the pain of the wound running through him. He reared up to his full height, throwing off the orks, letting his bolter fall on its strap and catching one by the neck. He dashed the ork's brains out against the engine block of the fallen bike beside him. Hot blood spattered over his face and he revelled in the feeling like the most vicious Blood Claw, letting himself forget the iron discipline of his calling and allowing the rage of a Fenrisian son to boil over.

Another ork fell to an elbow shattering the side of its face and the rune axe's blade carving up through its sternum. Ulli kicked down on another and stamped on its chest, grabbing the grip of his bolter and hammering three shots into it point blank.

Blood was thick and sticky underfoot. It misted in the air and ran down Ulli's face. It pooled in his eyes and he saw through it as if through a pane of red glass. In the back of his mind a wolf howled, exulting in the freedom it finally had to drive Ulli's fist and blade into the body of any ork that got within arm's length.

Through the melee, he glimpsed Tanngjost's twin blades puncturing torsos and eye sockets. He could hear, amid the orkish bellowing and snapping bones, the screeching of Fejor's chainblade against bone. But they felt far away, the combatants in three battles separated by an ocean of greenskin flesh. Ulli's battle was a cauldron of fury and blood, seething with broken bodies falling away from his axe.

The symbols on the blade glowed deep red now, drinking the fury in the air without Ulli having to will it. The weapon hungered in the hand of the wolf, coming alive with every spray of blood across its runes. Ulli rode the wave of it, and let the axe swing as if it were leading his hand and not the other way around.

He shouldered an ork against the fallen bike, and gloried in the breaking of its ribs. He kneed another in the jaw and whooped with joy as its fangs were driven up into the base of its brain.

The tide hammered home, body after body, corpse after corpse. Ulli lost sight of his packmates in the throng. There was nothing but the stink of torn bodies and the din of dying greenskins.

Ulli felt space open around him. He drew in a panting breath. His body finally told him how far he had pushed it. His throat was bubbling with blood from his torn lung, and the fires of pain ran up and down the channel punched through his chest. Every joint was wrenched and every muscle was pulled. The pain combined into a red veil that hung over his body, dulled by his augmentations and painkillers, heavy as stone.

The greenskins had stopped pressing forward. Their dead were waist-high around Ulli, and bodies tumbled off one another as he kicked himself free of them. He was slick with blood from head to toe.

The barricade and the wreck of the first ork's bike were buried in bodies. Blood was sprayed up the walls and dripped from the ceiling. Ulli looked around to see the passageway choked with greenskin corpses in both directions. A few groans and dying whimpers came from the bodies.

He could not see his battle-brothers. He called out their names, and his own voice was dull in his ears. There was no reply.

Ulli hauled greenskin bodies away, digging in the places he had seen his fellow Space Wolves last. He spotted a chainblade sticking up from the mass and hauled corpses aside to reveal Fejor Redblade, lying face down. Ulli turned him over and saw his breastplate had been carved open by an orkish cleaver or power claw, and the red ruin within had been torn by teeth and claws. Fejor's jaw was still clenched and set, for he had died denying the pain, fighting on without showing the enemy they had hurt him. His eyes were open. Ulli lifted Fejor off the ground and propped the body against the wall.

A sudden desperation seized Ulli. He dived into the bodies where Tanngjost had fought, where they were piled high and sliced apart by his twin blades. The wounds on the orkish bodies were still smouldering with the power of the runes Ulli had etched on Tanngjost's knives. Ulli's body complained as he dug in a frenzy, like a starving animal clawing through frozen earth.

Ulli's hand closed on ceramite – a gauntlet. He grabbed and pulled, and Tanngjost's body came free, heaved up through the broken limbs and sundered bodies. It was slick and dripping with ork blood.

Unlike Fejor, Tanngjost had died with his fury written across his face. His lips were drawn back, showing the elongated canines grown by every ageing Space Wolf. It could have been any one of a score of wounds that had finally killed him – cleaver wounds into his chest, one leg shattered and bent unnaturally, a deep cut to his scalp, punctures through his back and abdomen. Dried blood beaded, jewel-like, where he had bled and fought on.

Ulli held Tanngjost's body and shuddered. All the pain caught up to him at once. The red veil dissolved into a million points of pain spreading through his body, pooling in his joints and the wound in his chest, sparking through the back of his mind. For a moment it was overwhelming and Ulli felt he would pitch over into the mass of bodies, his augmented organs finally failing and his mind shutting down, and that he would die alongside his brothers there in Sacred Mountain.

But the Fenrisian cold would not melt away. It demanded Ulli rise and stay alive, just as it had done during his Blooding, just as when his heart had refused to stop beating when he was executed with the rest of the Vulture Tribe. Ulli did not die but threw back his head and howled, and the sound echoed down to the heart of Sacred Mountain and back again.

The sound of mourning scoured away the red veil. When Ulli opened his eyes the pain was gone, replaced with a deep chill that filled him. His skin prickled with sensitivity and his throat was raw with the cold air.

He laid Tanngjost Seven Fingers alongside Fejor Redblade. The gene-seed organs of both Space Wolves were still intact. Ulli let himself take solace in that. Whatever happened, the flesh of Russ would be taken from their throats and implanted into a new Space Wolf. Their spirits would never truly die.

The orks had stopped. Though the three Space Wolves had killed many indeed, it was just a fraction of the army that had remained after the avalanche. But they had stopped, and it was not at all like the greenskin to hold off in their assault when an enemy still lived. They should still be pouring in to defile the bodies of the Space Wolves, and charge on into Sacred Mountain to loot and destroy.

The dullness of Ulli's senses was gone, and his ears pricked when he heard a familiar sound. It was the roar of engines, the engines of a Stormwolf gunship that could carry a squad of Space Wolves into the heart of battle.

He heard bolter fire and the howling of Fenrisian wolves loosed at the prey. He heard a hunting horn sounded.

Ulli clambered free of the bodies and ran for the entrance to Sacred Mountain. The air was heavy with the stench of newly shed blood, and the rankness of greenskin flesh. The floor was slick with blood and frost. The bodies ran right up to the entrance where Fejor and Tanngjost had begun the fight before falling back. Framed against the stark blue sky, Ulli saw another drop pod falling towards the mountain slope, in the grey livery of the Space Wolves, with its landing jets firing.

The pod bore the markings of Ragnar Blackmane, the Wolf Lord of his Great Company. Reinforcements from below had arrived, in force, eager for revenge.

Ulli reached the entrance, and below him unfolded the whole scene.

The Space Wolves had landed scattered around the lower slopes, their drop pods deployed from a modified Thunderhawk gunship that circled above. They were fighting as they unbuckled their grav-harnesses and leapt from the pods. Grey Hunters formed firing lines mowing down the orks that had broken off their attack on the mountain to storm down the slopes towards the new threat. Blood Claws, with bright red and yellow markings on their armour, shrieked battle-cries and ran with chainswords drawn at the closest orks. A Dreadnought stomped free of its clamps and levelled its assault cannon at the greenskins.

Ulli spotted Lord Ragnar Blackmane himself leaping free of his grav-restraints and drawing his frost blade, which flashed like a bolt of lightning. Blackmane was accompanied by Ulrik, the eldest of the Wolf Priests, his face hidden by his wolf's skull helm, and a squad of Wolf Guard in Terminator armour hung with trophies and honours. Ulli's heart should have leapt to see his Wolf Lord come to bring destruction to the greenskins, but the deaths of his battle-brothers were too raw in his mind to let in any joy.

He heard a familiar howl, one that echoed around the peak even above the gunfire and war-cries from below. On the promontory stood Aesor Dragon's Head, his own frost blade raised, not in salute to Blackmane but in challenge. In the greenskin throng Ulli saw the ork leader stop in its charge forward and return the challenge, raising its cleaver high and bellowing a wordless response.

Aesor wanted his duel with the greenskin. He would die here fighting it, or defeat it and live on forever sustained by the corruption inside him. He could not lose.

Ulli knew the path the future would take if Aesor won. The Space Wolves would run to him and embrace him as a victorious brother, and they would all be exposed to that corruption – all those sons of Fenris who did not have the protection of a Rune Priest's psychic discipline. How many would fall to the corruption entering their minds through their greatest flaw? It would return to the Chapter, that corruption, perhaps to the Fang itself. And if the greenskin won the duel it would continue its campaign on Alaric Prime, escape the mountainside in the confusion of battle and take its machine-curse to the Imperial Knights fighting below.

Whoever won that duel, the Space Wolves and this world would suffer for it. Both Aesor and the greenskin had to lose.

They both had to die.

Ulli could not fight them himself. He was a poor opponent for Aesor or the ork at the best of times and now he was exhausted and wounded. His fellow Space Wolves were too far away to intervene, and even if they could, would they kill Aesor before they were exposed? Ulli had seen what Aesor had become. Blackmane and the rest of the Great Company had not. No Space Wolf would stay his hand when the kill was necessary – except if the kill were of one of his own. Even Ragnar Blackmane might hesitate.

Ulli had to do it himself, and this time his rune axe would not help him. He leaned against the rock, almost robbed of all his strength by the weight of what he had to do.

The ork bounded up to the promontory and bellowed a war-cry. Aesor howled in reply. The ork vaulted onto the rocky spur and slashed at Aesor, who parried and stepped aside. The duel had begun. There was no more time.

Ulli drew in a breath of the cold mountain air, felt it run like freezing water through his ruined lungs, and ran back into Sacred Mountain.

SEVEN

The datamedium cavern had escaped the bloodshed. The orks had not got that far before Blackmane's assault drew them away. The *Dominus Vult* still lay in its pooling blackness. The charred eye sockets of the dead baron watched Ulli as he limped into the chamber. The sounds of battle were little more here than a dull crackle of distant gunfire.

Ulli knelt on the floor and laid his axe beside him. He tried to divine some reaction to his presence, some flicker of recognition against his psychic sense.

'You tried to take my soul,' he said quietly. 'You were nearly successful. That was when you found your way into my mind with perfidy and deceit. Now, I bid you enter.'

He felt nothing. A drop of blackness, like glistening tar, dripped from the Imperial Knight's faceplate onto the crystal floor.

'My brother saved me,' continued Ulli. 'But he lies dead and I am alone. We both know you can break me. And we both know you cannot turn down a mind like this to ravage. An Imperial psyker, a Rune Priest of Fenris. How many of your kind ever claim a trophy like me?'

There was a response to that. A low whisper, a laugh or a curse, not a sound but a rumbling at the base of Ulli's skull.

If the machine-curse reached the Chapter, it would enter their minds through their pride – through the sin of every Space Marine. And it was also the sin of the daemon.

The chamber began to melt away. Darkness ran down the walls. The floor shifted under Ulli, deepening into the trash-choked base of a deep ravine. Skulls and long-withered bodies lay in the detritus and Ulli caught the familiar scent of carrion and smoke.

Sacred Mountain was gone, and Ulli was somewhere else.

There was a memory that Ulli kept locked away, using the mental techniques the Rune Priests had taught him. He had not forgotten it entirely, for it was much too important a part of him to abandon. But it was dangerous, and so he had placed it behind a barrier of mental steel, shut away as the keeper of a library might shut away a blasphemous work too valuable to burn.

It was a memory that at all times would create the heresy of doubt in Ulli's mind, except in those rarest cases when it would give him strength. Knowing the difference was a discipline he had learned in long sessions of meditation and sleep-doctrination, before the vigil of the Rune Priests who trained him.

The memory was one of the cold slab against his back, and the heat of the incinerator nearby. The sound of cracking bones and spitting fat in the flames. The sight, blurry and painful, of a stone ceiling above him, flickering orange.

He heard breathing beside him as the thrall, muscular and tanned deep bronze on his shirtless back, hauled another of the Vulture Clan dead into the incinerator.

Ulli had forced his eyes open all the way, and drawn in a weak, ragged breath in spite of the pain in his side. Bolter shell fragments, he would later learn, had lodged in his chest cavity and would need weeks of surgery to remove.

'Stop,' said a voice, deep and commanding. The thrall, one of the thousands who worked maintaining the Fang under the command of the Wolf Lords, halted and looked around uncertainly. 'My lord?' he asked.

'This one lives,' said the other voice. Ulli forced his head around and saw two Wolf Priests overseeing the disposal of the Vulture Clan bodies. One was the same who had shot him at the Valley of the Burning Stones, whose name he would later learn to be Vortigan Breakbone. The second wore a suit of polished black power armour with a wolf's-skull helm, the pale bone grinning down at Ulli as the second Wolf Priest regarded him.

Then, this Wolf Priest had been a vision from a nightmare, an otherworldly power sent to judge the dead. Now Ulli knew him to be Ulrik the Slayer, the most senior Wolf Priest of his generation.

'Damnation,' spat Vortigan. 'This one's stubborn. Be warned, Brother Ulrik, he's a witch-child.' Vortigan drew his combat knife, as long as a sword, but a dagger in his hand.

Ulli Vulturekin had not fully understood their words, but he knew well enough their meaning. He also knew that it was no use reasoning with the man who had killed him once already.

He turned to the wolf-skull helm and forced himself to meet its eyes. Lenses of red were set into its sockets, reflecting the furnace fire. 'Stop,' Ulli gasped, hoping this Wolf Priest would understand enough of his tribe's dialect. 'You do not know what I can do.'

'Then tell me,' replied the wolf's skull in a version of Fenrisian that Ulli Vulturekin could just understand. 'But be quick. My brother here has made up his mind about killing you, and I cannot stay him for long.'

Ulli swallowed, a painful movement that reminded him how severe the wounds inside must be. And then he told Ulrik the Slayer just what Ulli Vulturekin was.

Ulli held on to the memory as the new world formed around him. This time it was not taken to a place from his own mind. He was here on the machine-curse's terms, and it had laid out for him a vision of Hel such as the fieriest Imperial preachers would fear to conjure up.

Crevasses brimming with corpses criss-crossed the blasted landscape, reaching to the foot of the wall that bounded a massive dark city. The bodies writhed and pulsed with decay, bursting like pustules in eruptions of bile and filth, and they screamed in the drizzle of corrosive sludge that fell from a purple-black sky. Faces melted away. Hands reached out, were stripped to bone, and dissolved to nothing.

The city's towers and cathedrals were vast organs, heaving out over the edge of their confinement like rolls of corpulent belly. Lengths of entrails slithered into the seething death, fanged mouths sucking up the decaying gore. Banners showing the symbols of the carrion insect and the gouged eye hung from the highest spurs of bone, where flocks of enormously bloated flies hung like dark clouds.

Daemons leapt and cackled on the edges of the crevasses, dragging corpses out with hooked spears and throwing them onto the stones like landed fish to be gutted, cut up, and thrown back in. Some choice heads and organs were carried to lords of their kind who sat on palanquins, snatching up the finest and gulping them down. A few were taken by messenger-daemons to the gates of the city, to be passed on for the delectation of its rulers. Each daemon was a vision of decay, a corpse bloated and rotting but animated with a gleeful purpose, and each had a single yellow eye that bled malicious light.

'This is where you bring me?' called out Ulli, knowing the corruption could hear him. 'A world of daemons and decay? I am a Space Marine and a son of Fenris! I know no fear! And I saw worse than this before I left my crib. Do you seek to challenge me or to make me laugh?'

A tide rose through the rotting bodies and they swelled up into the air in a foetid column of flesh. A face formed in the mass, noseless, with three pits for eyes over a wide frog-like mouth. The whole thing was enormous, the size of a tall building.

'You lie, Ulli Vulturekin,' it said, though the voice was not truly sound but something conjured in Ulli's mind. 'You despair to know your mind will be lost in a place like this.'

'Not as much,' retorted Ulli, 'as I would despair to be a greenskin slave!'

The face creased with rage. The world the corruption had created flickered and shifted, as if in its anger it lost its concentration for a moment.

'What did it have to offer to bind you into service, daemon?' yelled Ulli.

'A million dead? A billion? A world for you to defile? And was it enough to make you kneel before the beast?'

The daemon's rage rained down as scalding blood. Its eye pits caught fire, flames consuming liquefying flesh. A Space Marine had pride, but the daemon – and the machine-curse was most definitely a daemon in information form – had rage. That was another of its sins, and it was inflamed by Ulli speaking of how the greenskin must have summoned it forth and bound it into service.

The world melted around Ulli. The sky ran down the horizon like wet paint. The walls sagged under their own weight, spilling the rancid offal of the city out onto the plain. Ulli planted his feet and willed stability around him, so he stood as an island in a churning sea.

The mass of corpses fell apart. Limbs rained down and vanished, drops of corruption in the swirl of bile that now made up the world. The noxious mass churned around Ulli and he dropped to one knee, driving the butt of his axe into the ground to steady himself.

'Now,' said Ulli through a grimace of concentration, 'I will show you a place of my own.'

In his mind's eye he created it, and around him it took shape. It was a place from his youth, the substance of another toxic memory he kept locked away even more closely than the first time he spoke with Ulrik the Slayer. A cave in the Valley of the Burning Stones, cut of sharp obsidian deep into the valley wall, stifling and hot. The heat came from the fire in the centre of the room, guttering with blackened bones.

Ulli had been here as a youth. He remembered most the smell of it – even before the enhancement of his senses the stench of the burning offerings had been dizzyingly intense. Ulli was kneeling in the cave just as he had been when the elders of the Vulture Clan had hauled him in there and gripped his shoulders to hold him still.

The elders were there now, shadowy figures half remembered. In the flames leaped a darkness – the darkness they had called forth with the ancient sorceries of his tribe. Even then, ignorant and afraid, Ulli had known the blasphemy of that sight, the long, spindly limbs forming from the air, the many eyes winking white in its substance, the spread of ragged wings behind it filling the cavern.

'They brought me here,' said Ulli, still tense with concentration. The memory was delicate and the machine-curse daemon was strong, and he could not let it unravel around him. 'They conjured it forth. The Spirit of the Burning Stones. One of your own kind. The daemon that enslaved the Vulture Tribe.'

Ulli stared into the eyes of the daemon forming in the fire. Drops of blackness spat and hissed in the fire. Trapped there in his memory was the machine-curse daemon, pinned in place by the force of Ulli's mind. Ulli had trained for this, for endless hours in the scriptoria and breaking halls of the Fang.

'No trick can stay me,' spat the daemon. 'This is my world, this place inside your head. I cannot be deceived, I who am deceit! I cannot be destroyed, I who am destruction!'

'Every one of my people was given to the Spirit of the Burning Stones,' continued Ulli. 'Brought here and possessed by it, then spat back out again with their minds in ruins. But not me. I resisted it. I looked it in the eye and I cast it out of me. I was the strongest witch-child they had ever borne, and the Spirit could not take me.' Ulli stood, his head reaching the ceiling of the cavern that had seemed so huge in his youth. 'And they feared me! I was marked for death when the Wolf Priests came for them! Do you understand now what I can do, daemon? I can crush your kind with the power of my soul, and you are trapped in here with me! Do you despair? Do you know fear?'

'Blasphemer!' spat the daemon back at him. It writhed in the flame, trying to break free. Ulli felt it struggling in the back of his head, pounding the inside of his skull. 'Wretch! Filth! The gods of the warp will tear–'

'I am the god of this place!' yelled Ulli, 'You are the broken slave of a greenskin beast! And I command you to burn!'

The flames leapt up. The chamber was full of fire. The obsidian walls and the Vulture Clan elders bled away and all that remained was the flame, raging white and blue-hot.

The daemon screamed. The sound filled Ulli's skull. It lost any shape, and with it any resemblance to the daemon Ulli Vulturekin had defied beneath the Valley of the Burning Stones. The machine-curse daemon broke apart into the information of which it was composed. Scraps of cogitator code fluttered in the fire like burning insects.

Ulli took the whole world inside him, encompassed in the obsidian cavern, and crunched it into a single diamond-hard point of knowledge. In there was contained the daemon, compressed into white-hot agony. Aside from that there was a void inside him, a pure and endless space where the daemon would find no purchase.

Ulli let his senses reel out. He had the scent of his prey already and it did not take him long to follow the trail up out of Sacred Mountain and onto the slope. He followed the stink of the corruption, the sweat and chain-blade oil of a Space Wolf – Aesor Dragon's Head, still fighting his duel with the greenskin lord.

And Ulli could sense the greenskin itself, the reeking hulk of alien muscle, its machinery belching thick smoke. Ulli perceived the burning red anger of the ork's mind and held on to it, drawing his consciousness closer, willing the connection to become stronger.

Ulli took the prison in which he had trapped the daemon, clutching it in a psychic fist. He drew it back and willed all the strength of his arm into that mental grip.

The strength Ulli called upon was what had caused Ulrik to spare his life.

It was the same quality that had denied his possession by the Spirit of the Burning Stones – the raw strength that pooled in Ulli's mind, a reservoir of power that he so rarely had the chance to tap. Most uses would destroy him, burning out his brain or tearing a hole through to the warp. But now, with the daemon in his grasp, he could use every drop of it.

Ulli rammed the daemon into the ork's mind. The daemon poured screaming into the ork, clashing with the furnace of hatred within the alien. The daemon took on its shape as the machine-curse and, without room in the ork's skull, it was forced into the only place it could go: the machinery built into the ork's body, the generators and weaponry grafted onto its spine and the back of its ribcage.

Ulli did not see what happened, but he felt it. He felt the daemon, uncaged and furious, course through the ork's half-mechanical body. He felt the ork's body prised apart by the force of it, the bones splintering, the organs pulping, skin and muscle tearing. Ulli could feel its pain and he felt in himself that savage joy of battle again, that spark of hot Fenrisian fury.

EPILOGUE

Ulli heard later what happened outside on the mountain slope. The other Space Wolves battling there witnessed Aesor Dragon's Head duck a swipe of the greenskin's cleaver and charge shoulder-first into the alien's midriff. The ork wrapped its massive arms around Aesor and the two wrestled, Aesor forcing its jaw open with one hand while the ork tried to crush the ceramite of Aesor's damaged armour. None of those watching could guess who would win, and struggling with the mass of greenskins further down the slope there was nothing even Wolf Lord Blackmane could do to intervene.

The machinery built in to the greenskin's body glowed deep red, and the sizzling of its flesh added to the smoke. The ork howled, a terrible sound that shook the mountain's peak, and flames licked from its body. Black corruption spurted from the joints of the machinery, spattering foulness across the icy rocks.

Aesor fought back, but the death grip was around him. The ork didn't have Aesor's skill as a master swordsman, but it was stronger than any Space Marine. Aesor couldn't break out of the hold and as the flames grew they caught on his hair and the wolf's-tail talismans hanging from his armour.

Then, with a sound like thunder breaking around the peak, the ork's body exploded. The greenskin and Aesor Dragon's Head vanished in a burst of flame and debris, and burning darkness that cast across the snow like a rain of black blood.

The greenskin horde bellowed in rage and grief to see their lord, who to them must have seemed invincible, destroyed in an instant. The Space Wolves echoed the sound as they howled in anger to see the death of the young and noble Aesor Dragon's Head.

It was the Space Wolves who used that anger the best. Ragnar Blackmane, who was fighting alongside the Dreadnought Karulf the Wizened, vaulted up onto the shoulder of the war machine and howled out his fury. The Space Wolves took up the call and leapt into the orks with renewed anger, vengeance adding strength to their arms. The orks were shocked and shattered, and fell back in ill-ordered mobs as Blackmane dived from Karulf's shoulder into the thick of them.

It was a few moments later that Ulli, exhausted, stumbled from the entrance to Sacred Mountain. He saw the blackened circle where Aesor and the greenskin had fought, and smelled the last wisps of the machine-curse daemon dissipating on the mountain wind. Ahead of him, down the slopes, the orks were in rout, fleeing from the Space Wolves and being chased down by the Blood Claws. Ulli held his axe out in front of him and used the last reserves of power inside him to will onto its blade the runes of hatred and rage, the purity of war, revenge and contempt.

The sun by then was low on the horizon, and the rocks around the peak cast long shadows. The burning runes made a pool of light around Ulli as he took up the hunter's howl. He let himself forget what he had done there on Sacred Mountain, the things he had seen, the memories he had dredged up, and replaced them with the hatred of the greenskin and every-thing it represented.

Ulli ran down the slope at the orks. His mind was full of nothing but the desire to destroy them. The Fenrisian joy of battle was all that mattered now, and it was with a great relief that he felt nothing else as he plunged into the fray.

An hour after the sun had set, the last ork was hunted down around the mountain peak and despatched by a Blood Claw's chainsword. Ulli heard the sound of it dying as he cleaned the blood off his axe in the snow heaped up by one of the Stormwolf gunships. Ulli took a handful of the snow and rubbed it across his face to wash the worst of the ork blood out of his eyes. It was thick and gelid in his hair, smeared across his armour, and its taste was like a mouthful of metal.

A shadow approached, cast by the moon hanging high in the clear sky. Wolf Lord Blackmane approached. He was no older than Ulli, for Ragnar Blackmane's rise to Wolf Lord had been faster than any in memory and the men of Fenris called him the Young King. His face was tanned and noble, the hair pulled back in a topknot of braids, and in spite of his youth his canines were already as prominent as those of a Long Fang.

'Brother Ulli Iceclaw,' said Ragnar. 'You fought well today. Before we reached you, and afterwards. The Knights of Alaric Prime and your broth-ers alike owe you much.'

'What victories we won here were not without their price,' replied Ulli. He scraped a gobbet of blood from his eye with his thumb. 'I cannot take solace in a battle well fought when of my brothers who came to this moun-tain, only I lived. I do not know whether to rejoice that I live, or mourn those who did not.'

'There will be a place for both,' said Lord Blackmane.

'How did you find us?' asked Ulli.

'I am not the one to answer that,' replied Blackmane. He pointed to a band of Blood Claws returning from the hunt. 'Brother! Come forth.'

A familiar figure walked out of the Blood Claws – this one was not a Blood Claw, but wore the pack markings of a Grey Hunter, with the eagle's wings badge of the sky hunter on one knee guard.

'Sigrund!' cried Ulli, and jumped to his feet to embrace the pilot of the *Skjaldi's Lament*. 'I thought you lost, my brother. I thought I saw you die.'

'Indeed you did,' said Sigrund. 'But the *Lament* did not let death take me all the way. She lodged in a crevasse halfway down. Her vox-booster still worked and the last thing she did before she died was tell Lord Blackmane here that my brothers needed help.' Sigrund had a broad face, always smiling, and hair shorn close to allow for the cranial jacks with which he interfaced with the controls of his gunship. His face fell a little as he looked up towards the peak. 'Did they die well?' he asked.

'They did,' said Ulli.

'And is what they say true of Aesor? I did not see it myself, but you were closer.'

'What do they say?' asked Ulli.

'That he died that glorious death we always fated for him.'

Ulli's eyes passed across the battlefield strewn with ork bodies, the dense drift of snow at the bottom of the slope where hundreds more were buried by the avalanche. It passed across Lord Blackmane – and behind him, watching from a distance, the black armour and skull-helm of Ulrik the Slayer.

'It is true,' he said. 'The greenskin had harried us all the way up the mountain and slain Saehrimnar and Starkad, but in Aesor it met a foe it could not beat, and it knew it. It must have overloaded the machinery grafted to its body to destroy the both of them. An act of spite from the alien, but an act that proved Aesor was a greater warrior than any ork.'

'Then that is what will be inscribed upon his cairn!' said Blackmane, turning to the Blood Claws. 'And sung of in the Great Hall when we come to tell the tale of Aesor Dragon's Head! He struck fear into the alien too brutal to know fear!'

The Blood Claws cheered at his words, one brandishing the greenskin head he had taken as a trophy of the hunt. They were the last party to return – the force was embarking onto the gunships that had swept in as the second wave, to carry them back down the mountain to the lower slopes where the battle for Alaric Prime was being fought.

Ulli finished wiping the worst of the blood off his axe. The runes on it had grown dim now, but once he joined the main force below, they would have to glow bright again.

It would be good to fight down there. It would be good to let himself forget.

* * *

The battle lines had stayed fluid throughout the day. The orks had launched berserk charges from the landing sites of their crude landing craft, each time met by a counterattack from the squadrons of Imperial Knights who charged under the banners of Alaric Prime's great houses. The Space Wolves had struck hard and fast into the flanks of the orks, deployed by gunship and drop pod and whisked away when the harvest of dead greenskins was reaped. But there were more orks with new landing sites established by the hour, and whole tribes were gathering ready to charge towards the Imperial lines. They were testing the Knights and the Space Wolves, spending greenskin lives to see the war machines in battle. The real fight for Alaric Prime would come later, after these opening moves had yielded no victor. The real battle would be close and vicious, a fight at which both greenskin and Space Wolf excelled.

The battle lines shifted as Blackmane watched through the port of the gunship. A wedge of orks, led by salvaged Imperial tanks and orkish war machines, was grinding across the battlefield in a pall of filthy smoke. Facing them was a phalanx of Imperial Knights, holding their ground in close order as they waited for the command to charge.

Watching the battle beside Ragnar was Ulrik the Slayer, wearing his wolf's-skull helm as he always did. It was his mark as a Wolf Priest, the barrier between him and the rest of his Chapter, a symbol of how he must remain apart from them as the Rune Priests did, for it was his duty to judge them.

'I had heard that Ulli Iceclaw was ill-starred,' said Ragnar Blackmane as he watched the battle unfolding. 'I do not listen to such rumours. They are foul and base things, not becoming of battle-brothers. But I am glad they will be dispelled now, when the rest of the Chapter learns of what he did on Sacred Mountain today.'

'It was always his burden,' replied Ulrik. He carried the only part of Aesor Dragon's Head the Space Wolves had recovered from the battlefield – the hilt of his shattered frost blade, the fat uncut emerald gleaming in the centre. 'And he was the only one who could throw it off.'

'Would that Aesor had lived also,' said Blackmane. 'There was no limit to how high he could have risen. He could have succeeded any one of the Wolf Lords, save perhaps Grimnar. But even the Old Wolf will not last forever, and it is men like Aesor who will vie for his post when he is gone. We have lost more than a Space Wolf in him, keen though we feel that loss. We have lost the hero of the Imperium he could have become.'

'He will serve on as an example of his heroism,' said Ulrik. 'Even in death, a Space Wolf fights on.'

'To think that Ulli alone should survive of all that pack,' continued Blackmane. 'I was certain that if any one of them were to return to us, it would be Aesor.'

The gemstone set into the broken frost blade's hilt appeared cracked.

On closer inspection, however, it was riddled with dark threads, slowly squirming their way through the emerald. On the hilt, the black marks where Aesor's fingers had gripped the sword looked like scorches inflicted when the ork detonated itself – but they, too, were liquid darkness, as if something had left a stain of living corruption there.

'I am not so surprised the Rune Priest is still among us,' replied Ulrik, glancing down at the blade. 'I know what Ulli Iceclaw can do.'

ICECLAW

Ben Counter

The bunker was small and dark, the only light coming from a fire that crackled quietly in a grate on the wall. Two Space Wolves stood near the roaring flames, one clad in storm-grey battleplate carved with eldritch runes, and the other the black of the Wolf Priests.

'So, Ulli Iceclaw,' said the Wolf Priest, 'I hear you gave a good day's battle. I wish I had witnessed it myself. The fight for Alaric Prime will demand many such days from all of us.'

'My thanks, Wolf Priest. But you did not call me forth to congratulate me. Ulrik the Slayer does not give his time to such small talk.'

Ulrik smiled, revealing sharp fangs.

'I do not. And you know why I must speak with you.'

'About Lord Ragnar,' said Ulli.

'You were at his side. You saw it all. It is my duty as senior Wolf Priest to examine the conduct of all Space Wolves, even the Wolf Lords – or Rune Priests like yourself.'

'Of course, Ulrik. And yet the consequences of what I witnessed do not sit easy with me.'

'I will deal with the consequences,' growled Ulrik. 'Think only of the truth.'

Ulli Iceclaw sighed heavily. Very well. The greenskins had come at us not just on the ground, but from the air...'

We held a ridge of ruins and shell craters. A whole tribe of greenskins was arrayed against us. Tens of thousands of them seethed towards us in waves, as if the foothills had become an ocean of greenskin flesh. The Cadians held our flank and fended them off with las-fire, and we did the same with our bolters. And at the heart of our line stood Wolf Lord Ragnar Blackmane.

'Space Wolves! The ork is cunning and without number, but he is still an animal! He has but one tactic in this battle, to spend the lives of his fellow greenskins to find a weak point in our line! But he will not find it where the sons of Fenris hold their ground!'

All the warriors of Fenris around us cheered, and I too was caught up in the Young Wolf's fury.

'And you men of Cadia! They will not find it where you stand, either. For there walks the Scorched Knight!'

Dyros Kamata, the Scorched Knight. He alone had stood proud of the Knightly Houses' politicking and pledged himself and his war machine to the fight when the first orks landed. Ragnar Blackmane saw in Kamata a fellow hunter and asked that the Scorched Knight fight alongside him in person. Kamata spoke through his steed's vox-emitters.

'*The greenskins thought they would find good hunting on Alaric Prime, Lord Blackmane. But now an Imperial Knight stands alongside Space Wolves and Guardsmen of Cadia, and none of us are used to being the prey!*'

Ragnar grinned.

'For every Imperial loss, Baron Kamata, I will take ten orkish heads. Can you keep up with that?'

'*I have never turned down a hunter's wager yet, Blackmane!*'

There is much scorn I could pour on the Knightly Houses, for their politics slowed the response to the greenskin invasion and cost many lives. But they produced a warrior of the Scorched Knight's calibre, and so I cannot show them too much disdain. It was then that I received the vox-report from our Stormwolf wings in the air.

'Lord Blackmane,' I reported. 'Thunderfall Squadron is pursuing a wing of ork aircraft. It's a bombing run. We have accounted for half their number but they will still hit us hard.'

'Then the greenskin attacks were to keep us in place while they hit us from the air,' Ragnar replied. 'It passes for a plan by their standards. But it will not work. Space Wolves, Cadians – take cover!'

There were more aircraft than the orks should ever have been able to field on Alaric Prime. The greenskin technology was possessed of some kind of mad genius that made those rusting crates airworthy. Dozens of bombers bore down on us. Hundreds of bombs fell.

They hit the Cadians. I could hear the men burning. They lost hundreds in moments. Good men, brave men. I saw Lord Ragnar silhouetted by the firestorm as the worst of it rained down. And then the vox-net opened up, and I heard the voice of the Scorched Knight.

'*Lord Blackmane, my power plant is ruptured. Plasma is leaking into the thorax and the hatch is jammed. It's not looking too good from where I'm sitting.*'

'Hold fast,' growled Ragnar. 'I shall be with you soon. My Blood Claws can make it. We will get you out of there.'

'*Everything around me is burning. My life is not worth the Space Wolves who will be lost if the plant goes critical. We had a fine hunt, Ragnar.*'

'Lord Blackmane does not abandon his brothers. Hold fast and survive. We will be there! Damn it, fetch me a jump pack!'

'*It was always going to end this way, Ragnar,*' said the baron. '*This Knight has served me well but she does make for a tempting target. I'm amazed I–*'

Static drowned his words and we could hear sirens blaring within the cockpit of the Scorched Knight.

'No!' screamed Ragnar as the Knight exploded.

When the smoke blew off the ridge, the destruction was terrible. Hundreds of Cadians had not reached shelter in time. They lay dead or dying in burning craters. But the most awful sight was the Scorched Knight. It still stood, but the upper half of its chest was a melted ruin. The cockpit was gone. Dyros Kamata was dead.

When I think back, I still cannot read what I saw on Lord Blackmane's face. It was as if his eyes were flecks of ice and his skin was of cold iron. For a moment there was just silence. Then he turned to me.

'Rune Priest, place the mark upon my blade. Frostfang hungers.'

'What rune should I strike, my lord?'

'Vengeance.'

'The greenskins are massing for another charge,' I warned him.

'Then be quick about it.'

It seemed I had placed a thousand runes on the weapons of my battle-brothers while we fought for that ridge. I pictured a symbol of chill hatred, and I laid my hand on Frostfang's blade. The rune burned there in cold fire. I could feel the same rune burning across the heart of Lord Blackmane.

I could see the orks approaching, thousands of them in a green tide. In their midst was their warlord, a towering creature riding a tank festooned with gun turrets and blades. I could see its fangs bared as it grinned. I could see, through my psyker's eye, the alien's joy at the prospect of slaughtering Space Wolf and Cadian alike.

'Sons of Fenris!' bellowed Ragnar. 'The greenskin thinks we are defeated! He thinks we are weak! But all he has done is stoke in us the rage the whole galaxy has learned to fear! Ten ork heads are not enough for one Imperial corpse. I will not take ten! I will not take a hundred, nor a thousand. This rage will not be quelled until every greenskin on Alaric Prime is dead!'

I have seen the volcanoes that rise from the oceans of Fenris in the Season of Fire. I have witnessed storms that bring down mountains. But I have never witnessed such rage as burned inside Ragnar Blackmane then. And though I am a Rune Priest and must always strive to keep my soul in check, I felt it too. Blackmane's rage is no mere anger. It is a force that floods into every Space Wolf. I wanted nothing more than to leap into the fray and kill every ork I could see. Forgive me, that anger burned in me.

Ulrik looked thoughtful. His snarling wolf-helm, reputed to be that worn by Leman Russ himself, sat on the table beside him. He stroked it absent-mindedly as he spoke.

'But what then, Ulli? What of Blackmane?'

'The Great Wolf Grimnar was behind our lines, leading the battle along-side the Imperial commanders. I had access to the command vox and I heard his response...'

'Blackmane! I have reports of an air attack on your position. What is our situation?' The Great Wolf sounded tense.

'The wounds have done no more than bloody our claws, Great Wolf. I am giving the order to charge.'

'No, Blackmane. Your orders are to hold that ridge. If the orks break through the whole Imperial line could fall.'

'The orks have taken our lives for too long. The time has come to slaughter them!'

'Ragnar, hold your position! Ragnar Blackmane, in the name of Russ and the Allfather, your liege lord commands you to hold your position!'

The vox-channel went dead. I looked in Ragnar's face and knew that our lord's orders would go unheeded.

'I go now to extract the price of our dead in greenskin flesh. Who is with me?'

He was answered by a chorus of howls and oaths.

'Then charge, sons of Fenris! By fire and blade, by tooth and claw! Charge!'

Even as the Cadians were pulling their wounded from the rubble, we abandoned their side and joined Ragnar's charge. Brother Einar's Swift-claws leapt into the saddles of their bikes and roared after him. The Skyclaws hurtled in his wake on their jump packs. Even the Grey Hunters and Long Fangs, whose rage should have been tempered by the discipline of a veteran, ran from cover to join the fight. And of course, I was amongst them.

'It was the death of the Scorched Knight that spurred Blackmane's anger?' asked Ulrik.

'So it seemed,' replied Ulli. 'But I am not certain.'

'How so, Rune Priest?'

'Whenever Lord Blackmane was near, I could feel that rage inside him, under the surface. It was quiet while he kept it caged, but it was always there. I wonder now if it needed much reason to be unleashed. When the Scorched Knight fell, was it a terrible enough blow that it could only be answered with such anger? Or did the rage itself simply use Kamata's death as a trigger to take Ragnar over?'

'But what of the battle that followed?' prompted the Wolf Priest.

Ulli hesitated before answering, and when he did, his voice was dark.

'It was slaughter...'

'What vermin are these that stand before me? I am Ragnar Blackmane! I am the Young King of Fenris! What senseless animal thinks he can look upon me and live?'

The greenskins were without number and I could see no end of them. I told Blackmane so.

'Then cut them down until there are few enough to count!' he shouted. 'Stand by my side, Rune Priest, and should I die here, live on that the Chapter might know of what I did!'

He lashed out with his frost blade, hewing an ork in two.

'That one tasted sweet, but Frostfang is still thirsty!'

Another greenskin fell to his blade, then another.

'These aliens know our greatness, Ulli Iceclaw. See how they throw themselves on our blades!'

One large beast wielding a huge chain-toothed axe growled a challenge at the Young Wolf, who laughed in response.

'This one thinks he's clever. He's not so quick to charge in. He wants to find an opening. But Frostfang isn't my only weapon. These are the fangs and teeth of a Fenrisian!'

Ragnar leapt and drove Frostfang's whirring teeth through the haft of the ork's axe. It shattered and the alien roared in anger, throwing himself at the Wolf Lord.

'A blade through the gut is too good for you, greenskin. A broken neck is all you get!'

He took the beast in a headlock and snapped its neck with an audible crack. Behind him another, even larger, brute raised a crude sword, aimed for Ragnar's back.

'Behind you, Lord Ragnar!' I shouted as I fired a volley of bolt pistol rounds that turned the ork to mush. 'They're pressing in on all sides!'

Through the clamour of combat, I heard another sound, the rumbling of engines. I glanced around and saw an immense shape closing on us.

'It's the war machine. The warlord's heading right for us.'

Ragnar grinned. 'Ulli, Blood Claws, keep them off me. This one's mine.'

The warlord was one of the biggest of its kind I have ever seen. Only the strongest and most vicious orks ever get to lead a whole tribe to war.

Lord Ragnar vaulted onto the tank and ran at it as if there was nothing else he wanted in this galaxy but to kill that greenskin. It wielded a giant hammer. I was sure Ragnar would have to evade it or be crushed flat, but he caught the weapon on his chest and wrenched it out of the ork's hands.

Then Frostfang flashed, and those hands were sliced off. The warlord stared down at the stumps of its wrists, and that moment of shock was the opening Ragnar needed for the kill. Frostfang sawed through the warlord's neck and its head came free of its shoulders. Ragnar held the head up high, so all the tribe could see what had become of their leader.

'*This* is the one you followed across the stars, to despoil this world? *This* is the lord who made you cower? Look at it now, greenskins, and know what you are. You are prey!'

* * *

'So,' said Ulli, 'Lord Ragnar had made good on his promise of revenge. Many orks lay dead and their leader was among the slain.

'But then I saw how much we had paid. Of Einar's Swiftclaw pack, half lay dead, dragged down off their bikes and butchered on the ground. As I watched a Grey Hunter, cut off from his pack, was surrounded, beaten down and torn apart. We had paid for this with Space Wolf lives. And there was worse to come.'

'Ragnar, we are surrounded,' I told him. 'The orks have flooded in behind us and cut us off from the ridge. The Cadians could not hold our flank, we have pushed forwards too far.'

'Then we fight on, Rune Priest.' His tone brooked no argument, but I could see the danger we were in.

'Even Ragnar Blackmane cannot kill them all.'

'Then we die well.'

'But what of the people of Alaric Prime?' I argued. 'What of all the dead from defeats that would have been victories, had we not died here? For revenge on this day, you have sacrificed our future. Half your Great Company stands here, surrounded by foes we cannot defeat. Was it worth throwing their lives away, to brandish one orkish head?'

Ulrik looked startled by this. 'You spoke thus to him?' he asked.

'I knew I had gone too far,' said Ulli, shaking his head. 'It was my duty to follow my Wolf Lord into the jaws of hell, not curse him as a headstrong fool. But I could see nothing then save the bodies of my brother Space Wolves trampled in the mud.'

'What did Blackmane say in reply?'

'Nothing...'

He fixed me with a stare that could freeze an ocean. But then the greenskins found heart again. I felt their anger rise to a crescendo, and they charged.

In the shadow of that war machine, I fought back to back with my Space Wolf brothers, and in moments my axe was heavy with gore. The ork bodies piled up into a rampart of the dead. But though we might each kill ten of them, a hundred, eventually they took one of ours.

I saw Brother Halfrad of Gundar's Grey Hunters pack, his head split open down to the collar by an ork's cleaver. The Blood Claws howled and counter-charged whenever they opened up enough space, but each time they fell back with one of their number wounded or dead.

I lost sight of Lord Ragnar, so dense was the press of orks around us. Then, above the gunfire and the cries of the wounded, I heard the sound of engines.

Three Stormwolf gunships, wearing the livery of the Great Wolf Logan Grimnar, swooped down from the sky. And leaning from the ramp I saw Grimnar himself, the Axe Morkai in his hand.

'Blackmane!' shouted the Great Wolf. 'I see once more the alpha wolf must drag the headstrong whelp out of trouble! Much as I would love for you to learn your lesson, I cannot let my brothers die out here surrounded. My Wolf Guard will cut a path for you back to our lines. I trust you can show enough sense at least to follow it!'

'The Great Wolf brought with him three packs of Wolf Guard, Grimnar's own personal troops in Terminator armour,' said Ulli, watching the flickering of the firelight. 'They were amongst the best warriors in our Chapter. Our ranks cheered as they leapt down from their gunships.'

'And did you cheer as well, Ulli Iceclaw?' asked Ulrik, curiosity in his voice. 'Were you as relieved as your battle-brothers?'

The Rune Priest sighed. 'I do not know, Wolf Priest. True, where we had faced death we now had a chance. But with the certainty of death removed, my thoughts had leave to go elsewhere, and I saw how troubled I was. Ragnar was my Wolf Lord, the Young King of Fenris. We idolised him. Already, my brothers and I had memorised his sagas and sought to emulate the skill and fury he showed in battle. But now, I saw something else in Ragnar Blackmane.'

'You speak of Blackmane's rage. The rage that had cost so many lives, and brought a whole Great Company so close to destruction.'

'My brothers lay dead. The Imperial line was compromised. All that could have been avoided. Had we held our ground, we could have weathered whatever storm the orks threw at us. The cost would have been high, but we would have held. Imperial command had a plan to shatter the army of orks that faced us. Now whatever that plan was, it was in tatters, for we had not played our part. Instead we had followed a leader driven by headstrong anger, and many of us lay butchered in the mud because of it. This mighty lord of Fenris, in whom I had seen the very exemplar of our Chapter, now seemed to me no more than a berserker who would lead us all to a fruitless death.'

'I have served as Wolf Priest for many years, Ulli. Since before you were ever made a Space Wolf. And in that time my purpose has been to minister to the spiritual needs of my brethren, to watch for the sins of the mind that might lead them down a wayward path. And of those sins, one of the gravest is doubt. What you saw in Blackmane's conduct planted that doubt in you. That is what I must fight, just as you fought the greenskins.'

Ulli struggled for a moment to find the words. 'But how can I forget the sight of my battle-brothers torn apart by orkish hands? How can I ignore the despair I felt, to know that we would die there for nothing?'

'Go on, Ulli Iceclaw,' urged Ulrik gently. 'Your tale does not end there.'

Ulli shook his head. 'No. No it does not.'

* * *

Grimnar and his Wolf Guard landed beside us. With a roar of assault cannon and storm bolters, they forced back the first ranks of the orks. The Stormwolves circled overhead, strafing the orks or picking out their war machines with pinpoint fire. Then Grimnar held the Axe Morkai aloft so all could see it.

'With me, sons of Fenris!' the Great Wolf roared. 'We will cut a bloody canyon through this greenskin flesh!'

'Fight beside me, Ulli!' laughed Ragnar. 'The rune you placed on my blade still burns bright. It will take plenty more ork blood to douse that fire.'

And so I fought. I had lost count of the orks I had killed, though they numbered a pittance compared to Blackmane's tally. We forged through the ork ranks, following the bloody wake of Grimnar and the Wolf Guard.

Even as the greenskins reeled, I saw one of the Wolf Guard fall. He was pulled down by a mass of orks who used crude cutting torches to carve his armour apart. One of our finest, lost to the Chapter because Ragnar Blackmane had given in to his rage.

We were within sight of the Imperial line. The Cadians had suffered badly and their fortifications were aflame, but they were still manned. The remains of the Scorched Knight still burned. We were close. I let the hope kindle in my hearts that we would survive this. But this battle was not over.

A great shadow passed over us. I looked up to see an enormous war machine flying above us in a mockery of logic. From its hull hung hundreds of gibbets, each containing an Imperial Guard prisoner, stripped of his wargear, bleeding and left there to die for the amusement of the orks. Its gun turrets blazed and our Stormwolves had to back away or be blasted from the sky.

'What you saw was called the Skygouger,' said Ulrik. 'It had led attacks on Imperial positions since the beginning of the war for Alaric Prime. Already it had gained a reputation like death itself, for wherever it went it left just corpses. Imperial command had tried to track it, but some xenos technology made it invisible to our augurs. It was only seen when the orks wished to inflict punishment on Imperial forces, and they summoned it to punish the Space Wolves.'

'The Skygouger,' mused Ulli. 'So that is what they called it. To us it seemed a final insult. That orks can even build something that flies is obscene enough. That it should intercept us just when our line was within sight – that seemed calculated to drain us of hope. Perhaps the timing was deliberate. Perhaps the orks wanted us to know hope, and then have it snatched away, so we would be weakened in the final moments by despair.'

'But Space Marines do not know despair,' said Ulrik.

'No, Wolf Priest. We do not. But the orks were going to try their best to make us know it...'

Their assault forces launched from the Skygouger in their dozens. They were jump pack troops in black-painted armour. Where most greenskins fought with wildness and savagery, these were disciplined and ruthless. They fell upon our Grey Hunters and Blood Claws, avoiding the guns and blades of Grimnar's Wolf Guard.

Cannons on the Skygouger rained fire, forcing our formation apart so the greenskin assault could isolate and butcher us. I saw the Great Wolf surrounded by seven or eight of them, keeping them at bay with great swings of the Axe Morkai. The rest of the orks took heart from the Skygouger's appearance and they massed once more, ready to swarm and finish us off.

'No!' shouted Ragnar. 'Not now, not when we are so close! It will not end this way, my brothers!' He gestured to a nearby Space Wolf. 'You, Skyclaw. You are wounded. Can you fight?'

The young warrior shook his head. His right arm had been crushed and though I knew that he would fight on with his teeth if needs be, the day's battle was over for him.

'Then give me your jump pack,' growled Ragnar.

'Lord Blackmane, what are you doing?' I asked.

'If I am to fall here it will not be in the mud, on my knees. It will be taking the fight to the enemy, as a Space Wolf should!'

'You will die,' I told him.

'Not so, for I will not be alone. There lies another fallen brother. He will not fight any more, but his wargear can still serve. Take his jump pack and follow me. The rune on my blade has grown dull and I have need of a Rune Priest. Your Wolf Lord has spoken, Ulli Iceclaw.'

I buckled on the jump pack. I knew what insanity this was, but my Wolf Lord *had* spoken.

'Was that the only reason you followed him?' asked Ulrik.

Ulli considered the question. 'In truth, Wolf Priest? I cannot say.'

The Skygouger had drifted low to drop off its troops, low enough for a bound of the jump pack to reach it. Ragnar leapt before me. I barely made it onto the war machine. The hull of the Skygouger was crawling with ork drop troops massing for the next wave. Ragnar dived into them, full of the fury that had caused him to abandon our lines.

I felt, kindling in my heart again, that same fury. I had not thought it possible, for I had seen the cost of such recklessness, but I could not deny it. My mind was full of the battle-brothers who had died that day – the Blood Claws and Grey Hunters slain as the orks surrounded us, the Wolf Guard who had followed Grimnar's rescue mission, all butchered by greenskin hands. And I wanted what Ragnar wanted. I wanted to kill them all.

He howled and it filled my heart with joy to hear it.

'What alien eyes are worthy to look on a Space Wolf?' I growled at an ork who approached with an axe in each hand. 'Look well, for it is the last thing you will see! This is my Rune Axe, an extension of this psyker's mind. I hear your kind can fight on with a severed limb. But how can you fight when I sever your soul?'

I brought the blade down and siphoned a portion of my power through it, obliterating the greenskin.

'That is the fate of all your kind,' I told its remains. 'To be turned to red mist and ash!'

'Well fought, Rune Priest! We must bring this metal beast down.'

Blackmane reached the prow of the Skygouger. He tore the canopy off the cockpit.

The ork pilot barely had time to show surprise before Frostfang took his head. I followed Lord Blackmane inside the hull. The stench was awful, of rotting meat and sweat. Gnawed bones and body parts were everywhere. The Skygouger had taken hundreds of Imperial Guard prisoners and this was where they had died. Stunted versions of the greenskins scurried away at our approach. Orks tried to bar our way but Blackmane was possessed with a rage, and so was I.

'It is an honour greater than you xenos filth deserve to die on Frost-fang's blade!'

He gave it that honour regardless.

'We should let one of you live, to tell the other greenskin filth of what happens when you make war on the Space Wolves,' I laughed at my opponent. 'But not you.'

I hacked it down and turned to find another, but Ragnar had made short, bloody work of them.

'Press on, Rune Priest,' he ordered. 'We need to find something this hulk cannot fly without.'

But I did not see the shape in the shadows, looming up from the depths of the Skygouger's hold. It hit me before I could react.

It was an ork, one of their leaders by its size, perhaps even huger than the warlord Ragnar had slain. Around its neck hung a hundred dog tags torn from Guardsmen's necks. It had taken their medals, too, and wore them on its armoured chest in mockery of the brave men it had killed. On its head was a Cadian officer's cap, still stained with the blood of the man who had worn it. The ork's limbs were clad in black steel and each hand was a mechanical claw to tear and crush.

The greenskin howled, as if in mockery of the noble howls of our Chapter, and beckoned Ragnar forward. The Wolf Lord leapt.

Blackmane and the ork commander clashed, and they were matched in strength. In the confines of the Skygouger there was only room to wrestle. In the open, Ragnar's swordsmanship might have cut the ork to pieces and left him open for the killing blow. But here it was face to face, the claws seeking to grab and crush as the ork's bulk pinned Blackmane to the ground. My head swam and my body would not respond as I wished. I crawled closer.

'Ulli,' Ragnar roared, 'if this creature bests me, return to the Chapter. Tell them how I died.'

But this time, I did not obey. I placed my hand on the side of Ragnar's breastplate. I willed there a rune of defiance, of honour and fury, a symbol of the high kings of Fenris from an age remembered only by the stones. I dredged up every drop of will I had. My body was spent, but my mind was still a weapon. And as the claws crushed home, the rune flared bright.

The ork's claw bit into Ragnar's armour, and there was a great pulse of energy. The greenskin roared in agony and anger.

'Fenrisian guile beats xenos brawn,' growled the Wolf Lord. 'And Space Wolf steel beats everything!'

Frostfang pierced the greenskin's heart. I saw the light go out in its eyes. I felt the rage-filled fires of its life extinguished as it fell to the deck. Ragnar paused to help me to my feet, and rampaged on through the carrier.

The greenskins were dismayed to see their commander fall and they fled before us as Lord Blackmane tore engines and fuel lines apart. I felt the Skygouger lurch.

'Come, Rune Priest. It is time to leave,' said Ragnar.

As we leapt from the carrier and our jump packs slowed our descent, I watched the Skygouger falling in flames. It crashed into the heart of the orks.

I saw a thousand of them die in the storm of flame and wreckage that followed.

The orks fled from us. The Great Wolf led the way back to the Imperial lines, with Lord Ragnar fighting by his side. When we reached our positions on the ridge, I saw the Cadians rejoicing that the Skygouger had fallen and the orks had been so thoroughly beaten.

'But you did not rejoice, Ulli Iceclaw,' said Ulrik, looking intently at the Rune Priest. 'Though your battle-brothers cheered the deaths of so many greenskins, I see no joy in your face.'

'No, Wolf Priest. I thought only of my brothers who had fallen, and of how the rage of Ragnar Blackmane was scarcely less responsible for their deaths than the greenskins.'

'But you do not have the perspective of a Wolf Priest. You saw Ragnar's rage bring the Space Wolves to the edge of defeat. But what did you see when Ragnar boarded the Skygouger? You felt that same rage then, and you saw what it did to the enemy. Do you think anyone else could have brought down the Skygouger? It was Ragnar's rage that made it possible. That anger cost us many lives, but it also brought us a victory where nothing else could have.'

Ulli considered this. 'Then it is no surprise for you to hear of what his rage can do.'

Ulrik shook his head slowly. 'It is not. Long ago, we looked on the young Ragnar Blackmane, promoted to the Wolf Guard directly from the Blood Claws, an unheard-of feat. We knew what would happen if he ever rose to the position of Wolf Lord, of how many of our brothers would pay for his anger with their lives. But we also saw how many victories it would bring us, how many enemies would fall before it who would otherwise survive. And we decided the price of his recklessness was worth the victories it would bring us.'

There was a long silence broken only by the crackling of the fire.

'I see,' said Ulli at last. 'I have but one question for you, Ulrik, if I may.'

'Speak on, Rune Priest.'

'You say the Wolf Priests made a decision on Ragnar's fitness to serve as a Wolf Lord. But if the cost became too high, if the Chapter suffers too greatly from his rages... could that decision be reversed?'

Klaxons sounded from outside and Ulrik looked up.

'The orks are charging again,' he said. 'Look fast, Rune Priest. We need all battle-brothers on the line.'

The question went unanswered. Ulli thought he might be glad of that.

Outside, Ulli watched Ragnar Blackmane as he addressed the warriors of his Great Company.

'Sons of Fenris,' the Young Wolf began. 'The orks will not stop until this world is barren and despoiled. But when the smoke has cleared and the blood soaked into the earth, it is the Space Wolves who will be standing atop a mountain of orkish dead!'

He howled, and his Wolves howled with him.

ARJAC ROCKFIST

Ben Counter

Let the fire burn low.

The time for feasting is done. You have all had your fill. Yes, even you Blood Claws, you young and violent pups who revel as hard as you fight! Even you. By day I am a mere thrall, my task to fix your wargear, maintain the Fang, labour in your forges and armouries, and do the drudge work that lets the Space Wolves focus entirely on war. But now, as the suns of Fenris drift us into twilight, as the shadows of the Great Hall gather like palls of night sky above us, now I am the voice that all must heed. Did not Leman Russ himself tell tales such as these, of the Emperor and the Great Crusade? Did he not command to heed the tellers of stories, be they mighty Wolf Lord or humble serf? So stoke not the fire until I am done, and let words take flight in the glow of its embers.

My tale this night is of Arjac Rockfist.

Yes, well might you cheer. Arjac, the mightiest of us all! A giant even among the Space Marines, the Anvil and the Hammer of Fenris! Many kegs of ale have been drained in toast to him. Even you Long Fangs, you who grumble and shake your heads at the antics of the Blood Claws, even you Grey Hunters who call yourself the backbone of our Chapter, even you will celebrate his name. Yes, Arjac Rockfist, Grimnar's Champion! Many are the foes of the Allfather who curse his name in *hel*.

But this is not a tale of the crushing of the unrighteous at the far ends of the galaxy. No, this tale takes place here, on Fenris, the cold and heartless mother that gave birth to us all, home to the tribes which whelped each one of you. It unfolds in this very place, at the Fang, throne of Leman Russ, fortress of the Space Wolves. My words will take us even to this spot, the Great Hall.

Who will pour me a mug? I have much to say and my throat becomes dry. Thank you, Brother Hef. Now, let me see.

Yes, Arjac! Arjac was strong before he ever became a Space Wolf, before the Wolf Priests ever singled him out for elevation to your number. He was a child of prodigious strength and size, and the fathers of his people told him he would be a warrior. And indeed he was a terror on the battlefield. But truly his home was not there, but in the forge. There his great strength could bend the shafts of fangtree wood into yokes for the Fenrisian drakes that pulled his chieftain's chariot.

His hammer blows could tame blades of titansteel into shape, and only with his sternness and strength of arm could the steeds of the mountain valleys be shoed for the cavalry of his people. Though many enemies fell to his hand in his youth, it was by his labour in the forges that his people were victorious and thrived.

Barely had Arjac returned from his Blooding when the Iron Priests near demanded he be apprenticed to them, to work hammer and anvil in the Forge Hills that form the lower slopes of the Fang.

His master then was Hengis Blackhand, High Iron Priest, and Arjac learned quickly. While his fellow Blood Claws, like all you raucous whelps, feasted and tested their strength, and the Wolf Priests were pressed to keep them from putting one another in the apothecarion, Arjac read the treatises on weapon-craft he hoped would make him worthy of the greatest relics in the Chapter armoury. He spent his time on Mars, that world of forges, as all who aspire to forge and repair the machines of war must do. Even among their strange rituals and inhuman Magi he was a prodigy of the anvil!

The Magi of the Red World claimed he had in him the potential to himself be High Iron Priest one day, though that would be centuries of labour and learning in the future. Many are the tales I could tell of his time at Mars, but for now I will speak of a time after he returned, apprentice to the High Iron Priest.

Everyone will be tested. This is the lesson that Fenris teaches us. We are tested first when we are born squealing and naked into her clutches, when she challenges us merely to survive. As we approach manhood we must pass her thousand tests of resolve and strength, of valour, intelligence, temperance and fury.

A Space Wolf is tested in another thousand trials, the greatest of which is the Blooding. You passed that test – I did not, as is evidenced by the limp with which I walk and the humble trappings of a thrall I wear instead of the carapace and armour of a Space Marine. And so it was that Arjac was tested, too. Hengis Blackhand summoned Arjac to the Heart Forge, that lava-fed pit of fire, the only place where Fenris's fury can be kindled sufficient to forge the hardest and sharpest frost blade. Arjac attended his master there above the lava pit, ringed as it still is by its hundred anvils, on the lower slope of the Fang.

'Arjac,' said Lord Hengis. 'Long have you laboured here, remaking the torn armour and broken blades of our Chapter. Your work is fine and long-serving. Your blades are honed sharp, and folded strong. But this is work for thralls. You may do the work of twenty men at the forge, but a Space Marine is worth a hundred men in battle. It is no great shame for a Space Wolf to labour at the anvil – indeed, each Iron Priest must do so for a year and a day before he is granted his servo-harness – but you, Arjac, are wasted on mundane wargear when the forge thralls could do that work.'

'I value the service I can do to my Chapter,' said Arjac, 'and the honour that is done to me when my battle-brothers trust in the arms I have worked. But if you command that I withdraw from the forges and join my brothers in their revelry and brawling, then I shall, though I will miss the heat of the fires and the ringing of the anvil.'

'No, Arjac, I do not ask that of you.'

Some of you knew High Iron Priest Hengis, those older among you. He was broad of girth and full of beard, which was red-brown and worn in braids. His face was ruddy and his voice as deep as the mountain's own rumble. He clapped Arjac on the back heartily, as was his way. 'I ask that you take on the task of remaking the ancient relics of the Chapter, those that have lain broken for centuries now. Though we yearn to return such relics to the battlefield, the reverence in which we hold them bids us to leave them be and not disturb their spirits with an imperfect remaking. But you, Arjac, have such a fineness of touch, such an understanding of steel, that perhaps you might be the first of us to take on this task. But to be sure, you must be tested.'

'I will submit to any test, and may the Allfather guide me and the wolves of the night sky look with favour on it,' said Arjac, for he was humble and would not say that he relished such a task or the opportunity to prove himself. How many of you, when given such a task, would celebrate that you had been chosen, or would cry out with words unsoft that no man might perform it better than you, or that the obstacle before you is as nothing? Most of you, I have no doubt. Not Arjac.

Hengis bade the forge thralls forth, carrying between them a suit of armour. It was Terminator armour, such as is granted to the most honoured of Wolf Guard.

Blessed are you who have earned the right to wear it! You are champions among champions. The armour was ancient, its grey ceramite plates inlaid with the most intricate knot work in brass and silver. Wolves hunted their prey through the spiralling pattern, battleships did war upon Fenris's oceans, and the stars in the sky formed the constellations under which we were all born. Such was the workmanship of the armour presented to Arjac Rockfist.

'This is the armour of Wolf Lord Torjek Granitebrow,' said Hengis. 'He was lost in the assault on Brehan IV, and though his body was recovered his armour never functioned again. See, how the servos are charred and useless! Alas, none have been able to repair them, for their riddles elude us. And these ceramite plates, on the shoulder and the greave. See how they are split and torn! Yet to repair it seamlessly is beyond any of us, for the work is so fine and intricate. To you, Arjac Rockfist, I give this task. Repair the armour of Torjek Granitebrow, and return it to our armouries that it might be granted to a hero of our future. This is the test I set before you.'

Arjac knelt and bowed in thanks, and took the armour and laid it on the anvil beside him. Without a word more he set about his work.

Some of you have heard of Torjek Granitebrow, for I have told his tale before, and much is the drinking and feasting on that occasion for it is a hearty and glorious tale indeed. Quiet, be calm! I shall tell that tale again, fear not, just not now. Now I speak of Arjac.

Arjac was thus presented with a stern test indeed. For many days he contemplated the armour of Torjek Granitebrow, seeking to understand it as much as to examine it. For many more days he performed the rituals learned on Mars to the machine-spirit of that armour, seeking to earn its respect and gain permission to work it. Never did he leave the edge of the Heart Forge, bathed in the heat welling up from Fenris's very core.

How did he fix the servos? He meditated on them, following the path of every wire and circuit, until he could retrace them all in his mind. And he listened thereby to the wishes of the machine-spirit and followed them, rewiring the circuits with hands dexterous in spite of their size. Through turning his perception inwards, he unravelled that mystery.

And how did he forge the plates of the armour back into shape, without destroying the workmanship of that past age? He used his bare hands. Mighty hands, with a grip stronger than any man born to Fenris before or since, hands themselves forged upon the anvil as sure as any of his blades. With bloody and calloused fingers he forced the ceramite back into shape, and so the wounds were rendered invisible, the repairs seamless. Both meditation and reforging took months, during which time Arjac remained in the Heart Forge fed and watered by the forge thralls who had such great respect for the blacksmith as well as reverence for the warrior.

Thus it was that Arjac returned to the Great Hall of the Fang, where you sit now, where High Iron Priest Blackhand was feasting alongside the Great Wolf Logan Grimnar. They were celebrating battles to come, for at that time the Chapter was about to embark on the Calunian Crusade. Arjac was still smeared with soot, his skin singed from the Heart Forge's heat, and he placed the armour of Torjek Granitebrow on the feasting table.

For an hour Blackhand examined the armour, a critical eye scouring every rivet and weld.

'What do you see?' asked Great Wolf Grimnar, at length.

'I see the armour of Torjek Granitebrow,' replied Hengis Blackhand.

Though few words, they were enough. Before, Hengis had seen a wreck, the corpse of mighty wargear inhabited by a miserable machine-spirit encased in ruined and unloving ceramite. But now it was a suit of armour again, a weapon of war, such as it had been before Torjek fell.

Great was the cheer! Gone was the ale! The return of the relic to the Chapter vaults was a good portent for the crusade to come, and so the Space Wolves waxed merry. Arjac Rockfist did not feast with them, though he spilled a mug of ale in honour of the fallen and accepted the plaudits of his battle-brothers with grace. He was a humble man, as I have said.

'Feast and sing, Brother Arjac,' said Great Wolf Grimnar. 'This is a great day, and a great feat of yours that we applaud.'

'I am glad that I have served my Chapter,' said Arjac, 'and truly it is this that makes me happy. But these are the achievements of but one man. It is when we all fight together and win some mighty victory that I truly feel the most joy. When we have won our crusade and many foes of the Allfather are ground beneath our feet, then perhaps I shall sing of our greatness.'

'Alas, Brother Arjac!' cried Grimnar. 'I must bring you news that you will not relish. For you will not join us on our crusade.'

Who can say whether Arjac felt sorrow in that moment? None save Arjac himself, who does not discuss such things, at least not with a lowly thrall such as I. He did not show it, but instead bowed his head in deference to the authority of the Great Wolf. 'Then how,' said he, 'shall I serve instead?'

It was Hengis Blackhand who answered. 'The armour of Torjek Granitebrow was a test for you, as you have no doubt concluded yourself. But it was a test to decide if you were to be given another very specific task. Tell me, Brother Arjac, what manner of relic, were it wielded today, would bring the greatest dread to our enemies?'

'There is no relic that causes such fear,' said Arjac without hesitation. 'Save that which is wielded by a Space Wolf in battle. The battle-brother who bears it is the true cause of our enemies' dread. So I will say that which the greatest of us carries, and that is the Axe Morkai borne by our Great Wolf Grimnar.' At this Arjac bowed his head in deference to Grimnar, who looked on.

'And so it shall be!' bellowed Hengis. 'For great was the sorrow when, upon the Chapter's last voyage into war, the Axe Morkai was shattered!'

Who among you here has heard that tale? Ah, not a few of you I see. Yes, for my tale takes place shortly after the duel our Great Wolf had with the Mad Butcher of the Gorgavian Maw, that lord of the greenskins who, like all before him and since, thought himself the one to unite the orkish hordes and dominate the galaxy. His quest ended beneath the blade of the Axe Morkai!

Alas, that greenskin warlord was blessed by his savage gods with a skull thicker than the armour of a Rhino tank. The axe shattered even as the ork's skull was crushed. So the Great Wolf was victorious, but the Axe Morkai, that mighty relic he had carried for centuries, was broken.

'A weapon for the Great Wolf,' said Grimnar. 'For I seek to wield it again. Our foes tremble when they hear the howling of our pack approach, and I would give the keenest edge to their fear when I brandish the Axe Morkai before we charge. From the shards of the axe the relic will rise anew, and its spirit will once more taste the blood of our enemies!'

Who can say what thoughts might run through the mind of a Space Wolf who is given a work of such great import, and yet must withdraw from the sacred battlefield to see it done? Again, only Arjac can say, and again, a thrall such as I has no right to ask. The answer will be found in you, Space Wolves, who so love to fight.

By answer, Arjac said only this: 'Then I must leave this gathering, and go to the armoury. For the Axe Morkai's machine-spirit will be eager to see its new birth. With your leave, Great Wolf, and yours, High Iron Priest.'

So Arjac watched the Space Wolves Chapter leaving in their Thunderhawk gunships as he worked in the forges of the Fang's lower slopes. What a heartening sight, to see the Chapter aloft, heading for the fleet in orbit that they might go to war! But Arjac must have felt such sorrow to see them go without him, and yet taken comfort from the knowledge that he would create a legacy for the whole Chapter in the reforging of the Axe Morkai.

At that time, the Fang was held by a ceremonial guard of a single Grey Hunters squad. This was Squad Fornjot, whose heraldry you can see there among the hundreds hung about the Great Hall. There, above the fireplace. The skeletal paw over the three mountains, on a field of yellow and red. The personal heraldry of the pack leader, Fornjot Halfenhelm. He was sorrowful also, as were the brothers of his pack, for they would be denied their part in the Calunian Crusade. But his orders were from the Great Wolf, and he was obedient as any wolf must be to the alpha of his pack.

'Whatever you require of my Grey Hunters,' said Fornjot to Arjac, as he visited the forge slopes, 'I shall see to it that one of us or the thralls shall provide it to you.'

'Then I have a task that only one of your pack may fulfil,' said Arjac. 'Look upon the shards of the Axe Morkai upon this anvil. Have you heard tell of its origin?'

'I have,' said Fornjot. 'It was once carried by a champion of Chaos, beholden to the Fell Powers. He was defeated by the Great Wolf in his youth, when but a young warrior of our Chapter. He took the axe as a trophy and has carried it ever since.'

'Indeed,' said Arjac. 'But that is not all there is to the tale. First the axe had to be tamed, for it was tainted with the sins of he who had carried it before. None can say what innocent blood was shed, or what terrible blasphemies it witnessed. The Great Wolf wrestled with its machine-spirit for a hundred days, they say, before the axe was cleansed and safe for him to carry. And so it must be purified again, and reconsecrated, before it can be remade.'

'And how can such corruption be held at bay?' asked Fornjot. He looked at the shattered weapon with eyes anew, for now he understood why the Great Wolf had carried it – to show that even the debasement of the Dark Gods and their followers cannot stay the hand of a Space Wolf.

'Anointment with the blood of a Space Wolf shall consecrate this blade,' said Fornjot. 'But not just any battle-brother. I must do as Lord Grimnar did when he first conquered the weapon's corrupted spirit, and anoint it with the blood of the Primarch Leman Russ himself! A vial of it lies in the gene-seed vault, and I need it to continue my work.'

'Then I shall bring it myself,' said Fornjot. 'Ha! This at least is some consolation! Still I would rather be fighting, for I love nothing more than to rend unrighteous flesh with my claws and my teeth! But to carry a relic such as Russ's own blood will be something.' Fornjot flashed a savage smile. Perhaps he had never truly left the ways of the Blood Claw, aggressive and headstrong, behind him, and perhaps that was why his Wolf Lord had selected him to lead a Grey Hunters pack. While the Grey Hunter should be level-headed and serve as an example to the Blood Claw pups, yet they must also keep that steel and blood-hunger in their souls.

Do you think it an insult that a thrall should tell a hall full of Space Wolves how a Space Wolf should fight? From your growls I suppose that it must be. But I can say these things, and you must hear them. Such is the privilege of the tellers of tales.

So Fornjot brought a vial of Russ's blood to the Heart Forge, where Arjac worked. The Axe Morkai lay on his anvil as Arjac contemplated it. Though it was shattered, its great crescent blade deeply cracked and its starmetal haft split apart, still it seemed a terrible thing, the killing power of a storm or a volcano's eruption bound in the shape of a weapon. In the carvings along the trophy halls you can see it, held in the Great Wolf's paw as he smites legions of greenskins or armies of traitors. This was what Arjac contemplated as he made ready to activate the Axe Morkai's power field and study its spirit.

Fornjot's pack was a reliable and sturdy band, not given to riotous feasting or brawling among themselves as some are. Fornjot himself, as I have said, was their spirit of savagery, and they held his predator's instincts back as much as he led them. Brother Vidfinn carried the pack's meltagun, for he had once faced an Abyssal Wurm on his Blooding and had not taken one step back from it. Thus it was that they trusted him to stand his ground even as the greatest engines of war approached close enough to use his weapon. Truly there was nothing that elicited more than a raised eyebrow from Brother Vidfinn, be it alien, abomination or act of blasphemy.

Brother Anvakyr was a war-poet and wrote down the pack's exploits. Fast with words was he, faster even than with his boltgun, though he was a fine enough shot.

Brothers Dvarnn and Brokkyr had been brought to the Fang on the same day, from the same tribe, and some wondered if they were literally brothers. Each one carried a lightning claw which had been forged and wielded as a pair, and when they fought, they did so in concert, with the same certainty that the right hand feels of the left.

Their packmate was Svalin, and if Fornjot was the pack's savagery, Svalin was their reason. A veteran who had not passed into the ranks of the Long Fangs or been elevated to the Wolf Guard, he wished to live out his days as a Grey Hunter where his wisdom would serve as the pack's keenest weapon.

This, then, was Pack Fornjot, the only Space Wolves in the Fang save Arjac Rockfist. And we must not forget the Chapter thralls who laboured there also. How easy it is for you to forget them entirely! As if we were invisible spirits that tended to your fortress-monastery, like the nixies and trolls of Fenrisian myth!

Do you think that we blink into existence to clean up the wreckage of your feasting, or polish the trophies of the paw prints you leave on them, or mop the blood from the duelling circles? No! The Fang is our home just as it is yours, though you see us not when we go by. Though many had left with the Chapter on their crusade, still there were countless thralls in the Fang when Pack Fornjot had watch over it.

On the battlements of the Fang stood Brother Anvakyr. His wargear rites and duelling drills completed, he had now the sliver of the day that a Space Marine has to himself, where his own thoughts might hold court.

Anvakyr came here often, to the defences and sally ports that stud the upper slopes of the Fang, where all the majesty of Fenris unfolds for a hundred miles. In the light of the dusk the crevasses of the foothills were edged in the red of the dying sun. The polar lights hung in shimmering curtains, like waterfalls of many-coloured fire that poured over the stars just starting to emerge. Distant glaciers seemed covered in fields of red. And the ocean lapped at the lowest slopes where the forges smouldered, for on one side the Fang is a sheer cliff that looms over the black depths. The air was cold and good, and Anvakyr loved to inhale the tales of Fenris told in the chill air.

'I shall write of this night,' said he. 'How it is that alone, when war is distant and even one's packmates are at bay, then the truth of the universe can reach us. Just a syllable here, a note there, of what creation we truly inhabit, can reach us if we let it. Crone-Mother Fenris! I was born into cruel arms, your arms. Yet the galaxy is cruel, and so you taught me well. Father Fenris! I was raised a short cast away from death, your death, the death of your storms and your predators. But this galaxy is full of death, and so you taught me well. Brother Fenris! I was born into sorrow, for you watched over many good men and women lost, when I was spared. But this galaxy is full of sorrows, and through it I survived, for I was ordained to serve as a Space Marine. And so, Brother Fenris, you taught me well.'

'Yes,' said Brother Anvakyr, 'I will write that down.'

But as he spoke, yet the instincts of the wolf did not leave him. Taught to him by Fenris, honed by the Wolf Priests and the sleep-taught lessons of our Chapter, they howled in his head.

Anvakyr knew in that moment he was not alone. He did not know what manner of enemy was upon him, be it razorhawk or Peak Render, but he knew it was no Space Wolf or thrall.

'Show yourself!' he cried, drawing his chainblade keen. 'What fool is this, that thinks he can creep up on a Space Wolf? I hear you, the clicking of your claws on stone, or perhaps of a form armoured in scale or bone. I can smell you! Xenos, you are, for this stink is not of Fenris. And soon I will see you, and when that happens I will gut you alive! Show yourself, and at least die in open fight, if your kind has any honour to gain from it!'

No answer came. But the stink was clear. It was not the smell of the ocean or the mountains, or the winter wind. It was nothing that had ever been tracked by a predator across the snowdrifts of Fenris, nor ridden the storms of her skies. It was an alien.

Brother Anvakyr whirled around, seeking to perceive with his eyes what his nose told him was approaching. Upon the battlements he was alone, and he spied nothing living save for the birds of prey circling the peak overhead.

It was from above that it came. The rock of the Fang, caked in ice and streaked in grey and black, shifted and came alive – first like a rockfall, then like a sinuous predator rushing down the sheer rock as swiftly and surely as if it was on level ground.

Anvakyr's nose told him it was coming. His ears picked out its claws on stone. He did not see it in time. He brought his chainblade up by instinct as it fell upon him.

Would that I could give Anvakyr a good death! Every Space Wolf should die one, a magnificent final stand atop a heap of the enemy dead, or a sacrifice of legend where he gives his life to save his brethren. These are the deaths that are supposed to end the best stories.

But alas, though I tell a tale, yet this tale must have some truth in it, and to give Brother Anvakyr a glorious death would be to deny that truth. You are not children. Though you hiss and snarl at me, you can cope with that truth, and you should hear it.

Brother Anvakyr did not die well. He will stand at the end of time, alongside Leman Russ in the battle where all the incarnations of Chaos will be scattered and driven from the galaxy. But he did not die well. So mourn him.

The thralls who came to the battlements with the dawn, to tend to the defence guns that loomed from their mountainside ports, found Brother Anvakyr's body. His head was a ruin, frozen into a red bloom, his skull split several ways asunder. Claw gouges on the stone beside him told of the fury and swiftness with which death had come to him. His chainblade was still in his hand, and alas, on its teeth were no shreds of frozen alien flesh. He had died before he could strike any blow of his own. Yes, howl! Remember him with that dread keening! But soon, as is the way of things, let your sorrow become anger, for that was the anger that flooded the Fang.

The body was borne back into the Fang before the predators of the sky could fall on it. Fornjot carried it, for he was the leader of Anvakyr's pack. Anvakyr was laid out under a shroud in the apothecarion. Fornjot bade all his brothers kneel by the body, and spoke a prayer seeing Anvakyr swiftly to the End Times.

'And now,' said Fornjot, 'comes revenge. What beast did this, I do not know. But I do know that we will hunt it down. Chase it! Corner it! Butcher it and hang its carcass in the trophy hall! Dvarnn and Brokkyr, spread the word among the thralls that a predator has taken a Space Wolf. Whatever they see or hear that is out of place, I must hear of it. Svalin, go to the forge slopes and bring back Arjac Rockfist, for there he works. I would have another wolf in my pack for this hunt. The rest, stay with me, and we will prowl the Fang with our eyes open and our noses keen. Go! To the hunt, go!'

Word spread swiftly. Though you might not pay it any mind, the thralls of the Fang are drilled well in responding to a crisis such as an intruder in the Fang. We have our own leaders, our own patterns of readiness and war. Indeed, I myself was there, although then I was but young, barely recovered from my failed Blooding, and I played no part in what follows.

I remember there was no panic, just determination, just the knowledge that we were without the Chapter and had to act in the defence of the Fang ourselves. We broke open the arms lockers and each thrall took an auto-gun and a combat blade. Thane Morgharn was my superior and he had our maintenance crew watch the vents and tunnels, the places for pumping of water and waste where a predator might make entrance to the Fang.

We were brave, for one does not come to the notice of the Space Wolves without being among the most valiant of his tribe. But we knew we were not Space Wolves. If a hunter that could kill a Space Wolf fell amongst us, we would probably die. I felt then the fear of death, that final obstacle that can only be overcome when a pup becomes a Space Wolf.

It was known even then that we faced not a mundane intruder, such as some beast wandered in from the ice fields beyond the Fang. Our augurs, maintained and watched by us thralls, had not detected the life signs of any intruder, nor had the sensors scattered through the Fang that should have picked up the pheromones of a xenos. I know now why that was, for the intruder was a thing of cunning and deceit, in form created to fool all but the nose of a Space Wolf. But back then we fancied the Fang had become home to a ghost of Fenris's past, one of the ancient kings who had clawed his way up from a frozen grave, mad with grief and anger. Would that it had been so! Rather would I have had us prey to a furious spectre than the predator truly among us. But I get ahead of myself.

Arjac had made progress in his work on the Axe Morkai. The shards of the Steel Glacier's blade had been removed from the haft, rearranged and assembled as Morkai's new blade, and Arjac had begun the work of forging them into a single arc of deadly steel.

He looked up as Brother Svalin approached through the snows that lay on the forge slopes. Working at the forges outside the Fang, between this great fortress and the ever-churning sea, Arjac had not yet heard of the commotion within.

'Brother Arjac!' cried Svalin. 'One of us is lost. Brother Anvakyr of our pack. A predator has killed him, an alien by the smell of it. We are naught but one pack in the whole Fang. All are needed to hunt it down.'

Arjac was much beloved by the thralls who laboured on the forge slopes. Hundreds of them worked there – I might say lived there – hammering ceramite into shape, forging new components for boltguns. Arjac went to them and told them of what had happened, and that he was needed within the fortress.

'Let us join you in the hunt!' said Thane Darskaan, a master among the forge thralls who had assisted the Iron Priests for more than forty years. 'Every one of us has forged his own weapon as a condition of our apprenticehood, and we would wield them in revenge.'

'No,' said Arjac. 'You will stay here and man the forges, and watch for this enemy. If it flees through the forge slopes, it must not have an easy escape.'

Arjac took as a weapon the hammer with which he had worked on the Axe Morkai – in his youth among the Fenrisian tribes, he had learned there was no distinction between tool and weapon. He carried also a shield which hung above the Heart Forge. It was the masterpiece of a long-dead thrall, who had created it to show the pinnacle of his skills, and it was as strong as it was ornate. No thrall could carry it. In the hands of a Space Wolf it would be heavy and unwieldy, quite unsuitable for battle. But even then

Arjac was renowned for his strength, and he hefted it as lightly as if it was made of wood and hide.

'Brother Svalin,' said Arjac when he was thus armed. 'Where lies the quarry?'

And so Pack Fornjot and Arjac Rockfist set about hunting the xenos intruder through the Fang. The thralls held their ground and let the Space Wolves stalk their enemy. The alien was swift and cunning, and certainly deadly enough to slay even a Space Marine as it had showed. But like all aliens, like all unrighteous and unnatural things, it had a weakness from which it could not hide. The stench of the xenos. All you who have faced the alien know it! Let the Ultramarines consult their volumes of lore for how to seek the alien, let the Dark Angels torment answers from all they see and let the Blood Angels write poetry and drink blood. A Space Wolf will have already cornered his prey, for Leman Russ taught us to follow our noses! I know you can scarce imagine that there are Space Marines who cannot trail the foulest xenos by its stench, but it is true that our fellows in other Chapters are blind to everything their noses tell them. That is why they cannot hunt like a Space Wolf, as Pack Fornjot and Arjac hunted their quarry through the Fang.

Arjac and Fornjot both followed the same scent trail, one that wound through the lower levels of the Fang into the cells and workshops of the thralls. The stench may have evaded the pheromone sensors of the Fang, but to the Space Wolves it was clear as the path the shining moon leaves on a calm sea. The thralls waited at every intersection, grim-faced with their guns in their hands, for in that warren they might be attacked from any direction. In the youth of the Fang, when the mountain first grew from the surface of Fenris, those tunnels had been burrowed by lava that forced its way up. Now they were trackless and twisting, an excellent ground for an enemy to flee.

'What manner of xenos do we face?' asked Fornjot as he and Arjac followed the trail, though it wound through awkward turns and often leapt through narrow tunnels from one floor to the next where a man could not climb. 'I have not smelled its like before.'

'The body of Anvakyr tells us that it is swift and strong,' said Arjac. 'But

716   BEN COUNTER

more than that. It lies in ambush like the Rime Spider, which lurks in ice caves to leap upon pack beasts and travellers. It is clever and patient, but springs to the kill when the time is right. Without such qualities it would never have taken Anvakyr as swiftly as it did. It will seek to ambush us, I do not doubt, so we must be ready for it and strike first.'

'Accursed luck!' snarled Fornjot. 'I have lost the trail. This place is like a nest of worms! It could have gone in a dozen directions from here.'

'I have lost the trail as well,' said Arjac. 'Hurry! The longer we flounder here, the more of our blood shall stain the Fang!'

Thus the two, along with the other members of Fornjot's pack, spread out through the lava warrens, seeking to pick up the scent trail again, always watching for places the unseen foe could spring at them. And a frustration came upon them, for nothing is as grave an insult to the hunter as the foe that gives them the slip.

'Wait, Brother Fornjot!' said Arjac, as he and Fornjot ran through the warrens trying to pick up the trail. 'Let us pause for just a moment, and listen.'

'I will waste no time!' retorted Fornjot, but with a simple gesture, a hand on his shoulder pad, Arjac silenced him.

Dimly could be heard the sound of screaming.

Arjac and Fornjot followed the sound now, and with every second it seemed another voice was raised in terror and pain. They heard gunfire, and now, as they got closer, the crunch of bone and wet tearing of flesh. Ahead was an intersection of tunnels and Arjac saw now that the thralls had watched every exit except that which lay directly above them, a narrow passage winding to a level above. It was impossible for a man to climb up, and so they had not watched it as they had the passageways to the front and rear. But it was from there that death had come upon them, and it had been swift indeed.

The two Space Wolves saw blood on the stone walls, a gore that clung in wet clumps. A body had been ripped almost in two, stomach and chest laid open. A head had been torn from another corpse. One thrall still lived, his lower half a ruin, his last moments spent picking with trembling hands at the innards that pulsed from him. They were Chapter thralls, most of them dead before they had fired but a shot.

'Does it kill to survive,' said Fornjot as he witnessed this carnage, 'or because it hungers?'

'Or,' said Arjac, 'because it knows nothing but killing?'

Fornjot wrinkled his nose. 'Its stench is strong,' he said. 'We have missed its escape, but it is close.'

Fornjot went armed with a lightning claw, and with a bolt pistol. Both had once been carried by Daegal Mountainclaw, his pack leader, and by the Wolf Guard Haarald Forkenbeard before him. They were fine wargear and had served the Chapter well before that day.

'Where are you?' demanded Fornjot. 'I owe you a brother's death, alien!

Though I cannot tear my rage from your flesh, yet it will be some consolation to make you suffer a fraction of the pain I feel!' A tear of rage glittered
on Fornjot's cheek. 'I will put out your eyes, if you have them! I will cook
your meat and tear it with my teeth, and spit it upon the floor!'

Fornjot now turned to Arjac, who had said nothing. 'Why do you speak
not?' demanded Fornjot. 'Do you not feel hate for the thing that killed
Brother Anvakyr?'

'I feel hate, my brother,' said Arjac. 'But I will not waste it speaking of
it to an alien, who does not understand the hate that makes us human.'

'Whatever it might be, it dies,' said Fornjot.

How shall I speak of the speed with which it struck? No striking snake or
diving sea-eagle was ever so swift. From the mouth of a tunnel overhead it
darted, its hide speckled dark like the rock around it. Arjac saw it, but could
command no response from his arm before it was upon Brother Fornjot.

In the gloom, Arjac could make out not its shape nor any suggestion
of its species, for it was so swift and camouflaged so keenly it seemed to
be the surrounding rocks taking shape and leaping upon Fornjot. He had
but an impression of size, power, speed, sharpness and savagery of purpose. It struck not like the rampaging sporebear, with its clubbing fists of
bony spurs, nor like the frost wolf which clamps home with its jaws and
shakes its prey apart. Compared to such predators of Fenris it was a surgeon, with such purity and efficiency of movement and power that Fornjot
was impaled on claw or mandible and lifted off his feet before Arjac could
take a step forwards or cast his hammer forth.

Fornjot disappeared overhead, dragged up into the lava shaft. There Arjac
could not pursue, for this alien predator, whatever it might be, moved as
swiftly along a sheer wall or ceiling as along the floor. But Arjac did not
despair, for he knew Fornjot and the voice he gave to his defiance.

'I will suck out your eyeballs!' yelled Fornjot, even surely as his flesh was
rent. 'And dance on your guts!'

Arjac followed Fornjot's voice, taking twisting turn and switchback, ever
heading upwards. Many were the threats that Fornjot made, most of them
foul and base in nature but justified by the obscenity that is an alien on
the sacred ground of the Fang.

'Stand fast! Do not pursue!' called out Arjac to the thralls he passed by,
for he knew that if a Space Wolf could be taken by the creature then a
thrall had no hope against it. No, it had to be he, Arjac, who faced it. He
hoped Fornjot's pack-brothers were close behind, but he could not pause
for them to catch up.

Fornjot's words became cries of anger and pain, and threatened to grow
distant and quiet as the predator outpaced Arjac. Arjac knew the Fang well,
but the alien had the use of the tunnels that looped up and down, beyond
the capacity of a Space Marine to traverse. Here and there gunshots rang
out as thralls took shots at the beast as it passed, but Arjac knew that none

of them would find a fatal mark. The beast had to be his, and his alone, or two battle-brothers would go unavenged.

Arjac burst through into a hall of the Wolf Priests, where the altars to the unkind winds of Fenris stood to be placated with libations and prayer. The image of Leman Russ presided over the chapel, his mighty shoulders the pillars that supported the ceiling, his eyes set with dark glares of obsidian.

Here the wolf packs prayed under the Wolf Priests' ministrations to the ancient spirits of Fenris, to our home world's ancestors and our fallen packmates. A priest of the Ecclesiarchy might see this place and think us heathens, for we hold our own rites where they would have us genuflect in rote to an image of the Allfather. But a Space Wolf does not give his faith like a tithe upon demand. He prays because he seeks to commune with the mighty spirits of his Chapter, with the savage soul of his home world! Yes, spit upon the floor at the mention of the Ecclesiarchy dogs, but save the worst of your anger for the alien.

In this chapel Arjac caught up with the alien. It crouched upon the image of Leman Russ. Go there to this day and you will see the marks of its claws, the scars of the acid it belched, disfiguring still the primarch's image! Though its colours shifted to match its surroundings, Arjac had his first true sight of the alien and saw its four long, wicked claws, as long as a man is tall, and on the lower two impaled the body of Fornjot.

Fornjot was alive. He fought to draw breath, to spit one final hateful oath at the alien, one final promise of a gory and dishonourable death for its trespasses. But the final two claws punched through his body, through his armour as if it was no stronger than skin, and with a single terrible effort of its limbs the alien ripped Fornjot in three.

The eyes set into the alien's skull, reddish, glinting spheres, many in number, focused on Arjac for a moment, as if issuing a challenge or seeking to mock the death of Brother Fornjot.

Arjac drew back his arm and hurled his hammer. The alien was quick, and the hammer missed. Look again on the image of Leman Russ in the chapel and you will see the chunk missing from his breastplate, where Arjac's hammer splintered the stone! The alien was upon the ceiling, and Arjac was without a weapon to cast before it slithered up the statue, through a fissure in the rock of the ceiling, and into the trackless strata of the Fang.

Arjac walked across the chapel, unable to meet the obsidian gaze of Leman Russ. He stood over the body of Fornjot and howled in grief and anger, and in shame that he had failed to save the life of his battle-brother.

Howl, as he did! There, see the arms of this brave pack leader, and cleanse your souls of the uncleanness of his death with the purity of his dying rage! But do not give in to your sorrow, for Fornjot did not die as prey, but as a fellow predator struggling for his revenge. He had struck one final blow, even as his body was pierced by the alien's claws. One of them lodged in his body, and as he was torn apart it snapped off and remained jammed in his ribcage.

Arjac looked upon his dead brother and saw the claw. He knelt and tore it from the body. The thralls who followed the sounds of death found him there, the alien's claw in hand, tears in his eyes and sorrow on his face, as he bowed his head over the corpse of Brother Fornjot.

The beast had fled, as the xenos is wont to do, like a scurrying animal afraid of the predator. Alas, the Fang is ancient and vast, and though it serves us well as our fortress and our warrior-monastery there are many tunnels and caverns unmapped or forgotten where a creature of base cunning could hide. The thralls sent out parties to locate it, searching for its leavings or a trail of its blood, but they could find it not.

Pack Fornjot carried their leader from the thralls' warrens, bearing his corpse on their shoulders. Wordlessly they bore him to the Chapter apothecarion, and with Arjac they stood about his corpse. There he was laid out on the slab, among the autosurgeons and the thrall orderlies that could do nothing to help him now.

'Svalin,' said Vidfinn at last. 'You should speak. Were any of us to fall, it would be Fornjot himself who would speak of the fallen's valour. Should Fornjot be lost, the duty would surely fall to Anvakyr. But both are gone, and you, Svalin, as the oldest, are best to give voice to our sorrow.'

What could Svalin say? He was not a man given to speeches or sagas. No, he was a simple warrior, who aspired to nothing more than a life of righteous war.

'Fornjot will be mourned,' said Svalin, 'for as long as we shall live. And we shall speak of him to our brothers, so he shall live on in word and memory forever, until we meet him again at Russ's side. More than words will pass on. His wargear will be distributed among the newest Blood Claws, and more than that, his gene-seed, the very flesh of the primarch, will be implanted into a new battle-brother and help turn him from a mere man into a Space Marine. There is no more glorious legacy. That is all there is to say, save for to bid our brother farewell.'

And so, in the absence of a Wolf Priest, the thrall orderlies set to removing the wargear and the gene-seed from Brother Fornjot's corpse, as they had to Anvakyr but a day before.

'To think,' said Svalin to Arjac, 'that when a Space Wolf imagines death, he sees only death in combat with the foes of mankind, in a hail of bullets or a flurry of claws, atop a mountain of the enemy's dead. And yet two of our brothers have been lost not in the fires of war but slain by deceit by a faceless foe. We should be the predators, not the prey! We are the hunters, not the quarry! How difficult it is to understand that a Space Wolf might die thus!'

'Is a man judged,' said Arjac, 'by his death alone? Does a death not in battle erase a lifetime's service? Anvakyr was not just a fine soldier, but a rare soul. I cannot imagine the way a mind must work to spin words such as he did. His death will go unsung of, but does that make his life similarly worthy of forgetting? And Fornjot will never cease to be your pack leader, though he did not die leading you in battle as any pack leader would wish. It is impossible now, when his death is so raw to you, but in time perhaps you will come to remember him in life and not in death.'

'I hope you speak true,' said Svalin. 'And a Space Wolf, any soldier, must learn to accept the deaths of his brothers in battle or succumb himself to despair. But it is easy to speak of such things and not so simple to believe them, when the body still lies before us torn and bloody.'

Then one of the orderlies spoke up. He was, like all of us, a man who goes about the Fang ignored by the Space Wolves, and spoke up now in a voice so quiet even Svalin's enhanced hearing barely registered him.

'Brother Svalin,' said the thrall, whose name none recorded. 'We are troubled. Please, come and see.'

The thralls led Svalin to the table on which Fornjot's corpse lay. It was a pitiful sight, a state to which no warrior should ever be reduced. He was torn into three, the claws of the alien having separated his shoulders and head from his torso, and cut his body in two at the height of the navel. His armour had yet to be removed, and the ceramite had been sheared clean through. The thrall indicated the incision the thralls had already opened up in Fornjot's throat.

'Where is my brother's gene-seed?' demanded Svalin, for he was looking into the part of the throat that served as the seat of that organ.

'It is gone,' said the thrall. 'It was not there when we searched for it. But there is a wound inside the mouth where something has punched down through the tongue, and something has extracted the gene-seed through there.'

'Did the xenos do this?' asked Svalin, his face darkening as he turned to Arjac.

'I cannot tell,' said Arjac. 'His death was swift and the alien camouflaged by some xenos trick. Yet it had mouthparts like an insect, I think, and certainly could have done this.'

Svalin drove a fist into the slab on which his dead brother lay, and the stone cracked. 'Is it not enough to slay us where we should reign as lords?' he cried. 'Is it not enough? Must our dead be stripped of their legacy, too?

Must not only one brother die, but the ascension of another be denied? I thought this alien was a beast, an animal that hunted by instinct and not malice, and yet it does to our dead that which is most hateful to us!'

Svalin tore an autosurgeon unit off the ceiling, that device of many limbs and sharp blades which can knit together sundered flesh and organ. He hurled it across the apothecarion, and thralls scattered from him. He knelt on the floor and tore at his hair, and his fingers drew blood. He howled so loud and long that the whole Fang shook with it, and flocks of mountain raptors took flight in alarm.

Vidfinn stood forth. 'This rage we all feel,' he said, and true, even this unshockable warrior had flinty tears in his eyes. 'And it shall find its channel in the pursuit of the hunt. Arm yourself, Brother Svalin, take up bolter and chainsword once more. No corner of the Fang will be left unscoured. The hunt will continue and the prey will be taken.' His voice was glacial and his fist clenched. He did not cry out or rage as Svalin had done. For Vidfinn, hatred was something silent and steely, and colder than the ocean depths.

Pack Fornjot set about their grim and bloody work, but Arjac Rockfist did not join them, not right away. In their sorrow and anger they did not admonish him for not running alongside them in the hunt. They forgot him, as men are wont to do, for in spite of his size and the fabled strength of his arm Arjac speaks little and shouts less, and in the fires of their wrath the other Space Wolves ignored him. Instead Arjac went to the trophy hall of the Fang.

How many tales have I told that made some reference to that hall? Every great exploit of our Chapter's heroes put a new exhibit in the trophy hall. How often do I speak of some foe vanquished, and add that you still can see the claw of this ork warlord or the skull of that eldar pirate, hung among the banners and captive arms? A teller of tales such as I must know the trophy hall as well as he knows his own stories, for surely some Blood Claw will find him in passing and say to him, 'This trophy I saw among the spoils of our conquests, what story lies behind it?'

Indeed, to me the place is not merely a room of captured objects, but a history book telling the tale of our Chapter. The tooth of the Lion, Primarch of the Dark Angels, knocked out of his smirking head by Russ's own fist? It is in the trophy hall, preserved in the heart of a fat ruby set into a sceptre. The war crown of Salvardis the Silver, cohort of Ahriman of the Thousand Sons, beaten by Wolf Lord Gorri Sunderblade into divulging the darkest secrets of that traitor legion? It is mounted on the wall, surrounded by a blessed cage that keeps its baleful energies locked away. Truly there is not a single shell casing or banner scrap that does not have its own saga behind it. Find me in an accommodating mood, as I wander through that hall, and I could bend your ear for hours with the tales that come to me unbidden.

Arjac, then, went to this hall, and to a corner of it where there stood a skeleton. On one side of this skeleton was hung the wargear of a Venenum Assassin, who infiltrated the Fang to assassinate Wolf Lord Gunnar White-of-Claw and was instead uncovered and killed. On the other side was the skull of the Beast of Karchadan, a xenos of immense cunning whose vast brain was once held within that misshapen globe of bone. But the skeleton that Arjac sought out had none of the history of these relics.

The skeleton stood rather taller than a Space Wolf, and spoke of an alien creature of great strength with its torso armoured in bone and its limbs strong of sinew. It resembled something like a huge lizard that walked on two legs, something like an insect with its exoskeleton, but with a great

723

deal about it that could only be alien. It had great slashing claws, and Arjac examined these very closely.

He had with him the claw that he had taken from the body of Pack Leader Fornjot, the claw broken off from the predator that had invaded the Fang. Even now Pack Fornjot was seeking to track the beast down, but Arjac was pursuing his own hunt here.

The claw was very similar to that of the skeleton in the trophy room. The tip of the skeleton's claw was broken off, and in cross-section Arjac saw that they were identical. Arjac thought long on this, for it presented a conundrum.

The skeleton in the trophy room was of a tyranid. Who among you has faced the tyranids, the minions of the accursed Kraken whose hive fleets darken the skies of the Imperium? Yes, your faces crease with the anger of those memories, you stare down into your tankards and recall the seething on the horizon as the tyranids swarmed forth. Is there any xenos so hateful?

And yet, this truth was a strange one. For if the intruder in the Fang was a tyranid, it was far from its fellows. Fenris lies far from the invasion routes of the tyranid hive fleets, and though our world has been embattled in its history it was never preyed upon by the Kraken. How could a tyranid come to be on Fenris? No hive fleet could approach without the Chapter having good warning of it, for in Fenris's solar system hang monitoring stations and planetary defence platforms that ensure we will never be blind to an approaching foe. And moreover the tyranid is a creature that attacks in hordes, great swarms without number to overwhelm the enemy with their untold billions. A single tyranid is a thing unheard-of on the battlefield. Like the vermin they are, they are never found alone.

Brother Vidfinn meanwhile descended into the pits of the Fang, those nameless levels below the generatoria and the ancient tribal tombs, where the refuse of the fortress gathered in the dark. Shoulder-deep in ancient filth, he sought the beast. Brother Svalin clambered the upper slopes, seeking the alien even as raptors circled him as if he were prey. Dvarnn and Brokkyr went among the thralls, leading them in scouring the living places and dusty old halls of the fortress, the titanic armaplas gates and the mighty battlements that no foe had ever breached. But they had been breached now, by a lone killer, and it was holy work to expunge the intruder.

Arjac still did not join them. How, you might say, could he refrain from the hunt when the quarry was still abroad, when there were sons of Fenris to be avenged? Because, my brothers, there is more than one way to hunt.

Indeed, a Blood Claw only knows one, for what is there to him save charging headlong into the enemy and rending it with tooth and claw? And it is good that he knows only this, for it makes him strong in the thick of battle. But he who lives to serve as a Long Fang, or who comes to lead his battle-brothers in the Wolf Guard, knows that the hunt is not always pursued on foot. Sometimes, the quarry must be hunted through the forests of the mind and across the endless glacier of reason.

Yes, scoff if you will. Why would you listen to a thrall, a man maimed in his Blooding and fit only to mop the floor after your feasting? But remember. Leman Russ stood in this very hall, before this very hearth, and decreed that the man who sat before it and span the sagas of Fenris would be heeded whoever he might be. Thus I must be shown the same respect you would show Bjorn the Fell-Handed if he awoke and lumbered in here, with all the thunder and majesty of his ancient Dreadnought form. So jeer and heckle all you will, I know you still must listen.

Arjac went seeking not the beast, for if it could be found Pack Fornjot would surely find it. Instead he went seeking knowledge. Now, there is plenty of knowledge in the Fang. Since the days of the Great Crusade the Iron Priests and Rune-crafters have gathered information on the foes of the Allfather, and written sagas of our history. But we are not scholars! We are not librarians! In the Fang lie countless chambers and vaults where such knowledge was kept, from data-slates to ancient tomes and tablets of granite inscribed with the legends of Fenris. It is no easy task to seek out a particular answer in the Fang, and the Rune Priests who knew best where to find them were away on the Calunian Crusade. But Arjac sought it anyway.

For a day and a night Arjac laboured in the libraries of the Fang. Though it was no onerous task of the body, as working at the anvil might be, nevertheless it was taxing on the mind. Arjac wrought his wargear not just with his hands, though, but with keenness of perception and quickness of wits. Finally, by the light of a guttering candle, he read the name Kryptmann on the spine of a cracked and ancient book bound with xenos scale and blessed iron bands.

As the dawn of Fenris broke, her pale light flowing across the glaciers and breaking against the slopes of the Fang, the hunters gathered here, in this hall. There was no feast laid out for them that day. They were solemn, and still in mourning. Arjac joined them there, and with him he had brought two items. One was covered in a sheet stained with oil and ash, laid out on one of the feasting tables. The other was the book of Kryptmann.

'Alas,' said Brother Svalin, who with Fornjot's death had acted as pack leader in the hunt. 'The quarry eludes us! Though swift we were, and rageful, there was no foe that would stand before us to be fought. The alien is a creature devoid of honour, even of hatred, and so is frustrating to hunt. Even the savage beast of glacier and valley will turn on you when it is wounded, or cornered. This accursed thing lies silent, waiting for another victim, and will not be brought to battle.'

'We have not yet finished the hunt,' retorted Brother Dvarnn. 'We will pursue it ever more fiercely! Let us be bloody and righteous! Tear the Fang apart, leave it no hiding place!'

'My brother speaks my own mind,' said Brokkyr, for the two were always in agreement. 'We are but a few, and so we must make up our number with the fires of our fury!'

'No,' said Arjac, and the other Space Wolves were silent. With just that word he caused all to turn to him, as if an elder of the pack, grey-pelted and massive, had walked in to take over the hunt. 'This is the book of Kryptmann,' he said, holding up the tome. 'He was an inquisitor who made study of the Kraken when the hive fleets first plagued the Imperium.'

'The Kraken?' asked Vidfinn. 'Speak on, Brother Arjac. No tyranid has ever been seen within light centuries of Fenris.'

'And yet I believe it is a tyranid we face,' said Arjac. 'As unlikely as it might be, we can all agree the enemy is no native of Fenris, and in the form and composition of its body it resembles a tyranid more than anything. But the tyranid is not so simple a foe as we imagine. It is not a simple scavenger, aimed at our galaxy by some cosmic accident. No, its presence here is a deliberate act of predation, planned over thousands of years drifting in interstellar space.

'This was Kryptmann's theory, as I have read. On the world of Tiamet, explorators encountered aliens resembling the tyranids four millennia before Hive Fleet Behemoth. On Ouroboris, but centuries later, our own Chapter attended to a xenos invasion where they recorded the form of the tyranid, though they did not give it that name.

'Kryptmann believed the tyranids had sent organisms ahead of the hive fleets to scout our galaxy, and call through the hive mind that we were fit for invasion, and that some such organisms had been present in our galaxy for thousands of years before the hive fleets. Many examples he cited, from Ymgarl to Balthusas. What if Fenris is another on that list? A world visited by a tyranid scout, one that now hunts us?'

Now, this was quite something to be said. It flew in the face of what the Space Marines taught of fighting the Kraken, for Kryptmann was not a man well respected by the Chapter Masters as is often the case with agents of the Inquisition. But the Space Wolves are not so closed-minded as our brother Chapters, and Pack Fornjot did not shout down Arjac's assertions out of hand as might have happened in another fortress-monastery.

'If what you say is true,' said Brother Svalin, 'and I do not say it is – if what you say is true, how does it help us kill it?'

'That is the second question I asked myself,' said Arjac. 'The first question was, why did it come to the Fang?'

Pack Fornjot thought on this, and none of them could be certain of an answer. Nevertheless, Brother Brokkyr spoke up.

'The tyranid craves biomass,' he said. 'The material of muscle and bone, and of all living things on a world. There are hundreds of thralls in the Fang for it to consume.'

'Indeed, brother, it is this biomass they want,' said Arjac. 'This much I learned from Kryptmann's book, too. But the alien we hunt is not one of the great harvester-beasts vomited from the bellies of the hive fleets to strip a world of its life. No, it more closely resembles the creature named the lictor by the inquisitors of the Ordo Xenos, a scout and assassin that takes no part in the digestion of a planet. And there are places on Fenris far more tempting for a hungering tyranid. Why not the tundra where thunder million-head herds of storm elk? Or the places where the fathom whales come to spawn, thousands of them teeming upon the polar shores? There are no Space Wolves there to defend its quarry. And yet, here it is. It wants something that can only be found in the Fang, something craved by the tyranid hive fleets of which this creature is the herald.'

'Then what?' asked Brokkyr and Dvarnn as one.

'The blood of the Allfather,' said Arjac. 'The flesh of the primarch. The gene-seed.'

I see hands touch your throats. Yes, the gene-seed, that organ grown from the genetic template of Leman Russ who was, in turn, made after the Emperor. Each gene-seed organ is a relic of the primarch and of the Allfather, as sacred as the bones of the most famous of saints. And it is a weapon as potent as any you might carry into battle, for it is what makes your transformation into a Space Wolf possible. That feeling you have now, that sense of the blasphemous when the flesh of Russ is threatened by the predations of the alien, that is perhaps the closest a Space Marine can come to feeling fear.

Though the institutions of the Imperium have long sought to test and probe it, our store of gene-seed has remained sacrosanct, for the use only of our Wolf Priests. The Inquisition has demanded entry to the Fang's gene-seed vault and the Ecclesiarchy declaimed our jealousy of it, but none have laid hand or eye on it except the Space Wolves.

Those of you who have seen the vault know of its antiquity and majesty, as sacred as the most honoured temple, a monument to the primarch and the Emperor. Those who have not, know that it is reached through the apothecarion, down a processional lined with the armour of great Space Wolves who asked that their wargear guard over our most precious resource.

The vault itself is within the heart of the mountain, carved into the metal that runs down the spine of the Fang, an alloy of fantastic strength forged in some volcanic event an aeon ago. And within, past the great circular stone which only a Dreadnought can roll aside, is the vault kept chill and clung with frozen mist where the gene-seed waits in a thousand glass vessels for the next Space Wolf to be selected from the sons of Fenris.

'Think,' said Arjac, 'of what we know. An organism such as this hunter is a vanguard and a herald. It seeks out worlds and, when it has found one suitable, it sends out a mental signal to the hive mind of its parent fleet, to summon the tyranids in their numberless hordes. Perhaps on a more

populous world, or one covered in living jungle or otherwise teeming with
life, it would seek out the greatest concentration of life. But on Fenris the
tyranid looks not for quantity of biomass, but quality. The purest genetic
matter with the greatest potential, that can be used even in the smallest amounts to create ever greater warriors for the hive fleets. On Fenris,
there is only one thing the tyranid could seek. It wants the gene-seed of
the Space Marines. That is why it tore the gene-seed out of Brother Fornjot. That is why it came to the Fang in the first place.'

Brother Svalin it was who stood forwards now. 'You did not answer my
brother here,' he said. 'How do we kill it?'

'We lure it to the gene-seed vault,' said Arjac. 'There we know it will
be. There we can fight it as one, on our terms, in ambush. There we can
avenge our brothers.'

'Lead it to the vault?' said Vidfinn, and though it was a rare thing to be
seen his face was flushed with anger. 'Bring it to such sacred ground and
give it the very thing it craves? Can we risk the Chapter's very existence,
the creation of future Space Wolves, with such recklessness?'

Arjac did not anger as Vidfinn did, but remained calm. 'Can we allow it to
roam at will, to kill us one by one, until there is none to oppose it? And then
let it find the vault on its own? How long will that take? And can the thralls
stop it from getting in? Only we can kill it, my brothers, and only together.
This is the only way.'

Would that the Great Wolf was there, and his Wolf Lords and all the
mighty war-packs of the Chapter! But Arjac and Pack Fornjot were alone
save the thralls who, valiant though they were, could not hope to stand
against a hunter that had made the Space Marines its prey. And Vidfinn
cast his eyes down, like the packmate who has challenged the alpha and
found the alpha not willing to back down. There were no words spoken
and no triumph on Arjac's face. The pack knew he was correct. There was
only one way – lure the hunter to the vault, and there kill it, before it killed
all of them.

'And we do not fight with empty hands, my brothers,' said Arjac. The second object that Arjac had brought with him lay under the sheet. Now he
took the sheet away to reveal there the Axe Morkai.

The Axe Morkai had been remade, and yet was not the lesser for it. The
weapon that Arjac Rockfist now carried was the equal of any seen in the
Fang within the memory of the living. The Axe Morkai had a two-headed
blade, each a brutal hard-edged shape that spoke of nothing but death. Into
its blade was etched the wolf rampant that was the Great Wolf's heraldry,
and a square-cut emerald the size of a fist was set between the blade's
halves. It was too large for any to wield without the enhanced strength of
Terminator armour – save for Arjac himself.

Arjac led Pack Fornjot to the head of the processional leading to the
gene-seed vault, where glowered the images of past Great Wolves as if

judging all who walked by. 'It is good that you are armed for once,' said Svalin. 'I had envisioned you engaging this beast with fists and teeth.'

'And so I shall, if needs be,' replied Arjac, though Svalin's words had been meant in grim jest.

From the apothecarion came Dvarnn and Brokkyr, each one bearing a lightning claw that together formed the matched pair. 'The path is clear to the vault,' Brokkyr said. 'The blast doors are open from here to the Great Hall. All that remains is to open the vault itself.'

Arjac walked to the door of the vault. It was not a door in truth, but a circular slab of rock that lay in front of the vault entrance. The names of long-dead Wolf Priests were carved into the slab, along with their hundreds of heraldries.

Arjac leaned the Axe Morkai against the wall, at the feet of one of the suits of armour. He placed his shoulder against the edge of the slab and pushed.

None but a Dreadnought had ever shifted that door. But against the might of Arjac, it shifted. The brothers of Pack Fornjot ran to help him, when they saw the stone first move. Together, Arjac's strength the greater part of their effort, they rolled the stone aside and opened the door to the gene-seed vault.

Now arrived Vidfinn, who had been organising the thralls to guard the approaches down which the beast might flee, and so Pack Fornjot's survivors were assembled. Vidfinn normally carried the meltagun, but that is a weapon most fell against the tanks and armoured vehicles of the enemy. This beast was no such thing, and so from the armouries he had brought a boltgun with many examples of the artificer's art, rapid firing and loaded with shells each containing a reservoir of vicious acid. Such Hellfire shells are praised by those who fight primarily against the alien, the spawn of the Kraken in particular.

'Brothers of Fornjot,' said Svalin, 'pray now to the souls of our Chapter's fallen. Pray now to the ancestor-souls of Fenris, to Leman Russ and the warriors of the Great Crusade, to the Crone Fenris herself, the Allfather who gave us purpose, to every battle-brother who has passed from our sight and to Brother Fornjot. We have no time to spill blood in sacrifice or to feast and toast their honour. Instead, let your prayers suffice. Let those honoured dead speak to us of their ways of war, whisper to us the weaknesses of the enemy and the strengths of our own arm. Let them lend us strength. Let them witness our vengeance, and salute our victory when we join them at the end of time!'

Each brother made his own prayer, letting his thoughts turn for a moment inwards to the memories of Fenris's ancestors. But the majority of his mind was set like a hunter's trap, assembled as they were in the processional where surely their enemy would approach.

'There,' hissed Brother Vidfinn. 'I see it. I smell it. It approaches.'

The alien was disguised, and had evolved the shifting colours of its skin to match the stone of the Fang perfectly. But a Space Wolf could smell it out, and the faintest hint of movement was all the confirmation a Space Wolf needed. The xenos was scurrying along the ribbed and vaulted ceiling, slinking with speed and darting grace over every contour.

Vidfinn dropped to one knee and opened fire. Bark, bolter! Cry out like the scream of the raptor, like the shriek of the snow-blind geist and the wendigore that hunt upon the glacier! Vidfinn's aim was true and the alien was struck, the wet thump of each shot accompanied by a spray of the alien's iridescent blood.

But it did not die. No, it drove on, even as chunks of chitin and flesh fell from it. Dvarnn leapt forwards, for the alien's speed was such that Vidfinn could not fire another volley before the alien was upon them. Dvarnn's claw, upon his left hand, sliced up to meet the alien as it dropped towards him.

In its shape it reflected the tyranid creatures that you may have fought against, but with a form all of its own. The forms of the lizard and the insect, such as is common to the many varieties of tyranid, were present, but also something of the ocean predator, of the eyeless things that on occasion will rise up from the depths to prey on the longships of our peoples. The Space Wolves had a glimpse of a long and fleshy abdomen, that undulated like the fronds of a sea creature or the swaying of an ice cobra to power it forwards. But its foreparts were all claws and blades, and they struck as fast as Dvarnn's claw.

And with less time than it took to think, less time that it took for the instincts of the predator to take hold of a Space Wolf's mind, Brother Dvarnn was dead. Twin blades unfolded from the side of the alien's head – not the talons it bore on its forelimbs, which Dvarnn could parry and bat aside, but another pair of razored mandibles that closed around Dvarnn's neck. Dvarnn's head flew from his shoulders, and before it had even hit the floor the alien had scrabbled away and rushed up one wall, smearing its foul ichor across the armour of a long-dead hero.

Imagine the cry that Brokkyr let out! They were brothers, not just in battle but by blood. Svalin grabbed Brokkyr by the edge of the shoulder guard, for he knew that Brokkyr would give his life just to die in the same moment as his oldest friend. Brokkyr fought him off and rushed the alien, the power field around his own claw flashing with the weapon's caged power.

Brokkyr survived the first exchanges, the fury of his charge knocking the alien off the wall. It squirmed and thrashed on the floor, spraying gore and lashing blades from every direction. Arjac waded in, swinging the Axe Morkai in a great arc. Bladed limbs were severed. Brokkyr dived onto the alien and plunged his blade into the centre of the alien's mass. The power field discharged with a flash like the lightning that spans the mountain peaks.

But the speed! The unnatural speed, as if the xenos did not exist wholly in our world, but partly in the realm of the unhallowed dead where mortal hands could not reach it! The ever-shifting camouflage of its scaly hide kept it shifting out of sight, a trick of the light that fooled even a Space Marine's keen eye. Brokkyr's claw impacted against the stony floor and blasted a crater there at his feet, as the alien slithered faster than the wink of an eye out of his reach.

And thus Brother Brokkyr died. His wish was granted, for he would not live on without his battle-brother Dvarnn. A tentacle lashed around his neck and wrenched his head back. From the alien's jaws emerged a segmented tongue tipped with a pincer, striking like a snake at Brokkyr's throat. Brokkyr's claw was up in front of his face, fending off the jaws, but one of the alien's claw-blades lanced through his torso. The edge, as hard as a diamond and honed as a sabrewolf's fang, cut through the ceramite of Brokkyr's armour and impaled him straight through. Another blade lashed up and sliced off his other arm at the elbow. Brokkyr cried out, not with pain but with anger.

And on fought Arjac! The Axe Morkai fell down like a pendulum, its head arcing down to cut off the elongated mouthpiece threatening to tear the throat from Brokkyr. The alien leapt onto the wall and brought Brokkyr with it. It gnashed on Brokkyr's body, cracking open the ceramite that guarded his torso. The wet meat inside was exposed and lanced through by another blade, opening up Brokkyr like a fresh kill to be gutted.

Cover again your fangs, and sheath your claws. This was the death of Brokkyr, and none of it may I omit.

Vidfinn's bolter hit home and xenos blood spurted. Arjac grabbed a limb and wrenched it free, and it came away in a fountain of such gore. But even the flight of a bullet seemed too long a span to catch out the alien and it ran along the wall, evading Arjac's axe and flying for the gene-seed vault.

Svalin stood in its way. Svalin, that most blooded of Pack Fornjot, who stood as steadfast as a mountain with chainsword raised! He struck out, and the beast parried him. And then it was gone, trailing tentacles, throwing Svalin into the air. By the time he landed, the alien was at the vault's threshold.

Arjac gave chase. For all his size, his strength gave him speed, and he was on the alien's heels. As it raised its foul head, drooling mandibles parted to gobble down the first of the vault's gene-seed, Arjac reached it and plunged a hand into the writhing flesh of its spine. He hefted it in the air, all its weight, and slammed it down!

Thus, as I cast down my cup, so did the alien predator hit the stony floor! Bones broke! Carapace cracked and foul blood flowed! And to hear the beast scream, you would have thought that all the damned of Fenris's dead had returned from the blizzard-bound north of their banishment!

The beast reared up. Arjac was ready. The Axe Morkai now was held in both his hands, and he drew it back as does a woodsman about to fell a mighty tree.

The beast roared, and became in colouration the same as its surroundings, blending into the freezing mist and grey stone. It was too fast for a normal man to follow, but to Arjac's eye surely it happened so slowly he had time for a thousand thoughts to form.

From a dozen foul orifices along its abdomen, the alien sprayed a fog of mind-befuddling pheromones. Gasping with the effort of pursuit, Arjac gulped down a lungful of the alien poison. The room shivered and shuddered, and in that moment all distance and speed became impossible to judge.

Arjac struck, and struck well. But the blade of the Axe Morkai was aimed at the place the alien had been a half-second before, and where now it was not. Reactions slowed, Arjac could not drive his blow home and the blade shrieked past the alien's body.

With no body to impact, the axe swung wild. Its blade impacted against the stone which Arjac had rolled aside from the entrance to the vault. And, driven by the great strength of Arjac Rockfist, the axe blade shattered.

What a sound! Like the crack of a lightning bolt. The stone split, sundered as if by the hand of a giant. Splinters of the shattered axe rained down.

Arjac let out a great roar of anger and grief. The weapon lost, the beast alive, his dead battle-brothers unavenged.

Shards of the axe were embedded in the beast. Weakened and knowing it faced a great warrior, it took flight, scurrying along the ceiling of the processional, chased by Vidfinn's gunfire. Arjac ran after it, armed now with nothing but his hands and his teeth, as if to wrestle the beast into submission. But it outpaced him and disappeared through the apothecarion, using some vent or narrow passageway to make its escape.

Arjac looked for a moment on the face of Brother Fornjot who lay there on the slab in the apothecarion, still with the empty wound in his throat where the beast had taken his gene-seed. With hot tears in his eyes he returned to the vault entrance, where Brokkyr and Dvarnn also lay dead.

What can I speak of the grief of Arjac Rockfist and the two survivors of Pack Fornjot? You have all lost battle-brothers. You have all seen those who to you were dear, shot or cut down on the battlefield. Think now to the Space Wolf you most admired, whose strength gave you strength, and who was lost. Think how you howled long into the night! Think of the mead you have spilled upon the floor of this hall in their memory. We all deal with such sorrow in our own way. Some will tear at their hair and inflict scars upon themselves in memory of the wounds that felled their brother. Some will pen sagas of their bravery. Some remain quiet, and do not speak of their grief. Such is the domain of each man over himself, a place where none can intrude. This was the grief that Arjac and his battle-brothers felt.

Arjac, Svalin and Vidfinn took the gene-seed from Brokkyr and Dvarnn that very hour. At least, the alien had not had time to take the organ from them. Then they took their four fallen brothers to the basalt vaults, far in the igneous depths of the Fang beneath the lava vents and rockworm warrens. In that time Space Wolves who lost their lives on Fenris, and those aspirants lost in the Blooding, were so interred, and there you may see them now, their bones buried beneath cairns of black volcanic glass and their armaments lain on top. There you might also see the offerings of wolf's tooth necklaces and prayers to their ancestor-souls, for whenever I tell this story there are some who go to that deep, dark place to pay them homage. At the end of time, they will be there to thank you.

As they finished this sorrowful work, there came to them a lowly thrall much like myself.

'My lords,' he said, 'I have news. The Great Company of Hengis Blackhand returns! His fleet has just passed through the outer reaches of our system, as marked by the monitoring station that watches over deep space. He sends tidings of victory over pirates that sought to waylay them, but also of anger that a warp storm has prevented a part of the Chapter's fleet from joining the crusade. Thus he returns to Fenris.'

'My thanks, thrall,' said Arjac, dismissing him.

'You speak thanks, but I think you do not feel it,' said Svalin. 'For Hengis it was who bade you forge the Axe Morkai, which lies shattered. His anger will be great to know it has been lost.'

'What was lost,' said Arjac, 'has been lost. Without the shards of the blade that are embedded in the beast, the axe cannot be remade. Yes, I am shamed that I will not present the Axe Morkai to the Great Wolf. But this is nothing compared to the shame that brothers were lost where I might have protected them.'

'I saw the beast,' said Svalin, 'and mighty it was. None of us could have bested it, not all of us together.'

'I am mighty,' replied Arjac most grimly. 'Do they not say so? I bore the weapon once carried by our Great Wolf. It was I who devised the plan to kill the beast. And yet I could not finish it.'

'You cannot carry on your shoulders every ill that befalls the Space Wolves,' said Svalin.

'They fall on the shoulders of us all,' said Arjac, 'and I am among us. It is not by choice I feel their weight. And now the Axe Morkai is lost, and there will be nothing that greets our returning battle-brothers but sorrow.'

And so Hengis Blackhand returned to the Fang. Hengis rode the *Savage Steed*, the gunship he had himself fitted out as he rose through the ranks of the Iron Priests. The *Steed* descended through the clouds that gathered about the peak of the Fang, and landed on the landing pad among the aerie of the raptors where the air was thin and a man's breath was but icy vapours. There are among us thralls whose duties are the ritual greeting of the returning warrior, and though they were at their post, when Lord Hengis Blackhand descended from the belly of the *Savage Steed* he was greeted by but two Space Wolves, brothers Svalin and Vidfinn of Pack Fornjot.

Imagine now the slight that Hengis felt. For one, he had left Fenris seeking battle, but had been foiled in his hopes by the vagaries of the warp. Already his temper was short, and while he was a man of heartiness and joy when all was right the foulness of his temper could more than equal his rough good humour. Indeed, he spat on the ground as he disembarked, and only then did he see the paucity of the welcome that awaited him.

'You!' he barked at Brother Svalin, the more senior of rank. 'Where is Brother Fornjot? And where is Arjac Rockfist, with the Axe Morkai for my inspection? The Great Wolf's Company, and the rest of my men, are close behind me, and I would have the weapon pass before my exacting eye before Lord Grimnar sees it.'

'Brother Fornjot lies dead and cold,' said Svalin. 'And the rest of our pack also. We laid them beneath the lava vaults. The Axe Morkai is shattered. Dread news we must bring you, Lord Hengis. The Fang is no more inviolate against our enemies and the honour of the Chapter has been made filthy by the predations of the alien.'

Lord Hengis, when he heard this, strode forward and struck Brother Svalin a mighty blow. And well he might! For the Fang was sacred ground, the impenetrable heart of Mother Fenris where, for all the violence and cruelty of our world, no evil could be permitted to enter. The Axe Morkai was a relic beyond value, and the loss of four battle-brothers while within the walls of the Fang was an insult as much as it was a tragedy. Svalin was thrown to the ground of the aerie, and the raptors, who had not stirred from their roosts even at the roar of the gunship's engines, took flight in alarm at the bellow of Lord Hengis's anger! The thralls quailed, and we thralls are not cowards. Brother Vidfinn, though he had never shown aught but scorn for the enemy in battle, could not meet the High Iron Priest's eye.

'For all this I will demand answers of you,' spat Lord Hengis, 'and afterwards so will the Great Wolf. But for now I ask you again. Where is Arjac Rockfist?'

And Brother Svalin could not answer. Nor could Vidfinn or the thralls gathered there, for they did not know.

Arjac was a man who rarely spoke when it was not needed, and those of you who know him will say that indeed he is the same to this day. He had spoken nothing since the laying to rest of Fornjot and his packmates, and so Svalin had assumed that Arjac would join him to acknowledge the arrival of Hengis. But Arjac had not done so, for to him there were more pressing matters than this issue of protocol. He had rolled the stone back to seal the gene-seed vault and so the Chapter's genetic future was not imperilled by the tyranid predator, and indeed the beast had been chased into the Fang's depths, so he had made right the threat to the gene-seed that had been necessary to bring the beast to battle. Yet, he did not think the matter settled. He had, instead, set off on his own to hunt the alien.

Arjac did this alone, and who am I to say why? No one, it is true, but I will try none the less. Perhaps he felt such responsibility for the death of his brothers and of the Axe Morkai that he went about a kind of penance, to hunt the prey that a whole pack could not bring down. Perhaps he believed that, like many a stealthy predator, he could only take his quarry alone. In any case, Arjac descended to the lower levels of the Fang, beneath the halls walked by you Space Wolves but above the ancient subterranean layers where the dead and their relics lie. He went to those places you might never have seen, where many thralls live and work, and where are stored the mundane supplies that keep the Fang functioning as fortress and a city in miniature.

He had seen the many transformations of body the beast had achieved in its battle with Arjac and his fellow Space Wolves, and it had caused him to think. I know this because all was reported shortly after to the Great Wolf, but that happens later in my tale and I am running ahead of myself.

Arjac thought that to achieve the strange mutations and remakings of its form, the alien needed raw materials, in the form of the biomass the alien tyranids crave so much. When they descend on a world they strip it of all the biomass there is, the material that makes up the plants and animals found thereon. Thus is the tyranid a parasite, for it must spend biomass to win more, and thus is locked in an endless cycle of predation like the locust.

The predator in the Fang had found biomass for the battle by taking the bodies of thralls it had killed, but it had expended much and so Arjac knew it would go hunting for more. Its animal cunning suggested it would realise the upper levels of the Fang would have lean pickings for it, and so he sought it among the places where only thralls might be found.

Now, there are thralls among us who have never seen a Space Wolf save the Wolf Priest who sent them on their Blooding. Wounded or exhausted by their trial, they lose consciousness and wake in those parts of the Fang where Space Wolves do not go, their duty to the Chapter now not as a warrior but working in the generatoria or the workshops, trading with the people of Fenris or seeing to the many needs of a Chapter that you, of course, care nothing about. And so many were the excited whispers that met Arjac's ears as he wandered the dormitories and chapels, the assembly halls, the kitchens and the armament shops, stalking for any sign of the predator.

There is in the Fang an apothecarion where the sick and wounded thralls are cared for. Quite different are its needs than the apothecarion that you might visit, for our physiologies are of mere men and not of a superhuman Space Marine. No need is there in the thralls' hospital for the cracking open of a breastplate of bone, or for a surgeon to operate on two hearts at once. Had they succeeded in their Blooding the healers who plied their art there might have become Wolf Priests one day, but as it was they spent their lives seeing to the injuries and sicknesses of the other thralls, for the Fang is not as safe a place for us as it is for you and oft does one of us need the healer's art.

There was at that time a single doctor in this apothecarion, named Thelrid of the Ice Bear people. Some of you hail from that same people, who hunt through the chill caverns of the Frozen Sky glacier. This Thelrid was tending to a thrall whose arm had been crushed in the gears of a generator, and when Arjac entered the hospital this Thelrid held up a hand to silence the newcomer while he finished setting the thrall's broken bones.

It was only when his work was done that Thelrid saw he had silenced a Space Marine, and he all but fell to his knees. 'My apologies, Lord Space Wolf,' he said, 'I was engrossed in healing this man.'

'Think not of it,' said Arjac Rockfist. 'We all have our duties. I, like you, am here to see my duty done.'

'Then speak of what you would have of me.'

'I hunt a predator,' said Arjac. 'A killer, and it is hungry. Tell me, for you would know better than any in the Fang, have there been found this last day any dead, violently slain, for which a cause has not been found?'

Thelrid's face turned grim and he nodded, and walked to the back of the thrall's hospital where lay the beds on which the long-term sick and injured lay. Most slept. Behind a curtain lay more beds, separated from the rest, and to these Thelrid walked. Thelrid was an elderly man and walked with a limp, but still the old red and black tattoos and the tangled braids in his beard spoke of his youth among the hunters of the Ice Bear people.

'Here,' he said, drawing back the sheet from one bed. 'He was found but eight hours ago. We have yet to give a name to him. A tally must be taken of all the thralls, and the only name left unclaimed will surely be this man. As you can see, it is the only way we will know who he was.'

Thelrid spoke truth, for the man's face was gravely ruined. The lower half was torn open, the wound running from the jaw to the upper chest.

'I had believed,' said Thelrid, 'that this man had befallen some accident among the machinery of the generators, for he was found wedged in a vent

741

that draws hot air from the turbine hall. But your being here, Lord Space Wolf, tells me that it is not by accident that he died.'

'I believe not,' said Arjac. 'His throat has been torn open.'

'Either at the moment of his death,' said Thelrid, 'or in the moments immediately thereafter. A wolf might go for the throat, but I have seen many bodies of those killed by wolves on their Blooding and these are not the marks of a wolf's fang. No, the killing blow was dealt by an instrument far longer and keener. I had thought it the violence of another man that did this, for while murder among thralls is rare it has not been unknown in our history. But is this the mark of the predator you seek?'

'These other wounds, this gash in the torso as if from the sweep of a great curved blade, and the crushing of this arm as if in the coils of a snake. These are the marks it leaves. Yes, healer of thralls, the predator has been here, and I think it is here still. I pray you, if any more are found like this, send word to me, and let your messenger use the name of Arjac Rockfist if he is challenged. I would know where the predator hunts, and if it hunts still.'

'I shall, Lord Arjac,' said Thelrid.

So much for Thelrid. He does not appear further in my tale. He was a fine man, though. I knew him before he died at the end of a long life in service to the Chapter. But who among you has heard his name, or seen the thrall's hospital where he gave so many years to you? Think on him when next you take to battle, for without him, and men like him, your Chapter would be stuck wandering the snows of Fenris with neither fortress nor fleet.

Arjac Rockfist returned to the halls of the Fang many hours later, for he had found nothing of the alien intruder save the corpse it had left in its wake. The Space Wolf packs led by High Iron Priest Hengis Blackhand had all returned to the Fang by that time, and were feasting to commiserate their lack of battle or were making offerings in the shrines to the ancestor-spirits of the Chapter.

A pack of Wolf Guard were duelling in the armament halls, for it was bad luck to go to war and yet not shed blood and this ill fate might be staved off by striking one another in a duel. Hengis himself was the highest ranking Space Wolf among those who had returned and he held court here in the Great Hall. His temper at that time was foul indeed.

Arjac entered the hall, and Hengis rose in anger from his seat at the head of the table. Neither mead nor meat nor song had eased his temper. 'Arjac Rockfist!' he bellowed. 'I have heard of the failings that fell upon the custodians of the Fang in our absence, but not from you! I have heard how the gene-seed stock was put at risk, how battle-brothers and thralls have lost their lives, and yet it is only now that you stand before me! And I hear also that the Axe Morkai is shattered, and the task which I left you, in good faith that you were the best man to complete it, has been undone. Explain yourself, Space Wolf!'

'I see Svalin and Vidfinn have told you all that happened,' replied Arjac.

'Their explanation sounds thorough, and it will have to do for now. I say this not to slight you, High Iron Priest, but because the danger is not yet done. The alien is loose in the Fang – this much you know, and no doubt you have seen to it that the Space Wolves you bring back hunt it as we speak. But there is more, and far worse.'

Lord Hengis kept his calm for just a moment longer, enough for him to gesture to Arjac to continue.

'The alien is a tyranid,' said Arjac. 'But it has about it a cunning not common to the tyranid warrior-beast. It seeks our gene-seed even now, it hungers for it. It has slain thralls in the lower levels and torn open their throats, seeking the organ.'

'Then you have been among the lowly thralls instead of explaining your failings to your betters,' said Hengis, his voice smouldering and his face grown dark.

'I believe,' said Arjac, 'that this tyranid is seeking to gauge the presence of gene-seed at the Fang, and ascertain whether it should summon more of its kind to harvest it. This is the way of the tyranid – first for its van-guard creatures to locate a source of biomass, and then to summon the fleets and armies of the hive mind. Many worlds have been lost in this way. Perhaps Fenris does not seem a tempting target for the tyranids, for she is chill and great swathes of her are devoid of life. But this tyranid came to the Fang because it had detected the gene-seed kept here, and now it has confirmed the presence of such valuable biomass it will surely seek to bring more of its kind here. I have read the work of Inquisitor Kryptmann, and he described creatures resembling our intruder and the function they served in the hive fleets. I am certain I speak true of its purpose, and of the danger that falls upon the Fang.'

'There has never been a tyranid sighted within light years of Fenris,' retorted Hengis. 'And yet you would have a great hive fleet fall from the sky upon us?'

'I believe, Lord Hengis,' said Arjac, 'that this creature did not come from the sky.'

'I will hear no more,' said Hengis Blackhand. 'You seek to shift the blame for the deaths of your brothers with this talk of alien fleets invading us from nowhere. You are withdrawn from duty until the Great Wolf and his com-pany arrive, when he will hear the trial to decide what punishment should fall on you for your failings.'

'I understand,' said Arjac, and he was not unbowed. 'May I ask leave to withdraw to the forges, where I might continue my work?'

'Do so,' said Hengis. 'Better that you remain not in the Fang, but on the forge slopes where the brothers will not have to hear of your excuses.'

You might think that I am being unkind to High Iron Priest Hengis Black-hand. He was, after all, a hero of our Chapter. In battle he was a boon to his allies and a bane to his enemies. But a man can be both a hero, and yet also a man quick to anger and short of sight whose hotness of temper, such a potent weapon in war, could be a liability in peace. And he was confronted here by what appeared to be a terrible catastrophe and failing among the battle-brothers he had trusted to act as stewards to the Fang while the Chapter was away. Indeed, to him it must have seemed that Arjac was shirking his duties in failing to acknowledge Hengis's return, was avoiding the taking of responsibility for the deaths in the Fang, and was seeking to protect himself from the worst of the Iron Priest's ire. I do not judge him too harshly, and indeed he is a greater man than I could ever imagine being, though I put in his mouth words born of the anger that overtakes reason.

Thus did Arjac Rockfist, barred from seeking the alien predator any further, indeed withdrew to the forges of the lower slopes. He brought with him the fragments that remained of the Axe Morkai, though the blade was incomplete. A shard of it was still, as far as he knew, embedded in the alien. But still he went to work dismantling the parts of the broken Axe Morkai, and undoing that puzzle of workmanship he had so diligently put together.

And what of the alien? Lord Hengis did not shirk his duty in hunting it down. Indeed, he tasked each one of the Wolf Guard with assembling a hunt, choosing men from the Great Company to follow him into the endless warrens of the Fang. Some went to the dark igneous caves beneath the lava vents, where the cairns of the dead lie still. Some scoured the upper peak, fending off the raptors and braving the winds of icy razors. Three of them roamed the foothills, those deep crevasses and unkind expanses where you all underwent your Blooding. There they found glacier wurms and rot spectres, but no tyranid. Nor did those battle-brothers who went hunting in all other corners of the Fang, delving into cells and chapels not used for centuries, places where old bones mouldered and the deeds of wars now forgotten were etched upon the walls.

Down on the forge slopes, Arjac laboured. In the ruddy glow of the Heart Forge he salvaged what he could of the Axe Morkai, always whispering prayers to beg forgiveness from the weapon's great machine-spirit. He worked upon the Voidstone Anvil, which had been carved from a meteor by Fenris's mighty ancestor-lords in an age long since passed, and in the heat of the molten fire that bubbled up from Fenris's own furious heart.

The snow fell heavy on that morning, when Arjac spent his third day of ceaseless labour. It seemed to all who knew of it that Arjac sought a kind of penance, pouring all his sorrow and guilt into the remaking of the Axe Morkai. And, of course, it was a fruitless task, for the blade was incomplete and the weapon could never be remade. It was a punishment Arjac Rockfist inflicted on himself, to forge what should have been a great weapon for the armouries of the Fang and yet never to see it completed.

Through the snow walked Thane Darskaan, the master of the thralls who worked in the Forge Hills. He was wrapped heavily in furs against the chill, though Arjac himself had stripped off his armour and wore only his novice's habit, and the sweat glistened on his chest.

'Lord Arjac,' he said. 'I see you work once more. Though we would all have the circumstances changed, it is good that you are among us again.'

'No good can come of my failings,' said Arjac.

'There are those among the thralls, and I dare say among your own battle-brothers, who believe Lord Hengis is wrong,' said Darskaan. 'And that he should heed your wisdom in the hunting of the beast. You have faced it, after all. You puzzled out when and where it would strike, and you were right.'

Arjac stood up from the Voidstone Anvil then, and laid down the hammer with which he had been beating the imperfect blade of the Axe Morkai. 'Thane Darskaan,' he said. 'I hear your words and I am grateful for them. You have ever been my friend, and glad I am that our Chapter is served by such as you. But I cannot accept such sentiment as you offer me. Lord Hengis is my master, and his word is as the snarl of the pack's alpha wolf. If he wills that I return to the Heart Forge and join not the hunt, then that is what I must do, and thoughts and words to the contrary are for nought.'

'And is every alpha right?' asked Darskaan. 'Though my words are dangerous, still I must speak them. A wolf might deny the leader of his pack, and triumph, and win the right to go his own way. Have not the Space Wolves themselves clashed often with the organisations of the Imperium, who stand according to Imperial law above the Chapter?'

'You would have me defy Lord Hengis?' asked Arjac.

'If it is the right thing to do,' said Darskaan, 'then yes. But then, I am just a thrall. What can I know?'

Arjac made to answer. No doubt it was to say something that exemplified his wisdom and humility, for such was his way of speech. But he was given to pause, and turn his face to the sky, and hold out a hand for silence.

'What do you hear?' asked Darskaan, for he could hear nothing save the chill wind and the distant roar of the Heart Forge's fires from below.

'It is not what I hear,' said Arjac. 'It is what I smell.'

'Then what?'

Arjac's brow creased in concentration. 'The ocean,' he said. 'The salt and the spray, whipped from the cresting waves by the wind. And the decay of its very depths, those lightless places where a thousand years of shipwrecks might be found, where eyeless things squirm through the bones of Fenrisians that lie centuries drowned. I can smell the salt tears in the brine, shed over the cruelty of Fenris's sea. And the stench of the unknown life that teems there, that will sometimes rise to drag down a hundred screaming sailors with tentacle and fang. That is what I smell, all the chill and forgotten evil that sinks to the depths of our heartless world, and it rises.'

Arjac cast down his tools and turned to his armour, which he had stacked up beside the great anvil. 'Darskaan,' he said, 'bring the forge thralls together. Arm them, and ensure you have taken the name of each man so none is left unaccounted for. I must go to the Fang, but soon I shall return.'

Arjac donned his armour, and took down the hammer which he had used as a weapon before he wielded the Axe Morkai. He stood on the lip of the Heart Forge's great pit, and he glanced across the forge slopes that stretched down towards the sea.

You may have been on the Forge Hills yourself, perhaps in apprenticeship to the Iron Priests or to see to the making of your arms and armour. If you walked down to the lowest of the hills, where great heaps of spoil from the kilns and forges lie darkening the fields of snow, and if the day was clear, you might have seen the ocean. There lie the terrible black rocks, sharp and jagged as a glacier wurm's teeth, that form the first defence of the Fang. In ages past, when the Fang was the seat of the kings of this region, invading fleets were wrecked there, and traitors were chained there to be dashed to pieces upon the rising tide. One whole side of the Fang is guarded by those vicious rocks. And for a moment the snows parted, and Arjac could see clear across the Forge Hills to that unkind shore.

The sea was grey slate, tormented by the winds that shrieked down from the heights of the Fang. The rocks were slick and obsidian black, sharp as broken glass. And from those depths reached the first tendrils of the Kraken.

From the depths it rose. A jointed limb, like that of a great insect, that ended in a pair of pincers. Behind it emerged the hulking carapace of its body, encrusted with eyes made huge and pale by the lightlessness of the depths.

Upon a far battlefield you may have seen its like, you who have fought the minions of the Kraken, and you would recognise the lumbering strength of the carnifex, the screamer-killer, living war engines of the hive mind. But this had about it something of the sea, beyond the encrustations of barnacles and coral that clung to its hide. Fronds of glowing flesh hung from its joints, the means by which it might illuminate its prey on the ocean floor. Its eyes were on stalks like those of a crab. Anemones and smaller parasites clung all over it, eager to feed from the scraps it cast about itself. And the stench of it had welled up from the very chasms of the deep.

Another rose, its brother in form but different as brothers are, this one a fiddler with one huge claw dragging across the rocks beneath it. More shapes were breaking the surface of the waves.

Smaller creatures were teeming around the Kraken as they rose. You have seen the hordes without number of the tyranids, either in the illuminations of battle histories or in the flesh as you did battle with them. These lesser things were no less deadly for their size was compensated for by their number. Six-legged and swift, they carried weapons grown from organisms slaved into their primitive minds that fired grubs or shards of bone.

In dozens, then hundreds, they chittered and seethed from the surf. Some of the Kraken spawn had bodies studded with human skulls, gathered from the debris to make their carapaces, as if in mockery of Fenris herself and the fury of her storms. Here and there an ingot of gold or a gemstone winked, detritus from a treasure-laden ship that carried some ancient king's wealth to the bottom of the sea.

The Kraken were huge, and festooned with natural weaponry. Their spawn were legion, squirming or scuttling over the rocks in their thousands. More and more of them emerged, as great an army as had ever besieged the Fang since the Plague of Unbelief, and nought but Arjac Rockfist and the five hundred thralls of the Forge Hills stood before them.

'I will return!' called Arjac to Thane Darskaan. 'This I swear!' And Arjac ran towards the Fang, striding through the snow even as the chittering and shrieking of the Kraken spawn army reached his ears.

When Arjac reached the Fang, already the Space Wolves were on the walls. The thrall sentries had alerted the battle-brothers and they were massing to witness the spring tide of foulness suddenly rising from the sea.

Arjac reached the battlements and sought out Hengis Blackhand, who by virtue of being the highest ranking Space Wolf there was its commander now that it was at war.

'Arjac,' snarled Hengis. 'Take your position among the battle-brothers. You are returned to duty to fight.'

'I hear,' said Arjac. 'What is our plan of defence?'

'The Forge Hills are abandoned,' said Hengis. 'There the enemy shall find few pickings among the thralls. When they reach our walls, we will hold them, and the xenos shall be dashed to pieces against our fury.'

'Then I plead,' said Arjac, 'do not abandon the men out there. Though thralls they be, they are brave. Each one would stand as a battle-brother to us were it not for a single slip during the Blooding. And there is not one among them who has not excelled himself with a lifetime of service to the Chapter, to the Allfather and to the ancestors of Fenris.'

'If I open the doors to the Fang, the enemy will seek to enter thereby,' replied Hengis, unmoved. 'See, the horde moves swiftly! They will be upon us before the thralls have been evacuated. No, I will not put the lives of Space Wolves in peril for the sake of the Forge Hills thralls, valiant men as they may be.'

Arjac Rockfist thought upon this, and for a moment too long for the liking of Hengis Blackhand. 'Do you have ought to say to me, Arjac, about my orders?' Hengis demanded.

'No, my lord,' said Arjac, eyes cast down in humility. 'I ask only leave to go to the armouries and seek out a weapon. I have only this hammer, which

I use in my work upon the Voidstone Anvil. It has earned my trust, but it is not a weapon, certainly not for the defending of our fortress.'

'Go,' said Hengis, 'but be back on the walls shortly.'

And so Hengis oversaw the manning of the Fang's battlements. He had twenty Wolf Guard resplendent in their Terminator armour, each man a fortification in his own right. Eighty more Space Wolves, Grey Hunters and Blood Claws, took their places. The Grey Hunters were arranged for mass volley fire from their bolters, with Hengis's drill masters walking up and down their line to see that their fields of fire overlapped such that no living thing might make it through them.

The Wolf Priest Gunnar Skyfire, who still preaches the tales of Russ's exploits in the chapels of the Fang, had the task of keeping the Blood Claws in check so they might not charge down from the Fang's battlements too early into the approaching horde. Well do you all know those days, either because you left them behind you or you live them still, when a steady old hand was needed to hold you back, lest your headstrong fury take you too quickly into the thick of battle!

Also on the walls were Svalin and Vidfinn, their helms cast aside and their faces painted for battle, for they sought now not glory but revenge for their lost packmates. Thralls manned the defence guns, waiting for the command to fire, which Hengis would give the moment the horde passed within range.

But the horde was vast. Still the ocean disgorged its forgotten army. Hulking things with swollen, fleshy bodies bigger than a Land Raider tank clambered onto the rocks and disgorged tall plumes of poisonous spores, turning the sky black. Dense clouds of such corrosive poison were caught on the wind off the ocean, and the venom raked at the side of the Fang like a great caustic claw. Sacs of bilious acid were flung from beasts evolved into slithering war machines, burning great holes in the emplacements and rendering mighty rockcrete battlements as unto heaps of sand. Many were the thralls caught in the open before the orders were given to take cover. Many were the tales of sorrow written in those first few moments.

The Space Wolves held fast. Ceramite armour of ancient design, created

750

in the depths of the Imperium's forge-worlds, was proof against the first volley from the horde. And so Hengis gave no order for the battle-brothers to withdraw, and instead bade them sight at the horde down the barrels of their boltguns and missile launchers, ready for the moment when the enemy slithered and crawled into range.

But then, as Hengis cast his eyes down at the battlefield, he saw something that gave flame to his already well-stoked anger. For one of the blast doors at the base of the walls was opening.

'Who is this that sallies forth from our fortress?' bellowed Lord Hengis. 'Who has defied my order, and, seeks instead of doing his duty upon the walls of the Fang, walks out to face the horde? Who is it that throws his life away, hoping to receive some fleeting glory in return? It is no hero that walks out alone. No, it is a fool, a wastrel – a traitor say I, for he has abandoned his duty to his Chapter!'

The Space Wolves gathered at the battlements' edge to see. And in shock, they saw that the Space Wolf who was the object of Hengis's anger was Arjac Rockfist.

'He seeks death,' cried out one Space Wolf, 'to atone for the loss of the Axe Morkai!'

'No,' said another, 'it is in guilt at the deaths of Pack Fornjot that he invites the xenos to butcher him on the field of battle!'

Another, older and wiser, called out, 'Nay! He wishes to fight and die alongside the thralls of the Forge Hills. For Arjac was never one of us, never quick to laugh and to feast. No, he was scornful of the mighty warrior the Chapter made of him, and he dressed up such scorn in the guise of humility. See how he walks towards the forges, where stand the thralls with whom he spent so much more time than with his battle-brothers! See his eyes downcast! He knows he was never truly a Space Wolf. Thus our doubts of him, that have been unspoken yet shared by many, are proven well-founded!'

And many others echoed these words. For in part, it was true. Was Arjac like a Space Wolf? Was he like any of you? He boasted not of his victories, and yet even Leman Russ himself spoke greatly of his might and triumphs, and even in the face of the Allfather proclaimed his strength and ferocity. All the heroes of our Chapter have shown neither shame nor restraint in boasting of whatever heroic deed has earned them their plaudits last – all save, it seems, Arjac Rockfist. And how many of you have clashed fists with your battle-brothers in arguing who has fought the hardest or taken the most prestigious trophy in battle, and felt the hand of the Wolf Priest on them hauling them out of the brawl before one of them is sent to the apothecarion? Every one of you here has at one time beaten his chest and proclaimed, 'I am the greatest among us here, and I will fight any who says I am not!' But Arjac never had. And so it was some darkness in him, some doubt unbecoming of a Space Marine, that many of our Chapter saw in Arjac as he walked out that day in defiance of Lord Hengis's orders.

And still, the horde grew. Who among you has fought the hated tyranid, face to face, smelled its corruption and tasted the blasphemy of it on the air? Ah, many of you here. Then you think you know what Arjac might have seen gushing up from the ocean, crawling across the rocks in an obscene tide of reeking, oozing flesh. But those who have seen more than one campaign against the tyranid know that never does the tyranid appear on two battlefields in the same form. It is ever changing, wearing the deceit of the alien in the mutability of its flesh.

Many are the Imperial Guard warmasters and writers of battle-tomes who have sought to categorise the tyranid into genus and species, taking note of its form and behaviour and describing each organism as if to force it to fit into a neat definition. Comforting it would be if a soldier could open a book, and count the tentacles and orifices of the beast before him, and say, 'Ah! I face this beast, and not this beast or that, and now I know its capabilities and what must be done to destroy it!' But the tyranid gives us no such comfort. For it always changes.

The organisms of one hive fleet are different from the next, and one fleet's warriors and war-beasts will be different the next battle they fight. When the field is chill, they swathe their bulk in fat and hide to keep the steaming heat of their bodies from being drawn away by the cold. When it is hot, they are lean, bleeding off excess heat on long vanes of bone or trailing fronds of skin. Where the environment is caustic, their hides are scaled as if with stone. Where ground is scarce, they evolve wings and take to the air. Where it is plentiful and porous, they grow shovel-like jaws and great earth-moving claws to burrow through the earth. And the beasts that assailed the Fang had evolved to survive in the most hostile place that Mother Fenris ever conceived – the lightless depths of her oceans, where the Kraken and leviathan dwell.

Arjac Rockfist reached the first of the forges, where Thane Darskaan was leading the thralls who stood therein, anticipating the enemy's approach. The thane and his men wore now protective hoods and coveralls, which were more frequently donned when dangerous chemicals or radiation leaked from the generators and fuel stores. Now it served to give them some protection against the clouds of corrosive venom issuing from the gullets of the alien horde, and yet Arjac saw draped among the anvils and quenching troughs the bodies of those who had been caught in the open by that first bilious assault. Dissolved to the bone they were, their flesh and organs a bubbling soup of foulness. How grisly and ill-starred a death for such valiant sons of Fenris!

'I am glad that you return to us,' said Thane Darskaan. 'And yet I fear that for your abandoning of the walls, Lord Hengis will become as sure an enemy to you as any alien fiend.'

'You may be right,' said Arjac. 'But if I should survive to see his ire, it means the battle has been won, and I would then welcome his wrath.'

Arjac joined the men holding that forge, which was used for the fashioning of ceramite plates for the armour of the Chapter's vehicles. They were armed with autoguns and shotguns, and with the tools of their forges. They were strong and brave men, muscles honed working the anvils of their tribes, many of them formidable warriors in the most ferocious tribes of Fenris. Truly, they were men who would not flee or flinch, nor give in to despair. And yet, when they saw the magnitude of the enemy that approached, was there something in their hearts, hidden and shamed, that quailed at the sight?

I myself was a young man there and, all the ancestors be praised, I stood not in the forges that day but among the thralls loading the shells into the defence cannons on the cliffs of the Fang. And even so I felt fear. Yes, fear, though I am ashamed of it. The sound of the horde, the stench of it, sent recoiling within me everything that made me human. And yet the thralls of the forge slopes stood shoulder to shoulder with Arjac Rockfist.

'From whence did the enemy come to the Fang?' asked Thane Darskaan, awe and disgust alike in his voice. 'There is no predator ever sighted on Fenris's oceans that matches such a thing. Sea serpents and leviathan whales I have heard of, seen even from a distance. But not this.'

'It is in the depths that they evolved,' said Arjac. 'Who knows when the tyranid vanguard creatures first came to Fenris? Perhaps a few decades ago, perhaps in the unknown past before the Dark Age when man had never set foot on Fenris. But their orders from the hive mind were clear. Wait and grow, until such time as Fenris becomes a worthy source of biomass for the hive fleets to harvest.

'One hunter this horde sent forth, to seek out such biomass, and it found its goal in the gene-seed vaults. It could not capture the gene-seed alone, for I and my brothers fought it to a standstill, and found not what it desired among the thralls. So it broadcast a psychic signal to its fellow creatures in the depths, summoning them to take by numbers and force what the organism could not take alone by cunning and stealth.

'And what better place to breed an army of predators than Fenris's ocean depths? We have seen but a fraction of the monsters that live down there. To survive – nay, to thrive in those lightless waters, against the wrath of Fenris's native predators, that has honed these alien intruders into killers of a quality that even Fenris has rarely bred.'

'The Crone Fenris's fury turned against us,' said Darskaan. 'Corrupted by the alien, her ferocity turned to filth. Bless this alien for giving us so much to hate about him! Fear is a distant and pathetic thing compared to that hate. But tell me, Brother Arjac, what orders should I give to my fellow thralls?'

Arjac thought upon this, for a moment. Indeed, it is the mark of a leader in war that he does not despair, that he does not look at the battle that cannot be won and give no order. For even in the bedlam of defeat, there is something to be eked out by discipline and steadfastness, even if it be but fitting deaths for the doomed. 'Have them hold their ground,' he said. 'The enemy will seek to close and to kill us with fang and claw. Do not charge in, no matter how glorious a death you seek. But do not fall back when overwhelmed. Let the fires of your forges be a weapon, and stoke their flames to immolate the enemy when they overrun you.'

'I understand,' said Darskaan. 'Truly my suspicions have been confirmed, and Lord Hengis has given the command that we be left out here to die and the doors to the Fang to be held closed.'

'There is anger in your voice, Darskaan,' said Arjac Rockfist.

'The High Iron Priest's orders are his orders,' said Darskaan. 'However the pack's leader wills it, so it shall be.'

'Now is not the time for meekness, Thane Darskaan. Now, of all times, you must be free to speak your mind.'

'In that case,' said Thane Darskaan, 'I think that Hengis Blackhand is a witch-begotten swine not fit to lick the fleas from the mangiest alley-cur, and if he were to stride into my forge and proclaim his valour in fighting alongside us I would spit on his boots.'

And I know that is what he said, for Arjac Rockfist told me himself.

At the foot of the Forge Hills, where the rocks of the forge pit walls were pitted with spray from the salt ocean, the Kraken spawn crashed into the first forges like a great wave of corrupted flesh. Thralls bellowed their oaths to the ancestors of Fenris as they took aim and fired every clip of ammunition they had. They could not miss, for there was but one single great target that loomed up foul and terrible. Who can say what tales of heroism were written there, how many men scorned the inevitability of death and hurled curses at it even as they blazed fire into the tyranid organisms swarming forth? None, I fear, for not one man survived those first few seconds who was within reach of a claw or a fang.

The smaller six-legged beasts, called 'gaunts by the Imperial Guard, were cut down by the dozen. Such is the way of the hive mind, to send waves of the creatures it considers disposable in its cold, inhuman reckoning. In the ocean they had evolved without eyes, sensing through fronds of feelers that waved around their needle-toothed jaws. Autogun rounds punched through the barnacled armour that covered their torsos and ripped off their many limbs. The aliens' blood was pale and bluish, the colour of an overcast sky, and it fell as dense as the rains that come with the spring thaw.

The first of the aliens leapt into the forge pits, and died. Shotguns blasted them apart at a few paces' range, and the thralls wiped the gore from the faceplates of their protective gear. But with every one that died, it seemed a dozen more sprinted forth from the horde. Jaws snapped and severed men's limbs even as the aliens died. Some bore long talons in place of front limbs, which cut men in two. Others had twin tentacles that twined around thralls' throats, and sent them into terrible dying spasms as the venom cells that covered them pierced their coveralls and sent agonising poison into their veins.

One mighty warrior-thrall, his face bescarred from the wounds of his failed Blooding, roared and hauled over his head a great cask of fuel. It was used, a few drops at a time, to make flare the fires that burned in the smouldering hearths of his forge pit. This thrall, whose name was Imrak the Bear, had made it his task to immolate the attackers in the flames of the forge, and even as they surrounded him he made ready to smash the cask into the burning coals and end his own life, and those of a hundred xenos, in the roaring flames.

But through the seething horde leapt another creature, something very different to the attack-beasts that made up the first assault. It was lithe and quick, powered on long muscular limbs, its body long and hunched, twin-bladed limbs reaching from its shoulder and two more forelimbs tipped with talons hurling thralls out of its way. Its eyes were wide and filmy, as if to drink in all the light from the dimness of the ocean depths. In place of mouthparts, it had a nest of tendrils that dripped with corrosive venom. It was a cousin to the predator of the Fang, the lictor xenotype of stealthy assassin-beast.

Imrak drew back his arm to hurl the fuel casket. But even before it could leave his hand, the leaping xenos had transfixed his mighty body with one of its blades. Imrak stood there, spine cut and body unresponsive, as the alien's taloned hand gripped him by the chin and turned his head this way and that, as if the alien was examining him with the curiosity of a creature first encountering an example of another species. Then, as it turned away, it twisted Imrak's head off his shoulders with a flick of its wrist. It raised its head, sent out a terrible keening cry that set its maw-tendrils quivering, and the attack-beasts seethed across the forge as the last of its defenders were dragged down.

Woe that Imrak the Bear was denied the death he deserved! I had known of Imrak the Bear when I served in those times, and to us it seemed that he could never die. He was huge of body and of spirit, and often he would mockingly wrestle the other thralls when they got to drinking, always laughing as he pinned his opponents to the ground, always celebrating each bout with a hearty laugh and joke with the man he had defeated. And yet this immortal man was dead, ripped apart by a creature that thought no more of him than you or I might think about the microscopic things that slither across the ground beneath our feet.

Arjac Rockfist witnessed this with the keenness of eye of a Space Marine. He knew that for men to die such deaths bred despair in the hearts of soldiers. Though there were many thralls in the Forge Hills, numbering all those who laboured there, he knew then that the manner of this battle depended on him. The thralls would look to him, a Space Marine, a Space Wolf and a friend to the forge thralls. He could not promise them victory. He could not promise survival. He could promise them only the chance to die like men of Fenris.

'I must reach the Heart Forge,' Arjac said to Thane Darskaan. 'It is much I ask, of you, my friend, and all of you. But I cannot do it alone. When the great war-beasts of the horde are embattled, I must make my way to that great pit where the fires of Fenris's heart rage, and I ask the cover from your guns to help me do it.'

'Everything I have, I will give,' said Thane Darskaan. 'I can vouch for my brothers here, too.'

And behind the first wave of attack-beasts rose the battle-hulks, grinding through the surf much like the war machines of other races might rumble on wheels or tracks, weighed down by armour and guns. These carnifex beasts resembled crustaceans of appalling size, gnarled and misshapen, their towering bulk surmounted with cannons of muscle and bone.

Each one was unique in its form, covered with scars gained in battle with the countless leviathans of Fenris's ocean, carapaces home to colonies of barnacle and anemone that dripped streams of noisome ooze. They squatted down on their shovel-like claws and fired huge chunks of coral at the forges, each porous boulder filled with acid. Men dived for cover as the living artillery hit home, shattering the sturdy structures of the forges. The stone blocks that shored up the walls of the pits tumbled, crushing body and limb. Men were struck by shards of coral and impaled, or showered with acid that burned at their skin as keen as the hottest forge flame.

Another beast, far larger, was in form like a gargantuan sea worm with a tentacled maw and pincered tail. Skeletons of drowned sailors were embedded in the coral growths covering the armour plates on its back. It was like the trygon beast of tyranid battle-lore, such as you may have seen burrowing up from the ground to devour man and vehicle in a frenzy. This one disgorged the lesser gaunt-beasts, curled up and writhing as if newly-born, vomiting them over the defences to land among thralls who died to their birth-throes. The trygon reared high above the horde, like a banner of a Great Company might stand above our own battle lines.

One forge exploded, whether through the bedlam of battle or the deliberate efforts of the doomed defenders I cannot say. In the great plume of flame, charred bodies of man and xenos fell. Through the smoke stumbled the few survivors, burned and dragging broken limbs or clutching bloody wounds, hoping to reach the next set of defences behind them. But volleys of acid-drenched artillery fire landed among them, shredding and dissolving their exposed flesh, and none survived to tell of how that first conflagration was triggered.

And now, from the alien mass, rose four towering shapes, the generals of the horde. For the hive mind cedes a portion of its command to the mightiest organisms, who transmit its orders through psychic means. The Imperial Guard fighting the tyranid focus on such creatures, to disrupt the alien armies and force them to act only on their unguided animal instincts. Arjac stood proud of the forge in which he and Darskaan stood, clambering up onto one of the anvils for a better view. Through the poisonous fog the generals loomed, and he knew that their appearance was what he had been waiting for.

One was like a huge, glistening brain held within a cage of bone, supported by the atrophied body of a tyranid beast that had lost its limbs as it evolved. It hovered above the ground by some bestial witchcraft, and from the greyish mass of that brain spat fiery bolts of power that burst among the fleeing thralls. This was the zoanthrope, psychic artillery and conduit of the hive mind's will, again in form adapted to the oceans with fins and rancid gills. A second was the malefactor, rarely seen in recent centuries but a mainstay of the earliest hive fleet invasions, with a slug-like body armoured in dense bone and a pair of enormous shovel-claws that gouged at the snowy rock to drag itself along. It was a machine of destruction, its claws solid masses of bone with which it demolished the walls of the forges so the lesser beasts could pour through. It, too, directed the xenos around it, for at its psychic command the 'gaunts surged through the breaches it tore.

The third xenos general was a foul thing, a dactylis as the battle-manuals have it, with a bulbous body far larger than a tank. Its rear limbs were vestigial but the front pair were long and many-jointed, ending in dextrous hands unwholesomely similar to those of a human in shape though far larger. With these hands it plucked the eggs from a bubbling mass of fertile flesh on its back, and hurled them to fall like artillery shells. Swarms of immature tyranids burst forth where the eggs landed, filling their short lives with a fury of hunger as they stripped men to the bone in their lust for flesh.

But it was the fourth that Arjac Rockfist knew he had to face. It was the fourth that had given Arjac cause to abandon the battlements and stand with the thralls in the path of the enemy.

In size it rivalled the demi-titans the Adeptus Mechanicus once fielded in whole regiments, now consigned to the defence of a few forge-worlds as their numbers fell. On four massive legs it walked, its body plated in bone armour, its head encased save for the massive jaws that lowered down to scoop up mouthfuls of the 'gaunts that scurried before it. Squealing they disappeared down its gullet to fuel it as it lumbered. A pair of forelimbs plucked other stragglers from the befouled snow to swallow them or cast them aside, tyranids and thralls alike. Indeed, its mass was that of a mighty siege engine – and yet it was not just for the purpose of raw destruction that the hive mind employed this general.

The annals of battle-lore record, in a few sketchy and ill-observed instances, the presence of such beasts on battlefields from long past. They were known as the mistresses of the tyranid hordes, the dominatrices who communed directly with the hive mind and directed the flow of battle. In a throne upon the beast's back resided a tyranid queen, bloated and unfit for war herself but capable of transmitting the hive mind's will over great leagues of battlefront.

No such queen was enthroned there now, but in that cradle of muscle and bone instead reigned the lictor, the predator, the same creature that had entered the halls and murdered its fill of Space Wolves. It was unquestionably the same creature, selected by the hive mind to direct the horde as it assaulted the Fang, for it alone had seen the defences up close and scuttled along the halls of our fortress home.

Across the battlefield, did the eyes of Arjac and lictor meet? Was there a mutual recognition there, for each had seen in the other the ultimate foe, the prey at the end of its greatest hunt? Perhaps. But in the alien mind of the predator there was room for no respect, no honour such as the hunter shows to the prey who has evaded him over miles of tundra. No, there was only the desire to consume, for such is the sole purpose of the tyranid.

Arjac vaulted the defences of the forge pit. Thane Darskaan and the other thralls, some two hundred men who had gathered in the forges of the upper slopes, followed in his wake. Arjac held up his hammer, the smith's tool he had adopted as a weapon, and it was like a banner of the Chapter raised high.

The thralls who looked on from the battlements of the Fang cheered when they saw Arjac taking to the battlefield. Though Lord Hengis looked ill upon them, still they cared not, for they felt keenly the deaths of their fellow thralls doomed by the decision to close the doors of the Fang.

'If he seeks death,' bellowed Hengis, 'then he has it! See the futility of his loss! All that has been given to him, the wargear of ancient mark, the years of training and psycho-doctrination, the very gene-seed of Leman Russ, Arjac Rockfist wastes in his desire to atone!'

The Space Wolves watching did not raise their voices in agreement or scorn. Though many had cast doubts on Arjac, now they watched him charging across the embattled Forge Hills they could find nothing in their hearts that bade them echo Lord Hengis's words. I know this because I have spoken with the battle-brothers who were there, and heard of their shame that they had mocked their fellow Space Wolf minutes earlier. For each Space Wolf has within him the predator, the wolf-spirit of Fenris the Chapter seeks to nurture and unleash, and there was not one predator heart that did not wish its owner, too, was down there with Arjac, weapon held high, rushing towards the towering lord-beasts of the Kraken spawn horde.

The first of the tyranid lords towered ahead – the dactylis that cast its living artillery all about. Thralls were taking cover but finding scant protection from the assault, for this general was softening up a string of fortified forges ready to send a torrent of 'gaunts in to overrun them.

Arjac sought not cover nor pause as he rushed at it. The thralls dived for safety, slowing themselves down and making of themselves easy targets. But Arjac did not. It was as if the mortars fell not around him, the flame washed not against his armoured body. He reached within a few paces of the beast, and as he passed into its shadow he leapt.

No, he did not strike at its head, for there lay its weapons, its clawed mandibles and the terrible circular maw of its mouth. He hit the edge of its carapace, which was much like bone and much like rock, the edge impacting against his chest. He found handholds in the gnarled mass and dragged himself on top of the creature. A man would have been cut to pieces by the sharp protrusions of shattered coral and barnacle, but Arjac's armour held firm. A man would have been thrown off by the bucking of the beast beneath him, but Arjac's grip was strong.

Arjac clambered to the centre of the beast's back, where the bone formed a ridge around the bubbling, steaming mass of fecundity that birthed its living ammunition. Thousands of embryonic tyranids writhed there, clawing and gnashing their tiny maws, their sole purpose to devour everything around them before their lives were spent.

Truly it is written in the Codex Astartes that every enemy has a weak point, and that a victor must exploit that point. So it was that Arjac Rockfist plunged a fist into the hole he had smashed, down into the boiling mass of ichor and sinew. He ignored the scalding billows of steam and the sudden tilting of the carapace as the beast tried to throw him off. Tyranid spawn hatched and leapt at him, but Arjac swatted away those that threatened to gain purchase on his face and ignored the rest, trusting in his armour to hold firm against the needles of their teeth. Deeper he reached as the foul mass of flesh rose up around him like a tide of alien bodies. His hand found resistance in the murk, something stringy that sought to cling to the beast's inside, and his fingers closed around it.

Great was Arjac's strength. Gritted were his teeth. From the crater in the beast's back, he tore a long slithering section of its spine.

The dactylis screeched, a sound that even from the malformed throat of the alien spoke of fear and pain. It tilted like a longship holed below the waterline, the edge of its carapace grinding into the blood-streaked earth of the Forge Hills. Still it lived, but Arjac had ripped from it the means by which its alien mind commanded its limbs and organs. Its forelimbs lay immobile and useless, the final egg-sac rolling from its fingers. Its many eyes rolled as if in terror. It heaved, trying to force itself up and forwards again, but the greater part of its strength was gone.

'Finish it!' yelled Arjac to the thralls who fought alongside Thane Darskaan. 'Show it how we welcome its kind to Fenris! But take not too long! The Heart Forge is my destination, and I would not go there alone!'

Arjac waded now into the throng. With every swing of his blacksmith's hammer he shattered the exoskeleton skull of an attack-beast. The 'gaunts tried to swarm him, a dozen of them piling on him and seeking to tear open his armour with their claws, but with a shrug of his mighty shoulders he threw them off and struck all about him. Broken xenos bodies were tossed aside like snowflakes on the winter wind. The snow beneath his feet turned purple-black with their blood. His armour was spattered with it, the grey of his armour clotted black to the elbow. He strode on, crushing bodies under his boots. A leaping hunter-beast, long limbs powering it across the battlefield, hurtled towards Arjac swift as an arrow. But Arjac was quicker and slammed his hammer down, crunching it into the alien's back as he sidestepped its charge. The alien was driven into the ground and Arjac stamped down on its neck. Vertebrae crunched and the beast fell still, save for the death-spasm of its claws.

The thralls lent their fire to Arjac, autoguns picking off attack-beasts as they rushed to fill the breach Arjac left. Thane Darskaan took to the lead himself, carrying a twin-barrelled autogun that he himself had pieced together from the finest components. Its stock was inscribed with scenes of Fenris's savagery, the hunting wolf and the diving raptor. Such was the weapon with which he led the thralls even as he stood in the open, heedless of danger, scorning the enemy with his valour.

So it was that Arjac Rockfist reached the Heart Forge. Alas, the thralls that had defended it lay dead, overcome by a great blast of bilious acid and the survivors slain by the waves of attack-beasts. Arjac vaulted into the pit and bellowed in anger to see the thralls who had worked at his side mangled and eaten away. He grabbed one beast by the throat and hurled it into the pit of molten stone from where the Heart Forge drew its fires. He laid another one onto the Voidstone Anvil and battered it with his hammer, as if it was iron upon which he worked.

Over the Heart Forge rose the second of the alien lords, the zoanthrope with its pulsating brain. A legion of 'gaunts scuttled beneath it, bodyguards and mind-slaves to it, and its glistening eyes focused on Arjac as it made ready to unleash a bolt of the hive mind's own wrath.

I have spoken before of the shield that hung above the Voidstone Anvil. Arjac leapt onto the anvil now and snatched down the shield. He crouched behind it as a glistening arrow of the foulest witchcraft arced from the malformed brain of the beast. A man would have been thrown off his feet by its impact, tossed into the forge's very fires like an ember on the hot air. But Arjac was more than a man! He held fast, and that beautiful shield held too – such was its workmanship. The zoanthrope, surely in its hateful mind expecting this obstacle to have been cleared from its path, perhaps failed to notice that Arjac yet stood in its way. Something like surprise caused its jaw to hang open and its eyes to roll as Arjac ran through the front rank of its 'gaunts and jumped at it.

The zoanthrope's body was withered and without limbs, but it had a tail that hung down to steady itself or to fend off attackers with the bony blade on its tip. This Arjac grabbed in one hand, letting the shield fall beneath him. He clambered up the zoanthrope as a man might climb a sheer cliff. The beast was protected by a field of psychic energy which caused the bullets and las-blasts from the thralls to glance off it, but it could do nothing against an assailant within the field with a hammer and a strong grip to do his work! Nor could the 'gaunts shoot Arjac down with bone shards or ravenous grubs, though they tried, seeing the fire from the fleshy guns spark against the field and strike not.

Arjac splintered the bony cage around the zoanthrope's brain. How the alien cried out, its psychic scream echoing to the very peak of the Fang! I can hear it even now, just as I heard it then, a terrible howl inside my head. Sometimes it comes to me when I am halfway between sleep and waking, and the shriek of fear I know will never leave me.

Such was the violence that Arjac did to the zoanthrope's brain that clods of the pink-grey stuff rained down across the Heart Forge. Clouds of blood-steam rose where they fell into the flames. The hive mind's signal, which had until then driven the tyranid horde on, was splintered and confused now, and the 'gaunts around the zoanthrope ran this way and that without reason or plan. The zoanthrope drifted down towards the ground and Arjac leapt down, again taking hold of the alien's tail.

What better fate for the hateful xenos than to be purified in the flame? I can think of none, and neither could Arjac. He dragged the alien by the tail to the edge of the Heart Forge's pit of flame, that shaft of molten rock that lead all the way to the wrathful heart of Fenris. With a cry of anger he hefted the beast above his head! With a roar of effort he hurled it down into the fire!

Arjac Rockfist had taken back the Heart Forge. From the walls of the Fang rose a cheer, led by the thralls who saw their fellow men of Fenris bringing the battle back into the teeth of the Kraken spawn. And yet the alien tide was but set back a few steps, and surely would flow forth and drown Arjac in a tide of xenos flesh.

Arjac was not there simply to win a symbolic victory, to write a last saga of defiance before death overtook him. No, every step he had taken since he opened the doors of the Fang had been to this end. He found his place of work, where were stored all the many tools he had used to forge the ill-fated Axe Morkai. Here were fittings he had examined and discarded, there were the caches of precious metals and gemstones with which he had hoped to make the Great Wolf's weapon magnificent. But among them was the most vital tool of all, without which he would have been loath to handle the once-tainted weapon let alone hope to reforge it.

Arjac had now in his hand the vial of Leman Russ's blood, sacred relic of the primarch, the greatness of our Chapter distilled into a few drops of liquid. With this he had purified the Axe Morkai before its remaking.

'See!' cried the battle-brothers on the walls. 'Brother Arjac seeks to recover a great relic from the jaws of the Kraken! Though he will surely fail, for the alien horde surrounds him once more even now, yet we must applaud his valour to keep xenos claws off the very flesh of the primarch!'

'Yet futile is this gesture,' growled High Iron Priest Hengis, who in spite of his scorn of Arjac was compelled to look on also. 'The relic is lost, and Arjac with it. Better we had lost the relic than lost both, but thanks to Arjac's recklessness and conceit it is both we have lost.'

Brothers Svalin and Vidfinn looked on also. They did not cheer, or marvel at the valour shown in the battle below. 'Would that I was down there,' said Brother Svalin. 'Though Hengis's orders are sound in holding the walls instead of engaging the enemy outside, yet still I yearn to fight, to feel blood on my face, to tear at the Kraken with claws and teeth!'

'And I say, curses on Arjac,' cried Brother Vidfinn, 'who took to the battlefield alone, and did not bring us with him! For I would have joined him in a heartbeat.'

'Blame not Arjac,' retorted Svalin. 'Curses upon our own lack of boldness, that bade us not defy Hengis ourselves!'

Arjac stood upon the Voidstone Anvil, where the better part of the Kraken spawn horde could see him, as could the thralls and the Space Wolves on the walls. Did Arjac glance behind him, to the battlements of the Fang where Hengis Blackhand looked on? Perhaps he did. Or perhaps he was looking for the survivors of Pack Fornjot, to show them that he had not forgotten them or their fallen pack-brothers.

Arjac then pulled the stopper from the vial of sacred blood and held it aloft. The genetic signature of the Primarch Leman Russ was carried on the air, and even through the venomous fog and clouds of corrosive spores. That trace of greatness, of strength and fury, of might and battle-wisdom unequalled in all the history of mankind, reached the scent receptors of the xenos, and one among them bellowed when it recognised it. For this was something akin to the signature of the Space Wolves' own gene-seed but in a form far more concentrated and powerful.

The lictor, riding on the towering fourth general of the alien horde, had sought out the gene-seed of the Fang and sampled its power from the battle-brothers it had slain. It had emerged first from the sea, then brought forth all the Kraken spawn of the ocean, to claim that gene-seed so it might be passed on to the hive fleet. And yet now it was presented with a prize far greater, the essence of a primarch. And of course it could not resist.

Ah, my mug runs dry. Who will fill it? Yes, yes, I hear your displeasure, your hissing and name-calling. But you cannot expect me to do Arjac Rockfist justice with a dry throat, can you? Surely you would not deny this old thrall a taste of the Fang's finest? Ah, thank you. Brother Myrikk, I see, pack leader and man of great honour and courage! I salute you, and drink to you. As for the rest of you, learn patience! It is not a virtue given enough mind by the Wolf Priests and their teachings, I see.

Now, where was I? Of course! Arjac and the hunter. You knew, of course, that Arjac and the hunter-beast would clash again. It is not the way of the saga to leave such battles unfinished, so when two mortal enemies fight and both walk away, you can be sure the tale will lead them back to face one another again. I can imagine what you must be anticipating. Blood! Fury! Alien limbs hitting the ground in fountains of gore! The hero Space Wolf atop a mound of the dead, streaked in their blood, his axe clotted with their torn meat, roaring at the sky! I have told a lot of stories like that. They are good stories. Half my mind is a library for such sagas, and no doubt tomorrow I will tell one just like I told another yesterday. But today, the tale I tell is not quite the same. It is very similar. It has plenty of death and bloodshed, as Space Wolves are wont to enjoy in their sagas, and true the enemy is the hated alien and the hero is the valiant Space Wolf, but... ah, well, perhaps it is the same. The longer in fang among you might see something the young whelps do not. We shall see.

Now, Arjac was in the centre of the battlefield. The thralls who had followed in his wake were scattered, diving into cover under the assault of the attack-beasts still pulsing forwards like a tide of flesh from the sea. Arjac would surely fall, for he was alone and the xenos could send more and more alien killers at him until he was overwhelmed. If it came to that, they could crush him under the weight of their dead, for the tyranid cares not for the lives of its organisms as it will merely harvest their biomass again once they have won the field.

Arjac knew this, and yet he did not falter, he did not seek cover or head back to the Fang, to be saved by the protection of its stone walls. The lictor, his nemesis that he had sworn and failed to slay, fixed its many eyes on him, and trumpeted its lust for the primarch's gene-seed as its mount trampled its own kind to get to it. Indeed, it was as powerful a lure for the tyranid as Arjac could have used. The hunter-beast had first come to the Fang following the faintest traces of the gene-seed's scent and it was so sensitive to the signature that its senses were overwhelmed, all instincts subsumed by the need to acquire this prize.

'The pain of my brothers,' cried out Arjac, though he cared not if the lictor could understand him, 'the shame of my Chapter's loss, the deceit of a thousand years lying in wait and the blasphemy of your quest to take the blood of Russ's sons and make it your own! All these things I shall repay!'

The beast as a whole was immense, its mass approaching that of the bio-titans such as those recorded on the fields of Ichar IV. Even against the walls of the Fang it would be a formidable weapon, and keeping it from breaching the fortress was by no means a certainty for the Space Wolves on the battlements. Now it was a hunter, bearing down on a single quarry, but in form it was a living siege weapon, a breaching tower, that could bore through the walls and make way for thousands of attack-beasts. And most surely it would kill Arjac Rockfist, and end the resistance of all on the Forge Hills.

Brother Svalin saw the titanic beast and the lictor riding it bearing down on Arjac and a thought occurred to him, in some ways ridiculous but in others so completely logical and typical of Arjac's ways that it had to be the case. Svalin left his post, leaving Brother Vidfinn behind, and ran in to the interior of the Fang. Such was the fixation on Arjac's fate that no Space Wolf saw him go, save for Lord Hengis who noted Svalin's flight from the battlements with anger. Surely he was minded to deal with Svalin when the battle was done, if indeed it was won and the Fang did not fall to the beast.

'Everything,' bellowed Arjac as the beast's shadow passed over him, 'I repay!'

The great maw of the general-beast opened wide. The lictor leered down from above, maw-tendrils quivering as perhaps it anticipated the taste of Arjac's corpse transmitted through the connections that bound it to the general. Arjac did nought but stoppered again the vial of Russ's blood. Then the beast's mouth closed over Arjac Rockfist.

Arjac had no chance to fight. He might as well have battled the void of space or the pull of a planet's gravity. He was simply gone, vanished into the tunnel of the beast's gullet, where churned an ocean of bilious acid and countless lesser creatures to devour and dissolve him.

The hush on the battlements, a moment before of anticipation, was now the dead silence of grief. Arjac Rockfist was dead.

The fire has gone cold. You may not feel the chill but these old bones do.

How the lofty halls of the Fang let in a draught! Ah, but I see, a few embers are glowing still. Pause a moment while I rake them over.

There, that is better. A little warmth now, for I have lost track of time and outside the walls the sun has set and the night birds are wheeling about the aeries, looking for prey.

Thane Darskaan fell, for a tyranid 'gaunt, all talons and swift speed, rushed at him from behind and cut a deep gash across his back. It cut through sinew and lung and he fell to his knees. He hammered fire into the beast at point-blank range, but as it fell he surely knew his wound was a mortal one. He looked up, but the sun was blotted out by the clouds of spores and by the towering form of the beast that had swallowed Arjac whole.

The beast swayed, its mouth lolling open. A torrent of gore and broken bodies spilled forth. A front leg buckled and its head slammed into the snowy earth beside the Heart Forge. Then its body toppled to the side, landing with the force of an avalanche as all strength left it.

Thane Darskaan died then, but with a smile on his face, for a victory had been won and the beast was slain.

Within the Fang, Brother Svalin of Pack Fornjot reached the trophy hall where countless prizes won from the Chapter's defeated foes were displayed. There he ran to one trophy in particular, one he recalled seeing before and which he knew was close to the tyranid exoskeleton that Arjac had used in his study of the lictor.

The thought that had occurred to him regarded the wargear captured from a spy who had entered the Fang some centuries before to slay the then Great Wolf by stealth and treachery – an Imperial Assassin of the Venenum Temple, a master poisoner who had been caught in his endeavour and rent asunder by the Wolf Lord's fury. What force of the Imperium had sought to slay the Wolf Lord was never known, but the Assassin's death and displaying of his wargear was enough, it seems, to have dissuaded further killers from being sent to the Fang.

Svalin found this wargear and looked through it, scattering the synskin suit and the many concealed weapons and instruments of death on the floor in his search. Brother Vidfinn appeared in the doorway of the trophy room, confusion on his face.

'What are you doing, Svalin?' he demanded. 'Have you lost your mind? You are too strong a soul, too old and steadfast, to go mad with grief.'

'It is not madness that brought me here,' replied Svalin. 'No, I have proven that to myself for the poison vial is not here!'

'The poison vial?'

'Indeed, brother. The receptacle of poison with which the Assassin, whose gear this is, sought to poison the Great Wolf all those years ago. It was displayed proudly here to show we fear no weapon, even that of subterfuge and treachery, but now it is gone!'

'Then who took it?' said Vidfinn. 'And why does it matter?'

'Arjac took it,' said Svalin. 'And it matters because it is the only way for him to fell the beast.'

The two returned to the battlements and they saw that the general-beast had fallen. And Svalin wept, for he knew now what Arjac had done. He had taken the Venenum Assassin's poison, and then used the blood of Leman Russ to lure forth the beast and let it swallow him alive. The poison was thereby transferred to the beast, and it had fallen thereby. And now the Kraken spawn were in disarray, allowing the pockets of thrall survivors to regroup and hold the forges.

The lictor was bound to the general-beast, their nervous systems one, so it could direct the monstrosity and transmit through it the hive mind's will. Through those connections had also coursed the poison. Still clinging to the back of the fallen beast the lictor spasmed out its last moments, its muscles and tendons dissolving, torrents of foul gore spilling from between the joints of its armour. The claws that had killed Anvakyr, Fornjot, Dvarnn and Brokkyr hung limp and useless, and the jaws that had rent their flesh yawed open as the blood dribbled from its mandibles. Thus the hunter died, a weakened and pathetic thing, robbed of the Kraken spawn's fury. I can only hope it felt whatever in a tyranid passes for despair as its body dissolved from within and it came apart in an upwelling of foulness and gore.

With its death the hive mind was silent and the tyranids heard it not, and no more were directed in their assault but now fell to the behaviour of animals.

In the sky above, bright streaks of fire appeared, burning through the spore clouds. They were the trails of drop pods, falling from Fenris's orbit.

'The Great Wolf has arrived!' one battle-brother cried. 'Logan Grimnar has reached Fenris!'

'Iron Priest Hengis Blackhand!' came a transmission from the Great Wolf himself, who was even at that moment hurtling towards the ground in his pod. 'What is this I see? A xenos army in disarray, ripe for the killing, and yet you crouch behind the battlements for shelter? For shame, son of Fenris! Bring forth the axe and the fury, bring battle to the foe! For though I am happy to drive them back alone, yet we should fight side by side. So leave the safety of the Fang and join me in the slaughter!'

The whole Great Company of Logan Grimnar descended onto the battlefield, for the Great Wolf, like Lord Hengis, had been foiled by the warp storm and turned back to Fenris. He arrived too late to face the Kraken as they emerged, but made landfall in that moment when the alien horde was at its weakest.

'Onward, brothers!' yelled Lord Hengis. 'Thralls, throw open the doors! Space Wolves, onward! Bring axe and chainblade, bolter and flamer! Bring the pride of Fenris! Bring hatred and rage, brothers! Bring victory!'

Perhaps Lord Hengis's words rang hollow among the Space Wolves who had witnessed Arjac and the fall of the beast. But they showed it not in their conduct in battle, rushing from the Fang to do bloody work upon the hated tyranid! Logan Grimnar and his men landed in the heart of the throng, their drop pods splitting open and a hundred Space Wolves leaping out.

Only the final lord of the Kraken spawn, the malefactor with its mighty bone claws, gave any cohesion to the horde. About it the attack-beasts formed up and charged in waves, regrouping and charging again. But it was alone, and for once the number of the horde grew thin, for the attack-beasts charged now into the massed guns of two Great Companies' worth and were withered away.

Logan Grimnar himself charged at the Kraken spawn lord and shattered one of its claws with his frost blade, rolling out from beneath the second claw before it came crashing down on top of him. Indeed, it was glorious to see him bring up his blade and drive it through the beast over and over again until he stood knee-deep in its gore and the last of its life pumped out onto the ground.

Great was the righteous slaughter! Unlovely were the screeches of the alien doomed, foul was the stink of their burned and riven bodies! The sea was black with their blood, the surf a foul purple, the sky overcast with a green-black pall. The fires of the forges leapt high, fed by the heaps of xenos corpses. The survivors of the Forge Hills thralls, who would surely have been slain to a man without Arjac Rockfist, exacted their own bloody vengeance on the alien with bayonet and autogun, executing the squealing remnants of the horde that remained when the Space Wolves had butchered their path through the army's heart.

The Great Wolf Logan Grimnar sought out Hengis Blackhand. Lord Hengis had fought mightily, but he raged still, finding no happiness in the execution of his enemies which had theretofore brought him such great joy. Scowling he lopped the head off a 'gaunt with his axe, even as Grimnar found him and clapped him on the shoulder.

'Great is the day!' said Logan Grimnar. 'The enemy has been thrown back from our walls, and if a single one of these tentacled heathens lives to writhe back into the sea then they have been fortunate indeed. But tell me, Hengis, where is Arjac Rockfist? Though this frost blade has served me well, yet I long to take the Axe Morkai in my hand once more!'

'Arjac Rockfist is dead,' said Hengis Blackhand. 'And the Axe Morkai is shattered, its blade broken and never to be reforged.' And Lord Hengis spoke unto Logan Grimnar all the sorry tale of what had happened at the Fang since the Chapter left for the Calunian Crusade, the loss of Pack Fornjot's battle-brothers, the gambit at the gene-seed vault and the depravity of the alien hunter who had brought the Kraken spawn army from the sea.

The Great Wolf was much stricken with sorrow. Without a word of reply to Hengis's tale, Grimnar strode across the battlefield to where the immense corpse of the horde's general lay steaming in the chill. The blood poured out of it was freezing into a great purplish slick and the carrion-birds of the mountain peaks were already descending, tasting its corrupting flesh, and wheeling away in scorn of its foulness.

Grimnar clambered on top of the corpse. The Space Wolves looked on, none willing to disturb the Great Wolf in his obvious grief. Grimnar plunged his frost blade into the corpse and, with a mighty swing of his sword arm, slit open the body. The Great Wolf strode into the wound there opened, sinking first to the knee, then to the waist, in the foul and noisome entrails of that unnatural beast.

For a long while the Great Wolf was gone, somewhere inside the corpse of the beast. The battle-brothers looked on first with reverence, then with concern. But eventually the corpse stirred and the head was hacked open from within, the beast's mandibles sheared away by blows of the Great Wolf's frost blade. And from the sundered head strode the Great Wolf, covered in gore and bilious filth, and on his shoulder he carried the body of Arjac Rockfist.

Grimnar laid the body out on the bloodstained snow, and wiped the filth from Arjac's acid-blistered face. He looked up at the Space Wolves watching around him.

'Why do you look on?' he shouted at them. 'Where is a Wolf Priest? Here lies a brother stricken, and he must be helped!'

The Space Wolves who had seen Arjac swallowed whole knew he was dead. Those who had seen only the aftermath had taken one look at the fallen beast, and known that only by mortal sacrifice could a single man, even a Space Wolf, have laid it low. Perhaps they thought the Great Wolf was showing some weakness for the first time in his service to the Chapter, that in some strange wrench of grief he had lost his mind and saw life where there was none. But they dared not defy an order from the Great Wolf's own mouth, and so a Wolf Priest ran to Arjac's side and those battle-brothers versed in the apothecarion's arts joined him.

'By the twin suns of Fenris!' cried one. 'One heart yet beats!'

'The eye's pupil recoils at the light!' said another.

'See!' shouted a third. 'He draws breath!'

'Then bring him to the apothecarion!' ordered the Great Wolf. 'Why do you gawp and delay? Faugh! I will carry him myself, then. With me, brothers!'

Logan Grimnar, the Great Wolf, bore Arjac Rockfist into the Fang, and to the apothecarion. With disbelief the battle-brothers looked upon the scene as Arjac was hooked up to the monitoring devices, and there indeed leapt a spark of light along with his heartbeat. It was as if they witnessed a miracle to see his chest rise and fall when his bile-scarred armour was unbolted.

Logan Grimnar knew something that the other Space Wolves did not. A mighty warrior he might be, but that alone is not what makes a great man into a legend such as the Great Wolf. It is his wisdom that makes him who he is, that causes every Space Wolf to bow in deference to his command, that makes even kings and mighty lords of the Imperium give pause to vent their arrogance when he is present. What Logan Grimnar knew then, you too can see. Simply turn around.

There, at the back of the hall, in the shadows, beneath the banner of Lykki Clovenhelm. Do you see him? You did not see him when he came in, for it was a particularly bloody and battle-filled part of my tale when you were all rapt waiting for the next gory detail. No, you did not notice him, even though he outstrips many of you by a full head in height, even though in the Terminator armour he earned of late he weighs as much as a fully laden thunderwolf.

There sits Arjac Rockfist, in silent deference to the role of the story-teller. I have no doubt he knew not I was telling his tale, and that he would avoid hearing it if such were possible. But he could not leave during its telling, for to do so would be an insult to the teller of tales, and unlike some of you he respects that ancient Fenrisian office, honoured as it was by Leman Russ in the Chapter's earliest days. You can see now what Logan Grimnar saw.

You can see the humility of Arjac Rockfist. Did I not tell you he was humble? And did you not forget that detail as soon as it left my tongue, for you care only to hear of strength and rage and battle-prowess? But Logan Grimnar was wiser than you are, and he remembered. He knew that Arjac Rockfist did not trumpet his greatness at every opportunity, that he kept it quiet and was silent when his battle-brothers would crow for hours about the sagas they had carved on the bones of their enemies. Logan Grimnar, unlike perhaps Lord Hengis, remembered the great strength and mighty constitution of Arjac Rockfist. He remembered that Arjac was lost in a terrible blizzard during his Blooding, alone and all but naked, and that he survived the terrible chill when any other would have perished. If any of you had done that you would remind us of it at every turn, but not Arjac. But Logan Grimnar remembered regardless.

Arjac had survived the sting of the psychneuein wasp. He had contracted the Vileheart Pox, concocted by the witches of the Plague God, and had defeated the disease. He had not mentioned ever again such great feats of resilience, but Grimnar remembered. And so when the Great Wolf heard that Arjac had poisoned himself to in turn infect the hunter-beast with the Venenum's lethal potion, he knew better than to assume, as all others did, that Arjac Rockfist was dead.

That humility you can see in Arjac Rockfist now. Such it is that I am ashamed to bring your attention to him, for though he would never say it I feel he would dearly love for this story to end so he did not have to suffer the hearing of it any more.

There is on Rockfist's palm a scar, deep and livid, that has never healed. Ask him how he received it and he will tell you it was inflicted during the battle of the Forge Hills, and say no more of it. But the truth of it is that when he was lain out in the apothecarion, and his armour was removed, the apothecaries found that his hand was still clutched around something. They could not loosen his grip so they had to take his gauntlet off segment by segment. When it was done, it was revealed that he was clutching a shard of metal – the missing piece of the Axe Morkai's blade, the one that had been lost, lodged in the body of the lictor.

Arjac had climbed through the guts of the general and torn it from within the lictor in its bony cradle, before the poison and the forces of the beast's digestion had rendered him unconscious. He had clutched it so tight that it had cut deep into his palm, and such was its keenness that the wound has never fully closed.

And in his other hand he held the vial of Leman Russ's blood, intact. The Wolf Priests took it and restored it to the Chapter vaults, where it lies to this day, a great relic of our Chapter's past. As for his own weapon, the blacksmith's hammer, that was found in the remains of the beast's corpse and Arjac wielded it from then on, adapting it himself upon the Voidstone Anvil and using it in place of the relics offered to him from the armoury.

Those of you who have seen the Great Wolf in battle will know well the final detail I have to make right. The Axe Morkai was shattered, but its pieces were now recovered. Arjac Rockfist, when he awoke on the apothecarion slab, asked firstly who had fallen in the battle, and secondly that he be given leave to return to the Heart Forge and help rebuild it so he could once more forge the Axe Morkai. The Axe Morkai is the axe that rarely leaves the hand of Logan Grimnar, and in his employ it is an echo of Leman Russ's own fury.

Now the fire has died completely, but it is of no matter. The night's chill has retreated, and I feel the rays of dawn must have broken over the mountains. It is thanks to Arjac Rockfist, though he would never admit it, that the sun shines down through ice-clear skies and not dimly through clouds of spore and venom. For the Fang stands, never breached again by the Kraken spawn. They failed at the battle of the Forge Hills and they have never returned, though the lookouts have watched the ocean ever since.

You Space Wolves may not need to sleep as mere men do, but I am a mere man and the long night has put an ache in my bones. I would sleep, after I finish this last mug. I must bid you good night and good day, and retreat to my lodgings down in the humble lower levels where once a terrible predator hunted us thralls.

And pray you, brothers, ask not Arjac Rockfist about the tale I have told. Part of the reason I have told it to you is that you might know the tale of those days and will not have to question Arjac about the acid scars on the seaward wall of the Fang, the memorials to the fallen thralls in the Forge Hills, and the blacksmith's hammer, much altered and enhanced, he now carries into battle.

There are other reasons I have told you the saga of Arjac Rockfist. You will have to work those out for yourselves. For now, my mug is dry and I would sleep. Feast now, tell your own tales of battle and heroism. But remember, boast not too much of your exploits, for perhaps the greatest hero among you has no need to boast of anything.

TWELVE WOLVES

Ben Counter

Why is it Arjac Rockfist that speaks to you now? You are used to the Wolf Priests sitting here in the saga teller's place, or perhaps one of the thralls who keeps the many tales of the Fang to be recounted on the longest Fenrisian night. And true enough, I speak rarely enough, for our Wolf Lords are masters of war and I will only offer them my counsel if they seek it out. But those same Wolf Lords bade me take my place here before you, for they would have you listen to others you would not.

For good or ill, with justice or not, I am ascribed a weight of authority among you young ones. I cannot say I have sought it, nor that I believe it really exists, but perhaps the great size for which I am inevitably famed gives my words greater weight. The Terminator armour of a Wolf Guard, such as I wear, itself lends me the gravity of its age and bulk. Whatever the case, there is a tale that would be told to the Blood Claws among you, and it is a tale that must be understood. You are less likely, I am told, to squabble and heckle if I am the teller. True or not, here I sit, as I am bidden.

I hear you now, throaty and raucous, demanding to hear a saga of some great battle or feat of arms that will fill your hearts with fire. Lord Russ fighting the One-Eyed traitor, you cry! The many crimes of the Dark Angels, you demand, so that we might feast and drink and remember our grudges! But my purpose here is not to serve this feasting throng with whatever bloody tale they desire. No, I have gathered you by this roaring fire, in the Great Hall of the Fang where generations of Space Wolves have celebrated their victories and toasted their dead, because there is a lesson I have to impart.

You forget I can hear your sighs! I have the same predator's senses as you. What use, you whisper, is a saga not dripping with the blood of foes and thundering with the sound of chainblade on heretic flesh? Arjac Rockfist is not such a fool that he thinks he can keep the attention of wayward pups like you with a tale free of bloodshed and glory. My tale is from the Wolf Priests themselves, the guardians of your spirits, and they know better than to impart lessons that will not be heeded.

* * *

It is in a great battle of the past, then, that my tale takes place. Those attentive young wolves will know of the Age of Apostasy, one of the direst lessons that mankind has ever had to learn, during which the corrupt clergy of the Imperial Creed sought to seize power for themselves. It is a long and grim story in its own right that I will not tell here. Suffice it to say that it was a time of blindness, fear and chaos, when the Imperium of Man sought to crumble in a way not threatened since the dark times of Horus. Among the many tales of sorrow in this time, I speak of the Plague of Unbelief, when a wicked man named Cardinal Bucharis carved out an empire of his own, throwing off Imperial authority to rule as a king!

Bucharis, while a bold and cunning man, was a fool. For as his empire grew, conquered by renegades of the Imperial Guard and armies of mercenary cutthroats, he came to the threshold of Fenris. Arrogant in the extreme, Bucharis did not halt there and turn back, afeared of the Space Wolves who called it their home then as we do now. No, he sent his armies to Fenris, to conquer its savage peoples and force the Space Wolves to cede their world to him!

Ah, yes, you laugh. Who could have thought that an Apostate Cardinal and a host of mere men could defeat the Space Wolves on their home world? But it happened that at this time very few Space Wolves were at the Fang, with most of them having joined the Wolf Lord Kyrl Grimblood on a crusade elsewhere in the galaxy. The Space Wolves left there to face Bucharis's villains numbered little more than a single Great Company, along with the newly-blooded novices and the thralls who dwell within the Fang. Bucharis, meanwhile, bled the garrisons of his empire white to flood Fenris with soldiers and lay siege to the Fang. Do not think that the Fang was impregnable to them! Any fortress, even this ancient and formidable mountain hold, can fall.

In the third month of this siege two Space Wolves were abroad in the valleys and foothills around the Fang. They were patrolling to disrupt and observe the enemy forces, as the sons of Fenris were wont to do at that time in the battle. One of them, and his name was Daegalan, was a Long Fang such as those battered, leather-coloured brothers who watch us even now from the back of the hall. They have heard this tale many times, but take note, young Blood Claws and novices, that they still listen, for they understand its lesson well. The other was much like you. His name was Hrothgar, and he was a Blood Claw as most of you are. Daegalan was wise and stern, and had taken Hrothgar as a student to teach him the ways of war that, with the Fang and the Chapter in great peril, he had to learn very quickly.

Imagine a mountain ridge at night, bare flint as sharp as knives clad in ice that glinted under the many stars and moons of the Crone Fenris. It overlooked a wide, rocky valley, cleared of snow by tanks and shored up by engineers, like a black serpent winding between the flinty blades of the Fang's foothills. Now you are there, the story can begin.

Two Astartes made their way up to the lip of this ridge. One of them wore a wolf skin cloak about his shoulders, and across his back was slung a missile launcher. This was Daegalan. His face was like a mask of tanned leather, so deeply lined it might have been carved with a knife, his grey-streaked hair whipping around his head in the night's chill wind. He wore on his shoulder pad the symbol of Wolf Lord Hef Icenheart, who at that time was directing the defence of the Fang from its granite halls. The other, with the red slash marks painted on his shoulder pad, was Hrothgar. The scars, where the organs of an Astartes were implanted, were still red on his shaven scalp. His chainsword was in his hand, for it rarely left, and his armour was unadorned with markings of past campaigns.

'See, young cub,' said Daegalan. 'This is the place where our enemy creeps, like vermin, thinking he is hidden from our eyes. Look down, and tell me what you see.'

Hrothgar looked over the edge of the ridge into the valley. The night's darkness was no hindrance to the eyes of an Astartes. He saw a track laid along the bottom of the valley, along which could be wheeled the huge siege guns and war machines which Bucharis's armies hoped would shake the sides of the Fang and bring its defences down. Slave labour on the worlds the Cardinal had captured had created countless such machines and they filled the bellies of spacecraft supplying his war on Fenris. Indeed, it was the mission of the two Astartes to locate and disrupt the bringing of these war machines to a location where they could fire on the Fang.

Many Guardsmen, from the renegade Rigellian regiments who had thrown their lot in with Bucharis, guarded the tracks, knowing that soon the precious war machines would come trundling along it.

'I count twenty of the enemy,' said Hrothgar. 'Imperial Guard all, they are reasonably trained – not the equal of a Space Wolf, of course, but dangerous if they can fire upon us in great numbers. See, Long Fang, they have assembled defences of flak-weave and ammunition crates, and they seem ready for an attack by such as us. They know the importance of their mission.'

'Good,' said Daegalan, 'for a first glance. But our task here is to destroy these enemies. What can you see that will ensure they fall?'

'This one, 'said Hrothgar, 'is the officer that leads them. See the medals and badges of rank on his uniform? That silver skull on his chest is granted by the heretic Cardinal to followers who show great ruthlessness in leading the troops. Upon one sleeve are the marks of his rank. In his hand is a map case, surely marking out the route of these tracks. This man must die first, for with their leader dead, the others will fall into disarray.'

Daegalan smiled at this, and showed the grand canine teeth that are the mark of a true Long Fang. May you who listen to this one day sport such fangs as these, sharp and white, to tell the tale of your years spent fighting with the Sons of Russ! 'Young Blood Claw,' said Daegalan, 'can it be that

even with the eyes of an Astartes you are so blind? You must learn the lessons of the Twelve Wolves of Fenris, those great beasts who even now hunt
through the mountains and snowy plains of our world. Each wolf is taken
as the totem of one of our Great Companies, and for good reason.' Daegalan here tapped the symbol of his Great Company on his shoulder pad. 'I
wear the symbol of Wolf Lord Iceheart. He took as his totem Torvald the
Far-Sighted, the wolf whose eyes miss nothing. This wolf of Fenris teaches
us to observe our enemy, much as we would love to get our claws around
his throat first, for it is in looking ahead that the victory can sometimes be
won before a blow is struck.

'Look again. The man you see is indeed an officer, and no doubt a ruthless one at that. But there is another. There, seated on an ammunition
crate, his lasgun propped up by his side. See him? He is reading from a
book. Even these old eyes can read its title. It is the *Collected Visions*, a
book written by the Apostate Cardinal himself, serving as a collection of
his madness and heresies. Only the most devout of his followers, when the
night is this cold and the mission is this crucial, would read it so earnestly.
This man may not be the officer who leads these soldiers on paper, but he
leads them in reality. He is their spiritual heart, the one to whom they turn
for true leadership. This man must die first, for when it is shown that the
most devout of them is no more than meat and bone beneath our claws,
then all their hope shall flee them.'

Hrothgar thought upon this, and he saw the truth in the Long Fang's
words.

'Then let us fight,' said the Blood Claw. 'The reader of books shall die
first, beneath these very hands!'

'Alas, I have but two missiles left,' said Daegalan, 'otherwise I would sow
fire and death among them from up here. I shall fight alongside you, then.
When you tear the heart from them, I shall slay the rest, including that
officer to whom you paid so much attention.'

With this Hrothgar vaulted down from the ridge and crashed with a snarl
into the heart of the enemy. He charged for the spiritual leader, and was
upon him before the other Guardsmen had even raised their lasguns! At
that time the Space Wolves were sorely lacking of ammunition for their
guns and power packs for their chainswords, and so it was with his hands
that Hrothgar hauled the reader of books into the air and dashed his brains
out against the rocks.

'He is dead!' came the cry from the Guardsmen. 'He who assured us the
divine Cardinal would deliver us, he whose survival proved to us the sure-
ness of our victory! He is dead!' And they wailed in much terror.

Daegalan was among them now. He was not as fast as the Blood Claw,
but he surpassed him in strength and cunning. He fought with his knife,
and plunged it up to the hilt in the skull of the first Guardsman who faced
him. Another died, head cracked open by the swinging of his fist, and then

another, speared through the midriff. The officer, who was shouting and trying to steel the hearts of his men, fell next, knocked to the ground and crushed beneath Daegalan's armour-shod feet.

It was in but the space of a few heartbeats, as a non-Astartes might reckon it, that the enemy were torn asunder and scattered. Those that were not dead cursed their fates and fled into the snowy wilderness, eager to face the teeth and claws of the Crone Fenris rather than spend another moment in that blood-spattered valley.

The hot breath of the two Astartes was white in the cold as they panted like predators sated from the hunt. But this hunt was not finished. For from down the tracks came the sound of steel feet on the rocks, and the roaring voice of an engine. And before the Astartes could ready themselves, from the frozen darkness lumbered a Sentinel walker.

Many of you have seen such a thing, and perhaps even fought alongside them, for they are commonly used by the armies of the Imperial Guard. This, however, was different. Its two legs were reinforced with sturdy armour plates and its cab, in which its traitor driver cowered, was as heavily plated as a tank. It had been made with techniques forgotten to the masters of the forge worlds today, and it bore as its weapon a pair of autocannon. This was no mere spindly scouting machine! This was an engine of destruction.

'Despair not!' shouted the headstrong Hrothgar as this monster came into view. 'You shall not have to face this machine, old man, wizened and decrepit as you are! I shall ensure this traitor's eyes are on me alone. All you need do, venerable one, is fire that missile launcher of yours!'

Daegalan had it in mind to scold the Blood Claw for his insolence, but it was not the time for such things.

Hrothgar ran into view of the Sentinel. He fired off shots from his bolt pistol, and the Sentinel turned to hunt him through the valley's shadows. But Hrothgar was fast and valiant, and even as the Sentinel's mighty guns opened fire he sprinted from rock to rock, from flinty fissure to deep shadow, and every shell spat by the Sentinel's guns was wasted against unyielding stone. At that time it happened a flurry of snow was blown up by Fenris's icy breath and Hrothgar ventured closer still, diving between the metal feet of the Sentinel, knowing that he was too fast and his movements too unpredictable for the machine's pilot to fire upon him with accuracy.

So infuriated was the pilot of the Sentinel that he forgot, as lesser soldiers than Astartes are wont to do, the true threat he was facing. For Daegalan the Long Fang had indeed taken aim with his missile launcher, the only weapon the Astartes had between them that might pierce the machine's armour. With a roar the missile fired, and with a vicious bark it exploded. The rear of the Sentinel was torn clear away, and the pilot mortally wounded. Exposed to the cold night, the blood from his many wounds froze. But he did not have long to suffer this fate, for Hrothgar the Blood Claw climbed up the legs of the Sentinel and tore out the traitor's spine with his bare hands.

'You may think,' said Daegalan, 'to have angered this old Long Fang with your insolence, but in truth you have expounded the lesson of another of Fenris's wolves – or rather, two of them, for they are Freki and Geri, the Twin Wolves who were companions of Leman Russ himself. See how this enemy, a match for both of us, was destroyed by the fruits of our brotherhood! When wolves fight as a pack, as one, they slay foes that would confound them if they merely attacked as individuals. You have learned well, though you did not know it, the lesson of the Twin Wolves!'

With that, the two Astartes set about destroying the tracks, and for many days as a result the walls of the Fang were spared the bombardment of Bucharis's war machines, and the lives of many Space Wolves were surely spared.

Now, it was about this time that the Apostate Cardinal, accursed Bucharis himself, was upon Fenris directing the siege of the Fang. You already know that he was a man possessed of great arrogance and blindness to the rage he inflamed in those who suffered under his conquest. He was also a wrathful man, much given to extravagant punishments and feats of cruelty when angered. Having heard from a subordinate that his war machines (which he expected to shatter the Fang and slay all those within) would be delayed by the actions of the Astartes, he flew into a rage. He supposed that a great host of Space Wolves had done this deed, and that with their destruction the defenders of the Fang would be greatly weakened in number. A foolish man, I hear you cry! Indeed he was, but he was also a very dangerous man, whose foolishness lay not in an inability to achieve his goals but in ignorance of the consequences his cruelty would have. You know, of course, that Bucharis was eventually to meet an end as befits a man like him, but that is a story for another time.

Many units of the Imperial Guard were sent to punish the host of Astartes that Bucharis believed to be abroad in the foothills of the Fang. They were men picked by Bucharis's warmaster, the renegade Colonel Gasto, from the regiments of Rigellians he commanded. They had been well versed in the beliefs of Bucharis, which were heretical in the extreme and shall not be spoken of by this humble tongue. They believed Bucharis's lies that the Imperium had fallen and that only by obeying Bucharis could they hope to survive its collapse. Gasto gave them tanks and heavy weapons, and the kind of murderous cutthroat mercenaries that Bucharis had swayed to his cause to lead them.

These men and machines left the great siege encampment of the Rigellian Guard and headed for the Fang, ordered on pain of death to destroy the Astartes.

Meanwhile, Daegalan the Long Fang and Hrothgar the Blood Claw were making their way back to the Fang, for their mission was completed.

Though it was now daylight a storm had fallen over the area and Fenris was breathing ice across the flinty hills. Terrible gales blew and showers of ice fell like daggers.

'Remember,' said Daegalan as he led Hrothgar up the slippery slope of a barren hill, 'that cruel weather such as this makes every blasted and inhospitable place the domain of Haegr, the Mountain Wolf. For he endures all, indeed, he thrives in such inhospitable climes. It is to him that we must look, for is it not so that the physical endurance of an Astartes is a weapon in itself, and that by taking this hazardous path we make better time towards the Fang and further confound our enemies?'

Hrothgar did not answer this, for while he was young and vigorous, the Long Fang was so much inured to hardships and gnarled by Fenris's icy winds that the old Astartes did not feel the cold as much as the Blood Claw. But he did indeed recall the Mountain Wolf and, knowing that the sons of Fenris are made of stern stuff, he shrugged off his discomfort and the two made good speed over the hills.

It was at the pinnacle of the next hill that a break in the storm gave them a glimpse of the Fang. It was the first time they had seen it in many days. Daegalan bade his companion to stop, and look for a moment upon the Fang itself.

'This tooth of ice and stone, this spear piercing the white sky, does this not fill your heart with gladness, young Blood Claw?'

'Indeed,' said Hrothgar, 'I am now struck by the majesty of it. It gladdens me to think of the despair our foes must suffer when they see it, for those are the slopes they must climb! Those are the walls they must breach!' And all of you have looked on the Fang and imagined how any foe might hope to silence the guns that stud its sides or climb the sheer slopes that guard its doors more surely than any army.

'Then you feel,' said Daegalan, 'the howl of Thengir in your veins! For he is the King Wolf, the monarch of Fenris, and everything under his domain is alight with glory and majesty. So you see, ignorant and insolent young cub, that another of Fenris's wolves has a lesson to teach us today.'

Hrothgar did indeed hear Thengir, like a distant howl, speaking of the kingly aspect of the Fang as it rules over all the mountains of Fenris.

'And mark also the Wolf Who Stalks Between Stars,' continued Daegalan, 'as you look above the Fang to the moons that hang in the sky. The Stalker Between Stars was the totem of Leman Russ himself, and even now his symbol adorns the Great Wolf's own pack. Our pawprints may be found even on distant worlds and the farthest-flung corners of the Imperium. So long as we, like that wolf, hunt abroad among the stars, then Fenris is not merely the ground beneath our feet but also any place where the Sons of Fenris have trod, where the Space Wolves have brought fang and fire to their enemies!'

Hrothgar's hearts swelled with pride as he thought of the mark the Space

Wolves had left upon the galaxy beyond Fenris. But the Astartes could not tarry for long, and quickly made their way on.

Soon Daegalan saw the white tongues of engine exhausts nearby, and knew that the traitor Guard were close. He led Hrothgar into a winding valley, deep and dark even when the sun broke through the blizzards. Many such valleys lead through the foothills of the Fang, chill and black, and within their depths lurk many of the most deadly things with which Mother Fenris has populated her world.

'I can tell,' said Daegalan after some time, 'your frustration, young Blood Claw. You wish to get to grips with the foe and cover your armour with their blood! But remember, if you will, that another wolf stalks beside us. Ranek, the Hidden Wolf, goes everywhere unseen, silent and cunning. In just such a way do we also stalk unseen. Do not scorn the Hidden Wolf, young one! For his claws are as sharp as any other, and when he strikes from the shadows the wound is doubly deep!'

Hrothgar was a little consoled by this as he listened to the engines of the enemy's tanks and the voices of the soldiers raised as they called to one another. They could not traverse the foothills of the Fang as surely as a Space Wolf, and many of them were lost as they stumbled into gorges or fell through thin ice. Driven by their fear of Bucharis they made good time but paid for it in lives, and with every step the force became more ragged. Hrothgar imagined slaying them as he emerged from hiding, and he smiled.

'Now you think of killing them by the dozen,' continued Daegalan, for he never passed by the opportunity to instruct a younger Astartes. 'But ask yourself, in this butchery you imagine, is there any place for me, your battle-brother? You need not reply, for of course there is not. I do not admonish you this, Blood Claw. Quite the opposite, I commend you to the spirit of Lokyar, the Lone Wolf. While the Twin Wolves teach us of brotherhood, Lokyar reminds us that sometimes we must fight alone. He is the totem of our Wolf Scouts, those solitary killers, and now he may be your totem, too, for it is Lokyar whose path you tread as you imagine yourself diving into our enemy alone.'

Now our two Astartes came to the head of the valley, where it reached the surface. They espied before them fearsome barricades set up by the traitor Guard, the bayonets of the heretics glinting in the sun that now broke through the storm clouds. Dozens of them were waiting for the Astartes, and they were trembling for they believed that a host of Astartes would stream from the black valley.

'Ah, may we give thanks to Mother Fenris,' said Hrothgar the Blood Claw, 'for she has guided our friends to meet us! What a grand reunion this shall be! I shall embrace our friends with these bloody hands and I shall give them all gifts of a happy death!'

'Now I see the battle favours the youthful and the heedless of danger,' said Daegalan in reply, 'and is content to leave the old and cunning behind.

Go, Brother Hrothgar! Bestow upon them the welcome your young wolf's heart lusts for! And remember the Iron Wolf, too, for he watches over the artificers of our Chapter forge wherein your armour was smelted. Trust in him that your battlegear will turn aside their laser fire and their bullets, and run with him into battle!'

Hrothgar recalled, indeed, the Iron Wolf, whose pelt can turn aside even the teeth of the kraken who haunt the oceans of Fenris. And he ran from the darkness of the valley. The soldiers opened fire as one and bolts of red laser fell around the Blood Claw like a rain of burning blood. But his armour held firm, the Iron Wolf's teachings having guided well the artificers of the Fang.

Ah, how I wish I had the words to describe Hrothgar in that bloody hour! His armour was red to the elbow and the screams of his enemies were like a blizzard gale howling through the mountains. He leapt the barriers the traitors had set up and even as he landed, men were dying around him. He drew his chainsword and its teeth chewed through muscle and bone. One heretic he spitted through the throat, throwing him off with a flick of a wrist, and a heartbeat later a skull was staved in by a strike from his gauntleted fist. He cut them apart and crushed them underfoot. He threw them aside and hurled them against the rocks. He took the lasgun from one and stabbed him through the stomach with his own bayonet. Some traitors even fell to their own laser fire as the men around them fired blindly, seeing in their terror a Space Wolf charging from every shadow.

Daegalan followed Hrothgar into the fray. Some leader amongst the traitors called out for a counterattack and bullied a few men into charging at Hrothgar with their bayonets lowered. Daegalan fell amongst them, his combat knife reaping a terrible toll. He cut arms and heads from bodies, and when he was faced by the officer alone he grabbed the heretic fool with both arms. He crushed the life out of the man, holding him fast in a terrible embrace.

The Guardsmen fled, but Hrothgar was not done. Some he followed behind outcrops of rock where they sought to hide. He hauled them out, as a hunter's hounds might drag an unwilling prey from a burrow, and killed them there on the ground. When they tried to snipe at him from some high vantage point he trusted in his armour to scorn their fire and clambered to meet them, holding them above his head and throwing them down to be dashed to pieces against the rocks below.

When the traitors bled, their blood froze around their wounds, for the Crone Fenris had granted the Space Wolves a day bright yet as cold as any that had ever passed around the Fang. Blood fell like a harvest of frozen rubies. Now Daegalan and Hrothgar rested in the centre of this field of bloody jewels, as bright and plentiful as if our world herself was bleeding. They were exhausted by their killing and they panted like wolves after the kill, their breath white in the cold. They were covered in blood, their faces spattered with it, their pack emblems and Great Company totems almost hidden. Silently, each gave thanks to Fenris herself for the hunt, and even to Cardinal Bucharis for his foolishness and arrogance, for it was he who had sent them such prey.

Above them loomed the Fang, wherein their battle-brothers waited to receive the news of their success. Prey lay dead all around them, and the majesty of Fenris was all about. What more could a Space Wolf ask for? It was indeed a good day, and may you young pups have many such hunts ahead of you.

'Well fought, my brother,' said Daegalan. 'It is well that the Apostate Cardinal stumbled upon Fenris, for without his ill fortune we would not have such hunts upon our very doorstep!'

'He should have a statue in the Hall of Echoes,' agreed Hrothgar. 'Was there ever a man who did more for the glory of the Space Wolves? I think I shall toast him with a barrel of mead when we celebrate this hunt.'

They laughed at that, and it was to this sound that the rumble of engines grew closer and a shadow fell over them. For the mercenaries who led the Guardsmen were hard-bitten and foul-minded men, well versed in the low cunning of war, and they had prepared a trap for the Astartes.

The force the Space Wolves had slaughtered were just the vanguard of the army sent to punish them. Bucharis had sent in his fear ten times that number, sorely stretching the forces that besieged the Fang elsewhere. They had with them tanks: Reaper-class war machines such as can no longer be made by the forge worlds of the Mechanicus. Six of these machines had survived the journey, and they all rumbled into view now, their guns aiming at the place where the two Astartes stood.

The Guardsmen, though sorely pressed by the harsh journey through the foothills, still numbered hundreds, and they had brought many heavy weapons with which to destroy the Astartes from afar – for they feared to face the claws and teeth of the Space Wolves up close, and rightly so. Their leaders, Bucharis's chosen mercenaries, were strong and brutal men who wore pieces of uniform and armour from a dozen places they had plundered, and all wore the scars of war like banners proclaiming their savagery. They, too, were afraid of the Astartes, but they turned their fear into brutality and so the men under them obeyed them out of terror.

One such man addressed the two Space Wolves through the vox-caster of his tank. By the standards of such men, it was a bold thing to do indeed!

'Astartes!' he called to them. 'Noble sons of Fenris! The honoured Lord Bucharis, monarch of his galactic empire, has no quarrel with the Space Wolves. He seeks only to grant protection to those within the fold of his generosity. For the Imperium has fallen, and Terra lies aflame and ruined. Lord Bucharis promises safety and sanity for those who kneel to him!

'But we do not ask you to kneel. How could we, mere men, demand such of the Adeptus Astartes? No, we ask only that Lord Bucharis count Fenris among the worlds of his empire. What do you care for this grim and frozen place, its savage peoples and its bitter oceans? To the Space Wolves, of course, we shall leave the Fang, and the right to rule yourselves, excepting a few minor and quite necessary obeisances to Lord Bucharis's undoubted majesty. So you see, there is no need for you to fight any more. There is nothing left for you to prove. Stand down and place yourselves within our custody, and we shall deliver you safely unto the Fang where you can pass on word of Lord Bucharis's matchless generosity.'

The two Space Wolves, of course, saw through these lies. They knew the Imperium was eternal, and had not fallen, and moreover they believed no more than you do that Bucharis meant anything but destroy the Space Wolves and take the Fang for himself. No doubt he wished to install himself in our great fortress, and to use as his throne room the hall wherein Leman Russ himself once held court! The only answer to such a speech lies at the tip of a wolf's claws, or in the gnashing of his fangs!

'Now, young wolf,' said Daegalan, 'we face our death. How blessed are we that we can look it in the face as it comes for us. And moreover, we die on Fenris, on the ground upon which we were born, and first ran with our packs in the snow. This is the world that forged us into the Space Marines we are, that gave us the strength and ferocity to be accepted into the ranks of the Space Wolves. Now we shall repay that honour by choosing this very ground for our deaths! How blessed are we, Blood Claw, and how blessed am I that it is beside my brother that I die.

'And do not think that we shall die alone. For I hear the snarling of Lakkan, the Runed Wolf, upon the wind. Once Lakkan walked across Fenris, and wise men read the symbols he left in his footprints. These men were the first Rune Priests and those who still follow the path of Lakkan even now watch us from the Fang. They scry out our deeds, and they shall record them, and give thanks as we do that we die a death so fine.'

Daegalan now drew his bolt pistol. He had but a single magazine of bolt shells, for at that time the Sons of Fenris were sorely pressed for ammunition with their fortress besieged. Hrothgar, in turn, drew once more his chainsword. Its teeth were clotted with the frozen blood of traitors, but soon, he knew, he would plunge it into a warm body and thaw out that blood so its teeth could gnash again.

'I do not seek death,' said the Blood Claw, 'as easily as you do, old man.'

'Your saga shall be a fine one,' replied Daegalan, 'though it is short.'

'Perhaps you are right,' said Hrothgar, and in that moment the guns of the tanks were levelled at the place where they stood in the field of blood rubies. 'You are a Long Fang, after all, and wise. But I fear that in all you have taught me you have made a single error.'

'And what might that be, Blood Claw?' said Daegalan. 'What omission have I made that is so grave I must hear of it now, in the moment of my death?'

Now a strange countenance came upon Hrothgar the Blood Claw. His teeth flashed like fangs and his eyes turned into the flinty black orbs of the hunting wolf. 'You have spoken of the wolves of Fenris that follow us and impart to us their lessons. Twelve of them you have described to me, each one mirroring an aspect of Fenris or of the teachings the Wolf Priests have passed down to us. These lessons were well earned, and I thank you for them, Brother Daegalan. But I am wiser than you in but one aspect.'

'Speak of it, you cur!' demanded Daegalan with much impatience, for the guns of the traitor tanks were now aimed at them, awaiting the order to fire, as were the heavy weapons of the Guardsmen.

'I have counted twelve Fenrisian wolves in your teachings, each one taken as the totem of a Great Company of the Space Wolves. But here you are mistaken. For I know that in truth, there are not twelve wolves. There are thirteen.'

It is time, I fear, for this old tongue to lie still. The night draws on. Time stands not still and we shall all have our duties in the hour before dawn to attend to, be they in the sparring-hall or among the forges. So raise a drink, brothers, to Daegalan and his teachings!

Ah, so you wish the story to continue? I have no doubt you foresee great bloodshed of the kind you love to hear. And there was bloodshed after that moment, it is true. Terrible it was, perhaps worse than any that fell upon the face of the Crone Fenris during the besieging of the Fang. But it is not for me to speak of it. I hear you groan, and a few even flash your fangs in anger! But look to the Long Fangs who sit at the back of the hall. Do they growl their displeasure? No, for they know the truth. A Wolf Guard I may be, but it is not my place to speak of what happened in that place. Even the most ancient among the children of Russ, the mighty Dreadnoughts who have marched to war for a thousand years or more, would not speak of it.

There is, however, a legend told among the people of Gathalamor, the world where the Apostate Bucharis first came to prominence. They are a fearful and religious people, for upon them has fallen the burden of redeeming their world from the stain the Apostate left upon it. But sometimes they speak of legends forbidden by the cardinals of their world, and among them is this one, brought back, it is said, by the few survivors of the armies who fought on Fenris.

Once an army was sent by Bucharis to destroy the Space Wolves who had been sowing much death and confusion among the besieging forces. The army cornered their but found, much to their delight, that they faced not a Great Company or even a single pack, but a single Space Wolf.

In some versions of the tale there was not one Space Wolf, but two. The difference matters not.

Now the soldiers drove their tanks into range and took aim at this Space Wolf. And they awaited only the order to open fire, which would surely have been given but a moment later. But then they were struck by a great and monstrous fear, such as rarely enters the hearts even of the most cowardly of men.

The Space Wolf was a Space Wolf no more. In fact, he appeared as nothing that could once have been a man. A bestial countenance overcame him, and the winds howled as if Fenris herself was recoiling in disgust. Talons grew from his fingers. His armour warped and split as his body deformed, shoulders broadening and spine hunching over in the aspect of a beast. The soldiers cried that a daemon had come into their midst, and men fled the sight of it. Even the gunners in their tanks did not think themselves safe from the horror unfolding in front of them.

And then there came the slaughter. The beast charged and butchered men with every stroke of its gory claws. It tore open the hulls of their tanks and ripped out the men inside. In its frenzy it feasted on them, and strips of bloody skin and meat hung from its inhuman fangs. Men went mad with the force of its onslaught. The leaders of that army fired on their own men to keep them from fleeing but the beast fell on them next and the last moments of their life were filled with terror and the agony of claws through their flesh.

The soldiers were thrown to the winds of Fenris and scattered. Some say that none survived, either torn down by the beast or frozen to death as they cowered from it. Others insist that a single man survived to tell the tale, but that he was driven hopelessly mad and the legend of the Beast of Fenris was all that ever escaped his quivering lips.

But this is a tale told by other men, far from the Fang and the proud sons of Fenris who dwell therein, and I shall dwell upon it no more.

Now it came that many days later, when the battle had waxed and waned as battles do, a pack of Grey Hunters ventured forth from the Fang to drive off the traitor Guardsmen who were thought to be encamped in the foothills. There they came across a place like a field of rubies, where frozen blood lay scattered across the snowy rocks with such great abandon that it seemed a great battle had been fought there, though the pack-mates knew of no such battle.

'Look!' cried one Space Wolf. 'Someone yet lives! He is clad in the armour of a Space Wolf and yet he is not one, for see, his bearing is that of an animal and his face bears no trace of the human we all were before becoming Space Marines.'

The pack leader bade his battle-brothers to cover him with their boltguns as he went to see what they had found. As he approached he saw countless bodies torn asunder, many with the marks of teeth in their frozen flesh, and still others dead in the ruins of their tanks.

The figure in the centre of the battlefield indeed wore the power armour of a Space Wolf, but split apart and ruined as if rent from within. He crouched panting in the cold, as if fresh from a hunt. His form was not that of a human, but of a beast.

'He is touched by the Wulfen,' said the pack leader. 'The Thirteenth Wolf of Fenris has walked here, and its inhumanity has found a place to dwell inside this Blood Claw. Some flaw in his gene-seed went unnoticed during his novicehood, and now it has come to the fore in this place of bloodshed.'

Another Space Wolf cried out. 'There lies another of our battle-brothers, dead beside him! What appalling wounds he has suffered! What monstrous force must have torn his armour so, and what claws must have ripped at his flesh!'

'Indeed,' said the pack leader, 'this noble brother was a Long Fang, one of that wise and hardy breed, and he shall be borne by us to a proper place of resting within the Fang. Alas, I knew him – he is Brother Daegalan, I recognise him by his pack markings. But see, the claws of the survivor made these wounds! His teeth have gnashed at Daegalan's armour, and even upon his bones.'

The pack was much dismayed at this. 'What Space Wolf could turn on his brother?' they asked.

'Mark well the path of the Wulfen,' said the pack leader sternly. 'His is the way of deviant and frenzied bloodshed. He cares not from whom the blood flows as long as the hunting is good. This ill-fated Long Fang is testament to that – when this Blood Claw ran out of foes to slay, under the Wulfen's influence he turned upon his brother.'

The pack spoke prayers to mighty Russ and to the ancestors of the Chapter, and all those interred in the Fang, to watch over them and protect them from such a fate as suffered by the two battle-brothers.

You might think that a beast such as they found should have been put down, but imagine for a moment you were confronted by such a sight. It would surely be impossible for you to kill one such as Hrothgar, for though a warped and pitiable thing he was still a Son of Fenris and to slay him was still to slay a brother. So the pack brought Daegalan's body and Hrothgar, still living, to the Fang. I have heard it said they led him by a chain like an animal, or that they called upon a Wolf Priest to administer a powerful concoction that sedated him long enough to be carried to the Fang.

And so it came to be that Daegalan the Long Fang was given his rightful place among the packmates who had fallen over the decades, and there he lies still. As for Hrothgar, well, he was interred in a similar way, this time in a cell hollowed out from the rock of the Fang's very heart where from the lightless cold none can hope to escape.

Hush! Cease the sound of clinking tankards. Ignore the crackling of the fire. Can you hear it? That scratching at the walls? That is Brother Hrothgar, scrabbling at the boundaries of his cell, for he is now but an animal and yearns to run in the snows of Fenris, hunting beast and brother alike. But sometimes he remembers who he once was, and the Long Fang who fought alongside him, and then he lets out a terrible mournful howl. You can hear it in the longest of Fenris's nights, echoing around the heart of the Fang.

Now, my tale has come to an end. Perhaps now you understand why I have told you this, why the telling of it was entrusted to Arjac Rockfist. None but a Space Wolf may know of it. In tales such as this is a power than cannot be entrusted to any soul but a battle-brother of Fenris.

And perhaps a few of you have even understood the lesson that lies at its heart. The rest will have to listen for Hrothgar's claws, for Hrothgar's howl, and perhaps the truth will come to you.

Remember always, whether you hunt in the wilds that the Crone Fenris tends, or you stalk between the stars, the thirteen wolves hunt beside you.

THUNDER
FROM FENRIS

Nick Kyme

'No son of Russ should die like this.'

Afger Ironmane was crouched in the snow. He regarded the mangled corpse lying next to him forlornly.

It was Barek Thunderborn, a fellow Space Wolf, his brother.

Steam was rising from the carcass of Barek's beloved wolf-mount, Gerik. The monstrous beast had been torn apart.

The drifts had lessened in the last hour, and rolled slowly across the tundra. Even so, they had begun to settle over Barek's corpse. The Space Wolf's blood, still warm from his recent slaying, created dark-red blossoms in the veiling snow. It did little to hide the lacerations in his battle-plate. Nor did it smother his grievous wounds. Cooling intestines were heaped just below Barek's groin and trailed a half metre from the murder site.

'Slain by one of his own.' Afger bit back his anger, but his gauntleted fist was clenched. Snow dappled his armour, turning blue-grey into dirty white. It piled on his pauldrons, only to loosen and cascade off as he got up. Clods of snow clung to his beard too, the black and iron-grey streaks powdered white.

'We don't know that for sure, brother.'

Skeln Icehowl was standing farther away. His voice was deep, like the rumble of slow-moving icebergs. He patted his giant wolf-mount Fenrir as it bristled at the stench of blood.

Like his battle-brother, Skeln wore the blue-grey power armour of the Space Wolves. And also like his brother, it was festooned with fetishes and totems honouring their liege-lord Leman Russ and the fierce warrior-pride of the Wolf Guard of Fenris. A fanged necklace hung around Skeln's gorget, and a pelt of thick fur draped down his armoured back. Runic talismans dangled off leather thongs attached to his breastplate, which carried the gilt sigil of a winged, lupine skull.

Skeln's blond beard was less wild than Afger's and wreathed by snow. He carried a scar across his forehead and above his left eye – a relic of an earlier battle. Both warriors had a feral cast to their features, the echo of their namesake, and went unhooded, preferring to feel the icy caress of the weather.

'It was Hagni,' disputed Afger. 'What else could tear Barek Thunderborn apart like this?' He gestured to the butchered remains. With Barek's power amour split like paper, his flesh torn and organs ripped from his body, Skeln found an argument difficult to come by. Instead he snarled, showing long canines. His massive wolf-mount bared its own fangs in empathy.

Afger and Skeln hailed from a rarefied, some said mythical, brotherhood within the Space Wolves. They rode thunderwolves, the greatest of all the Fenrisian wolves, as a man would ride a horse. Such creatures were massive, more monster than wolf, easily twice as large as a Terran bear and many times more ferocious. Thick fur was as strong as steel wire. Long fangs were sharp and broad like swords. Few could master such beasts as those that stalked the Mountains of the Maelstrom, and even then they were not wholly tamed.

'The Scions of Pestilence are dead. Our mission is ended,' muttered Skeln. 'Hagni must be found and captured.'

'He is wulfen!' Afger was vehement. 'He must be killed.'

'No, Afger,' Skeln's voice was firm. 'The Wolf Priests will judge him. It is not for us to decide.'

'Barek Thunderborn lies dead and it is not for us to decide? Hagni is our brother no longer. He slew a thunderwolf, Skeln.'

'I won't condemn him, Afger. What if it was you we hunted?'

Afger thumped his breastplate. Nearby, his wolf-mount, Skoll, growled and pawed the ground.

'Then I would welcome death as release from dishonour.'

Fenrir snarled, hackles rising on its muscled neck. A sharp word from Skeln quelled his mount's ire to a low growl. Any retort would have to wait, as the sound of an approaching vehicle interrupted them.

Both Space Wolves turned and saw a Chimera armoured troop carrier rumbling towards them across a snow-choked road. Several kilometres behind it, south of the Space Wolves' position, loomed a dark bastion. It was the Imperial command post of the Cadian 154th, the 'Fusiliers', and the slab-sided Chimera tank that ground to a halt before the Wolves belonged to the regiment's commanding officer, Colonel Vorin Ekhart.

The rear hatch squealed opened on half-frozen hinges, landing with a dull *thunk*, and a jowly man in the olive drab of the Cadians stepped out.

Colonel Ekhart rubbed his gloved hands together, his breath ghosting the air, as he tried to ward off the cold. Neither the storm coat he wore, nor the thick moustaches framing his upper lip, could keep him from shivering.

'Your men are as grey as the weather, colonel,' remarked Skeln, appraising the bedraggled state of the Kasrkin storm troopers accompanying him.

Ekhart looked skyward to a blanket of oppressive platinum, and shrugged.

Skeln's shadow eclipsed the officer, the Space Wolf half again as tall and almost twice as wide. To his credit, Ekhart didn't look intimidated.

'A long campaign and this damnable cold,' he uttered by way of explanation. 'A few weeks for you, my lord, has been the best part of a year on Skorbad for my men and I.'

The colonel stole a furtive glance at Fenrir, who lathed the air with its long, pink tongue, and tried not to show his disquiet. He was dwarfed by the monstrous wolf. Ekhart would barely be a morsel to a beast like that. Even faced with it now, the colonel couldn't quite believe his eyes. He hadn't known such creatures even existed, until he'd seen one. Thunderwolf – the name was mythic, almost otherworldly. Yet here two of them stood, like monsters from some elder age, their masters no less impressive and god-like.

Skeln bared his fangs, grinning, though the gesture failed to reach his eyes.

'Fenrir...' he warned in a low growl, before the beast backed down and stopped trying to taste the human meat. 'The Scions of Pestilence are all dead, colonel,' Skeln continued. 'You'll be leaving this rock soon enough, bound for fresh fields and greater glories in the name of the Allfather.'

Skorbad had been in the clutch of a deadly Chaos plague when the Space Wolves had arrived. A cult of Nurgle, one of the Ruinous Powers and the entity that revelled in disease and despoliation, had arisen in one of Skorbad's monolithic cities. Infection spread quickly, the plague's victims sickening and dying, before stirring into horrific un-life as mindless flesh-eaters. The Cadians had done their best to staunch its spread but had been unable to locate and destroy the plague's propagators, a war band of Chaos renegades called the Scions of Pestilence – in truth, bloated monstrosities swelled by Father Nurgle's corruption.

In three short weeks, the Wolf Guard had trawled the cities of Skorbad, found the renegades and despatched them one by one. Hordes of zombies still haunted the deepest ruins but were waning, and aimless without their Chaos pack masters. The Space Wolves' role in the conflict was over, until Hagni had turned. So far, only the Space Wolves knew of it.

As for the Cadians, they were to consolidate their position and then hand over control to Skorbad's Defence Forces, who would mop up what was left of the zombie hordes. The less enviable task of putting back together the shattered world's infrastructure was the job of its governor and his bureaucratic staff.

Ekhart made the sign of the aquila at the Space Wolf's utterance of the name the sons of Russ used for the Immortal Emperor of Mankind.

'Indeed, and I'll not be sorry to leave this place either,' he then replied. 'We caught your coded vox echo over our instruments, and I wanted to come out personally to express my gratitude for–' the colonel stopped abruptly for a sharp intake of breath. 'Throne of Earth!' he swore. 'Is that...?' Colonel Ekhart had noticed the visceral remains of Barek, just visible beneath the falling snow.

'Aye, it is,' Skeln uttered solemnly, not turning to follow the colonel's gaze.

Ekhart was shaking his head. Somewhere behind him, a Kasrkin threw up. 'How could...?' There was a tremble in the colonel's voice.

To witness one of the Emperor's Adeptus Astartes, a fearsome Space Wolf at that, killed in such a way was disturbing. Something that could do that, something that could kill one of the mythical wolves must be...

'A beast,' answered Afger, having stayed silent until then. He locked eyes with Skeln, 'One that must be hunted and slain in turn.'

Ekhart averted his gaze to focus on Skeln. His tone was incredulous.

'I thought you said the Scions of Pestilence were dead.'

'They are,' replied Skeln, turning away, not deigning to elaborate.

'I have heard tales...' Ekhart began.

Skeln glared back at him.

The colonel licked his lips nervously.

'Of Space Wolves becoming beasts.'

The curse of the wulfen was the secret burden of the Space Wolves, a genetic flaw handed down by their progenitor that could manifest at any time. Rumours abound, as they always did, but this was one ugly truth to be kept by the Chapter, and the Chapter alone.

'Go back to your bastion and lock the gates,' snarled Afger, losing patience. Mounting up, he reined Skoll towards the open tundra. Kilometres distant the black silhouette of Helspire, one of the largest of Skorbad's cities, blighted the horizon. Hagni would be seeking refuge after his kill. 'We have lingered here long enough, brother,' Afger said to Skeln, who nodded.

'Will you...?' Ekhart ventured, taking an involuntary step back. His storm troopers levelled their lasguns, as they imagined monsters in the warriors before them.

'You'd be dead before you'd pull the trigger,' said a rasping voice.

A Kasrkin put up his hands as he felt the sharp caress of metal at his neck.

A third Space Wolf emerged out of the drifts that had grown more belligerent as they'd been talking, having crept up on Colonel Ekhart's party.

Skeln scowled, but was inwardly impressed at his brother's stealth.

'Thorgard,' he said.

The Space Wolf lowered his wolf claw and laughed. He hadn't ignited the blades; at such close proximity, the electrical charge alone would have sheared the Kasrkin's head off.

Thorgard had a closely-cropped beard with a long mane of ruddy hair, plaited with rune stones and bound by bronze rings. His humour was booming, and showed his perfect white fangs.

'Your men were sleeping, colonel. Perhaps you should find some better bodyguards,' he said good-naturedly, tramping past them with a feral glint in his eyes. 'Brother,' he added, the grin just for Skeln as he walked on.

Thorgard's face saddened as he regarded Barek, but was quickly impassive.

'The Allfather will judge him, now. It's out of our hands.'

Afger growled something under his breath, unimpressed at his brother's antics.

Skeln ignored their bickering, his attention on Ekhart who had yet to lower his guard.

'Our will is strong, colonel,' he assured him. 'You need have no fear of us.'

'Can you be certain of that?' asked Ekhart, craning his neck as Skeln mounted Fenrir.

Skeln noticed Thorgard's beast pad over to him from where he'd left it hiding amongst the snow so he could play his trick. Its name was Magnin, and it bowed its head to allow Thorgard to straddle it.

Facing the colonel, Skeln's eyes were dark hollows. 'Do as Afger said: go back to your bastion. Lock the gates.'

He urged Fenrir with a firm command and went to join his brothers, leaving Ekhart no less uneasy.

They had tarried long enough. Barek's slayer must be found and stopped, one way or another. Skeln only hoped there was some of Hagni left to bring back.

Colonel Ekhart shuddered as he watched the thunderwolves lope away. It wasn't from the cold, either.

A terrible, wracking cough gripped him. It felt like burning acid in his lungs. When Ekhart took his hand away from his mouth, there were traces of blood on his glove.

'Sir?' said the sergeant of the Kasrkin, about to go to his colonel's aid before being waved away.

'It's nothing,' Ekhart lied. 'Into the Chimera,' he added, before about facing. 'We'll wait for the landers at the bastion and lock our gates.'

'They're surrounded,' hissed Afger, sliding up his bolter to sight down its barrel. 'I count sixteen left. Estimate thirty dead.'

'Enemies?' Skeln's voice inquired from below.

'At least sixty... maybe more.'

Following Hagni's trail, the Wolf Guard had entered Helspire without incident. On the way, Thorgard had told them of his discovery of Warg, Hagni's thunderwolf, ripped apart like Barek and half-buried by a forlorn roadside. Skeln hoped shame had compelled Hagni to try and conceal the carcass, that some of the warrior yet remained within the flesh of the beast. Shreds of armour had littered the trail, too, discarded by Hagni as he outgrew it, shed like old skin as he metamorphosed beneath.

As it had eclipsed the Space Wolves, the long shadow of Helspire had been a blanket over Skeln's thoughts. Entering the darkness of the city, he became alert and set his troubles aside.

The sprawling cityscape was ghostlike and silent. Shadowed avenues held potential threats at every turn, huge towers loomed forbiddingly, watching, waiting. Ruins filled the broken streets and plazas, stark evidence of the brutal fight that had unfolded here. It proved little impediment to the monstrous beasts rode by the Wolf Guard. None challenged them. Most of Helspire's populace was either dead, in hiding or had already fled elsewhere. It made hearing the crack of las-fire and the frantic shouts of Cadians easy to discern. The battle din echoed loudly in the empty city. Tracking it to its source had been even easier.

What might once have been a public auditorium stretched out below Afger. One of its columns, no longer supporting the vaulted ceiling, had half-collapsed. Crashed into the wall and held fast, it offered a high vantage point. Skoll had crawled stealthily up the column and lay on its belly as Afger leaned over to survey the scene beneath him.

There was only room for one thunderwolf at the column's broken summit, so Skeln waited some fifteen metres or so below with Thorgard and their mounts, hidden by the ruins.

Afger saw a ring of battered-looking Cadian Guardsmen, pulling ever tighter; snapping off sporadic bursts with whatever was left in their weapons' power packs. Converging on them, a shambling horde of flesh-eaters, their bodies rank with decomposition. The whiff of decay made the Space Wolf's olfactory senses rankle. The wretched plague victims shuffled on broken limbs, old wounds ragged and dark in their dirty uniforms. Some clutched lasguns like clubs, in parody of their former lives and compelled by degrading muscle memory. Others merely reached with taloned fingers, their sharpened nails piercing their gloves; dried blood masking their grotesque and hungering faces.

'To be killed by your former comrades in arms...' Afger whispered, shaking his head, then realised what he was saying. He held his tongue as another Cadian was dragged screaming into the mob and slowly devoured. The rest were fighting hard. They wanted to live.

'Skeln,' uttered Afger, 'High and low.'

Turning to Thorgard, Skeln found his brother was already gone.

'On my way,' Thorgard's voice came through the comm-bead in Skeln's ear. Always a step ahead was Thorgard.

Skeln mentally traced a route for Fenrir through the ruins that would bring them to the auditorium floor.

'We are ready, Afger.'

A second's pause went by.

'Now,' snarled Afger.

Skoll got to its haunches and leapt off the column, a howling battle-cry on the lips of man and monster.

They fell amongst the zombie horde and laid about them with fury. Skoll crushed three of the plague creatures as it landed, dashing out their putrid brains with sweeps of its claws. It seized another in iron-hard jaws, biting it in two and casting aside the remains like unwanted meat. The legs stayed inert, but the zombie's torso began to crawl along the ground, driven by keening hunger.

Afger paid it no heed. Unleashing his bolter, he gunned down a slavering zombie pack, their bodies exploding as the mass-reactive shells blasted them apart. Gore spattered his armour and Skoll's brawny, half-cybernetic flanks. Man and beast revelled in it, this baptism of blood, howling for more carnage.

As the creatures moved on Afger, this new prey taking the pressure off the still firing Cadians, Skeln roared into view. He drove Fenrir headlong into the diseased masses, the thunderwolf using its bulk and power to batter through them. Rotting corpses were tossed aside, smashed like kindling against pounding surf, before Fenrir slowed and the real slaughter began.

A zombie leapt at Skeln, having launched itself from a high pile of rubble, only for the Space Wolf to arrest its flight with a blazing retort of fire from his bolt pistol. The creature was held in mid-air, caught in the explosive web from Skeln's weapon. The muzzle flare lit its gruesome features in monochrome before it disintegrated against the bolt pistol's power.

A half-second and Skeln swung his weapon around to dispatch another zombie trying to rake Fenrir's exposed flanks. Decaying talons met adamantium skin and shattered, before Skeln killed it. The monstrous wolf had just torn the head off another plague creature and was spitting out the saliva-drenched skull when Thorgard appeared on the far side of the auditorium, wolf claws crackling.

He sheared through a half-dozen zombies as Magnin carried him low across the floor. Heads, limbs and torsos fell like macabre rain in his wake.

The Space Wolves were three points of a triangle, herding the diminishing zombie horde together, what was left of the Cadians standing at the edge of the corral's bloody perimeter.

Each time the thunderwolves drove in to the zombie horde they tore out again, wreaking carnage, slaying any stragglers and tightening the noose before charging back in. It was savage and furious, but not an iota of rage was wasted. Every shot was a kill, every blade stroke left a dismembered corpse behind it.

Sixty soon became thirty, then twenty as the Space Wolves butchered with controlled ferocity.

'For the Allfather!' roared Afger, his snarling face framed by the flare of his bolter's thunder.

Thorgard echoed him then leapt up onto his beast's back, balancing on its broad shoulders for a moment like an acrobat at a carnival before catapulting into the zombies. Lightning arcs tore strips in the half-darkness, describing the deadly passage of Thorgard's wolf claws. Magnin peeled off, loping around the edge of the plague-ridden masses, biting off heads and shredding bodies with its claws.

Skeln had drawn his rune-etched power axe and stormed in, straddling

Fenrir's back. He howled savagely, hacking down to bifurcate a zombie's skull before decapitating another with the upswing. Cutting the last of the creatures down, he reined Fenrir in. Even then, the thunderwolf worried at the ruined corpses of the twice dead.

It had lasted only minutes, yet the desolation of dismembered bodies swathed the auditorium floor.

Afger was breathing hard, not from exertion but from the feral rage still fuelling him. He eyed the eight Cadian survivors and motioned to Skeln.

'What should we do about them?'

The humans were cowering, awestruck and fearful at the same time, faced with the monstrous thunderwolves and their riders. Several were injured, already showing signs of infection. A Space Wolf's biology was engineered to withstand such contagions. A Cadian's was not.

Skeln's body language was resigned as he dropped down off Fenrir and stalked over to the Guardsmen.

'We can take no chances.'

To succumb to such a flesh plague was horrendous. Skeln could scarcely imagine the dishonour in it should his brothers be susceptible to it; should they ever turn. At least the wulfen curse was pure; at least it embraced the unfettered feral rage that lurked at every Space Wolf's core. But this... it was ignoble, debased. Grace of Russ that they should be spared such a fate.

Some of the Cadians pleaded for death. Some got to their knees.

The Space Wolf levelled his bolt pistol. A few of the men closed their eyes, their lips moving silently.

'Receive the Emperor's Peace,' Skeln muttered sadly.

A bark of fire silenced any screams and eclipsed the Guardsmen's lives forever.

'It had to be done, brother,' Thorgard said to Skeln as he was tramping back again.

Skeln mounted up.

'Aye.'

Afger turned his back on the carnage of the dead Cadians. It was a pity they could not save them, but many more would die if they did not find Hagni soon.

'The plague worsens,' Afger stated flatly. A burst from his bolter slew the zombie torso labouring to claw across the floor towards them. Eerie silence followed for a moment after.

'Ekhart's soldiers,' he sneered, evidently unimpressed. 'I wonder how many more have fallen?'

'It is a small matter,' replied Skeln. 'Infected or fully turned, we have to despatch any we come across until Hagni is found. Though the Scions are slain, the plague must not be allowed to spread.' He fixed Afger with an icy glare. 'Mercy guides our hand in this, not revenge. You'd do well to remember that, brother.'

Afger snarled and turned away.

'Lead on, Thorgard,' he growled a moment later.

Skeln regarded the dead Cadians again, the ones he had been forced to kill.

How many did you butcher, Hagni?

Thorgard had the wulfen's trail again. The hunt was back on.

Thorgard sat alone, in the lee of a ruined meat-farm outhouse. It was towards the heart of Helspire and had been badly damaged in the fighting, little more than a broken corner of prefabricated rockcrete with the skeletons of other structures and the shells of destroyed Chimeras half-buried in the snow nearby. A Cadian platoon had come this way, but had got no farther.

The drifts had worsened in the last few hours. An almost total white-out smothered the horizon. Visibility was abysmally poor, even for the Space Wolves' acute senses.

Thorgard's head was bowed, as if in contemplation, oblivious to the snow flurries dancing around his head and clinging to his beard like arctic limpets. He'd built a fire, using his body and the ruin to shield it from the ice winds rolling across the urban tundra, and flensed the meat from some shaggy-haired bovine, indigenous to Skorbad and somehow missed in the evacuation. It was messy work; blood painted the ground around him and gave off a coppery stink.

A hundred metres away, two Wolves were watching.

'Hagni may be a beast, but he hasn't lost his instincts,' hissed Afger. 'The wulfen won't take the bait. Why do you insist on trying to snare him, Skeln?'

The other Space Wolf crouched alongside him in a ruined warehouse structure. Skeln was staring intently at the perimeter Thorgard had made, at the traps and foils he had set, hidden well in the snow and rubble. They kept low and to the shadows, Fenrir and Skoll lurking just behind their masters.

Of Magnin, there was no sign. Like its rider, the thunderwolf was adept at stealth – an uncanny feat for a monstrous beast that was nearly two and half metres from claw to shoulder.

'His fate is not ours to decide,' Skeln replied at length. He glared at Afger. 'I've told you this already, brother. I won't give up on Hagni. Not yet.'

Due to the escalating drifts, the trail had grown cold in more ways than one. Hagni's wulfen scent was no longer redolent on the breeze. His tracks had disappeared, as well as any other signs of his passing.

'You must be prepared to kill him, Skeln. If Thorgard or I fail, you must do it!'

Skeln grunted and went back to surveying Thorgard's concealed deterrents.

'Only if there's no other choice,' he muttered.

Something niggled at the back of Skeln's mind. Hagni was leading them further into disputed territory, where the punitive influence of the Imperial Guard had not reached fully. On the way, they'd seen entire platoons frozen solid, grimaces etched permanently on the troopers' faces under the ice. Convoys of vehicles, Chimeras and even battle tanks, were left by the roadside – empty and abandoned. Was Hagni even fleeing from them? Or was it the wulfen that, even now, laid the trap and not the Wolf Guard?

Skeln had no more time to ponder.

Shadows smeared the snowy fog, grey against the drifts. They were heading for Thorgard.

Afger bared his fangs and scowled. Even in the snow storm, he was close enough to detect the stench of putrefaction. The wind rose abruptly, intensifying to a shrieking gale. Thorgard huddled close to the fire, but made no move, as the shadows approached. A spurt of crimson laced the ground as he sheared away another scrap of raw meat. The shadows jerked and quickened.

They were just a few metres away now... drawn by the blood.

A form emerged, its crooked fingers reaching, shuffling close to Thorgard on bent, misshapen limbs. It was not alone; not nearly alone.

A hundred metres away, Afger reached for his bolter.

Skeln laid a hand on his shoulder.

'What if he cannot hear them?' the twitchy Wolf Guard rasped.

The wind had built to a scream. It buffeted Thorgard's plaits, tossing them around like vipers. Still he flensed, occasionally devouring a strip of the raw meat.

'He'll move.' Skeln's tone was reassuring, but he reached for his bolt pistol anyway.

Just a metre away – still, Thorgard seemed oblivious.

Could he not scent the creatures?

'He'll move...' The confidence in Skeln's voice was waning rapidly. The zombie was almost within touching distance... 'Arse of Russ!' he swore, powering to his feet and wrenching his bolt pistol free–

–just as Thorgard leapt up, a backhand slash with his wolf claw cutting first through the reaching zombie's wrist, then driving on into its upper torso and scything through its neck. Its head bounced onto the ground and Thorgard kicked it into the face of another assailant, before launching forward, claws wide, to cleave the plague creature in two.

Thorgard decapitated four more in as many seconds, grinning wildly at the shredded corpses at his feet, and it was over before it had begun. The zombies' lighter body mass had evidently failed to set off the snares meant for Hagni, but had not been so silent as to fool Thorgard.

Now only fifty metres away and slowing to a walk, Skeln sighed with relief. He and Afger were about to relax when the grey shadows returned. As the zombies appeared in their droves, it became clear by their uniforms what had happened to the crews of the vehicle convoy.

'Now we go!' roared Skeln.

Together they plunged into the drifts, weapons booming.

Thorgard rushed forward and bisected a creature from groin to sternum, using his momentum to push through it and leaving the two ragged body hunks flapping impotently, a metre of gore-slicked snow between them.

To his left a zombie stuttered, its advance halted by the staccato fire of Afger's bolter. A second burst spun it on its broken ankle and pitched the creature back.

An exploding cranium painted Thorgard's power armour in thick, dead blood and brain matter. The zombie collapsed to its knees like a puppet without its strings and slumped headless in the slushed snow.

The muzzle flash had barely died from Skeln's bolt pistol as he drew his power axe and went hand-to-hand. Still a few metres from Thorgard, the other Space Wolf found it hard to maintain his brother's frenetic pace.

Afger sensibly kept his distance, using his bolter's range to protect his battle-brothers' flanks. Fenrir and Skoll barrelled past him on either side as he took up a ready stance and switched to rapid fire. As the pair of snarling thunderwolves hit, Magnin rose out of a snow mound, shawled white and growling for blood. The creatures tore into the undead tank crews, ripping off limbs and raking bodies. Any normal enemy would have fled before such carnage, but the plague zombies had long since forgotten fear. They knew nothing now but the urge to feed, the maddening hunger for flesh that was never slaked.

Skeln hacked through a zombie's spinal column, just as three more of the creatures rammed into him. He was rocked on his heels but kept his footing, splitting the skull of one with his elbow and shredding the other two with a close-range burst of his bolt pistol.

'Ha!' Thorgard bellowed, surrounded by plague creatures. 'Now *this* is sport!' He drove a wolf claw into the torso of one, tearing the blades upward and shattering its clavicle. With the other hand, he swiped off a zombie's head before crushing it to the ground with a heavy boot. One leapt onto his back, scratching at his neck and gorget. Thorgard reached around to seize it and throw it off when another zombie fired a shot into his torso, an old memory triggering the lasgun in its grasp.

Grimacing, the Space Wolf was about to slash it when he found his arm pinned by another creature. A fourth had mounted his right pauldron and was gnawing at the ceramite.

'Not like this!' Thorgard raged. 'Teeth of Russ, my end will be worthy of a saga!'

Heat singed his face as Afger's bolter shells tore into the zombies clambering over him. The one clinging to his pauldron was torn off, claws still embedded in the ceramite, whilst the creature pinning Thorgard's arm was struck in the back. The ammo storm rolled up its spine to burst open

its head like a rotten fruit. As Thorgard yanked the zombie off his back and
then punched his fist through the lasgunner, Magnin leapt to its master's
defence, crushing another two.

'We cannot slay them all.' Afger's voice was tinny and cracked with static
as it came through on the comm-bead in Skeln's ear.

'Agreed,' he replied. 'Mount up and break through.' Afger cut the link
when Skeln had finally caught up to Thorgard. 'It seems your lure was too
effective, brother.'

Some of the other Space Wolf's eagerness had diminished.

'I had hoped for larger prey,' he confessed.

Skeln howled and Fenrir bounded to his side, after finishing a zombie
with a savage twist of its jaws.

'We're done here,' he told Thorgard as he climbed atop the monstrous
thunderwolf's back. They'd cleared a bloody gap in the horde but had only
seconds until the next wave of plague creatures were upon them.

Thorgard nodded reluctantly. He was summoning Magnin when Afger's
voice crashed in on the comm-bead.

'There!' he cried, 'There, I see the beast! Hagni is abroad and in my sight!'

Afger was pointing, even as he slung himself across Skoll's shoulders
and urged the thunderwolf to charge.

Skeln and Thorgard followed his outstretched finger to a dark silhouette crouched on the horizon line. Though distant, the Wolf Guard made
out hulking shoulders and a broad back, hirsute with fur. Skeln thought he
caught a shimmer from a pauldron hanging loosely off the beast's shoulder.

There could be no doubt. It was Hagni; now more beast than man.

Howling a battle-cry, Afger hammered past the other two Space Wolves,
intent on his prey. Skoll used its muscled bulk to heave zombies out of its
way, crushing bodies beneath it as drove inexorably forwards.

By the time Skeln and Thorgard had spurred their mounts, Afger was
well ahead of them. They too battered their way through the plague mob,
cutting a bloody path to the open ground ahead. Soon, the horde was
floundering behind them and an arctic waste beckoned where the chase
was on for Hagni.

'Damn you, Afger,' hissed Skeln, eyes locked onto his brother, now even
farther in front of them.

Hagni's silhouette had not yet moved. It merely watched its brothers'
approach. At this rate, Afger would reach it well before Skeln and Thorgard.
He seemed hell-bent on facing the wulfen alone. And despite the fact he
rode Skoll, Skeln recalled all too well the butchered remains of Barek and
his thunderwolf. Alone, Afger faced a very uncertain victory.

A sudden cracking arrested Skeln's thoughts, and a chill entered his spine.

'Skeln!' said Thorgard. He was looking downward, already slowing. 'The
ice!'

The snowy tundra they traversed was not solid ground at all. It was a lake, frozen stiff by the cold weather, but now breaking up with the heavy foot-falls of the thunderwolves. Skeln saw the ground webbing beneath Fenrir's massive paws. An ominous cracking sound followed it.

'Hold!' he roared, reining the monstrous beast in and stalling the pursuit. Opening up a channel, he shouted into the comm-bead.

'Afger! Slow down, the ice is cracking.'

'I have him. The beast won't escape again.'

'Afger–'

–wasn't listening. He severed the link and rode on harder.

'I'm sorry Skeln,' he muttered, 'Barek must be avenged.' He peered down the end of his bolter, bringing Hagni into his sights–

'You are mine, wulfen...'

–when the beast slipped away and was gone.

'No!'

That was when the ground fell away and icy water rose up around them. Weighed down by armour and augmetics, man and beast were dragged into stygian gloom.

Darkness surrounded him, together with a sense of lightness that Afger had not felt for some time. The rage, the grief at Barek's death, the burning desire for vengeance, all of it seemed muted by the cold. And for a moment, just the briefest of moments, Afger almost gave in.

Something strong and vice-like seized his wrist. He was travelling upwards again. He saw the vague suggestion of light. Air rushed his lungs and raucous noise clamoured into being as Afger breached the freezing surface of the water.

'Hold on,' snarled the voice of Skeln, beard dripping icy wet from when he'd plunged in to grab him.

'Thorgard, I have him,' he growled, and the other Wolf Guard came into view. He'd removed his wolf claw gauntlets – they lay on the ice nearby – and leaned over to grasp Afger's power generator.

'No,' Afger roared, thrashing. 'Leave me! Follow Hagni! Avenge Barek!'

Skeln wasn't listening. Together, he and Thorgard hauled Afger up and onto the fragile ice bank.

Skoll had not been so fortunate. The thunderwolf's sheer bulk, its cybernetic body fashioned by the Iron Priests, had sunk it like an anchor. With nothing to cling to, the great beast had drowned in the black depths of the lake. It was a poor end for such a noble creature.

Afger's expression told Skeln that Skoll's former master thought so too.

For a short while, they sat on the ice, not daring to move should it crack again and swallow them all this time. The zombie hordes were far enough away not to trouble them.

Skeln glared at Afger, his gaze murderous. Thorgard tentatively retrieved his gauntlets. Afger merely lay on his back and stared into the sky. Cold and pitiless, it echoed the feeling in his hollow heart.

Afger had not spoken for over an hour after the incident on the lake. He felt the loss of Skoll keenly, so strong was their bond. The separation of a limb would have been easier to take. When he did finally give voice, now running alongside Skeln on Fenrir's back, it was clear his mood had not improved.

'You should have let me sink and gone after the wulfen,' he growled.

Skeln's retort was biting.

'You've lost your mount, and we are two brothers down already, Afger. I will not lose another in a vain and foolish sacrifice.'

'I would not have drowned,' Afger snapped.

Skeln looked down at him.

'No, brother, but you would have given up.'

Afger's shadowed expression betrayed his shame.

Thorgard had found Hagni's trail again soon after leaving the ice lake, now far behind them, and was leading the Wolf Guard down into the catacombs of Helspire, the urbanisation of the city growing around them suddenly like a virus.

Here, the city was at its darkest. These were its sinks, its bowels, the very bones of its construction. Streets and avenues became tunnels, towers morphed into the sweating columns of foundation stones and the platinum sky was replaced by the rockcrete underbelly of the roads above. A sewer stink pervaded, sullying the icy crispness of the air. Stagnant heat lingered, emanating from the buried fusion generators that ran the benighted city's power grid.

Thorgard sniffed the air, finding the wulfen's scent. There was something else, too, something he couldn't place.

'It's strange...' he muttered, oblivious to his brothers' arguing.

'What is?' asked Skeln.

'Since killing Barek, Hagni has had many days to get ahead of us. I expected to track him to a lair, not to see him out in the open, especially so blatantly. It's as if he wants to be caught.'

Afger bristled.

'He begs for death.'

Skeln's eyes became cold, hard bergs. His anger made him rasp.

'No Space Wolf would ever desire that. No Space Wolf would ever die without a fight.'

Chastened, Afger realised he had spoken out of turn.

'Sorry, brother,' he admitted. 'I am not myself.'

Skoll's death had hit him hard.

'But what other explanation is there?'

'No, it doesn't feel like that,' offered Thorgard, challenging Afger's earlier remark. 'There is no sport in this. I've seen whelpling aspirants harder to track. Hagni allows us to catch up, only to then flee.'

'He's getting careless then, that's all,' said Afger, 'and hungry. There is only dead flesh here, no fresh meat to sate the beast.'

Skeln was silent and stern. That was when he noticed the sigils daubed on the walls and the rank, pervading stench growing stronger. They were deep into the heart of Helspire now and reaching the end of a long, broad sewer conduit. A chamber loomed ahead, a sickly oval of light announcing it.

'There's something else here,' hissed Thorgard suddenly, reining Magnin to a stop and speaking Skeln's thoughts aloud. 'Very large, very strong. Its scent mingles with the wulfen's...'

Thorgard turned to face his brothers.

'Hagni wasn't trying to flee or merely running wild–'

'He was leading us,' said Skeln.

'There may be some of Hagni left after all...' hissed Afger.

Skeln ignored him.

'But leading us to what?'

Thorgard ignited his wolf claws. Their electrical glow framed his face in an eerie light.

'Brothers...'

Misshapen forms were shuffling into the dirty oval of light. In the chamber beyond, Skeln knew in his core they would find Hagni, and whatever it was he had been leading them to.

Skeln had drawn his weapons, Afger too.

'Thunderwolves!' he roared, glaring at the approaching zombies, 'For Fenris and Leman Russ!'

Howling, the Space Wolves charged down the tunnel, making for the opening and whatever waited for them beyond it.

Skeln's uppercut smashed a plague creature aside, tearing open its torso and spilling diseased innards. He hung down along Fenrir's flank like a trick-rider from the old clan gatherings of his former life, when he was still human. Another was flung into the tunnel wall, its bones shattered by the force of Fenrir's swipe. Afger raked three more with controlled bursts from his bolter. The explosive rounds turned the creatures into little more than a visceral mist. Thorgard cut down the rest; by the end of it, his scything wolf claws were slick and red.

'A vanguard, nothing more,' he breathed. The actinic glare from his blades pooled deep shadows around his wild eyes. He was ready for more.

Skeln snarled at the miasma of pestilence coming from the chamber entrance.

Howling, and the deep bellowing of something large and unnatural, emanated from it. It was a wolf fighting a monster.

'Steel yourselves, brothers,' Skeln growled, and passed through the dirty oval of light riding Fenrir.

* * *

The chamber was a confluence of sewer pipes. Rusted openings in the walls disgorged filth. It pooled in a deep basin in the middle of the room. Wallowing in the dark morass was a pustulant giant.

Sloth-like and disgusting, burgeoning rolls of putrescent-yellow flab ruptured the creature's armour. The fragments of ceramite that still clung to its grotesque bulk were adhered by rivulets of puss, bursting from the boils and sores infesting its blubbery flesh. Horrid and distended, the beast's mouth was a gaping maw. Several tongues lolled from one encrusted corner. They licked and probed at the sores lasciviously, tendril-like and sentient. Filled with ranks of needle-like teeth, its mouth was like that of a bloated shark.

Skeln saw the potential in those fangs to inflict the wounds that had killed Barek Thunderborn and hope flared that Hagni could still be saved. He wrinkled his nose at the noisome stench emanating from the thing's corpulent body. Fat flies buzzed around it in a swarm.

Facing it across a river of pestilence was Hagni.

He was not as Skeln remembered him. Hagni's armour hung off his body in scraps. His lupine form, now covered in thick fur, had simply outgrown it. Fangs were like daggers in his long mouth, stitched around a slightly protruding snout. Sinew throbbed like cords of steel across a brawny body stretched and made more muscular by the changes wrought by the wulfen curse. Horrific as it was, it was as nothing compared to the other monster in the room.

It was one of the Scions of Pestilence, now swelled by plague and decay, favoured by its dark lord and mutated into a hideous plague-spawn, unrecognisable from the traitors the Space Wolves had hunted previously. Even now, before their eyes, it seemed to be growing, absorbing the filth from the tainted sewer pipes. It had not always been this size, and explained how the creature had managed to kill Barek Thunderborn and slip away undetected... almost undetected. The Space Wolves had somehow missed it, but Hagni, turned to wulfen, his preternatural senses enhanced, had not. He could not defeat it alone; there was enough of the Space Wolf remaining to realise this, or perhaps it was merely instinct that had compelled Hagni to seek out allies and draw them to this fight. Skeln hoped for the former.

Skeln processed this in a half-second, before baring his fangs and howling–

'Slay it!'

A ripple of explosive fire stitched the plague-spawn's bloated body and a burble of what might have been pain bubbled from its swollen lips. A stream of corruption belched from the creature's maw by way of riposte, but Fenrir was already moving. An acid-hiss erupted behind Skeln, head down, as his thunderwolf bounded away from the deadly spray. Afger stormed forwards at the same time, working his way through the mire to the plague-spawn's left.

Zombies stirred in the wretched muck, corpses surfacing like gruesome buoys, animated by the plague-spawn's presence. Afger shot them down as he moved, shredding them to pieces as he kept an eye on Hagni.

The wulfen ignored him and launched itself upon the creature, raking its rancid flanks. Flesh tore away, wretched and thin with decomposition. Black, sap-like blood started to mat Hagni's fur as he clawed at it. Like a geyser exploding from the earth, the wulfen was struck in the face by a plume of bile. The force of it pitched Hagni off the plague-spawn's body and sent him careening into the chamber wall.

Thorgard rode Magnin down the creature's right flank. Its tongues lashed out like serpents, jabbing at the thunderwolf. The fleshy muscle was laced with barbs and tiny mouths, fang-filled and drooling pus.

Despite its bulk, Magnin turned and weaved to evade the probing tongues. One nicked Thorgard's pauldron, leaving an acidic scar, as his thunderwolf jinked to the side. He followed its course as it seized a zombie shambling behind them, ripping the creature off its feet and hauling it forwards with a predatory jerk. Swept up in an eye blink into the plague-spawn's maw, the zombie's rotten bones crunched as it was devoured.

Head down, Thorgard urged Magnin on.

Skeln ducked another putrid stream from the plague-spawn's mouth. He had torn out his bolt pistol and the muzzle burned white-hot with the flare of his weapon's fire. The mass-reactive shells bit deep, sinking, as if in rubber, below the creature's flesh. Explosions rippled beneath the sickly skin, bulging like tumours, but the plague-spawn's epidermis just stretched to compensate, any damage that had been inflicted regenerated instantly.

Frenzied bolter fire from Afger's position suggested Skeln's battle-brother was similarly frustrated.

Skeln unsheathed his power axe and fed a ripple of energy across the rune-etched blade. It was time to get in close.

For Hagni, getting in close was the only way he knew how to fight. Dazed but unbowed, he shook away the wretched bile gumming his fur and drove at the creature again. As wulfen, Hagni was even larger than his Wolf Guard brethren. At over three metres tall, he was a monster. Yet even Hagni was small compared to the plague-spawn, so grotesquely swollen as it was by Nurgle's taint.

Leaping onto the creature's back, Hagni slashed and gored, searching for vital organs amidst the blubbery mass. The wulfen was elbow-deep in putrid blood and viscera, but the folds of flab, like fleshy armour, were too thick for him to inflict any serious harm.

Below, Thorgard raced along the plague-spawn's flank, wolf claws spitting lightning. The stink of burning flesh was redolent in the air, but the long grooves he carved in the creature's side merely oozed and closed up again, a roll of flab melting down over them.

Skeln was getting dizzy. The vile stench emanating off the creature made the air thick with its contagion. Fat flies buzzed around his face, trying to infest his mouth, ears and nostrils as he sought to get in close. He hacked

810   NICK KYME

away a tendril-like tongue and heard a deep yelp of agony from across
the chamber. Though his view was occluded by the spawn's bulk, Skeln
recognised the cry of Thorgard's thunderwolf. Magnin was wounded, possibly even dead.

'Thorgard!' he bellowed down the comm-feed.

Crackling static and a half-heard roar of anguish returned to him.

'Brother, answer me!'

Skeln was pinned by the lashing tongues, oozing fronds attached to the
pair that assailed him like the stingers of some rancid cnidaria. He couldn't
get to Thorgard. He couldn't help his brother.

Another channel opened up in his ear.

'This isn't working–' snarled Afger.

Bolter fire interrupted him.

'We need to burn it!'

'With what? We have no flamer, no incendiaries, we–' Skeln had detected
something, a distinctive tang in the mire of sewerage. He fended off a probing tongue, the plague-spawn burbling with laughter. A moment's respite
allowed him to cast about the chamber.

Pipes, everywhere pipes...

Skeln allowed himself a grim smile as he found what he was looking for.

A shadow eclipsed him as the plague-spawn leaned down, the shifting
of its mass releasing noxious gases trapped within the rolls of flab. Skeln
fought not to gag and reined Fenrir back. The tongue tendrils recoiled and
Skeln urged his mount away. Fenrir turned and leapt, narrowly avoiding
the burst of corruption vomited from the spawn's distended mouth. It was
still drooling acid as its burbled laughter came again.

But now Skeln was no longer penned in. He used this freedom of movement to ride Fenrir around the plague-spawn's side, searching for Thorgard,
following a pipe kept at the periphery of his vision.

Magnin was dead. The noble beast lay on its side, a brackish liquid
trickling from its maw and pooling around its snout. Three deep puncture
wounds were visible in its flank, having entered flesh. They were dark and
infected from where the plague-spawn's tongues had raked it.

Whatever poison was harboured by the plague-spawn, it was more deadly
and virulent than that carried by the zombies. If it could kill a mythical
thunderwolf, it could kill Skeln and his brothers too.

A desperate roar seized Skeln's attention and his gaze was drawn upward
to where Thorgard and Hagni had mounted the plague-spawn's back and
were tearing at it with their claws.

Lost to grief and vengeance, Thorgard was no further use right now.

A loud crack, followed a shallow *crump* and the tang of explosive, came
from the opposite end of the chamber.

'Afger?' Skeln hoped at least one of his battle-brothers still had something left.

'Bolter's dry... switching to grenades...' came the fragmented response.

'Is it working?'

Fenrir had slowed so Skeln could reload his bolt pistol. Last clip.

Thorgard and Hagni were keeping the creature occupied, eliciting bellows of pain as they tore into its blubbery hide.

Several seconds elapsed before Afger answered. Another explosive rocked the chamber. He sounded annoyed.

'What do you think?'

Skeln reined Fenrir around, tracing the pipe he had seen earlier to the source of its rupture. He let rip a desultory burst, downing a pair of zombies creeping towards him, before fixing his attention back on the broken pipe.

'Hang on to whatever grenades you've got left. We're going to need a spark for our accelerant.'

'What are you talking about, Skeln?' Afger spoke between thrusts. He'd drawn his combat blade.

'Can't you smell it, brother? The tainted water, just below the reek of decay...'

'Promethium,' replied Afger a moment later.

Skeln reached the ruptured pipe. It was one of Skorbad's main fuel lines, fed from its major pumping station. Volatile liquid exuded from it in a slow but steady trickle. They'd need more. Much more.

Skeln jumped down off Fenrir's back. The thunderwolf turned, guarding its master's blindside as Skeln sheathed his weapons. He'd have to tear a wider opening in the broken pipe – he couldn't risk a spark before the tainted water was saturated.

Digging his gauntleted fingers around the ragged hole, he heaved and pulled. The metal screeched but gave instantly. Corruption had ravaged it, degrading the tough housing of the pipe. Promethium was gushing freely now. It lapped onto the floor and spilled eagerly into the morass where the plague-spawn was languishing.

Skeln turned, leaping onto Fenrir's back again. He unclipped a grenade from his belt. The thunderwolf was barrelling towards a sewer-slicked column at the edge of the room.

'Find cover,' he growled to Afger.

Reaching the column, Skeln swivelled his torso and pressed the detonator stud on the grenade. Its parabola took it across the chamber where – a second before it splashed down – it exploded, igniting the promethium drowning the tainted pool.

A burst of incendiary lit up the room, fire sweeping through the water in a purging wave. Through the inferno's glare, Skeln thought he saw two figures leap free, obscured by smoke and rising flame.

The plague-spawn bucked and thrashed, powerless to heave its monstrous girth away from the burning pool, its efforts only splashing fiery promethium over its waxy skin. It burned, and as it burned, seemed to shrink. Like a diseased candle against the attentions of a blowtorch, the Scion of Pestilence melted away, shrieking rage and denial.

A curtain of fire was left flickering across the surface of the pool; the roaring promethium flames had died quickly. A dark green sludge, polluting the already tainted water, was all that remained of the plague-spawn. Cleansing fire had destroyed it.

Relieved to see Afger alive and well, across the other side of the chamber, Skeln then looked for Thorgard. Another tunnel lay across from them, opposite where the Space Wolves had entered. Diminishing boot steps echoed from the shadows there.

Thorgard was alive, but he had gone after Hagni.

Skeln met Afger's gaze and the two of them raced towards the tunnel mouth.

Fenrir slowed, keeping pace with the other Wolf Guard, then charged into the gloom of the tunnel.

'He is a fool!' snarled Afger. 'Alone, he is no match for it.'

'He is blinded by grief. Magnin is dead, Thorgard wants to finish the mission to honour his mount's sacrifice,' Skeln countered, adding, 'Besides, I remember you were determined to face the beast alone, too.'

Afger sniffed his contempt.

'So you now acknowledge it is a beast?'

Skeln's reply was prevented by a scream up ahead.

It was Thorgard.

Fenrir rode on faster–

But was too late.

Thorgard's half-eviscerated body was lying in the centre of the tunnel, wet and bloody. His torn throat hung open like a second mouth, fixed in a dark red scream.

Afger snarled, walking over to take up one of his fallen brother's wolf claw gauntlets. He winced as he stooped down, gingerly touching his chest.

'It's nothing,' he growled, before Skeln could say a word. Swiftly, Afger changed the subject back to the wulfen. 'It's of the killing mind, now. Hagni is lost to us,' he said, removing his old gauntlet and pulling the weapon onto his fist.

Skeln was silent, but didn't linger with Fenrir. There was no time for remorse. The wulfen must be stopped.

The trail was easy to follow. Fenrir tracked the wulfen by the scent of Thorgard's blood still on the beast. The tunnel took them back up into the snow drifts and arctic tundra of Skorbad. Crimson droplets dotted the landscape at long, loping intervals.

Skeln knew this road, and realised where the wulfen was headed.

'It returns to its old hunting ground,' muttered Afger, running alongside them.

Skeln urged Fenrir on and allowed the howling ice-winds to smother his thoughts.

In less than an hour, the bastion loomed on the horizon.

'Something is wrong,' said Skeln.

The Imperial command post was dark, as if it had lost all power. Smoke trailed from unseen fires behind the walls and there were no visible sentries. As the Space Wolves drew nearer, they saw the gate was wide open and streaked with bloodstains. A Chimera had slewed to a stop a few metres away, the vehicle's exit ramp yawning. There was more blood here too.

Two hundred metres of open ground lay between the Space Wolves and the bastion.

Afger was incredulous.

'Not even the wulfen could've got so far ahead and done all of this...'

Skeln eyed the silent battlements. His gaze narrowed.

'It didn't.'

Shambling into view where they had laid crumpled and inert, figures wearing the olive drab of the Cadian 154th and cradling lasguns in crooked fingers appeared. Old memories compelled them. The plague had come here, and now the bastion had an undead garrison. In his last act, before the feral aspect of the wulfen had claimed his mind, Hagni had led them here.

Afger grimaced, gripping his chest again, but kept his pain hidden. In the sewer chamber, there hadn't been enough time to reach cover...

A spark of melancholy flickered suddenly within him. The end of the road was near.

'I wish Barek and Thorgard were with us.'

'So do I,' the solemnity in Skeln's voice turned to anger, 'We finish this.' He outstretched his hand, beckoning to his brother.

Afger seemed reluctant.

'You'll never reach the bastion alive on foot, and I need your bolter and blade with me, brother.'

Skeln gestured again.

After a moment, Afger took his hand, seizing Skeln by the wrist and swinging up and onto Fenrir's broad back.

Skeln spurred Fenrir on just as the zombie-Cadians were levelling their guns.

'The last charge of the thunderwolves, brother.'

'Let it be a worthy end, then.'

'I'll see you in the halls of Russ, Afger.'

For the first time in weeks, Afger smiled.

'Aye, that you may.'

Skeln kicked Fenrir's flanks and the beast began to charge.

If there had been anyone alive to see it, the deed would have been worthy of a saga or two.

Skeln and Afger howled together as las-bolts filled the air around them.

Fenrir died just before they reached the wall. An autocannon burst had opened up its torso in a red mist and the great beast collapsed in the snow, leaving a crimson smear behind it. Their armour punctured and torn by las-blasts, the Wolf Guard burst into the bastion and commenced slaying everything inside.

A ragged firing line, a crippled mockery of disorder, opposed them as they barrelled through the gates. Bolters flaring, the Space Wolves swept the zombies aside and then split up, intent on destruction.

Skeln took the stairway to the battlements. Zombies fell like suicides, heaved from his path as he rose up the steps. He savaged with his fangs, tearing open throats, and split torsos with his power axe to reach the summit. The battlements became a field of slaughter, a reaping of cleaved limbs and staved-in skulls. Russ's name bellowed loud above the carnage, piercing the blood-red night.

Fires began below. Promethium storage sheds were set ablaze by Afger's bolter. Explosions cracked, billowing black smoke. Bodies were heaped onto the conflagrations, like heretics onto a pyre. He went to his fists, snapping spines across his knee, wrenching bones from decaying sockets. Afger carved a red ruin with Thorgard's wolf claw, anointing it in old blood to honour its fallen keeper.

Skeln's bolt pistol had long been empty when he noticed the wulfen amongst the horde, clawing and shredding with abandon, reunited with its former brothers for one last fight. He'd lost sight of Hagni after that, the need for killing preventing any pursuit.

The Space Wolves were gored and burned, but in less than twenty bloody minutes, the entire Cadian garrison was destroyed. Skeln had not seen Ekhart in the mob, but then could have missed him easily. A haze had fallen upon the Space Wolf, blood-red and frenzied. There was no way to identify any individual amongst the heaped body parts.

Heaving air into his lungs, Skeln was standing at the bastion's perimeter as it burned. After they'd vanquished the undead Cadians, he and Afger had spread the fires. The roaring flames cast a sombre light on the mound where Skeln had buried Fenrir. He'd wept as he'd done it, Afger looking on, honouring them with stoic silence.

In the aftermath, there was no sign of Hagni. Skeln assumed the beast had loped away once the killing was done. But it was not ended. There was no monster to lead them to, no fight save the one that was left between former brothers. Hagni knew it as well as Skeln did. A reckoning was near.

'Time to move, brother,' Skeln said to Afger.

The wulfen was still loose. It was all they had left now to stop it.

'Brother,' Skeln repeated when there was no answer. He turned...

Afger was slumped against the hull of the abandoned Chimera. His arms hung down by his sides and his cold eyes were glassy.

For the first time, Skeln noticed the wound in his torso. It was deep and mortal. Afger had held on long enough to finish the fight and see his foes burn. He was with the Allfather now, feasting in the halls of Russ.

'Be at peace, brother,' Skeln whispered, closing Afger's eyes.

All dead now, except for him – a lone wolf with but one duty left to it.

Skeln took off his left pauldron, stripped away the arm greave and vambrace of his power armour to leave his skin bare. With a tooth from his fang necklace, Skeln carved the runes of Barek, Thorgard and Afger in his flesh. At the end, he added Hagni.

The bolt pistol was empty, so he dumped it along with his gun belt. Hefting his power axe, he ignited the blade and trudged into the ice wastes.

Somewhere in the drifts, Hagni was waiting.

'Wulfen!' His challenge echoed across the tundra.

A few moments later, a feral howl answered.

ON THE HEELS OF MORKAI

Nick Kyme

At the lake, they finally catch up to him.

Though he can't see them, he knows they are close. He hears their snorting breath, smells the reek of their fur, damp with sweat and blood.

They scent him too and howl in anticipation of the hunt.

He runs, forcing tired muscles into a kilometres-eating stride that has him halfway across the glittering slab before his pursuers can match him.

A forest encroaches on the lake. It is dense and thick, foul with bracken, hellspines and beasts. In Fenrisian, the lake is called *rjalka domra*, which means 'mawdoom'. His pursuers will not venture onto its frozen expanse, preferring the forest and its denizens.

Something dies and the sound of its scream echoes across the ice lake, causing a shadow lurking beneath its frozen surface to stir.

He doesn't slow, but watches the dark shadow begin to uncoil below him. He has his saw-edged *seax* tucked in his belt, but is naked of his armour and carries no other weapon, save tooth and claw.

Boosting into a sprint, he pumps with his arms, weaves around the jagged spikes of ice jutting from the frozen plain, which is far from flat. All the while, the lurker below awakens and his hunters track him.

The shore looms, a short scrub of ice-rimed tundra that quickly gives way to swathes of near-impenetrable forest.

Something large and innately predatory presses against the *rjalka domra* and cracks start to web its surface. A dirty black membrane, pulsing with hibernation hunger, pushes up to the metres-thick ice and attempts a breach. Short, questing tendrils spill out like geysers of oil from the main, gelatinous mass of the lurker and probe for weak points.

Still he runs, keeping the knife at hand.

The shore draws closer, but he knows he will not reach it in time. His tongue lolls from his mouth, drawing in air, making his body work harder and faster. From within, the black wolf stirs and he embraces the spirit of Morkai, body and soul.

An almighty *crack* heralds the emergence of the lurker. Three of its tendrils have broken free of its ice prison and are blindly seeking food.

He rolls beneath the first, trusting in his momentum to carry him over the slickness underfoot. The second he vaults in a lupine crouch, gripping with bare toes and using his thighs to propel him. The third he cuts and does so savagely. A shriek emanates from beneath, muffled through the frost. He lets it echo in his wake, scrambling ashore and leaving *rjalka domra* behind.

There is no time to slow, no chance for breath or rest. The hunters are almost upon, his encounter at the lake negating any lead he might have had on them.

Now he sees them, blurring through a lattice of coal-black trees as they fall in either side of him.

Fangs glisten in the penumbral twilight. Eyes possessed of feral intelligence flash like captured firelight. Their bodies, glimpsed only in part, are muscled and loping. One is the hue of umber, large and vital; the other is smaller with fur like a winter storm, dark grey and white. She is the leader and howls to her packmate.

He grins savagely in what might be reckless abandon.

The pups of Asaheim look even more feral by the light of the moon.

Silver limns his body, casting it in a pellucid veneer. It shines off his densely-packed muscles, creates pearls from the half-frozen droplets of sweat dappling his skin. His hair, a long and unkempt mane, flows around his bulky shoulders like mercury.

The forest wanes, passing by in a furious explosion of branches, bracken and steel-thick trunks. Overhead, a jagged cliff thrusts up through the canopy, parting it like a veil.

Reaching the boulder-strewn scree at its base, he begins to climb.

The hunters are on his heels, snapping and growling.

Hand over hand, taking fat fistfuls of rock, he powers up the barren cliff face.

Below, the hunters give chase.

Though he doesn't look, he knows they are close. The stink of their breath, redolent with the casual kill they'd slain earlier, washes over him.

The summit of the rise beckons, a four hundred and forty metre sprint climb, sapping strength from already weary limbs.

He relishes it, embraces it, lets the black wolf have its fill of his pain.

So close now, the hunters are almost at his back. A single leap and...

With a massive effort, he crests the rise, heaving his body onto the plateau but gazing straight into the retinal lenses of a power armoured warrior.

Clad in winter grey, festooned with fetishes and a vast pelt sprawled languidly across his pauldrons, he recognises the rune priest at once.

'Vyargir, *hjolda*!'

The pair of wolves scramble onto the plateau a moment later, mewling disconsolately.

He turns to them, pressing two meaty fists to his hips. A thick sheen of sweat evaporates off his body into the freezing night, but he barely notices.

'Timba, Mia,' he says, his tone paternal. 'We shall run again, and next time you might beat me.' His smiling face turns to granite when he faces Vyargir the Runewrought.

'So then, brother?'

Vyargir bows, his ancient armour growling as the servos go to work and he manages to kneel.

'Lord Wolfborn, the Rout is waiting. Word has come, a plea for us to murder-make.'

Canis Wolfborn smiles a feral smile, baring teeth like daggers that shine in the moonlight.

Behind Vyargir Runewrought another figure stirs, a massive beast of such size and immensity that its presence fills the cliff-top. Sighting the other wolves, it snarls.

The pups Timba and Mia quail before it, recognising its dominance.

'Fregir...' the Wolf Lord warns his mount, patting its shaggy, iron-hard hide.

'What is our answer, Lord Wolfborn?'

'It augurs well, this murder-make?'

'Aye, the runes are cast and favour it.'

Canis grins again, meeting the collective gaze of his beloved wolves.

'Then there can be but one answer,' he says, before lord and wolves both throw back their heads and howl at the night.

REPARATION

Andy Smillie

Thorolf coughed, sending flecks of blood and filmy matter onto the dirt. Touching a hand to his aching ribs, he scolded himself for allowing the human to get so close. Human, the term barely applied to the gene-bulked creature growling at him from across the arena. The man's, if he had been a man, musculature was swollen to insane proportions, his head lost between boulder-like shoulders. His nervous system had been replaced by a network of cables that poked through pallid skin like rusting veins, and his legs were powered by pistons sunk into the meat of enlarged thighs. In a century of warfare, Thorolf had yet to encounter such a nightmarish union of flesh and science. The chrono-gladiator had been quicker than his bulk belied, steaming into Thorolf to deliver a punch to the Space Marine's midriff that would have killed him if it were not for the hardened bone structure and numerous implants his Chapter's Apothecaries had gifted him. Even now, Thorolf knew his enhanced physiology was working to heal the internal injuries he'd sustained; his twin hearts pumping fresh blood to areas of trauma while his Haemastamen implant helped filter away dead cells.

'We must keep our distance.'

Thorolf turned to look at his cell mate as auditory devices fashioned into the walls of the arena translated the lanky, blue-skinned xenos's words into Gothic.

The chrono-gladiator rushed forward again, steam hissing from metallic vents sunk into its spinal column. Thorolf dived forward, throwing himself into a roll to evade the brute's charge. The tau side-stepped left, flowing around the gladiator to slash a wide gash in its midriff as it thumped past. Thorolf was begrudgingly impressed; the tau wielded his weapon, a long pole-arm with a curved blade at each end, with enviable dexterity.

Ignorant of the wound, the chrono-gladiator reset itself and came at them again.

'Aim for the cabling!' Thorolf shouted to the tau and rushed forward to meet the chrono-gladiator head on, baiting him.

ANDY SMILLIE

Nodding in affirmation, the tau circled round behind their opponent, whipping his blade up in a tight arc to slash through a host of the putrid tubes feeding the chrono-gladiator's nervous system. Chemical-laden fluid spurted out from the severed cables, which writhed like pained serpents, spraying onto the tau's exposed abdomen. Screaming in pain as the chemicals seared into his flesh, the tau dropped his weapon and stumbled backwards.

Pivoting with a speed that belied its size, the chrono-gladiator sunk a hammer-like fist into the tau's jaw. The blow shattered the aliens mandible, caved the side of his face in, flipping him backwards through the air like a spent round.

Breathing heavily, the chrono-gladiator turned to face Thorolf. It fought to take a step forward as a shudder permeated its body, the vital fluid balancing its tortured musculature spilling out onto the ground.

Thorolf moved backwards, drawing the chrono-gladiator away from the tau, before darting around the walking-weapon to scoop up the tau's pole-arm. Sticking one of the bladed-ends in the ground and snapping it off, the Space Marine fashioned himself a spear.

'Your body has suffered enough. It's time your soul bore some of the burden,' Thorolf spat, hefting the spear and running full tilt at the chrono-gladiator.

The brute braced itself, flexing its biceps as it prepared to rip Thorolf in half.

A hair's-breadth outside striking range, Thorolf threw the spear. The weapon hit home before the chrono-gladiator could react, punching into the soft flesh of the brute's throat. Thorolf followed it in, diving elbow first into the chrono-gladiator and knocking it to the ground.

The Space Marine recovered first, righting himself and driving the spear further through the gladiator's neck, pinning it to the ground.

Dark ichor ran from the gladiator's mouth as it reached for the spear but again Thorolf was faster, hammering his fists into the brute's deltoids and smashing its shoulder joints. With both of its arms disabled, the gladiator's legs flayed helplessly, its torso twitching in shock as it died.

'The Emperor protects,' exhausted, Thorolf rolled off his opponent's corpse and stumbled to the exit.

'Space Marine... I live,' the tau cried out as Thorolf moved past him.

Thorolf stopped and closed his eyes, 'In His sight.' Straightening, he turned and walked to the tau. 'No xenos, you do not.'

The tau looked up, his eyes full of confusion, 'I... I thought we had a bond, as warriors.'

'If that were true, I would be as guilty of heresy as those I hunt.' The Space Marine raised his blade.

Thorolf ran his hand up over the smooth metal of his cell wall, bringing it to rest on a blackened, pockmarked section. Closing his eyes, he traced the contours, his fingers remembering how he'd made each of them. Thorolf's thoughts turned to the strangled cries of the chrono-gladiator as its retarded throat tried to give voice to its death. He spat on the wall. The metal hissed under the saliva as the acid liquid burned a fresh imperfection into the metal. Satisfied, Thorolf knelt in prayer and offered thanks to the Holy Throne and God Emperor that he yet lived to continue his mission.

Thorolf stared uneasily at the hunchbacks. Their childlike, smiling faces jarred with their weeping skin in a way that made Thorolf wish was able to adjust his eyes the way he could the optic lenses of his battle helm.

He had little way of knowing how long it had been since his fight with the chrono-gladiator, but he was certain it wasn't time for another appearance in the arena. Perhaps, he thought, this was an oddity of the tournament. Since his imprisonment, he knew that time had flowed strangely. It seemed fragmented and inconsistent, days indistinguishable from hours, seconds stretched out that they might fill eternity. He sighed, through gritted teeth; time was yet another constant that the eldar had taken from him. Running his hand across the black body suit that they had replaced his power armour with, Thorolf visualised the armoured grooves of his sacred breast-plate, his fingers able to trace the line of every chink where the reinforced ceramite had been tested in saving his life. Inwardly, the Space Marine promised himself that he would don his armour again.

He looked past his jailors towards the open cell door and waited for the bastardised female to enter. She did not.

A body flew from the darkness beyond the door, hurled like a doll by someone or something far stronger than even the stimm-pumped chrono-gladiator. It landed hard on the floor between the hunchbacks, twitched and coughed up a smattering of blood. Thorolf took one look at the prone figure, immediately recognising the enhanced musculature of a fellow Space Marine. Without a word the hunchbacks turned and exited, the door locking behind them.

Thorolf moved to check the figure's vitals –

'Stay back,' the new arrival snarled through bloodied teeth and pushed his torso off the ground.

'Easy, brother, we are both playthings of the same captors. I bring no harm.' Thorolf spread his hands in conciliation and retreated to the far wall.

The Space Marine seemed appeased, and slid back against the opposite wall. 'Where are we?'

Thorolf looked at the naked Space Marine, studying the tapestry of angry scars that criss-crossed the pale flesh of his torso. Tell-tale puncture marks studded the Space Marine's body, souvenirs left by the pain racks that had tortured his nervous system. Thorolf felt his muscles bunch as he remembered his own ordeal at the hands of their jailors. By contrast, the newcomer's face was untouched; baring none of the signs of warfare Thorolf would have expected to see on one of the Emperor's shock troops. It reminded Thorolf of the hunchbacks, wracked of body and beautiful of visage. His mind recoiled at the twisted work of the eldar surgeons.

'We are on Damorragh,' Thorolf spoke with hushed clarity, like a preacher consoling his flock. He sought the beads of his faith as he spoke but they had been stripped from him along with the rest of his wargear when the eldar had taken him. The warrior monk sighed and made a mental note to beg the Emperor's forgiveness for uttering the xenos word. 'It is an arena world of the pirate eldar.'

The newcomer was about to speak when Thorolf interrupted him, 'I think brother, it is my turn to ask a question.'

The other Space Marine nodded.

'Who do you serve?'

Anger flashed across the Space Marine's face, 'And why is it that I should tell you? Which Legion do you serve?'

'I seek no advantage over you, brother. I am Thorolf Icewalkdr, son of Russ.'

'Space Wolf,' the Space Marine spat, doing a poor job of hiding his distaste for the children of Fenris. The newcomer considered the other Space Marine. It seemed at odds with what he knew of Russ' descendants that Thorolf had spoken so plainly rather than aggrandising his Chapter in a torrent of audacious boasts. 'You speak well for a berserker.'

Thorolf felt the Space Marine's eyes on him. He wondered just how bestial he must look to him, his hair twisting in blood-matted locks down to his shoulders, an unkempt beard clinging to his face.

'Now,' Thorolf's voice hardened, 'I would know who it is that shares this cell.'

'I am Ecanus of the Dark Angels.'

Thorolf stared the Dark Angel in the eyes; he could detect no taint of Chaos upon him. 'I fought alongside a Dark Angel once.'

'What?'

Thorolf lowered his eyes, 'Ramiel was my first cell mate. He was a mighty warrior. I honour him with each breath I take in the arena, my body a monument to his legacy.'

'Where are your fangs, wolf?' Ecanus snapped, distracted.

Thorolf clenched his teeth in annoyance, 'It would bid you well to watch your tone, son of Jonson.' He paused and rubbed a hand against his mouth, 'Their infernal surgeons took great joy in filing away my lord's gift. A pain and an affront I will wash clean with blood.' Thorolf let his gaze drift to the kill markings on the wall.

Ecanus followed his gaze. 'Leave it to a Space Wolf to tally kills. You and your brethren's idea of honour is more akin to the feudal barbarism of backwater savages.'

Thorolf's face softened, 'It is not glory that they recount. Each mark serves to remind me of the penance I must face when this is over.'

'This will never be over, Wolf. I have emerged champion from two of these infernal games, only to find myself here, at the beginning of a fresh nightmare.'

'In death brother, in death shall it be over.'

'Hmm,' Ecanus sniffed. 'Perhaps it will be you and I who fight next.'

'Perhaps,' answered Thorolf softly. 'The eldar take great pleasure in watching the arena tear apart the bond of brotherhood.'

'Ramiel?'

Thorolf nodded, 'I killed him.' He met Ecanus's gaze. The Dark Angel brow was creased with rage, his eyes murderous. 'Fear not brother, should we make it far enough in this forsaken tournament then I have no doubt that we shall be pitted against one another. You will have your chance to restore Ramiel's honour...' Thorolf shuffled down onto the ground and closed his eyes, 'but for now, there are plenty enough xenos and mutated abominations for us to dull our blades on.'

The grind of gears and rattle of chain-fed levers woke Thorolf. He could have enabled his Catalepsean Node to cut in; allowing parts of his brain to switch off while the others maintained alertness. But in truth he needed to rest fully. The demands the recent past had placed on his body were nothing to what his mind had been forced to endure. He sat up as the brass door to his cell ground open. A lithe figured entered, the symmetry of her long, curved limbs and perfect bosom at odds with the vertical grille that replaced her face. Thorolf stayed on the ground as two of her kin entered, and flanked her to either side. They were badly hunched, the musculature in their chest's overdeveloped to such an extent it threatened to snap their backs. Their bodies were revolting, sheathed in a sickly skin with pores that dripped with virulent toxins. Yet by the standards of most cultures their faces would have been considered beautiful.

'Stand.' The female hissed the command through her grille-face.

The word rasped through the air, both distorted and clear. Had it not been for his Lyman's Ear, which worked to filter out the harshness of the sound, it would have ripped into Thorolf's skull like a saw blade. As it was, he felt wetness on his cheeks as blood trickled from his ears. He stood and waited for the hunched males to step forward, keeping his gaze fixed on the perverse ugliness of the female as they shackled his wrists with heavy chains.

'Follow.' The female turned sharply, her barbed hair cutting the air as she exited.

Thorolf ground his teeth as he fought against the nausea her voice induced, and allowed himself to be led from the cell by the hunchbacks.

* * *

The corridor stank of death. On the battlefield, Thorolf had smelt almost every death imaginable: the acrid taste of dirt mixed with bone as explosive rounds blew men apart; the sharp tang of laser fire as it lanced through their flesh; and the choking smell of promethium that burned them to ash and boiled away the air they breathed. But the death-smell in the corridor was far more putrid than anything a soldier was capable of inflicting on his enemies. The air tasted of depravity, of death wrought for the enjoyment of butchers. Thorolf tried hard not to breathe too deeply, his enhanced senses choked by the reek of dozens of foul toxins and pollutants. Down there, in the depths of an alien contrived hell, you died over a long time, when elaborate tortures had broken your spirit, and decay and rot had wasted your body. Death here was not a means to an end, an acceptable part of winning a war. It was manufactured for its own sake.

The hunchbacks led Thorolf along a snaking corridor of tarnished metal and smooth stone, lit by ghoulish faces that hung from the ceiling like lanterns. The eyes and mouths cast a drab light on the studded panels of the walkway. Each time he'd been led from his cell, Thorolf had tried to get his bearings. He'd tried to keep track of the twists in the corridor by counting the lanterns, then by remembering the shape of the other cells they passed. But it was no use, each time the corridor looked different, turned in a different direction. It was as impossible to fathom as it was for him to deny the hundred years of training and instinct that forced him to continue to try.

At the bottom of a metal incline, the female turned and spoke, 'Stillness.'

Thorolf remained where he was as the hunchbacks ambled forward and removed his chains.

'Go,' the female motioned towards the ramp with an elongated arm that ended in knife-like fingers.

Thorolf fixed his gaze ahead and started up the incline. The surface, which at first had seemed smooth and featureless, was covered in an intricate design and script; carved into the metal with a craftsmanship that Thorolf doubted even his Chapter's finest artisans could match. Blood ran in the relief between the symbols, tracing a grim outline around them. Thorolf felt his pulse quicken as he realised the arena he was about to enter was of more significance than the ones he'd fought in previously. At the top of the ramp Thorolf was met by an enormous circular metallic door large enough for his Chapter's holy Land Raiders to drive through two abreast. He waited.

With a whisper, the circular door opened, its petal-like segments peeling apart to reveal an equally massive spiked gate. Light flooded in, and Thorolf was forced to cover his eyes until they adjusted. Then came the noise, a thunderous cacophony of jeering voices calling Thorolf to battle.

'Within dark and forgotten regions hide the enemies of the Emperor. Be resolute. You have received his gifts so that you may enter such places and cleanse them,' Thorolf let the mantra slow the beating of his twin hearts, and ease the tension from his shoulders.

The gate vibrated angrily as unseen machines hoisted it up into the vaulted ceiling. Thorolf took a long breath and strode forward; whatever it was that awaited him, he would bring it the Emperor's forgiveness.

Thorolf stepped onto the arena floor, a steel platform covered in coarse, spiked gravel, to an explosion of noise from the crowd. He ignored them, thankful for the heat of the planet's three suns as they burned down on him. The coliseum was by far the largest he had fought in. Tiered galleries surrounded the fighting pit, towering up into the blood-stained sky to where even Thorolf's enhanced eyes could make out no more than a vague outline. No wall separated the crowd from the gladiators, allowing a privileged few to be sprayed with the blood of a combatant as an opponent's blade opened his flesh. Between each row of seated spectators a pole of spiked iron stood in the ground, the head of a fallen gladiator impaled upon its tip.

At the opposite side of the arena, Thorolf saw his opponent – an ork. He had killed hundreds of the green beast's kin on the field of battle, given the order to bombard thousands more out of existence from the deck of an orbiting battle-barge. But here, without the protection of his blessed armour, the cleansing rounds of his boltgun or the reassuring weight of the crozius arcanum, the hulking greenskin seemed a far harder proposition. Even hunched, the beast stood head and shoulders above Thorolf. Stood upright, it would have been double his height. The Ork gripped a makeshift mace in each of its oversized fists, metal poles with stone blocks chained to their tops.

Thorolf hefted the saw-blade he'd taken from the armoury in his right hand. 'Pit the might of your faith against the strength of the foe and you will cease their onslaught,' Thorolf knelt in prayer, sanctifying his temporary weapon the way he would have honoured his own battlegear.

The air above the centre of the arena sparked and distorted. Thorolf turned his attention upwards as the light folded in on itself creating a dark spot from which an obsidian balcony materialised. The platform was devoid of any thrusters, and Thorolf assumed it was held aloft by the same advanced anti-grav technology the eldar used on their skimming battle tanks. The crowd fell silent as the doors stood in the centre of the balcony swung open.

A single figure emerged onto the platform. Thorolf recognised him by the blood-soaked flesh cloak that hung across his shoulders. The Orator, the grotesque narrator of Damorragh's arenas, was clad in crimson armour that dripped with thick blood pumped over its surface by hidden nozzles. With the skin of his bald scalp scraped back in a taut flesh-lock, his eyelids pinned back to reveal pallid, weeping eyes, and his mouth sewn shut by barbed wire, he was as frightening a spectacle as anything the arena could muster.

'Citizens of Damorragh, warriors of the Bladed Lotus, raise your blades and kneel,' the Orator's lips stayed sewn shut as he spoke. Instead, the hundreds of ghoulish faces impaled around the arena gave voice to his words, their lifeless jaws moving in unnatural unison.

A hundred thousand barbed weapons glinted in the sun as the assembled masses obeyed.

'Archon K'shaic,' the Orator made a sweeping gesture with his arms, flicking blood from his armour into the air. The droplets hung suspended for a fraction too long, a morbid collage painted with the blood of the archon's enemies. To Thorolf they formed a crimson serpent, and he felt his insides bunch at the unnatural liquid.

K'shaic stepped through the doors to deafening applause; the interlocking plates of his midnight black armour shifting like scuttle beetles. The blood-master of the depraved arena world raised a gauntleted hand and took his seat at the front of the balcony.

Once more, the Orator spoke through the mouths of the dead. 'Here in Xelaic Prime, most blood-spattered of our inglorious amphitheatres, the tournament of the Razor Vein dawns. Let us greet it with the blood of a lab-grown man-thing and the entrails of a barbarous ork.'

Thorolf tried to block out the voices, but they washed over him in a nauseous wave that flooded his mind. He looked around for some way of silencing them but saw no cables or antenna linking the heads to the Orator. Thorolf dared not think of the debased technology the aliens used to accomplish such a bonding with the dead.

'Emperor protects,' he said, turning his thoughts away from the macabre.

From across the arena, the ork bellowed a thunderous roar, its mouth opening wide enough to swallow Thorolf's head whole. He remained kneeling and closed his eyes. Enraged by its prey's insensate reaction, the greenskin beat its chest and charged towards the Space Marine. Thorolf felt the ground tremble under the ork's quickening footsteps. It rushed onward, and his nose picked up the beast's foul breath. Thorolf shifted his weight to the front of his feet. The Ork's sweat filled his senses. He heard the crunch of gravel as the beast turned on its foot, swinging a mace at his face. Thorolf sprang up and backwards in a tight arc, his blade flashing out to slice up the ork's midsection and rip though its eye. The beast howled and stumbled backwards.

Thorolf landed and rolled sideways, away from the ork's enraged thrashing. On his feet, he darted inside the beast's reach, chopping its right hand off at the wrist with a downward stroke. Turning in place he brought it back up to block the mace held in the ork's left, though the force of the blow threw him flat on his back. Thorolf rolled sideways as the ork brought a foot down to trample him, reaching up to cut the tendons behind the beast's knees. Unable to stand, the ork fell forward, catching itself on its remaining hand. Thorolf leapt to his feet and dragged his blade two-handed through the ork's neck. Showered in blood, Thorolf tore his blade free, locking eyes with the archon as the ork's head flopped backwards onto its shoulders.

'Our stances are not as dissimilar as I would have expected Space Wolf; you fight with more grace than I credited you with.'

Thorolf had no idea how Ecanus had observed his fight with the ork, and he was too weary to investigate further, 'Ramiel. I fought many bouts alongside him.' Thorolf eased his body onto the ground, 'A true warrior must learn from his allies and adapt to his enemy.'

Ecanus said nothing.

He was awake when they came for Ecanus. Though his eyes were shut, Thorolf had allowed his Catalepsean Node to keep part of his brain alert, forgoing a measure of rest to keep a mind on his new cell mate. Judging by the stench, a pair of hunchbacks had entered the cell, though Thorolf didn't detect the female. He picked up a new scent as a harsh male voice ordered Ecanus to stand. It reminded Thorolf of the deep rumble the deceleration thrusters on a drop-pod made seconds before impact. He felt pressure build in his ears until he was sure they would burst. Fighting the urge to vomit, Thorolf continued to listen as the hunchbacks shackled the Dark Angel, chains rattling as they led him off into the corridor. Thorolf waited for three breaths but the door didn't close.

Thorolf opened his eyes, and rose to a crouch. Awake, he tensed and relaxed his muscles, bringing his body to combat readiness. Yet he still found himself caught by surprise when the female appeared in the doorway. She fixed Thorolf with her oval eyes, each a single black jewel promising infinite pleasure, and leaned into the cell. Unable to do otherwise, he held her gaze.

The female ran her palm over the wall sending a snaking current across its surface. The metal of the wall shifted like water, rippling away from the current's touch. Thorolf watched as the energy settled in a pool above his head height. The grey of the wall dissolved and fell away in droplets to reveal a dark, fathomless rectangle. A moment later and a fighting pit swam into view. Through the eldritch lens Thorolf felt the heat of the suns and tasted the outside air. Somehow, the female had opened a portal onto the arena itself.

'Watch.'

The word drifted from her face-grille like thoughts and seeped into Thorolf's mind. Despite himself, he took comfort in the warm embrace of her voice. The female retracted her arm, the door springing closed behind her.

'Emperor forgive me,' Thorolf bowed his head, ashamed of his weakness. He let a drop of his acid-saliva fall onto his forearm, keeping his lips sealed as it bubbled away his flesh.

Through the portal, Thorolf watched a blue humanoid enter the arena.

He had his back to him, a long blade held by his side. Beyond the tau, Thorolf could just make out Ecanus clutching a trident-like spear in both hands. Thorolf had encountered the tau twice in his lifetime; they were exceptional marksmen and employed powerful ranged weaponry, but he doubted they could match Ecanus in combat. The tau stepped forward and Thorolf caught sight of four more of its kin, all similarly armed and pacing towards Ecanus. That evened things up.

Thorolf could see the crowd cheering, willing blood to be spilt, and the Orator floating above the arena his arms outstretched in pantomime. Yet he could hear nothing. *Watch*, the female voice surfaced in Thorolf's mind; she was being literal. He stared at the portal as it bobbed within the wall of his cell, and shuddered at the erroneousness of the alien technology.

Thorolf's captors had never allowed him to watch a match before. Perhaps they wanted him to see what nightmares awaited him, so that they may revel in his fear; or they wanted him to watch his brother Space Marine die, and gorge themselves on his anguish. Even in the darkest corners of his heart, Thorolf knew no fear, and the Dark Angel's death would be an inconvenience at best – his would-be tormentors would fail on both accounts.

Ecanus's spear struck the lead tau in the chest and pitched him backwards. Thorolf flinched as a spatter of blood shot through the portal to land on his face.

Thorolf wiped his brow, rubbing the sticky tau blood between his forefinger and thumb, 'Emperor protects.'

The fallen tau's body was blocking his view of part of the arena, but Thorolf could make out Ecanus surrounded by the remaining tau. Ecanus sprang into motion, and in a blur of tangled limbs fought his way through the circle of tau, to emerge on the side closest to Thorolf. The Dark Angel was bleeding from several slashes on his arms and back but seemed untroubled. Two more of the tau lay dead in his wake, each missing an arm and a leg. Ecanus now gripped their blades in his hands. The last of the tau approached him cautiously. The Dark Angel strode forward, blocking the tau to his left's downward stroke with a rising sweep of his own blade. Reversing the motion, he severed the tau's arm at the elbow, before taking a half step forward and pushing the blade through the alien's throat. Ecanus left the blade in place and spun on the spot, kicking the final tau in the head as it rushed in to attack. The Dark Angel caught the dazed tau's weapon hand and muttered something before bending the weaker creatures arm back until it pierced its chest with its own blade.

Blood dripping from him like a macabre sweat, his muscular frame fighting for breath, Ecanus looked more feral than any Space Wolf Thorolf had ever encountered.

Abruptly, the portal closed and the limits of Thorolf's world reasserted themselves.

* * *

'The lion and the wolf, together,' Ecanus held out his hand, 'what would our ancestors make of this?'

Thorolf ignored Ecanus's jibe and clasped the Dark Angel's hand.

Surprised that his mention of the rivalry between their two Chapters hadn't promoted as much as a growl or toothed grin from his opposite, Ecanus clasped the Space Wolves hand for a second too long.

Thorolf was about to speak when a tremor rocked the ground beneath his feat, forcing him to steady himself. The arena floor continued to rumble, giving birth to four obsidian columns that pushed up through the ground like the stems of some infernal plant, dislodged rock tumbling from them as they rose. The pillars stood equidistant from one another, creating a smaller arena within the confines of the larger fighting pit. Each was covered in bronzed spikes and etched with burning runes that spat blood into the air.

'Citizens of Damorragh,' the Orator appeared in the air between the four pillars, his arms outstretched like the master of a blasphemous orchestra. 'Archon K'shaic welcomes you all to the final stages of the Razor Vein.' The crowd answered the Orator with a screaming roar, several of them cutting their own flesh in honour of the tournament. 'Two of mankind's super-humans,' the Orator swept his arm out to encompass Ecanus and Thorolf, blood flowing from his armour to form a toothed serpent in the air. 'Those considered the height of human evolution...' the ghoulish vox-faces conveyed every nuance of the Orator's mocking tone, '...against this monster.' the Orator pointed a blood-slicked arm at the ogryn.

Thorolf stared past the bleeding columns towards their opponent and sighed. The ogryn's bulk was greater than even his and Ecanus's muscular frames combined. A particularly resilient species of abhuman, Thorolf had once watched an ogryn stagger from a burning Chimera armoured transport, its skin running from its skeleton like melted rubber as it charged into the fray, bent on exacting vengeance from its would be killers. The abhuman had barrelled into a group of cultists who tried in vain to scrabble away. Using its weapon like a meat-hammer, the ogryn beat them to death with blunt, callous strikes. Concentrated lasfire and small-arms munitions had blasted chunks off the abhuman's flesh as the cultists rallied, yet still it had fought on, cracking their treacherous bones until a barking heavy weapon round exploded its head in a shower of teeth and bone.

Thorolf studied the ogryn's confident gait as it began pacing towards him, a massive halberd clutched in one over-sized fist, a flail of chain wrapped around the other like an improvised knuckle-duster. He took one look at the saw-blade in his own hand and found himself longing for the arcing power of the weapon of his office, the peerless relic his captors had taken from him.

'An abhuman, a bastard flaw of their species.' the Orator continued, turning in the air to include more of the crowd. 'Today, we shall see who evolution truly favours – the genetic misfit or this pair of lab-grown dolls.'

'*You do not fight like a wolf.*' As the Orator brought the fight to a start, Thorolf remembered the words Ecanus had spoken three fights ago, after watching him kill a vicious, bird-like xenos. '*I have fought alongside Space Wolves before and you lack their ferocity. You attack with poise and intent, never with instinct.*'

'*You brother, are not the only warrior with a keen eye.*' Thorolf had replied. '*The eldar are well versed in how we of the Fang wage battle. I would have been slain like a youngling whelp had I not adapted my approach.*' Thorolf hadn't been sure if Ecanus had believed him. He still wasn't.

'Vlka Fenryka!' Thorolf beat his chest and advanced to the orgyn's right. He motioned for Ecanus to circle left, knowing full well their best chance lay in attacking from both sides at once. But the ogryn moved with them, side-stepping and turning so that Thorolf always blocked Ecanus's line of attack and vice versa. *Clever,* thought Thorolf, what the abhuman lacked in intelligence his genetic disposition for fighting seemed more than capable of compensating for.

'You are an oddity of creation, a stain on the Emperor's divine canvas...' Thorolf spat as he continued to circle the ogryn. The abhuman's face folded in rage but it didn't break from the stand-off as Thorolf had hoped. It wasn't inconceivable that the abhuman had undergone some form of neural enhancement at the hands of the eldar. 'I will take your life in penance for the sin of your birth.' Thorolf stepped in to attack but the ogryn was ready, striking out with the halberd. Wrong footed, Thorolf pivoted out the way, the halberd's blade slicing through the air where his throat had been a moment before, and dropped into a roll.

Thorolf got to his feet as Ecanus's impaler speared past him and into the ogryn's shoulder, stopping the abhuman's advance and giving the Space Wolf time to recover. Untroubled, the ogryn grunted in annoyance, pulling the spear out and tossing it away.

'We must attack together.' Ecanus pointed towards the ogryn, 'From this side.'

Thorolf followed Ecanus's gaze – behind the abhuman a glistening spike jutted out from the nearest of the columns. 'I understand, brother.'

Together, Thorolf and Ecanus strode towards the ogryn. Thorolf relaxed his body and lowered his weapon, baiting the abhuman. The ogryn didn't waste the opportunity, striking out with the halberd in a long-reaching slash that would have been impossible if it weren't for the abhuman's weaponised biceps. Thorolf's blade was raised in an instant. Blocking the halberd, Thorolf rolled along its length, inside the orgyn's reach. At the same time Ecanus rushed in and pinned the abhuman's other arm.

'All-Father, grant me strength!' Thorolf hammered his shoulder in under the ogryn's arm and tried to drive him back. The abhuman resisted, his feet fixed in place.

'He's too strong,' Ecanus snarled.

'Wound it!' Thorolf swung the ridge of his hand up and into the soft meat of the monster's throat, bruising its windpipe.

Ecanus followed suit, delivering three swift punches to the ogryn's body, the punch-dagger clutched in his fist digging deep into the abhuman's flesh.

Thorolf felt the resistance lessen, the muscles in his legs flexing as they edged the ogryn backwards.

'Now!' Ecanus yelled.

Thorolf pushed with every ounce of the holy strength the Emperor had gifted him, the screaming pain in his muscles drowned out by the roar of defiance in his throat.

Together, the Space Marines powered the ogryn backwards, driving him onto the spike. Thorolf felt the abhuman go slack as the serrated metal punched through its abdomen, shredding its organs as it drove through them. Thorolf kept pushing, tearing the ogryn along the length of the spike until its back was against the pillar. Exhausted, Thorolf let go and staggered away from the eviscerated ogryn.

The abhuman glanced down at the spike protruding from his chest. It was sticking out from his midriff like the misplaced tusk of a metal beast.

Thorolf looked round as a guttural sound rumbled from the ogryn's damaged throat, blood spilling over its lips with every tortured syllable. He watched as the abhuman reached up with its hands and gripped the spike, and strained to hear a rasping curse, as the ogryn pulled its ruined body, hand-over-hand to the end of the spike.

'Emperor's mercy,' Thorolf stared in disbelief as the ogryn inched its way off the spine of metal. 'Will this abomination not find peace?' Breathing hard, he turned his blade over and readied himself for another attack.

For the briefest of moments, Ecanus took his eyes off of the ogryn to glance at Thorolf. The elegant piousness of the Space Wolf continued to unsettle him. It was not the way of the Fenrisians. A rising roar from the crowd drew Ecanus's attention back to the abhuman, his doubts pushed aside by decades of conditioning as he readied his weapon.

The attack never came. Free from the skewer, the ogryn fell to its knees, its midriff torn apart, its shredded entrails spilling to the ground. Twice it tried to rise, gurgling bloodied chunks as it sought to voice its frustration, until even its enduring constitution gave way to the inevitable, the last of its innards escaping through the grievous wound in its torso. With a final grimace, the ogryn fell forward onto its face and lay still, the earth beneath its body stained dark by an expanding pool of blood.

'His will,' Thorolf lowered his blade and walked to Ecanus, 'You fought well, brother.'

'As did you. Though it seems as well that you don't give into your more impulsive nature too often, that clumsy abhuman would have had your head had I not intervened.'

Thorolf grinned, 'Aye, it is as you say, brother.' He fought to keep the smile from his face. Thorolf had hoped that the Dark Angel would interpret his carelessness as the act of an enraged, impetuous Space Wolf. Thorolf clamped his fist against his chest, 'You have my thanks.'

Ecanus's reply was lost in the maelstrom of directional air as a platfrom shot down from the upper reaches of the amphitheatre and threw the two Space Marines flat with a decelerating burst from its engines.

Thorolf was aware of the crowd going berserk, chanting words of hate as he suffered for their amusement. Even with his enhanced hearing, he was unable to tell where the roar of the thrusters ended and their bloodthirsty shrieking began. Pinned to the ground, Thorolf managed to crane his neck round far enough to catch a glimpse of the platform. A discus of sublime metal that was at the same time transparent and pitch black, the platform seemed to blink in and out of focus. Holding it aloft were three monstrous faces that spewed flame downward, each a tortured sculpture of the terrible beasts that stalked the arena. Though Thorolf suspected their purpose was more decorative than functional, the platform likely calling upon the same esoteric anti-grav technology that the rest of the eldar vehicles used to stay aloft. Thorolf felt the pressure on him wane as the thrusters died, the platform drifting to the ground to his left. Able to move, Thorolf sprang to his feet and took up a guard position next to Ecanus.

Two hulking figures stepped off the platforms. Each head and shoulders taller than the ogryn, they gripped two-handed axes in immense fists and left depressions in the ground as they walked. Under ragged robes of dyed flesh, taut translucent skin strived to contain their swollen musculature. Implanted pipes and hoses fed coloured liquids directly into their organs, which glowed with a sickly hue beneath a re-engineered skeleton. Errant cables snaked from sparking backpacks and shocked their nervous system into a constant state of readiness, further increasing their lethality.

Thorolf dropped his guard. He knew with certainty that without the augmentative abilities of their power armour, he and Ecanus were no match for the colossal arrivals. Clearly, whoever else was waiting on the platform was taking no chances that the gladiators might try and kill them.

The lead brute pointed toward the platform, motioning for the Space Marines to board.

Thorolf stepped forward, stopping short as one of the brutes caught his arm. He let out a cry of pain, dropping to one knee as he felt his skin burning beneath the vat-creation's icy grip. Thorolf dropped his blade and the crushing hand let him go. He tested his arm, splaying and tensing his fingers, checking for broken bones and severed tendons. Nothing; his arm was fine. Where his senses told him that his radius and ulna should have been broken, the tendons severed, his limb useless, reality asserted otherwise. Thorolf glanced up at the brute, inwardly shuddering at the adeptness with which the eldar administered pain, and joined Ecanus on the platform.

The brutes stepped on behind Thorolf and the platform sped upwards, activated by the weight of their immense physiques. The crowd applauded as it roared up past the highest balconies of the arena, carried aloft on pillars of blood-red flame. Thorolf tensed the muscles in his legs, ready to adjust for any pitch or yaw that might toss him over the edge. He needn't have bothered – for all its seemingly abrupt, crude acceleration, the dais maintained a perfect horizontal alignment as it climbed. Thorolf experienced none of the discomfort he'd have expected from such rapid acceleration, his breathing normal and his feet as steady on the platform as they were on the ground. Confident in his footing, Thorolf relaxed, noticing for the first time the intricate detail forged into the floor. The prostrate bodies of a human, an orc, a tau, an eldar and several creatures Thorolf had never encountered were strewn across the platform, their macabre mouths fixed in a moment of pain, gutted by a barbed vine that looped around the platform and tore through their bodies.

'Watch,' the word came from nowhere.

Thorolf spun in place, his eyes searching the platform for... the female. She was on the platform. *How*? The thought hung in his mind like a slab of ceramite, slowing his wits. *How had he not seen her*? *What unholy alliance of light and dark had worked to keep her from him*?

'Watch,' the female repeated her command and walked to the edge of the platform, pointing a slender limb down towards the arena.

Thorolf swallowed the temptation to shove her off and followed her gaze to the arena below. Impossibly, he could see everything – the Orator, his arms sweeping the air as he spoke; two eldar, one in pale bone armour wielding a sword that throbbed with eldritch current, the other in hues of green clutching an elegant chainsword; facing them the arena champion, Khalys Dzhar, who was all but naked save for the leather holsters and bandoliers that held her array of knives. Unsurprisingly, Thorolf could hear nothing.

'You two next,' the female motioned to Thorolf and Ecanus, and withdraw to the rear of the platform.

The meaning was clear; she wanted the Space Marines to watch Khalys slay the eldar, to quiver as they awaited their own turn to cross swords with the arena's champion. Thorolf would give her no such satisfaction. He was an instrument of the Emperor, he feared no evil, his faith armour against the horrors of the universe. The wych Khalys was but one more stepping-stone on the path to his quarry. Thorolf turned away from the arena...

'She is not unbeatable.'

Thorolf turned back, annoyed that Ecanus had mistaken his disinterest for concern.

'She wastes energy with her flourishes. Her obsession with violence makes her unable simply to strike, to kill. For her there is too much pleasure to be gleaned from the moment.'

Thorolf watched Khalys slip a blade into the green-armoured eldar's neck as Ecanus spoke.

'It is slight, minute even, but there is a lull in her concentration.' Ecanus pointed at the wych's face and it zoomed into focus. 'See, as she cuts and tastes blood, she relishes the sensation. We can exploit that.'

'Warriors of the Bladed Lotus,' the Orator swept off the Archon's balcony into the air, a mist of red gore billowing in his wake like a vengeful cape. 'Much blood has been spilt for your pleasure. Now, it is you who must give yours.'

'A razor through our veins! A blade through the heart of our foe!' As one, the warriors of the Bladed Lotus recited the oath. Drawing ceremonial daggers from ornate clasps fastened around their wrists; they slashed their hands, squeezing three drops of blood each into a thin channel that spiralled down through the galleries of the amphitheatre. The crowd fell silent as the blood trickled downwards to pool in the skull of an onyx gargoyle.

'Drink!'

Khalys bowed to the Orator and walked beneath the gargoyle. The beast's stone mouth opened, bathing Khalys in the crimson liquid. She opened her mouth wide, relishing the baptism as the blood fell across her face and flooded her throat.

'And so it begins, the end of the Razor Vein,' the Orator broke the silence that had descended upon the arena.

Without pause, Khalys turned and paced towards the Space Marines. She had sought no respite after killing the eldar, stopping only to accept a frenzied roar of approval as the crowd celebrated their champion. Droplets of the green-armoured warrior's blood still adorned her unblemished skin, reminding Thorolf of the tell-tale markings carried by the most venomous snakes of his home world.

Ecanus sensed the other Space Marine's disquiet, 'Remember, brother, she can be killed.' The Dark Angel shook the tension from his body and tested the weight of the impaler he carried in his right hand.

'As the Emperor wills it,' affirmed Thorolf adopting an aggressive posture with his blade.

Khalys smiled and stopped. Sheathing her twin blades, she held her empty hands up to the archon. The crowd met her display with ecstasy, eager to see her kill the so called super-humans with her bare hands.

Thorolf thrust his blade at her midsection. She stepped to the side, patting away his arm with her palm before skipping her knee into his jaw. Thorolf staggered backwards, teeth loose in his mouth. Ecanus made to attack Khalys' exposed back but she was quicker, twisting in mid-air to kick him in the head. The blow flipped him; he landed hard on his shoulder.

Thorolf struck out with a flurry of arcing cuts, but the wych weaved between his blows, stepping inside his guard to strike him in the throat before hooking her hand under his arm and throwing him to the ground. Khalys moved to finish the prone Space Marine, but Ecanus interceded, stabbing the tip of his impaler toward her. She turned just in time and leapt over the weapon. Ecanus pressed his attack but the wych cartwheeled off to the side, whipping her feet into the side of his head as she danced past.

The crowd roared with amusement as the Space Marines flailed around like children, unable to land a blow on the dextrous wych.

Khalys attacked again. Pushing through her toes, she let her lithe calf muscles propel her through the air, the ridge of her outstretched foot aimed at Thorolf's throat. Ecanus read her move. Pivoting on his back foot he kicked Thorolf hard in the abdomen. The Space Wolf bent double as the blow, robbing Khalys of her target, unbalancing her. Ecanus let the momentum of his strike carry him round, swinging his rear leg up like the blade of a grav-copter to kick the wych in the face as she landed.

Khalys moved with the blow, folding into a roll that took her clear of the Space Marines and up to her feet. She touched a hand to her jaw and licked her tongue around the inside of her mouth, delighting in the metallic tang of her chemical-filled blood. With a smile that didn't reach her eyes, Khalys unsheathed her knives.

'No more games wych,' Ecnaus spat.

Khalys snarled and leapt at the Dark Angel. Ecanus gripped his impaler by the edge of the haft and whipped it out in a long-arcing strike. Khalys bent at the waist, curving her body underneath his swing. Rising, she disarmed Ecanus, slashing a dagger across his forearm and driving the other into the side of his neck. The wych finished with a flourish, kicking Ecanus in the face with the exact same kick he'd struck her with.

Thorolf looked up from all fours. Kahlys had paused to savour the Dark Angel's blood. It had been for less than a heartbeat, but for an instant she wasn't in motion.

Khalys was poised to finish Ecanus as he struggled with the wound in his neck.

Thorolf sprinted headlong at the wych. She turned as he knew she would. He fed her blades the outsides of his forearms. Devoid of vital arteries, her blows would not be fatal.

Blood splashed across Khalys's face. She moved around the charging Space Marine, though slower than she might have, her mouth open as she relished the fruit of his veins. Thorolf twisted as he past her, and spat a gobbet of acid-saliva onto her face.

Khalys screamed as the searing liquid burnt at her flesh. She lashed out like a rabid dog, her twin blades seeking vengeance.

Thorolf swept low, avoiding her desperate attack, and ripped his blade across her abdomen.

He stared at Khalys as she bled out on the ground in front of him. The wych's once perfect features burned away by his saliva, her lithe body ruined by the vengeful teeth of his blade. Ecanus had been right, Khalys technique was as flawed as her debased soul. Thorolf caught the Dark Angel's hand as he moved to finish Khalys.

'The champion of this accursed arena does not deserve the All-father's mercy. She will die in pain.'

'As you wish,' Ecanus dipped his head in acknowledgement.

'Emperor, eternal saviour and redeemer, it is by your hand and unfailing wisdom that we have been spared this fate.' Thorolf closed his eyes in prayer.

Ecanus stared at Khalys in silent satisfaction as the last of her life-force ebbed away. The wych's veins pulsed like flashes of lightning beneath her taut flesh as the cocktail of stimms and combat drugs in her system continued to burn. Khalys's flesh began to bubble and run as the excess adrenaline and frenzon in her blood melted her organs. Within moments all that remained was a pool of toxic ichor.

Ecanus ignored the jubilant roaring of the crowd and held his hand out towards Thorolf. 'It has been an honour to fight by your side, brother.'

Thorolf looked Ecanus in the eyes and grasped his arm in a warrior fashion, clasping his hand around the other Space Marine's forearm. 'It is my sacred duty to save your soul from the Dark Gods of Chaos,' Thorolf stared into Ecanus's eyes as he spoke, feeling the Dark Angel's grip loosen as realisation set in, 'and I will save your soul, even if you die in the process.'

The nagging feeling Ecanus had pushed to the recesses of his mind burst to the surface like a blazing comet, illuminating the truth that had until now eluded him. Past the unruly, matted hair, the unwashed skin, and the careful lies, Ecanus saw Thorolf for the first time. The other Space Marine was not a wolf but a lion, a Dark Angel.

'You...' Ecanus's mouth hung open as understanding dawned.

Thorolf brought his knee up and drove his foot into Ecanus's chest. Ecanus let the force of the blow carry him and rolled backwards to his feet. 'I am Interrogator Chaplain Ramiel,' Thorolf spoke, revealing his true identity, 'member of the most sacred brotherhood of the Inner Circle, son of the Lion and avenging blade of the Angels.' Ramiel pointed his blade at Ecanus, 'You are a traitorous cur, a shameful stain upon our Chapter's honour and I have come to offer redemption.'

Ecanus bared his teeth in a snarl, 'I will spit upon your corpse, pawn of Jonson.' Ecanus sprang at Ramiel, unfettered rage dulling the pain from his wounds.

Ramiel stepped off Ecanus's line of attack, avoiding the punch-dagger that was aimed at his primary heart, and sliced his blade down towards Ecanus's thigh. The Fallen countered without pause, pivoting away from the blade, swinging his leg up over the sword stroke to kick the Chaplain in the jaw. Ramiel staggered, recovering in time to block the cross Ecanus threw at his nose. Too late, Ramiel realised Ecanus had wanted him to block it.

The Fallen rode the momentum of the Chaplain's parry, folding his arm in on itself and bringing his elbow smashing through Ramiel's guard and into his face. Ramiel felt the sickening crunch as his cheekbone broke, dropping his blade as he struggled to stay upright. Ecanus allowed him no reprieve, spinning tightly to deliver a powerful back-kick that broke the Chaplain's ribs and sent him sprawling into the dirt. Ramiel wheezed heavily as his lungs struggled to draw breath.

The crowd erupted in violence-fuelled ecstasy, drinking in the animosity between the two combatants.

'I have crossed the depths of space and ripped the hearts from warriors far mightier than you before you'd even deemed to crawl from your mother's foetid womb,' spat Ecanus as he paced towards Ramiel.

Ramiel felt his strength slipping, he needed to buy some time, recover and then–

Fight now, heal later.

Brother-Sergeant Sariel's voice filled the Chaplain's head. Sariel was a member of the Deathwatch, the best of the most elite warriors the Dark Angels could muster. He had helped Ramiel from his knees once before, back on Tervanaous IV when a tyranid bio-weapon had devoured most of Ramiel's abdomen. Ramiel took heart from his old sergeant's words, Sariel's memory surfacing in the Chaplain's mind to help him once more. Emboldened, Ramiel threw himself at Ecanus.

Caught off guard by his opponent's sudden resurgence, Ecanus swung a clumsy punch at the Chaplain's face. Ramiel caught the attack, wrapping his right arm around Ecanus's left and using his other to hook the Fallen's neck, pulling him into a headbutt that began when Ramiel had leapt from the ground and ended when it dented Ecanus's brow and caved-in his right eye socket. Ramiel kept a hold of Ecanus, firing one knee and then the other into his gut, winding him. Grunting with effort, the Chaplain hurled the Fallen Angel across one of the barbed sections the arena floor. The carpet of microscopic blades ripped open Ecanus's skin as he tumbled over it, leaving him bleeding from hundreds of small lacerations.

'The will of the righteous cannot be denied,' Ramiel let the catechism invigorate him.

Ecanus's head swam, Ramiel's blow had been severe and his body was struggling to heal the myriad incisions puncturing his body. He looked up and saw the Chaplain, blade in hand, advancing. Behind him, Ecanus could just make out the glint of an impaler in the dirt. Standing, he winced as the damnable arena stabbed into his feet.

'Time to die, Chaplain,' Ecanus skipped forward and flipped over Ramiel's sword stroke. Landing behind the Chaplain, Ecanus scooped up the impaler with his foot; catching it he lunged at the Chaplain.

Ramiel had read Ecanus's move, his clumsy sword stroke a lure. Turning on the balls of his feet, he side-stepped the impaler's tip, grabbed its haft and pulled Ecanus onto his outstretched blade. Ramiel felt the Fallen's body judder and spasm as the blade punctured his primary heart.

'Let the blood of the unclean act as an offering to the Lion's shade.'

The Chaplain ignored Ecanus's desperate hands as they tried to push him away. Ripping the blade across Ecanus's chest, Ramiel scythed it through the secondary heart and tore it out through the shoulder. The Fallen's body fell at Ramiel's feet in a ruined heap.

'The unworthy shall be crushed from the Emperor's sight.' Ramiel stamped his foot down hard on Ecanus's skull, cracking it into the dirt.

The crowd erupted in a torrent of cheering; their sickening ovation amplified to a numbing crescendo by the distended mouths of the cadaver heads encircling the arena.

Archon K'shaic stood, silencing the applauding masses.

'Champion of Xelaic,' the Orator began. 'Through blood and death you have earned your freedom.'

Ramiel stood immobile and waited for the punchline.

'You will accompany my master to the depths of Commorragh, where you will fight for even greater glory and perhaps even, immortality.'

The crowd approved. Braying like savages, they banged gauntleted fists against armoured chests and roared in pleasured excitement.

Ramiel's jaw tightened in anger. He would no more continue to kill for the entertainment of K'shaic and his depraved race than he would have allowed Ecanus to live. The Chaplain closed his eyes for a moment, finding solace in the darkness and offering a prayer to the Emperor for strength. He felt the weight of the impaler clutched in his right hand, it was perfectly balanced. Opening his eyes Ramiel let his enhanced senses filter out the crowd. Their jeering faded away to a wash of noise, like waves rolling onto a distant beach. The army of pendants and the grotesque sheets of flapping skin blurring out of focus until only the archon remained visible – a dark spot at the end of a white tunnel Ramiel formed in his mind.

'I am the Emperor's wrath!' cried Ramiel, and in one fluid motion the Chaplain stepped forward, his arm shooting up to launch the impaler at K'shaic's chest.

The impaler flew true, covering the distance to the archon in a heartbeat and striking him full in the chest. The blow triggered a burst of light like the shattering of a minute star, momentarily eclipsing the archon and his attendants. In the after-flare, Ramiel saw K'shaic still standing – the archon had used some form of displacement field to swap places with the Orator.

A thousand lifeless mouths cried out in symphony as the Orator looked down at the haft of the impaler protruding from his chest, its spear tip buried in his black heart.

K'shaic watched dispassionately as the mouthless creature collapsed in a pool of thick blood. The cries of the Orator's familiars tailed off as the last of its blood ran onto the barbed floor of the balcony. The archon nodded in mock respect towards the Chaplain, with a wicked smile that revealed two rows of dagger teeth.

'His loyal servant unto death,' Ramiel reached for where his rosarius should be sitting on his chest and awaited eternity.

DEFENDER
OF HONOUR

Cavan Scott

The smell of blood was all it took.

Turin Strongheart was back on the battlefield, ears ringing from the explosion. The blast had sent him crashing into the burned-out husk of a Whirlwind tank. He'd slid into the mire, slick fingers wrestling with his twisted helm. With a cry of frustration he ripped the now useless lump of ceramite from his head, throwing it aside.

Brother Ironblade had been in front of him, running full pelt at the ork lines, when his body had been enveloped in a brilliant flash of light. The damned greenskins had buried mines in the very ground they were walking upon themselves. Suicidal xenos wretches. Ironblade's body took the brunt of the explosion, shielding Strongheart. Another brother was fallen.

The Space Wolf reached up, grabbing hold of the side of the Whirlwind and hauling himself back to his feet, the sounds of the battle rising to a crescendo. Screams, bolter fire, the roar of demolisher cannons, merging together, flattened out into one cacophonous note. Strongheart scanned the ground for his bolter. Where had it fallen? He would not end up like Ironblade. He would not die a worthless death.

Something glinted in the mud before him, illuminated by the sudden flash of a frag grenade. There it was, sinking steadily in the bog. Strongheart was pushing himself away from the Whirlwind when he was hit in the chest with the force of a pile driver.

The impact sent him spinning away from his bolter. Strongheart crashed to the ground, tumbling over and over, praying that he wouldn't trigger another of the hidden mines. When he finally came to rest, the monstrosity that had fired the weapon at him was filling his vision, a mass of wires and crudely implanted robotic appendages. The ork charged, steam billowing from every cybernetic joint, bile streaming from a maw crammed with far too many metal teeth. Without a weapon, Strongheart dropped down and put his shoulder into the beast's plated chest. He would use the brute's momentum against itself.

At least that was the plan. It was like hitting a Rhino. Strongheart's feet slipped back in the wet mud and he tumbled forward, throwing out an arm to avoid plunging face-down in the muck. Before he could recover, the ork was upon him, metallic claws attempting to prise the armour from his back. His left cheek exploded in pain as barbed steel met exposed flesh. Try as he might, he couldn't get a purchase, couldn't shove the fiend from him. The attack was animalistic, frenzied. Overpowering.

This couldn't be the end. Not here. Not like this.

'Brother?'

Strongheart blinked and snapped back to the here and now. The heat of the battle was instantly replaced by biting cold, a sickening smell of copper and rust filling his nostrils.

'Brother Strongheart?'

He looked up into the grizzled face before him. The features were heavily scarred, and the eyes that glared out from beneath a strong brow intense. A face that every member of the Space Wolves knew, a face that was carved into their very hearts. As much the reason they fought as their devotion to the All-Father.

Logan Grimnar, the Great Wolf.

'I am sorry, Fangfather,' Strongheart said, crouched on his haunches. 'I was distracted.'

'You were thinking of battle,' Grimnar growled, his voice like a pack of Fenrisian wolves, the very same creatures that were emblazoned on their heavy pauldrons. 'I could see it in your eyes.'

'The battle of Mactalas,' Strongheart acknowledged, shifting uncomfortably beneath the Great Wolf's steady gaze.

Grimnar nodded, snow tumbling from his long, greying beard. 'Understandable. We lost many that day, but we took more in Russ's name. A hundred orks for every brother who lost his life.'

'Victory, Jarl.'

'Victory,' Grimnar repeated, quieter than before, his keen eyes now resting on the large, metal fang that hung around Strongheart's neck. His trophy.

The breath of the ork on his face. The beast bearing down on him, crushing him. Scrabbling in the mud for his gun, feeling its grip in his hand.

'So, brother,' Grimnar prompted, 'the carcass...'

Strongheart glanced at the body he was crouched beside, the spilled guts of the great white bear steaming in the sub-zero temperatures. The smell was overwhelming. Rust and copper. A stink Strongheart had smelled a hundred, if not a thousand, times before.

'A fresh kill.'

'But not fresh enough. The killer's tracks have been covered.'

Strongheart nodded. The snow was coming down hard, hissing against the heat of their power armour. Winter in Asaheim. Fenris at her most brutal.

'But we know what slew the beast?'

At any other time, Strongheart would have smiled at the question. As if Grimnar didn't know the answer. He was the greatest hunter the Space Wolves had ever produced, save Russ himself. A test then.

'The bones here are broken, but these...' Strongheart indicated the blood-stained ribs jutting from the bear's open torso.

'Melted,' Grimnar rumbled, flexing his fingers against the Axe Morkai, his legendary weapon, 'as if by acid.'

'The blood of a snow troll. It must have been injured in the fight.'

'And is no doubt licking its wounds as we speak.'

Grimnar threw his head back and took a deep breath through his hooked nose, the bones beaded into his mane clattered together. 'We have its scent,' the venerable Space Wolf stated flatly, looking up at the mountain that rose into low cloud, 'and soon shall have our prize.'

'A good hunt,' Strongheart acknowledged, rising to his feet.

Had his voice just wavered? He couldn't be sure. The Great Wolf turned to face him, ancient eyes narrowing.

'A good hunt,' the Jarl repeated, before his face split into a grin, long canines flashing. Laughing, Grimnar slapped Strongheart's arm with a blow that would have shattered a human's arm. 'Worthy of a hero, eh, Strongheart? Come, let us finish this.'

The two Space Marines started towards the foot of the mountain.

It had happened at the feast. By the time the company had returned to Fenris, preparations for the customary celebrations were already underway. Yes, they had lost many taking the city of Mactalas back from the orks, but they had been triumphant. The cost had been high, but the enemy had been vanquished.

It was always the same. Grimnar decreed that the fallen would be honoured, not with bowed heads and mournful hymns, but meat and ale and hearty songs. They had died warriors. Heroes forevermore. Their names would be remembered.

Strongheart had been a hero too, albeit one of the living, breathing variety. The story of his victory had spread, how he had slain the berserker ork that had tried to kill him, a brute twice the size of a Space Marine. His brothers gathered around, eager to see the metal fang that hung from Strongheart's neck, to hear how he'd reached into the alien's filthy mouth and ripped it free with his bare hands.

And the stories had reached Jarl Grimnar's table. The Fangfather had appeared in front of Strongheart, praising the Space Marine for his valour, inviting him on a hunting expedition. Just the two of them. Strongheart had seen the envy in his brothers' eyes. Unworthy of them. Unworthy of the Chapter.

Not that he could see anything now. The blizzard had hit as they'd started their ascent, clinging onto the side of the mountain. A complete whiteout.

'Jarl Grimnar,' Strongheart called, but there was no answer. The Fang-father had shouted, once, moments before and then there had been silence. Thoughts raced through Strongheart's mind. What if the Great Wolf had fallen? What if the mountain had succeeded where the enemies of the Imperium had failed for centuries? What if Grimnar was dead?

The ork's eyes blazing with hatred. Its body crushing him. Unable to even breathe.

Strongheart took a step forward, raising his hand as if he could some-how swat away the storm. Then the ground disappeared beneath him. He was falling, bouncing off rock and ice, down into *hel* itself.

The Space Wolf crashed into the ground, his power armour absorbing most of the impact. He blinked, his augmented eyes adjusting immedi-ately to the gloom of the cavern, weak light spilling down from the crack he had fallen through, high above.

Had Grimnar suffered the same fate?

The report of a bolt being fired. Something warm splattering over him, burning against his slashed cheek. The stench of violent death.

Strongheart took a breath, tasting the scent that permeated the cave. A vile musk, mixed with excrement and blood. Near. Very near.

The growl from his left had Strongheart on his feet in an instant. He reached down for his chainsword, but his gloved hand found only rock. It could have fallen anywhere as he had tumbled into the cave. Left with his fists then. That would be enough.

Movement from behind. Strongheart turned, but a moment too late. A massive paw caught him in the face, scythe-like claws gouging out his right eye, opening his cheek, finishing what the ork started.

Like steel through flesh.

The force of the blow sent Strongheart spinning, and he felt something crack in his spine as his massive body twisted.

Then he was falling back, the weight of his armour dragging him down. The back of his head cracked painfully against a boulder. Above him the snow troll blared, lips drawn back to reveal monumental teeth, its coarse fur the colour of Strongheart's own power armour, stained red by the blood that flowed from deep gashes in its side and arms. The bear had fought well. Better than he.

A roar filled the cave, not from the snow troll but from behind the mon-ster. As Strongheart recoiled, the giant turned, but not fast enough. One minute it was whole, a mountain of rage, muscle and hair, and the next its head had split down the middle, blood gushing like a fountain.

Grimnar drove Morkai down, cleaving deep into the snow troll's chest, the two sides of its body peeling away to frame the imposing bulk of the Great Wolf, magnificent in a haze of blood.

And then the corpse was crashing to the ground, Grimnar stepping over the twitching body, Morkai swinging back into the air, ready to bite for a second time.

The prone Space Wolf raised a hand, a futile defence against the legendary frost blades. The Fangfather bellowed, bringing the axe down where it bedded into the boulder behind Strongheart with a sound like thunder. Strongheart's shout of alarm caught in a throat thick with blood. He just stared, with his one remaining eye, up into a face twisted into a mask of pure disgust.

'What was his name?' Grimnar's voice was calm and measured and all the more dreadful because of it. Only his eyes betrayed the fury that boiled in his chest. 'Tell me you know his name.'

Strongheart choked, desperately trying to speak. 'Jarl, I...'

'Tell me!'

He shook his head, waves of pain accompanying the gesture. 'I don't know who you mean.'

Grimnar bent over the Space Wolf, leaning heavily on Morkai, eyes like blazing coals. 'I was there,' he snarled, 'when the ork attacked. I saw you fight. I saw you fall.'

'My lord...'

'I was too far away to offer assistance, had my own battles to win, but saw him rush forward, emptying his pistol into the beast. The Blood Claw who saved your miserable hide.'

All at once, Strongheart could see the new recruit's face. The pale skin free of scars, the shock of red hair. Unseeing eyes, staring up into the rain.

'And that's not all I saw that day, is it, Strongheart?'

The scene replayed in Strongheart's mind. The confusion. The noise. The ork bucking in its death-throes, slashing out with those infernal claws, striking the Blood Claw across the throat, damn near severing his neck. Strongheart would never know if the bolt from the Blood Claw's gun was the result of his hand spasming in death, or a last act of defiance.

Grimnar reached down, fingers curling around the metal tooth that rested on Strongheart's heaving chest.

'What did you do?' the Fangfather asked, his strong voice quiet. 'Pulled your memento from the ork's corpse as your brother lay dying beside you?'

Grimnar glanced down at the bisected carcass at his feet.

'Will you claim this kill as well?'

Bubbles of blood burst on Strongheart's lips as his mouth worked silently. Grimnar didn't wait for an answer. He drew himself up, the chain snapping around Strongheart's neck.

'I will seek out the name of the Blood Claw,' he promised, holding the tooth in his hand, 'and hang this trophy in the Great Hall in his memory. Those who praised you will know the truth. They will know how *worthy* you are. And you will face them, Turin Strongheart. You shall face them, when you return from this place.'

'My lord,' Strongheart managed finally. 'It was one battle, one mistake. I–'

Shards of rock stung Strongheart's cheek as Grimnar pulled Morkai free, cutting his excuses dead. Without another word, the Fangfather turned and strode from the cave, the expression etched into his face far worse than any rebuke. Strongheart listened to his heavy footsteps fade, snow drifting down steadily from the fissure high above.

Covering their tracks.

IN HRONDIR'S TOMB

Mark Clapham

It was the smell he registered first, before the sight or the sound. It was a hot scent, hotter than the sparks coming off his chainblade as it cut through armour, or the warmth of the Tau commander's blood as the blade dug through the battlesuit and into his flesh.

It was a static smell of air being agitated, of a very heavy weapon powering up, somewhere nearby. A mortal human, or even a Space Marine of a different Chapter, might not have picked the scent out from the many smells of battle.

Anvindr Godrichsson was a wolf brother, and his senses were more finely attuned. His nostrils twitched at the tang of it, catching the scent over the foul aroma of alien gore before him.

He glanced up, for little more than half a second. The sky was a grey blur of falling rain and rising smoke, but Anvindr could see a great, dark shape moving between buildings, a solid ring of light glowing through the mist.

A Tau gunship, its railgun powering up.

'To shelter,' Anvindr called to his squad, his voice ringing out through the ruins. He extracted his blood-slicked chainblade from the chest plate of the fallen commander, and dropped to the ground from his position astride the chest of the alien's battlesuit.

A Space Wolf feared nothing; the Adeptus Astartes fled from no enemy, but there was no glory or honour in meekly allowing a weapon like that to reduce you to a paste. The Tau were notorious for their desire to kill from a distance rather than engage in close combat, and Anvindr would be damned if they would succeed with his pack.

Anvindr's pack responded to his call without question, although Tormodr approached with bad grace as usual, a scowl across his face and a desultory huff of fire spurting from his flamer. Tormodr moved as fast as any of them, the heavy boots of his armour barely glancing off the rubble as he sprung over an incline into Anvindr's field of vision, yet he still managed to seem like he was dragging his feet.

Then the rest, all Grey Hunters of the Fourth Company of the *Vlka Fenryka*, known commonly as Space Wolves: Sindri, eyes gleaming with youth in spite of all his decades, his hair a shock of blond curls, unusual for a Fenrisian; Liulfr, heavy even for a Space Marine, as much immovable object as unstoppable force; and finally Gulbrandr, his skin pale but his hair and beard raven black. They all wore the colours of their Chapter, blue-grey power armour edged with gold, augmented with honour markings and the fur of significant kills.

Although all of them had their eyes out for a safe place of cover, it was Gulbrandr, sharp-eyed as ever, who let out a high whistle, pointing ahead.

They ran as the railgun fired its first shots, the blasts tearing into a city that had already been devastated by ground-level warfare. As the large railgun fired upon the retreating Wolves, buildings already gutted by fire and ordnance were shook to their foundations, and began to crumble altogether.

The Wolves ran through a city that threatened to bury them alive.

Then, following Gulbrandr's lead, they were on a steep, gravel-strewn slope at an angle to the city streets, sliding down towards a weathered stone archway some distance below ground level. Anvindr dug in his heels, controlling his descent as the weight of his armoured body dragged him downwards, throwing up scree in his wake.

Surrounding the archway were a few squat industrial vehicles and stacks of crates, as well as a series of crude arc lights, dull in the afternoon haze.

As the Wolves reached level ground, moving from a controlled slide to a run without a stumble or pause, a blast from the railgun impacted nearby, throwing Anvindr forward. Without his power armour he would have fallen. He wore no helmet, and so closed his eyes against the blazing light and heat that scorched his skin.

Still running, he opened his eyes, ears ringing, just in time to see another blast consume the archway they were running under. As they ran under the archway they did so through a rain of rubble; the arch itself collapsed over them, shaken to pieces by the hammering detonations.

The falling wall of shattered rock consumed them in darkness.

His ears still filled with the roar of the explosion, his field of vision obscured by rock dust, Anvindr found himself falling forward, struck in the right pauldron by some unseen chunk of rock. He controlled his fall enough to drop to one knee, steadying himself. He braced himself for further blows, but none came, just a gentle rain of fragments.

Then there was silence, or something like it. The rock fall had totally blocked the way they had come in, cutting off any noise from the surface, although Anvindr could still feel the periodic vibration from explosions above ground.

Anvindr checked himself. One pauldron dented, but otherwise just scrapes to his power armour, and light burns and scratches over his exposed face. He pulled himself to his feet, dust and small pieces of rock falling from his armour as he did so.

As the dust settled, he could make out a large chamber lit by a string of arc lights. The walls were polished stone, but featureless. Around Anvindr, his brothers were recovering themselves. Gulbrandr stood in front, entirely unscathed, and was looking ahead to the chamber's one exit, a corridor leading downwards. Anvindr ignored him, and turned to see Tormodr rising from the ground, shaking chunks of rock from his pelts while brushing aside a mocking hand of assistance from Sindri. Both seemed battered but intact, although Tormodr's arm hung limp at his side.

Of Liulfr, there was initially no sign. Where once the chamber led out to the daylight, a sloped wall of broken rock now blocked the way. There was no trace of Liulfr at all, just that wall of rock.

Anvindr approached the rockslide, ears and nose pricked, searching for the slightest sign. Within seconds he was on his knees, rolling away a stone as tall as himself. Sindri and Tormodr aided him in the work, while Gulbrandr hung back, keeping watch.

All this, they did wordlessly, united in a common objective. They uncovered a gloved hand, the fingers twitching at the air as the rocks holding it down were removed, then the rest of an armoured arm, and Liulfr's head and shoulders. Liulfr's helmet had buckled and split down one side of his face, and he blinked away dust and took a ragged breath as his face was exposed. His cheek was broken and his face bloodied, but he was alive.

'Real darkness,' said Liulfr with a cough of blood. 'I'd forgotten what it was like. Shame to have it broken by faces such as yours.' He laughed to himself, coughing blood again, then grunted.

'We'd have left you in peace if those furs didn't smell so much,' said Anvindr, nodding at the torn strips of pelt around the shoulders of Liulfr's battered armour. 'A noseless hive dweller could catch the scent of those, rockslide or not.'

During this exchange, Anvindr had been looking at his fellow Wolf closely, and this last insult was delivered with relief. Liulfr was pinned, a giant slab of rock having crushed his lower body. Anvindr knew the look of a brother whose thread was at its end, and Liulfr did not have that look. He would live.

He would not, however, be moving anywhere, as the Wolves discovered when they cleared a space around Liulfr. The rock slab that held him down was huge, taller than the chamber they were in and half as wide. Even the collective strength of the four other Wolves would not be enough to shift it.

Anvindr's mind was just teasing towards what exactly they might need to aid Liulfr when he heard the sound of someone approaching. The others had heard it too: Anvindr turned to see Gulbrandr already taking a firing position, his boltgun aimed down the tunnel. As footsteps drew closer,

Anvindr saw Gulbrandr relax his grip and give a barely perceptible nod: friend, not foe.

The man who emerged up the incline of the tunnel was an Imperial Guardsman, wearing the uniform of the Lacusian Guard, dark green with silver trim. As he approached he looked first at Gulbrandr, towering over him, then at the rest of the Wolves, then at the collapsed archway.

'My lords,' said the Lacusian formally. He looked past the Wolves to see the extent of the rockslide that had sealed the entrance.

'Who are you?' asked Anvindr.

'Could you come with me, lords?' asked the Lacusian, having finished his inspection.

Anvindr bristled at the evasion. He had expected a straight answer. In his experience most Guardsmen, even the sternest veterans, were intimidated by the presence of the Adeptus Astartes, as well they should. Was this man not afraid to defy a Space Marine?

No, Anvindr thought, looking at the Guardsman before him. It wasn't that the man wasn't intimidated by Anvindr. It was that there was someone or something else that intimidated him more.

'Very well,' grunted Anvindr, nodding for the Lacusian to lead the way.

Leaving Liulfr, the Wolves followed their mortal guide further down the tunnel, which remained broad enough for two Space Marines to walk shoulder-to-shoulder. The Lacusian walked with a slight limp, the sound of grinding gears as his right foot touched the ground indicating an augmetic leg.

Curved corridors broke off from the tunnel as it levelled out, but the Guardsman led them straight ahead. As they passed these corridors, Anvindr could see hollows in the curved stone walls, facing inwards towards their destination. Some of the alcoves were lit with lamps or small fires, and he could hear and smell human life nearby. People were living down here. The war on Beltrasse had raged for months before the Wolves arrived to drive back the Tau, and these were the refugees.

They were led into a wide octagonal chamber, the ceiling of which rose to a high dome. Lights strung around the chamber all pointed to the centre, where a huge stone cube sat on a raised dais. Machinery of a kind Anvindr did not recognise was scattered around the chamber, connected by bundles of cable.

The Lacusian who led them there stepped aside as they entered, and Anvindr climbed the steps of the dais. Carved into one side of the cube was a representation, crude but instantly recognisable, of a Space Marine in Terminator armour, seated with his hands resting on his knees.

The rest of the chamber was as unadorned as the tunnel that had led them there, the polished stone unmarked by any text. However, one word was carved beneath the engraving of the Space Marine:

HRONDIR

Anvindr looked back at the carving. The markings on one shoulder could have been part of a horned skull motif, seen from the side.

'His name was Hrondir, of the Exorcists Chapter of loyal Adeptus Astartes,' pronounced a smooth, clipped voice, as a newcomer entered the chamber. It was a supremely confident voice and the appearance matched: the man who entered was tall, taller than virtually any mortal, but shorter than a Space Marine. He was dark-skinned with chiselled, sharp cheeked features and piercing eyes, beneath one of which was a tattoo of a stylised letter 'I' that glowed slightly in the firelight. He wore a plain black robe thrown back over the shoulders of heavy gold armour, the plates of which were inscribed with curved lettering and ornate patterns. A long-handled hammer hung from his belt.

Anvindr recognised the man for what he was: an inquisitor. To Anvindr, it was obvious from his armour, but knowledge of the Inquisition's existence was privileged information, and few would recognise an inquisitor by sight.

The inquisitor was accompanied by another man, wearing black robes trimmed with silver. The second mortal was shorter, paler and seemed to almost disappear when stood beside his grandiosely clothed companion. He didn't speak, but instead carried a data-slate which he periodically glanced at.

'I am Montiyf, and this is Hrondir's tomb,' said the inquisitor, making a sweeping gesture. 'He fell here some three centuries ago, in a battle to save Beltrasse, and the people built this tomb in his honour. As the decades wore on, the catacombs of the tomb were expanded to house the other dead from that battle, so that they might be closer to where Hrondir sits within his sarcophagus, as is the local tradition.'

'Three centuries,' repeated Anvindr, still examining the carving on the great cube, Hrondir's sarcophagus. Had it been that long?

'Yes,' said the inquisitor redundantly, scrutinising Anvindr for a few seconds. He then turned to the Guardsman who had led the Wolves into Hrondir's tomb. 'Galvern, what is your report?'

'My lord,' the Lacusian nodded crisply, and Anvindr could see the hold that the inquisitor had over him. 'The entrance has been completely sealed by a rockslide, but otherwise the integrity of the tomb is intact.'

'Heavy fire from a Tau gunship brought down the archway,' added Anvindr. 'My brothers and I sought temporary shelter here. We will return to the surface once the threat has passed.'

'If the entrance is blocked then that will not be possible,' said the inquisitor. 'This is a tomb; there is only one entrance, captain. Fortunately it is a very well built and deep tomb, and is unlikely to suffer any further damage from the Tau.'

Anvindr shrugged off the inquisitor's acknowledgement of his rank, as it wasn't difficult to read his shoulder markings.

'If this is a tomb, why are you down here, inquisitor...?' asked Anvindr.

'Inquisitor Montiyf of the Ordo Malleus,' finished the man, gesturing to his companion. 'This is Interrogator Pranix, and we are here to learn what we can from Hrondir's victory, to study the enemies he defeated here. As battle-brothers of the honoured Sixth Chapter, you will of course understand the need to learn from a defeated enemy.'

Anvindr did not understand how Montiyf expected to discover anything about a long-dead enemy by skulking around a featureless tomb, but presumably the banks of equipment served some purpose in this respect. It was none of Anvindr's concern, regardless.

'We are here to fight the Tau,' said Anvindr. 'Is there no way back to the surface?'

It would, he thought, be intolerable to rot away down in such a hole, immortal life steadily slipping away in the dark. A perilously dull end to a long life of glorious battle.

'You will get to fight the xenos again soon enough,' said Montiyf. 'My retinue are following another lead, but they know our position and are due to liaise with me in nine days. Once they find the entrance has collapsed they will requisition whatever is needed to dig us out. Until then, the labyrinth of tunnels surrounding the main tomb is large, and there have been over a hundred civilians sheltering down here. They have water, air and food supplies, it should not be difficult to requisition whatever you need.'

Anvindr grunted again. He turned his attention back to the carving of Hrondir.

'I knew him,' said Anvindr.

'You knew Captain Hrondir?' asked Montiyf. The inquisitor, for all his pomp and threat, could not help but appear surprised.

Anvindr nodded. Although he was no *skjald*, he could tell what was expected of him, and cleared his throat to tell the tale.

They had fought side by side in the sinking city of Majohah, slaughtering heretic after heretic through flooded streets. Anvindr was a Blood Claw then, he and his young brothers meeting the fanatical savagery of the cultists with a youthful bloodlust of their own.

As the rising waters broke through crumbling walls in polluted torrents, so wave after wave of men and women, their souls bargained away to unspeakable forces, would burst out of buildings or from beneath the waters to assault the Wolves.

The Wolves cut their threads by the hundreds, and Anvindr was at the heart of it, slashing his chainblade back and forth through hordes of fanatics, slicing through corrupted flesh and chopping away at mutated limbs.

For Anvindr and the Wolves, Majohah was a slow, bloody matter of week after week of slaughtering a blighted population. Whether the

Wolves hunted down their enemy, or the enemy attacked them, made no difference.

The Exorcists arrived with a different mission. While the Wolves were spread across the city, killing heretics wherever they were found, the red-armoured Exorcists cut through it in a straight line, moving in on the Great Cathedra at the heart of Majohah.

Anvindr was one of the Wolves drawn into the Exorcists' assault on the Cathedra. They besieged the desecrated temple for three days, and it was there that Anvindr met Hrondir and the other Terminators of his squad.

The Exorcists were secretive and, compared to the hot-tempered Blood Claws, reserved in their mood, but Anvindr had found them to be determined and relentless warriors. Between his slow, incomprehensible chants and other rituals, Hrondir, looming over Anvindr in his Terminator armour, had spoken a little of his home world of Banish.

When one wall of the Cathedra fell, and the defences scattered, the Exorcists insisted on going in alone, leaving the Wolves to return to their primary mission. Anvindr watched Hrondir and the others cross the flooded square and charge through the breach, but within minutes Anvindr had an enemy by the throat and was preoccupied.

However, in the hours that followed the Exorcists entering the Cathedra, the air above that part of the city was disturbed, storm clouds turning in on themselves unnaturally. The Wolves, out in the streets, sniffed the air and knew something pivotal was going on at the city's heart.

Then it was done. The sky settled. Their mission complete, the Exorcists departed.

The Wolves fought on, but without the presence of whatever the Exorcists had confronted in the Cathedra, the enemy's will to fight was gone. The Wolves showed them no mercy, and the heretics fought for their lives as best they could, but within days they were all dead.

The city's descent halted, the floodwaters left to grow stagnant without further replenishment. The Wolves left Majohah in peace of a sort, a part-flooded ruin devoid of life, its streets clogged with the bloated, tainted bodies of its former residents.

Anvindr left out some details: the chants, the lights in the sky. The mortal, Galvern, was still in earshot, and Anvindr had no desire to see him purged for hearing of matters the Inquisition would rather he did not know. But he kept much of the story intact, the valour of Hrondir and that the battle turned the tide.

As Anvindr had told his story, more mortals had entered the chamber, cautiously keeping their distance from both the inquisitor and the Wolves. By the time the retelling was complete, he had an audience; a few more Guardsmen, standing respectfully to attention in his presence, but mainly civilians, hovering nervously at the edge of the room, rapt to his speech.

'To these people, Hrondir is a myth,' explained Montiyf. 'No official

account was ever written down, and even this tomb was lost for over a
hundred years. Hrondir's name has been passed down by word of mouth,
little more than a folk tale, and now you are here, talking of meeting Hrondir
in your own lifetime. To them, you have stepped out of a legend.'

In the tomb, time passed painfully slowly for the Wolves. Unable to hunt
or fight, without even space to properly train, they instead searched every
inch of the catacombs to find something that might aid their escape, or
help free Liulfr. The web of tunnels sprawling out from the central chamber
where Hrondir lay at rest led to dozens of small chambers, and the Wolves
searched every one.

Many were occupied by civilians who had descended into the tomb to
shelter from the war above. Others had been turned into makeshift supply rooms, or housed water recycling equipment or generators. Some had
been left as they had been found, containing nothing but funerary relics.
The Beltrassens did not entomb their dead lying down, instead burying
them seated, so that they might face the afterlife with dignity, and many
of the rooms had square stone sarcophagi set into alcoves.

The Wolves found little of use. They found cracks or pores in the stone
that allowed air or a trickle of water into the tomb, but no hidden tunnels,
nor any heavy equipment that could help free Liulfr. In spite of this, they
continued to prowl the corridors, searching for an advantage.

Even this endless pacing was impeded by the presence of so many
mortals. The Wolves could see perfectly well in the low light of the darker
tunnels, so carried no light source with them.

When a mortal came walking from the opposite direction, that mortal would walk straight into the towering Space Marines, if not given due
warning. Most of the Wolves adopted a terse 'make way' to scatter any
mortals in their path, with the exception of Sindri, who found it amusing
to stay silent and watch the coming mortal bounce off his heavy armour.

For all his sport, even Sindri was not cruel, and he would catch any mortal who fell before they hurt themselves, his reflexes responding before the
mortal had any real idea of what had happened.

While the Guardsmen at least had some military training and physical
aptitude, the fragility and clumsiness of the civilian mortals retained a fascination for Anvindr. Even in the distant days of his childhood, before the
Sky Warriors had made him one of their own, Anvindr had been made of
stronger stuff than these city dwellers. Fenrisian young learned survival
fast, and Anvindr had been a hunter from virtually the moment he took
his first steps.

As a Grey Hunter, so far removed from those beginnings, these mortals
with their fast breaths and heartbeats, so involved in the transient concerns
of their short lives, were a mystery to him. They fluttered around him like
moths, and he tried not to break them.

* * *

Blood and scraps of bone.

The chamber was one of many similar rooms, featureless except for three small podiums, each of which held a smooth-surfaced reliquary box. Two were in place, while one had been knocked to the floor. It remained intact, whatever bones or other remains it contained kept safely inside.

The mortals who had rested in this chamber were not so lucky. Blood splattered the walls and floor, and within the streaks of dried blood were scraps of bone, cloth and other, thicker, matter, the shredded remains of skin and organs.

The room was small, at least to Anvindr, and while the mortals walked in and out with ease, he had to duck to enter. Montiyf was standing, arms folded so that Anvindr could see the ruby-eyed skulls engraved on his gauntlets, while Pranix squatted closer to the floor, examining a streak of gore and tapping his data-slate.

'I am not yours to summon,' Anvindr growled to Montiyf. It had been three days since the Wolves had entered the tomb, and Montiyf had sent one of the Lacusians to request Anvindr's presence.

Anvindr didn't expect any response to this from the inquisitor, any acknowledgement that the Wolves were not a resource at the inquisitor's disposal, and he didn't get any beyond an impassive glare.

'What happened here?' Anvindr asked.

'We do not know,' said Montiyf. 'Five people were in this room. This is all that is left of them.'

'You are sure all five?' asked Anvindr. 'One didn't turn on the others?' Mortal men killed each other for foolish reasons, Anvindr knew this.

'We have checked the entire tomb, lord,' said Pranix, with soft formality. He had attached a brass rod to his data-slate with a line of copper wire, and embedded one end in a smear of gore on the ground. 'This is all that remains of any of them.'

'Then someone else?' asked Anvindr, frustrated. 'Grief, these petty crimes are no concern of mine, and I don't see why the Inquisition cares either.'

'If this were a normal crime,' said Montiyf, running one gloved finger down the tattoo beneath his eye. 'But look at the remains. Does this strike you as something a normal human could do? Fast enough that no one even heard a scream?'

Anvindr gave a non-committal grunt. There were plenty of things that could kill this fast, beasts and xenos that could rend flesh in a flurry of claws or weapons. Anvindr had seen it happen.

In the heat of battle, he had been that killer himself.

'There are fears that some savage beast did this, although there is nowhere for such an animal to hide,' said Montiyf. Anvindr could feel the inquisitor's gaze on him. 'Unless that beast lurked beneath a human skin, a hidden animal rage.'

'You can reassure the mortals, this was not one of us,' said Anvindr, not rising to the inquisitor's coy insinuations. 'We are not animals.'

Anvindr crossed the room, looked more closely at a streak of blood on the wall and opened up his senses. He could smell human blood and a touch of bile, but those fluids didn't smell fresh, nor did they have the dead scent of stale, dried blood. He rubbed at one of the blood stains with his fingers. His fingers came away stained with powder, the dust leaving a hint of something in the air.

'This blood was hot as it spilled,' Anvindr said. 'Very hot; these stains are burnt.'

'We must be alert,' said Inquisitor Montiyf, and with that he left the room. Pranix remained, and Anvindr lingered, thinking of the ways to kill a man, and what might cause such damage, shredding flesh and leaving blood stains burnt into the walls.

A weapon? Someone would have heard.

A psyker? Anvindr had seen mental powers tear an enemy to pieces, or burn them from the inside out. The Inquisition were known for their psychic powers.

Deep in thought, Anvindr picked up the fallen reliquary from the floor. It rattled slightly, the sound of bone fragments moving within. The box seemed tiny in Anvindr's giant hand, the remains of a mortal life in his palm. He placed the featureless box back on its featureless podium.

'No names,' he said, largely to himself.

Pranix looked up from his data-slate. 'Lord?'

'There are no names, apart from Hrondir's,' said Anvindr. 'The people who built this tomb made all this effort to lay their dead here, all these boxes and chambers, yet they didn't mark down the names of the dead?'

Pranix didn't say anything, but continued to watch Anvindr as he walked away.

'He insults us!' complained Gulbrandr, after Anvindr reported the deaths, and his conversation with the inquisitor. 'As if we were beasts who needed to chew down on these tiny mortals.'

The four Wolves had taken one of the larger chambers in the tomb for themselves, a long room with a long stone altar in the centre. Gulbrandr prowled the room, whilst Tormodr sat in one corner and Sindri leaned nonchalantly against a wall.

'He did not say he believed this,' said Anvindr. 'But I am sure some of the mortals do.'

'Let them run scared of us,' said Sindri. 'Weak little things. Why should we care if a few of them die? This whole world is in ruins.'

'That depends what killed them,' said Anvindr. 'And how we can kill it.'

'If there is something worth hunting down here after all, then that changes everything,' said Sindri, grinning widely.

* * *

A day later, another mortal died. This time, screams were heard, but by the time any witness arrived, the room from which the scream came was empty.

It was rapidly established that a young woman had gone missing, and a search was organised.

It was Gulbrandr who found the body, collapsed in an alcove at the opposite end of the catacombs. Skinned and gutted, an unnatural heat rose from the corpse.

Of the killer, they could find no sign.

'He's gone,' said Sindri.

It was now four days since they had entered the tomb.

Liulfr would not be able to heal fully until his legs were freed, but his condition was stable, and he certainly didn't need monitoring, his own remarkable physiology keeping him healthy and in minimal pain even while pinned.

Nonetheless, the Wolves chose to visit Liulfr regularly, recounting old war stories while making futile attempts to discover a way of freeing Liulfr without causing a larger rockslide.

It had been Sindri's turn to visit Liulfr, but he returned within minutes of departing.

'If this is one of your jests...' Anvindr began, but he could see from Sindri's expression that he wasn't joking.

'I must see this for myself,' said Anvindr.

Liulfr was indeed gone, almost without a trace. Scree had rolled down to fill the gap where Liulfr had been pinned under the stone column, and in spite of digging through the gravel Anvindr couldn't find even a fragment of ceramite. If Liulfr had somehow been dragged away, there would at least be some part of him left behind.

Instead, there was nothing to mark where Liulfr had been, except a scattering of blackened stones, scarred from exposure to a great and sudden heat.

'Perhaps he freed himself,' said Montiyf, when told the news of Liulfr's disappearance. 'The explosions above may have shaken the rock above him, allowing your brother to manoeuvre himself free.'

'And walk away on broken legs?' scoffed Anvindr. 'Why even try to drag himself away, when Liulfr knew we would come to him in good time? No, if Liulfr had dragged himself loose, he would have waited for one of his pack to find him.'

'Then what would you suggest happened?' asked Montiyf.

The inquisitor and the Wolf circled each other slowly, stood before Hrondir's sarcophagus. Montiyf's hammer and Anvindr's chainblade stayed hanging from their respective belts, but each had a hand free, ready to defend themselves.

'There are ways to move flesh through walls, to pull that which is solid through matter,' said Anvindr.

'A sorcerer?' asked Montiyf, an eyebrow raised. Matters of daemonic heresy were the business of the Ordo Malleus, and Anvindr was pushing into Montiyf's territory by even discussing them.

'Or a psyker,' said Anvindr. 'Such power can leave a tang in the air, and create a great excess of heat.'

Anvindr raised one hand in a closed fist, and then opened it to reveal blackened stones in his palm.

It was an accusation, albeit an indirect one. Many inquisitors were psykers, and those abilities could stretch from the reading of mortal minds to the manipulation of objects, and even greater distortions of reality. And the greater those powers, the more likely the psyker would succumb to the dark forces drawn to his unnatural talents.

Tension hung in the air between the two. They were not alone – while the chamber had been cleared so that Anvindr could speak about matters that the inquisitor would execute most subjects of the Imperium for even knowing about, the rest of Anvindr's pack were present, as was Pranix. While the Wolves outnumbered the representatives of the Inquisition, and their Chapter was known for its defiance, to attack an inquisitor was nonetheless almost unthinkable, treasonous.

Unless that inquisitor had been corrupted by the very forces he was sworn to destroy.

Montiyf was about to speak when a mortal cry echoed from a nearby corridor. There was a momentary exchange of glances between Anvindr and Montiyf, then a nodding agreement to temporarily postpone their conversation.

As the Wolves ran from the chamber, the inquisitor and his interrogator close behind, there was no one to see an icy film develop on the surface of Hrondir's sarcophagus, then evaporate into the air as quickly as it had formed.

The man whose cry they had heard stood, back pressed into the stone wall, shuddering in horror, his eyes locked on the smouldering mass on the floor before him.

'It just appeared,' the man said, then proceeded to repeat those three words again and again, staring at the bloody, burning mass. Steam filled the air, and in the dimly lit corridor it was hard to see what was actually there.

Anvindr had his bolter drawn as he approached the twitching shape on the ground, ready to confront whatever horror had materialised, but rapidly lowered his weapon.

'Liulfr,' he said. 'It's Liulfr.'

The Wolves gathered around their fallen comrade. His armour had been battered and burnt, and was still hot to the touch, dented all over and even cracked in places. The livery of his ceramite plate was blackened beyond recognition, and the pelts he wore around his shoulders were little more than crisped wisps of ashen matter.

From the waist down Liulfr's legs were indeed crushed, mangled within flattened armour, and where the armour was most cracked burnt flesh was visible beneath.

Liulfr's head was a scorched-red mass of bruised and burnt flesh, the hair entirely gone and the eyes and mouth reduced to crumpled slits.

As Anvindr leaned over to check Liulfr's breathing, his mouth and eyes snapped open. His eyes were bloodshot but intact, and a bruised tongue wet burnt-dry lips.

'Fought it,' he said, with considerable effort. 'It dragged me into the dark, but I fought it every step. I wouldn't let it take me, tried to free him.'

This message delivered, Liulfr slumped back, eyes staring blankly.

Liulfr was dead.

The Wolves carried Liulfr to their chamber, and laid him out on the altar.

'Tried to free who?' asked Sindri, breaking the mournful silence that had fallen across them all. 'He makes no sense.'

'He was taken somewhere,' said Anvindr. 'Pulled away by magic to some-where dark, then returned.'

'This is work for a rune priest, not for us,' rumbled Tormodr.

'Well, there are no priests here,' said Anvindr. 'So it falls to us whether it pleases us or not.'

Anvindr was no inquisitor, nor one of the Adeptus Arbites: he did not sift for truth or search out secrets.

He was a Sky Warrior, a hunter, one of the *Vlka Fenryka*. His earliest memories were of the hunt, of the endless icy wastes of Fenris, tracking the distant shape of an animal as the cold winds tore through layers of furs. He knew how to seek out prey, to kill, to be aware of a predator's eyes on you, and strike at them first.

As a young man he had become aware of being observed, and when he sought out his observers they took him away to the *Aett*, where he was ele-vated to the ranks of the Sky Warriors.

He had hunted and fought and killed ever since, it was his nature from birth and it would be with him until his death; an endless cycle.

The enemy he faced now seemed to break that simple cycle of his exist-ence, to defy face-to-face confrontation, to leave no trail to follow. It was a riddle, and Anvindr had no use for riddles. It was for Montiyf to unpick such things, and Montiyf showed no sign of understanding any more than Anvindr.

Unless Anvindr was wrong to consider this different to any other threat. There was an enemy, one which ventured from its lair. If it could not be caught while it hunted, then it would need to be found in its den and struck at there.

Perhaps it was all that simple, and there was no mystery, just the hunt.

And if there was no mystery, perhaps there were no riddles to be resolved, and the one person who should have known what was happening, who had been strangely idle, had the knowledge that was expected of them. Perhaps everything was exactly as it should be, and all Anvindr needed to do was resolve the problem in the best way he knew.

'Hrondir is at the heart of this,' Anvindr called out to Montiyf as he entered the central chamber of the tomb. The inquisitor and his interrogator were alone, poring over readings on their equipment. 'We have been looking for enemies in the shadows, but this place is no mystery, it is devoted to the memory of one man alone. Whatever is attacking us, it relates to Hrondir. I don't know how, but I think you do.'

'I do?' asked Montiyf.

'Why else would you be here?' said Anvindr. 'Research on a dead enemy, in the middle of a Tau invasion? No, the Exorcists have always been close to the Inquisition. If your Ordo didn't send Hrondir here then they at least knew what he faced, and knew enough to come here the moment this tomb was uncovered.'

'These are matters for the Inqui–' Montiyf began.

'Enough,' Anvindr barked. 'Keep your secrets from these mortals, but whatever stalks these halls cut the thread of Liulfr, a brother of the *Vlka Fenryka*. I will not waste time on protocol while a threat like that exists. So speak, so that we may kill this thing and be done with it.'

There was a long silence. Anvindr's pack had followed him into the chamber, and stood quietly nearby.

Then Montiyf spoke, evenly and surely, as if Anvindr hadn't needed to wring the truth out of him.

'Hrondir came here alone,' said Montiyf. 'The forces of Chaos sought to break into this sector, and the Exorcists and my ordo were spread thin striking at the gravest heresies wherever they erupted. Hrondir was the last of his squad. By what accounts we have left from that time, he responded to reports of some daemonic emergence here on Beltrasse.'

Montiyf circled the dais at the centre of the room, and the great stone sarcophagus that dominated the chamber.

'It took three decades to purify this sector, but we were thorough,' Montiyf continued. 'No report was left unchecked, no matter how long it took, so decades after Hrondir was sent to Beltrasse the planet was revisited, to see what became of him. This world was clean of heresy, and all that could be gleaned were stories of a single Space Marine destroying a great evil.'

Montiyf gestured to the chamber they were in. 'This tomb was already buried and forgotten by then, so there was little to be done to follow up the stories. But concerns lingered still, that Beltrasse had too neatly forgotten what occurred here. So when the tomb was uncovered in a Tau attack, we returned. And the events of recent days show that we were right to do so.'

'Hrondir's mission remains incomplete,' said Anvindr. 'The daemon still lives.'

'Not necessarily,' said Montiyf. 'Hrondir may have dealt with the enemy as best he could. If the evil could not be killed, there are other ways to win such battles.'

'Witchcraft,' Anvindr said.

'There are rituals,' said Montiyf. 'But these are many, and we do not know which one. But I am certain that whatever lives here in the tomb, it is not fully manifest. It is restrained, or else it would have killed us all days ago and unleashed itself upon the world above.'

Restrained. Something about the word itched at Anvindr's brain. What had Liulfr said, about being trapped in the darkness? As if the daemon had been drawn back to some cell, and took its victims there with it before reaching out once more to deposit the remains back where it found them. Only Liulfr had fought, and been released with a last breath left in him.

'There are no hidden rooms or spaces here?' asked Anvindr, already knowing the answer.

It was Interrogator Pranix who answered, rather than his master.

'None,' said Pranix. 'We have scanned every bit of wall, floor and ceiling. This tomb is buried deep in stony ground.'

'Then where could this beast be hiding... except in there?' Anvindr pointed to the sarcophagus. 'Why else would you be watching that box so closely if the daemon were not in there? The Beltrassens must have known the daemon lay with Hrondir, that's why this tomb bears not a single word or image or name apart from his, so that the daemon could take no hold of them. So why haven't you opened the sarcophagus yet?'

'Because we do not know enough. We have not gathered enough information on this creature,' said Montiyf. 'To act prematurely would be foolhardy.'

'Is that why you have been scouring the scene after every attack, so that you can gather more data while this thing wreaks havoc?' said Anvindr, turning to Pranix.

'An unfortunate necessity,' said Pranix. He barely raised his voice but there was steel behind his words, an absolute self-possession. 'We could not afford to act prematurely, until we knew exactly–'

'So you kept your silence while one of us died?' snarled Anvindr in exasperation, his rage barely contained.

Pranix didn't respond, but neither did he flinch in the face of Anvindr's anger.

Anvindr looked between inquisitor and interrogator, both absolutely certain in their authority. He ground his teeth, fangs digging into the inside of his mouth. Then, with a snarl of released anger, he turned to his pack.

'Well, if caution is the word of the day,' said Anvindr. 'We know what we must do, brothers?'

Montiyf and Pranix made no move to stop the Wolves as they surrounded the stone sarcophagus and searched for a way to open it, instead stepping back and preparing themselves for whatever came next. In his peripheral vision Anvindr could see Montiyf detaching the gold hammer from where it hung from his belt, adjusting his grip on its ornate handle.

It was Sindri who found that the front panel of the sarcophagus, the one bearing Hrondir's likeness and name, could be slowly eased out. Tormodr and Gulbrandr did the heavy lifting, while Anvindr and Sindri stepped back, weapons raised.

Tormodr and Gulbrandr moved the slab aside, resting it against the side of the sarcophagus. Dead air seeped out of the interior, a musty smell but with something else, a more recent stink of burnt flesh and hot blood.

There was a moment of absolute stillness, as the Wolves waited for something to emerge. But nothing did.

Anvindr approached the sarcophagus, bolter raised.

As opposed to the spartan stone of the rest of the tomb, the interior of the sarcophagus was covered with writing, some in languages Anvindr didn't understand, scratched on every surface. The text was accompanied by arcane signs and symbols, many of which Anvindr did recognise, as marks of warding to hold back evil.

Hold back, or hold in?

The stone interior was blackened by scorch marks, but the set of Terminator armour that occupied the sarcophagus still bore its fierce red livery, the horned skull still displayed on one shoulder.

Matching the engraving on the front of the sarcophagus, Hrondir had been laid to rest seated, his fully armoured body sat on a stone throne strong enough to hold the armour's vast weight. The helmet was down over Hrondir's face, and his hands rested, palms down, in his lap.

'Stay back,' said Anvindr, stepping towards Hrondir. He reached around the armour's helmet, finding the release clasps. There was a hiss of released air as the helmet lifted away.

The exposed head was well-preserved. Pallid, dried skin had shrunk over the skull, the eyelids sunken. The emaciated features were recognisably Hrondir's, and even in death his wide jaw was set in a caricature of stoic determination.

Anvindr's eyes narrowed, his ears pricked, checking for any sign of life. There was not the murmur of even the slowest heartbeat or breath, no movement at all, but there was still something there. Hrondir was not alive, but neither was he quite dead, in a way that Anvindr could not understand.

'He is dead... but not dead?' said Anvindr, realising how absurd this was while standing in Hrondir's tomb.

'A tiny spark of his life essence still holds on,' said Montiyf. 'His body is long dead, but some part of his soul lingers.'

As Anvindr stepped away from Hrondir's body, determined to ask Montiyf to explain himself, his heavy boot knocked something aside, a chip of hard material that bounced off the interior wall of the sarcophagus and spun at Anvindr's feet.

He looked down to see it was a chip of ceramite spinning to a halt. A curved piece of armour plate, painted in the colour of his own Chapter.

A piece of Liulfr's armour.

And then Anvindr was hit by an incredible rush of force, a surge of heat and violence in the air strong enough to throw even a fully armoured Space Marine off his feet and across the chamber.

Anvindr hit the wall hard, falling to the floor in a shower of stone fragments. He landed on his feet, bolter already raised.

He could see it now, a blur in the air coalescing before the body of Hrondir. It made his eyes itch to look at it, an amorphous blob of fiery, semi-transparent matter, straining to pull itself into existence, the shadows of teeth and claws slashing the air around it.

'For Russ!' shouted Anvindr, squeezing the trigger of his bolter to unleash a storm of explosive bolts. Sindri and Gulbrandr fired too, and the daemonic presence squirmed under fire.

Then, it was gone.

'Too easy?' asked Sindri, keeping his bolter raised.

'Far too easy,' agreed Anvindr. 'Inquisitor?'

'Agreed,' said Montiyf. 'It will return.'

'It's anchored,' said Pranix.

'Speak sense,' snapped Anvindr.

'The inquisitor said some of Hrondir's soul remained,' said Pranix. 'Hrondir must have been unable to kill the daemon outright, so instead he bound it to his own soul. Even in death that bond still holds, Hrondir's soul is bound to his body, pulling the daemon back to its cell.'

The inquisitor pointed to Hrondir's body. 'You can see it, the force holding it here.'

Anvindr looked. Hrondir's armour seemed lit with a light blue, flickering glow, traces of psychic energy rippling across the surfaces of the ancient armour. The light crackled, as if responding to some opposing force.

'Pranix is right,' said Montiyf. 'That's the daemon's anchor.'

The blue light burst forth with a wave of cold air, a brief frost forming around the edges of the sarcophagus, and the daemonic presence reappeared. It was not alone: Anvindr could see Galvern, the first Guardsman they had encountered in the tomb, twisting in the air before Hrondir's seated figure. Galvern was in agony, his body covered in flames, cuts appearing on his skin as the very air around him attacked with daemonic force.

Anvindr felt rising anger. This must have been what happened to Liulfr and the others, warped to the inside of Hrondir's sarcophagus to be mauled by this daemon, the remains then returned to where they had come from once its foul work was done.

Anvindr had had enough.

'Gulbrandr,' he called to the best shot in the pack. 'Mercy kill.'

Gulbrandr nodded, fired his bolter once and Galvern's head exploded. Galvern's body went limp, and there was a high screech as the daemon tore the body limb from limb, frustrated at having its game cut short.

The daemon itself seemed unaffected by the bolt having penetrated its body to reach Galvern. Instead it dropped to the floor, and disappeared once again, only to emerge at Gulbrandr's feet, consuming him in a wave of heat.

Gulbrandr struggled against the semi-visible creature that clawed at him with burning, translucent limbs, but it was like wrestling a liquid. Tormodr and Sindri rushed to help, the latter revving his chainblade, which he brought down on to the creature.

Sindri swore as the creature flowed around the blade and it bounced off the chest plate of Gulbrandr's armour.

'Great Russ,' said Sindri. 'We're more likely to kill him than it.'

'Stand back,' shouted Montiyf, stepping forward. His eyes were faintly glowing with energy, which crackled around the hammer in his grip. He swung the hammer just short of Gulbrandr so that it swept through the creature's mass without hitting the Space Marine, and the creature recoiled from the psychic charge, disappearing into the floor once again.

It reappeared back in Hrondir's sarcophagus. Gulbrandr dropped to one knee, his flesh steaming from contact with the thing, his face a mass of bloody cuts.

'It doesn't seem scratched,' said Anvindr bitterly. 'How do we even hurt this thing?'

'We need to cut it loose,' said Pranix. Anvindr registered that he, too, had a flicker of psychic energy running through him. 'Destroy the anchor, release Hrondir's spirit and the daemon will manifest fully in our world. The body is untouched, so the daemon must have been unable to set itself free, but that rite won't prevent anyone else from doing it. Once unleashed, the creature will be far more dangerous than it is now, but it will be vulnerable to attack. Together, we may be able to defeat it.'

It was Anvindr's turn to swear, uttering under his breath a very old, very obscure Fenrisian curse from his youth about bearing the children from a rival tribe. Montiyf and Pranix had let Liulfr die while they kept their secrets, but the Ordo Malleus knew more about fighting daemons than anyone. The Wolves would need them to destroy the monster that killed Liulfr.

'Very well,' said Anvindr. 'Tormodr, I want you to give my old friend Hrondir a long overdue cremation. The rest of you, draw that thing out.'

Anvindr, Gulbrandr and Sindri opened fire on the creature, which flowed away from the sarcophagus to avoid their shots, slipping in and out of existence as it rolled around the chamber. The Wolves maintained fire, driving it back.

With the creature distracted, Tormodr ran up the steps into the sarcophagus. Hrondir's helmet sat loosely on his shoulders, as Anvindr hadn't locked it back into place, so it came off easily as Tormodr pulled it away, revealing the Exorcist's withered head.

'Apologies, brother,' said Tormodr, aiming his flamer and letting loose a gout of flame that consumed Hrondir's head. The ancient flesh was dry as paper, and the fire not only burned away the skin from his head, but descended down the collar into the armour, burning away the rest of his body.

The Terminator armour fell forward, thick black smoke pouring out of the neck. It crashed to the ground spilling dark cindered fragments across the floor. Anvindr thought he saw a mist of blue energy rise from the ashes, and then dissipate altogether.

The daemon roared, and what had been a ghostly shape in the air began to coalesce into something solid but unstable, a rippling mass of horribly real, pustulant flesh. Pores expanded on the repellent flesh, exhaling foetid air as tubular masses became limbs, razor-edged tips scratching the stone floor as it found purpose. Other limbs expanded and thrashed, while a mass of glassy eyes burst from the centre of the daemon's body like pustules.

The daemon's eyes held Anvindr's gaze and he felt a hot sensation behind his eyes, the touch of Chaos trying to find purchase on his mind.

It would take no hold of him.

'Now!' bellowed Anvindr, opening fire on the thing, the cacophony of gunfire rising as the rest of the pack opened fire too.

Anvindr concentrated his fire on that mass of eyes, and boiling ichor sprayed from the wounds as the foul eyeballs were destroyed. However the creature was still in flux, still expanding, and other eyes opened up over its body just as extra limbs flailed around the chamber. Each limb rippled with spines and teeth, the flesh flowing like liquid, so it was hard to tell where the flesh ended and the slime that dripped from it began.

One such limb slashed at Gulbrandr, and a razor-edged claw scythed through the ceramite of his chest plate as if it were old vellum, drawing blood and throwing him backwards. Where the daemon's claw had cut flesh, the edge of the wound began to blacken with decay.

The creature shifted forward, its flailing limbs dragging it across the chamber at terrifying speed in spite of its bulk, raising a mass of claws to deliver a killing blow to Gulbrandr. The daemon seemed unperturbed by the bolts still exploding all over its body, but was driven back as Montiyf and Pranix stepped into the fray, unleashing a blast of psychic energy that drove back the monster.

The daemon swerved to find another victim to satiate its bloodlust, but found Tormodr and his flamer instead. While previously the creature had coursed with the unnatural heat of its incursion upon reality, now it was a thing of vulnerable flesh, and it howled as Tormodr set it alight.

Anvindr seized Gulbrandr's arm to prevent him from falling. Steam was rising from his infected wound, and there was a lost, unfocussed look in his eyes.

'Look at me, brother,' Anvindr said, and Gulbrandr's eyes locked on to his. 'Do not let it take a hold of you, fight it.'

Gulbrandr nodded, focus returning to his eyes, and shook off Anvindr's supporting arm, raising his bolter to open fire once more.

The daemon was still trying to expand its mass, but the hail of bolter fire was tearing its flesh apart as it did so. The Wolves, along with the inquisitor, attacked the daemon while evading its thrashing limbs, but they were merely holding it in check, not destroying it.

'We must take it apart,' said Montiyf, raising his hammer. Anvindr nodded, raising his own chainblade in reply, and they moved in on the creature.

The creature lashed out at them as they closed, but Anvindr jumped over a low-swiping limb to land close to the creature's torso, while Montiyf smacked aside a claw with his hammer. Anvindr drove his chainblade into the creature's eyes while Montiyf brought his hammer down on the creature's head, each blow accompanied by a release of psychic power.

Pranix moved in with a psychic blast of his own, while Tormodr had his own chainblade free, and even Gulbrandr staggered over with a long knife drawn, his other arm held across his bleeding chest.

As Sindri approached a flailing claw caught him behind the knee, a claw that shifted into a tendril and dragged him to the floor, pulling him towards a mouth that opened up in the daemon's side. As he was dragged towards the daemon, Sindri kept his bolter level, firing ahead as the tendril crushed the power armour and began to dig into his flesh.

Anvindr could feel the malign presence as his chainsword rose and fell, hacking and smashing at vile flesh. Doubts and heresies began to sprout in his mind, bursting forth like an infection. That Hrondir had sold his soul to this daemon to sustain it, that it was a god, the only true god, that it was life, that it could not die.

Lies and heresies from a desperate entity. Anvindr drove his chainsword deeper into the amorphous flesh, and a howl rang out. Beside him, Montiyf brought his hammer down again with another psychic flash. The vile flesh of the thing began to bubble and disintegrate, mouths forming to let out a piteous, monstrous whine.

The creature's screams rang out through the catacombs. In the subchambers of the tomb, mortals sat in the darkness, trickles of blood dripping from their ears at the sound of a daemon being dispatched back to hell.

* * *

Anvindr and his pack barely spoke to Montiyf and Pranix in the days that followed, nor when the blockade of the tomb entrance was cleared and they stepped out into the light. While they had come together to destroy the daemon, Anvindr knew that Pranix could have done more to confront the creature earlier, rather than allowing Liulfr to die as part of his strategy.

Anvindr and Tormodr would rejoin the battle against the Tau immediately, but Gulbrandr and Sindri would be out of action for a while. It left a bad taste in Anvindr's mouth, but he held his tongue. The Inquisition was a dangerous enemy to make, and Anvindr had a war of his own to fight. He decided to redirect his anger at the Tau.

Before they left the tomb, Anvindr removed the pieces of Hrondir's armour from his sarcophagus. He did not know how, but he would find a way to return them to Banish, so that they might be worn once more by a brother of the Exorcists Chapter.

'They resent us,' said Pranix, watching the Wolves walk away. 'They believe we could have acted sooner, and that our reticence let their brother die.'

Montiyf raised an eyebrow.

'You were right to counsel caution,' he said. 'An excellent strategy, Pranix, and your suggestion to destroy the anchor turned the course of battle. I fear you will be leaving my retinue soon.'

'Leaving?' asked Interrogator Pranix.

'Of course,' replied Montiyf. 'I will be recommending your raising to the role of inquisitor, Pranix. You have demonstrated the correct qualities.'

'Thank you,' said Pranix. He didn't meet Montiyf's eye.

Inquisitor Montiyf felt a slight sense of disquiet at the coolness of his interrogator's thanks, the slight suspicion that he expected no less than to be raised to the Inquisition. That this was Pranix's decision, not Montiyf's.

Then he dismissed the thought. He could hear Tau heavy ordnance not far away. The daemon was dead and it was time for them to withdraw.

Soon, they would depart the planet altogether, and leave Beltrasse to the Wolves.

ENGAGE
THE ENEMY

Lee Lightner

Thokar, wolf priest of Fenris, transmitted his acceptance of the wolf lord's command, although he didn't expect his master to give it more than a glance. The wolf lord demanded quick obedience and such formalities were not to his taste. Thokar surveyed the Space Marines around him. Grey power armour glinted under the bright lights of the battle-barge. Contrasting their boltguns and grenades, pelts and skulls of Fenrisian wolves hung from their chest plates, shoulder pads and anywhere else the Space Wolves could fit them. Beneath his helm, Thokar smiled.

'For Fenris! For Russ! For the Emperor!' shouted the Space Wolves, raising their fists. The wolf priest lowered his black gauntleted hand as the others moved to the Thunderhawk. For other Chapters, war cries might be ceremony, but those words echoed like thunder in the hearts of his Wolves.

Thokar watched each of his battle-brothers, seeing not the armoured and invincible warriors of the Imperium, but the individual warriors that he had chosen. So many times he'd searched for the bravest warriors of Fenris. He remembered the reverence in the eyes of mortals as they looked upon the Space Wolves as armoured gods. Each of these Grey Hunters had once been a Fenrisian warrior, struggling to survive in a land of eternal danger. The skills, the loyalty and the heart of these few had proven them worthy of travel to the Fang, the fortress of the Space Wolves. Thokar had guided each one through the terrifying initiation process, implanting them with the gene-seed of the Chapter. Many warriors had not survived, but others accepted the gene-seed transformation into the Emperor's finest. Inside each one of them, the predator – the wolf within – stirred, awaiting the fight.

Thokar strode aboard the Thunderhawk, anticipating the descent to the war torn world below. Even the wolf priest in his long centuries had never seen a war like this one. The battles of Armageddon under the command of the Great Wolf, Logan Grimnar, paled in comparison to the massive conflict caused by the Black Crusade. Abbadon the Despoiler, most terrible living lord of Chaos, had led his Traitor Legions out of the Eye of Terror in such numbers that they threatened to consume the Imperium. Not since the Horus Heresy had mankind seen such conflict.

The machine spirits within the Thunderhawk roared as the landing craft descended to the dark jungles. To the east, the wolf priest saw explosions as battle continued in a burning city. The jolts of the descent mimicked the excitement in his blood. He was ready for combat, and he could sense that his packs were ready as well. The Thunderhawk came down with a hard landing, bursts of promethium flame clearing the jungle around the vessel.

Thokar nodded to his Grey Hunters and loyal Wolf Guard. They knew their roles: one team of Grey Hunters would scout ahead. Wulfric, a member of the Wolf Guard and an old friend, loved the hunt. He led Pack Morkai, while Pack Ranulf kept close to Thokar. The wolf priest stepped onto the planet's surface. Behind him, the ramp to the Thunderhawk closed.

The Space Wolves moved with a singular purpose. Within seconds, the first squad of Grey Hunters had vanished. Pack Morkai had to move quickly, time was precious. Although the wolf priest had every bit of faith in the crew of the Thunderhawk, he knew that this enemy might detect the landing of even a single flier. Thokar only hoped that the Iron Warriors hadn't already entrenched and trapped the jungle floor. Long minutes passed as the Space Marines moved through the jungle. The wolf priest waited for the first call from Wulfric and his lead pack.

'My lord, we have discovered the aftermath of a battle. Someone has claimed a few of our kills,' said Wulfric, with a hint of a grin in his voice.

The wolf priest nodded to the Grey Hunters around him. 'The first of our enemies have fallen.'

'Hold your position.' The wolf priest gestured to Pack Ranulf. No words were spoken; none were needed. In the matter of Chaos, they could not take chances. Bolters at the ready, the wolf priest led Pack Ranulf cautiously through the jungle to Wulfric's position.

The wolf priest's senses sharpened, focussing on this new world. Of the hundreds of smells in the jungle air, Thokar picked out several that did not belong in this environment. The oily and metallic odours of machinery were mixed with familiar scents, reminding him somehow of his own Wolves.

When Thokar reached the site, the jungle had already reclaimed most of the battlefield. Creeper vines, blood ferns and assorted insectoids covered the metallic and gold plated armour of the Traitor Marines. The smell of death permeated everything. Wulfric glanced at Thokar, then stepped back to allow the wolf priest's examination. The events of the battle unfolded in Thokar's mind as he pieced together the remains.

'We have the position covered. The plans for ambush are proceeding apace.' Champion Dalloc flexed his power claw, admiring the way the energy crackled and sizzled from his fingertips.

'Sir, we have motion in the undergrowth.' The squad raised their bolters.

'Assume fire pattern omega,' stated Dalloc calmly. 'Expect indigenous predators.' He never glanced at his men; thousands of years of training made their drill flawless.

'Sir, nothing in the north quadr–'

Something moved toward Dalloc, a blur of speed, fast enough that even his enhanced vision couldn't lock on it.

'Fire at will!' commanded Dalloc. In an instant, the jungle exploded with bolter fire. As the sound of the guns died, inhumanly strong claws tore apart the champion's helmet and fangs ripped off the front of his face.

The jungle cried out with growls and the sound of splintering metal. Dalloc's power claw lay on the ground, quiet and lifeless.

The wolf priest carefully picked up the power claw. Claw marks completely covered the armour, which lay nearby. His sharp eyes spotted a strand of fur across the metal. He carefully picked it up, twisting it in his fingers. Thokar knew the scent. The hair was that of a Fenrisian wolf and, yet, something wasn't right. There was a vaguely human scent mixed in as well. Strange, it reminded him of...

The wolf priest quickly activated his comm. 'Defender of Russ, a Space Wolf has succumbed to the curse of our gene-seed. All of my Wolves are present. Are any men missing, especially from the ranks of the Blood Claws or Wolf Guard?'

'Wolf Priest Thokar, we have no reports of anyone succumbing to the gene-seed. There are no Wulfen in your area. Are you certain of your findings?'

'Not entirely. I will report back when I know more.'

Thokar signalled his men to move forward. They spread out, vanishing from sight. Only the wolf priest's acute senses told him that the Grey Hunters maintained their formation.

As Thokar pushed his way through the jungle, the hairs on his neck rose. The smell of rot assailed him, overcoming the other smells of the planet.

'We've found the remains of a vehicle,' came a call over the vox.

A fallen Chaos Dreadnought lay in a charred section of jungle, surrounded by dozens of small fires, as if part of a foul ritual. The sarcophagus was missing, the metal edges around it thin and flaking. Thokar knew a melta weapon at close range had vaporized the metal.

The wolf priest knelt down beside the remnants of the infernal machine. The hairs on the back of his neck remained standing as he examined the blasphemous runes etched across the Dreadnought's metal surface. Small gargoyles, spikes and plated skulls hung from the fallen giant. He muttered a quick prayer to Russ. A single hit had destroyed the Dreadnought. Only the Emperor's finest, the Space Marines, were so accurate. There were no Space Marines, assigned here... and a lone Wulfen couldn't have done this. This attack was recent, happening within moments of the first attack they had discovered.

'A highly coordinated assault... even through this jungle. So fast that even these Chaos Marines were caught unprepared,' observed the wolf priest. The colours of the enemy were unmistakable. Though little could be certain about Chaos, the wolf priest knew his ancient lore. Before their fall, the Iron Warriors had been master tacticians. Of all Space Marine Chapters from ancient times, the Iron Warriors had been unsurpassed in siege warfare. Now, ten thousand years later, after giving themselves to the powers of Chaos, no one knew the limits of their abilities. Yet, Thokar noted, someone had caught the enemy off guard.

Drawing on his decades of experience, Thokar paced over to the spot from which the melta shot should have come. The boot prints he found were unmistakable... power armour, a few different types, from different eras. They could be Traitor Marines. Yet their scents reminded him of Fenris. However they had arrived, the Iron Warriors' attackers had left no trail. They had used teleporters. Space Wolves did not teleport, they had a healthy mistrust of such technology. Still, the scents of Fenris were unmistakable to Thokar. Space Wolves had been here.

Bolter shells illustrated where the Iron Warriors had returned fire against their attackers. Crushed plants indicated that some of their number fell during the initial attack, only to have bodies removed later. The wolf priest found an unusual shell, larger than the others. It was an autocannon round fired from another direction.

'Thokar, come see this,' Wulfric gestured. As Thokar strode through the undergrowth, he noted with approval that the Grey Hunters stayed watchful, instinctively creating a perimeter.

The remains of a massive Chaos war engine lay burned and crumpled in the creeper vines. At first, Thokar mistook the machine for another Dreadnought. Although it was obviously a walker, the infernal device had six legs and a turret mounted atop them, more akin to a tank. The scent of sulphur, and a sickly smell of decay mixed with the acrid aromas of spent shells and oil, hung around it.

'What in the frozen hells is it?' asked Wulfric.

The wolf priest raised a hand. An autocannon hung off the shattered turret. Even more impressively, the main gun appeared to be a battlecannon. Thokar had heard reports of such creations. This was a construct of daemons. The rear armour of the turret showed signs of plasma blasts. Exact hits, obviously from close range. Yet these blasts weren't enough to destroy the war engine. A single strike, possibly from a power fist, had shattered the heart of the machine. The faintest scent of blood and... wolves came from the power claws found at the end of each of the Chaos machine's legs. Thokar noted the faintest flakes of grey ceramite on two of the claws, a slightly darker shade than his Wolves wore. The paint could have come from any of a number of Space Marine Chapters, but this colour meant something to Thokar.

'Space Wolves used to wear this colour,' whispered the wolf priest. 'Ten thousand years ago.'

Thokar felt his heart rate increase as the words left his mouth. He strode around the war machine, and then he found bootprints. No prints came or went, although autocannon shells and bolter rounds lay all around. He saw the impression of a power armour-clad body in the soft earth, but there was no body. There had been two. One had fallen, but it was as if both had vanished.

The thought that two men would have attempted to take on a tank-sized monstrosity like this one spoke of men pushing the limits of courage. What was more, the blast strikes suggested that they knew where to shoot the strange vehicle. They must have fought such things before.

Thokar felt a sense of religious awe flow through him. By Russ! How could he have ever guessed? If what he was seeing were true, there was only one explanation. The lost 13th Company had survived over ten thousand years in the Eye of Terror. What could sustain even the Emperor's finest for ten thousand years in pure Chaos, surrounded by enemies?

Thokar looked around at the Grey Hunters he could see, and scented the ones he could not. He felt the determination and the focus in each one. The wolf priest also felt the Wulfen growl deep within his own soul. It would not let him die or fail. What if the entire Chapter had given themselves to the Wulfen?

Icy sweat broke out on Thokar's brow. What sort of foe had the Iron Warriors faced?

Thokar nodded to his Wolf Guard. It was time to find the objective. Wilderness Outpost Delta was their mission, although it paled in comparison to what the wolf priest had discovered. If it were true... Thokar shuddered inwardly, unsure whether to feel elation or fear. He had personally killed recruits on Fenris, lost to the Wulfen. Only the strongest Space Wolves, Wolf Guard or older, could survive attaining the Mark of the Wulfen.

'More bodies, sir. We're very close,' came Wulfric's voice.

Thokar saw the blood drenched, torn remains. These were the ones he had seen evidence of earlier, the ones who had been near the Dreadnought. He recognised the scents. They had fallen back into an ambush.

'Let me see...' Thokar knelt over the remains.

The attack had been different this time. Although the carnage was substantial, the claw and teeth marks were absent. This time, more conventional weapons had been brought to bear: power weapons, a power fist and something else. He carefully examined the cuts in the power armour. He could have identified an axe slash even before he had donned the mantle of Blood Claw, and the weapon had cleanly cut the armour, leaving the edges ice-cold. Only a Frostaxe, a sacred weapon of the Space Wolves, left these marks. The weapon had struck with wild abandon in a frenzy, a definite sign of the Wulfen.

'Sir,' said the Wolf Guard. 'There is no sign of the body of a champion. We are almost at the objective.'

'Indeed. Move on,' ordered Thokar, already piecing together what had happened. He had a vision in his mind of what must have occurred shortly before their arrival.

Champion Kurnos ordered the retreat. Adaric's squad was not responding. These weren't ordinary Space Wolves. There was only one explanation: the 13th Company, the Space Wolves who had followed them into the Eye of Terror itself.

Suddenly, the air shimmered around his squad. A rune priest appeared before them, accompanied by a squad clad in bits of power armour from a dozen Chaos Chapters. Before Kurnos could shout orders, his attackers launched a savage assault. The rune priest fought with unmatched fury. Kurnos felt strangely detached as claws severed his right arm. He closed his eyes and waited for death.

Death never came. Instead, strong hands wrestled his helm off and jerked back his head. A pair of bright, yellow eyes stared down. They were not the eyes of a man, but the eyes of a wolf.

'Tell us, Iron Warrior, will your commanders come for you?' growled the Space Marine. 'Call them.' Kurnos heard the hum of the power weapon as it sectioned off his knees. The attackers dragged him across the ground, writhing in agony.

'Iron within, iron...' Kurnos started the mantra of his Legion.

'This is your emergency beacon. Live long enough to signal them, not to speak,' growled his attacker. Razor claws sliced apart his tongue. Dimly aware of his shock, Kurnos realised that he lay on the floor in the outpost. The 13th Company had set an ambush. He was bait. As Kurnos heard his emergency beacon go off, the iron within him turned to rust.

Incomplete trenches, half-used razor wire, unassembled gun emplacements and bodies of Iron Warriors littered the area around Wilderness Outpost Delta. The wolf scent was strong here. This was the site of a Wulfen attack.

'Seize the objective,' ordered Thokar in a tone that brooked obedience.

'There are slain Iron Warrior Terminators scattered inside,' called Uller, one of Pack Morkai's Grey Hunters. The wolf priest was prepared for the carnage.

The exterior of Wilderness Outpost Delta was standard rockcrete, covered in camouflage netting to hide the communications array. Thokar had seen the same building on half a hundred worlds. Inside lay the corpses of five Iron Warriors in Terminator armour, and a sixth in power armour.

Wulfric led Pack Morkai back outside, while Pack Ranulf stayed with Thokar. Blood splatter decorated the interior of the room. Thokar knelt over one of the dead Terminators. The wiring attaching the corpse's backup power supply sparked.

'Something over here, sir,' said Bran. 'Looks like part of a skull.'

Thokar nodded to the Grey Hunter. This was the end of the story as he had seen it.

The air shimmered as five of the warsmith's Chosen materialised from the warp inside Wilderness Outpost Delta. The Terminators dwarfed other Space Marines. Their armour was the most ancient and ensorcelled of their Chapter. They had no equals, and only bent their knees to the warsmith himself. They looked down on Kurnos's twitching form. He saw daemonic faces leering at him from within the glossy dark metal of their armour.

Kurnos struggled to warn the Chosen, but it was too late. The Wolves were inside, power fists smashing against the Terminators. A chill ran through Kurnos as the Frostaxe stole the heat from the room, then sliced open the sacred Terminator armour, as easily as it cut the flesh within. The Chosen of Chaos, the warsmith's Terminators, were no more.

'A transport has landed,' said one of the bestial Marines.

'You've earned this,' another of them growled to Kurnos.

Kurnos looked up and the claws took off the top of his head.

Wulfric and Pack Morkai reacted as one. Somewhere high above the range of human hearing, they each heard a familiar sound, a sound that they had heard a thousand times before, on a hundred different worlds. In every case, on every world, it came with the same deadly result.

'Incoming ordnance!' howled Wulfric over the comm.

The wolf priest and Pack Ranulf disappeared in smoke, fire and debris as the first of the artillery rounds impacted dead centre on the outpost. A geyser of dirt, rock, concrete and ceramite armour fragments erupted as the second round hit home. Ancient power armour failed to save two members of Pack Morkai as their remains rained down on their brothers. Shells struck all around them.

Wulfric triggered his comm. 'Thokar... Thokar... Please respond...'

Static answered the Wolf Guard. Wulfric's anger built in his heart. His wolf priest should not die on this backwater world. He howled in rage.

Wulfric heard movement behind him. He spun, drawing his power sword. Thokar stood over him, dirt smeared across his black armour.

'Wulfric, we have work to do. Control yourself until we can get to grips with the enemy,' Thokar said with a half grin.

Wulfric took the moment to control his own inner beast. Relief replaced rage on his face. 'Russ be praised. I thought we'd lost you!'

The wolf priest spoke reassuringly. 'It will take more than Iron Warrior artillery to kill me.'

'Uller, establish a flanking position to the east. Keep Pack Morkai in the cover of the jungle, at the clearing's edge. Wulfric, stay with me. They will come upwind from the north,' ordered the wolf priest. 'Wulfric, we're the bait.'

The surviving Space Wolves took up positions among their fallen in the ruins of the wilderness outpost, making good use of the rockcrete as cover. They waited. The jungle fell silent.

Thokar mentally reviewed his plan. Iron Warriors bombarded their enemies to soften them before an assault. When the Chaos Marines broke cover, they would open fire. In that instant, Uller and Pack Morkai would return fire from the jungle, giving Thokar, Wulfric and the survivors of Pack Ranulf the opportunity to seize the initiative and take the fight to them.

A skirmish line of iron behemoths broke from the thick jungle. Stepping into the midday sun, they wore armour from a different time and place, holy relics from ten thousand years past, now polluted with Chaos symbols and unholy markings. It sickened Thokar that these gifts of the Emperor were now bastardised tools of Chaos.

Boltgun rounds exploded around Thokar and the Wolf Guard. The few surviving chunks of Wilderness Outpost Delta blew apart, sandblasting the Space Wolves hiding in cover. Brother Sven looked up, only to catch a bolter round in his helmet. Thokar cursed the young and bold.

Pack Morkai opened fire from the jungle. The Iron Warriors paused for a fraction of a moment, confused by the attack from an unexpected quarter. That fraction of a moment was enough of a signal for the Space Wolves to charge from the ruin.

Raising his plasma pistol, Thokar exploded from behind his cover. 'For Russ!' he shouted. Each Space Wolf in turn added their own battle-cry to Thokar's until 'For Russ' resounded above the bolter shots.

The Wolves tore into the Iron Warriors like predators on prey. Pack Morkai swiftly joined their brothers. Throughout the vastness of space, few could match the fury of a Space Wolf assault. Today, the Iron Warriors would learn this lesson. The Wolves asked no quarter and offered none. Bolt pistol rounds met ceramite and chainswords bit deep, first into armour and then into corrupted flesh. The Iron Warriors fell in droves.

Thokar briefly paused as the torn corpse of an Iron Warrior slipped from the grasp of his power fist. 'Regroup and prepare to move....' Thokar started, then realised that something was distinctly wrong.

'Russ protect us!' shouted Wulfric beside him.

Thokar knew the unmistakable scent. Whenever the Iron Priests evoked the Holy Litanies of the Machine God, they anointed their great machines with oil. Trees crashed into the clearing from the south as twin abominations charged. The Iron Warriors had flanked them!

Thokar had underestimated his foes, perhaps lulled into false security by the carnage they had encountered earlier. The Chaos Dreadnoughts roared with madness as they lumbered toward the Space Wolves. Two squads of Iron Warriors followed, spraying bolter fire as they advanced.

'Pull back. Use the cover of the jungle,' Thokar ordered. The wolf priest hoped that the thick foliage might neutralise the Iron Warriors' numbers and superior firepower.

A small ball of energy cut off the withdrawal, appearing in front of the tree line. The energy pulsed once, then expanded into a sphere several feet in diameter. Lightning swirled across the sphere's surface, then the sphere vanished with a thunderclap. Iron Warrior Terminators stood in place of the energy. As the Space Wolves paused, twin bolters and reaper autocannons sent the souls of three members of Pack Morkai to their ancestors. The Iron Warriors had them surrounded.

One of the Terminators raised a hand and the firing stopped. His armour was far more ornate than the others, decorated with longer spikes holding many skulls and the helms of a dozen Chapters of Space Marines, including the Space Wolves. Faces twisted across the surfaces of his metal armour like trapped souls trying to escape.

'What do we have here? Pups of Leman Russ, pet dog of the False Emperor!' the warsmith spat the words like venom. 'You have a choice: renounce your failed Emperor or beg for a swift death!'

Before Thokar could retort, howls echoed from all around, faintly at first, then growing rapidly in volume and intensity. The warsmith paused and turned his head, trying to locate the source of the sounds.

'Thokar, behind us!' Wulfric warned.

Thokar glanced back at the Iron Warriors and their ancient war machines. Behind the forces of Chaos, the landscape distorted as a vortex of energy formed, flinging bolts of lightning in all directions. Shadowy figures materialised.

Immediately, one Chaos Dreadnaught collapsed. A pack with the markings of Long Fangs, the most experienced Space Wolves, poured nuclear fire into the remaining Dreadnought from meltaguns. The war machine exploded, engulfing several Iron Warriors in a blossom of destruction.

Thokar seized the moment. 'Pack Morkai, aid our reinforcements. Wulfric, everyone else, take the Terminators. The warsmith is mine!' he shouted, and the Space Wolves attacked.

Even as Thokar swung his power fist into a Terminator, new combatants joined the assault. A snarling mass of fangs and teeth leapt upon the enemy. The primal fury of the Wulfen amazed even the veteran wolf priest. His new allies were more beast than Space Marine, clad only in remnants of power armour. A few held weapons, but these were secondary to claws and teeth as they gouged out crimson chunks from beneath the pewter and gold Chaos Marines.

Distracted for a second, Thokar barely evaded an attack. It was the warsmith. Thokar cursed as a second blow caught him squarely in the chest, throwing him backward into a crater left from the bombardment. Pain seared through Thokar's ribs. The warsmith loomed over the wolf priest, glaring down at him from the crater's edge. Thokar slowly rose to his feet, growling with defiance as energy rippled from his power fist.

'Your time is over, wolf!' declared the warsmith.

'Your pitiful existence is all that will end today, betrayer!' responded the wolf priest.

The ancient warriors collided. Thokar, filled with rage, deflected or dodged every one of the warsmith's attacks. The power fist was an ancient weapon, slow and cumbersome to wield. In lesser hands, that would have been a liability. Thokar used its weight to his advantage, holding back, luring the warsmith closer. The master of the Iron Warriors swung his power sword in a killing blow, overcome with confidence. Only as his weight shifted into the swing did he realise that Thokar had feinted, tricking him into overextending his attack. The wolf priest had an opening. His power fist only needed one. The warsmith's helmet exploded under the impact. Victory belonged to the wolf priest.

Searing pain flooded through Thokar's left arm. Instinctively, he ducked and twisted to his right and brought his power fist around. With a sickening crack, a Wulfen's chest splattered.

The 13th Company survivors surrounded the remaining Space Wolves. There was no question in Thokar's mind now as to the fate of the 13th Great Company. Their time in the Eye of Terror had unleashed the beast within. The wolf priest saw no remaining humanity in their feral yellow eyes. The Space Wolves hesitantly levelled their weapons at the Wulfen. They had all had reached same conclusion. They faced fellow Sons of Russ; they didn't want to fire on their own. Some even lowered their weapons, apparently choosing destruction over betraying their lost brothers.

'Hold, my brothers!' The command came in ancient Fenrisian.

Instantly, the Wulfen submitted and withdrew to the edge of the clearing. A grizzled ancient figure, tall even by Space Wolf standards, with a snow-white beard hanging from a cracked, weathered face, stood at the tree line. The figure wore black armour from a time before the Great Betrayal, from the Time of Russ. He was a wolf priest.

The Wulfen disappeared into the jungle. When the last one had gone, the old priest slowly turned to face the Space Wolves.

'Lord priest...' Thokar began. If there were any words beyond that they were lost to him.

With a last glance to Thokar and a slight smile, the wolf priest disappeared as well. The silence within the clearing was deafening.

Thokar's comm crackled. 'Commissar Thaddeus Palentine at your service, Lord Chaplain. We are your relief. Is the area secure for our landing?'

'This is Thokar, wolf priest of Russ,' stated Thokar, efficiently introducing himself and correcting the commissar simultaneously.

'I'm afraid we missed all the fun. Our intelligence indicates that you were horribly outnumbered,' observed the commissar.

'Russ was with us today,' offered Thokar.

'We've had scattered reports of bestial creatures wearing fragments of Space Marine power armour. We were hoping that maybe you and your men could shed some light on these matters,' said Commissar Palentine.

'Have you ever battled Chaos? They are all mindless beasts wearing power armour,' Thokar spat. 'We have Khorne Berserkers in the area, frenzied, skull-rending killers. This area isn't safe for your men. We'll handle things. Go where you are needed. The Space Wolves will handle it from here.'

'I see...' replied the commissar. 'Very well.' The comm signal died.

'Not that I would ever challenge you, wolf priest, but I'm not sure I understand what you said to the commissar,' Wulfric stated.

Thokar sighed. 'I lied, Wulfric. Our brothers have returned after centuries of existence within the Eye. You saw them. They can never return to Fenris. The Great Wolf can never welcome them back. However, we can ensure that they do not become hunted, hunted by those who they set out to defend ten thousand years ago. So, I gave the commissar what he was looking for: an answer.'

As the wolf priest and Wolf Guard walked back toward the ruins of the outpost, the ancient yellow eyes of a predator tracked them.

HOLLOW
BEGINNINGS

Mark Clapham

The ork fortress had been an ugly sight to begin with, and setting it on fire hadn't improved the view. A scrap-built mass of metal the size of a town squatted on the dusty, lifeless plain, and a swampish lake of filth and toxic waste formed a shallow moat around its jagged perimeter. Its towers and parapets clawed the air, twisted black digits scraping against the reddish blue sky.

The fortress was the base of operations for Stumpgutz, ork warboss and plague of the Alixind system. Now it was aflame, artillery guns in the nearby hills having battered the fortress with incendiary shells for a day and a night. The guns were silent now, but the fires still raged.

It was a terrible place in the throes of dying, and it refused to die quietly or well. Clouds of noxious black smoke, hanging in the windless air above the fortress, lingered so high they almost seemed to touch the four visible moons in the sky above.

As flames licked the unstable walls and teetering battlements, burning chunks began to fall off and tumble down the walls, the orkish architecture fatally undermined by the heat.

It was an ugly sight on an unlovely world. Durrl had been the warboss' first landing place within the system, his first clawhold in a twenty-year campaign against the Imperium. The planet bore the scars of occupation, its cities wrecked and cannibalised to feed the ork war machine, the majority of the population having fled or died years before.

Now it would make a fitting grave, or maybe a funeral pyre, for Stumpgutz and his ambitions. So thought Captain Anju Badya as she looked across at the burning fortress, a rough scarf wrapped around her mouth and nose to hold back the stench from the fiery ruin. Her horse moved restlessly beneath her; it was a disciplined beast of good Tallarn stock, but even a well-trained animal became uneasy in such a place.

Captain Badya was a rider in the Tallarn 14th, her regimental fatigues complemented by a long overcoat and a red sash at the waist, from which hung a gilt-edged blade. She sat tall in her saddle, and from between the layers of headscarf, her piercing green eyes surveyed the area around her, watching for any movement. It was hard, tense work as the plain was littered with debris and shrouded in smoke. Badya had one hand ready to grab her lasrifle at all times.

The Tallarn 14th, along with an alliance of other forces from the Imperium, had driven Stumpgutz's forces back to the plains of Durrl, and were here to finish the job. The fire was building in intensity, and while the main structures still stood, the increasing damage was causing some of the inhabitants to flee. The orks were ferocious and incredibly dangerous, but also deeply stupid, and only now, at the last stand, was it becoming clear to some of them that Stumpgutz was finished.

Badya's squad, and others patrolling the plains surrounding the fortress, were there to ensure no orks escaped the stronghold's demise. She could hear distant gunfire, orkish bellows and human screams as distant comrades engaged the enemy.

'Captain?' asked Ejad, one of the younger riders under her command.

'I hear them,' said Badya, speaking loud enough that the rest of the squad could hear her as they rode behind, her voice hoarse from the dry desert air. 'You know what to do. We stay on our patrol pattern. Any back-up comes in from the perimeter. If we ride to the rescue, we might let some of these greenskins through.'

'Yes, captain,' said Ejad.

Was he disappointed or relieved that they didn't have to plunge into the smoke to save fellow Tallarns under attack? Badya neither knew nor cared. They had their orders: patrol, kill anything they find and call for support from the perimeter if things went south.

Badya had added her own orders for her squad: stay back, engage from as much distance as possible. Orks were stupid, but they were also savage beasts, squat green creatures with vicious teeth and thick, muscular limbs that could tear a human being apart with one hand. Tallarn riders were highly mobile and usually very able sharp shooters, even on the move, and Badya intended to fire on any orks they encountered from afar.

As the wreckage of a burnt-out ork vehicle exploded, a green fist punched the smouldering metal out of the way. Badya's hopes were crushed. An ork burst through the obstruction, raising a stumpy pistol and firing at the nearest Tallarn, an older woman called Khai. The shot tore a lump of flesh from the flanks of Khai's mount and the beast bucked in agony, throwing Khai out of the saddle.

Badya didn't wait to see Khai hit the ground. She began to ride in as wide an arc as the debris-strewn plain would allow, staying as clear as she could of the wrecked vehicle from which she could now see a second ork emerging.

As she rode, Badya leaned low in her saddle, cradling her lasrifle under one arm and lifting it so that she had the barrel level. She adjusted the rifle in her grip, compensating for the rhythmic motion of the horse beneath her as she aimed at the first ork, which was now shambling towards the fallen Khai, pistol lowered in meaty hands.

She didn't attempt anything clever while firing mounted, no head shots or other feats of marksmanship. Instead Badya tightened her grip on her lasrifle and muttered some familiar words of reassurance so that her horse knew what was about to happen, then she fired three las shots in close succession, all aimed at the ork's torso. The movement of the running horse made her grip loosen a little, and one of the shots went wide but two hit their target. One shot winged the ork, causing it to drop its pistol, while another hit it square in the chest.

The ork rocked backwards and roared in protest, but it didn't go down. Meanwhile Ejad was trying to ride away from the second ork, firing on it from dangerously close range, while a third emerged from the hole. Was there some kind of tunnel in there, or did the wrecked vehicle mask a channel leading back to the fortress? Badya didn't have time to think. All around her Tallarns were engaging with orks, las shots wounding but not killing the monsters as they attacked.

Badya aimed her lasgun at the first ork once more, but before she could fire, Khai, with one arm limp at her side from falling off her horse, lifted herself up from the ground and fired her hellgun. The kickback from firing it one-handed was enough to throw Khai backwards, but it was close range enough to blow a hole in the ork's face.

Finally, the creature died.

Badya changed targets. The third ork had killed Barro's horse with one neck-breaking punch, and had used its other hand to break Barro's own neck in a stranglehold. The horse had fallen but Barro still hung from the ork's grip, body dangling limply like a doll. Badya resisted the urge to avenge him and searched for someone she could assist who was still alive.

Ejad was still on horseback but had been cornered by the second ork, and Badya rode straight for him, firing as she came. The ork turned its attention to her, tiny black eyes staring with animal hatred.

The ork pulled Ejad off his horse and threw him at Badya.

Ejad hit Badya hard and the two of them fell backwards off Badya's horse, which panicked and ran away. They landed hard, and Badya felt Ejad shake in agony as one of his bones broke.

Her own body ached from multiple impacts. Badya pushed Ejad off her, ignoring his cries of agony, and searched for her lasrifle. The rest of her squad were coming to the rescue, but the ork that had thrown Ejad was running at them both now, gun raised and drool dripping from its huge yellow teeth.

Badya's ears were ringing, so she barely heard the roar of engines before it happened.

An armoured blue-grey Rhino crashed into view, the squat vehicle throwing up clouds of dust as its tracks ploughed through the sands. The Rhino made a direct line for the ork approaching Badya, crushing it beneath its tracks, and the other greenskins had no time to react when its mounted storm bolter opened up on them, a furious barrage of fire bringing the survivors down in one sweep.

Before their bodies had even hit the ground the Rhino had gone, crashing through the wrecked ork vehicle and rolling off some kind of crude lowered road cutting through the plain that Badya had suspected was there. In the distance she could see the breach from which the orks had escaped the burning fortress.

Still on her knees, she watched from afar as five towering figures emerged from the Rhino, clad in armour the same colour as the Rhino itself and augmented with the furs of great beasts. All five were a head or two taller than a normal human, and broad to match – Space Marines, the Adeptus Astartes, favoured warriors of the Emperor himself.

The five Space Marines disappeared into the depths of the fortress. Its job done, their transport returned to base, leaving a cloud of dust behind it once more. As the Tallarns of Badya's squad pulled together, assisting their wounded and wary of a further ork attack, the Rhino simply rolled past them without pause. The Space Marines clearly had their own mission to attend to, and didn't stop for the Tallarns who cheered them on, grateful for their intervention.

Captain Anju Badya whistled for her horse to return to her and looked up again at the hulking fortress, its charred structures licked by fiercer and fiercer flames. A place even orks would flee.

Only Space Wolves would choose to go the other way.

'Thank you for your gracious welcome,' said Sindri, ramming a chainblade into the side of an attacking ork. 'You do us honour with your hospitality.'

'You forget your place, Sindri,' shouted Anvindr Godrichsson, pack leader, over the roar of his own bolter. 'I have command, it is for me to relay gratitude to our hosts.'

'Apologies,' said Sindri, bowing to Anvindr at the same time as an ork swung a red-painted hammer through the space his head had just occupied. 'Here, you may do the honours.' He slashed the back of the ork's right knee with his chainblade, shoving the creature into Anvindr's line of fire to be gunned down.

'I am grateful,' grunted Anvindr, concentrating fire as three more orks rushed at him, 'but please keep any more to yourself.'

Within seconds of entering the fortress, Anvindr and his pack had been surrounded by orks. They had come almost immediately after the pack climbed through the breach in the outer wall, that uncanny ork talent of sniffing out the chance of a fight drawing them from the hive-like corridors of the fortress to face down the incoming Space Marines. While Sindri spoke with his usual infuriating levity, Anvindr acknowledged that the other Wolf was correct – the orks had prepared a substantial welcome for the Space Marines.

One of the approaching orks came at Anvindr with an axe, and Anvindr shot it down before it even got close, a bolt-round exploding within the ork's chest in a mist of red blood and green scraps of flesh. Before that body had even hit the ground the other two were about to strike, chunky ork pistols raised to fire at near point-blank range. Anvindr grabbed one of the orks by its gun hand and pulled the great beast forward and down, enough for Anvindr to bring his knee up hard, breaking the ork's arm and causing it to drop its gun.

He now had the ork in a hold close to him, the creature's jaws dangerously close to his face. Anvindr was helmless, and the breath coming from the ork's yellow-toothed mouth was rank as it pushed forward to try and bite his face off. Even against a Space Marine in full power armour, the ork was strong, struggling in Anvindr's grip, but Anvindr had swung the beast between him and the other ork, which simply tried to fire straight through its comrade.

The ork took four or five 'friendly fire' shots to the back, dying with a look of annoyance in its tiny black eyes.

As Anvindr pushed the body away he raised his bolter again, firing twice before the other ork could get a clear shot, killing it instantly. Then he locked his bolter to the leg of his armour and unleashed his chainsword. As more orks charged at him, he wielded the blade back and forth, hacking through limbs and occasionally grinding against pieces of crude armour.

Around him, the rest of Anvindr's pack was equally busy. They were brothers of the *Vlka Fenryka*, whom the rest of the Imperium called Space Wolves. They had fought so long together, for so many countless winters, that they worked side-by-side like a single organism, staying out of each other's way without ever needing to look, pack instincts driving them forward together as one.

Anvindr was leader of this pack. Like any of his kind he was far taller than a human, and his heavy features were framed by long hair and matching beard, both streaked white and oily with smoke. Signs of age and marks of long service covered Anvindr's body and armour: scars and dents on skin and plate, grey in the beard and lengthening teeth in his jaws, furs and other trophies hanging from his shoulders.

The others fought nearby.

There was Sindri, of course, agile even in full power armour, spinning between opponents, ducking under the arm of one ork to run him through with his chainblade, then bringing it around to cut straight through the knees of another. His blond curls were unusual for a Fenrisian, and even as the decades passed there was something in him that remained unaging.

Although this meant he lacked the growing fangs and other traditional signs of a wolf brother's maturity, there was no denying his warrior spirit.

Then there was Gulbrandr, steady as ever with a series of well-placed, thoughtful shots from his bolter that always found their mark, not letting an ork even get close to him. His once raven-black hair and beard showed thin streaks of white, but his impassive expression remained the same as it always had.

At the edge of the group was great Tormodr, heavy even for a fully-armoured Space Marine, wielding his flamer back and forth, roasting countless orks as they crawled out of holes in the wall.

And finally there was red-headed Hoenir, whose presence always surprised Anvindr, even after decades of fighting by his side. Although Hoenir, last survivor of his own pack, had joined Anvindr's many years ago after their own loss, Anvindr still found a part of him always expected long-lost Liulfr to be there instead. Hoenir was no Blood Claw, and was a brother of many battles standing, but he would always be partially a newcomer.

One of Hoenir's hands was encased in a great, red-painted power fist, and Anvindr saw him pick up an ork by the criss-crossed ammunition belts the creature wore across its chest and slam it hard into an already prone ork on the floor, killing both of them.

'For Russ and for Fenris,' shouted Hoenir, raising his bloodied power fist.

'For Fenris!' boomed Tormodr, and the others echoed the sentiment, even ever-terse Gulbrandr.

'I think we're thinning their numbers,' said Sindri.

He was right. The numbers of orks attacking them seemed to be subsiding, with Anvindr able to count the time between his kills in seconds. However, this was not necessarily reason to celebrate – the smoke was thickening and the air was getting hotter around them. There may have been fewer orks attacking, but the fire consuming the fortress was also getting nearer.

'We need to move now, while we have the chance,' Anvindr called to his pack, striking another ork aside.

'This way,' said Gulbrandr, indicating an opening in the wall near him. They were all hunters, but the smoke and carnage could spin even a Space Wolf around. Gulbrandr, however, never lost his bearings, and would lead them where they needed to go – straight to the centre of the fortress. Ork hierarchies were simple, and their target would be close to that centre.

Anvindr had looked at the fortress from afar that morning, watching the bombardment from the Imperial cannon, and had decided that the long campaign that he, his brothers and thousands of other souls of the Imperium had fought in could not end like this – not with the uncertainty of a pile of anonymous ash.

Victory required someone to take the head of the warboss, even if it was just hacked from its scorched corpse. Proof of death was required, a trophy to take for the glory of the Emperor, and Anvindr decided that he and his squad would be the ones to take it.

So the artillery guns had been silenced, Anvindr and his pack had crossed the plain, and here they were in smoke and darkness and raging flame.

Initially they made slow progress, fighting every step through corridors that threatened to collapse around them, changing course as one potential route turned out to be blocked by wreckage, but otherwise staying true to their objective. Howls of orkish pain echoed from afar, but the number of orks seeking out the Wolves to attack them lessened as they got closer to the centre of the fortress.

The orks that did try to block their path fought savagely, but in isolation they were no match for the pack fighting as one.

Eventually Anvindr and his pack found themselves in a larger corridor lined with skulls and other trophies. It was ugly rubbish, crudely attached to the walls, but the meaning of such trophies was clear – these were the displays of the great warboss, whose throne room they approached.

The chamber they entered was more or less round and as tall as the fortress itself, the walls tapering to an opening high above. Any sunlight that reached down from that far was watery, thinned out by the oily smoke that clogged the air. Burning embers tumbled down from somewhere above, as did some larger chunks of flaming rubble.

The walls were littered with long spikes holding skeletons or other trophies, while others were bare. The central focus of the chamber was a crude balcony overlooking the chamber, on which a throne of scrap metal could be seen.

That throne sat empty, and as Anvindr had no idea what Stumpgutz looked like, he could not tell whether the warboss was amongst the horde before them.

His instinct told him that none of the orks before him was Stumpgutz, and that he would know the warboss when he saw it. Rumour was that long ago a captain of the White Consuls had got close to killing him, and had cut through the warboss' legs at the knee. Those rumours also said that Stumpgutz wore that Space Marine's helmet on one shoulder and his skull on the other – trophies of its eventual victory over the Imperium's finest.

Neither Anvindr nor anyone else in the Imperium had any idea how the renamed Stumpgutz had managed to not only maintain his rule while suffering such a disability, but increase his power. Orks were dumb but treacherous, and wouldn't hesitate to depose an injured or crippled leader. For Stumpgutz to prosper, the warboss would have to be something much more than the orks under his command.

The mass of orks that filled the throne room surged towards Anvindr and his Wolves as one tumultuous green mass of savage muscle. Looming over the horde were four great orks, presumably Stumpgutz's bodyguards, dressed from head to foot in crude armour plating, with bucket-like helmets over their heads, wielding hatchets as well as stubby, over-sized pistols.

The gretchin and common orks were the first to reach the Wolves, who found themselves engaging ork warriors hand-to-hand while kicking away the smaller, dome-headed creatures trying to stab at the joints in their power armour.

'Sindri, help me give Tormodr space to clear this rabble,' shouted Anvindr, slamming a boot down on the skull of one gretchin while elbowing an ork in its thick jaw. 'Hoenir, Gulbrandr, take the first chance to engage those big brutes. I want a path to the boss.'

The Wolves all stepped back a little, forming a circle around Tormodr, then as the big wolf readied his flamer, Sindri and Anvindr surged forward, slashing wildly with their chainswords, sweeping low to hack through the skulls of gretchin and the knees of orks, pushing back the forward line.

'Make way, make way!' said Sindri, slashing back and forth. 'Brother Tormodr has some difficult buttons to adjust. Give him space.'

Tormodr boomed some filthy words relating to Sindri's tribal ancestry, then shouted 'Clear!'

Anvindr and Sindri rolled out of the way, letting the ork rabble surge forward over their injured and dead comrades, only for Tormodr to flame the lot of them. The ork advance faltered and tripped over itself, the dead and the dying blocking the way of those trying to both advance and retreat, and the flame scorched them *all* while the other Wolves fired into the carnage.

'The smell...' said Sindri in disgust. Anvindr grunted. He hated it too, but it was not very... *wolf-like* to express the sentiment that way. Typical Sindri.

Tormodr's roasting of the orks was interrupted by a shot from one of the over-sized pistols wielded by the helmeted ork guards, which exploded near Tormodr's feet with enough force to knock the huge Wolf brother backwards, his flamer setting part of the high ceiling alight.

The pack were already returning fire, with Gulbrandr firing precise bolt-rounds over the heads of the shorter orks, but these seemed to do limited damage to the ork guards' thick armour. One took a well-placed bolt from Gulbrandr to the chest, only to keep walking with just a dent in his plate to show for it.

'Get close and take these down now, quickly,' bellowed Anvindr. 'I want that boss.'

'Nice easy orders,' shouted Sindri back. 'Should only take a second.'

Then the guards were upon them, shoving through the blackened remains that littered the throne room, kicking aside charred corpses. Anvindr ran towards the nearest ork, which thrust its crude dagger towards him. Anvindr lunged to the side, the thick blade cutting the air beside him. Gripping the handle of the ork weapon in one hand, Anvindr lunged forward with his chainsword, aiming for the weak point between the ork's armour and helmet. The chainsword found some initial purchase, digging in between the lip of the helmet and the chestplate to open up a gap, but began to grind with a hail of sparks. As Anvindr held the dagger out of the way, the ork brought its gun arm around to try and shoot Anvindr at point-blank range.

Anvindr pushed back, letting go of both the chainsword and hatchet, and the ork stumbled without Anvindr to push against. Anvindr drew his bolter and fired just next to where the chainsword was jammed in place. The bolt-round found the point where the chainsword had created a small gap, and there was a muted thud as it exploded within the confines of the helmet. Blood dribbled from the helmet's eye slits as the ork collapsed to the ground.

Anvindr twisted his chainsword to pull it free and turned to see the rest of the pack overcoming the other ork guards – one was staggering around, smoke pouring out of the seams of its armour after Tormodr set it alight, while Hoenir had torn the helmet off another with his power fist, finishing it off with a bolt pistol.

'Do you think the warboss is one of these?' shouted Hoenir.

Anvindr was about to answer when the double doors at the far end of the throne room were kicked open by a towering greenskin far taller than any present, a grotesquely over-sized ork wearing a mass of armour plating and furs, the skull of a Space Marine on one shoulder and a battered helmet on the other. The ork's huge green hands were encrusted with barbed rings, and were wrapped around the shaft of a long, two-bladed axe.

Stumpgutz.

'Great Russ!' exclaimed Sindri, lost for anything smart to say.

'Now we know how this thing stayed boss for so long,' said Anvindr.

Stumpgutz did not walk in on the legs of an ork, that part of the legend was true. Instead he strode in on two long, pneumatic legs that dripped with oil, released hissing steam from the knees and ended in boot-shaped artificial feet that looked like they could kick a hole in a Rhino.

Anvindr raised his bolter but Stumpgutz jumped, his pneumatic legs carrying him a quarter of the way across the chamber in one leap. He landed with an impact that rocked the whole room, throwing up dust that mingled with the thickening smoke from the fires consuming the fortress.

Stumpgutz went straight for Anvindr, swinging the giant axe around in a long arc, catching the barrel of Anvindr's gun. It was barely a scratch, but the incredible force of the axe blow was enough to wrench the bolter out of Anvindr's hands and nearly pull him off his feet.

As Anvindr righted himself, revving up his chainsword, Stumpgutz was already swiping at the others with his axe, the great warboss stomping back and forth across the throne room with mechanical strides that shook the very ground, bolt-rounds exploding around it. Gulbrandr managed to hit the warboss in the shoulder, causing a howl of rage from the giant ork, but otherwise none of the Wolves' shots managed to hit home. They were on the defensive.

'Anvindr!' warned Hoenir, and Anvindr saw the axe swing in his direction once more. He leapt over the huge, flat axe head, then prepared for the return swing, bracing himself against the ground and raising his chainsword. While the previous swing had cut low, this one came in high, and would have taken Anvindr's head clean off his shoulders if he had had nothing to raise in his defence.

As it was, the chainsword barely stopped the axe. The two weapons clashed with an impact that shuddered through Anvindr's body, every muscle straining as he struggled to hold his chainsword firm. The force of the blow pushed him backwards, his boots scuffing the dirt. The teeth of the weapon screamed against the rough metal of the axe head, sparks flying and machinery grinding.

'Yield, you green wretch!' shouted Anvindr as he forced every iota of his strength into pushing the chainsword.

Stumpgutz roared and twisted the handle in its grip, applying both hands to the job, turning the axe to force it downwards and letting gravity add to the pressure on Anvindr. Teeth began to fly off the chainsword and it sputtered. The chain broke and suddenly Stumpgutz's axe was cleaving through the metal of the chainsword itself, an increasingly thin strip of metal and component parts between the axe and Anvindr's skull.

'Now, while I hold him back,' said Anvindr to his pack.

Gulbrandr was first to move in for the kill, but Stumpgutz lashed out with one of his mechanical legs, kicking the Wolf in his helmless head so hard his jaw shattered, the bottom half of his face crumpling beneath the blow. The impact knocked him aside, but before he was out of sight Anvindr saw a copious spurt of blood come from his ruined face.

There was no time to worry about Gulbrandr, as both Hoenir and Tormodr were running to Anvindr's aid. Hoenir used the body of a dead ork as a step to launch himself into the air, raising his power fist high.

'For Russ!' shouted Hoenir. Anvindr's chainsword was about to break in two when Hoenir dropped, bringing his power fist down where Stumpgutz's wrists overlapped, causing the ork to release the weapon with a howl. Stumpgutz battered Hoenir aside with one huge hand, tremendously strong even with a damaged wrist, but by then Tormodr was in close with his flamer.

'Burn, xenos filth,' he rumbled, a torrent of promethium from his flamer causing the ork to bellow further still, stumbling backwards across the chamber, unsteady on his tall artificial legs.

Anvindr knew this was his moment, while Stumpgutz was off-balance. He ran straight at the warboss, firing a burst from his bolter, and this time Stumpgutz was too busy trying to stay on his feet to dodge. Bolter-rounds slammed into Warboss Stumpgutz's head and torso, some deflected by armour but others exploding within vulnerable flesh. He stumbled again, managing to control his descent enough to land on one knee rather than fall flat.

Then Sindri was in close, rolling beneath the wild flail of an arm by Stumpgutz, swinging upwards to jam his own chainsword into the warboss' neck.

'Hold him!' cried Sindri, and as Stumpgutz scrambled to grab him and pull the Space Wolf away, one long arm was seized by Hoenir's power fist while another was held by Tormodr, who wrapped himself around it to hold it back. Stumpgutz's bionic legs scraped back and forth against the rocky floor but couldn't help him escape.

He roared with rage, unleashing a torrent of incomprehensible orkish insults.

As his brothers held the warboss down, Anvindr ran up to Sindri and put his hands over Sindri's on the chainsword.

'Together!' he cried, adding his strength, helping Sindri to force the chainblade deep into the sinew of the warboss' neck. Blood poured down the blade, the motion of the teeth dispersing it as a fine red spray.

Then any resistance against the chainblade was gone, and with a judder Warboss Stumpgutz, scourge of the Alixind System, finally died.

The ork's limbs went limp, allowing Tormodr and Hoenir to let go, dropping them to the floor. Anvindr let go of Sindri and stepped back.

'They never die easily, do they?' sighed Hoenir, flat on his back.

Sindri put his booted foot to the dead ork's chin and used it as leverage to pull his chainsword free.

'Anvindr,' Sindri said with a smile twitching at the corner of his mouth, 'will you have the honour of taking the head yourself?'

Sindri gestured towards the dead warboss, then gave an exaggerated look of shock at where Anvindr's chainsword lay broken on the floor.

'Careless,' he said, shaking his head sadly. 'Careless, to break your weapon like that.'

'I recognise my failing,' replied Anvindr drily, 'and will be sure to correct it.'

Then he remembered Gulbrandr.

'Take the head,' Anvindr told Sindri, running over to where Gulbrandr had fallen. He could not believe that in his moment of victory he had briefly forgotten one of his pack was down. What was victory if the pack did not claim it as one?

Gulbrandr was lying still on the filthy ground, face down so that Anvindr could not see his injuries, just the pool of blood spreading beneath him.

Anvindr was about to turn Gulbrandr over on to his back when a gauntlet on his shoulder stopped him.

'Easy,' said Sindri. 'I saw the blow, turn him over without care and you might worsen the wound.'

'Didn't I order you to take the beast's head?' Anvindr spat.

There was a revving of Sindri's chainsword from across the chamber, the grinding of the sword digging into thick muscle and bone.

'Young Hoenir is fit to the task,' said Sindri. 'I felt over-dressed still holding my sword, now you have chosen to discard yours. Let's turn our brother together.'

Anvindr nodded, and he and Sindri carefully turned Gulbrandr over, Sindri reaching under to support Gulbrandr's neck at the back as Anvindr shifted the bulk of his armoured weight.

It was an ugly wound. Stumpgutz's powerful kick had indeed crushed Gulbrandr's jaw and torn open part of his neck, a wound that continued to bleed, albeit slower than before. His eyes were closed, the lids grey.

'Brother?' asked Sindri. 'Do you still live?'

There was a grunt and a cough from Gulbrandr, blood trickling down from the centre of his mouth. He didn't open his eyes, but tried to speak, finding that the words would not come from his broken face. Gulbrandr collapsed into a further series of coughs, spitting blood.

'Silence brother, the boss is dead,' said Anvindr. 'Do not try and speak, let us help you stand.'

Anvindr and Sindri helped Gulbrandr to his feet. He was a dead weight.

Around them, the smoke in the throne room was thickening. Anvindr heard a rumble and a creak from somewhere nearby. A large flaming pylon toppled from high above, and landed nearby with a crash and shower of cinders.

'Hoenir, get that head,' said Anvindr. 'Tormodr, come help carry Gulbrandr. We need to leave before this place collapses in on itself.'

They regrouped following the attack that had left Barro dead. Captain Anju Badya and her squad had spent hours riding back and forth searching for escaping orks. There had been the occasional individual greenskin, but the squad had not been overrun again.

Their patrols had brought them to a position with a clear view of the fortress. Most of that structure was now a skeleton of blackened wreckage, with only a few visible fires burning.

Captain Badya hadn't seen any ork survivors in a while.

One of her riders whistled for her attention. She turned to watch as a large section of exterior wall collapsed like an avalanche, a stretch covering perhaps a sixth of the fortress perimeter just falling in on itself, huge chunks of blackened metal rolling across the plain, followed by an expanding cloud of ash.

'Nothing's walking out of there,' said Khai, wounded but still alive.

It was then that they saw the figures, the same five that had disappeared into the fortress earlier.

Five Space Wolves, one of whom was carrying one of his fellows on his back, while another carried the largest ork head that Captain Anju Badya had ever seen.

'Ejad,' shouted Badya. 'Ride to the Wolves and tell them that their brothers return, and they have both their prize and injured.'

Ejad nodded wordlessly, pulled on the reins of his horse and rode away back towards camp.

With the head retrieved, the cannons resumed firing for a few hours to pound the remains of Warboss Stumpgutz's fortress into the ground, and then all was silence on the plain of Durrl. The Alixind campaign was over.

As night fell, celebrations began in the encampments of the Imperium forces. For the last months of the campaign, the Tallarn 14th and the Fourth Company of the Space Wolves had been encamped here in a sprawling temporary city of tents and mobile support units. Now the campfires burned high, and desert riders and Wolf brothers alike gathered to celebrate their victory.

They did so separately in their own ways. The Tallarns, as was their way, sat close around the fires, conserving warmth against the hard desert night, talking in low whispers of comrades lost in battles both recent and long ago.

The Space Wolves had their own traditions.

'My money is on the youngster,' said Sindri, in between gulps from a large tankard. 'Tormodr may have strength on his side, but Hoenir has youth.'

'Youth?' replied Anvindr, snorting. 'Hoenir has exactly as many winters behind him as you.'

'And am I not still young, even after all these decades?' demanded Sindri in mock outrage.

Yes, you are, thought Anvindr, looking upon Sindri's unlined face in the firelight. But he didn't say that out loud.

With Anvindr silent, Sindri looked elsewhere for support. He turned as if to find Gulbrandr, who usually sat back from the fire, then remembered that Gulbrandr wasn't there. He was recovering, and would continue to recover, but his absence was felt around the fire. They were a close pack, whatever their differences, and any absence amongst them was always felt.

'Brother Gulbrandr would support me,' said Sindri stubbornly.

'When he wakes, you will already have been proven wrong,' said Anvindr.

Gulbrandr had been lucky. A blow that hard would cut the thread of a normal human, but Gulbrandr was a Space Marine and would recover once his jaw had been rebuilt.

Sindri was about to object to Anvindr, but the fight began before he could speak. Tormodr and Hoenir were wearing most of their armour, but without their helmets or the pelts and adornments that might provide treacherous handholds. They ran at each other and fell into a grappling hold, both trying to bring the other to the ground. When they clashed it was with a great clang and a shriek of metal as their breastplates smashed into each other then ground together.

Sindri made a gagging noise, as if his drink was foul.

'That sound!' he exclaimed over the metallic grinding. 'It's like knives sharpening in my skull, a stink for the ears.'

Anvindr couldn't help laughing.

Hoenir had the advantage, as Sindri had said he would. Hoenir had a better footing, and beneath Tormodr's thick grey moustache his mouth was set in a grimace of effort as he tried to maintain his position.

It seemed to be all over as Tormodr lost his footing and began to be pulled over by Hoenir, but then Tormodr stepped right into a stronger position, and allowed Hoenir's own momentum to cause the red-headed warrior to slip forward. Tormodr took advantage of that momentum to grab Hoenir by the waist and pitch him face forward into the fire with a crunch of burning timber.

Leaving Hoenir face down in the flames, Tormodr walked over to where Sindri sat, plucked the tankard from his grasp, and drained the contents in one swig. He then dropped the empty tankard in Sindri's lap.

'Gracious in victory as ever,' said Sindri, calling for a kaerl to refill his cup.

Tormodr chuckled his deep, low laugh and reached out a hand to help Hoenir stand up.

'One day, brother, one day,' said Hoenir, shaking burning embers from his hair. His skin was red from the fire, but already healing. He gratefully accepted Anvindr's cup, and took a deep swig. He rolled the liquid around his mouth and stared thoughtfully into the cup.

'Foul,' he said. 'Absolutely foul.'

'Big words,' said Sindri, 'from a man who just tasted burning coals.'

'If you wish to take on mighty Tormodr,' said Hoenir, 'I am sure he will oblige.'

Tormodr grunted his assent.

Sindri shook his head.

'No need,' he said. 'After today's victory we should not be contesting each other, brothers. We should be revelling in our glory! The humans lost this whole system to the greenskins, and we came from the heavens to take it back. We have slain their nightmares, and delivered the head of the monster. No wonder they look upon us as gods.'

'We are not gods,' said Anvindr uneasily. 'We just have a sliver of god-like power gifted to us.'

'True,' conceded Sindri.

'Besides,' said Anvindr, 'the mortals fought this campaign as much as we did, and have died in many greater numbers. We could not have won this campaign without the Tallarns or–'

'True, true, all true,' said Sindri. 'The humans die easily, albeit sometimes bravely– this is true.' Sindri paused for effect. 'But were they the ones that brought back the warboss' head?'

Anvindr laughed aloud, and so suddenly that he was surprised by the sound of the deep and rolling laughter that came out of him.

'No, we took the warboss' head,' he told Sindri once his own laughter had subsided. 'We definitely did that.'

'Then let us celebrate our great victory,' said Sindri, raising his cup. 'As conquerors of this system, who came and took the head of the monster.'

Sindri's voice was loud enough to reach other campfires, and when Anvindr's pack cheered together it could be heard echoed by other packs through the dark of the encampment.

Anvindr sat back and watched his pack, or at least most of them, celebrate. Sindri was right to mark the moment. It had been a long campaign, and they had fought well. In an endless life of battle, this had been a good and notable victory to be spoken of and remembered, passed down in the verbal records of the Vlka Fenryka. There was something in Sindri's manner and humour, his dismissive attitude to lesser mortals and his jokes about being a god, that rankled Anvindr – but then that was just Sindri's way. He was a natural joker, a taunter and a mocker, and in spite of that he had saved Anvindr and every other member of his pack a hundred times over. Let him have his ways.

They had all survived this campaign, even Gulbrandr. That was a reason to celebrate and enjoy each other's company, regardless of faults. The pack fought on.

The one loss the pack had suffered, that of Liulfr, had been long ago but still ached at Anvindr like an old wound in the cold. He still blamed Liulfr's death on the Inquisitor's lackey, Interrogator Pranix. It had been Pranix's scheming and keeping of secrets that had prevented Anvindr and his Wolves from sooner defeating the daemon hidden within Hrondir's tomb, and Anvindr blamed Pranix more for Liulfr's death than the daemon itself.

Anvindr shook his head. This was a night for celebrating recent victories, not for dwelling on ancient defeats.

Something broke the darkness of the sky above, a fiery streak that passed overhead and disappeared past the line of tents behind them.

'See?' asked Sindri. 'The heavens drop stars from the sky in our honour.'

'Perhaps,' rumbled Tormodr. 'But only if stars fire their afterburners to slow their descent.'

'A ship?' asked Anvindr.

Tormodr nodded. 'One that must have landed not far from here, on that path of descent.'

'Let's go find this ship before the mortals do,' said Anvindr, reaching to pick up the scabbard containing his chainsword, before remembering with a curse that he didn't have it anymore. He checked his bolter instead before re-holstering it. 'If Sindri's right and the heavens honour us, it is only fair we should get there first.'

The Wolves had to cut through the Imperial Guard encampments in order to exit the camp on the side the meteor fell. Uniformed men and women rushed out of their way as the four giant Space Marines stomped through their camp and towered over them.

At the perimeter, a group of Cadians were preparing to move out to where they had seen the ship land, and Anvindr spoke to their lieutenant.

'We'll engage first,' he told the mortal. 'Inform your commanders and the Wolf Lord, so that the camp may prepare.'

'Yes, my lord,' said the Cadian, and as he went to relay his reports they set out into the desert.

They found it over a bluff, a small space vehicle stuck in the desert sands, embedded at an angle and covered in scars and scorch marks from entering the atmosphere. It was rounded and crude, an unwieldy vehicle, but it bore the aquila and ornamental skull insignia of a vehicle of the Imperium, as well as an unusual sigil with nine interlinked spheres.

'Lacusian,' said Sindri, indicating the linked spheres. 'Remember them?'

'Remind me,' snapped Anvindr. So many worlds and armies he had encountered, he lost track. So old now…

'Lacusians. The Hollow Worlds,' said Sindri. 'That's their mark. Their guard wore green jackets. They were everywhere when we fought the tau.'

Anvindr remembered now. The Hollow Worlds, a system of artificial planets. He had never been there, but Imperial Guard regiments from those worlds had fought alongside the Wolves against the tau, a campaign that had ended for Anvindr in Hrondir's tomb.

Allies, then. But what was a ship bearing the marks of both the Hollow Worlds and the Inquisition doing here?

The Wolves circled the ship, which was still white-hot from re-entry. Shortly, a rectangular panel in one side of the ship opened and a feeble glow came from inside: the red pulse of emergency lighting. Silhouetted within that dim light was a very dishevelled, but definitely human, man.

Anvindr tentatively lowered his bolter. The man had very little hair on his head, but wore a short, unkempt beard. Anvindr knew little of the ageing patterns of normal humans, but considered this man to be neither a child nor elderly. Beneath the beard, the dirty clothes and the overgrown fingernails, there was also something he recognised about this man.

His memory took him back to when he had stood in Hrondir's tomb, with the Inquisitor Montiyf and the young Interrogator in his plain robes. This man was older, balder, carrying slightly more weight, but the eyes and manner, those were unmistakable. Anvindr found himself almost unconsciously lifting his bolter back up, taking a bead on the man before him. Sindri had been right in spite of himself, this was a portent of some kind, or a gift from the stars.

'Captain Godrichsson,' croaked the man, his voice clearly unused for a long time.

'Interrogator,' growled Anvindr through clenched teeth. The rank of captain was one the Space Wolves did not use, and this man knew it.

'Inquisitor now,' said the man, leaning on the interior frame of the ship hatch. He was clearly physically weak from his journey, and could not move out of the ship until the exterior had cooled sufficiently to touch. He was stuck standing where he was, in Anvindr's sights.

'Pranix,' the Space Wolf hissed, his finger tightening around the trigger of his bolter.

'Pranix?' asked Hoenir. 'That Pranix?'

'Aye,' grumbled Tormodr, raising his flamer.

'So it is,' said Sindri, quietly for once, without humour.

They all looked to Anvindr who looked to Hoenir, the only one of them who had not met Pranix before in Hrondir's tomb. The only one with no reason to have let a grudge stew for long decades.

'I am with you in whatever you decide,' said Hoenir, also raising his weapon.

'Nine worlds,' croaked Pranix, with something that might have been a parched laugh. 'Nine worlds fallen to the tyrant, and you think I'm the enemy?' He leaned forwards, head low, and let out a chuckle, then threw back his head and laughed hysterically.

Anvindr realised the Inquisitor was delirious. Perhaps that was what stayed his hand. Or perhaps it was the memory that he had not acted against Pranix when he had the chance, all those years ago, and it had only been in the intervening decades that his resentment had stewed into murderous hatred. Had he lost his way?

'I have wasted my journey,' said Pranix, possibly to himself, but audible to Anvindr's enhanced hearing. 'All is lost.'

Then he collapsed backwards into the ship doorway.

Anvindr cursed, lowering his gun.

'Help me get him out of there,' he barked to Sindri.

'What?' demanded Sindri, outraged, his weapon still raised.

'Just do it, damn you,' shouted Anvindr, advancing on the ship, though he sympathised with Sindri's bafflement.

Anvindr had wanted to kill this man for so long, but the nature of Pranix's arrival, fleeing some great enemy of the Imperium, overrode Anvindr's own desires. The Hollow Worlds, fallen to some tyrant? That could not be ignored, regardless of personal enmities.

Like it or not, and Anvindr hated it, one thing was certain – for now at least.

If they were to find out what calamity had occurred, if they were to rectify it and save the Hollow Worlds for the Emperor... they needed Inquisitor Pranix alive.

STORMSEEKER

Alec Worley

The huge wolf pelt hung like a rancid curtain. It was ragged and infested with maggots, the whole thing as moist as the day it had been peeled from the flanks of a dead Fenrisian wolf. Anvarr Rustmane unpinned the final rivet and the heavy pelt flopped into his waiting arms, unveiling the bulkhead that housed the sacred engine of his Stormwolf gunship. Pipes and cables pulsed like arteries, their junction box embossed with the emblem of a glowering wolf's head.

The immense Iron Priest recited a memorial prayer of the Adeptus Mechanicus, folding the stinking pelt as reverently as if it were the banner of a Wolf Lord. As Anvarr had explained to those of his brothers who had grumbled about the smell, the Stormwolf's machine-spirit had insisted the pelt remained untreated, so the trophy could better permeate the gunship with its feral aura.

The assortment of charms and relics that adorned Anvarr's battered blue-grey power armour clinked in the darkness, the significance of these mementoes unfathomable to all but the Iron Priest himself. The matted ropes of rust-red hair that ran down his back presented a tapestry of fangs, spikes of bone, cogs, spent bolter casings, lengths of relay wiring tied in elaborate knots. Each braid offered a chronicle of battles past. Anvarr's mane clattered as he bowed his head before the engine and raised the folded pelt before him, backing away and down the Stormwolf's hold as he concluded his prayer. The Iron Priest glanced up as he reached the open ramp, and the embossed wolf's head seemed to glare back at him from the gloom.

Anvarr frowned and handed the pelt to a waiting servitor before emerging onto the busy flight deck of the strike cruiser, the *Ragnarök*. His battle-brothers surged about him, the boots of their power armour clattering as they hurried between the docked aircraft that loomed like rows of monoliths either side of them. To Anvarr's preternatural senses, the flight deck reeked of bio-enhanced adrenaline, as dozens of hearts pounded in anticipation of clashing with a hated foe.

Hailing from the Deathwolves Company, Anvarr and his detachment had been stationed in this sector to hunt a pair of elusive dark eldar pirates. The xenos had been raiding the vast mining cities located upon the sun-scorched death world of Vityris. Hardened by generations of crystal-mining beneath the planet's blistering sun, the colonists had apparently proved to be durable material for the pain-farms of Commorragh, the degenerate stronghold of the dark eldar.

The Deathwolves had hunted for weeks without detecting any sign of their quarry. Then, less than an hour ago, a scout pack had reported that one of these pirates, along with his entire raiding party, had captured a remote research station overlooking a network of canyons. It appeared the xenos were stranded there, although the scouts knew not how. After weeks of frustration, Anvarr was eager to join his pack in combat, but knew the hunt could not commence in earnest just yet.

'Brother?' said a voice beside him.

It was Eadric, the youngest of the Iron Priest pilots in Anvarr's assault wing.

'This is all I could find,' he said, presenting a handful of totems: bundles of bones, fangs suspended from strips of leather, and a huge severed paw bearing claws the size of ork cleavers.

'Trinkets!' spat Anvarr. 'The machine-spirit requires a tribute of suitable magnitude! That pelt was torn from the beast's back after I slew it with my bare hands! Have the Rune Priests nothing else for us?'

'Nothing that can be prepared without the proper ceremony,' Eadric said.

'You'll have to fly without, Anvarr,' said another voice.

Anvarr turned, his braids clinking, as he faced his fellow alpha.

Skaldr Frostbiter mag-locked his chainsword and bolt pistol to his belt, the weapons having just received blessings from the Iron Priests Kaarle and Varg. Frostbiter, a Pack Leader of the Wolf Guard, was a fine Space Marine, a blonde-bearded giant whose radiant charisma inspired all those around him, although he smiled far too much for Anvarr's liking.

'My Stormwolf's machine-spirit has just told me the pelt is no longer a worthy tribute,' Anvarr said. 'I need a replacement, or else disaster will befall this hunt, I promise you.'

Skaldr exchanged a glance with Eadric.

'I need a proper totem,' Anvarr said impatiently. 'A relic fragment. Anything! Perhaps you have a trophy I might borrow, brother...?'

'Anvarr, we need to make planetfall within the next fifteen minutes. The *Ragnarök* has jammed the research station's comms relay. We must strike before the xenos hear us coming.'

Anvarr stared at him, incredulous.

'But to fly without tribute is an invitation to disaster,' he spluttered, his voice rising, spit flecking his beard. 'An insult to the Omnissiah, neglect of the sacred mechanics of fate itself. To break with ritual is to break with faith, brother...'

Skaldr placed a calming hand on Anvarr's shoulder.

'And I have faith that you will honour the Allfather with your skill, Anvarr,' he said calmly. 'You are not one for boasts, Rustmane, which is why perhaps you need reminding that you stand among the finest pilots in our Chapter.'

A pack of Blood Claws approached them, reckless wild-haired whelps. They jostled and laughed as they filed into the hold of Anvarr's Stormwolf.

'It is time,' Skaldr said, slapping Anvarr's pauldron. 'Fear not, brother,' he said, departing with yet another smile. 'Sometimes valour is tribute enough.'

Anvarr kept his curses to himself as he turned to the three Iron Priests under his command.

'Very well,' he growled. 'I doubt compliments alone are honour enough for the Omnissiah, but the Deathwolves have xenos to kill. To your ships then, brothers.'

Eadric, Kaarle and Varg nodded and hurried to their ships as Anvarr looked away and whistled. From across the flight deck loped Cogfang, Anvarr's cyberwolf. The hulking creature had once been a coal-black Fenrisian Ironpelt, whose pack had fought alongside the Deathwolves on several campaigns. After an invigorating clash with a horde of World Eaters, Anvarr had found the beast dying upon the battlefield, a chainaxe buried in its chest and a dead Traitor Marine still clamped in its jaws. Anvarr had taken his find as a sign from the Omnissiah that he should save the life of this valiant beast. Cogfang's bionic front leg clanked as he ascended the ramp, saliva trailing from the serrated iron trap that replaced his lower jaw as he followed his grumbling master inside the Stormwolf.

The Blood Claws were cursing and arguing as they locked themselves to the walls of the hold. Anvarr shoved past them. When the Iron Priest reached the bulkhead, Cogfang sat on his haunches, his head almost level with his master's shoulders. Anvarr produced a clay cup carved with runes and filled it with a pungent measure of mjod from a metal decanter built into Cogfang's throat. The cyberwolf yawned – a strange metallic whine – and shook itself, rattling the cybernetic cables that wormed through its pelt. Its bionic eye cast a bloody glow over the Iron Priest's face as he murmured a prayer of contrition, dipping his fingers in the cup and painting runes around the engine bulkhead.

A hush had descended upon the hold and Anvarr felt the eyes of his young passengers upon him. It amused him to think of the stories that circulated around the feast halls on the many occasions he declined to attend, that Anvarr Rustmane communed as much with the voices in his head as with the spirits of the armoury. He concluded his ritual by raising his cup to the engine then tipping what was left of the Fenrisian liquor down his throat. The mjod scorched his tongue and warmed his chest, filling his nose with a perfume of fermented honey and frost-nettle.

He caught the eye of the nearest Blood Claw. Nudged by his fellows,

the whelp looked as though he were about to comment but had thought
better of it.

'Mjod is a sacrament, little brother,' Anvarr said, smiling to himself. 'It
helps me commune with the machine-spirits.'

As he downed another measure from Cogfang's decanter, his ears
twitched at the sound of an amused whisper.

'Clearly he and the spirits have much to say.'

Anvarr paused as he ascended the ladder into the cockpit, casting his
red-rimmed eyes over the two ranks of Blood Claws.

'Aye, we have much to discuss,' Anvarr said. 'Flying this vessel without
proper tribute to the machine-spirit is a heinous offence, tantamount to
flying under a curse, some might say. Unless I can convince it that you are
a cargo worthy of being borne into battle, it may allow a fan blade to snap
or a fuel line to leak and we'll die in flames before we reach the battlefield.
And so your names shall go unheard in the sagas to come.'

The Blood Claws were silent.

'But rest assured, little brothers,' Anvarr laughed. 'Should we burn, my
guts shall be filled with drink enough to light our passage all the way to hel.'

Anvarr's yellow eyes flashed like coins as the ramp lifted and darkness
enveloped them all.

'Fangs of Russ!'

Anvarr voxed the Blood Claws in the hold beneath.

'Save your songs for the feasting halls, damn you!'

The whelps had been singing battle hymns ever since leaving the strike
cruiser. Perhaps they were honouring the Stormwolf in their own crude
way, but their howling distracted him from reciting his own murmured
entreaties to the machine-spirit.

The hurtling Stormwolf emerged into the planet's atmosphere, and
the rippling sheet of fire that covered the canopy gradually disappeared,
revealing the gunship's long, shuddering snout and a piercing sun beyond.
Canyons veined the rust-red mesa far below, cracking the landscape as
though some waking behemoth strained beneath its surface. The sun
gleamed viciously upon lakes of shattered crystal, the remains of countless glass bodies that formed in the upper atmosphere and rained upon
the planet's surface. Anvarr felt the engine behind him growl like a restless beast. He shifted uncomfortably.

The ship trembled and rattled as Anvarr continued his descent, shaking
on his pilot's throne as he absorbed a weight of acceleration that would
have crushed the chest of an ordinary man. Atmospheric and positional
data scrolled and flickered across the Iron Priest's vision, the gene-implants
in his brain feeding him a constant stream of information from the ship's
sensor array. Four arrowheads bleeped before his eyes in a steady diamond
formation. Kaarle and Varg's Stormfangs flew abeam on Anvarr's flanks.

They each carried a unit of Long Fangs, white-haired veterans all, as prodigious and majestic as the great lascannons they bore into battle. Eadric
remained steady on Anvarr's tail, his Stormwolf carrying another unit of
eager young Blood Claws.

'There's Skaldr,' voxed Kaarle.

The Iron Priest looked up to see four golden dots emerging like comets
from the clouds ahead. Anvarr voxed the *Ragnarök*.

'Drop pods sighted,' he said.

'Received, Assault Wing,' the *Ragnarök* replied. 'Drop pods will reach
the target in thirty seconds.'

'Too late, I fear, to save those poor wretches who were manning the
research station,' Kaarle voxed.

'Indeed,' Varg said. 'Any the xenos have left alive will be welcoming death
by now. May Russ guide us in granting them vengeance.'

Anvarr continued his dive, leading his assault wing towards a magnificent
canyon, slowing to cruising speed as he levelled out high above a river of
crystal shards that ran along the floor of the chasm. He leaned on the sticks
and the canyon walls rose either side of him, the level mesa disappearing
from view. With a blink-click, he dismissed part of his tactical display and
snapped a row of switches above his head, activating the sensor relays in
the Stormwolf's prow. Anvarr's helmet filled with the hot scent of the outside world, the smoky smell of arid rock, the hot tang of seared crystal.

'Snouts to the wind, brothers,' he voxed, accelerating slightly ahead of
the pack and dipping low enough above the crystal river for his thrusters
to carve a glittering spray as he passed. Although initiated in the mys-
teries of the Cult Mechanicus, Anvarr remained a Space Wolf, his Canis
Helix gifting him with the senses of an apex predator. He read the land as
it flowed beneath him, detecting every subtle pattern wrought by wind
and sun, devouring every secret as he rode the curve of the canyon walls.

As the Space Wolves' briefing had explained, the surface of this death
world was beset with what the mining colonies called 'shard-devils'. Stirred
into life by columns of superheated air, these vast swirling towers guzzled
loose rocks and crystal debris and spat them in all directions. Anvarr
scanned the trail ahead for the telltale sign of whirling dust that heralded
the arrival of such a maelstrom.

The Iron Priest led his pack down a fork in the canyon, following the
buffeting wind like a wolf tracking prey. Streamers of smoke appeared
ahead, lining the sky atop a sheer canyon wall ahead. As Anvarr slowed,
he detected not only the familiar musk of bolter fire, but also the sour oily
stench of the xenos. Acting as one, the Space Wolf assault wing angled
their thrusters, their ships rising out of the canyon and looming over the
smoking research station.

The four empty drop pods surrounded the station like the pinnacles of
a castle. Skaldr and his Wolf Guard had broken into the various bunkers

and would be deep in the underground tunnels by now, exterminating the cornered xenos with blade and bolter. Occasionally a lithe black figure would spring like a spider from an exit hatch and flee towards the outlying crags, crying out as it stumbled through ankle-deep drifts of razor-sharp crystal debris.

'Ready yourselves, whelps,' Anvarr voxed his Blood Claws as the rest of the assault wing fanned into position behind the drop pods.

'Be grateful the machine-spirit has deemed you worthy of being carried into battle,' he roared. 'Now, destroy the xenos filth as your brothers drive them into your arms. Blood your blades and win yourselves honour enough for a ride home!'

The youngsters yelled and whooped in reply. Cogfang howled among them, his cry ringing through the Stormwolf's hull like an alarm as a red warning rune flashed on Anvarr's tac-display.

Something was closing in on him from behind, moving at unthinkable speed. The Iron Priest felt the engine judder beneath him, and could have sworn he heard a ghostly laugh.

Clad in elegant black carapace, Iruthyr Xynariis, Archon of the Kabal of the Forked Tongue, stalked towards the invading savages like a huge venomous insect. He was grateful for the opportunity to vent his displeasure. His raiding party's webway portals had shattered upon entry to this world. Sabotaged. Agents of the Book of Sorrows, his rival Kabal, were the obvious culprits. As if this were not humiliation enough, he had been forced not only to abort his latest raid, but also to take refuge in this stinking human burrow.

Three armoured apes blocked his exit from the control room, their maskless faces grimacing amid flashes of booming gunfire. Iruthyr vaulted over an exploding control console and scuttled over toppled furniture as a trail of blasts chased him across the room, destroying an entire wall of surveillance monitors. A short while ago, Iruthyr and his exhausted raiders had been availing themselves of the humans that had been stationed here, feasting on their tortured screams. Then the apes' assault pods had landed overhead, shaking the bunkers' foundations and spoiling the meticulous flesh-peeling he had been performing upon a shrieking captive.

Iruthyr rose from behind cover and fired his splinter pistol twice and with seeming carelessness. Spikes of poisoned crystal punctured the eyes of the two bearded savages closing in on him. Iruthyr slithered between them as they toppled to the floor, their blue-grey power armour clattering as the bodies inside convulsed in agony. The dark eldar sidestepped another clumsy burst of gunfire and slid his huskblade into the shooter's throat. Iruthyr shuddered with pleasure, feeling his muscles invigorated by the pain radiating from his victim. He watched the ape's face shrink into a withered brown skull before withdrawing the blade and sprinting through the nearby exit, splinter pistol in hand.

The corridor outside rang with nearby bolter blasts as Iruthyr bounded through a set of double doors and into the elevated tunnel that led to the station's hangar bay. Here his beloved Razorwing jetfighter sat undamaged, fully fuelled, its missiles unspent. Dust hissed against a porthole beside him as a booming shadow passed overhead.

He peered outside and saw a huge blue-grey vessel, a gunship by the look of it. Its ramp yawned in mid-air, disgorging several wild-eyed apes wearing bulky jump packs, each waving a chainsword as they leapt one by one from the gunship. Through the opposite window, Iruthyr saw another gunship circling nearby, flanked by two more, each with a huge ice-blue cannon embedded in its snout. Iruthyr felt a flicker of disbelief as he considered the possibility that his raiding party – veterans of countless incursions, selected from among the finest mercenaries and murder-artists of Commorragh – could actually be slaughtered by these brainless animals.

One of the gunships exploded in mid-air.

Iruthyr flinched as a ball of fire tore the vessel apart in a shower of debris and burning bodies. Three bat-like shadows streaked overhead as the shattered gunship sank, crashing to the ground with a boom that shook the corridor.

Iruthyr's communicator crackled into life.

'Brother?' a familiar voice purred. 'Are you there?'

'Izabella,' Iruthyr gasped.

'You sound surprised.'

Iruthyr fumbled for an answer to the contrary as he watched the remaining gunships scatter, the streaking shadows driving them into the air with volleys of disintegrator fire. Clearly, the apes had not expected a rescue attempt either.

'After all this time,' Izabella said. 'After everything we have built together, have you not yet learned that the Kabal of the Forked Tongue stands for the two of us, or it does not stand at all?'

Iruthyr heard approaching cries and ran down the corridor as more explosive rounds tore open the wall beside him. He turned to see another gaggle of apes pounding towards him.

Iruthyr ducked as he heard the familiar whine of an approaching monoscythe missile. The projectile pierced an overhead skylight and detonated in the midst of his enemies, bursting into a sizzling halo that decapitated the apes and destroyed the surrounding walls. Long-haired heads rolled for an instant on a dwindling shelf of energy, then dropped to the floor.

'I have another present for you, brother,' Izabella said as her twin scrambled to his feet. 'Captured saboteurs of the Book of Sorrows. I have

prepared them as part of a pain-feast to celebrate your return to Commorragh. But first, won't you join me in this little appetizer...?'

Iruthyr laughed as he ran towards the hangar bay.

Another burst of disintegrator fire slammed into the Stormwolf's snout,
punching the ship into a spin that turned the world outside Anvarr's canopy into a whirl of smoke and flashing gunfire. The Iron Priest grunted as
he heaved at the sticks, arresting his turn in time to lance the air where
he calculated his enemy would appear, but his las-bolts strafed nothing
but empty sky. Another shadow screamed past him as Kaarle's and Varg's
enraged curses crackled over the vox. The wreckage of Eadric's Stormwolf
smoked nearby as Anvarr struggled to dismiss the thought that his failure
to honour the machine-spirit had not gone unnoticed by the Omnissiah,
and that his brothers were now paying the price for his dishonour.

He voxed the two gunships as he saw a red arrowhead on his tac-display
streak towards him from behind, preparing to fire upon his exposed tail.

'They're trying to scatter us,' he said. 'But they're moving too fast to be
accurate.'

He heaved his Stormwolf to one side, avoiding another blazing disintegrator beam as the crescent-winged jetfighter sliced past him. The craft was
sleek and black, veined with green, its barbed fins like those of a venomous fish. Razorwings, the xenos called them, named after some predatory
alien bird. Anvarr blasted after it with his heavy bolters, but the jet merely
twirled aside, peeling away to commence another run.

Anvarr wheeled hard, the battleground rising into a wall beside him.
The xenos were swarming now. Those that had escaped the bunker were
leaping aboard open-topped skiffs, which must have arrived alongside the
fighters. The skiffs' crews helped their comrades aboard, handing them
masks to protect their eyes from the crystal splinters churned into clouds
by the aircraft that thundered above them. The rescued xenos took up position and fired their rifles at the bunkers where Skaldr's Wolf Guard now
crouched, pinned behind cover. Small-arms fire rattled upon the ceramite hide of Anvarr's prowling Stormwolf as the Razorwing dived overhead.

He glanced at his tac-display. Every time Kaarle and Varg moved to
deploy their troops behind the xenos' skiffs, a Razorwing dived at them,
seemingly out of nowhere, and cut them off. Even if the gunships could
land, their troops would likely be cut down by the swooping fighters. His
assault wing was being worn down and prised apart.

'Abort deployment,' Anvarr growled over the vox. He swung his Stormwolf hard to port. Kaarle's Stormfang reeled into view on the other side
of the station, dodging twin beams of disintegrator fire from the Razorwing above him.

'Ignore the ground for now,' Anvarr voxed. 'Let us tear these three little
birds from the sky first. For Eadric! For the Allfather!'

Anvarr charged towards the distant Stormfang, intent upon destroying the xenos fighter bearing down on Kaarle's gunship, heedless of the other fighter the Iron Priest knew was closing on his own tail. The heavy snout of his Stormwolf dipped as he accelerated, the battleground rising to meet him, rifle-fire sparking on his armoured canopy. His augmented brain engaged in myriad calculations, Anvarr felt the engine rumble beneath him. He commenced a prayer of invocation to the machine-spirit, surrendering himself to instinct as he corrected his approach, training his attention upon the area behind Kaarle's Stormfang where the xenos fighter would appear. As he closed in, he realised he had not taken fire from the Razorwing behind him.

A shadow enveloped the cockpit. Anvarr looked up to see the fighter hovering upside down above him. Unlike the ships of its two wingmen, the fighter was not black, but a livid purple, its canopy wavering a few feet from his own. The dark eldar pilot was female. She wore no flight helmet, her red and black hair hanging in a ponytail as she gazed down at the Iron Priest, oblivious to the streaking gunfire that surrounded them. He was close enough to see that her hooded eyes regarded him with a mingled look of curiosity and disgust, as though he were a dead animal about to be dissected.

Anvarr concluded his prayer to the machine-spirit as he brought two sets of weapons to bear.

'I'll give you something to watch,' he growled. The helfrost turret whirred into life above his head and he sensed the heavy bolters lock at his sides, feeling their weight as though he held them in his own hands.

He thumbed both fire buttons a split second before the xenos fighter appeared in his sights, expecting to hit the ship dead centre, destroying it with a single blow.

Both weapons stalled and the fighter flashed past unmolested. Anvarr cursed aloud, glaring in rage as the fighter released another burst from its disintegrators, destroying a rack of missiles in the flank of Kaarle's Stormfang.

He commenced a prayer of entreaty as he pulled up after it, but the xenos fighter was faster and rose out of sight. The machine-spirit had refused Anvarr's plea, allowing the ammunition feeds to become misaligned, or perhaps static to have impeded the targeting relays, denying him glory and perhaps costing his packmates their lives. Such was the price of his failure.

The purple Razorwing followed him, still hovering above his head. Anvarr punched the inside of his canopy, cursing with rage. The dark eldar woman laughed as she pulled back, dazzling Anvarr as sunlight flooded his cockpit. She corkscrewed into position behind him, chasing him as he climbed after the other fighter, which curved back to continue its attack upon Kaarle.

Anvarr bared his fangs as the speeding fighter wavered into his sights. He slowed enough to achieve a target lock, although he knew he would need to accelerate if he had any hope of evading the blast about to tear into his tail. Anvarr fired his heavy bolters and prayed.

Shuddering thunder answered him as the bolters pounded long lines of explosive rounds into the fighter's path, stitching fire across its left wing as it zipped past. An explosion threw Anvarr forward in his seat. Warning runes glimmered on his tac-display as the ship dipped to one side. He had lost one of his thrusters. Another was badly damaged. As he pulled aside, he saw the fighter he had wounded roll directly in front of his packmate's Stormfang. The vessel's helfrost cannon spat a dazzling blast that enveloped the black Razorwing, freezing it white. The xenos fighter tumbled to the rocky ground where it shattered like porcelain.

Anvarr turned his helfrost turret to face the fighter behind him. He fired wildly, thanking the machine-spirit for not disabling the weapon permanently. The disintegrator bolts that lanced the air either side of him ceased as the purple Razorwing peeled away in search of easier prey. The Iron Priest gave chase as quickly as his shattered thruster array would allow.

'My thanks, Anvarr,' Kaarle voxed. 'I shall sing your sagas louder than thunder.'

Anvarr grunted.

'Deploy your troops to the south-west,' he said.

Kaarle retreated, leaving Anvarr to cruise after the purple Razorwing. The Iron Priest fired his las-cannons at the fighter's rear, but the vessel dodged every volley, rolling aside each time as if pestered by insects.

'Anvarr!'

It was Skaldr.

'We grow lonely down here behind cover,' he voxed. 'Any chance of some company, brother?'

'Kaarle's sending you a bellyful of Long Fangs,' Anvarr replied. 'They shall bite the xenos' flanks shortly.'

The purple Razorwing had joined its remaining wingman in attacking Varg's smoking Stormfang, the two fighters like moths battering a dying flame.

'Tell the elders to hurry,' Skaldr voxed. 'The xenos seem to think there are enough of them to take us alive. I would hate to have to prove them wrong.'

'Give us time enough to kill the rest of these vermin,' Anvarr said. 'Just two of them left now.'

A third xenos fighter flashed before him, rocketing up from the station below, forcing Anvarr into a tight swerve. As he swung back to face Varg's besieged gunship, he saw the purple Razorwing break away and race to meet the newcomer, another Razorwing of the same hue. Anvarr braced himself, expecting the pair to collide head-on, but the twin fighters snapped into a climb at the last second, spinning skywards in perfect unison. The other Razorwing joined the greeting display and the three ships peeled apart at the apex of their climb, curling backwards like the petals of a blossoming rose, then dived back down towards the crippled Stormfang.

Anvarr's damaged thruster shrieked as he accelerated, firing madly at the three descending fighters. Kaarle joined the barrage, his own Stormfang closing at Anvarr's flank, his cargo of Long Fangs safely deployed.

Together the Space Wolf ships lanced the air relentlessly, firing bolt after bolt of helfrost above their injured packmate, eventually scattering all three fighters, forcing them to flee like startled crows. A pair of missiles had already sizzled out from beneath one of the Razorwings, but the projectiles detonated either side of Varg's gunship, exploding into haloes of energy that showered the wounded vessel with rocks and dust.

Anvarr and Kaarle had saved Varg's Stormfang from complete destruction, but its thrusters were already ruined, leaking columns of smoke as the vessel lowered majestically. The Stormfang's snout ploughed through the crags in the direction of the dark eldar skiffs, threatening to topple onto its side before eventually grinding to a halt on its belly. Anvarr and Kaarle circled the grounded ship, like wolves guarding a kill. Anvarr targeted the approaching skiffs as Kaarle prowled the air above him, protecting his alpha against the Razorwings' next attack.

Anvarr saw Varg's Long Fangs batter open the rear exit of the crashed Stormfang, their faces streaked with blood. Their life signs scrolled and glimmered in his tac-display. Varg's did not.

The air above him suddenly streamed with heavy bolter fire as Kaarle drove off the weaving Razorwings. Anvarr pummelled the dark eldar skiffs with las-fire, covering the wounded Long Fangs as they limped and stumbled behind the cover of the rocks. His ship's tac-display was a riot of warning runes, while Kaarle's Stormfang appeared relatively intact. But the three Razorwings threatened to slip past them both and turn the advancing Long Fangs into a crater. A xenos skiff exploded amid bolts of heavy las-fire as the Long Fangs claimed their first kill. Anvarr felt a rush of battle-hunger and gained altitude to join Kaarle.

He prayed again, imploring the machine-spirit for forgiveness, turned and was blessed with the sight of the two purple Razorwings nearing his target-lock. He fired helfrost and bolters together, targeting both fighters at once.

His weapons seized once again.

Defiance and rage burned within the Iron Priest as he surged after the fighters. If skill and valour in battle was the price demanded by the machine-spirit, then Anvarr Rustmane, Iron Priest of the Deathwolves, was prepared to give more than suitable tribute.

He voxed his remaining wingman.

'Our brothers on the ground look bored, Kaarle,' he growled. 'Let's give them a display such as would inspire Russ himself!'

Kaarle howled down the vox in agreement, and the Space Wolf ships loped after the streaking Razorwings.

Skaldr Frostbiter broke cover, several of his packmates howling behind him. As he ran, the Pack Leader emptied the clip of his bolt pistol into the xenos pirates that clustered behind the spent drop pod. He beheaded the last of them with a backhand swipe of his chainsword as he skidded into cover behind the ceramite plating of the downed gunship. His packmates joined him as he looked up at the Space Wolf ships tearing after the xenos fighters above them. White bolts of helfrost and golden spears of disintegrator fire criss-crossed beneath the glaring sun as the Iron Priests fought to prevent the enemy from loosing their missiles upon the Space Wolves below.

More dark eldar pounced upon Skaldr's men from the nearby crags, wearing horned masks and twirling strange two-handed swords that flashed in the sun. Skaldr's chainsword sparked as he parried a sweeping blow at his neck, grabbing the creature and slamming his forehead into its mask, shattering the skull beneath. Another blow glanced off his pauldron and he charged at his attacker, aiming to drive his shoulder into the creature's chest. But the nimble xenos dodged aside, spilling him onto the ground. Before the dark eldar blade could meet Skaldr's neck, a thick las-bolt exploded from the xenos' chest, spraying ash and blackened bone.

The pack of wounded Long Fangs who had clambered from the ruined Stormfang were crouched atop a nearby ridge. They pumped heavy las-fire into the retreating xenos swordsmen as Skaldr and his packmates recovered and crouched behind the drop pod, their advance momentarily secure. The Long Fangs turned and directed their fire at the xenos skiffs pinning the rest of the Wolf Guard within the bunkers. Their las-fire ripped into the jagged craft of the dark eldar, shattering their black carapace and scattering their screaming riders, each of whom was then calmly blasted into smoking pieces. The veteran Space Wolves held the line, shielding their flank with an outcrop of rock, their faces weary, almost bored by their own mastery of battle.

Skaldr needed to order the rest of his Wolf Guard forward to support the Long Fangs, before the xenos could regroup and overwhelm them with their superior weight of numbers. He went to vox his command when he was thrown to the ground by a blast of air. Silence fell for an instant and Skaldr assumed he had been deafened. Then the clamour of rifle and bolter fire returned as he got to his feet and peered through a cloud of glittering dust.

Where the Long Fangs had crouched seconds ago, a deep and immaculate bowl had appeared in the rock, its surface smooth and crackling with residual energy. One of his packmates was pointing at two flyers retreating in the distance. Skaldr's tac-display magnified the image, revealing two black ships fleeing side by side across the shimmering mesa. They were narrower than the broad-winged fighters, with long sharp beaks like those of carrion crows.

Skaldr voxed Anvarr.

'Voidravens!'

'I see them,' growled Anvarr, pelting a Razorwing with las-fire as he glanced at his tac-display. The two bombers were slowing into a climb, preparing to make another supersonic run across the battlefield. Anvarr and his wing-man could barely contain three fast-moving ships, let alone five.

The Voidravens curled back towards the battlefield.

Apart from Skaldr and his Wolf Guard, the only other ground troops out in the open were the pack of Long Fangs whom Kaarle had deployed earlier. The veterans were plodding towards the crater to replace their fallen broth-ers and maintain the line. If the Voidravens hit them, the xenos ground troops would eventually overrun the Wolf Guard pinned inside the bunkers.

Anvarr's Stormwolf shuddered as another blast smashed into his snout. It would be a miracle if there were any Blood Claws left alive in the hold. He returned fire, the fighter swerving to avoid his volley. Anvarr knew that attempting to save his brothers on the ground would mean abandoning Kaarle to the Razorwings. Not even a Stormfang pilot of his brother's feroc-ity could prevent three agile xenos fighters from tearing him apart.

The Voidravens accelerated, commencing their run towards Skaldr and the Long Fangs.

Kaarle voxed him.

'Save them, brother,' he laughed. 'And sing them the saga of Kaarle Grey-wing upon your return.'

'I shall,' Anvarr said. 'Louder than thunder, brother.'

Kaarle's Stormfang unleashed a stream of bolter fire, herding one of the Razorwings into a sharp turn, freeing Anvarr to plunge towards the approaching Voidravens.

Anvarr circled the research station as Kaarle fought to keep the Razor-wings occupied. The bombers were still kilometres away, but their distance to the battlefield was shrinking faster than Anvarr believed possible. He scanned the rocks and bunkers before him with the eyes of a hunter, seek-ing any elevation or cover that might provide a tactical advantage.

He voxed Skaldr.

'Do you have any Sky Claws left?'

'One.'

'Get him onto the roof of that high bunker to the north-west. And tell those Long Fangs to cover the airspace above that comms relay on the other side.'

Skaldr directed his troops as the Voidravens closed in, hurtling low over the mesa, carving waves of crystal dust in their wake. Anvarr swooped low, grazing the ground as he hid behind a long wall of crumbled rock, rifle-fire scuttling across his Stormwolf's hide as he calculated the speed of his approach, matching it to the lunatic velocity of the oncoming Voidravens.

He was laughing now, drunk with feral adrenaline as he raced behind the rock wall to meet the bombers. When his Stormwolf lay a shattered wreck, perhaps then the machine-spirit would be appeased by his valour.

As the Voidravens reached the edge of the battlefield, Anvarr raised his Stormwolf from behind the cover of the rocks, spraying las-bolts at the two bombers screaming towards him, seconds from collision.

As the Space Wolf gunship reared into their path, the dark eldar pilots reacted with predictable precision. Performing a miracle of control and timing, they slowed from a scream to a shriek, Anvarr having given them just enough time to bank into a hard turn – one left, the other right. The Stormwolf redirected them like a stone diverting a stream.

Anvarr hit the tail of a fleeing Voidraven, clipping its fins with a stream of las-bolts. The other bomber banked above the station's shattered comms relay, where waited Skaldr's Long Fangs. They caught the ship in a web of heavy las-fire, punching through its exposed belly and driving it into the rocks in a glorious bloom of fire.

Khanvir Marugaard heard his wingman's ship detonate behind him. Khanvir was wrestling with the sticks of his own bomber, struggling to ride its momentum and slow the vessel enough to make another turn. He cruised low across the ground, past a high bunker and felt the bomber rock as if with an impact. He had taken las-fire from that gunship. Perhaps it had damaged a stabiliser.

Khanvir pulled into another turn, steering towards the apes on the ground that had destroyed his wingman. He went to arm his void-lances when something smashed through the canopy, impaling his chest and pinning him to his seat. The dark eldar stared in disbelief at the whirring blade protruding from his body and thought he could make out a face grinning down at him from the other side of the shattered canopy. Then the blade revved faster and a churning fountain of his own blood obscured Khanvir's view.

Skaldr was reloading his bolt pistol when he saw the lone Sky Claw leap from the canopy of the second bomber before it crashed to the ground. The whelp cannonballed into the rocks, rolling several dozen feet before crashing to a halt. Skaldr almost laughed as moments later the battered warrior got to his feet, grinning through a mouthful of blood and twirling the pilot's severed head above his own.

A second explosion bellowed overhead and a shrieking cheer arose among the dark eldar. Anvarr's valiant wingman had finally fallen, his Stormfang a blazing wreck as it slumped into the crags below. The three Razorwings that had torn it apart now circled the battlefield, surveying their outnumbered prey. The replacement Long Fangs were still trudging into position on the rocks nearby, readying their smoking lascannons.

Skaldr activated his chainsword as he voxed what remained of his warriors.

'Advance, Wolves of Fenris,' he howled. 'Better to die with fangs bared than–'

Something struck him in the throat. He grunted and dropped to one knee, his body shivering uncontrollably. Skaldr knew he had been hit by a poisoned shard fired from a xenos splinter rifle. His face contorted into a grimace of agony as the arcane toxin boiled his nervous system. He watched, helpless, as his Wolf Guard scattered from the bunkers and ran towards the dark eldar, bolters blazing. The black-armoured xenos and their craft swarmed like beetles over the crags to meet them, their ghostly faces gleeful. One of the circling Razorwings despatched a missile that exploded amid the ragged Space Wolf vanguard, expelling a disc of energy that sliced their legs out from under them. The dark eldar still clearly hoped to take them alive. But the xenos were arrogant indeed if they believed a pack of cornered Space Wolves could be rounded up like cattle.

Skaldr rose to his feet, his head swimming, his every nerve aflame as his augmented biology fought the invading poison. A pack of Blood Claws trampled past him, hooting wild battle songs, chainswords in hand. Anvarr's deployment. The Iron Priest's Stormwolf surged into the sky behind them, hurling las-bolts at the circling Razorwings. He caught one of them, punching a black hole in its wing, as all three detached like bats from a cave roof and chased the Stormwolf from the battlefield with spears of disintegrator fire.

The Pack Leader went to murmur private words of thanks after the indomitable Iron Priest, but the words refused to form on his lips. The Stormwolf disappeared into the canyon with the three Razorwings in pursuit. Skaldr shook his head and staggered after his battle-brothers, resolved to meet his death among them.

Anvarr gunned the juddering Stormwolf down the canyon through which he and the rest of his ill-fated assault wing had entered, casting aside sheets of crystal spray as he veered down a fork in the path ahead. The Razorwings raced after him without slowing. The passage ahead was strung with natural arches, sculpted by the crystal-toothed winds. The Stormwolf's damaged thrusters threaded a line of smoke through the rock formations as Anvarr dipped and dodged between them, occasionally scraping a wing or swerving clumsily to avoid a collision. Behind him, the Razorwings swooped and twisted with ease, flowing over the landscape like water.

A bolt of fire flashed past and destroyed a rocky bridge ahead of him. He swerved to avoid a curtain of tumbling stone, dodging deeper into the canyon network before his pursuers could fire again. Anvarr drank in the odour of baking rock cooled by the coursing winds, his mask feeding his predatory senses all the tactical data he required. The smell of hot stone intensified and he broke away down a slot canyon as spikes of fire exploded behind him. The Razorwings stood on their sides as they followed him, one after the other, relentless as the canyon winds that threatened to wrench the sticks from Anvarr's hands and fling his Stormwolf into the rocks. The Iron Priest fled deeper and deeper into the rocky maze, chasing the scent of burning stone carried upon a gathering wind as the dark eldar closed in behind him.

Iruthyr cackled with excitement, nestling in the darkness of his cockpit as he chased the battered gunship down yet another canyon, this one cradling a wide river of crystal debris that sparkled beneath the blazing sun.

'Sister, I'll give you fifty slaves if you can shear off its wing,' he laughed, his ghoulish features bathed green by the glowing runes on his console. He steadied his fighter against a strengthening wind.

'Too easy,' she replied. 'I would prefer we destroy what is left of his thrusters and when he crawls from the wreckage, then we can play. Disintegrators only. Let's say sixty slaves a limb...?'

'As you wish, sister,' Iruthyr said, his targeting icon hovering into place over the rear of the fleeing ship.

The ape's gunship suddenly accelerated, the gathering wind snatching away the black smoke now churning from its thrusters as it vanished through a gap in the canyon wall. Focused only upon his prey, Iruthyr dived after it, his fighter shaking. He noticed an air pressure warning flashing on his console.

'Pull up,' Izabella screamed through the comm. 'The savage has led us into a trap.'

Iruthyr pulled up, abandoning the hunt, his fighter convulsing now as a whirling storm of shards raked his fighter like the claws of some ravenous beast, tearing into its hull. He struggled to follow his sister's Razorwing as she accelerated into a steady climb above him, her wings also ragged with damage.

They rocketed from the canyon and soared side by side above the mesa as chunks of rock streaked across the sky amid a glittering mist of crystal shards. Their wingman's black fighter was visible ahead, the mercenary evidently seeking to abandon the twin Archons to their fate. As Iruthyr and his sister did their best to dodge the raining debris, a boulder crashed into the black Razorwing like an asteroid, smashing the fighter to pieces. Iruthyr ducked to avoid the oncoming slipstream of debris and saw the pilot himself tumbling towards him as the shard-infested wind whipped the flesh from his bones.

Gore sprayed Iruthyr's canopy, blinding him, his fighter tipping as something smashed onto his wing. He fought to arrest his spin as dust and wind scoured the canopy clear, revealing sky and earth tumbling one over the other. He managed to level out, his sister still beside him. Together they climbed hard, their engines grinding, until they were free of the sucking wind. He gazed down at a vast twirling column of air, its tail wriggling through the canyon miles below as it rained destruction about the mesa.

Izabella snarled over the comm.

'A curse on this world.'

Iruthyr glanced at his data display. His hull was in shreds, although both disintegrators remained functional.

'Agreed,' he said. 'Enough games. Let us return to the field, finish the apes and be gone.'

Iruthyr and his sister followed the canyon back to the battlefield, leaving the hurricane far behind them. His tattered fighter trembled as he neared the station where the battle continued to rage. He armed his disintegrators, his sister abeam as they commenced a steady descent.

Las-fire flashed at his back. Checking what remained of his sensor readout, Iruthyr saw the smoking gunship thundering close behind them, as if the storm itself had followed them from the canyon.

Anvarr had followed his hunter's nose back through the maze of canyons as surely as he had found his way into its boiling heart, luring his arrogant pursuers into the nearest shard-devil. But he had clipped several more rocks on the way back as he squirmed through the canyons, sheltering from the rain of rock and crystal fragments crashing overhead. Entire plates of ceramite had been prised from the Stormwolf's hull, exposing pipes and cabling to the elements. He was down to two thrusters, one of which threatened to collapse every time he manoeuvred and spoiled his aim when he had tried to take out one of the Razorwings. The xenos fighters did not give him another chance.

As they reached the smoking battlefield, they peeled off either side of him, curling as smoothly as their damaged wings would allow, preparing to fire upon Anvarr from either side as he approached.

His damaged thruster finally surrendered and the Stormwolf slumped to one side, threatening to drop from the sky. The Razorwings fired, their disintegrators slicing the ground as they flew towards him, ready to cut the ruined Stormwolf in half.

The beams flashed before Anvarr's eyes as he murmured a prayer to the machine-spirit, aiming his heavy bolters to the left, his helfrost cannons to the right. The engine purred beneath him as he fired.

The heavy bolters boomed at his flank as twin spikes of helfrost flashed overhead.

Anvarr Rustmane did not flinch as both weapons hit their marks and the shattered fighters screamed past his canopy, crashing to the ground behind him.

He ignored them and sped towards the battlefield, destroying a dark eldar skiff with las-fire and crushing a unit of squealing xenos beneath the belly of his Stormwolf as he ploughed the ruined gunship to a stop.

Anvarr detached his helm, sporadic rifle-fire crackling against the buckled hull as he clambered down the cockpit ladder to the hold where Cogfang awaited him, his master's thunder hammer held ready in his slavering jaws. Anvarr slung the weapon over his shoulder as he booted the malfunctioning ramp to the ground, then raised it over his head, announcing his arrival to the power-armoured warriors battling outside amid the sweltering dust.

'For Russ! For the Allfather!'

He whistled three times at Cogfang, who comprehended his master's instruction and bounded away. Anvarr dared a glance at the embossed wolf's head on the bulkhead behind him, then pounded towards his brothers to join them in glory.

Iruthyr Xynariis limped towards his sister's crashed Razorwing. He had driven his own crippled ship into a deep drift of crystal shards that had worked their way through the plates of his armour and chewed his flesh as he ran. Izabella still lay in her cockpit. He clambered onto the downed fighter and heaved open the broken canopy to find her looking up at him, breathing hard, her legs pinned and broken by the crushed console. He paused for a moment, invigorated by his sister's pain, the shrieks of his dying raiders carried by the hot winds.

She seized him by the collar of his flightsuit and yanked him towards her. Iruthyr realised she had a barbed knife at his throat.

'The Kabal of the Forked Tongue stands for the two of us,' she gasped. 'Or it does not stand at all.'

'Come, sister...' he said, reaching for the huskblade at his belt.

A low metallic growl startled the twins. They looked up to see a massive half-mechanised wolf standing on the prow of the ruined Razorwing, saliva leaking from its iron jaw as it watched them.

Iruthyr and his sister faltered, undecided whether to defend themselves or slit each other's throats. The cyberwolf proved more decisive.

The sky darkened into a starfield with the *Ragnarök* visible a short distance away. Anvarr growled into the vox once again.

'Throne of Earth! Cease your blasted singing, I said!'

The victory songs rising from the hold continued regardless, hardly improved by Cogfang's piercing howls.

Skaldr laughed over the vox from the Thunderhawk that had been sent to pick him up.

'You had better get used it, brother,' he said. 'Tonight the Deathwolves will honour Anvarr Rustmane with hours of song and oceans of mjod.'

The great blonde Pack Leader had acquitted himself well this day. He had shaken off a dose of dark eldar poison to cut down scores of Kabalite pirates, later joking that his half-drunken state had only served to improve his swing. Skaldr's deeds would certainly be worth a mention in the sagas, no doubt something else for him to smile about.

Anvarr scowled as his passengers launched into another song. The Storm-wolf's makeshift repairs were holding up well, but hours more work awaited the Iron Priest upon docking. At least he had found a replacement totem that would properly honour the machine-spirit for today's blessing.

In the hold below, the three surviving Blood Claws raised beakers of mjod to their grumbling Iron Priest, and to the slack-faced heads of the dark eldar twins pinned to the engine bulkhead by their long black hair. The eyes of the metal wolf's head gleamed.

ABOUT THE AUTHORS

David Annandale is the author of the Warhammer Horror novel T*he House of Night and Chain* and the novella *The Faith and the Flesh*, which features in the portmanteau *The Wicked and the Damned*. His work for the Horus Heresy series includes the novels *Ruinstorm* and *The Damnation of Pythos*, and the Primarchs novels *Roboute Guilliman: Lord of Ultramar* and *Vulkan: Lord of Drakes*. For Warhammer 40,000 he has written *Warlord: Fury of the God-Machine*, the Yarrick series, and several stories involving the Grey Knights, as well as titles for The Beast Arises and the Space Marine Battles series. For Warhammer Age of Sigmar he has written *Neferata: Mortarch of Blood* and *Neferata: The Dominion of Bones*. David lectures at a Canadian university, on subjects ranging from English literature to horror films and video games.

Mark Clapham was born and raised in Yorkshire, studied and worked in London for over a decade, and is now an itinerant writer and editor based in Exeter, Devon. He is the author of the Warhammer 40,000 novel *Iron Guard*, and his short stories have appeared in the *Fear the Alien* anthology and the monthly magazine *Hammer and Bolter*.

Ben Counter has two Horus Heresy novels to his name – *Galaxy in Flames* and *Battle for the Abyss*. He is the author of the Soul Drinkers series and *The Grey Knights Omnibus*. For Space Marine Battles, he has written *The World Engine* and *Malodrax*, and has turned his attention to the Space Wolves with the novella *Arjac Rockfist: Anvil of Fenris* as well as a number of short stories. He is a fanatical painter of miniatures, a pursuit that has won him his most prized possession: a prestigious Golden Demon award. He lives in Portsmouth, England.

Aaron Dembski-Bowden is the author of the Horus Heresy novels *The Master of Mankind*, *Betrayer* and *The First Heretic*, as well as the novella *Aurelian* and the audio drama *Butcher's Nails*, for the same series. He has also written the Warhammer 40,000 novel *Spear of the Emperor*, the popular Night Lords series, the Space Marine Battles book *Armageddon*, the novels *The Talon of Horus* and *Black Legion*, the Grey Knights novel *The Emperor's Gift* and numerous short stories. He lives and works in Northern Ireland.

Nick Kyme is the author of the Horus Heresy novels *Old Earth*, *Deathfire*, *Vulkan Lives* and *Sons of the Forge*, the novellas *Promethean Sun* and *Scorched Earth*, and the audio dramas *Red-Marked*, *Censure* and *Nightfane*. His novella *Feat of Iron* was a *New York Times* bestseller in the Horus Heresy collection, The Primarchs. Nick is well known for his popular Salamanders novels, including *Rebirth*, the Sicarius novels *Damnos* and *Knights of Macragge*, and numerous short stories. He has also written fiction set in the world of Warhammer, most notably the Warhammer Chronicles novel *The Great Betrayal* and the Age of Sigmar story 'Borne by the Storm', included in the novel *War Storm*. More recently he has scripted the Age of Sigmar audio drama *The Imprecations of Daemons*. He lives and works in Nottingham.

Lee Lightner is the penname for two authors who live in Baltimore, USA. Lifelong friends, they are both avid Space Wolf fans, and have written the Warhammer 40,000 novels *Sons of Fenris* and *Wolf's Honour*.

Cavan Scott has written the Space Marine Battles novella *Plague Harvest*, along with the Warhammer 40,000 short stories 'Doom Flight', 'Trophies', 'Sanctus Reach: Death Mask', 'Flayed' and 'Logan Grimnar: Defender of Honour'. He lives and works in Bristol.

Andy Smillie is best known for his visceral Flesh Tearers novellas, *Sons of Wrath* and *Flesh of Cretacia*, and the novel *Trial by Blood*. He has also written a host of short stories starring this brutal Chapter of Space Marines and a number of audio dramas including and *The Kauyon, Blood in the Machine, Deathwolf, From the Blood, Hunger* and *The Assassination of Gabriel Seth*.

Alec Worley is a well-known comics and science fiction and fantasy author, with numerous publications to his name. He is an avid fan of Warhammer 40,000 and has written many short stories for Black Library including 'Stormseeker', 'Whispers' and 'Repentia'. He has recently forayed into Black Library Horror with the audio drama *Perdition's Flame* and his novella *The Nothings*, featured in the anthology *Maledictions*. He lives and works in London.

YOUR
NEXT READ

BELISARIUS CAWL: THE GREAT WORK
by Guy Haley

In the wake of the Great Rift, Belisarius Cawl turns his attention to the abandoned
world of Sotha. Once home to the Scythes of the Emperor, it also hides
a long-buried secret… and an ancient evil.

Glittering debris surrounded the corpse of the planet. Grey as old bone, drier than dust, a shroud of shining particulates gathered solemnly around the corpse as it proceeded about the sun. The track the world ran was the most amenable to life, and yet life was absent entirely.

The broken remains of a single void station hung at equatorial high anchor, its decaying orbit recently stabilised. The soft shine of atmospheric shields closing the breaches in one section was just visible against the sun's glare. Three ships occupied the orbital's near space. Between the station and the world was a light cruiser bearing rich heraldry of yellow and black. Crossed scythes of gold on a sable background adorned its stern shield plates. In the glare of the sun the scars all over its hull were starkly visible. The scrollwork upon its hammerhead prow bore the name *Sterope*, one of the ten legendary steeds of Sotha.

Closest to the orbital was a small vessel of the Mechanicus tech-priests. Much of it was bare metal, the rest painted in the rich reds of Mars. It had no name displayed, but several identification plates bore the same number string – 0-101-0. Small in size, it was nevertheless packed with manufacturing facilities and dock points, and a constant stream of drone craft passed between the ship and the station.

The vessel furthest out was a larger Space Marine strike cruiser of new design, fresh from the shipyard, and free of damage or alterations to its original plan. Its deep blue livery was unmarred, the horned ultima displayed in many places remaining crisply white. It was a young yet fierce ship, and was named the *Lord of Vespator*, for it bore the ruler of that world as he travelled throughout his kingdom.

A hangar door opened in the side of the *Lord of Vespator*. A single gunship emerged. Exhaust stabbing from the engines made a blade of blue plasma fire and the ship's hull shone as bright as a jewelled hilt, so that it resembled a sword thrown handle-first to a beleaguered warrior battling a monster.

But the weapon came too late. The monster had triumphed. The world was dead.

So did Decimus Felix, Tetrarch of Ultramar, come to survey the ruin of his domain.

'A tight fit,' said Daelus. The Techmarine altered the ship's path with minute adjustments to the flightsticks. Felix looked out through the armourglass blister. The cockpit was set high back above the transport bays, and the ceiling passed within inches of his face, close enough that he could examine the damage to the metal, and name the bioweapons responsible.

Only Daelus' skill saw the Overlord squeeze into the hangar. His left hand moved swiftly over the ship's array of buttons. Jets fringed the blocky double hull with bursts of light and vapour in response.

'This is not ideal,' said Felix.

'I've landed in tighter spaces, my lord,' said Daelus, tense with concentration. 'Not many, I'll admit.'

Daelus' crew consisted of a further Primaris Marine in the red of the forge and three Chapter serfs. They were far too preoccupied with landing to speak to the tetrarch, but peered at their instruments nervously. Troncus, the Techmarine co-pilot, was immobile. Only the tiny movements of his hands as he corrected Daelus' few errors showed that a living being occupied his armour.

Proximity alarms trilled from several quarters. The prow lights hit a solid wall.

'Emperor's will, this is getting worse!' Daelus said.

The landing bay had suffered catastrophic damage. Efforts to patch it up had shrunk its space by half. A wall of plasteel plating fixed in place with metallite foams divided the bay. Bracing girders holding the wall upright angled into the hangar, making Daelus' task all the more difficult.

'Nearly got it,' the pilot said, more to himself than to anyone else.

Felix watched ruptured metal pass by. The Aegida had possessed many landing decks. The monsters of Hive Fleet Kraken had wrecked them all as they boarded. Only this smaller docking portal had been returned to operational use.

The Overlord's power core whined up and down as Troncus adjusted the energy flow in preparation for landing. The ship swayed. Troncus looked at the pilot.

'That's not my fault,' Daelus said to his unspoken rebuke. 'Grav-plating's no good in here,' he grumbled. 'Nothing's good in here. Troncus, run landing sequence. This is the best position we're going to get.'

Felix's ear beads clicked. Daelus had opened an unencrypted vox channel.

'Sergeant Cominus,' Daelus said. 'I'm setting down.'

'Ready. Open the forward hatches,' Cominus voxed back.

'Depressurising holds. There's no atmosphere. I'm sure you've got your helmets on.'

'I need not remind you I find your levity irritating, Daelus.'

'He's no fun, that one,' said Daelus, making sure Cominus heard before he shut the channel.

'He serves well,' said Felix.

'He could smile while he was doing it,' said Daelus. 'Life does not all have to be drill and duty, not even for us.'

The atmospheric retention field was out, leaving the hangar open to space. Daelus joggled the flight sticks against the outrush of air expelled from the twin passenger compartments. The ramps opened as the vessel's engines gave out one last burst. The starboard wing squealed noisily down the partition wall, causing Felix to grit his teeth.

'I said it was tight,' Daelus muttered.

Before the Overlord settled onto its landing claws, eight Space Marines ran out, bolt rifles at the ready, and took up guard at various points of the hangar. Each wore Mark X Intercessor pattern power armour in differing heraldries, but all were united by their richly decorated left pauldrons, where the sigil of the Tetrarch of Vespator was displayed on golden plating. Cominus was more obvious for his manner than the bright red and white wargear he wore or his sergeant's insignia. He stood in front of the Overlord's nose, directing Felix's bodyguard with a flurry of battle-sign, his bolt rifle held upright.

The engines wheezed. The ship sank down on its hydraulics and ceased moving.

'That's it, we're in,' Daelus said. Troncus clicked a dozen buttons. The serfs visibly relaxed and began post-flight checks. The power plant quieted to a hum. Daelus' armour sighed as it disconnected from the umbilicus set into the back of the seat. The armour was heavy on him without power, but he turned round naturally enough, and angled his helm to look up at Felix.

'Welcome to the Aegida Orbital, my lord. Welcome to Sotha.'

3117209875 1043